The Upton Sinclair Collection

By

Upton Sinclair

ISBN: 9781789431964

Contents

THE JUNGLE

THE METROPOLIS

THE MONEYCHANGERS

KING COAL

THEY CALL ME CARPENTER

THE JUNGLE

CHAPTER 1

It was four o'clock when the ceremony was over and the carriages began to arrive. There had been a crowd following all the way, owing to the exuberance of Marija Berczynskas. The occasion rested heavily upon Marija's broad shoulders—it was her task to see that all things went in due form, and after the best home traditions; and, flying wildly hither and thither, bowling every one out of the way, and scolding and exhorting all day with her tremendous voice, Marija was too eager to see that others conformed to the proprieties to consider them herself. She had left the church last of all, and, desiring to arrive first at the hall, had issued orders to the coachman to drive faster. When that personage had developed a will of his own in the matter, Marija had flung up the window of the carriage, and, leaning out, proceeded to tell him her opinion of him, first in Lithuanian, which he did not understand, and then in Polish, which he did. Having the advantage of her in altitude, the driver had stood his ground and even ventured to attempt to speak; and the result had been a furious altercation, which, continuing all the way down Ashland Avenue, had added a new swarm of urchins to the cortege at each side street for half a mile.

This was unfortunate, for already there was a throng before the door. The music had started up, and half a block away you could hear the dull "broom, broom" of a cello, with the squeaking of two fiddles which vied with each other in intricate and altitudinous gymnastics. Seeing the throng, Marija abandoned precipitately the debate concerning the ancestors of her coachman, and, springing from the moving carriage, plunged in and proceeded to clear a way to the hall. Once within, she turned and began to push the other way, roaring, meantime, "Eik! Eik! Uzdaryk-duris!" in tones which made the orchestral uproar sound like fairy music.

"Z. Graiczunas, Pasilinksminimams darzas. Vynas. Sznapsas. Wines and Liquors. Union Headquarters"—that was the way the signs ran. The reader, who perhaps has never held much converse in the language of far-off Lithuania, will be glad of the explanation that the place was the rear room of a saloon in that part of Chicago known as "back of the yards." This information is definite and suited to the matter of fact; but how pitifully inadequate it would have seemed to one who understood that it was also the supreme hour of ecstasy in the life of one of

God's gentlest creatures, the scene of the wedding feast and the joy-transfiguration of little Ona Lukoszaite!

She stood in the doorway, shepherded by Cousin Marija, breathless from pushing through the crowd, and in her happiness painful to look upon. There was a light of wonder in her eyes and her lids trembled, and her otherwise wan little face was flushed. She wore a muslin dress, conspicuously white, and a stiff little veil coming to her shoulders. There were five pink paper roses twisted in the veil, and eleven bright green rose leaves. There were new white cotton gloves upon her hands, and as she stood staring about her she twisted them together feverishly. It was almost too much for her—you could see the pain of too great emotion in her face, and all the tremor of her form. She was so young—not quite sixteen—and small for her age, a mere child; and she had just been married—and married to Jurgis[1], of all men, to Jurgis Rudkus, he with the white flower in the buttonhole of his new black suit, he with the mighty shoulders and the giant hands.

Ona was blue-eyed and fair, while Jurgis had great black eyes with beetling brows, and thick black hair that curled in waves about his ears—in short, they were one of those incongruous and impossible married couples with which Mother Nature so often wills to confound all prophets, before and after. Jurgis could take up a two-hundred-and-fifty-pound quarter of beef and carry it into a car without a stagger, or even a thought; and now he stood in a far corner, frightened as a hunted animal, and obliged to moisten his lips with his tongue each time before he could answer the congratulations of his friends.

Gradually there was effected a separation between the spectators and the guests—a separation at least sufficiently complete for working purposes. There was no time during the festivities which ensued when there were not groups of onlookers in the doorways and the corners; and if any one of these onlookers came sufficiently close, or looked sufficiently hungry, a chair was offered him, and he was invited to the feast. It was one of the laws of the veselija that no one goes hungry; and, while a rule made in the forests of Lithuania is hard to apply in the stockyards district of Chicago, with its quarter of a million inhabitants, still they did their best, and the children who ran in from the street, and even the dogs, went out again happier. A charming informality was one of the characteristics of this celebration. The men wore their hats, or, if they wished, they took them off, and their coats with them; they ate when and where they pleased, and moved as often as they pleased. There were to be speeches and singing, but no one had to listen who did not care to; if he wished, meantime, to speak or sing himself, he was perfectly free. The resulting medley of sound distracted no one, save possibly alone the babies, of which there were present a number equal to the total possessed by all the guests invited. There was no other place for the babies to be, and so part of the preparations for the evening consisted of a collection of cribs and carriages in one corner. In these the babies slept, three or four together, or wakened together, as the case might be. Those who were still older, and could reach

---

[1] Pronounced Yoorghis

the tables, marched about munching contentedly at meat bones and bologna sausages.

The room is about thirty feet square, with whitewashed walls, bare save for a calendar, a picture of a race horse, and a family tree in a gilded frame. To the right there is a door from the saloon, with a few loafers in the doorway, and in the corner beyond it a bar, with a presiding genius clad in soiled white, with waxed black mustaches and a carefully oiled curl plastered against one side of his forehead. In the opposite corner are two tables, filling a third of the room and laden with dishes and cold viands, which a few of the hungrier guests are already munching. At the head, where sits the bride, is a snow-white cake, with an Eiffel tower of constructed decoration, with sugar roses and two angels upon it, and a generous sprinkling of pink and green and yellow candies. Beyond opens a door into the kitchen, where there is a glimpse to be had of a range with much steam ascending from it, and many women, old and young, rushing hither and thither. In the corner to the left are the three musicians, upon a little platform, toiling heroically to make some impression upon the hubbub; also the babies, similarly occupied, and an open window whence the populace imbibes the sights and sounds and odors.

Suddenly some of the steam begins to advance, and, peering through it, you discern Aunt Elizabeth, Ona's stepmother—Teta Elzbieta, as they call her—bearing aloft a great platter of stewed duck. Behind her is Kotrina, making her way cautiously, staggering beneath a similar burden; and half a minute later there appears old Grandmother Majauszkiene, with a big yellow bowl of smoking potatoes, nearly as big as herself. So, bit by bit, the feast takes form—there is a ham and a dish of sauerkraut, boiled rice, macaroni, bologna sausages, great piles of penny buns, bowls of milk, and foaming pitchers of beer. There is also, not six feet from your back, the bar, where you may order all you please and do not have to pay for it. "Eiksz! Graicziau!" screams Marija Berczynskas, and falls to work herself—for there is more upon the stove inside that will be spoiled if it be not eaten.

So, with laughter and shouts and endless badinage and merriment, the guests take their places. The young men, who for the most part have been huddled near the door, summon their resolution and advance; and the shrinking Jurgis is poked and scolded by the old folks until he consents to seat himself at the right hand of the bride. The two bridesmaids, whose insignia of office are paper wreaths, come next, and after them the rest of the guests, old and young, boys and girls. The spirit of the occasion takes hold of the stately bartender, who condescends to a plate of stewed duck; even the fat policeman—whose duty it will be, later in the evening, to break up the fights—draws up a chair to the foot of the table. And the children shout and the babies yell, and every one laughs and sings and chatters—while above all the deafening clamor Cousin Marija shouts orders to the musicians.

The musicians—how shall one begin to describe them? All this time they have been there, playing in a mad frenzy—all of this scene must be read, or said, or sung, to music. It is the music which makes it what it is; it is the music which changes the place from the rear room of a saloon in back of the yards to a fairy place, a wonderland, a little corner of the high mansions of the sky.

The little person who leads this trio is an inspired man. His fiddle is out of tune, and there is no rosin on his bow, but still he is an inspired man—the hands of the muses have been laid upon him. He plays like one possessed by a demon, by a whole horde of demons. You can feel them in the air round about him, capering frenetically; with their invisible feet they set the pace, and the hair of the leader of the orchestra rises on end, and his eyeballs start from their sockets, as he toils to keep up with them.

Tamoszius Kuszleika is his name, and he has taught himself to play the violin by practicing all night, after working all day on the "killing beds." He is in his shirt sleeves, with a vest figured with faded gold horseshoes, and a pink-striped shirt, suggestive of peppermint candy. A pair of military trousers, light blue with a yellow stripe, serve to give that suggestion of authority proper to the leader of a band. He is only about five feet high, but even so these trousers are about eight inches short of the ground. You wonder where he can have gotten them or rather you would wonder, if the excitement of being in his presence left you time to think of such things.

For he is an inspired man. Every inch of him is inspired—you might almost say inspired separately. He stamps with his feet, he tosses his head, he sways and swings to and fro; he has a wizened-up little face, irresistibly comical; and, when he executes a turn or a flourish, his brows knit and his lips work and his eyelids wink—the very ends of his necktie bristle out. And every now and then he turns upon his companions, nodding, signaling, beckoning frantically—with every inch of him appealing, imploring, in behalf of the muses and their call.

For they are hardly worthy of Tamoszius, the other two members of the orchestra. The second violin is a Slovak, a tall, gaunt man with black-rimmed spectacles and the mute and patient look of an overdriven mule; he responds to the whip but feebly, and then always falls back into his old rut. The third man is very fat, with a round, red, sentimental nose, and he plays with his eyes turned up to the sky and a look of infinite yearning. He is playing a bass part upon his cello, and so the excitement is nothing to him; no matter what happens in the treble, it is his task to saw out one long-drawn and lugubrious note after another, from four o'clock in the afternoon until nearly the same hour next morning, for his third of the total income of one dollar per hour.

Before the feast has been five minutes under way, Tamoszius Kuszleika has risen in his excitement; a minute or two more and you see that he is beginning to edge over toward the tables. His nostrils are dilated and his breath comes fast— his demons are driving him. He nods and shakes his head at his companions, jerking at them with his violin, until at last the long form of the second violinist also rises up. In the end all three of them begin advancing, step by step, upon the banqueters, Valentinavyczia, the cellist, bumping along with his instrument between notes. Finally all three are gathered at the foot of the tables, and there Tamoszius mounts upon a stool.

CHAPTER 1

Now he is in his glory, dominating the scene. Some of the people are eating, some are laughing and talking—but you will make a great mistake if you think there is one of them who does not hear him. His notes are never true, and his fiddle buzzes on the low ones and squeaks and scratches on the high; but these things they heed no more than they heed the dirt and noise and squalor about them—it is out of this material that they have to build their lives, with it that they have to utter their souls. And this is their utterance; merry and boisterous, or mournful and wailing, or passionate and rebellious, this music is their music, music of home. It stretches out its arms to them, they have only to give themselves up. Chicago and its saloons and its slums fade away—there are green meadows and sunlit rivers, mighty forests and snow-clad hills. They behold home landscapes and childhood scenes returning; old loves and friendships begin to waken, old joys and griefs to laugh and weep. Some fall back and close their eyes, some beat upon the table. Now and then one leaps up with a cry and calls for this song or that; and then the fire leaps brighter in Tamoszius' eyes, and he flings up his fiddle and shouts to his companions, and away they go in mad career. The company takes up the choruses, and men and women cry out like all possessed; some leap to their feet and stamp upon the floor, lifting their glasses and pledging each other. Before long it occurs to some one to demand an old wedding song, which celebrates the beauty of the bride and the joys of love. In the excitement of this masterpiece Tamoszius Kuszleika begins to edge in between the tables, making his way toward the head, where sits the bride. There is not a foot of space between the chairs of the guests, and Tamoszius is so short that he pokes them with his bow whenever he reaches over for the low notes; but still he presses in, and insists relentlessly that his companions must follow. During their progress, needless to say, the sounds of the cello are pretty well extinguished; but at last the three are at the head, and Tamoszius takes his station at the right hand of the bride and begins to pour out his soul in melting strains.

Little Ona is too excited to eat. Once in a while she tastes a little something, when Cousin Marija pinches her elbow and reminds her; but, for the most part, she sits gazing with the same fearful eyes of wonder. Teta Elzbieta is all in a flutter, like a hummingbird; her sisters, too, keep running up behind her, whispering, breathless. But Ona seems scarcely to hear them—the music keeps calling, and the far-off look comes back, and she sits with her hands pressed together over her heart. Then the tears begin to come into her eyes; and as she is ashamed to wipe them away, and ashamed to let them run down her cheeks, she turns and shakes her head a little, and then flushes red when she sees that Jurgis is watching her. When in the end Tamoszius Kuszleika has reached her side, and is waving his magic wand above her, Ona's cheeks are scarlet, and she looks as if she would have to get up and run away.

In this crisis, however, she is saved by Marija Berczynskas, whom the muses suddenly visit. Marija is fond of a song, a song of lovers' parting; she wishes to hear it, and, as the musicians do not know it, she has risen, and is proceeding to teach them. Marija is short, but powerful in build. She works in a canning factory, and all day long she handles cans of beef that weigh fourteen pounds. She has a broad Slavic face, with prominent red cheeks. When she opens her mouth, it is tragical, but you cannot help thinking of a horse. She wears a blue flannel shirt-waist, which is now rolled up at the sleeves, disclosing her brawny arms; she has a carving fork in her hand, with which she pounds on the table to mark the time. As she roars her song, in a voice of which it is enough to say that it leaves no portion of the room vacant, the three musicians follow her, laboriously and note by note, but averaging one note behind; thus they toil through stanza after stanza of a lovesick swain's lamentation:—

> "Sudiev' kvietkeli, tu brangiausis;
> Sudiev' ir laime, man biednam,
> Matau—paskyre teip Aukszcziausis,
> Jog vargt ant svieto reik vienam!"

When the song is over, it is time for the speech, and old Dede Antanas rises to his feet. Grandfather Anthony, Jurgis' father, is not more than sixty years of age, but you would think that he was eighty. He has been only six months in America, and the change has not done him good. In his manhood he worked in a cotton mill, but then a coughing fell upon him, and he had to leave; out in the country the trouble disappeared, but he has been working in the pickle rooms at Durham's, and the breathing of the cold, damp air all day has brought it back. Now as he rises he is seized with a coughing fit, and holds himself by his chair and turns away his wan and battered face until it passes.

Generally it is the custom for the speech at a veselija to be taken out of one of the books and learned by heart; but in his youthful days Dede Antanas used to be a scholar, and really make up all the love letters of his friends. Now it is understood that he has composed an original speech of congratulation and benediction, and this is one of the events of the day. Even the boys, who are romping about the room, draw near and listen, and some of the women sob and wipe their aprons in their eyes. It is very solemn, for Antanas Rudkus has become possessed of the idea that he has not much longer to stay with his children. His speech leaves them all so tearful that one of the guests, Jokubas Szedvilas, who keeps a delicatessen store on Halsted Street, and is fat and hearty, is moved to rise and say that things may not be as bad as that, and then to go on and make a little speech of his own, in which he showers congratulations and prophecies of happiness upon the bride and groom, proceeding to particulars which greatly delight the young men, but which cause Ona to blush more furiously than ever. Jokubas possesses what his wife complacently describes as "poetiszka vaidintuve"—a poetical imagination.

Now a good many of the guests have finished, and, since there is no pretense of ceremony, the banquet begins to break up. Some of the men gather about the bar; some wander about, laughing and singing; here and there will be a little group, chanting merrily, and in sublime indifference to the others and to the orchestra as well. Everybody is more or less restless—one would guess that something is on their minds. And so it proves. The last tardy diners are scarcely given time to finish, before the tables and the debris are shoved into the corner, and the chairs and the babies piled out of the way, and the real celebration of the evening begins. Then Tamoszius Kuszleika, after replenishing himself with a pot of beer, returns to his platform, and, standing up, reviews the scene; he taps authoritatively upon the side of his violin, then tucks it carefully under his chin, then waves his bow in an elaborate flourish, and finally smites the sounding strings and closes his eyes, and floats away in spirit upon the wings of a dreamy waltz. His companion follows, but with his eyes open, watching where he treads, so to speak; and finally Valentinavyczia, after waiting for a little and beating with his foot to get the time, casts up his eyes to the ceiling and begins to saw—"Broom! broom! broom!"

The company pairs off quickly, and the whole room is soon in motion. Apparently nobody knows how to waltz, but that is nothing of any consequence—there is music, and they dance, each as he pleases, just as before they sang. Most of them prefer the "two-step," especially the young, with whom it is the fashion. The older people have dances from home, strange and complicated steps which they execute with grave solemnity. Some do not dance anything at all, but simply hold each other's hands and allow the undisciplined joy of motion to express itself with their feet. Among these are Jokubas Szedvilas and his wife, Lucija, who together keep the delicatessen store, and consume nearly as much as they sell; they are too fat to dance, but they stand in the middle of the floor, holding each other fast in their arms, rocking slowly from side to side and grinning seraphically, a picture of toothless and perspiring ecstasy.

Of these older people many wear clothing reminiscent in some detail of home—an embroidered waistcoat or stomacher, or a gaily colored handkerchief, or a coat with large cuffs and fancy buttons. All these things are carefully avoided by the young, most of whom have learned to speak English and to affect the latest style of clothing. The girls wear ready-made dresses or shirt waists, and some of them look quite pretty. Some of the young men you would take to be Americans, of the type of clerks, but for the fact that they wear their hats in the room. Each of these younger couples affects a style of its own in dancing. Some hold each other tightly, some at a cautious distance. Some hold their hands out stiffly, some drop them loosely at their sides. Some dance springily, some glide softly, some move with grave dignity. There are boisterous couples, who tear wildly about the room, knocking every one out of their way. There are nervous couples, whom these frighten, and who cry, "Nusfok! Kas yra?" at them as they pass. Each couple is paired for the evening—you will never see them change about. There is Alena Jasaityte, for instance, who has danced unending hours with Juozas Raczius, to whom she is engaged. Alena is the beauty of the evening, and she would be really beautiful if she were not so proud. She wears a white shirtwaist, which represents, perhaps, half a week's labor painting cans. She holds her skirt with her hand as she dances, with stately precision, after the manner of the grandes dames. Juozas is driving one of Durham's wagons, and is making big wages. He affects a "tough" aspect, wearing his hat on one side and keeping a cigarette in his mouth all the evening. Then there is Jadvyga Marcinkus, who is also beautiful, but humble. Jadvyga likewise paints cans, but then she has an invalid mother and three little sisters to support by it, and so she does not spend her wages for shirtwaists. Jadvyga is small and delicate, with jet-black eyes and hair, the latter twisted into a little knot and tied on the top of her head. She wears an old white dress which she has made herself and worn to parties for the past five years; it is high-waisted— almost under her arms, and not very becoming,—but that does not trouble Jadvyga, who is dancing with her Mikolas. She is small, while he is big and powerful; she nestles in his arms as if she would hide herself from view, and leans her head upon his shoulder. He in turn has clasped his arms tightly around her, as if he would carry her away; and so she dances, and will dance the entire evening, and would dance forever, in ecstasy of bliss. You would smile, perhaps, to see them—but you would not smile if you knew all the story. This is the fifth year, now, that Jadvyga has been engaged to Mikolas, and her heart is sick. They would have been married in the beginning, only Mikolas has a father who is drunk all day, and he is the only other man in a large family. Even so they might have managed it (for Mikolas is a skilled man) but for cruel accidents which have almost taken the heart out of them. He is a beef-boner, and that is a dangerous trade, especially when you are on piecework and trying to earn a bride. Your hands are slippery, and your knife is slippery, and you are toiling like mad, when somebody happens to speak to you, or you strike a bone. Then your hand slips up on the blade, and there is a fearful gash. And that would not be so bad, only for the deadly contagion. The cut may heal, but you never can tell. Twice now; within the last three years, Mikolas has been lying at home with blood poisoning—once for three months and once for nearly seven. The last time, too, he lost his job, and that meant six weeks more of standing at the doors of the packing houses, at six o'clock on bitter winter mornings, with a foot of snow on the ground and more in the air. There are learned people who can tell you out of the statistics that beef-boners make forty cents an hour, but, perhaps, these people have never looked into a beef-boner's hands.

When Tamoszius and his companions stop for a rest, as perforce they must, now and then, the dancers halt where they are and wait patiently. They never seem to tire; and there is no place for them to sit down if they did. It is only for a minute, anyway, for the leader starts up again, in spite of all the protests of the other two. This time it is another sort of a dance, a Lithuanian dance. Those who prefer to, go on with the two-step, but the majority go through an intricate series of motions, resembling more fancy skating than a dance. The climax of it is a furious prestissimo, at which the couples seize hands and begin a mad whirling. This is quite irresistible, and every one in the room joins in, until the place becomes a maze of flying skirts and bodies quite dazzling to look upon. But the sight of sights at this moment is Tamoszius Kuszleika. The old fiddle squeaks and shrieks in protest, but Tamoszius has no mercy. The sweat starts out on his forehead, and he bends over like a cyclist on the last lap of a race. His body shakes and throbs like a runaway steam engine, and the ear cannot follow the flying showers of notes—there is a pale blue mist where you look to see his bowing arm.

With a most wonderful rush he comes to the end of the tune, and flings up his hands and staggers back exhausted; and with a final shout of delight the dancers fly apart, reeling here and there, bringing up against the walls of the room.

After this there is beer for every one, the musicians included, and the revelers take a long breath and prepare for the great event of the evening, which is the acziavimas. The acziavimas is a ceremony which, once begun, will continue for three or four hours, and it involves one uninterrupted dance. The guests form a great ring, locking hands, and, when the music starts up, begin to move around in a circle. In the center stands the bride, and, one by one, the men step into the enclosure and dance with her. Each dances for several minutes—as long as he pleases; it is a very merry proceeding, with laughter and singing, and when the guest has finished, he finds himself face to face with Teta Elzbieta, who holds the hat. Into it he drops a sum of money—a dollar, or perhaps five dollars, according to his power, and his estimate of the value of the privilege. The guests are expected to pay for this entertainment; if they be proper guests, they will see that there is a neat sum left over for the bride and bridegroom to start life upon.

Most fearful they are to contemplate, the expenses of this entertainment. They will certainly be over two hundred dollars and maybe three hundred; and three hundred dollars is more than the year's income of many a person in this room. There are able-bodied men here who work from early morning until late at night, in ice-cold cellars with a quarter of an inch of water on the floor—men who for six or seven months in the year never see the sunlight from Sunday afternoon till the next Sunday morning—and who cannot earn three hundred dollars in a year. There are little children here, scarce in their teens, who can hardly see the top of the work benches—whose parents have lied to get them their places—and who do not make the half of three hundred dollars a year, and perhaps not even the third of it. And then to spend such a sum, all in a single day of your life, at a wedding feast! (For obviously it is the same thing, whether you spend it at once for your own wedding, or in a long time, at the weddings of all your friends.)

It is very imprudent, it is tragic—but, ah, it is so beautiful! Bit by bit these poor people have given up everything else; but to this they cling with all the power of their souls—they cannot give up the veselija! To do that would mean, not merely to be defeated, but to acknowledge defeat—and the difference between these two things is what keeps the world going. The veselija has come down to them from a far-off time; and the meaning of it was that one might dwell within the cave and gaze upon shadows, provided only that once in his lifetime he could break his chains, and feel his wings, and behold the sun; provided that once in his lifetime he might testify to the fact that life, with all its cares and its terrors, is no such great thing after all, but merely a bubble upon the surface of a river, a thing that one may toss about and play with as a juggler tosses his golden balls, a thing that one may quaff, like a goblet of rare red wine. Thus having known himself for the master of things, a man could go back to his toil and live upon the memory all his days.

Endlessly the dancers swung round and round—when they were dizzy they swung the other way. Hour after hour this had continued—the darkness had fallen and the room was dim from the light of two smoky oil lamps. The musicians had spent all their fine frenzy by now, and played only one tune, wearily, ploddingly. There were twenty bars or so of it, and when they came to the end they began again. Once every ten minutes or so they would fail to begin again, but instead would sink back exhausted; a circumstance which invariably brought on a painful and terrifying scene, that made the fat policeman stir uneasily in his sleeping place behind the door.

It was all Marija Berczynskas. Marija was one of those hungry souls who cling with desperation to the skirts of the retreating muse. All day long she had been in a state of wonderful exaltation; and now it was leaving—and she would not let it go. Her soul cried out in the words of Faust, "Stay, thou art fair!" Whether it was by beer, or by shouting, or by music, or by motion, she meant that it should not go. And she would go back to the chase of it—and no sooner be fairly started than her chariot would be thrown off the track, so to speak, by the stupidity of those thrice accursed musicians. Each time, Marija would emit a howl and fly at them, shaking her fists in their faces, stamping upon the floor, purple and incoherent with rage. In vain the frightened Tamoszius would attempt to speak, to plead the limitations of the flesh; in vain would the puffing and breathless ponas Jokubas insist, in vain would Teta Elzbieta implore. "Szalin!" Marija would scream. "Palauk! isz kelio! What are you paid for, children of hell?" And so, in sheer terror, the orchestra would strike up again, and Marija would return to her place and take up her task.

She bore all the burden of the festivities now. Ona was kept up by her excitement, but all of the women and most of the men were tired—the soul of Marija was alone unconquered. She drove on the dancers—what had once been the ring had now the shape of a pear, with Marija at the stem, pulling one way and pushing the other, shouting, stamping, singing, a very volcano of energy. Now and then some one coming in or out would leave the door open, and the night air was chill; Marija as she passed would stretch out her foot and kick the doorknob, and slam would go the door! Once this procedure was the cause of a calamity of which Sebastijonas Szedvilas was the hapless victim. Little Sebastijonas, aged three, had been wandering about oblivious to all things, holding turned up over his mouth a bottle of liquid known as "pop," pink-colored, ice-cold, and delicious. Passing through the doorway the door smote him full, and the shriek which followed brought the dancing to a halt. Marija, who threatened horrid murder a hundred times a day, and would weep over the injury of a fly, seized little Sebastijonas in her arms and bid fair to smother him with kisses. There was a long rest for the orchestra, and plenty of refreshments, while Marija was making her peace with her victim, seating him upon the bar, and standing beside him and holding to his lips a foaming schooner of beer.

In the meantime there was going on in another corner of the room an anxious conference between Teta Elzbieta and Dede Antanas, and a few of the more intimate friends of the family. A trouble was come upon them. The veselija is a compact, a compact not expressed, but therefore only the more binding upon all. Every one's share was different—and yet every one knew perfectly well what his share was, and strove to give a little more. Now, however, since they had come to the new country, all this was changing; it seemed as if there must be some subtle poison in the air that one breathed here—it was affecting all the young men at once. They would come in crowds and fill themselves with a fine dinner, and then sneak off. One would throw another's hat out of the window, and both would go out to get it, and neither could be seen again. Or now and then half a dozen of them would get together and march out openly, staring at you, and making fun of you to your face. Still others, worse yet, would crowd about the bar, and at the expense of the host drink themselves sodden, paying not the least attention to any one, and leaving it to be thought that either they had danced with the bride already, or meant to later on.

All these things were going on now, and the family was helpless with dismay. So long they had toiled, and such an outlay they had made! Ona stood by, her eyes wide with terror. Those frightful bills—how they had haunted her, each item gnawing at her soul all day and spoiling her rest at night. How often she had named them over one by one and figured on them as she went to work—fifteen dollars for the hall, twenty-two dollars and a quarter for the ducks, twelve dollars for the musicians, five dollars at the church, and a blessing of the Virgin besides—and so on without an end! Worst of all was the frightful bill that was still to come from Graiczunas for the beer and liquor that might be consumed. One could never get in advance more than a guess as to this from a saloon-keeper—and then, when the time came he always came to you scratching his head and saying that he had guessed too low, but that he had done his best—your guests had gotten so very drunk. By him you were sure to be cheated unmercifully, and that even though you thought yourself the dearest of the hundreds of friends he had. He would begin to serve your guests out of a keg that was half full, and finish with one that was half empty, and then you would be charged for two kegs of beer. He would agree to serve a certain quality at a certain price, and when the time came you and your friends would be drinking some horrible poison that could not be described. You might complain, but you would get nothing for your pains but a ruined evening; while, as for going to law about it, you might as well go to heaven at once. The saloon-keeper stood in with all the big politics men in the district; and when you had once found out what it meant to get into trouble with such people, you would know enough to pay what you were told to pay and shut up.

What made all this the more painful was that it was so hard on the few that had really done their best. There was poor old ponas Jokubas, for instance—he had already given five dollars, and did not every one know that Jokubas Szedvilas had just mortgaged his delicatessen store for two hundred dollars to meet several months' overdue rent? And then there was withered old poni Aniele—who was a widow, and had three children, and the rheumatism besides, and did washing for the tradespeople on Halsted Street at prices it would break your heart to hear named. Aniele had given the entire profit of her chickens for several months. Eight of them she owned, and she kept them in a little place fenced around on her backstairs. All day long the children of Aniele were raking in the dump for food for these chickens; and sometimes, when the competition there was too fierce, you might see them on Halsted Street walking close to the gutters, and with their mother following to see that no one robbed them of their finds. Money could not tell the value of these chickens to old Mrs. Jukniene—she valued them different-ly, for she had a feeling that she was getting something for nothing by means of them—that with them she was getting the better of a world that was getting the better of her in so many other ways. So she watched them every hour of the day, and had learned to see like an owl at night to watch them then. One of them had been stolen long ago, and not a month passed that some one did not try to steal another. As the frustrating of this one attempt involved a score of false alarms, it will be understood what a tribute old Mrs. Jukniene brought, just because Teta Elzbieta had once loaned her some money for a few days and saved her from be-ing turned out of her house.

More and more friends gathered round while the lamentation about these things was going on. Some drew nearer, hoping to overhear the conversation, who were themselves among the guilty—and surely that was a thing to try the patience of a saint. Finally there came Jurgis, urged by some one, and the story was retold to him. Jurgis listened in silence, with his great black eyebrows knitted. Now and then there would come a gleam underneath them and he would glance about the room. Perhaps he would have liked to go at some of those fellows with his big clenched fists; but then, doubtless, he realized how little good it would do him. No bill would be any less for turning out any one at this time; and then there would be the scandal—and Jurgis wanted nothing except to get away with Ona and to let the world go its own way. So his hands relaxed and he merely said qui-etly: "It is done, and there is no use in weeping, Teta Elzbieta." Then his look turned toward Ona, who stood close to his side, and he saw the wide look of terror in her eyes. "Little one," he said, in a low voice, "do not worry—it will not matter to us. We will pay them all somehow. I will work harder." That was always what Jurgis said. Ona had grown used to it as the solution of all difficulties—"I will work harder!" He had said that in Lithuania when one official had taken his pass-port from him, and another had arrested him for being without it, and the two had divided a third of his belongings. He had said it again in New York, when the smooth-spoken agent had taken them in hand and made them pay such high pric-es, and almost prevented their leaving his place, in spite of their paying. Now he said it a third time, and Ona drew a deep breath; it was so wonderful to have a husband, just like a grown woman—and a husband who could solve all problems, and who was so big and strong!

The last sob of little Sebastijonas has been stifled, and the orchestra has once more been reminded of its duty. The ceremony begins again—but there are few now left to dance with, and so very soon the collection is over and promiscuous dances once more begin. It is now after midnight, however, and things are not as they were before. The dancers are dull and heavy—most of them have been drinking hard, and have long ago passed the stage of exhilaration. They dance in mo-monotonous measure, round after round, hour after hour, with eyes fixed upon vacancy, as if they were only half conscious, in a constantly growing stupor. The men grasp the women very tightly, but there will be half an hour together when neither will see the other's face. Some couples do not care to dance, and have retired to the corners, where they sit with their arms enlaced. Others, who have been drinking still more, wander about the room, bumping into everything; some are in groups of two or three, singing, each group its own song. As time goes on there is a variety of drunkenness, among the younger men especially. Some stagger about in each other's arms, whispering maudlin words—others start quarrels upon the slightest pretext, and come to blows and have to be pulled apart. Now the fat policeman wakens definitely, and feels of his club to see that it is ready for business. He has to be prompt—for these two-o'clock-in-the-morning fights, if they once get out of hand, are like a forest fire, and may mean the whole reserves at the station. The thing to do is to crack every fighting head that you see, before there are so many fighting heads that you cannot crack any of them. There is but scant account kept of cracked heads in back of the yards, for men who have to crack the heads of animals all day seem to get into the habit, and to practice on their friends, and even on their families, between times. This makes it a cause for congratulation that by modern methods a very few men can do the painfully necessary work of head-cracking for the whole of the cultured world.

There is no fight that night—perhaps because Jurgis, too, is watchful—even more so than the policeman. Jurgis has drunk a great deal, as any one naturally would on an occasion when it all has to be paid for, whether it is drunk or not; but he is a very steady man, and does not easily lose his temper. Only once there is a tight shave—and that is the fault of Marija Berczynskas. Marija has apparently concluded about two hours ago that if the altar in the corner, with the deity in soiled white, be not the true home of the muses, it is, at any rate, the nearest substitute on earth attainable. And Marija is just fighting drunk when there come to her ears the facts about the villains who have not paid that night. Marija goes on the warpath straight off, without even the preliminary of a good cursing, and when she is pulled off it is with the coat collars of two villains in her hands. Fortunately, the policeman is disposed to be reasonable, and so it is not Marija who is flung out of the place.

All this interrupts the music for not more than a minute or two. Then again the merciless tune begins—the tune that has been played for the last half-hour without one single change. It is an American tune this time, one which they have picked up on the streets; all seem to know the words of it—or, at any rate, the first line of it, which they hum to themselves, over and over again without rest: "In the good old summertime—in the good old summertime! In the good old summertime—in the good old summertime!" There seems to be something hypnotic about this, with its endlessly recurring dominant. It has put a stupor upon every one who hears it, as well as upon the men who are playing it. No one can get away from it, or even think of getting away from it; it is three o'clock in the morning, and they have danced out all their joy, and danced out all their strength, and all the strength that unlimited drink can lend them—and still there is no one among them who has the power to think of stopping. Promptly at seven o'clock this same Monday morning they will every one of them have to be in their places at Durham's or Brown's or Jones's, each in his working clothes. If one of them be a minute late, he will be docked an hour's pay, and if he be many minutes late, he will be apt to find his brass check turned to the wall, which will send him out to join the hungry mob that waits every morning at the gates of the packing houses, from six o'clock until nearly half-past eight. There is no exception to this rule, not even little Ona—who has asked for a holiday the day after her wedding day, a holiday without pay, and been refused. While there are so many who are anxious to work as you wish, there is no occasion for incommoding yourself with those who must work otherwise.

Little Ona is nearly ready to faint—and half in a stupor herself, because of the heavy scent in the room. She has not taken a drop, but every one else there is literally burning alcohol, as the lamps are burning oil; some of the men who are sound asleep in their chairs or on the floor are reeking of it so that you cannot go near them. Now and then Jurgis gazes at her hungrily—he has long since forgotten his shyness; but then the crowd is there, and he still waits and watches the door, where a carriage is supposed to come. It does not, and finally he will wait no longer, but comes up to Ona, who turns white and trembles. He puts her shawl about her and then his own coat. They live only two blocks away, and Jurgis does not care about the carriage.

There is almost no farewell—the dancers do not notice them, and all of the children and many of the old folks have fallen asleep of sheer exhaustion. Dede Antanas is asleep, and so are the Szedvilases, husband and wife, the former snoring in octaves. There is Teta Elzbieta, and Marija, sobbing loudly; and then there is only the silent night, with the stars beginning to pale a little in the east. Jurgis, without a word, lifts Ona in his arms, and strides out with her, and she sinks her head upon his shoulder with a moan. When he reaches home he is not sure whether she has fainted or is asleep, but when he has to hold her with one hand while he unlocks the door, he sees that she has opened her eyes.

"You shall not go to Brown's today, little one," he whispers, as he climbs the stairs; and she catches his arm in terror, gasping: "No! No! I dare not! It will ruin us!"

But he answers her again: "Leave it to me; leave it to me. I will earn more money—I will work harder."

CHAPTER 2

Jurgis talked lightly about work, because he was young. They told him stories about the breaking down of men, there in the stockyards of Chicago, and of what had happened to them afterward—stories to make your flesh creep, but Jurgis would only laugh. He had only been there four months, and he was young, and a giant besides. There was too much health in him. He could not even imagine how it would feel to be beaten. "That is well enough for men like you," he would say, "silpnas, puny fellows—but my back is broad."

Jurgis was like a boy, a boy from the country. He was the sort of man the bosses like to get hold of, the sort they make it a grievance they cannot get hold of. When he was told to go to a certain place, he would go there on the run. When he had nothing to do for the moment, he would stand round fidgeting, dancing, with the overflow of energy that was in him. If he were working in a line of men, the line always moved too slowly for him, and you could pick him out by his impatience and restlessness. That was why he had been picked out on one important occasion; for Jurgis had stood outside of Brown and Company's "Central Time Station" not more than half an hour, the second day of his arrival in Chicago, before he had been beckoned by one of the bosses. Of this he was very proud, and it made him more disposed than ever to laugh at the pessimists. In vain would they all tell him that there were men in that crowd from which he had been chosen who had stood there a month—yes, many months—and not been chosen yet. "Yes," he would say, "but what sort of men? Broken-down tramps and good-for-nothings, fellows who have spent all their money drinking, and want to get more for it. Do you want me to believe that with these arms"—and he would clench his fists and hold them up in the air, so that you might see the rolling muscles—"that with these arms people will ever let me starve?"

"It is plain," they would answer to this, "that you have come from the country, and from very far in the country." And this was the fact, for Jurgis had never seen a city, and scarcely even a fair-sized town, until he had set out to make his fortune in the world and earn his right to Ona. His father, and his father's father before him, and as many ancestors back as legend could go, had lived in that part of Lithuania known as Brelovicz, the Imperial Forest. This is a great tract of a hundred thousand acres, which from time immemorial has been a hunting preserve of the nobility. There are a very few peasants settled in it, holding title from ancient times; and one of these was Antanas Rudkus, who had been reared himself, and had reared his children in turn, upon half a dozen acres of cleared land in the midst of a wilderness. There had been one son besides Jurgis, and one sister. The former had been drafted into the army; that had been over ten years ago, but since that day nothing had ever been heard of him. The sister was married, and her husband had bought the place when old Antanas had decided to go with his son.

It was nearly a year and a half ago that Jurgis had met Ona, at a horse fair a hundred miles from home. Jurgis had never expected to get married—he had laughed at it as a foolish trap for a man to walk into; but here, without ever having spoken a word to her, with no more than the exchange of half a dozen smiles, he found himself, purple in the face with embarrassment and terror, asking her parents to sell her to him for his wife—and offering his father's two horses he had been sent to the fair to sell. But Ona's father proved as a rock—the girl was yet a child, and he was a rich man, and his daughter was not to be had in that way. So Jurgis went home with a heavy heart, and that spring and summer toiled and tried hard to forget. In the fall, after the harvest was over, he saw that it would not do, and tramped the full fortnight's journey that lay between him and Ona.

He found an unexpected state of affairs—for the girl's father had died, and his estate was tied up with creditors; Jurgis' heart leaped as he realized that now the prize was within his reach. There was Elzbieta Lukoszaite, Teta, or Aunt, as they called her, Ona's stepmother, and there were her six children, of all ages. There was also her brother Jonas, a dried-up little man who had worked upon the farm. They were people of great consequence, as it seemed to Jurgis, fresh out of the woods; Ona knew how to read, and knew many other things that he did not know, and now the farm had been sold, and the whole family was adrift—all they owned in the world being about seven hundred rubles which is half as many dollars. They would have had three times that, but it had gone to court, and the judge had decided against them, and it had cost the balance to get him to change his decision.

Ona might have married and left them, but she would not, for she loved Teta Elzbieta. It was Jonas who suggested that they all go to America, where a friend of his had gotten rich. He would work, for his part, and the women would work, and some of the children, doubtless—they would live somehow. Jurgis, too, had heard of America. That was a country where, they said, a man might earn three rubles a day; and Jurgis figured what three rubles a day would mean, with prices as they were where he lived, and decided forthwith that he would go to America and marry, and be a rich man in the bargain. In that country, rich or poor, a man was free, it was said; he did not have to go into the army, he did not have to pay out his money to rascally officials—he might do as he pleased, and count himself as good as any other man. So America was a place of which lovers and young people dreamed. If one could only manage to get the price of a passage, he could count his troubles at an end.

It was arranged that they should leave the following spring, and meantime Jurgis sold himself to a contractor for a certain time, and tramped nearly four hundred miles from home with a gang of men to work upon a railroad in Smolensk. This was a fearful experience, with filth and bad food and cruelty and overwork; but Jurgis stood it and came out in fine trim, and with eighty rubles sewed up in his coat. He did not drink or fight, because he was thinking all the time of Ona; and for the rest, he was a quiet, steady man, who did what he was told to, did not lose his temper often, and when he did lose it made the offender anxious that he should not lose it again. When they paid him off he dodged the company gamblers and dramshops, and so they tried to kill him; but he escaped, and tramped it home, working at odd jobs, and sleeping always with one eye open.

So in the summer time they had all set out for America. At the last moment there joined them Marija Berczynskas, who was a cousin of Ona's. Marija was an orphan, and had worked since childhood for a rich farmer of Vilna, who beat her regularly. It was only at the age of twenty that it had occurred to Marija to try her strength, when she had risen up and nearly murdered the man, and then come away.

There were twelve in all in the party, five adults and six children—and Ona, who was a little of both. They had a hard time on the passage; there was an agent who helped them, but he proved a scoundrel, and got them into a trap with some officials, and cost them a good deal of their precious money, which they clung to with such horrible fear. This happened to them again in New York—for, of course, they knew nothing about the country, and had no one to tell them, and it was easy for a man in a blue uniform to lead them away, and to take them to a hotel and keep them there, and make them pay enormous charges to get away. The law says that the rate card shall be on the door of a hotel, but it does not say that it shall be in Lithuanian.

It was in the stockyards that Jonas' friend had gotten rich, and so to Chicago the party was bound. They knew that one word, Chicago and that was all they needed to know, at least, until they reached the city. Then, tumbled out of the cars without ceremony, they were no better off than before; they stood staring down the vista of Dearborn Street, with its big black buildings towering in the distance, unable to realize that they had arrived, and why, when they said "Chicago," people no longer pointed in some direction, but instead looked perplexed, or laughed, or went on without paying any attention. They were pitiable in their helplessness; above all things they stood in deadly terror of any sort of person in official uniform, and so whenever they saw a policeman they would cross the street and hurry by. For the whole of the first day they wandered about in the midst of deafening confusion, utterly lost; and it was only at night that, cowering in the doorway of a house, they were finally discovered and taken by a policeman to the station. In the morning an interpreter was found, and they were taken and put upon a car, and taught a new word—"stockyards." Their delight at discovering that they were to get out of this adventure without losing another share of their possessions it would not be possible to describe.

They sat and stared out of the window. They were on a street which seemed to run on forever, mile after mile—thirty-four of them, if they had known it—and each side of it one uninterrupted row of wretched little two-story frame buildings. Down every side street they could see, it was the same—never a hill and never a hollow, but always the same endless vista of ugly and dirty little wooden buildings. Here and there would be a bridge crossing a filthy creek, with hard-baked mud shores and dingy sheds and docks along it; here and there would be a railroad crossing, with a tangle of switches, and locomotives puffing, and rattling freight cars filing by; here and there would be a great factory, a dingy building with innumerable windows in it, and immense volumes of smoke pouring from the chimneys, darkening the air above and making filthy the earth beneath. But after each of these interruptions, the desolate procession would begin again—the procession of dreary little buildings.

A full hour before the party reached the city they had begun to note the perplexing changes in the atmosphere. It grew darker all the time, and upon the earth the grass seemed to grow less green. Every minute, as the train sped on, the colors of things became dingier; the fields were grown parched and yellow, the landscape hideous and bare. And along with the thickening smoke they began to notice another circumstance, a strange, pungent odor. They were not sure that it was unpleasant, this odor; some might have called it sickening, but their taste in odors was not developed, and they were only sure that it was curious. Now, sitting in the trolley car, they realized that they were on their way to the home of it—that they had traveled all the way from Lithuania to it. It was now no longer something far off and faint, that you caught in whiffs; you could literally taste it, as well as smell it—you could take hold of it, almost, and examine it at your leisure. They were divided in their opinions about it. It was an elemental odor, raw and crude; it was rich, almost rancid, sensual, and strong. There were some who drank it in as if it were an intoxicant; there were others who put their handkerchiefs to their faces. The new emigrants were still tasting it, lost in wonder, when suddenly the car came to a halt, and the door was flung open, and a voice shouted—"Stockyards!"

They were left standing upon the corner, staring; down a side street there were two rows of brick houses, and between them a vista: half a dozen chimneys, tall as the tallest of buildings, touching the very sky—and leaping from them half a dozen columns of smoke, thick, oily, and black as night. It might have come from the center of the world, this smoke, where the fires of the ages still smolder. It came as if self-impelled, driving all before it, a perpetual explosion. It was inexhaustible; one stared, waiting to see it stop, but still the great streams rolled out. They spread in vast clouds overhead, writhing, curling; then, uniting in one giant river, they streamed away down the sky, stretching a black pall as far as the eye could reach.

Then the party became aware of another strange thing. This, too, like the color, was a thing elemental; it was a sound, a sound made up of ten thousand little sounds. You scarcely noticed it at first—it sunk into your consciousness, a vague disturbance, a trouble. It was like the murmuring of the bees in the spring, the whisperings of the forest; it suggested endless activity, the rumblings of a world in motion. It was only by an effort that one could realize that it was made by animals, that it was the distant lowing of ten thousand cattle, the distant grunting of ten thousand swine.

They would have liked to follow it up, but, alas, they had no time for adventures just then. The policeman on the corner was beginning to watch them; and so, as usual, they started up the street. Scarcely had they gone a block, however, before Jonas was heard to give a cry, and began pointing excitedly across the street. Before they could gather the meaning of his breathless ejaculations he had bounded away, and they saw him enter a shop, over which was a sign: "J. Szedvilas, Delicatessen." When he came out again it was in company with a very stout gentleman in shirt sleeves and an apron, clasping Jonas by both hands and laughing hilariously. Then Teta Elzbieta recollected suddenly that Szedvilas had been the name of the mythical friend who had made his fortune in America. To find that he had been making it in the delicatessen business was an extraordinary piece of good fortune at this juncture; though it was well on in the morning, they had not breakfasted, and the children were beginning to whimper.

Thus was the happy ending to a woeful voyage. The two families literally fell upon each other's necks—for it had been years since Jokubas Szedvilas had met a man from his part of Lithuania. Before half the day they were lifelong friends. Jokubas understood all the pitfalls of this new world, and could explain all of its mysteries; he could tell them the things they ought to have done in the different emergencies—and what was still more to the point, he could tell them what to do now. He would take them to poni Aniele, who kept a boardinghouse the other side of the yards; old Mrs. Jukniene, he explained, had not what one would call choice accommodations, but they might do for the moment. To this Teta Elzbieta hastened to respond that nothing could be too cheap to suit them just then; for they were quite terrified over the sums they had had to expend. A very few days of practical experience in this land of high wages had been sufficient to make clear to them the cruel fact that it was also a land of high prices, and that in it the poor man was almost as poor as in any other corner of the earth; and so there vanished in a night all the wonderful dreams of wealth that had been haunting Jurgis. What had made the discovery all the more painful was that they were spending, at American prices, money which they had earned at home rates of wages—and so were really being cheated by the world! The last two days they had all but starved themselves—it made them quite sick to pay the prices that the railroad people asked them for food.

Yet, when they saw the home of the Widow Jukniene they could not but recoil, even so, in all their journey they had seen nothing so bad as this. Poni Aniele had a four-room flat in one of that wilderness of two-story frame tenements that lie "back of the yards." There were four such flats in each building, and each of the four was a "boardinghouse" for the occupancy of foreigners—Lithuanians, Poles, Slovaks, or Bohemians. Some of these places were kept by private persons, some were cooperative. There would be an average of half a dozen boarders to each room—sometimes there were thirteen or fourteen to one room, fifty or sixty to a flat. Each one of the occupants furnished his own accommodations—that is, a mattress and some bedding. The mattresses would be spread upon the floor in rows—and there would be nothing else in the place except a stove. It was by no means unusual for two men to own the same mattress in common, one working by day and using it by night, and the other working at night and using it in the daytime. Very frequently a lodging house keeper would rent the same beds to double shifts of men.

Mrs. Jukniene was a wizened-up little woman, with a wrinkled face. Her home was unthinkably filthy; you could not enter by the front door at all, owing to the mattresses, and when you tried to go up the backstairs you found that she had walled up most of the porch with old boards to make a place to keep her chickens. It was a standing jest of the boarders that Aniele cleaned house by letting the chickens loose in the rooms. Undoubtedly this did keep down the vermin, but it seemed probable, in view of all the circumstances, that the old lady regarded it rather as feeding the chickens than as cleaning the rooms. The truth was that she had definitely given up the idea of cleaning anything, under pressure of an attack of rheumatism, which had kept her doubled up in one corner of her room for over a week; during which time eleven of her boarders, heavily in her debt, had concluded to try their chances of employment in Kansas City. This was July, and the fields were green. One never saw the fields, nor any green thing whatever, in Packingtown; but one could go out on the road and "hobo it," as the men phrased it, and see the country, and have a long rest, and an easy time riding on the freight cars.

Such was the home to which the new arrivals were welcomed. There was nothing better to be had—they might not do so well by looking further, for Mrs. Jukniene had at least kept one room for herself and her three little children, and now offered to share this with the women and the girls of the party. They could get bedding at a secondhand store, she explained; and they would not need any, while the weather was so hot—doubtless they would all sleep on the sidewalk such nights as this, as did nearly all of her guests. "Tomorrow," Jurgis said, when they were left alone, "tomorrow I will get a job, and perhaps Jonas will get one also; and then we can get a place of our own."

Later that afternoon he and Ona went out to take a walk and look about them, to see more of this district which was to be their home. In back of the yards the dreary two-story frame houses were scattered farther apart, and there were great spaces bare—that seemingly had been overlooked by the great sore of a city as it spread itself over the surface of the prairie. These bare places were grown up with dingy, yellow weeds, hiding innumerable tomato cans; innumerable children played upon them, chasing one another here and there, screaming and fighting. The most uncanny thing about this neighborhood was the number of the children; you thought there must be a school just out, and it was only after long acquaintance that you were able to realize that there was no school, but that these were the children of the neighborhood—that there were so many children to the block in Packingtown that nowhere on its streets could a horse and buggy move faster than a walk!

It could not move faster anyhow, on account of the state of the streets. Those through which Jurgis and Ona were walking resembled streets less than they did a miniature topographical map. The roadway was commonly several feet lower than the level of the houses, which were sometimes joined by high board walks; there were no pavements—there were mountains and valleys and rivers, gullies and ditches, and great hollows full of stinking green water. In these pools the children played, and rolled about in the mud of the streets; here and there one noticed them digging in it, after trophies which they had stumbled on. One wondered about this, as also about the swarms of flies which hung about the scene, literally blackening the air, and the strange, fetid odor which assailed one's nostrils, a ghastly odor, of all the dead things of the universe. It impelled the visitor to questions and then the residents would explain, quietly, that all this was "made" land, and that it had been "made" by using it as a dumping ground for the city garbage. After a few years the unpleasant effect of this would pass away, it was said; but meantime, in hot weather—and especially when it rained—the flies were apt to be annoying. Was it not unhealthful? the stranger would ask, and the residents would answer, "Perhaps; but there is no telling."

A little way farther on, and Jurgis and Ona, staring open-eyed and wondering, came to the place where this "made" ground was in process of making. Here was a great hole, perhaps two city blocks square, and with long files of garbage wagons creeping into it. The place had an odor for which there are no polite words; and it was sprinkled over with children, who raked in it from dawn till dark. Sometimes visitors from the packing houses would wander out to see this "dump," and they would stand by and debate as to whether the children were eating the food they got, or merely collecting it for the chickens at home. Apparently none of them ever went down to find out.

Beyond this dump there stood a great brickyard, with smoking chimneys. First they took out the soil to make bricks, and then they filled it up again with garbage, which seemed to Jurgis and Ona a felicitous arrangement, characteristic of an enterprising country like America. A little way beyond was another great hole, which they had emptied and not yet filled up. This held water, and all summer it stood there, with the near-by soil draining into it, festering and stewing in the sun; and then, when winter came, somebody cut the ice on it, and sold it to the people of the city. This, too, seemed to the newcomers an economical arrangement; for they did not read the newspapers, and their heads were not full of troublesome thoughts about "germs."

They stood there while the sun went down upon this scene, and the sky in the west turned blood-red, and the tops of the houses shone like fire. Jurgis and Ona were not thinking of the sunset, however—their backs were turned to it, and all their thoughts were of Packingtown, which they could see so plainly in the distance. The line of the buildings stood clear-cut and black against the sky; here and there out of the mass rose the great chimneys, with the river of smoke streaming away to the end of the world. It was a study in colors now, this smoke; in the sunset light it was black and brown and gray and purple. All the sordid suggestions of the place were gone—in the twilight it was a vision of power. To the two who stood watching while the darkness swallowed it up, it seemed a dream of wonder, with its talc of human energy, of things being done, of employment for thousands upon thousands of men, of opportunity and freedom, of life and love and joy. When they came away, arm in arm, Jurgis was saying, "Tomorrow I shall go there and get a job!"

CHAPTER 3

In his capacity as delicatessen vender, Jokubas Szedvilas had many acquaintances. Among these was one of the special policemen employed by Durham, whose duty it frequently was to pick out men for employment. Jokubas had never tried it, but he expressed a certainty that he could get some of his friends a job through this man. It was agreed, after consultation, that he should make the effort with old Antanas and with Jonas. Jurgis was confident of his ability to get work for himself, unassisted by any one. As we have said before, he was not mistaken in this. He had gone to Brown's and stood there not more than half an hour before one of the bosses noticed his form towering above the rest, and signaled to him. The colloquy which followed was brief and to the point:

"Speak English?"

"No; Lit-uanian." (Jurgis had studied this word carefully.)

"Job?"

"Je." (A nod.)

"Worked here before?"

"No 'stand."

(Signals and gesticulations on the part of the boss. Vigorous shakes of the head by Jurgis.)

"Shovel guts?"

"No 'stand." (More shakes of the head.)

"Zarnos. Pagaiksztis. Szluofa!" (Imitative motions.)

"Je."

"See door. Durys?" (Pointing.)

"Je."

"To-morrow, seven o'clock. Understand? Rytoj! Prieszpietys! Septyni!"

"Dekui, tamistai!" (Thank you, sir.) And that was all. Jurgis turned away, and then in a sudden rush the full realization of his triumph swept over him, and he gave a yell and a jump, and started off on a run. He had a job! He had a job! And he went all the way home as if upon wings, and burst into the house like a cyclone, to the rage of the numerous lodgers who had just turned in for their daily sleep.

Meantime Jokubas had been to see his friend the policeman, and received encouragement, so it was a happy party. There being no more to be done that day, the shop was left under the care of Lucija, and her husband sallied forth to show his friends the sights of Packingtown. Jokubas did this with the air of a country gentleman escorting a party of visitors over his estate; he was an old-time resident, and all these wonders had grown up under his eyes, and he had a personal pride in them. The packers might own the land, but he claimed the landscape, and there was no one to say nay to this.

They passed down the busy street that led to the yards. It was still early morning, and everything was at its high tide of activity. A steady stream of employees was pouring through the gate—employees of the higher sort, at this hour, clerks and stenographers and such. For the women there were waiting big two-horse wagons, which set off at a gallop as fast as they were filled. In the distance there was heard again the lowing of the cattle, a sound as of a far-off ocean calling. They followed it, this time, as eager as children in sight of a circus menagerie—which, indeed, the scene a good deal resembled. They crossed the railroad tracks, and then on each side of the street were the pens full of cattle; they would have stopped to look, but Jokubas hurried them on, to where there was a stairway and a raised gallery, from which everything could be seen. Here they stood, staring, breathless with wonder.

There is over a square mile of space in the yards, and more than half of it is occupied by cattle pens; north and south as far as the eye can reach there stretches a sea of pens. And they were all filled—so many cattle no one had ever dreamed existed in the world. Red cattle, black, white, and yellow cattle; old cattle and young cattle; great bellowing bulls and little calves not an hour born; meek-eyed milch cows and fierce, long-horned Texas steers. The sound of them here was as of all the barnyards of the universe; and as for counting them—it would have taken all day simply to count the pens. Here and there ran long alleys, blocked at intervals by gates; and Jokubas told them that the number of these gates was twenty-five thousand. Jokubas had recently been reading a newspaper article which was full of statistics such as that, and he was very proud as he repeated them and made his guests cry out with wonder. Jurgis too had a little of this sense of pride. Had he not just gotten a job, and become a sharer in all this activity, a cog in this marvelous machine? Here and there about the alleys galloped men upon horseback, booted, and carrying long whips; they were very busy, calling to each other, and to those who were driving the cattle. They were drovers and stock raisers, who had come from far states, and brokers and commission merchants, and buyers for all the big packing houses.

Here and there they would stop to inspect a bunch of cattle, and there would be a parley, brief and businesslike. The buyer would nod or drop his whip, and that would mean a bargain; and he would note it in his little book, along with hundreds of others he had made that morning. Then Jokubas pointed out the place where the cattle were driven to be weighed, upon a great scale that would weigh a hundred thousand pounds at once and record it automatically. It was near to the east entrance that they stood, and all along this east side of the yards ran the railroad tracks, into which the cars were run, loaded with cattle. All night long this had been going on, and now the pens were full; by tonight they would all be empty, and the same thing would be done again.

"And what will become of all these creatures?" cried Teta Elzbieta.

"By tonight," Jokubas answered, "they will all be killed and cut up; and over there on the other side of the packing houses are more railroad tracks, where the cars come to take them away."

There were two hundred and fifty miles of track within the yards, their guide went on to tell them. They brought about ten thousand head of cattle every day, and as many hogs, and half as many sheep—which meant some eight or ten million live creatures turned into food every year. One stood and watched, and little by little caught the drift of the tide, as it set in the direction of the packing houses. There were groups of cattle being driven to the chutes, which were roadways about fifteen feet wide, raised high above the pens. In these chutes the stream of animals was continuous; it was quite uncanny to watch them, pressing on to their fate, all unsuspicious a very river of death. Our friends were not poetical, and the sight suggested to them no metaphors of human destiny; they thought only of the wonderful efficiency of it all. The chutes into which the hogs went climbed high up—to the very top of the distant buildings; and Jokubas explained that the hogs went up by the power of their own legs, and then their weight carried them back through all the processes necessary to make them into pork.

"They don't waste anything here," said the guide, and then he laughed and added a witticism, which he was pleased that his unsophisticated friends should take to be his own: "They use everything about the hog except the squeal." In front of Brown's General Office building there grows a tiny plot of grass, and this, you may learn, is the only bit of green thing in Packingtown; likewise this jest about the hog and his squeal, the stock in trade of all the guides, is the one gleam of humor that you will find there.

After they had seen enough of the pens, the party went up the street, to the mass of buildings which occupy the center of the yards. These buildings, made of brick and stained with innumerable layers of Packingtown smoke, were painted all over with advertising signs, from which the visitor realized suddenly that he had come to the home of many of the torments of his life. It was here that they made those products with the wonders of which they pestered him so—by placards that defaced the landscape when he traveled, and by staring advertisements in the newspapers and magazines—by silly little jingles that he could not get out of his mind, and gaudy pictures that lurked for him around every street corner. Here was where they made Brown's Imperial Hams and Bacon, Brown's Dressed Beef, Brown's Excelsior Sausages! Here was the headquarters of Durham's Pure Leaf Lard, of Durham's Breakfast Bacon, Durham's Canned Beef, Potted Ham, Deviled Chicken, Peerless Fertilizer!

Entering one of the Durham buildings, they found a number of other visitors waiting; and before long there came a guide, to escort them through the place. They make a great feature of showing strangers through the packing plants, for it is a good advertisement. But Ponas Jokubas whispered maliciously that the visitors did not see any more than the packers wanted them to. They climbed a long series of stairways outside of the building, to the top of its five or six stories. Here was the chute, with its river of hogs, all patiently toiling upward; there was a place for them to rest to cool off, and then through another passageway they went into a room from which there is no returning for hogs.

It was a long, narrow room, with a gallery along it for visitors. At the head there was a great iron wheel, about twenty feet in circumference, with rings here and there along its edge. Upon both sides of this wheel there was a narrow space, into which came the hogs at the end of their journey; in the midst of them stood a great burly Negro, bare-armed and bare-chested. He was resting for the moment, for the wheel had stopped while men were cleaning up. In a minute or two, however, it began slowly to revolve, and then the men upon each side of it sprang to work. They had chains which they fastened about the leg of the nearest hog, and the other end of the chain they hooked into one of the rings upon the wheel. So, as the wheel turned, a hog was suddenly jerked off his feet and borne aloft.

At the same instant the car was assailed by a most terrifying shriek; the visitors started in alarm, the women turned pale and shrank back. The shriek was followed by another, louder and yet more agonizing—for once started upon that journey, the hog never came back; at the top of the wheel he was shunted off upon a trolley, and went sailing down the room. And meantime another was swung up, and then another, and another, until there was a double line of them, each dangling by a foot and kicking in frenzy—and squealing. The uproar was appalling, perilous to the eardrums; one feared there was too much sound for the room to hold—that the walls must give way or the ceiling crack. There were high squeals and low squeals, grunts, and wails of agony; there would come a momentary lull, and then a fresh outburst, louder than ever, surging up to a deafening climax. It was too much for some of the visitors—the men would look at each other, laughing nervously, and the women would stand with hands clenched, and the blood rushing to their faces, and the tears starting in their eyes.

Meantime, heedless of all these things, the men upon the floor were going about their work. Neither squeals of hogs nor tears of visitors made any difference to them; one by one they hooked up the hogs, and one by one with a swift stroke they slit their throats. There was a long line of hogs, with squeals and lifeblood ebbing away together; until at last each started again, and vanished with a splash into a huge vat of boiling water.

It was all so very businesslike that one watched it fascinated. It was porkmaking by machinery, porkmaking by applied mathematics. And yet somehow the most matter-of-fact person could not help thinking of the hogs; they were so innocent, they came so very trustingly; and they were so very human in their protests—and so perfectly within their rights! They had done nothing to deserve it; and it was adding insult to injury, as the thing was done here, swinging them up in this cold-blooded, impersonal way, without a pretense of apology, without the homage of a tear. Now and then a visitor wept, to be sure; but this slaughtering machine ran on, visitors or no visitors. It was like some horrible crime committed in a dungeon, all unseen and unheeded, buried out of sight and of memory.

One could not stand and watch very long without becoming philosophical, without beginning to deal in symbols and similes, and to hear the hog squeal of the universe. Was it permitted to believe that there was nowhere upon the earth, or above the earth, a heaven for hogs, where they were requited for all this suffering? Each one of these hogs was a separate creature. Some were white hogs, some were black; some were brown, some were spotted; some were old, some young; some were long and lean, some were monstrous. And each of them had an individuality of his own, a will of his own, a hope and a heart's desire; each was full of self-confidence, of self-importance, and a sense of dignity. And trusting and strong in faith he had gone about his business, the while a black shadow hung over him and a horrid Fate waited in his pathway. Now suddenly it had swooped upon him, and had seized him by the leg. Relentless, remorseless, it was; all his protests, his screams, were nothing to it—it did its cruel will with him, as if his wishes, his feelings, had simply no existence at all; it cut his throat and watched him gasp out his life. And now was one to believe that there was nowhere a god of hogs, to whom this hog personality was precious, to whom these hog squeals and agonies had a meaning? Who would take this hog into his arms and comfort him, reward him for his work well done, and show him the meaning of his sacrifice? Perhaps some glimpse of all this was in the thoughts of our humble-minded Jurgis, as he turned to go on with the rest of the party, and muttered: "Dieve—but I'm glad I'm not a hog!"

The carcass hog was scooped out of the vat by machinery, and then it fell to the second floor, passing on the way through a wonderful machine with numerous scrapers, which adjusted themselves to the size and shape of the animal, and sent it out at the other end with nearly all of its bristles removed. It was then again strung up by machinery, and sent upon another trolley ride; this time passing between two lines of men, who sat upon a raised platform, each doing a certain single thing to the carcass as it came to him. One scraped the outside of a leg; another scraped the inside of the same leg. One with a swift stroke cut the throat; another with two swift strokes severed the head, which fell to the floor and vanished through a hole. Another made a slit down the body; a second opened the body wider; a third with a saw cut the breastbone; a fourth loosened the entrails; a fifth pulled them out—and they also slid through a hole in the floor. There were men to scrape each side and men to scrape the back; there were men to clean the carcass inside, to trim it and wash it. Looking down this room, one saw, creeping slowly, a line of dangling hogs a hundred yards in length; and for every yard there was a man, working as if a demon were after him. At the end of this hog's progress every inch of the carcass had been gone over several times; and then it was rolled into the chilling room, where it stayed for twenty-four hours, and where a stranger might lose himself in a forest of freezing hogs.

Before the carcass was admitted here, however, it had to pass a government inspector, who sat in the doorway and felt of the glands in the neck for tuberculosis.

This government inspector did not have the manner of a man who was worked to death; he was apparently not haunted by a fear that the hog might get by him before he had finished his testing. If you were a sociable person, he was quite willing to enter into conversation with you, and to explain to you the deadly nature of the ptomaines which are found in tubercular pork; and while he was talking with you you could hardly be so ungrateful as to notice that a dozen carcasses were passing him untouched. This inspector wore a blue uniform, with brass buttons, and he gave an atmosphere of authority to the scene, and, as it were, put the stamp of official approval upon the things which were done in Durham's.

Jurgis went down the line with the rest of the visitors, staring open-mouthed, lost in wonder. He had dressed hogs himself in the forest of Lithuania; but he had never expected to live to see one hog dressed by several hundred men. It was like a wonderful poem to him, and he took it all in guilelessly—even to the conspicuous signs demanding immaculate cleanliness of the employees. Jurgis was vexed when the cynical Jokubas translated these signs with sarcastic comments, offering to take them to the secret rooms where the spoiled meats went to be doctored.

The party descended to the next floor, where the various waste materials were treated. Here came the entrails, to be scraped and washed clean for sausage casings; men and women worked here in the midst of a sickening stench, which caused the visitors to hasten by, gasping. To another room came all the scraps to be "tanked," which meant boiling and pumping off the grease to make soap and lard; below they took out the refuse, and this, too, was a region in which the visitors did not linger. In still other places men were engaged in cutting up the carcasses that had been through the chilling rooms. First there were the "splitters," the most expert workmen in the plant, who earned as high as fifty cents an hour, and did not a thing all day except chop hogs down the middle. Then there were "cleaver men," great giants with muscles of iron; each had two men to attend him—to slide the half carcass in front of him on the table, and hold it while he chopped it, and then turn each piece so that he might chop it once more. His cleaver had a blade about two feet long, and he never made but one cut; he made it so neatly, too, that his implement did not smite through and dull itself—there was just enough force for a perfect cut, and no more. So through various yawning holes there slipped to the floor below—to one room hams, to another forequarters, to another sides of pork. One might go down to this floor and see the pickling rooms, where the hams were put into vats, and the great smoke rooms, with their airtight iron doors. In other rooms they prepared salt pork—there were whole cellars full of it, built up in great towers to the ceiling. In yet other rooms they were putting up meats in boxes and barrels, and wrapping hams and bacon in oiled paper, sealing and labeling and sewing them. From the doors of these rooms went men with loaded trucks, to the platform where freight cars were waiting to be filled; and one went out there and realized with a start that he had come at last to the ground floor of this enormous building.

Then the party went across the street to where they did the killing of beef—where every hour they turned four or five hundred cattle into meat. Unlike the place they had left, all this work was done on one floor; and instead of there being one line of carcasses which moved to the workmen, there were fifteen or twenty lines, and the men moved from one to another of these. This made a scene of intense activity, a picture of human power wonderful to watch. It was all in one great room, like a circus amphitheater, with a gallery for visitors running over the center.

Along one side of the room ran a narrow gallery, a few feet from the floor; into which gallery the cattle were driven by men with goads which gave them electric shocks. Once crowded in here, the creatures were prisoned, each in a separate pen, by gates that shut, leaving them no room to turn around; and while they stood bellowing and plunging, over the top of the pen there leaned one of the "knockers," armed with a sledge hammer, and watching for a chance to deal a blow. The room echoed with the thuds in quick succession, and the stamping and kicking of the steers. The instant the animal had fallen, the "knocker" passed on to another; while a second man raised a lever, and the side of the pen was raised, and the animal, still kicking and struggling, slid out to the "killing bed." Here a man put shackles about one leg, and pressed another lever, and the body was jerked up into the air. There were fifteen or twenty such pens, and it was a matter of only a couple of minutes to knock fifteen or twenty cattle and roll them out. Then once more the gates were opened, and another lot rushed in; and so out of each pen there rolled a steady stream of carcasses, which the men upon the killing beds had to get out of the way.

The manner in which they did this was something to be seen and never forgotten. They worked with furious intensity, literally upon the run—at a pace with which there is nothing to be compared except a football game. It was all highly specialized labor, each man having his task to do; generally this would consist of only two or three specific cuts, and he would pass down the line of fifteen or twenty carcasses, making these cuts upon each. First there came the "butcher," to bleed them; this meant one swift stroke, so swift that you could not see it—only the flash of the knife; and before you could realize it, the man had darted on to the next line, and a stream of bright red was pouring out upon the floor. This floor was half an inch deep with blood, in spite of the best efforts of men who kept shoveling it through holes; it must have made the floor slippery, but no one could have guessed this by watching the men at work.

The carcass hung for a few minutes to bleed; there was no time lost, however, for there were several hanging in each line, and one was always ready. It was let down to the ground, and there came the "headsman," whose task it was to sever the head, with two or three swift strokes. Then came the "floorsman," to make the first cut in the skin; and then another to finish ripping the skin down the center; and then half a dozen more in swift succession, to finish the skinning. After they were through, the carcass was again swung up; and while a man with a stick examined the skin, to make sure that it had not been cut, and another rolled it up and tumbled it through one of the inevitable holes in the floor, the beef proceeded on its journey. There were men to cut it, and men to split it, and men to gut it and scrape it clean inside. There were some with hose which threw jets of boiling water upon it, and others who removed the feet and added the final touches. In the end, as with the hogs, the finished beef was run into the chilling room, to hang its appointed time.

The visitors were taken there and shown them, all neatly hung in rows, labeled conspicuously with the tags of the government inspectors—and some, which had been killed by a special process, marked with the sign of the kosher rabbi, certifying that it was fit for sale to the orthodox. And then the visitors were taken to the other parts of the building, to see what became of each particle of the waste material that had vanished through the floor; and to the pickling rooms, and the salting rooms, the canning rooms, and the packing rooms, where choice meat was prepared for shipping in refrigerator cars, destined to be eaten in all the four corners of civilization. Afterward they went outside, wandering about among the mazes of buildings in which was done the work auxiliary to this great industry. There was scarcely a thing needed in the business that Durham and Company did not make for themselves. There was a great steam power plant and an electricity plant. There was a barrel factory, and a boiler-repair shop. There was a building to which the grease was piped, and made into soap and lard; and then there was a factory for making lard cans, and another for making soap boxes. There was a building in which the bristles were cleaned and dried, for the making of hair cushions and such things; there was a building where the skins were dried and tanned, there was another where heads and feet were made into glue, and another where bones were made into fertilizer. No tiniest particle of organic matter was wasted in Durham's. Out of the horns of the cattle they made combs, buttons, hairpins, and imitation ivory; out of the shinbones and other big bones they cut knife and toothbrush handles, and mouthpieces for pipes; out of the hoofs they cut hairpins and buttons, before they made the rest into glue. From such things as feet, knuckles, hide clippings, and sinews came such strange and unlikely products as gelatin, isinglass, and phosphorus, bone black, shoe blacking, and bone oil. They had curled-hair works for the cattle tails, and a "wool pullery" for the sheepskins; they made pepsin from the stomachs of the pigs, and albumen from the blood, and violin strings from the ill-smelling entrails. When there was nothing else to be done with a thing, they first put it into a tank and got out of it all the tallow and grease, and then they made it into fertilizer. All these industries were gathered into buildings near by, connected by galleries and railroads with the main establishment; and it was estimated that they had handled nearly a quarter of a billion of animals since the founding of the plant by the elder Durham a generation and more ago. If you counted with it the other big plants—and they were now really all one—it was, so Jokubas informed them, the greatest aggregation of labor and capital ever gathered in one place. It employed thirty thousand men; it supported directly two hundred and fifty thousand people in its neighborhood, and indirectly it supported half a million. It sent its products to every country in the civilized world, and it furnished the food for no less than thirty million people!

To all of these things our friends would listen open-mouthed—it seemed to them impossible of belief that anything so stupendous could have been devised by mortal man. That was why to Jurgis it seemed almost profanity to speak about the place as did Jokubas, skeptically; it was a thing as tremendous as the universe—the laws and ways of its working no more than the universe to be questioned or understood. All that a mere man could do, it seemed to Jurgis, was to take a thing like this as he found it, and do as he was told; to be given a place in it and a share in its wonderful activities was a blessing to be grateful for, as one was grateful for the sunshine and the rain. Jurgis was even glad that he had not seen the place before meeting with his triumph, for he felt that the size of it would have overwhelmed him. But now he had been admitted—he was a part of it all! He had the feeling that this whole huge establishment had taken him under its protection, and had become responsible for his welfare. So guileless was he, and ignorant of the nature of business, that he did not even realize that he had become an employee of Brown's, and that Brown and Durham were supposed by all the world to be deadly rivals—were even required to be deadly rivals by the law of the land, and ordered to try to ruin each other under penalty of fine and imprisonment!

CHAPTER 4

Promptly at seven the next morning Jurgis reported for work. He came to the door that had been pointed out to him, and there he waited for nearly two hours. The boss had meant for him to enter, but had not said this, and so it was only when on his way out to hire another man that he came upon Jurgis. He gave him a good cursing, but as Jurgis did not understand a word of it he did not object. He followed the boss, who showed him where to put his street clothes, and waited while he donned the working clothes he had bought in a secondhand shop and brought with him in a bundle; then he led him to the "killing beds." The work which Jurgis was to do here was very simple, and it took him but a few minutes to learn it. He was provided with a stiff besom, such as is used by street sweepers, and it was his place to follow down the line the man who drew out the smoking entrails from the carcass of the steer; this mass was to be swept into a trap, which was then closed, so that no one might slip into it. As Jurgis came in, the first cattle of the morning were just making their appearance; and so, with scarcely time to look about him, and none to speak to any one, he fell to work. It was a sweltering day in July, and the place ran with steaming hot blood—one waded in it on the floor. The stench was almost overpowering, but to Jurgis it was nothing. His whole soul was dancing with joy—he was at work at last! He was at work and earning money! All day long he was figuring to himself. He was paid the fabulous sum of seventeen and a half cents an hour; and as it proved a rush day and he worked until nearly seven o'clock in the evening, he went home to the family with the tidings that he had earned more than a dollar and a half in a single day!

At home, also, there was more good news; so much of it at once that there was quite a celebration in Aniele's hall bedroom. Jonas had been to have an interview with the special policeman to whom Szedvilas had introduced him, and had been taken to see several of the bosses, with the result that one had promised him a job the beginning of the next week. And then there was Marija Berczynskas, who, fired with jealousy by the success of Jurgis, had set out upon her own responsibility to get a place. Marija had nothing to take with her save her two brawny arms and the word "job," laboriously learned; but with these she had marched about Packingtown all day, entering every door where there were signs of activity. Out of some she had been ordered with curses; but Marija was not afraid of man or devil, and asked every one she saw—visitors and strangers, or work-people like herself, and once or twice even high and lofty office personages, who stared at her as if they thought she was crazy. In the end, however, she had reaped her reward. In one of the smaller plants she had stumbled upon a room where scores of women and girls were sitting at long tables preparing smoked beef in cans; and wandering through room after room, Marija came at last to the place where the sealed cans were being painted and labeled, and here she had the good fortune to encounter the "forelady." Marija did not understand then, as she was destined to understand later, what there was attractive to a "forelady" about the combination of a face full of boundless good nature and the muscles of a dray horse; but the woman had told her to come the next day and she would perhaps give her a chance to learn the trade of painting cans. The painting of cans being skilled piecework, and paying as much as two dollars a day, Marija burst in upon the family with the yell of a Comanche Indian, and fell to capering about the room so as to frighten the baby almost into convulsions.

Better luck than all this could hardly have been hoped for; there was only one of them left to seek a place. Jurgis was determined that Teta Elzbieta should stay at home to keep house, and that Ona should help her. He would not have Ona working—he was not that sort of a man, he said, and she was not that sort of a woman. It would be a strange thing if a man like him could not support the family, with the help of the board of Jonas and Marija. He would not even hear of letting the children go to work—there were schools here in America for children, Jurgis had heard, to which they could go for nothing. That the priest would object to these schools was something of which he had as yet no idea, and for the present his mind was made up that the children of Teta Elzbieta should have as fair a chance as any other children. The oldest of them, little Stanislovas, was but thirteen, and small for his age at that; and while the oldest son of Szedvilas was only twelve, and had worked for over a year at Jones's, Jurgis would have it that Stanislovas should learn to speak English, and grow up to be a skilled man.

So there was only old Dede Antanas; Jurgis would have had him rest too, but he was forced to acknowledge that this was not possible, and, besides, the old man would not hear it spoken of—it was his whim to insist that he was as lively as any boy. He had come to America as full of hope as the best of them; and now he was the chief problem that worried his son. For every one that Jurgis spoke to assured him that it was a waste of time to seek employment for the old man in Packingtown. Szedvilas told him that the packers did not even keep the men who had grown old in their own service—to say nothing of taking on new ones. And not only was it the rule here, it was the rule everywhere in America, so far as he knew. To satisfy Jurgis he had asked the policeman, and brought back the message that the thing was not to be thought of. They had not told this to old Anthony, who had consequently spent the two days wandering about from one part of the yards to another, and had now come home to hear about the triumph of the others, smiling bravely and saying that it would be his turn another day.

Their good luck, they felt, had given them the right to think about a home; and sitting out on the doorstep that summer evening, they held consultation about it, and Jurgis took occasion to broach a weighty subject. Passing down the avenue to work that morning he had seen two boys leaving an advertisement from house to house; and seeing that there were pictures upon it, Jurgis had asked for one, and had rolled it up and tucked it into his shirt. At noontime a man with whom he had been talking had read it to him and told him a little about it, with the result that Jurgis had conceived a wild idea.

He brought out the placard, which was quite a work of art. It was nearly two feet long, printed on calendered paper, with a selection of colors so bright that they shone even in the moonlight. The center of the placard was occupied by a house, brilliantly painted, new, and dazzling. The roof of it was of a purple hue, and trimmed with gold; the house itself was silvery, and the doors and windows red. It was a two-story building, with a porch in front, and a very fancy scrollwork around the edges; it was complete in every tiniest detail, even the doorknob, and there was a hammock on the porch and white lace curtains in the windows. Underneath this, in one corner, was a picture of a husband and wife in loving embrace; in the opposite corner was a cradle, with fluffy curtains drawn over it, and a smiling cherub hovering upon silver-colored wings. For fear that the significance of all this should be lost, there was a label, in Polish, Lithuanian, and German—"Dom. Namai. Heim." "Why pay rent?" the linguistic circular went on to demand. "Why not own your own home? Do you know that you can buy one for less than your rent? We have built thousands of homes which are now occupied by happy families."—So it became eloquent, picturing the blissfulness of married life in a house with nothing to pay. It even quoted "Home, Sweet Home," and made bold to translate it into Polish—though for some reason it omitted the Lithuanian of this. Perhaps the translator found it a difficult matter to be sentimental in a language in which a sob is known as a gukcziojimas and a smile as a nusiszypsojimas.

Over this document the family pored long, while Ona spelled out its contents. It appeared that this house contained four rooms, besides a basement, and that it might be bought for fifteen hundred dollars, the lot and all. Of this, only three hundred dollars had to be paid down, the balance being paid at the rate of twelve dollars a month. These were frightful sums, but then they were in America, where people talked about such without fear. They had learned that they would have to pay a rent of nine dollars a month for a flat, and there was no way of doing better, unless the family of twelve was to exist in one or two rooms, as at present. If they paid rent, of course, they might pay forever, and be no better off; whereas, if they could only meet the extra expense in the beginning, there would at last come a time when they would not have any rent to pay for the rest of their lives.

They figured it up. There was a little left of the money belonging to Teta Elzbieta, and there was a little left to Jurgis. Marija had about fifty dollars pinned up somewhere in her stockings, and Grandfather Anthony had part of the money he had gotten for his farm. If they all combined, they would have enough to make the first payment; and if they had employment, so that they could be sure of the future, it might really prove the best plan. It was, of course, not a thing even to be talked of lightly; it was a thing they would have to sift to the bottom. And yet, on the other hand, if they were going to make the venture, the sooner they did it the better, for were they not paying rent all the time, and living in a most horrible way besides? Jurgis was used to dirt—there was nothing could scare a man who had been with a railroad gang, where one could gather up the fleas off the floor of the sleeping room by the handful. But that sort of thing would not do for Ona. They must have a better place of some sort soon—Jurgis said it with all the assurance of a man who had just made a dollar and fifty-seven cents in a single day. Jurgis was at a loss to understand why, with wages as they were, so many of the people of this district should live the way they did.

The next day Marija went to see her "forelady," and was told to report the first of the week, and learn the business of can-painter. Marija went home, singing out loud all the way, and was just in time to join Ona and her stepmother as they were setting out to go and make inquiry concerning the house. That evening the three made their report to the men—the thing was altogether as represented in the circular, or at any rate so the agent had said. The houses lay to the south, about a mile and a half from the yards; they were wonderful bargains, the gentleman had assured them—personally, and for their own good. He could do this, so he explained to them, for the reason that he had himself no interest in their sale—he was merely the agent for a company that had built them. These were the last, and the company was going out of business, so if any one wished to take advantage of this wonderful no-rent plan, he would have to be very quick. As a matter of fact there was just a little uncertainty as to whether there was a single house left; for the agent had taken so many people to see them, and for all he knew the company might have parted with the last. Seeing Teta Elzbieta's evident grief at this news, he added, after some hesitation, that if they really intended to make a purchase, he would send a telephone message at his own expense, and have one of the houses kept. So it had finally been arranged—and they were to go and make an inspection the following Sunday morning.

That was Thursday; and all the rest of the week the killing gang at Brown's worked at full pressure, and Jurgis cleared a dollar seventy-five every day. That was at the rate of ten and one-half dollars a week, or forty-five a month. Jurgis was not able to figure, except it was a very simple sum, but Ona was like lightning at such things, and she worked out the problem for the family. Marija and Jonas were each to pay sixteen dollars a month board, and the old man insisted that he could do the same as soon as he got a place—which might be any day now. That would make ninety-three dollars. Then Marija and Jonas were between them to take a third share in the house, which would leave only eight dollars a month for Jurgis to contribute to the payment. So they would have eighty-five dollars a month—or, supposing that Dede Antanas did not get work at once, seventy dollars a month—which ought surely to be sufficient for the support of a family of twelve.

An hour before the time on Sunday morning the entire party set out. They had the address written on a piece of paper, which they showed to some one now and then. It proved to be a long mile and a half, but they walked it, and half an hour or so later the agent put in an appearance. He was a smooth and florid personage, elegantly dressed, and he spoke their language freely, which gave him a great advantage in dealing with them. He escorted them to the house, which was one of a long row of the typical frame dwellings of the neighborhood, where architecture is a luxury that is dispensed with. Ona's heart sank, for the house was not as it was shown in the picture; the color scheme was different, for one thing, and then it did not seem quite so big. Still, it was freshly painted, and made a considerable show. It was all brand-new, so the agent told them, but he talked so incessantly that they were quite confused, and did not have time to ask many questions. There were all sorts of things they had made up their minds to inquire about, but when the time came, they either forgot them or lacked the courage. The other houses in the row did not seem to be new, and few of them seemed to be occupied. When they ventured to hint at this, the agent's reply was that the purchasers would be moving in shortly. To press the matter would have seemed to be doubting his word, and never in their lives had any one of them ever spoken to a person of the class called "gentleman" except with deference and humility.

The house had a basement, about two feet below the street line, and a single story, about six feet above it, reached by a flight of steps. In addition there was an attic, made by the peak of the roof, and having one small window in each end. The street in front of the house was unpaved and unlighted, and the view from it consisted of a few exactly similar houses, scattered here and there upon lots grown up with dingy brown weeds. The house inside contained four rooms, plastered white; the basement was but a frame, the walls being unplastered and the floor not laid. The agent explained that the houses were built that way, as the purchasers generally preferred to finish the basements to suit their own taste. The attic was also unfinished—the family had been figuring that in case of an emergency they could rent this attic, but they found that there was not even a floor, nothing but joists, and beneath them the lath and plaster of the ceiling below. All of this, however, did not chill their ardor as much as might have been expected, because of the volubility of the agent. There was no end to the advantages of the house, as he set them forth, and he was not silent for an instant; he showed them everything, down to the locks on the doors and the catches on the windows, and how to work them. He showed them the sink in the kitchen, with running water and a faucet, something which Teta Elzbieta had never in her wildest dreams hoped to possess. After a discovery such as that it would have seemed ungrateful to find any fault, and so they tried to shut their eyes to other defects.

Still, they were peasant people, and they hung on to their money by instinct; it was quite in vain that the agent hinted at promptness—they would see, they would see, they told him, they could not decide until they had had more time. And so they went home again, and all day and evening there was figuring and debating. It was an agony to them to have to make up their minds in a matter such as this. They never could agree all together; there were so many arguments upon each side, and one would be obstinate, and no sooner would the rest have convinced him than it would transpire that his arguments had caused another to waver. Once, in the evening, when they were all in harmony, and the house was as good as bought, Szedvilas came in and upset them again. Szedvilas had no use for property owning. He told them cruel stories of people who had been done to death in this "buying a home" swindle. They would be almost sure to get into a tight place and lose all their money; and there was no end of expense that one could never foresee; and the house might be good-for-nothing from top to bottom—how was a poor man to know? Then, too, they would swindle you with the contract—and how was a poor man to understand anything about a contract? It was all nothing but robbery, and there was no safety but in keeping out of it. And pay rent? asked Jurgis. Ah, yes, to be sure, the other answered, that too was robbery. It was all robbery, for a poor man. After half an hour of such depressing conversation, they had their minds quite made up that they had been saved at the brink of a precipice; but then Szedvilas went away, and Jonas, who was a sharp little man, reminded them that the delicatessen business was a failure, according to its proprietor, and that this might account for his pessimistic views. Which, of course, reopened the subject!

The controlling factor was that they could not stay where they were—they had to go somewhere. And when they gave up the house plan and decided to rent, the prospect of paying out nine dollars a month forever they found just as hard to face. All day and all night for nearly a whole week they wrestled with the problem, and then in the end Jurgis took the responsibility. Brother Jonas had gotten his job, and was pushing a truck in Durham's; and the killing gang at Brown's continued to work early and late, so that Jurgis grew more confident every hour, more certain of his mastership. It was the kind of thing the man of the family had to decide and carry through, he told himself. Others might have failed at it, but he was not the failing kind—he would show them how to do it. He would work all day, and all night, too, if need be; he would never rest until the house was paid for and his people had a home. So he told them, and so in the end the decision was made.

They had talked about looking at more houses before they made the purchase; but then they did not know where any more were, and they did not know any way of finding out. The one they had seen held the sway in their thoughts; whenever they thought of themselves in a house, it was this house that they thought of. And so they went and told the agent that they were ready to make the agreement. They knew, as an abstract proposition, that in matters of business all men are to be accounted liars; but they could not but have been influenced by all they had heard from the eloquent agent, and were quite persuaded that the house was something they had run a risk of losing by their delay. They drew a deep breath when he told them that they were still in time.

They were to come on the morrow, and he would have the papers all drawn up. This matter of papers was one in which Jurgis understood to the full the need of caution; yet he could not go himself—every one told him that he could not get a holiday, and that he might lose his job by asking. So there was nothing to be done but to trust it to the women, with Szedvilas, who promised to go with them. Jurgis spent a whole evening impressing upon them the seriousness of the occasion—and then finally, out of innumerable hiding places about their persons and in their baggage, came forth the precious wads of money, to be done up tightly in a little bag and sewed fast in the lining of Teta Elzbieta's dress.

Early in the morning they sallied forth. Jurgis had given them so many instructions and warned them against so many perils, that the women were quite pale with fright, and even the imperturbable delicatessen vender, who prided himself upon being a businessman, was ill at ease. The agent had the deed all ready, and invited them to sit down and read it; this Szedvilas proceeded to do—a painful and laborious process, during which the agent drummed upon the desk. Teta Elzbieta was so embarrassed that the perspiration came out upon her forehead in beads; for was not this reading as much as to say plainly to the gentleman's face that they doubted his honesty? Yet Jokubas Szedvilas read on and on; and presently there developed that he had good reason for doing so. For a horrible suspicion had begun dawning in his mind; he knitted his brows more and more as he read. This was not a deed of sale at all, so far as he could see—it provided only for the renting of the property! It was hard to tell, with all this strange legal jargon, words he had never heard before; but was not this plain—"the party of the first part hereby covenants and agrees to rent to the said party of the second part!" And then again—"a monthly rental of twelve dollars, for a period of eight years and four months!" Then Szedvilas took off his spectacles, and looked at the agent, and stammered a question.

The agent was most polite, and explained that that was the usual formula; that it was always arranged that the property should be merely rented. He kept trying to show them something in the next paragraph; but Szedvilas could not get by the word "rental"—and when he translated it to Teta Elzbieta, she too was thrown into a fright. They would not own the home at all, then, for nearly nine years! The agent, with infinite patience, began to explain again; but no explanation would do now. Elzbieta had firmly fixed in her mind the last solemn warning of Jurgis: "If there is anything wrong, do not give him the money, but go out and get a lawyer." It was an agonizing moment, but she sat in the chair, her hands clenched like death, and made a fearful effort, summoning all her powers, and gasped out her purpose.

Jokubas translated her words. She expected the agent to fly into a passion, but he was, to her bewilderment, as ever imperturbable; he even offered to go and get a lawyer for her, but she declined this. They went a long way, on purpose to find a man who would not be a confederate. Then let any one imagine their dismay, when, after half an hour, they came in with a lawyer, and heard him greet the agent by his first name! They felt that all was lost; they sat like prisoners summoned to hear the reading of their death warrant. There was nothing more that they could do—they were trapped! The lawyer read over the deed, and when he had read it he informed Szedvilas that it was all perfectly regular, that the deed was a blank deed such as was often used in these sales. And was the price as agreed? the old man asked—three hundred dollars down, and the balance at twelve dollars a month, till the total of fifteen hundred dollars had been paid? Yes, that was correct. And it was for the sale of such and such a house—the house and lot and everything? Yes,—and the lawyer showed him where that was all written. And it was all perfectly regular—there were no tricks about it of any sort? They were poor people, and this was all they had in the world, and if there was anything wrong they would be ruined. And so Szedvilas went on, asking one trembling question after another, while the eyes of the women folks were fixed upon him in mute agony. They could not understand what he was saying, but they knew that upon it their fate depended. And when at last he had questioned until there was no more questioning to be done, and the time came for them to make up their minds, and either close the bargain or reject it, it was all that poor Teta Elzbieta could do to keep from bursting into tears. Jokubas had asked her if she wished to sign; he had asked her twice—and what could she say? How did she know if this lawyer were telling the truth—that he was not in the conspiracy? And yet, how could she say so—what excuse could she give? The eyes of every one in the room were upon her, awaiting her decision; and at last, half blind with her tears, she began fumbling in her jacket, where she had pinned the precious money. And she brought it out and unwrapped it before the men. All of this Ona sat watching, from a corner of the room, twisting her hands together, meantime, in a fever of fright. Ona longed to cry out and tell her stepmother to stop, that it was all a trap; but there seemed to be something clutching her by the throat, and she could not make a sound. And so Teta Elzbieta laid the money on the table, and the agent picked it up and counted it, and then wrote them a receipt for it and passed them the deed. Then he gave a sigh of satisfaction, and rose and shook hands with them all, still as smooth and polite as at the beginning. Ona had a dim recollection of the lawyer telling Szedvilas that his charge was a dollar, which occasioned some debate, and more agony; and then, after they had paid that, too, they went out into the street, her stepmother clutching the deed in her hand. They were so weak from fright that they could not walk, but had to sit down on the way.

So they went home, with a deadly terror gnawing at their souls; and that evening Jurgis came home and heard their story, and that was the end. Jurgis was sure that they had been swindled, and were ruined; and he tore his hair and cursed like a madman, swearing that he would kill the agent that very night. In the end he seized the paper and rushed out of the house, and all the way across the yards to Halsted Street. He dragged Szedvilas out from his supper, and together they rushed to consult another lawyer. When they entered his office the lawyer sprang up, for Jurgis looked like a crazy person, with flying hair and bloodshot eyes. His companion explained the situation, and the lawyer took the paper and began to read it, while Jurgis stood clutching the desk with knotted hands, trembling in every nerve.

Once or twice the lawyer looked up and asked a question of Szedvilas; the other did not know a word that he was saying, but his eyes were fixed upon the lawyer's face, striving in an agony of dread to read his mind. He saw the lawyer look up and laugh, and he gave a gasp; the man said something to Szedvilas, and Jurgis turned upon his friend, his heart almost stopping.

"Well?" he panted.

"He says it is all right," said Szedvilas.

"All right!"

"Yes, he says it is just as it should be." And Jurgis, in his relief, sank down into a chair.

"Are you sure of it?" he gasped, and made Szedvilas translate question after question. He could not hear it often enough; he could not ask with enough variations. Yes, they had bought the house, they had really bought it. It belonged to them, they had only to pay the money and it would be all right. Then Jurgis covered his face with his hands, for there were tears in his eyes, and he felt like a fool. But he had had such a horrible fright; strong man as he was, it left him almost too weak to stand up.

The lawyer explained that the rental was a form—the property was said to be merely rented until the last payment had been made, the purpose being to make it easier to turn the party out if he did not make the payments. So long as they paid, however, they had nothing to fear, the house was all theirs.

Jurgis was so grateful that he paid the half dollar the lawyer asked without winking an eyelash, and then rushed home to tell the news to the family. He found Ona in a faint and the babies screaming, and the whole house in an uproar—for it had been believed by all that he had gone to murder the agent. It was hours before the excitement could be calmed; and all through that cruel night Jurgis would wake up now and then and hear Ona and her stepmother in the next room, sobbing softly to themselves.

CHAPTER 5

They had bought their home. It was hard for them to realize that the wonderful house was theirs to move into whenever they chose. They spent all their time thinking about it, and what they were going to put into it. As their week with Aniele was up in three days, they lost no time in getting ready. They had to make some shift to furnish it, and every instant of their leisure was given to discussing this.

A person who had such a task before him would not need to look very far in Packingtown—he had only to walk up the avenue and read the signs, or get into a streetcar, to obtain full information as to pretty much everything a human creature could need. It was quite touching, the zeal of people to see that his health and happiness were provided for. Did the person wish to smoke? There was a little discourse about cigars, showing him exactly why the Thomas Jefferson Five-cent Perfecto was the only cigar worthy of the name. Had he, on the other hand, smoked too much? Here was a remedy for the smoking habit, twenty-five doses for a quarter, and a cure absolutely guaranteed in ten doses. In innumerable ways such as this, the traveler found that somebody had been busied to make smooth his paths through the world, and to let him know what had been done for him. In Packingtown the advertisements had a style all of their own, adapted to the peculiar population. One would be tenderly solicitous. "Is your wife pale?" it would inquire. "Is she discouraged, does she drag herself about the house and find fault with everything? Why do you not tell her to try Dr. Lanahan's Life Preservers?" Another would be jocular in tone, slapping you on the back, so to speak. "Don't be a chump!" it would exclaim. "Go and get the Goliath Bunion Cure." "Get a move on you!" would chime in another. "It's easy, if you wear the Eureka Two-fifty Shoe."

Among these importunate signs was one that had caught the attention of the family by its pictures. It showed two very pretty little birds building themselves a home; and Marija had asked an acquaintance to read it to her, and told them that it related to the furnishing of a house. "Feather your nest," it ran—and went on to say that it could furnish all the necessary feathers for a four-room nest for the ludicrously small sum of seventy-five dollars. The particularly important thing about this offer was that only a small part of the money need be had at once—the rest one might pay a few dollars every month. Our friends had to have some furniture, there was no getting away from that; but their little fund of money had sunk so low that they could hardly get to sleep at night, and so they fled to this as their deliverance. There was more agony and another paper for Elzbieta to sign, and then one night when Jurgis came home, he was told the breathless tidings that the furniture had arrived and was safely stowed in the house: a parlor set of four pieces, a bedroom set of three pieces, a dining room table and four chairs, a toilet set with beautiful pink roses painted all over it, an assortment of crockery, also with pink roses—and so on. One of the plates in the set had been found broken when they unpacked it, and Ona was going to the store the first thing in the morning to make them change it; also they had promised three saucepans, and there had only two come, and did Jurgis think that they were trying to cheat them?

The next day they went to the house; and when the men came from work they ate a few hurried mouthfuls at Aniele's, and then set to work at the task of carrying their belongings to their new home. The distance was in reality over two miles, but Jurgis made two trips that night, each time with a huge pile of mattresses and bedding on his head, with bundles of clothing and bags and things tied up inside. Anywhere else in Chicago he would have stood a good chance of being arrested; but the policemen in Packingtown were apparently used to these informal movings, and contented themselves with a cursory examination now and then. It was quite wonderful to see how fine the house looked, with all the things in it, even by the dim light of a lamp: it was really home, and almost as exciting as the placard had described it. Ona was fairly dancing, and she and Cousin Marija took Jurgis by the arm and escorted him from room to room, sitting in each chair by turns, and then insisting that he should do the same. One chair squeaked with his great weight, and they screamed with fright, and woke the baby and brought everybody running. Altogether it was a great day; and tired as they were, Jurgis and Ona sat up late, contented simply to hold each other and gaze in rapture about the room. They were going to be married as soon as they could get everything settled, and a little spare money put by; and this was to be their home—that little room yonder would be theirs!

It was in truth a never-ending delight, the fixing up of this house. They had no money to spend for the pleasure of spending, but there were a few absolutely necessary things, and the buying of these was a perpetual adventure for Ona. It must always be done at night, so that Jurgis could go along; and even if it were only a pepper cruet, or half a dozen glasses for ten cents, that was enough for an expedition. On Saturday night they came home with a great basketful of things, and spread them out on the table, while every one stood round, and the children climbed up on the chairs, or howled to be lifted up to see. There were sugar and salt and tea and crackers, and a can of lard and a milk pail, and a scrubbing brush, and a pair of shoes for the second oldest boy, and a can of oil, and a tack hammer, and a pound of nails. These last were to be driven into the walls of the kitchen and the bedrooms, to hang things on; and there was a family discussion as to the place where each one was to be driven. Then Jurgis would try to hammer, and hit his fingers because the hammer was too small, and get mad because Ona had refused to let him pay fifteen cents more and get a bigger hammer; and Ona would be invited to try it herself, and hurt her thumb, and cry out, which necessitated the thumb's being kissed by Jurgis. Finally, after every one had had a try, the nails would be driven, and something hung up. Jurgis had come home with a big packing box on his head, and he sent Jonas to get another that he had bought. He meant to take one side out of these tomorrow, and put shelves in them, and make them into bureaus and places to keep things for the bedrooms. The nest which had been advertised had not included feathers for quite so many birds as there were in this family.

They had, of course, put their dining table in the kitchen, and the dining room was used as the bedroom of Teta Elzbieta and five of her children. She and the two youngest slept in the only bed, and the other three had a mattress on the floor. Ona and her cousin dragged a mattress into the parlor and slept at night, and the three men and the oldest boy slept in the other room, having nothing but the very level floor to rest on for the present. Even so, however, they slept soundly—it was necessary for Teta Elzbieta to pound more than once on the door at a quarter past five every morning. She would have ready a great pot full of steaming black coffee, and oatmeal and bread and smoked sausages; and then she would fix them their dinner pails with more thick slices of bread with lard between them—they could not afford butter—and some onions and a piece of cheese, and so they would tramp away to work.

This was the first time in his life that he had ever really worked, it seemed to Jurgis; it was the first time that he had ever had anything to do which took all he had in him. Jurgis had stood with the rest up in the gallery and watched the men on the killing beds, marveling at their speed and power as if they had been wonderful machines; it somehow never occurred to one to think of the flesh-and-blood side of it—that is, not until he actually got down into the pit and took off his coat. Then he saw things in a different light, he got at the inside of them. The pace they set here, it was one that called for every faculty of a man—from the instant the first steer fell till the sounding of the noon whistle, and again from half-past twelve till heaven only knew what hour in the late afternoon or evening, there was never one instant's rest for a man, for his hand or his eye or his brain. Jurgis saw how they managed it; there were portions of the work which determined the pace of the rest, and for these they had picked men whom they paid high wages, and whom they changed frequently. You might easily pick out these pacemakers, for they worked under the eye of the bosses, and they worked like men possessed. This was called "speeding up the gang," and if any man could not keep up with the pace, there were hundreds outside begging to try.

Yet Jurgis did not mind it; he rather enjoyed it. It saved him the necessity of flinging his arms about and fidgeting as he did in most work. He would laugh to himself as he ran down the line, darting a glance now and then at the man ahead of him. It was not the pleasantest work one could think of, but it was necessary work; and what more had a man the right to ask than a chance to do something useful, and to get good pay for doing it?

So Jurgis thought, and so he spoke, in his bold, free way; very much to his surprise, he found that it had a tendency to get him into trouble. For most of the men here took a fearfully different view of the thing. He was quite dismayed when he first began to find it out—that most of the men hated their work. It seemed strange, it was even terrible, when you came to find out the universality of the sentiment; but it was certainly the fact—they hated their work. They hated the bosses and they hated the owners; they hated the whole place, the whole neighborhood—even the whole city, with an all-inclusive hatred, bitter and fierce. Women and little children would fall to cursing about it; it was rotten, rotten as hell—everything was rotten. When Jurgis would ask them what they meant, they would begin to get suspicious, and content themselves with saying, "Never mind, you stay here and see for yourself."

One of the first problems that Jurgis ran upon was that of the unions. He had had no experience with unions, and he had to have it explained to him that the men were banded together for the purpose of fighting for their rights. Jurgis asked them what they meant by their rights, a question in which he was quite sincere, for he had not any idea of any rights that he had, except the right to hunt for a job, and do as he was told when he got it. Generally, however, this harmless question would only make his fellow workingmen lose their tempers and call him a fool. There was a delegate of the butcher-helpers' union who came to see Jurgis to en-roll him; and when Jurgis found that this meant that he would have to part with some of his money, he froze up directly, and the delegate, who was an Irishman and only knew a few words of Lithuanian, lost his temper and began to threaten him. In the end Jurgis got into a fine rage, and made it sufficiently plain that it would take more than one Irishman to scare him into a union. Little by little he gathered that the main thing the men wanted was to put a stop to the habit of "speeding-up"; they were trying their best to force a lessening of the pace, for there were some, they said, who could not keep up with it, whom it was killing. But Jurgis had no sympathy with such ideas as this—he could do the work himself, and so could the rest of them, he declared, if they were good for anything. If they couldn't do it, let them go somewhere else. Jurgis had not studied the books, and he would not have known how to pronounce "laissez faire"; but he had been round the world enough to know that a man has to shift for himself in it, and that if he gets the worst of it, there is nobody to listen to him holler.

Yet there have been known to be philosophers and plain men who swore by Malthus in the books, and would, nevertheless, subscribe to a relief fund in time of a famine. It was the same with Jurgis, who consigned the unfit to destruction, while going about all day sick at heart because of his poor old father, who was wandering somewhere in the yards begging for a chance to earn his bread. Old Antanas had been a worker ever since he was a child; he had run away from home when he was twelve, because his father beat him for trying to learn to read. And he was a faithful man, too; he was a man you might leave alone for a month, if only you had made him understand what you wanted him to do in the meantime. And now here he was, worn out in soul and body, and with no more place in the world than a sick dog. He had his home, as it happened, and some one who would care for him if he never got a job; but his son could not help thinking, suppose this had not been the case. Antanas Rudkus had been into every building in Packingtown by this time, and into nearly every room; he had stood mornings among the crowd of applicants till the very policemen had come to know his face and to tell him to go home and give it up. He had been likewise to all the stores and saloons for a mile about, begging for some little thing to do; and everywhere they had ordered him out, sometimes with curses, and not once even stopping to ask him a question.

So, after all, there was a crack in the fine structure of Jurgis' faith in things as they are. The crack was wide while Dede Antanas was hunting a job—and it was yet wider when he finally got it. For one evening the old man came home in a great state of excitement, with the tale that he had been approached by a man in one of the corridors of the pickle rooms of Durham's, and asked what he would pay to get a job. He had not known what to make of this at first; but the man had gone on with matter-of-fact frankness to say that he could get him a job, provided that he were willing to pay one-third of his wages for it. Was he a boss? Antanas had asked; to which the man had replied that that was nobody's business, but that he could do what he said.

Jurgis had made some friends by this time, and he sought one of them and asked what this meant. The friend, who was named Tamoszius Kuszleika, was a sharp little man who folded hides on the killing beds, and he listened to what Jurgis had to say without seeming at all surprised. They were common enough, he said, such cases of petty graft. It was simply some boss who proposed to add a little to his income. After Jurgis had been there awhile he would know that the plants were simply honeycombed with rottenness of that sort—the bosses grafted off the men, and they grafted off each other; and some day the superintendent would find out about the boss, and then he would graft off the boss. Warming to the subject, Tamoszius went on to explain the situation. Here was Durham's, for instance, owned by a man who was trying to make as much money out of it as he could, and did not care in the least how he did it; and underneath him, ranged in ranks and grades like an army, were managers and superintendents and foremen, each one driving the man next below him and trying to squeeze out of him as much work as possible. And all the men of the same rank were pitted against each other; the accounts of each were kept separately, and every man lived in terror of losing his job, if another made a better record than he. So from top to bottom the place was simply a seething caldron of jealousies and hatreds; there was no loyalty or decency anywhere about it, there was no place in it where a man counted for anything against a dollar. And worse than there being no decency, there was not even any honesty. The reason for that? Who could say? It must have been old Durham in the beginning; it was a heritage which the self-made merchant had left to his son, along with his millions.

Jurgis would find out these things for himself, if he stayed there long enough; it was the men who had to do all the dirty jobs, and so there was no deceiving them; and they caught the spirit of the place, and did like all the rest. Jurgis had come there, and thought he was going to make himself useful, and rise and become a skilled man; but he would soon find out his error—for nobody rose in Packingtown by doing good work. You could lay that down for a rule—if you met a man who was rising in Packingtown, you met a knave. That man who had been sent to Jurgis' father by the boss, he would rise; the man who told tales and spied upon his fellows would rise; but the man who minded his own business and did his work—why, they would "speed him up" till they had worn him out, and then they would throw him into the gutter.

Jurgis went home with his head buzzing. Yet he could not bring himself to believe such things—no, it could not be so. Tamoszius was simply another of the grumblers. He was a man who spent all his time fiddling; and he would go to parties at night and not get home till sunrise, and so of course he did not feel like work. Then, too, he was a puny little chap; and so he had been left behind in the race, and that was why he was sore. And yet so many strange things kept coming to Jurgis' notice every day!

He tried to persuade his father to have nothing to do with the offer. But old Antanas had begged until he was worn out, and all his courage was gone; he wanted a job, any sort of a job. So the next day he went and found the man who had spoken to him, and promised to bring him a third of all he earned; and that same day he was put to work in Durham's cellars. It was a "pickle room," where there was never a dry spot to stand upon, and so he had to take nearly the whole of his first week's earnings to buy him a pair of heavy-soled boots. He was a "squeedgie" man; his job was to go about all day with a long-handled mop, swabbing up the floor. Except that it was damp and dark, it was not an unpleasant job, in summer.

Now Antanas Rudkus was the meekest man that God ever put on earth; and so Jurgis found it a striking confirmation of what the men all said, that his father had been at work only two days before he came home as bitter as any of them, and cursing Durham's with all the power of his soul. For they had set him to cleaning out the traps; and the family sat round and listened in wonder while he told them what that meant. It seemed that he was working in the room where the men prepared the beef for canning, and the beef had lain in vats full of chemicals, and men with great forks speared it out and dumped it into trucks, to be taken to the cooking room. When they had speared out all they could reach, they emptied the vat on the floor, and then with shovels scraped up the balance and dumped it into the truck. This floor was filthy, yet they set Antanas with his mop slopping the "pickle" into a hole that connected with a sink, where it was caught and used over again forever; and if that were not enough, there was a trap in the pipe, where all the scraps of meat and odds and ends of refuse were caught, and every few days it was the old man's task to clean these out, and shovel their contents into one of the trucks with the rest of the meat!

This was the experience of Antanas; and then there came also Jonas and Marija with tales to tell. Marija was working for one of the independent packers, and was quite beside herself and outrageous with triumph over the sums of money she was making as a painter of cans. But one day she walked home with a pale-faced little woman who worked opposite to her, Jadvyga Marcinkus by name, and Jadvyga told her how she, Marija, had chanced to get her job. She had taken the place of an Irishwoman who had been working in that factory ever since any one could remember. For over fifteen years, so she declared. Mary Dennis was her name, and a long time ago she had been seduced, and had a little boy; he was a cripple, and an epileptic, but still he was all that she had in the world to love, and they had lived in a little room alone somewhere back of Halsted Street, where the Irish were. Mary had had consumption, and all day long you might hear her coughing as she worked; of late she had been going all to pieces, and when Marija came, the "forelady" had suddenly decided to turn her off. The forelady had to come up to a certain standard herself, and could not stop for sick people, Jadvyga explained. The fact that Mary had been there so long had not made any difference to her—it was doubtful if she even knew that, for both the forelady and the superintendent were new people, having only been there two or three years themselves. Jadvyga did not know what had become of the poor creature; she would have gone to see her, but had been sick herself. She had pains in her back all the time, Jadvyga explained, and feared that she had womb trouble. It was not fit work for a woman, handling fourteen-pound cans all day.

It was a striking circumstance that Jonas, too, had gotten his job by the misfortune of some other person. Jonas pushed a truck loaded with hams from the smoke rooms on to an elevator, and thence to the packing rooms. The trucks were all of iron, and heavy, and they put about threescore hams on each of them, a load of more than a quarter of a ton. On the uneven floor it was a task for a man to start one of these trucks, unless he was a giant; and when it was once started he naturally tried his best to keep it going. There was always the boss prowling about, and if there was a second's delay he would fall to cursing; Lithuanians and Slovaks and such, who could not understand what was said to them, the bosses were wont to kick about the place like so many dogs. Therefore these trucks went for the most part on the run; and the predecessor of Jonas had been jammed against the wall by one and crushed in a horrible and nameless manner.

All of these were sinister incidents; but they were trifles compared to what Jurgis saw with his own eyes before long. One curious thing he had noticed, the very first day, in his profession of shoveler of guts; which was the sharp trick of the floor bosses whenever there chanced to come a "slunk" calf. Any man who knows anything about butchering knows that the flesh of a cow that is about to calve, or has just calved, is not fit for food. A good many of these came every day to the packing houses—and, of course, if they had chosen, it would have been an easy matter for the packers to keep them till they were fit for food. But for the saving of time and fodder, it was the law that cows of that sort came along with the others, and whoever noticed it would tell the boss, and the boss would start up a conversation with the government inspector, and the two would stroll away. So in a trice the carcass of the cow would be cleaned out, and entrails would have vanished; it was Jurgis' task to slide them into the trap, calves and all, and on the floor below they took out these "slunk" calves, and butchered them for meat, and used even the skins of them.

One day a man slipped and hurt his leg; and that afternoon, when the last of the cattle had been disposed of, and the men were leaving, Jurgis was ordered to remain and do some special work which this injured man had usually done. It was late, almost dark, and the government inspectors had all gone, and there were only a dozen or two of men on the floor. That day they had killed about four thousand cattle, and these cattle had come in freight trains from far states, and some of them had got hurt. There were some with broken legs, and some with gored sides; there were some that had died, from what cause no one could say; and they were all to be disposed of, here in darkness and silence. "Downers," the men called them; and the packing house had a special elevator upon which they were raised to the killing beds, where the gang proceeded to handle them, with an air of businesslike nonchalance which said plainer than any words that it was a matter of everyday routine. It took a couple of hours to get them out of the way, and in the end Jurgis saw them go into the chilling rooms with the rest of the meat, being carefully scattered here and there so that they could not be identified. When he came home that night he was in a very somber mood, having begun to see at last how those might be right who had laughed at him for his faith in America.

CHAPTER 6

Jurgis and Ona were very much in love; they had waited a long time—it was now well into the second year, and Jurgis judged everything by the criterion of its helping or hindering their union. All his thoughts were there; he accepted the family because it was a part of Ona. And he was interested in the house because it was to be Ona's home. Even the tricks and cruelties he saw at Durham's had little meaning for him just then, save as they might happen to affect his future with Ona.

The marriage would have been at once, if they had had their way; but this would mean that they would have to do without any wedding feast, and when they suggested this they came into conflict with the old people. To Teta Elzbieta especially the very suggestion was an affliction. What! she would cry. To be married on the roadside like a parcel of beggars! No! No!—Elzbieta had some traditions behind her; she had been a person of importance in her girlhood—had lived on a big estate and had servants, and might have married well and been a lady, but for the fact that there had been nine daughters and no sons in the family. Even so, however, she knew what was decent, and clung to her traditions with desperation. They were not going to lose all caste, even if they had come to be unskilled laborers in Packingtown; and that Ona had even talked of omitting a *veselija* was enough to keep her stepmother lying awake all night. It was in vain for them to say that they had so few friends; they were bound to have friends in time, and then the friends would talk about it. They must not give up what was right for a little money—if they did, the money would never do them any good, they could depend upon that. And Elzbieta would call upon Dede Antanas to support her; there was a fear in the souls of these two, lest this journey to a new country might somehow undermine the old home virtues of their children. The very first Sunday they had all been taken to mass; and poor as they were, Elzbieta had felt it advisable to invest a little of her resources in a representation of the babe of Bethlehem, made in plaster, and painted in brilliant colors. Though it was only a foot high, there was a shrine with four snow-white steeples, and the Virgin standing with her child in her arms, and the kings and shepherds and wise men bowing down before him. It had cost fifty cents; but Elzbieta had a feeling that money spent for such things was not to be counted too closely, it would come back in hidden ways. The piece was beautiful on the parlor mantel, and one could not have a home without some sort of ornament.

The cost of the wedding feast would, of course, be returned to them; but the problem was to raise it even temporarily. They had been in the neighborhood so short a time that they could not get much credit, and there was no one except Szedvilas from whom they could borrow even a little. Evening after evening Jurgis and Ona would sit and figure the expenses, calculating the term of their separation. They could not possibly manage it decently for less than two hundred dollars, and even though they were welcome to count in the whole of the earnings of Marija and Jonas, as a loan, they could not hope to raise this sum in less than four or five months. So Ona began thinking of seeking employment herself, saying that if she had even ordinarily good luck, she might be able to take two months off the time. They were just beginning to adjust themselves to this necessity, when out of the clear sky there fell a thunderbolt upon them—a calamity that scattered all their hopes to the four winds.

About a block away from them there lived another Lithuanian family, consisting of an elderly widow and one grown son; their name was Majauszkis, and our friends struck up an acquaintance with them before long. One evening they came over for a visit, and naturally the first subject upon which the conversation turned was the neighborhood and its history; and then Grandmother Majauszkiene, as the old lady was called, proceeded to recite to them a string of horrors that fairly froze their blood. She was a wrinkled-up and wizened personage—she must have been eighty—and as she mumbled the grim story through her toothless gums, she seemed a very old witch to them. Grandmother Majauszkiene had lived in the midst of misfortune so long that it had come to be her element, and she talked about starvation, sickness, and death as other people might about weddings and holidays.

The thing came gradually. In the first place as to the house they had bought, it was not new at all, as they had supposed; it was about fifteen years old, and there was nothing new upon it but the paint, which was so bad that it needed to be put on new every year or two. The house was one of a whole row that was built by a company which existed to make money by swindling poor people. The family had paid fifteen hundred dollars for it, and it had not cost the builders five hundred, when it was new. Grandmother Majauszkiene knew that because her son belonged to a political organization with a contractor who put up exactly such houses. They used the very flimsiest and cheapest material; they built the houses a dozen at a time, and they cared about nothing at all except the outside shine. The family could take her word as to the trouble they would have, for she had been through it all—she and her son had bought their house in exactly the same way. They had fooled the company, however, for her son was a skilled man, who made as high as a hundred dollars a month, and as he had had sense enough not to marry, they had been able to pay for the house.

Grandmother Majauszkiene saw that her friends were puzzled at this remark; they did not quite see how paying for the house was "fooling the company." Evidently they were very inexperienced. Cheap as the houses were, they were sold with the idea that the people who bought them would not be able to pay for them. When they failed—if it were only by a single month—they would lose the house and all that they had paid on it, and then the company would sell it over again. And did they often get a chance to do that? Dieve! (Grandmother Majauszkiene raised her hands.) They did it—how often no one could say, but certainly more than half of the time. They might ask any one who knew anything at all about Packingtown as to that; she had been living here ever since this house was built, and she could tell them all about it. And had it ever been sold before? Susimilkie! Why, since it had been built, no less than four families that their informant could name had tried to buy it and failed. She would tell them a little about it.

The first family had been Germans. The families had all been of different nationalities—there had been a representative of several races that had displaced each other in the stockyards. Grandmother Majauszkiene had come to America with her son at a time when so far as she knew there was only one other Lithuanian family in the district; the workers had all been Germans then—skilled cattle butchers that the packers had brought from abroad to start the business. Afterward, as cheaper labor had come, these Germans had moved away. The next were the Irish—there had been six or eight years when Packingtown had been a regular Irish city. There were a few colonies of them still here, enough to run all the unions and the police force and get all the graft; but most of those who were working in the packing houses had gone away at the next drop in wages—after the big strike. The Bohemians had come then, and after them the Poles. People said that old man Durham himself was responsible for these immigrations; he had sworn that he would fix the people of Packingtown so that they would never again call a strike on him, and so he had sent his agents into every city and village in Europe to spread the tale of the chances of work and high wages at the stockyards. The people had come in hordes; and old Durham had squeezed them tighter and tighter, speeding them up and grinding them to pieces and sending for new ones. The Poles, who had come by tens of thousands, had been driven to the wall by the Lithuanians, and now the Lithuanians were giving way to the Slovaks. Who there was poorer and more miserable than the Slovaks, Grandmother Majauszkiene had no idea, but the packers would find them, never fear. It was easy to bring them, for wages were really much higher, and it was only when it was too late that the poor people found out that everything else was higher too. They were like rats in a trap, that was the truth; and more of them were piling in every day. By and by they would have their revenge, though, for the thing was getting beyond human endurance, and the people would rise and murder the packers. Grandmother Majauszkiene was a socialist, or some such strange thing; another son of hers was working in the mines of Siberia, and the old lady herself had made speeches in her time—which made her seem all the more terrible to her present auditors.

They called her back to the story of the house. The German family had been a good sort. To be sure there had been a great many of them, which was a common failing in Packingtown; but they had worked hard, and the father had been a steady man, and they had a good deal more than half paid for the house. But he had been killed in an elevator accident in Durham's.

Then there had come the Irish, and there had been lots of them, too; the husband drank and beat the children—the neighbors could hear them shrieking any night. They were behind with their rent all the time, but the company was good to them; there was some politics back of that, Grandmother Majauszkiene could not say just what, but the Laffertys had belonged to the "War Whoop League," which was a sort of political club of all the thugs and rowdies in the district; and if you belonged to that, you could never be arrested for anything. Once upon a time old Lafferty had been caught with a gang that had stolen cows from several of the poor people of the neighborhood and butchered them in an old shanty back of the yards and sold them. He had been in jail only three days for it, and had come out laughing, and had not even lost his place in the packing house. He had gone all to ruin with the drink, however, and lost his power; one of his sons, who was a good man, had kept him and the family up for a year or two, but then he had got sick with consumption.

That was another thing, Grandmother Majauszkiene interrupted herself—this house was unlucky. Every family that lived in it, some one was sure to get consumption. Nobody could tell why that was; there must be something about the house, or the way it was built—some folks said it was because the building had been begun in the dark of the moon. There were dozens of houses that way in Packingtown. Sometimes there would be a particular room that you could point out—if anybody slept in that room he was just as good as dead. With this house it had been the Irish first; and then a Bohemian family had lost a child of it—though, to be sure, that was uncertain, since it was hard to tell what was the matter with children who worked in the yards. In those days there had been no law about the age of children—the packers had worked all but the babies. At this remark the family looked puzzled, and Grandmother Majauszkiene again had to make an explanation—that it was against the law for children to work before they were sixteen. What was the sense of that? they asked. They had been thinking of letting little Stanislovas go to work. Well, there was no need to worry, Grandmother Majauszkiene said—the law made no difference except that it forced people to lie about the ages of their children. One would like to know what the lawmakers expected them to do; there were families that had no possible means of support except the children, and the law provided them no other way of getting a living. Very often a man could get no work in Packingtown for months, while a child could go and get a place easily; there was always some new machine, by which the packers could get as much work out of a child as they had been able to get out of a man, and for a third of the pay.

To come back to the house again, it was the woman of the next family that had died. That was after they had been there nearly four years, and this woman had had twins regularly every year—and there had been more than you could count when they moved in. After she died the man would go to work all day and leave them to shift for themselves—the neighbors would help them now and then, for they would almost freeze to death. At the end there were three days that they were alone, before it was found out that the father was dead. He was a "floorsman" at Jones's, and a wounded steer had broken loose and mashed him against a pillar. Then the children had been taken away, and the company had sold the house that very same week to a party of emigrants.

So this grim old women went on with her tale of horrors. How much of it was exaggeration—who could tell? It was only too plausible. There was that about consumption, for instance. They knew nothing about consumption whatever, except that it made people cough; and for two weeks they had been worrying about a coughing-spell of Antanas. It seemed to shake him all over, and it never stopped; you could see a red stain wherever he had spit upon the floor.

And yet all these things were as nothing to what came a little later. They had begun to question the old lady as to why one family had been unable to pay, trying to show her by figures that it ought to have been possible; and Grandmother Majauszkiene had disputed their figures—"You say twelve dollars a month; but that does not include the interest."

Then they stared at her. "Interest!" they cried.

"Interest on the money you still owe," she answered.

"But we don't have to pay any interest!" they exclaimed, three or four at once. "We only have to pay twelve dollars each month."

And for this she laughed at them. "You are like all the rest," she said; "they trick you and eat you alive. They never sell the houses without interest. Get your deed, and see."

Then, with a horrible sinking of the heart, Teta Elzbieta unlocked her bureau and brought out the paper that had already caused them so many agonies. Now they sat round, scarcely breathing, while the old lady, who could read English, ran over it. "Yes," she said, finally, "here it is, of course: 'With interest thereon monthly, at the rate of seven per cent per annum.'"

And there followed a dead silence. "What does that mean?" asked Jurgis finally, almost in a whisper.

"That means," replied the other, "that you have to pay them seven dollars next month, as well as the twelve dollars."

Then again there was not a sound. It was sickening, like a nightmare, in which suddenly something gives way beneath you, and you feel yourself sinking, sinking, down into bottomless abysses. As if in a flash of lightning they saw themselves—victims of a relentless fate, cornered, trapped, in the grip of destruction. All the fair structure of their hopes came crashing about their ears.—And all the time the old woman was going on talking. They wished that she would be still; her voice sounded like the croaking of some dismal raven. Jurgis sat with his hands clenched and beads of perspiration on his forehead, and there was a great lump in Ona's throat, choking her. Then suddenly Teta Elzbieta broke the silence with a wail, and Marija began to wring her hands and sob, "Ai! Ai! Beda man!"

All their outcry did them no good, of course. There sat Grandmother Majauszkiene, unrelenting, typifying fate. No, of course it was not fair, but then fairness had nothing to do with it. And of course they had not known it. They had not been intended to know it. But it was in the deed, and that was all that was necessary, as they would find when the time came.

Somehow or other they got rid of their guest, and then they passed a night of lamentation. The children woke up and found out that something was wrong, and they wailed and would not be comforted. In the morning, of course, most of them had to go to work, the packing houses would not stop for their sorrows; but by seven o'clock Ona and her stepmother were standing at the door of the office of the agent. Yes, he told them, when he came, it was quite true that they would have to pay interest. And then Teta Elzbieta broke forth into protestations and reproaches, so that the people outside stopped and peered in at the window. The agent was as bland as ever. He was deeply pained, he said. He had not told them, simply because he had supposed they would understand that they had to pay interest upon their debt, as a matter of course.

So they came away, and Ona went down to the yards, and at noontime saw Jurgis and told him. Jurgis took it stolidly—he had made up his mind to it by this time. It was part of fate; they would manage it somehow—he made his usual answer, "I will work harder." It would upset their plans for a time; and it would perhaps be necessary for Ona to get work after all. Then Ona added that Teta Elzbieta had decided that little Stanislovas would have to work too. It was not fair to let Jurgis and her support the family—the family would have to help as it could. Previously Jurgis had scouted this idea, but now knit his brows and nodded his head slowly—yes, perhaps it would be best; they would all have to make some sacrifices now.

So Ona set out that day to hunt for work; and at night Marija came home saying that she had met a girl named Jasaityte who had a friend that worked in one of the wrapping rooms in Brown's, and might get a place for Ona there; only the forelady was the kind that takes presents—it was no use for any one to ask her for a place unless at the same time they slipped a ten-dollar bill into her hand. Jurgis was not in the least surprised at this now—he merely asked what the wages of the place would be. So negotiations were opened, and after an interview Ona came home and reported that the forelady seemed to like her, and had said that, while she was not sure, she thought she might be able to put her at work sewing covers on hams, a job at which she would earn as much as eight or ten dollars a week. That was a bid, so Marija reported, after consulting her friend; and then there was an anxious conference at home. The work was done in one of the cellars, and Jurgis did not want Ona to work in such a place; but then it was easy work, and one could not have everything. So in the end Ona, with a ten-dollar bill burning a hole in her palm, had another interview with the forelady.

Meantime Teta Elzbieta had taken Stanislovas to the priest and gotten a certificate to the effect that he was two years older than he was; and with it the little boy now sallied forth to make his fortune in the world. It chanced that Durham had just put in a wonderful new lard machine, and when the special policeman in front of the time station saw Stanislovas and his document, he smiled to himself and told him to go—"Czia! Czia!" pointing. And so Stanislovas went down a long stone corridor, and up a flight of stairs, which took him into a room lighted by electricity, with the new machines for filling lard cans at work in it. The lard was finished on the floor above, and it came in little jets, like beautiful, wriggling, snow-white snakes of unpleasant odor. There were several kinds and sizes of jets, and after a certain precise quantity had come out, each stopped automatically, and the wonderful machine made a turn, and took the can under another jet, and so on, until it was filled neatly to the brim, and pressed tightly, and smoothed off. To attend to all this and fill several hundred cans of lard per hour, there were necessary two human creatures, one of whom knew how to place an empty lard can on a certain spot every few seconds, and the other of whom knew how to take a full lard can off a certain spot every few seconds and set it upon a tray.

And so, after little Stanislovas had stood gazing timidly about him for a few minutes, a man approached him, and asked what he wanted, to which Stanislovas said, "Job." Then the man said "How old?" and Stanislovas answered, "Sixtin." Once or twice every year a state inspector would come wandering through the packing plants, asking a child here and there how old he was; and so the packers were very careful to comply with the law, which cost them as much trouble as was now involved in the boss's taking the document from the little boy, and glancing at it, and then sending it to the office to be filed away. Then he set some one else at a different job, and showed the lad how to place a lard can every time the empty arm of the remorseless machine came to him; and so was decided the place in the universe of little Stanislovas, and his destiny till the end of his days. Hour after hour, day after day, year after year, it was fated that he should stand upon a certain square foot of floor from seven in the morning until noon, and again from half-past twelve till half-past five, making never a motion and thinking never a thought, save for the setting of lard cans. In summer the stench of the warm lard would be nauseating, and in winter the cans would all but freeze to his naked little fingers in the unheated cellar. Half the year it would be dark as night when he went in to work, and dark as night again when he came out, and so he would never know what the sun looked like on weekdays. And for this, at the end of the week, he would carry home three dollars to his family, being his pay at the rate of five cents per hour—just about his proper share of the total earnings of the million and three-quarters of children who are now engaged in earning their livings in the United States.

And meantime, because they were young, and hope is not to be stifled before its time, Jurgis and Ona were again calculating; for they had discovered that the wages of Stanislovas would a little more than pay the interest, which left them just about as they had been before! It would be but fair to them to say that the little boy was delighted with his work, and at the idea of earning a lot of money; and also that the two were very much in love with each other.

CHAPTER 7

All summer long the family toiled, and in the fall they had money enough for Jurgis and Ona to be married according to home traditions of decency. In the latter part of November they hired a hall, and invited all their new acquaintances, who came and left them over a hundred dollars in debt.

It was a bitter and cruel experience, and it plunged them into an agony of despair. Such a time, of all times, for them to have it, when their hearts were made tender! Such a pitiful beginning it was for their married life; they loved each other so, and they could not have the briefest respite! It was a time when everything cried out to them that they ought to be happy; when wonder burned in their hearts, and leaped into flame at the slightest breath. They were shaken to the depths of them, with the awe of love realized—and was it so very weak of them that they cried out for a little peace? They had opened their hearts, like flowers to the springtime, and the merciless winter had fallen upon them. They wondered if ever any love that had blossomed in the world had been so crushed and trampled!

Over them, relentless and savage, there cracked the lash of want; the morning after the wedding it sought them as they slept, and drove them out before daybreak to work. Ona was scarcely able to stand with exhaustion; but if she were to lose her place they would be ruined, and she would surely lose it if she were not on time that day. They all had to go, even little Stanislovas, who was ill from overindulgence in sausages and sarsaparilla. All that day he stood at his lard machine, rocking unsteadily, his eyes closing in spite of him; and he all but lost his place even so, for the foreman booted him twice to waken him.

It was fully a week before they were all normal again, and meantime, with whining children and cross adults, the house was not a pleasant place to live in. Jurgis lost his temper very little, however, all things considered. It was because of Ona; the least glance at her was always enough to make him control himself. She was so sensitive—she was not fitted for such a life as this; and a hundred times a day, when he thought of her, he would clench his hands and fling himself again at the task before him. She was too good for him, he told himself, and he was afraid, because she was his. So long he had hungered to possess her, but now that the time had come he knew that he had not earned the right; that she trusted him so was all her own simple goodness, and no virtue of his. But he was resolved that she should never find this out, and so was always on the watch to see that he did not betray any of his ugly self; he would take care even in little matters, such as his manners, and his habit of swearing when things went wrong. The tears came so easily into Ona's eyes, and she would look at him so appealingly—it kept Jurgis quite busy making resolutions, in addition to all the other things he had on his mind. It was true that more things were going on at this time in the mind of Jurgis than ever had in all his life before.

He had to protect her, to do battle for her against the horror he saw about them. He was all that she had to look to, and if he failed she would be lost; he would wrap his arms about her, and try to hide her from the world. He had learned the ways of things about him now. It was a war of each against all, and the devil take the hindmost. You did not give feasts to other people, you waited for them to give feasts to you. You went about with your soul full of suspicion and hatred; you understood that you were environed by hostile powers that were trying to get your money, and who used all the virtues to bait their traps with. The store-keepers plastered up their windows with all sorts of lies to entice you; the very fences by the wayside, the lampposts and telegraph poles, were pasted over with lies. The great corporation which employed you lied to you, and lied to the whole country—from top to bottom it was nothing but one gigantic lie.

So Jurgis said that he understood it; and yet it was really pitiful, for the struggle was so unfair—some had so much the advantage! Here he was, for instance, vowing upon his knees that he would save Ona from harm, and only a week later she was suffering atrociously, and from the blow of an enemy that he could not possibly have thwarted. There came a day when the rain fell in torrents; and it being December, to be wet with it and have to sit all day long in one of the cold cellars of Brown's was no laughing matter. Ona was a working girl, and did not own waterproofs and such things, and so Jurgis took her and put her on the street-car. Now it chanced that this car line was owned by gentlemen who were trying to make money. And the city having passed an ordinance requiring them to give transfers, they had fallen into a rage; and first they had made a rule that transfers could be had only when the fare was paid; and later, growing still uglier, they had made another—that the passenger must ask for the transfer, the conductor was not allowed to offer it. Now Ona had been told that she was to get a transfer; but it was not her way to speak up, and so she merely waited, following the conductor about with her eyes, wondering when he would think of her. When at last the time came for her to get out, she asked for the transfer, and was refused. Not knowing what to make of this, she began to argue with the conductor, in a language of which he did not understand a word. After warning her several times, he pulled the bell and the car went on—at which Ona burst into tears. At the next corner she got out, of course; and as she had no more money, she had to walk the rest of the way to the yards in the pouring rain. And so all day long she sat shivering, and came home at night with her teeth chattering and pains in her head and back. For two weeks afterward she suffered cruelly—and yet every day she had to drag herself to her work. The forewoman was especially severe with Ona, because she believed that she was obstinate on account of having been refused a holiday the day after her wedding. Ona had an idea that her "forelady" did not like to have her girls marry—perhaps because she was old and ugly and unmarried herself.

There were many such dangers, in which the odds were all against them. Their children were not as well as they had been at home; but how could they know that there was no sewer to their house, and that the drainage of fifteen years was in a cesspool under it? How could they know that the pale-blue milk that they bought around the corner was watered, and doctored with formaldehyde besides? When the children were not well at home, Teta Elzbieta would gather herbs and cure them; now she was obliged to go to the drugstore and buy extracts—and how was she to know that they were all adulterated? How could they find out that their tea and coffee, their sugar and flour, had been doctored; that their canned peas had been colored with copper salts, and their fruit jams with aniline dyes? And even if they had known it, what good would it have done them, since there was no place within miles of them where any other sort was to be had? The bitter winter was coming, and they had to save money to get more clothing and bedding; but it would not matter in the least how much they saved, they could not get anything to keep them warm. All the clothing that was to be had in the stores was made of cotton and shoddy, which is made by tearing old clothes to pieces and weaving the fiber again. If they paid higher prices, they might get frills and fanciness, or be cheated; but genuine quality they could not obtain for love nor money. A young friend of Szedvilas', recently come from abroad, had become a clerk in a store on Ashland Avenue, and he narrated with glee a trick that had been played upon an unsuspecting countryman by his boss. The customer had desired to purchase an alarm clock, and the boss had shown him two exactly similar, telling him that the price of one was a dollar and of the other a dollar seventy-five. Upon being asked what the difference was, the man had wound up the first halfway and the second all the way, and showed the customer how the latter made twice as much noise; upon which the customer remarked that he was a sound sleeper, and had better take the more expensive clock!

There is a poet who sings that

> "Deeper their heart grows and nobler their bearing,
> Whose youth in the fires of anguish hath died."

But it was not likely that he had reference to the kind of anguish that comes with destitution, that is so endlessly bitter and cruel, and yet so sordid and petty, so ugly, so humiliating—unredeemed by the slightest touch of dignity or even of pathos. It is a kind of anguish that poets have not commonly dealt with; its very words are not admitted into the vocabulary of poets—the details of it cannot be told in polite society at all. How, for instance, could any one expect to excite sympathy among lovers of good literature by telling how a family found their home alive with vermin, and of all the suffering and inconvenience and humiliation they were put to, and the hard-earned money they spent, in efforts to get rid of them? After long hesitation and uncertainty they paid twenty-five cents for a big package of insect powder—a patent preparation which chanced to be ninety-five per cent gypsum, a harmless earth which had cost about two cents to prepare.

Of course it had not the least effect, except upon a few roaches which had the misfortune to drink water after eating it, and so got their inwards set in a coating of plaster of Paris. The family, having no idea of this, and no more money to throw away, had nothing to do but give up and submit to one more misery for the rest of their days.

Then there was old Antanas. The winter came, and the place where he worked was a dark, unheated cellar, where you could see your breath all day, and where your fingers sometimes tried to freeze. So the old man's cough grew every day worse, until there came a time when it hardly ever stopped, and he had become a nuisance about the place. Then, too, a still more dreadful thing happened to him; he worked in a place where his feet were soaked in chemicals, and it was not long before they had eaten through his new boots. Then sores began to break out on his feet, and grow worse and worse. Whether it was that his blood was bad, or there had been a cut, he could not say; but he asked the men about it, and learned that it was a regular thing—it was the saltpeter. Every one felt it, sooner or later, and then it was all up with him, at least for that sort of work. The sores would never heal—in the end his toes would drop off, if he did not quit. Yet old Antanas would not quit; he saw the suffering of his family, and he remembered what it had cost him to get a job. So he tied up his feet, and went on limping about and coughing, until at last he fell to pieces, all at once and in a heap, like the One-Horse Shay. They carried him to a dry place and laid him on the floor, and that night two of the men helped him home. The poor old man was put to bed, and though he tried it every morning until the end, he never could get up again. He would lie there and cough and cough, day and night, wasting away to a mere skeleton. There came a time when there was so little flesh on him that the bones began to poke through—which was a horrible thing to see or even to think of. And one night he had a choking fit, and a little river of blood came out of his mouth. The family, wild with terror, sent for a doctor, and paid half a dollar to be told that there was nothing to be done. Mercifully the doctor did not say this so that the old man could hear, for he was still clinging to the faith that tomorrow or next day he would be better, and could go back to his job. The company had sent word to him that they would keep it for him—or rather Jurgis had bribed one of the men to come one Sunday afternoon and say they had. Dede Antanas continued to believe it, while three more hemorrhages came; and then at last one morning they found him stiff and cold. Things were not going well with them then, and though it nearly broke Teta Elzbieta's heart, they were forced to dispense with nearly all the decencies of a funeral; they had only a hearse, and one hack for the women and children; and Jurgis, who was learning things fast, spent all Sunday making a bargain for these, and he made it in the presence of witnesses, so that when the man tried to charge him for all sorts of incidentals, he did not have to pay. For twenty-five years old Antanas Rudkus and his son had dwelt in the forest together, and it was hard to part in this way; perhaps it was just as well that Jurgis had to give all his attention to the task of having a funeral without being bankrupted, and so had no time to indulge in memories and grief.

Now the dreadful winter was come upon them. In the forests, all summer long, the branches of the trees do battle for light, and some of them lose and die; and then come the raging blasts, and the storms of snow and hail, and strew the ground with these weaker branches. Just so it was in Packingtown; the whole district braced itself for the struggle that was an agony, and those whose time was come died off in hordes. All the year round they had been serving as cogs in the great packing machine; and now was the time for the renovating of it, and the replacing of damaged parts. There came pneumonia and grippe, stalking among them, seeking for weakened constitutions; there was the annual harvest of those whom tuberculosis had been dragging down. There came cruel, cold, and biting winds, and blizzards of snow, all testing relentlessly for failing muscles and impoverished blood. Sooner or later came the day when the unfit one did not report for work; and then, with no time lost in waiting, and no inquiries or regrets, there was a chance for a new hand.

The new hands were here by the thousands. All day long the gates of the packing houses were besieged by starving and penniless men; they came, literally, by the thousands every single morning, fighting with each other for a chance for life. Blizzards and cold made no difference to them, they were always on hand; they were on hand two hours before the sun rose, an hour before the work began. Sometimes their faces froze, sometimes their feet and their hands; sometimes they froze all together—but still they came, for they had no other place to go. One day Durham advertised in the paper for two hundred men to cut ice; and all that day the homeless and starving of the city came trudging through the snow from all over its two hundred square miles. That night forty score of them crowded into the station house of the stockyards district—they filled the rooms, sleeping in each other's laps, toboggan fashion, and they piled on top of each other in the corridors, till the police shut the doors and left some to freeze outside. On the morrow, before daybreak, there were three thousand at Durham's, and the police reserves had to be sent for to quell the riot. Then Durham's bosses picked out twenty of the biggest; the "two hundred" proved to have been a printer's error.

Four or five miles to the eastward lay the lake, and over this the bitter winds came raging. Sometimes the thermometer would fall to ten or twenty degrees below zero at night, and in the morning the streets would be piled with snowdrifts up to the first-floor windows. The streets through which our friends had to go to their work were all unpaved and full of deep holes and gullies; in summer, when it rained hard, a man might have to wade to his waist to get to his house; and now in winter it was no joke getting through these places, before light in the morning and after dark at night. They would wrap up in all they owned, but they could not wrap up against exhaustion; and many a man gave out in these battles with the snowdrifts, and lay down and fell asleep.

And if it was bad for the men, one may imagine how the women and children fared. Some would ride in the cars, if the cars were running; but when you are making only five cents an hour, as was little Stanislovas, you do not like to spend that much to ride two miles. The children would come to the yards with great shawls about their ears, and so tied up that you could hardly find them—and still there would be accidents. One bitter morning in February the little boy who worked at the lard machine with Stanislovas came about an hour late, and screaming with pain. They unwrapped him, and a man began vigorously rubbing his ears; and as they were frozen stiff, it took only two or three rubs to break them short off. As a result of this, little Stanislovas conceived a terror of the cold that was almost a mania. Every morning, when it came time to start for the yards, he would begin to cry and protest. Nobody knew quite how to manage him, for threats did no good—it seemed to be something that he could not control, and they feared sometimes that he would go into convulsions. In the end it had to be arranged that he always went with Jurgis, and came home with him again; and often, when the snow was deep, the man would carry him the whole way on his shoulders. Sometimes Jurgis would be working until late at night, and then it was pitiful, for there was no place for the little fellow to wait, save in the doorways or in a corner of the killing beds, and he would all but fall asleep there, and freeze to death.

There was no heat upon the killing beds; the men might exactly as well have worked out of doors all winter. For that matter, there was very little heat anywhere in the building, except in the cooking rooms and such places—and it was the men who worked in these who ran the most risk of all, because whenever they had to pass to another room they had to go through ice-cold corridors, and sometimes with nothing on above the waist except a sleeveless undershirt. On the killing beds you were apt to be covered with blood, and it would freeze solid; if you leaned against a pillar, you would freeze to that, and if you put your hand upon the blade of your knife, you would run a chance of leaving your skin on it. The men would tie up their feet in newspapers and old sacks, and these would be soaked in blood and frozen, and then soaked again, and so on, until by nighttime a man would be walking on great lumps the size of the feet of an elephant. Now and then, when the bosses were not looking, you would see them plunging their feet and ankles into the steaming hot carcass of the steer, or darting across the room to the hot-water jets. The cruelest thing of all was that nearly all of them—all of those who used knives—were unable to wear gloves, and their arms would be white with frost and their hands would grow numb, and then of course there would be accidents. Also the air would be full of steam, from the hot water and the hot blood, so that you could not see five feet before you; and then, with men rushing about at the speed they kept up on the killing beds, and all with butcher knives, like razors, in their hands—well, it was to be counted as a wonder that there were not more men slaughtered than cattle.

And yet all this inconvenience they might have put up with, if only it had not been for one thing—if only there had been some place where they might eat. Jurgis had either to eat his dinner amid the stench in which he had worked, or else to rush, as did all his companions, to any one of the hundreds of liquor stores which stretched out their arms to him. To the west of the yards ran Ashland Avenue, and here was an unbroken line of saloons—"Whiskey Row," they called it; to the north was Forty-seventh Street, where there were half a dozen to the block, and at the angle of the two was "Whiskey Point," a space of fifteen or twenty acres, and containing one glue factory and about two hundred saloons.

One might walk among these and take his choice: "Hot pea-soup and boiled cabbage today." "Sauerkraut and hot frankfurters. Walk in." "Bean soup and stewed lamb. Welcome." All of these things were printed in many languages, as were also the names of the resorts, which were infinite in their variety and appeal. There was the "Home Circle" and the "Cosey Corner"; there were "Firesides" and "Hearthstones" and "Pleasure Palaces" and "Wonderlands" and "Dream Castles" and "Love's Delights." Whatever else they were called, they were sure to be called "Union Headquarters," and to hold out a welcome to workingmen; and there was always a warm stove, and a chair near it, and some friends to laugh and talk with. There was only one condition attached,—you must drink. If you went in not intending to drink, you would be put out in no time, and if you were slow about going, like as not you would get your head split open with a beer bottle in the bargain. But all of the men understood the convention and drank; they believed that by it they were getting something for nothing—for they did not need to take more than one drink, and upon the strength of it they might fill themselves up with a good hot dinner. This did not always work out in practice, however, for there was pretty sure to be a friend who would treat you, and then you would have to treat him. Then some one else would come in—and, anyhow, a few drinks were good for a man who worked hard. As he went back he did not shiver so, he had more courage for his task; the deadly brutalizing monotony of it did not afflict him so,—he had ideas while he worked, and took a more cheerful view of his circumstances. On the way home, however, the shivering was apt to come on him again; and so he would have to stop once or twice to warm up against the cruel cold. As there were hot things to eat in this saloon too, he might get home late to his supper, or he might not get home at all. And then his wife might set out to look for him, and she too would feel the cold; and perhaps she would have some of the children with her—and so a whole family would drift into drinking, as the current of a river drifts downstream. As if to complete the chain, the packers all paid their men in checks, refusing all requests to pay in coin; and where in Packingtown could a man go to have his check cashed but to a saloon, where he could pay for the favor by spending a part of the money?

From all of these things Jurgis was saved because of Ona. He never would take but the one drink at noontime; and so he got the reputation of being a surly fellow, and was not quite welcome at the saloons, and had to drift about from one to another. Then at night he would go straight home, helping Ona and Stanislovas, or often putting the former on a car. And when he got home perhaps he would have to trudge several blocks, and come staggering back through the snowdrifts with a bag of coal upon his shoulder. Home was not a very attractive place—at least not this winter. They had only been able to buy one stove, and this was a small one, and proved not big enough to warm even the kitchen in the bitterest weather. This made it hard for Teta Elzbieta all day, and for the children when they could not get to school. At night they would sit huddled round this stove, while they ate their supper off their laps; and then Jurgis and Jonas would smoke a pipe, after which they would all crawl into their beds to get warm, after putting out the fire to save the coal. Then they would have some frightful experiences with the cold. They would sleep with all their clothes on, including their overcoats, and put over them all the bedding and spare clothing they owned; the children would sleep all crowded into one bed, and yet even so they could not keep warm. The outside ones would be shivering and sobbing, crawling over the others and trying to get down into the center, and causing a fight. This old house with the leaky weatherboards was a very different thing from their cabins at home, with great thick walls plastered inside and outside with mud; and the cold which came upon them was a living thing, a demon-presence in the room. They would waken in the midnight hours, when everything was black; perhaps they would hear it yelling outside, or perhaps there would be deathlike stillness—and that would be worse yet. They could feel the cold as it crept in through the cracks, reaching out for them with its icy, death-dealing fingers; and they would crouch and cower, and try to hide from it, all in vain. It would come, and it would come; a grisly thing, a specter born in the black caverns of terror; a power primeval, cosmic, shadowing the tortures of the lost souls flung out to chaos and destruction. It was cruel iron-hard; and hour after hour they would cringe in its grasp, alone, alone. There would be no one to hear them if they cried out; there would be no help, no mercy. And so on until morning—when they would go out to another day of toil, a little weaker, a little nearer to the time when it would be their turn to be shaken from the tree.

CHAPTER 8

Yet even by this deadly winter the germ of hope was not to be kept from sprouting in their hearts. It was just at this time that the great adventure befell Marija.

The victim was Tamoszius Kuszleika, who played the violin. Everybody laughed at them, for Tamoszius was petite and frail, and Marija could have picked him up and carried him off under one arm. But perhaps that was why she fascinated him; the sheer volume of Marija's energy was overwhelming. That first night at the wedding Tamoszius had hardly taken his eyes off her; and later on, when he came to find that she had really the heart of a baby, her voice and her violence ceased to terrify him, and he got the habit of coming to pay her visits on Sunday afternoons. There was no place to entertain company except in the kitchen, in the midst of the family, and Tamoszius would sit there with his hat between his knees, never saying more than half a dozen words at a time, and turning red in the face before he managed to say those; until finally Jurgis would clap him upon the back, in his hearty way, crying, "Come now, brother, give us a tune." And then Tamoszius' face would light up and he would get out his fiddle, tuck it under his chin, and play. And forthwith the soul of him would flame up and become eloquent—it was almost an impropriety, for all the while his gaze would be fixed upon Marija's face, until she would begin to turn red and lower her eyes. There was no resisting the music of Tamoszius, however; even the children would sit awed and wondering, and the tears would run down Teta Elzbieta's cheeks. A wonderful privilege it was to be thus admitted into the soul of a man of genius, to be allowed to share the ecstasies and the agonies of his inmost life.

Then there were other benefits accruing to Marija from this friendship—benefits of a more substantial nature. People paid Tamoszius big money to come and make music on state occasions; and also they would invite him to parties and festivals, knowing well that he was too good-natured to come without his fiddle, and that having brought it, he could be made to play while others danced. Once he made bold to ask Marija to accompany him to such a party, and Marija accepted, to his great delight—after which he never went anywhere without her, while if the celebration were given by friends of his, he would invite the rest of the family also. In any case Marija would bring back a huge pocketful of cakes and sandwiches for the children, and stories of all the good things she herself had managed to consume. She was compelled, at these parties, to spend most of her time at the refreshment table, for she could not dance with anybody except other women and very old men; Tamoszius was of an excitable temperament, and afflicted with a frantic jealousy, and any unmarried man who ventured to put his arm about the ample waist of Marija would be certain to throw the orchestra out of tune.

It was a great help to a person who had to toil all the week to be able to look forward to some such relaxation as this on Saturday nights. The family was too poor and too hardworked to make many acquaintances; in Packingtown, as a rule, people know only their near neighbors and shopmates, and so the place is like a myriad of little country villages. But now there was a member of the family who was permitted to travel and widen her horizon; and so each week there would be new personalities to talk about,—how so-and-so was dressed, and where she worked, and what she got, and whom she was in love with; and how this man had jilted his girl, and how she had quarreled with the other girl, and what had passed between them; and how another man beat his wife, and spent all her earnings upon drink, and pawned her very clothes. Some people would have scorned this talk as gossip; but then one has to talk about what one knows.

It was one Saturday night, as they were coming home from a wedding, that Tamoszius found courage, and set down his violin case in the street and spoke his heart; and then Marija clasped him in her arms. She told them all about it the next day, and fairly cried with happiness, for she said that Tamoszius was a lovely man. After that he no longer made love to her with his fiddle, but they would sit for hours in the kitchen, blissfully happy in each other's arms; it was the tacit convention of the family to know nothing of what was going on in that corner.

They were planning to be married in the spring, and have the garret of the house fixed up, and live there. Tamoszius made good wages; and little by little the family were paying back their debt to Marija, so she ought soon to have enough to start life upon—only, with her preposterous softheartedness, she would insist upon spending a good part of her money every week for things which she saw they needed. Marija was really the capitalist of the party, for she had become an expert can painter by this time—she was getting fourteen cents for every hundred and ten cans, and she could paint more than two cans every minute. Marija felt, so to speak, that she had her hand on the throttle, and the neighborhood was vocal with her rejoicings.

Yet her friends would shake their heads and tell her to go slow; one could not count upon such good fortune forever—there were accidents that always happened. But Marija was not to be prevailed upon, and went on planning and dreaming of all the treasures she was going to have for her home; and so, when the crash did come, her grief was painful to see.

For her canning factory shut down! Marija would about as soon have expected to see the sun shut down—the huge establishment had been to her a thing akin to the planets and the seasons. But now it was shut! And they had not given her any explanation, they had not even given her a day's warning; they had simply posted a notice one Saturday that all hands would be paid off that afternoon, and would not resume work for at least a month! And that was all that there was to it—her job was gone!

It was the holiday rush that was over, the girls said in answer to Marija's inquiries; after that there was always a slack. Sometimes the factory would start up on half time after a while, but there was no telling—it had been known to stay closed until way into the summer. The prospects were bad at present, for truckmen who worked in the storerooms said that these were piled up to the ceilings, so that the firm could not have found room for another week's output of cans. And they had turned off three-quarters of these men, which was a still worse sign, since it meant that there were no orders to be filled. It was all a swindle, can-painting, said the girls—you were crazy with delight because you were making twelve or fourteen dollars a week, and saving half of it; but you had to spend it all keeping alive while you were out, and so your pay was really only half what you thought.

Marija came home, and because she was a person who could not rest without danger of explosion, they first had a great house cleaning, and then she set out to search Packingtown for a job to fill up the gap. As nearly all the canning establishments were shut down, and all the girls hunting work, it will be readily understood that Marija did not find any. Then she took to trying the stores and saloons, and when this failed she even traveled over into the far-distant regions near the lake front, where lived the rich people in great palaces, and begged there for some sort of work that could be done by a person who did not know English.

The men upon the killing beds felt also the effects of the slump which had turned Marija out; but they felt it in a different way, and a way which made Jurgis understand at last all their bitterness. The big packers did not turn their hands off and close down, like the canning factories; but they began to run for shorter and shorter hours. They had always required the men to be on the killing beds and ready for work at seven o'clock, although there was almost never any work to be done till the buyers out in the yards had gotten to work, and some cattle had come over the chutes. That would often be ten or eleven o'clock, which was bad enough, in all conscience; but now, in the slack season, they would perhaps not have a thing for their men to do till late in the afternoon. And so they would have to loaf around, in a place where the thermometer might be twenty degrees below zero! At first one would see them running about, or skylarking with each other, trying to keep warm; but before the day was over they would become quite chilled through and exhausted, and, when the cattle finally came, so near frozen that to move was an agony. And then suddenly the place would spring into activity, and the merciless "speeding-up" would begin!

There were weeks at a time when Jurgis went home after such a day as this with not more than two hours' work to his credit—which meant about thirty-five cents. There were many days when the total was less than half an hour, and others when there was none at all. The general average was six hours a day, which meant for Jurgis about six dollars a week; and this six hours of work would be done after standing on the killing bed till one o'clock, or perhaps even three or four o'clock, in the afternoon. Like as not there would come a rush of cattle at the very end of the day, which the men would have to dispose of before they went home, often working by electric light till nine or ten, or even twelve or one o'clock, and without a single instant for a bite of supper. The men were at the mercy of the cattle. Perhaps the buyers would be holding off for better prices—if they could scare the shippers into thinking that they meant to buy nothing that day, they could get their own terms. For some reason the cost of fodder for cattle in the yards was much above the market price—and you were not allowed to bring your own fodder! Then, too, a number of cars were apt to arrive late in the day, now that the roads were blocked with snow, and the packers would buy their cattle that night, to get them cheaper, and then would come into play their ironclad rule, that all cattle must be killed the same day they were bought. There was no use kicking about this—there had been one delegation after another to see the packers about it, only to be told that it was the rule, and that there was not the slightest chance of its ever being altered. And so on Christmas Eve Jurgis worked till nearly one o'clock in the morning, and on Christmas Day he was on the killing bed at seven o'clock.

All this was bad; and yet it was not the worst. For after all the hard work a man did, he was paid for only part of it. Jurgis had once been among those who scoffed at the idea of these huge concerns cheating; and so now he could appreciate the bitter irony of the fact that it was precisely their size which enabled them to do it with impunity. One of the rules on the killing beds was that a man who was one minute late was docked an hour; and this was economical, for he was made to work the balance of the hour—he was not allowed to stand round and wait. And on the other hand if he came ahead of time he got no pay for that—though often the bosses would start up the gang ten or fifteen minutes before the whistle. And this same custom they carried over to the end of the day; they did not pay for any fraction of an hour—for "broken time." A man might work full fifty minutes, but if there was no work to fill out the hour, there was no pay for him. Thus the end of every day was a sort of lottery—a struggle, all but breaking into open war between the bosses and the men, the former trying to rush a job through and the latter trying to stretch it out. Jurgis blamed the bosses for this, though the truth to be told it was not always their fault; for the packers kept them frightened for their lives—and when one was in danger of falling behind the standard, what was easier than to catch up by making the gang work awhile "for the church"? This was a savage witticism the men had, which Jurgis had to have explained to him. Old man Jones was great on missions and such things, and so whenever they were doing some particularly disreputable job, the men would wink at each other and say, "Now we're working for the church!"

One of the consequences of all these things was that Jurgis was no longer perplexed when he heard men talk of fighting for their rights. He felt like fighting now himself; and when the Irish delegate of the butcher-helpers' union came to him a second time, he received him in a far different spirit. A wonderful idea it now seemed to Jurgis, this of the men—that by combining they might be able to make a stand and conquer the packers! Jurgis wondered who had first thought of it; and when he was told that it was a common thing for men to do in America, he got the first inkling of a meaning in the phrase "a free country." The delegate explained to him how it depended upon their being able to get every man to join and stand by the organization, and so Jurgis signified that he was willing to do his share. Before another month was by, all the working members of his family had union cards, and wore their union buttons conspicuously and with pride. For fully a week they were quite blissfully happy, thinking that belonging to a union meant an end to all their troubles.

But only ten days after she had joined, Marija's canning factory closed down, and that blow quite staggered them. They could not understand why the union had not prevented it, and the very first time she attended a meeting Marija got up and made a speech about it. It was a business meeting, and was transacted in English, but that made no difference to Marija; she said what was in her, and all the pounding of the chairman's gavel and all the uproar and confusion in the room could not prevail. Quite apart from her own troubles she was boiling over with a general sense of the injustice of it, and she told what she thought of the packers, and what she thought of a world where such things were allowed to happen; and then, while the echoes of the hall rang with the shock of her terrible voice, she sat down again and fanned herself, and the meeting gathered itself together and proceeded to discuss the election of a recording secretary.

Jurgis too had an adventure the first time he attended a union meeting, but it was not of his own seeking. Jurgis had gone with the desire to get into an inconspicuous corner and see what was done; but this attitude of silent and open-eyed attention had marked him out for a victim. Tommy Finnegan was a little Irishman, with big staring eyes and a wild aspect, a "hoister" by trade, and badly cracked. Somewhere back in the far-distant past Tommy Finnegan had had a strange experience, and the burden of it rested upon him. All the balance of his life he had done nothing but try to make it understood. When he talked he caught his victim by the buttonhole, and his face kept coming closer and closer—which was trying, because his teeth were so bad. Jurgis did not mind that, only he was frightened. The method of operation of the higher intelligences was Tom Finnegan's theme, and he desired to find out if Jurgis had ever considered that the representation of things in their present similarity might be altogether unintelligible upon a more elevated plane. There were assuredly wonderful mysteries about the developing of these things; and then, becoming confidential, Mr. Finnegan proceeded to tell of some discoveries of his own. "If ye have iver had onything to do wid shperrits," said he, and looked inquiringly at Jurgis, who kept shaking his head. "Niver mind, niver mind," continued the other, "but their influences may be operatin' upon ye; it's shure as I'm tellin' ye, it's them that has the reference to the immejit surroundin's that has the most of power. It was vouchsafed to me in me youthful days to be acquainted with shperrits" and so Tommy Finnegan went on, expounding a system of philosophy, while the perspiration came out on Jurgis' forehead, so great was his agitation and embarrassment. In the end one of the men, seeing his plight, came over and rescued him; but it was some time before he was able to find any one to explain things to him, and meanwhile his fear lest the strange little Irishman should get him cornered again was enough to keep him dodging about the room the whole evening.

He never missed a meeting, however. He had picked up a few words of English by this time, and friends would help him to understand. They were often very turbulent meetings, with half a dozen men declaiming at once, in as many dialects of English; but the speakers were all desperately in earnest, and Jurgis was in earnest too, for he understood that a fight was on, and that it was his fight. Since the time of his disillusionment, Jurgis had sworn to trust no man, except in his own family; but here he discovered that he had brothers in affliction, and allies. Their one chance for life was in union, and so the struggle became a kind of crusade. Jurgis had always been a member of the church, because it was the right thing to be, but the church had never touched him, he left all that for the women. Here, however, was a new religion—one that did touch him, that took hold of every fiber of him; and with all the zeal and fury of a convert he went out as a missionary. There were many nonunion men among the Lithuanians, and with these he would labor and wrestle in prayer, trying to show them the right. Sometimes they would be obstinate and refuse to see it, and Jurgis, alas, was not always patient! He forgot how he himself had been blind, a short time ago—after the fashion of all crusaders since the original ones, who set out to spread the gospel of Brotherhood by force of arms.

CHAPTER 9

One of the first consequences of the discovery of the union was that Jurgis became desirous of learning English. He wanted to know what was going on at the meetings, and to be able to take part in them, and so he began to look about him, and to try to pick up words. The children, who were at school, and learning fast, would teach him a few; and a friend loaned him a little book that had some in it, and Ona would read them to him. Then Jurgis became sorry that he could not read himself; and later on in the winter, when some one told him that there was a night school that was free, he went and enrolled. After that, every evening that he got home from the yards in time, he would go to the school; he would go even if he were in time for only half an hour. They were teaching him both to read and to speak English—and they would have taught him other things, if only he had had a little time.

Also the union made another great difference with him—it made him begin to pay attention to the country. It was the beginning of democracy with him. It was a little state, the union, a miniature republic; its affairs were every man's affairs, and every man had a real say about them. In other words, in the union Jurgis learned to talk politics. In the place where he had come from there had not been any politics—in Russia one thought of the government as an affliction like the lightning and the hail. "Duck, little brother, duck," the wise old peasants would whisper; "everything passes away." And when Jurgis had first come to America he had supposed that it was the same. He had heard people say that it was a free country—but what did that mean? He found that here, precisely as in Russia, there were rich men who owned everything; and if one could not find any work, was not the hunger he began to feel the same sort of hunger?

When Jurgis had been working about three weeks at Brown's, there had come to him one noontime a man who was employed as a night watchman, and who asked him if he would not like to take out naturalization papers and become a citizen. Jurgis did not know what that meant, but the man explained the advantages. In the first place, it would not cost him anything, and it would get him half a day off, with his pay just the same; and then when election time came he would be able to vote—and there was something in that. Jurgis was naturally glad to accept, and so the night watchman said a few words to the boss, and he was excused for the rest of the day. When, later on, he wanted a holiday to get married he could not get it; and as for a holiday with pay just the same—what power had wrought that miracle heaven only knew! However, he went with the man, who picked up several other newly landed immigrants, Poles, Lithuanians, and Slovaks, and took them all outside, where stood a great four-horse tallyho coach, with fifteen or twenty men already in it. It was a fine chance to see the sights of the city, and the party had a merry time, with plenty of beer handed up from inside. So they drove downtown and stopped before an imposing granite building, in which they interviewed an official, who had the papers all ready, with only the names to be filled in. So each man in turn took an oath of which he did not understand a word, and then was presented with a handsome ornamented document with a big red seal and the shield of the United States upon it, and was told that he had become a citizen of the Republic and the equal of the President himself.

A month or two later Jurgis had another interview with this same man, who told him where to go to "register." And then finally, when election day came, the packing houses posted a notice that men who desired to vote might remain away until nine that morning, and the same night watchman took Jurgis and the rest of his flock into the back room of a saloon, and showed each of them where and how to mark a ballot, and then gave each two dollars, and took them to the polling place, where there was a policeman on duty especially to see that they got through all right. Jurgis felt quite proud of this good luck till he got home and met Jonas, who had taken the leader aside and whispered to him, offering to vote three times for four dollars, which offer had been accepted.

And now in the union Jurgis met men who explained all this mystery to him; and he learned that America differed from Russia in that its government existed under the form of a democracy. The officials who ruled it, and got all the graft, had to be elected first; and so there were two rival sets of grafters, known as political parties, and the one got the office which bought the most votes. Now and then, the election was very close, and that was the time the poor man came in. In the stockyards this was only in national and state elections, for in local elections the Democratic Party always carried everything. The ruler of the district was therefore the Democratic boss, a little Irishman named Mike Scully. Scully held an important party office in the state, and bossed even the mayor of the city, it was said; it was his boast that he carried the stockyards in his pocket. He was an enormously rich man—he had a hand in all the big graft in the neighborhood. It was Scully, for instance, who owned that dump which Jurgis and Ona had seen the first day of their arrival. Not only did he own the dump, but he owned the brick factory as well, and first he took out the clay and made it into bricks, and then he had the city bring garbage to fill up the hole, so that he could build houses to sell to the people. Then, too, he sold the bricks to the city, at his own price, and the city came and got them in its own wagons. And also he owned the other hole near by, where the stagnant water was; and it was he who cut the ice and sold it; and what was more, if the men told truth, he had not had to pay any taxes for the water, and he had built the ice-house out of city lumber, and had not had to pay anything for that. The newspapers had got hold of that story, and there had been a scandal; but Scully had hired somebody to confess and take all the blame, and then skip the country. It was said, too, that he had built his brick-kiln in the same way, and that the workmen were on the city payroll while they did it; however, one had to press closely to get these things out of the men, for it was not their business, and Mike Scully was a good man to stand in with. A note signed by him was equal to a job any time at the packing houses; and also he employed a good many men himself, and worked them only eight hours a day, and paid them the highest wages. This gave him many friends—all of whom he had gotten together into the "War Whoop League," whose clubhouse you might see just outside of the yards. It was the biggest clubhouse, and the biggest club, in all Chicago; and they had prizefights every now and then, and cockfights and even dogfights. The policemen in the district all belonged to the league, and instead of suppressing the fights, they sold tickets for them. The man that had taken Jurgis to be naturalized was one of these "Indians," as they were called; and on election day there would be hundreds of them out, and all with big wads of money in their pockets and free drinks at every saloon in the district. That was another thing, the men said—all the saloon-keepers had to be "Indians," and to put up on demand, otherwise they could not do business on Sundays, nor have any gambling at all. In the same way Scully had all the jobs in the fire department at his disposal, and all the rest of the city graft in the stockyards district; he was building a block of flats somewhere up on Ashland Avenue, and the man who was overseeing it for him was drawing pay as a city inspector of sewers. The city inspector of water pipes had been dead and buried for over a year, but somebody was still drawing his pay. The city inspector of sidewalks was a barkeeper at the War Whoop Cafe—and maybe he could make it uncomfortable for any tradesman who did not stand in with Scully!

Even the packers were in awe of him, so the men said. It gave them pleasure to believe this, for Scully stood as the people's man, and boasted of it boldly when election day came. The packers had wanted a bridge at Ashland Avenue, but they had not been able to get it till they had seen Scully; and it was the same with "Bubbly Creek," which the city had threatened to make the packers cover over, till Scully had come to their aid. "Bubbly Creek" is an arm of the Chicago River, and forms the southern boundary of the yards: all the drainage of the square mile of packing houses empties into it, so that it is really a great open sewer a hundred or two feet wide. One long arm of it is blind, and the filth stays there forever and a day. The grease and chemicals that are poured into it undergo all sorts of strange transformations, which are the cause of its name; it is constantly in motion, as if huge fish were feeding in it, or great leviathans disporting themselves in its depths. Bubbles of carbonic acid gas will rise to the surface and burst, and make rings two or three feet wide. Here and there the grease and filth have caked solid, and the creek looks like a bed of lava; chickens walk about on it, feeding, and many times an unwary stranger has started to stroll across, and vanished temporarily. The packers used to leave the creek that way, till every now and then the surface would catch on fire and burn furiously, and the fire department would have to come and put it out. Once, however, an ingenious stranger came and started to gather this filth in scows, to make lard out of; then the packers took the cue, and got out an injunction to stop him, and afterward gathered it themselves. The banks of "Bubbly Creek" are plastered thick with hairs, and this also the packers gather and clean.

And there were things even stranger than this, according to the gossip of the men. The packers had secret mains, through which they stole billions of gallons of the city's water. The newspapers had been full of this scandal—once there had even been an investigation, and an actual uncovering of the pipes; but nobody had been punished, and the thing went right on. And then there was the condemned meat industry, with its endless horrors. The people of Chicago saw the government inspectors in Packingtown, and they all took that to mean that they were protected from diseased meat; they did not understand that these hundred and sixty-three inspectors had been appointed at the request of the packers, and that they were paid by the United States government to certify that all the diseased meat was kept in the state. They had no authority beyond that; for the inspection of meat to be sold in the city and state the whole force in Packingtown consisted of three henchmen of the local political machine![1]

And shortly afterward one of these, a physician, made the discovery that the carcasses of steers which had been condemned as tubercular by the government inspectors, and which therefore contained ptomaines, which are deadly poisons, were left upon an open platform and carted away to be sold in the city; and so he insisted that these carcasses be treated with an injection of kerosene—and was ordered to resign the same week! So indignant were the packers that they went farther, and compelled the mayor to abolish the whole bureau of inspection; so that since then there has not been even a pretense of any interference with the graft. There was said to be two thousand dollars a week hush money from the tubercular steers alone; and as much again from the hogs which had died of cholera on the trains, and which you might see any day being loaded into boxcars and

---

[1] Rules and Regulations for the Inspection of Livestock and Their Products. United States Department of Agriculture, Bureau of Animal Industries, Order No. 125:—
Section 1. Proprietors of slaughterhouses, canning, salting, packing, or rendering establishments engaged in the slaughtering of cattle, sheep, or swine, or the packing of any of their products, the carcasses or products of which are to become subjects of interstate or foreign commerce, shall make application to the Secretary of Agriculture for inspection of said animals and their products
Section 15. Such rejected or condemned animals shall at once be removed by the owners from the pens containing animals which have been inspected and found to be free from disease and fit for human food, and shall be disposed of in accordance with the laws, ordinances, and regulations of the state and municipality in which said rejected or condemned animals are located
Section 25. A microscopic examination for trichinae shall be made of all swine products exported to countries requiring such examination. No microscopic examination will be made of hogs slaughtered for interstate trade, but this examination shall be confined to those intended for the export trade.

hauled away to a place called Globe, in Indiana, where they made a fancy grade of lard.

Jurgis heard of these things little by little, in the gossip of those who were obliged to perpetrate them. It seemed as if every time you met a person from a new department, you heard of new swindles and new crimes. There was, for instance, a Lithuanian who was a cattle butcher for the plant where Marija had worked, which killed meat for canning only; and to hear this man describe the animals which came to his place would have been worthwhile for a Dante or a Zola. It seemed that they must have agencies all over the country, to hunt out old and crippled and diseased cattle to be canned. There were cattle which had been fed on "whisky-malt," the refuse of the breweries, and had become what the men called "steerly"—which means covered with boils. It was a nasty job killing these, for when you plunged your knife into them they would burst and splash foul-smelling stuff into your face; and when a man's sleeves were smeared with blood, and his hands steeped in it, how was he ever to wipe his face, or to clear his eyes so that he could see? It was stuff such as this that made the "embalmed beef" that had killed several times as many United States soldiers as all the bullets of the Spaniards; only the army beef, besides, was not fresh canned, it was old stuff that had been lying for years in the cellars.

Then one Sunday evening, Jurgis sat puffing his pipe by the kitchen stove, and talking with an old fellow whom Jonas had introduced, and who worked in the canning rooms at Durham's; and so Jurgis learned a few things about the great and only Durham canned goods, which had become a national institution. They were regular alchemists at Durham's; they advertised a mushroom-catsup, and the men who made it did not know what a mushroom looked like. They advertised "potted chicken,"—and it was like the boardinghouse soup of the comic papers, through which a chicken had walked with rubbers on. Perhaps they had a secret process for making chickens chemically—who knows? said Jurgis' friend; the things that went into the mixture were tripe, and the fat of pork, and beef suet, and hearts of beef, and finally the waste ends of veal, when they had any. They put these up in several grades, and sold them at several prices; but the contents of the cans all came out of the same hopper. And then there was "potted game" and "potted grouse," "potted ham," and "deviled ham"—de-vyled, as the men called it. "De-vyled" ham was made out of the waste ends of smoked beef that were too small to be sliced by the machines; and also tripe, dyed with chemicals so that it would not show white; and trimmings of hams and corned beef; and potatoes, skins and all; and finally the hard cartilaginous gullets of beef, after the tongues had been cut out. All this ingenious mixture was ground up and flavored with spices to make it taste like something. Anybody who could invent a new imitation had been sure of a fortune from old Durham, said Jurgis' informant; but it was hard to think of anything new in a place where so many sharp wits had been at work for so long; where men welcomed tuberculosis in the cattle they were feeding, because it made them fatten more quickly; and where they bought up all the old rancid butter left over in the grocery stores of a continent, and "oxidized" it by a forced-air process, to take away the odor, rechurned it with skim milk, and sold it in bricks in the cities! Up to a year or two ago it had been the custom to kill horses in the yards—ostensibly for fertilizer; but after long agitation the newspapers had been able to make the public realize that the horses were being canned. Now it was against the law to kill horses in Packingtown, and the law was really complied with—for the present, at any rate. Any day, however, one might see sharp-horned and shaggy-haired creatures running with the sheep and yet what a job you would have to get the public to believe that a good part of what it buys for lamb and mutton is really goat's flesh!

There was another interesting set of statistics that a person might have gathered in Packingtown—those of the various afflictions of the workers. When Jurgis had first inspected the packing plants with Szedvilas, he had marveled while he listened to the tale of all the things that were made out of the carcasses of animals, and of all the lesser industries that were maintained there; now he found that each one of these lesser industries was a separate little inferno, in its way as horrible as the killing beds, the source and fountain of them all. The workers in each of them had their own peculiar diseases. And the wandering visitor might be skeptical about all the swindles, but he could not be skeptical about these, for the worker bore the evidence of them about on his own person—generally he had only to hold out his hand.

There were the men in the pickle rooms, for instance, where old Antanas had gotten his death; scarce a one of these that had not some spot of horror on his person. Let a man so much as scrape his finger pushing a truck in the pickle rooms, and he might have a sore that would put him out of the world; all the joints in his fingers might be eaten by the acid, one by one. Of the butchers and floorsmen, the beef-boners and trimmers, and all those who used knives, you could scarcely find a person who had the use of his thumb; time and time again the base of it had been slashed, till it was a mere lump of flesh against which the man pressed the knife to hold it. The hands of these men would be criss-crossed with cuts, until you could no longer pretend to count them or to trace them. They would have no nails,—they had worn them off pulling hides; their knuckles were swollen so that their fingers spread out like a fan. There were men who worked in the cooking rooms, in the midst of steam and sickening odors, by artificial light; in these rooms the germs of tuberculosis might live for two years, but the supply was renewed every hour. There were the beef-luggers, who carried two-hundred-pound quarters into the refrigerator-cars; a fearful kind of work, that began at four o'clock in the morning, and that wore out the most powerful men in a few years. There were those who worked in the chilling rooms, and whose special disease was rheumatism; the time limit that a man could work in the chilling rooms was said to be five years. There were the wool-pluckers, whose hands went to pieces even sooner than the hands of the pickle men; for the pelts of the sheep had to be painted with acid to loosen the wool, and then the pluckers had to pull out this wool with their bare hands, till the acid had eaten their fingers off. There were those who made the tins for the canned meat; and their hands, too, were a maze of cuts, and each cut represented a chance for blood poisoning. Some worked at the stamping machines, and it was very seldom that one could work long there at the pace that was set, and not give out and forget himself and have a part of his hand chopped off. There were the "hoisters," as they were called, whose task it was to press the lever which lifted the dead cattle off the floor. They ran along upon a rafter, peering down through the damp and the steam; and as old Durham's architects had not built the killing room for the convenience of the hoisters, at every few feet they would have to stoop under a beam, say four feet above the one they ran on; which got them into the habit of stooping, so that in a few years they would be walking like chimpanzees. Worst of any, however, were the fertilizer men, and those who served in the cooking rooms. These people could not be shown to the visitor,—for the odor of a fertilizer man would scare any ordinary visitor at a hundred yards, and as for the other men, who worked in tank rooms full of steam, and in some of which there were open vats near the level of the floor, their peculiar trouble was that they fell into the vats; and when they were fished out, there was never enough of them left to be worth exhibiting,— sometimes they would be overlooked for days, till all but the bones of them had gone out to the world as Durham's Pure Leaf Lard!

CHAPTER 10

During the early part of the winter the family had had money enough to live and a little over to pay their debts with; but when the earnings of Jurgis fell from nine or ten dollars a week to five or six, there was no longer anything to spare. The winter went, and the spring came, and found them still living thus from hand to mouth, hanging on day by day, with literally not a month's wages between them and starvation. Marija was in despair, for there was still no word about the reopening of the canning factory, and her savings were almost entirely gone. She had had to give up all idea of marrying then; the family could not get along without her—though for that matter she was likely soon to become a burden even upon them, for when her money was all gone, they would have to pay back what they owed her in board. So Jurgis and Ona and Teta Elzbieta would hold anxious conferences until late at night, trying to figure how they could manage this too without starving.

Such were the cruel terms upon which their life was possible, that they might never have nor expect a single instant's respite from worry, a single instant in which they were not haunted by the thought of money. They would no sooner escape, as by a miracle, from one difficulty, than a new one would come into view. In addition to all their physical hardships, there was thus a constant strain upon their minds; they were harried all day and nearly all night by worry and fear. This was in truth not living; it was scarcely even existing, and they felt that it was too little for the price they paid. They were willing to work all the time; and when people did their best, ought they not to be able to keep alive?

There seemed never to be an end to the things they had to buy and to the unforeseen contingencies. Once their water pipes froze and burst; and when, in their ignorance, they thawed them out, they had a terrifying flood in their house. It happened while the men were away, and poor Elzbieta rushed out into the street screaming for help, for she did not even know whether the flood could be stopped, or whether they were ruined for life. It was nearly as bad as the latter, they found in the end, for the plumber charged them seventy-five cents an hour, and seventy-five cents for another man who had stood and watched him, and included all the time the two had been going and coming, and also a charge for all sorts of material and extras. And then again, when they went to pay their January's installment on the house, the agent terrified them by asking them if they had

had the insurance attended to yet. In answer to their inquiry he showed them a clause in the deed which provided that they were to keep the house insured for one thousand dollars, as soon as the present policy ran out, which would happen in a few days. Poor Elzbieta, upon whom again fell the blow, demanded how much it would cost them. Seven dollars, the man said; and that night came Jurgis, grim and determined, requesting that the agent would be good enough to inform him, once for all, as to all the expenses they were liable for. The deed was signed now, he said, with sarcasm proper to the new way of life he had learned—the deed was signed, and so the agent had no longer anything to gain by keeping quiet. And Jurgis looked the fellow squarely in the eye, and so the fellow wasted no time in conventional protests, but read him the deed. They would have to renew the insurance every year; they would have to pay the taxes, about ten dollars a year; they would have to pay the water tax, about six dollars a year—(Jurgis silently resolved to shut off the hydrant). This, besides the interest and the monthly installments, would be all—unless by chance the city should happen to decide to put in a sewer or to lay a sidewalk. Yes, said the agent, they would have to have these, whether they wanted them or not, if the city said so. The sewer would cost them about twenty-two dollars, and the sidewalk fifteen if it were wood, twenty-five if it were cement.

So Jurgis went home again; it was a relief to know the worst, at any rate, so that he could no more be surprised by fresh demands. He saw now how they had been plundered; but they were in for it, there was no turning back. They could only go on and make the fight and win—for defeat was a thing that could not even be thought of.

When the springtime came, they were delivered from the dreadful cold, and that was a great deal; but in addition they had counted on the money they would not have to pay for coal—and it was just at this time that Marija's board began to fail. Then, too, the warm weather brought trials of its own; each season had its trials, as they found. In the spring there were cold rains, that turned the streets into canals and bogs; the mud would be so deep that wagons would sink up to the hubs, so that half a dozen horses could not move them. Then, of course, it was impossible for any one to get to work with dry feet; and this was bad for men that were poorly clad and shod, and still worse for women and children. Later came midsummer, with the stifling heat, when the dingy killing beds of Durham's became a very purgatory; one time, in a single day, three men fell dead from sunstroke. All day long the rivers of hot blood poured forth, until, with the sun beating down, and the air motionless, the stench was enough to knock a man over; all the old smells of a generation would be drawn out by this heat—for there was never any washing of the walls and rafters and pillars, and they were caked with the filth of a lifetime. The men who worked on the killing beds would come to reek with foulness, so that you could smell one of them fifty feet away; there was simply no such thing as keeping decent, the most careful man gave it up in the end, and wallowed in uncleanness. There was not even a place where a man could wash his hands, and the men ate as much raw blood as food at dinnertime. When they were at work they could not even wipe off their faces—they were as helpless as newly born babes in that respect; and it may seem like a small matter, but when the sweat began to run down their necks and tickle them, or a fly to bother them, it was a torture like being burned alive. Whether it was the slaughterhouses or the dumps that were responsible, one could not say, but with the hot weather there descended upon Packingtown a veritable Egyptian plague of flies; there could be no describing this—the houses would be black with them. There was no escaping; you might provide all your doors and windows with screens, but their buzzing outside would be like the swarming of bees, and whenever you opened the door they would rush in as if a storm of wind were driving them.

Perhaps the summertime suggests to you thoughts of the country, visions of green fields and mountains and sparkling lakes. It had no such suggestion for the people in the yards. The great packing machine ground on remorselessly, without thinking of green fields; and the men and women and children who were part of it never saw any green thing, not even a flower. Four or five miles to the east of them lay the blue waters of Lake Michigan; but for all the good it did them it might have been as far away as the Pacific Ocean. They had only Sundays, and then they were too tired to walk. They were tied to the great packing machine, and tied to it for life. The managers and superintendents and clerks of Packingtown were all recruited from another class, and never from the workers; they scorned the workers, the very meanest of them. A poor devil of a bookkeeper who had been working in Durham's for twenty years at a salary of six dollars a week, and might work there for twenty more and do no better, would yet consider himself a gentleman, as far removed as the poles from the most skilled worker on the killing beds; he would dress differently, and live in another part of the town, and come to work at a different hour of the day, and in every way make sure that he never rubbed elbows with a laboring man. Perhaps this was due to the repulsiveness of the work; at any rate, the people who worked with their hands were a class apart, and were made to feel it.

In the late spring the canning factory started up again, and so once more Marija was heard to sing, and the love-music of Tamoszius took on a less melancholy tone. It was not for long, however; for a month or two later a dreadful calamity fell upon Marija. Just one year and three days after she had begun work as a can-painter, she lost her job.

It was a long story. Marija insisted that it was because of her activity in the union. The packers, of course, had spies in all the unions, and in addition they made a practice of buying up a certain number of the union officials, as many as they thought they needed. So every week they received reports as to what was going on, and often they knew things before the members of the union knew them. Any one who was considered to be dangerous by them would find that he was not a favorite with his boss; and Marija had been a great hand for going after the foreign people and preaching to them. However that might be, the known facts were that a few weeks before the factory closed, Marija had been cheated out of her pay for three hundred cans. The girls worked at a long table, and behind them walked a woman with pencil and notebook, keeping count of the number they finished. This woman was, of course, only human, and sometimes made mistakes; when this happened, there was no redress—if on Saturday you got less money than you had earned, you had to make the best of it. But Marija did not understand this, and made a disturbance. Marija's disturbances did not mean anything, and while she had known only Lithuanian and Polish, they had done no harm, for people only laughed at her and made her cry. But now Marija was able to call names in English, and so she got the woman who made the mistake to disliking her. Probably, as Marija claimed, she made mistakes on purpose after that; at any rate, she made them, and the third time it happened Marija went on the warpath and took the matter first to the forelady, and when she got no satisfaction there, to the superintendent. This was unheard-of presumption, but the superintendent said he would see about it, which Marija took to mean that she was going to get her money; after waiting three days, she went to see the superintendent again. This time the man frowned, and said that he had not had time to attend to it; and when Marija, against the advice and warning of every one, tried it once more, he ordered her back to her work in a passion. Just how things happened after that Marija was not sure, but that afternoon the forelady told her that her services would not be any longer required. Poor Marija could not have been more dumfounded had the woman knocked her over the head; at first she could not believe what she heard, and then she grew furious and swore that she would come anyway, that her place belonged to her. In the end she sat down in the middle of the floor and wept and wailed.

It was a cruel lesson; but then Marija was headstrong—she should have listened to those who had had experience. The next time she would know her place, as the forelady expressed it; and so Marija went out, and the family faced the problem of an existence again.

It was especially hard this time, for Ona was to be confined before long, and Jurgis was trying hard to save up money for this. He had heard dreadful stories of the midwives, who grow as thick as fleas in Packingtown; and he had made up his mind that Ona must have a man-doctor. Jurgis could be very obstinate when he wanted to, and he was in this case, much to the dismay of the women, who felt that a man-doctor was an impropriety, and that the matter really belonged to them. The cheapest doctor they could find would charge them fifteen dollars, and perhaps more when the bill came in; and here was Jurgis, declaring that he would pay it, even if he had to stop eating in the meantime!

Marija had only about twenty-five dollars left. Day after day she wandered about the yards begging a job, but this time without hope of finding it. Marija could do the work of an able-bodied man, when she was cheerful, but discouragement wore her out easily, and she would come home at night a pitiable object. She learned her lesson this time, poor creature; she learned it ten times over. All the family learned it along with her—that when you have once got a job in Packingtown, you hang on to it, come what will.

Four weeks Marija hunted, and half of a fifth week. Of course she stopped paying her dues to the union. She lost all interest in the union, and cursed herself for a fool that she had ever been dragged into one. She had about made up her mind that she was a lost soul, when somebody told her of an opening, and she went and got a place as a "beef-trimmer." She got this because the boss saw that she had the muscles of a man, and so he discharged a man and put Marija to do his work, paying her a little more than half what he had been paying before.

When she first came to Packingtown, Marija would have scorned such work as this. She was in another canning factory, and her work was to trim the meat of those diseased cattle that Jurgis had been told about not long before. She was shut up in one of the rooms where the people seldom saw the daylight; beneath her were the chilling rooms, where the meat was frozen, and above her were the cooking rooms; and so she stood on an ice-cold floor, while her head was often so hot that she could scarcely breathe. Trimming beef off the bones by the hundred-weight, while standing up from early morning till late at night, with heavy boots on and the floor always damp and full of puddles, liable to be thrown out of work indefinitely because of a slackening in the trade, liable again to be kept overtime in rush seasons, and be worked till she trembled in every nerve and lost her grip on her slimy knife, and gave herself a poisoned wound—that was the new life that unfolded itself before Marija. But because Marija was a human horse she merely laughed and went at it; it would enable her to pay her board again, and keep the family going. And as for Tamoszius—well, they had waited a long time, and they could wait a little longer. They could not possibly get along upon his wages alone, and the family could not live without hers. He could come and visit her, and sit in the kitchen and hold her hand, and he must manage to be content with that. But day by day the music of Tamoszius' violin became more passionate and heart-breaking; and Marija would sit with her hands clasped and her cheeks wet and all her body a-tremble, hearing in the wailing melodies the voices of the unborn generations which cried out in her for life.

Marija's lesson came just in time to save Ona from a similar fate. Ona, too, was dissatisfied with her place, and had far more reason than Marija. She did not tell half of her story at home, because she saw it was a torment to Jurgis, and she was afraid of what he might do. For a long time Ona had seen that Miss Henderson, the forelady in her department, did not like her. At first she thought it was the old-time mistake she had made in asking for a holiday to get married. Then she concluded it must be because she did not give the forelady a present occasional-ly—she was the kind that took presents from the girls, Ona learned, and made all sorts of discriminations in favor of those who gave them. In the end, however, Ona discovered that it was even worse than that. Miss Henderson was a newcom-er, and it was some time before rumor made her out; but finally it transpired that she was a kept woman, the former mistress of the superintendent of a department in the same building. He had put her there to keep her quiet, it seemed—and that not altogether with success, for once or twice they had been heard quarreling. She had the temper of a hyena, and soon the place she ran was a witch's caldron.

There were some of the girls who were of her own sort, who were willing to toady to her and flatter her; and these would carry tales about the rest, and so the furies were unchained in the place. Worse than this, the woman lived in a bawdy-house downtown, with a coarse, red-faced Irishman named Connor, who was the boss of the loading-gang outside, and would make free with the girls as they went to and from their work. In the slack seasons some of them would go with Miss Henderson to this house downtown—in fact, it would not be too much to say that she managed her department at Brown's in conjunction with it. Sometimes women from the house would be given places alongside of decent girls, and after other decent girls had been turned off to make room for them. When you worked in this woman's department the house downtown was never out of your thoughts all day—there were always whiffs of it to be caught, like the odor of the Packing-town rendering plants at night, when the wind shifted suddenly. There would be stories about it going the rounds; the girls opposite you would be telling them and winking at you. In such a place Ona would not have stayed a day, but for starvation; and, as it was, she was never sure that she could stay the next day. She understood now that the real reason that Miss Henderson hated her was that she was a decent married girl; and she knew that the talebearers and the toadies hated her for the same reason, and were doing their best to make her life miserable.

But there was no place a girl could go in Packingtown, if she was particular about things of this sort; there was no place in it where a prostitute could not get along better than a decent girl. Here was a population, low-class and mostly for-eign, hanging always on the verge of starvation, and dependent for its opportunities of life upon the whim of men every bit as brutal and unscrupulous as the old-time slave drivers; under such circumstances immorality was exactly as inevitable, and as prevalent, as it was under the system of chattel slavery. Things that were quite unspeakable went on there in the packing houses all the time, and were taken for granted by everybody; only they did not show, as in the old slavery times, because there was no difference in color between master and slave.

One morning Ona stayed home, and Jurgis had the man-doctor, according to his whim, and she was safely delivered of a fine baby. It was an enormous big boy, and Ona was such a tiny creature herself, that it seemed quite incredible. Jurgis would stand and gaze at the stranger by the hour, unable to believe that it had really happened.

The coming of this boy was a decisive event with Jurgis. It made him irrevo-cably a family man; it killed the last lingering impulse that he might have had to go out in the evenings and sit and talk with the men in the saloons. There was nothing he cared for now so much as to sit and look at the baby. This was very curious, for Jurgis had never been interested in babies before. But then, this was a very unusual sort of a baby. He had the brightest little black eyes, and little black ringlets all over his head; he was the living image of his father, everybody said— and Jurgis found this a fascinating circumstance. It was sufficiently perplexing that this tiny mite of life should have come into the world at all in the manner that it had; that it should have come with a comical imitation of its father's nose was simply uncanny.

Perhaps, Jurgis thought, this was intended to signify that it was his baby; that it was his and Ona's, to care for all its life. Jurgis had never possessed anything nearly so interesting—a baby was, when you came to think about it, assuredly a marvelous possession. It would grow up to be a man, a human soul, with a personality all its own, a will of its own! Such thoughts would keep haunting Jurgis, filling him with all sorts of strange and almost painful excitements. He was wonderfully proud of little Antanas; he was curious about all the details of him—the washing and the dressing and the eating and the sleeping of him, and asked all sorts of absurd questions. It took him quite a while to get over his alarm at the incredible shortness of the little creature's legs.

Jurgis had, alas, very little time to see his baby; he never felt the chains about him more than just then. When he came home at night, the baby would be asleep, and it would be the merest chance if he awoke before Jurgis had to go to sleep himself. Then in the morning there was no time to look at him, so really the only chance the father had was on Sundays. This was more cruel yet for Ona, who ought to have stayed home and nursed him, the doctor said, for her own health as well as the baby's; but Ona had to go to work, and leave him for Teta Elzbieta to feed upon the pale blue poison that was called milk at the corner grocery. Ona's confinement lost her only a week's wages—she would go to the factory the second Monday, and the best that Jurgis could persuade her was to ride in the car, and let him run along behind and help her to Brown's when she alighted. After that it would be all right, said Ona, it was no strain sitting still sewing hams all day; and if she waited longer she might find that her dreadful forelady had put some one else in her place. That would be a greater calamity than ever now, Ona continued, on account of the baby. They would all have to work harder now on his account. It was such a responsibility—they must not have the baby grow up to suffer as they had. And this indeed had been the first thing that Jurgis had thought of himself—he had clenched his hands and braced himself anew for the struggle, for the sake of that tiny mite of human possibility.

And so Ona went back to Brown's and saved her place and a week's wages; and so she gave herself some one of the thousand ailments that women group under the title of "womb trouble," and was never again a well person as long as she lived. It is difficult to convey in words all that this meant to Ona; it seemed such a slight offense, and the punishment was so out of all proportion, that neither she nor any one else ever connected the two. "Womb trouble" to Ona did not mean a specialist's diagnosis, and a course of treatment, and perhaps an operation or two; it meant simply headaches and pains in the back, and depression and heartsickness, and neuralgia when she had to go to work in the rain. The great majority of the women who worked in Packingtown suffered in the same way, and from the same cause, so it was not deemed a thing to see the doctor about; instead Ona would try patent medicines, one after another, as her friends told her about them. As these all contained alcohol, or some other stimulant, she found that they all did her good while she took them; and so she was always chasing the phantom of good health, and losing it because she was too poor to continue.

CHAPTER 11

During the summer the packing houses were in full activity again, and Jurgis made more money. He did not make so much, however, as he had the previous summer, for the packers took on more hands. There were new men every week, it seemed—it was a regular system; and this number they would keep over to the next slack season, so that every one would have less than ever. Sooner or later, by this plan, they would have all the floating labor of Chicago trained to do their work. And how very cunning a trick was that! The men were to teach new hands, who would some day come and break their strike; and meantime they were kept so poor that they could not prepare for the trial!

But let no one suppose that this superfluity of employees meant easier work for any one! On the contrary, the speeding-up seemed to be growing more savage all the time; they were continually inventing new devices to crowd the work on— it was for all the world like the thumbscrew of the medieval torture chamber. They would get new pacemakers and pay them more; they would drive the men on with new machinery—it was said that in the hog-killing rooms the speed at which the hogs moved was determined by clockwork, and that it was increased a little every day. In piecework they would reduce the time, requiring the same work in a shorter time, and paying the same wages; and then, after the workers had accustomed themselves to this new speed, they would reduce the rate of payment to correspond with the reduction in time! They had done this so often in the canning establishments that the girls were fairly desperate; their wages had gone down by a full third in the past two years, and a storm of discontent was brewing that was likely to break any day. Only a month after Marija had become a beef-trimmer the canning factory that she had left posted a cut that would divide the girls' earnings almost squarely in half; and so great was the indignation at this that they marched out without even a parley, and organized in the street outside. One of the girls had read somewhere that a red flag was the proper symbol for oppressed workers, and so they mounted one, and paraded all about the yards, yelling with rage. A new union was the result of this outburst, but the impromptu strike went to pieces in three days, owing to the rush of new labor. At the end of it the girl who had carried the red flag went downtown and got a position in a great department store, at a salary of two dollars and a half a week.

Jurgis and Ona heard these stories with dismay, for there was no telling when their own time might come. Once or twice there had been rumors that one of the big houses was going to cut its unskilled men to fifteen cents an hour, and Jurgis knew that if this was done, his turn would come soon. He had learned by this time that Packingtown was really not a number of firms at all, but one great firm, the Beef Trust. And every week the managers of it got together and compared notes, and there was one scale for all the workers in the yards and one standard of efficiency. Jurgis was told that they also fixed the price they would pay for beef on the hoof and the price of all dressed meat in the country; but that was something he did not understand or care about.

The only one who was not afraid of a cut was Marija, who congratulated herself, somewhat naively, that there had been one in her place only a short time before she came. Marija was getting to be a skilled beef-trimmer, and was mounting to the heights again. During the summer and fall Jurgis and Ona managed to pay her back the last penny they owed her, and so she began to have a bank account. Tamoszius had a bank account also, and they ran a race, and began to figure upon household expenses once more.

The possession of vast wealth entails cares and responsibilities, however, as poor Marija found out. She had taken the advice of a friend and invested her savings in a bank on Ashland Avenue. Of course she knew nothing about it, except that it was big and imposing—what possible chance has a poor foreign working girl to understand the banking business, as it is conducted in this land of frenzied finance? So Marija lived in a continual dread lest something should happen to her bank, and would go out of her way mornings to make sure that it was still there. Her principal thought was of fire, for she had deposited her money in bills, and was afraid that if they were burned up the bank would not give her any others. Jurgis made fun of her for this, for he was a man and was proud of his superior knowledge, telling her that the bank had fireproof vaults, and all its millions of dollars hidden safely away in them.

However, one morning Marija took her usual detour, and, to her horror and dismay, saw a crowd of people in front of the bank, filling the avenue solid for half a block. All the blood went out of her face for terror. She broke into a run, shouting to the people to ask what was the matter, but not stopping to hear what they answered, till she had come to where the throng was so dense that she could no longer advance. There was a "run on the bank," they told her then, but she did not know what that was, and turned from one person to another, trying in an agony of fear to make out what they meant. Had something gone wrong with the bank? Nobody was sure, but they thought so. Couldn't she get her money? There was no telling; the people were afraid not, and they were all trying to get it. It was too early yet to tell anything—the bank would not open for nearly three hours. So in a frenzy of despair Marija began to claw her way toward the doors of this building, through a throng of men, women, and children, all as excited as herself. It was a scene of wild confusion, women shrieking and wringing their hands and fainting, and men fighting and trampling down everything in their way. In the midst of the melee Marija recollected that she did not have her bankbook, and could not get her money anyway, so she fought her way out and started on a run for home. This was fortunate for her, for a few minutes later the police reserves arrived.

In half an hour Marija was back, Teta Elzbieta with her, both of them breathless with running and sick with fear. The crowd was now formed in a line, extending for several blocks, with half a hundred policemen keeping guard, and so there was nothing for them to do but to take their places at the end of it. At nine o'clock the bank opened and began to pay the waiting throng; but then, what good did that do Marija, who saw three thousand people before her—enough to take out the last penny of a dozen banks?

To make matters worse a drizzling rain came up, and soaked them to the skin; yet all the morning they stood there, creeping slowly toward the goal—all the afternoon they stood there, heartsick, seeing that the hour of closing was coming, and that they were going to be left out. Marija made up her mind that, come what might, she would stay there and keep her place; but as nearly all did the same, all through the long, cold night, she got very little closer to the bank for that. Toward evening Jurgis came; he had heard the story from the children, and he brought some food and dry wraps, which made it a little easier.

The next morning, before daybreak, came a bigger crowd than ever, and more policemen from downtown. Marija held on like grim death, and toward afternoon she got into the bank and got her money—all in big silver dollars, a handkerchief full. When she had once got her hands on them her fear vanished, and she wanted to put them back again; but the man at the window was savage, and said that the bank would receive no more deposits from those who had taken part in the run. So Marija was forced to take her dollars home with her, watching to right and left, expecting every instant that some one would try to rob her; and when she got home she was not much better off. Until she could find another bank there was nothing to do but sew them up in her clothes, and so Marija went about for a week or more, loaded down with bullion, and afraid to cross the street in front of the house, because Jurgis told her she would sink out of sight in the mud. Weighted this way she made her way to the yards, again in fear, this time to see if she had lost her place; but fortunately about ten per cent of the working people of Packingtown had been depositors in that bank, and it was not convenient to discharge that many at once. The cause of the panic had been the attempt of a policeman to arrest a drunken man in a saloon next door, which had drawn a crowd at the hour the people were on their way to work, and so started the "run."

About this time Jurgis and Ona also began a bank account. Besides having paid Jonas and Marija, they had almost paid for their furniture, and could have that little sum to count on. So long as each of them could bring home nine or ten dollars a week, they were able to get along finely. Also election day came round again, and Jurgis made half a week's wages out of that, all net profit. It was a very close election that year, and the echoes of the battle reached even to Packingtown. The two rival sets of grafters hired halls and set off fireworks and made speeches, to try to get the people interested in the matter. Although Jurgis did not under-stand it all, he knew enough by this time to realize that it was not supposed to be right to sell your vote. However, as every one did it, and his refusal to join would not have made the slightest difference in the results, the idea of refusing would have seemed absurd, had it ever come into his head.

Now chill winds and shortening days began to warn them that the winter was coming again. It seemed as if the respite had been too short—they had not had time enough to get ready for it; but still it came, inexorably, and the hunted look began to come back into the eyes of little Stanislovas. The prospect struck fear to the heart of Jurgis also, for he knew that Ona was not fit to face the cold and the snowdrifts this year. And suppose that some day when a blizzard struck them and the cars were not running, Ona should have to give up, and should come the next day to find that her place had been given to some one who lived nearer and could be depended on?

It was the week before Christmas that the first storm came, and then the soul of Jurgis rose up within him like a sleeping lion. There were four days that the Ashland Avenue cars were stalled, and in those days, for the first time in his life, Jurgis knew what it was to be really opposed. He had faced difficulties before, but they had been child's play; now there was a death struggle, and all the furies were unchained within him. The first morning they set out two hours before dawn, Ona wrapped all in blankets and tossed upon his shoulder like a sack of meal, and the little boy, bundled nearly out of sight, hanging by his coat-tails. There was a rag-ing blast beating in his face, and the thermometer stood below zero; the snow was never short of his knees, and in some of the drifts it was nearly up to his armpits. It would catch his feet and try to trip him; it would build itself into a wall before him to beat him back; and he would fling himself into it, plunging like a wounded buffalo, puffing and snorting in rage. So foot by foot he drove his way, and when at last he came to Durham's he was staggering and almost blind, and leaned against a pillar, gasping, and thanking God that the cattle came late to the killing beds that day. In the evening the same thing had to be done again; and because Jurgis could not tell what hour of the night he would get off, he got a saloon-keeper to let Ona sit and wait for him in a corner. Once it was eleven o'clock at night, and black as the pit, but still they got home.

That blizzard knocked many a man out, for the crowd outside begging for work was never greater, and the packers would not wait long for any one. When it was over, the soul of Jurgis was a song, for he had met the enemy and conquered, and felt himself the master of his fate.—So it might be with some monarch of the forest that has vanquished his foes in fair fight, and then falls into some cowardly trap in the night-time.

A time of peril on the killing beds was when a steer broke loose. Sometimes, in the haste of speeding-up, they would dump one of the animals out on the floor before it was fully stunned, and it would get upon its feet and run amuck. Then there would be a yell of warning—the men would drop everything and dash for the nearest pillar, slipping here and there on the floor, and tumbling over each other. This was bad enough in the summer, when a man could see; in wintertime it was enough to make your hair stand up, for the room would be so full of steam that you could not make anything out five feet in front of you. To be sure, the steer was generally blind and frantic, and not especially bent on hurting any one; but think of the chances of running upon a knife, while nearly every man had one in his hand! And then, to cap the climax, the floor boss would come rushing up with a rifle and begin blazing away!

It was in one of these melees that Jurgis fell into his trap. That is the only word to describe it; it was so cruel, and so utterly not to be foreseen. At first he hardly noticed it, it was such a slight accident—simply that in leaping out of the way he turned his ankle. There was a twinge of pain, but Jurgis was used to pain, and did not coddle himself. When he came to walk home, however, he realized that it was hurting him a great deal; and in the morning his ankle was swollen out nearly double its size, and he could not get his foot into his shoe. Still, even then, he did nothing more than swear a little, and wrapped his foot in old rags, and hobbled out to take the car. It chanced to be a rush day at Durham's, and all the long morning he limped about with his aching foot; by noontime the pain was so great that it made him faint, and after a couple of hours in the afternoon he was fairly beaten, and had to tell the boss. They sent for the company doctor, and he examined the foot and told Jurgis to go home to bed, adding that he had probably laid himself up for months by his folly. The injury was not one that Durham and Company could be held responsible for, and so that was all there was to it, so far as the doctor was concerned.

Jurgis got home somehow, scarcely able to see for the pain, and with an awful terror in his soul, Elzbieta helped him into bed and bandaged his injured foot with cold water and tried hard not to let him see her dismay; when the rest came home at night she met them outside and told them, and they, too, put on a cheerful face, saying it would only be for a week or two, and that they would pull him through.

When they had gotten him to sleep, however, they sat by the kitchen fire and talked it over in frightened whispers. They were in for a siege, that was plainly to be seen. Jurgis had only about sixty dollars in the bank, and the slack season was upon them. Both Jonas and Marija might soon be earning no more than enough to pay their board, and besides that there were only the wages of Ona and the pittance of the little boy. There was the rent to pay, and still some on the furniture; there was the insurance just due, and every month there was sack after sack of coal. It was January, midwinter, an awful time to have to face privation. Deep snows would come again, and who would carry Ona to her work now? She might lose her place—she was almost certain to lose it. And then little Stanislovas began to whimper—who would take care of him?

It was dreadful that an accident of this sort, that no man can help, should have meant such suffering. The bitterness of it was the daily food and drink of Jurgis. It was of no use for them to try to deceive him; he knew as much about the situation as they did, and he knew that the family might literally starve to death. The worry of it fairly ate him up—he began to look haggard the first two or three days of it.

In truth, it was almost maddening for a strong man like him, a fighter, to have to lie there helpless on his back. It was for all the world the old story of Prometheus bound. As Jurgis lay on his bed, hour after hour there came to him emotions that he had never known before. Before this he had met life with a welcome—it had its trials, but none that a man could not face. But now, in the nighttime, when he lay tossing about, there would come stalking into his chamber a grisly phantom, the sight of which made his flesh curl and his hair to bristle up. It was like seeing the world fall away from underneath his feet; like plunging down into a bottomless abyss into yawning caverns of despair. It might be true, then, after all, what others had told him about life, that the best powers of a man might not be equal to it! It might be true that, strive as he would, toil as he would, he might fail, and go down and be destroyed! The thought of this was like an icy hand at his heart; the thought that here, in this ghastly home of all horror, he and all those who were dear to him might lie and perish of starvation and cold, and there would be no ear to hear their cry, no hand to help them! It was true, it was true,—that here in this huge city, with its stores of heaped-up wealth, human creatures might be hunted down and destroyed by the wild-beast powers of nature, just as truly as ever they were in the days of the cave men!

Ona was now making about thirty dollars a month, and Stanislovas about thirteen. To add to this there was the board of Jonas and Marija, about forty-five dollars. Deducting from this the rent, interest, and installments on the furniture, they had left sixty dollars, and deducting the coal, they had fifty. They did without everything that human beings could do without; they went in old and ragged clothing, that left them at the mercy of the cold, and when the children's shoes wore out, they tied them up with string. Half invalid as she was, Ona would do herself harm by walking in the rain and cold when she ought to have ridden; they bought literally nothing but food—and still they could not keep alive on fifty dollars a month. They might have done it, if only they could have gotten pure food, and at fair prices; or if only they had known what to get—if they had not been so pitifully ignorant! But they had come to a new country, where everything was different, including the food. They had always been accustomed to eat a great deal of smoked sausage, and how could they know that what they bought in America was not the same—that its color was made by chemicals, and its smoky flavor by more chemicals, and that it was full of "potato flour" besides? Potato flour is the waste of potato after the starch and alcohol have been extracted; it has no more food value than so much wood, and as its use as a food adulterant is a penal offense in Europe, thousands of tons of it are shipped to America every year. It was amazing what quantities of food such as this were needed every day, by eleven hungry persons. A dollar sixty-five a day was simply not enough to feed them, and there was no use trying; and so each week they made an inroad upon the pitiful little bank account that Ona had begun. Because the account was in her name, it was possible for her to keep this a secret from her husband, and to keep the heartsickness of it for her own.

It would have been better if Jurgis had been really ill; if he had not been able to think. For he had no resources such as most invalids have; all he could do was to lie there and toss about from side to side. Now and then he would break into cursing, regardless of everything; and now and then his impatience would get the better of him, and he would try to get up, and poor Teta Elzbieta would have to plead with him in a frenzy. Elzbieta was all alone with him the greater part of the time. She would sit and smooth his forehead by the hour, and talk to him and try to make him forget. Sometimes it would be too cold for the children to go to school, and they would have to play in the kitchen, where Jurgis was, because it was the only room that was half warm. These were dreadful times, for Jurgis would get as cross as any bear; he was scarcely to be blamed, for he had enough to worry him, and it was hard when he was trying to take a nap to be kept awake by noisy and peevish children.

Elzbieta's only resource in those times was little Antanas; indeed, it would be hard to say how they could have gotten along at all if it had not been for little Antanas. It was the one consolation of Jurgis' long imprisonment that now he had time to look at his baby. Teta Elzbieta would put the clothes-basket in which the baby slept alongside of his mattress, and Jurgis would lie upon one elbow and watch him by the hour, imagining things. Then little Antanas would open his eyes—he was beginning to take notice of things now; and he would smile—how he would smile! So Jurgis would begin to forget and be happy because he was in a world where there was a thing so beautiful as the smile of little Antanas, and because such a world could not but be good at the heart of it. He looked more like his father every hour, Elzbieta would say, and said it many times a day, because she saw that it pleased Jurgis; the poor little terror-stricken woman was planning all day and all night to soothe the prisoned giant who was intrusted to her care. Jurgis, who knew nothing about the age-long and everlasting hypocrisy of woman, would take the bait and grin with delight; and then he would hold his finger in front of little Antanas' eyes, and move it this way and that, and laugh with glee to see the baby follow it. There is no pet quite so fascinating as a baby; he would look into Jurgis' face with such uncanny seriousness, and Jurgis would start and cry: "Palauk! Look, Muma, he knows his papa! He does, he does! Tu mano szirdele, the little rascal!"

CHAPTER 12

For three weeks after his injury Jurgis never got up from bed. It was a very obstinate sprain; the swelling would not go down, and the pain still continued. At the end of that time, however, he could contain himself no longer, and began trying to walk a little every day, laboring to persuade himself that he was better. No arguments could stop him, and three or four days later he declared that he was going back to work. He limped to the cars and got to Brown's, where he found that the boss had kept his place—that is, was willing to turn out into the snow the poor devil he had hired in the meantime. Every now and then the pain would force Jurgis to stop work, but he stuck it out till nearly an hour before closing. Then he was forced to acknowledge that he could not go on without fainting; it almost broke his heart to do it, and he stood leaning against a pillar and weeping like a child. Two of the men had to help him to the car, and when he got out he had to sit down and wait in the snow till some one came along.

So they put him to bed again, and sent for the doctor, as they ought to have done in the beginning. It transpired that he had twisted a tendon out of place, and could never have gotten well without attention. Then he gripped the sides of the bed, and shut his teeth together, and turned white with agony, while the doctor pulled and wrenched away at his swollen ankle. When finally the doctor left, he told him that he would have to lie quiet for two months, and that if he went to work before that time he might lame himself for life.

Three days later there came another heavy snowstorm, and Jonas and Marija and Ona and little Stanislovas all set out together, an hour before daybreak, to try to get to the yards. About noon the last two came back, the boy screaming with pain. His fingers were all frosted, it seemed. They had had to give up trying to get to the yards, and had nearly perished in a drift. All that they knew how to do was to hold the frozen fingers near the fire, and so little Stanislovas spent most of the day dancing about in horrible agony, till Jurgis flew into a passion of nervous rage and swore like a madman, declaring that he would kill him if he did not stop. All that day and night the family was half-crazed with fear that Ona and the boy had lost their places; and in the morning they set out earlier than ever, after the little fellow had been beaten with a stick by Jurgis. There could be no trifling in a case like this, it was a matter of life and death; little Stanislovas could not be expected to realize that he might a great deal better freeze in the snowdrift than lose his job at the lard machine. Ona was quite certain that she would find her place gone, and was all unnerved when she finally got to Brown's, and found that the forelady herself had failed to come, and was therefore compelled to be lenient.

One of the consequences of this episode was that the first joints of three of the little boy's fingers were permanently disabled, and another that thereafter he always had to be beaten before he set out to work, whenever there was fresh snow on the ground. Jurgis was called upon to do the beating, and as it hurt his foot he did it with a vengeance; but it did not tend to add to the sweetness of his temper. They say that the best dog will turn cross if he be kept chained all the time, and it was the same with the man; he had not a thing to do all day but lie and curse his fate, and the time came when he wanted to curse everything.

This was never for very long, however, for when Ona began to cry, Jurgis could not stay angry. The poor fellow looked like a homeless ghost, with his cheeks sunken in and his long black hair straggling into his eyes; he was too discouraged to cut it, or to think about his appearance. His muscles were wasting away, and what were left were soft and flabby. He had no appetite, and they could not afford to tempt him with delicacies. It was better, he said, that he should not eat, it was a saving. About the end of March he had got hold of Ona's bankbook, and learned that there was only three dollars left to them in the world.

But perhaps the worst of the consequences of this long siege was that they lost another member of their family; Brother Jonas disappeared. One Saturday night he did not come home, and thereafter all their efforts to get trace of him were futile. It was said by the boss at Durham's that he had gotten his week's money and left there. That might not be true, of course, for sometimes they would say that when a man had been killed; it was the easiest way out of it for all concerned. When, for instance, a man had fallen into one of the rendering tanks and had been made into pure leaf lard and peerless fertilizer, there was no use letting the fact out and making his family unhappy. More probable, however, was the theory that Jonas had deserted them, and gone on the road, seeking happiness. He had been discontented for a long time, and not without some cause. He paid good board, and was yet obliged to live in a family where nobody had enough to eat. And Marija would keep giving them all her money, and of course he could not but feel that he was called upon to do the same. Then there were crying brats, and all sorts of misery; a man would have had to be a good deal of a hero to stand it all without grumbling, and Jonas was not in the least a hero—he was simply a weatherbeaten old fellow who liked to have a good supper and sit in the corner by the fire and smoke his pipe in peace before he went to bed. Here there was not room by the fire, and through the winter the kitchen had seldom been warm enough for comfort. So, with the springtime, what was more likely than that the wild idea of escaping had come to him? Two years he had been yoked like a horse to a half-ton truck in Durham's dark cellars, with never a rest, save on Sundays and four holidays in the year, and with never a word of thanks—only kicks and blows and curses, such as no decent dog would have stood. And now the winter was over, and the spring winds were blowing—and with a day's walk a man might put the smoke of Packingtown behind him forever, and be where the grass was green and the flowers all the colors of the rainbow!

But now the income of the family was cut down more than one-third, and the food demand was cut only one-eleventh, so that they were worse off than ever. Also they were borrowing money from Marija, and eating up her bank account, and spoiling once again her hopes of marriage and happiness. And they were even going into debt to Tamoszius Kuszleika and letting him impoverish himself. Poor Tamoszius was a man without any relatives, and with a wonderful talent besides, and he ought to have made money and prospered; but he had fallen in love, and so given hostages to fortune, and was doomed to be dragged down too.

So it was finally decided that two more of the children would have to leave school. Next to Stanislovas, who was now fifteen, there was a girl, little Kotrina, who was two years younger, and then two boys, Vilimas, who was eleven, and Nikalojus, who was ten. Both of these last were bright boys, and there was no reason why their family should starve when tens of thousands of children no older were earning their own livings. So one morning they were given a quarter apiece and a roll with a sausage in it, and, with their minds top-heavy with good advice, were sent out to make their way to the city and learn to sell newspapers. They came back late at night in tears, having walked for the five or six miles to report that a man had offered to take them to a place where they sold newspapers, and had taken their money and gone into a store to get them, and nevermore been seen. So they both received a whipping, and the next morning set out again. This time they found the newspaper place, and procured their stock; and after wandering about till nearly noontime, saying "Paper?" to every one they saw, they had all their stock taken away and received a thrashing besides from a big newsman upon whose territory they had trespassed. Fortunately, however, they had already sold some papers, and came back with nearly as much as they started with.

After a week of mishaps such as these, the two little fellows began to learn the ways of the trade—the names of the different papers, and how many of each to get, and what sort of people to offer them to, and where to go and where to stay away from. After this, leaving home at four o'clock in the morning, and running about the streets, first with morning papers and then with evening, they might come home late at night with twenty or thirty cents apiece—possibly as much as forty cents. From this they had to deduct their carfare, since the distance was so great; but after a while they made friends, and learned still more, and then they would save their carfare. They would get on a car when the conductor was not looking, and hide in the crowd; and three times out of four he would not ask for their fares, either not seeing them, or thinking they had already paid; or if he did ask, they would hunt through their pockets, and then begin to cry, and either have their fares paid by some kind old lady, or else try the trick again on a new car. All this was fair play, they felt. Whose fault was it that at the hours when working-men were going to their work and back, the cars were so crowded that the conductors could not collect all the fares? And besides, the companies were thieves, people said—had stolen all their franchises with the help of scoundrelly politicians!

Now that the winter was by, and there was no more danger of snow, and no more coal to buy, and another room warm enough to put the children into when they cried, and enough money to get along from week to week with, Jurgis was less terrible than he had been. A man can get used to anything in the course of time, and Jurgis had gotten used to lying about the house. Ona saw this, and was very careful not to destroy his peace of mind, by letting him know how very much pain she was suffering. It was now the time of the spring rains, and Ona had often to ride to her work, in spite of the expense; she was getting paler every day, and sometimes, in spite of her good resolutions, it pained her that Jurgis did not notice it. She wondered if he cared for her as much as ever, if all this misery was not wearing out his love. She had to be away from him all the time, and bear her own troubles while he was bearing his; and then, when she came home, she was so worn out; and whenever they talked they had only their worries to talk of—truly it was hard, in such a life, to keep any sentiment alive. The woe of this would flame up in Ona sometimes—at night she would suddenly clasp her big husband in her arms and break into passionate weeping, demanding to know if he really loved her. Poor Jurgis, who had in truth grown more matter-of-fact, under the endless pressure of penury, would not know what to make of these things, and could only try to recollect when he had last been cross; and so Ona would have to forgive him and sob herself to sleep.

The latter part of April Jurgis went to see the doctor, and was given a bandage to lace about his ankle, and told that he might go back to work. It needed more than the permission of the doctor, however, for when he showed up on the killing floor of Brown's, he was told by the foreman that it had not been possible to keep his job for him. Jurgis knew that this meant simply that the foreman had found some one else to do the work as well and did not want to bother to make a change. He stood in the doorway, looking mournfully on, seeing his friends and companions at work, and feeling like an outcast. Then he went out and took his place with the mob of the unemployed.

This time, however, Jurgis did not have the same fine confidence, nor the same reason for it. He was no longer the finest-looking man in the throng, and the bosses no longer made for him; he was thin and haggard, and his clothes were seedy, and he looked miserable. And there were hundreds who looked and felt just like him, and who had been wandering about Packingtown for months begging for work. This was a critical time in Jurgis' life, and if he had been a weaker man he would have gone the way the rest did. Those out-of-work wretches would stand about the packing houses every morning till the police drove them away, and then they would scatter among the saloons. Very few of them had the nerve to face the rebuffs that they would encounter by trying to get into the buildings to interview the bosses; if they did not get a chance in the morning, there would be nothing to do but hang about the saloons the rest of the day and night. Jurgis was saved from all this—partly, to be sure, because it was pleasant weather, and there was no need to be indoors; but mainly because he carried with him always the pitiful little face of his wife. He must get work, he told himself, fighting the battle with despair every hour of the day. He must get work! He must have a place again and some money saved up, before the next winter came.

But there was no work for him. He sought out all the members of his union—Jurgis had stuck to the union through all this—and begged them to speak a word for him. He went to every one he knew, asking for a chance, there or anywhere. He wandered all day through the buildings; and in a week or two, when he had been all over the yards, and into every room to which he had access, and learned that there was not a job anywhere, he persuaded himself that there might have been a change in the places he had first visited, and began the round all over; till finally the watchmen and the "spotters" of the companies came to know him by sight and to order him out with threats. Then there was nothing more for him to do but go with the crowd in the morning, and keep in the front row and look eager, and when he failed, go back home, and play with little Kotrina and the baby.

The peculiar bitterness of all this was that Jurgis saw so plainly the meaning of it. In the beginning he had been fresh and strong, and he had gotten a job the first day; but now he was second-hand, a damaged article, so to speak, and they did not want him. They had got the best of him—they had worn him out, with their speeding-up and their carelessness, and now they had thrown him away! And Jurgis would make the acquaintance of others of these unemployed men and find that they had all had the same experience. There were some, of course, who had wandered in from other places, who had been ground up in other mills; there were others who were out from their own fault—some, for instance, who had not been able to stand the awful grind without drink. The vast majority, however, were simply the worn-out parts of the great merciless packing machine; they had toiled there, and kept up with the pace, some of them for ten or twenty years, until finally the time had come when they could not keep up with it any more. Some had been frankly told that they were too old, that a sprier man was needed; others had given occasion, by some act of carelessness or incompetence; with most, however, the occasion had been the same as with Jurgis. They had been overworked and underfed so long, and finally some disease had laid them on their backs; or they had cut themselves, and had blood poisoning, or met with some other accident. When a man came back after that, he would get his place back only by the courtesy of the boss. To this there was no exception, save when the accident was one for which the firm was liable; in that case they would send a slippery lawyer to see him, first to try to get him to sign away his claims, but if he was too smart for that, to promise him that he and his should always be provided with work. This promise they would keep, strictly and to the letter—for two years. Two years was the "statute of limitations," and after that the victim could not sue.

What happened to a man after any of these things, all depended upon the circumstances. If he were of the highly skilled workers, he would probably have enough saved up to tide him over. The best paid men, the "splitters," made fifty cents an hour, which would be five or six dollars a day in the rush seasons, and one or two in the dullest. A man could live and save on that; but then there were only half a dozen splitters in each place, and one of them that Jurgis knew had a family of twenty-two children, all hoping to grow up to be splitters like their father. For an unskilled man, who made ten dollars a week in the rush seasons and five in the dull, it all depended upon his age and the number he had dependent upon him. An unmarried man could save, if he did not drink, and if he was absolutely selfish—that is, if he paid no heed to the demands of his old parents, or of his little brothers and sisters, or of any other relatives he might have, as well as of the members of his union, and his chums, and the people who might be starving to death next door.

CHAPTER 13

During this time that Jurgis was looking for work occurred the death of little Kristoforas, one of the children of Teta Elzbieta. Both Kristoforas and his brother, Juozapas, were cripples, the latter having lost one leg by having it run over, and Kristoforas having congenital dislocation of the hip, which made it impossible for him ever to walk. He was the last of Teta Elzbieta's children, and perhaps he had been intended by nature to let her know that she had had enough. At any rate he was wretchedly sick and undersized; he had the rickets, and though he was over three years old, he was no bigger than an ordinary child of one. All day long he would crawl around the floor in a filthy little dress, whining and fretting; because the floor was full of drafts he was always catching cold, and snuffling because his nose ran. This made him a nuisance, and a source of endless trouble in the family. For his mother, with unnatural perversity, loved him best of all her children, and made a perpetual fuss over him—would let him do anything undisturbed, and would burst into tears when his fretting drove Jurgis wild.

And now he died. Perhaps it was the smoked sausage he had eaten that morning—which may have been made out of some of the tubercular pork that was condemned as unfit for export. At any rate, an hour after eating it, the child had begun to cry with pain, and in another hour he was rolling about on the floor in convulsions. Little Kotrina, who was all alone with him, ran out screaming for help, and after a while a doctor came, but not until Kristoforas had howled his last howl. No one was really sorry about this except poor Elzbieta, who was inconsolable. Jurgis announced that so far as he was concerned the child would have to be buried by the city, since they had no money for a funeral; and at this the poor woman almost went out of her senses, wringing her hands and screaming with grief and despair. Her child to be buried in a pauper's grave! And her stepdaughter to stand by and hear it said without protesting! It was enough to make Ona's father rise up out of his grave to rebuke her! If it had come to this, they might as well give up at once, and be buried all of them together! . . . In the end Marija said that she would help with ten dollars; and Jurgis being still obdurate, Elzbieta went in tears and begged the money from the neighbors, and so little Kristoforas had a mass and a hearse with white plumes on it, and a tiny plot in a graveyard with a wooden cross to mark the place. The poor mother was not the same for months after that; the mere sight of the floor where little Kristoforas had crawled about would make her weep. He had never had a fair chance, poor little fellow, she would say. He had been handicapped from his birth. If only she had heard about it in time, so that she might have had that great doctor to cure him of his lameness! . . . Some time ago, Elzbieta was told, a Chicago billionaire had paid a fortune to bring a great European surgeon over to cure his little daughter of the same disease from which Kristoforas had suffered. And because this surgeon had to have bodies to demonstrate upon, he announced that he would treat the children of the poor, a piece of magnanimity over which the papers became quite eloquent. Elzbieta, alas, did not read the papers, and no one had told her; but perhaps it was as well, for just then they would not have had the carfare to spare to go every day to wait upon the surgeon, nor for that matter anybody with the time to take the child.

All this while that he was seeking for work, there was a dark shadow hanging over Jurgis; as if a savage beast were lurking somewhere in the pathway of his life, and he knew it, and yet could not help approaching the place. There are all stages of being out of work in Packingtown, and he faced in dread the prospect of reaching the lowest. There is a place that waits for the lowest man—the fertilizer plant!

The men would talk about it in awe-stricken whispers. Not more than one in ten had ever really tried it; the other nine had contented themselves with hearsay evidence and a peep through the door. There were some things worse than even starving to death. They would ask Jurgis if he had worked there yet, and if he meant to; and Jurgis would debate the matter with himself. As poor as they were, and making all the sacrifices that they were, would he dare to refuse any sort of work that was offered to him, be it as horrible as ever it could? Would he dare to go home and eat bread that had been earned by Ona, weak and complaining as she was, knowing that he had been given a chance, and had not had the nerve to take it?—And yet he might argue that way with himself all day, and one glimpse into the fertilizer works would send him away again shuddering. He was a man, and he would do his duty; he went and made application—but surely he was not also required to hope for success!

The fertilizer works of Durham's lay away from the rest of the plant. Few visitors ever saw them, and the few who did would come out looking like Dante, of whom the peasants declared that he had been into hell. To this part of the yards came all the "tankage" and the waste products of all sorts; here they dried out the bones,—and in suffocating cellars where the daylight never came you might see men and women and children bending over whirling machines and sawing bits of bone into all sorts of shapes, breathing their lungs full of the fine dust, and doomed to die, every one of them, within a certain definite time. Here they made the blood into albumen, and made other foul-smelling things into things still more foul-smelling. In the corridors and caverns where it was done you might lose yourself as in the great caves of Kentucky. In the dust and the steam the electric lights would shine like far-off twinkling stars—red and blue-green and purple stars, according to the color of the mist and the brew from which it came. For the odors of these ghastly charnel houses there may be words in Lithuanian, but there are none in English. The person entering would have to summon his courage as for a cold-water plunge. He would go in like a man swimming under water; he would put his handkerchief over his face, and begin to cough and choke; and then, if he were still obstinate, he would find his head beginning to ring, and the veins in his forehead to throb, until finally he would be assailed by an overpowering blast of ammonia fumes, and would turn and run for his life, and come out half-dazed.

On top of this were the rooms where they dried the "tankage," the mass of brown stringy stuff that was left after the waste portions of the carcasses had had the lard and tallow dried out of them. This dried material they would then grind to a fine powder, and after they had mixed it up well with a mysterious but inoffensive brown rock which they brought in and ground up by the hundreds of carloads for that purpose, the substance was ready to be put into bags and sent out to the world as any one of a hundred different brands of standard bone phosphate. And then the farmer in Maine or California or Texas would buy this, at say twenty-five dollars a ton, and plant it with his corn; and for several days after the operation the fields would have a strong odor, and the farmer and his wagon and the very horses that had hauled it would all have it too. In Packingtown the fertilizer is pure, instead of being a flavoring, and instead of a ton or so spread out on several acres under the open sky, there are hundreds and thousands of tons of it in one building, heaped here and there in haystack piles, covering the floor several inches deep, and filling the air with a choking dust that becomes a blinding sandstorm when the wind stirs.

It was to this building that Jurgis came daily, as if dragged by an unseen hand. The month of May was an exceptionally cool one, and his secret prayers were granted; but early in June there came a record-breaking hot spell, and after that there were men wanted in the fertilizer mill.

The boss of the grinding room had come to know Jurgis by this time, and had marked him for a likely man; and so when he came to the door about two o'clock this breathless hot day, he felt a sudden spasm of pain shoot through him—the boss beckoned to him! In ten minutes more Jurgis had pulled off his coat and overshirt, and set his teeth together and gone to work. Here was one more difficulty for him to meet and conquer!

His labor took him about one minute to learn. Before him was one of the vents of the mill in which the fertilizer was being ground—rushing forth in a great brown river, with a spray of the finest dust flung forth in clouds. Jurgis was given a shovel, and along with half a dozen others it was his task to shovel this fertilizer into carts. That others were at work he knew by the sound, and by the fact that he sometimes collided with them; otherwise they might as well not have been there, for in the blinding dust storm a man could not see six feet in front of his face. When he had filled one cart he had to grope around him until another came, and if there was none on hand he continued to grope till one arrived. In five minutes he was, of course, a mass of fertilizer from head to feet; they gave him a sponge to tie over his mouth, so that he could breathe, but the sponge did not prevent his lips and eyelids from caking up with it and his ears from filling solid. He looked like a brown ghost at twilight—from hair to shoes he became the color of the building and of everything in it, and for that matter a hundred yards outside it. The building had to be left open, and when the wind blew Durham and Company lost a great deal of fertilizer.

Working in his shirt sleeves, and with the thermometer at over a hundred, the phosphates soaked in through every pore of Jurgis' skin, and in five minutes he had a headache, and in fifteen was almost dazed. The blood was pounding in his brain like an engine's throbbing; there was a frightful pain in the top of his skull, and he could hardly control his hands. Still, with the memory of his four months' siege behind him, he fought on, in a frenzy of determination; and half an hour later he began to vomit—he vomited until it seemed as if his inwards must be torn into shreds. A man could get used to the fertilizer mill, the boss had said, if he would make up his mind to it; but Jurgis now began to see that it was a question of making up his stomach.

At the end of that day of horror, he could scarcely stand. He had to catch himself now and then, and lean against a building and get his bearings. Most of the men, when they came out, made straight for a saloon—they seemed to place fertilizer and rattlesnake poison in one class. But Jurgis was too ill to think of drinking—he could only make his way to the street and stagger on to a car. He had a sense of humor, and later on, when he became an old hand, he used to think it fun to board a streetcar and see what happened. Now, however, he was too ill to notice it—how the people in the car began to gasp and sputter, to put their hand-kerchiefs to their noses, and transfix him with furious glances. Jurgis only knew that a man in front of him immediately got up and gave him a seat; and that half a minute later the two people on each side of him got up; and that in a full minute the crowded car was nearly empty—those passengers who could not get room on the platform having gotten out to walk.

Of course Jurgis had made his home a miniature fertilizer mill a minute after entering. The stuff was half an inch deep in his skin—his whole system was full of it, and it would have taken a week not merely of scrubbing, but of vigorous exercise, to get it out of him. As it was, he could be compared with nothing known to men, save that newest discovery of the savants, a substance which emits energy for an unlimited time, without being itself in the least diminished in power. He smelled so that he made all the food at the table taste, and set the whole family to vomiting; for himself it was three days before he could keep anything upon his stomach—he might wash his hands, and use a knife and fork, but were not his mouth and throat filled with the poison?

And still Jurgis stuck it out! In spite of splitting headaches he would stagger down to the plant and take up his stand once more, and begin to shovel in the blinding clouds of dust. And so at the end of the week he was a fertilizer man for life—he was able to eat again, and though his head never stopped aching, it ceased to be so bad that he could not work.

So there passed another summer. It was a summer of prosperity, all over the country, and the country ate generously of packing house products, and there was plenty of work for all the family, in spite of the packers' efforts to keep a superfluity of labor. They were again able to pay their debts and to begin to save a little sum; but there were one or two sacrifices they considered too heavy to be made for long—it was too bad that the boys should have to sell papers at their age. It was utterly useless to caution them and plead with them; quite without knowing it, they were taking on the tone of their new environment. They were learning to swear in voluble English; they were learning to pick up cigar stumps and smoke them, to pass hours of their time gambling with pennies and dice and cigarette cards; they were learning the location of all the houses of prostitution on the "Levee," and the names of the "madames" who kept them, and the days when they gave their state banquets, which the police captains and the big politicians all attended. If a visiting "country customer" were to ask them, they could show him which was "Hinkydink's" famous saloon, and could even point out to him by name the different gamblers and thugs and "hold-up men" who made the place their headquarters. And worse yet, the boys were getting out of the habit of coming home at night. What was the use, they would ask, of wasting time and energy and a possible carfare riding out to the stockyards every night when the weather was pleasant and they could crawl under a truck or into an empty doorway and sleep exactly as well? So long as they brought home a half dollar for each day, what mattered it when they brought it? But Jurgis declared that from this to ceasing to come at all would not be a very long step, and so it was decided that Vilimas and Nikalojus should return to school in the fall, and that instead Elzbieta should go out and get some work, her place at home being taken by her younger daughter.

Little Kotrina was like most children of the poor, prematurely made old; she had to take care of her little brother, who was a cripple, and also of the baby; she had to cook the meals and wash the dishes and clean house, and have supper ready when the workers came home in the evening. She was only thirteen, and small for her age, but she did all this without a murmur; and her mother went out, and after trudging a couple of days about the yards, settled down as a servant of a "sausage machine."

Elzbieta was used to working, but she found this change a hard one, for the reason that she had to stand motionless upon her feet from seven o'clock in the morning till half-past twelve, and again from one till half-past five. For the first few days it seemed to her that she could not stand it—she suffered almost as much as Jurgis had from the fertilizer, and would come out at sundown with her head fairly reeling. Besides this, she was working in one of the dark holes, by electric light, and the dampness, too, was deadly—there were always puddles of water on the floor, and a sickening odor of moist flesh in the room. The people who worked here followed the ancient custom of nature, whereby the ptarmigan is the color of dead leaves in the fall and of snow in the winter, and the chameleon, who is black when he lies upon a stump and turns green when he moves to a leaf.

The men and women who worked in this department were precisely the color of the "fresh country sausage" they made.

The sausage-room was an interesting place to visit, for two or three minutes, and provided that you did not look at the people; the machines were perhaps the most wonderful things in the entire plant. Presumably sausages were once chopped and stuffed by hand, and if so it would be interesting to know how many workers had been displaced by these inventions. On one side of the room were the hoppers, into which men shoveled loads of meat and wheelbarrows full of spices; in these great bowls were whirling knives that made two thousand revolutions a minute, and when the meat was ground fine and adulterated with potato flour, and well mixed with water, it was forced to the stuffing machines on the other side of the room. The latter were tended by women; there was a sort of spout, like the nozzle of a hose, and one of the women would take a long string of "casing" and put the end over the nozzle and then work the whole thing on, as one works on the finger of a tight glove. This string would be twenty or thirty feet long, but the woman would have it all on in a jiffy; and when she had several on, she would press a lever, and a stream of sausage meat would be shot out, taking the casing with it as it came. Thus one might stand and see appear, miraculously born from the machine, a wriggling snake of sausage of incredible length. In front was a big pan which caught these creatures, and two more women who seized them as fast as they appeared and twisted them into links. This was for the uninitiated the most perplexing work of all; for all that the woman had to give was a single turn of the wrist; and in some way she contrived to give it so that instead of an endless chain of sausages, one after another, there grew under her hands a bunch of strings, all dangling from a single center. It was quite like the feat of a prestidigitator—for the woman worked so fast that the eye could literally not follow her, and there was only a mist of motion, and tangle after tangle of sausages appearing. In the midst of the mist, however, the visitor would suddenly notice the tense set face, with the two wrinkles graven in the forehead, and the ghastly pallor of the cheeks; and then he would suddenly recollect that it was time he was going on. The woman did not go on; she stayed right there—hour after hour, day after day, year after year, twisting sausage links and racing with death. It was piecework, and she was apt to have a family to keep alive; and stern and ruthless economic laws had arranged it that she could only do this by working just as she did, with all her soul upon her work, and with never an instant for a glance at the well-dressed ladies and gentlemen who came to stare at her, as at some wild beast in a menagerie.

CHAPTER 14

With one member trimming beef in a cannery, and another working in a sausage factory, the family had a first-hand knowledge of the great majority of Packingtown swindles. For it was the custom, as they found, whenever meat was so spoiled that it could not be used for anything else, either to can it or else to chop it up into sausage. With what had been told them by Jonas, who had worked in the pickle rooms, they could now study the whole of the spoiled-meat industry on the inside, and read a new and grim meaning into that old Packingtown jest—that they use everything of the pig except the squeal.

Jonas had told them how the meat that was taken out of pickle would often be found sour, and how they would rub it up with soda to take away the smell, and sell it to be eaten on free-lunch counters; also of all the miracles of chemistry which they performed, giving to any sort of meat, fresh or salted, whole or chopped, any color and any flavor and any odor they chose. In the pickling of hams they had an ingenious apparatus, by which they saved time and increased the capacity of the plant—a machine consisting of a hollow needle attached to a pump; by plunging this needle into the meat and working with his foot, a man could fill a ham with pickle in a few seconds. And yet, in spite of this, there would be hams found spoiled, some of them with an odor so bad that a man could hardly bear to be in the room with them. To pump into these the packers had a second and much stronger pickle which destroyed the odor—a process known to the workers as "giving them thirty per cent." Also, after the hams had been smoked, there would be found some that had gone to the bad. Formerly these had been sold as "Number Three Grade," but later on some ingenious person had hit upon a new device, and now they would extract the bone, about which the bad part generally lay, and insert in the hole a white-hot iron. After this invention there was no longer Number One, Two, and Three Grade—there was only Number One Grade. The packers were always originating such schemes—they had what they called "boneless hams," which were all the odds and ends of pork stuffed into casings; and "California hams," which were the shoulders, with big knuckle joints, and nearly all the meat cut out; and fancy "skinned hams," which were made of the oldest hogs, whose skins were so heavy and coarse that no one would buy them—that is, until they had been cooked and chopped fine and labeled "head cheese!"

CHAPTER 14

It was only when the whole ham was spoiled that it came into the department of Elzbieta. Cut up by the two-thousand-revolutions-a-minute flyers, and mixed with half a ton of other meat, no odor that ever was in a ham could make any difference. There was never the least attention paid to what was cut up for sausage; there would come all the way back from Europe old sausage that had been rejected, and that was moldy and white—it would be dosed with borax and glycerine, and dumped into the hoppers, and made over again for home consumption. There would be meat that had tumbled out on the floor, in the dirt and sawdust, where the workers had tramped and spit uncounted billions of consumption germs. There would be meat stored in great piles in rooms; and the water from leaky roofs would drip over it, and thousands of rats would race about on it. It was too dark in these storage places to see well, but a man could run his hand over these piles of meat and sweep off handfuls of the dried dung of rats. These rats were nuisances, and the packers would put poisoned bread out for them; they would die, and then rats, bread, and meat would go into the hoppers together. This is no fairy story and no joke; the meat would be shoveled into carts, and the man who did the shoveling would not trouble to lift out a rat even when he saw one—there were things that went into the sausage in comparison with which a poisoned rat was a tidbit. There was no place for the men to wash their hands before they ate their dinner, and so they made a practice of washing them in the water that was to be ladled into the sausage. There were the butt-ends of smoked meat, and the scraps of corned beef, and all the odds and ends of the waste of the plants, that would be dumped into old barrels in the cellar and left there. Under the system of rigid economy which the packers enforced, there were some jobs that it only paid to do once in a long time, and among these was the cleaning out of the waste barrels. Every spring they did it; and in the barrels would be dirt and rust and old nails and stale water—and cartload after cartload of it would be taken up and dumped into the hoppers with fresh meat, and sent out to the public's breakfast. Some of it they would make into "smoked" sausage—but as the smoking took time, and was therefore expensive, they would call upon their chemistry department, and preserve it with borax and color it with gelatine to make it brown. All of their sausage came out of the same bowl, but when they came to wrap it they would stamp some of it "special," and for this they would charge two cents more a pound.

Such were the new surroundings in which Elzbieta was placed, and such was the work she was compelled to do. It was stupefying, brutalizing work; it left her no time to think, no strength for anything. She was part of the machine she tended, and every faculty that was not needed for the machine was doomed to be crushed out of existence. There was only one mercy about the cruel grind—that it gave her the gift of insensibility. Little by little she sank into a torpor—she fell silent. She would meet Jurgis and Ona in the evening, and the three would walk home together, often without saying a word. Ona, too, was falling into a habit of silence—Ona, who had once gone about singing like a bird. She was sick and miserable, and often she would barely have strength enough to drag herself home.

And there they would eat what they had to eat, and afterward, because there was only their misery to talk of, they would crawl into bed and fall into a stupor and never stir until it was time to get up again, and dress by candlelight, and go back to the machines. They were so numbed that they did not even suffer much from hunger, now; only the children continued to fret when the food ran short.

Yet the soul of Ona was not dead—the souls of none of them were dead, but only sleeping; and now and then they would waken, and these were cruel times. The gates of memory would roll open—old joys would stretch out their arms to them, old hopes and dreams would call to them, and they would stir beneath the burden that lay upon them, and feel its forever immeasurable weight. They could not even cry out beneath it; but anguish would seize them, more dreadful than the agony of death. It was a thing scarcely to be spoken—a thing never spoken by all the world, that will not know its own defeat.

They were beaten; they had lost the game, they were swept aside. It was not less tragic because it was so sordid, because it had to do with wages and grocery bills and rents. They had dreamed of freedom; of a chance to look about them and learn something; to be decent and clean, to see their child grow up to be strong. And now it was all gone—it would never be! They had played the game and they had lost. Six years more of toil they had to face before they could expect the least respite, the cessation of the payments upon the house; and how cruelly certain it was that they could never stand six years of such a life as they were living! They were lost, they were going down—and there was no deliverance for them, no hope; for all the help it gave them the vast city in which they lived might have been an ocean waste, a wilderness, a desert, a tomb. So often this mood would come to Ona, in the nighttime, when something wakened her; she would lie, afraid of the beating of her own heart, fronting the blood-red eyes of the old primeval terror of life. Once she cried aloud, and woke Jurgis, who was tired and cross. After that she learned to weep silently—their moods so seldom came together now! It was as if their hopes were buried in separate graves.

Jurgis, being a man, had troubles of his own. There was another specter following him. He had never spoken of it, nor would he allow any one else to speak of it—he had never acknowledged its existence to himself. Yet the battle with it took all the manhood that he had—and once or twice, alas, a little more. Jurgis had discovered drink.

He was working in the steaming pit of hell; day after day, week after week—until now, there was not an organ of his body that did its work without pain, until the sound of ocean breakers echoed in his head day and night, and the buildings swayed and danced before him as he went down the street. And from all the unending horror of this there was a respite, a deliverance—he could drink! He could forget the pain, he could slip off the burden; he would see clearly again, he would be master of his brain, of his thoughts, of his will. His dead self would stir in him, and he would find himself laughing and cracking jokes with his companions—he would be a man again, and master of his life.

It was not an easy thing for Jurgis to take more than two or three drinks. With the first drink he could eat a meal, and he could persuade himself that that was economy; with the second he could eat another meal—but there would come a time when he could eat no more, and then to pay for a drink was an unthinkable extravagance, a defiance of the age-long instincts of his hunger-haunted class. One day, however, he took the plunge, and drank up all that he had in his pockets, and went home half "piped," as the men phrase it. He was happier than he had been in a year; and yet, because he knew that the happiness would not last, he was savage, too with those who would wreck it, and with the world, and with his life; and then again, beneath this, he was sick with the shame of himself. Afterward, when he saw the despair of his family, and reckoned up the money he had spent, the tears came into his eyes, and he began the long battle with the specter.

It was a battle that had no end, that never could have one. But Jurgis did not realize that very clearly; he was not given much time for reflection. He simply knew that he was always fighting. Steeped in misery and despair as he was, merely to walk down the street was to be put upon the rack. There was surely a saloon on the corner—perhaps on all four corners, and some in the middle of the block as well; and each one stretched out a hand to him each one had a personality of its own, allurements unlike any other. Going and coming—before sunrise and after dark—there was warmth and a glow of light, and the steam of hot food, and perhaps music, or a friendly face, and a word of good cheer. Jurgis developed a fondness for having Ona on his arm whenever he went out on the street, and he would hold her tightly, and walk fast. It was pitiful to have Ona know of this—it drove him wild to think of it; the thing was not fair, for Ona had never tasted drink, and so could not understand. Sometimes, in desperate hours, he would find himself wishing that she might learn what it was, so that he need not be ashamed in her presence. They might drink together, and escape from the horror—escape for a while, come what would.

So there came a time when nearly all the conscious life of Jurgis consisted of a struggle with the craving for liquor. He would have ugly moods, when he hated Ona and the whole family, because they stood in his way. He was a fool to have married; he had tied himself down, had made himself a slave. It was all because he was a married man that he was compelled to stay in the yards; if it had not been for that he might have gone off like Jonas, and to hell with the packers. There were few single men in the fertilizer mill—and those few were working only for a chance to escape. Meantime, too, they had something to think about while they worked,—they had the memory of the last time they had been drunk, and the hope of the time when they would be drunk again. As for Jurgis, he was expected to bring home every penny; he could not even go with the men at noontime—he was supposed to sit down and eat his dinner on a pile of fertilizer dust.

This was not always his mood, of course; he still loved his family. But just now was a time of trial. Poor little Antanas, for instance—who had never failed to win him with a smile—little Antanas was not smiling just now, being a mass of fiery red pimples. He had had all the diseases that babies are heir to, in quick succession, scarlet fever, mumps, and whooping cough in the first year, and now he was down with the measles. There was no one to attend him but Kotrina; there was no doctor to help him, because they were too poor, and children did not die of the measles—at least not often. Now and then Kotrina would find time to sob over his woes, but for the greater part of the time he had to be left alone, barricaded upon the bed. The floor was full of drafts, and if he caught cold he would die. At night he was tied down, lest he should kick the covers off him, while the family lay in their stupor of exhaustion. He would lie and scream for hours, almost in convulsions; and then, when he was worn out, he would lie whimpering and wailing in his torment. He was burning up with fever, and his eyes were running sores; in the daytime he was a thing uncanny and impish to behold, a plaster of pimples and sweat, a great purple lump of misery.

Yet all this was not really as cruel as it sounds, for, sick as he was, little Antanas was the least unfortunate member of that family. He was quite able to bear his sufferings—it was as if he had all these complaints to show what a prodigy of health he was. He was the child of his parents' youth and joy; he grew up like the conjurer's rosebush, and all the world was his oyster. In general, he toddled around the kitchen all day with a lean and hungry look—the portion of the family's allowance that fell to him was not enough, and he was unrestrainable in his demand for more. Antanas was but little over a year old, and already no one but his father could manage him.

It seemed as if he had taken all of his mother's strength—had left nothing for those that might come after him. Ona was with child again now, and it was a dreadful thing to contemplate; even Jurgis, dumb and despairing as he was, could not but understand that yet other agonies were on the way, and shudder at the thought of them.

For Ona was visibly going to pieces. In the first place she was developing a cough, like the one that had killed old Dede Antanas. She had had a trace of it ever since that fatal morning when the greedy streetcar corporation had turned her out into the rain; but now it was beginning to grow serious, and to wake her up at night. Even worse than that was the fearful nervousness from which she suffered; she would have frightful headaches and fits of aimless weeping; and sometimes she would come home at night shuddering and moaning, and would fling herself down upon the bed and burst into tears. Several times she was quite beside herself and hysterical; and then Jurgis would go half-mad with fright. Elzbieta would explain to him that it could not be helped, that a woman was subject to such things when she was pregnant; but he was hardly to be persuaded, and would beg and plead to know what had happened. She had never been like this before, he would argue—it was monstrous and unthinkable. It was the life she had to live, the accursed work she had to do, that was killing her by inches. She was not fitted for it—no woman was fitted for it, no woman ought to be allowed to do such work; if the world could not keep them alive any other way it ought to kill them at once and be done with it. They ought not to marry, to have children; no workingman ought to marry—if he, Jurgis, had known what a woman was like, he would have had his eyes torn out first. So he would carry on, becoming half hysterical himself, which was an unbearable thing to see in a big man; Ona would pull herself together and fling herself into his arms, begging him to stop, to be still, that she would be better, it would be all right. So she would lie and sob out her grief upon his shoulder, while he gazed at her, as helpless as a wounded animal, the target of unseen enemies.

CHAPTER 15

The beginning of these perplexing things was in the summer; and each time Ona would promise him with terror in her voice that it would not happen again—but in vain. Each crisis would leave Jurgis more and more frightened, more disposed to distrust Elzbieta's consolations, and to believe that there was some terrible thing about all this that he was not allowed to know. Once or twice in these outbreaks he caught Ona's eye, and it seemed to him like the eye of a hunted animal; there were broken phrases of anguish and despair now and then, amid her frantic weeping. It was only because he was so numb and beaten himself that Jurgis did not worry more about this. But he never thought of it, except when he was dragged to it—he lived like a dumb beast of burden, knowing only the moment in which he was.

The winter was coming on again, more menacing and cruel than ever. It was October, and the holiday rush had begun. It was necessary for the packing machines to grind till late at night to provide food that would be eaten at Christmas breakfasts; and Marija and Elzbieta and Ona, as part of the machine, began working fifteen or sixteen hours a day. There was no choice about this—whatever work there was to be done they had to do, if they wished to keep their places; besides that, it added another pittance to their incomes. So they staggered on with the awful load. They would start work every morning at seven, and eat their dinners at noon, and then work until ten or eleven at night without another mouthful of food. Jurgis wanted to wait for them, to help them home at night, but they would not think of this; the fertilizer mill was not running overtime, and there was no place for him to wait save in a saloon. Each would stagger out into the darkness, and make her way to the corner, where they met; or if the others had already gone, would get into a car, and begin a painful struggle to keep awake. When they got home they were always too tired either to eat or to undress; they would crawl into bed with their shoes on, and lie like logs. If they should fail, they would certainly be lost; if they held out, they might have enough coal for the winter.

A day or two before Thanksgiving Day there came a snowstorm. It began in the afternoon, and by evening two inches had fallen. Jurgis tried to wait for the women, but went into a saloon to get warm, and took two drinks, and came out and ran home to escape from the demon; there he lay down to wait for them, and instantly fell asleep. When he opened his eyes again he was in the midst of a nightmare, and found Elzbieta shaking him and crying out. At first he could not realize what she was saying—Ona had not come home. What time was it, he asked. It was morning—time to be up. Ona had not been home that night! And it was bitter cold, and a foot of snow on the ground.

Jurgis sat up with a start. Marija was crying with fright and the children were wailing in sympathy—little Stanislovas in addition, because the terror of the snow was upon him. Jurgis had nothing to put on but his shoes and his coat, and in half a minute he was out of the door. Then, however, he realized that there was no need of haste, that he had no idea where to go. It was still dark as midnight, and the thick snowflakes were sifting down—everything was so silent that he could hear the rustle of them as they fell. In the few seconds that he stood there hesitating he was covered white.

He set off at a run for the yards, stopping by the way to inquire in the saloons that were open. Ona might have been overcome on the way; or else she might have met with an accident in the machines. When he got to the place where she worked he inquired of one of the watchmen—there had not been any accident, so far as the man had heard. At the time office, which he found already open, the clerk told him that Ona's check had been turned in the night before, showing that she had left her work.

After that there was nothing for him to do but wait, pacing back and forth in the snow, meantime, to keep from freezing. Already the yards were full of activity; cattle were being unloaded from the cars in the distance, and across the way the "beef-luggers" were toiling in the darkness, carrying two-hundred-pound quarters of bullocks into the refrigerator cars. Before the first streaks of daylight there came the crowding throngs of workingmen, shivering, and swinging their dinner pails as they hurried by. Jurgis took up his stand by the time-office window, where alone there was light enough for him to see; the snow fell so quick that it was only by peering closely that he could make sure that Ona did not pass him.

Seven o'clock came, the hour when the great packing machine began to move. Jurgis ought to have been at his place in the fertilizer mill; but instead he was waiting, in an agony of fear, for Ona. It was fifteen minutes after the hour when he saw a form emerge from the snow mist, and sprang toward it with a cry. It was she, running swiftly; as she saw him, she staggered forward, and half fell into his outstretched arms.

"What has been the matter?" he cried, anxiously. "Where have you been?"

It was several seconds before she could get breath to answer him. "I couldn't get home," she exclaimed. "The snow—the cars had stopped."

"But where were you then?" he demanded.

"I had to go home with a friend," she panted—"with Jadvyga."

Jurgis drew a deep breath; but then he noticed that she was sobbing and trembling—as if in one of those nervous crises that he dreaded so. "But what's the matter?" he cried. "What has happened?"

"Oh, Jurgis, I was so frightened!" she said, clinging to him wildly. "I have been so worried!"

They were near the time station window, and people were staring at them. Jurgis led her away. "How do you mean?" he asked, in perplexity.

"I was afraid—I was just afraid!" sobbed Ona. "I knew you wouldn't know where I was, and I didn't know what you might do. I tried to get home, but I was so tired. Oh, Jurgis, Jurgis!"

He was so glad to get her back that he could not think clearly about anything else. It did not seem strange to him that she should be so very much upset; all her fright and incoherent protestations did not matter since he had her back. He let her cry away her tears; and then, because it was nearly eight o'clock, and they would lose another hour if they delayed, he left her at the packing house door, with her ghastly white face and her haunted eyes of terror.

There was another brief interval. Christmas was almost come; and because the snow still held, and the searching cold, morning after morning Jurgis half carried his wife to her post, staggering with her through the darkness; until at last, one night, came the end.

It lacked but three days of the holidays. About midnight Marija and Elzbieta came home, exclaiming in alarm when they found that Ona had not come. The two had agreed to meet her; and, after waiting, had gone to the room where she worked; only to find that the ham-wrapping girls had quit work an hour before, and left. There was no snow that night, nor was it especially cold; and still Ona had not come! Something more serious must be wrong this time.

They aroused Jurgis, and he sat up and listened crossly to the story. She must have gone home again with Jadvyga, he said; Jadvyga lived only two blocks from the yards, and perhaps she had been tired. Nothing could have happened to her— and even if there had, there was nothing could be done about it until morning. Jurgis turned over in his bed, and was snoring again before the two had closed the door.

In the morning, however, he was up and out nearly an hour before the usual time. Jadvyga Marcinkus lived on the other side of the yards, beyond Halsted Street, with her mother and sisters, in a single basement room—for Mikolas had recently lost one hand from blood poisoning, and their marriage had been put off forever. The door of the room was in the rear, reached by a narrow court, and Jurgis saw a light in the window and heard something frying as he passed; he knocked, half expecting that Ona would answer.

Instead there was one of Jadvyga's little sisters, who gazed at him through a crack in the door. "Where's Ona?" he demanded; and the child looked at him in perplexity. "Ona?" she said.

"Yes," said Jurgis, "isn't she here?"

"No," said the child, and Jurgis gave a start. A moment later came Jadvyga, peering over the child's head. When she saw who it was, she slid around out of sight, for she was not quite dressed. Jurgis must excuse her, she began, her mother was very ill—

"Ona isn't here?" Jurgis demanded, too alarmed to wait for her to finish.

"Why, no," said Jadvyga. "What made you think she would be here? Had she said she was coming?"

"No," he answered. "But she hasn't come home—and I thought she would be here the same as before."

"As before?" echoed Jadvyga, in perplexity.

"The time she spent the night here," said Jurgis.

"There must be some mistake," she answered, quickly. "Ona has never spent the night here."

He was only half able to realize the words. "Why—why—" he exclaimed. "Two weeks ago. Jadvyga! She told me so the night it snowed, and she could not get home."

"There must be some mistake," declared the girl, again; "she didn't come here."

He steadied himself by the door-sill; and Jadvyga in her anxiety—for she was fond of Ona—opened the door wide, holding her jacket across her throat. "Are you sure you didn't misunderstand her?" she cried. "She must have meant somewhere else. She—"

"She said here," insisted Jurgis. "She told me all about you, and how you were, and what you said. Are you sure? You haven't forgotten? You weren't away?"

"No, no!" she exclaimed—and then came a peevish voice—"Jadvyga, you are giving the baby a cold. Shut the door!" Jurgis stood for half a minute more, stammering his perplexity through an eighth of an inch of crack; and then, as there was really nothing more to be said, he excused himself and went away.

He walked on half dazed, without knowing where he went. Ona had deceived him! She had lied to him! And what could it mean—where had she been? Where was she now? He could hardly grasp the thing—much less try to solve it; but a hundred wild surmises came to him, a sense of impending calamity overwhelmed him.

Because there was nothing else to do, he went back to the time office to watch again. He waited until nearly an hour after seven, and then went to the room where Ona worked to make inquiries of Ona's "forelady." The "forelady," he found, had not yet come; all the lines of cars that came from downtown were stalled—there had been an accident in the powerhouse, and no cars had been running since last night. Meantime, however, the ham-wrappers were working away, with some one else in charge of them. The girl who answered Jurgis was busy, and as she talked she looked to see if she were being watched. Then a man came up, wheeling a truck; he knew Jurgis for Ona's husband, and was curious about the mystery.

"Maybe the cars had something to do with it," he suggested—"maybe she had gone down-town."

"No," said Jurgis, "she never went down-town."

"Perhaps not," said the man. Jurgis thought he saw him exchange a swift glance with the girl as he spoke, and he demanded quickly. "What do you know about it?"

But the man had seen that the boss was watching him; he started on again, pushing his truck. "I don't know anything about it," he said, over his shoulder. "How should I know where your wife goes?"

Then Jurgis went out again and paced up and down before the building. All the morning he stayed there, with no thought of his work. About noon he went to the police station to make inquiries, and then came back again for another anxious vigil. Finally, toward the middle of the afternoon, he set out for home once more.

He was walking out Ashland Avenue. The streetcars had begun running again, and several passed him, packed to the steps with people. The sight of them set Jurgis to thinking again of the man's sarcastic remark; and half involuntarily he found himself watching the cars—with the result that he gave a sudden startled exclamation, and stopped short in his tracks.

Then he broke into a run. For a whole block he tore after the car, only a little ways behind. That rusty black hat with the drooping red flower, it might not be Ona's, but there was very little likelihood of it. He would know for certain very soon, for she would get out two blocks ahead. He slowed down, and let the car go on.

She got out: and as soon as she was out of sight on the side street Jurgis broke into a run. Suspicion was rife in him now, and he was not ashamed to shadow her: he saw her turn the corner near their home, and then he ran again, and saw her as she went up the porch steps of the house. After that he turned back, and for five minutes paced up and down, his hands clenched tightly and his lips set, his mind in a turmoil. Then he went home and entered.

As he opened the door, he saw Elzbieta, who had also been looking for Ona, and had come home again. She was now on tiptoe, and had a finger on her lips. Jurgis waited until she was close to him.

"Don't make any noise," she whispered, hurriedly.

"What's the matter'?" he asked. "Ona is asleep," she panted. "She's been very ill. I'm afraid her mind's been wandering, Jurgis. She was lost on the street all night, and I've only just succeeded in getting her quiet."

"When did she come in?" he asked.

"Soon after you left this morning," said Elzbieta.

"And has she been out since?"

"No, of course not. She's so weak, Jurgis, she—"

And he set his teeth hard together. "You are lying to me," he said.

Elzbieta started, and turned pale. "Why!" she gasped. "What do you mean?"

But Jurgis did not answer. He pushed her aside, and strode to the bedroom door and opened it.

Ona was sitting on the bed. She turned a startled look upon him as he entered. He closed the door in Elzbieta's face, and went toward his wife. "Where have you been?" he demanded.

She had her hands clasped tightly in her lap, and he saw that her face was as white as paper, and drawn with pain. She gasped once or twice as she tried to answer him, and then began, speaking low, and swiftly. "Jurgis, I—I think I have been out of my mind. I started to come last night, and I could not find the way. I walked—I walked all night, I think, and—and I only got home—this morning."

"You needed a rest," he said, in a hard tone. "Why did you go out again?"

He was looking her fairly in the face, and he could read the sudden fear and wild uncertainty that leaped into her eyes. "I—I had to go to—to the store," she gasped, almost in a whisper, "I had to go—"

"You are lying to me," said Jurgis. Then he clenched his hands and took a step toward her. "Why do you lie to me?" he cried, fiercely. "What are you doing that you have to lie to me?"

"Jurgis!" she exclaimed, starting up in fright. "Oh, Jurgis, how can you?"

"You have lied to me, I say!" he cried. "You told me you had been to Jadvyga's house that other night, and you hadn't. You had been where you were last night—somewheres downtown, for I saw you get off the car. Where were you?"

It was as if he had struck a knife into her. She seemed to go all to pieces. For half a second she stood, reeling and swaying, staring at him with horror in her eyes; then, with a cry of anguish, she tottered forward, stretching out her arms to him. But he stepped aside, deliberately, and let her fall. She caught herself at the side of the bed, and then sank down, burying her face in her hands and bursting into frantic weeping.

There came one of those hysterical crises that had so often dismayed him. Ona sobbed and wept, her fear and anguish building themselves up into long climaxes. Furious gusts of emotion would come sweeping over her, shaking her as the tempest shakes the trees upon the hills; all her frame would quiver and throb with them—it was as if some dreadful thing rose up within her and took possession of her, torturing her, tearing her. This thing had been wont to set Jurgis quite beside himself; but now he stood with his lips set tightly and his hands clenched—she might weep till she killed herself, but she should not move him this time—not an inch, not an inch. Because the sounds she made set his blood to running cold and his lips to quivering in spite of himself, he was glad of the diversion when Teta Elzbieta, pale with fright, opened the door and rushed in; yet he turned upon her with an oath. "Go out!" he cried, "go out!" And then, as she stood hesitating, about to speak, he seized her by the arm, and half flung her from the room, slamming the door and barring it with a table. Then he turned again and faced Ona, crying—"Now, answer me!"

Yet she did not hear him—she was still in the grip of the fiend. Jurgis could see her outstretched hands, shaking and twitching, roaming here and there over the bed at will, like living things; he could see convulsive shudderings start in her body and run through her limbs. She was sobbing and choking—it was as if there were too many sounds for one throat, they came chasing each other, like waves upon the sea. Then her voice would begin to rise into screams, louder and louder until it broke in wild, horrible peals of laughter. Jurgis bore it until he could bear it no longer, and then he sprang at her, seizing her by the shoulders and shaking her, shouting into her ear: "Stop it, I say! Stop it!"

She looked up at him, out of her agony; then she fell forward at his feet. She caught them in her hands, in spite of his efforts to step aside, and with her face upon the floor lay writhing. It made a choking in Jurgis' throat to hear her, and he cried again, more savagely than before: "Stop it, I say!"

This time she heeded him, and caught her breath and lay silent, save for the gasping sobs that wrenched all her frame. For a long minute she lay there, perfectly motionless, until a cold fear seized her husband, thinking that she was dying. Suddenly, however, he heard her voice, faintly: "Jurgis! Jurgis!"

"What is it?" he said.

He had to bend down to her, she was so weak. She was pleading with him, in broken phrases, painfully uttered: "Have faith in me! Believe me!"

"Believe what?" he cried.

"Believe that I—that I know best—that I love you! And do not ask me—what you did. Oh, Jurgis, please, please! It is for the best—it is—"

He started to speak again, but she rushed on frantically, heading him off. "If you will only do it! If you will only—only believe me! It wasn't my fault—I couldn't help it—it will be all right—it is nothing—it is no harm. Oh, Jurgis—please, please!"

She had hold of him, and was trying to raise herself to look at him; he could feel the palsied shaking of her hands and the heaving of the bosom she pressed against him. She managed to catch one of his hands and gripped it convulsively, drawing it to her face, and bathing it in her tears. "Oh, believe me, believe me!" she wailed again; and he shouted in fury, "I will not!"

But still she clung to him, wailing aloud in her despair: "Oh, Jurgis, think what you are doing! It will ruin us—it will ruin us! Oh, no, you must not do it! No, don't, don't do it. You must not do it! It will drive me mad—it will kill me—no, no, Jurgis, I am crazy—it is nothing. You do not really need to know. We can be happy—we can love each other just the same. Oh, please, please, believe me!"

Her words fairly drove him wild. He tore his hands loose, and flung her off. "Answer me," he cried. "God damn it, I say—answer me!"

She sank down upon the floor, beginning to cry again. It was like listening to the moan of a damned soul, and Jurgis could not stand it. He smote his fist upon the table by his side, and shouted again at her, "Answer me!"

She began to scream aloud, her voice like the voice of some wild beast: "Ah! Ah! I can't! I can't do it!"

"Why can't you do it?" he shouted.

"I don't know how!"

He sprang and caught her by the arm, lifting her up, and glaring into her face. "Tell me where you were last night!" he panted. "Quick, out with it!"

Then she began to whisper, one word at a time: "I—was in—a house—downtown—"

"What house? What do you mean?"

She tried to hide her eyes away, but he held her. "Miss Henderson's house," she gasped. He did not understand at first. "Miss Henderson's house," he echoed.

And then suddenly, as in an explosion, the horrible truth burst over him, and he reeled and staggered back with a scream. He caught himself against the wall, and put his hand to his forehead, staring about him, and whispering, "Jesus! Jesus!"

An instant later he leaped at her, as she lay groveling at his feet. He seized her by the throat. "Tell me!" he gasped, hoarsely. "Quick! Who took you to that place?"

She tried to get away, making him furious; he thought it was fear, of the pain of his clutch—he did not understand that it was the agony of her shame. Still she answered him, "Connor."

"Connor," he gasped. "Who is Connor?"

"The boss," she answered. "The man—"

He tightened his grip, in his frenzy, and only when he saw her eyes closing did he realize that he was choking her. Then he relaxed his fingers, and crouched, waiting, until she opened her lids again. His breath beat hot into her face.

"Tell me," he whispered, at last, "tell me about it."

She lay perfectly motionless, and he had to hold his breath to catch her words. "I did not want—to do it," she said; "I tried—I tried not to do it. I only did it—to save us. It was our only chance."

Again, for a space, there was no sound but his panting. Ona's eyes closed and when she spoke again she did not open them. "He told me—he would have me turned off. He told me he would—we would all of us lose our places. We could never get anything to do—here—again. He—he meant it—he would have ruined us."

Jurgis' arms were shaking so that he could scarcely hold himself up, and lurched forward now and then as he listened. "When—when did this begin?" he gasped.

"At the very first," she said. She spoke as if in a trance. "It was all—it was their plot—Miss Henderson's plot. She hated me. And he—he wanted me. He used to speak to me—out on the platform. Then he began to—to make love to me. He offered me money. He begged me—he said he loved me. Then he threatened me. He knew all about us, he knew we would starve. He knew your boss—he knew Marija's. He would hound us to death, he said—then he said if I would—if I—we would all of us be sure of work—always. Then one day he caught hold of me—he would not let go—he—he—"

"Where was this?"

"In the hallway—at night—after every one had gone. I could not help it. I thought of you—of the baby—of mother and the children. I was afraid of him—afraid to cry out."

A moment ago her face had been ashen gray, now it was scarlet. She was beginning to breathe hard again. Jurgis made not a sound.

"That was two months ago. Then he wanted me to come—to that house. He wanted me to stay there. He said all of us—that we would not have to work. He made me come there—in the evenings. I told you—you thought I was at the factory. Then—one night it snowed, and I couldn't get back. And last night—the cars were stopped. It was such a little thing—to ruin us all. I tried to walk, but I couldn't. I didn't want you to know. It would have—it would have been all right. We could have gone on—just the same—you need never have known about it. He was getting tired of me—he would have let me alone soon. I am going to have a baby—I am getting ugly. He told me that—twice, he told me, last night. He kicked me—last night—too. And now you will kill him—you—you will kill him—and we shall die."

All this she had said without a quiver; she lay still as death, not an eyelid moving. And Jurgis, too, said not a word. He lifted himself by the bed, and stood up. He did not stop for another glance at her, but went to the door and opened it. He did not see Elzbieta, crouching terrified in the corner. He went out, hatless, leaving the street door open behind him. The instant his feet were on the sidewalk he broke into a run.

He ran like one possessed, blindly, furiously, looking neither to the right nor left. He was on Ashland Avenue before exhaustion compelled him to slow down, and then, noticing a car, he made a dart for it and drew himself aboard. His eyes were wild and his hair flying, and he was breathing hoarsely, like a wounded bull; but the people on the car did not notice this particularly—perhaps it seemed natural to them that a man who smelled as Jurgis smelled should exhibit an aspect to correspond. They began to give way before him as usual. The conductor took his nickel gingerly, with the tips of his fingers, and then left him with the platform to himself. Jurgis did not even notice it—his thoughts were far away. Within his soul it was like a roaring furnace; he stood waiting, waiting, crouching as if for a spring.

He had some of his breath back when the car came to the entrance of the yards, and so he leaped off and started again, racing at full speed. People turned and stared at him, but he saw no one—there was the factory, and he bounded through the doorway and down the corridor. He knew the room where Ona worked, and he knew Connor, the boss of the loading-gang outside. He looked for the man as he sprang into the room.

The truckmen were hard at work, loading the freshly packed boxes and barrels upon the cars. Jurgis shot one swift glance up and down the platform—the man was not on it. But then suddenly he heard a voice in the corridor, and started for it with a bound. In an instant more he fronted the boss.

He was a big, red-faced Irishman, coarse-featured, and smelling of liquor. He saw Jurgis as he crossed the threshold, and turned white. He hesitated one second, as if meaning to run; and in the next his assailant was upon him. He put up his hands to protect his face, but Jurgis, lunging with all the power of his arm and body, struck him fairly between the eyes and knocked him backward. The next moment he was on top of him, burying his fingers in his throat.

To Jurgis this man's whole presence reeked of the crime he had committed; the touch of his body was madness to him—it set every nerve of him a-tremble, it aroused all the demon in his soul. It had worked its will upon Ona, this great beast—and now he had it, he had it! It was his turn now! Things swam blood before him, and he screamed aloud in his fury, lifting his victim and smashing his head upon the floor.

The place, of course, was in an uproar; women fainting and shrieking, and men rushing in. Jurgis was so bent upon his task that he knew nothing of this, and scarcely realized that people were trying to interfere with him; it was only when half a dozen men had seized him by the legs and shoulders and were pulling at him, that he understood that he was losing his prey. In a flash he had bent down and sunk his teeth into the man's cheek; and when they tore him away he was dripping with blood, and little ribbons of skin were hanging in his mouth.

They got him down upon the floor, clinging to him by his arms and legs, and still they could hardly hold him. He fought like a tiger, writhing and twisting, half flinging them off, and starting toward his unconscious enemy. But yet others rushed in, until there was a little mountain of twisted limbs and bodies, heaving and tossing, and working its way about the room. In the end, by their sheer weight, they choked the breath out of him, and then they carried him to the company police station, where he lay still until they had summoned a patrol wagon to take him away.

CHAPTER 16

When Jurgis got up again he went quietly enough. He was exhausted and half-dazed, and besides he saw the blue uniforms of the policemen. He drove in a patrol wagon with half a dozen of them watching him; keeping as far away as possible, however, on account of the fertilizer. Then he stood before the sergeant's desk and gave his name and address, and saw a charge of assault and battery entered against him. On his way to his cell a burly policeman cursed him because he started down the wrong corridor, and then added a kick when he was not quick enough; nevertheless, Jurgis did not even lift his eyes—he had lived two years and a half in Packingtown, and he knew what the police were. It was as much as a man's very life was worth to anger them, here in their inmost lair; like as not a dozen would pile on to him at once, and pound his face into a pulp. It would be nothing unusual if he got his skull cracked in the melee—in which case they would report that he had been drunk and had fallen down, and there would be no one to know the difference or to care.

So a barred door clanged upon Jurgis and he sat down upon a bench and buried his face in his hands. He was alone; he had the afternoon and all of the night to himself.

At first he was like a wild beast that has glutted itself; he was in a dull stupor of satisfaction. He had done up the scoundrel pretty well—not as well as he would have if they had given him a minute more, but pretty well, all the same; the ends of his fingers were still tingling from their contact with the fellow's throat. But then, little by little, as his strength came back and his senses cleared, he began to see beyond his momentary gratification; that he had nearly killed the boss would not help Ona—not the horrors that she had borne, nor the memory that would haunt her all her days. It would not help to feed her and her child; she would certainly lose her place, while he—what was to happen to him God only knew.

Half the night he paced the floor, wrestling with this nightmare; and when he was exhausted he lay down, trying to sleep, but finding instead, for the first time in his life, that his brain was too much for him. In the cell next to him was a drunken wife-beater and in the one beyond a yelling maniac. At midnight they opened the station house to the homeless wanderers who were crowded about the door, shivering in the winter blast, and they thronged into the corridor outside of the cells. Some of them stretched themselves out on the bare stone floor and fell to snoring, others sat up, laughing and talking, cursing and quarreling. The air was fetid with their breath, yet in spite of this some of them smelled Jurgis and called down the torments of hell upon him, while he lay in a far corner of his cell, counting the throbbings of the blood in his forehead.

They had brought him his supper, which was "duffers and dope"—being hunks of dry bread on a tin plate, and coffee, called "dope" because it was drugged to keep the prisoners quiet. Jurgis had not known this, or he would have swallowed the stuff in desperation; as it was, every nerve of him was a-quiver with shame and rage. Toward morning the place fell silent, and he got up and began to pace his cell; and then within the soul of him there rose up a fiend, red-eyed and cruel, and tore out the strings of his heart.

It was not for himself that he suffered—what did a man who worked in Durham's fertilizer mill care about anything that the world might do to him! What was any tyranny of prison compared with the tyranny of the past, of the thing that had happened and could not be recalled, of the memory that could never be effaced! The horror of it drove him mad; he stretched out his arms to heaven, crying out for deliverance from it—and there was no deliverance, there was no power even in heaven that could undo the past. It was a ghost that would not drown; it followed him, it seized upon him and beat him to the ground. Ah, if only he could have foreseen it—but then, he would have foreseen it, if he had not been a fool! He smote his hands upon his forehead, cursing himself because he had ever allowed Ona to work where she had, because he had not stood between her and a fate which every one knew to be so common. He should have taken her away, even if it were to lie down and die of starvation in the gutters of Chicago's streets! And now—oh, it could not be true; it was too monstrous, too horrible.

It was a thing that could not be faced; a new shuddering seized him every time he tried to think of it. No, there was no bearing the load of it, there was no living under it. There would be none for her—he knew that he might pardon her, might plead with her on his knees, but she would never look him in the face again, she would never be his wife again. The shame of it would kill her—there could be no other deliverance, and it was best that she should die.

This was simple and clear, and yet, with cruel inconsistency, whenever he escaped from this nightmare it was to suffer and cry out at the vision of Ona starving. They had put him in jail, and they would keep him here a long time, years maybe. And Ona would surely not go to work again, broken and crushed as she was. And Elzbieta and Marija, too, might lose their places—if that hell fiend Connor chose to set to work to ruin them, they would all be turned out. And even if he did not, they could not live—even if the boys left school again, they could surely not pay all the bills without him and Ona. They had only a few dollars now—they had just paid the rent of the house a week ago, and that after it was two weeks overdue. So it would be due again in a week! They would have no money to pay it then—and they would lose the house, after all their long, heartbreaking struggle. Three times now the agent had warned him that he would not tolerate another delay. Perhaps it was very base of Jurgis to be thinking about the house when he had the other unspeakable thing to fill his mind; yet, how much he had suffered for this house, how much they had all of them suffered! It was their one hope of respite, as long as they lived; they had put all their money into it—and they were working people, poor people, whose money was their strength, the very substance of them, body and soul, the thing by which they lived and for lack of which they died.

And they would lose it all; they would be turned out into the streets, and have to hide in some icy garret, and live or die as best they could! Jurgis had all the night—and all of many more nights—to think about this, and he saw the thing in its details; he lived it all, as if he were there. They would sell their furniture, and then run into debt at the stores, and then be refused credit; they would borrow a little from the Szedvilases, whose delicatessen store was tottering on the brink of ruin; the neighbors would come and help them a little—poor, sick Jadvyga would bring a few spare pennies, as she always did when people were starving, and Tamoszius Kuszleika would bring them the proceeds of a night's fiddling. So they would struggle to hang on until he got out of jail—or would they know that he was in jail, would they be able to find out anything about him? Would they be allowed to see him—or was it to be part of his punishment to be kept in ignorance about their fate?

His mind would hang upon the worst possibilities; he saw Ona ill and tortured, Marija out of her place, little Stanislovas unable to get to work for the snow, the whole family turned out on the street. God Almighty! would they actually let them lie down in the street and die? Would there be no help even then—would they wander about in the snow till they froze? Jurgis had never seen any dead bodies in the streets, but he had seen people evicted and disappear, no one knew where; and though the city had a relief bureau, though there was a charity organization society in the stockyards district, in all his life there he had never heard of either of them. They did not advertise their activities, having more calls than they could attend to without that.

—So on until morning. Then he had another ride in the patrol wagon, along with the drunken wife-beater and the maniac, several "plain drunks" and "saloon fighters," a burglar, and two men who had been arrested for stealing meat from the packing houses. Along with them he was driven into a large, white-walled room, stale-smelling and crowded. In front, upon a raised platform behind a rail, sat a stout, florid-faced personage, with a nose broken out in purple blotches.

Our friend realized vaguely that he was about to be tried. He wondered what for—whether or not his victim might be dead, and if so, what they would do with him. Hang him, perhaps, or beat him to death—nothing would have surprised Jurgis, who knew little of the laws. Yet he had picked up gossip enough to have it occur to him that the loud-voiced man upon the bench might be the notorious Justice Callahan, about whom the people of Packingtown spoke with bated breath.

"Pat" Callahan—"Growler" Pat, as he had been known before he ascended the bench—had begun life as a butcher boy and a bruiser of local reputation; he had gone into politics almost as soon as he had learned to talk, and had held two offices at once before he was old enough to vote. If Scully was the thumb, Pat Callahan was the first finger of the unseen hand whereby the packers held down the people of the district. No politician in Chicago ranked higher in their confidence; he had been at it a long time—had been the business agent in the city council of old Durham, the self-made merchant, way back in the early days, when the whole city of Chicago had been up at auction. "Growler" Pat had given up holding city offices very early in his career—caring only for party power, and giving the rest of his time to superintending his dives and brothels. Of late years, however, since his children were growing up, he had begun to value respectability, and had had himself made a magistrate; a position for which he was admirably fitted, because of his strong conservatism and his contempt for "foreigners."

Jurgis sat gazing about the room for an hour or two; he was in hopes that some one of the family would come, but in this he was disappointed. Finally, he was led before the bar, and a lawyer for the company appeared against him. Connor was under the doctor's care, the lawyer explained briefly, and if his Honor would hold the prisoner for a week—"Three hundred dollars," said his Honor, promptly.

Jurgis was staring from the judge to the lawyer in perplexity. "Have you any one to go on your bond?" demanded the judge, and then a clerk who stood at Jurgis' elbow explained to him what this meant. The latter shook his head, and before he realized what had happened the policemen were leading him away again. They took him to a room where other prisoners were waiting and here he stayed until court adjourned, when he had another long and bitterly cold ride in a patrol wagon to the county jail, which is on the north side of the city, and nine or ten miles from the stockyards.

Here they searched Jurgis, leaving him only his money, which consisted of fifteen cents. Then they led him to a room and told him to strip for a bath; after which he had to walk down a long gallery, past the grated cell doors of the inmates of the jail. This was a great event to the latter—the daily review of the new arrivals, all stark naked, and many and diverting were the comments. Jurgis was required to stay in the bath longer than any one, in the vain hope of getting out of him a few of his phosphates and acids. The prisoners roomed two in a cell, but that day there was one left over, and he was the one.

The cells were in tiers, opening upon galleries. His cell was about five feet by seven in size, with a stone floor and a heavy wooden bench built into it. There was no window—the only light came from windows near the roof at one end of the court outside. There were two bunks, one above the other, each with a straw mattress and a pair of gray blankets—the latter stiff as boards with filth, and alive with fleas, bedbugs, and lice. When Jurgis lifted up the mattress he discovered beneath it a layer of scurrying roaches, almost as badly frightened as himself.

Here they brought him more "duffers and dope," with the addition of a bowl of soup. Many of the prisoners had their meals brought in from a restaurant, but Jurgis had no money for that. Some had books to read and cards to play, with candles to burn by night, but Jurgis was all alone in darkness and silence. He could not sleep again; there was the same maddening procession of thoughts that lashed him like whips upon his naked back. When night fell he was pacing up and down his cell like a wild beast that breaks its teeth upon the bars of its cage. Now and then in his frenzy he would fling himself against the walls of the place, beating his hands upon them. They cut him and bruised him—they were cold and merciless as the men who had built them.

In the distance there was a church-tower bell that tolled the hours one by one. When it came to midnight Jurgis was lying upon the floor with his head in his arms, listening. Instead of falling silent at the end, the bell broke into a sudden clangor. Jurgis raised his head; what could that mean—a fire? God! Suppose there were to be a fire in this jail! But then he made out a melody in the ringing; there were chimes. And they seemed to waken the city—all around, far and near, there were bells, ringing wild music; for fully a minute Jurgis lay lost in wonder, before, all at once, the meaning of it broke over him—that this was Christmas Eve!

Christmas Eve—he had forgotten it entirely! There was a breaking of floodgates, a whirl of new memories and new griefs rushing into his mind. In far Lithuania they had celebrated Christmas; and it came to him as if it had been yesterday—himself a little child, with his lost brother and his dead father in the cabin—in the deep black forest, where the snow fell all day and all night and buried them from the world. It was too far off for Santa Claus in Lithuania, but it was not too far for peace and good will to men, for the wonder-bearing vision of the Christ Child. And even in Packingtown they had not forgotten it—some gleam of it had never failed to break their darkness. Last Christmas Eve and all Christmas Day Jurgis had toiled on the killing beds, and Ona at wrapping hams, and still they had found strength enough to take the children for a walk upon the avenue, to see the store windows all decorated with Christmas trees and ablaze with electric lights. In one window there would be live geese, in another marvels in sugar—pink and white canes big enough for ogres, and cakes with cherubs upon them; in a third there would be rows of fat yellow turkeys, decorated with rosettes, and rabbits and squirrels hanging; in a fourth would be a fairyland of toys—lovely dolls with pink dresses, and woolly sheep and drums and soldier hats. Nor did they have to go without their share of all this, either. The last time they had had a big basket with them and all their Christmas marketing to do—a roast of pork and a cabbage and some rye bread, and a pair of mittens for Ona, and a rubber doll that squeaked, and a little green cornucopia full of candy to be hung from the gas jet and gazed at by half a dozen pairs of longing eyes.

Even half a year of the sausage machines and the fertilizer mill had not been able to kill the thought of Christmas in them; there was a choking in Jurgis' throat as he recalled that the very night Ona had not come home Teta Elzbieta had taken him aside and shown him an old valentine that she had picked up in a paper store for three cents—dingy and shopworn, but with bright colors, and figures of angels and doves. She had wiped all the specks off this, and was going to set it on the mantel, where the children could see it. Great sobs shook Jurgis at this memory—they would spend their Christmas in misery and despair, with him in prison and Ona ill and their home in desolation. Ah, it was too cruel! Why at least had they not left him alone—why, after they had shut him in jail, must they be ringing Christmas chimes in his ears!

But no, their bells were not ringing for him—their Christmas was not meant for him, they were simply not counting him at all. He was of no consequence—he was flung aside, like a bit of trash, the carcass of some animal. It was horrible, horrible! His wife might be dying, his baby might be starving, his whole family might be perishing in the cold—and all the while they were ringing their Christmas chimes! And the bitter mockery of it—all this was punishment for him! They put him in a place where the snow could not beat in, where the cold could not eat through his bones; they brought him food and drink—why, in the name of heaven, if they must punish him, did they not put his family in jail and leave him outside—why could they find no better way to punish him than to leave three weak women and six helpless children to starve and freeze? That was their law, that was their justice!

Jurgis stood upright; trembling with passion, his hands clenched and his arms upraised, his whole soul ablaze with hatred and defiance. Ten thousand curses upon them and their law! Their justice—it was a lie, it was a lie, a hideous, brutal lie, a thing too black and hateful for any world but a world of nightmares. It was a sham and a loathsome mockery. There was no justice, there was no right, anywhere in it—it was only force, it was tyranny, the will and the power, reckless and unrestrained! They had ground him beneath their heel, they had devoured all his substance; they had murdered his old father, they had broken and wrecked his wife, they had crushed and cowed his whole family; and now they were through with him, they had no further use for him—and because he had interfered with them, had gotten in their way, this was what they had done to him! They had put him behind bars, as if he had been a wild beast, a thing without sense or reason, without rights, without affections, without feelings. Nay, they would not even have treated a beast as they had treated him! Would any man in his senses have trapped a wild thing in its lair, and left its young behind to die?

These midnight hours were fateful ones to Jurgis; in them was the beginning of his rebellion, of his outlawry and his unbelief. He had no wit to trace back the social crime to its far sources—he could not say that it was the thing men have called "the system" that was crushing him to the earth; that it was the packers, his masters, who had bought up the law of the land, and had dealt out their brutal will to him from the seat of justice. He only knew that he was wronged, and that the world had wronged him; that the law, that society, with all its powers, had declared itself his foe. And every hour his soul grew blacker, every hour he dreamed new dreams of vengeance, of defiance, of raging, frenzied hate.

> The vilest deeds, like poison weeds,
>   Bloom well in prison air;
> It is only what is good in Man
>   That wastes and withers there;
> Pale Anguish keeps the heavy gate,
>   And the Warder is Despair.

THE JUNGLE

So wrote a poet, to whom the world had dealt its justice—

> I know not whether Laws be right,
>   Or whether Laws be wrong;
> All that we know who lie in gaol
>   Is that the wall is strong.
> And they do well to hide their hell,
>   For in it things are done
> That Son of God nor son of Man
>   Ever should look upon!

CHAPTER 17

At seven o'clock the next morning Jurgis was let out to get water to wash his cell—a duty which he performed faithfully, but which most of the prisoners were accustomed to shirk, until their cells became so filthy that the guards interposed. Then he had more "duffers and dope," and afterward was allowed three hours for exercise, in a long, cement-walked court roofed with glass. Here were all the inmates of the jail crowded together. At one side of the court was a place for visitors, cut off by two heavy wire screens, a foot apart, so that nothing could be passed in to the prisoners; here Jurgis watched anxiously, but there came no one to see him.

Soon after he went back to his cell, a keeper opened the door to let in another prisoner. He was a dapper young fellow, with a light brown mustache and blue eyes, and a graceful figure. He nodded to Jurgis, and then, as the keeper closed the door upon him, began gazing critically about him.

"Well, pal," he said, as his glance encountered Jurgis again, "good morning."

"Good morning," said Jurgis.

"A rum go for Christmas, eh?" added the other.

Jurgis nodded.

The newcomer went to the bunks and inspected the blankets; he lifted up the mattress, and then dropped it with an exclamation. "My God!" he said, "that's the worst yet."

He glanced at Jurgis again. "Looks as if it hadn't been slept in last night. Couldn't stand it, eh?"

"I didn't want to sleep last night," said Jurgis.

"When did you come in?"

"Yesterday."

The other had another look around, and then wrinkled up his nose. "There's the devil of a stink in here," he said, suddenly. "What is it?"

"It's me," said Jurgis.

"You?"

"Yes, me."

"Didn't they make you wash?"

"Yes, but this don't wash."

"What is it?"

"Fertilizer."

"Fertilizer! The deuce! What are you?"

"I work in the stockyards—at least I did until the other day. It's in my clothes."

"That's a new one on me," said the newcomer. "I thought I'd been up against 'em all. What are you in for?"

"I hit my boss."

"Oh—that's it. What did he do?"

"He—he treated me mean."

"I see. You're what's called an honest workingman!"

"What are you?" Jurgis asked.

"I?" The other laughed. "They say I'm a cracksman," he said.

"What's that?" asked Jurgis.

"Safes, and such things," answered the other.

"Oh," said Jurgis, wonderingly, and stated at the speaker in awe. "You mean you break into them—you—you—"

"Yes," laughed the other, "that's what they say."

He did not look to be over twenty-two or three, though, as Jurgis found afterward, he was thirty. He spoke like a man of education, like what the world calls a "gentleman."

"Is that what you're here for?" Jurgis inquired.

"No," was the answer. "I'm here for disorderly conduct. They were mad because they couldn't get any evidence.

"What's your name?" the young fellow continued after a pause. "My name's Duane—Jack Duane. I've more than a dozen, but that's my company one." He seated himself on the floor with his back to the wall and his legs crossed, and went on talking easily; he soon put Jurgis on a friendly footing—he was evidently a man of the world, used to getting on, and not too proud to hold conversation with a mere laboring man. He drew Jurgis out, and heard all about his life all but the one unmentionable thing; and then he told stories about his own life. He was a great one for stories, not always of the choicest. Being sent to jail had apparently not disturbed his cheerfulness; he had "done time" twice before, it seemed, and he took it all with a frolic welcome. What with women and wine and the excitement of his vocation, a man could afford to rest now and then.

Naturally, the aspect of prison life was changed for Jurgis by the arrival of a cell mate. He could not turn his face to the wall and sulk, he had to speak when he was spoken to; nor could he help being interested in the conversation of Duane— the first educated man with whom he had ever talked. How could he help listening with wonder while the other told of midnight ventures and perilous escapes, of feastings and orgies, of fortunes squandered in a night? The young fellow had an amused contempt for Jurgis, as a sort of working mule; he, too, had felt the world's injustice, but instead of bearing it patiently, he had struck back, and struck hard. He was striking all the time—there was war between him and society. He was a genial freebooter, living off the enemy, without fear or shame. He was not always victorious, but then defeat did not mean annihilation, and need not break his spirit.

Withal he was a goodhearted fellow—too much so, it appeared. His story came out, not in the first day, nor the second, but in the long hours that dragged by, in which they had nothing to do but talk and nothing to talk of but themselves. Jack Duane was from the East; he was a college-bred man—had been studying electrical engineering. Then his father had met with misfortune in business and killed himself; and there had been his mother and a younger brother and sister. Also, there was an invention of Duane's; Jurgis could not understand it clearly, but it had to do with telegraphing, and it was a very important thing—there were fortunes in it, millions upon millions of dollars. And Duane had been robbed of it by a great company, and got tangled up in lawsuits and lost all his money. Then somebody had given him a tip on a horse race, and he had tried to retrieve his fortune with another person's money, and had to run away, and all the rest had come from that. The other asked him what had led him to safe-breaking—to Jurgis a wild and appalling occupation to think about. A man he had met, his cell mate had replied—one thing leads to another. Didn't he ever wonder about his family, Jurgis asked. Sometimes, the other answered, but not often—he didn't allow it. Thinking about it would make it no better. This wasn't a world in which a man had any business with a family; sooner or later Jurgis would find that out also, and give up the fight and shift for himself.

Jurgis was so transparently what he pretended to be that his cell mate was as open with him as a child; it was pleasant to tell him adventures, he was so full of wonder and admiration, he was so new to the ways of the country. Duane did not even bother to keep back names and places—he told all his triumphs and his failures, his loves and his griefs. Also he introduced Jurgis to many of the other prisoners, nearly half of whom he knew by name. The crowd had already given Jurgis a name—they called him "he stinker." This was cruel, but they meant no harm by it, and he took it with a good-natured grin.

Our friend had caught now and then a whiff from the sewers over which he lived, but this was the first time that he had ever been splashed by their filth. This jail was a Noah's ark of the city's crime—there were murderers, "hold-up men" and burglars, embezzlers, counterfeiters and forgers, bigamists, "shoplifters," "confidence men," petty thieves and pickpockets, gamblers and procurers, brawlers, beggars, tramps and drunkards; they were black and white, old and young, Americans and natives of every nation under the sun. There were hardened criminals and innocent men too poor to give bail; old men, and boys literally not yet in their teens. They were the drainage of the great festering ulcer of society; they were hideous to look upon, sickening to talk to. All life had turned to rottenness and stench in them—love was a beastliness, joy was a snare, and God was an imprecation. They strolled here and there about the courtyard, and Jurgis listened to them. He was ignorant and they were wise; they had been everywhere and tried everything. They could tell the whole hateful story of it, set forth the inner soul of a city in which justice and honor, women's bodies and men's souls, were for sale in the marketplace, and human beings writhed and fought and fell upon each other like wolves in a pit; in which lusts were raging fires, and men were fuel, and humanity was festering and stewing and wallowing in its own corruption. Into this wild-beast tangle these men had been born without their consent, they had taken part in it because they could not help it; that they were in jail was no disgrace to them, for the game had never been fair, the dice were loaded. They were swindlers and thieves of pennies and dimes, and they had been trapped and put out of the way by the swindlers and thieves of millions of dollars.

To most of this Jurgis tried not to listen. They frightened him with their savage mockery; and all the while his heart was far away, where his loved ones were calling. Now and then in the midst of it his thoughts would take flight; and then the tears would come into his eyes—and he would be called back by the jeering laughter of his companions.

He spent a week in this company, and during all that time he had no word from his home. He paid one of his fifteen cents for a postal card, and his companion wrote a note to the family, telling them where he was and when he would be tried. There came no answer to it, however, and at last, the day before New Year's, Jurgis bade good-by to Jack Duane. The latter gave him his address, or rather the address of his mistress, and made Jurgis promise to look him up. "Maybe I could help you out of a hole some day," he said, and added that he was sorry to have him go. Jurgis rode in the patrol wagon back to Justice Callahan's court for trial.

One of the first things he made out as he entered the room was Teta Elzbieta and little Kotrina, looking pale and frightened, seated far in the rear. His heart began to pound, but he did not dare to try to signal to them, and neither did Elzbieta. He took his seat in the prisoners' pen and sat gazing at them in helpless agony. He saw that Ona was not with them, and was full of foreboding as to what that might mean. He spent half an hour brooding over this—and then suddenly he straightened up and the blood rushed into his face. A man had come in—Jurgis could not see his features for the bandages that swathed him, but he knew the burly figure. It was Connor! A trembling seized him, and his limbs bent as if for a spring. Then suddenly he felt a hand on his collar, and heard a voice behind him: "Sit down, you son of a—!"

He subsided, but he never took his eyes off his enemy. The fellow was still alive, which was a disappointment, in one way; and yet it was pleasant to see him, all in penitential plasters. He and the company lawyer, who was with him, came and took seats within the judge's railing; and a minute later the clerk called Jurgis' name, and the policeman jerked him to his feet and led him before the bar, gripping him tightly by the arm, lest he should spring upon the boss.

Jurgis listened while the man entered the witness chair, took the oath, and told his story. The wife of the prisoner had been employed in a department near him, and had been discharged for impudence to him. Half an hour later he had been violently attacked, knocked down, and almost choked to death. He had brought witnesses—

"They will probably not be necessary," observed the judge and he turned to Jurgis. "You admit attacking the plaintiff?" he asked.

"Him?" inquired Jurgis, pointing at the boss.

"Yes," said the judge. "I hit him, sir," said Jurgis.

"Say 'your Honor,'" said the officer, pinching his arm hard.

"Your Honor," said Jurgis, obediently.

"You tried to choke him?"

"Yes, sir, your Honor."

"Ever been arrested before?"

"No, sir, your Honor."

"What have you to say for yourself?"

Jurgis hesitated. What had he to say? In two years and a half he had learned to speak English for practical purposes, but these had never included the statement that some one had intimidated and seduced his wife. He tried once or twice, stammering and balking, to the annoyance of the judge, who was gasping from the odor of fertilizer. Finally, the prisoner made it understood that his vocabulary was inadequate, and there stepped up a dapper young man with waxed mustaches, bidding him speak in any language he knew.

Jurgis began; supposing that he would be given time, he explained how the boss had taken advantage of his wife's position to make advances to her and had threatened her with the loss of her place. When the interpreter had translated this, the judge, whose calendar was crowded, and whose automobile was ordered for a certain hour, interrupted with the remark: "Oh, I see. Well, if he made love to your wife, why didn't she complain to the superintendent or leave the place?"

Jurgis hesitated, somewhat taken aback; he began to explain that they were very poor—that work was hard to get—

"I see," said Justice Callahan; "so instead you thought you would knock him down." He turned to the plaintiff, inquiring, "Is there any truth in this story, Mr. Connor?"

"Not a particle, your Honor," said the boss. "It is very unpleasant—they tell some such tale every time you have to discharge a woman—"

"Yes, I know," said the judge. "I hear it often enough. The fellow seems to have handled you pretty roughly. Thirty days and costs. Next case."

Jurgis had been listening in perplexity. It was only when the policeman who had him by the arm turned and started to lead him away that he realized that sentence had been passed. He gazed round him wildly. "Thirty days!" he panted and then he whirled upon the judge. "What will my family do?" he cried frantically. "I have a wife and baby, sir, and they have no money—my God, they will starve to death!"

"You would have done well to think about them before you committed the assault," said the judge dryly, as he turned to look at the next prisoner.

Jurgis would have spoken again, but the policeman had seized him by the collar and was twisting it, and a second policeman was making for him with evidently hostile intentions. So he let them lead him away. Far down the room he saw Elzbieta and Kotrina, risen from their seats, staring in fright; he made one effort to go to them, and then, brought back by another twist at his throat, he bowed his head and gave up the struggle. They thrust him into a cell room, where other prisoners were waiting; and as soon as court had adjourned they led him down with them into the "Black Maria," and drove him away.

This time Jurgis was bound for the "Bridewell," a petty jail where Cook County prisoners serve their time. It was even filthier and more crowded than the county jail; all the smaller fry out of the latter had been sifted into it—the petty thieves and swindlers, the brawlers and vagrants. For his cell mate Jurgis had an Italian fruit seller who had refused to pay his graft to the policeman, and been arrested for carrying a large pocketknife; as he did not understand a word of English our friend was glad when he left. He gave place to a Norwegian sailor, who had lost half an ear in a drunken brawl, and who proved to be quarrelsome, cursing Jurgis because he moved in his bunk and caused the roaches to drop upon the lower one. It would have been quite intolerable, staying in a cell with this wild beast, but for the fact that all day long the prisoners were put at work breaking stone.

Ten days of his thirty Jurgis spent thus, without hearing a word from his family; then one day a keeper came and informed him that there was a visitor to see him. Jurgis turned white, and so weak at the knees that he could hardly leave his cell.

The man led him down the corridor and a flight of steps to the visitors' room, which was barred like a cell. Through the grating Jurgis could see some one sitting in a chair; and as he came into the room the person started up, and he saw that it was little Stanislovas. At the sight of some one from home the big fellow nearly went to pieces—he had to steady himself by a chair, and he put his other hand to his forehead, as if to clear away a mist. "Well?" he said, weakly.

Little Stanislovas was also trembling, and all but too frightened to speak. "They—they sent me to tell you—" he said, with a gulp.

"Well?" Jurgis repeated. He followed the boy's glance to where the keeper was standing watching them. "Never mind that," Jurgis cried, wildly. "How are they?"

"Ona is very sick," Stanislovas said; "and we are almost starving. We can't get along; we thought you might be able to help us."

Jurgis gripped the chair tighter; there were beads of perspiration on his forehead, and his hand shook. "I—can't help you," he said.

"Ona lies in her room all day," the boy went on, breathlessly. "She won't eat anything, and she cries all the time. She won't tell what is the matter and she won't go to work at all. Then a long time ago the man came for the rent. He was very cross. He came again last week. He said he would turn us out of the house. And then Marija—"

A sob choked Stanislovas, and he stopped. "What's the matter with Marija?" cried Jurgis.

"She's cut her hand!" said the boy. "She's cut it bad, this time, worse than before. She can't work and it's all turning green, and the company doctor says she may—she may have to have it cut off. And Marija cries all the time—her money is nearly all gone, too, and we can't pay the rent and the interest on the house; and we have no coal and nothing more to eat, and the man at the store, he says—"

The little fellow stopped again, beginning to whimper. "Go on!" the other panted in frenzy—"Go on!"

"I—I will," sobbed Stanislovas. "It's so—so cold all the time. And last Sunday it snowed again—a deep, deep snow—and I couldn't—couldn't get to work."

"God!" Jurgis half shouted, and he took a step toward the child. There was an old hatred between them because of the snow—ever since that dreadful morning when the boy had had his fingers frozen and Jurgis had had to beat him to send him to work. Now he clenched his hands, looking as if he would try to break through the grating. "You little villain," he cried, "you didn't try!"

"I did—I did!" wailed Stanislovas, shrinking from him in terror. "I tried all day—two days. Elzbieta was with me, and she couldn't either. We couldn't walk at all, it was so deep. And we had nothing to eat, and oh, it was so cold! I tried, and then the third day Ona went with me—"

"Ona!"

"Yes. She tried to get to work, too. She had to. We were all starving. But she had lost her place—"

Jurgis reeled, and gave a gasp. "She went back to that place?" he screamed. "She tried to," said Stanislovas, gazing at him in perplexity. "Why not, Jurgis?"

The man breathed hard, three or four times. "Go—on," he panted, finally.

"I went with her," said Stanislovas, "but Miss Henderson wouldn't take her back. And Connor saw her and cursed her. He was still bandaged up—why did you hit him, Jurgis?" (There was some fascinating mystery about this, the little fellow knew; but he could get no satisfaction.)

Jurgis could not speak; he could only stare, his eyes starting out. "She has been trying to get other work," the boy went on; "but she's so weak she can't keep up. And my boss would not take me back, either—Ona says he knows Connor, and that's the reason; they've all got a grudge against us now. So I've got to go down-town and sell papers with the rest of the boys and Kotrina—"

"Kotrina!"

"Yes, she's been selling papers, too. She does best, because she's a girl. Only the cold is so bad—it's terrible coming home at night, Jurgis. Sometimes they can't come home at all—I'm going to try to find them tonight and sleep where they do, it's so late and it's such a long ways home. I've had to walk, and I didn't know where it was—I don't know how to get back, either. Only mother said I must come, because you would want to know, and maybe somebody would help your family when they had put you in jail so you couldn't work. And I walked all day to get here—and I only had a piece of bread for breakfast, Jurgis. Mother hasn't any work either, because the sausage department is shut down; and she goes and begs at houses with a basket, and people give her food. Only she didn't get much yesterday; it was too cold for her fingers, and today she was crying—"

So little Stanislovas went on, sobbing as he talked; and Jurgis stood, gripping the table tightly, saying not a word, but feeling that his head would burst; it was like having weights piled upon him, one after another, crushing the life out of him. He struggled and fought within himself—as if in some terrible nightmare, in which a man suffers an agony, and cannot lift his hand, nor cry out, but feels that he is going mad, that his brain is on fire—

Just when it seemed to him that another turn of the screw would kill him, little Stanislovas stopped. "You cannot help us?" he said weakly.

Jurgis shook his head.

"They won't give you anything here?"

He shook it again.

"When are you coming out?"

"Three weeks yet," Jurgis answered.

And the boy gazed around him uncertainly. "Then I might as well go," he said.

Jurgis nodded. Then, suddenly recollecting, he put his hand into his pocket and drew it out, shaking. "Here," he said, holding out the fourteen cents. "Take this to them."

And Stanislovas took it, and after a little more hesitation, started for the door. "Good-by, Jurgis," he said, and the other noticed that he walked unsteadily as he passed out of sight.

For a minute or so Jurgis stood clinging to his chair, reeling and swaying; then the keeper touched him on the arm, and he turned and went back to breaking stone.

CHAPTER 18

Jurgis did not get out of the Bridewell quite as soon as he had expected. To his sentence there were added "court costs" of a dollar and a half—he was supposed to pay for the trouble of putting him in jail, and not having the money, was obliged to work it off by three days more of toil. Nobody had taken the trouble to tell him this—only after counting the days and looking forward to the end in an agony of impatience, when the hour came that he expected to be free he found himself still set at the stone heap, and laughed at when he ventured to protest. Then he concluded he must have counted wrong; but as another day passed, he gave up all hope—and was sunk in the depths of despair, when one morning after breakfast a keeper came to him with the word that his time was up at last. So he doffed his prison garb, and put on his old fertilizer clothing, and heard the door of the prison clang behind him.

He stood upon the steps, bewildered; he could hardly believe that it was true,—that the sky was above him again and the open street before him; that he was a free man. But then the cold began to strike through his clothes, and he started quickly away.

There had been a heavy snow, and now a thaw had set in; fine sleety rain was falling, driven by a wind that pierced Jurgis to the bone. He had not stopped for his-overcoat when he set out to "do up" Connor, and so his rides in the patrol wagons had been cruel experiences; his clothing was old and worn thin, and it never had been very warm. Now as he trudged on the rain soon wet it through; there were six inches of watery slush on the sidewalks, so that his feet would soon have been soaked, even had there been no holes in his shoes.

Jurgis had had enough to eat in the jail, and the work had been the least trying of any that he had done since he came to Chicago; but even so, he had not grown strong—the fear and grief that had preyed upon his mind had worn him thin. Now he shivered and shrunk from the rain, hiding his hands in his pockets and hunching his shoulders together. The Bridewell grounds were on the outskirts of the city and the country around them was unsettled and wild—on one side was the big drainage canal, and on the other a maze of railroad tracks, and so the wind had full sweep.

After walking a ways, Jurgis met a little ragamuffin whom he hailed: "Hey, sonny!" The boy cocked one eye at him—he knew that Jurgis was a "jailbird" by his shaven head. "Wot yer want?" he queried.

"How do you go to the stockyards?" Jurgis demanded.

"I don't go," replied the boy.

Jurgis hesitated a moment, nonplussed. Then he said, "I mean which is the way?"

"Why don't yer say so then?" was the response, and the boy pointed to the northwest, across the tracks. "That way."

"How far is it?" Jurgis asked. "I dunno," said the other. "Mebbe twenty miles or so."

"Twenty miles!" Jurgis echoed, and his face fell. He had to walk every foot of it, for they had turned him out of jail without a penny in his pockets.

Yet, when he once got started, and his blood had warmed with walking, he forgot everything in the fever of his thoughts. All the dreadful imaginations that had haunted him in his cell now rushed into his mind at once. The agony was almost over—he was going to find out; and he clenched his hands in his pockets as he strode, following his flying desire, almost at a run. Ona—the baby—the family—the house—he would know the truth about them all! And he was coming to the rescue—he was free again! His hands were his own, and he could help them, he could do battle for them against the world.

For an hour or so he walked thus, and then he began to look about him. He seemed to be leaving the city altogether. The street was turning into a country road, leading out to the westward; there were snow-covered fields on either side of him. Soon he met a farmer driving a two-horse wagon loaded with straw, and he stopped him.

"Is this the way to the stockyards?" he asked.

The farmer scratched his head. "I dunno jest where they be," he said. "But they're in the city somewhere, and you're going dead away from it now."

Jurgis looked dazed. "I was told this was the way," he said.

"Who told you?"

"A boy."

"Well, mebbe he was playing a joke on ye. The best thing ye kin do is to go back, and when ye git into town ask a policeman. I'd take ye in, only I've come a long ways an' I'm loaded heavy. Git up!"

So Jurgis turned and followed, and toward the end of the morning he began to see Chicago again. Past endless blocks of two-story shanties he walked, along wooden sidewalks and unpaved pathways treacherous with deep slush holes. Every few blocks there would be a railroad crossing on the level with the sidewalk, a deathtrap for the unwary; long freight trains would be passing, the cars clanking and crashing together, and Jurgis would pace about waiting, burning up with a fever of impatience. Occasionally the cars would stop for some minutes, and wagons and streetcars would crowd together waiting, the drivers swearing at each other, or hiding beneath umbrellas out of the rain; at such times Jurgis would dodge under the gates and run across the tracks and between the cars, taking his life into his hands.

He crossed a long bridge over a river frozen solid and covered with slush. Not even on the river bank was the snow white—the rain which fell was a diluted solution of smoke, and Jurgis' hands and face were streaked with black. Then he came into the business part of the city, where the streets were sewers of inky blackness, with horses sleeping and plunging, and women and children flying across in panic-stricken droves. These streets were huge canyons formed by towering black buildings, echoing with the clang of car gongs and the shouts of drivers; the people who swarmed in them were as busy as ants—all hurrying breathlessly, never stopping to look at anything nor at each other. The solitary trampish-looking foreigner, with water-soaked clothing and haggard face and anxious eyes, was as much alone as he hurried past them, as much unheeded and as lost, as if he had been a thousand miles deep in a wilderness.

A policeman gave him his direction and told him that he had five miles to go. He came again to the slum districts, to avenues of saloons and cheap stores, with long dingy red factory buildings, and coal-yards and railroad tracks; and then Jurgis lifted up his head and began to sniff the air like a startled animal—scenting the far-off odor of home. It was late afternoon then, and he was hungry, but the dinner invitations hung out of the saloons were not for him.

So he came at last to the stockyards, to the black volcanoes of smoke and the lowing cattle and the stench. Then, seeing a crowded car, his impatience got the better of him and he jumped aboard, hiding behind another man, unnoticed by the conductor. In ten minutes more he had reached his street, and home.

He was half running as he came round the corner. There was the house, at any rate—and then suddenly he stopped and stared. What was the matter with the house?

Jurgis looked twice, bewildered; then he glanced at the house next door and at the one beyond—then at the saloon on the corner. Yes, it was the right place, quite certainly—he had not made any mistake. But the house—the house was a different color!

He came a couple of steps nearer. Yes; it had been gray and now it was yellow! The trimmings around the windows had been red, and now they were green! It was all newly painted! How strange it made it seem!

Jurgis went closer yet, but keeping on the other side of the street. A sudden and horrible spasm of fear had come over him. His knees were shaking beneath him, and his mind was in a whirl. New paint on the house, and new weatherboards, where the old had begun to rot off, and the agent had got after them! New shingles over the hole in the roof, too, the hole that had for six months been the bane of his soul—he having no money to have it fixed and no time to fix it himself, and the rain leaking in, and overflowing the pots and pans he put to catch it, and flooding the attic and loosening the plaster. And now it was fixed! And the broken windowpane replaced! And curtains in the windows! New, white curtains, stiff and shiny!

Then suddenly the front door opened. Jurgis stood, his chest heaving as he struggled to catch his breath. A boy had come out, a stranger to him; a big, fat, rosy-cheeked youngster, such as had never been seen in his home before.

Jurgis stared at the boy, fascinated. He came down the steps whistling, kicking off the snow. He stopped at the foot, and picked up some, and then leaned against the railing, making a snowball. A moment later he looked around and saw Jurgis, and their eyes met; it was a hostile glance, the boy evidently thinking that the other had suspicions of the snowball. When Jurgis started slowly across the street toward him, he gave a quick glance about, meditating retreat, but then he concluded to stand his ground.

Jurgis took hold of the railing of the steps, for he was a little unsteady. "What—what are you doing here?" he managed to gasp.

"Go on!" said the boy.

"You—" Jurgis tried again. "What do you want here?"

"Me?" answered the boy, angrily. "I live here."

"You live here!" Jurgis panted. He turned white and clung more tightly to the railing. "You live here! Then where's my family?"

The boy looked surprised. "Your family!" he echoed.

And Jurgis started toward him. "I—this is my house!" he cried.

"Come off!" said the boy; then suddenly the door upstairs opened, and he called: "Hey, ma! Here's a fellow says he owns this house."

A stout Irishwoman came to the top of the steps. "What's that?" she demanded.

Jurgis turned toward her. "Where is my family?" he cried, wildly. "I left them here! This is my home! What are you doing in my home?"

The woman stared at him in frightened wonder, she must have thought she was dealing with a maniac—Jurgis looked like one. "Your home!" she echoed.

"My home!" he half shrieked. "I lived here, I tell you."

"You must be mistaken," she answered him. "No one ever lived here. This is a new house. They told us so. They—"

"What have they done with my family?" shouted Jurgis, frantically.

A light had begun to break upon the woman; perhaps she had had doubts of what "they" had told her. "I don't know where your family is," she said. "I bought the house only three days ago, and there was nobody here, and they told me it was all new. Do you really mean you had ever rented it?"

"Rented it!" panted Jurgis. "I bought it! I paid for it! I own it! And they—my God, can't you tell me where my people went?"

She made him understand at last that she knew nothing. Jurgis' brain was so confused that he could not grasp the situation. It was as if his family had been wiped out of existence; as if they were proving to be dream people, who never had existed at all. He was quite lost—but then suddenly he thought of Grandmother Majauszkiene, who lived in the next block. She would know! He turned and started at a run.

Grandmother Majauszkiene came to the door herself. She cried out when she saw Jurgis, wild-eyed and shaking. Yes, yes, she could tell him. The family had moved; they had not been able to pay the rent and they had been turned out into the snow, and the house had been repainted and sold again the next week. No, she had not heard how they were, but she could tell him that they had gone back to Aniele Jukniene, with whom they had stayed when they first came to the yards. Wouldn't Jurgis come in and rest? It was certainly too bad—if only he had not got into jail—

And so Jurgis turned and staggered away. He did not go very far round the corner he gave out completely, and sat down on the steps of a saloon, and hid his face in his hands, and shook all over with dry, racking sobs.

Their home! Their home! They had lost it! Grief, despair, rage, overwhelmed him—what was any imagination of the thing to this heartbreaking, crushing reality of it—to the sight of strange people living in his house, hanging their curtains to his windows, staring at him with hostile eyes! It was monstrous, it was unthinkable—they could not do it—it could not be true! Only think what he had suffered for that house—what miseries they had all suffered for it—the price they had paid for it!

The whole long agony came back to him. Their sacrifices in the beginning, their three hundred dollars that they had scraped together, all they owned in the world, all that stood between them and starvation! And then their toil, month by month, to get together the twelve dollars, and the interest as well, and now and then the taxes, and the other charges, and the repairs, and what not! Why, they had put their very souls into their payments on that house, they had paid for it with their sweat and tears—yes, more, with their very lifeblood. Dede Antanas had died of the struggle to earn that money—he would have been alive and strong today if he had not had to work in Durham's dark cellars to earn his share. And Ona, too, had given her health and strength to pay for it—she was wrecked and ruined because of it; and so was he, who had been a big, strong man three years ago, and now sat here shivering, broken, cowed, weeping like a hysterical child. Ah! they had cast their all into the fight; and they had lost, they had lost! All that they had paid was gone—every cent of it. And their house was gone—they were back where they had started from, flung out into the cold to starve and freeze!

Jurgis could see all the truth now—could see himself, through the whole long course of events, the victim of ravenous vultures that had torn into his vitals and devoured him; of fiends that had racked and tortured him, mocking him, meantime, jeering in his face. Ah, God, the horror of it, the monstrous, hideous, demoniacal wickedness of it! He and his family, helpless women and children, struggling to live, ignorant and defenseless and forlorn as they were—and the enemies that had been lurking for them, crouching upon their trail and thirsting for their blood! That first lying circular, that smooth-tongued slippery agent! That trap of the extra payments, the interest, and all the other charges that they had not the means to pay, and would never have attempted to pay! And then all the tricks of the packers, their masters, the tyrants who ruled them—the shutdowns and the scarcity of work, the irregular hours and the cruel speeding-up, the lowering of wages, the raising of prices! The mercilessness of nature about them, of heat and cold, rain and snow; the mercilessness of the city, of the country in which they lived, of its laws and customs that they did not understand! All of these things had worked together for the company that had marked them for its prey and was waiting for its chance. And now, with this last hideous injustice, its time had come, and it had turned them out bag and baggage, and taken their house and sold it again! And they could do nothing, they were tied hand and foot—the law was against them, the whole machinery of society was at their oppressors' command! If Jurgis so much as raised a hand against them, back he would go into that wild-beast pen from which he had just escaped!

To get up and go away was to give up, to acknowledge defeat, to leave the strange family in possession; and Jurgis might have sat shivering in the rain for hours before he could do that, had it not been for the thought of his family. It might be that he had worse things yet to learn—and so he got to his feet and started away, walking on, wearily, half-dazed.

To Aniele's house, in back of the yards, was a good two miles; the distance had never seemed longer to Jurgis, and when he saw the familiar dingy-gray shanty his heart was beating fast. He ran up the steps and began to hammer upon the door.

The old woman herself came to open it. She had shrunk all up with her rheumatism since Jurgis had seen her last, and her yellow parchment face stared up at him from a little above the level of the doorknob. She gave a start when she saw him. "Is Ona here?" he cried, breathlessly.

"Yes," was the answer, "she's here."

"How—" Jurgis began, and then stopped short, clutching convulsively at the side of the door. From somewhere within the house had come a sudden cry, a wild, horrible scream of anguish. And the voice was Ona's. For a moment Jurgis stood half-paralyzed with fright; then he bounded past the old woman and into the room.

It was Aniele's kitchen, and huddled round the stove were half a dozen women, pale and frightened. One of them started to her feet as Jurgis entered; she was haggard and frightfully thin, with one arm tied up in bandages—he hardly realized that it was Marija. He looked first for Ona; then, not seeing her, he stared at the women, expecting them to speak. But they sat dumb, gazing back at him, panic-stricken; and a second later came another piercing scream.

It was from the rear of the house, and upstairs. Jurgis bounded to a door of the room and flung it open; there was a ladder leading through a trap door to the garret, and he was at the foot of it when suddenly he heard a voice behind him, and saw Marija at his heels. She seized him by the sleeve with her good hand, panting wildly, "No, no, Jurgis! Stop!"

"What do you mean?" he gasped.

"You mustn't go up," she cried.

Jurgis was half-crazed with bewilderment and fright. "What's the matter?" he shouted. "What is it?"

Marija clung to him tightly; he could hear Ona sobbing and moaning above, and he fought to get away and climb up, without waiting for her reply. "No, no," she rushed on. "Jurgis! You mustn't go up! It's—it's the child!"

"The child?" he echoed in perplexity. "Antanas?"

Marija answered him, in a whisper: "The new one!"

And then Jurgis went limp, and caught himself on the ladder. He stared at her as if she were a ghost. "The new one!" he gasped. "But it isn't time," he added, wildly.

Marija nodded. "I know," she said; "but it's come."

And then again came Ona's scream, smiting him like a blow in the face, making him wince and turn white. Her voice died away into a wail—then he heard her sobbing again, "My God—let me die, let me die!" And Marija hung her arms about him, crying: "Come out! Come away!"

She dragged him back into the kitchen, half carrying him, for he had gone all to pieces. It was as if the pillars of his soul had fallen in—he was blasted with horror. In the room he sank into a chair, trembling like a leaf, Marija still holding him, and the women staring at him in dumb, helpless fright.

And then again Ona cried out; he could hear it nearly as plainly here, and he staggered to his feet. "How long has this been going on?" he panted.

"Not very long," Marija answered, and then, at a signal from Aniele, she rushed on: "You go away, Jurgis you can't help—go away and come back later. It's all right—it's—"

"Who's with her?" Jurgis demanded; and then, seeing Marija hesitating, he cried again, "Who's with her?"

"She's—she's all right," she answered. "Elzbieta's with her."

"But the doctor!" he panted. "Some one who knows!"

He seized Marija by the arm; she trembled, and her voice sank beneath a whisper as she replied, "We—we have no money." Then, frightened at the look on his face, she exclaimed: "It's all right, Jurgis! You don't understand—go away—go away! Ah, if you only had waited!"

Above her protests Jurgis heard Ona again; he was almost out of his mind. It was all new to him, raw and horrible—it had fallen upon him like a lightning stroke. When little Antanas was born he had been at work, and had known nothing about it until it was over; and now he was not to be controlled. The frightened women were at their wits' end; one after another they tried to reason with him, to make him understand that this was the lot of woman. In the end they half drove him out into the rain, where he began to pace up and down, bareheaded and frantic. Because he could hear Ona from the street, he would first go away to escape the sounds, and then come back because he could not help it. At the end of a quarter of an hour he rushed up the steps again, and for fear that he would break in the door they had to open it and let him in.

There was no arguing with him. They could not tell him that all was going well—how could they know, he cried—why, she was dying, she was being torn to pieces! Listen to her—listen! Why, it was monstrous—it could not be allowed—

there must be some help for it! Had they tried to get a doctor? They might pay him afterward—they could promise—

"We couldn't promise, Jurgis," protested Marija. "We had no money—we have scarcely been able to keep alive."

"But I can work," Jurgis exclaimed. "I can earn money!"

"Yes," she answered—"but we thought you were in jail. How could we know when you would return? They will not work for nothing."

Marija went on to tell how she had tried to find a midwife, and how they had demanded ten, fifteen, even twenty-five dollars, and that in cash. "And I had only a quarter," she said. "I have spent every cent of my money—all that I had in the bank; and I owe the doctor who has been coming to see me, and he has stopped because he thinks I don't mean to pay him. And we owe Aniele for two weeks' rent, and she is nearly starving, and is afraid of being turned out. We have been borrowing and begging to keep alive, and there is nothing more we can do—"

"And the children?" cried Jurgis.

"The children have not been home for three days, the weather has been so bad. They could not know what is happening—it came suddenly, two months before we expected it."

Jurgis was standing by the table, and he caught himself with his hand; his head sank and his arms shook—it looked as if he were going to collapse. Then suddenly Aniele got up and came hobbling toward him, fumbling in her skirt pocket. She drew out a dirty rag, in one corner of which she had something tied.

"Here, Jurgis!" she said, "I have some money. Palauk! See!"

She unwrapped it and counted it out—thirty-four cents. "You go, now," she said, "and try and get somebody yourself. And maybe the rest can help—give him some money, you; he will pay you back some day, and it will do him good to have something to think about, even if he doesn't succeed. When he comes back, maybe it will be over."

And so the other women turned out the contents of their pocketbooks; most of them had only pennies and nickels, but they gave him all. Mrs. Olszewski, who lived next door, and had a husband who was a skilled cattle butcher, but a drinking man, gave nearly half a dollar, enough to raise the whole sum to a dollar and a quarter. Then Jurgis thrust it into his pocket, still holding it tightly in his fist, and started away at a run.

CHAPTER 19

"Madame Haupt Hebamme", ran a sign, swinging from a second-story window over a saloon on the avenue; at a side door was another sign, with a hand pointing up a dingy flight of stairs. Jurgis went up them, three at a time.

Madame Haupt was frying pork and onions, and had her door half open to let out the smoke. When he tried to knock upon it, it swung open the rest of the way, and he had a glimpse of her, with a black bottle turned up to her lips. Then he knocked louder, and she started and put it away. She was a Dutchwoman, enormously fat—when she walked she rolled like a small boat on the ocean, and the dishes in the cupboard jostled each other. She wore a filthy blue wrapper, and her teeth were black.

"Vot is it?" she said, when she saw Jurgis.

He had run like mad all the way and was so out of breath he could hardly speak. His hair was flying and his eyes wild—he looked like a man that had risen from the tomb. "My wife!" he panted. "Come quickly!" Madame Haupt set the frying pan to one side and wiped her hands on her wrapper.

"You vant me to come for a case?" she inquired.

"Yes," gasped Jurgis.

"I haf yust come back from a case," she said. "I haf had no time to eat my dinner. Still—if it is so bad—"

"Yes—it is!" cried he.

"Vell, den, perhaps—vot you pay?"

"I—I—how much do you want?" Jurgis stammered.

"Tventy-five dollars." His face fell. "I can't pay that," he said.

The woman was watching him narrowly. "How much do you pay?" she demanded.

"Must I pay now—right away?"

"Yes; all my customers do."

"I—I haven't much money," Jurgis began in an agony of dread. "I've been in—in trouble—and my money is gone. But I'll pay you—every cent—just as soon as I can; I can work—"

"Vot is your work?"

"I have no place now. I must get one. But I—"

"How much haf you got now?"

He could hardly bring himself to reply. When he said "A dollar and a quarter," the woman laughed in his face.

"I vould not put on my hat for a dollar and a quarter," she said.

"It's all I've got," he pleaded, his voice breaking. "I must get some one—my wife will die. I can't help it—I—"

Madame Haupt had put back her pork and onions on the stove. She turned to him and answered, out of the steam and noise: "Git me ten dollars cash, und so you can pay me the rest next mont'."

"I can't do it—I haven't got it!" Jurgis protested. "I tell you I have only a dollar and a quarter."

The woman turned to her work. "I don't believe you," she said. "Dot is all to try to sheat me. Vot is de reason a big man like you has got only a dollar und a quarter?"

"I've just been in jail," Jurgis cried—he was ready to get down upon his knees to the woman—"and I had no money before, and my family has almost starved."

"Vere is your friends, dot ought to help you?"

"They are all poor," he answered. "They gave me this. I have done everything I can—"

"Haven't you got notting you can sell?"

"I have nothing, I tell you—I have nothing," he cried, frantically.

"Can't you borrow it, den? Don't your store people trust you?" Then, as he shook his head, she went on: "Listen to me—if you git me you vill be glad of it. I vill save your wife und baby for you, and it vill not seem like mooch to you in de end. If you loose dem now how you tink you feel den? Und here is a lady dot knows her business—I could send you to people in dis block, und dey vould tell you—"

Madame Haupt was pointing her cooking-fork at Jurgis persuasively; but her words were more than he could bear. He flung up his hands with a gesture of despair and turned and started away. "It's no use," he exclaimed—but suddenly he heard the woman's voice behind him again—

"I vill make it five dollars for you."

She followed behind him, arguing with him. "You vill be foolish not to take such an offer," she said. "You von't find nobody go out on a rainy day like dis for less. Vy, I haf never took a case in my life so sheap as dot. I couldn't pay mine room rent—"

Jurgis interrupted her with an oath of rage. "If I haven't got it," he shouted, "how can I pay it? Damn it, I would pay you if I could, but I tell you I haven't got it. I haven't got it! Do you hear me I haven't got it!"

He turned and started away again. He was halfway down the stairs before Madame Haupt could shout to him: "Vait! I vill go mit you! Come back!"

He went back into the room again.

"It is not goot to tink of anybody suffering," she said, in a melancholy voice. "I might as vell go mit you for noffing as vot you offer me, but I vill try to help you. How far is it?"

"Three or four blocks from here."

"Tree or four! Und so I shall get soaked! Gott in Himmel, it ought to be vorth more! Vun dollar und a quarter, und a day like dis!—But you understand now— you vill pay me de rest of twenty-five dollars soon?"

"As soon as I can."

"Some time dis mont'?"

"Yes, within a month," said poor Jurgis. "Anything! Hurry up!"

"Vere is de dollar und a quarter?" persisted Madame Haupt, relentlessly.

Jurgis put the money on the table and the woman counted it and stowed it away. Then she wiped her greasy hands again and proceeded to get ready, complaining all the time; she was so fat that it was painful for her to move, and she grunted and gasped at every step. She took off her wrapper without even taking the trouble to turn her back to Jurgis, and put on her corsets and dress. Then there was a black bonnet which had to be adjusted carefully, and an umbrella which was mislaid, and a bag full of necessaries which had to be collected from here and there—the man being nearly crazy with anxiety in the meantime. When they were on the street he kept about four paces ahead of her, turning now and then, as if he could hurry her on by the force of his desire. But Madame Haupt could only go so far at a step, and it took all her attention to get the needed breath for that.

They came at last to the house, and to the group of frightened women in the kitchen. It was not over yet, Jurgis learned—he heard Ona crying still; and meantime Madame Haupt removed her bonnet and laid it on the mantelpiece, and got out of her bag, first an old dress and then a saucer of goose grease, which she proceeded to rub upon her hands. The more cases this goose grease is used in, the better luck it brings to the midwife, and so she keeps it upon her kitchen mantelpiece or stowed away in a cupboard with her dirty clothes, for months, and sometimes even for years.

Then they escorted her to the ladder, and Jurgis heard her give an exclamation of dismay. "Gott in Himmel, vot for haf you brought me to a place like dis? I could not climb up dot ladder. I could not git troo a trap door! I vill not try it—vy, I might kill myself already. Vot sort of a place is dot for a woman to bear a child in—up in a garret, mit only a ladder to it? You ought to be ashamed of yourselves!" Jurgis stood in the doorway and listened to her scolding, half drowning out the horrible moans and screams of Ona.

At last Aniele succeeded in pacifying her, and she essayed the ascent; then, however, she had to be stopped while the old woman cautioned her about the floor of the garret. They had no real floor—they had laid old boards in one part to make a place for the family to live; it was all right and safe there, but the other part of the garret had only the joists of the floor, and the lath and plaster of the ceiling below, and if one stepped on this there would be a catastrophe. As it was half dark up above, perhaps one of the others had best go up first with a candle. Then there were more outcries and threatening, until at last Jurgis had a vision of a pair of elephantine legs disappearing through the trap door, and felt the house shake as Madame Haupt started to walk. Then suddenly Aniele came to him and took him by the arm.

"Now," she said, "you go away. Do as I tell you—you have done all you can, and you are only in the way. Go away and stay away."

"But where shall I go?" Jurgis asked, helplessly.

"I don't know where," she answered. "Go on the street, if there is no other place—only go! And stay all night!"

In the end she and Marija pushed him out of the door and shut it behind him. It was just about sundown, and it was turning cold—the rain had changed to snow, and the slush was freezing. Jurgis shivered in his thin clothing, and put his hands into his pockets and started away. He had not eaten since morning, and he felt weak and ill; with a sudden throb of hope he recollected he was only a few blocks from the saloon where he had been wont to eat his dinner. They might have mercy on him there, or he might meet a friend. He set out for the place as fast as he could walk.

"Hello, Jack," said the saloon-keeper, when he entered—they call all foreigners and unskilled men "Jack" in Packingtown. "Where've you been?"

Jurgis went straight to the bar. "I've been in jail," he said, "and I've just got out. I walked home all the way, and I've not a cent, and had nothing to eat since this morning. And I've lost my home, and my wife's ill, and I'm done up."

The saloon-keeper gazed at him, with his haggard white face and his blue trembling lips. Then he pushed a big bottle toward him. "Fill her up!" he said.

Jurgis could hardly hold the bottle, his hands shook so.

"Don't be afraid," said the saloon-keeper, "fill her up!"

So Jurgis drank a large glass of whisky, and then turned to the lunch counter, in obedience to the other's suggestion. He ate all he dared, stuffing it in as fast as he could; and then, after trying to speak his gratitude, he went and sat down by the big red stove in the middle of the room.

It was too good to last, however—like all things in this hard world. His soaked clothing began to steam, and the horrible stench of fertilizer to fill the room. In an hour or so the packing houses would be closing and the men coming in from their work; and they would not come into a place that smelt of Jurgis. Also it was Saturday night, and in a couple of hours would come a violin and a cornet, and in the rear part of the saloon the families of the neighborhood would dance and feast upon wienerwurst and lager, until two or three o'clock in the morning. The saloon-keeper coughed once or twice, and then remarked, "Say, Jack, I'm afraid you'll have to quit."

He was used to the sight of human wrecks, this saloon-keeper; he "fired" dozens of them every night, just as haggard and cold and forlorn as this one. But they were all men who had given up and been counted out, while Jurgis was still in the fight, and had reminders of decency about him. As he got up meekly, the other reflected that he had always been a steady man, and might soon be a good customer again. "You've been up against it, I see," he said. "Come this way."

In the rear of the saloon were the cellar stairs. There was a door above and another below, both safely padlocked, making the stairs an admirable place to stow away a customer who might still chance to have money, or a political light whom it was not advisable to kick out of doors.

So Jurgis spent the night. The whisky had only half warmed him, and he could not sleep, exhausted as he was; he would nod forward, and then start up, shivering with the cold, and begin to remember again. Hour after hour passed, until he could only persuade himself that it was not morning by the sounds of music and laughter and singing that were to be heard from the room. When at last these ceased, he expected that he would be turned out into the street; as this did not happen, he fell to wondering whether the man had forgotten him.

In the end, when the silence and suspense were no longer to be borne, he got up and hammered on the door; and the proprietor came, yawning and rubbing his eyes. He was keeping open all night, and dozing between customers.

"I want to go home," Jurgis said. "I'm worried about my wife—I can't wait any longer."

"Why the hell didn't you say so before?" said the man. "I thought you didn't have any home to go to." Jurgis went outside. It was four o'clock in the morning, and as black as night. There were three or four inches of fresh snow on the ground, and the flakes were falling thick and fast. He turned toward Aniele's and started at a run.

There was a light burning in the kitchen window and the blinds were drawn. The door was unlocked and Jurgis rushed in.

Aniele, Marija, and the rest of the women were huddled about the stove, exactly as before; with them were several newcomers, Jurgis noticed—also he noticed that the house was silent.

"Well?" he said.

No one answered him, they sat staring at him with their pale faces. He cried again: "Well?"

And then, by the light of the smoky lamp, he saw Marija who sat nearest him, shaking her head slowly. "Not yet," she said.

And Jurgis gave a cry of dismay. "Not yet?"

Again Marija's head shook. The poor fellow stood dumfounded. "I don't hear her," he gasped.

"She's been quiet a long time," replied the other.

There was another pause—broken suddenly by a voice from the attic: "Hello, there!"

Several of the women ran into the next room, while Marija sprang toward Jurgis. "Wait here!" she cried, and the two stood, pale and trembling, listening. In a few moments it became clear that Madame Haupt was engaged in descending the ladder, scolding and exhorting again, while the ladder creaked in protest. In a moment or two she reached the ground, angry and breathless, and they heard her coming into the room. Jurgis gave one glance at her, and then turned white and reeled. She had her jacket off, like one of the workers on the killing beds. Her hands and arms were smeared with blood, and blood was splashed upon her clothing and her face.

She stood breathing hard, and gazing about her; no one made a sound. "I haf done my best," she began suddenly. "I can do noffing more—dere is no use to try."

Again there was silence.

"It ain't my fault," she said. "You had ought to haf had a doctor, und not vaited so long—it vas too late already ven I come." Once more there was deathlike stillness. Marija was clutching Jurgis with all the power of her one well arm.

Then suddenly Madame Haupt turned to Aniele. "You haf not got something to drink, hey?" she queried. "Some brandy?"

Aniele shook her head.

"Herr Gott!" exclaimed Madame Haupt. "Such people! Perhaps you vill give me someting to eat den—I haf had noffing since yesterday morning, und I haf vorked myself near to death here. If I could haf known it vas like dis, I vould never haf come for such money as you gif me." At this moment she chanced to look round, and saw Jurgis: She shook her finger at him. "You understand me," she said, "you pays me dot money yust de same! It is not my fault dat you send for me so late I can't help your vife. It is not my fault if der baby comes mit one arm first, so dot I can't save it. I haf tried all night, und in dot place vere it is not fit for dogs to be born, und mit notting to eat only vot I brings in mine own pockets."

Here Madame Haupt paused for a moment to get her breath; and Marija, seeing the beads of sweat on Jurgis's forehead, and feeling the quivering of his frame, broke out in a low voice: "How is Ona?"

"How is she?" echoed Madame Haupt. "How do you tink she can be ven you leave her to kill herself so? I told dem dot ven they send for de priest. She is young, und she might haf got over it, und been vell und strong, if she had been treated right. She fight hard, dot girl—she is not yet quite dead."

And Jurgis gave a frantic scream. "Dead!"

"She vill die, of course," said the other angrily. "Der baby is dead now."

The garret was lighted by a candle stuck upon a board; it had almost burned itself out, and was sputtering and smoking as Jurgis rushed up the ladder. He could make out dimly in one corner a pallet of rags and old blankets, spread upon the floor; at the foot of it was a crucifix, and near it a priest muttering a prayer. In a far corner crouched Elzbieta, moaning and wailing. Upon the pallet lay Ona.

She was covered with a blanket, but he could see her shoulders and one arm lying bare; she was so shrunken he would scarcely have known her—she was all but a skeleton, and as white as a piece of chalk. Her eyelids were closed, and she lay still as death. He staggered toward her and fell upon his knees with a cry of anguish: "Ona! Ona!"

She did not stir. He caught her hand in his, and began to clasp it frantically, calling: "Look at me! Answer me! It is Jurgis come back—don't you hear me?"

There was the faintest quivering of the eyelids, and he called again in frenzy: "Ona! Ona!"

Then suddenly her eyes opened one instant. One instant she looked at him—there was a flash of recognition between them, he saw her afar off, as through a dim vista, standing forlorn. He stretched out his arms to her, he called her in wild despair; a fearful yearning surged up in him, hunger for her that was agony, desire that was a new being born within him, tearing his heartstrings, torturing him. But it was all in vain—she faded from him, she slipped back and was gone. And a wail of anguish burst from him, great sobs shook all his frame, and hot tears ran down his cheeks and fell upon her. He clutched her hands, he shook her, he caught her in his arms and pressed her to him but she lay cold and still—she was gone—she was gone!

The word rang through him like the sound of a bell, echoing in the far depths of him, making forgotten chords to vibrate, old shadowy fears to stir—fears of the dark, fears of the void, fears of annihilation. She was dead! She was dead! He would never see her again, never hear her again! An icy horror of loneliness seized him; he saw himself standing apart and watching all the world fade away from him—a world of shadows, of fickle dreams. He was like a little child, in his fright and grief; he called and called, and got no answer, and his cries of despair echoed through the house, making the women downstairs draw nearer to each other in fear. He was inconsolable, beside himself—the priest came and laid his hand upon his shoulder and whispered to him, but he heard not a sound. He was gone away himself, stumbling through the shadows, and groping after the soul that had fled.

So he lay. The gray dawn came up and crept into the attic. The priest left, the women left, and he was alone with the still, white figure—quieter now, but moaning and shuddering, wrestling with the grisly fiend. Now and then he would raise himself and stare at the white mask before him, then hide his eyes because he could not bear it. Dead! dead! And she was only a girl, she was barely eighteen! Her life had hardly begun—and here she lay murdered—mangled, tortured to death!

It was morning when he rose up and came down into the kitchen—haggard and ashen gray, reeling and dazed. More of the neighbors had come in, and they stared at him in silence as he sank down upon a chair by the table and buried his face in his arms.

A few minutes later the front door opened; a blast of cold and snow rushed in, and behind it little Kotrina, breathless from running, and blue with the cold. "I'm home again!" she exclaimed. "I could hardly—"

And then, seeing Jurgis, she stopped with an exclamation. Looking from one to another she saw that something had happened, and she asked, in a lower voice: "What's the matter?"

Before anyone could reply, Jurgis started up; he went toward her, walking unsteadily. "Where have you been?" he demanded.

"Selling papers with the boys," she said. "The snow—"

"Have you any money?" he demanded.

"Yes."

"How much?"

"Nearly three dollars, Jurgis."

"Give it to me."

Kotrina, frightened by his manner, glanced at the others. "Give it to me!" he commanded again, and she put her hand into her pocket and pulled out a lump of coins tied in a bit of rag. Jurgis took it without a word, and went out of the door and down the street.

Three doors away was a saloon. "Whisky," he said, as he entered, and as the man pushed him some, he tore at the rag with his teeth and pulled out half a dollar. "How much is the bottle?" he said. "I want to get drunk."

CHAPTER 20

But a big man cannot stay drunk very long on three dollars. That was Sunday morning, and Monday night Jurgis came home, sober and sick, realizing that he had spent every cent the family owned, and had not bought a single instant's forgetfulness with it.

Ona was not yet buried; but the police had been notified, and on the morrow they would put the body in a pine coffin and take it to the potter's field. Elzbieta was out begging now, a few pennies from each of the neighbors, to get enough to pay for a mass for her; and the children were upstairs starving to death, while he, good-for-nothing rascal, had been spending their money on drink. So spoke Aniele, scornfully, and when he started toward the fire she added the information that her kitchen was no longer for him to fill with his phosphate stinks. She had crowded all her boarders into one room on Ona's account, but now he could go up in the garret where he belonged—and not there much longer, either, if he did not pay her some rent.

Jurgis went without a word, and, stepping over half a dozen sleeping boarders in the next room, ascended the ladder. It was dark up above; they could not afford any light; also it was nearly as cold as outdoors. In a corner, as far away from the corpse as possible, sat Marija, holding little Antanas in her one good arm and trying to soothe him to sleep. In another corner crouched poor little Juozapas, wailing because he had had nothing to eat all day. Marija said not a word to Jurgis; he crept in like a whipped cur, and went and sat down by the body.

Perhaps he ought to have meditated upon the hunger of the children, and upon his own baseness; but he thought only of Ona, he gave himself up again to the luxury of grief. He shed no tears, being ashamed to make a sound; he sat motionless and shuddering with his anguish. He had never dreamed how much he loved Ona, until now that she was gone; until now that he sat here, knowing that on the morrow they would take her away, and that he would never lay eyes upon her again—never all the days of his life. His old love, which had been starved to death, beaten to death, awoke in him again; the floodgates of memory were lifted—he saw all their life together, saw her as he had seen her in Lithuania, the first day at the fair, beautiful as the flowers, singing like a bird. He saw her as he had married her, with all her tenderness, with her heart of wonder; the very words she had spoken seemed to ring now in his ears, the tears she had shed to be wet upon his cheek. The long, cruel battle with misery and hunger had hardened and embittered him, but it had not changed her—she had been the same hungry soul to the end, stretching out her arms to him, pleading with him, begging him for love and tenderness. And she had suffered—so cruelly she had suffered, such agonies, such infamies—ah, God, the memory of them was not to be borne. What a monster of wickedness, of heartlessness, he had been! Every angry word that he had ever spoken came back to him and cut him like a knife; every selfish act that he had done—with what torments he paid for them now! And such devotion and awe as welled up in his soul—now that it could never be spoken, now that it was too late, too late! His bosom-was choking with it, bursting with it; he crouched here in the darkness beside her, stretching out his arms to her—and she was gone forever, she was dead! He could have screamed aloud with the horror and despair of it; a sweat of agony beaded his forehead, yet he dared not make a sound—he scarcely dared to breathe, because of his shame and loathing of himself.

Late at night came Elzbieta, having gotten the money for a mass, and paid for it in advance, lest she should be tempted too sorely at home. She brought also a bit of stale rye bread that some one had given her, and with that they quieted the children and got them to sleep. Then she came over to Jurgis and sat down beside him.

She said not a word of reproach—she and Marija had chosen that course before; she would only plead with him, here by the corpse of his dead wife. Already Elzbieta had choked down her tears, grief being crowded out of her soul by fear. She had to bury one of her children—but then she had done it three times before, and each time risen up and gone back to take up the battle for the rest. Elzbieta was one of the primitive creatures: like the angleworm, which goes on living though cut in half; like a hen, which, deprived of her chickens one by one, will mother the last that is left her. She did this because it was her nature—she asked no questions about the justice of it, nor the worth-whileness of life in which destruction and death ran riot.

And this old common-sense view she labored to impress upon Jurgis, pleading with him with tears in her eyes. Ona was dead, but the others were left and they must be saved. She did not ask for her own children. She and Marija could care for them somehow, but there was Antanas, his own son. Ona had given Antanas to him—the little fellow was the only remembrance of her that he had; he must treasure it and protect it, he must show himself a man. He knew what Ona would have had him do, what she would ask of him at this moment, if she could speak to him. It was a terrible thing that she should have died as she had; but the life had been too hard for her, and she had to go. It was terrible that they were not able to bury her, that he could not even have a day to mourn her—but so it was. Their fate was pressing; they had not a cent, and the children would perish—some money must be had. Could he not be a man for Ona's sake, and pull himself together? In a little while they would be out of danger—now that they had given up the house they could live more cheaply, and with all the children working they could get along, if only he would not go to pieces. So Elzbieta went on, with feverish intensity. It was a struggle for life with her; she was not afraid that Jurgis would go on drinking, for he had no money for that, but she was wild with dread at the thought that he might desert them, might take to the road, as Jonas had done.

But with Ona's dead body beneath his eyes, Jurgis could not well think of treason to his child. Yes, he said, he would try, for the sake of Antanas. He would give the little fellow his chance—would get to work at once, yes, tomorrow, without even waiting for Ona to be buried. They might trust him, he would keep his word, come what might.

And so he was out before daylight the next morning, headache, heartache, and all. He went straight to Graham's fertilizer mill, to see if he could get back his job. But the boss shook his head when he saw him—no, his place had been filled long ago, and there was no room for him.

"Do you think there will be?" Jurgis asked. "I may have to wait."

"No," said the other, "it will not be worth your while to wait—there will be nothing for you here."

Jurgis stood gazing at him in perplexity. "What is the matter?" he asked. "Didn't I do my work?"

The other met his look with one of cold indifference, and answered, "There will be nothing for you here, I said."

Jurgis had his suspicions as to the dreadful meaning of that incident, and he went away with a sinking at the heart. He went and took his stand with the mob of hungry wretches who were standing about in the snow before the time station. Here he stayed, breakfastless, for two hours, until the throng was driven away by the clubs of the police. There was no work for him that day.

Jurgis had made a good many acquaintances in his long services at the yards—there were saloonkeepers who would trust him for a drink and a sandwich, and members of his old union who would lend him a dime at a pinch. It was not a question of life and death for him, therefore; he might hunt all day, and come again on the morrow, and try hanging on thus for weeks, like hundreds and thousands of others. Meantime, Teta Elzbieta would go and beg, over in the Hyde Park district, and the children would bring home enough to pacify Aniele, and keep them all alive.

It was at the end of a week of this sort of waiting, roaming about in the bitter winds or loafing in saloons, that Jurgis stumbled on a chance in one of the cellars of Jones's big packing plant. He saw a foreman passing the open doorway, and hailed him for a job.

"Push a truck?" inquired the man, and Jurgis answered, "Yes, sir!" before the words were well out of his mouth.

"What's your name?" demanded the other.

"Jurgis Rudkus."

"Worked in the yards before?"

"Yes."

"Whereabouts?"

"Two places—Brown's killing beds and Durham's fertilizer mill."

"Why did you leave there?"

"The first time I had an accident, and the last time I was sent up for a month."

"I see. Well, I'll give you a trial. Come early tomorrow and ask for Mr. Thomas."

So Jurgis rushed home with the wild tidings that he had a job—that the terrible siege was over. The remnants of the family had quite a celebration that night; and in the morning Jurgis was at the place half an hour before the time of opening. The foreman came in shortly afterward, and when he saw Jurgis he frowned.

"Oh," he said, "I promised you a job, didn't I?"

"Yes, sir," said Jurgis.

"Well, I'm sorry, but I made a mistake. I can't use you."

Jurgis stared, dumfounded. "What's the matter?" he gasped.

"Nothing," said the man, "only I can't use you."

There was the same cold, hostile stare that he had had from the boss of the fertilizer mill. He knew that there was no use in saying a word, and he turned and went away.

Out in the saloons the men could tell him all about the meaning of it; they gazed at him with pitying eyes—poor devil, he was blacklisted! What had he done? they asked—knocked down his boss? Good heavens, then he might have known! Why, he stood as much chance of getting a job in Packingtown as of being chosen mayor of Chicago. Why had he wasted his time hunting? They had him on a secret list in every office, big and little, in the place. They had his name by this time in St. Louis and New York, in Omaha and Boston, in Kansas City and St. Joseph. He was condemned and sentenced, without trial and without appeal; he could never work for the packers again—he could not even clean cattle pens or drive a truck in any place where they controlled. He might try it, if he chose, as hundreds had tried it, and found out for themselves. He would never be told anything about it; he would never get any more satisfaction than he had gotten just now; but he would always find when the time came that he was not needed. It would not do for him to give any other name, either—they had company "spotters" for just that purpose, and he wouldn't keep a job in Packingtown three days. It was worth a fortune to the packers to keep their blacklist effective, as a warning to the men and a means of keeping down union agitation and political discontent.

Jurgis went home, carrying these new tidings to the family council. It was a most cruel thing; here in this district was his home, such as it was, the place he was used to and the friends he knew—and now every possibility of employment in it was closed to him. There was nothing in Packingtown but packing houses; and so it was the same thing as evicting him from his home.

He and the two women spent all day and half the night discussing it. It would be convenient, downtown, to the children's place of work; but then Marija was on the road to recovery, and had hopes of getting a job in the yards; and though she did not see her old-time lover once a month, because of the misery of their state, yet she could not make up her mind to go away and give him up forever. Then, too, Elzbieta had heard something about a chance to scrub floors in Durham's offices and was waiting every day for word. In the end it was decided that Jurgis should go downtown to strike out for himself, and they would decide after he got a job. As there was no one from whom he could borrow there, and he dared not beg for fear of being arrested, it was arranged that every day he should meet one of the children and be given fifteen cents of their earnings, upon which he could keep going. Then all day he was to pace the streets with hundreds and thousands of other homeless wretches inquiring at stores, warehouses, and factories for a chance; and at night he was to crawl into some doorway or underneath a truck, and hide there until midnight, when he might get into one of the station houses, and spread a newspaper upon the floor, and lie down in the midst of a throng of "bums" and beggars, reeking with alcohol and tobacco, and filthy with vermin and disease.

So for two weeks more Jurgis fought with the demon of despair. Once he got a chance to load a truck for half a day, and again he carried an old woman's valise and was given a quarter. This let him into a lodging-house on several nights when he might otherwise have frozen to death; and it also gave him a chance now and then to buy a newspaper in the morning and hunt up jobs while his rivals were watching and waiting for a paper to be thrown away. This, however, was really not the advantage it seemed, for the newspaper advertisements were a cause of much loss of precious time and of many weary journeys. A full half of these were "fakes," put in by the endless variety of establishments which preyed upon the helpless ignorance of the unemployed. If Jurgis lost only his time, it was because he had nothing else to lose; whenever a smooth-tongued agent would tell him of the wonderful positions he had on hand, he could only shake his head sorrowfully and say that he had not the necessary dollar to deposit; when it was explained to him what "big money" he and all his family could make by coloring photographs, he could only promise to come in again when he had two dollars to invest in the outfit.

In the end Jurgis got a chance through an accidental meeting with an old-time acquaintance of his union days. He met this man on his way to work in the giant factories of the Harvester Trust; and his friend told him to come along and he would speak a good word for him to his boss, whom he knew well. So Jurgis trudged four or five miles, and passed through a waiting throng of unemployed at the gate under the escort of his friend. His knees nearly gave way beneath him when the foreman, after looking him over and questioning him, told him that he could find an opening for him.

How much this accident meant to Jurgis he realized only by stages; for he found that the harvester works were the sort of place to which philanthropists and reformers pointed with pride. It had some thought for its employees; its workshops were big and roomy, it provided a restaurant where the workmen could buy good food at cost, it had even a reading room, and decent places where its girl-hands could rest; also the work was free from many of the elements of filth and repulsiveness that prevailed at the stockyards. Day after day Jurgis discovered these things—things never expected nor dreamed of by him—until this new place came to seem a kind of a heaven to him.

It was an enormous establishment, covering a hundred and sixty acres of ground, employing five thousand people, and turning out over three hundred thousand machines every year—a good part of all the harvesting and mowing machines used in the country. Jurgis saw very little of it, of course—it was all specialized work, the same as at the stockyards; each one of the hundreds of parts of a mowing machine was made separately, and sometimes handled by hundreds of men. Where Jurgis worked there was a machine which cut and stamped a certain piece of steel about two square inches in size; the pieces came tumbling out upon a tray, and all that human hands had to do was to pile them in regular rows, and change the trays at intervals. This was done by a single boy, who stood with eyes and thought centered upon it, and fingers flying so fast that the sounds of the bits of steel striking upon each other was like the music of an express train as one hears it in a sleeping car at night. This was "piece-work," of course; and besides it was made certain that the boy did not idle, by setting the machine to match the highest possible speed of human hands. Thirty thousand of these pieces he handled every day, nine or ten million every year—how many in a lifetime it rested with the gods to say. Near by him men sat bending over whirling grindstones, putting the finishing touches to the steel knives of the reaper; picking them out of a basket with the right hand, pressing first one side and then the other against the stone and finally dropping them with the left hand into another basket. One of these men told Jurgis that he had sharpened three thousand pieces of steel a day for thirteen years. In the next room were wonderful machines that ate up long steel rods by slow stages, cutting them off, seizing the pieces, stamping heads upon them, grinding them and polishing them, threading them, and finally dropping them into a basket, all ready to bolt the harvesters together. From yet another machine came tens of thousands of steel burs to fit upon these bolts. In other places all these various parts were dipped into troughs of paint and hung up to dry, and then slid along on trolleys to a room where men streaked them with red and yellow, so that they might look cheerful in the harvest fields.

Jurgis's friend worked upstairs in the casting rooms, and his task was to make the molds of a certain part. He shoveled black sand into an iron receptacle and pounded it tight and set it aside to harden; then it would be taken out, and molten iron poured into it. This man, too, was paid by the mold—or rather for perfect castings, nearly half his work going for naught. You might see him, along with dozens of others, toiling like one possessed by a whole community of demons; his arms working like the driving rods of an engine, his long, black hair flying wild, his eyes starting out, the sweat rolling in rivers down his face. When he had shoveled the mold full of sand, and reached for the pounder to pound it with, it was after the manner of a canoeist running rapids and seizing a pole at sight of a submerged rock. All day long this man would toil thus, his whole being centered upon the purpose of making twenty-three instead of twenty-two and a half cents an hour; and then his product would be reckoned up by the census taker, and jubilant captains of industry would boast of it in their banquet halls, telling how our workers are nearly twice as efficient as those of any other country. If we are the greatest nation the sun ever shone upon, it would seem to be mainly because we have been able to goad our wage-earners to this pitch of frenzy; though there are a few other things that are great among us including our drink-bill, which is a billion and a quarter of dollars a year, and doubling itself every decade.

There was a machine which stamped out the iron plates, and then another which, with a mighty thud, mashed them to the shape of the sitting-down portion of the American farmer. Then they were piled upon a truck, and it was Jurgis's task to wheel them to the room where the machines were "assembled." This was child's play for him, and he got a dollar and seventy-five cents a day for it; on Saturday he paid Aniele the seventy-five cents a week he owed her for the use of her garret, and also redeemed his overcoat, which Elzbieta had put in pawn when he was in jail.

This last was a great blessing. A man cannot go about in midwinter in Chicago with no overcoat and not pay for it, and Jurgis had to walk or ride five or six miles back and forth to his work. It so happened that half of this was in one direction and half in another, necessitating a change of cars; the law required that transfers be given at all intersecting points, but the railway corporation had gotten round this by arranging a pretense at separate ownership. So whenever he wished to ride, he had to pay ten cents each way, or over ten per cent of his income to this power, which had gotten its franchises long ago by buying up the city council, in the face of popular clamor amounting almost to a rebellion. Tired as he felt at night, and dark and bitter cold as it was in the morning, Jurgis generally chose to walk; at the hours other workmen were traveling, the streetcar monopoly saw fit to put on so few cars that there would be men hanging to every foot of the backs of them and often crouching upon the snow-covered roof. Of course the doors could never be closed, and so the cars were as cold as outdoors; Jurgis, like many others, found it better to spend his fare for a drink and a free lunch, to give him strength to walk.

These, however, were all slight matters to a man who had escaped from Durham's fertilizer mill. Jurgis began to pick up heart again and to make plans. He had lost his house but then the awful load of the rent and interest was off his shoulders, and when Marija was well again they could start over and save. In the shop where he worked was a man, a Lithuanian like himself, whom the others spoke of in admiring whispers, because of the mighty feats he was performing. All day he sat at a machine turning bolts; and then in the evening he went to the public school to study English and learn to read. In addition, because he had a family of eight children to support and his earnings were not enough, on Saturdays and Sundays he served as a watchman; he was required to press two buttons at opposite ends of a building every five minutes, and as the walk only took him two minutes, he had three minutes to study between each trip. Jurgis felt jealous of this fellow; for that was the sort of thing he himself had dreamed of, two or three years ago. He might do it even yet, if he had a fair chance—he might attract attention and become a skilled man or a boss, as some had done in this place. Suppose that Marija could get a job in the big mill where they made binder twine—then they would move into this neighborhood, and he would really have a chance. With a hope like that, there was some use in living; to find a place where you were treated like a human being—by God! he would show them how he could appreciate it. He laughed to himself as he thought how he would hang on to this job!

And then one afternoon, the ninth of his work in the place, when he went to get his overcoat he saw a group of men crowded before a placard on the door, and when he went over and asked what it was, they told him that beginning with the morrow his department of the harvester works would be closed until further notice!

CHAPTER 21

That was the way they did it! There was not half an hour's warning—the works were closed! It had happened that way before, said the men, and it would happen that way forever. They had made all the harvesting machines that the world needed, and now they had to wait till some wore out! It was nobody's fault—that was the way of it; and thousands of men and women were turned out in the dead of winter, to live upon their savings if they had any, and otherwise to die. So many tens of thousands already in the city, homeless and begging for work, and now several thousand more added to them!

Jurgis walked home-with his pittance of pay in his pocket, heartbroken, overwhelmed. One more bandage had been torn from his eyes, one more pitfall was revealed to him! Of what help was kindness and decency on the part of employers—when they could not keep a job for him, when there were more harvesting machines made than the world was able to buy! What a hellish mockery it was, anyway, that a man should slave to make harvesting machines for the country, only to be turned out to starve for doing his duty too well!

It took him two days to get over this heart-sickening disappointment. He did not drink anything, because Elzbieta got his money for safekeeping, and knew him too well to be in the least frightened by his angry demands. He stayed up in the garret however, and sulked—what was the use of a man's hunting a job when it was taken from him before he had time to learn the work? But then their money was going again, and little Antanas was hungry, and crying with the bitter cold of the garret. Also Madame Haupt, the midwife, was after him for some money. So he went out once more.

For another ten days he roamed the streets and alleys of the huge city, sick and hungry, begging for any work. He tried in stores and offices, in restaurants and hotels, along the docks and in the railroad yards, in warehouses and mills and factories where they made products that went to every corner of the world. There were often one or two chances—but there were always a hundred men for every chance, and his turn would not come. At night he crept into sheds and cellars and doorways—until there came a spell of belated winter weather, with a raging gale, and the thermometer five degrees below zero at sundown and falling all night. Then Jurgis fought like a wild beast to get into the big Harrison Street police station, and slept down in a corridor, crowded with two other men upon a single step.

He had to fight often in these days to fight for a place near the factory gates, and now and again with gangs on the street. He found, for instance, that the business of carrying satchels for railroad passengers was a pre-empted one—whenever he essayed it, eight or ten men and boys would fall upon him and force him to run for his life. They always had the policeman "squared," and so there was no use in expecting protection.

That Jurgis did not starve to death was due solely to the pittance the children brought him. And even this was never certain. For one thing the cold was almost more than the children could bear; and then they, too, were in perpetual peril from rivals who plundered and beat them. The law was against them, too—little Vilimas, who was really eleven, but did not look to be eight, was stopped on the streets by a severe old lady in spectacles, who told him that he was too young to be working and that if he did not stop selling papers she would send a truant officer after him. Also one night a strange man caught little Kotrina by the arm and tried to persuade her into a dark cellar-way, an experience which filled her with such terror that she was hardly to be kept at work.

At last, on a Sunday, as there was no use looking for work, Jurgis went home by stealing rides on the cars. He found that they had been waiting for him for three days—there was a chance of a job for him.

It was quite a story. Little Juozapas, who was near crazy with hunger these days, had gone out on the street to beg for himself. Juozapas had only one leg, having been run over by a wagon when a little child, but he had got himself a broomstick, which he put under his arm for a crutch. He had fallen in with some other children and found the way to Mike Scully's dump, which lay three or four blocks away. To this place there came every day many hundreds of wagon-loads of garbage and trash from the lake front, where the rich people lived; and in the heaps the children raked for food—there were hunks of bread and potato peelings and apple cores and meat bones, all of it half frozen and quite unspoiled. Little Juozapas gorged himself, and came home with a newspaper full, which he was feeding to Antanas when his mother came in. Elzbieta was horrified, for she did not believe that the food out of the dumps was fit to eat. The next day, however, when no harm came of it and Juozapas began to cry with hunger, she gave in and said that he might go again. And that afternoon he came home with a story of how while he had been digging away with a stick, a lady upon the street had called him. A real fine lady, the little boy explained, a beautiful lady; and she wanted to know all about him, and whether he got the garbage for chickens, and why he walked with a broomstick, and why Ona had died, and how Jurgis had come to go to jail, and what was the matter with Marija, and everything. In the end she had asked where he lived, and said that she was coming to see him, and bring him a new crutch to walk with. She had on a hat with a bird upon it, Juozapas added, and a long fur snake around her neck.

She really came, the very next morning, and climbed the ladder to the garret, and stood and stared about her, turning pale at the sight of the blood stains on the floor where Ona had died. She was a "settlement worker," she explained to Elzbieta—she lived around on Ashland Avenue. Elzbieta knew the place, over a feed store; somebody had wanted her to go there, but she had not cared to, for she thought that it must have something to do with religion, and the priest did not like her to have anything to do with strange religions. They were rich people who came to live there to find out about the poor people; but what good they expected it would do them to know, one could not imagine. So spoke Elzbieta, naively, and the young lady laughed and was rather at a loss for an answer—she stood and gazed about her, and thought of a cynical remark that had been made to her, that she was standing upon the brink of the pit of hell and throwing in snowballs to lower the temperature.

Elzbieta was glad to have somebody to listen, and she told all their woes—what had happened to Ona, and the jail, and the loss of their home, and Marija's accident, and how Ona had died, and how Jurgis could get no work. As she listened the pretty young lady's eyes filled with tears, and in the midst of it she burst into weeping and hid her face on Elzbieta's shoulder, quite regardless of the fact that the woman had on a dirty old wrapper and that the garret was full of fleas. Poor Elzbieta was ashamed of herself for having told so woeful a tale, and the other had to beg and plead with her to get her to go on. The end of it was that the young lady sent them a basket of things to eat, and left a letter that Jurgis was to take to a gentleman who was superintendent in one of the mills of the great steel-works in South Chicago. "He will get Jurgis something to do," the young lady had said, and added, smiling through her tears—"If he doesn't, he will never marry me."

The steel-works were fifteen miles away, and as usual it was so contrived that one had to pay two fares to get there. Far and wide the sky was flaring with the red glare that leaped from rows of towering chimneys—for it was pitch dark when Jurgis arrived. The vast works, a city in themselves, were surrounded by a stockade; and already a full hundred men were waiting at the gate where new hands were taken on. Soon after daybreak whistles began to blow, and then suddenly thousands of men appeared, streaming from saloons and boardinghouses across the way, leaping from trolley cars that passed—it seemed as if they rose out of the ground, in the dim gray light. A river of them poured in through the gate—and then gradually ebbed away again, until there were only a few late ones running, and the watchman pacing up and down, and the hungry strangers stamping and shivering.

Jurgis presented his precious letter. The gatekeeper was surly, and put him through a catechism, but he insisted that he knew nothing, and as he had taken the precaution to seal his letter, there was nothing for the gatekeeper to do but send it to the person to whom it was addressed. A messenger came back to say that Jurgis should wait, and so he came inside of the gate, perhaps not sorry enough that there were others less fortunate watching him with greedy eyes. The great mills were getting under way—one could hear a vast stirring, a rolling and rumbling and hammering. Little by little the scene grew plain: towering, black buildings here and there, long rows of shops and sheds, little railways branching everywhere, bare gray cinders underfoot and oceans of billowing black smoke above. On one side of the grounds ran a railroad with a dozen tracks, and on the other side lay the lake, where steamers came to load.

Jurgis had time enough to stare and speculate, for it was two hours before he was summoned. He went into the office building, where a company timekeeper interviewed him. The superintendent was busy, he said, but he (the timekeeper) would try to find Jurgis a job. He had never worked in a steel mill before? But he was ready for anything? Well, then, they would go and see.

So they began a tour, among sights that made Jurgis stare amazed. He wondered if ever he could get used to working in a place like this, where the air shook with deafening thunder, and whistles shrieked warnings on all sides of him at once; where miniature steam engines came rushing upon him, and sizzling, quivering, white-hot masses of metal sped past him, and explosions of fire and flaming sparks dazzled him and scorched his face. The men in these mills were all black with soot, and hollow-eyed and gaunt; they worked with fierce intensity, rushing here and there, and never lifting their eyes from their tasks. Jurgis clung to his guide like a scared child to its nurse, and while the latter hailed one foreman after another to ask if they could use another unskilled man, he stared about him and marveled.

He was taken to the Bessemer furnace, where they made billets of steel—a dome-like building, the size of a big theater. Jurgis stood where the balcony of the theater would have been, and opposite, by the stage, he saw three giant caldrons, big enough for all the devils of hell to brew their broth in, full of something white and blinding, bubbling and splashing, roaring as if volcanoes were blowing through it—one had to shout to be heard in the place. Liquid fire would leap from these caldrons and scatter like bombs below—and men were working there, seeming careless, so that Jurgis caught his breath with fright. Then a whistle would toot, and across the curtain of the theater would come a little engine with a carload of something to be dumped into one of the receptacles; and then another whistle would toot, down by the stage, and another train would back up—and suddenly, without an instant's warning, one of the giant kettles began to tilt and topple, flinging out a jet of hissing, roaring flame. Jurgis shrank back appalled, for he thought it was an accident; there fell a pillar of white flame, dazzling as the sun, swishing like a huge tree falling in the forest. A torrent of sparks swept all the way across the building, overwhelming everything, hiding it from sight; and then Jurgis looked through the fingers of his hands, and saw pouring out of the caldron a cascade of living, leaping fire, white with a whiteness not of earth, scorching the eyeballs. Incandescent rainbows shone above it, blue, red, and golden lights played about it; but the stream itself was white, ineffable. Out of regions of wonder it streamed, the very river of life; and the soul leaped up at the sight of it, fled back upon it, swift and resistless, back into far-off lands, where beauty and terror dwell. Then the great caldron tilted back again, empty, and Jurgis saw to his relief that no one was hurt, and turned and followed his guide out into the sunlight.

They went through the blast furnaces, through rolling mills where bars of steel were tossed about and chopped like bits of cheese. All around and above giant machine arms were flying, giant wheels were turning, great hammers crashing; traveling cranes creaked and groaned overhead, reaching down iron hands and seizing iron prey—it was like standing in the center of the earth, where the machinery of time was revolving.

By and by they came to the place where steel rails were made; and Jurgis heard a toot behind him, and jumped out of the way of a car with a white-hot ingot upon it, the size of a man's body. There was a sudden crash and the car came to a halt, and the ingot toppled out upon a moving platform, where steel fingers and arms seized hold of it, punching it and prodding it into place, and hurrying it into the grip of huge rollers. Then it came out upon the other side, and there were more crashings and clatterings, and over it was flopped, like a pancake on a gridiron, and seized again and rushed back at you through another squeezer. So amid deafening uproar it clattered to and fro, growing thinner and flatter and longer. The ingot seemed almost a living thing; it did not want to run this mad course, but it was in the grip of fate, it was tumbled on, screeching and clanking and shivering in protest. By and by it was long and thin, a great red snake escaped from purgatory; and then, as it slid through the rollers, you would have sworn that it was alive—it writhed and squirmed, and wriggles and shudders passed out through its tail, all but flinging it off by their violence. There was no rest for it until it was cold and black—and then it needed only to be cut and straightened to be ready for a railroad.

It was at the end of this rail's progress that Jurgis got his chance. They had to be moved by men with crowbars, and the boss here could use another man. So he took off his coat and set to work on the spot.

It took him two hours to get to this place every day and cost him a dollar and twenty cents a week. As this was out of the question, he wrapped his bedding in a bundle and took it with him, and one of his fellow workingmen introduced him to a Polish lodging-house, where he might have the privilege of sleeping upon the floor for ten cents a night. He got his meals at free-lunch counters, and every Saturday night he went home—bedding and all—and took the greater part of his money to the family. Elzbieta was sorry for this arrangement, for she feared that it would get him into the habit of living without them, and once a week was not very often for him to see his baby; but there was no other way of arranging it. There was no chance for a woman at the steelworks, and Marija was now ready for work again, and lured on from day to day by the hope of finding it at the yards.

In a week Jurgis got over his sense of helplessness and bewilderment in the rail mill. He learned to find his way about and to take all the miracles and terrors for granted, to work without hearing the rumbling and crashing. From blind fear he went to the other extreme; he became reckless and indifferent, like all the rest of the men, who took but little thought of themselves in the ardor of their work. It was wonderful, when one came to think of it, that these men should have taken an interest in the work they did—they had no share in it—they were paid by the hour, and paid no more for being interested. Also they knew that if they were hurt they would be flung aside and forgotten—and still they would hurry to their task by dangerous short cuts, would use methods that were quicker and more effective in spite of the fact that they were also risky. His fourth day at his work Jurgis saw a man stumble while running in front of a car, and have his foot mashed off, and before he had been there three weeks he was witness of a yet more dreadful accident. There was a row of brick furnaces, shining white through every crack with the molten steel inside. Some of these were bulging dangerously, yet men worked before them, wearing blue glasses when they opened and shut the doors. One morning as Jurgis was passing, a furnace blew out, spraying two men with a shower of liquid fire. As they lay screaming and rolling upon the ground in agony, Jurgis rushed to help them, and as a result he lost a good part of the skin from the inside of one of his hands. The company doctor bandaged it up, but he got no other thanks from any one, and was laid up for eight working days without any pay.

Most fortunately, at this juncture, Elzbieta got the long-awaited chance to go at five o'clock in the morning and help scrub the office floors of one of the packers. Jurgis came home and covered himself with blankets to keep warm, and divided his time between sleeping and playing with little Antanas. Juozapas was away raking in the dump a good part of the time, and Elzbieta and Marija were hunting for more work.

Antanas was now over a year and a half old, and was a perfect talking machine. He learned so fast that every week when Jurgis came home it seemed to him as if he had a new child. He would sit down and listen and stare at him, and give vent to delighted exclamations—"Palauk! Muma! Tu mano szirdele!" The little fellow was now really the one delight that Jurgis had in the world—his one hope, his one victory. Thank God, Antanas was a boy! And he was as tough as a pine knot, and with the appetite of a wolf. Nothing had hurt him, and nothing could hurt him; he had come through all the suffering and deprivation unscathed—only shriller-voiced and more determined in his grip upon life. He was a terrible child to manage, was Antanas, but his father did not mind that—he would watch him and smile to himself with satisfaction. The more of a fighter he was the better—he would need to fight before he got through.

Jurgis had got the habit of buying the Sunday paper whenever he had the money; a most wonderful paper could be had for only five cents, a whole armful, with all the news of the world set forth in big headlines, that Jurgis could spell out slowly, with the children to help him at the long words. There was battle and murder and sudden death—it was marvelous how they ever heard about so many entertaining and thrilling happenings; the stories must be all true, for surely no man could have made such things up, and besides, there were pictures of them all, as real as life. One of these papers was as good as a circus, and nearly as good as a spree—certainly a most wonderful treat for a workingman, who was tired out and stupefied, and had never had any education, and whose work was one dull, sordid grind, day after day, and year after year, with never a sight of a green field nor an hour's entertainment, nor anything but liquor to stimulate his imagination. Among other things, these papers had pages full of comical pictures, and these were the main joy in life to little Antanas. He treasured them up, and would drag them out and make his father tell him about them; there were all sorts of animals among them, and Antanas could tell the names of all of them, lying upon the floor for hours and pointing them out with his chubby little fingers. Whenever the story was plain enough for Jurgis to make out, Antanas would have it repeated to him, and then he would remember it, prattling funny little sentences and mixing it up with other stories in an irresistible fashion. Also his quaint pronunciation of words was such a delight—and the phrases he would pick up and remember, the most outlandish and impossible things! The first time that the little rascal burst out with "God damn," his father nearly rolled off the chair with glee; but in the end he was sorry for this, for Antanas was soon "God-damning" everything and everybody.

And then, when he was able to use his hands, Jurgis took his bedding again and went back to his task of shifting rails. It was now April, and the snow had given place to cold rains, and the unpaved street in front of Aniele's house was turned into a canal. Jurgis would have to wade through it to get home, and if it was late he might easily get stuck to his waist in the mire. But he did not mind this much—it was a promise that summer was coming. Marija had now gotten a place as beef-trimmer in one of the smaller packing plants; and he told himself that he had learned his lesson now, and would meet with no more accidents—so that at last there was prospect of an end to their long agony. They could save money again, and when another winter came they would have a comfortable place; and the children would be off the streets and in school again, and they might set to work to nurse back into life their habits of decency and kindness. So once more Jurgis began to make plans and dream dreams.

And then one Saturday night he jumped off the car and started home, with the sun shining low under the edge of a bank of clouds that had been pouring floods of water into the mud-soaked street. There was a rainbow in the sky, and another in his breast—for he had thirty-six hours' rest before him, and a chance to see his family. Then suddenly he came in sight of the house, and noticed that there was a crowd before the door. He ran up the steps and pushed his way in, and saw Aniele's kitchen crowded with excited women. It reminded him so vividly of the time when he had come home from jail and found Ona dying, that his heart almost stood still. "What's the matter?" he cried.

A dead silence had fallen in the room, and he saw that every one was staring at him. "What's the matter?" he exclaimed again.

And then, up in the garret, he heard sounds of wailing, in Marija's voice. He started for the ladder—and Aniele seized him by the arm. "No, no!" she exclaimed. "Don't go up there!"

"What is it?" he shouted.

And the old woman answered him weakly: "It's Antanas. He's dead. He was drowned out in the street!"

CHAPTER 22

Jurgis took the news in a peculiar way. He turned deadly pale, but he caught himself, and for half a minute stood in the middle of the room, clenching his hands tightly and setting his teeth. Then he pushed Aniele aside and strode into the next room and climbed the ladder.

In the corner was a blanket, with a form half showing beneath it; and beside it lay Elzbieta, whether crying or in a faint, Jurgis could not tell. Marija was pacing the room, screaming and wringing her hands. He clenched his hands tighter yet, and his voice was hard as he spoke.

"How did it happen?" he asked.

Marija scarcely heard him in her agony. He repeated the question, louder and yet more harshly. "He fell off the sidewalk!" she wailed. The sidewalk in front of the house was a platform made of half-rotten boards, about five feet above the level of the sunken street.

"How did he come to be there?" he demanded.

"He went—he went out to play," Marija sobbed, her voice choking her. "We couldn't make him stay in. He must have got caught in the mud!"

"Are you sure that he is dead?" he demanded.

"Ai! ai!" she wailed. "Yes; we had the doctor."

Then Jurgis stood a few seconds, wavering. He did not shed a tear. He took one glance more at the blanket with the little form beneath it, and then turned suddenly to the ladder and climbed down again. A silence fell once more in the room as he entered. He went straight to the door, passed out, and started down the street.

When his wife had died, Jurgis made for the nearest saloon, but he did not do that now, though he had his week's wages in his pocket. He walked and walked, seeing nothing, splashing through mud and water. Later on he sat down upon a step and hid his face in his hands and for half an hour or so he did not move. Now and then he would whisper to himself: "Dead! Dead!"

Finally, he got up and walked on again. It was about sunset, and he went on and on until it was dark, when he was stopped by a railroad crossing. The gates were down, and a long train of freight cars was thundering by. He stood and watched it; and all at once a wild impulse seized him, a thought that had been lurking within him, unspoken, unrecognized, leaped into sudden life. He started down the track, and when he was past the gate-keeper's shanty he sprang forward and swung himself on to one of the cars.

By and by the train stopped again, and Jurgis sprang down and ran under the car, and hid himself upon the truck. Here he sat, and when the train started again, he fought a battle with his soul. He gripped his hands and set his teeth together—he had not wept, and he would not—not a tear! It was past and over, and he was done with it—he would fling it off his shoulders, be free of it, the whole business, that night. It should go like a black, hateful nightmare, and in the morning he would be a new man. And every time that a thought of it assailed him—a tender memory, a trace of a tear—he rose up, cursing with rage, and pounded it down.

He was fighting for his life; he gnashed his teeth together in his desperation. He had been a fool, a fool! He had wasted his life, he had wrecked himself, with his accursed weakness; and now he was done with it—he would tear it out of him, root and branch! There should be no more tears and no more tenderness; he had had enough of them—they had sold him into slavery! Now he was going to be free, to tear off his shackles, to rise up and fight. He was glad that the end had come—it had to come some time, and it was just as well now. This was no world for women and children, and the sooner they got out of it the better for them. Whatever Antanas might suffer where he was, he could suffer no more than he would have had he stayed upon earth. And meantime his father had thought the last thought about him that he meant to; he was going to think of himself, he was going to fight for himself, against the world that had baffled him and tortured him!

So he went on, tearing up all the flowers from the garden of his soul, and setting his heel upon them. The train thundered deafeningly, and a storm of dust blew in his face; but though it stopped now and then through the night, he clung where he was—he would cling there until he was driven off, for every mile that he got from Packingtown meant another load from his mind.

Whenever the cars stopped a warm breeze blew upon him, a breeze laden with the perfume of fresh fields, of honeysuckle and clover. He snuffed it, and it made his heart beat wildly—he was out in the country again! He was going to live in the country! When the dawn came he was peering out with hungry eyes, getting glimpses of meadows and woods and rivers. At last he could stand it no longer, and when the train stopped again he crawled out. Upon the top of the car was a brakeman, who shook his fist and swore; Jurgis waved his hand derisively, and started across the country.

Only think that he had been a countryman all his life; and for three long years he had never seen a country sight nor heard a country sound! Excepting for that one walk when he left jail, when he was too much worried to notice anything, and for a few times that he had rested in the city parks in the winter time when he was out of work, he had literally never seen a tree! And now he felt like a bird lifted up and borne away upon a gale; he stopped and stared at each new sight of wonder—at a herd of cows, and a meadow full of daisies, at hedgerows set thick with June roses, at little birds singing in the trees.

Then he came to a farm-house, and after getting himself a stick for protection, he approached it. The farmer was greasing a wagon in front of the barn, and Jurgis went to him. "I would like to get some breakfast, please," he said.

"Do you want to work?" said the farmer.

"No," said Jurgis. "I don't."

"Then you can't get anything here," snapped the other.

"I meant to pay for it," said Jurgis.

"Oh," said the farmer; and then added sarcastically, "We don't serve breakfast after 7 A.M."

"I am very hungry," said Jurgis gravely; "I would like to buy some food."

"Ask the woman," said the farmer, nodding over his shoulder. The "woman" was more tractable, and for a dime Jurgis secured two thick sandwiches and a piece of pie and two apples. He walked off eating the pie, as the least convenient thing to carry. In a few minutes he came to a stream, and he climbed a fence and walked down the bank, along a woodland path. By and by he found a comfortable spot, and there he devoured his meal, slaking his thirst at the stream. Then he lay for hours, just gazing and drinking in joy; until at last he felt sleepy, and lay down in the shade of a bush.

When he awoke the sun was shining hot in his face. He sat up and stretched his arms, and then gazed at the water sliding by. There was a deep pool, sheltered and silent, below him, and a sudden wonderful idea rushed upon him. He might have a bath! The water was free, and he might get into it—all the way into it! It would be the first time that he had been all the way into the water since he left Lithuania!

When Jurgis had first come to the stockyards he had been as clean as any workingman could well be. But later on, what with sickness and cold and hunger and discouragement, and the filthiness of his work, and the vermin in his home, he had given up washing in winter, and in summer only as much of him as would go into a basin. He had had a shower bath in jail, but nothing since—and now he would have a swim!

The water was warm, and he splashed about like a very boy in his glee. Afterward he sat down in the water near the bank, and proceeded to scrub himself—soberly and methodically, scouring every inch of him with sand. While he was doing it he would do it thoroughly, and see how it felt to be clean. He even scrubbed his head with sand, and combed what the men called "crumbs" out of his long, black hair, holding his head under water as long as he could, to see if he could not kill them all. Then, seeing that the sun was still hot, he took his clothes from the bank and proceeded to wash them, piece by piece; as the dirt and grease went floating off downstream he grunted with satisfaction and soused the clothes again, venturing even to dream that he might get rid of the fertilizer.

He hung them all up, and while they were drying he lay down in the sun and had another long sleep. They were hot and stiff as boards on top, and a little damp on the underside, when he awakened; but being hungry, he put them on and set out again. He had no knife, but with some labor he broke himself a good stout club, and, armed with this, he marched down the road again.

Before long he came to a big farmhouse, and turned up the lane that led to it. It was just supper-time, and the farmer was washing his hands at the kitchen door. "Please, sir," said Jurgis, "can I have something to eat? I can pay." To which the farmer responded promptly, "We don't feed tramps here. Get out!"

Jurgis went without a word; but as he passed round the barn he came to a freshly ploughed and harrowed field, in which the farmer had set out some young peach trees; and as he walked he jerked up a row of them by the roots, more than a hundred trees in all, before he reached the end of the field. That was his answer, and it showed his mood; from now on he was fighting, and the man who hit him would get all that he gave, every time.

Beyond the orchard Jurgis struck through a patch of woods, and then a field of winter grain, and came at last to another road. Before long he saw another farmhouse, and, as it was beginning to cloud over a little, he asked here for shelter as well as food. Seeing the farmer eying him dubiously, he added, "I'll be glad to sleep in the barn."

"Well, I dunno," said the other. "Do you smoke?"

"Sometimes," said Jurgis, "but I'll do it out of doors." When the man had assented, he inquired, "How much will it cost me? I haven't very much money."

"I reckon about twenty cents for supper," replied the farmer. "I won't charge ye for the barn."

So Jurgis went in, and sat down at the table with the farmer's wife and half a dozen children. It was a bountiful meal—there were baked beans and mashed potatoes and asparagus chopped and stewed, and a dish of strawberries, and great, thick slices of bread, and a pitcher of milk. Jurgis had not had such a feast since his wedding day, and he made a mighty effort to put in his twenty cents' worth.

They were all of them too hungry to talk; but afterward they sat upon the steps and smoked, and the farmer questioned his guest. When Jurgis had explained that he was a workingman from Chicago, and that he did not know just whither he was bound, the other said, "Why don't you stay here and work for me?"

"I'm not looking for work just now," Jurgis answered.

"I'll pay ye good," said the other, eying his big form—"a dollar a day and board ye. Help's terrible scarce round here."

"Is that winter as well as summer?" Jurgis demanded quickly.

"N—no," said the farmer; "I couldn't keep ye after November—I ain't got a big enough place for that."

"I see," said the other, "that's what I thought. When you get through working your horses this fall, will you turn them out in the snow?" (Jurgis was beginning to think for himself nowadays.)

"It ain't quite the same," the farmer answered, seeing the point. "There ought to be work a strong fellow like you can find to do, in the cities, or some place, in the winter time."

"Yes," said Jurgis, "that's what they all think; and so they crowd into the cities, and when they have to beg or steal to live, then people ask 'em why they don't go into the country, where help is scarce." The farmer meditated awhile.

"How about when your money's gone?" he inquired, finally. "You'll have to, then, won't you?"

"Wait till she's gone," said Jurgis; "then I'll see."

He had a long sleep in the barn and then a big breakfast of coffee and bread and oatmeal and stewed cherries, for which the man charged him only fifteen cents, perhaps having been influenced by his arguments. Then Jurgis bade farewell, and went on his way.

Such was the beginning of his life as a tramp. It was seldom he got as fair treatment as from this last farmer, and so as time went on he learned to shun the houses and to prefer sleeping in the fields. When it rained he would find a deserted building, if he could, and if not, he would wait until after dark and then, with his stick ready, begin a stealthy approach upon a barn. Generally he could get in before the dog got scent of him, and then he would hide in the hay and be safe until morning; if not, and the dog attacked him, he would rise up and make a retreat in battle order. Jurgis was not the mighty man he had once been, but his arms were still good, and there were few farm dogs he needed to hit more than once.

Before long there came raspberries, and then blackberries, to help him save his money; and there were apples in the orchards and potatoes in the ground—he learned to note the places and fill his pockets after dark. Twice he even managed to capture a chicken, and had a feast, once in a deserted barn and the other time in a lonely spot alongside of a stream. When all of these things failed him he used his money carefully, but without worry—for he saw that he could earn more whenever he chose. Half an hour's chopping wood in his lively fashion was enough to bring him a meal, and when the farmer had seen him working he would sometimes try to bribe him to stay.

But Jurgis was not staying. He was a free man now, a buccaneer. The old wanderlust had got into his blood, the joy of the unbound life, the joy of seeking, of hoping without limit. There were mishaps and discomforts—but at least there was always something new; and only think what it meant to a man who for years had been penned up in one place, seeing nothing but one dreary prospect of shanties and factories, to be suddenly set loose beneath the open sky, to behold new landscapes, new places, and new people every hour! To a man whose whole life had consisted of doing one certain thing all day, until he was so exhausted that he could only lie down and sleep until the next day—and to be now his own master, working as he pleased and when he pleased, and facing a new adventure every hour!

Then, too, his health came back to him, all his lost youthful vigor, his joy and power that he had mourned and forgotten! It came with a sudden rush, bewildering him, startling him; it was as if his dead childhood had come back to him, laughing and calling! What with plenty to eat and fresh air and exercise that was taken as it pleased him, he would waken from his sleep and start off not knowing what to do with his energy, stretching his arms, laughing, singing old songs of home that came back to him. Now and then, of course, he could not help but think of little Antanas, whom he should never see again, whose little voice he should never hear; and then he would have to battle with himself. Sometimes at night he would waken dreaming of Ona, and stretch out his arms to her, and wet the ground with his tears. But in the morning he would get up and shake himself, and stride away again to battle with the world.

He never asked where he was nor where he was going; the country was big enough, he knew, and there was no danger of his coming to the end of it. And of course he could always have company for the asking—everywhere he went there were men living just as he lived, and whom he was welcome to join. He was a stranger at the business, but they were not clannish, and they taught him all their tricks—what towns and villages it was best to keep away from, and how to read the secret signs upon the fences, and when to beg and when to steal, and just how to do both. They laughed at his ideas of paying for anything with money or with work—for they got all they wanted without either. Now and then Jurgis camped out with a gang of them in some woodland haunt, and foraged with them in the neighborhood at night. And then among them some one would "take a shine" to him, and they would go off together and travel for a week, exchanging reminiscences.

Of these professional tramps a great many had, of course, been shiftless and vicious all their lives. But the vast majority of them had been workingmen, had fought the long fight as Jurgis had, and found that it was a losing fight, and given up. Later on he encountered yet another sort of men, those from whose ranks the tramps were recruited, men who were homeless and wandering, but still seeking work—seeking it in the harvest fields. Of these there was an army, the huge surplus labor army of society; called into being under the stern system of nature, to do the casual work of the world, the tasks which were transient and irregular, and yet which had to be done. They did not know that they were such, of course; they only knew that they sought the job, and that the job was fleeting. In the early summer they would be in Texas, and as the crops were ready they would follow north with the season, ending with the fall in Manitoba. Then they would seek out the big lumber camps, where there was winter work; or failing in this, would drift to the cities, and live upon what they had managed to save, with the help of such transient work as was there the loading and unloading of steamships and drays, the digging of ditches and the shoveling of snow. If there were more of them on hand than chanced to be needed, the weaker ones died off of cold and hunger, again according to the stern system of nature.

It was in the latter part of July, when Jurgis was in Missouri, that he came upon the harvest work. Here were crops that men had worked for three or four months to prepare, and of which they would lose nearly all unless they could find others to help them for a week or two. So all over the land there was a cry for labor—agencies were set up and all the cities were drained of men, even college boys were brought by the carload, and hordes of frantic farmers would hold up trains and carry off wagon-loads of men by main force. Not that they did not pay them well—any man could get two dollars a day and his board, and the best men could get two dollars and a half or three.

The harvest-fever was in the very air, and no man with any spirit in him could be in that region and not catch it. Jurgis joined a gang and worked from dawn till dark, eighteen hours a day, for two weeks without a break. Then he had a sum of money that would have been a fortune to him in the old days of misery—but what could he do with it now? To be sure he might have put it in a bank, and, if he were fortunate, get it back again when he wanted it. But Jurgis was now a home-less man, wandering over a continent; and what did he know about banking and drafts and letters of credit? If he carried the money about with him, he would surely be robbed in the end; and so what was there for him to do but enjoy it while he could? On a Saturday night he drifted into a town with his fellows; and because it was raining, and there was no other place provided for him, he went to a saloon. And there were some who treated him and whom he had to treat, and there was laughter and singing and good cheer; and then out of the rear part of the saloon a girl's face, red-cheeked and merry, smiled at Jurgis, and his heart thumped suddenly in his throat. He nodded to her, and she came and sat by him, and they had more drink, and then he went upstairs into a room with her, and the wild beast rose up within him and screamed, as it has screamed in the Jungle from the dawn of time. And then because of his memories and his shame, he was glad when others joined them, men and women; and they had more drink and spent the night in wild rioting and debauchery. In the van of the surplus-labor army, there followed another, an army of women, they also struggling for life under the stern system of nature. Because there were rich men who sought pleasure, there had been ease and plenty for them so long as they were young and beautiful; and later on, when they were crowded out by others younger and more beautiful, they went out to follow upon the trail of the workingmen. Sometimes they came of them-selves, and the saloon-keepers shared with them; or sometimes they were handled by agencies, the same as the labor army. They were in the towns in harvest time, near the lumber camps in the winter, in the cities when the men came there; if a regiment were encamped, or a railroad or canal being made, or a great exposition getting ready, the crowd of women were on hand, living in shanties or saloons or tenement rooms, sometimes eight or ten of them together.

In the morning Jurgis had not a cent, and he went out upon the road again. He was sick and disgusted, but after the new plan of his life, he crushed his feelings down. He had made a fool of himself, but he could not help it now—all he could do was to see that it did not happen again. So he tramped on until exercise and fresh air banished his headache, and his strength and joy returned. This happened to him every time, for Jurgis was still a creature of impulse, and his pleasures had not yet become business. It would be a long time before he could be like the ma-jority of these men of the road, who roamed until the hunger for drink and for women mastered them, and then went to work with a purpose in mind, and stopped when they had the price of a spree.

On the contrary, try as he would, Jurgis could not help being made miserable by his conscience. It was the ghost that would not down. It would come upon him in the most unexpected places—sometimes it fairly drove him to drink.

One night he was caught by a thunderstorm, and he sought shelter in a little house just outside of a town. It was a working-man's home, and the owner was a Slav like himself, a new emigrant from White Russia; he bade Jurgis welcome in his home language, and told him to come to the kitchen-fire and dry himself. He had no bed for him, but there was straw in the garret, and he could make out. The man's wife was cooking the supper, and their children were playing about on the floor. Jurgis sat and exchanged thoughts with him about the old country, and the places where they had been and the work they had done. Then they ate, and afterward sat and smoked and talked more about America, and how they found it. In the middle of a sentence, however, Jurgis stopped, seeing that the woman had brought a big basin of water and was proceeding to undress her youngest baby. The rest had crawled into the closet where they slept, but the baby was to have a bath, the workingman explained. The nights had begun to be chilly, and his mother, ignorant as to the climate in America, had sewed him up for the winter; then it had turned warm again, and some kind of a rash had broken out on the child. The doctor had said she must bathe him every night, and she, foolish woman, believed him.

Jurgis scarcely heard the explanation; he was watching the baby. He was about a year old, and a sturdy little fellow, with soft fat legs, and a round ball of a stomach, and eyes as black as coals. His pimples did not seem to bother him much, and he was wild with glee over the bath, kicking and squirming and chuckling with delight, pulling at his mother's face and then at his own little toes. When she put him into the basin he sat in the midst of it and grinned, splashing the water over himself and squealing like a little pig. He spoke in Russian, of which Jurgis knew some; he spoke it with the quaintest of baby accents—and every word of it brought back to Jurgis some word of his own dead little one, and stabbed him like a knife. He sat perfectly motionless, silent, but gripping his hands tightly, while a storm gathered in his bosom and a flood heaped itself up behind his eyes. And in the end he could bear it no more, but buried his face in his hands and burst into tears, to the alarm and amazement of his hosts. Between the shame of this and his woe Jurgis could not stand it, and got up and rushed out into the rain.

He went on and on down the road, finally coming to a black woods, where he hid and wept as if his heart would break. Ah, what agony was that, what despair, when the tomb of memory was rent open and the ghosts of his old life came forth to scourge him! What terror to see what he had been and now could never be—to see Ona and his child and his own dead self stretching out their arms to him, calling to him across a bottomless abyss—and to know that they were gone from him forever, and he writhing and suffocating in the mire of his own vileness!

CHAPTER 23

Early in the fall Jurgis set out for Chicago again. All the joy went out of tramping as soon as a man could not keep warm in the hay; and, like many thousands of others, he deluded himself with the hope that by coming early he could avoid the rush. He brought fifteen dollars with him, hidden away in one of his shoes, a sum which had been saved from the saloon-keepers, not so much by his conscience, as by the fear which filled him at the thought of being out of work in the city in the winter time.

He traveled upon the railroad with several other men, hiding in freight cars at night, and liable to be thrown off at any time, regardless of the speed of the train. When he reached the city he left the rest, for he had money and they did not, and he meant to save himself in this fight. He would bring to it all the skill that practice had brought him, and he would stand, whoever fell. On fair nights he would sleep in the park or on a truck or an empty barrel or box, and when it was rainy or cold he would stow himself upon a shelf in a ten-cent lodging-house, or pay three cents for the privileges of a "squatter" in a tenement hallway. He would eat at free lunches, five cents a meal, and never a cent more—so he might keep alive for two months and more, and in that time he would surely find a job. He would have to bid farewell to his summer cleanliness, of course, for he would come out of the first night's lodging with his clothes alive with vermin. There was no place in the city where he could wash even his face, unless he went down to the lake front— and there it would soon be all ice.

First he went to the steel mill and the harvester works, and found that his places there had been filled long ago. He was careful to keep away from the stockyards—he was a single man now, he told himself, and he meant to stay one, to have his wages for his own when he got a job. He began the long, weary round of factories and warehouses, tramping all day, from one end of the city to the other, finding everywhere from ten to a hundred men ahead of him. He watched the newspapers, too—but no longer was he to be taken in by smooth-spoken agents. He had been told of all those tricks while "on the road."

In the end it was through a newspaper that he got a job, after nearly a month of seeking. It was a call for a hundred laborers, and though he thought it was a "fake," he went because the place was near by. He found a line of men a block long, but as a wagon chanced to come out of an alley and break the line, he saw his chance and sprang to seize a place. Men threatened him and tried to throw him out, but he cursed and made a disturbance to attract a policeman, upon which they subsided, knowing that if the latter interfered it would be to "fire" them all.

An hour or two later he entered a room and confronted a big Irishman behind a desk.

"Ever worked in Chicago before?" the man inquired; and whether it was a good angel that put it into Jurgis's mind, or an intuition of his sharpened wits, he was moved to answer, "No, sir."

"Where do you come from?"

"Kansas City, sir."

"Any references?"

"No, sir. I'm just an unskilled man. I've got good arms."

"I want men for hard work—it's all underground, digging tunnels for tele-phones. Maybe it won't suit you."

"I'm willing, sir—anything for me. What's the pay?"

"Fifteen cents an hour."

"I'm willing, sir."

"All right; go back there and give your name."

So within half an hour he was at work, far underneath the streets of the city. The tunnel was a peculiar one for telephone wires; it was about eight feet high, and with a level floor nearly as wide. It had innumerable branches—a perfect spi-der web beneath the city; Jurgis walked over half a mile with his gang to the place where they were to work. Stranger yet, the tunnel was lighted by electricity, and upon it was laid a double-tracked, narrow-gauge railroad!

But Jurgis was not there to ask questions, and he did not give the matter a thought. It was nearly a year afterward that he finally learned the meaning of this whole affair. The City Council had passed a quiet and innocent little bill allowing a company to construct telephone conduits under the city streets; and upon the strength of this, a great corporation had proceeded to tunnel all Chicago with a system of railway freight-subways. In the city there was a combination of em-ployers, representing hundreds of millions of capital, and formed for the purpose of crushing the labor unions. The chief union which troubled it was the teamsters'; and when these freight tunnels were completed, connecting all the big factories and stores with the railroad depots, they would have the teamsters' union by the throat. Now and then there were rumors and murmurs in the Board of Aldermen, and once there was a committee to investigate—but each time another small for-tune was paid over, and the rumors died away; until at last the city woke up with a start to find the work completed. There was a tremendous scandal, of course; it was found that the city records had been falsified and other crimes committed, and some of Chicago's big capitalists got into jail—figuratively speaking. The aldermen declared that they had had no idea of it all, in spite of the fact that the main entrance to the work had been in the rear of the saloon of one of them.

It was in a newly opened cut that Jurgis worked, and so he knew that he had an all-winter job. He was so rejoiced that he treated himself to a spree that night, and with the balance of his money he hired himself a place in a tenement room, where he slept upon a big homemade straw mattress along with four other workingmen. This was one dollar a week, and for four more he got his food in a boardinghouse near his work. This would leave him four dollars extra each week, an unthinkable sum for him. At the outset he had to pay for his digging tools, and also to buy a pair of heavy boots, since his shoes were falling to pieces, and a flannel shirt, since the one he had worn all summer was in shreds. He spent a week meditating whether or not he should also buy an overcoat. There was one belonging to a Hebrew collar button peddler, who had died in the room next to him, and which the landlady was holding for her rent; in the end, however, Jurgis decided to do without it, as he was to be underground by day and in bed at night.

This was an unfortunate decision, however, for it drove him more quickly than ever into the saloons. From now on Jurgis worked from seven o'clock until half-past five, with half an hour for dinner; which meant that he never saw the sunlight on weekdays. In the evenings there was no place for him to go except a barroom; no place where there was light and warmth, where he could hear a little music or sit with a companion and talk. He had now no home to go to; he had no affection left in his life—only the pitiful mockery of it in the camaraderie of vice. On Sundays the churches were open—but where was there a church in which an ill-smelling workingman, with vermin crawling upon his neck, could sit without seeing people edge away and look annoyed? He had, of course, his corner in a close though unheated room, with a window opening upon a blank wall two feet away; and also he had the bare streets, with the winter gales sweeping through them; besides this he had only the saloons—and, of course, he had to drink to stay in them. If he drank now and then he was free to make himself at home, to gamble with dice or a pack of greasy cards, to play at a dingy pool table for money, or to look at a beer-stained pink "sporting paper," with pictures of murderers and half-naked women. It was for such pleasures as these that he spent his money; and such was his life during the six weeks and a half that he toiled for the merchants of Chicago, to enable them to break the grip of their teamsters' union.

In a work thus carried out, not much thought was given to the welfare of the laborers. On an average, the tunneling cost a life a day and several manglings; it was seldom, however, that more than a dozen or two men heard of any one accident. The work was all done by the new boring machinery, with as little blasting as possible; but there would be falling rocks and crushed supports, and premature explosions—and in addition all the dangers of railroading. So it was that one night, as Jurgis was on his way out with his gang, an engine and a loaded car dashed round one of the innumerable right-angle branches and struck him upon the shoulder, hurling him against the concrete wall and knocking him senseless.

When he opened his eyes again it was to the clanging of the bell of an ambulance. He was lying in it, covered by a blanket, and it was threading its way slowly through the holiday-shopping crowds. They took him to the county hospital, where a young surgeon set his arm; then he was washed and laid upon a bed in a ward with a score or two more of maimed and mangled men.

Jurgis spent his Christmas in this hospital, and it was the pleasantest Christmas he had had in America. Every year there were scandals and investigations in this institution, the newspapers charging that doctors were allowed to try fantastic experiments upon the patients; but Jurgis knew nothing of this—his only complaint was that they used to feed him upon tinned meat, which no man who had ever worked in Packingtown would feed to his dog. Jurgis had often wondered just who ate the canned corned beef and "roast beef" of the stockyards; now he began to understand—that it was what you might call "graft meat," put up to be sold to public officials and contractors, and eaten by soldiers and sailors, prisoners and inmates of institutions, "shantymen" and gangs of railroad laborers.

Jurgis was ready to leave the hospital at the end of two weeks. This did not mean that his arm was strong and that he was able to go back to work, but simply that he could get along without further attention, and that his place was needed for some one worse off than he. That he was utterly helpless, and had no means of keeping himself alive in the meantime, was something which did not concern the hospital authorities, nor any one else in the city.

As it chanced, he had been hurt on a Monday, and had just paid for his last week's board and his room rent, and spent nearly all the balance of his Saturday's pay. He had less than seventy-five cents in his pockets, and a dollar and a half due him for the day's work he had done before he was hurt. He might possibly have sued the company, and got some damages for his injuries, but he did not know this, and it was not the company's business to tell him. He went and got his pay and his tools, which he left in a pawnshop for fifty cents. Then he went to his landlady, who had rented his place and had no other for him; and then to his boardinghouse keeper, who looked him over and questioned him. As he must certainly be helpless for a couple of months, and had boarded there only six weeks, she decided very quickly that it would not be worth the risk to keep him on trust.

So Jurgis went out into the streets, in a most dreadful plight. It was bitterly cold, and a heavy snow was falling, beating into his face. He had no overcoat, and no place to go, and two dollars and sixty-five cents in his pocket, with the certainty that he could not earn another cent for months. The snow meant no chance to him now; he must walk along and see others shoveling, vigorous and active—and he with his left arm bound to his side! He could not hope to tide himself over by odd jobs of loading trucks; he could not even sell newspapers or carry satchels, because he was now at the mercy of any rival. Words could not paint the terror that came over him as he realized all this. He was like a wounded animal in the forest; he was forced to compete with his enemies upon unequal terms. There would be no consideration for him because of his weakness—it was no one's business to help him in such distress, to make the fight the least bit easier for him. Even if he took to begging, he would be at a disadvantage, for reasons which he was to discover in good time.

In the beginning he could not think of anything except getting out of the awful cold. He went into one of the saloons he had been wont to frequent and bought a drink, and then stood by the fire shivering and waiting to be ordered out. According to an unwritten law, the buying a drink included the privilege of loafing for just so long; then one had to buy another drink or move on. That Jurgis was an old customer entitled him to a somewhat longer stop; but then he had been away two weeks, and was evidently "on the bum." He might plead and tell his "hard luck story," but that would not help him much; a saloon-keeper who was to be moved by such means would soon have his place jammed to the doors with "hoboes" on a day like this.

So Jurgis went out into another place, and paid another nickel. He was so hungry this time that he could not resist the hot beef stew, an indulgence which cut short his stay by a considerable time. When he was again told to move on, he made his way to a "tough" place in the "Levee" district, where now and then he had gone with a certain rat-eyed Bohemian workingman of his acquaintance, seeking a woman. It was Jurgis's vain hope that here the proprietor would let him remain as a "sitter." In low-class places, in the dead of winter, saloon-keepers would often allow one or two forlorn-looking bums who came in covered with snow or soaked with rain to sit by the fire and look miserable to attract custom. A workingman would come in, feeling cheerful after his day's work was over, and it would trouble him to have to take his glass with such a sight under his nose; and so he would call out: "Hello, Bub, what's the matter? You look as if you'd been up against it!" And then the other would begin to pour out some tale of misery, and the man would say, "Come have a glass, and maybe that'll brace you up." And so they would drink together, and if the tramp was sufficiently wretched-looking, or good enough at the "gab," they might have two; and if they were to discover that they were from the same country, or had lived in the same city or worked at the same trade, they might sit down at a table and spend an hour or two in talk—and before they got through the saloon-keeper would have taken in a dollar. All of this might seem diabolical, but the saloon-keeper was in no wise to blame for it. He was in the same plight as the manufacturer who has to adulterate and misrepresent his product. If he does not, some one else will; and the saloon-keeper, unless he is also an alderman, is apt to be in debt to the big brewers, and on the verge of being sold out.

The market for "sitters" was glutted that afternoon, however, and there was no place for Jurgis. In all he had to spend six nickels in keeping a shelter over him that frightful day, and then it was just dark, and the station houses would not open until midnight! At the last place, however, there was a bartender who knew him and liked him, and let him doze at one of the tables until the boss came back; and also, as he was going out, the man gave him a tip—on the next block there was a religious revival of some sort, with preaching and singing, and hundreds of hoboes would go there for the shelter and warmth.

Jurgis went straightway, and saw a sign hung out, saying that the door would open at seven-thirty; then he walked, or half ran, a block, and hid awhile in a doorway and then ran again, and so on until the hour. At the end he was all but frozen, and fought his way in with the rest of the throng (at the risk of having his arm broken again), and got close to the big stove.

By eight o'clock the place was so crowded that the speakers ought to have been flattered; the aisles were filled halfway up, and at the door men were packed tight enough to walk upon. There were three elderly gentlemen in black upon the platform, and a young lady who played the piano in front. First they sang a hymn, and then one of the three, a tall, smooth-shaven man, very thin, and wearing black spectacles, began an address. Jurgis heard smatterings of it, for the reason that terror kept him awake—he knew that he snored abominably, and to have been put out just then would have been like a sentence of death to him.

The evangelist was preaching "sin and redemption," the infinite grace of God and His pardon for human frailty. He was very much in earnest, and he meant well, but Jurgis, as he listened, found his soul filled with hatred. What did he know about sin and suffering—with his smooth, black coat and his neatly starched collar, his body warm, and his belly full, and money in his pocket—and lecturing men who were struggling for their lives, men at the death grapple with the demon powers of hunger and cold!—This, of course, was unfair; but Jurgis felt that these men were out of touch with the life they discussed, that they were unfitted to solve its problems; nay, they themselves were part of the problem— they were part of the order established that was crushing men down and beating them! They were of the triumphant and insolent possessors; they had a hall, and a fire, and food and clothing and money, and so they might preach to hungry men, and the hungry men must be humble and listen! They were trying to save their souls—and who but a fool could fail to see that all that was the matter with their souls was that they had not been able to get a decent existence for their bodies?

At eleven the meeting closed, and the desolate audience filed out into the snow, muttering curses upon the few traitors who had got repentance and gone up on the platform. It was yet an hour before the station house would open, and Jurgis had no overcoat—and was weak from a long illness. During that hour he nearly perished. He was obliged to run hard to keep his blood moving at all—and then he came back to the station house and found a crowd blocking the street before the door! This was in the month of January, 1904, when the country was on the verge of "hard times," and the newspapers were reporting the shutting down of factories every day—it was estimated that a million and a half men were thrown out of work before the spring. So all the hiding places of the city were crowded, and before that station house door men fought and tore each other like savage beasts. When at last the place was jammed and they shut the doors, half the crowd was still outside; and Jurgis, with his helpless arm, was among them. There was no choice then but to go to a lodging-house and spend another dime. It really broke his heart to do this, at half-past twelve o'clock, after he had wasted the night at the meeting and on the street. He would be turned out of the lodging-house promptly at seven—they had the shelves which served as bunks so contrived that they could be dropped, and any man who was slow about obeying orders could be tumbled to the floor.

This was one day, and the cold spell lasted for fourteen of them. At the end of six days every cent of Jurgis' money was gone; and then he went out on the streets to beg for his life.

He would begin as soon as the business of the city was moving. He would sally forth from a saloon, and, after making sure there was no policeman in sight, would approach every likely-looking person who passed him, telling his woeful story and pleading for a nickel or a dime. Then when he got one, he would dart round the corner and return to his base to get warm; and his victim, seeing him do this, would go away, vowing that he would never give a cent to a beggar again. The victim never paused to ask where else Jurgis could have gone under the circumstances—where he, the victim, would have gone. At the saloon Jurgis could not only get more food and better food than he could buy in any restaurant for the same money, but a drink in the bargain to warm him up. Also he could find a comfortable seat by a fire, and could chat with a companion until he was as warm as toast. At the saloon, too, he felt at home. Part of the saloon-keeper's business was to offer a home and refreshments to beggars in exchange for the proceeds of their foragings; and was there any one else in the whole city who would do this— would the victim have done it himself?

Poor Jurgis might have been expected to make a successful beggar. He was just out of the hospital, and desperately sick-looking, and with a helpless arm; also he had no overcoat, and shivered pitifully. But, alas, it was again the case of the honest merchant, who finds that the genuine and unadulterated article is driven to the wall by the artistic counterfeit. Jurgis, as a beggar, was simply a blundering amateur in competition with organized and scientific professionalism. He was just out of the hospital—but the story was worn threadbare, and how could he prove it? He had his arm in a sling—and it was a device a regular beggar's little boy would have scorned. He was pale and shivering—but they were made up with cosmetics, and had studied the art of chattering their teeth. As to his being without an overcoat, among them you would meet men you could swear had on nothing but a ragged linen duster and a pair of cotton trousers—so cleverly had they concealed the several suits of all-wool underwear beneath. Many of these professional mendicants had comfortable homes, and families, and thousands of dollars in the bank; some of them had retired upon their earnings, and gone into the business of fitting out and doctoring others, or working children at the trade. There were some who had both their arms bound tightly to their sides, and padded stumps in their sleeves, and a sick child hired to carry a cup for them. There were some who had no legs, and pushed themselves upon a wheeled platform—some who had been favored with blindness, and were led by pretty little dogs. Some less fortunate had mutilated themselves or burned themselves, or had brought horrible sores upon themselves with chemicals; you might suddenly encounter upon the street a man holding out to you a finger rotting and discolored with gangrene—or one with livid scarlet wounds half escaped from their filthy bandages. These desperate ones were the dregs of the city's cesspools, wretches who hid at night in the rain-soaked cellars of old ramshackle tenements, in "stale-beer dives" and opium joints, with abandoned women in the last stages of the harlot's progress—women who had been kept by Chinamen and turned away at last to die. Every day the police net would drag hundreds of them off the streets, and in the detention hospital you might see them, herded together in a miniature inferno, with hideous, beastly faces, bloated and leprous with disease, laughing, shouting, screaming in all stages of drunkenness, barking like dogs, gibbering like apes, raving and tearing themselves in delirium.

CHAPTER 24

In the face of all his handicaps, Jurgis was obliged to make the price of a lodging, and of a drink every hour or two, under penalty of freezing to death. Day after day he roamed about in the arctic cold, his soul filled full of bitterness and despair. He saw the world of civilization then more plainly than ever he had seen it before; a world in which nothing counted but brutal might, an order devised by those who possessed it for the subjugation of those who did not. He was one of the latter; and all outdoors, all life, was to him one colossal prison, which he paced like a pent-up tiger, trying one bar after another, and finding them all beyond his power. He had lost in the fierce battle of greed, and so was doomed to be exterminated; and all society was busied to see that he did not escape the sentence. Everywhere that he turned were prison bars, and hostile eyes following him; the well-fed, sleek policemen, from whose glances he shrank, and who seemed to grip their clubs more tightly when they saw him; the saloon-keepers, who never ceased to watch him while he was in their places, who were jealous of every moment he lingered after he had paid his money; the hurrying throngs upon the streets, who were deaf to his entreaties, oblivious of his very existence—and savage and contemptuous when he forced himself upon them. They had their own affairs, and there was no place for him among them. There was no place for him anywhere—every direction he turned his gaze, this fact was forced upon him: Everything was built to express it to him: the residences, with their heavy walls and bolted doors, and basement windows barred with iron; the great warehouses filled with the products of the whole world, and guarded by iron shutters and heavy gates; the banks with their unthinkable billions of wealth, all buried in safes and vaults of steel.

And then one day there befell Jurgis the one adventure of his life. It was late at night, and he had failed to get the price of a lodging. Snow was falling, and he had been out so long that he was covered with it, and was chilled to the bone. He was working among the theater crowds, flitting here and there, taking large chances with the police, in his desperation half hoping to be arrested. When he saw a blue-coat start toward him, however, his heart failed him, and he dashed down a side street and fled a couple of blocks. When he stopped again he saw a man coming toward him, and placed himself in his path.

"Please, sir," he began, in the usual formula, "will you give me the price of a lodging? I've had a broken arm, and I can't work, and I've not a cent in my pocket. I'm an honest working-man, sir, and I never begged before! It's not my fault, sir—"

Jurgis usually went on until he was interrupted, but this man did not interrupt, and so at last he came to a breathless stop. The other had halted, and Jurgis suddenly noticed that he stood a little unsteadily. "Whuzzat you say?" he queried suddenly, in a thick voice.

Jurgis began again, speaking more slowly and distinctly; before he was half through the other put out his hand and rested it upon his shoulder. "Poor ole chappie!" he said. "Been up—hic—up—against it, hey?"

Then he lurched toward Jurgis, and the hand upon his shoulder became an arm about his neck. "Up against it myself, ole sport," he said. "She's a hard ole world."

They were close to a lamppost, and Jurgis got a glimpse of the other. He was a young fellow—not much over eighteen, with a handsome boyish face. He wore a silk hat and a rich soft overcoat with a fur collar; and he smiled at Jurgis with benignant sympathy. "I'm hard up, too, my goo' fren'," he said. "I've got cruel parents, or I'd set you up. Whuzzamatter whizyer?"

"I've been in the hospital."

"Hospital!" exclaimed the young fellow, still smiling sweetly, "thass too bad! Same's my Aunt Polly—hic—my Aunt Polly's in the hospital, too—ole auntie's been havin' twins! Whuzzamatter whiz you?"

"I've got a broken arm—" Jurgis began.

"So," said the other, sympathetically. "That ain't so bad—you get over that. I wish somebody'd break my arm, ole chappie—damfidon't! Then they'd treat me better—hic—hole me up, ole sport! Whuzzit you wamme do?"

"I'm hungry, sir," said Jurgis.

"Hungry! Why don't you hassome supper?"

"I've got no money, sir."

"No money! Ho, ho—less be chums, ole boy—jess like me! No money, either—a'most busted! Why don't you go home, then, same's me?"

"I haven't any home," said Jurgis.

"No home! Stranger in the city, hey? Goo' God, thass bad! Better come home wiz me—yes, by Harry, thass the trick, you'll come home an' hassome supper—hic—wiz me! Awful lonesome—nobody home! Guv'ner gone abroad—Bubby on's honeymoon—Polly havin' twins—every damn soul gone away! Nuff—hic—nuff to drive a feller to drink, I say! Only ole Ham standin' by, passin' plates—damfican eat like that, no sir! The club for me every time, my boy, I say. But then they won't lemme sleep there—guv'ner's orders, by Harry—home every night, sir! Ever hear anythin' like that? 'Every mornin' do?' I asked him. 'No, sir, every night, or no allowance at all, sir.' Thass my guv'ner—'nice as nails, by Harry! Tole ole Ham to watch me, too—servants spyin' on me—whuzyer think that, my fren'? A nice, quiet—hic—goodhearted young feller like me, an' his daddy can't go to Europe—hup!—an' leave him in peace! Ain't that a shame, sir? An' I gotter go home every evenin' an' miss all the fun, by Harry! Thass whuzzamatter now—thass why I'm here! Hadda come away an' leave Kitty—hic—left her cryin', too—whujja think of that, ole sport? 'Lemme go, Kittens,' says I—'come early an' often—I go where duty—hic—calls me. Farewell, farewell, my own true love—farewell, farewehell, my—own true—love!'"

This last was a song, and the young gentleman's voice rose mournful and wailing, while he swung upon Jurgis's neck. The latter was glancing about nervously, lest some one should approach. They were still alone, however.

"But I came all right, all right," continued the youngster, aggressively, "I can—hic—I can have my own way when I want it, by Harry—Freddie Jones is a hard man to handle when he gets goin'! 'No, sir,' says I, 'by thunder, and I don't need anybody goin' home with me, either—whujja take me for, hey? Think I'm drunk, dontcha, hey?—I know you! But I'm no more drunk than you are, Kittens,' says I to her. And then says she, 'Thass true, Freddie dear' (she's a smart one, is Kitty), 'but I'm stayin' in the flat, an' you're goin' out into the cold, cold night!' 'Put it in a pome, lovely Kitty,' says I. 'No jokin', Freddie, my boy,' says she. 'Lemme call a cab now, like a good dear'—but I can call my own cabs, dontcha fool yourself—and I know what I'm a-doin', you bet! Say, my fren', whatcha say—willye come home an' see me, an' hassome supper? Come 'long like a good feller—don't be haughty! You're up against it, same as me, an' you can unerstan' a feller; your heart's in the right place, by Harry—come 'long, ole chappie, an' we'll light up the house, an' have some fizz, an' we'll raise hell, we will—whoop-la! S'long's I'm inside the house I can do as I please—the guv'ner's own very orders, b'God! Hip! hip!"

They had started down the street, arm in arm, the young man pushing Jurgis along, half dazed. Jurgis was trying to think what to do—he knew he could not pass any crowded place with his new acquaintance without attracting attention and being stopped. It was only because of the falling snow that people who passed here did not notice anything wrong.

Suddenly, therefore, Jurgis stopped. "Is it very far?" he inquired.

"Not very," said the other, "Tired, are you, though? Well, we'll ride—whatcha say? Good! Call a cab!"

And then, gripping Jurgis tight with one hand, the young fellow began searching his pockets with the other. "You call, ole sport, an' I'll pay," he suggested. "How's that, hey?"

And he pulled out from somewhere a big roll of bills. It was more money than Jurgis had ever seen in his life before, and he stared at it with startled eyes.

"Looks like a lot, hey?" said Master Freddie, fumbling with it. "Fool you, though, ole chappie—they're all little ones! I'll be busted in one week more, sure thing—word of honor. An' not a cent more till the first—hic—guv'ner's orders—hic—not a cent, by Harry! Nuff to set a feller crazy, it is. I sent him a cable, this af'noon—thass one reason more why I'm goin' home. 'Hangin' on the verge of starvation,' I says—'for the honor of the family—hic—sen' me some bread. Hunger will compel me to join you—Freddie.' Thass what I wired him, by Harry, an' I mean it—I'll run away from school, b'God, if he don't sen' me some."

After this fashion the young gentleman continued to prattle on—and meantime Jurgis was trembling with excitement. He might grab that wad of bills and be out of sight in the darkness before the other could collect his wits. Should he do it? What better had he to hope for, if he waited longer? But Jurgis had never committed a crime in his life, and now he hesitated half a second too long. "Freddie" got one bill loose, and then stuffed the rest back into his trousers' pocket.

"Here, ole man," he said, "you take it." He held it out fluttering. They were in front of a saloon; and by the light of the window Jurgis saw that it was a hundred-dollar bill! "You take it," the other repeated. "Pay the cabbie an' keep the change—I've got—hic—no head for business! Guv'ner says so hisself, an' the guv'ner knows—the guv'ner's got a head for business, you bet! 'All right, guv'ner,' I told him, 'you run the show, and I'll take the tickets!' An' so he set Aunt Polly to watch me—hic—an' now Polly's off in the hospital havin' twins, an' me out raisin' Cain! Hello, there! Hey! Call him!"

A cab was driving by; and Jurgis sprang and called, and it swung round to the curb. Master Freddie clambered in with some difficulty, and Jurgis had started to follow, when the driver shouted: "Hi, there! Get out—you!"

Jurgis hesitated, and was half obeying; but his companion broke out: "Whuzzat? Whuzzamatter wiz you, hey?"

And the cabbie subsided, and Jurgis climbed in. Then Freddie gave a number on the Lake Shore Drive, and the carriage started away. The youngster leaned back and snuggled up to Jurgis, murmuring contentedly; in half a minute he was sound asleep, Jurgis sat shivering, speculating as to whether he might not still be able to get hold of the roll of bills. He was afraid to try to go through his companion's pockets, however; and besides the cabbie might be on the watch. He had the hundred safe, and he would have to be content with that.

At the end of half an hour or so the cab stopped. They were out on the water-front, and from the east a freezing gale was blowing off the ice-bound lake. "Here we are," called the cabbie, and Jurgis awakened his companion.

Master Freddie sat up with a start.

"Hello!" he said. "Where are we? Whuzzis? Who are you, hey? Oh, yes, sure nuff! Mos' forgot you—hic—ole chappie! Home, are we? Lessee! Br-r-r—it's cold! Yes—come 'long—we're home—it ever so—hic—humble!"

Before them there loomed an enormous granite pile, set far back from the street, and occupying a whole block. By the light of the driveway lamps Jurgis could see that it had towers and huge gables, like a medieval castle. He thought that the young fellow must have made a mistake—it was inconceivable to him that any person could have a home like a hotel or the city hall. But he followed in silence, and they went up the long flight of steps, arm in arm.

"There's a button here, ole sport," said Master Freddie. "Hole my arm while I find her! Steady, now—oh, yes, here she is! Saved!"

A bell rang, and in a few seconds the door was opened. A man in blue livery stood holding it, and gazing before him, silent as a statue.

They stood for a moment blinking in the light. Then Jurgis felt his companion pulling, and he stepped in, and the blue automaton closed the door. Jurgis's heart was beating wildly; it was a bold thing for him to do—into what strange unearthly place he was venturing he had no idea. Aladdin entering his cave could not have been more excited.

The place where he stood was dimly lighted; but he could see a vast hall, with pillars fading into the darkness above, and a great staircase opening at the far end of it. The floor was of tesselated marble, smooth as glass, and from the walls strange shapes loomed out, woven into huge portieres in rich, harmonious colors, or gleaming from paintings, wonderful and mysterious-looking in the half-light, purple and red and golden, like sunset glimmers in a shadowy forest.

The man in livery had moved silently toward them; Master Freddie took off his hat and handed it to him, and then, letting go of Jurgis' arm, tried to get out of his overcoat. After two or three attempts he accomplished this, with the lackey's help, and meantime a second man had approached, a tall and portly personage, solemn as an executioner. He bore straight down upon Jurgis, who shrank away nervously; he seized him by the arm without a word, and started toward the door with him. Then suddenly came Master Freddie's voice, "Hamilton! My fren' will remain wiz me."

The man paused and half released Jurgis. "Come 'long ole chappie," said the other, and Jurgis started toward him.

"Master Frederick!" exclaimed the man.

"See that the cabbie—hic—is paid," was the other's response; and he linked his arm in Jurgis'. Jurgis was about to say, "I have the money for him," but he restrained himself. The stout man in uniform signaled to the other, who went out to the cab, while he followed Jurgis and his young master.

They went down the great hall, and then turned. Before them were two huge doors.

"Hamilton," said Master Freddie.

"Well, sir?" said the other.

"Whuzzamatter wizze dinin'-room doors?"

"Nothing is the matter, sir."

"Then why dontcha openum?"

The man rolled them back; another vista lost itself in the darkness. "Lights," commanded Master Freddie; and the butler pressed a button, and a flood of brilliant incandescence streamed from above, half-blinding Jurgis. He stared; and little by little he made out the great apartment, with a domed ceiling from which the light poured, and walls that were one enormous painting—nymphs and dryads dancing in a flower-strewn glade—Diana with her hounds and horses, dashing headlong through a mountain streamlet—a group of maidens bathing in a forest pool—all life-size, and so real that Jurgis thought that it was some work of enchantment, that he was in a dream palace. Then his eye passed to the long table in the center of the hall, a table black as ebony, and gleaming with wrought silver and gold. In the center of it was a huge carven bowl, with the glistening gleam of ferns and the red and purple of rare orchids, glowing from a light hidden somewhere in their midst.

"This's the dinin' room," observed Master Freddie. "How you like it, hey, ole sport?"

He always insisted on having an answer to his remarks, leaning over Jurgis and smiling into his face. Jurgis liked it.

"Rummy ole place to feed in all 'lone, though," was Freddie's comment— "rummy's hell! Whuzya think, hey?" Then another idea occurred to him and he went on, without waiting: "Maybe you never saw anythin—hic—like this 'fore? Hey, ole chappie?"

"No," said Jurgis.

"Come from country, maybe—hey?"

"Yes," said Jurgis.

"Aha! I thosso! Lossa folks from country never saw such a place. Guv'ner brings 'em—free show—hic—reg'lar circus! Go home tell folks about it. Ole man Jones's place—Jones the packer—beef-trust man. Made it all out of hogs, too, damn ole scoundrel. Now we see where our pennies go—rebates, an' private car lines—hic—by Harry! Bully place, though—worth seein'! Ever hear of Jones the packer, hey, ole chappie?"

Jurgis had started involuntarily; the other, whose sharp eyes missed nothing, demanded: "Whuzzamatter, hey? Heard of him?"

And Jurgis managed to stammer out: "I have worked for him in the yards."

"What!" cried Master Freddie, with a yell. "You! In the yards? Ho, ho! Why, say, thass good! Shake hands on it, ole man—by Harry! Guv'ner ought to be here—glad to see you. Great fren's with the men, guv'ner—labor an' capital, commun'ty 'f int'rests, an' all that—hic! Funny things happen in this world, don't they, ole man? Hamilton, lemme interduce you—fren' the family—ole fren' the guv'ner's—works in the yards. Come to spend the night wiz me, Hamilton—have a hot time. Me fren', Mr.—whuzya name, ole chappie? Tell us your name."

"Rudkus—Jurgis Rudkus."

"My fren', Mr. Rednose, Hamilton—shake han's."

The stately butler bowed his head, but made not a sound; and suddenly Master Freddie pointed an eager finger at him. "I know whuzzamatter wiz you, Hamilton—lay you a dollar I know! You think—hic—you think I'm drunk! Hey, now?"

And the butler again bowed his head. "Yes, sir," he said, at which Master Freddie hung tightly upon Jurgis's neck and went into a fit of laughter. "Hamilton, you damn ole scoundrel," he roared, "I'll 'scharge you for impudence, you see 'f I don't! Ho, ho, ho! I'm drunk! Ho, ho!"

The two waited until his fit had spent itself, to see what new whim would seize him. "Whatcha wanta do?" he queried suddenly. "Wanta see the place, ole chappie? Wamme play the guv'ner—show you roun'? State parlors—Looee Cans— Looee Sez—chairs cost three thousand apiece. Tea room Maryanntnet—picture of shepherds dancing—Ruysdael—twenty-three thousan'! Ballroom—balc'ny pillars—hic—imported—special ship—sixty-eight thousan'! Ceilin' painted in Rome—whuzzat feller's name, Hamilton—Mattatoni? Macaroni? Then this place—silver bowl—Benvenuto Cellini—rummy ole Dago! An' the organ—thirty thousan' dollars, sir—starter up, Hamilton, let Mr. Rednose hear it. No—never mind—clean forgot—says he's hungry, Hamilton—less have some supper. Only—hic—don't less have it here—come up to my place, ole sport—nice an' cosy. This way—steady now, don't slip on the floor. Hamilton, we'll have a cole spread, an' some fizz—don't leave out the fizz, by Harry. We'll have some of the eighteen-thirty Madeira. Hear me, sir?"

"Yes, sir," said the butler, "but, Master Frederick, your father left orders—"

And Master Frederick drew himself up to a stately height. "My father's orders were left to me—hic—an' not to you," he said. Then, clasping Jurgis tightly by the neck, he staggered out of the room; on the way another idea occurred to him, and he asked: "Any—hic—cable message for me, Hamilton?"

"No, sir," said the butler.

"Guv'ner must be travelin'. An' how's the twins, Hamilton?"

"They are doing well, sir."

"Good!" said Master Freddie; and added fervently: "God bless 'em, the little lambs!"

They went up the great staircase, one step at a time; at the top of it there gleamed at them out of the shadows the figure of a nymph crouching by a fountain, a figure ravishingly beautiful, the flesh warm and glowing with the hues of life. Above was a huge court, with domed roof, the various apartments opening into it. The butler had paused below but a few minutes to give orders, and then followed them; now he pressed a button, and the hall blazed with light. He opened a door before them, and then pressed another button, as they staggered into the apartment.

It was fitted up as a study. In the center was a mahogany table, covered with books, and smokers' implements; the walls were decorated with college trophies and colors—flags, posters, photographs and knickknacks—tennis rackets, canoe paddles, golf clubs, and polo sticks. An enormous moose head, with horns six feet across, faced a buffalo head on the opposite wall, while bear and tiger skins covered the polished floor. There were lounging chairs and sofas, window seats covered with soft cushions of fantastic designs; there was one corner fitted in Persian fashion, with a huge canopy and a jeweled lamp beneath. Beyond, a door opened upon a bedroom, and beyond that was a swimming pool of the purest marble, that had cost about forty thousand dollars.

Master Freddie stood for a moment or two, gazing about him; then out of the next room a dog emerged, a monstrous bulldog, the most hideous object that Jurgis had ever laid eyes upon. He yawned, opening a mouth like a dragon's; and he came toward the young man, wagging his tail. "Hello, Dewey!" cried his master. "Been havin' a snooze, ole boy? Well, well—hello there, whuzzamatter?" (The dog was snarling at Jurgis.) "Why, Dewey—this' my fren', Mr. Rednose—

ole fren' the guv'ner's! Mr. Rednose, Admiral Dewey; shake han's—hic. Ain't he a daisy, though—blue ribbon at the New York show—eighty-five hundred at a clip! How's that, hey?"

The speaker sank into one of the big armchairs, and Admiral Dewey crouched beneath it; he did not snarl again, but he never took his eyes off Jurgis. He was perfectly sober, was the Admiral.

The butler had closed the door, and he stood by it, watching Jurgis every second. Now there came footsteps outside, and, as he opened the door a man in livery entered, carrying a folding table, and behind him two men with covered trays. They stood like statues while the first spread the table and set out the contents of the trays upon it. There were cold pates, and thin slices of meat, tiny bread and butter sandwiches with the crust cut off, a bowl of sliced peaches and cream (in January), little fancy cakes, pink and green and yellow and white, and half a dozen ice-cold bottles of wine.

"Thass the stuff for you!" cried Master Freddie, exultantly, as he spied them. "Come 'long, ole chappie, move up."

And he seated himself at the table; the waiter pulled a cork, and he took the bottle and poured three glasses of its contents in succession down his throat. Then he gave a long-drawn sigh, and cried again to Jurgis to seat himself.

The butler held the chair at the opposite side of the table, and Jurgis thought it was to keep him out of it; but finally he understand that it was the other's intention to put it under him, and so he sat down, cautiously and mistrustingly. Master Freddie perceived that the attendants embarrassed him, and he remarked with a nod to them, "You may go."

They went, all save the butler.

"You may go too, Hamilton," he said.

"Master Frederick—" the man began.

"Go!" cried the youngster, angrily. "Damn you, don't you hear me?"

The man went out and closed the door; Jurgis, who was as sharp as he, observed that he took the key out of the lock, in order that he might peer through the keyhole.

Master Frederick turned to the table again. "Now," he said, "go for it."

Jurgis gazed at him doubtingly. "Eat!" cried the other. "Pile in, ole chappie!"

"Don't you want anything?" Jurgis asked.

"Ain't hungry," was the reply—"only thirsty. Kitty and me had some candy—you go on."

So Jurgis began, without further parley. He ate as with two shovels, his fork in one hand and his knife in the other; when he once got started his wolf-hunger got the better of him, and he did not stop for breath until he had cleared every plate. "Gee whiz!" said the other, who had been watching him in wonder.

Then he held Jurgis the bottle. "Lessee you drink now," he said; and Jurgis took the bottle and turned it up to his mouth, and a wonderfully unearthly liquid ecstasy poured down his throat, tickling every nerve of him, thrilling him with joy. He drank the very last drop of it, and then he gave vent to a long-drawn "Ah!"

"Good stuff, hey?" said Freddie, sympathetically; he had leaned back in the big chair, putting his arm behind his head and gazing at Jurgis.

And Jurgis gazed back at him. He was clad in spotless evening dress, was Freddie, and looked very handsome—he was a beautiful boy, with light golden hair and the head of an Antinous. He smiled at Jurgis confidingly, and then started talking again, with his blissful insouciance. This time he talked for ten minutes at a stretch, and in the course of the speech he told Jurgis all of his family history. His big brother Charlie was in love with the guileless maiden who played the part of "Little Bright-Eyes" in "The Kaliph of Kamskatka." He had been on the verge of marrying her once, only "the guv'ner" had sworn to disinherit him, and had presented him with a sum that would stagger the imagination, and that had staggered the virtue of "Little Bright-Eyes." Now Charlie had got leave from college, and had gone away in his automobile on the next best thing to a honeymoon. "The guv'ner" had made threats to disinherit another of his children also, sister Gwendolen, who had married an Italian marquis with a string of titles and a dueling record. They lived in his chateau, or rather had, until he had taken to firing the breakfast dishes at her; then she had cabled for help, and the old gentleman had gone over to find out what were his Grace's terms. So they had left Freddie all alone, and he with less than two thousand dollars in his pocket. Freddie was up in arms and meant serious business, as they would find in the end—if there was no other way of bringing them to terms he would have his "Kittens" wire that she was about to marry him, and see what happened then.

So the cheerful youngster rattled on, until he was tired out. He smiled his sweetest smile at Jurgis, and then he closed his eyes, sleepily. Then he opened them again, and smiled once more, and finally closed them and forgot to open them.

For several minutes Jurgis sat perfectly motionless, watching him, and reveling in the strange sensation of the champagne. Once he stirred, and the dog growled; after that he sat almost holding his breath—until after a while the door of the room opened softly, and the butler came in.

He walked toward Jurgis upon tiptoe, scowling at him; and Jurgis rose up, and retreated, scowling back. So until he was against the wall, and then the butler came close, and pointed toward the door. "Get out of here!" he whispered.

Jurgis hesitated, giving a glance at Freddie, who was snoring softly. "If you do, you son of a—" hissed the butler, "I'll mash in your face for you before you get out of here!"

And Jurgis wavered but an instant more. He saw "Admiral Dewey" coming up behind the man and growling softly, to back up his threats. Then he surrendered and started toward the door.

They went out without a sound, and down the great echoing staircase, and through the dark hall. At the front door he paused, and the butler strode close to him.

"Hold up your hands," he snarled. Jurgis took a step back, clinching his one well fist.

"What for?" he cried; and then understanding that the fellow proposed to search him, he answered, "I'll see you in hell first."

"Do you want to go to jail?" demanded the butler, menacingly. "I'll have the police—"

"Have 'em!" roared Jurgis, with fierce passion. "But you won't put your hands on me till you do! I haven't touched anything in your damned house, and I'll not have you touch me!"

So the butler, who was terrified lest his young master should waken, stepped suddenly to the door, and opened it. "Get out of here!" he said; and then as Jurgis passed through the opening, he gave him a ferocious kick that sent him down the great stone steps at a run, and landed him sprawling in the snow at the bottom.

CHAPTER 25

Jurgis got up, wild with rage, but the door was shut and the great castle was dark and impregnable. Then the icy teeth of the blast bit into him, and he turned and went away at a run.

When he stopped again it was because he was coming to frequented streets and did not wish to attract attention. In spite of that last humiliation, his heart was thumping fast with triumph. He had come out ahead on that deal! He put his hand into his trousers' pocket every now and then, to make sure that the precious hundred-dollar bill was still there.

Yet he was in a plight—a curious and even dreadful plight, when he came to realize it. He had not a single cent but that one bill! And he had to find some shelter that night he had to change it!

Jurgis spent half an hour walking and debating the problem. There was no one he could go to for help—he had to manage it all alone. To get it changed in a lodging-house would be to take his life in his hands—he would almost certainly be robbed, and perhaps murdered, before morning. He might go to some hotel or railroad depot and ask to have it changed; but what would they think, seeing a "bum" like him with a hundred dollars? He would probably be arrested if he tried it; and what story could he tell? On the morrow Freddie Jones would discover his loss, and there would be a hunt for him, and he would lose his money. The only other plan he could think of was to try in a saloon. He might pay them to change it, if it could not be done otherwise.

He began peering into places as he walked; he passed several as being too crowded—then finally, chancing upon one where the bartender was all alone, he gripped his hands in sudden resolution and went in.

"Can you change me a hundred-dollar bill?" he demanded.

The bartender was a big, husky fellow, with the jaw of a prize fighter, and a three weeks' stubble of hair upon it. He stared at Jurgis. "What's that youse say?" he demanded.

"I said, could you change me a hundred-dollar bill?"

"Where'd youse get it?" he inquired incredulously.

"Never mind," said Jurgis; "I've got it, and I want it changed. I'll pay you if you'll do it."

The other stared at him hard. "Lemme see it," he said.

"Will you change it?" Jurgis demanded, gripping it tightly in his pocket.

"How the hell can I know if it's good or not?" retorted the bartender. "Whatcher take me for, hey?"

Then Jurgis slowly and warily approached him; he took out the bill, and fumbled it for a moment, while the man stared at him with hostile eyes across the counter. Then finally he handed it over.

The other took it, and began to examine it; he smoothed it between his fingers, and held it up to the light; he turned it over, and upside down, and edgeways. It was new and rather stiff, and that made him dubious. Jurgis was watching him like a cat all the time.

"Humph," he said, finally, and gazed at the stranger, sizing him up—a ragged, ill-smelling tramp, with no overcoat and one arm in a sling—and a hundred-dollar bill! "Want to buy anything?" he demanded.

"Yes," said Jurgis, "I'll take a glass of beer."

"All right," said the other, "I'll change it." And he put the bill in his pocket, and poured Jurgis out a glass of beer, and set it on the counter. Then he turned to the cash register, and punched up five cents, and began to pull money out of the drawer. Finally, he faced Jurgis, counting it out—two dimes, a quarter, and fifty cents. "There," he said.

For a second Jurgis waited, expecting to see him turn again. "My ninety-nine dollars," he said.

"What ninety-nine dollars?" demanded the bartender.

"My change!" he cried—"the rest of my hundred!"

"Go on," said the bartender, "you're nutty!"

And Jurgis stared at him with wild eyes. For an instant horror reigned in him—black, paralyzing, awful horror, clutching him at the heart; and then came rage, in surging, blinding floods—he screamed aloud, and seized the glass and hurled it at the other's head. The man ducked, and it missed him by half an inch; he rose again and faced Jurgis, who was vaulting over the bar with his one well arm, and dealt him a smashing blow in the face, hurling him backward upon the floor. Then, as Jurgis scrambled to his feet again and started round the counter after him, he shouted at the top of his voice, "Help! help!"

Jurgis seized a bottle off the counter as he ran; and as the bartender made a leap he hurled the missile at him with all his force. It just grazed his head, and shivered into a thousand pieces against the post of the door. Then Jurgis started back, rushing at the man again in the middle of the room. This time, in his blind frenzy, he came without a bottle, and that was all the bartender wanted—he met him halfway and floored him with a sledgehammer drive between the eyes. An instant later the screen doors flew open, and two men rushed in—just as Jurgis was getting to his feet again, foaming at the mouth with rage, and trying to tear his broken arm out of its bandages.

"Look out!" shouted the bartender. "He's got a knife!" Then, seeing that the two were disposed to join the fray, he made another rush at Jurgis, and knocked aside his feeble defense and sent him tumbling again; and the three flung themselves upon him, rolling and kicking about the place.

A second later a policeman dashed in, and the bartender yelled once more—"Look out for his knife!" Jurgis had fought himself half to his knees, when the policeman made a leap at him, and cracked him across the face with his club. Though the blow staggered him, the wild-beast frenzy still blazed in him, and he got to his feet, lunging into the air. Then again the club descended, full upon his head, and he dropped like a log to the floor.

The policeman crouched over him, clutching his stick, waiting for him to try to rise again; and meantime the barkeeper got up, and put his hand to his head. "Christ!" he said, "I thought I was done for that time. Did he cut me?"

"Don't see anything, Jake," said the policeman. "What's the matter with him?"

"Just crazy drunk," said the other. "A lame duck, too—but he 'most got me under the bar. Youse had better call the wagon, Billy."

"No," said the officer. "He's got no more fight in him, I guess—and he's only got a block to go." He twisted his hand in Jurgis's collar and jerked at him. "Git up here, you!" he commanded.

But Jurgis did not move, and the bartender went behind the bar, and after stowing the hundred-dollar bill away in a safe hiding place, came and poured a glass of water over Jurgis. Then, as the latter began to moan feebly, the policeman got him to his feet and dragged him out of the place. The station house was just around the corner, and so in a few minutes Jurgis was in a cell.

He spent half the night lying unconscious, and the balance moaning in torment, with a blinding headache and a racking thirst. Now and then he cried aloud for a drink of water, but there was no one to hear him. There were others in that same station house with split heads and a fever; there were hundreds of them in the great city, and tens of thousands of them in the great land, and there was no one to hear any of them.

In the morning Jurgis was given a cup of water and a piece of bread, and then hustled into a patrol wagon and driven to the nearest police court. He sat in the pen with a score of others until his turn came.

The bartender—who proved to be a well-known bruiser—was called to the stand. He took the oath and told his story. The prisoner had come into his saloon after midnight, fighting drunk, and had ordered a glass of beer and tendered a dollar bill in payment. He had been given ninety-five cents' change, and had demanded ninety-nine dollars more, and before the plaintiff could even answer had hurled the glass at him and then attacked him with a bottle of bitters, and nearly wrecked the place.

Then the prisoner was sworn—a forlorn object, haggard and unshorn, with an arm done up in a filthy bandage, a cheek and head cut, and bloody, and one eye purplish black and entirely closed. "What have you to say for yourself?" queried the magistrate.

"Your Honor," said Jurgis, "I went into his place and asked the man if he could change me a hundred-dollar bill. And he said he would if I bought a drink. I gave him the bill and then he wouldn't give me the change."

The magistrate was staring at him in perplexity. "You gave him a hundred-dollar bill!" he exclaimed.

"Yes, your Honor," said Jurgis.

"Where did you get it?"

"A man gave it to me, your Honor."

"A man? What man, and what for?"

"A young man I met upon the street, your Honor. I had been begging."

There was a titter in the courtroom; the officer who was holding Jurgis put up his hand to hide a smile, and the magistrate smiled without trying to hide it. "It's true, your Honor!" cried Jurgis, passionately.

"You had been drinking as well as begging last night, had you not?" inquired the magistrate. "No, your Honor—" protested Jurgis. "I—"

"You had not had anything to drink?"

"Why, yes, your Honor, I had—"

"What did you have?"

"I had a bottle of something—I don't know what it was—something that burned—"

There was again a laugh round the courtroom, stopping suddenly as the magistrate looked up and frowned. "Have you ever been arrested before?" he asked abruptly.

The question took Jurgis aback. "I—I—" he stammered.

"Tell me the truth, now!" commanded the other, sternly.

"Yes, your Honor," said Jurgis.

"How often?"

"Only once, your Honor."

"What for?"

"For knocking down my boss, your Honor. I was working in the stockyards, and he—"

"I see," said his Honor; "I guess that will do. You ought to stop drinking if you can't control yourself. Ten days and costs. Next case."

Jurgis gave vent to a cry of dismay, cut off suddenly by the policeman, who seized him by the collar. He was jerked out of the way, into a room with the convicted prisoners, where he sat and wept like a child in his impotent rage. It seemed monstrous to him that policemen and judges should esteem his word as nothing in comparison with the bartender's—poor Jurgis could not know that the owner of the saloon paid five dollars each week to the policeman alone for Sunday privileges and general favors—nor that the pugilist bartender was one of the most trusted henchmen of the Democratic leader of the district, and had helped only a few months before to hustle out a record-breaking vote as a testimonial to the magistrate, who had been made the target of odious kid-gloved reformers.

Jurgis was driven out to the Bridewell for the second time. In his tumbling around he had hurt his arm again, and so could not work, but had to be attended by the physician. Also his head and his eye had to be tied up—and so he was a pretty-looking object when, the second day after his arrival, he went out into the exercise court and encountered—Jack Duane!

The young fellow was so glad to see Jurgis that he almost hugged him. "By God, if it isn't 'the Stinker'!" he cried. "And what is it—have you been through a sausage machine?"

"No," said Jurgis, "but I've been in a railroad wreck and a fight." And then, while some of the other prisoners gathered round he told his wild story; most of them were incredulous, but Duane knew that Jurgis could never have made up such a yarn as that.

"Hard luck, old man," he said, when they were alone; "but maybe it's taught you a lesson."

"I've learned some things since I saw you last," said Jurgis mournfully. Then he explained how he had spent the last summer, "hoboing it," as the phrase was. "And you?" he asked finally. "Have you been here ever since?"

"Lord, no!" said the other. "I only came in the day before yesterday. It's the second time they've sent me up on a trumped-up charge—I've had hard luck and can't pay them what they want. Why don't you quit Chicago with me, Jurgis?"

"I've no place to go," said Jurgis, sadly.

"Neither have I," replied the other, laughing lightly. "But we'll wait till we get out and see."

In the Bridewell Jurgis met few who had been there the last time, but he met scores of others, old and young, of exactly the same sort. It was like breakers upon a beach; there was new water, but the wave looked just the same. He strolled about and talked with them, and the biggest of them told tales of their prowess, while those who were weaker, or younger and inexperienced, gathered round and listened in admiring silence. The last time he was there, Jurgis had thought of little but his family; but now he was free to listen to these men, and to realize that he was one of them—that their point of view was his point of view, and that the way they kept themselves alive in the world was the way he meant to do it in the future.

And so, when he was turned out of prison again, without a penny in his pocket, he went straight to Jack Duane. He went full of humility and gratitude; for Duane was a gentleman, and a man with a profession—and it was remarkable that he should be willing to throw in his lot with a humble workingman, one who had even been a beggar and a tramp. Jurgis could not see what help he could be to him; but he did not understand that a man like himself—who could be trusted to stand by any one who was kind to him—was as rare among criminals as among any other class of men.

The address Jurgis had was a garret room in the Ghetto district, the home of a pretty little French girl, Duane's mistress, who sewed all day, and eked out her living by prostitution. He had gone elsewhere, she told Jurgis—he was afraid to stay there now, on account of the police. The new address was a cellar dive, whose proprietor said that he had never heard of Duane; but after he had put Jurgis through a catechism he showed him a back stairs which led to a "fence" in the rear of a pawnbroker's shop, and thence to a number of assignation rooms, in one of which Duane was hiding.

Duane was glad to see him; he was without a cent of money, he said, and had been waiting for Jurgis to help him get some. He explained his plan—in fact he spent the day in laying bare to his friend the criminal world of the city, and in showing him how he might earn himself a living in it. That winter he would have a hard time, on account of his arm, and because of an unwonted fit of activity of the police; but so long as he was unknown to them he would be safe if he were careful. Here at "Papa" Hanson's (so they called the old man who kept the dive) he might rest at ease, for "Papa" Hanson was "square"—would stand by him so long as he paid, and gave him an hour's notice if there were to be a police raid. Also Rosensteg, the pawnbroker, would buy anything he had for a third of its value, and guarantee to keep it hidden for a year.

There was an oil stove in the little cupboard of a room, and they had some supper; and then about eleven o'clock at night they sallied forth together, by a rear entrance to the place, Duane armed with a slingshot. They came to a residence district, and he sprang up a lamppost and blew out the light, and then the two dodged into the shelter of an area step and hid in silence.

Pretty soon a man came by, a workingman—and they let him go. Then after a long interval came the heavy tread of a policeman, and they held their breath till he was gone. Though half-frozen, they waited a full quarter of an hour after that—and then again came footsteps, walking briskly. Duane nudged Jurgis, and the instant the man had passed they rose up. Duane stole out as silently as a shadow, and a second later Jurgis heard a thud and a stifled cry. He was only a couple of feet behind, and he leaped to stop the man's mouth, while Duane held him fast by the arms, as they had agreed. But the man was limp and showed a tendency to fall, and so Jurgis had only to hold him by the collar, while the other, with swift fingers, went through his pockets—ripping open, first his overcoat, and then his coat, and then his vest, searching inside and outside, and transferring the contents into his own pockets. At last, after feeling of the man's fingers and in his necktie, Duane whispered, "That's all!" and they dragged him to the area and dropped him in. Then Jurgis went one way and his friend the other, walking briskly.

The latter arrived first, and Jurgis found him examining the "swag." There was a gold watch, for one thing, with a chain and locket; there was a silver pencil, and a matchbox, and a handful of small change, and finally a card-case. This last Duane opened feverishly—there were letters and checks, and two theater-tickets, and at last, in the back part, a wad of bills. He counted them—there was a twenty, five tens, four fives, and three ones. Duane drew a long breath. "That lets us out!" he said.

After further examination, they burned the card-case and its contents, all but the bills, and likewise the picture of a little girl in the locket. Then Duane took the watch and trinkets downstairs, and came back with sixteen dollars. "The old scoundrel said the case was filled," he said. "It's a lie, but he knows I want the money."

They divided up the spoils, and Jurgis got as his share fifty-five dollars and some change. He protested that it was too much, but the other had agreed to divide even. That was a good haul, he said, better than average.

When they got up in the morning, Jurgis was sent out to buy a paper; one of the pleasures of committing a crime was the reading about it afterward. "I had a pal that always did it," Duane remarked, laughing—"until one day he read that he had left three thousand dollars in a lower inside pocket of his party's vest!"

There was a half-column account of the robbery—it was evident that a gang was operating in the neighborhood, said the paper, for it was the third within a week, and the police were apparently powerless. The victim was an insurance agent, and he had lost a hundred and ten dollars that did not belong to him. He had chanced to have his name marked on his shirt, otherwise he would not have been identified yet. His assailant had hit him too hard, and he was suffering from concussion of the brain; and also he had been half-frozen when found, and would lose three fingers on his right hand. The enterprising newspaper reporter had taken all this information to his family, and told how they had received it.

Since it was Jurgis's first experience, these details naturally caused him some worriment; but the other laughed coolly—it was the way of the game, and there was no helping it. Before long Jurgis would think no more of it than they did in the yards of knocking out a bullock. "It's a case of us or the other fellow, and I say the other fellow, every time," he observed.

"Still," said Jurgis, reflectively, "he never did us any harm."

"He was doing it to somebody as hard as he could, you can be sure of that," said his friend.

Duane had already explained to Jurgis that if a man of their trade were known he would have to work all the time to satisfy the demands of the police. Therefore it would be better for Jurgis to stay in hiding and never be seen in public with his pal. But Jurgis soon got very tired of staying in hiding. In a couple of weeks he was feeling strong and beginning to use his arm, and then he could not stand it any longer. Duane, who had done a job of some sort by himself, and made a truce with the powers, brought over Marie, his little French girl, to share with him; but even that did not avail for long, and in the end he had to give up arguing, and take Jurgis out and introduce him to the saloons and "sporting houses" where the big crooks and "holdup men" hung out.

And so Jurgis got a glimpse of the high-class criminal world of Chicago. The city, which was owned by an oligarchy of business men, being nominally ruled by the people, a huge army of graft was necessary for the purpose of effecting the transfer of power. Twice a year, in the spring and fall elections, millions of dollars were furnished by the business men and expended by this army; meetings were held and clever speakers were hired, bands played and rockets sizzled, tons of documents and reservoirs of drinks were distributed, and tens of thousands of votes were bought for cash. And this army of graft had, of course, to be maintained the year round. The leaders and organizers were maintained by the business men directly—aldermen and legislators by means of bribes, party officials out of the campaign funds, lobbyists and corporation lawyers in the form of salaries, contractors by means of jobs, labor union leaders by subsidies, and newspaper proprietors and editors by advertisements. The rank and file, however, were either foisted upon the city, or else lived off the population directly. There was the police department, and the fire and water departments, and the whole balance of the civil list, from the meanest office boy to the head of a city department; and for the horde who could find no room in these, there was the world of vice and crime, there was license to seduce, to swindle and plunder and prey. The law forbade Sunday drinking; and this had delivered the saloon-keepers into the hands of the police, and made an alliance between them necessary. The law forbade prostitution; and this had brought the "madames" into the combination. It was the same with the gambling-house keeper and the poolroom man, and the same with any other man or woman who had a means of getting "graft," and was willing to pay over a share of it: the green-goods man and the highwayman, the pickpocket and the sneak thief, and the receiver of stolen goods, the seller of adulterated milk, of stale fruit and diseased meat, the proprietor of unsanitary tenements, the fake doctor and the usurer, the beggar and the "pushcart man," the prize fighter and the professional slugger, the race-track "tout," the procurer, the white-slave agent, and the expert seducer of young girls. All of these agencies of corruption were banded together, and leagued in blood brotherhood with the politician and the police; more often than not they were one and the same person,—the police captain would own the brothel he pretended to raid, the politician would open his headquarters in his saloon. "Hinkydink" or "Bathhouse John," or others of that ilk, were proprietors of the most notorious dives in Chicago, and also the "gray wolves" of the city council, who gave away the streets of the city to the business men; and those who patronized their places were the gamblers and prize fighters who set the law at defiance, and the burglars and holdup men who kept the whole city in terror. On election day all these powers of vice and crime were one power; they could tell within one per cent what the vote of their district would be, and they could change it at an hour's notice.

A month ago Jurgis had all but perished of starvation upon the streets; and now suddenly, as by the gift of a magic key, he had entered into a world where money and all the good things of life came freely. He was introduced by his friend to an Irishman named "Buck" Halloran, who was a political "worker" and on the inside of things. This man talked with Jurgis for a while, and then told him that he had a little plan by which a man who looked like a workingman might make some easy money; but it was a private affair, and had to be kept quiet. Jurgis expressed himself as agreeable, and the other took him that afternoon (it was Saturday) to a place where city laborers were being paid off. The paymaster sat in a little booth, with a pile of envelopes before him, and two policemen standing by. Jurgis went, according to directions, and gave the name of "Michael

O'Flaherty," and received an envelope, which he took around the corner and delivered to Halloran, who was waiting for him in a saloon. Then he went again; and gave the name of "Johann Schmidt," and a third time, and give the name of "Serge Reminitsky." Halloran had quite a list of imaginary workingmen, and Jurgis got an envelope for each one. For this work he received five dollars, and was told that he might have it every week, so long as he kept quiet. As Jurgis was excellent at keeping quiet, he soon won the trust of "Buck" Halloran, and was introduced to others as a man who could be depended upon.

This acquaintance was useful to him in another way, also before long Jurgis made his discovery of the meaning of "pull," and just why his boss, Connor, and also the pugilist bartender, had been able to send him to jail. One night there was given a ball, the "benefit" of "One-eyed Larry," a lame man who played the violin in one of the big "high-class" houses of prostitution on Clark Street, and was a wag and a popular character on the "Levee." This ball was held in a big dance hall, and was one of the occasions when the city's powers of debauchery gave themselves up to madness. Jurgis attended and got half insane with drink, and began quarreling over a girl; his arm was pretty strong by then, and he set to work to clean out the place, and ended in a cell in the police station. The police station being crowded to the doors, and stinking with "bums," Jurgis did not relish staying there to sleep off his liquor, and sent for Halloran, who called up the district leader and had Jurgis bailed out by telephone at four o'clock in the morning. When he was arraigned that same morning, the district leader had already seen the clerk of the court and explained that Jurgis Rudkus was a decent fellow, who had been indiscreet; and so Jurgis was fined ten dollars and the fine was "suspended"—which meant that he did not have to pay for it, and never would have to pay it, unless somebody chose to bring it up against him in the future.

Among the people Jurgis lived with now money was valued according to an entirely different standard from that of the people of Packingtown; yet, strange as it may seem, he did a great deal less drinking than he had as a workingman. He had not the same provocations of exhaustion and hopelessness; he had now something to work for, to struggle for. He soon found that if he kept his wits about him, he would come upon new opportunities; and being naturally an active man, he not only kept sober himself, but helped to steady his friend, who was a good deal fonder of both wine and women than he.

One thing led to another. In the saloon where Jurgis met "Buck" Halloran he was sitting late one night with Duane, when a "country customer" (a buyer for an out-of-town merchant) came in, a little more than half "piped." There was no one else in the place but the bartender, and as the man went out again Jurgis and Duane followed him; he went round the corner, and in a dark place made by a combination of the elevated railroad and an unrented building, Jurgis leaped forward and shoved a revolver under his nose, while Duane, with his hat pulled over his eyes, went through the man's pockets with lightning fingers. They got his watch and his "wad," and were round the corner again and into the saloon before he could shout more than once. The bartender, to whom they had tipped the wink, had the cellar door open for them, and they vanished, making their way by a secret entrance to a brothel next door. From the roof of this there was access to three similar places beyond. By means of these passages the customers of any one place could be gotten out of the way, in case a falling out with the police chanced to lead to a raid; and also it was necessary to have a way of getting a girl out of reach in case of an emergency. Thousands of them came to Chicago answering advertisements for "servants" and "factory hands," and found themselves trapped by fake employment agencies, and locked up in a bawdy-house. It was generally enough to take all their clothes away from them; but sometimes they would have to be "doped" and kept prisoners for weeks; and meantime their parents might be telegraphing the police, and even coming on to see why nothing was done. Occasionally there was no way of satisfying them but to let them search the place to which the girl had been traced.

For his help in this little job, the bartender received twenty out of the hundred and thirty odd dollars that the pair secured; and naturally this put them on friendly terms with him, and a few days later he introduced them to a little "sheeny" named Goldberger, one of the "runners" of the "sporting house" where they had been hidden. After a few drinks Goldberger began, with some hesitation, to narrate how he had had a quarrel over his best girl with a professional "cardsharp," who had hit him in the jaw. The fellow was a stranger in Chicago, and if he was found some night with his head cracked there would be no one to care very much. Jurgis, who by this time would cheerfully have cracked the heads of all the gamblers in Chicago, inquired what would be coming to him; at which the Jew became still more confidential, and said that he had some tips on the New Orleans races, which he got direct from the police captain of the district, whom he had got out of a bad scrape, and who "stood in" with a big syndicate of horse owners. Duane took all this in at once, but Jurgis had to have the whole race-track situation explained to him before he realized the importance of such an opportunity.

There was the gigantic Racing Trust. It owned the legislatures in every state in which it did business; it even owned some of the big newspapers, and made public opinion—there was no power in the land that could oppose it unless, perhaps, it were the Poolroom Trust. It built magnificent racing parks all over the country, and by means of enormous purses it lured the people to come, and then it organized a gigantic shell game, whereby it plundered them of hundreds of millions of dollars every year. Horse racing had once been a sport, but nowadays it was a business; a horse could be "doped" and doctored, undertrained or overtrained; it could be made to fall at any moment—or its gait could be broken by lashing it with the whip, which all the spectators would take to be a desperate effort to keep it in the lead. There were scores of such tricks; and sometimes it was the owners who played them and made fortunes, sometimes it was the jockeys and trainers, sometimes it was outsiders, who bribed them—but most of the time it was the chiefs of the trust. Now for instance, they were having winter racing in New Orleans and a syndicate was laying out each day's program in advance, and its agents in all the Northern cities were "milking" the poolrooms. The word came by long-distance telephone in a cipher code, just a little while before each race; and any man who could get the secret had as good as a fortune. If Jurgis did not believe it, he could try it, said the little Jew—let them meet at a certain house on the morrow and make a test. Jurgis was willing, and so was Duane, and so they went to one of the high-class poolrooms where brokers and merchants gambled (with society women in a private room), and they put up ten dollars each upon a horse called "Black Beldame," a six to one shot, and won. For a secret like that they would have done a good many sluggings—but the next day Goldberger informed them that the offending gambler had got wind of what was coming to him, and had skipped the town.

There were ups and downs at the business; but there was always a living, inside of a jail, if not out of it. Early in April the city elections were due, and that meant prosperity for all the powers of graft. Jurgis, hanging round in dives and gambling houses and brothels, met with the heelers of both parties, and from their conversation he came to understand all the ins and outs of the game, and to hear of a number of ways in which he could make himself useful about election time. "Buck" Halloran was a "Democrat," and so Jurgis became a Democrat also; but he was not a bitter one—the Republicans were good fellows, too, and were to have a pile of money in this next campaign. At the last election the Republicans had paid four dollars a vote to the Democrats' three; and "Buck" Halloran sat one night playing cards with Jurgis and another man, who told how Halloran had been charged with the job voting a "bunch" of thirty-seven newly landed Italians, and how he, the narrator, had met the Republican worker who was after the very same gang, and how the three had effected a bargain, whereby the Italians were to vote half and half, for a glass of beer apiece, while the balance of the fund went to the conspirators!

Not long after this, Jurgis, wearying of the risks and vicissitudes of miscellaneous crime, was moved to give up the career for that of a politician. Just at this time there was a tremendous uproar being raised concerning the alliance between the criminals and the police. For the criminal graft was one in which the business men had no direct part—it was what is called a "side line," carried by the police. "Wide open" gambling and debauchery made the city pleasing to "trade," but burglaries and holdups did not. One night it chanced that while Jack Duane was drilling a safe in a clothing store he was caught red-handed by the night watchman, and turned over to a policeman, who chanced to know him well, and who took the responsibility of letting him make his escape. Such a howl from the newspapers followed this that Duane was slated for sacrifice, and barely got out of town in time. And just at that juncture it happened that Jurgis was introduced to a man named Harper whom he recognized as the night watchman at Brown's, who had been instrumental in making him an American citizen, the first year of his arrival at the yards. The other was interested in the coincidence, but did not remember Jurgis—he had handled too many "green ones" in his time, he said. He sat in a dance hall with Jurgis and Halloran until one or two in the morning, exchanging experiences. He had a long story to tell of his quarrel with the superintendent of his department, and how he was now a plain workingman, and a good union man as well. It was not until some months afterward that Jurgis understood that the quarrel with the superintendent had been prearranged, and that Harper was in reality drawing a salary of twenty dollars a week from the packers for an inside report of his union's secret proceedings. The yards were seething with agitation just then, said the man, speaking as a unionist. The people of Packingtown had borne about all that they would bear, and it looked as if a strike might begin any week.

After this talk the man made inquiries concerning Jurgis, and a couple of days later he came to him with an interesting proposition. He was not absolutely certain, he said, but he thought that he could get him a regular salary if he would come to Packingtown and do as he was told, and keep his mouth shut. Harper—"Bush" Harper, he was called—was a right-hand man of Mike Scully, the Democratic boss of the stockyards; and in the coming election there was a peculiar situation. There had come to Scully a proposition to nominate a certain rich brewer who lived upon a swell boulevard that skirted the district, and who coveted the big badge and the "honorable" of an alderman. The brewer was a Jew, and had no brains, but he was harmless, and would put up a rare campaign fund. Scully had accepted the offer, and then gone to the Republicans with a proposition. He was not sure that he could manage the "sheeny," and he did not mean to take any chances with his district; let the Republicans nominate a certain obscure but amiable friend of Scully's, who was now setting tenpins in the cellar of an Ashland Avenue saloon, and he, Scully, would elect him with the "sheeny's" money, and the Republicans might have the glory, which was more than they would get otherwise. In return for this the Republicans would agree to put up no candidate the following year, when Scully himself came up for reelection as the other alderman from the ward. To this the Republicans had assented at once; but the hell of it was—so Harper explained—that the Republicans were all of them fools—a man had to be a fool to be a Republican in the stockyards, where Scully was king. And they didn't know how to work, and of course it would not do for the Democratic workers, the noble redskins of the War Whoop League, to support the Republican openly. The difficulty would not have been so great except for another fact—there had been a curious development in stockyards politics in the last year or two, a new party having leaped into being. They were the Socialists; and it was a devil of a mess, said "Bush" Harper. The one image which the word "Socialist" brought to Jurgis was of poor little Tamoszius Kuszleika, who had called himself one, and would go out with a couple of other men and a soap-box, and shout himself hoarse on a street corner Saturday nights. Tamoszius had tried to explain to Jurgis what it was all about, but Jurgis, who was not of an imaginative turn, had never quite got it straight; at present he was content with his companion's explanation that the Socialists were the enemies of American institutions—could not be bought, and would not combine or make any sort of a "dicker." Mike Scully was very much worried over the opportunity which his last deal gave to them—the stockyards Democrats were furious at the idea of a rich capitalist for their candidate, and while they were changing they might possibly conclude that a Socialist firebrand was preferable to a Republican bum. And so right here was a chance for Jurgis to make himself a place in the world, explained "Bush" Harper; he had been a union man, and he was known in the yards as a workingman; he must have hundreds of acquaintances, and as he had never talked politics with them he might come out as a Republican now without exciting the least suspicion. There were barrels of money for the use of those who could deliver the goods; and Jurgis might count upon Mike Scully, who had never yet gone back on a friend. Just what could he do? Jurgis asked, in some perplexity, and the other explained in detail. To begin with, he would have to go to the yards and work, and he mightn't relish that; but he would have what he earned, as well as the rest that came to him. He would get active in the union again, and perhaps try to get an office, as he, Harper, had; he would tell all his friends the good points of Doyle, the Republican nominee, and the bad ones of the "sheeny"; and then Scully would furnish a meeting place, and he would start the "Young Men's Republican Association," or something of that sort, and have the rich brewer's best beer by the hogshead, and fireworks and speeches, just like the War Whoop League. Surely Jurgis must know hundreds of men who would like that sort of fun; and there would be the regular Republican leaders and workers to help him out, and they would deliver a big enough majority on election day.

When he had heard all this explanation to the end, Jurgis demanded: "But how can I get a job in Packingtown? I'm blacklisted."

At which "Bush" Harper laughed. "I'll attend to that all right," he said.

And the other replied, "It's a go, then; I'm your man." So Jurgis went out to the stockyards again, and was introduced to the political lord of the district, the boss of Chicago's mayor. It was Scully who owned the brick-yards and the dump and the ice pond—though Jurgis did not know it. It was Scully who was to blame for the unpaved street in which Jurgis's child had been drowned; it was Scully who had put into office the magistrate who had first sent Jurgis to jail; it was Scully who was principal stockholder in the company which had sold him the ramshackle tenement, and then robbed him of it. But Jurgis knew none of these things— any more than he knew that Scully was but a tool and puppet of the packers. To him Scully was a mighty power, the "biggest" man he had ever met.

He was a little, dried-up Irishman, whose hands shook. He had a brief talk with his visitor, watching him with his ratlike eyes, and making up his mind about him; and then he gave him a note to Mr. Harmon, one of the head managers of Durham's—

"The bearer, Jurgis Rudkus, is a particular friend of mine, and I would like you to find him a good place, for important reasons. He was once indiscreet, but you will perhaps be so good as to overlook that."

Mr. Harmon looked up inquiringly when he read this. "What does he mean by 'indiscreet'?" he asked.

"I was blacklisted, sir," said Jurgis.

At which the other frowned. "Blacklisted?" he said. "How do you mean?" And Jurgis turned red with embarrassment.

He had forgotten that a blacklist did not exist. "I—that is—I had difficulty in getting a place," he stammered.

"What was the matter?"

"I got into a quarrel with a foreman—not my own boss, sir—and struck him."

"I see," said the other, and meditated for a few moments. "What do you wish to do?" he asked.

"Anything, sir," said Jurgis—"only I had a broken arm this winter, and so I have to be careful."

"How would it suit you to be a night watchman?"

"That wouldn't do, sir. I have to be among the men at night."

"I see—politics. Well, would it suit you to trim hogs?"

"Yes, sir," said Jurgis.

And Mr. Harmon called a timekeeper and said, "Take this man to Pat Murphy and tell him to find room for him somehow."

And so Jurgis marched into the hog-killing room, a place where, in the days gone by, he had come begging for a job. Now he walked jauntily, and smiled to himself, seeing the frown that came to the boss's face as the timekeeper said, "Mr. Harmon says to put this man on." It would overcrowd his department and spoil the record he was trying to make—but he said not a word except "All right."

And so Jurgis became a workingman once more; and straightway he sought out his old friends, and joined the union, and began to "root" for "Scotty" Doyle. Doyle had done him a good turn once, he explained, and was really a bully chap; Doyle was a workingman himself, and would represent the workingmen—why did they want to vote for a millionaire "sheeny," and what the hell had Mike Scully ever done for them that they should back his candidates all the time? And meantime Scully had given Jurgis a note to the Republican leader of the ward, and he had gone there and met the crowd he was to work with. Already they had hired a big hall, with some of the brewer's money, and every night Jurgis brought in a dozen new members of the "Doyle Republican Association." Pretty soon they had a grand opening night; and there was a brass band, which marched through the streets, and fireworks and bombs and red lights in front of the hall; and there was an enormous crowd, with two overflow meetings—so that the pale and trembling candidate had to recite three times over the little speech which one of Scully's henchmen had written, and which he had been a month learning by heart. Best of all, the famous and eloquent Senator Spareshanks, presidential candidate, rode out in an automobile to discuss the sacred privileges of American citizenship, and protection and prosperity for the American workingman. His inspiriting address was quoted to the extent of half a column in all the morning newspapers, which also said that it could be stated upon excellent authority that the unexpected popularity developed by Doyle, the Republican candidate for alderman, was giving great anxiety to Mr. Scully, the chairman of the Democratic City Committee.

The chairman was still more worried when the monster torchlight procession came off, with the members of the Doyle Republican Association all in red capes and hats, and free beer for every voter in the ward—the best beer ever given away in a political campaign, as the whole electorate testified. During this parade, and at innumerable cart-tail meetings as well, Jurgis labored tirelessly. He did not make any speeches—there were lawyers and other experts for that—but he helped to manage things; distributing notices and posting placards and bringing out the crowds; and when the show was on he attended to the fireworks and the beer. Thus in the course of the campaign he handled many hundreds of dollars of the Hebrew brewer's money, administering it with naive and touching fidelity. Toward the end, however, he learned that he was regarded with hatred by the rest of the "boys," because he compelled them either to make a poorer showing than he or to do without their share of the pie. After that Jurgis did his best to please them, and to make up for the time he had lost before he discovered the extra bungholes of the campaign barrel.

He pleased Mike Scully, also. On election morning he was out at four o'clock, "getting out the vote"; he had a two-horse carriage to ride in, and he went from house to house for his friends, and escorted them in triumph to the polls. He voted half a dozen times himself, and voted some of his friends as often; he brought bunch after bunch of the newest foreigners—Lithuanians, Poles, Bohemians, Slovaks—and when he had put them through the mill he turned them over to another man to take to the next polling place. When Jurgis first set out, the captain of the precinct gave him a hundred dollars, and three times in the course of the day he came for another hundred, and not more than twenty-five out of each lot got stuck in his own pocket. The balance all went for actual votes, and on a day of Democratic landslides they elected "Scotty" Doyle, the ex-tenpin setter, by nearly a thousand plurality—and beginning at five o'clock in the afternoon, and ending at three the next morning, Jurgis treated himself to a most unholy and horrible "jag." Nearly every one else in Packingtown did the same, however, for there was universal exultation over this triumph of popular government, this crushing defeat of an arrogant plutocrat by the power of the common people.

CHAPTER 26

After the elections Jurgis stayed on in Packingtown and kept his job. The agitation to break up the police protection of criminals was continuing, and it seemed to him best to "lay low" for the present. He had nearly three hundred dollars in the bank, and might have considered himself entitled to a vacation; but he had an easy job, and force of habit kept him at it. Besides, Mike Scully, whom he consulted, advised him that something might "turn up" before long.

Jurgis got himself a place in a boardinghouse with some congenial friends. He had already inquired of Aniele, and learned that Elzbieta and her family had gone downtown, and so he gave no further thought to them. He went with a new set, now, young unmarried fellows who were "sporty." Jurgis had long ago cast off his fertilizer clothing, and since going into politics he had donned a linen collar and a greasy red necktie. He had some reason for thinking of his dress, for he was making about eleven dollars a week, and two-thirds of it he might spend upon his pleasures without ever touching his savings.

Sometimes he would ride down-town with a party of friends to the cheap theaters and the music halls and other haunts with which they were familiar. Many of the saloons in Packingtown had pool tables, and some of them bowling alleys, by means of which he could spend his evenings in petty gambling. Also, there were cards and dice. One time Jurgis got into a game on a Saturday night and won prodigiously, and because he was a man of spirit he stayed in with the rest and the game continued until late Sunday afternoon, and by that time he was "out" over twenty dollars. On Saturday nights, also, a number of balls were generally given in Packingtown; each man would bring his "girl" with him, paying half a dollar for a ticket, and several dollars additional for drinks in the course of the festivities, which continued until three or four o'clock in the morning, unless broken up by fighting. During all this time the same man and woman would dance together, half-stupefied with sensuality and drink.

Before long Jurgis discovered what Scully had meant by something "turning up." In May the agreement between the packers and the unions expired, and a new agreement had to be signed. Negotiations were going on, and the yards were full of talk of a strike. The old scale had dealt with the wages of the skilled men only; and of the members of the Meat Workers' Union about two-thirds were unskilled men. In Chicago these latter were receiving, for the most part, eighteen and a half cents an hour, and the unions wished to make this the general wage for the next year. It was not nearly so large a wage as it seemed—in the course of the negotiations the union officers examined time checks to the amount of ten thousand dollars, and they found that the highest wages paid had been fourteen dollars a week, and the lowest two dollars and five cents, and the average of the whole, six dollars and sixty-five cents. And six dollars and sixty-five cents was hardly too much for a man to keep a family on, considering the fact that the price of dressed meat had increased nearly fifty per cent in the last five years, while the price of "beef on the hoof" had decreased as much, it would have seemed that the packers ought to be able to pay it; but the packers were unwilling to pay it—they rejected the union demand, and to show what their purpose was, a week or two after the agreement expired they put down the wages of about a thousand men to sixteen and a half cents, and it was said that old man Jones had vowed he would put them to fifteen before he got through. There were a million and a half of men in the country looking for work, a hundred thousand of them right in Chicago; and were the packers to let the union stewards march into their places and bind them to a contract that would lose them several thousand dollars a day for a year? Not much!

All this was in June; and before long the question was submitted to a referendum in the unions, and the decision was for a strike. It was the same in all the packing house cities; and suddenly the newspapers and public woke up to face the gruesome spectacle of a meat famine. All sorts of pleas for a reconsideration were made, but the packers were obdurate; and all the while they were reducing wages, and heading off shipments of cattle, and rushing in wagon-loads of mattresses and cots. So the men boiled over, and one night telegrams went out from the union headquarters to all the big packing centers—to St. Paul, South Omaha, Sioux City, St. Joseph, Kansas City, East St. Louis, and New York—and the next day at noon between fifty and sixty thousand men drew off their working clothes and marched out of the factories, and the great "Beef Strike" was on.

Jurgis went to his dinner, and afterward he walked over to see Mike Scully, who lived in a fine house, upon a street which had been decently paved and lighted for his especial benefit. Scully had gone into semi-retirement, and looked nervous and worried. "What do you want?" he demanded, when he saw Jurgis.

"I came to see if maybe you could get me a place during the strike," the other replied.

And Scully knit his brows and eyed him narrowly. In that morning's papers Jurgis had read a fierce denunciation of the packers by Scully, who had declared that if they did not treat their people better the city authorities would end the matter by tearing down their plants. Now, therefore, Jurgis was not a little taken aback when the other demanded suddenly, "See here, Rudkus, why don't you stick by your job?"

Jurgis started. "Work as a scab?" he cried.

"Why not?" demanded Scully. "What's that to you?"

"But—but—" stammered Jurgis. He had somehow taken it for granted that he should go out with his union. "The packers need good men, and need them bad," continued the other, "and they'll treat a man right that stands by them. Why don't you take your chance and fix yourself?"

"But," said Jurgis, "how could I ever be of any use to you—in politics?"

"You couldn't be it anyhow," said Scully, abruptly.

"Why not?" asked Jurgis.

"Hell, man!" cried the other. "Don't you know you're a Republican? And do you think I'm always going to elect Republicans? My brewer has found out already how we served him, and there is the deuce to pay."

Jurgis looked dumfounded. He had never thought of that aspect of it before. "I could be a Democrat," he said.

"Yes," responded the other, "but not right away; a man can't change his politics every day. And besides, I don't need you—there'd be nothing for you to do. And it's a long time to election day, anyhow; and what are you going to do meantime?"

"I thought I could count on you," began Jurgis.

"Yes," responded Scully, "so you could—I never yet went back on a friend. But is it fair to leave the job I got you and come to me for another? I have had a hundred fellows after me today, and what can I do? I've put seventeen men on the city payroll to clean streets this one week, and do you think I can keep that up forever? It wouldn't do for me to tell other men what I tell you, but you've been on the inside, and you ought to have sense enough to see for yourself. What have you to gain by a strike?"

"I hadn't thought," said Jurgis.

"Exactly," said Scully, "but you'd better. Take my word for it, the strike will be over in a few days, and the men will be beaten; and meantime what you can get out of it will belong to you. Do you see?"

And Jurgis saw. He went back to the yards, and into the workroom. The men had left a long line of hogs in various stages of preparation, and the foreman was directing the feeble efforts of a score or two of clerks and stenographers and office boys to finish up the job and get them into the chilling rooms. Jurgis went straight up to him and announced, "I have come back to work, Mr. Murphy."

The boss's face lighted up. "Good man!" he cried. "Come ahead!"

"Just a moment," said Jurgis, checking his enthusiasm. "I think I ought to get a little more wages."

"Yes," replied the other, "of course. What do you want?"

Jurgis had debated on the way. His nerve almost failed him now, but he clenched his hands. "I think I ought to have' three dollars a day," he said.

"All right," said the other, promptly; and before the day was out our friend discovered that the clerks and stenographers and office boys were getting five dollars a day, and then he could have kicked himself!

So Jurgis became one of the new "American heroes," a man whose virtues merited comparison with those of the martyrs of Lexington and Valley Forge. The resemblance was not complete, of course, for Jurgis was generously paid and comfortably clad, and was provided with a spring cot and a mattress and three substantial meals a day; also he was perfectly at ease, and safe from all peril of life and limb, save only in the case that a desire for beer should lead him to venture outside of the stockyards gates. And even in the exercise of this privilege he was not left unprotected; a good part of the inadequate police force of Chicago was suddenly diverted from its work of hunting criminals, and rushed out to serve him. The police, and the strikers also, were determined that there should be no violence; but there was another party interested which was minded to the contrary—and that was the press. On the first day of his life as a strikebreaker Jurgis quit work early, and in a spirit of bravado he challenged three men of his acquaintance to go outside and get a drink. They accepted, and went through the big Halsted Street gate, where several policemen were watching, and also some union pickets, scanning sharply those who passed in and out. Jurgis and his companions went south on Halsted Street; past the hotel, and then suddenly half a dozen men started across the street toward them and proceeded to argue with them concerning the error of their ways. As the arguments were not taken in the proper spirit, they went on to threats; and suddenly one of them jerked off the hat of one of the four and flung it over the fence. The man started after it, and then, as a cry of "Scab!" was raised and a dozen people came running out of saloons and doorways, a second man's heart failed him and he followed. Jurgis and the fourth stayed long enough to give themselves the satisfaction of a quick exchange of blows, and then they, too, took to their heels and fled back of the hotel and into the yards again. Meantime, of course, policemen were coming on a run, and as a crowd gathered other police got excited and sent in a riot call. Jurgis knew nothing of this, but went back to "Packers' Avenue," and in front of the "Central Time Station" he saw one of his companions, breathless and wild with excitement, narrating to an ever growing throng how the four had been attacked and surrounded by a howling mob, and had been nearly torn to pieces. While he stood listening, smiling cynically, several dapper young men stood by with notebooks in their hands, and it was not more than two hours later that Jurgis saw newsboys running about with armfuls of newspapers, printed in red and black letters six inches high:

VIOLENCE IN THE YARDS! STRIKEBREAKERS SURROUNDED BY FRENZIED MOB!

If he had been able to buy all of the newspapers of the United States the next morning, he might have discovered that his beer-hunting exploit was being perused by some two score millions of people, and had served as a text for editorials in half the staid and solemn business-men's newspapers in the land.

Jurgis was to see more of this as time passed. For the present, his work being over, he was free to ride into the city, by a railroad direct from the yards, or else to spend the night in a room where cots had been laid in rows. He chose the latter, but to his regret, for all night long gangs of strikebreakers kept arriving. As very few of the better class of workingmen could be got for such work, these specimens of the new American hero contained an assortment of the criminals and thugs of the city, besides Negroes and the lowest foreigners—Greeks, Roumanians, Sicilians, and Slovaks. They had been attracted more by the prospect of disorder than by the big wages; and they made the night hideous with singing and carousing, and only went to sleep when the time came for them to get up to work.

In the morning before Jurgis had finished his breakfast, "Pat" Murphy ordered him to one of the superintendents, who questioned him as to his experience in the work of the killing room. His heart began to thump with excitement, for he divined instantly that his hour had come—that he was to be a boss!

Some of the foremen were union members, and many who were not had gone out with the men. It was in the killing department that the packers had been left most in the lurch, and precisely here that they could least afford it; the smoking and canning and salting of meat might wait, and all the by-products might be wasted—but fresh meats must be had, or the restaurants and hotels and brownstone houses would feel the pinch, and then "public opinion" would take a startling turn.

An opportunity such as this would not come twice to a man; and Jurgis seized it. Yes, he knew the work, the whole of it, and he could teach it to others. But if he took the job and gave satisfaction he would expect to keep it—they would not turn him off at the end of the strike? To which the superintendent replied that he might safely trust Durham's for that—they proposed to teach these unions a lesson, and most of all those foremen who had gone back on them. Jurgis would receive five dollars a day during the strike, and twenty-five a week after it was settled.

So our friend got a pair of "slaughter pen" boots and "jeans," and flung himself at his task. It was a weird sight, there on the killing beds—a throng of stupid black Negroes, and foreigners who could not understand a word that was said to them, mixed with pale-faced, hollow-chested bookkeepers and clerks, half-fainting for the tropical heat and the sickening stench of fresh blood—and all struggling to dress a dozen or two cattle in the same place where, twenty-four hours ago, the old killing gang had been speeding, with their marvelous precision, turning out four hundred carcasses every hour!

The Negroes and the "toughs" from the Levee did not want to work, and every few minutes some of them would feel obliged to retire and recuperate. In a couple of days Durham and Company had electric fans up to cool off the rooms for them, and even couches for them to rest on; and meantime they could go out and find a shady corner and take a "snooze," and as there was no place for any one in particular, and no system, it might be hours before their boss discovered them. As for the poor office employees, they did their best, moved to it by terror; thirty of them had been "fired" in a bunch that first morning for refusing to serve, besides a number of women clerks and typewriters who had declined to act as waitresses.

It was such a force as this that Jurgis had to organize. He did his best, flying here and there, placing them in rows and showing them the tricks; he had never given an order in his life before, but he had taken enough of them to know, and he soon fell into the spirit of it, and roared and stormed like any old stager. He had not the most tractable pupils, however. "See hyar, boss," a big black "buck" would begin, "ef you doan' like de way Ah does dis job, you kin get somebody else to do it." Then a crowd would gather and listen, muttering threats. After the first meal nearly all the steel knives had been missing, and now every Negro had one, ground to a fine point, hidden in his boots.

There was no bringing order out of such a chaos, Jurgis soon discovered; and he fell in with the spirit of the thing—there was no reason why he should wear himself out with shouting. If hides and guts were slashed and rendered useless there was no way of tracing it to any one; and if a man lay off and forgot to come back there was nothing to be gained by seeking him, for all the rest would quit in the meantime. Everything went, during the strike, and the packers paid. Before long Jurgis found that the custom of resting had suggested to some alert minds the possibility of registering at more than one place and earning more than one five dollars a day. When he caught a man at this he "fired" him, but it chanced to be in a quiet corner, and the man tendered him a ten-dollar bill and a wink, and he took them. Of course, before long this custom spread, and Jurgis was soon making quite a good income from it.

In the face of handicaps such as these the packers counted themselves lucky if they could kill off the cattle that had been crippled in transit and the hogs that had developed disease. Frequently, in the course of a two or three days' trip, in hot weather and without water, some hog would develop cholera, and die; and the rest would attack him before he had ceased kicking, and when the car was opened there would be nothing of him left but the bones. If all the hogs in this carload were not killed at once, they would soon be down with the dread disease, and there would be nothing to do but make them into lard. It was the same with cattle that were gored and dying, or were limping with broken bones stuck through their flesh—they must be killed, even if brokers and buyers and superintendents had to take off their coats and help drive and cut and skin them. And meantime, agents of the packers were gathering gangs of Negroes in the country districts of the far South, promising them five dollars a day and board, and being careful not to mention there was a strike; already carloads of them were on the way, with special rates from the railroads, and all traffic ordered out of the way. Many towns and cities were taking advantage of the chance to clear out their jails and workhouses—in Detroit the magistrates would release every man who agreed to leave town within twenty-four hours, and agents of the packers were in the courtrooms to ship them right. And meantime trainloads of supplies were coming in for their accommodation, including beer and whisky, so that they might not be tempted to go outside. They hired thirty young girls in Cincinnati to "pack fruit," and when they arrived put them at work canning corned beef, and put cots for them to sleep in a public hallway, through which the men passed. As the gangs came in day and night, under the escort of squads of police, they stowed away in unused workrooms and storerooms, and in the car sheds, crowded so closely together that the cots touched. In some places they would use the same room for eating and sleeping, and at night the men would put their cots upon the tables, to keep away from the swarms of rats.

But with all their best efforts, the packers were demoralized. Ninety per cent of the men had walked out; and they faced the task of completely remaking their labor force—and with the price of meat up thirty per cent, and the public clamoring for a settlement. They made an offer to submit the whole question at issue to arbitration; and at the end of ten days the unions accepted it, and the strike was called off. It was agreed that all the men were to be re-employed within forty-five days, and that there was to be "no discrimination against union men."

This was an anxious time for Jurgis. If the men were taken back "without discrimination," he would lose his present place. He sought out the superintendent, who smiled grimly and bade him "wait and see." Durham's strikebreakers were few of them leaving.

Whether or not the "settlement" was simply a trick of the packers to gain time, or whether they really expected to break the strike and cripple the unions by the plan, cannot be said; but that night there went out from the office of Durham and Company a telegram to all the big packing centers, "Employ no union leaders." And in the morning, when the twenty thousand men thronged into the yards, with their dinner pails and working clothes, Jurgis stood near the door of the hog-trimming room, where he had worked before the strike, and saw a throng of eager men, with a score or two of policemen watching them; and he saw a superintendent come out and walk down the line, and pick out man after man that pleased him; and one after another came, and there were some men up near the head of the line who were never picked—they being the union stewards and delegates, and the men Jurgis had heard making speeches at the meetings. Each time, of course, there were louder murmurings and angrier looks. Over where the cattle butchers were waiting, Jurgis heard shouts and saw a crowd, and he hurried there. One big butcher, who was president of the Packing Trades Council, had been passed over five times, and the men were wild with rage; they had appointed a committee of three to go in and see the superintendent, and the committee had made three attempts, and each time the police had clubbed them back from the door. Then there were yells and hoots, continuing until at last the superintendent came to the door. "We all go back or none of us do!" cried a hundred voices. And the other shook his fist at them, and shouted, "You went out of here like cattle, and like cattle you'll come back!"

Then suddenly the big butcher president leaped upon a pile of stones and yelled: "It's off, boys. We'll all of us quit again!" And so the cattle butchers declared a new strike on the spot; and gathering their members from the other plants, where the same trick had been played, they marched down Packers' Avenue, which was thronged with a dense mass of workers, cheering wildly. Men who had already got to work on the killing beds dropped their tools and joined them; some galloped here and there on horseback, shouting the tidings, and within half an hour the whole of Packingtown was on strike again, and beside itself with fury.

There was quite a different tone in Packingtown after this—the place was a seething caldron of passion, and the "scab" who ventured into it fared badly. There were one or two of these incidents each day, the newspapers detailing them, and always blaming them upon the unions. Yet ten years before, when there were no unions in Packingtown, there was a strike, and national troops had to be called, and there were pitched battles fought at night, by the light of blazing freight trains. Packingtown was always a center of violence; in "Whisky Point," where there were a hundred saloons and one glue factory, there was always fighting, and always more of it in hot weather. Any one who had taken the trouble to consult the station house blotter would have found that there was less violence that summer than ever before—and this while twenty thousand men were out of work, and with nothing to do all day but brood upon bitter wrongs. There was no one to picture the battle the union leaders were fighting—to hold this huge army in rank, to keep it from straggling and pillaging, to cheer and encourage and guide a hundred thousand people, of a dozen different tongues, through six long weeks of hunger and disappointment and despair.

Meantime the packers had set themselves definitely to the task of making a new labor force. A thousand or two of strikebreakers were brought in every night, and distributed among the various plants. Some of them were experienced workers,—butchers, salesmen, and managers from the packers' branch stores, and a few union men who had deserted from other cities; but the vast majority were "green" Negroes from the cotton districts of the far South, and they were herded into the packing plants like sheep. There was a law forbidding the use of buildings as lodginghouses unless they were licensed for the purpose, and provided with proper windows, stairways, and fire escapes; but here, in a "paint room," reached only by an enclosed "chute," a room without a single window and only one door, a hundred men were crowded upon mattresses on the floor. Up on the third story of the "hog house" of Jones's was a storeroom, without a window, into which they crowded seven hundred men, sleeping upon the bare springs of cots, and with a second shift to use them by day. And when the clamor of the public led to an investigation into these conditions, and the mayor of the city was forced to order the enforcement of the law, the packers got a judge to issue an injunction forbidding him to do it!

Just at this time the mayor was boasting that he had put an end to gambling and prize fighting in the city; but here a swarm of professional gamblers had leagued themselves with the police to fleece the strikebreakers; and any night, in the big open space in front of Brown's, one might see brawny Negroes stripped to the waist and pounding each other for money, while a howling throng of three or four thousand surged about, men and women, young white girls from the country rubbing elbows with big buck Negroes with daggers in their boots, while rows of woolly heads peered down from every window of the surrounding factories. The ancestors of these black people had been savages in Africa; and since then they had been chattel slaves, or had been held down by a community ruled by the traditions of slavery. Now for the first time they were free—free to gratify every passion, free to wreck themselves. They were wanted to break a strike, and when it was broken they would be shipped away, and their present masters would never see them again; and so whisky and women were brought in by the carload and sold to them, and hell was let loose in the yards. Every night there were stabbings and shootings; it was said that the packers had blank permits, which enabled them to ship dead bodies from the city without troubling the authorities. They lodged men and women on the same floor; and with the night there began a saturnalia of debauchery—scenes such as never before had been witnessed in America. And as the women were the dregs from the brothels of Chicago, and the men were for the most part ignorant country Negroes, the nameless diseases of vice were soon rife; and this where food was being handled which was sent out to every corner of the civilized world.

The "Union Stockyards" were never a pleasant place; but now they were not only a collection of slaughterhouses, but also the camping place of an army of fifteen or twenty thousand human beasts. All day long the blazing midsummer sun beat down upon that square mile of abominations: upon tens of thousands of cattle crowded into pens whose wooden floors stank and steamed contagion; upon bare, blistering, cinder-strewn railroad tracks, and huge blocks of dingy meat factories, whose labyrinthine passages defied a breath of fresh air to penetrate them; and there were not merely rivers of hot blood, and car-loads of moist flesh, and rendering vats and soap caldrons, glue factories and fertilizer tanks, that smelt like the craters of hell—there were also tons of garbage festering in the sun, and the greasy laundry of the workers hung out to dry, and dining rooms littered with food and black with flies, and toilet rooms that were open sewers.

And then at night, when this throng poured out into the streets to play—fighting, gambling, drinking and carousing, cursing and screaming, laughing and singing, playing banjoes and dancing! They were worked in the yards all the seven days of the week, and they had their prize fights and crap games on Sunday nights as well; but then around the corner one might see a bonfire blazing, and an old, gray-headed Negress, lean and witchlike, her hair flying wild and her eyes blazing, yelling and chanting of the fires of perdition and the blood of the "Lamb," while men and women lay down upon the ground and moaned and screamed in convulsions of terror and remorse.

Such were the stockyards during the strike; while the unions watched in sullen despair, and the country clamored like a greedy child for its food, and the packers went grimly on their way. Each day they added new workers, and could be more stern with the old ones—could put them on piecework, and dismiss them if they did not keep up the pace. Jurgis was now one of their agents in this process; and he could feel the change day by day, like the slow starting up of a huge machine. He had gotten used to being a master of men; and because of the stifling heat and the stench, and the fact that he was a "scab" and knew it and despised himself. He was drinking, and developing a villainous temper, and he stormed and cursed and raged at his men, and drove them until they were ready to drop with exhaustion.

Then one day late in August, a superintendent ran into the place and shouted to Jurgis and his gang to drop their work and come. They followed him outside, to where, in the midst of a dense throng, they saw several two-horse trucks waiting, and three patrol-wagon loads of police. Jurgis and his men sprang upon one of the trucks, and the driver yelled to the crowd, and they went thundering away at a gallop. Some steers had just escaped from the yards, and the strikers had got hold of them, and there would be the chance of a scrap!

They went out at the Ashland Avenue gate, and over in the direction of the "dump." There was a yell as soon as they were sighted, men and women rushing out of houses and saloons as they galloped by. There were eight or ten policemen on the truck, however, and there was no disturbance until they came to a place where the street was blocked with a dense throng. Those on the flying truck yelled a warning and the crowd scattered pell-mell, disclosing one of the steers lying in its blood. There were a good many cattle butchers about just then, with nothing much to do, and hungry children at home; and so some one had knocked out the steer—and as a first-class man can kill and dress one in a couple of minutes, there were a good many steaks and roasts already missing. This called for punishment, of course; and the police proceeded to administer it by leaping from the truck and cracking at every head they saw. There were yells of rage and pain, and the terrified people fled into houses and stores, or scattered helter-skelter down the street. Jurgis and his gang joined in the sport, every man singling out his victim, and striving to bring him to bay and punch him. If he fled into a house his pursuer would smash in the flimsy door and follow him up the stairs, hitting every one who came within reach, and finally dragging his squealing quarry from under a bed or a pile of old clothes in a closet.

Jurgis and two policemen chased some men into a bar-room. One of them took shelter behind the bar, where a policeman cornered him and proceeded to whack him over the back and shoulders, until he lay down and gave a chance at his head. The others leaped a fence in the rear, balking the second policeman, who was fat; and as he came back, furious and cursing, a big Polish woman, the owner of the saloon, rushed in screaming, and received a poke in the stomach that doubled her up on the floor. Meantime Jurgis, who was of a practical temper, was helping himself at the bar; and the first policeman, who had laid out his man, joined him, handing out several more bottles, and filling his pockets besides, and then, as he started to leave, cleaning off all the balance with a sweep of his club. The din of the glass crashing to the floor brought the fat Polish woman to her feet again, but another policeman came up behind her and put his knee into her back and his hands over her eyes—and then called to his companion, who went back and broke open the cash drawer and filled his pockets with the contents. Then the three went outside, and the man who was holding the woman gave her a shove and dashed out himself. The gang having already got the carcass on to the truck, the party set out at a trot, followed by screams and curses, and a shower of bricks and stones from unseen enemies. These bricks and stones would figure in the accounts of the "riot" which would be sent out to a few thousand newspapers within an hour or two; but the episode of the cash drawer would never be mentioned again, save only in the heartbreaking legends of Packingtown.

It was late in the afternoon when they got back, and they dressed out the remainder of the steer, and a couple of others that had been killed, and then knocked off for the day. Jurgis went downtown to supper, with three friends who had been on the other trucks, and they exchanged reminiscences on the way. Afterward they drifted into a roulette parlor, and Jurgis, who was never lucky at gambling, dropped about fifteen dollars. To console himself he had to drink a good deal, and he went back to Packingtown about two o'clock in the morning, very much the worse for his excursion, and, it must be confessed, entirely deserving the calamity that was in store for him.

As he was going to the place where he slept, he met a painted-cheeked woman in a greasy "kimono," and she put her arm about his waist to steady him; they turned into a dark room they were passing—but scarcely had they taken two steps before suddenly a door swung open, and a man entered, carrying a lantern. "Who's there?" he called sharply. And Jurgis started to mutter some reply; but at the same instant the man raised his light, which flashed in his face, so that it was possible to recognize him. Jurgis stood stricken dumb, and his heart gave a leap like a mad thing. The man was Connor!

Connor, the boss of the loading gang! The man who had seduced his wife—who had sent him to prison, and wrecked his home, ruined his life! He stood there, staring, with the light shining full upon him.

Jurgis had often thought of Connor since coming back to Packingtown, but it had been as of something far off, that no longer concerned him. Now, however, when he saw him, alive and in the flesh, the same thing happened to him that had happened before—a flood of rage boiled up in him, a blind frenzy seized him. And he flung himself at the man, and smote him between the eyes—and then, as he fell, seized him by the throat and began to pound his head upon the stones.

The woman began screaming, and people came rushing in. The lantern had been upset and extinguished, and it was so dark they could not see a thing; but they could hear Jurgis panting, and hear the thumping of his victim's skull, and they rushed there and tried to pull him off. Precisely as before, Jurgis came away with a piece of his enemy's flesh between his teeth; and, as before, he went on fighting with those who had interfered with him, until a policeman had come and beaten him into insensibility.

And so Jurgis spent the balance of the night in the stockyards station house. This time, however, he had money in his pocket, and when he came to his senses he could get something to drink, and also a messenger to take word of his plight to "Bush" Harper. Harper did not appear, however, until after the prisoner, feeling very weak and ill, had been hailed into court and remanded at five hundred dollars' bail to await the result of his victim's injuries. Jurgis was wild about this, because a different magistrate had chanced to be on the bench, and he had stated that he had never been arrested before, and also that he had been attacked first—

and if only someone had been there to speak a good word for him, he could have been let off at once.

But Harper explained that he had been downtown, and had not got the message. "What's happened to you?" he asked.

"I've been doing a fellow up," said Jurgis, "and I've got to get five hundred dollars' bail."

"I can arrange that all right," said the other—"though it may cost you a few dollars, of course. But what was the trouble?"

"It was a man that did me a mean trick once," answered Jurgis.

"Who is he?"

"He's a foreman in Brown's or used to be. His name's Connor."

And the other gave a start. "Connor!" he cried. "Not Phil Connor!"

"Yes," said Jurgis, "that's the fellow. Why?"

"Good God!" exclaimed the other, "then you're in for it, old man! I can't help you!"

"Not help me! Why not?"

"Why, he's one of Scully's biggest men—he's a member of the War-Whoop League, and they talked of sending him to the legislature! Phil Connor! Great heavens!"

Jurgis sat dumb with dismay.

"Why, he can send you to Joliet, if he wants to!" declared the other.

"Can't I have Scully get me off before he finds out about it?" asked Jurgis, at length.

"But Scully's out of town," the other answered. "I don't even know where he is—he's run away to dodge the strike."

That was a pretty mess, indeed. Poor Jurgis sat half-dazed. His pull had run up against a bigger pull, and he was down and out! "But what am I going to do?" he asked, weakly.

"How should I know?" said the other. "I shouldn't even dare to get bail for you—why, I might ruin myself for life!"

Again there was silence. "Can't you do it for me," Jurgis asked, "and pretend that you didn't know who I'd hit?"

"But what good would that do you when you came to stand trial?" asked Harper. Then he sat buried in thought for a minute or two. "There's nothing—unless it's this," he said. "I could have your bail reduced; and then if you had the money you could pay it and skip."

"How much will it be?" Jurgis asked, after he had had this explained more in detail.

"I don't know," said the other. "How much do you own?"

"I've got about three hundred dollars," was the answer.

"Well," was Harper's reply, "I'm not sure, but I'll try and get you off for that. I'll take the risk for friendship's sake—for I'd hate to see you sent to state's prison for a year or two."

And so finally Jurgis ripped out his bankbook—which was sewed up in his trousers—and signed an order, which "Bush" Harper wrote, for all the money to be paid out. Then the latter went and got it, and hurried to the court, and explained to the magistrate that Jurgis was a decent fellow and a friend of Scully's, who had been attacked by a strike-breaker. So the bail was reduced to three hundred dollars, and Harper went on it himself; he did not tell this to Jurgis, however—nor did he tell him that when the time for trial came it would be an easy matter for him to avoid the forfeiting of the bail, and pocket the three hundred dollars as his reward for the risk of offending Mike Scully! All that he told Jurgis was that he was now free, and that the best thing he could do was to clear out as quickly as possible; and so Jurgis overwhelmed with gratitude and relief, took the dollar and fourteen cents that was left him out of all his bank account, and put it with the two dollars and quarter that was left from his last night's celebration, and boarded a streetcar and got off at the other end of Chicago.

CHAPTER 27

Poor Jurgis was now an outcast and a tramp once more. He was crippled—he was as literally crippled as any wild animal which has lost its claws, or been torn out of its shell. He had been shorn, at one cut, of all those mysterious weapons whereby he had been able to make a living easily and to escape the consequences of his actions. He could no longer command a job when he wanted it; he could no longer steal with impunity—he must take his chances with the common herd. Nay worse, he dared not mingle with the herd—he must hide himself, for he was one marked out for destruction. His old companions would betray him, for the sake of the influence they would gain thereby; and he would be made to suffer, not merely for the offense he had committed, but for others which would be laid at his door, just as had been done for some poor devil on the occasion of that assault upon the "country customer" by him and Duane.

And also he labored under another handicap now. He had acquired new standards of living, which were not easily to be altered. When he had been out of work before, he had been content if he could sleep in a doorway or under a truck out of the rain, and if he could get fifteen cents a day for saloon lunches. But now he desired all sorts of other things, and suffered because he had to do without them. He must have a drink now and then, a drink for its own sake, and apart from the food that came with it. The craving for it was strong enough to master every other consideration—he would have it, though it were his last nickel and he had to starve the balance of the day in consequence.

Jurgis became once more a besieger of factory gates. But never since he had been in Chicago had he stood less chance of getting a job than just then. For one thing, there was the economic crisis, the million or two of men who had been out of work in the spring and summer, and were not yet all back, by any means. And then there was the strike, with seventy thousand men and women all over the country idle for a couple of months—twenty thousand in Chicago, and many of them now seeking work throughout the city. It did not remedy matters that a few days later the strike was given up and about half the strikers went back to work; for every one taken on, there was a "scab" who gave up and fled. The ten or fifteen thousand "green" Negroes, foreigners, and criminals were now being turned loose to shift for themselves. Everywhere Jurgis went he kept meeting them, and he was in an agony of fear lest some one of them should know that he was "wanted." He would have left Chicago, only by the time he had realized his danger he was almost penniless; and it would be better to go to jail than to be caught out in the country in the winter time.

At the end of about ten days Jurgis had only a few pennies left; and he had not yet found a job—not even a day's work at anything, not a chance to carry a satchel. Once again, as when he had come out of the hospital, he was bound hand and foot, and facing the grisly phantom of starvation. Raw, naked terror possessed him, a maddening passion that would never leave him, and that wore him down more quickly than the actual want of food. He was going to die of hunger! The fiend reached out its scaly arms for him—it touched him, its breath came into his face; and he would cry out for the awfulness of it, he would wake up in the night, shuddering, and bathed in perspiration, and start up and flee. He would walk, begging for work, until he was exhausted; he could not remain still—he would wander on, gaunt and haggard, gazing about him with restless eyes. Everywhere he went, from one end of the vast city to the other, there were hundreds of others like him; everywhere was the sight of plenty and the merciless hand of authority waving them away. There is one kind of prison where the man is behind bars, and everything that he desires is outside; and there is another kind where the things are behind the bars, and the man is outside.

When he was down to his last quarter, Jurgis learned that before the bakeshops closed at night they sold out what was left at half price, and after that he would go and get two loaves of stale bread for a nickel, and break them up and stuff his pockets with them, munching a bit from time to time. He would not spend a penny save for this; and, after two or three days more, he even became sparing of the bread, and would stop and peer into the ash barrels as he walked along the streets, and now and then rake out a bit of something, shake it free from dust, and count himself just so many minutes further from the end.

So for several days he had been going about, ravenous all the time, and growing weaker and weaker, and then one morning he had a hideous experience, that almost broke his heart. He was passing down a street lined with warehouses, and a boss offered him a job, and then, after he had started to work, turned him off because he was not strong enough. And he stood by and saw another man put into his place, and then picked up his coat, and walked off, doing all that he could to keep from breaking down and crying like a baby. He was lost! He was doomed! There was no hope for him! But then, with a sudden rush, his fear gave place to rage. He fell to cursing. He would come back there after dark, and he would show that scoundrel whether he was good for anything or not!

He was still muttering this when suddenly, at the corner, he came upon a green-grocery, with a tray full of cabbages in front of it. Jurgis, after one swift glance about him, stooped and seized the biggest of them, and darted round the corner with it. There was a hue and cry, and a score of men and boys started in chase of him; but he came to an alley, and then to another branching off from it and leading him into another street, where he fell into a walk, and slipped his cabbage under his coat and went off unsuspected in the crowd. When he had gotten a safe distance away he sat down and devoured half the cabbage raw, stowing the balance away in his pockets till the next day.

Just about this time one of the Chicago newspapers, which made much of the "common people," opened a "free-soup kitchen" for the benefit of the unemployed. Some people said that they did this for the sake of the advertising it gave them, and some others said that their motive was a fear lest all their readers should be starved off; but whatever the reason, the soup was thick and hot, and there was a bowl for every man, all night long. When Jurgis heard of this, from a fellow "hobo," he vowed that he would have half a dozen bowls before morning; but, as it proved, he was lucky to get one, for there was a line of men two blocks long before the stand, and there was just as long a line when the place was finally closed up.

This depot was within the danger line for Jurgis—in the "Levee" district, where he was known; but he went there, all the same, for he was desperate, and beginning to think of even the Bridewell as a place of refuge. So far the weather had been fair, and he had slept out every night in a vacant lot; but now there fell suddenly a shadow of the advancing winter, a chill wind from the north and a driving storm of rain. That day Jurgis bought two drinks for the sake of the shelter, and at night he spent his last two pennies in a "stale-beer dive." This was a place kept by a Negro, who went out and drew off the old dregs of beer that lay in barrels set outside of the saloons; and after he had doctored it with chemicals to make it "fizz," he sold it for two cents a can, the purchase of a can including the privilege of sleeping the night through upon the floor, with a mass of degraded outcasts, men and women.

All these horrors afflicted Jurgis all the more cruelly, because he was always contrasting them with the opportunities he had lost. For instance, just now it was election time again—within five or six weeks the voters of the country would select a President; and he heard the wretches with whom he associated discussing it, and saw the streets of the city decorated with placards and banners—and what words could describe the pangs of grief and despair that shot through him?

For instance, there was a night during this cold spell. He had begged all day, for his very life, and found not a soul to heed him, until toward evening he saw an old lady getting off a streetcar and helped her down with her umbrellas and bundles and then told her his "hard-luck story," and after answering all her suspicious questions satisfactorily, was taken to a restaurant and saw a quarter paid down for a meal. And so he had soup and bread, and boiled beef and potatoes and beans, and pie and coffee, and came out with his skin stuffed tight as a football. And then, through the rain and the darkness, far down the street he saw red lights flaring and heard the thumping of a bass drum; and his heart gave a leap, and he made for the place on the run—knowing without the asking that it meant a political meeting.

The campaign had so far been characterized by what the newspapers termed "apathy." For some reason the people refused to get excited over the struggle, and it was almost impossible to get them to come to meetings, or to make any noise when they did come. Those which had been held in Chicago so far had proven most dismal failures, and tonight, the speaker being no less a personage than a candidate for the vice-presidency of the nation, the political managers had been trembling with anxiety. But a merciful providence had sent this storm of cold rain—and now all it was necessary to do was to set off a few fireworks, and thump awhile on a drum, and all the homeless wretches from a mile around would pour in and fill the hall! And then on the morrow the newspapers would have a chance to report the tremendous ovation, and to add that it had been no "silk-stocking" audience, either, proving clearly that the high tariff sentiments of the distinguished candidate were pleasing to the wage-earners of the nation.

So Jurgis found himself in a large hall, elaborately decorated with flags and bunting; and after the chairman had made his little speech, and the orator of the evening rose up, amid an uproar from the band—only fancy the emotions of Jurgis upon making the discovery that the personage was none other than the famous and eloquent Senator Spareshanks, who had addressed the "Doyle Republican Association" at the stockyards, and helped to elect Mike Scully's ten-pin setter to the Chicago Board of Aldermen!

In truth, the sight of the senator almost brought the tears into Jurgis's eyes. What agony it was to him to look back upon those golden hours, when he, too, had a place beneath the shadow of the plum tree! When he, too, had been of the elect, through whom the country is governed—when he had had a bung in the campaign barrel for his own! And this was another election in which the Republicans had all the money; and but for that one hideous accident he might have had a share of it, instead of being where he was!

The eloquent senator was explaining the system of protection; an ingenious device whereby the workingman permitted the manufacturer to charge him higher prices, in order that he might receive higher wages; thus taking his money out of his pocket with one hand, and putting a part of it back with the other. To the senator this unique arrangement had somehow become identified with the higher verities of the universe. It was because of it that Columbia was the gem of the ocean; and all her future triumphs, her power and good repute among the nations, depended upon the zeal and fidelity with which each citizen held up the hands of those who were toiling to maintain it. The name of this heroic company was "the Grand Old Party"—

And here the band began to play, and Jurgis sat up with a violent start. Singular as it may seem, Jurgis was making a desperate effort to understand what the senator was saying—to comprehend the extent of American prosperity, the enormous expansion of American commerce, and the Republic's future in the Pacific and in South America, and wherever else the oppressed were groaning. The reason for it was that he wanted to keep awake. He knew that if he allowed himself to fall asleep he would begin to snore loudly; and so he must listen—he must be interested! But he had eaten such a big dinner, and he was so exhausted, and the hall was so warm, and his seat was so comfortable! The senator's gaunt form began to grow dim and hazy, to tower before him and dance about, with figures of exports and imports. Once his neighbor gave him a savage poke in the ribs, and he sat up with a start and tried to look innocent; but then he was at it again, and men began to stare at him with annoyance, and to call out in vexation. Finally one of them called a policeman, who came and grabbed Jurgis by the collar, and jerked him to his feet, bewildered and terrified. Some of the audience turned to see the commotion, and Senator Spareshanks faltered in his speech; but a voice shouted cheerily: "We're just firing a bum! Go ahead, old sport!" And so the crowd roared, and the senator smiled genially, and went on; and in a few seconds poor Jurgis found himself landed out in the rain, with a kick and a string of curses.

He got into the shelter of a doorway and took stock of himself. He was not hurt, and he was not arrested—more than he had any right to expect. He swore at himself and his luck for a while, and then turned his thoughts to practical matters. He had no money, and no place to sleep; he must begin begging again.

He went out, hunching his shoulders together and shivering at the touch of the icy rain. Coming down the street toward him was a lady, well dressed, and protected by an umbrella; and he turned and walked beside her. "Please, ma'am," he began, "could you lend me the price of a night's lodging? I'm a poor working-man—"

Then, suddenly, he stopped short. By the light of a street lamp he had caught sight of the lady's face. He knew her.

It was Alena Jasaityte, who had been the belle of his wedding feast! Alena Jasaityte, who had looked so beautiful, and danced with such a queenly air, with Juozas Raczius, the teamster! Jurgis had only seen her once or twice afterward, for Juozas had thrown her over for another girl, and Alena had gone away from Packingtown, no one knew where. And now he met her here!

She was as much surprised as he was. "Jurgis Rudkus!" she gasped. "And what in the world is the matter with you?"

"I—I've had hard luck," he stammered. "I'm out of work, and I've no home and no money. And you, Alena—are you married?"

"No," she answered, "I'm not married, but I've got a good place."

They stood staring at each other for a few moments longer. Finally Alena spoke again. "Jurgis," she said, "I'd help you if I could, upon my word I would, but it happens that I've come out without my purse, and I honestly haven't a penny with me: I can do something better for you, though—I can tell you how to get help. I can tell you where Marija is."

Jurgis gave a start. "Marija!" he exclaimed.

"Yes," said Alena; "and she'll help you. She's got a place, and she's doing well; she'll be glad to see you."

It was not much more than a year since Jurgis had left Packingtown, feeling like one escaped from jail; and it had been from Marija and Elzbieta that he was escaping. But now, at the mere mention of them, his whole being cried out with joy. He wanted to see them; he wanted to go home! They would help him—they would be kind to him. In a flash he had thought over the situation. He had a good excuse for running away—his grief at the death of his son; and also he had a good excuse for not returning—the fact that they had left Packingtown. "All right," he said, "I'll go."

So she gave him a number on Clark Street, adding, "There's no need to give you my address, because Marija knows it." And Jurgis set out, without further ado. He found a large brownstone house of aristocratic appearance, and rang the basement bell. A young colored girl came to the door, opening it about an inch, and gazing at him suspiciously.

"What do you want?" she demanded.

"Does Marija Berczynskas live here?" he inquired.

"I dunno," said the girl. "What you want wid her?"

"I want to see her," said he; "she's a relative of mine."

The girl hesitated a moment. Then she opened the door and said, "Come in." Jurgis came and stood in the hall, and she continued: "I'll go see. What's yo' name?"

"Tell her it's Jurgis," he answered, and the girl went upstairs. She came back at the end of a minute or two, and replied, "Dey ain't no sich person here."

Jurgis's heart went down into his boots. "I was told this was where she lived!" he cried. But the girl only shook her head. "De lady says dey ain't no sich person here," she said.

And he stood for a moment, hesitating, helpless with dismay. Then he turned to go to the door. At the same instant, however, there came a knock upon it, and the girl went to open it. Jurgis heard the shuffling of feet, and then heard her give a cry; and the next moment she sprang back, and past him, her eyes shining white with terror, and bounded up the stairway, screaming at the top of her lungs: "Police! Police! We're pinched!"

Jurgis stood for a second, bewildered. Then, seeing blue-coated forms rushing upon him, he sprang after the Negress. Her cries had been the signal for a wild uproar above; the house was full of people, and as he entered the hallway he saw them rushing hither and thither, crying and screaming with alarm. There were men and women, the latter clad for the most part in wrappers, the former in all stages of dishabille. At one side Jurgis caught a glimpse of a big apartment with plush-covered chairs, and tables covered with trays and glasses. There were playing cards scattered all over the floor—one of the tables had been upset, and bottles of wine were rolling about, their contents running out upon the carpet. There was a young girl who had fainted, and two men who were supporting her; and there were a dozen others crowding toward the front door.

Suddenly, however, there came a series of resounding blows upon it, causing the crowd to give back. At the same instant a stout woman, with painted cheeks and diamonds in her ears, came running down the stairs, panting breathlessly: "To the rear! Quick!"

She led the way to a back staircase, Jurgis following; in the kitchen she pressed a spring, and a cupboard gave way and opened, disclosing a dark passageway. "Go in!" she cried to the crowd, which now amounted to twenty or thirty, and they began to pass through. Scarcely had the last one disappeared, however, before there were cries from in front, and then the panic-stricken throng poured out again, exclaiming: "They're there too! We're trapped!"

"Upstairs!" cried the woman, and there was another rush of the mob, women and men cursing and screaming and fighting to be first. One flight, two, three—and then there was a ladder to the roof, with a crowd packed at the foot of it, and one man at the top, straining and struggling to lift the trap door. It was not to be stirred, however, and when the woman shouted up to unhook it, he answered: "It's already unhooked. There's somebody sitting on it!"

And a moment later came a voice from downstairs: "You might as well quit, you people. We mean business, this time."

So the crowd subsided; and a few moments later several policemen came up, staring here and there, and leering at their victims. Of the latter the men were for the most part frightened and sheepish-looking. The women took it as a joke, as if they were used to it—though if they had been pale, one could not have told, for the paint on their cheeks. One black-eyed young girl perched herself upon the top of the balustrade, and began to kick with her slippered foot at the helmets of the policemen, until one of them caught her by the ankle and pulled her down. On the floor below four or five other girls sat upon trunks in the hall, making fun of the procession which filed by them. They were noisy and hilarious, and had evidently been drinking; one of them, who wore a bright red kimono, shouted and screamed in a voice that drowned out all the other sounds in the hall—and Jurgis took a glance at her, and then gave a start, and a cry, "Marija!"

She heard him, and glanced around; then she shrank back and half sprang to her feet in amazement. "Jurgis!" she gasped.

For a second or two they stood staring at each other. "How did you come here?" Marija exclaimed.

"I came to see you," he answered.

"When?"

"Just now."

"But how did you know—who told you I was here?"

"Alena Jasaityte. I met her on the street."

Again there was a silence, while they gazed at each other. The rest of the crowd was watching them, and so Marija got up and came closer to him. "And you?" Jurgis asked. "You live here?"

"Yes," said Marija, "I live here." Then suddenly came a hail from below: "Get your clothes on now, girls, and come along. You'd best begin, or you'll be sorry—it's raining outside."

"Br-r-r!" shivered some one, and the women got up and entered the various doors which lined the hallway.

"Come," said Marija, and took Jurgis into her room, which was a tiny place about eight by six, with a cot and a chair and a dressing stand and some dresses hanging behind the door. There were clothes scattered about on the floor, and hopeless confusion everywhere—boxes of rouge and bottles of perfume mixed with hats and soiled dishes on the dresser, and a pair of slippers and a clock and a whisky bottle on a chair.

Marija had nothing on but a kimono and a pair of stockings; yet she proceeded to dress before Jurgis, and without even taking the trouble to close the door. He had by this time divined what sort of a place he was in; and he had seen a great deal of the world since he had left home, and was not easy to shock—and yet it gave him a painful start that Marija should do this. They had always been decent people at home, and it seemed to him that the memory of old times ought to have ruled her. But then he laughed at himself for a fool. What was he, to be pretending to decency!

"How long have you been living here?" he asked.

"Nearly a year," she answered.

"Why did you come?"

"I had to live," she said; "and I couldn't see the children starve."

He paused for a moment, watching her. "You were out of work?" he asked, finally.

"I got sick," she replied, "and after that I had no money. And then Stanislovas died—"

"Stanislovas dead!"

"Yes," said Marija, "I forgot. You didn't know about it."

"How did he die?"

"Rats killed him," she answered.

Jurgis gave a gasp. "Rats killed him!"

"Yes," said the other; she was bending over, lacing her shoes as she spoke. "He was working in an oil factory—at least he was hired by the men to get their beer. He used to carry cans on a long pole; and he'd drink a little out of each can, and one day he drank too much, and fell asleep in a corner, and got locked up in the place all night. When they found him the rats had killed him and eaten him nearly all up."

Jurgis sat, frozen with horror. Marija went on lacing up her shoes. There was a long silence.

Suddenly a big policeman came to the door. "Hurry up, there," he said.

"As quick as I can," said Marija, and she stood up and began putting on her corsets with feverish haste.

"Are the rest of the people alive?" asked Jurgis, finally.

"Yes," she said.

"Where are they?"

"They live not far from here. They're all right now."

"They are working?" he inquired.

"Elzbieta is," said Marija, "when she can. I take care of them most of the time—I'm making plenty of money now."

Jurgis was silent for a moment. "Do they know you live here—how you live?" he asked.

"Elzbieta knows," answered Marija. "I couldn't lie to her. And maybe the children have found out by this time. It's nothing to be ashamed of—we can't help it."

"And Tamoszius?" he asked. "Does he know?"

Marija shrugged her shoulders. "How do I know?" she said. "I haven't seen him for over a year. He got blood poisoning and lost one finger, and couldn't play the violin any more; and then he went away."

Marija was standing in front of the glass fastening her dress. Jurgis sat staring at her. He could hardly believe that she was the same woman he had known in the old days; she was so quiet—so hard! It struck fear to his heart to watch her.

Then suddenly she gave a glance at him. "You look as if you had been having a rough time of it yourself," she said.

"I have," he answered. "I haven't a cent in my pockets, and nothing to do."

"Where have you been?"

"All over. I've been hoboing it. Then I went back to the yards—just before the strike." He paused for a moment, hesitating. "I asked for you," he added. "I found you had gone away, no one knew where. Perhaps you think I did you a dirty trick running away as I did, Marija—"

"No," she answered, "I don't blame you. We never have—any of us. You did your best—the job was too much for us." She paused a moment, then added: "We were too ignorant—that was the trouble. We didn't stand any chance. If I'd known what I know now we'd have won out."

"You'd have come here?" said Jurgis.

"Yes," she answered; "but that's not what I meant. I meant you—how differently you would have behaved—about Ona."

Jurgis was silent; he had never thought of that aspect of it.

"When people are starving," the other continued, "and they have anything with a price, they ought to sell it, I say. I guess you realize it now when it's too late. Ona could have taken care of us all, in the beginning." Marija spoke without emotion, as one who had come to regard things from the business point of view.

"I—yes, I guess so," Jurgis answered hesitatingly. He did not add that he had paid three hundred dollars, and a foreman's job, for the satisfaction of knocking down "Phil" Connor a second time.

The policeman came to the door again just then. "Come on, now," he said. "Lively!"

"All right," said Marija, reaching for her hat, which was big enough to be a drum major's, and full of ostrich feathers. She went out into the hall and Jurgis followed, the policeman remaining to look under the bed and behind the door.

"What's going to come of this?" Jurgis asked, as they started down the steps.

"The raid, you mean? Oh, nothing—it happens to us every now and then. The madame's having some sort of time with the police; I don't know what it is, but maybe they'll come to terms before morning. Anyhow, they won't do anything to you. They always let the men off."

"Maybe so," he responded, "but not me—I'm afraid I'm in for it."

"How do you mean?"

"I'm wanted by the police," he said, lowering his voice, though of course their conversation was in Lithuanian. "They'll send me up for a year or two, I'm afraid."

"Hell!" said Marija. "That's too bad. I'll see if I can't get you off."

Downstairs, where the greater part of the prisoners were now massed, she sought out the stout personage with the diamond earrings, and had a few whispered words with her. The latter then approached the police sergeant who was in charge of the raid. "Billy," she said, pointing to Jurgis, "there's a fellow who came in to see his sister. He'd just got in the door when you knocked. You aren't taking hoboes, are you?"

The sergeant laughed as he looked at Jurgis. "Sorry," he said, "but the orders are every one but the servants."

So Jurgis slunk in among the rest of the men, who kept dodging behind each other like sheep that have smelled a wolf. There were old men and young men, college boys and gray-beards old enough to be their grandfathers; some of them wore evening dress—there was no one among them save Jurgis who showed any signs of poverty.

When the roundup was completed, the doors were opened and the party marched out. Three patrol wagons were drawn up at the curb, and the whole neighborhood had turned out to see the sport; there was much chaffing, and a universal craning of necks. The women stared about them with defiant eyes, or laughed and joked, while the men kept their heads bowed, and their hats pulled over their faces. They were crowded into the patrol wagons as if into streetcars, and then off they went amid a din of cheers. At the station house Jurgis gave a Polish name and was put into a cell with half a dozen others; and while these sat and talked in whispers, he lay down in a corner and gave himself up to his thoughts.

Jurgis had looked into the deepest reaches of the social pit, and grown used to the sights in them. Yet when he had thought of all humanity as vile and hideous, he had somehow always excepted his own family that he had loved; and now this sudden horrible discovery—Marija a whore, and Elzbieta and the children living off her shame! Jurgis might argue with himself all he chose, that he had done worse, and was a fool for caring—but still he could not get over the shock of that sudden unveiling, he could not help being sunk in grief because of it. The depths of him were troubled and shaken, memories were stirred in him that had been sleeping so long he had counted them dead. Memories of the old life—his old hopes and his old yearnings, his old dreams of decency and independence! He saw Ona again, he heard her gentle voice pleading with him. He saw little Antanas, whom he had meant to make a man. He saw his trembling old father, who had blessed them all with his wonderful love. He lived again through that day of horror when he had discovered Ona's shame—God, how he had suffered, what a madman he had been! How dreadful it had all seemed to him; and now, today, he had sat and listened, and half agreed when Marija told him he had been a fool! Yes—told him that he ought to have sold his wife's honor and lived by it!—And then there was Stanislovas and his awful fate—that brief story which Marija had narrated so calmly, with such dull indifference! The poor little fellow, with his frostbitten fingers and his terror of the snow—his wailing voice rang in Jurgis's ears, as he lay there in the darkness, until the sweat started on his forehead. Now and then he would quiver with a sudden spasm of horror, at the picture of little Stanislovas shut up in the deserted building and fighting for his life with the rats!

All these emotions had become strangers to the soul of Jurgis; it was so long since they had troubled him that he had ceased to think they might ever trouble him again. Helpless, trapped, as he was, what good did they do him—why should he ever have allowed them to torment him? It had been the task of his recent life to fight them down, to crush them out of him; never in his life would he have suffered from them again, save that they had caught him unawares, and overwhelmed him before he could protect himself. He heard the old voices of his soul, he saw its old ghosts beckoning to him, stretching out their arms to him! But they were far-off and shadowy, and the gulf between them was black and bottomless; they would fade away into the mists of the past once more. Their voices would die, and never again would he hear them—and so the last faint spark of manhood in his soul would flicker out.

CHAPTER 28

After breakfast Jurgis was driven to the court, which was crowded with the prisoners and those who had come out of curiosity or in the hope of recognizing one of the men and getting a case for blackmail. The men were called up first, and reprimanded in a bunch, and then dismissed; but, Jurgis, to his terror, was called separately, as being a suspicious-looking case. It was in this very same court that he had been tried, that time when his sentence had been "suspended"; it was the same judge, and the same clerk. The latter now stared at Jurgis, as if he half thought that he knew him; but the judge had no suspicions—just then his thoughts were upon a telephone message he was expecting from a friend of the police captain of the district, telling what disposition he should make of the case of "Polly" Simpson, as the "madame" of the house was known. Meantime, he listened to the story of how Jurgis had been looking for his sister, and advised him dryly to keep his sister in a better place; then he let him go, and proceeded to fine each of the girls five dollars, which fines were paid in a bunch from a wad of bills which Madame Polly extracted from her stocking.

Jurgis waited outside and walked home with Marija. The police had left the house, and already there were a few visitors; by evening the place would be running again, exactly as if nothing had happened. Meantime, Marija took Jurgis upstairs to her room, and they sat and talked. By daylight, Jurgis was able to observe that the color on her cheeks was not the old natural one of abounding health; her complexion was in reality a parchment yellow, and there were black rings under her eyes.

"Have you been sick?" he asked.

"Sick?" she said. "Hell!" (Marija had learned to scatter her conversation with as many oaths as a longshoreman or a mule driver.) "How can I ever be anything but sick, at this life?"

She fell silent for a moment, staring ahead of her gloomily. "It's morphine," she said, at last. "I seem to take more of it every day."

"What's that for?" he asked.

"It's the way of it; I don't know why. If it isn't that, it's drink. If the girls didn't booze they couldn't stand it any time at all. And the madame always gives them dope when they first come, and they learn to like it; or else they take it for headaches and such things, and get the habit that way. I've got it, I know; I've tried to quit, but I never will while I'm here."

"How long are you going to stay?" he asked.

"I don't know," she said. "Always, I guess. What else could I do?"

"Don't you save any money?"

"Save!" said Marija. "Good Lord, no! I get enough, I suppose, but it all goes. I get a half share, two dollars and a half for each customer, and sometimes I make twenty-five or thirty dollars a night, and you'd think I ought to save something out of that! But then I am charged for my room and my meals—and such prices as you never heard of; and then for extras, and drinks—for everything I get, and some I don't. My laundry bill is nearly twenty dollars each week alone—think of that! Yet what can I do? I either have to stand it or quit, and it would be the same anywhere else. It's all I can do to save the fifteen dollars I give Elzbieta each week, so the children can go to school."

Marija sat brooding in silence for a while; then, seeing that Jurgis was interested, she went on: "That's the way they keep the girls—they let them run up debts, so they can't get away. A young girl comes from abroad, and she doesn't know a word of English, and she gets into a place like this, and when she wants to go the madame shows her that she is a couple of hundred dollars in debt, and takes all her clothes away, and threatens to have her arrested if she doesn't stay and do as she's told. So she stays, and the longer she stays, the more in debt she gets. Often, too, they are girls that didn't know what they were coming to, that had hired out for housework. Did you notice that little French girl with the yellow hair, that stood next to me in the court?"

Jurgis answered in the affirmative.

"Well, she came to America about a year ago. She was a store clerk, and she hired herself to a man to be sent here to work in a factory. There were six of them, all together, and they were brought to a house just down the street from here, and this girl was put into a room alone, and they gave her some dope in her food, and when she came to she found that she had been ruined. She cried, and screamed, and tore her hair, but she had nothing but a wrapper, and couldn't get away, and they kept her half insensible with drugs all the time, until she gave up. She never got outside of that place for ten months, and then they sent her away, because she didn't suit. I guess they'll put her out of here, too—she's getting to have crazy fits, from drinking absinthe. Only one of the girls that came out with her got away, and she jumped out of a second-story window one night. There was a great fuss about that—maybe you heard of it."

"I did," said Jurgis, "I heard of it afterward." (It had happened in the place where he and Duane had taken refuge from their "country customer." The girl had become insane, fortunately for the police.)

"There's lots of money in it," said Marija—"they get as much as forty dollars a head for girls, and they bring them from all over. There are seventeen in this place, and nine different countries among them. In some places you might find even more. We have half a dozen French girls—I suppose it's because the madame speaks the language. French girls are bad, too, the worst of all, except for the Japanese. There's a place next door that's full of Japanese women, but I wouldn't live in the same house with one of them."

Marija paused for a moment or two, and then she added: "Most of the women here are pretty decent—you'd be surprised. I used to think they did it because they liked to; but fancy a woman selling herself to every kind of man that comes, old or young, black or white—and doing it because she likes to!"

"Some of them say they do," said Jurgis.

"I know," said she; "they say anything. They're in, and they know they can't get out. But they didn't like it when they began—you'd find out—it's always misery! There's a little Jewish girl here who used to run errands for a milliner, and got sick and lost her place; and she was four days on the streets without a mouthful of food, and then she went to a place just around the corner and offered herself, and they made her give up her clothes before they would give her a bite to eat!"

Marija sat for a minute or two, brooding somberly. "Tell me about yourself, Jurgis," she said, suddenly. "Where have you been?"

So he told her the long story of his adventures since his flight from home; his life as a tramp, and his work in the freight tunnels, and the accident; and then of Jack Duane, and of his political career in the stockyards, and his downfall and subsequent failures. Marija listened with sympathy; it was easy to believe the tale of his late starvation, for his face showed it all. "You found me just in the nick of time," she said. "I'll stand by you—I'll help you till you can get some work."

"I don't like to let you—" he began.

"Why not? Because I'm here?"

"No, not that," he said. "But I went off and left you—"

"Nonsense!" said Marija. "Don't think about it. I don't blame you."

"You must be hungry," she said, after a minute or two. "You stay here to lunch—I'll have something up in the room."

She pressed a button, and a colored woman came to the door and took her order. "It's nice to have somebody to wait on you," she observed, with a laugh, as she lay back on the bed.

As the prison breakfast had not been liberal, Jurgis had a good appetite, and they had a little feast together, talking meanwhile of Elzbieta and the children and old times. Shortly before they were through, there came another colored girl, with the message that the "madame" wanted Marija—"Lithuanian Mary," as they called her here.

"That means you have to go," she said to Jurgis.

So he got up, and she gave him the new address of the family, a tenement over in the Ghetto district. "You go there," she said. "They'll be glad to see you."

But Jurgis stood hesitating.

"I—I don't like to," he said. "Honest, Marija, why don't you just give me a little money and let me look for work first?"

"How do you need money?" was her reply. "All you want is something to eat and a place to sleep, isn't it?"

"Yes," he said; "but then I don't like to go there after I left them—and while I have nothing to do, and while you—you—"

"Go on!" said Marija, giving him a push. "What are you talking?—I won't give you money," she added, as she followed him to the door, "because you'll drink it up, and do yourself harm. Here's a quarter for you now, and go along, and they'll be so glad to have you back, you won't have time to feel ashamed. Good-by!"

So Jurgis went out, and walked down the street to think it over. He decided that he would first try to get work, and so he put in the rest of the day wandering here and there among factories and warehouses without success. Then, when it was nearly dark, he concluded to go home, and set out; but he came to a restaurant, and went in and spent his quarter for a meal; and when he came out he changed his mind—the night was pleasant, and he would sleep somewhere outside, and put in the morrow hunting, and so have one more chance of a job. So he started away again, when suddenly he chanced to look about him, and found that he was walking down the same street and past the same hall where he had listened to the political speech the night before. There was no red fire and no band now, but there was a sign out, announcing a meeting, and a stream of people pouring in through the entrance. In a flash Jurgis had decided that he would chance it once more, and sit down and rest while making up his mind what to do. There was no one taking tickets, so it must be a free show again.

He entered. There were no decorations in the hall this time; but there was quite a crowd upon the platform, and almost every seat in the place was filled. He took one of the last, far in the rear, and straightway forgot all about his surroundings. Would Elzbieta think that he had come to sponge off her, or would she understand that he meant to get to work again and do his share? Would she be decent to him, or would she scold him? If only he could get some sort of a job before he went— if that last boss had only been willing to try him!

—Then suddenly Jurgis looked up. A tremendous roar had burst from the throats of the crowd, which by this time had packed the hall to the very doors. Men and women were standing up, waving handkerchiefs, shouting, yelling. Evidently the speaker had arrived, thought Jurgis; what fools they were making of themselves! What were they expecting to get out of it anyhow—what had they to do with elections, with governing the country? Jurgis had been behind the scenes in politics.

He went back to his thoughts, but with one further fact to reckon with—that he was caught here. The hall was now filled to the doors; and after the meeting it would be too late for him to go home, so he would have to make the best of it outside. Perhaps it would be better to go home in the morning, anyway, for the children would be at school, and he and Elzbieta could have a quiet explanation. She always had been a reasonable person; and he really did mean to do right. He would manage to persuade her of it—and besides, Marija was willing, and Marija was furnishing the money. If Elzbieta were ugly, he would tell her that in so many words.

So Jurgis went on meditating; until finally, when he had been an hour or two in the hall, there began to prepare itself a repetition of the dismal catastrophe of the night before. Speaking had been going on all the time, and the audience was clapping its hands and shouting, thrilling with excitement; and little by little the sounds were beginning to blur in Jurgis's ears, and his thoughts were beginning to run together, and his head to wobble and nod. He caught himself many times, as usual, and made desperate resolutions; but the hall was hot and close, and his long walk and is dinner were too much for him—in the end his head sank forward and he went off again.

And then again someone nudged him, and he sat up with his old terrified start! He had been snoring again, of course! And now what? He fixed his eyes ahead of him, with painful intensity, staring at the platform as if nothing else ever had interested him, or ever could interest him, all his life. He imagined the angry exclamations, the hostile glances; he imagined the policeman striding toward him—reaching for his neck. Or was he to have one more chance? Were they going to let him alone this time? He sat trembling; waiting—

And then suddenly came a voice in his ear, a woman's voice, gentle and sweet, "If you would try to listen, comrade, perhaps you would be interested."

Jurgis was more startled by that than he would have been by the touch of a policeman. He still kept his eyes fixed ahead, and did not stir; but his heart gave a great leap. Comrade! Who was it that called him "comrade"?

He waited long, long; and at last, when he was sure that he was no longer watched, he stole a glance out of the corner of his eyes at the woman who sat beside him. She was young and beautiful; she wore fine clothes, and was what is called a "lady." And she called him "comrade"!

He turned a little, carefully, so that he could see her better; then he began to watch her, fascinated. She had apparently forgotten all about him, and was looking toward the platform. A man was speaking there—Jurgis heard his voice vaguely; but all his thoughts were for this woman's face. A feeling of alarm stole over him as he stared at her. It made his flesh creep. What was the matter with her, what could be going on, to affect any one like that? She sat as one turned to stone, her hands clenched tightly in her lap, so tightly that he could see the cords standing out in her wrists. There was a look of excitement upon her face, of tense effort, as of one struggling mightily, or witnessing a struggle. There was a faint quivering of her nostrils; and now and then she would moisten her lips with feverish haste. Her bosom rose and fell as she breathed, and her excitement seemed to mount higher and higher, and then to sink away again, like a boat tossing upon ocean surges. What was it? What was the matter? It must be something that the man was saying, up there on the platform. What sort of a man was he? And what sort of thing was this, anyhow?—So all at once it occurred to Jurgis to look at the speaker.

It was like coming suddenly upon some wild sight of nature—a mountain forest lashed by a tempest, a ship tossed about upon a stormy sea. Jurgis had an unpleasant sensation, a sense of confusion, of disorder, of wild and meaningless uproar. The man was tall and gaunt, as haggard as his auditor himself; a thin black beard covered half of his face, and one could see only two black hollows where the eyes were. He was speaking rapidly, in great excitement; he used many gestures—as he spoke he moved here and there upon the stage, reaching with his long arms as if to seize each person in his audience. His voice was deep, like an organ; it was some time, however, before Jurgis thought of the voice—he was too much occupied with his eyes to think of what the man was saying. But suddenly it seemed as if the speaker had begun pointing straight at him, as if he had singled him out particularly for his remarks; and so Jurgis became suddenly aware of his voice, trembling, vibrant with emotion, with pain and longing, with a burden of things unutterable, not to be compassed by words. To hear it was to be suddenly arrested, to be gripped, transfixed.

"You listen to these things," the man was saying, "and you say, 'Yes, they are true, but they have been that way always.' Or you say, 'Maybe it will come, but not in my time—it will not help me.' And so you return to your daily round of toil, you go back to be ground up for profits in the world-wide mill of economic might! To toil long hours for another's advantage; to live in mean and squalid homes, to work in dangerous and unhealthful places; to wrestle with the specters of hunger and privation, to take your chances of accident, disease, and death. And each day the struggle becomes fiercer, the pace more cruel; each day you have to toil a little harder, and feel the iron hand of circumstance close upon you a little tighter. Months pass, years maybe—and then you come again; and again I am here to plead with you, to know if want and misery have yet done their work with you, if injustice and oppression have yet opened your eyes! I shall still be waiting—there is nothing else that I can do. There is no wilderness where I can hide from these things, there is no haven where I can escape them; though I travel to the ends of the earth, I find the same accursed system—I find that all the fair and noble impulses of humanity, the dreams of poets and the agonies of martyrs, are shackled and bound in the service of organized and predatory Greed! And therefore I cannot rest, I cannot be silent; therefore I cast aside comfort and happiness, health and good repute—and go out into the world and cry out the pain of my spirit! Therefore I am not to be silenced by poverty and sickness, not by hatred and obloquy, by threats and ridicule—not by prison and persecution, if they should come—not by any power that is upon the earth or above the earth, that was, or is, or ever can be created. If I fail tonight, I can only try tomorrow; knowing that the fault must be mine—that if once the vision of my soul were spoken upon earth, if once the anguish of its defeat were uttered in human speech, it would break the stoutest barriers of prejudice, it would shake the most sluggish soul to action! It would abash the most cynical, it would terrify the most selfish; and the voice of mockery would be silenced, and fraud and falsehood would slink back into their dens, and the truth would stand forth alone! For I speak with the voice of the millions who are voiceless! Of them that are oppressed and have no comforter! Of the disinherited of life, for whom there is no respite and no deliverance, to whom the world is a prison, a dungeon of torture, a tomb! With the voice of the little child who toils tonight in a Southern cotton mill, staggering with exhaustion, numb with agony, and knowing no hope but the grave! Of the mother who sews by candlelight in her tenement garret, weary and weeping, smitten with the mortal hunger of her babes! Of the man who lies upon a bed of rags, wrestling in his last sickness and leaving his loved ones to perish! Of the young girl who, somewhere at this moment, is walking the streets of this horrible city, beaten and starving, and making her choice between the brothel and the lake! With the voice of those, whoever and wherever they may be, who are caught beneath the wheels of the Juggernaut of Greed! With the voice of humanity, calling for deliverance! Of the everlasting soul of Man, arising from the dust; breaking its way out of its prison—rending the bands of oppression and ignorance—groping its way to the light!"

The speaker paused. There was an instant of silence, while men caught their breaths, and then like a single sound there came a cry from a thousand people. Through it all Jurgis sat still, motionless and rigid, his eyes fixed upon the speaker; he was trembling, smitten with wonder.

Suddenly the man raised his hands, and silence fell, and he began again.

"I plead with you," he said, "whoever you may be, provided that you care about the truth; but most of all I plead with working-man, with those to whom the evils I portray are not mere matters of sentiment, to be dallied and toyed with, and then perhaps put aside and forgotten—to whom they are the grim and relentless realities of the daily grind, the chains upon their limbs, the lash upon their backs, the iron in their souls. To you, working-men! To you, the toilers, who have made this land, and have no voice in its councils! To you, whose lot it is to sow that others may reap, to labor and obey, and ask no more than the wages of a beast of burden, the food and shelter to keep you alive from day to day. It is to you that I come with my message of salvation, it is to you that I appeal. I know how much it is to ask of you—I know, for I have been in your place, I have lived your life, and there is no man before me here tonight who knows it better. I have known what it is to be a street-waif, a bootblack, living upon a crust of bread and sleeping in cellar stairways and under empty wagons. I have known what it is to dare and to aspire, to dream mighty dreams and to see them perish—to see all the fair flowers of my spirit trampled into the mire by the wild-beast powers of my life. I know what is the price that a working-man pays for knowledge—I have paid for it with food and sleep, with agony of body and mind, with health, almost with life itself; and so, when I come to you with a story of hope and freedom, with the vision of a new earth to be created, of a new labor to be dared, I am not surprised that I find you sordid and material, sluggish and incredulous. That I do not despair is because I know also the forces that are driving behind you—because I know the raging lash of poverty, the sting of contempt and mastership, 'the insolence of office and the spurns.' Because I feel sure that in the crowd that has come to me tonight, no matter how many may be dull and heedless, no matter how many may have come out of idle curiosity, or in order to ridicule—there will be some one man whom pain and suffering have made desperate, whom some chance vision of wrong and horror has startled and shocked into attention. And to him my words will come like a sudden flash of lightning to one who travels in darkness—revealing the way before him, the perils and the obstacles—solving all problems, making all difficulties clear! The scales will fall from his eyes, the shackles will be torn from his limbs—he will leap up with a cry of thankfulness, he will stride forth a free man at last! A man delivered from his self-created slavery! A man who will never more be trapped—whom no blandishments will cajole, whom no threats will frighten; who from tonight on will move forward, and not backward, who will study and understand, who will gird on his sword and take his place in the army of his comrades and brothers. Who will carry the good tidings to others, as I have carried them to him—priceless gift of liberty and light that is neither mine nor his, but is the heritage of the soul of man! Working-men, working-men—comrades! open your eyes and look about you! You have lived so long in the toil and heat that your senses are dulled, your souls are numbed; but realize once in your lives this world in which you dwell—tear off the rags of its customs and conventions—behold it as it is, in all its hideous nakedness! Realize it, realize it! Realize that out upon the plains of Manchuria tonight two hostile armies are facing each other—that now, while we are seated here, a million human beings may be hurled at each other's throats, striving with the fury of maniacs to tear each other to pieces! And this in the twentieth century, nineteen hundred years since the Prince of Peace was born on earth! Nineteen hundred years that his words have been preached as divine, and here two armies of men are rending and tearing each other like the wild beasts of the forest! Philosophers have reasoned, prophets have denounced, poets have wept and pleaded—and still this hideous Monster roams at large! We have schools and colleges, newspapers and books; we have searched the heavens and the earth, we have weighed and probed and reasoned—and all to equip men to destroy each other! We call it War, and pass it by—but do not put me off with platitudes and conventions—come with me, come with me—realize it! See the bodies of men pierced by bullets, blown into pieces by bursting shells! Hear the crunching of the bayonet, plunged into human flesh; hear the groans and shrieks of agony, see the faces of men crazed by pain, turned into fiends by fury and hate! Put your hand upon that piece of flesh—it is hot and quivering—just now it was a part of a man! This blood is still steaming—it was driven by a human heart! Almighty God! and this goes on—it is systematic, organized, premeditated! And we know it, and read of it, and take it for granted; our papers tell of it, and the presses are not stopped—our churches know of it, and do not close their doors—the people behold it, and do not rise up in horror and revolution!

"Or perhaps Manchuria is too far away for you—come home with me then, come here to Chicago. Here in this city to-night ten thousand women are shut up in foul pens, and driven by hunger to sell their bodies to live. And we know it, we make it a jest! And these women are made in the image of your mothers, they may be your sisters, your daughters; the child whom you left at home tonight, whose laughing eyes will greet you in the morning—that fate may be waiting for her! To-night in Chicago there are ten thousand men, homeless and wretched, willing to work and begging for a chance, yet starving, and fronting in terror the awful winter cold! Tonight in Chicago there are a hundred thousand children wearing out their strength and blasting their lives in the effort to earn their bread! There are a hundred thousand mothers who are living in misery and squalor, struggling to earn enough to feed their little ones! There are a hundred thousand old people, cast off and helpless, waiting for death to take them from their torments! There are a million people, men and women and children, who share the curse of the wage-slave; who toil every hour they can stand and see, for just enough to keep them alive; who are condemned till the end of their days to monotony and weariness, to hunger and misery, to heat and cold, to dirt and disease, to ignorance and drunkenness and vice! And then turn over the page with me, and gaze upon the other side of the picture. There are a thousand—ten thousand, maybe—who are the masters of these slaves, who own their toil. They do nothing to earn what they receive, they do not even have to ask for it—it comes to them of itself, their only care is to dispose of it. They live in palaces, they riot in luxury and extravagance—such as no words can describe, as makes the imagination reel and stagger, makes the soul grow sick and faint. They spend hundreds of dollars for a pair of shoes, a handkerchief, a garter; they spend millions for horses and automobiles and yachts, for palaces and banquets, for little shiny stones with which to deck their bodies. Their life is a contest among themselves for supremacy in ostentation and recklessness, in the destroying of useful and necessary things, in the wasting of the labor and the lives of their fellow creatures, the toil and anguish of the nations, the sweat and tears and blood of the human race! It is all theirs—it comes to them; just as all the springs pour into streamlets, and the streamlets into rivers, and the rivers into the oceans—so, automatically and inevitably, all the wealth of society comes to them. The farmer tills the soil, the miner digs in the earth, the weaver tends the loom, the mason carves the stone; the clever man invents, the shrewd man directs, the wise man studies, the inspired man sings—and all the result, the products of the labor of brain and muscle, are gathered into one stupendous stream and poured into their laps! The whole of society is in their grip, the whole labor of the world lies at their mercy—and like fierce wolves they rend and destroy, like ravening vultures they devour and tear! The whole power of mankind belongs to them, forever and beyond recall—do what it can, strive as it will, humanity lives for them and dies for them! They own not merely the labor of society, they have bought the governments; and everywhere they use their raped and stolen power to intrench themselves in their privileges, to dig wider and deeper the channels through which the river of profits flows to them!—And you, workingmen, workingmen! You have been brought up to it, you plod on like beasts of burden, thinking only of the day and its pain—yet is there a man among you who can believe that such a system will continue forever—is there a man here in this audience tonight so hardened and debased that he dare rise up before me and say that he believes it can continue forever; that the product of the labor of society, the means of existence of the human race, will always belong to idlers and parasites, to be spent for the gratification of vanity and lust—to be spent for any purpose whatever, to be at the disposal of any individual will whatever—that somehow, somewhere, the labor of humanity will not belong to humanity, to be used for the purposes of humanity, to be controlled by the will of humanity? And if this is ever to be, how is it to be—what power is there that will bring it about? Will it be the task of your masters, do you think—will they write the charter of your liberties? Will they forge you the sword of your deliverance, will they marshal you the army and lead it to the fray? Will their wealth be spent for the purpose—will they build colleges and churches to teach you, will they print papers to herald your progress, and organize political parties to guide and carry on the struggle? Can you not see that the task is your task—yours to dream, yours to resolve, yours to execute? That if ever it is carried out, it will be in the face of every obstacle that wealth and mastership can oppose—in the face of ridicule and slander, of hatred and persecution, of the bludgeon and the jail? That it will be by the power of your naked bosoms, opposed to the rage of oppression! By the grim and bitter teaching of blind and merciless affliction! By the painful gropings of the untutored mind, by the feeble stammerings of the uncultured voice! By the sad and lonely hunger of the spirit; by seeking and striving and yearning, by heartache and despairing, by agony and sweat of blood! It will be by money paid for with hunger, by knowledge stolen from sleep, by thoughts communicated under the shadow of the gallows! It will be a movement beginning in the far-off past, a thing obscure and unhonored, a thing easy to ridicule, easy to despise; a thing unlovely, wearing the aspect of vengeance and hate—but to you, the working-man, the wage-slave, calling with a voice insistent, imperious—with a voice that you cannot escape, wherever upon the earth you may be! With the voice of all your wrongs, with the voice of all your desires; with the voice of your duty and your hope—of everything in the world that is worth while to you! The voice of the poor, demanding that poverty shall cease! The voice of the oppressed, pronouncing the doom of oppression! The voice of power, wrought out of suffering—of resolution, crushed out of weakness—of joy and courage, born in the bottomless pit of anguish and despair! The voice of Labor, despised and outraged; a mighty giant, lying prostrate—mountainous, colossal, but blinded, bound, and ignorant of his strength. And now a dream of resistance haunts him, hope battling with fear; until suddenly he stirs, and a fetter snaps—and a thrill shoots through him, to the farthest ends of his huge body, and in a flash the dream becomes an act! He starts, he lifts himself; and the bands are shattered, the burdens roll off him—he rises—towering, gigantic; he springs to his feet, he shouts in his new-born exultation—"

And the speaker's voice broke suddenly, with the stress of his feelings; he stood with his arms stretched out above him, and the power of his vision seemed to lift him from the floor. The audience came to its feet with a yell; men waved their arms, laughing aloud in their excitement. And Jurgis was with them, he was shouting to tear his throat; shouting because he could not help it, because the stress of his feeling was more than he could bear. It was not merely the man's words, the torrent of his eloquence. It was his presence, it was his voice: a voice with strange intonations that rang through the chambers of the soul like the clanging of a bell—that gripped the listener like a mighty hand about his body, that shook him and startled him with sudden fright, with a sense of things not of earth, of mysteries never spoken before, of presences of awe and terror! There was an unfolding of vistas before him, a breaking of the ground beneath him, an upheaving, a stirring, a trembling; he felt himself suddenly a mere man no longer—there were powers within him undreamed of, there were demon forces contending, age-long wonders struggling to be born; and he sat oppressed with pain and joy, while a tingling stole down into his finger tips, and his breath came hard and fast. The sentences of this man were to Jurgis like the crashing of thunder in his soul; a flood of emotions surged up in him—all his old hopes and longings, his old griefs and rages and despairs. All that he had ever felt in his whole life seemed to come back to him at once, and with one new emotion, hardly to be described. That he should have suffered such oppressions and such horrors was bad enough; but that he should have been crushed and beaten by them, that he should have submitted, and forgotten, and lived in peace—ah, truly that was a thing not to be put into words, a thing not to be borne by a human creature, a thing of terror and madness! "What," asks the prophet, "is the murder of them that kill the body, to the murder of them that kill the soul?" And Jurgis was a man whose soul had been murdered, who had ceased to hope and to struggle—who had made terms with degradation and despair; and now, suddenly, in one awful convulsion, the black and hideous fact was made plain to him! There was a falling in of all the pillars of his soul, the sky seemed to split above him—he stood there, with his clenched hands upraised, his eyes bloodshot, and the veins standing out purple in his face, roaring in the voice of a wild beast, frantic, incoherent, maniacal. And when he could shout no more he still stood there, gasping, and whispering hoarsely to himself: "By God! By God! By God!"

CHAPTER 29

The man had gone back to a seat upon the platform, and Jurgis realized that his speech was over. The applause continued for several minutes; and then some one started a song, and the crowd took it up, and the place shook with it. Jurgis had never heard it, and he could not make out the words, but the wild and wonderful spirit of it seized upon him—it was the "Marseillaise!" As stanza after stanza of it thundered forth, he sat with his hands clasped, trembling in every nerve. He had never been so stirred in his life—it was a miracle that had been wrought in him. He could not think at all, he was stunned; yet he knew that in the mighty upheaval that had taken place in his soul, a new man had been born. He had been torn out of the jaws of destruction, he had been delivered from the thraldom of despair; the whole world had been changed for him—he was free, he was free! Even if he were to suffer as he had before, even if he were to beg and starve, nothing would be the same to him; he would understand it, and bear it. He would no longer be the sport of circumstances, he would be a man, with a will and a purpose; he would have something to fight for, something to die for, if need be! Here were men who would show him and help him; and he would have friends and allies, he would dwell in the sight of justice, and walk arm in arm with power.

The audience subsided again, and Jurgis sat back. The chairman of the meeting came forward and began to speak. His voice sounded thin and futile after the other's, and to Jurgis it seemed a profanation. Why should any one else speak, after that miraculous man—why should they not all sit in silence? The chairman was explaining that a collection would now be taken up to defray the expenses of the meeting, and for the benefit of the campaign fund of the party. Jurgis heard; but he had not a penny to give, and so his thoughts went elsewhere again.

He kept his eyes fixed on the orator, who sat in an armchair, his head leaning on his hand and his attitude indicating exhaustion. But suddenly he stood up again, and Jurgis heard the chairman of the meeting saying that the speaker would now answer any questions which the audience might care to put to him. The man came forward, and some one—a woman—arose and asked about some opinion the speaker had expressed concerning Tolstoy. Jurgis had never heard of Tolstoy, and did not care anything about him. Why should any one want to ask such questions, after an address like that? The thing was not to talk, but to do; the thing was to get bold of others and rouse them, to organize them and prepare for the fight!

But still the discussion went on, in ordinary conversational tones, and it brought Jurgis back to the everyday world. A few minutes ago he had felt like seizing the hand of the beautiful lady by his side, and kissing it; he had felt like flinging his arms about the neck of the man on the other side of him. And now he began to realize again that he was a "hobo," that he was ragged and dirty, and smelled bad, and had no place to sleep that night!

And so, at last, when the meeting broke up, and the audience started to leave, poor Jurgis was in an agony of uncertainty. He had not thought of leaving—he had thought that the vision must last forever, that he had found comrades and brothers. But now he would go out, and the thing would fade away, and he would never be able to find it again! He sat in his seat, frightened and wondering; but others in the same row wanted to get out, and so he had to stand up and move along. As he was swept down the aisle he looked from one person to another, wistfully; they were all excitedly discussing the address—but there was nobody who offered to discuss it with him. He was near enough to the door to feel the night air, when desperation seized him. He knew nothing at all about that speech he had heard, not even the name of the orator; and he was to go away—no, no, it was preposterous, he must speak to some one; he must find that man himself and tell him. He would not despise him, tramp as he was!

So he stepped into an empty row of seats and watched, and when the crowd had thinned out, he started toward the platform. The speaker was gone; but there was a stage door that stood open, with people passing in and out, and no one on guard. Jurgis summoned up his courage and went in, and down a hallway, and to the door of a room where many people were crowded. No one paid any attention to him, and he pushed in, and in a corner he saw the man he sought. The orator sat in a chair, with his shoulders sunk together and his eyes half closed; his face was ghastly pale, almost greenish in hue, and one arm lay limp at his side. A big man with spectacles on stood near him, and kept pushing back the crowd, saying, "Stand away a little, please; can't you see the comrade is worn out?"

So Jurgis stood watching, while five or ten minutes passed. Now and then the man would look up, and address a word or two to those who were near him; and, at last, on one of these occasions, his glance rested on Jurgis. There seemed to be a slight hint of inquiry about it, and a sudden impulse seized the other. He stepped forward.

"I wanted to thank you, sir!" he began, in breathless haste. "I could not go away without telling you how much—how glad I am I heard you. I—I didn't know anything about it all—"

The big man with the spectacles, who had moved away, came back at this moment. "The comrade is too tired to talk to any one—" he began; but the other held up his hand.

"Wait," he said. "He has something to say to me." And then he looked into Jurgis's face. "You want to know more about Socialism?" he asked.

Jurgis started. "I—I—" he stammered. "Is it Socialism? I didn't know. I want to know about what you spoke of—I want to help. I have been through all that."

"Where do you live?" asked the other.

"I have no home," said Jurgis, "I am out of work."

"You are a foreigner, are you not?"

"Lithuanian, sir."

The man thought for a moment, and then turned to his friend. "Who is there, Walters?" he asked. "There is Ostrinski—but he is a Pole—"

"Ostrinski speaks Lithuanian," said the other. "All right, then; would you mind seeing if he has gone yet?"

The other started away, and the speaker looked at Jurgis again. He had deep, black eyes, and a face full of gentleness and pain. "You must excuse me, comrade," he said. "I am just tired out—I have spoken every day for the last month. I will introduce you to some one who will be able to help you as well as I could—"

The messenger had had to go no further than the door, he came back, followed by a man whom he introduced to Jurgis as "Comrade Ostrinski." Comrade Ostrinski was a little man, scarcely up to Jurgis's shoulder, wizened and wrinkled, very ugly, and slightly lame. He had on a long-tailed black coat, worn green at the seams and the buttonholes; his eyes must have been weak, for he wore green spectacles that gave him a grotesque appearance. But his handclasp was hearty, and he spoke in Lithuanian, which warmed Jurgis to him.

"You want to know about Socialism?" he said. "Surely. Let us go out and take a stroll, where we can be quiet and talk some."

And so Jurgis bade farewell to the master wizard, and went out. Ostrinski asked where he lived, offering to walk in that direction; and so he had to explain once more that he was without a home. At the other's request he told his story; how he had come to America, and what had happened to him in the stockyards, and how his family had been broken up, and how he had become a wanderer. So much the little man heard, and then he pressed Jurgis's arm tightly. "You have been through the mill, comrade!" he said. "We will make a fighter out of you!"

Then Ostrinski in turn explained his circumstances. He would have asked Jurgis to his home—but he had only two rooms, and had no bed to offer. He would have given up his own bed, but his wife was ill. Later on, when he understood that otherwise Jurgis would have to sleep in a hallway, he offered him his kitchen floor, a chance which the other was only too glad to accept. "Perhaps tomorrow we can do better," said Ostrinski. "We try not to let a comrade starve."

Ostrinski's home was in the Ghetto district, where he had two rooms in the basement of a tenement. There was a baby crying as they entered, and he closed the door leading into the bedroom. He had three young children, he explained, and a baby had just come. He drew up two chairs near the kitchen stove, adding that Jurgis must excuse the disorder of the place, since at such a time one's domestic arrangements were upset. Half of the kitchen was given up to a workbench, which was piled with clothing, and Ostrinski explained that he was a "pants finisher." He brought great bundles of clothing here to his home, where he and his wife worked on them. He made a living at it, but it was getting harder all the time, because his eyes were failing. What would come when they gave out he could not tell; there had been no saving anything—a man could barely keep alive by twelve or fourteen hours' work a day. The finishing of pants did not take much skill, and anybody could learn it, and so the pay was forever getting less. That was the competitive wage system; and if Jurgis wanted to understand what Socialism was, it was there he had best begin. The workers were dependent upon a job to exist from day to day, and so they bid against each other, and no man could get more than the lowest man would consent to work for. And thus the mass of the people were always in a life-and-death struggle with poverty. That was "competition," so far as it concerned the wage-earner, the man who had only his labor to sell; to those on top, the exploiters, it appeared very differently, of course—there were few of them, and they could combine and dominate, and their power would be unbreakable. And so all over the world two classes were forming, with an unbridged chasm between them—the capitalist class, with its enormous fortunes, and the proletariat, bound into slavery by unseen chains. The latter were a thousand to one in numbers, but they were ignorant and helpless, and they would remain at the mercy of their exploiters until they were organized—until they had become "class-conscious." It was a slow and weary process, but it would go on— it was like the movement of a glacier, once it was started it could never be stopped. Every Socialist did his share, and lived upon the vision of the "good time coming,"—when the working class should go to the polls and seize the powers of government, and put an end to private property in the means of production. No matter how poor a man was, or how much he suffered, he could never be really unhappy while he knew of that future; even if he did not live to see it himself, his children would, and, to a Socialist, the victory of his class was his victory. Also he had always the progress to encourage him; here in Chicago, for instance, the movement was growing by leaps and bounds. Chicago was the industrial center of the country, and nowhere else were the unions so strong; but their organizations did the workers little good, for the employers were organized, also; and so the strikes generally failed, and as fast as the unions were broken up the men were coming over to the Socialists.

Ostrinski explained the organization of the party, the machinery by which the proletariat was educating itself. There were "locals" in every big city and town, and they were being organized rapidly in the smaller places; a local had anywhere from six to a thousand members, and there were fourteen hundred of them in all, with a total of about twenty-five thousand members, who paid dues to support the organization. "Local Cook County," as the city organization was called, had eighty branch locals, and it alone was spending several thousand dollars in the campaign. It published a weekly in English, and one each in Bohemian and German; also there was a monthly published in Chicago, and a cooperative publishing house, that issued a million and a half of Socialist books and pamphlets every year. All this was the growth of the last few years—there had been almost nothing of it when Ostrinski first came to Chicago.

Ostrinski was a Pole, about fifty years of age. He had lived in Silesia, a member of a despised and persecuted race, and had taken part in the proletarian movement in the early seventies, when Bismarck, having conquered France, had turned his policy of blood and iron upon the "International." Ostrinski himself had twice been in jail, but he had been young then, and had not cared. He had had more of his share of the fight, though, for just when Socialism had broken all its barriers and become the great political force of the empire, he had come to America, and begun all over again. In America every one had laughed at the mere idea of Socialism then—in America all men were free. As if political liberty made wage slavery any the more tolerable! said Ostrinski.

The little tailor sat tilted back in his stiff kitchen chair, with his feet stretched out upon the empty stove, and speaking in low whispers, so as not to waken those in the next room. To Jurgis he seemed a scarcely less wonderful person than the speaker at the meeting; he was poor, the lowest of the low, hunger-driven and miserable—and yet how much he knew, how much he had dared and achieved, what a hero he had been! There were others like him, too—thousands like him, and all of them workingmen! That all this wonderful machinery of progress had been created by his fellows—Jurgis could not believe it, it seemed too good to be true.

That was always the way, said Ostrinski; when a man was first converted to Socialism he was like a crazy person—he could not' understand how others could fail to see it, and he expected to convert all the world the first week. After a while he would realize how hard a task it was; and then it would be fortunate that other new hands kept coming, to save him from settling down into a rut. Just now Jurgis would have plenty of chance to vent his excitement, for a presidential campaign was on, and everybody was talking politics. Ostrinski would take him to the next meeting of the branch local, and introduce him, and he might join the party. The dues were five cents a week, but any one who could not afford this might be excused from paying. The Socialist party was a really democratic political organization—it was controlled absolutely by its own membership, and had no bosses. All of these things Ostrinski explained, as also the principles of the party. You might say that there was really but one Socialist principle—that of "no compromise," which was the essence of the proletarian movement all over the world. When a Socialist was elected to office he voted with old party legislators for any measure that was likely to be of help to the working class, but he never forgot that these concessions, whatever they might be, were trifles compared with the great purpose—the organizing of the working class for the revolution. So far, the rule in America had been that one Socialist made another Socialist once every two years; and if they should maintain the same rate they would carry the country in 1912— though not all of them expected to succeed as quickly as that.

The Socialists were organized in every civilized nation; it was an international political party, said Ostrinski, the greatest the world had ever known. It numbered thirty million of adherents, and it cast eight million votes. It had started its first newspaper in Japan, and elected its first deputy in Argentina; in France it named members of cabinets, and in Italy and Australia it held the balance of power and turned out ministries. In Germany, where its vote was more than a third of the total vote of the empire, all other parties and powers had united to fight it. It would not do, Ostrinski explained, for the proletariat of one nation to achieve the victory, for that nation would be crushed by the military power of the others; and so the Socialist movement was a world movement, an organization of all mankind to establish liberty and fraternity. It was the new religion of humanity—or you might say it was the fulfillment of the old religion, since it implied but the literal application of all the teachings of Christ.

Until long after midnight Jurgis sat lost in the conversation of his new acquaintance. It was a most wonderful experience to him—an almost supernatural experience. It was like encountering an inhabitant of the fourth dimension of space, a being who was free from all one's own limitations. For four years, now, Jurgis had been wondering and blundering in the depths of a wilderness; and here, suddenly, a hand reached down and seized him, and lifted him out of it, and set him upon a mountain-top, from which he could survey it all—could see the paths from which he had wandered, the morasses into which he had stumbled, the hiding places of the beasts of prey that had fallen upon him. There were his Packingtown experiences, for instance—what was there about Packingtown that Ostrinski could not explain! To Jurgis the packers had been equivalent to fate; Ostrinski showed him that they were the Beef Trust. They were a gigantic combination of capital, which had crushed all opposition, and overthrown the laws of the land, and was preying upon the people. Jurgis recollected how, when he had first come to Packingtown, he had stood and watched the hog-killing, and thought how cruel and savage it was, and come away congratulating himself that he was not a hog; now his new acquaintance showed him that a hog was just what he had been—one of the packers' hogs. What they wanted from a hog was all the profits that could be got out of him; and that was what they wanted from the working-man, and also that was what they wanted from the public. What the hog thought of it, and what he suffered, were not considered; and no more was it with labor, and no more with the purchaser of meat. That was true everywhere in the world, but it was especially true in Packingtown; there seemed to be something about the work of slaughtering that tended to ruthlessness and ferocity—it was literally the fact that in the methods of the packers a hundred human lives did not balance a penny of profit. When Jurgis had made himself familiar with the Socialist literature, as he would very quickly, he would get glimpses of the Beef Trust from all sorts of aspects, and he would find it everywhere the same; it was the incarnation of blind and insensate Greed. It was a monster devouring with a thousand mouths, trampling with a thousand hoofs; it was the Great Butcher—it was the spirit of Capitalism made flesh. Upon the ocean of commerce it sailed as a pirate ship; it had hoisted the black flag and declared war upon civilization. Bribery and corruption were its everyday methods. In Chicago the city government was simply one of its branch offices; it stole billions of gallons of city water openly, it dictated to the courts the sentences of disorderly strikers, it forbade the mayor to enforce the building laws against it. In the national capital it had power to prevent inspection of its product, and to falsify government reports; it violated the rebate laws, and when an investigation was threatened it burned its books and sent its criminal agents out of the country. In the commercial world it was a Juggernaut car; it wiped out thousands of businesses every year, it drove men to madness and suicide. It had forced the price of cattle so low as to destroy the stock-raising industry, an occupation upon which whole states existed; it had ruined thousands of butchers who had refused to handle its products. It divided the country into districts, and fixed the price of meat in all of them; and it owned all the refrigerator cars, and levied an enormous tribute upon all poultry and eggs and fruit and vegetables. With the millions of dollars a week that poured in upon it, it was reaching out for the control of other interests, railroads and trolley lines, gas and electric light franchises—it already owned the leather and the grain business of the country. The people were tremendously stirred up over its encroachments, but nobody had any remedy to suggest; it was the task of Socialists to teach and organize them, and prepare them for the time when they were to seize the huge machine called the Beef Trust, and use it to produce food for human beings and not to heap up fortunes for a band of pirates. It was long after midnight when Jurgis lay down upon the floor of Ostrinski's kitchen; and yet it was an hour before he could get to sleep, for the glory of that joyful vision of the people of Packingtown marching in and taking possession of the Union Stockyards!

CHAPTER 30

Jurgis had breakfast with Ostrinski and his family, and then he went home to Elzbieta. He was no longer shy about it—when he went in, instead of saying all the things he had been planning to say, he started to tell Elzbieta about the revolution! At first she thought he was out of his mind, and it was hours before she could really feel certain that he was himself. When, however, she had satisfied herself that he was sane upon all subjects except politics, she troubled herself no further about it. Jurgis was destined to find that Elzbieta's armor was absolutely impervious to Socialism. Her soul had been baked hard in the fire of adversity, and there was no altering it now; life to her was the hunt for daily bread, and ideas existed for her only as they bore upon that. All that interested her in regard to this new frenzy which had seized hold of her son-in-law was whether or not it had a tendency to make him sober and industrious; and when she found he intended to look for work and to contribute his share to the family fund, she gave him full rein to convince her of anything. A wonderfully wise little woman was Elzbieta; she could think as quickly as a hunted rabbit, and in half an hour she had chosen her life-attitude to the Socialist movement. She agreed in everything with Jurgis, except the need of his paying his dues; and she would even go to a meeting with him now and then, and sit and plan her next day's dinner amid the storm.

For a week after he became a convert Jurgis continued to wander about all day, looking for work; until at last he met with a strange fortune. He was passing one of Chicago's innumerable small hotels, and after some hesitation he concluded to go in. A man he took for the proprietor was standing in the lobby, and he went up to him and tackled him for a job.

"What can you do?" the man asked.

"Anything, sir," said Jurgis, and added quickly: "I've been out of work for a long time, sir. I'm an honest man, and I'm strong and willing—"

The other was eying him narrowly. "Do you drink?" he asked.

"No, sir," said Jurgis.

"Well, I've been employing a man as a porter, and he drinks. I've discharged him seven times now, and I've about made up my mind that's enough. Would you be a porter?"

"Yes, sir."

"It's hard work. You'll have to clean floors and wash spittoons and fill lamps and handle trunks—"

"I'm willing, sir."

"All right. I'll pay you thirty a month and board, and you can begin now, if you feel like it. You can put on the other fellow's rig."

And so Jurgis fell to work, and toiled like a Trojan till night. Then he went and told Elzbieta, and also, late as it was, he paid a visit to Ostrinski to let him know of his good fortune. Here he received a great surprise, for when he was describing the location of the hotel Ostrinski interrupted suddenly, "Not Hinds's!"

"Yes," said Jurgis, "that's the name."

To which the other replied, "Then you've got the best boss in Chicago—he's a state organizer of our party, and one of our best-known speakers!"

So the next morning Jurgis went to his employer and told him; and the man seized him by the hand and shook it. "By Jove!" he cried, "that lets me out. I didn't sleep all last night because I had discharged a good Socialist!"

So, after that, Jurgis was known to his "boss" as "Comrade Jurgis," and in return he was expected to call him "Comrade Hinds." "Tommy" Hinds, as he was known to his intimates, was a squat little man, with broad shoulders and a florid face, decorated with gray side whiskers. He was the kindest-hearted man that ever lived, and the liveliest—inexhaustible in his enthusiasm, and talking Socialism all day and all night. He was a great fellow to jolly along a crowd, and would keep a meeting in an uproar; when once he got really waked up, the torrent of his eloquence could be compared with nothing save Niagara.

Tommy Hinds had begun life as a blacksmith's helper, and had run away to join the Union army, where he had made his first acquaintance with "graft," in the shape of rotten muskets and shoddy blankets. To a musket that broke in a crisis he always attributed the death of his only brother, and upon worthless blankets he blamed all the agonies of his own old age. Whenever it rained, the rheumatism would get into his joints, and then he would screw up his face and mutter: "Capitalism, my boy, capitalism! 'Ecrasez l'infame!'" He had one unfailing remedy for all the evils of this world, and he preached it to every one; no matter whether the person's trouble was failure in business, or dyspepsia, or a quarrelsome mother-in-law, a twinkle would come into his eyes and he would say, "You know what to do about it—vote the Socialist ticket!"

Tommy Hinds had set out upon the trail of the Octopus as soon as the war was over. He had gone into business, and found himself in competition with the fortunes of those who had been stealing while he had been fighting. The city government was in their hands and the railroads were in league with them, and honest business was driven to the wall; and so Hinds had put all his savings into Chicago real estate, and set out singlehanded to dam the river of graft. He had been a reform member of the city council, he had been a Greenbacker, a Labor Unionist, a Populist, a Bryanite—and after thirty years of fighting, the year 1896 had served to convince him that the power of concentrated wealth could never be controlled, but could only be destroyed. He had published a pamphlet about it, and set out to organize a party of his own, when a stray Socialist leaflet had revealed to him that others had been ahead of him. Now for eight years he had been fighting for the party, anywhere, everywhere—whether it was a G.A.R. reunion, or a hotel-keepers' convention, or an Afro-American business-men's banquet, or a Bible society picnic, Tommy Hinds would manage to get himself invited to explain the relations of Socialism to the subject in hand. After that he would start off upon a tour of his own, ending at some place between New York and Oregon; and when he came back from there, he would go out to organize new locals for the state committee; and finally he would come home to rest—and talk Socialism in Chicago. Hinds's hotel was a very hot-bed of the propaganda; all the employees were party men, and if they were not when they came, they were quite certain to be before they went away. The proprietor would get into a discussion with some one in the lobby, and as the conversation grew animated, others would gather about to listen, until finally every one in the place would be crowded into a group, and a regular debate would be under way. This went on every night—when Tommy Hinds was not there to do it, his clerk did it; and when his clerk was away campaigning, the assistant attended to it, while Mrs. Hinds sat behind the desk and did the work. The clerk was an old crony of the proprietor's, an awkward, rawboned giant of a man, with a lean, sallow face, a broad mouth, and whiskers under his chin, the very type and body of a prairie farmer. He had been that all his life—he had fought the railroads in Kansas for fifty years, a Granger, a Farmers' Alliance man, a "middle-of-the-road" Populist. Finally, Tommy Hinds had revealed to him the wonderful idea of using the trusts instead of destroying them, and he had sold his farm and come to Chicago.

That was Amos Struver; and then there was Harry Adams, the assistant clerk, a pale, scholarly-looking man, who came from Massachusetts, of Pilgrim stock. Adams had been a cotton operative in Fall River, and the continued depression in the industry had worn him and his family out, and he had emigrated to South Carolina. In Massachusetts the percentage of white illiteracy is eight-tenths of one per cent, while in South Carolina it is thirteen and six-tenths per cent; also in South Carolina there is a property qualification for voters—and for these and other reasons child labor is the rule, and so the cotton mills were driving those of Massachusetts out of the business. Adams did not know this, he only knew that the Southern mills were running; but when he got there he found that if he was to live, all his family would have to work, and from six o'clock at night to six o'clock in the morning. So he had set to work to organize the mill hands, after the fashion in Massachusetts, and had been discharged; but he had gotten other work, and stuck at it, and at last there had been a strike for shorter hours, and Harry Adams had attempted to address a street meeting, which was the end of him. In the states of the far South the labor of convicts is leased to contractors, and when there are not convicts enough they have to be supplied. Harry Adams was sent up by a judge who was a cousin of the mill owner with whose business he had interfered; and though the life had nearly killed him, he had been wise enough not to murmur, and at the end of his term he and his family had left the state of South

Carolina—hell's back yard, as he called it. He had no money for carfare, but it was harvest-time, and they walked one day and worked the next; and so Adams got at last to Chicago, and joined the Socialist party. He was a studious man, reserved, and nothing of an orator; but he always had a pile of books under his desk in the hotel, and articles from his pen were beginning to attract attention in the party press.

Contrary to what one would have expected, all this radicalism did not hurt the hotel business; the radicals flocked to it, and the commercial travelers all found it diverting. Of late, also, the hotel had become a favorite stopping place for Western cattlemen. Now that the Beef Trust had adopted the trick of raising prices to induce enormous shipments of cattle, and then dropping them again and scooping in all they needed, a stock raiser was very apt to find himself in Chicago without money enough to pay his freight bill; and so he had to go to a cheap hotel, and it was no drawback to him if there was an agitator talking in the lobby. These Western fellows were just "meat" for Tommy Hinds—he would get a dozen of them around him and paint little pictures of "the System." Of course, it was not a week before he had heard Jurgis's story, and after that he would not have let his new porter go for the world. "See here," he would say, in the middle of an argument, "I've got a fellow right here in my place who's worked there and seen every bit of it!" And then Jurgis would drop his work, whatever it was, and come, and the other would say, "Comrade Jurgis, just tell these gentlemen what you saw on the killing-beds." At first this request caused poor Jurgis the most acute agony, and it was like pulling teeth to get him to talk; but gradually he found out what was wanted, and in the end he learned to stand up and speak his piece with enthusiasm. His employer would sit by and encourage him with exclamations and shakes of the head; when Jurgis would give the formula for "potted ham," or tell about the condemned hogs that were dropped into the "destructors" at the top and immediately taken out again at the bottom, to be shipped into another state and made into lard, Tommy Hinds would bang his knee and cry, "Do you think a man could make up a thing like that out of his head?"

And then the hotel-keeper would go on to show how the Socialists had the only real remedy for such evils, how they alone "meant business" with the Beef Trust. And when, in answer to this, the victim would say that the whole country was getting stirred up, that the newspapers were full of denunciations of it, and the government taking action against it, Tommy Hinds had a knock-out blow all ready. "Yes," he would say, "all that is true—but what do you suppose is the reason for it? Are you foolish enough to believe that it's done for the public? There are other trusts in the country just as illegal and extortionate as the Beef Trust: there is the Coal Trust, that freezes the poor in winter—there is the Steel Trust, that doubles the price of every nail in your shoes—there is the Oil Trust, that keeps you from reading at night—and why do you suppose it is that all the fury of the press and the government is directed against the Beef Trust?" And when to this the victim would reply that there was clamor enough over the Oil Trust, the other would continue: "Ten years ago Henry D. Lloyd told all the truth about the

Standard Oil Company in his Wealth versus Commonwealth; and the book was allowed to die, and you hardly ever hear of it. And now, at last, two magazines have the courage to tackle 'Standard Oil' again, and what happens? The newspapers ridicule the authors, the churches defend the criminals, and the government—does nothing. And now, why is it all so different with the Beef Trust?"

Here the other would generally admit that he was "stuck"; and Tommy Hinds would explain to him, and it was fun to see his eyes open. "If you were a Socialist," the hotel-keeper would say, "you would understand that the power which really governs the United States today is the Railroad Trust. It is the Railroad Trust that runs your state government, wherever you live, and that runs the United States Senate. And all of the trusts that I have named are railroad trusts—save only the Beef Trust! The Beef Trust has defied the railroads—it is plundering them day by day through the Private Car; and so the public is roused to fury, and the papers clamor for action, and the government goes on the war-path! And you poor common people watch and applaud the job, and think it's all done for you, and never dream that it is really the grand climax of the century-long battle of commercial competition—the final death grapple between the chiefs of the Beef Trust and 'Standard Oil,' for the prize of the mastery and ownership of the United States of America!"

Such was the new home in which Jurgis lived and worked, and in which his education was completed. Perhaps you would imagine that he did not do much work there, but that would be a great mistake. He would have cut off one hand for Tommy Hinds; and to keep Hinds's hotel a thing of beauty was his joy in life. That he had a score of Socialist arguments chasing through his brain in the meantime did not interfere with this; on the contrary, Jurgis scrubbed the spittoons and polished the banisters all the more vehemently because at the same time he was wrestling inwardly with an imaginary recalcitrant. It would be pleasant to record that he swore off drinking immediately, and all the rest of his bad habits with it; but that would hardly be exact. These revolutionists were not angels; they were men, and men who had come up from the social pit, and with the mire of it smeared over them. Some of them drank, and some of them swore, and some of them ate pie with their knives; there was only one difference between them and all the rest of the populace—that they were men with a hope, with a cause to fight for and suffer for. There came times to Jurgis when the vision seemed far-off and pale, and a glass of beer loomed large in comparison; but if the glass led to another glass, and to too many glasses, he had something to spur him to remorse and resolution on the morrow. It was so evidently a wicked thing to spend one's pennies for drink, when the working class was wandering in darkness, and waiting to be delivered; the price of a glass of beer would buy fifty copies of a leaflet, and one could hand these out to the unregenerate, and then get drunk upon the thought of the good that was being accomplished. That was the way the movement had been made, and it was the only way it would progress; it availed nothing to know of it, without fighting for it—it was a thing for all, not for a few! A corollary of this proposition of course was, that any one who refused to receive the new gospel was personally responsible for keeping Jurgis from his heart's desire; and this, alas, made him uncomfortable as an acquaintance. He met some neighbors with whom Elzbieta had made friends in her neighborhood, and he set out to make Socialists of them by wholesale, and several times he all but got into a fight.

It was all so painfully obvious to Jurgis! It was so incomprehensible how a man could fail to see it! Here were all the opportunities of the country, the land, and the buildings upon the land, the railroads, the mines, the factories, and the stores, all in the hands of a few private individuals, called capitalists, for whom the people were obliged to work for wages. The whole balance of what the people produced went to heap up the fortunes of these capitalists, to heap, and heap again, and yet again—and that in spite of the fact that they, and every one about them, lived in unthinkable luxury! And was it not plain that if the people cut off the share of those who merely "owned," the share of those who worked would be much greater? That was as plain as two and two makes four; and it was the whole of it, absolutely the whole of it; and yet there were people who could not see it, who would argue about everything else in the world. They would tell you that governments could not manage things as economically as private individuals; they would repeat and repeat that, and think they were saying something! They could not see that "economical" management by masters meant simply that they, the people, were worked harder and ground closer and paid less! They were wage-earners and servants, at the mercy of exploiters whose one thought was to get as much out of them as possible; and they were taking an interest in the process, were anxious lest it should not be done thoroughly enough! Was it not honestly a trial to listen to an argument such as that?

And yet there were things even worse. You would begin talking to some poor devil who had worked in one shop for the last thirty years, and had never been able to save a penny; who left home every morning at six o'clock, to go and tend a machine, and come back at night too tired to take his clothes off; who had never had a week's vacation in his life, had never traveled, never had an adventure, never learned anything, never hoped anything—and when you started to tell him about Socialism he would sniff and say, "I'm not interested in that—I'm an individualist!" And then he would go on to tell you that Socialism was "paternalism," and that if it ever had its way the world would stop progressing. It was enough to make a mule laugh, to hear arguments like that; and yet it was no laughing matter, as you found out—for how many millions of such poor deluded wretches there were, whose lives had been so stunted by capitalism that they no longer knew what freedom was! And they really thought that it was "individualism" for tens of thousands of them to herd together and obey the orders of a steel magnate, and produce hundreds of millions of dollars of wealth for him, and then let him give them libraries; while for them to take the industry, and run it to suit themselves, and build their own libraries—that would have been "Paternalism"!

Sometimes the agony of such things as this was almost more than Jurgis could bear; yet there was no way of escape from it, there was nothing to do but to dig away at the base of this mountain of ignorance and prejudice. You must keep at the poor fellow; you must hold your temper, and argue with him, and watch for your chance to stick an idea or two into his head. And the rest of the time you must sharpen up your weapons—you must think out new replies to his objections, and provide yourself with new facts to prove to him the folly of his ways.

So Jurgis acquired the reading habit. He would carry in his pocket a tract or a pamphlet which some one had loaned him, and whenever he had an idle moment during the day he would plod through a paragraph, and then think about it while he worked. Also he read the newspapers, and asked questions about them. One of the other porters at Hinds's was a sharp little Irishman, who knew everything that Jurgis wanted to know; and while they were busy he would explain to him the geography of America, and its history, its constitution and its laws; also he gave him an idea of the business system of the country, the great railroads and corporations, and who owned them, and the labor unions, and the big strikes, and the men who had led them. Then at night, when he could get off, Jurgis would attend the Socialist meetings. During the campaign one was not dependent upon the street corner affairs, where the weather and the quality of the orator were equally uncertain; there were hall meetings every night, and one could hear speakers of national prominence. These discussed the political situation from every point of view, and all that troubled Jurgis was the impossibility of carrying off but a small part of the treasures they offered him.

There was a man who was known in the party as the "Little Giant." The Lord had used up so much material in the making of his head that there had not been enough to complete his legs; but he got about on the platform, and when he shook his raven whiskers the pillars of capitalism rocked. He had written a veritable encyclopedia upon the subject, a book that was nearly as big as himself—And then there was a young author, who came from California, and had been a salmon fisher, an oyster-pirate, a longshoreman, a sailor; who had tramped the country and been sent to jail, had lived in the Whitechapel slums, and been to the Klondike in search of gold. All these things he pictured in his books, and because he was a man of genius he forced the world to hear him. Now he was famous, but wherever he went he still preached the gospel of the poor. And then there was one who was known at the "millionaire Socialist." He had made a fortune in business, and spent nearly all of it in building up a magazine, which the post office department had tried to suppress, and had driven to Canada. He was a quiet-mannered man, whom you would have taken for anything in the world but a Socialist agitator. His speech was simple and informal—he could not understand why any one should get excited about these things. It was a process of economic evolution, he said, and he exhibited its laws and methods. Life was a struggle for existence, and the strong overcame the weak, and in turn were overcome by the strongest. Those who lost in the struggle were generally exterminated; but now and then they had been known to save themselves by combination—which was a new and higher kind of strength. It was so that the gregarious animals had overcome the predaceous; it was so, in human history, that the people had mastered the kings. The workers were simply the citizens of industry, and the Socialist movement was the expression of their will to survive. The inevitability of the revolution depended upon this fact, that they had no choice but to unite or be exterminated; this fact, grim and inexorable, depended upon no human will, it was the law of the economic process, of which the editor showed the details with the most marvelous precision.

And later on came the evening of the great meeting of the campaign, when Jurgis heard the two standard-bearers of his party. Ten years before there had been in Chicago a strike of a hundred and fifty thousand railroad employees, and thugs had been hired by the railroads to commit violence, and the President of the United States had sent in troops to break the strike, by flinging the officers of the union into jail without trial. The president of the union came out of his cell a ruined man; but also he came out a Socialist; and now for just ten years he had been traveling up and down the country, standing face to face with the people, and pleading with them for justice. He was a man of electric presence, tall and gaunt, with a face worn thin by struggle and suffering. The fury of outraged manhood gleamed in it—and the tears of suffering little children pleaded in his voice. When he spoke he paced the stage, lithe and eager, like a panther. He leaned over, reaching out for his audience; he pointed into their souls with an insistent finger. His voice was husky from much speaking, but the great auditorium was as still as death, and every one heard him.

And then, as Jurgis came out from this meeting, some one handed him a paper which he carried home with him and read; and so he became acquainted with the "Appeal to Reason." About twelve years previously a Colorado real-estate speculator had made up his mind that it was wrong to gamble in the necessities of life of human beings: and so he had retired and begun the publication of a Socialist weekly. There had come a time when he had to set his own type, but he had held on and won out, and now his publication was an institution. It used a carload of paper every week, and the mail trains would be hours loading up at the depot of the little Kansas town. It was a four-page weekly, which sold for less than half a cent a copy; its regular subscription list was a quarter of a million, and it went to every crossroads post office in America.

The "Appeal" was a "propaganda" paper. It had a manner all its own—it was full of ginger and spice, of Western slang and hustle: It collected news of the doings of the "plutes," and served it up for the benefit of the "American working-mule." It would have columns of the deadly parallel—the million dollars' worth of diamonds, or the fancy pet-poodle establishment of a society dame, beside the fate of Mrs. Murphy of San Francisco, who had starved to death on the streets, or of John Robinson, just out of the hospital, who had hanged himself in New York because he could not find work. It collected the stories of graft and misery from the daily press, and made a little pungent paragraphs out of them. "Three banks of Bungtown, South Dakota, failed, and more savings of the workers swallowed up!" "The mayor of Sandy Creek, Oklahoma, has skipped with a hundred thousand dollars. That's the kind of rulers the old partyites give you!" "The president of the

Florida Flying Machine Company is in jail for bigamy. He was a prominent opponent of Socialism, which he said would break up the home!" The "Appeal" had what it called its "Army," about thirty thousand of the faithful, who did things for it; and it was always exhorting the "Army" to keep its dander up, and occasionally encouraging it with a prize competition, for anything from a gold watch to a private yacht or an eighty-acre farm. Its office helpers were all known to the "Army" by quaint titles—"Inky Ike," "the Bald-headed Man," "the Redheaded Girl," "the Bulldog," "the Office Goat," and "the One Hoss."

But sometimes, again, the "Appeal" would be desperately serious. It sent a correspondent to Colorado, and printed pages describing the overthrow of American institutions in that state. In a certain city of the country it had over forty of its "Army" in the headquarters of the Telegraph Trust, and no message of importance to Socialists ever went through that a copy of it did not go to the "Appeal." It would print great broadsides during the campaign; one copy that came to Jurgis was a manifesto addressed to striking workingmen, of which nearly a million copies had been distributed in the industrial centers, wherever the employers' associations had been carrying out their "open shop" program. "You have lost the strike!" it was headed. "And now what are you going to do about it?" It was what is called an "incendiary" appeal—it was written by a man into whose soul the iron had entered. When this edition appeared, twenty thousand copies were sent to the stockyards district; and they were taken out and stowed away in the rear of a little cigar store, and every evening, and on Sundays, the members of the Packingtown locals would get armfuls and distribute them on the streets and in the houses. The people of Packingtown had lost their strike, if ever a people had, and so they read these papers gladly, and twenty thousand were hardly enough to go round. Jurgis had resolved not to go near his old home again, but when he heard of this it was too much for him, and every night for a week he would get on the car and ride out to the stockyards, and help to undo his work of the previous year, when he had sent Mike Scully's ten-pin setter to the city Board of Aldermen.

It was quite marvelous to see what a difference twelve months had made in Packingtown—the eyes of the people were getting opened! The Socialists were literally sweeping everything before them that election, and Scully and the Cook County machine were at their wits' end for an "issue." At the very close of the campaign they bethought themselves of the fact that the strike had been broken by Negroes, and so they sent for a South Carolina fire-eater, the "pitchfork senator," as he was called, a man who took off his coat when he talked to workingmen, and damned and swore like a Hessian. This meeting they advertised extensively, and the Socialists advertised it too—with the result that about a thousand of them were on hand that evening. The "pitchfork senator" stood their fusillade of questions for about an hour, and then went home in disgust, and the balance of the meeting was a strictly party affair. Jurgis, who had insisted upon coming, had the time of his life that night; he danced about and waved his arms in his excitement—and at the very climax he broke loose from his friends, and got out into the aisle, and proceeded to make a speech himself! The senator had been denying that the Democratic party was corrupt; it was always the Republicans who bought the votes, he said—and here was Jurgis shouting furiously, "It's a lie! It's a lie!" After which he went on to tell them how he knew it—that he knew it because he had bought them himself! And he would have told the "pitchfork senator" all his experiences, had not Harry Adams and a friend grabbed him about the neck and shoved him into a seat.

CHAPTER 31

One of the first things that Jurgis had done after he got a job was to go and see Marija. She came down into the basement of the house to meet him, and he stood by the door with his hat in his hand, saying, "I've got work now, and so you can leave here."

But Marija only shook her head. There was nothing else for her to do, she said, and nobody to employ her. She could not keep her past a secret—girls had tried it, and they were always found out. There were thousands of men who came to this place, and sooner or later she would meet one of them. "And besides," Marija added, "I can't do anything. I'm no good—I take dope. What could you do with me?"

"Can't you stop?" Jurgis cried.

"No," she answered, "I'll never stop. What's the use of talking about it—I'll stay here till I die, I guess. It's all I'm fit for." And that was all that he could get her to say—there was no use trying. When he told her he would not let Elzbieta take her money, she answered indifferently: "Then it'll be wasted here—that's all." Her eyelids looked heavy and her face was red and swollen; he saw that he was annoying her, that she only wanted him to go away. So he went, disappointed and sad.

Poor Jurgis was not very happy in his home-life. Elzbieta was sick a good deal now, and the boys were wild and unruly, and very much the worse for their life upon the streets. But he stuck by the family nevertheless, for they reminded him of his old happiness; and when things went wrong he could solace himself with a plunge into the Socialist movement. Since his life had been caught up into the current of this great stream, things which had before been the whole of life to him came to seem of relatively slight importance; his interests were elsewhere, in the world of ideas. His outward life was commonplace and uninteresting; he was just a hotel-porter, and expected to remain one while he lived; but meantime, in the realm of thought, his life was a perpetual adventure. There was so much to know—so many wonders to be discovered! Never in all his life did Jurgis forget the day before election, when there came a telephone message from a friend of Harry Adams, asking him to bring Jurgis to see him that night; and Jurgis went, and met one of the minds of the movement.

The invitation was from a man named Fisher, a Chicago millionaire who had given up his life to settlement work, and had a little home in the heart of the city's slums. He did not belong to the party, but he was in sympathy with it; and he said that he was to have as his guest that night the editor of a big Eastern magazine, who wrote against Socialism, but really did not know what it was. The millionaire suggested that Adams bring Jurgis along, and then start up the subject of "pure food," in which the editor was interested.

Young Fisher's home was a little two-story brick house, dingy and weather-beaten outside, but attractive within. The room that Jurgis saw was half lined with books, and upon the walls were many pictures, dimly visible in the soft, yellow light; it was a cold, rainy night, so a log fire was crackling in the open hearth. Seven or eight people were gathered about it when Adams and his friend arrived, and Jurgis saw to his dismay that three of them were ladies. He had never talked to people of this sort before, and he fell into an agony of embarrassment. He stood in the doorway clutching his hat tightly in his hands, and made a deep bow to each of the persons as he was introduced; then, when he was asked to have a seat, he took a chair in a dark corner, and sat down upon the edge of it, and wiped the perspiration off his forehead with his sleeve. He was terrified lest they should expect him to talk.

There was the host himself, a tall, athletic young man, clad in evening dress, as also was the editor, a dyspeptic-looking gentleman named Maynard. There was the former's frail young wife, and also an elderly lady, who taught kindergarten in the settlement, and a young college student, a beautiful girl with an intense and earnest face. She only spoke once or twice while Jurgis was there—the rest of the time she sat by the table in the center of the room, resting her chin in her hands and drinking in the conversation. There were two other men, whom young Fisher had introduced to Jurgis as Mr. Lucas and Mr. Schliemann; he heard them address Adams as "Comrade," and so he knew that they were Socialists.

The one called Lucas was a mild and meek-looking little gentleman of clerical aspect; he had been an itinerant evangelist, it transpired, and had seen the light and become a prophet of the new dispensation. He traveled all over the country, living like the apostles of old, upon hospitality, and preaching upon street-corners when there was no hall. The other man had been in the midst of a discussion with the editor when Adams and Jurgis came in; and at the suggestion of the host they resumed it after the interruption. Jurgis was soon sitting spellbound, thinking that here was surely the strangest man that had ever lived in the world.

Nicholas Schliemann was a Swede, a tall, gaunt person, with hairy hands and bristling yellow beard; he was a university man, and had been a professor of phi-losophy—until, as he said, he had found that he was selling his character as well as his time. Instead he had come to America, where he lived in a garret room in this slum district, and made volcanic energy take the place of fire. He studied the composition of food-stuffs, and knew exactly how many proteids and carbohy-drates his body needed; and by scientific chewing he said that he tripled the value of all he ate, so that it cost him eleven cents a day. About the first of July he would leave Chicago for his vacation, on foot; and when he struck the harvest fields he would set to work for two dollars and a half a day, and come home when he had another year's supply—a hundred and twenty-five dollars. That was the nearest approach to independence a man could make "under capitalism," he explained; he would never marry, for no sane man would allow himself to fall in love until after the revolution.

He sat in a big arm-chair, with his legs crossed, and his head so far in the shadow that one saw only two glowing lights, reflected from the fire on the hearth. He spoke simply, and utterly without emotion; with the manner of a teacher setting forth to a group of scholars an axiom in geometry, he would enunciate such propositions as made the hair of an ordinary person rise on end. And when the auditor had asserted his non-comprehension, he would proceed to elucidate by some new proposition, yet more appalling. To Jurgis the Herr Dr. Schliemann assumed the proportions of a thunderstorm or an earthquake. And yet, strange as it might seem, there was a subtle bond between them, and he could follow the argument nearly all the time. He was carried over the difficult places in spite of himself; and he went plunging away in mad career—a very Mazeppa-ride upon the wild horse Speculation.

Nicholas Schliemann was familiar with all the universe, and with man as a small part of it. He understood human institutions, and blew them about like soap bubbles. It was surprising that so much destructiveness could be contained in one human mind. Was it government? The purpose of government was the guarding of property-rights, the perpetuation of ancient force and modern fraud. Or was it marriage? Marriage and prostitution were two sides of one shield, the predatory man's exploitation of the sex-pleasure. The difference between them was a difference of class. If a woman had money she might dictate her own terms: equality, a life contract, and the legitimacy—that is, the property-rights—of her children. If she had no money, she was a proletarian, and sold herself for an existence. And then the subject became Religion, which was the Archfiend's deadliest weapon. Government oppressed the body of the wage-slave, but Religion oppressed his mind, and poisoned the stream of progress at its source. The working-man was to fix his hopes upon a future life, while his pockets were picked in this one; he was brought up to frugality, humility, obedience—in short to all the pseudo-virtues of capitalism. The destiny of civilization would be decided in one final death struggle between the Red International and the Black, between Socialism and the Roman Catholic Church; while here at home, "the stygian midnight of American evangelicalism—"

And here the ex-preacher entered the field, and there was a lively tussle. "Comrade" Lucas was not what is called an educated man; he knew only the Bible, but it was the Bible interpreted by real experience. And what was the use, he asked, of confusing Religion with men's perversions of it? That the church was in the hands of the merchants at the moment was obvious enough; but already there were signs of rebellion, and if Comrade Schliemann could come back a few years from now—

"Ah, yes," said the other, "of course, I have no doubt that in a hundred years the Vatican will be denying that it ever opposed Socialism, just as at present it denies that it ever tortured Galileo."

"I am not defending the Vatican," exclaimed Lucas, vehemently. "I am defending the word of God—which is one long cry of the human spirit for deliverance from the sway of oppression. Take the twenty-fourth chapter of the Book of Job, which I am accustomed to quote in my addresses as 'the Bible upon the Beef Trust'; or take the words of Isaiah—or of the Master himself! Not the elegant prince of our debauched and vicious art, not the jeweled idol of our society churches—but the Jesus of the awful reality, the man of sorrow and pain, the outcast, despised of the world, who had nowhere to lay his head—"

"I will grant you Jesus," interrupted the other.

"Well, then," cried Lucas, "and why should Jesus have nothing to do with his church—why should his words and his life be of no authority among those who profess to adore him? Here is a man who was the world's first revolutionist, the true founder of the Socialist movement; a man whose whole being was one flame of hatred for wealth, and all that wealth stands for,—for the pride of wealth, and the luxury of wealth, and the tyranny of wealth; who was himself a beggar and a tramp, a man of the people, an associate of saloon-keepers and women of the town; who again and again, in the most explicit language, denounced wealth and the holding of wealth: 'Lay not up for yourselves treasures on earth!'—'Sell that ye have and give alms!'—'Blessed are ye poor, for yours is the kingdom of Heaven!'—'Woe unto you that are rich, for ye have received your consolation!'— 'Verily, I say unto you, that a rich man shall hardly enter into the kingdom of Heaven!' Who denounced in unmeasured terms the exploiters of his own time: 'Woe unto you, scribes and pharisees, hypocrites!'—'Woe unto you also, you lawyers!'—'Ye serpents, ye generation of vipers, how can ye escape the damnation of hell?' Who drove out the business men and brokers from the temple with a whip! Who was crucified—think of it—for an incendiary and a disturber of the social order! And this man they have made into the high priest of property and smug respectability, a divine sanction of all the horrors and abominations of modern commercial civilization! Jeweled images are made of him, sensual priests burn incense to him, and modern pirates of industry bring their dollars, wrung from the toil of helpless women and children, and build temples to him, and sit in cushioned seats and listen to his teachings expounded by doctors of dusty divinity—"

"Bravo!" cried Schliemann, laughing. But the other was in full career—he had talked this subject every day for five years, and had never yet let himself be stopped. "This Jesus of Nazareth!" he cried. "This class-conscious working-man! This union carpenter! This agitator, law-breaker, firebrand, anarchist! He, the sovereign lord and master of a world which grinds the bodies and souls of human beings into dollars—if he could come into the world this day and see the things that men have made in his name, would it not blast his soul with horror? Would he not go mad at the sight of it, he the Prince of Mercy and Love! That dreadful night when he lay in the Garden of Gethsemane and writhed in agony until he sweat blood—do you think that he saw anything worse than he might see tonight upon the plains of Manchuria, where men march out with a jeweled image of him before them, to do wholesale murder for the benefit of foul monsters of sensuality and cruelty? Do you not know that if he were in St. Petersburg now, he would take the whip with which he drove out the bankers from his temple—"

Here the speaker paused an instant for breath. "No, comrade," said the other, dryly, "for he was a practical man. He would take pretty little imitation lemons, such as are now being shipped into Russia, handy for carrying in the pockets, and strong enough to blow a whole temple out of sight."

Lucas waited until the company had stopped laughing over this; then he began again: "But look at it from the point of view of practical politics, comrade. Here is an historical figure whom all men reverence and love, whom some regard as divine; and who was one of us—who lived our life, and taught our doctrine. And now shall we leave him in the hands of his enemies—shall we allow them to stifle and stultify his example? We have his words, which no one can deny; and shall we not quote them to the people, and prove to them what he was, and what he taught, and what he did? No, no, a thousand times no!—we shall use his authority to turn out the knaves and sluggards from his ministry, and we shall yet rouse the people to action!—"

Lucas halted again; and the other stretched out his hand to a paper on the table. "Here, comrade," he said, with a laugh, "here is a place for you to begin. A bishop whose wife has just been robbed of fifty thousand dollars' worth of diamonds! And a most unctuous and oily of bishops! An eminent and scholarly bishop! A philanthropist and friend of labor bishop—a Civic Federation decoy duck for the chloroforming of the wage-working-man!"

To this little passage of arms the rest of the company sat as spectators. But now Mr. Maynard, the editor, took occasion to remark, somewhat naively, that he had always understood that Socialists had a cut-and-dried program for the future of civilization; whereas here were two active members of the party, who, from what he could make out, were agreed about nothing at all. Would the two, for his enlightenment, try to ascertain just what they had in common, and why they belonged to the same party? This resulted, after much debating, in the formulating of two carefully worded propositions: First, that a Socialist believes in the common ownership and democratic management of the means of producing the necessities of life; and, second, that a Socialist believes that the means by which this is to be brought about is the class conscious political organization of the wage-earners. Thus far they were at one; but no farther. To Lucas, the religious zealot, the co-operative commonwealth was the New Jerusalem, the kingdom of Heaven, which is "within you." To the other, Socialism was simply a necessary step toward a far-distant goal, a step to be tolerated with impatience. Schliemann called himself a "philosophic anarchist"; and he explained that an anarchist was one who believed that the end of human existence was the free development of every personality, unrestricted by laws save those of its own being. Since the same kind of match would light every one's fire and the same-shaped loaf of bread would fill every one's stomach, it would be perfectly feasible to submit industry to the control of a majority vote. There was only one earth, and the quantity of material things was limited. Of intellectual and moral things, on the other hand, there was no limit, and one could have more without another's having less; hence "Communism in material production, anarchism in intellectual," was the formula of modern proletarian thought. As soon as the birth agony was over, and the wounds of society had been healed, there would be established a simple system whereby each man was credited with his labor and debited with his purchases; and after that the processes of production, exchange, and consumption would go on automatically, and without our being conscious of them, any more than a man is conscious of the beating of his heart. And then, explained Schliemann, society would break up into independent, self-governing communities of mutually congenial persons; examples of which at present were clubs, churches, and political parties. After the revolution, all the intellectual, artistic, and spiritual activities of men would be cared for by such "free associations"; romantic novelists would be supported by those who liked to read romantic novels, and impressionist painters would be supported by those who liked to look at impressionist pictures—and the same with preachers and scientists, editors and actors and musicians. If any one wanted to work or paint or pray, and could find no one to maintain him, he could support himself by working part of the time. That was the case at present, the only difference being that the competitive wage system compelled a man to work all the time to live, while, after the abolition of privilege and exploitation, any one would be able to support himself by an hour's work a day. Also the artist's audience of the present was a small minority of people, all debased and vulgarized by the effort it had cost them to win in the commercial battle, of the intellectual and artistic activities which would result when the whole of mankind was set free from the nightmare of competition, we could at present form no conception whatever.

And then the editor wanted to know upon what ground Dr. Schliemann asserted that it might be possible for a society to exist upon an hour's toil by each of its members. "Just what," answered the other, "would be the productive capacity of society if the present resources of science were utilized, we have no means of ascertaining; but we may be sure it would exceed anything that would sound reasonable to minds inured to the ferocious barbarities of capitalism. After the triumph of the international proletariat, war would of course be inconceivable; and who can figure the cost of war to humanity—not merely the value of the lives and the material that it destroys, not merely the cost of keeping millions of men in idleness, of arming and equipping them for battle and parade, but the drain upon the vital energies of society by the war attitude and the war terror, the brutality and ignorance, the drunkenness, prostitution, and crime it entails, the industrial impotence and the moral deadness? Do you think that it would be too much to say that two hours of the working time of every efficient member of a community goes to feed the red fiend of war?"

And then Schliemann went on to outline some of the wastes of competition: the losses of industrial warfare; the ceaseless worry and friction; the vices—such as drink, for instance, the use of which had nearly doubled in twenty years, as a consequence of the intensification of the economic struggle; the idle and unproductive members of the community, the frivolous rich and the pauperized poor; the law and the whole machinery of repression; the wastes of social ostentation, the milliners and tailors, the hairdressers, dancing masters, chefs and lackeys. "You understand," he said, "that in a society dominated by the fact of commercial competition, money is necessarily the test of prowess, and wastefulness the sole criterion of power. So we have, at the present moment, a society with, say, thirty per cent of the population occupied in producing useless articles, and one per cent occupied in destroying them. And this is not all; for the servants and panders of the parasites are also parasites, the milliners and the jewelers and the lackeys have also to be supported by the useful members of the community. And bear in mind also that this monstrous disease affects not merely the idlers and their menials, its poison penetrates the whole social body. Beneath the hundred thousand women of the elite are a million middle-class women, miserable because they are not of the elite, and trying to appear of it in public; and beneath them, in turn, are five million farmers' wives reading 'fashion papers' and trimming bonnets, and shop-girls and serving-maids selling themselves into brothels for cheap jewelry and imitation seal-skin robes. And then consider that, added to this competition in display, you have, like oil on the flames, a whole system of competition in selling! You have manufacturers contriving tens of thousands of catchpenny devices, store-keepers displaying them, and newspapers and magazines filled up with advertisements of them!"

"And don't forget the wastes of fraud," put in young Fisher.

"When one comes to the ultra-modern profession of advertising," responded Schliemann—"the science of persuading people to buy what they do not want— he is in the very center of the ghastly charnel house of capitalist destructiveness, and he scarcely knows which of a dozen horrors to point out first. But consider the waste in time and energy incidental to making ten thousand varieties of a thing for purposes of ostentation and snobbishness, where one variety would do for use! Consider all the waste incidental to the manufacture of cheap qualities of goods, of goods made to sell and deceive the ignorant; consider the wastes of adulteration,—the shoddy clothing, the cotton blankets, the unstable tenements, the ground-cork life-preservers, the adulterated milk, the aniline soda water, the potato-flour sausages—"

"And consider the moral aspects of the thing," put in the ex-preacher.

"Precisely," said Schliemann; "the low knavery and the ferocious cruelty incidental to them, the plotting and the lying and the bribing, the blustering and bragging, the screaming egotism, the hurrying and worrying. Of course, imitation and adulteration are the essence of competition—they are but another form of the phrase 'to buy in the cheapest market and sell in the dearest.' A government official has stated that the nation suffers a loss of a billion and a quarter dollars a year through adulterated foods; which means, of course, not only materials wasted that might have been useful outside of the human stomach, but doctors and nurses for people who would otherwise have been well, and undertakers for the whole human race ten or twenty years before the proper time. Then again, consider the waste of time and energy required to sell these things in a dozen stores, where one would do. There are a million or two of business firms in the country, and five or ten times as many clerks; and consider the handling and rehandling, the accounting and reaccounting, the planning and worrying, the balancing of petty profit and loss. Consider the whole machinery of the civil law made necessary by these processes; the libraries of ponderous tomes, the courts and juries to interpret them, the lawyers studying to circumvent them, the pettifogging and chicanery, the hatreds and lies! Consider the wastes incidental to the blind and haphazard production of commodities—the factories closed, the workers idle, the goods spoiling in storage; consider the activities of the stock manipulator, the paralyzing of whole industries, the overstimulation of others, for speculative purposes; the assignments and bank failures, the crises and panics, the deserted towns and the starving populations! Consider the energies wasted in the seeking of markets, the sterile trades, such as drummer, solicitor, bill-poster, advertising agent. Consider the wastes incidental to the crowding into cities, made necessary by competition and by monopoly railroad rates; consider the slums, the bad air, the disease and the waste of vital energies; consider the office buildings, the waste of time and material in the piling of story upon story, and the burrowing underground! Then take the whole business of insurance, the enormous mass of administrative and clerical labor it involves, and all utter waste—"

"I do not follow that," said the editor. "The Cooperative Commonwealth is a universal automatic insurance company and savings bank for all its members. Capital being the property of all, injury to it is shared by all and made up by all. The bank is the universal government credit-account, the ledger in which every individual's earnings and spendings are balanced. There is also a universal government bulletin, in which are listed and precisely described everything which the commonwealth has for sale. As no one makes any profit by the sale, there is no longer any stimulus to extravagance, and no misrepresentation; no cheating, no adulteration or imitation, no bribery or 'grafting.'"

"How is the price of an article determined?"

"The price is the labor it has cost to make and deliver it, and it is determined by the first principles of arithmetic. The million workers in the nation's wheat fields have worked a hundred days each, and the total product of the labor is a billion bushels, so the value of a bushel of wheat is the tenth part of a farm labor-day. If we employ an arbitrary symbol, and pay, say, five dollars a day for farm work, then the cost of a bushel of wheat is fifty cents."

"You say 'for farm work,'" said Mr. Maynard. "Then labor is not to be paid alike?"

"Manifestly not, since some work is easy and some hard, and we should have millions of rural mail carriers, and no coal miners. Of course the wages may be left the same, and the hours varied; one or the other will have to be varied continually, according as a greater or less number of workers is needed in any particular industry. That is precisely what is done at present, except that the transfer of the workers is accomplished blindly and imperfectly, by rumors and advertisements, instead of instantly and completely, by a universal government bulletin."

"How about those occupations in which time is difficult to calculate? What is the labor cost of a book?"

"Obviously it is the labor cost of the paper, printing, and binding of it—about a fifth of its present cost."

"And the author?"

"I have already said that the state could not control intellectual production. The state might say that it had taken a year to write the book, and the author might say it had taken thirty. Goethe said that every bon mot of his had cost a purse of gold. What I outline here is a national, or rather international, system for the providing of the material needs of men. Since a man has intellectual needs also, he will work longer, earn more, and provide for them to his own taste and in his own way. I live on the same earth as the majority, I wear the same kind of shoes and sleep in the same kind of bed; but I do not think the same kind of thoughts, and I do not wish to pay for such thinkers as the majority selects. I wish such things to be left to free effort, as at present. If people want to listen to a certain preacher, they get together and contribute what they please, and pay for a church and support the preacher, and then listen to him; I, who do not want to listen to him, stay away, and it costs me nothing. In the same way there are magazines about Egyptian coins, and Catholic saints, and flying machines, and athletic records, and I know nothing about any of them. On the other hand, if wage slavery were abolished, and I could earn some spare money without paying tribute to an exploiting capitalist, then there would be a magazine for the purpose of interpreting and popularizing the gospel of Friedrich Nietzsche, the prophet of Evolution, and also of Horace Fletcher, the inventor of the noble science of clean eating; and incidentally, perhaps, for the discouraging of long skirts, and the scientific breeding of men and women, and the establishing of divorce by mutual consent."

Dr. Schliemann paused for a moment. "That was a lecture," he said with a laugh, "and yet I am only begun!"

"What else is there?" asked Maynard.

"I have pointed out some of the negative wastes of competition," answered the other. "I have hardly mentioned the positive economies of co-operation. Allowing five to a family, there are fifteen million families in this country; and at least ten million of these live separately, the domestic drudge being either the wife or a wage slave. Now set aside the modern system of pneumatic house-cleaning, and the economies of co-operative cooking; and consider one single item, the washing of dishes. Surely it is moderate to say that the dish-washing for a family of five takes half an hour a day; with ten hours as a day's work, it takes, therefore, half a million able-bodied persons—mostly women to do the dish-washing of the country. And note that this is most filthy and deadening and brutalizing work; that it is a cause of anemia, nervousness, ugliness, and ill-temper; of prostitution, suicide, and insanity; of drunken husbands and degenerate children—for all of which things the community has naturally to pay. And now consider that in each of my little free communities there would be a machine which would wash and dry the dishes, and do it, not merely to the eye and the touch, but scientifically— sterilizing them—and do it at a saving of all the drudgery and nine-tenths of the time! All of these things you may find in the books of Mrs. Gilman; and then take Kropotkin's Fields, Factories, and Workshops, and read about the new science of agriculture, which has been built up in the last ten years; by which, with made soils and intensive culture, a gardener can raise ten or twelve crops in a season, and two hundred tons of vegetables upon a single acre; by which the population of the whole globe could be supported on the soil now cultivated in the United States alone! It is impossible to apply such methods now, owing to the ignorance and poverty of our scattered farming population; but imagine the problem of providing the food supply of our nation once taken in hand systematically and rationally, by scientists! All the poor and rocky land set apart for a national timber reserve, in which our children play, and our young men hunt, and our poets dwell! The most favorable climate and soil for each product selected; the exact require- ments of the community known, and the acreage figured accordingly; the most improved machinery employed, under the direction of expert agricultural chem- ists! I was brought up on a farm, and I know the awful deadliness of farm work; and I like to picture it all as it will be after the revolution. To picture the great po- tato-planting machine, drawn by four horses, or an electric motor, ploughing the furrow, cutting and dropping and covering the potatoes, and planting a score of acres a day! To picture the great potato-digging machine, run by electricity, per- haps, and moving across a thousand-acre field, scooping up earth and potatoes, and dropping the latter into sacks! To every other kind of vegetable and fruit han- dled in the same way—apples and oranges picked by machinery, cows milked by electricity—things which are already done, as you may know. To picture the har- vest fields of the future, to which millions of happy men and women come for a summer holiday, brought by special trains, the exactly needful number to each place! And to contrast all this with our present agonizing system of independent small farming,—a stunted, haggard, ignorant man, mated with a yellow, lean, and sad-eyed drudge, and toiling from four o'clock in the morning until nine at night, working the children as soon as they are able to walk, scratching the soil with its primitive tools, and shut out from all knowledge and hope, from all their benefits of science and invention, and all the joys of the spirit—held to a bare existence by competition in labor, and boasting of his freedom because he is too blind to see his chains!"

Dr. Schliemann paused a moment. "And then," he continued, "place beside this fact of an unlimited food supply, the newest discovery of physiologists, that most of the ills of the human system are due to overfeeding! And then again, it has been proven that meat is unnecessary as a food; and meat is obviously more diffi- cult to produce than vegetable food, less pleasant to prepare and handle, and more likely to be unclean. But what of that, so long as it tickles the palate more strongly?"

"How would Socialism change that?" asked the girl-student, quickly. It was the first time she had spoken.

"So long as we have wage slavery," answered Schliemann, "it matters not in the least how debasing and repulsive a task may be, it is easy to find people to perform it. But just as soon as labor is set free, then the price of such work will begin to rise. So one by one the old, dingy, and unsanitary factories will come down—it will be cheaper to build new; and so the steamships will be provided with stoking machinery, and so the dangerous trades will be made safe, or substitutes will be found for their products. In exactly the same way, as the citizens of our Industrial Republic become refined, year by year the cost of slaughterhouse products will increase; until eventually those who want to eat meat will have to do their own killing—and how long do you think the custom would survive then?— To go on to another item—one of the necessary accompaniments of capitalism in a democracy is political corruption; and one of the consequences of civic administration by ignorant and vicious politicians, is that preventable diseases kill off half our population. And even if science were allowed to try, it could do little, because the majority of human beings are not yet human beings at all, but simply machines for the creating of wealth for others. They are penned up in filthy houses and left to rot and stew in misery, and the conditions of their life make them ill faster than all the doctors in the world could heal them; and so, of course, they remain as centers of contagion, poisoning the lives of all of us, and making happiness impossible for even the most selfish. For this reason I would seriously maintain that all the medical and surgical discoveries that science can make in the future will be of less importance than the application of the knowledge we already possess, when the disinherited of the earth have established their right to a human existence."

And here the Herr Doctor relapsed into silence again. Jurgis had noticed that the beautiful young girl who sat by the center-table was listening with something of the same look that he himself had worn, the time when he had first discovered Socialism. Jurgis would have liked to talk to her, he felt sure that she would have understood him. Later on in the evening, when the group broke up, he heard Mrs. Fisher say to her, in a low voice, "I wonder if Mr. Maynard will still write the same things about Socialism"; to which she answered, "I don't know—but if he does we shall know that he is a knave!"

And only a few hours after this came election day—when the long campaign was over, and the whole country seemed to stand still and hold its breath, awaiting the issue. Jurgis and the rest of the staff of Hinds's Hotel could hardly stop to finish their dinner, before they hurried off to the big hall which the party had hired for that evening.

But already there were people waiting, and already the telegraph instrument on the stage had begun clicking off the returns. When the final accounts were made up, the Socialist vote proved to be over four hundred thousand—an increase of something like three hundred and fifty per cent in four years. And that was doing well; but the party was dependent for its early returns upon messages from the locals, and naturally those locals which had been most successful were the ones which felt most like reporting; and so that night every one in the hall believed that the vote was going to be six, or seven, or even eight hundred thousand. Just such an incredible increase had actually been made in Chicago, and in the state; the vote of the city had been 6,700 in 1900, and now it was 47,000; that of Illinois had been 9,600, and now it was 69,000! So, as the evening waxed, and the crowd piled in, the meeting was a sight to be seen. Bulletins would be read, and the people would shout themselves hoarse—and then some one would make a speech, and there would be more shouting; and then a brief silence, and more bulletins. There would come messages from the secretaries of neighboring states, reporting their achievements; the vote of Indiana had gone from 2,300 to 12,000, of Wisconsin from 7,000 to 28,000; of Ohio from 4,800 to 36,000! There were telegrams to the national office from enthusiastic individuals in little towns which had made amazing and unprecedented increases in a single year: Benedict, Kansas, from 26 to 260; Henderson, Kentucky, from 19 to 111; Holland, Michigan, from 14 to 208; Cleo, Oklahoma, from 0 to 104; Martin's Ferry, Ohio, from 0 to 296—and many more of the same kind. There were literally hundreds of such towns; there would be reports from half a dozen of them in a single batch of telegrams. And the men who read the despatches off to the audience were old campaigners, who had been to the places and helped to make the vote, and could make appropriate comments: Quincy, Illinois, from 189 to 831—that was where the mayor had arrested a Socialist speaker! Crawford County, Kansas, from 285 to 1,975; that was the home of the "Appeal to Reason"! Battle Creek, Michigan, from 4,261 to 10,184; that was the answer of labor to the Citizens' Alliance Movement!

And then there were official returns from the various precincts and wards of the city itself! Whether it was a factory district or one of the "silk-stocking" wards seemed to make no particular difference in the increase; but one of the things which surprised the party leaders most was the tremendous vote that came rolling in from the stockyards. Packingtown comprised three wards of the city, and the vote in the spring of 1903 had been 500, and in the fall of the same year, 1,600. Now, only one year later, it was over 6,300—and the Democratic vote only 8,800! There were other wards in which the Democratic vote had been actually surpassed, and in two districts, members of the state legislature had been elected. Thus Chicago now led the country; it had set a new standard for the party, it had shown the workingmen the way!

—So spoke an orator upon the platform; and two thousand pairs of eyes were fixed upon him, and two thousand voices were cheering his every sentence. The orator had been the head of the city's relief bureau in the stockyards, until the sight of misery and corruption had made him sick. He was young, hungry-looking, full of fire; and as he swung his long arms and beat up the crowd, to Jurgis he seemed the very spirit of the revolution. "Organize! Organize! Organize!"—that was his cry. He was afraid of this tremendous vote, which his party had not expected, and which it had not earned. "These men are not Socialists!" he cried. "This election will pass, and the excitement will die, and people will forget about it; and if you forget about it, too, if you sink back and rest upon your oars, we shall lose this vote that we have polled to-day, and our enemies will laugh us to scorn! It rests with you to take your resolution—now, in the flush of victory, to find these men who have voted for us, and bring them to our meetings, and organize them and bind them to us! We shall not find all our campaigns as easy as this one. Everywhere in the country tonight the old party politicians are studying this vote, and setting their sails by it; and nowhere will they be quicker or more cunning than here in our own city. Fifty thousand Socialist votes in Chicago means a municipal-ownership Democracy in the spring! And then they will fool the voters once more, and all the powers of plunder and corruption will be swept into office again! But whatever they may do when they get in, there is one thing they will not do, and that will be the thing for which they were elected! They will not give the people of our city municipal ownership—they will not mean to do it, they will not try to do it; all that they will do is give our party in Chicago the greatest opportunity that has ever come to Socialism in America! We shall have the sham reformers self-stultified and self-convicted; we shall have the radical Democracy left without a lie with which to cover its nakedness! And then will begin the rush that will never be checked, the tide that will never turn till it has reached its flood—that will be irresistible, overwhelming—the rallying of the outraged workingmen of Chicago to our standard! And we shall organize them, we shall drill them, we shall marshal them for the victory! We shall bear down the opposition, we shall sweep if before us—and Chicago will be ours! Chicago will be ours! CHICAGO WILL BE OURS!"

THE METROPOLIS

CHAPTER I

"Return at ten-thirty," the General said to his chauffeur, and then they entered the corridor of the hotel.

Montague gazed about him, and found himself trembling just a little with anticipation. It was not the magnificence of the place. The quiet uptown hotel would have seemed magnificent to him, fresh as he was from the country; but, he did not see the marble columns and the gilded carvings-he was thinking of the men he was to meet. It seemed too much to crowd into one day-first the vision of the whirling, seething city, the centre of all his hopes of the future; and then, at night, this meeting, overwhelming him with the crowded memories of everything that he held precious in the past.

There were groups of men in faded uniforms standing about in the corridors. General Prentice bowed here and there as they retired and took the elevator to the reception-rooms. In the doorway they passed a stout little man with stubby white moustaches, and the General stopped, exclaiming, "Hello, Major!" Then he added: "Let me introduce Mr. Allan Montague. Montague, this is Major Thorne."

A look of sudden interest flashed across the Major's face. "General Montague's son?" he cried. And then he seized the other's hand in both of his, exclaiming, "My boy! my boy! I'm glad to see you!"

Now Montague was no boy—he was a man of thirty, and rather sedate in his appearance and manner; there was enough in his six feet one to have made two of the round and rubicund little Major. And yet it seemed to him quite proper that the other should address him so. He was back in his boyhood to-night—he was a boy whenever anyone mentioned the name of Major Thorne.

"Perhaps you have heard your father speak of me?" asked the Major, eagerly; and Montague answered, "A thousand times."

He was tempted to add that the vision that rose before him was of a stout gentleman hanging in a grape-vine, while a whole battery of artillery made him their target.

Perhaps it was irreverent, but that was what Montague had always thought of, ever since he had first laughed over the tale his father told. It had happened one January afternoon in the Wilderness, during the terrible battle of Chancellorsville, when Montague's father had been a rising young staff-officer, and it had fallen to his lot to carry to Major Thorne what was surely the most terrifying order that ever a cavalry officer received. It was in the crisis of the conflict, when the Army of the Potomac was reeling before the onslaught of Stonewall Jackson's columns. There was no one to stop them-and yet they must be stopped, for the whole right wing of the army was going. So that cavalry regiment had charged full tilt through the thickets, and into a solid wall of infantry and artillery. The crash of their volley was blinding—and horses wore fairly shot to fragments; and the Major's horse, with its lower jaw torn off, had plunged madly away and left its rider hanging in the aforementioned grape-vine. After he had kicked himself loose, it was to find himself in an arena where pain-maddened horses and frenzied men raced about amid a rain of minie-balls and canister. And in this inferno the gallant Major had captured a horse, and rallied the remains of his shattered command, and held the line until help came-and then helped to hold it, all through the afternoon and the twilight and the night, against charge after charge.—And now to stand and gaze at this stout and red-nosed little personage, and realize that these mighty deeds had been his!

Then, even while Montague was returning his hand-clasp and telling him of his pleasure, the Major's eye caught some one across the room, and he called eagerly, "Colonel Anderson! Colonel Anderson!"

And this was the heroic Jack Anderson! "Parson" Anderson, the men had called him, because he always prayed before everything he did. Prayers at each mess,—a prayer-meeting in the evening,—and then rumour said the Colonel prayed on while his men slept. With his battery of artillery trained to perfection under three years of divine guidance, the gallant Colonel had stood in the line of battle at Cold Harbour—name of frightful memory!—and when the enemy had swarmed out of their intrenchments and swept back the whole line just beyond him, his battery had stood like a cape in a storm-beaten ocean, attacked on two sides at once; and for the half-hour that elapsed before infantry support came up, the Colonel had ridden slowly up and down his line, repeating in calm and godly accents, "Give 'em hell, boys—give 'em hell!"—The Colonel's hand trembled now as he held it out, and his voice was shrill and cracked as he told what pleasure it gave him to meet General Montague's son.

"Why have we never seen you before?" asked Major Thorne. Montague replied that he had spent all his life in Mississippi—his father having married a Southern woman after the war. Once every year the General had come to New York to attend the reunion of the Loyal Legion of the State; but some one had had to stay at home with his mother, Montague explained.

There were perhaps a hundred men in the room, and he was passed about from group to group. Many of them had known his father intimately. It seemed almost uncanny to him to meet them in the body; to find them old and feeble, white-haired and wrinkled. As they lived in the chambers of his memory, they were in their mighty youth-heroes, transfigured and radiant, not subject to the power of time.

Life on the big plantation had been a lonely one, especially for a Southern-born man who had fought in the Union army. General Montague had been a person of quiet tastes, and his greatest pleasure had been to sit with his two boys on his knees and "fight his battles o'er again." He had collected all the literature of the corps which he had commanded—a whole library of it, in which Allan had learned to find his way as soon as he could read. He had literally been brought up on the war—for hours he would lie buried in some big illustrated history, until people came and called him away. He studied maps of campaigns and battle-fields, until they became alive with human passion and struggle; he knew the Army of the Potomac by brigade and division, with the names of commanders, and their faces, and their ways-until they lived and spoke, and the bare roll of their names had power to thrill him.—And now here were the men themselves, and all these scenes and memories crowding upon him in tumultuous throngs. No wonder that he was a little dazed, and could hardly find words to answer when he was spoken to.

But then came an incident which called him suddenly back to the world of the present. "There is Judge Ellis," said the General.

Judge Ellis! The fame of his wit and eloquence had reached even far Mississippi—was there any remotest corner of America where men had not heard of the silver tongue of Judge Ellis? "Cultivate him!" Montague's brother Oliver had laughed, when it was mentioned that the Judge would be present—"Cultivate him—he may be useful."

It was not difficult to cultivate one who was as gracious as Judge Ellis. He stood in the doorway, a smooth, perfectly groomed gentleman, conspicuous in the uniformed assembly by his evening dress. The Judge was stout and jovial, and cultivated Dundreary whiskers and a beaming smile. "General Montague's son!" he exclaimed, as he pressed the young man's hands. "Why, why—I'm surprised! Why have we never seen you before?"

Montague explained that he had only been in New York about six hours. "Oh, I see," said the Judge. "And shall you remain long?"

"I have come to stay," was the reply.

"Well, well!" said the other, cordially. "Then we may see more of you. Are you going into business?"

"I am a lawyer," said Montague. "I expect to practise."

The Judge's quick glance had been taking the measure of the tall, handsome man before him, with his raven-black hair and grave features. "You must give us a chance to try your mettle," he said; and then, as others approached to meet him, and he was forced to pass on, he laid a caressing hand on Montague's arm, whispering, with a sly smile, "I mean it."

Montague felt his heart beat a little faster. He had not welcomed his brother's suggestion—there was nothing of the sycophant in him; but he meant to work and to succeed, and he knew what the favour of a man like Judge Ellis would mean to him. For the Judge was the idol of New York's business and political aristocracy, and the doorways of fortune yielded at his touch.

There were rows of chairs in one of the rooms, and here two or three hundred men were gathered. There were stands of battle-flags in the corners, each one of them a scroll of tragic history, to one like Montague, who understood. His eye roamed over them while the secretary was reading minutes of meetings and other routine announcements. Then he began to study the assemblage. There were men with one arm and men with one leg—one tottering old soldier ninety years of age, stone blind, and led about by his friends. The Loyal Legion was an officers' organization, and to that extent aristocratic; but worldly success counted for nothing in it—some of its members were struggling to exist on their pensions, and were as much thought of as a man like General Prentice, who was president of one of the city's largest banks, and a rich man, even in New York's understanding of that term.

The presiding officer introduced "Colonel Robert Selden, who will read the paper of the evening: 'Recollections of Spottsylvania.'" Montague started at the name—for "Bob" Selden had been one of his father's messmates, and had fought all through the Peninsula Campaign at his side.

He was a tall, hawk-faced man with a grey imperial. The room was still as he arose, and after adjusting his glasses, he began to read his story. He recalled the situation of the Army of the Potomac in the spring of 1864; for three years it had marched and fought, stumbling through defeat after defeat, a mighty weapon, lacking only a man who could wield it. Now at last the man had come—one who would put them into the battle and give them a chance to fight. So they had marched into the Wilderness, and there Lee struck them, and for three days they groped in a blind thicket, fighting hand to hand, amid suffocating smoke. The Colonel read in a quiet, unassuming voice; but one could see that he had hold of his hearers by the light that crossed their features when he told of the army's recoil from the shock, and of the wild joy that ran through the ranks when they took up their march to the left, and realized that this time they were not going back.—So they came to the twelve days' grapple of the Spottsylvania Campaign.

There was still the Wilderness thicket; the enemy's intrenchments, covering about eight miles, lay in the shape of a dome, and at the cupola of it were breastworks of heavy timbers banked with earth, and with a ditch and a tangle of trees in front. The place was the keystone of the Confederate arch, and the name of it was "the Angle"—"Bloody Angle!" Montague heard the man who sat next to him draw in his breath, as if a spasm of pain had shot through him.

At dawn two brigades had charged and captured the place. The enemy returned to the attack, and for twenty hours thereafter the two armies fought, hurling regiment after regiment and brigade after brigade into the trenches. There was a pouring rain, and the smoke hung black about them; they could only see the flashes of the guns, and the faces of the enemy, here and there.

The Colonel described the approach of his regiment. They lay down for a moment in a swamp, and the minie-balls sang like swarming bees, and split the blades of the grass above them. Then they charged, over ground that ran with human blood. In the trenches the bodies of dead and dying men lay three deep, and were trampled out of sight in the mud by the feet of those who fought. They would crouch behind the works, lifting their guns high over their heads, and firing into the throngs on the other side; again and again men sprang upon the breast-works and fired their muskets, and then fell dead. They dragged up cannon, one after another, and blew holes through the logs, and raked the' ground with charges of canister.

While the Colonel read, still in his calm, matter-of-fact voice, you might see men leaning forward in their chairs, hands clenched, teeth set. They knew! They knew! Had there ever before been a time in history when breastworks had been charged by artillery? Twenty-four men in the crew of one gun, and only two un-hurt! One iron sponge-bucket with thirty-nine bullet holes shot through it! And then blasts of canister sweeping the trenches, and blowing scores of living and dead men to fragments! And into this hell of slaughter new regiments charging, in lines four deep! And squad after squad of the enemy striving to surrender, and shot to pieces by their own comrades as they clambered over the blood-soaked walls! And heavy timbers in the defences shot to splinters! Huge oak trees—one of them twenty-four inches in diameter—crashing down upon the combatants, gnawed through by rifle-bullets! Since the world began had men ever fought like that?

Then the Colonel told of his own wound in the shoulder, and how, toward dusk, he had crawled away; and how he became lost, and strayed into the enemy's line, and was thrust into a batch of prisoners and marched to the rear. And then of the night that he spent beside a hospital camp in the Wilderness, where hundreds of wounded and dying men lay about on the rain-soaked ground, moaning, screaming, praying to be killed. Again the prisoners were moved, having been ordered to march to the railroad; and on the way the Colonel went blind from suf-fering and exhaustion, and staggered and fell in the road. You could have heard a pin drop in the room, in the pause between sentences in his story, as he told how the guard argued with him to persuade him to go on. It was their duty to kill him if he refused, but they could not bring themselves to do it. In the end they left the job to one, and he stood and cursed the officer, trying to get up his courage; and finally fired his gun into the air, and went off and left him.

Then he told how an old negro had found him, and how he lay delirious; and how, at last, the army marched his way. He ended his narrative the simple sen-tence: "It was not until the siege of Petersburg that I was able to rejoin my Command."

There was a murmur of applause; and then silence. Suddenly, from somewhere in the room, came the sound of singing—"Mine eyes have seen the glory of the coming of the Lord!" The old battle-hymn seemed to strike the very mood of the meeting; the whole throng took it up, and they sang it, stanza by stanza. It was rolling forth like a mighty organ-chant as they came to the fervid closing:—

"He hath sounded forth the trumpet that shall never call retreat; He is sifting out the hearts of men before his judgment seat; Oh! be swift, my soul, to answer Him; be jubilant, my feet,—Our God is marching on!"

There was a pause again; and the presiding officer rose and said that, owing to the presence of a distinguished guest, they would forego one of their rules, and invite Judge Ellis to say a few words. The Judge came forward, and bowed his acknowledgment of their welcome. Then, perhaps feeling a need of relief after the sombre recital, the Judge took occasion to apologize for his own temerity in addressing a roomful of warriors; and somehow he managed to make that remind him of a story of an army mule, a very amusing story; and that reminded him of another story, until, when he stopped and sat down, every one in the room broke into delighted applause.

They went in to dinner. Montague sat by General Prentice, and he, in turn, by the Judge; the latter was reminded of more stories during the dinner, and kept every one near him laughing. Finally Montague was moved to tell a story himself—about an old negro down home, who passed himself off for an Indian. The Judge was so good as to consider this an immensely funny story, and asked permission to tell it himself. Several times after that he leaned over and spoke to Montague, who felt a slight twinge of guilt as he recalled his brother's cynical advice, "Cultivate him!" The Judge was so willing to be cultivated, however, that it gave one's conscience little chance.

They went back to the meeting-room again; chairs were shifted, and little groups formed, and cigars and pipes brought out. They moved the precious battle-flags forward, and some one produced a bugle and a couple of drums; then the walls of the place shook, as the whole company burst forth:—

"Bring the good old bugle, boys! we'll sing another song—Sing it with a spirit that will start the world along—Sing it as we used to sing it, fifty thousand strong,—While we were marching through Georgia!"

It was wonderful to witness the fervour with which they went through this rollicking chant—whose spirit we miss because we hear it too often. They were not skilled musicians—they could only sing loud; but the fire leaped into their eyes, and they swayed with the rhythm, and sang! Montague found himself watching the old blind soldier, who sat beating his foot in time, upon his face the look of one who sees visions.

And then he noticed another man, a little, red-faced Irishman, one of the drummers. The very spirit of the drum seemed to have entered into him—into his hands and his feet, his eyes and his head, and his round little body. He played a long roll between the verses, and it seemed as if he must surely be swept away upon the wings of it. Catching Montague's eye, he nodded and smiled; and after that, every once in a while their eyes would meet and exchange a greeting. They sang "The Loyal Legioner" and "The Army Bean" and "John Brown's Body" and "Tramp, tramp, tramp, the boys are marching"; all the while the drum rattled and thundered, and the little drummer laughed and sang, the very incarnation of the care-free spirit of the soldier!

They stopped for a while, and the little man came over and was introduced. Lieutenant O'Day was his name; and after he had left, General Prentice leaned over to Montague and told him a story. "That little man," he said, "began as a drummer-boy in my regiment, and went all through the war in my brigade; and two years ago I met him on the street one cold winter night, as thin as I am, and shivering in a summer overcoat. I took him to dinner with me and watched him eat, and I made up my mind there was something wrong. I made him take me home, and do you know, the man was starving! He had a little tobacco shop, and he'd got into trouble—the trust had taken away his trade. And he had a sick wife, and a daughter clerking at six dollars a week!"

The General went on to tell of his struggle to induce the little man to accept his aid—to accept a loan of a few hundreds of dollars from Prentice, the banker! "I never had anything hurt me so in all my life," he said. "Finally I took him into the bank—and now you can see he has enough to eat!"

They began to sing again, and Montague sat and thought over the story. It seemed to him typical of the thing that made this meeting beautiful to him—of the spirit of brotherhood and service that reigned here.—They sang "We are tenting to-night on the old camp ground"; they sang "Benny Havens, Oh!" and "A Soldier No More"; they sang other songs of tenderness and sorrow, and men felt a trembling in their voices and a mist stealing over their eyes. Upon Montague a spell was falling.

Over these men and their story there hung a mystery—a presence of wonder, that discloses itself but rarely to mortals, and only to those who have dreamed and dared. They had not found it easy to do their duty; they had had their wives and children, their homes and friends and familiar places; and all these they had left to serve the Republic. They had taught themselves a new way of life—they had forged themselves into an iron sword of war. They had marched and fought in dust and heat, in pouring rains and driving, icy blasts; they had become men grim and terrible in spirit-men with limbs of steel, who could march or ride for days and nights, who could lie down and sleep upon the ground in rain-storms and winter snows, who were ready to leap at a word and seize their muskets and rush into the cannon's mouth. They had learned to stare into the face of death, to meet its fiery eyes; to march and eat and sleep, to laugh and play and sing, in its presence—to carry their life in their hands, and toss it about as a juggler tosses a ball. And this for Freedom: for the star-crowned goddess with the flaming eyes, who trod upon the mountain-tops and called to them in the shock and fury of the battle; whose trailing robes they followed through the dust and cannon-smoke; for a glimpse of whose shining face they had kept the long night vigils and charged upon the guns in the morning; for a touch of whose shimmering robe they had wasted in prison pens, where famine and loathsome pestilence and raving madness stalked about in the broad daylight.

And now this army of deliverance, with its waving banners and its prancing horses and its rumbling cannon, had marched into the shadow-world. The very ground that it had trod was sacred; and one who fingered the dusty volumes which held the record of its deeds would feel a strange awe come upon him, and thrill with a sudden fear of life—that was so fleeting and so little to be understood. There were boyhood memories in Montague's mind, of hours of consecration, when the vision had descended upon him, and he had sat with face hidden in his hands.

It was for the Republic that these men had suffered; for him and his children—that a government of the people, by the people, for the people, might not perish from the earth. And with the organ-music of the Gettysburg Address echoing within him, the boy laid his soul upon the altar of his country. They had done so much for him—and now, was there anything that he could do? A dozen years had passed since then, and still he knew that deep within him—deeper than all other purposes, than all thoughts of wealth and fame and power—was the purpose that the men who had died for the Republic should find him worthy of their trust.

The singing had stopped, and Judge Ellis was standing before him. The Judge was about to go, and in his caressing voice he said that he would hope to see Montague again. Then, seeing that General Prentice was also standing up, Montague threw off the spell that had gripped him, and shook hands with the little drummer, and with Selden and Anderson and all the others of his dream people. A few minutes later he found himself outside the hotel, drinking deep draughts of the cold November air.

Major Thorne had come out with them; and learning that the General's route lay uptown, he offered to walk with Montague to his hotel.

They set out, and then Montague told the Major about the figure in the grape-vine, and the Major laughed and told how it had felt. There had been more adventures, it seemed; while he was hunting a horse he had come upon two mules loaded with ammunition and entangled with their harness about a tree; he had rushed up to seize them—when a solid shot had struck the tree and exploded the ammunition and blown the mules to fragments. And then there was the story of the charge late in the night, which had recovered the lost ground, and kept Stonewall Jackson busy up to the very hour of his tragic death. And there was the story of Andersonville, and the escape from prison. Montague could have walked the streets all night, exchanging these war-time reminiscences with the Major.

Absorbed in their talk, they came to an avenue given up to the poorer class of people; with elevated trains rattling by overhead, and rows of little shops along it. Montague noticed a dense crowd on one of the corners, and asked what it meant.

"Some sort of a meeting," said the Major.

They came nearer, and saw a torch, with a man standing near it, above the heads of the crowd.

"It looks like a political meeting," said Montague, "but it can't be, now—just after election."

"Probably it's a Socialist," said the Major. "They're at it all the time."

They crossed the avenue, and then they could see plainly. The man was lean and hungry-looking, and he had long arms, which he waved with prodigious violence. He was in a frenzy of excitement, pacing this way and that, and leaning over the throng packed about him. Because of a passing train the two could not hear a sound.

"A Socialist!" exclaimed Montague, wonderingly. "What do they want?"

"I'm not sure," said the other. "They want to overthrow the government."

The train passed, and then the man's words came to them: "They force you to build palaces, and then they put you into tenements! They force you to spin fine raiment, and then they dress you in rags! They force you to build jails, and then they lock you up in them! They force you to make guns, and then they shoot you with them! They own the political parties, and they name the candidates, and trick you into voting for them—and they call it the law! They herd you into armies and send you to shoot your brothers—and they call it order! They take a piece of coloured rag and call it the flag and teach you to let yourself be shot—and they call it patriotism! First, last, and all the time, you do the work and they get the benefit—they, the masters and owners, and you—fools—fools—fools!"

The man's voice had mounted to a scream, and he flung his hands into the air and broke into jeering laughter. Then came another train, and Montague could not hear him; but he could see that he was rushing on in the torrent of his denunciation.

Montague stood rooted to the spot; he was shocked to the depths of his being—he could scarcely contain himself as he stood there. He longed to spring forward to beard the man where he stood, to shout him down, to rebuke him before the crowd.

The Major must have seen his agitation, for he took his arm and led him back from the throng, saying: "Come! We can't help it."

"But—but—," he protested, "the police ought to arrest him."

"They do sometimes," said the Major, "but it doesn't do any good."

They walked on, and the sounds of the shrill voice died away. "Tell me," said Montague, in a low voice, "does that go on very often?"

"Around the corner from where I live," said the other, "it goes on every Saturday night."

"And do the people listen?" he asked.

"Sometimes they can't keep the street clear," was the reply.

And again they walked in silence. At last Montague asked, "What does it mean?"

The Major shrugged his shoulders. "Perhaps another civil war," said he.

CHAPTER II

Allan Montague's father had died about five years before. A couple of years later his younger brother, Oliver, had announced his intention of seeking a career in New York. He had no profession, and no definite plans; but his father's friends were men of influence and wealth, and the doors were open to him. So he had turned his share of the estate into cash and departed.

Oliver was a gay and pleasure-loving boy, with all the material of a prodigal son in him; his brother had more than half expected to see him come back in a year or two with empty pockets. But New York had seemed to agree with Oliver. He never told what he was doing—what he wrote was simply that he was managing to keep the wolf from the door. But his letters hinted at expensive ways of life; and at Christmas time, and at Cousin Alice's birthday, he would send home presents which made the family stare.

Montague had always thought of himself as a country lawyer and planter. But two months ago a fire had swept away the family mansion, and then on top of that had come an offer for the land; and with Oliver telegraphing several times a day in his eagerness, they had taken the sudden resolution to settle up their affairs and move to New York.

There were Montague and his mother, and Cousin Alice, who was nineteen, and old "Mammy Lucy," Mrs. Montague's servant. Oliver had met them at Jersey City, radiant with happiness. He looked just as much of a boy as ever, and just as beautiful; excepting that he was a little paler, New York had not changed him at all. There was a man in uniform from the hotel to take charge of their baggage, and a big red touring-car for them; and now they were snugly settled in their apartments, with the younger brother on duty as counsellor and guide.

Montague had come to begin life all over again. He had brought his money, and he expected to invest it, and to live upon the income until he had begun to earn something. He had worked hard at his profession, and he meant to work in New York, and to win his way in the end. He knew almost nothing about the city—he faced it with the wide-open eyes of a child.

One began to learn quickly, he found. It was like being swept into a maelstrom: first the hurrying throngs on the ferry-boat, and then the cabmen and the newsboys shouting, and the cars with clanging gongs; then the swift motor, gliding between trucks and carriages and around corners where big policemen shepherded the scurrying populace; and then Fifth Avenue, with its rows of shops and towering hotels; and at last a sudden swing round a corner—and their home.

"I have picked a quiet family place for you," Oliver had said, and that had greatly pleased his brother. But he had stared in dismay when he entered this latest "apartment hotel"—which catered for two or three hundred of the most exclusive of the city's aristocracy—and noted its great arcade, with massive doors of bronze, and its entrance-hall, trimmed with Caen stone and Italian marble, and roofed with a vaulted ceiling painted by modern masters. Men in livery bore their wraps and bowed the way before them; a great bronze elevator shot them to the proper floor; and they went to their rooms down a corridor walled with blood-red marble and paved with carpet soft as a cushion. Here were six rooms of palatial size, with carpets, drapery, and furniture of a splendour quite appalling to Montague.

As soon as the man who bore their wraps had left the room, he turned upon his brother.

"Oliver," he said, "how much are we paying for all this?"

Oliver smiled. "You are not paying anything, old man," he replied. "You're to be my guests for a month or two, until you get your bearings."

"That's very good of you," said the other; "—we'll talk about it later. But meantime, tell me what the apartment costs."

And then Montague encountered his first full charge of New York dynamite. "Six hundred dollars a week," said Oliver.

He started as if his brother had struck him. "Six hundred dollars a week!" he gasped.

"Yes," said the other, quietly.

It was fully a minute before he could find his breath. "Brother," he exclaimed, "you're mad!"

"It is a very good bargain," smiled the other; "I have some influence with them."

Again there was a pause, while Montague groped for words. "Oliver," he exclaimed, "I can't believe you! How could you think that we could pay such a price?"

"I didn't think it," said Oliver; "I told you I expected to pay it myself."

"But how could we let you pay it for us?" cried the other. "Can you fancy that *I* will ever earn enough to pay such a price?"

"Of course you will," said Oliver. "Don't be foolish, Allan—you'll find it's easy enough to make money in New York. Leave it to me, and wait awhile."

But the other was not to be put off. He sat down on the embroidered silk bedspread, and demanded abruptly, "What do you expect my income to be a year?"

"I'm sure I don't know," laughed Oliver; "nobody takes the time to add up his income. You'll make what you need, and something over for good measure. This one thing you'll know for certain—the more you spend, the more you'll be able to make."

And then, seeing that the sober look was not to be expelled from his brother's face, Oliver seated himself and crossed his legs, and proceeded to set forth the paradoxical philosophy of extravagance. His brother had come into a city of millionaires. There was a certain group of people—"the right set," was Oliver's term for them—and among them he would find that money was as free as air. So far as his career was concerned, he would find that there was nothing in all New York so costly as economy. If he did not live like a gentleman, he would find himself excluded from the circle of the elect—and how he would manage to exist then was a problem too difficult for his brother to face.

And so, as quickly as he could, he was to bring himself to a state of mind where things did not surprise him; where he did what others did and paid what others paid, and did it serenely, as if he had done it all his life. He would soon find his place; meantime all he had to do was to put himself into his brother's charge. "You'll find in time that I have the strings in my hands," the latter added. "Just take life easy, and let me introduce you to the right people."

All of which sounded very attractive. "But are you sure," asked Montague, "that you understand what I'm here for? I don't want to get into the Four Hundred, you know—I want to practise law."

"In the first place," replied Oliver, "don't talk about the Four Hundred—it's vulgar and silly; there's no such thing. In the next place, you're going to live in New York, and you want to know the right people. If you know them, you can practise law, or practise billiards, or practise anything else that you fancy. If you don't know them, you might as well go practise in Dahomey, for all you can accomplish. You might come on here and start in for yourself, and in twenty years you wouldn't get as far as you can get in two weeks, if you'll let me attend to it."

Montague was nearly five years his brother's senior, and at home had taken a semi-paternal attitude toward him. Now, however, the situation seemed to have reversed itself. With a slight smile of amusement, he subsided, and proceeded to put himself into the attitude of a docile student of the mysteries of the Metropolis.

They agreed that they would say nothing about these matters to the others. Mrs. Montague was half blind, and would lead her placid, indoor existence with old Mammy Lucy. As for Alice, she was a woman, and would not trouble herself with economics; if fairy godmothers chose to shower gifts upon her, she would take them.

Alice was built to live in a palace, anyway, Oliver said. He had cried out with delight when he first saw her. She had been sixteen when he left, and tall and thin; now she was nineteen, and with the pale tints of the dawn in her hair and face. In the auto, Oliver had turned and, stared at her, and pronounced the cryptic judgment, "You'll go!"

Just now she was wandering about the rooms, exclaiming with wonder. Everything here was so quiet and so harmonious that at first one's suspicions were lulled. It was simplicity, but of a strange and perplexing kind—simplicity elaborately studied. It was luxury, but grown assured of itself, and gazing down upon itself with aristocratic disdain. And after a while this began to penetrate the vulgarest mind, and to fill it with awe; one cannot remain long in an apartment which is trimmed and furnished in rarest Circassian walnut, and "papered" with hand-embroidered silk cloth, without feeling some excitement—even though there be no one to mention that the furniture has cost eight thousand dollars per room, and that the wall covering has been imported from Paris at a cost of seventy dollars per yard.

Montague also betook himself to gazing about. He noted the great double windows, with sashes of bronze; the bronze fire-proof doors; the bronze electric candles and chandeliers, from which the room was flooded with a soft radiance at the touch of a button; the "duchesse" and "marquise" chairs, with upholstery matching the walls; the huge leather "slumber-couch," with adjustable lamp at its head. When one opened the door of the dressing-room closet, it was automatically filled with light; there was an adjustable three-sided mirror, at which one could study his own figure from every side. There was a little bronze box near the bed, in which one might set his shoes, and with a locked door opening out into the hall, so that the floor-porter could get them without disturbing one. Each of the bathrooms was the size of an ordinary man's parlour, with floor and walls of snow-white marble, and a door composed of an imported plate-glass mirror. There was a great porcelain tub, with glass handles upon the wall by which you could help yourself out of it, and a shower-bath with linen duck curtains, which were changed every day; and a marble slab upon which you might lie to be rubbed by the masseur who would come at the touch of a button.

There was no end to the miracles of this establishment, as Montague found in the course of time. There was no chance that the antique bronze clock on the mantel might go wrong, for it was electrically controlled from the office. You did not open the window and let in the dust, for the room was automatically ventilated, and you turned a switch marked "hot" and "cold." The office would furnish you a guide who would show you the establishment; and you might see your bread being kneaded by electricity, upon an opal glass table, and your eggs being tested by electric light; you might peer into huge refrigerators, ventilated by electric fans, and in which each tiny lamb chop reposed in a separate holder. Upon your own floor was a pantry, provided with hot and cold storage-rooms and an air-tight dumb-waiter; you might have your own private linen and crockery and plate, and your own family butler, if you wished. Your children, however, would not be permitted in the building, even though you were dying—this was a small concession which you made to a host who had invested a million dollars and a half in furniture alone.

A few minutes later the telephone bell rang, and Oliver answered it and said, "Send him up."

"Here's the tailor," he remarked, as he hung up the receiver.

"Whose tailor?" asked his brother.

"Yours," said he.

"Do I have to have some new clothes?" Montague asked.

"You haven't any clothes at present," was the reply.

Montague was standing in front of the "costumer," as the elaborate mirror was termed. He looked himself over, and then he looked at his brother. Oliver's clothing was a little like the Circassian walnut; at first you thought that it was simple, and even a trifle careless—it was only by degrees you realized that it was original and distinguished, and very expensive.

"Won't your New York friends make allowance for the fact that I am fresh from the country?" asked Montague, quizzically.

"They might," was the reply. "I know a hundred who would lend me money, if I asked them. But I don't ask them."

"Then how soon shall I be able to appear?" asked Montague, with visions of himself locked up in the room for a week or two.

"You are to have three suits to-morrow morning," said Oliver. "Genet has promised."

"Suits made to order?" gasped the other, in perplexity.

"He never heard of any other sort of suits," said Oliver, with grave rebuke in his voice.

M. Genet had the presence of a Russian grand duke, and the manner of a court chamberlain. He brought a subordinate to take Montague's measure, while he himself studied his colour-scheme. Montague gathered from the conversation that he was going to a house-party in the country the next morning, and that he would need a dress-suit, a hunting-suit, and a "morning coat." The rest might wait until his return. The two discussed him and his various "points" as they might have discussed a horse; he possessed distinction, he learned, and a great deal could be done with him—with a little skill he might be made into a personality. His French was not in training, but he managed to make out that it was M. Genet's opinion that the husbands of New York would tremble when he made his appearance among them.

When the tailor had left, Alice came in, with her face shining from a cold bathing. "Here you are decking yourselves out!" she cried. "And what about me?"

"Your problem is harder," said Oliver, with a laugh; "but you begin this afternoon. Reggie Mann is going to take you with him, and get you some dresses."

"What!" gasped Alice. "Get me some dresses! A man?"

"Of course," said the other. "Reggie Mann advises half the women in New York about their clothes."

"Who is he? A tailor?" asked the girl.

Oliver was sitting on the edge of the canapé, swinging one leg over the other; and he stopped abruptly and stared, and then sank back, laughing softly to himself. "Oh, dear me!" he said. "Poor Reggie!"

Then, realizing that he would have to begin at the beginning, he proceeded to explain that Reggie Mann was a cotillion leader, the idol of the feminine side of society. He was the special pet and protege of the great Mrs. de Graffenried, of whom they had surely heard—Mrs. de Graffenried, who was acknowledged to be the mistress of society at Newport, and was destined some day to be mistress in New York. Reggie and Oliver were "thick," and he had stayed in town on purpose to attend to her attiring—having seen her picture, and vowed that he would make a work of art out of her. And then Mrs. Robbie Walling would give her a dance; and all the world would come to fall at her feet.

"You and I are going out to 'Black Forest,' the Wallings' shooting-lodge, to-morrow," Oliver added to his brother. "You'll meet Mrs. Robbie there. You've heard of the Wallings, I hope."

"Yes," said Montague, "I'm not that ignorant."

"All right," said the other, "we're to motor down. I'm going to take you in my racing-car, so you'll have an experience. We'll start early."

"I'll be ready," said Montague; and when his brother replied that he would be at the door at eleven, he made another amused note as to the habits of New Yorkers.

The price which he paid at the hotel included the services of a valet or a maid for each of them, and so when their baggage arrived they had nothing to do. They went to lunch in one of the main dining-rooms of the hotel, a room with towering columns of dark-green marble and a maze of palms and flowers. Oliver did the ordering; his brother noticed that the simple meal cost them about fifteen dollars, and he wondered if they were to eat at that rate all the time.

Then Montague mentioned the fact that before leaving home he had received a telegram from General Prentice, asking him to go with him that evening to the meeting of the Loyal Legion. Montague wondered, half amused, if his brother would deem his old clothing fit for such a function. But Oliver replied that it would not matter what he wore there; he would not meet anyone who counted, except Prentice himself. The General and his family were prominent in society, it appeared, and were to be cultivated. But Oliver shrewdly forbore to elaborate upon this, knowing that his brother would be certain to talk about old times, which would be the surest possible method of lodging himself in the good graces of General Prentice.

After luncheon came Reggie Mann, dapper and exquisite, with slender little figure and mincing gait, and the delicate hands and soft voice of a woman. He was dressed for the afternoon parade, and wore a wonderful scarlet orchid in his buttonhole. Montague's hand he shook at his shoulder's height; but when Alice came in he did not shake hands with her. Instead, he stood and gazed, and gazed again, and lifting his hands a little with excess of emotion, exclaimed, "Oh, perfect! perfect!"

"And Ollie, I told you so!" he added, eagerly. "She is tall enough to wear satin! She shall have the pale blue Empire gown—she shall have the pale blue Empire gown if I have to pay for it myself! And oh, what times we shall have with that hair! And the figure—Reval will simply go wild!"

So Reggie prattled on, with his airy grace; he took her hand and studied it, and then turned her about to survey her figure, while Alice blushed and strove to laugh to hide her embarrassment. "My dear Miss Montague," he exclaimed, "I bring all Gotham and lay it at your feet! Ollie, your battle is won! Won without firing a shot! I know the very man for her—his father is dying, and he will have four millions in Transcontinental alone. And he is as handsome as Antinous and as fascinating as Don Juan! Allons! we may as well begin with the trousseau this afternoon!"

CHAPTER III

Oliver was not rooming with them; he had his own quarters at the club, which he did not wish to leave. But the next morning, about twenty minutes after the hour he had named, he was at the door, and Montague went down.

Oliver's car was an imported French racer. It had only two seats, open in front, with a rumble behind for the mechanic. It was long and low and rakish, a most wicked-looking object; whenever it stopped on the street a crowd gathered to stare at it. Oliver was clad in a black bearskin coat, covering his feet, and with cap and gloves to match; he wore goggles, pushed up over his forehead. A similar costume lay ready in his brother's seat.

The suits of clothing had come, and were borne in his grips by his valet. "We can't carry them with us," said Oliver. "He'll have to take them down by train." And while his brother was buttoning up the coat, he gave the address; then Montague clambered in, and after a quick glance over his shoulder, Oliver pressed a lever and threw over the steering-wheel, and they whirled about and sped down the street.

Sometimes, at home in Mississippi, one would meet automobiling parties, generally to the damage of one's harness and temper. But until the day before, when he had stepped off the ferry, Montague had never ridden in a motor-car. Riding in this one was like travelling in a dream—it slid along without a sound, or the slightest trace of vibration; it shot forward, it darted to right or to left, it slowed up, it stopped, as if of its own will—the driver seemed to do nothing. Such things as car tracks had no effect upon it at all, and serious defects in the pavement caused only the faintest swelling motion; it was only when it leaped ahead like a living thing that one felt the power of it, by the pressure upon his back.

They went at what seemed to Montague a breakneck pace through the city streets, dodging among trucks and carriages, grazing cars, whirling round corners, taking the wildest of chances. Oliver seemed always to know what the other fellow would do; but the thought that he might do something different kept his companion's heart pounding in a painful way. Once the latter cried out as a man leapt for his life; Oliver laughed, and said, without turning his head, "You'll get used to it by and by."

They went down Fourth Avenue and turned into the Bowery. Elevated trains pounded overhead, and a maze of gin-shops, dime-museums, cheap lodginghouses, and clothing-stores sped past them. Once or twice Oliver's hawk-like glance detected a blue uniform ahead, and then they slowed down to a decorous pace, and the other got a chance to observe the miserable population of the neighbourhood. It was a cold November day, and an "out of work" time, and wretched outcast men walked with shoulders drawn forward and hands in their pockets.

"Where in the world are we going?" Montague asked.

"To Long Island," said the other. "It's a beastly ride—this part of it—but it's the only way. Some day we'll have an overhead speedway of our own, and we won't have to drive through this mess."

They turned off at the approach to the Williamsburg Bridge, and found the street closed for repairs. They had to make a detour of a block, and they turned with a vicious sweep and plunged into the very heart of the tenement district. Narrow, filthy streets, with huge, canon-like blocks of buildings, covered with rusty iron fire-escapes and decorated with soap-boxes and pails and laundry and babies; narrow stoops, crowded with playing children; grocery-shops, clothing-shops, saloons; and a maze of placards and signs in English and German and Yiddish. Through the throngs Oliver drove, his brows knitted with impatience and his horn honking angrily. "Take it easy,"—protested Montague; but the other answered, "Bah!" Children screamed and darted out of the way, and men and women started back, scowling and muttering; when a blockade of wagons and push-carts forced them to stop, the children gathered about and jeered, and a group of hoodlums loafing by a saloon flung ribaldry at them; but Oliver never turned his eyes from the road ahead.

And at last they were out on the bridge. "Slow vehicles keep to the right," ran the sign, and so there was a lane for them to the left. They sped up the slope, the cold air beating upon them like a hurricane. Far below lay the river, with tugs and ferry-boats ploughing the wind-beaten grey water, and a city spread out on either bank—a wilderness of roofs, with chimneys sticking up and white jets of steam spouting everywhere. Then they sped down the farther slope, and into Brooklyn.

There was an asphalted avenue, lined with little residences. There was block upon block of them, mile after mile of them—Montague had never, seen so many houses in his life before, and nearly all poured out of the same mould.

Many other automobiles were speeding out by this avenue, and they raced with one another. The one which was passed the most frequently got the dust and smell; and so the universal rule was that when you were behind you watched for a clear track, and then put on speed, and went to the front; but then just when you had struck a comfortable pace, there was a whirring and a puffing at your left, and your rival came stealing past you. If you were ugly, you put on speed yourself, and forced him to fall back, or to run the risk of trouble with vehicles coming the other way. For Oliver there seemed to be but one rule,—pass everything.

They came to the great Ocean Driveway. Here were many automobiles, nearly all going one way, and nearly all racing. There were two which stuck to Oliver and would not be left behind—one, two, three—one, two, three—they passed and repassed. Their dust was blinding, and the continual odour was sickening; and so

Oliver set his lips tight, and the little dial on the indicator began to creep ahead, and they whirled away down the drive. "Catch us this time!" he muttered.

A few seconds later Oliver gave a sudden exclamation, as a policeman, concealed behind a bush at the roadside, sprang out and hailed them. The policeman had a motor-cycle, and Oliver shouted to the mechanic, "Pull the cord!" His brother turned, alarmed and perplexed, and saw the man reach down to the floor of the car. He saw the policeman leap upon the cycle and start to follow. Then he lost sight of him in the clouds of dust.

For perhaps five minutes they tore on, tense and silent, at a pace that Montague had never equalled in an express train. Vehicles coming the other way would leap into sight, charging straight at them, it seemed, and shooting past a hand's breadth away. Montague had just about made up his mind that one such ride would last him for a lifetime, when he noticed that they were slacking up. "You can let go the cord," said Oliver. "He'll never catch us now."

"What is the cord?" asked the other.

"It's tied to the tag with our number on, in back. It swings it up so it can't be seen."

They were turning off into a country road, and Montague sank back and laughed till the tears ran down his cheeks. "Is that a common trick?" he asked.

"Quite," said the other. "Mrs. Robbie has a trough of mud in their garage, and her driver sprinkles the tag every time before she goes out. You have to do something, you know, or you'd be taken up all the time."

"Have you ever been arrested?"

"I've only been in court once," said Oliver. "I've been stopped a dozen times."

"What did they do the other times—warn you?"

"Warn me?" laughed Oliver. "What they did was to get in with me and ride a block or two, out of sight of the crowd; and then I slipped them a ten-dollar bill and they got out."

To which Montague responded, "Oh, I see!"

They turned into a broad macadamized road, and here were more autos, and more dust, and more racing. Now and then they crossed a trolley or a railroad track, and here was always a warning sign; but Oliver must have had some occult way of knowing that the track was clear, for he never seemed to slow up. Now and then they came to villages, and did reduce speed; but from the pace at which they went through, the villagers could not have suspected it.

And then came another adventure. The road was in repair, and was very bad, and they were picking their way, when suddenly a young man who had been walking on a side path stepped out before them, and drew a red handkerchief from his pocket, and faced them, waving it. Oliver muttered an oath.

"What's the matter?" cried his brother.

"We're arrested!" he exclaimed.

"What!" gasped the other. "Why, we were not going at all."

"I know," said Oliver; "but they've got us all the same."

He must have made up his mind at one glance that the case was hopeless, for he made no attempt to put on speed, but let the young man step aboard as they reached him.

"What is it?" Oliver demanded.

"I have been sent out by the Automobile Association," said the stranger, "to warn you that they have a trap set in the next town. So watch out."

And Oliver gave a gasp, and said, "Oh! Thank you!" The young man stepped off, and they went ahead, and he lay back in his seat and shook with laughter.

"Is that common?" his brother asked, between laughs.

"It happened to me once before," said Oliver. "But I'd forgotten it completely."

They proceeded very slowly; and when they came to the outskirts of the village they went at a funereal pace, while the car throbbed in protest. In front of a country store they saw a group of loungers watching them, and Oliver said, "There's the first part of the trap. They have a telephone, and somewhere beyond is a man with another telephone, and beyond that a man to stretch a rope across the road."

"What would they do with you?" asked the other.

"Haul you up before a justice of the peace, and fine you anywhere from fifty to two hundred and fifty dollars. It's regular highway robbery—there are some places that boast of never levying taxes; they get all their money out of us!"

Oliver pulled out his watch. "We're going to be late to lunch, thanks to these delays," he said. He added that they were to meet at the "Hawk's Nest," which he said was an "automobile joint."

Outside of the town they "hit it up" again; and half an hour later they came to a huge sign, "To the Hawk's Nest," and turned off. They ran up a hill, and came suddenly out of a pine-forest into view of a hostelry, perched upon the edge of a bluff overlooking the Sound. There was a broad yard in front, in which automobiles wheeled and sputtered, and a long shed that was lined with them.

Half a dozen attendants ran to meet them as they drew up at the steps. They all knew Oliver, and two fell to brushing his coat, and one got his cap, while the mechanic took the car to the shed. Oliver had a tip for each of them; one of the things that Montague observed was that in New York you had to carry a pocketful of change, and scatter it about wherever you went. They tipped the man who carried their coats and the boy who opened the door. In the washrooms they tipped the boys who filled the basins for them and those who gave them a second brushing.

The piazzas of the inn were crowded with automobiling parties, in all sorts of strange costumes. It seemed to Montague that most of them were flashy people— the men had red faces and the women had loud voices; he saw one in a sky-blue coat with bright scarlet facing. It occurred to him that if these women had not worn such large hats, they would not have needed quite such a supply of the bright-coloured veiling which they wound over the hats and tied under their chins, or left to float about in the breeze.

The dining-room seemed to have been built in sections, rambling about on the summit of the cliff. The side of it facing the water was all glass, and could be taken down. The ceiling was a maze of streamers and Japanese lanterns, and here and there were orange-trees and palms and artificial streams and fountains. Every table was crowded, it seemed; one was half-deafened by the clatter of plates, the voices and laughter, and the uproar of a negro orchestra of banjos, mandolins, and guitars. Negro waiters flew here and there, and a huge, stout head-waiter, who was pirouetting and strutting, suddenly espied Oliver, and made for him with smiles of welcome.

"Yes, sir—just come in, sir," he said, and led the way down the room, to where, in a corner, a table had been set for sixteen or eighteen people. There was a shout, "Here's Ollie!"—and a pounding of glasses and a chorus of welcome— "Hello, Ollie! You're late, Ollie! What's the matter—car broke down?"

Of the party, about half were men and half women. Montague braced himself for the painful ordeal of being introduced to sixteen people in succession, but this was considerately spared him. He shook hands with Robbie Walling, a tall and rather hollow-chested young man, with slight yellow moustaches; and with Mrs. Robbie, who bade him welcome, and presented him with the freedom of the company.

Then he found himself seated between two young ladies, with a waiter leaning over him to take his order for the drinks. He said, a little hesitatingly, that he would like some whisky, as he was about frozen, upon which the girl on his right, remarked, "You'd better try a champagne cocktail—you'll get your results quicker." She added, to the waiter, "Bring a couple of them, and be quick about it."

"You had a cold ride, no doubt, in that low car," she went on, to Montague. "What made you late?"

"We had some delays," he answered. "Once we thought we were arrested."

"Arrested!" she exclaimed; and others took up the word, crying, "Oh, Ollie! tell us about it!"

Oliver told the tale, and meantime his brother had a chance to look about him. All of the party were young—he judged that he was the oldest person there. They were not of the flashily dressed sort, but no one would have had to look twice to know that there was money in the crowd. They had had their first round of drinks, and started in to enjoy themselves. They were all intimates, calling each other by their first names. Montague noticed that these names always ended in "ie,"—there was Robbie and Freddie and Auggie and Clarrie and Bertie and Chappie; if their names could not be made to end properly, they had nicknames instead.

"Ollie" told how they had distanced the policeman; and Clarrie Mason (one of the younger sons of the once mighty railroad king) told of a similar feat which his car had performed. And then the young lady who sat beside him told how a fat Irish woman had skipped out of their way as they rounded a corner, and stood and cursed them from the vantage-point of the sidewalk.

The waiter came with the liquor, and Montague thanked his neighbour, Miss Price. Anabel Price was her name, and they called her "Billy"; she was a tall and splendidly formed creature, and he learned in due time that she was a famous athlete. She must have divined that he would feel a little lost in this crowd of intimates, and set to work to make him feel at home—an attempt in which she was not altogether successful.

They were bound for a shooting-lodge, and so she asked him if he were fond of shooting. He replied that he was; in answer to a further question he said that he had hunted chiefly deer and wild turkey. "Ah, then you are a real hunter!" said Miss Price. "I'm afraid you'll scorn our way."

"What do you do?" he inquired.

"Wait and you'll see," replied she; and added, casually, "When you get to be pally with us, you'll conclude we don't furnish."

Montague's jaw dropped just a little. He recovered himself, however, and said that he presumed so, or that he trusted not; afterward, when he had made inquiries and found out what he should have said, he had completely forgotten what he HAD said.—Down in a hotel in Natchez there was an old head-waiter, to whom Montague had once appealed to seat him next to a friend. At the next meal, learning that the request had been granted, he said to the old man, "I'm afraid you have shown me partiality"; to which the reply came, "I always tries to show it as much as I kin." Montague always thought of this whenever he recalled his first encounter with "Billy" Price.

The young lady on the other side of him now remarked that Robbie was ordering another "topsy-turvy lunch." He inquired what sort of a lunch that was; she told him that Robbie called it a "digestion exercise." That was the only remark that Miss de Millo addressed to him during the meal (Miss Gladys de Mille, the banker's daughter, known as "Baby" to her intimates). She was a stout and round-faced girl, who devoted herself strictly to the business of lunching; and Montague noticed at the end that she was breathing rather hard, and that her big round eyes seemed bigger than ever.

Conversation was general about the table, but it was not easy conversation to follow. It consisted mostly of what is known as "joshing," and involved acquaintance with intimate details of personalities and past events. Also, there was a great deal of slang used, which kept a stranger's wits on the jump. However, Montague concluded that all his deficiencies were made up for by his brother, whose sallies were the cause of the loudest laughter. Just now he seemed to the other more like the Oliver he had known of old—for Montague had already noted a change in him. At home there had never been any end to his gaiety and fun, and it was hard to get him to take anything seriously; but now he kept all his jokes for company, and when he was alone he was in deadly earnest. Apparently he was working hard over his pleasures.

Montague could understand how this was possible. Some one, for instance, had worked hard over the ordering of the lunch—to secure the maximum of explosive effect. It began with ice-cream, moulded in fancy shapes and then buried in white of egg and baked brown. Then there was a turtle soup, thick and green and greasy; and then—horror of horrors—a great steaming plum-pudding. It was served in a strange phenomenon of a platter, with six long, silver legs; and the waiter set it in front of Robbie Walling and lifted the cover with a sweeping gesture—and then removed it and served it himself. Montague had about made up his mind that this was the end, and begun to fill up on bread-and-butter, when there appeared cold asparagus, served in individual silver holders resembling andirons. Then—appetite now being sufficiently whetted—there came quail, in piping hot little casseroles—; and then half a grape-fruit set in a block of ice and filled with wine; and then little squab ducklings, bursting fat, and an artichoke; and then a *café parfait*; and then—as if to crown the audacity—huge thick slices of roast beef! Montague had given up long ago—he could keep no track of the deluge of food which poured forth. And between all the courses there were wines of precious brands, tumbled helter-skelter,—sherry and port, champagne and claret and liqueur. Montague watched poor "Baby" de Mille out of the corner of his eye, and pitied her; for it was evident that she could not resist the impulse to eat whatever was put before her, and she was visibly suffering. He wondered whether he might not manage to divert her by conversation, but he lacked the courage to make the attempt.

The meal was over at four o'clock. By that time most of the other parties were far on their way to New York, and the inn was deserted. They possessed themselves of their belongings, and one by one their cars whirled away toward "Black Forest."

Montague had been told that it was a "shooting-lodge." He had a vision of some kind of a rustic shack, and wondered dimly how so many people would be stowed away. When they turned off the main road, and his brother remarked, "Here we are," he was surprised to see a rather large building of granite, with an archway spanning the road. He was still more surprised when they whizzed through and went on.

"Where are we going?" he asked.

"To 'Black Forest,'" said Oliver.

"And what was that we passed?"

"That was the gate-keeper's lodge," was Oliver's reply.

CHAPTER IV

They ran for about three miles upon a broad macadamized avenue, laid straight as an arrow's flight through the forest; and then the sound of the sea came to them, and before them was a mighty granite pile, looming grim in the twilight, with a draw-bridge and moat, and four great castellated towers. "Black Forest" was built in imitation of a famous old fortress in Provence—only the fortress had forty small rooms, and its modern prototype had seventy large ones, and now every window was blazing with lights. A man does not let himself be caught twice in such a blunder; and having visited a "shooting-lodge" which had cost three-quarters of a million dollars and was set in a preserve of ten thousand acres, he was prepared for Adirondack "camps" which had cost half a million and Newport "cottages" which had cost a million or two.

Liveried servants took the car, and others opened the door and took their coats. The first thing they saw was a huge, fireplace, a fireplace a dozen feet across, made of great boulders, and with whole sections of a pine tree blazing in it. Underfoot was polished hardwood, with skins of bear and buffalo. The firelight flickered upon shields and battle-axes and broad-swords, hung upon the oaken pillars; while between them were tapestries, picturing the Song of Roland and the battle of Roncesvalles. One followed the pillars of the great hall to the vaulted roof, whose glass was glowing blood-red in the western light. A broad stairway ascended to the second floor, which opened upon galleries about the hall.

Montague went to the fire, and stood rubbing his hands before the grateful blaze. "Scotch or Irish, sir?" inquired a lackey, hovering at his side. He had scarcely given his order when the door opened and a second motor load of the party appeared, shivering and rushing for the fire. In a couple of minutes they were all assembled—and roaring with laughter over "Baby" de Mille's account of how her car had run over a dachshund. "Oh, do you know," she cried, "he simply POPPED!"

Half a dozen attendants hovered about, and soon the tables in the hall were covered with trays containing decanters and siphons. By this means everybody in the party was soon warmed up, and then in groups they scattered to amuse themselves.

There was a great hall for indoor tennis, and there were half a dozen squash-courts. Montague knew neither of these games, but he was interested in watching the water-polo in the swimming-tank, and in studying the appointments of this part of the building. The tank, with the walls and floor about it, were all of marble; there was a bronze gallery running about it, from which one might gaze into the green depths of the water. There were luxurious dressing-rooms for men and women, with hot and cold needle-baths, steam-rooms with rubbers in attendance and weighing and lifting machines, electric machines for producing "violet rays," and electric air-blasts for the drying of the women's hair.

He watched several games, in which men and women took part; and later on, when the tennis and other players appeared, he joined them in a plunge. Afterward, he entered one of the electric elevators and was escorted to his room, where he found his bag unpacked, and his evening attire laid out upon the bed.

It was about nine when the party went into the dining-room, which opened upon a granite terrace and loggia facing the sea. The room was finished in some rare black wood, the name of which he did not know; soft radiance suffused it, and the table was lighted by electric candles set in silver sconces, and veiled by silk shades. It gleamed with its load of crystal and silver, set off by scattered groups of orchids and ferns. The repast of the afternoon had been simply a lunch, it seemed—and now they had an elaborate dinner, prepared by Robbie Walling's famous ten-thousand-dollar chef. In contrast with the uproar of the inn was the cloistral stillness of this dining-room, where the impassive footmen seemed to move on padded slippers, and the courses appeared and vanished as if by magic. Montague did his best to accustom himself to the gowns of the women, which were cut lower than any he had ever seen in his life; but he hesitated every time he turned to speak to the young lady beside him, because he could look so deep down into her bosom, and it was difficult for him to realize that she did not mind it.

The conversation was the same as before, except that it was a little more general, and louder in tone; for the guests had become more intimate, and as Robbie Walling's wines of priceless vintage poured forth, they became a little "high." The young lady who sat on Montague's right was a Miss Vincent, a granddaughter of one of the sugar-kings; she was dark-skinned and slender, and had appeared at a recent lawn fete in the costume of an Indian maiden. The company amused itself by selecting an Indian name for her; all sorts of absurd ones were suggested, depending upon various intimate details of the young lady's personality and habits. Robbie caused a laugh by suggesting "Little Dewdrop"—it appeared that she had once been discovered writing a poem about a dewdrop; some one else suggested "Little Raindrop," and then Ollie brought down the house by exclaiming, "Little Raindrop in the Mud-puddle!" A perfect gale of laughter swept over the company, and it must have been a minute before they could recover their composure; in order to appreciate the humour of the sally it was necessary to know that Miss Vincent had "come a cropper" at the last meet of the Long Island Hunt Club, and been extricated from a slough several feet deep.

This was explained to Montague by the young lady on his left—the one whose half-dressed condition caused his embarrassment. She was only about twenty, with a wealth of golden hair and the bright, innocent face of a child; he had not yet learned her name, for every one called her "Cherub." Not long after this she made a remark across the table to Baby de Mille, a strange jumble of syllables, which sounded like English, yet was not. Miss de Mille replied, and several joined in, until there was quite a conversation going on. "Cherub" explained to him that "Baby" had invented a secret language, made by transposing letters; and that Ollie and Bertie were crazy to guess the key to it, and could not.

The dinner lasted until late. The wine-glasses continued to be emptied, and to be magically filled again. The laughter was louder, and now and then there were snatches of singing; women lolled about in their chairs-one beautiful boy sat gazing dreamily across the table at Montague, now and then closing his eyes, and opening them more and more reluctantly. The attendants moved about, impassive and silent as ever; no one else seemed to be cognizant of their existence, but Montague could not help noticing them, and wondering what they thought of it all.

When at last the party broke up, it was because the bridge-players wished to get settled for the evening. The others gathered in front of the fireplace, and smoked and chatted. At home, when one planned a day's hunting, he went to bed early and rose before dawn; but here, it seemed, there was game a-plenty, and the hunters had nothing to consider save their own comfort.

The cards were played in the vaulted "gun-room." Montague strolled through it, and his eye ran down the wall, lined with glass cases and filled with every sort of firearm known to the hunter. He recalled, with a twinge of self-abasement, that he had suggested bringing his shotgun along!

He joined a group in one corner, and lounged in the shadows, and studied "Billy" Price, whose conversation had so mystified him. "Billy," whose father was a banker, proved to be a devotee of horses; she was a veritable Amazon, the one passion of whose life was glory. Seeing her sitting in this group, smoking cigarettes, and drinking highballs, and listening impassively to risqué stories, one might easily draw base conclusions about Billy Price. But as a matter of fact she was made of marble; and the men, instead of falling in love with her, made her their confidante, and told her their troubles, and sought her sympathy and advice.

Some of this was explained to Montague by a young lady, who, as the evening wore on, came in and placed herself beside him. "My name is Betty Wyman," she said, "and you and I will have to be friends, because Ollie's my side partner."

Montague had to meet her advances; so had not much time to speculate as to what the term "side partner" might be supposed to convey. Betty was a radiant little creature, dressed in a robe of deep crimson, made of some soft and filmy and complicated material; there was a crimson rose in her hair, and a living glow of crimson in her cheeks. She was bright and quick, like a butterfly, full of strange whims and impulses; mischievous lights gleamed in her eyes and mischievous smiles played about her adorable little cherry lips. Some strange perfume haunted the filmy dress, and completed the bewilderment of the intended victim.

"I have a letter of introduction to a Mr. Wyman in New York," said Montague. "Perhaps he is a relative of yours."

"Is he a railroad president?" asked she; and when he answered in the affirmative, "Is he a railroad king?" she whispered, in a mocking, awe-stricken voice, "Is he rich—oh, rich as Solomon—and is he a terrible man, who eats people alive all the time?"

"Yes," said Montague—"that must be the one."

"Well," said Betty, "he has done me the honour to be my granddaddy; but don't you take any letter of introduction to him."

"Why not?" asked he, perplexed.

"Because he'll eat YOU," said the girl. "He hates Ollie."

"Dear me," said the other; and the girl asked, "Do you mean that the boy hasn't said a word about me?"

"No," said Montague—"I suppose he left it for you to do."

"Well," said Betty, "it's like a fairy story. Do you ever read fairy stories? In this story there was a princess—oh, the most beautiful princess! Do you understand?"

"Yes," said Montague. "She wore a red rose in her hair."

"And then," said the girl, "there was a young courtier—very handsome and gay; and they fell in love with each other. But the terrible old king—he wanted his daughter to wait a while, until he got through conquering his enemies, so that he might have time to pick out some prince or other, or maybe some ogre who was wasting his lands—do you follow me?"

"Perfectly," said he. "And then did the beautiful princess pine away?"

"Um—no," said Betty, pursing her lips. "But she had to dance terribly hard to keep from thinking about herself." Then she laughed, and exclaimed, "Dear me, we are getting poetical!" And next, looking sober again, "Do you know, I was half afraid to talk to you. Ollie tells me you're terribly serious. Are you?"

"I don't know," said Montague—but she broke in with a laugh, "We were talking about you at dinner last night. They had some whipped cream done up in funny little curliques, and Ollie said, 'Now, if my brother Allan were here, he'd be thinking about the man who fixed this cream, and how long it took him, and how he might have been reading "The Simple Life."' Is that true?"

"It involves a question of literary criticism"—said Montague.

"I don't want to talk about literature," exclaimed the other. In truth, she wanted nothing save to feel of his armour and find out if there were any weak spots through which he could be teased. Montague was to find in time that the adorable Miss Elizabeth was a very thorny species of rose—she was more like a gay-coloured wasp, of predatory temperament.

"Ollie says you want to go down town and work," she went on. "I think you're awfully foolish. Isn't it much nicer to spend your time in an imitation castle like this?"

"Perhaps," said he, "but I haven't any castle."

"You might get one," answered Betty. "Stay around awhile and let us marry you to a nice girl. They will all throw themselves at your feet, you know, for you have such a delicious melting voice, and you look romantic and exciting." (Montague made a note to inquire whether it was customary in New York to talk about you so frankly to your face.)

Miss Betty was surveying him quizzically meantime. "I don't know," she said. "On second thoughts, maybe you'll frighten the girls. Then it'll be the married women who'll fall in love with you. You'll have to watch out."

"I've already been told that by my tailor," said Montague, with a laugh.

"That would be a still quicker way of making your fortune," said she. "But I don't think you'd fit in the rôle of a tame cat."

"A *what*?" he exclaimed; and Miss Betty laughed.

"Don't you know what that is? Dear me—how charmingly naive! But perhaps you'd better get Ollie to explain for you."

That brought the conversation to the subject of slang; and Montague, in a sudden burst of confidence, asked for an interpretation of Miss Price's cryptic utterance. "She said"—he repeated slowly—"that when I got to be pally with her, I'd conclude she didn't furnish."

"Oh, yes," said Miss Wyman. "She just meant that when you knew her, you'd be disappointed. You see, she picks up all the race-track slang—one can't help it, you know. And last year she took her coach over to England, and so she's got all the English slang. That makes it hard, even for us."

And then Betty sailed in to entertain him with little sketches of other members of the party. A phenomenon that had struck Montague immediately was the extraordinary freedom with which everybody in New York discussed everybody else. As a matter of fact, one seldom discussed anything else; and it made not the least difference, though the person were one of your set,—though he ate your bread and salt, and you ate his,—still you would amuse yourself by pouring forth the most painful and humiliating and terrifying things about him.

There was poor Clarrie Mason: Clarrie, sitting in at bridge, with an expression of feverish eagerness upon his pale face. Clarrie always lost, and it positively broke his heart, though he had ten millions laid by on ice. Clarrie went about all day, bemoaning his brother, who had been kidnapped. Had Montague not heard about it? Well, the newspapers called it a marriage, but it was really a kidnapping. Poor Larry Mason was good-natured and weak in the knees, and he had been carried off by a terrible creature, three times as big as himself, and with a temper like—oh, there were no words for it! She had been an actress; and now she had carried Larry away in her talons, and was building a big castle to keep him in— for he had ten millions too, alas!

And then there was Bertie Stuyvesant, beautiful and winning—the boy who had sat opposite Montague at dinner. Bertie's father had been a coal man, and nobody knew how many millions he had left. Bertie was gay; last week he had invited them to a brook-trout breakfast—in November—and that had been a lark! Somebody had told him that trout never really tasted good unless you caught them yourself, and Bertie had suddenly resolved to catch them for that breakfast. "They have a big preserve up in the Adirondacks," said Betty; "and Bertie ordered his private train, and he and Chappie de Peyster and some others started that night;

they drove I don't know how many miles the next day, and caught a pile of trout—and we had them for breakfast the next morning! The best joke of all is that Chappie vows they were so full they couldn't fish, and that the trout were caught with nets! Poor Bertie—somebody'll have to separate him from that decanter now!"

From the hall there came loud laughter, with sounds of scuffling, and cries, "Let me have it!"—"That's Baby de Mille," said Miss Wyman. "She's always wanting to rough-house it. Robbie was mad the last time she was down here; she got to throwing sofa-cushions, and upset a vase."

"Isn't that supposed to be good form?" asked Montague.

"Not at Robbie's," said she. "Have you had a chance to talk with Robbie yet? You'll like him—he's serious, like you."

"What's he serious about?"

"About spending his money," said Betty. "That's the only thing he has to be serious about."

"Has he got so very much?"

"Thirty or forty millions," she replied; "but then, you see, a lot of it's in the inner companies of his railroad system, and it pays him fabulously. And his wife has money, too—she was a Miss Mason, you know, her father's one of the steel crowd. We've a saying that there are millionaires, and then multi-millionaires, and then Pittsburg millionaires. Anyhow, the two of them spend all their income in entertaining. It's Robbie's fad to play the perfect host—he likes to have lots of people round him. He does put up good times—only he's so very important about it, and he has so many ideas of what is proper! I guess most of his set would rather go to Mrs. Jack Warden's any day; I'd be there to-night, if it hadn't been for Ollie."

"Who's Mrs. Jack Warden?" asked Montague.

"Haven't you ever heard of her?" said Betty. "She used to be Mrs. van Ambridge, and then she got a divorce and married Warden, the big lumber man. She used to give 'boy and girl' parties, in the English fashion; and when we went there we'd do as we please—play tag all over the house, and have pillow-fights, and ransack the closets and get up masquerades! Mrs. Warden's as good-natured as an old cow. You'll meet her sometime—only don't you let her fool you with those soft eyes of hers. You'll find she doesn't mean it; it's just that she likes to have handsome men hanging round her."

At one o'clock a few of Robbie's guests went to bed, Montague among them. He left two tables of bridge fiends sitting immobile, the women with flushed faces and feverish hands, and the men with cigarettes dangling from their lips. There were trays and decanters beside each card-table; and in the hall he passed three youths staggering about in each other's arms and feebly singing snatches of "coon songs." Ollie and Betty had strolled away together to parts unknown.

Montague had entered his name in the order-book to be called at nine o'clock. The man who awakened him brought him coffee and cream upon a silver tray, and asked him if he would have anything stronger. He was privileged to have his breakfast in his room, if he wished; but he went downstairs, trying his best to feel natural in his elaborate hunting costume. No one else had appeared yet, but he found the traces of last night cleared away, and breakfast ready—served in English fashion, with urns of tea and coffee upon the buffet. The grave butler and his satellites were in attendance, ready to take his order for anything else under the sun that he fancied.

Montague preferred to go for a stroll upon the terrace, and to watch the sunlight sparkling upon the sea. The morning was beautiful—everything about the place was so beautiful that he wondered how men and women could live here and not feel the spell of it.

Billy Price came down shortly afterward, clad in a khaki hunting suit, with knee kilts and button-pockets and gun-pads and Cossack cartridge-loops. She joined him in a stroll down the beach, and talked to him about the coming winter season, with its leading personalities and events,—the Horse Show, which opened next week, and the prospects for the opera, and Mrs. de Graffenried's opening entertainment. When they came back it was eleven o'clock, and they found most of the guests assembled, nearly all of them looking a little pale and uncomfortable in the merciless morning light. As the two came in they observed Bertie Stuyvesant standing by the buffet, in the act of gulping down a tumbler of brandy. "Bertie has taken up the 'no breakfast fad,'" said Billy with an ironical smile.

Then began the hunt. The equipment of "Black Forest" included a granite building, steam-heated and elaborately fitted, in which an English expert and his assistants raised imported pheasants—magnificent bronze-coloured birds with long, floating black tails. Just before the opening of the season they were dumped by thousands into the covers—fat, and almost tame enough to be fed by hand; and now came the "hunters."

First they drew lots, for they were to hunt in pairs, a man and a woman. Montague drew Miss Vincent—"Little Raindrop in the Mud-puddle." Then Ollie, who was master of ceremonies, placed them in a long line, and gave them the direction; and at a signal they moved through the forest; Following each person were two attendants, to carry the extra guns and reload them; and out in front were men to beat the bushes and scare the birds into flight.

Now Montague's idea of hunting had been to steal through the bayou forests, and match his eyes against those of the wild turkey, and shoot off their heads with a rifle bullet. So, when one of these birds rose in front of him, he fired, and the bird dropped; and he could have done it for ever, he judged—only it was stupid slaughter, and it sickened him. However, if the creatures were not shot, they must inevitably perish in the winter snows; and he had heard that Robbie sent the game to the hospitals. Also, the score was being kept, and Miss Vincent, who was something of a shot herself, was watching him with eager excitement, being wild with desire to beat out Billy Price and Chappie de Peyster, who were the champion shots of the company. Baby de Mille, who was on his left, and who could not shoot at all, was blundering along, puffing for breath and eyeing him enviously; and the attendants at his back were trembling with delight and murmuring their applause. So he shot on, as long as the drive lasted, and again on their way back, over a new stretch of the country. Sometimes the birds would rise in pairs, and he would drop them both; and twice when a blundering flock took flight in his direction he seized a second gun and brought down a second pair. When the day's sport came to an end his score was fifteen better than his nearest competitor, and he and his partner had won the day.

They crowded round to congratulate him; first his partner, and then his rivals, and his host and hostess. Montague found that he had suddenly become a person of consequence. Some who had previously taken no notice of him now became aware of his existence; proud society belles condescended to make conversation with him, and Clarrie Mason, who hated de Peyster, made note of a way to annoy him. As for Oliver, he was radiant with delight. "When it came to horses and guns, I knew you'd make good," he whispered.

Leaving the game to be gathered up in carts, they made their way home, and there the two victors received their prizes. The man's consisted of a shaving set in a case of solid gold, set with diamonds. Montague was simply stunned, for the thing could not have cost less than one or two thousand dollars. He could not persuade himself that he had a right to accept of such hospitality, which he could never hope to return. He was to realize in time that Robbie lived for the pleasure of thus humiliating his fellow-men.

After luncheon, the party came to an end. Some set out to return as they had come; and others, who had dinner engagements, went back with their host in his private car, leaving their autos to be returned by the chauffeurs. Montague and his brother were among these; and about dusk, when the swarms of working people were pouring out of the city, they crossed the ferry and took a cab to their hotel.

CHAPTER V

They found their apartments looking as if they had been struck by a snow-storm-a storm of red and green and yellow, and all the colours that lie between. All day the wagons of fashionable milliners and costumiers had been stopping at the door, and their contents had found their way to Alice's room. The floors were ankle-deep in tissue paper and tape, and beds and couches and chairs were covered with boxes, in which lay wonderful symphonies of colour, half disclosed in their wrappings of gauze. In the midst of it all stood the girl, her eyes shining with excitement.

"Oh, Allan!" she cried, as they entered. "How am I ever to thank you?"

"You're not to thank me," Montague replied. "This is all Oliver's doings."

"Oliver!" exclaimed the girl, and turned to him. "How in the world could you do it?" she cried. "How will you ever get the money to pay for it all?"

"That's my problem," said the man, laughing. "All you have to think about is to look beautiful."

"If I don't," was her reply, "it won't be for lack of clothes. I never saw so many wonderful things in all my life as I've seen to-day."

"There's quite a show of them," admitted Oliver.

"And Reggie Mann! It was so queer, Allan! I never went shopping with a man before. And he's so—so matter-of-fact. You know, he bought me—everything!"

"That was what he was told to do," said Oliver. "Did you like him?"

"I don't know," said the girl. "He's queer—I never met a man like that before. But he was awfully kind; and the people just turned their stores inside out for us—half a dozen people hurrying about to wait on you at once!"

"You'll get used to such things," said Oliver; and then, stepping toward the bed, "Let's see what you got."

"Most of the things haven't come," said Alice. "The gowns all have to be fitted.—That one is for to-night," she added, as he lifted up a beautiful object made of rose-coloured chiffon.

Oliver studied it, and glanced once or twice at the girl. "I guess you can carry it," he said. "What sort of a cloak are you to wear?"

"Oh, the cloak!" cried Alice. "Oliver, I can't believe it's really to belong to me. I didn't know anyone but princesses wore such things."

The cloak was in Mrs. Montague's room, and one of the maids brought it in. It was an opera-wrap of grey brocade, lined with unborn baby lamb—a thing of a gorgeousness that made Montague literally gasp for breath.

"Did you ever see anything like it in your life?" cried Alice. "And Oliver, is it true that I have to have gloves and shoes and stockings—and a hat—to match every gown?"

"Of course." said Oliver. "If you were doing things right, you ought to have a cloak to match each evening gown as well."

"It seems incredible," said the girl. "Can it be right to spend so much money for things to wear?"

But Oliver was not discussing questions of ethics; he was examining sets of tinted crepe de chine lingerie, and hand-woven hose of spun silk. There were boxes upon boxes, and bureau drawers and closet shelves already filled up with hand-embroidered and lace-trimmed creations-chemises and corset-covers, night-robes of "handkerchief linen" lawn, lace handkerchiefs and veils, corsets of French coutil, dressing-jackets of pale-coloured silks, and negligees of soft batistes, trimmed with Valenciennes lace, or even with fur.

"You must have put in a full day," he said.

"I never looked at so many things in my life," said Alice. "And Mr. Mann never stopped to ask the price of a thing."

"I didn't think to tell him to," said Oliver, laughing.

Then the girl went in to dress—and Oliver faced about to find his brother sitting and staring hard at him.

"Tell me!" Montague exclaimed. "In God's name, what is all this to cost?"

"I don't know," said Oliver, impassively. "I haven't seen the bills. It'll be fifteen or twenty thousand, I guess."

Montague's hands clenched involuntarily, and he sat rigid. "How long will it all last her?" he asked.

"Why," said the other, "when she gets enough, it'll last her until spring, of course—unless she goes South during the winter."

"How much is it going to take to dress her for a year?"

"I suppose thirty or forty thousand," was the reply. "I don't expect to keep count."

Montague sat in silence. "You don't want to shut her up and keep her at home, do you?" inquired his brother, at last.

"Do you mean that other women spend that much on clothes?" he demanded.

"Of course," said Oliver, "hundreds of them. Some spend fifty thousand—I know several who go over a hundred."

"It's monstrous!" Montague exclaimed.

"Fiddlesticks!" was the other's response. "Why, thousands of people live by it—wouldn't know anything else to do."

Montague said nothing to that. "Can you afford to have Alice compete with such women indefinitely?" he asked.

"I have no idea of her doing it indefinitely," was Oliver's reply. "I simply propose to give her a chance. When she's married, her bills will be paid by her husband."

"Oh," said the other, "then this layout is just for her to be exhibited in."

"You may say that," answered Oliver,—"if you want to be foolish. You know perfectly well that parents who launch their daughters in Society don't figure on keeping up the pace all their lifetimes."

"We hadn't thought of marrying Alice off," said Montague.

To which his brother replied that the best physicians left all they could to nature. "Suppose," said he, "that we just introduce her in the right set, and turn her loose and let her enjoy herself—and then cross the next bridge when we come to it?"

Montague sat with knitted brows, pondering.' He was beginning to see a little daylight now. "Oliver," he asked suddenly, "are you sure the stakes in this game aren't too big?"

"How do you mean?" asked the other.

"Will you be able to stay in until the show-down? Until either Alice or myself begins to bring in some returns?"

"Never worry about that," said the other, with a laugh.

"But hadn't you better take me into your confidence?" Montague persisted. "How many weeks can you pay our rent in this place? Have you got the money to pay for all these clothes?"

"I've got it," laughed the other—"but that doesn't say I'm going to pay it."

"Don't you have to pay your bills? Can we do all this upon credit?"

Oliver laughed again. "You go at me like a prosecuting attorney," he said. "I'm afraid you'll have to inquire around and learn some respect for your brother." Then he added, seriously, "You see, Allan, people like Reggie or myself are in position to bring a great deal of custom to tradespeople, and so they are willing to go out of their way to oblige us. And we have commissions of all sorts coming to us, so it's never any question of cash."

"Oh!" exclaimed the other, opening his eyes, "I see! Is that the way you make money?"

"It's one of the ways we save it," said Oliver. "It comes to the same thing."

"Do people know it?"

"Why, of course. Why not?"

"I don't know," said Montague. "It sounds a little queer."

"Nothing of the kind," said Oliver. "Some of the best people in New York do it. Strangers come to the city, and they want to go to the right places, and they ask me, and I send them. Or take Robbie Walling, who keeps up five or six establishments, and spends several millions a year. He can't see to it all personally—if he did, he'd never do anything else. Why shouldn't he ask a friend to attend to things for him? Or again, a new shop opens, and they want Mrs. Walling's trade for the sake of the advertising, and they offer her a discount and me a commission. Why shouldn't I get her to try them?"

"It's quite intricate," commented the other. "The stores have more than one price, then?"

"They have as many prices as they have customers," was the answer. "Why shouldn't they? New York is full of raw rich people who value things by what they pay. And why shouldn't they pay high and be happy? That opera-cloak that Alice has—Reval promised it to me for two thousand, and I'll wager you she'd charge some woman from Butte, Montana, thirty-five hundred for one just like it."

Montague got up suddenly. "Stop," he said, waving his hands. "You take all the bloom off the butterfly's wings!"

He asked where they were going that evening, and Oliver said that they were invited to an informal dinner-party at Mrs. Winnie Duval's. Mrs. Winnie was the young widow who had recently married the founder of the great banking-house of Puval and Co.—so Oliver explained; she was a chum of his, and they would meet an interesting set there. She was going to invite her cousin, Charlie Carter—she wanted him to meet Alice. "Mrs. Winnie's always plotting to get Charlie to settle down," said Oliver, with a merry laugh.

He telephoned for his man to bring over his clothes, and he and his brother dressed. Then Alice came in, looking like the goddess of the dawn in the gorgeous rose-coloured gown. The colour in her cheeks was even brighter than usual; for she was staggered to find how low the gown was cut, and was afraid she was committing a faux pas. "Tell me about it," she stammered. "Mammy Lucy says I'm surely supposed to wear some lace, or a bouquet."

"Mammy Lucy isn't a Paris costumier," said Oliver, much amused. "Dear me—wait until you have seen Mrs. Winnie!"

Mrs. Winnie had kindly sent her limousine car for them, and it stood throbbing in front of the hotel-entrance, its acetylenes streaming far up the street. Mrs. Winnie's home was on Fifth Avenue, fronting the park. It occupied half a block, and had cost two millions to build and furnish. It was known as the "Snow Palace," being all of white marble.

At the curb a man in livery opened the door of the car, and in the vestibule another man in livery bowed the way. Lined up just inside the door was a corps of imposing personages, clad in scarlet waistcoats and velvet knee-breeches, with powdered wigs, and gold buttons, and gold buckles on their patent-leather pumps. These splendid creatures took their wraps, and then presented to Montague and Oliver a bouquet of flowers upon a silver salver, and upon another salver a tiny envelope bearing the name of their partner at this strictly "informal" dinner-party. Then the functionaries stood out of the way and permitted them to view the dazzling splendour of the entrance hall of the Snow Palace. There was a great marble staircase running up from the centre of the hall, with a carved marble gallery above, and a marble fireplace below. To decorate this mansion a real palace in the Punjab had been bought outright and plundered; there were mosaics of jade, and wonderful black marble, and rare woods, and strange and perplexing carvings.

The head butler stood at the entrance to the salon, pronouncing their names; and just inside was Mrs. Winnie.

Montague never forgot that first vision of her; she might have been a real princess out of the palace in the Punjab. She was a brunette, rich-coloured, full-throated and deep-bosomed, with scarlet lips, and black hair and eyes. She wore a court-gown of cloth of silver, with white kid shoes embroidered with jewelled flowers. All her life she had been collecting large turquoises, and these she had made into a tiara, and a neck ornament spreading over her chest, and a stomacher. Each of these stones was mounted with diamonds, and set upon a slender wire. So as she moved they quivered and shimmered, and the effect was dazzling, barbaric.

She must have seen that Montague was staggered, for she gave him a little extra pressure of the hand, and said, "I'm so glad you came. Ollie has told me all about you." Her voice was soft and melting, not so forbidding as her garb.

Montague ran the gauntlet of the other guests: Charlie Carter, a beautiful, dark-haired boy, having the features of a Greek god, but a sallow and unpleasant complexion; Major "Bob" Venable, a stout little gentleman with a red face and a heavy jowl; Mrs. Frank Landis, a merry-eyed young widow with pink cheeks and auburn hair; Willie Davis, who had been a famous half-back, and was now junior partner in the banking-house; and two young married couples, whose names Montague missed.

The name written on his card was Mrs. Alden. She came in just after him—a matron of about fifty, of vigorous aspect and ample figure, approaching what he had not yet learned to call embonpoint. She wore brocade, as became a grave dowager, and upon her ample bosom there lay an ornament the size of a man's hand, and made wholly out of blazing diamonds—the most imposing affair that Montague had ever laid eyes upon. She gave him her hand to shake, and made no attempt to disguise the fact that she was looking him over in the meantime.

"Madam, dinner is served," said the stately butler; and the glittering procession moved into the dining-room—a huge state apartment, finished in some lustrous jet-black wood, and with great panel paintings illustrating the Romaunt de la Rose. The table was covered with a cloth of French embroidery, and gleaming with its load of crystal and gold plate. At either end there were huge candlesticks of solid gold, and in the centre a mound of orchids and lilies of the valley, matching in colour the shades of the candelabra and the daintily painted menu cards.

"You are fortunate in coming to New York late in life," Mrs. Alden was saying to him. "Most of our young men are tired out before they have sense enough to enjoy anything. Take my advice and look about you—don't let that lively brother of yours set the pace for you."

In front of Mrs. Alden there was a decanter of Scotch whisky. "Will you have some?" she asked, as she took it up.

"No, I thank you," said he, and then wondered if perhaps he should not have said yes, as he watched the other select the largest of the half-dozen wine-glasses clustered at her place, and pour herself out a generous libation.

"Have you seen much of the city?" she asked, as she tossed it off—without as much as a quiver of an eyelash.

"No," said he. "They have not given me much time. They took me off to the country—to the Robert Wallings'."

"Ah," said Mrs. Alden; and Montague, struggling to make conversation, inquired, "Do you know Mr. Walling?"

"Quite well," said the other, placidly. "I used to be a Walling myself, you know."

"Oh," said Montague, taken aback; and then added, "Before you were married?"

"No," said Mrs. Alden, more placidly than ever, "before I was divorced."

There was a dead silence, and Montague sat gasping to catch his breath. Then suddenly he heard a faint subdued chuckle, which grew into open laughter; and he stole a glance at Mrs. Alden, and saw that her eyes were twinkling; and then he began to laugh himself. They laughed together, so merrily that others at the table began to look at them in perplexity.

So the ice was broken between them; which filled Montague with a vast relief. But he was still dimly touched with awe—for he realized that this must be the great Mrs. Billy Alden, whose engagement to the Duke of London was now the topic of the whole country. And that huge diamond ornament must be part of Mrs. Alden's million-dollar outfit of jewellery!

The great lady volunteered not to tell on him; and added generously that when he came to dinner with her she would post him concerning the company. "It's awkward for a stranger, I can understand," said she; and continued, grimly: "When people get divorces it sometimes means that they have quarrelled—and they don't always make it up afterward, either. And sometimes other people quarrel—almost as bitterly as if they had been married. Many a hostess has had her reputation ruined by not keeping track of such things."

So Montague made the discovery that the great Mrs. Billy, though. forbidding of aspect, was good-natured when she chose to be, and with a pretty wit. She was a woman with a mind of her own—a hard-fighting character, who had marshalled those about her, and taken her place at the head of the column. She had always counted herself a personage enough to do exactly as she pleased; through the course of the dinner she would take up the decanter of Scotch, and make a pass to help Montague—and then, when he declined, pour out imperturbably what she wanted. "I don't like your brother," she said to him, a little later. "He won't last; but he tells me you're different, so maybe I will like you. Come and see me sometime, and let me tell you what not to do in New York."

Then Montague turned to talk with his hostess, who sat on his right.

"Do you play bridge?" asked Mrs. Winnie, in her softest and most gracious tone.

"My brother has given me a book to study from," he answered. "But if he takes me about day and night, I don't know how I'm to manage it."

"Come and let me teach you," said Mrs. Winnie. "I mean it, really," she added. "I've nothing to do—at least that I'm not tired of. Only I don't believe you'd take long to learn all that I know."

"Aren't you a successful player?" he asked sympathetically.

"I don't believe anyone wants me to learn," said Mrs. Winnie.—"They'd rather come and get my money. Isn't that true, Major?"

Major Venable sat on her other hand, and he paused in the act of raising a spoonful of soup to his lips, and laughed, deep down in his throat—a queer little laugh that shook his fat cheeks and neck. "I may say," he said, "that I know several people to whom the status quo is satisfactory."

"Including yourself," said the lady, with a little moue. "The wretched man won sixteen hundred dollars from me last night; and he sat in his club window all afternoon, just to have the pleasure of laughing at me as I went by. I don't believe I'll play at all to-night—I'm going to make myself agreeable to Mr. Montague, and let you win from Virginia Landis for a change."

And then the Major paused again in his attack upon the soup. "My dear Mrs. Winnie," he said, "I can live for much more than one day upon sixteen hundred dollars!"

The Major was a famous club-man and bon vivant, as Montague learned later on. "He's an uncle of Mrs. Bobbie Walling's," said Mrs. Alden, in his ear. "And incidentally they hate each other like poison."

"That is so that I won't repeat my luckless question again?" asked Montague, with a smile.

"Oh, they meet," said the other. "You wouldn't be supposed to know that. Won't you have any Scotch?"

Montague's thoughts were so much taken up with the people at this repast that he gave little thought to the food. He noticed with surprise that they had real spring lamb—it being the middle of November. But he could not know that the six-weeks-old creatures from which it had come had been raised in cotton-wool and fed on milk with a spoon—and had cost a dollar and a half a pound. A little later, however, there was placed before him a delicately browned sweetbread upon a platter of gold, and then suddenly he began to pay attention. Mrs. Winnie had a coat of arms; he had noticed it upon her auto, and again upon the great bronze gates of the Snow Palace, and again upon the liveries of her footmen, and yet again upon the decanter of Scotch. And now—incredible and appalling—he observed it branded upon the delicately browned sweetbread!

After that, who would not have watched? There were large dishes of rare fruits upon the table—fruits which had been packed in cotton wool and shipped in cold storage from every corner of the earth. There were peaches which had come from South Africa (they had cost ten dollars apiece). There were bunches of Hamburg grapes, dark purple and bursting fat, which had been grown in a hot-house, wrapped in paper bags. There were nectarines and plums, and pomegranates and persimmons from Japan, and later on, little dishes of plump strawberries-raised in pots. There were quail which had come from Egypt, and a wonderful thing called "crab-flake a la Dewey," cooked in a chafing-dish, and served with mushrooms that had been grown in the tunnels of abandoned mines in Michigan. There was lettuce raised by electric light, and lima beans that had come from Porto Rico, and artichokes brought from France at a cost of one dollar each.—And all these extraordinary viands were washed down by eight or nine varieties of wines, from the cellar of a man who had made collecting them a fad for the last thirty years, who had a vineyard in France for the growing of his own champagne, and kept twenty thousand quarts of claret in storage all the time—and procured his Rhine wine from the cellar of the German Emperor, at a cost of twenty-five dollars a quart!

There were twelve people at dinner, and afterward they made two tables for bridge, leaving Charlie Carter to talk to Alice, and Mrs. Winnie to devote herself to Montague, according to her promise. "Everybody likes to see my house," she said. "Would you?" And she led the way from the dining-room into the great conservatory, which formed a central court extending to the roof of the building. She pressed a button, and a soft radiance streamed down from above, in the midst of which Mrs. Winnie stood, with her shimmering jewels a very goddess of the fire.

The conservatory was a place in which he could have spent the evening; it was filled with the most extraordinary varieties of plants. "They were gathered from all over the world," said Mrs. Winnie, seeing that he was staring at them. "My husband employed a connoisseur to hunt them out for him. He did it before we were married—he thought it would make me happy."

In the centre of the place there was a fountain, twelve or fourteen feet in height, and set in a basin of purest Carrara marble. By the touch of a button the pool was flooded with submerged lights, and one might see scores of rare and beautiful fish swimming about.

"Isn't it fine!" said Mrs. Winnie, and added eagerly, "Do you know, I come here at night, sometimes when I can't sleep, and sit for hours and gaze. All those living things; with their extraordinary forms-some of them have faces, and look like human beings! And I wonder what they think about, and if life seems as strange to them as it does to me."

She seated herself by the edge of the pool, and gazed in. "These fish were given to me by my cousin, Ned Carter. They call him Buzzie. Have you met him yet?—No, of course not. He's Charlie's brother, and he collects art things—the most unbelievable things. Once, a long time ago, he took a fad for goldfish—some goldfish are very rare and beautiful, you know—one can pay twenty-five and fifty dollars apiece for them. He got all the dealers had, and when he learned that there were some they couldn't get, he took a trip to Japan and China on purpose to get them. You know they raise them there, and some of them are sacred, and not allowed to be sold or taken out of the country. And he had all sorts of carved ivory receptacles for them, that he brought home with him—he had one beautiful marble basin about ten feet long, that had been stolen from the Emperor."

Over Montague's shoulder where he sat, there hung an orchid, a most curious creation, an explosion of scarlet flame. "That is the odonto-glossum," said Mrs. Winnie. "Have you heard of it?"

"Never," said the man.

"Dear me," said the other. "Such is fame!"

"Is it supposed to be famous?" he asked.

"Very," she replied. "There was a lot in the newspapers about it. You see Winton—that's my husband, you know—paid twenty-five thousand dollars to the man who created it; and that made a lot of foolish talk—people come from all over to look at it. I wanted to have it, because its shape is exactly like the coronet on my crest. Do you notice that?"

"Yes," said Montague. "It's curious."

"I'm very proud of my crest," continued Mrs. Winnie. "Of course there are vulgar rich people who have them made to order, and make them ridiculous; but ours is a real one. It's my own—not my husband's; the Duvals are an old French family, but they're not noble. I was a Morris, you know, and our line runs back to the old French ducal house of Montmorenci. And last summer, when we were motoring, I hunted up one of their chateaux; and see! I brought over this."

Mrs. Winnie pointed to a suit of armour, placed in a passage leading to the billiard-room. "I have had the lights fixed," she added. And she pressed a button, and all illumination vanished, save for a faint red glow just above the man in armour.

"Doesn't he look real?" said she. (He had his visor down, and a battle-axe in his mailed hands.) "I like to imagine that he may have been my twentieth great-grandfather. I come and sit here, and gaze at him and shiver. Think what a terrible time it must have been to live in—when men wore things like that! It couldn't be any worse to be a crab."

"You seem to be fond of strange emotions," said Montague, laughing.

"Maybe I am," said the other. "I like everything that's old and romantic, and makes you forget this stupid society world."

She stood brooding for a moment or two, gazing at the figure. Then she asked, abruptly, "Which do you like best, pictures or swimming?"

"Why," replied the man, laughing and perplexed, "I like them both, at times."

"I wondered which you'd rather see first," explained his escort; "the art gallery or the natatorium. I'm afraid you'll get tired before you've seen every thing."

"Suppose we begin with the art-gallery," said he. "There's not much to see in a swimming-pool."

"Ah, but ours is a very special one," said the lady.—"And some day, if you'll be very good, and promise not to tell anyone, I'll let you see my own bath. Perhaps they've told you, I have one in my own apartments, cut out of a block of the most wonderful green marble."

Montague showed the expected amount of astonishment.

"Of course that gave the dreadful newspapers another chance to gossip," said Mrs. Winnie, plaintively. "People found out what I had paid for it. One can't have anything beautiful without that question being asked."

And then followed a silence, while Mrs. Winnie waited for him to ask it. As he forebore to do so, she added, "It was fifty thousand dollars."

They were moving towards the elevator, where a small boy in the wonderful livery of plush and scarlet stood at attention. "Sometimes," she continued, "it seems to me that it is wicked to pay such prices for things. Have you ever thought about it?"

"Occasionally," Montague replied.

"Of course," said she, "it makes work for people; and I suppose they can't be better employed than in making beautiful things. But sometimes, when I think of all the poverty there is, I get unhappy. We have a winter place down South—one of those huge country-houses that look like exposition buildings, and have rooms for a hundred guests; and sometimes I go driving by myself, down to the mill towns, and go through them and talk to the children. I came to know some of them quite well—poor little wretches."

They stepped out of the elevator, and moved toward the art-gallery. "It used to make me so unhappy," she went on. "I tried to talk to my husband about it, but he wouldn't have it. 'I don't see why you can't be like other people,' he said—he's always repeating that to me. And what could I say?"

"Why not suggest that other people might be like you?" said the man, laughing.

"I wasn't clever enough," said she, regretfully.—"It's very hard for a woman, you know—with no one to understand. Once I went down to a settlement, to see what that was like. Do you know anything about settlements?"

"Nothing at all," said Montague.

"Well, they are people who go to live among the poor, and try to reform them. It takes a terrible lot of courage, I think. I give them money now and then, but I am never sure if it does any good. The trouble with poor people, it seems to me, is that there are so many of them."

"There are, indeed," said Montague, thinking of the vision he had seen from Oliver's racing-car.

Mrs. Winnie had seated herself upon a cushioned seat near the entrance to the darkened gallery. "I haven't been there for some time," she continued. "I've discovered something that I think appeals more to my temperament. I have rather a leaning toward the occult and the mystical, I'm afraid. Did you ever hear of the Babists?"

"No," said Montague.

"Well, that's a religious sect—from Persia, I think—and they are quite the rage. They are priests, you understand, and they give lectures, and teach you all about the immanence of the divine, and about reincarnation, and Karma, and all that. Do you believe any of those things?"

"I can't say that I know about them," said he.

"It is very beautiful and strange," added the other. "It makes you realize what a perplexing thing life is. They teach you how the universe is all one, and the soul is the only reality, and so bodily things don't matter. If I were a Babist, I believe that I could be happy, even if I had to work in a cotton-mill."

Then Mrs. Winnie rose up suddenly. "You'd rather look at the pictures, I know," she said; and she pressed a button, and a soft radiance flooded the great vaulted gallery.

"This is our chief pride in life," she said. "My husband's object has been to get one representative work of each of the great painters of the world. We got their masterpiece whenever we could. Over there in the corner are the old masters—don't you love to look at them?"

Montague would have liked to look at them very much; but he felt that he would rather it were some time when he did not have Mrs. Winnie by his side. Mrs. Winnie must have had to show the gallery quite frequently; and now her mind was still upon the Persian transcendentalists.

"That picture of the saint is a Botticelli," she said. "And do you know, the orange-coloured robe always makes me think of the swami. That is my teacher, you know—Swami Babubanana. And he has the most beautiful delicate hands, and great big brown eyes, so soft and gentle—for all the world like those of the gazelles in our place down South!"

Thus Mrs. Winnie, as she roamed from picture to picture, while the souls of the grave old masters looked down upon her in silence.

CHAPTER VI

Montague had now been officially pronounced complete by his tailor; and Reval had sent home the first of Alice's street gowns, elaborately plain, but fitting her conspicuously, and costing accordingly. So the next morning they were ready to be taken to call upon Mrs. Devon.

Of course Montague had heard of the Devons, but he was not sufficiently initiated to comprehend just what it meant to be asked to call. But when Oliver came in, a little before noon, and proceeded to examine his costume and to put him to rights, and insisted that Alice should have her hair done over, he began to realize that this was a special occasion. Oliver was in quite a state of excitement; and after they had left the hotel, and were driving up the Avenue, he explained to them that their future in Society depended upon the outcome of this visit. Calling upon Mrs. Devon, it seemed, was the American equivalent to being presented at court. For twenty-five years this grand lady had been the undisputed mistress of the Society of the metropolis; and if she liked them, they would be invited to her annual ball, which took place in January, and then for ever after their position would be assured. Mrs. Devon's ball was the one great event of the social year; about one thousand people were asked, while ten thousand disappointed ones gnashed their teeth in outer darkness.

All of which threw Alice into a state of trepidation.

"Suppose we don't suit her!" she said.

To that the other replied that their way had been made smooth by Reggie Mann, who was one of Mrs. Devon's favourites.

A century and more ago the founder of the Devon line had come to America, and invested his savings in land on Manhattan Island. Other people had toiled and built a city there, and generation after generation of the Devons had sat by and collected the rents, until now their fortune amounted to four or five hundred millions of dollars. They were the richest old family in America, and the most famous; and in Mrs. Devon, the oldest member of the line, was centred all its social majesty and dominion. She lived a stately and formal life, precisely like a queen; no one ever saw her save upon her raised chair of state, and she wore her jewels even at breakfast. She was the arbiter of social destinies, and the breakwater against which the floods of new wealth beat in vain. Reggie Mann told wonderful tales about the contents of her enormous mail—about wives and daughters of mighty rich men who flung themselves at her feet and pleaded abjectly for her favour—who laid siege to her house for months, and intrigued and pulled wires to get near her, and even bought the favour of her servants! If Reggie might be believed, great financial wars had been fought, and the stock-markets of the world convulsed more than once, because of these social struggles; and women of wealth and beauty had offered to sell themselves for the privilege which was so freely granted to them.

They came to the old family mansion and rang the bell, and the solemn butler ushered them past the grand staircase and into the front reception-room to wait. Perhaps five minutes later he came in and rolled back the doors, and they stood up, and beheld a withered old lady, nearly eighty years of age, bedecked with diamonds and seated upon a sort of throne. They approached, and Oliver introduced them, and the old lady held out a lifeless hand; and then they sat down.

Mrs. Devon asked them a few questions as to how much of New York they had seen, and how they liked it, and whom they had met; but most of the time she simply looked them over, and left the making of conversation to Oliver. As for Montague, he sat, feeling perplexed and uncomfortable, and wondering, deep down in him, whether it could really be America in which this was happening.

"You see," Oliver explained to them, when they were seated in their carriage again, "her mind is failing, and it's really quite difficult for her to receive."

"I'm glad I don't have to call on her more than once," was Alice's comment. "When do we know the verdict?"

"When you get a card marked 'Mrs. Devon at home,'" said Oliver. And he went on to tell them about the war which had shaken Society long ago, when the mighty dame had asserted her right to be "Mrs. Devon," and the only "Mrs. Devon." He told them also about her wonderful dinner-set of china, which had cost thirty thousand dollars, and was as fragile as a humming-bird's wing. Each piece bore her crest, and she had a china expert to attend to washing and packing it—no common hand was ever allowed to touch it. He told them, also, how Mrs. Devon's housekeeper had wrestled for so long, trying to teach the maids to arrange the furniture in the great reception-rooms precisely as the mistress ordered; until finally a complete set of photographs had been taken, so that the maids might do their work by chart.

Alice went back to the hotel, for Mrs. Robbie Walling was to call and take her home to lunch; and Montague and his brother strolled round to Reggie Mann's apartments, to report upon their visit.

Reggie received them in a pair of pink silk pyjamas, decorated with ribbons and bows, and with silk-embroidered slippers, set with pearls—a present from a feminine adorer. Montague noticed, to his dismay, that the little man wore a gold bracelet upon one arm! He explained that he had led a cotillion the night before—or rather this morning; he had got home at five o'clock. He looked quite white and tired, and there were the remains of a breakfast of brandy-and-soda on the table.

"Did you see the old girl?" he asked. "And how does she hold up?"

"She's game," said Oliver.

"I had the devil's own time getting you in," said the other. "It's getting harder every day."

"You'll excuse me," Reggie added, "if I get ready. I have an engagement." And he turned to his dressing-table, which was covered with an array of cosmetics and perfumes, and proceeded, in a matter-of-fact way, to paint his face. Meanwhile his valet was flitting silently here and there, getting ready his afternoon costume; and Montague, in spite of himself, followed the man with his eyes. A haberdasher's shop might have been kept going for quite a while upon the contents of Reggie's dressers. His clothing was kept in a room adjoining the dressing-room; Montague, who was near the door, could see the rosewood wardrobes, each devoted to a separate article of clothing-shirts, for instance, laid upon sliding racks, tier upon tier of them, of every material and colour. There was a closet fitted with shelves and equipped like a little shoe store—high shoes and low shoes, black ones, brown ones, and white ones, and each fitted over a last to keep its shape perfect. These shoes were all made to order according to Reggie's designs, and three or-four times a year there was a cleaning out, and those which had gone out of fashion became the prey of his "man." There was a safe in one closet, in which Reggie's jewellery was kept.

The dressing-room was furnished like a lady's boudoir, the furniture upholstered with exquisite embroidered silk, and the bed hung with curtains of the same material. There was a huge bunch of roses on the centre-table, and the odour of roses hung heavy in the room.

The valet stood at attention with a rack of neckties, from which Reggie critically selected one to match his shirt. "Are you going to take Alice with you down to the Havens's?" he was asking; and he added, "You'll meet Vivie Patton down there—she's had another row at home."

"You don't say so!" exclaimed Oliver.

"Yes," said the other. "Frank waited up all night for her, and he wept and tore his hair and vowed he would kill the Count. Vivie told him to go to hell."

"Good God!" said Oliver. "Who told you that?"

"The faithful Alphonse," said Reggie, nodding toward his valet. "Her maid told him. And Frank vows he'll sue—I half expected to see it in the papers this morning."

"I met Vivie on the street yesterday," said Oliver. "She looked as chipper as ever."

Reggie shrugged his shoulders. "Have you seen this week's paper?" he asked. "They've got another of Ysabel's suppressed poems in."—And then he turned toward Montague to explain that "Ysabel" was the pseudonym of a young débutante who had fallen under the spell of Baudelaire and Wilde, and had published a volume of poems of such furious eroticism that her parents were buying up stray copies at fabulous prices.

Then the conversation turned to the Horse Show, and for quite a while they talked about who was going to wear what. Finally Oliver rose, saying that they would have to get a bite to eat before leaving for the Havens's. "You'll have a good time," said Reggie. "I'd have gone myself, only I promised to stay and help Mrs. de Graffenried design a dinner. So long!"

Montague had heard nothing about the visit to the Havens's; but now, as they strolled down the Avenue, Oliver explained that they were to spend the weekend at Castle Havens. There was quite a party going up this Friday afternoon, and they would find one of the Havens's private cars waiting. They had nothing to do meantime, for their valets would attend to their packing, and Alice and her maid would meet them at the depot.

"Castle Havens is one of the show places of the country," Oliver added. "You'll see the real thing this time." And while they lunched, he went on to entertain his brother with particulars concerning the place and its owners. John had inherited the bulk of the enormous Havens fortune, and he posed as his father's successor in the Steel Trust. Some day some one of the big men would gobble him up; meantime he amused himself fussing over the petty details of administration. Mrs. Havens had taken a fancy to a rural life, and they had built this huge palace in the hills of Connecticut, and she wrote verses in which she pictured herself as a simple shepherdess—and all that sort of stuff. But no one minded that, because the place was grand, and there was always so much to do. They had forty or fifty polo ponies, for instance, and every spring the place was filled with polo men.

At the depot they caught sight of Charlie Carter, in his big red touring-car. "Are you going to the Havens's?" he said. "Tell them we're going to pick up Chauncey on the way."

"That's Chauncey Venable, the Major's nephew," said Oliver, as they strolled to the train. "Poor Chauncey—he's in exile!"

"How do you mean?" asked Montague.

"Why, he daren't come into New York," said the other. "Haven't you read about it in the papers? He lost one or two hundred thousand the other night in a gambling place, and the district attorney's trying to catch him."

"Does he want to put him in jail?" asked Montague.

"Heavens, no!" said Oliver. "Put a Venable in jail? He wants him for a witness against the gambler; and poor Chauncey is flitting about the country hiding with his friends, and wailing because he'll miss the Horse Show."

They boarded the palatial private car, and were introduced to a number of other guests. Among them was Major Venable; and while Oliver buried himself in the new issue of the fantastic-covered society journal, which contained the poem of the erotic "Ysabel," his brother chatted with the Major. The latter had taken quite a fancy to the big handsome stranger, to whom everything in the city was so new and interesting."

"Tell me what you thought of the Snow Palace," said he. "I've an idea that Mrs. Winnie's got quite a crush on you. You'll find her dangerous, my boy—she'll make you pay for your dinners before you get through!"

After the train was under way, the Major got himself surrounded with some apollinaris and Scotch, and then settled back to enjoy himself. "Did you see the 'drunken kid' at the ferry?" he asked. "(That's what our abstemious district attorney terms my precious young heir-apparent.) You'll meet him at the Castle—the Havens are good to him. They know how it feels, I guess; when John was a youngster his piratical uncle had to camp in Jersey for six months or so, to escape the strong arm of the law."

"Don't you know about it?" continued the Major, sipping at his beverage. "Sic transit gloria mundi! That was when the great Captain Kidd Havens was piling up the millions which his survivors are spending with such charming insouciance. He was plundering a railroad, and the original progenitor of the Wallings tried to buy the control away from him, and Havens issued ten or twenty millions of new stock overnight, in the face of a court injunction, and got away with most of his money. It reads like opera bouffe, you know—they had a regular armed camp across the river for about six months—until Captain Kidd went up to Albany with half a million dollars' worth of greenbacks in a satchel, and induced the legislature to legalize the proceedings. That was just after the war, you know, but I remember it as if it were yesterday. It seems strange to think that anyone shouldn't know about it."

"I know about Havens in a general way," said Montague.

"Yes," said the Major. "But I know in a particular way, because I've carried some of that railroad's paper all these years, and it's never paid any dividends since. It has a tendency to interfere with my appreciation of John's lavish hospitality."

Montague was reminded of the story of the Roman emperor who pointed out that money had no smell.

"Maybe not," said the Major. "But all the same, if you were superstitious, you might make out an argument from the Havens fortune. Take that poor girl who married the Count."

And the Major went on to picture the denouement of that famous international alliance, which, many years ago, had been the sensation of two continents. All Society had attended the gorgeous wedding, an archbishop had performed the ceremony, and the newspapers had devoted pages to describing the gowns and the jewels and the presents and all the rest of the magnificence. And the Count was a wretched little degenerate, who beat and kicked his wife, and flaunted his mistresses in her face, and wasted fourteen million dollars of her money in a couple of years. The mind could scarcely follow the orgies of this half-insane creature— he had spent two hundred thousand dollars on a banquet, and half as much again for a tortoise-shell wardrobe in which Louis the Sixteenth had kept his clothes! He had charged a diamond necklace to his wife, and taken two of the four rows of diamonds out of it before he presented it to her! He had paid a hundred thousand dollars a year to a jockey whom the Parisian populace admired, and a fortune for a palace in Verona, which he had promptly torn down, for the sake of a few painted ceilings. The Major told about one outdoor fete, which he had given upon a sudden whim: ten thousand Venetian lanterns, ten thousand metres of carpet; three thousand gilded chairs, and two or three hundred waiters in fancy costumes;

two palaces built in a lake, with sea-horses and dolphins, and half a dozen orchestras, and several hundred chorus—girls from the Grand Opera! And in between adventures such as these, he bought a seat in the Chamber of Deputies, and made speeches and fought duels in defence of the Holy Catholic Church—and wrote articles for the yellow journals of America. "And that's the fate of my lost dividends!" growled the Major.

There were several automobiles to meet the party at the depot, and they were whirled through a broad avenue up a valley, and past a little lake, and so to the gates of Castle Havens.

It was a tremendous building, a couple of hundred feet long. One entered into a main hall, perhaps fifty feet wide, with a great fireplace arid staircase of marble and bronze, and furniture of gilded wood and crimson velvet, and a huge painting, covering three of the walls, representing the Conquest of Peru. Each of the rooms was furnished in the style of a different period—one Louis Quatorze, one Louis Quinze, one Marie Antoinette, and so on. There was a drawing-room and a regal music-room; a dining-room in the Georgian style, and a billiard-room, also in the English fashion, with high wainscoting and open beams in the ceiling; and a library, and a morning-room and conservatory. Upstairs in the main suite of rooms was a royal bedstead, which alone was rumoured to have cost twenty-five thousand dollars; and you might have some idea of the magnificence of things when you learned that underneath the gilding of the furniture was the rare and precious Circassian walnut.

All this was beautiful. But what brought the guests to Castle Havens was the casino, so the Major had remarked. It was really a private athletic club—with tan-bark hippodrome, having a ring the size of that in Madison Square Garden, and a skylight roof, and thirty or forty arc-lights for night events. There were bowling-alleys, billiard and lounging-rooms, hand-ball, tennis and racket-courts, a completely equipped gymnasium, a shooting-gallery, and a swimming-pool with Turkish and Russian baths. In this casino alone there were rooms for forty guests.

Such was Castle Havens; it had cost three or four millions of dollars, and within the twelve-foot wall which surrounded its grounds lived two world-weary people who dreaded nothing so much as to be alone. There were always guests, and on special occasions there might be three or four score. They went whirling about the country in their autos; they rode and drove; they played games, outdoor and indoor, or gambled, or lounged and chatted, or wandered about at their own sweet will. Coming to one of these places was not different from staying at a great hotel, save that the company was selected, and instead of paying a bill, you gave twenty or thirty dollars to the servants when you left.

It was a great palace of pleasure, in which beautiful and graceful men and women played together in all sorts of beautiful and graceful ways. In the evenings great logs blazed in the fireplace in the hall, and there might be an informal dance—there was always music at hand. Now and then there would be a stately ball, with rich gowns and flashing jewels, and the grounds ablaze with lights, and a full orchestra, and special trains from the city. Or a whole theatrical company would be brought down to give an entertainment in the theatre; or a minstrel show, or a troupe of acrobats, or a menagerie of trained animals. Or perhaps there would be a great pianist, or a palmist, or a trance medium. Anyone at all would be welcome who could bring a new thrill—it mattered nothing at all, though the price might be several hundred dollars a minute.

Montague shook hands with his host and hostess, and with a number of others; among them Billy Price who forthwith challenged him, and carried him off to the shooting-gallery. Here he took a rifle, and proceeded to satisfy her as to his skill. This brought him to the notice of Siegfried Harvey, who was a famous cross-country rider and "polo-man." Harvey's father owned a score of copper-mines, and had named him after a race-horse; he was a big broad-shouldered fellow, a favourite of every one; and next morning, when he found that Montague sat a horse like one who was born to it, he invited him to come out to his place on Long Island, and see some of the fox-hunting.

Then, after he had dressed for dinner, Montague came downstairs, and found Betty Wyman, shining like Aurora in an orange-coloured cloud. She introduced him to Mrs. Vivie Patton, who was tall and slender and fascinating, and had told her husband to go to hell. Mrs. Vivie had black eyes that snapped and sparkled, and she was a geyser of animation in a perpetual condition of eruption. Montague wondered if she would have talked with him so gaily had she known what he knew about her domestic entanglements.

The company moved into the dining-room, where there was served another of those elaborate and enormously expensive meals which he concluded he was fated to eat for the rest of his life. Only, instead of Mrs. Billy Alden with her Scotch, there was Mrs. Vivie, who drank champagne in terrifying quantities; and afterward there was the inevitable grouping of the bridge fiends.

Among the guests there was a long-haired and wild-looking foreign personage, who was the "lion" of the evening, and sat with half a dozen admiring women about him. Now he was escorted to the music-room, and revealed the fact that he was a violin virtuoso. He played what was called "salon music"—music written especially for ladies and gentlemen to listen to after dinner; and also a strange contrivance called a concerto, put together to enable the player to exhibit within a brief space the utmost possible variety of finger gymnastics. To learn to perform these feats one had to devote his whole lifetime to practising them, just like any circus acrobat; and so his mind became atrophied, and a naive and elemental vanity was all that was left to him.

Montague stood for a while staring; and then took to watching the company, who chattered and laughed all through the performance. Afterward, he strolled into the billiard-room, where Billy Price and Chauncey Venable were having an exciting bout; and from there to the smoking-room, where the stout little Major had gotten a group of young bloods about him to play "Klondike." This was a game of deadly hazards, which they played without limit; the players themselves were silent and impassive, but the spectators who gathered about were tense with excitement.

In the morning Charlie Carter carried off Alice and Oliver and Betty in his auto; and Montague spent his time in trying some of Havens's jumping horses. The Horse Show was to open in New York on Monday, and there was an atmosphere of suppressed excitement because of this prospect; Mrs. Caroline Smythe, a charming young widow, strolled about with him and told him all about this Show, and the people who would take part in it.

And in the afternoon Major Venable took him for a stroll and showed him the grounds. He had been told what huge sums had been expended in laying them out; but after all, the figures were nothing compared with an actual view. There were hills and slopes, and endless vistas of green lawns and gardens, dotted with the gleaming white of marble staircases and fountains and statuary. There was a great Italian walk, leading by successive esplanades to an electric fountain with a basin sixty feet across, and a bronze chariot and marble horses. There were sunken gardens, with a fountain brought from the South of France, and Greek peristyles, and seats of marble, and vases and other treasures of art.

And then there were the stables; a huge Renaissance building, with a perfectly equipped theatre above. There was a model farm and dairy; a polo-field, and an enclosed riding-ring for the children; and dog-kennels and pigeon-houses, greenhouses and deer-parks—one was prepared for bear-pits and a menagerie. Finally, on their way back, they passed the casino, where musical chimes pealed out the quarter-hours. Montague stopped and gazed up at the tower from which the sounds had come.

The more he gazed, the more he found to gaze at The roof of this building had many gables, in the Queen Anne style; and from the midst of them shot up the tower, which was octagonal and solid, suggestive of the Normans. It was decorated with Christmas-wreaths in white stucco, and a few miscellaneous ornaments like the gilded tassels one sees upon plush curtains. Overtopping all of this was the dome of a Turkish mosque. Rising out of the dome was something that looked like a dove-cot; and out of this rose the slender white steeple of a Methodist country church. On top of that was a statue of Diana.

"What are you looking at?" asked the Major.

"Nothing," said Montague, as he moved on. "Has there ever been any insanity in the Havens family?"

"I don't know," replied the other, puzzled. "They say the old man never could sleep at night, and used to wander about alone in the park. I suppose he had things on his conscience."

They strolled away; and the Major's flood-gates of gossip were opened. There was an old merchant in New York, who had been Havens's private secretary. And Havens was always in terror of assassination, and so whenever they travelled abroad he and the secretary exchanged places. "The old man is big and imposing," said the Major, "and it's funny to hear him tell how he used to receive the visitors and be stared at by the crowds, while Havens, who was little and insignificant, would pretend to make himself useful. And then one day a wild-looking creature came into the Havens office, and began tearing the wrappings off some package that shone like metal—and quick as a flash he and Havens flung themselves down on the floor upon their faces. Then, as nothing happened, they looked up, and saw the puzzled stranger gazing over the railing at them. He had a patent churn, made of copper, which he wanted Havens to market for him!"

Montague could have wished that this party might last for a week or two, instead of only two days. He was interested in the life, and in those who lived it; all whom he met were people prominent in the social world, and some in the business world as well, and one could not have asked a better chance to study them.

Montague was taking his time and feeling his way slowly. But all the time that he was playing and gossiping he never lost from mind his real purpose, which was to find a place for himself in the world of affairs; and he watched for people from whose conversation he could get a view of this aspect of things. So he was interested when Mrs. Smythe remarked that among his fellow-guests was Vandam, an official of one of the great life-insurance companies. "Freddie" Vandam, as the lady called him, was a man of might in the financial world; and Montague said to himself that in meeting him he would really be accomplishing something. Crack shots and polo-players and four-in-hand experts were all very well, but he had his living to earn, and he feared that the problem was going to prove complicated.

So he was glad when chance brought him and young Vandam together, and Siegfried Harvey introduced them. And then Montague got the biggest shock which New York had given him yet.

It was not what Freddie Vandam said; doubtless he had a right to be interested in the Horse Show, since he was to exhibit many fine horses, and he had no reason to feel called upon to talk about anything more serious to a stranger at a house party. But it was the manner of the man, his whole personality. For Freddie was a man of fashion, with all the exaggerated and farcical mannerisms of the dandy of the comic papers. He wore a conspicuous and foppish costume, and posed with a little cane; he cultivated a waving pompadour, and his silky moustache and beard were carefully trimmed to points, and kept sharp by his active fingers. His conversation was full of French phrases and French opinions; he had been reared abroad, and had a whole-souled contempt for all things American-even dictating his business letters in French, and leaving it for his stenographer to translate them. His shirts were embroidered with violets and perfumed with violets—and there were bunches of violets at his horses' heads, so that he might get the odour as he drove!

There was a cruel saying about Freddie Vandam—that if only he had had a little more brains, he would have been half-witted. And Montague sat, and watched his mannerisms and listened to his inanities, with his mind in a state of bewilderment and dismay. When at last he got up and walked away, it was with a new sense of the complicated nature of the problem that confronted him. Who was there that could give him the key to this mystery—who could interpret to him a world in which a man such as this was in control of four or five hundred millions of trust funds?

CHAPTER VII

It was quite futile to attempt to induce anyone to talk about serious matters just now—for the coming week all Society belonged to the horse. The parties which went to church on Sunday morning talked about horses on the way, and the crowds that gathered in front of the church door to watch them descend from their automobiles, and to get "points" on their conspicuous costumes—these would read about horses all afternoon in the Sunday papers, and about the gowns which the women would wear at the show.

Some of the party went up on Sunday evening; Montague went with the rest on Monday morning, and had lunch with Mrs. Robbie Walling and Oliver and Alice. They had arrayed him in a frock coat and silk hat and fancy "spats"; and they took him and sat him in the front row of Robbie's box.

There was a great tan-bark arena, in which the horses performed; and then a railing, and a broad promenade for the spectators; and then, raised a few feet above, the boxes in which sat all Society. For the Horse Show had now become a great social function. Last year a visiting foreign prince had seen fit to attend it, and this year "everybody" would come.

Montague was rapidly getting used to things; he observed with a smile how easy it was to take for granted embroidered bed and table linen, and mural paintings, and private cars, and gold plate. At first it had seemed to him strange to be waited upon by a white woman, and by a white man quite unthinkable; but he was becoming accustomed to having silent and expressionless lackeys everywhere about him, attending to his slightest want. So he presumed that if he waited long enough, he might even get used to horses which had their tails cut off to stumps, and their manes to rows of bristles, and which had been taught to lift their feet in strange and eccentric ways, and were driven with burred bits in their mouths to torture them and make them step lively.

There were road-horses, coach-horses, saddle-horses and hunters, polo-ponies, stud-horses—every kind of horse that is used for pleasure, over a hundred different "classes" of them. They were put through their paces about the ring, and there was a committee which judged them, and awarded blue and red ribbons. Apparently their highly artificial kind of excellence was a real thing to the people who took part in the show; for the spectators thrilled with excitement, and applauded the popular victors. There was a whole set of conventions which were generally understood—there was even a new language. You were told that these "turnouts" were "nobby" and "natty"; they were "swagger" and "smart" and "swell."

However, the horse was really a small part of this show; before one had sat out an afternoon he realized that the function was in reality a show of Society. For six or seven hours during the day the broad promenade would be so packed with human beings that one moved about with difficulty; and this throng gazed towards the ring almost never—it stared up into the boxes. All the year round the discontented millions of the middle classes read of the doings of the "smart set"; and here they had a chance to come and see them-alive, and real, and dressed in their showiest costumes. Here was all the grand monde, in numbered boxes, and with their names upon the programmes, so that one could get them straight. Ten thousand people from other cities had come to New York on purpose to get a look. Women who lived in boarding-houses and made their own clothes, had come to get hints; all the dressmakers in town were present for the same purpose.. Society reporters had come, with notebooks in hand; and next morning the imitators of Society all over the United States would read about it, in such fashion as this: "Mrs. Chauncey Venable was becomingly gowned in mauve cloth, made with an Eton jacket trimmed with silk braid, and opening over a chemisette of lace. Her hat was of the same colour, draped with a great quantity of mauve and orange tulle, and surmounted with birds of paradise to match. Her furs were silver fox."

The most intelligent of the great metropolitan dailies would print columns of this sort of material; and as for the "yellow" journals, they would have discussions of the costumes by "experts," and half a page of pictures of the most conspicuous of the box-holders. While Montague sat talking with Mrs. Walling, half a dozen cameras were snapped at them; and once a young man with a sketch-book placed himself in front of them and went placidly to work.—Concerning such things the society dame had three different sets of emotions: first, the one which she showed in public, that of bored and contemptuous indifference; second, the one which she expressed to her friends, that of outraged but helpless indignation; and third, the one which she really felt, that of triumphant exultation over her rivals, whose pictures were not published and whose costumes were not described.

It was a great dress parade of society women. One who wished to play a proper part in it would spend at least ten thousand dollars upon her costumes for the week. It was necessary to have a different gown for the afternoon and evening of each day; and some, who were adepts at quick changes and were proud of it, would wear three or four a day, and so need a couple of dozen gowns for the show. And of course there had to be hats and shoes and gloves to match. There would be robes of priceless fur hung carelessly over the balcony to make a setting; and in the evening there would be pyrotechnical displays of jewels. Mrs. Virginia Landis wore a pair of simple pearl earrings, which she told the reporters had cost twenty thousand dollars; and there were two women who displayed four hundred thousand dollars' worth of diamonds—and each of them had hired a detective to hover about in the crowd and keep watch over her!

Nor must one suppose, because the horse was an inconspicuous part of the show, that he was therefore an inexpensive part. One man was to be seen here driving a four-in-hand of black stallions which had cost forty thousand; there were other men who drove only one horse, and had paid forty thousand for that. Half a million was a moderate estimate of the cost of the "string" which some would exhibit. And of course these horses were useless, save for show purposes, and to breed other horses like them. Many of them never went out of their stables except for exercise upon a track; and the cumbrous and enormous; expensive coaches were never by any possibility used elsewhere—when they were taken from place to place they seldom went upon their own wheels.

And there were people here who made their chief occupation in life the winning of blue ribbons at these shows. They kept great country estates especially for the horses, and had private indoor exhibition rings. Robbie Walling and Chauncey Venable were both such people; in the summer of next year another of the Wallings took a string across the water to teach the horse-show game to Society in London. He took twenty or thirty horses, under the charge of an expert manager and a dozen assistants; he sent sixteen different kinds of carriages, and two great coaches, and a ton of harness and other stuff. It required one whole deck of a steamer, and the expedition enabled him to get rid of six hundred thousand dollars.

All through the day, of course, Robbie was down in the ring with his trainers and his competitors, and Montague sat and kept his wife company. There was a steady stream of visitors, who came to congratulate her upon their successes, and to commiserate with Mrs. Chauncey Venable over the sufferings of the un-happy victim of a notoriety-seeking district attorney.

There was just one drawback to the Horse Show, as Montague gathered from the conversation that went on among the callers: it was public, and there was no way to prevent undesirable people from taking part. There were, it appeared, hordes of rich people in New York who were not in Society, and of whose existence Society was haughtily unaware; but these people might enter horses and win prizes, and even rent a box and exhibit their clothes. And they might induce the reporters to mention them—and of course the ignorant populace did not know the difference, and stared at them just as hard as at Mrs. Robbie or Mrs. Winnie. And so for a whole blissful week these people had all the sensations of being in Society! "It won't be very long before that will kill the Horse Show," said Mrs. Vivie Patton, with a snap of her black eyes.

There was Miss Yvette Simpkins, for instance; Society frothed at the mouth when her name was mentioned. Miss Yvette was the niece of a stock-broker who was wealthy, and she thought that she was in Society, and the foolish public thought so, too. Miss Yvette made a speciality of newspaper publicity; you were always seeing her picture, with some new "Worth creation," and the picture would be labelled "Miss Yvette Simpkins, the best-dressed woman in New York," or "Miss Yvette Simpkins, who is known as the best woman whip in Society." It was said that Miss Yvette, who was short and stout, and had a rosy German face, had paid five thousand dollars at one clip for photographs of herself in a new wardrobe; and her pictures were sent to the newspapers in bundles of a dozen at a time. Miss Yvette possessed over a million dollars' worth of diamonds—the finest in the country, according to the newspapers; she had spent a hundred and twenty-six thousand dollars this year upon her clothes, and she gave long interviews, in which she set forth the fact that a woman nowadays could not really be well dressed upon less than a hundred thousand a year. It was Miss Yvette's boast that she had never ridden in a street-car in her life.

Montague always had a soft spot in his heart for the unfortunate Miss Yvette, who laboured so hard to be a guiding light; for it chanced to be while she was in the ring, exhibiting her skill in driving tandem, that he met with a fateful encounter. Afterward, when he came to look back upon these early days, it seemed strange to him that he should have gone about this place, so careless and unsuspecting, while the fates were weaving strange destinies about him.

It was on Tuesday afternoon, and he sat in the box of Mrs. Venable, a sister-in-law of the Major. The Major, who was a care-free bachelor, was there himself, and also Betty Wyman, who was making sprightly comments on the passers-by; and there strolled into the box Chappie de Peyster, accompanied by a young lady.

So many people had stopped and been introduced and then passed on, that Montague merely glanced at her once. He noticed that she was tall and graceful, and caught her name, Miss Hegan.

The turnouts in the ring consisted of one horse harnessed in front of another; and Montague was wondering what conceivable motive could induce a human being to hitch and drive horses in that fashion. The conversation turned upon Miss Yvette, who was in the ring; and Betty remarked upon the airy grace with which she wielded the long whip she carried. "Did you see what the paper said about her this morning?" she asked. "' Miss Simpkins was exquisitely clad in purple velvet,' and so on! She looked for all the world like the Venus at the Hippodrome!"

"Why isn't she in Society?" asked Montague, curiously.

"She!" exclaimed Betty. "Why, she's a travesty!"

There was a moment's pause, preceding a remark by their young lady visitor. "I've an idea," said she, "that the real reason she never got into Society was that she was fond of her old father."

And Montague gave a short glance at the speaker, who was gazing fixedly into the ring. He heard the Major chuckle, and he thought that he heard Betty Wyman give a little sniff. A few moments later the young lady arose, and with some remark to Mrs. Venable about how well her costume became her, she passed on out of the box.

"Who is that?" asked Montague.

"That," the Major answered, "that's Laura Hegan—Jim Hegan's daughter."

"Oh!" said Montague, and caught his breath. Jim Hegan—Napoleon of finance—czar of a gigantic system of railroads, and the power behind the political thrones of many states.

"His only daughter, too," the Major added. "Gad, what a juicy morsel for somebody!"

"Well, she'll make him pay for all he gets, whoever he is!" retorted Betty, vindictively.

"You don't like her?" inquired Montague; and Betty replied promptly, "I do not!"

"Her daddy and Betty's granddaddy are always at swords' points," put in Major Venable.

"I have nothing to do with my granddaddy's quarrels," said the young lady. "I have troubles enough of my own."

"What is the matter with Miss Hegan?" asked Montague, laughing.

"She's an idea she's too good for the world she lives in," said Betty. "When you're with her, you feel as you will before the judgment throne."

"Undoubtedly a disturbing feeling," put in the Major.

"She never hands you anything but you find a pin hidden in it," went on the girl. "All her remarks are meant to be read backward, and my life is too short to straighten out their kinks. I like a person to say what they mean in plain English, and then I can either like them or not."

"Mostly not," said the Major, grimly; and added, "Anyway, she's beautiful."

"Perhaps," said the other. "So is the Jungfrau; but I prefer something more comfortable."

"What's Chappie de Peyster beauing her around for?" asked Mrs. Venable. "Is he a candidate?"

"Maybe his debts are troubling him again," said Mistress Betty. "He must be in a desperate plight.—Did you hear how Jack Audubon proposed to her?"

"Did Jack propose?" exclaimed the Major.

"Of course he did," said the girl. "His brother told me." Then, for Montague's benefit, she explained, "Jack Audubon is the Major's nephew, and he's a bookworm, and spends all his time collecting scarabs."

"What did he say to her?" asked the Major, highly amused.

"Why," said Betty, "he told her he knew she didn't love him; but also she knew that he didn't care anything about her money, and she might like to marry him so that other men would let her alone."

"Gad!" cried the old gentleman, slapping his knee. "A masterpiece!"

"Does she have so many suitors?" asked Montague; and the Major replied, "My dear boy—she'll have a hundred million dollars some day!"

At this point Oliver put in appearance, and Betty got up and went for a stroll with him; then Montague asked for light upon Miss Hegan's remark.

"What she said is perfectly true," replied the Major; "only it riled Betty. There's many a gallant dame cruising the social seas who has stowed her old relatives out of sight in the hold."

"What's the matter with old Simpkins?" asked the other.

"Just a queer boy," was the reply. "He has a big pile, and his one joy in life is the divine Yvette. It is really he who makes her ridiculous—he has a regular press agent for her, a chap he loads up with jewellery and cheques whenever he gets her picture into the papers."

The Major paused a moment to greet some acquaintance, and then resumed the conversation. Apparently he could gossip in this intimate fashion about any person whom you named. Old Simpkins had been very poor as a boy, it appeared, and he had never got over the memory of it. Miss Yvette spent fifty thousand at a clip for Paris gowns; but every day her old uncle would save up the lumps of sugar which came with the expensive lunch he had brought to his office. And when he had several pounds he would send them home by messenger!

This conversation gave Montague a new sense of the complicatedness of the world into which he had come. Miss Simpkins was "impossible"; and yet there was—for instance—that Mrs. Landis whom he had met at Mrs. Winnie Duval's. He had met her several times at the show; and he heard the Major and his sister-in-law chuckling over a paragraph in the society journal, to the effect that Mrs. Virginia van Rensselaer Landis had just returned from a successful hunting-trip in the far West. He did not see the humour of this, at least not until they had told him of another paragraph which had appeared some time before: stating that Mrs. Landis had gone to acquire residence in South Dakota, taking with her thirty-five trunks and a poodle; and that "Leanie" Hopkins, the handsome young stock-broker, had taken a six months' vow of poverty, chastity, and obedience.

And yet Mrs. Landis was "in" Society! And moreover, she spent nearly as much upon her clothes as Miss Yvette, and the clothes were quite as conspicuous; and if the papers did not print pages about them, it was not because Mrs. Landis was not perfectly willing. She was painted and made up quite as frankly as any chorus-girl on the stage. She laughed a great deal, and in a high key, and she and her friends told stories which made Montague wish to move out of the way.

Mrs. Landis had for some reason taken a fancy to Alice, and invited her home to lunch with her twice during the show. And after they had got home in the evening, the girl sat upon the bed in her fur-trimmed wrapper, and told Montague and his mother and Mammy Lucy all about her visit.

"I don't believe that woman has a thing to do or to think about in the world except to wear clothes!" she said. "Why, she has adjustable mirrors on ball-bearings, so that she can see every part of her skirts! And she gets all her gowns from Paris, four times a year—she says there are four seasons now, instead of two! I thought that my new clothes amounted to something, but my goodness, when I saw hers!"

Then Alice went on to describe the unpacking of fourteen trunks, which had just come up from the custom-house that day. Mrs. Virginia's couturiere had her photograph and her colouring (represented in actual paints) and a figure made up from exact measurements; and so every one of the garments would fit her perfectly. Each one came stuffed with tissue paper and held in place by a lattice-work of tape; and attached to each gown was a piece of the fabric, from which her shoe-maker would make shoes or slippers. There were street-costumes and opera-wraps, robes de chambre and tea-gowns, reception-dresses, and wonderful ball and dinner gowns. Most of these latter were to be embroidered with jewellery before they were worn, and imitation jewels were sewn on, to show how the real ones were to be placed. These garments were made of real lace or Parisian embroidery, and the prices paid for them were almost impossible to credit. Some of them were made of lace so filmy that the women who made them had to sit in damp cellars, because the sunlight would dry the fine threads and they would break; a single yard of the lace represented forty days of labour. There was a pastel "batiste de soie" Pompadour robe, embroidered with cream silk flowers, which had cost one thousand dollars. There was a hat to go with it, which had cost a hundred and twenty-five, and shoes of grey antelope-skin, buckled with mother-of-pearl, which had cost forty. There was a gorgeous and intricate ball-dress of pale green chiffon satin, with orchids embroidered in oxidized silver, and a long court train, studded with diamonds—and this had cost six thousand dollars without the jewels! And there was an auto-coat which had cost three thousand; and an opera-wrap made in Leipsic, of white unborn baby lamb, lined with ermine, which had cost twelve thousand—with a thousand additional for a hat to match! Mrs. Landis thought nothing of paying thirty-five dollars for a lace handkerchief, or sixty dollars for a pair of spun silk hose, or two hundred dollars for a pearl and gold-handled parasol trimmed with cascades of chiffon, and made, like her hats, one for each gown.

"And she insists that these things are worth the money," said Alice. "She says it's not only the material in them, but the ideas. Each costume is a study, like a picture. 'I pay for the creative genius of the artist,' she said to me—'for his ability to catch my ideas and apply them to my personality—my complexion and hair and eyes. Sometimes I design my own costumes, and so I know what hard work it is!'"

Mrs. Landis came from one of New York's oldest families, and she was wealthy in her own right; she had a palace on Fifth Avenue, and now that she had turned her husband out, she had nothing at all to put in it except her clothes. Alice told about the places in which she kept them—it was like a museum! There was a gown-room, made dust-proof, of polished hardwood, and with tier upon tier of long poles running across, and padded skirt-supporters hanging from them. Everywhere there was order and system—each skirt was numbered, and in a chiffonier-drawer of the same number you would find the waist—and so on with hats and stockings and gloves and shoes and parasols. There was a row of closets, having shelves piled up with dainty lace-trimmed and beribboned lingerie; there were two closets full of hats and three of shoes. "When she went West," said Alice, "one of her maids counted, and found that she had over four hundred pairs! And she actually has a cabinet with a card-catalogue to keep track of them. And all the shelves are lined with perfumed silk sachets, and she has tiny sachets sewed in every skirt and waist; and she has her own private perfume—she gave me some. She calls it Occur de Jeannette, and she says she designed it herself, and had it patented!"

And then Alice went on to describe the maid's work-room, which was also of polished hardwood, and dust-proof, and had a balcony for brushing clothes, and wires upon which to hang them, and hot and cold water, and a big ironing-table and an electric stove. "But there can't be much work to do," laughed the girl, "for she never wears a gown more than two or three times. Just think of paying several thousand dollars for a costume, and giving it to your poor relations after you have worn it only twice! And the worst of it is that Mrs. Landis says it's all nothing unusual; you'll find such arrangements in every home of people who are socially prominent. She says there are women who boast of never appearing twice in the same gown, and there's one dreadful personage in Boston who wears each costume once, and then has it solemnly cremated by her butler!"

"It is wicked to do such things," put in old Mrs. Montague, when she had heard this tale through. "I don't see how people can get any pleasure out of it."

"That's what I said," replied Alice.

"To whom did you say that?" asked Montague. "To Mrs. Landis?"

"No," said Alice, "to a cousin of hers. I was downstairs waiting for her, and this girl came in. And we got to talking about it, and I said that I didn't think I could ever get used to such things."

"What did she say?" asked the other.

"She answered me strangely," said the girl. "She's tall, and very stately, and I was a little bit afraid of her. She said, 'You'll get used to it. Everybody you know will be doing it, and if you try to do differently they'll take offence; and you won't have the courage to do without friends. You'll be meaning every day to stop, but you never will, and you'll go on until you die.'"

"What did you say to that?"

"Nothing," answered Alice. "Just then Mrs. Landis came in, and Miss Hegan went away."

"Miss Hegan?" echoed Montague.

"Yes," said the other. "That's her name—Laura Hegan. Have you met her?"

CHAPTER VIII

The Horse Show was held in Madison Square Garden, a building occupying a whole city block. It seemed to Montague that during the four days he attended he was introduced to enough people to fill it to the doors. Each one of the exquisite ladies and gentlemen extended to him a delicately gloved hand, and remarked what perfect weather they were having, and asked him how long he had been in New York, and what he thought of it. Then they would talk about the horses, and about the people who were present, and what they had on.

He saw little of his brother, who was squiring the Walling ladies most of the time; and Alice, too, was generally separated from him and taken care of by others. Yet he was never alone—there was always some young matron ready to lead him to her carriage and whisk him away to lunch or dinner.

Many times he wondered why people should be so kind to him, a stranger, and one who could do nothing for them in return. Mrs. Billy Alden undertook to explain it to him, one afternoon, as he sat in her box. There had to be some people to enjoy, it appeared, or there would be no fun in the game. "Everything is new and strange to you," said she, "and you're delicious and refreshing; you make these women think perhaps they oughtn't to be so bored after all! Here's a woman who's bought a great painting; she's told that it's great, but she doesn't understand it herself—all she knows is that it cost her a hundred thousand dollars. And now you come along, and to you it's really a painting—and don't you see how gratifying that is to her?"

"Oliver is always telling me it's bad form to admire," said the man, laughing.

"Yes?" said the other. "Well, don't you let that brother of yours spoil you. There are more than enough of blase people in town—you be yourself."

He appreciated the compliment, but added, "I'm afraid that when the novelty is worn off, people will be tired of me."

"You'll find your place," said Mrs. Alden—"the people you like and who like you." And she went on to explain that here he was being passed about among a number of very different "sets," with different people and different tastes. Society had become split up in that manner of late—each set being jealous and contemptuous of all the other sets. Because of the fact that they overlapped a little at the edges, it was possible for him to meet here a great many people who never met each other, and were even unaware of each other's existence.

CHAPTER VIII

And Mrs. Alden went on to set forth the difference between these "sets"; they ran from the most exclusive down to the most "yellow," where they shaded off into the disreputable rich—of whom, it seemed, there were hordes in the city. These included "sporting" and theatrical and political people, some of whom were very rich indeed; and these sets in turn shaded off into the criminals and the demi-monde—who might also easily be rich. "Some day," said Mrs. Alden "you should get my brother to tell you about all these people. He's been in politics, you know, and he has a racing-stable."

And Mrs. Alden told him about the subtle little differences in the conventions of these various sets of Society. There was the matter of women smoking, for instance. All women smoked, nowadays; but some would do it only in their own apartments, with their women friends; and some would retire to an out-of-the-way corner to do it; while others would smoke in their own dining-rooms, or wherever the men smoked. All agreed however, in never smoking "in public"—that is, where they would be seen by people not of their own set. Such, at any rate, had always been the rule, though a few daring ones were beginning to defy even that.

Such rules were very rigid, but they were purely conventional, they had nothing to do with right or wrong: a fact which Mrs. Alden set forth with her usual incisiveness. A woman, married or unmarried, might travel with a man all over Europe, and every one might know that she did it, but it would make no difference, so long as she did not do it in America. There was one young matron whom Montague would meet, a raging beauty, who regularly got drunk at dinner parties, and had to be escorted to her carriage by the butler. She moved in the most exclusive circles, and every one treated it as a joke. Unpleasant things like this did not hurt a person unless they got "out"—that is, unless they became a scandal in the courts or the newspapers. Mrs. Alden herself had a cousin (whom she cordially hated) who had gotten a divorce from her husband and married her lover forthwith and had for this been ostracized by Society. Once when she came to some semi-public affair, fifty women had risen at once and left the room! She might have lived with her lover, both before and after the divorce, and every one might have known it, and no one would have cared; but the convenances declared that she should not marry him until a year had elapsed after the divorce.

One thing to which Mrs. Alden could testify, as a result of a lifetime's observation, was the rapid rate at which these conventions, even the most essential of them, were giving way, and being replaced by a general "do as you please." Anyone could see that the power of women like Mrs. Devon, who represented the old regime, and were dignified and austere and exclusive, was yielding before the onslaught of new people, who were bizarre and fantastic and promiscuous and loud. And the younger sets cared no more about anyone—nor about anything under heaven, save to have a good time in their own harum-scarum ways. In the old days one always received a neatly-written or engraved invitation to dinner, worded in impersonal and formal style; but the other day Mrs. Alden had found a message which had been taken from the telephone: "Please come to dinner, but don't come unless you can bring a man, or we'll be thirteen at the table."

And along with this went a perfectly incredible increase in luxury and extravagance. "You are surprised at what you see here to-day," said she—"but take my word for it, if you were to come back five years later, you'd find all our present standards antiquated, and our present pace-makers sent to the rear. You'd find new hotels and theatres opening, and food and clothing and furniture that cost twice as much as they cost now. Not so long ago a private car was a luxury; now it's as much a necessity as an opera-box or a private ball-room, and people who really count have private trains. I can remember when our girls wore pretty muslin gowns in summer, and sent them to wash; now they wear what they call lingerie gowns, dimity en princesse, with silk embroidery and real lace and ribbons, that cost a thousand dollars apiece and won't wash. Years ago when I gave a dinner, I invited a dozen friends, and my own chef cooked it and my own servants served it. Now I have to pay my steward ten thousand a year, and nothing that I have is good enough. I have to ask forty or fifty people, and I call in a caterer, and he brings everything of his own, and my servants go off and get drunk. You used to get a good dinner for ten dollars a plate, and fifteen was something special; but now you hear of dinners that cost a thousand a plate! And it's not enough to have beautiful flowers on the table—you have to have 'scenery'; there must be a rural landscape for a background, and goldfish in the finger-bowls, and five thousand dollars' worth of Florida orchids on the table, and floral favours of roses that cost a hundred and fifty dollars a dozen. I attended a dinner at the Waldorf last year that had cost fifty thousand dollars; and when I ask those people to see me, I have to give them as good as I got. The other day I paid a thousand dollars for a table-cloth!"

"Why do you do it?" asked Montague, abruptly.

"God knows," said the other; "I don't. I sometimes wonder myself. I guess it's because I've nothing else to do. It's like the story they tell about my brother—he was losing money in a gambling-place in Saratoga, and some one said to him, 'Davy, why do you go there—don't you know the game is crooked?' 'Of course it's crooked,' said he, 'but, damn it, it's the only game in town!'"

"The pressure is more than anyone can stand," said Mrs. Alden, after a moment's thought. "It's like trying to swim against a current. You have to float, and do what every one expects you to do—your children and your friends and your servants and your tradespeople. All the world is in a conspiracy against you."

"It's appalling to me," said the man.

"Yes," said the other, "and there's never any end to it. You think you know it all, but you find you really know very little. Just think of the number of people there are trying to go the pace! They say there are seven thousand millionaires in this country, but I say there are twenty thousand in New York alone—or if they don't own a million, they're spending the income of it, which amounts to the same thing. You can figure that a man who pays ten thousand a year for rent is paying fifty thousand to live; and there's Fifth Avenue—two miles of it, if you count the uptown and downtown parts; and there's Madison Avenue, and half a dozen houses adjoining on every side street; and then there are the hotels and apartment houses, to say nothing of the West Side and Riverside Drive. And you meet these mobs of people in the shops and the hotels and the theatres, and they all want to be better dressed than you. I saw a woman here to-day that I never saw in my life before, and I heard her say she'd paid two thousand dollars for a lace handkerchief; and it might have been true, for I've been asked to pay ten thousand for a lace shawl at a bargain. It's a common enough thing to see a woman walking on Fifth Avenue with twenty or thirty thousand dollars' worth of furs on her. Fifty thousand is often paid for a coat of sable, and I know of one that cost two hundred thousand. I know women who have a dozen sets of furs—ermine, chinchilla, black fox, baby lamb, and mink and sable; and I know a man whose chauffeur quit him because he wouldn't buy him a ten-thousand-dollar fur coat! And once people used to pack their furs away and take care of them; but now they wear them about the street, or at the sea-shore, and you can fairly see them fade. Or else their cut goes out of fashion, and so they have to have new ones!"

All that was material for thought. It was all true—there was no question about that. It seemed to be the rule that whenever you questioned a tale of the extravagances of New York, you would hear the next day of something several times more startling. Montague was staggered at the idea of a two-hundred-thousand-dollar fur coat; and yet not long afterward there arrived in the city a titled Englishwoman, who owned a coat worth a million dollars, which hard-headed insurance companies had insured for half a million. It was made of the soft plumage of rare Hawaiian birds, and had taken twenty years to make; each feather was crescent-shaped, and there were wonderful designs in crimson and gold and black. Every day in the casual conversation of your acquaintances you heard of similar incredible things; a tiny antique Persian rug, which could be folded into an overcoat pocket, for ten thousand dollars; a set of five "art fans," each blade painted by a famous artist and costing forty-three thousand dollars; a crystal cup for eighty thousand; an edition de luxe of the works of Dickens for a hundred thousand; a ruby, the size of a pigeon's egg, for three hundred thousand. In some of these great New York palaces there were fountains which cost a hundred dollars a minute to run; and in the harbour there were yachts which cost twenty thousand a month to keep in commission.

And that same day, as it chanced, he learned of a brand-new kind of squandering. He went home to lunch with Mrs. Winnie Duval, and there met Mrs. Caroline Smythe, with whom he had talked at Castle Havens. Mrs. Smythe, whose husband had been a well-known Wall Street plunger, was soft and mushy, and very gushing in manner; and she asked him to come home to dinner with her, adding, "I'll introduce you to my babies."

From what Montague had so far seen, he judged that babies played a very small part in the lives of the women of Society; and so he was interested, and asked, "How many have you?"

"Only two, in town," said Mrs. Smythe. "I've just come up, you see."

"How old are they?" he inquired politely; and when the lady added, "About two years," he asked, "Won't they be in bed by dinner time?"

"Oh my, no!" said Mrs. Smythe. "The dear little lambs wait up for me. I always find them scratching at my chamber door and wagging their little tails."

Then Mrs. Winnie laughed merrily and said, "Why do you fool him?" and went on to inform Montague that Caroline's "babies" were griffons Bruxelloises. Griffons suggested to him vague ideas of dragons and unicorns and gargoyles; but he said nothing more, save to accept the invitation, and that evening he discovered that griffons Bruxelloises were tiny dogs, long-haired, yellow, and fluffy; and that for her two priceless treasures Mrs. Smythe had an expert nurse, to whom she paid a hundred dollars a month, and also a footman, and a special cuisine in which their complicated food was prepared. They had a regular dentist, and a physician, and gold plate to eat from. Mrs. Smythe also owned two long-haired St. Bernards of a very rare breed, and a fierce Great Dane, and a very fat Boston bull pup—the last having been trained to go for an airing all alone in her carriage, with a solemn coachman and footman to drive him.

Montague, deftly keeping the conversation upon the subject of pets, learned that all this was quite common. Many women in Society artificially made themselves barren, because of the inconvenience incidental to pregnancy and motherhood; and instead they lavished their affections upon cats and dogs. Some of these animals had elaborate costumes, rivalling in expensiveness those of their step-mothers. They wore tiny boots, which cost eight dollars a pair—house boots, and street boots lacing up to the knees; they had house-coats, walking-coats, dusters, sweaters, coats lined with ermine, and automobile coats with head and chest-protectors and hoods and goggles—and each coat fitted with a pocket for its tiny handkerchief of fine linen or lace! And they had collars set with rubies and pearls and diamonds—one had a collar that cost ten thousand dollars! Sometimes there would be a coat to match every gown of the owner. There were dog nurseries and resting-rooms, in which they might be left temporarily; and manicure parlours for cats, with a physician in charge. When these pets died, there was an expensive cemetery in Brooklyn especially for their interment; and they would be duly embalmed and buried in plush-lined casket, and would have costly marble monuments. When one of Mrs. Smythe's best loved pugs had fallen ill of congestion of the liver, she had had tan-bark put upon the street in front of her house; and when in spite of this the dog died, she had sent out cards edged in black, inviting her friends to a "memorial service." Also she showed Montague a number of books with very costly bindings, in which were demonstrated the unity, simplicity, and immortality of the souls of cats and dogs.

Apparently the sentimental Mrs. Smythe was willing to talk about these pets all through dinner; and so was her aunt, a thin and angular spinster, who sat on Montague's other side. And he was willing to listen—he wanted to know it all. There were umbrellas for dogs, to be fastened over their backs in wet weather; there were manicure and toilet sets, and silver medicine-chests, and jewel-studded whips. There were sets of engraved visiting-cards; there were wheel-chairs in which invalid cats and dogs might be taken for an airing. There were shows for cats and dogs, with pedigrees and prizes, and nearly as great crowds as the Horse

Show; Mrs. Smythe's St. Bernards were worth seven thousand dollars apiece, and there were bull-dogs worth twice that. There was a woman who had come all the way from the Pacific coast to have a specialist perform an operation upon the throat of her Yorkshire terrier! There was another who had built for her dog a tiny Queen Anne cottage, with rooms papered and carpeted and hung with lace curtains! Once a young man of fashion had come to the Waldorf and registered himself and "Miss Elsie Cochrane"; and when the clerk made the usual inquiries as to the relationship of the young lady, it transpired that Miss Elsie was a dog, arrayed in a prim little tea-gown, and requiring a room to herself. And then there was a tale of a cat which had inherited a life-pension from a forty-thousand-dollar estate; it had a two-floor apartment and several attendants, and sat at table and ate shrimps and Italian chestnuts, and had a velvet couch for naps, and a fur-lined basket for sleeping at night!

Four days of horses were enough for Montague, and on Friday morning, when Siegfried Harvey called him up and asked if he and Alice would come out to "The Roost" for the week-end, he accepted gladly. Charlie Carter was going, and volunteered to take them in his car; and so again they crossed the Williamsburg Bridge—"the Jewish passover," as Charlie called it—and went out on Long Island.

Montague was very anxious to get a "line" on Charlie Carter; for he had not been prepared for the startling promptness with which this young man had fallen at Alice's feet. It was so obvious, that everybody was smiling over it—he was with her every minute that he could arrange it, and he turned up at every place to which she was invited. Both Mrs. Winnie and Oliver were quite evidently complacent, but Montague was by no means the same. Charlie had struck him as a good-natured but rather weak youth, inclined to melancholy; he was never without a cigarette in his fingers, and there had been signs that he was not quite proof against the pitfalls which Society set about him in the shape of decanters and wine-cups: though in a world where the fragrance of spirits was never out of one's nostrils, and where people drank with such perplexing frequency, it was hard to know where to draw a line.

"You won't find my place like Havens's," Siegfried Harvey had said. "It is real country." Montague found it the most attractive of all the homes he had seen so far. It was a big rambling house, all in rustic style, with great hewn logs outside, and rafters within, and a winding oak stairway, and any number of dens and cosy corners, and broad window-seats with mountains of pillows. Everything here was built for comfort—there was a billiard-room and a smoking-room, and a real library with readable books and great chairs in which one sank out of sight. There were log fires blazing everywhere, and pictures on the walls that told of sport, and no end of guns and antlers and trophies of all sorts. But you were not to suppose that all this elaborate rusticity would be any excuse for the absence of attendants in livery, and a chef who boasted the cordon bleu, and a dinner-table resplendent with crystal and silver and orchids and ferns. After all, though the host called it a "small" place, he had invited twenty guests, and he had a hunter in his stables for each one of them.

But the most wonderful thing about "The Roost" was the fact that, at a touch of a button, all the walls of the lower rooms vanished into the second story, and there was one huge, log-lighted room, with violins tuning up and calling to one's feet. They set a fast pace here—the dancing lasted until three o'clock, and at dawn again they were dressed and mounted, and following the pink-coated grooms and the hounds across the frost-covered fields.

Montague was half prepared for a tame fox, but this was spared him. There was a real game, it seemed; and soon the pack gave tongue, and away went the hunt. It was the wildest ride that Montague ever had taken—over ditches and streams and innumerable rail-fences, and through thick coverts and densely populated barnyards; but he was in at the death, and Alice was only a few yards behind, to the immense delight of the company. This seemed to Montague the first real life he had met, and he thought to himself that these full-blooded and high-spirited men and women made a "set" into which he would have been glad to fit—save only that he had to earn his living, and they did not.

In the afternoon there was more riding, and walks in the crisp November air; and indoors, bridge and rackets and ping-pong, and a fast and furious game of roulette, with the host as banker. "Do I look much like a professional gambler?" he asked of Montague; and when the other replied that he had not yet met any New York gamblers, young Harvey went on to tell how he had gone to buy this apparatus (the sale of which was forbidden by law) and had been asked by the dealer how "strong" he wanted it!

Then in the evening there was more dancing, and on Sunday another hunt. That night a gambling mood seemed to seize the company—there were two bridge tables, and in another room the most reckless game of poker that Montague had ever sat in. It broke up at three in the morning, and one of the company wrote him a cheque for sixty-five hundred dollars; but even that could not entirely smooth his conscience, nor reconcile him to the fever that was in his blood.

Most important to him, however, was the fact that during the game he at last got to know Charlie Carter. Charlie did not play, for the reason that he was drunk, and one of the company told him so and refused to play with him; which left poor Charlie nothing to do but get drunker. This he did, and came and hung over the shoulders of the players, and told the company all about himself.

Montague was prepared to allow for the "wild oats" of a youngster with unlimited money, but never in his life had he heard or dreamed of anything like this boy. For half an hour he wandered about the table, and poured out a steady stream of obscenities; his mind was like a swamp, in which dwelt loathsome and hideous serpents which came to the surface at night and showed their flat heads and their slimy coils. In the heavens above or the earth beneath there was nothing sacred to him; there was nothing too revolting to be spewed out. And the company accepted the performance as an old story—the men would laugh, and push the boy away, and say, "Oh, Charlie, go to the devil!"

After it was all over, Montague took one of the company aside and asked him what it meant; to which the man replied: "Good God! Do you mean that nobody has told you about Charlie Carter?"

It appeared that Charlie was one of the "gilded youths" of the Tenderloin, whose exploits had been celebrated in the papers. And after the attendants had bundled him off to bed, several of the men gathered about the fire and sipped hot punch, and rehearsed for Montague's benefit some of his leading exploits.

Charlie was only twenty-three, it seemed; and when he was ten his father had died and left eight or ten millions in trust for him, in the care of a poor, foolish aunt whom he twisted about his finger. At the age of twelve he was a cigarette fiend, and had the run of the wine-cellar. When he went to a rich private school he took whole trunks full of cigarettes with him, and finally ran away to Europe, to acquire the learning of the brothels of Paris. And then he came home and struck the Tenderloin; and at three o'clock one morning he walked through a plate-glass window, and so the newspapers took him up. That had suddenly opened a new vista in life for Charlie—he became a devotee of fame; everywhere he went he was followed by newspaper reporters and a staring crowd. He carried wads as big round as his arm, and gave away hundred-dollar tips to bootblacks, and lost forty thousand dollars in a game of poker. He gave a fete to the demi-monde, with a jewelled Christmas tree in midsummer, and fifty thousand dollars' worth of splendour. But the greatest stroke of all was the announcement that he was going to build a submarine yacht and fill it with chorus-girls!—Now Charlie had sunk out of public attention, and his friends would not see him for days; he would be lying in a "sporting house" literally wallowing in champagne.

And all this, Montague realized, his brother must have known! And he had said not a word about it—because of the eight or ten millions which Charlie would have when he was twenty-five!

CHAPTER IX

In the morning they went home with others of the party by train. They could not wait for Charlie and his automobile, because Monday was the opening night of the Opera, and no one could miss that. Here Society would appear in its most gorgeous raiment, and, there would be a show of jewellery such as could be seen nowhere else in the world.

General Prentice and his wife had opened their town-house, and had invited them to dinner and to share their box; and so at about half-past nine o'clock Montague found himself seated in a great balcony of the shape of a horseshoe, with several hundred of the richest people in the city. There was another tier of boxes above, and three galleries above that, and a thousand or more people seated and standing below him. Upon the big stage there was an elaborate and showy play, the words of which were sung to the accompaniment of an orchestra.

Now Montague had never heard an opera, and he was fond of music. The second act had just begun when he came in, and all through it he sat quite spellbound, listening to the most ravishing strains that ever he had heard in his life. He scarcely noticed that Mrs. Prentice was spending her time studying the occupants of the other boxes through a jewelled lorgnette, or that Oliver was chattering to her daughter.

But after the act was over, Oliver got him alone outside the box, and whispered, "For God's sake, Allan, don't make a fool of yourself."

"Why, what's the matter?" asked the other.

"What will people think," exclaimed Oliver, "seeing you sitting there like a man in a dope dream?"

"Why," laughed the other, "they'll think I'm listening to the music."

To which Oliver responded, "People don't come to the Opera to listen to the music."

This sounded like a joke, but it was not. To Society the Opera was a great state function, an exhibition of far more exclusiveness and magnificence than the Horse Show; and Society certainly had the right to say, for it owned the opera-house and ran it. The real music-lovers who came, either stood up in the back, or sat in the fifth gallery, close to the ceiling, where the air was foul and hot. How much Society cared about the play was sufficiently indicated by the fact that all of the operas were sung in foreign languages, and sung so carelessly that the few who understood the languages could make but little of the words. Once there was a world-poet who devoted his life to trying to make the Opera an art; and in the battle with Society he all but starved to death. Now, after half a century, his genius had triumphed, and Society consented to sit for hours in darkness and listen to the domestic disputes of German gods and goddesses. But what Society really cared for was a play with beautiful costumes and scenery and dancing, and pretty songs to which one could listen while one talked; the story must be elemental and passionate, so that one could understand it in pantomime—say the tragic love of a beautiful and noble-minded courtesan for a gallant young man of fashion.

Nearly every one who came to the Opera had a glass, by means of which he could bring each gorgeously-clad society dame close to him, and study her at leisure. There were said to be two hundred million dollars' worth of diamonds in New York, and those that were not in the stores were very apt to be at this show; for here was where they could accomplish the purpose for which they existed— here was where all the world came to stare at them. There were nine prominent Society women, who among them displayed five million dollars' worth of jewels. You would see stomachers which looked like a piece of a coat of mail, and were made wholly of blazing diamonds. You would see emeralds and rubies and diamonds and pearls made in tiaras—that is to say, imitation crowns and coronets— and exhibited with a stout and solemn dowager for a pediment. One of the Wallings had set this fashion, and now every one of importance wore them. One lady to whom Montague was introduced made a speciality of pearls—two black pearl ear-rings at forty thousand dollars, a string at three hundred thousand, a brooch of pink pearls at fifty thousand, and two necklaces at a quarter of a million each!

This incessant repetition of the prices of things came to seem very sordid; but Montague found that there was no getting away from it. The people in Society who paid these prices affected to be above all such considerations, to be interested only in the beauty and artistic excellence of the things themselves; but one found that they always talked about the prices which other people had paid, and that somehow other people always knew what they had paid. They took care also to see that the public and the newspapers knew what they had paid, and knew everything else that they were doing. At this Opera, for instance, there was a diagram of the boxes printed upon the programme, and a list of all the box-holders, so that anyone could tell who was who. You might see these great dames in their gorgeous robes coming from their carriages, with crowds staring at them and detectives hovering about. And the bosom of each would be throbbing with a wild and wonderful vision of the moment when she would enter her box, and the music would be forgotten, and all eyes would be turned upon her; and she would lay aside her wraps, and flash upon the staring throngs, a vision of dazzling splendour.

Some of these jewels were family treasures, well known to New York for generations; and in such cases it was becoming the fashion to leave the real jewels in the safe-deposit vault, and to wear imitation stones exactly like them. From homes where the jewels were kept, detectives were never absent, and in many cases there were detectives watching the detectives; and yet every once in a while the newspapers would be full of a sensational story of a robbery. Then the unfortunates who chanced to be suspected would be seized by the police and subjected to what was jocularly termed the "third degree," and consisted of tortures as elaborate and cruel as any which the Spanish Inquisition had invented. The advertising value of this kind of thing was found to be so great that famous actresses also had costly jewels, and now and then would have them stolen.

That night, when they had got home, Montague had a talk with his cousin about Charlie Carter. He discovered a peculiar situation. It seemed that Alice already knew that Charlie had been "bad." He was sick and miserable; and her beauty and innocence had touched him and made him ashamed of himself, and he had hinted darkly at dreadful evils. Thus carefully veiled, and tinged with mystery and romance, Montague could understand how Charlie made an interesting and appealing figure. "He says I'm different from any girl he ever met," said Alice—a remark of such striking originality that her cousin could not keep back his smile.

Alice was not the least bit in love with him, and had no idea of being; and she said that she would accept no invitations, and never go alone with him; but she did not see how she could avoid him when she met him at other people's houses. And to this Montague had to assent.

General Prentice had inquired kindly as to what Montague had seen in New York, and how he was getting along. He added that he had talked about him to Judge Ellis, and that when he was ready to get to work, the Judge would perhaps have some suggestions to make to him. He approved, however, of Montague's plan of getting his bearings first; and said that he would introduce him and put him up at a couple of the leading clubs.

All this remained in Montague's mind; but there was no use trying to think of it at the moment. Thanksgiving was at hand, and in countless country mansions there would be gaieties under way. Bertie Stuyvesant had planned an excursion to his Adirondack camp, and had invited a score or so of young people, including the Montagues. This would be a new feature of the city's life, worth knowing about.

Their expedition began with a theatre-party. Bertie had engaged four boxes, and they met there, an hour or so after the performance had begun. This made no difference, however, for the play was like the opera-a number of songs and dances strung together, and with only plot enough to provide occasion for elaborate scenery and costumes. From the play they were carried to the Grand Central Station, and a little before midnight Bertie's private train set out on its journey.

This train was a completely equipped hotel. There was a baggage compartment and a dining-car and kitchen; and a drawing-room and library-car; and a bedroom-car—not with berths, such as the ordinary sleeping-car provides, but with comfortable bedrooms, furnished in white mahogany, and provided with running water and electric light. All these cars were built of steel, and automatically ventilated: and they were furnished in the luxurious fashion of everything with which Bertie Stuyvesant had anything to do. In the library-car there were velvet carpets upon the floor, and furniture of South American mahogany, and paintings upon the walls over which great artists had laboured for years.

Bertie's chef and servants were on board, and a supper was ready in the dining-car, which they ate while watching the Hudson by moonlight. And the next morning they reached their destination, a little station in the mountain wilderness. The train lay upon a switch, and so they had breakfast at their leisure, and then, bundled in furs, came out into the crisp pine-laden air of the woods. There was snow upon the ground, and eight big sleighs waiting; and for nearly three hours they drove in the frosty sunlight, through most beautiful mountain scenery. A good part of the drive was in Bertie's "preserve," and the road was private, as big signs notified one every hundred yards or so.

So at last they reached a lake, winding like a snake among towering hills, and with a huge baronial castle standing out upon the rocky shore. This imitation fortress was the "camp."

Bertie's father had built it, and visited it only half a dozen times in his life. Bertie himself had only been here twice, he said. The deer were so plentiful that in the winter they died in scores. Nevertheless there were thirty game-keepers to guard the ten thousand acres of forest, and prevent anyone's hunting in it. There were many such "preserves" in this Adirondack wilderness, so Montague was told; one man had a whole mountain fenced about with heavy iron railing, and had moose and elk and even wild boar inside. And as for the "camps," there were so many that a new style of architecture had been developed here—to say nothing of those which followed old styles, like this imported Rhine castle. One of Bertie's crowd had a big Swiss chalet; and one of the Wallings had a Japanese palace to which he came every August—a house which had been built from plans drawn in Japan, and by labourers imported especially from Japan. It was full of Japanese ware—furniture, tapestry, and mosaics; and the guides remembered with wonder the strange silent, brown-skinned little men who had laboured for days at carving a bit of wood, and had built a tiny pagoda-like tea-house with more bits of wood in it than a man could count in a week.

They had a luncheon of fresh venison and partridges and trout, and in the afternoon a hunt. The more active set out to track the deer in the snow; but most prepared to watch the lake-shore, while the game-keepers turned loose the dogs back in the hills. This "hounding" was against the law, but Bertie was his own law here—and at the worst there could simply be a small fine, imposed upon some of the keepers. They drove eight or ten deer to water; and as they fired as many as twenty shots at one deer, they had quite a lively time. Then at dusk they came back, in a fine glow of excitement, and spent the evening before the blazing logs, telling over their adventures.

The party spent two days and a half here, and on the last evening, which was Thanksgiving, they had a wild turkey which Bertie had shot the week before in Virginia, and were entertained by a minstrel show which had been brought up from New York the night before. The next afternoon they drove back to the train.

In the morning, when they reached the city, Alice found a note from Mrs. Winnie Duval, begging her and Montague to come to lunch and attend a private lecture by the Swami Babubanana, who would tell them all about the previous states of their souls. They went—though not without a protest from old Mrs. Montague, who declared it was "worse than Bob Ingersoll."

And then, in the evening, came Mrs. de Graffenried's opening entertainment, which was one of the great events of the social year. In the general rush of things Montague had not had a chance properly to realize it; but Reggie Mann and Mrs. de Graffenried had been working over it for weeks. When the Montagues arrived, they found the Riverside mansion—which was decorated in imitation of an Arabian palace—turned into a jungle of tropical plants.

They had come early at Reggie's request, and he introduced them to Mrs. de Graffenried, a tall and angular lady with a leathern complexion painfully painted; Mrs. de Graffenried was about fifty years of age, but like all the women of Society she was made up for thirty. Just at present there were beads of perspiration upon her forehead; something had gone wrong at the last moment, and so Reggie would have no time to show them the favours, as he had intended.

About a hundred and fifty guests were invited to this entertainment. A supper was served at little tables in the great ball-room, and afterward the guests wandered about the house while the tables were whisked out of the way and the room turned into a play-house. A company from one of the Broadway theatres would be bundled into cabs at the end of the performance, and by midnight they would be ready to repeat the performance at Mrs. de Graffenried's. Montague chanced to be near when this company arrived, and he observed that the guests had crowded up too close, and not left room enough for the actors. So the manager had placed them in a little ante-room, and when Mrs. de Graffenried observed this, she rushed at the man, and swore at him like a dragoon, and ordered the bewildered performers out into the main room.

But this was peering behind the scenes, and he was supposed to be watching the play. The entertainment was another "musical comedy" like the one he had seen a few nights before. On that occasion, however, Bertie Stuyvesant's sister had talked to him the whole time, while now he was let alone, and had a chance to watch the performance.

This was a very popular play; it had had a long run, and the papers told how its author had an income of a couple of hundred thousand dollars a year. And here was an audience of the most rich and influential people in the city; and they laughed and clapped, and made it clear that they were enjoying themselves heartily. And what sort of a play was it?

It was called "The Kaliph of Kamskatka." It had no shred of a plot; the Kaliph had seventeen wives, and there was an American drummer who wanted to sell him another—but then you did not need to remember this, for nothing came of it. There was nothing in the play which could be called a character—there was nothing which could be connected with any real emotion ever felt by human beings. Nor could one say that there was any incident—at least nothing happened because of anything else. Each event was a separate thing, like the spasmodic jerking in the face of an idiot. Of this sort of "action" there was any quantity—at an instant's notice every one on the stage would fall simultaneously into this condition of idiotic jerking. There was rushing about, shouting, laughing, exclaiming; the stage was in a continual uproar of excitement, which was without any reason or meaning. So it was impossible to think of the actors in their parts; one kept thinking of them as human beings—thinking of the awful tragedy of full-grown men and women being compelled by the pressure of hunger to dress up and paint themselves, and then come out in public and dance, stamp, leap about, wring their hands, make faces, and otherwise be "lively."

The costumes were of two sorts: one fantastic, supposed to represent the East, and the other a kind of reductio ad absurdum of fashionable garb. The leading man wore a "natty" outing-suit, and strutted with a little cane; his stock-in-trade was a jaunty air, a kind of perpetual flourish, and a wink that suggested the cunning of a satyr. The leading lady changed her costume several times in each act; but it invariably contained the elements of bare arms and bosom and back, and a skirt which did not reach her knees, and bright-coloured silk stockings, and slippers with heels two inches high. Upon the least provocation she would execute a little pirouette, which would reveal the rest of her legs, surrounded by a mass of lace ruffles. It is the nature of the human mind to seek the end of things; if this woman had worn a suit of tights and nothing else, she would have been as uninteresting as an underwear advertisement in a magazine; but this incessant not-quite-revealing of herself exerted a subtle fascination. At frequent intervals the orchestra would start up a jerky little tune, and the two "stars" would begin to sing in nasal voices some words expressive of passion; then the man would take the woman about the waist and dance and swing her about and bend her backward and gaze into her eyes—actions all vaguely suggestive of the relationship of sex. At the end of the verse a chorus would come gliding on, clad in any sort of costume which admitted of colour and the display of legs; the painted women of this chorus were never still for an instant—if they were not actually dancing, they were wriggling their legs, and jerking their bodies from side to side, and nodding their heads, and in all other possible ways being "lively."

But it was not the physical indecency of this show that struck Montague so much as its intellectual content. The dialogue of the piece was what is called "smart"; that is, it was full of a kind of innuendo which implied a secret understanding of evil between the actor and his audience—a sort of countersign which passed between them. After all, it would have been an error to say that there were no ideas in the play—there was one idea upon which all the interest of it was based; and Montague strove to analyze this idea and formulate it to himself. There are certain life principles-one might call them moral axioms—which are the result of the experience of countless ages of the human race, and upon the adherence to which the continuance of the race depends. And here was an audience by whom all these principles were—not questioned, nor yet disputed, nor yet denied—but to whom the denial was the axiom, something which it would be too banal to state flatly, but which it was elegant and witty to take for granted. In this audience there were elderly people, and married men and women, and young men and maidens; and a perfect gale of laughter swept through it at a story of a married woman whose lover had left her when he got married:—

"She must have been heartbroken," said the leading lady.

"She was desperate," said the leading man, with a grin.

"What did she do?" asked the lady "Go and shoot herself?"

"Worse than that," said the man. "She, went back to her husband and had a baby!"

But to complete your understanding of the significance of this play, you must bring yourself to realize that it was not merely a play, but a kind of a play; it had a name—a "musical comedy"—the meaning of which every one understood. Hundreds of such plays were written and produced, and "dramatic critics" went to see them and gravely discussed them, and many thousands of people made their livings by travelling over the country and playing them; stately theatres were built for them, and hundreds of thousands of people paid their money every night to see them. And all this no joke and no nightmare—but a thing that really existed. Men and women were doing these things—actual flesh-and-blood human beings.

Montague wondered, in an awestricken sort of way, what kind of human being it could be who had flourished the cane and made the grimaces in that play. Later on, when he came to know the "Tenderloin," he met this same actor, and he found that he had begun life as a little Irish "mick" who lived in a tenement, and whose mother stood at the head of the stairway and defended him with a rolling-pin against a policeman who was chasing him. He had discovered that he could make a living by his comical antics; but when he came home and told his mother that he had been offered twenty dollars a week by a show manager, she gave him a licking for lying to her. Now he was making three thousand dollars a week—more than the President of the United States and his Cabinet; but he was not happy, as he confided to Montague, because he did not know how to read, and this was a cause of perpetual humiliation. The secret desire of this little actor's heart was to play Shakespeare; he had "Hamlet" read to him, and pondered how to act it—all the time that he was flourishing his little cane and making his grimaces! He had chanced to be on the stage when a fire had broken out, and five or six hundred victims of greed were roasted to death. The actor had pleaded with the people to keep their seats, but all in vain; and all his life thereafter he went about with this vision of horror in his mind, and haunted by the passionate conviction that he had failed because of his lack of education—that if only he had been a man of culture, he would have been able to think of something to say to hold those terror-stricken people!

At three o'clock in the morning the performance came to an end, and then there were more refreshments; and Mrs. Vivie Patton came and sat by him, and they had a nice comfortable gossip. When Mrs. Vivie once got started at talking about people, her tongue ran on like a windmill.

There was Reggie Mann, meandering about and simpering at people. Reggie was in his glory at Mrs. de Graffenried's affairs. Reggie had arranged all this-he did the designing and the ordering, and contracted for the shows with the agents. You could bet that he had got his commission on them, too—though sometimes Mrs. de Graffenried got the shows to come for nothing, because of the advertising her name would bring. Commissions were Reggie's speciality—he had begun life as an auto agent. Montague didn't know what that was? An auto agent was a man who was for ever begging his friends to use a certain kind of car, so that he might make a living; and Reggie had made about thirty thousand a year in that way. He had come from Boston, where his reputation had been made by the fact that early one morning, as they were driving home from a celebration, he had dared a young society matron to take off her shoes and stockings, and get out and wade in the public fountain; and she had done it, and he had followed her. On the strength of the eclat of this he had been taken up by Mrs. Devon; and one day Mrs. Devon had worn a white gown, and asked him what he thought of it. "It needs but one thing to make it perfect," said Reggie, and taking a red rose, he pinned it upon her corsage. The effect was magical; every one exclaimed with delight, and so Reggie's reputation as an authority upon dress was made for ever. Now he was Mrs. de Graffenried's right-hand man, and they made up their pranks together. Once they had walked down the street in Newport with a big rag doll between them. And Reggie had given a dinner at which the guest of honour had been a monkey—surely Montague had heard of that, for it had been the sensation of the season. It was really the funniest thing imaginable; the monkey wore a suit of broad-cloth with collar and cuffs, and he shook hands with all the guests, and behaved himself exactly like a gentleman—except that he did not get drunk.

And then Mrs. Vivie pointed out the great Mrs. Ridgley-Clieveden, who was sitting with one of her favourites, a grave, black-bearded gentleman who had leaped into fame by inheriting fifty million dollars. "Mrs. R.-C." had taken him up, and ordered his engagement book for him, and he was solemnly playing the part of a social light. He had purchased an old New York mansion, upon the decoration of which three million dollars had been spent; and when he came down to business from Tuxedo, his private train waited all day for him with steam up. Mrs. Vivie told an amusing tale of a woman who had announced her engagement to him, and borrowed large sums of money upon the strength of it, before his denial came out. That had been a source of great delight to Mrs. de Graffenried, who was furiously jealous of "Mrs. R. C."

From the anecdotes that people told, Montague judged that Mrs. de Graffenried must be one of those new leaders of Society, who, as Mrs. Alden said, were inclined to the bizarre and fantastic. Mrs. de Graffenried spent half a million dollars every season to hold the position of leader of the Newport set, and you could always count upon her for new and striking ideas. Once she had given away as cotillion favours tiny globes with goldfish in them; again she had given a dance at which everybody got themselves up as different vegetables. She was fond of going about at Newport and inviting people haphazard to lunch—thirty or forty at a time—and then surprising them with a splendid banquet. Again she would give a big formal dinner, and perplex people by offering them something which they really cared to eat. "You see," explained Mrs. Vivie, "at these dinners we generally get thick green turtle soup, and omelettes with some sort of Florida water poured over them, and mushrooms cooked under glass, and real hand-made desserts; but Mrs. de Graffenried dares to have baked ham and sweet potatoes, or even real roast beef. You saw to-night that she had green corn; she must have arranged for that months ahead—we can never get it from Porto Rico until January. And you see this little dish of wild strawberries—they were probably transplanted and raised in a hothouse, and every single one wrapped separately before they were shipped."

All these labours had made Mrs. de Graffenried a tremendous power in the social world. She had a savage tongue, said Mrs. Vivie, and every one lived in terror of her; but once in a while she met her match. Once she had invited a comic opera star to sing for her guests, and all the men had crowded round this actress, and Mrs. de Graffenried had flown into a passion and tried to drive them away; and the actress, lolling back in her chair, and gazing up idly at Mrs. de Graffenried, had drawled, "Ten years older than God!" Poor Mrs. de Graffenried would carry that saying with her until she died.

Something reminiscent of this came under Montague's notice that same evening. At about four o'clock Mrs. Vivie wished to go home, and asked him to find her escort, the Count St. Elmo de Champignon—the man, by the way, for whom her husband was gunning. Montague roamed all about the house, and finally went downstairs, where a room had been set apart for the theatrical company to partake of refreshments. Mrs. de Graffenried's secretary was on guard at the door; but some of the boys had got into the room, and were drinking champagne and "making dates" with the chorus-girls. And here was Mrs. de Graffenried herself, pushing them bodily out of the room, a score and more of them—and among them Mrs. Vivie's Count!

Montague delivered his message, and then went upstairs to wait until his own party should be ready to leave. In the smoking-room were a number of men, also waiting; and among them he noticed Major Venable, in conversation with a man whom he did not know. "Come over here," the Major called; and Montague obeyed, at the same time noticing the stranger.

He was a tall, loose-jointed, powerfully built man, a small head and a very striking face: a grim mouth with drooping corners tightly set, and a hawk-like nose, and deep-set, peering eyes. "Have you met Mr. Hegan?" said the Major. "Hegan, this is Mr. Allan Montague." Jim Hegan! Montague repressed a stare and took the chair which they offered him. "Have a cigar," said Hegan, holding out his case.

"Mr. Montague has just come to New York," said the Major. "He is a Southerner, too."

"Indeed?" said Hegan, and inquired what State he came from. Montague replied, and added, "I had the pleasure of meeting your daughter last week, at the Horse Show."

That served to start a conversation; for Hegan came from Texas, and when he found that Montague knew about horses—real horses—he warmed to him. Then the Major's party called him away, and the other two were left to carry on the conversation.

It was very easy to chat with Hegan; and yet underneath, in the other's mind, there lurked a vague feeling of trepidation, as he realized that he was chatting with a hundred millions of dollars. Montague was new enough at the game to imagine that there ought to be something strange, some atmosphere of awe and mystery, about a man who was master of a dozen railroads and of the politics of half a dozen States. He was simple and very kindly in his manner, a plain man, interested in plain things. There was about him, as he talked, a trace of timidity, almost of apology, which Montague noticed and wondered at. It was only later, when he had time to think about it, that he realized that Hegan had begun as a farmer's boy in Texas, a "poor white"; and could it be that after all these years an instinct remained in him, so that whenever he met a gentleman of the old South he stood by with a little deference, seeming to beg pardon for his hundred millions of dollars?

And yet there was the power of the man. Even chatting about horses, you felt it; you felt that there was a part of him which did not chat, but which sat behind and watched. And strangest of all, Montague found himself fancying that behind the face that smiled was another face, that did not smile, but that was grim and set. It was a strange face, with its broad, sweeping eyebrows and its drooping mouth; it haunted Montague and made him feel ill at ease.

There came Laura Hegan, who greeted them in her stately way; and Mrs. Hegan, bustling and vivacious, costumed en grande dame. "Come and see me some time," said the man. "You won't be apt to meet me otherwise, for I don't go about much." And so they took their departure; and Montague sat alone and smoked and thought. The face still stayed with him; and now suddenly, in a burst of light, it came to him what it was: the face of a bird of prey—of the great wild, lonely eagle! You have seen it, perhaps, in a menagerie; sitting high up, submitting patiently, biding its time. But all the while the soul of the eagle is far away, ranging the wide spaces, ready for the lightning swoop, and the clutch with the cruel talons!

CHAPTER X

The next week was a busy one for the Montagues. The Robbie Wallings had come to town and opened their house, and the time drew near for the wonderful débutante dance at which Alice was to be formally presented to Society. And of course Alice must have a new dress for the occasion, and it must be absolutely the most beautiful dress ever known. In an idle moment her cousin figured out that it was to cost her about five dollars a minute to be entertained by the Wallings!

What it would cost the Wallings, one scarcely dared to think. Their ballroom would be turned into a flower-garden; and there would be a supper for a hundred guests, and still another supper after the dance, and costly favours for every figure. The purchasing of these latter had been entrusted to Oliver, and Montague heard with dismay what they were to cost. "Robbie couldn't afford to do anything second-rate," was the younger brother's only reply to his exclamations.

Alice divided her time between the Wallings and her costumiers, and every evening she came home with a new tale of important developments. Alice was new at the game, and could afford to be excited; and Mrs. Robbie liked to see her bright face, and to smile indulgently at her eager inquiries. Mrs. Robbie herself had given her orders to her steward and her florist and her secretary, and went on her way and thought no more about it. That was the way of the great ladies—or, at any rate, it was their pose.

The town-house of the Robbies was a stately palace occupying a block upon Fifth Avenue—one of the half-dozen mansions of the Walling family which were among the show places of the city. It would take a catalogue to list the establishments maintained by the Wallings—there was an estate in North Carolina, and another in the Adirondacks, and others on Long Island and in New Jersey. Also there were several in Newport—one which was almost never occupied, and which Mrs. Billy Alden sarcastically described as "a three-million-dollar castle on a desert."

Montague accompanied Alice once or twice, and had an opportunity to study Mrs. Robbie at home. There were thirty-eight servants in her establishment; it was a little state all in itself, with Mrs. Robbie as queen, and her housekeeper as prime minister, and under them as many different ranks and classes and castes as in a feudal principality. There had to be six separate dining-rooms for the various kinds of servants who scorned each other; there were servants' servants and servants of servants' servants. There were only three to whom the mistress was supposed to give orders—the butler, the steward, and the housekeeper; she did not even know the names of many of them, and they were changed so often, that, as she declared, she had to leave it to her detective to distinguish between employees and burglars.

Mrs. Robbie was quite a young woman, but it pleased her to pose as a care-worn matron, weary of the responsibilities of her exalted station. The ignorant looked on and pictured her as living in the lap of ease, endowed with every opportunity: in reality the meanest kitchen-maid was freer—she was quite worn thin with the burdens that fell upon her. The huge machine was for ever threatening to fall to pieces, and required the wisdom of Solomon and the patience of Job to keep it running. One paid one's steward a fortune, and yet he robbed right and left, and quarrelled with the chef besides. The butler was suspected of getting drunk upon rare and costly vintages, and the new parlour-maid had turned out to be a Sunday reporter in disguise. The man who had come every day for ten years to wind the clocks of the establishment was dead, and the one who took care of the bric-a-brac was sick, and the housekeeper was in a panic over the prospect of having to train another.

And even suppose that you escaped from these things, the real problems of your life had still to be faced. It was not enough to keep alive; you had your career—your duties as a leader of Society. There was the daily mail, with all the pitiful letters from people begging money—actually in one single week there were demands for two million dollars. There were geniuses with patent incubators and stove-lifters, and every time you gave a ball you stirred up swarms of anarchists and cranks. And then there were the letters you really had to answer, and the calls that had to be paid. These latter were so many that people in the same neighbourhood had arranged to have the same day at home; thus, if you lived on Madison Avenue you had Thursday; but even then it took a whole afternoon to leave your cards. And then there were invitations to be sent and accepted; and one was always making mistakes and offending somebody—people would become mortal enemies overnight, and expect all the world to know it the next morning. And now there were so many divorces and remarryings, with consequent changing of names; and some men knew about their wives' lovers and didn't care, and some did care, but didn't know—altogether it was like carrying a dozen chess games in your head. And then there was the hairdresser and the manicurist and the masseuse, and the tailor and the bootmaker and the jeweller; and then one absolutely had to glance through a newspaper, and to see one's children now and then.

All this Mrs. Robbie explained at luncheon; it was the rich man's burden, about which common people had no conception whatever. A person with a lot of money was like a barrel of molasses—all the flies in the neighbourhood came buzzing about. It was perfectly incredible, the lengths to which people would go to get invited to your house; not only would they write and beg you, they might attack your business interests, and even bribe your friends. And on the other hand, when people thought you needed them, the time you had to get them to come!

"Fancy," said Mrs. Robbie, "offering to give a dinner to an English countess, and having her try to charge you for coming!" And incredible as it might seem, some people had actually yielded to her, and the disgusting creature had played the social celebrity for a whole season, and made quite a handsome income out of it. There seemed to be no limit to the abjectness of some of the tuft-hunters in Society.

It was instructive to hear Mrs. Robbie denounce such evils; and yet—alas for human frailty—the next time that Montague called, the great lady was blazing with wrath over the tidings that a new foreign prince was coming to America, and that Mrs. Ridgely-Clieveden had stolen a march upon her and grabbed him. He was to be under her tutelage the entire time, and all the effulgence of his magnificence would be radiated upon that upstart house. Mrs. Robbie revenged herself by saying as many disagreeable things about Mrs. Ridgley-Clieveden as she could think of; winding up with the declaration that if she behaved with this prince as she had with the Russian grand duke, Mrs. Robbie Walling, for one, would cut her dead. And truly the details which Mrs. Robbie cited were calculated to suggest that her rival's hospitality was a reversion to the customs of primitive savagery.

The above is a fair sample of the kind of conversation that one heard whenever one visited any of the Wallings. Perhaps, as Mrs. Robbie said, it may have been their millions that made necessary their attitude toward other people; certain it was, at any rate, that Montague found them all most disagreeable people to know. There was always some tempest in a teapot over the latest machinations of their enemies. And then there was the whole dead mass of people who sponged upon them and toadied to them; and finally the barbarian hordes outside the magic circle of their acquaintance—some specimens of whom came up every day for ridicule. They had big feet and false teeth; they ate mush and molasses; they wore ready-made ties; they said: "Do you wish that I should do it?" Their grandfathers had been butchers and pedlars and other abhorrent things. Montague tried his best to like the Wallings, because of what they were doing for Alice; but after he had sat at their lunch-table and listened to a conversation such as this, he found himself in need of fresh air.

And then he would begin to wonder about his own relation to these people. If they talked about every one else behind their backs, certainly they must talk about him behind his. And why did they go out of their way to make him at home, and why were they spending their money to launch Alice in Society? In the beginning he had assumed that they did it out of the goodness of their hearts; but now that he had looked into their hearts, he rejected the explanation. It was not their way to shower princely gifts upon strangers; in general, the attitude of all the Wallings toward a stranger was that of the London hooligan—"'Eave a 'arf a brick at 'im!" They considered themselves especially appointed by Providence to protect Society from the vulgar newly rich who poured into the city, seeking for notoriety and recognition. They prided themselves upon this attitude—they called it their "exclusiveness"; and the exclusiveness of the younger generations of Wallings had become a kind of insanity.

Nor could the reason be that Alice was beautiful and attractive. One could have imagined it if Mrs. Robbie had been like—say, Mrs. Winnie Duval. It was easy to think of Mrs. Winnie taking a fancy to a girl, and spending half her fortune upon her. But from a hundred little things that he had seen, Montague had come to realize that the Robbie Wallings, with all their wealth and power and grandeur, were actually quite stingy. While all the world saw them scattering fortunes in their pathway, in reality they were keeping track of every dollar. And Robbie himself was liable to panic fits of economy, in which he went to the most absurd excesses—Montague once heard him haggling over fifty cents with a cabman. Lavish hosts though they both were, it was the literal truth that they never spent money upon anyone but themselves—the end and aim of their every action was the power and prestige of the Robbie Wallings.

"They do it because they are friends of mine," said Oliver, and evidently wished that to satisfy his brother. But it only shifted the problem and set him to watching Robbie and Oliver, and trying to make out the basis of their relationship. There was a very grave question concerned in this. Oliver had come to New York comparatively poor, and now he was rich—or, at any rate, he lived like a rich man. And his brother, whose scent was growing keener with every day of his stay in New York, had about made up his mind that Oliver got his money from Robbie Walling.

Here, again, the problem would have been simple, if it had been another person than Robbie; Montague would have concluded that his brother was a "hanger-on." There were many great families whose establishments were infested with such parasites. Siegfried Harvey, for instance, was a man who had always half a dozen young chaps hanging about him; good-looking and lively fellows, who hunted and played bridge, and amused the married women while their husbands were at work, and who, if ever they dropped a hint that they were hard up, might be reasonably certain of being offered a cheque. But if the Robbie Wallings were to write cheques, it must be for value received. And what could the value be?

"Ollie" was rather a little god among the ultra-swagger; his taste was a kind of inspiration. And yet his brother noticed that in such questions he always deferred instantly to the Wallings; and surely the Wallings were not people to be persuaded that they needed anyone to guide them in matters of taste. Again, Ollie was the very devil of a wit, and people were heartily afraid of him; and Montague had noticed that he never by any chance made fun of Robbie—that the fetiches of the house of Walling were always treated with respect. So he had wondered if by any chance Robbie was maintaining his brother in princely state for the sake of his ability to make other people uncomfortable. But he realized that the Robbies, in their own view of it, could have no more need of wit than a battleship has need of popguns. Oliver's position, when they were about, was rather that of the man who hardly ever dared to be as clever as he might, because of the restless jealousy of his friend.

It was a mystery; and it made the elder brother very uncomfortable. Alice was young and guileless, and a pleasant person to patronize; but he was a man of the world, and it was his business to protect her. He had always paid his own way through life, and he was very loath to put himself under obligations to people like the Wallings, whom he did not like, and who, he felt instinctively, could not like him.

But of course there was nothing he could do about it. The date for the great festivity was set; and the Wallings were affable and friendly, and Alice all a-tremble with excitement. The evening arrived, and with it came the enemies of the Wallings, dressed in their jewels and fine raiment. They had been asked because they were too important to be skipped, and they had come because the Wallings were too powerful to be ignored. They revenged themselves by consuming many courses of elaborate and costly viands; and they shook hands with Alice and beamed upon her, and then discussed her behind her back as if she were a French doll in a show-case. They decided unanimously that her elder cousin was a "stick," and that the whole family were interlopers and shameless adventurers; but it was understood that since the Robbie Wallings had seen fit to take them up, it would be necessary to invite them about.

At any rate, that was the way it all seemed to Montague, who had been brooding. To Alice it was a splendid festivity, to which exquisite people came to take delight in each other's society. There were gorgeous costumes and sparkling gems; there was a symphony of perfumes, intoxicating the senses, and a golden flood of music streaming by; there were laughing voices and admiring glances, and handsome partners with whom one might dance through the portals of fairy-land.—And then, next morning, there were accounts in all the newspapers, with descriptions of one's costume and then some of those present, and even the complete menus of the supper, to assist in preserving the memories of the wonderful occasion.

Now they were really in Society. A reporter called to get Alice's photo for the Sunday supplement; and floods of invitations came—and with them all the cares and perplexities about which Mrs. Robbie had told. Some of these invitations had to be declined, and one must know whom it was safe to offend. Also, there was a long letter from a destitute widow, and a proposal from a foreign count. Mrs. Robbie's secretary had a list of many hundreds of these professional beggars and blackmailers.

Conspicuous at the dance was Mrs. Winnie, in a glorious electric-blue silk gown. And she shook her fan at Montague, exclaiming, "You wretched man—you promised to come and see me!"

"I've been out of town," Montague protested.

"Well, come to dinner to-morrow night," said Mrs. Winnie. "There'll be some bridge fiends."

"You forget I haven't learned to play," he objected.

"Well, come anyhow," she replied. "We'll teach you. I'm no player myself, and my husband will be there, and he's good-natured; and my brother Dan—he'll have to be whether he likes it or not."

So Montague visited the Snow Palace again, and met Winton Duval, the banker,—a tall, military-looking man of about fifty, with a big grey moustache, and bushy eyebrows, and the head of a lion. His was one of the city's biggest banking-houses, and in alliance with powerful interests in the Street. At present he was going in for mines in Mexico and South America, and so he was very seldom at home. He was a man of most rigid habits—he would come back unexpectedly after a month's trip, and expect to find everything ready for him, both at home and in his office, as if he had just stepped round the corner. Montague observed that he took his menu-card and jotted down his comments upon each dish, and then sent it down to the chef. Other people's dinners he very seldom attended, and when his wife gave her entertainments, he invariably dined at the club.

He pleaded a business engagement for the evening; and as brother Dan did not appear, Montague did not learn any bridge. The other four guests settled down to the game, and Montague and Mrs. Winnie sat and chatted, basking before the fireplace in the great entrance-hall.

"Have you seen Charlie Carter?" was the first question she asked him.

"Not lately," he answered; "I met him at Harvey's."

"I know that," said she. "They tell me he got drunk."

"I'm afraid he did," said Montague.

"Poor boy!" exclaimed Mrs. Winnie. "And Alice saw him! He must be heart-broken!"

Montague said nothing. "You know," she went on, "Charlie really means well. He has honestly an affectionate nature."

She paused; and Montague Said, vaguely, "I suppose so."

"You don't like him," said the other. "I can see that. And I suppose now Alice will have no use for him, either. And I had it all fixed up for her to reform him!"

Montague smiled in spite of himself.

"Oh, I know," said she. "It wouldn't have been easy. But you've no idea what a beautiful boy Charlie used to be, until all the women set to work to ruin him."

"I can imagine it," said Montague; but he did not warm to the subject.

"You're just like my husband," said Mrs. Winnie, sadly. "You have no use at all for anything that's weak or unfortunate."

There was a pause. "And I suppose," she said finally, "you'll be turning into a business man also—with no time for anybody or anything. Have you begun yet?"

"Not yet," he answered. "I'm still looking round."

"I haven't the least idea about business," she confessed. "How does one begin at it?"

"I can't say I know that myself as yet," said Montague, laughing.

"Would you like to be a protege of my husband's?" she asked.

The proposition was rather sudden, but he answered, with a smile, "I should have no objections. What would he do with me?"

"I don't know that. But he can do whatever he wants down town. And he'd show you how to make a lot of money if I asked him to." Then Mrs. Winnie added, quickly, "I mean it—he could do it, really."

"I haven't the least doubt of it," responded Montague.

"And what's more," she went on, "you don't want to be shy about taking advantage of the opportunities that come to you. You'll find you won't get along in New York unless you go right in and grab what you can. People will be quick enough to take advantage of you."

"They have all been very kind to me so far," said he. "But when I get ready for business, I'll harden my heart."

Mrs. Winnie sat lost in meditation. "I think business is dreadful," she said. "So much hard work and worry! Why can't men learn to get along without it?"

"There are bills that have to be paid," Montague replied.

"It's our dreadfully extravagant way of life," exclaimed the other. "Sometimes I wish I had never had any money in my life."

"You would soon tire of it," said he. "You would miss this house."

"I should not miss it a bit," said Mrs. Winnie, promptly. "That is really the truth—I don't care for this sort of thing at all. I'd like to live simply, and without so many cares and responsibilities. And some day I'm going to do it, too—I really am. I'm going to get myself a little farm, away off somewhere in the country. And I'm going there to live and raise chickens and vegetables, and have my own flower-gardens, that I can take care of myself. It will all be plain and simple—" and then Mrs. Winnie stopped short, exclaiming, "You are laughing at me!"

"Not at all!" said Montague. "But I couldn't help thinking about the newspaper reporters—"

"There you are!" said she. "One can never have a beautiful dream, or try to do anything sensible—because of the newspaper reporters!"

If Montague had been meeting Mrs. Winnie Duval for the first time, he would have been impressed by her yearnings for the simple life; he would have thought it an important sign of the times. But alas, he knew by this time that his charming hostess had more flummery about her than anybody else he had encountered— and all of her own devising! Mrs. Winnie smoked her own private brand of cigarettes, and when she offered them to you, there were the arms of the old ducal house of Montmorenci on the wrappers! And when you got a letter from Mrs. Winnie, you observed a three-cent stamp upon the envelope—for lavender was her colour, and two-cent stamps were an atrocious red! So one might feel certain that it Mrs. Winnie ever went in for chicken-raising, the chickens would be especially imported from China or Patagonia, and the chicken-coops would be precise replicas of those in the old Chateau de Montmorenci which she had visited in her automobile.

But Mrs. Winnie was beautiful, and quite entertaining to talk to, and so he was respectfully sympathetic while she told him about her pastoral intentions. And then she told him about Mrs. Caroline Smythe, who had called a meeting of her friends at one of the big hotels, and organized a society and founded the "Bide-a-

Wee Home" for destitute cats. After that she switched off into psychic research—somebody had taken her to a seance, where grave college professors and ladies in spectacles sat round and waited for ghosts to materialize. It was Mrs. Winnie's first experience at this, and she was as excited as a child who has just found the key to the jam-closet. "I hardly knew whether to laugh or to be afraid," she said. "What would you think?"

"You may have the pleasure of giving me my first impressions of it," said Montague, with a laugh.

"Well," said she, "they had table-tipping—and it was the most uncanny thing to see the table go jumping about the room! And then there were raps—and one can't imagine how strange it was to see people who really believed they were getting messages from ghosts. It positively made my flesh creep. And then this woman—Madame Somebody-or-other—went into a trance—ugh! Afterward I talked with one of the men, and he told me about how his father had appeared to him in the night and told him he had just been drowned at sea. Have you ever heard of such a thing?"

"We have such a tradition in our family," said he.

"Every family seems to have," said Mrs. Winnie. "But, dear me, it made me so uncomfortable—I lay awake all night expecting to see my own father. He had the asthma, you know; and I kept fancying I heard him breathing."

They had risen and were strolling into the conservatory; and she glanced at the man in armour. "I got to fancying that his ghost might come to see me," she said. "I don't think I shall attend any more seances. My husband was told that I promised them some money, and he was furious—he's afraid it'll get into the papers." And Montague shook with inward laughter, picturing what a time the aristocratic and stately old banker must have, trying to keep his wife out of the papers!

Mrs. Winnie turned on the lights in the fountain, and sat by the edge, gazing at her fish. Montague was half expecting her to inquire whether he thought that they had ghosts; but she spared him this, going off on another line.

"I asked Dr. Parry about it," she said. "Have you met him?"

Dr. Parry was the rector of St. Cecilia's, the fashionable Fifth Avenue church which most of Montague's acquaintances attended. "I haven't been in the city over Sunday yet," he answered. "But Alice has met him."

"You must go with me some time," said she. "But about the ghosts—"

"What did he say?"

"He seemed to be shy of them," laughed Mrs. Winnie. "He said it had a tendency to lead one into dangerous fields. But oh! I forgot—I asked my swami also, and it didn't startle him. They are used to ghosts; they believe that souls keep coming back to earth, you know. I think if it was his ghost, I wouldn't mind seeing it—for he has such beautiful eyes. He gave me a book of Hindu legends—and there was such a sweet story about a young princess who loved in vain, and died of grief; and her soul went into a tigress; and she came in the night-time where her lover lay sleeping by the firelight, and she carried him off into the ghost-world. It was a most creepy thing—I sat out here and read it, and I could imagine the terrible tigress lurking in the shadows, with its stripes shining in the firelight, and its green eyes gleaming. You know that poem—we used to read it in school—'Tiger, tiger, burning bright!'"

It was not very easy for Montague to imagine a tigress in Mrs. Winnie's conservatory; unless, indeed, one were willing to take the proposition in a metaphorical sense. There are wild creatures which sleep in the heart of man, and which growl now and then, and stir their tawny limbs, and cause one to start and turn cold. Mrs. Winnie wore a dress of filmy softness, trimmed with red flowers which paled beside her own intenser colouring. She had a perfume of her own, with a strange exotic fragrance which touched the chorus of memory as only an odour can. She leaned towards him, speaking eagerly, with her soft white arms lying upon the basin's rim. So much loveliness could not be gazed at without pain; and a faint trembling passed through Montague, like a breeze across a pool. Perhaps it touched Mrs. Winnie also, for she fell suddenly silent, and her gaze wandered off into the darkness. For a minute or two there was stillness, save for the pulse of the fountain, and the heaving of her bosom keeping time with it.

And then in the morning Oliver inquired, "Where were you, last night?" And when his brother answered, "At Mrs. Winnie's," he smiled and said, "Oh!" Then he added, gravely, "Cultivate Mrs. Winnie—you can't do better at present."

CHAPTER XI

Montague accepted his friend's invitation to share her pew at St. Cecilia's, and next Sunday morning he and Alice went, and found Mrs. Winnie with her cousin. Poor Charlie had evidently been scrubbed and shined, both physically and morally, and got ready to appeal for "one more chance." While he shook hands with Alice, he was gazing at her with dumb and pleading eyes; he seemed to be profoundly grateful that she did not refuse to enter the pew with him.

A most interesting place was St. Cecilia's. Church-going was another of the customs of men and women which Society had taken up, like the Opera, and made into a state function. Here was a magnificent temple, with carved marble and rare woods, and jewels gleaming decorously in a dim religious light. At the door of this edifice would halt the carriages of Society, and its wives and daughters would alight, rustling with new silk petticoats and starched and perfumed linen, each one a picture, exquisitely gowned and bonneted and gloved, and carrying a demure little prayer-book. Behind them followed the patient men, all in new frock-coats and shiny silk hats; the men of Society were always newly washed and shaved, newly groomed and gloved, but now they seemed to be more so—they were full of the atmosphere of Sunday. Alas for those unregenerate ones, the infidels and the heathen who scoff in outer darkness, and know not the delicious feeling of Sunday—the joy of being washed and starched and perfumed, and made to be clean and comfortable and good, after all the really dreadful wickedness of six days of fashionable life!—And afterward the parade upon the Avenue, with the congregations of several score additional churches, and such a show of stylish costumes that half the city came to see!

Amid this exquisite assemblage at St. Cecilia's, the revolutionary doctrines of the Christian religion produced neither perplexity nor alarm. The chance investigator might have listened in dismay to solemn pronouncements of everlasting damnation, to statements about rich men and the eyes of needles, and the lilies of the field which did not spin. But the congregation of St. Cecilia's understood that these things were to be taken in a quixotic sense; sharing the view of the French marquis that the Almighty would think twice before damning a gentleman like him.

One had heard these phrases ever since childhood, and one accepted them as a matter of course. After all, these doctrines had come from the lips of a divine being, whom it would be presumptuous in a mere mortal to attempt to imitate. Such points one could but leave to those whose business it was to interpret them—the doctors and dignitaries of the church; and when one met them, one's heart was set at rest—for they were not iconoclasts and alarmists, but gentlemen of culture and tact. The bishop who presided in this metropolitan district was a stately personage, who moved in the best Society and belonged to the most exclusive clubs.

The pews in St. Cecilia's were rented, and they were always in great demand; it was one of the customs of those who hung upon the fringe of Society to come every Sunday, and bow and smile, and hope against hope for some chance opening. The stranger who came was dependent upon hospitality; but there were soft-footed and tactful ushers, who would find one a seat, if one were a presentable person. The contingency of an unpresentable person seldom arose, for the proletariat did not swarm at the gates of St. Cecilia's. Out of its liberal income the church maintained a "mission" upon the East Side, where young curates wrestled with the natural depravity of the lower classes—meantime cultivating a soul-stirring tone, and waiting until they should be promoted to a real church. Society was becoming deferential to its religious guides, and would have been quite shocked at the idea that it exerted any pressure upon them; but the young curates were painfully aware of a process of unnatural selection, whereby those whose manner and cut of coat were not pleasing were left a long time in the slums.—On one occasion there had been an amusing blunder; a beautiful new church was built at Newport, and an eloquent young minister was installed, and all Society attended the opening service—and sat and listened in consternation to an arraignment of its own follies and vices! The next Sunday, needless to say, Society was not present; and within half a year the church was stranded, and had to be dismantled and sold!

They had elaborate music at St. Cecilia's, so beautiful that Alice felt uncomfortable, and thought that it was perilously "high." At this Mrs. Winnie laughed, offering to take her to an afternoon service around the corner, where they had a full orchestra, and a harp, and opera music, and incense and genuflexions and confessionals. There were people, it seemed, who like to thrill themselves by dallying with the wickedness of "Romanism"; somewhat as a small boy tries to see how near he can walk to the edge of a cliff. The "father" at this church had a jewelled robe with a train so many yards long, and which had cost some incredible number of thousands of dollars; and every now and then he marched in a stately procession through the aisles, so that all the spectators might have a good look at it. There was a fierce controversy about these things in the church, and libraries of pamphlets were written, and intrigues and social wars were fought over them.

But Montague and Alice did not attend this service—they had promised themselves the very plebeian diversion of a ride in the subway; for so far they had not seen this feature of the city. People who lived in Society saw Madison and Fifth Avenues, where their homes were, with the churches and hotels scattered along them; and the shopping district just below, and the theatre district at one side, and the park to the north. Unless one went automobiling, that was all of the city one need ever see. When visitors asked about the Aquarium, and the Stock Exchange, and the Museum of Art, and Tammany Hall, and Ellis Island, where the immigrants came, the old New Yorkers would look perplexed, and say: "Dear me, do you really want to see those tilings? Why, I have been here all my life, and have never seen them!"

For the hordes of sightseers there had been provided a special contrivance, a huge automobile omnibus which seated thirty or forty people, and went from the Battery to Harlem with a young man shouting through a megaphone a description of the sights. The irreverent had nicknamed this the "yap-wagon"; and declared that the company maintained a fake "opium-joint" in Chinatown, and a fake "dive" in the Bowery, and hired tough-looking individuals to sit and be stared at by credulous excursionists from Oklahoma and Kalamazoo. Of course it would never have done for people who had just been passed into Society to climb upon a "yap-wagon"; but they were permitted to get into the subway, and were whirled with a deafening clatter through a long tunnel of steel and stone. And then they got out and climbed a steep hill like any common mortals, and stood and gazed at Grant's tomb: a huge white marble edifice upon a point overlooking the Hudson. Architecturally it was not a beautiful structure—but one was consoled by reflecting that the hero himself would not have cared about that. It might have been described as a soap-box with a cheese-box on top of it; and these homely and familiar articles were perhaps not altogether out of keeping with the character of the humblest great man who ever lived.

The view up the river was magnificent, quite the finest which the city had to offer; but it was ruined by a hideous gas-tank, placed squarely in the middle of it. And this, again, was not inappropriate—it was typical of all the ways of the city. It was a city which had grown up by accident, with nobody to care about it or to help it; it was huge and ungainly, crude, uncomfortable, and grotesque. There was nowhere in it a beautiful sight upon which a man could rest his eyes, without having them tortured by something ugly near by. At the foot of the slope of the River Drive ran a hideous freight-railroad; and across the river the beautiful Palisades were being blown to pieces to make paving stone—and meantime were covered with advertisements of land-companies. And if there was a beautiful building, there, was sure to be a tobacco advertisement beside it; if there was a beautiful avenue, there were trucks and overworked horses toiling in the harness; if there was a beautiful park, it was filled with wretched, outcast men. Nowhere was any order or system—everything was struggling for itself, and jarring and clashing with everything else; and this broke the spell of power which the Titan city would otherwise have produced. It seemed like a monstrous heap of wasted energies; a mountain in perpetual labour, and producing an endless series of abortions. The men and women in it were wearing themselves out with toil; but there was a spell laid upon them, so that, struggle as they might, they accomplished nothing.

Coming out of the church, Montague had met Judge Ellis; and the Judge had said, "I shall soon have something to talk over with you." So Montague gave him his address, and a day or two later came an invitation to lunch with him at his club.

The Judge's club took up a Fifth Avenue block, and was stately and imposing. It had been formed in the stress of the Civil War days; lean and hungry heroes had come home from battle and gone into business, and those who had succeeded had settled down here to rest. To see them now, dozing in huge leather-cushioned arm-chairs, you would have had a hard time to guess that they had ever been lean and hungry heroes. They were diplomats and statesmen, bishops and lawyers, great merchants and financiers—the men who had made the city's ruling-class for a century. Everything here was decorous and grave, and the waiters stole about with noiseless feet.

Montague talked with the Judge about New York and what he had seen of it, and the people he had met; and about his father, and the war; and about the recent election and the business outlook. And meantime they ordered luncheon; and when they had got to the cigars, the Judge coughed and said, "And now I have a matter of business to talk over with you."

Montague settled himself to listen. "I have a friend," the Judge explained—"a very good friend, who has asked me to find him a lawyer to undertake an important case. I talked the matter over with General Prentice, and he agreed with me that it would be a good idea to lay the matter before you."

"I am very much obliged to you," said Montague.

"The matter is a delicate one," continued the other. "It has to do with life insurance. Are you familiar with the insurance business?"

"Not at all."

"I had supposed not," said the Judge. "There are some conditions which are not generally known about, but which I may say, to put it mildly, are not altogether satisfactory. My friend is a large policy-holder in several companies, and he is not satisfied with the management of them. The delicacy of the situation, so far as I am concerned, is that the company with which he has the most fault to find is one in which I myself am a director. You understand?"

"Perfectly," said Montague. "What company is it?"

"The Fidelity," replied the other—and his companion thought in a flash of Freddie Vandam, whom he had met at Castle Havens! For the Fidelity was Freddie's company.

"The first thing that I have to ask you," continued the Judge, "is that, whether you care to take the case or not, you will consider my own intervention in the matter absolutely entre nous. My position is simply this: I have protested at the meetings of the directors of the company against what I consider an unwise policy—and my protests have been ignored. And when my friend asked me for advice, I gave it to him; but at the same time I am not in a position to be publicly quoted in connexion with the matter. You follow me?"

"Perfectly," said the other. "I will agree to what you ask."

"Very good. Now then, the condition is, in brief, this: the companies are accumulating an enormous surplus, which, under the law, belongs to the policy-holders; but the administrations of the various companies are withholding these dividends, for the sake of the banking-power which these accumulated funds afford to them and their associates. This is, as I hold, a very manifest injustice, and a most dangerous condition of affairs."

"I should say so!" responded Montague. He was amazed at such a statement, coming from such a source. "How could this continue?" he asked.

"It has continued for a long time," the Judge answered.

"But why is it not known?"

"It is perfectly well known to every one in the insurance business," was the answer. "The matter has never been taken up or published, simply because the interests involved have such enormous and widely extended power that no one has ever dared to attack them."

Montague sat forward, with his eyes riveted upon the Judge. "Go on," he said.

"The situation is simply this," said the other. "My friend, Mr. Hasbrook, wishes to bring a suit against the Fidelity Company to compel it to pay to him his proper share of its surplus. He wishes the suit pressed, and followed to the court of last resort."

"And do you mean to tell me," asked Montague, "that you would have any difficulty to find a lawyer in New York to undertake such a case?"

"No," said the other, "not exactly that. There are lawyers in New York who would undertake anything. But to find a lawyer of standing who would take it, and withstand all the pressure that would be brought to bear upon him—that might take some time."

"You astonish me, Judge."

"Financial interests in this city are pretty closely tied together, Mr. Montague. Of course there are law firms which are identified with interests opposed to those who control the company. It would be very easy to get them to take the case, but you can see that in that event my friend would be accused of bringing the suit in their interest; whereas he wishes it to appear, as it really is, a suit of an independent person, seeking the rights of the vast body of the policy-holders. For that reason, he wished to find a lawyer who was identified with no interest of any sort, and who was free to give his undivided attention to the issue. So I thought of you."

"I will take the case," said Montague instantly.

"It is my duty to warn you," said the Judge, gravely, "that you will be taking a very serious step. You must be prepared to face powerful, and, I am afraid, unscrupulous enemies. You may find that you have made it impossible for other and very desirable clients to deal with you. You may find your business interests, if you have any, embarrassed—your credit impaired, and so on. You must be prepared to have your character assailed, and your motives impugned in the public press. You may find that social pressure will be brought to bear on you. So it is a step from which most young men who have their careers to make would shrink."

Montague's face had turned a shade paler as he listened. "I am assuming," he said, "that the facts are as you have stated them to me—that an unjust condition exists."

"You may assume that."

"Very well." And Montague clenched his hand, and put it down upon the table. "I will take the case," he said.

For a few moments they sat in silence.

"I will arrange," said the Judge, at last, "for you and Mr. Hasbrook to meet. I must explain to you, as a matter of fairness, that he is a rich man, and will be able to pay you for your services. He is asking a great deal of you, and he should expect to pay for it."

Montague sat in thought. "I have not really had time to get my bearings in New York," he said at last. "I think I had best leave it to you to say what I should charge him."

"If I were in your position," the Judge answered, "I think that I should ask a retaining-fee of fifty thousand dollars. I believe he will expect to pay at least that."

Montague could scarcely repress a start. Fifty thousand dollars! The words made his head whirl round. But then, all of a sudden, he recalled his half-jesting resolve to play the game of business sternly. So he nodded his head gravely, and said, "Very well; I am much obliged to you."

After a pause, he added, "I hope that I may prove able to handle the case to your friend's satisfaction."

"Your ability remains for you to prove," said the Judge. "I have only been in position to assure him of your character."

"He must understand, of course," said Montague, "that I am a stranger, and that it will take me a while to study the situation."

"Of course he knows that. But you will find that Mr. Hasbrook knows a good deal about the law himself. And he has already had a lot of work done. You must understand that it is very easy to get legal advice about such a matter—what is sought is some one to take the conduct of the case."

"I see," said Montague; and the Judge added, with a smile, "Some one to get up on horseback, and draw the fire of the enemy!"

And then the great man was, as usual, reminded of a story; and then of more stories; until at last they rose from the table, and shook hands upon their bargain, and parted.

Fifty thousand dollars! Fifty thousand dollars! It was all Montague could do to keep from exclaiming it aloud on the street. He could hardly believe that it was a reality—if it had been a less-known person than Judge Ellis, he would have suspected that some one must be playing a joke upon him. Fifty thousand dollars was more than many a lawyer made at home in a lifetime; and simply as a retaining-fee in one case! The problem of a living had weighed on his soul ever since the first day in the city, and now suddenly it was solved; all in a few minutes, the way had been swept clear before him. He walked home as if upon air.

And then there was the excitement of telling the family about it. He had an idea that his brother might be alarmed if he were told about the seriousness of the case; and so he simply said that the Judge had brought him a rich client, and that it was an insurance case. Oliver, who knew and cared nothing about law, asked no questions, and contented himself with saying, "I told you how easy it was to make money in New York, if only you knew the right people!" As for Alice, she had known all along that her cousin was a great man, and that clients would come to him as soon as he hung out his sign.

His sign was not out yet, by the way; that was the next thing to be attended to. He must get himself an office at once, and some books, and begin to read up insurance law; and so, bright and early the next morning, he took the subway down town.

And here, for the first time, Montague saw the real New York. All the rest was mere shadow—the rest was where men slept and played, but there was where they fought out the battle of their lives. Here the fierce intensity of it smote him in the face—he saw the cruel waste and ruin of it, the wreckage of the blind, haphazard strife.

It was a city caught in a trap. It was pent in at one end of a narrow little island. It had been no one's business to foresee that it must some day outgrow this space; now men were digging a score of tunnels to set it free, but they had not begun these until the pressure had become unendurable, and now it had reached its climax. In the financial district, land had been sold for as much as four dollars a square inch. Huge blocks of buildings shot up to the sky in a few months—fifteen, twenty, twenty-five stories of them, and with half a dozen stories hewn out of the solid rock beneath; there was to be one building of forty-two stories, six hundred and fifty feet in height. And between them were narrow chasms of streets, where the hurrying crowds overflowed the sidewalks. Yet other streets were filled with trucks and heavy vehicles, with electric cars creeping slowly along, and little swirls and eddies of people darting across here and there.

These huge buildings were like beehives, swarming with life and activity, with scores of elevators shooting through them at bewildering speed. Everywhere was the atmosphere of rush; the spirit of it seized hold of one, and he began to hurry, even though he had no place to go. The man who walked slowly and looked about him was in the way—he was jostled here and there, and people eyed him with suspicion and annoyance.

Elsewhere on the island men did the work of the city; here they did the work of the world. Each room in these endless mazes of buildings was a cell in a mighty brain; the telephone wires were nerves, and by the whole huge organism the thinking and willing of a continent were done. It was a noisy place to the physical ear; but to the ear of the mind it roared with the roaring of a thousand Niagaras. Here was the Stock Exchange, where the scales of trade were held before the eyes of the country. Here was the clearing-house, where hundreds of millions of dollars were exchanged every day. Here were the great banks, the reservoirs into which the streams of the country's wealth were poured. Here were the brains of the great railroad systems, of the telegraph and telephone systems, of mines and mills and factories. Here were the centres of the country's trade; in one place the shipping trade, in another the jewellery trade, the grocery trade, the leather trade. A little farther up town was the clothing district, where one might see the signs of more Hebrews than all Jerusalem had ever held; in yet other districts were the newspaper offices, and the centre of the magazine and book-publishing business of the whole country. One might climb to the top of one of the great "sky-scrapers," and gaze down upon a wilderness of houses, with roofs as innumerable as tree-tops, and people looking like tiny insects below. Or one might go out into the harbour late upon a winter afternoon, and see it as a city of a million lights, rising like an incantation from the sea. Round about it was an unbroken ring of docks, with ferry-boats and tugs darting everywhere, and vessels which had come from every port in the world, emptying their cargoes into the huge maw of the Metropolis.

And of all this, nothing had been planned! All lay just as it had fallen, and men bore the confusion and the waste as best they could. Here were huge steel vaults, in which lay many billions of dollars' worth of securities, the control of the finances of the country; and a block or two in one direction were warehouses and gin-mills, and in another direction cheap lodging-houses and sweating-dens. And at a certain hour all this huge machine would come to a halt, and its millions of human units would make a blind rush for their homes. Then at the entrances to bridges and ferries and trams, would be seen sights of madness and terror; throngs of men and women swept hither and thither, pushing and struggling, shouting, cursing—fighting, now and then, in sudden panic fear. All decency was forgotten here—people would be mashed into cars like football players in a heap, and guards and policemen would jam the gates tight—or like as not be swept away themselves in the pushing, grunting, writhing mass of human beings. Women would faint and be trampled; men would come out with clothing torn to shreds, and sometimes with broken arms or ribs. And thinking people would gaze at the sight and shudder, wondering—how long a city could hold together, when the masses of its population were thus forced back, day after day, habitually, upon the elemental brute within them.

In this vast business district Montague would have felt utterly lost and helpless, if it had not been for that fifty thousand dollars, and the sense of mastery which it gave him. He sought out General Prentice, and under his guidance selected his suite of rooms, and got his furniture and books in readiness. And a day or two later, by appointment, came Mr. Hasbrook.

He was a wiry, nervous little man, who did not impress one as much of a personality; but he had the insurance situation at his fingers' ends—his grievance had evidently wrought upon him. Certainly, if half of what he alleged were true, it was time that the courts took hold of the affair.

Montague spent the whole day in consultation, going over every aspect of the case, and laying out his course of procedure. And then, at the end, Mr. Hasbrook remarked that it would be necessary for them to make some financial arrangement. And the other set his teeth together, and took a tight grip upon himself, and said, "Considering the importance of the case, and all the circumstances, I think I should have a retainer of fifty thousand dollars."

And the little man never turned a hair! "That will be perfectly satisfactory," he said. "I will attend to it at once." And the other's heart gave a great leap.

And sure enough, the next morning's mail brought the money, in the shape of a cashier's cheque from one of the big banks. Montague deposited it to his own account, and felt that the city was his!

And so he flung himself into the work. He went to his office every day, and he shut himself up in his own rooms in the evening. Mrs. Winnie was in despair because he would not come and learn bridge, and Mrs. Vivie Patton sought him in vain for a week-end party. He could not exactly say that while the others slept he was toiling upward in the night, for the others did not sleep in the night; but he could say that while they were feasting and dancing, he was delving into insurance law. Oliver argued in vain to make him realize that he could not live for ever upon one client; and that it was as important for a lawyer to be a social light as to win his first big case. Montague was so absorbed that he even failed to be thrilled when one morning he opened an invitation envelope, and read the fateful legend: "Mrs. Devon requests the honour of your company"—telling him that he had "passed" on that critical examination morning, and that he was definitely and irrevocably in Society!

CHAPTER XII

Montague was now a capitalist, and therefore a keeper of the gates of opportunity. It seemed as though the seekers for admission must have had some occult way of finding it out; almost immediately they began to lay siege to him.

About a week after his cheque arrived, Major Thorne, whom he had met the first evening at the Loyal Legion, called him up and asked to see him; and he came to Montague's room that evening, and after chatting awhile about old times, proceeded to unfold a business proposition. It seemed that the Major had a grandson, a young mechanical engineer, who had been labouring for a couple of years at a very important invention, a device for loading coal upon steamships and weighing it automatically in the process. It was a very complicated problem, needless to say, but it had been solved successfully, and patents had been applied for, and a working model constructed. But it had proved unexpectedly difficult to interest the officials of the great steamship companies in the device. There was no doubt about the practicability of the machine, or the economies it would effect; but the officials raised trivial objections, and caused delays, and offered prices that were ridiculously inadequate. So the young inventor had conceived the idea of organizing a company to manufacture the machines, and rent them upon a royalty. "I didn't know whether you would have any money," said Major Thorne, "—but I thought you might be in touch with others who could be got to look into the matter. There is a fortune in it for those who take it up."

Montague was interested, and he looked over the plans and descriptions which his friend had brought, and said that he would see the working model, and talk the proposition over with others. And so the Major took his departure.

The first person Montague spoke to about it was Oliver, with whom he chanced to be lunching, at the latter's club. This was the "All Night" club, a meeting-place of fast young Society men and millionaire Bohemians, who made a practice of going to bed at daylight, and had taken for their motto the words of Tennyson—"For men may come and men may go, but I go on for ever." It was not a proper club for his brother to join, Oliver considered; Montague's "game" was the heavy respectable, and the person to put him up was General Prentice. But he was permitted to lunch there with his brother to chaperon him—and also Reggie Mann, who happened in, fresh from talking over the itinerary of the foreign prince with Mrs. Ridgley-Clieveden, and bringing a diverting account of how Mrs. R.-C. had had a fisticuffs with her maid.

Montague mentioned the invention casually, and with no idea that his brother would have an opinion one way or the other. But Oliver had quite a vigorous opinion: "Good God, Allan, you aren't going to let yourself be persuaded into a thing like that!"

"But what do you know about it?" asked the other. "It may be a tremendous thing."

"Of course!" cried Oliver. "But what can you tell about it? You'll be like a child in other people's hands, and they'll be certain to rob you. And why in the world do you want to take risks when you don't have to?"

"I have to put my money somewhere," said Montague.

"His first fee is burning a hole in his pocket!" put in Reggie Mann, with a chuckle. "Turn it over to me, Mr. Montague; and let me spend it in a gorgeous entertainment for Alice; and the prestige of it will bring you more cases than you can handle in a lifetime!"

"He had much better spend it all for soda water than buy a lot of coal chutes with it," said Oliver: "Wait awhile, and let me find you some place to put your money, and you'll see that you don't have to take any risks."

"I had no idea of taking it up until I'd made certain of it," replied the other. "And those whose judgment I took would, of course, go in also."

The younger man thought for a moment. "You are going to dine with Major Venable to-night, aren't you?" he asked; and when the other answered in the affirmative, he continued, "Very well, then, ask him. The Major's been a capitalist for forty years, and if you can get him to take it up, why, you'll know you're safe."

Major Venable had taken quite a fancy to Montague—perhaps the old gentleman liked to have somebody to gossip with, to whom all his anecdotes were new. He had seconded Montague's name at the "Millionaires'," where he lived, and had asked him there to make the acquaintance of some of the other members. Before Montague parted with his brother, he promised that he would talk the matter over with the Major.

The Millionaires' was the show club of the city, the one which the ineffably rich had set apart for themselves. It was up by the park, in a magnificent white marble palace which had cost a million dollars. Montague felt that he had never really known the Major until he saw him here. The Major was excellent at all times and places, but in this club he became an edition de luxe of himself. He made his headquarters here, keeping his suite of rooms all the year round; and the atmosphere and surroundings of the place seemed to be a part of him.

Montague thought that the Major's face grew redder every day, and the purple veins in it purpler; or was it that the old gentleman's shirt bosom gleamed more brightly in the glare of the lights? The Major met him in the stately entrance hall, fifty feet square and all of Numidian marble, with a ceiling of gold, and a great bronze stairway leading to the gallery above. He apologized for his velvet slippers and for his hobbling walk—he was getting his accursed gout again. But he limped around and introduced his friend to the other millionaires—and then told scandal about them behind their backs.

The Major was the very type of a blue-blooded old aristocrat; he was all noblesse oblige to those within the magic circle of his intimacy—but alas for those outside it! Montague had never heard anyone bully servants as the Major did. "Here you!" he would cry, when something went wrong at the table. "Don't you know any better than to bring me a dish like that? Go and send me somebody who knows how to set a table!" And, strange to say, the servants all acknowledged his perfect right to bully them, and flew with terrified alacrity to do his bidding. Montague noticed that the whole staff of the club leaped into activity whenever the Major appeared; and when he was seated at the table, he led off in this fashion— "Now I want two dry Martinis. And I want them at once—do you understand me? Don't stop to get me any butter plates or finger-bowls—I want two cock-tails, just as quick as you can carry them!"

Dinner was an important event to Major Venable—the most important in life. The younger man humbly declined to make any suggestions, and sat and watched while his friend did all the ordering. They had some very small oysters, and an onion soup, and a grouse and asparagus, with some wine from the Major's own private store, and then a romaine salad. Concerning each one of these courses, the Major gave special injunctions, and throughout his conversation he scattered comments upon them: "This is good thick soup—lots of nourishment in onion soup. Have the rest of this?—I think the Burgundy is too cold. Sixty-five is as cold as Burgundy ought ever to be. I don't mind sherry as low as sixty.—They always cook a bird too much—Robbie Walling's chef is the only person I know who never makes a mistake with game."

All this, of course, was between comments upon the assembled millionaires. There was Hawkins, the corporation lawyer; a shrewd fellow, cold as a corpse. He was named for an ambassadorship—a very efficient man. Used to be old Wyman's confidential adviser and buy aldermen for him.—And the man at table with him was Harrison, publisher of the Star; administration newspaper, sound and conservative. Harrison was training for a cabinet position. He was a nice little man, and would make a fine splurge in Washington.—And that tall man coming in was Clarke, the steel magnate; and over there was Adams, a big lawyer also— prominent reformer—civic righteousness and all that sort of stuff. Represented the Oil Trust secretly, and went down to Trenton to argue against some reform measure, and took along fifty thousand dollars in bills in his valise. "A friend of mine got wind of what he was doing, and taxed him with it," said the Major, and laughed gleefully over the great lawyer's reply—"How did I know but I might have to pay for my own lunch?"—And the fat man with him—that was Jimmie Featherstone, the chap who had inherited a big estate. "Poor Jimmie's going all to pieces," the Major declared. "Goes down town to board meetings now and then— they tell a hair-raising story about him and old Dan Waterman. He had got up and started a long argument, when Waterman broke in, 'But at the earlier meeting you argued directly to the contrary, Mr. Featherstone!' 'Did I?' said Jimmie, looking bewildered. 'I wonder why I did that?' 'Well, Mr. Featherstone, since you ask me, I'll tell you,' said old Dan—he's savage as a wild boar, you know, and won't be delayed at meetings. 'The reason is that the last time you were drunker than you are now. If you would adopt a uniform standard of intoxication for the directors' meetings of this road, it would expedite matters considerably.'"

They had got as far as the romaine salad. The waiter came with a bowl of dressing—and at the sight of it, the old gentleman forgot Jimmie Featherstone. "Why are you bringing me that stuff?" he cried. "I don't want that! Take it away and get me some vinegar and oil."

The waiter fled in dismay, while the Major went on growling under his breath. Then from behind him came a voice: "What's the matter with you this evening, Venable? You're peevish!"

The Major looked up. "Hello, you old cormorant," said he. "How do you do these days?"

The old cormorant replied that he did very well. He was a pudgy little man, with a pursed-up, wrinkled face. "My friend Mr. Montague—Mr. Symmes," said the Major.

"I am very pleased to meet you, Mr. Montague," said Mr. Symmes, peering over his spectacles.

"And what are you doing with yourself these days?" asked the Major.

The other smiled genially. "Nothing much," said he. "Seducing my friends' wives, as usual."

"And who's the latest?"

"Read the newspapers, and you'll find out," laughed Symmes. "I'm told I'm being shadowed."

He passed on down the room, chuckling to himself; and the Major said, "That's Maltby Symmes. Have you heard of him?"

"No," said Montague.

"He gets into the papers a good deal. He was up in supplementary proceedings the other day—couldn't pay his liquor bill."

"A member of the Millionaires'?" laughed Montague.

"Yes, the papers made quite a joke out of it," said the other. "But you see he's run through a couple of fortunes; the last was his mother's—eleven millions, I believe. He's been a pretty lively old boy in his time."

The vinegar and oil had now arrived, and the Major set to work to dress the salad. This was quite a ceremony, and Montague took it with amused interest. The Major first gathered all the necessary articles together, and looked them all over and grumbled at them. Then he mixed the vinegar and the pepper and salt, a tablespoonful at a time, and poured it over the salad. Then very slowly and carefully the oil had to be poured on, the salad being poked and turned about so that it would be all absorbed. Perhaps it was because he was so busy narrating the escapades of Maltby Symmes that the old gentleman kneaded it about so long; all the time fussing over it like a hen-partridge with her chicks, and interrupting himself every sentence or two: "It was Lenore, the opera star, and he gave her about two hundred thousand dollars' worth of railroad shares. (Really, you know, romaine ought not to be served in a bowl at all, but in a square, flat dish, so that one could keep the ends quite dry.) And when they quarrelled, she found the old scamp had fooled her—the shares had never been transferred. (One is not supposed to use a fork at all, you know.) But she sued him, and he settled with her for about half the value. (If this dressing were done properly, there ought not to be any oil in the bottom of the dish at all.)"

This last remark meant that the process had reached its climax—that the long, crisp leaves were receiving their final affectionate overturnings. While the waiter stood at respectful attention, two or three pieces at a time were laid carefully upon the little silver plate intended for Montague. "And now," said the triumphant host, "try it! If it's good, it ought to be neither sweet nor bitter, but just right."—And he watched anxiously while Montague tasted it, saying, "If it's the least bit bitter, say so; and we'll send it out. I've told them about it often enough before."

But it was not bitter, and so the Major proceeded to help himself, after which the waiter whisked the bowl away. "I'm told that salad is the one vegetable we have from the Romans," said the old boy, as he munched at the crisp green leaves. "It's mentioned by Horace, you know.—As I was saying, all this was in Symmes's early days. But since his son's been grown up, he's married another chorus-girl."

After the salad the Major had another cocktail. In the beginning Montague had noticed that his hands shook and his eyes were watery; but now, after these copious libations, he was vigorous, and, if possible, more full of anecdotes than ever. Montague thought that it would be a good time to broach his inquiry, and so when the coffee had been served, he asked, "Have you any objections to talking business after dinner?"

"Not with you," said the Major. "Why? What is it?"

And then Montague told him about his friend's proposition, and described the invention. The other listened attentively to the end; and then, after a pause, Montague asked him, "What do you think of it?"

"The invention's no good," said the Major, promptly.

"How do you know?" asked the other.

"Because, if it had been, the companies would have taken it long ago, without paying him a cent."

"But he has it patented," said Montague.

"Patented hell!" replied the other. "What's a patent to lawyers of concerns of that size? They'd have taken it and had it in use from Maine to Texas; and when he sued, they'd have tied the case up in so many technicalities and quibbles that he couldn't have got to the end of it in ten years—and he'd have been ruined ten times over in the process."

"Is that really done?" asked Montague.

"Done!" exclaimed the Major. "It's done so often you might say it's the only thing that's done.—The people are probably trying to take you in with a fake."

"That couldn't possibly be so," responded the other. "The man is a friend—"

"I've found it an excellent rule never to do business with friends," said the Major, grimly.

"But listen," said Montague; and he argued long enough to convince his companion that that could not be the true explanation. Then the Major sat for a minute or two and pondered; and suddenly he exclaimed, "I have it! I see why they won't touch it!"

"What is it?"

"It's the coal companies! They're giving the steamships short weight, and they don't want the coal weighed truly!"

"But there's no sense in that," said Montague. "It's the steamship companies that won't take the machine."

"Yes," said the Major; "naturally, their officers are sharing the graft." And he laughed heartily at Montague's look of perplexity.

"Do you know anything about the business?" Montague asked.

"Nothing whatever," said the Major. "I am like the German who shut himself up in his inner consciousness and deduced the shape of an elephant from first principles. I know the game of big business from A to Z, and I'm telling you that if the invention is good and the companies won't take it, that's the reason; and I'll lay you a wager that if you were to make an investigation, some such thing as that is what you'd find! Last winter I went South on a steamer, and when we got near port, I saw them dumping a ton or two of good food overboard; and I made inquiries, and learned that one of the officials of the company ran a farm, and furnished the stuff—and the orders were to get rid of so much every trip!"

Montague's jaw had fallen. "What could Major Thorne do against such a combination?" he asked.

"I don't know," said the Major, shrugging his shoulders. "It's a case to take to a lawyer—one who knows the ropes. Hawkins over there would know what to tell you. I should imagine the thing he'd advise would be to call a strike of the men who handle the coal, and tie up the companies and bring them to terms."

"You're joking now!" exclaimed the other.

"Not at all," said the Major, laughing again. "It's done all the time. There's a building trust in this city, and the way it put all its rivals out of business was by having strikes called on their jobs."

"But how could it do that?"

"Easiest thing in the world. A labour leader is a man with a great deal of power, and a very small salary to live on. And even if he won't sell out—there are other ways. I could introduce you to a man right in this room who had a big strike on at an inconvenient time, and he had the president of the union trapped in a hotel with a woman, and the poor fellow gave in and called off the strike.'"

"I should think the strikers might sometimes get out of hand," said Montague.

"Sometimes they do," smiled the other. "There is a regular procedure for that case. Then you hire detectives and start violence, and call out the militia and put the strike leaders into jail."

Montague could think of nothing to say to that. The programme seemed to be complete.

"You see," the Major continued, earnestly, "I'm advising you as a friend, and I'm taking the point of view of a man who has money in his pocket. I've had some there always, but I've had to work hard to keep it there. All my life I've been surrounded by people who wanted to do me good; and the way they wanted to do it was to exchange my real money for pieces of paper which they'd had printed with fancy scroll-work and eagles and flags. Of course, if you want to look at the thing from the other side, why, then the invention is most ingenious, and trade is booming just now, and this is a great country, and merit is all you need in it—and everything else is just as it ought to be. It makes all the difference in the world, you know, whether a man is buying a horse or selling him!"

Montague had observed with perplexity that such incendiary talk as this was one of the characteristics of people in these lofty altitudes. It was one of the liberties accorded to their station. Editors and bishops and statesmen and all the rest of their retainers had to believe in the respectabilities, even in the privacy of their clubs—the people's ears were getting terribly sharp these days! But among the real giants of business you might have thought yourself in a society of revolutionists; they would tear up the mountain tops and hurl them at each other. When one of these old war-horses once got started, he would tell tales of deviltry to appall the soul of the hardiest muck-rake man. It was always the other fellow, of course; but then, if you pinned your man down, and if he thought that he could trust you—he would acknowledge that he had sometimes fought the enemy with the enemy's own weapons!

But of course one must understand that all this radicalism was for conversational purposes only. The Major, for instance, never had the slightest idea of doing anything about all the evils of which he told; when it came to action, he proposed to do just what he had done all his life—to sit tight on his own little pile. And the Millionaires' was an excellent place to learn to do it!

"See that old money-bags over there in the corner," said the Major. "He's a man you want to fix in your mind—old Henry S. Grimes. Have you heard of him?"

"Vaguely," said the other.

"He's Laura Hegan's uncle. She'll have his money also some day—but Lord, how he does hold on to it meantime! It's quite tragic, if you come to know him— he's frightened at his own shadow. He goes in for slum tenements, and I guess he evicts more people in a month than you could crowd into this building!"

Montague looked at the solitary figure at the table, a man with a wizened-up little face like a weasel's, and a big napkin tied around his neck. "That's so as to save his shirt-front for to-morrow," the Major explained. "He's really only about sixty, but you'd think he was eighty. Three times every day he sits here and eats a bowl of graham crackers and milk, and then goes out and sits rigid in an armchair for an hour. That's the regimen his doctors have put him on—angels and ministers of grace defend us!"

The old gentleman paused, and a chuckle shook his scarlet jowls. "Only think!" he said—"they tried to do that to me! But no, sir—when Bob Venable has to eat graham crackers and milk, he'll put in arsenic instead of sugar! That's the way with many a one of these rich fellows, though—you picture him living in Capuan luxury, when, as a matter of fact, he's a man with a torpid liver and a weak stomach, who is put to bed at ten o'clock with a hot-water bag and a flannel night-cap!"

The two had got up and were strolling toward the smoking-room; when suddenly at one side a door opened, and a group of men came out. At the head of them was an extraordinary figure, a big powerful body with a grim face. "Hello!" said the Major. "All the big bugs are here to-night. There must be a governors' meeting."

"Who is that?" asked his companion; and he answered, "That? Why, that's Dan Waterman."

Dan Waterman! Montague stared harder than ever, and now he identified the face with the pictures he had seen. Waterman, the Colossus of finance, the Croesus of copper and gold! How many trusts had Waterman organized! And how many puns had been made upon that name of his!

"Who are the other men?" Montague asked.

"Oh, they're just little millionaires," was the reply.

The "little millionaires" were following as a kind of body-guard; one of them, who was short and pudgy, was half running, to keep up with Waterman's heavy stride. When they came to the coat-room, they crowded the attendants away, and one helped the great man on with his coat, and another held his hat, and another his stick, and two others tried to talk to him. And Waterman stolidly buttoned his coat, and then seized his hat and stick, and without a word to anyone, bolted through the door.

It was one of the funniest sights that Montague had ever seen in his life, and he laughed all the way into the smoking-room. And, when Major Venable had settled himself in a big chair and bitten off the end of a cigar and lighted it, what flood-gates of reminiscence were opened!

For Dan Waterman was one of the Major's own generation, and he knew all his life and his habits. Just as Montague had seen him there, so he had been always; swift, imperious, terrible, trampling over all opposition; the most powerful men in the city quailed before the glare of his eyes. In the old days Wall Street had reeled in the shock of the conflicts between him and his most powerful rival.

And the Major went on to tell about Waterman's rival, and his life. He had been the city's traction-king, old Wyman had been made by him. He was the prince among political financiers; he had ruled the Democratic party in state and nation. He would give a quarter of a million at a time to the boss of Tammany Hall, and spend a million in a single campaign; on "dough-day," when the district leaders came to get the election funds, there would be a table forty feet long completely covered with hundred-dollar bills. He would have been the richest man in America, save that he spent his money as fast as he got it. He had had the most famous racing-stable in America; and a house on Fifth Avenue that was said to be the finest Italian palace in the world. Over three millions had been spent in decorating it; all the ceilings had been brought intact from palaces abroad, which he had bought and demolished! The Major told a story to show how such a man lost all sense of the value of money; he had once been sitting at lunch with him, when the editor of one of his newspapers had come in and remarked, "I told you we would need eight thousand dollars, and the check you send is for ten." "I know it," was the smiling answer—"but somehow I thought eight seemed harder to write than ten!"

"Old Waterman's quite a spender, too, when it comes to that," the Major went on. "He told me once that it cost him five thousand dollars a day for his ordinary expenses. And that doesn't include a million-dollar yacht, nor even the expenses of it.

"And think of another man I know of who spent a million dollars for a granite pier, so that he could land and see his mistress!—It's a fact, as sure as God made me! She was a well-known society woman, but she was poor, and he didn't dare to make her rich for fear of the scandal. So she had to live in a miserable fifty-thousand-dollar villa; and when other people's children would sneer at her children because they lived in a fifty-thousand-dollar villa, the answer would be, 'But you haven't got any pier!' And if you don't believe that—"

But here suddenly the Major turned, and observed a boy who had brought him some cigars, and who was now standing near by, pretending to straighten out some newspapers upon the table. "Here, sir!" cried the Major, "what do you mean—listening to what I'm saying! Out of the room with you now, you rascal!"

CHAPTER XIII

Another week-end came, and with it an invitation from the Lester Todds to visit them at their country place in New Jersey. Montague was buried in his books, but his brother routed him out with strenuous protests. His case be damned—was he going to ruin his career for one case? At all hazards, he must meet people—"people who counted." And the Todds were such, a big money crowd, and a power in the insurance world; if Montague were going to be an insurance lawyer, he could not possibly decline their invitation. Freddie Vandam would be a guest—and Montague smiled at the tidings that Betty Wyman would be there also. He had observed that his brother's week-end visits always happened at places where Betty was, and where Betty's granddaddy was not.

So Montague's man packed his grips, and Alice's maid her trunks; and they rode with a private-car party to a remote Jersey suburb, and were whirled in an auto up a broad shell road to a palace upon the top of a mountain. Here lived the haughty Lester Todds, and scattered about on the neighbouring hills, a set of the ultra-wealthy who had withdrawn to this seclusion. They were exceedingly "classy"; they affected to regard all the Society of the city with scorn, and had their own all-the-year-round diversions—an open-air horse show in summer, and in the fall fox-hunting in fancy uniforms.

The Lester Todds themselves were ardent pursuers of all varieties of game, and in various clubs and private preserves they followed the seasons, from Florida and North Carolina to Ontario, with occasional side trips to Norway, and New Brunswick, and British Columbia. Here at home they had a whole mountain of virgin forest, carefully preserved; and in the Renaissance palace at the summit—which they carelessly referred to as a "lodge"—you would find such articles de vertu as a ten-thousand-dollar table with a set of two-thousand-dollar chairs, and quite ordinary-looking rugs at ten and twenty thousand dollars each.—All these prices you might ascertain without any difficulty at all, because there were many newspaper articles describing the house to be read in an album in the hall. On Saturday afternoons Mrs. Todd welcomed the neighbours in a pastel grey reception-gown, the front of which contained a peacock embroidered in silk, with jewels in every feather, and a diamond solitaire for an eye; and in the evening there was a dance, and she appeared in a gown with several hundred diamonds sewn upon it, and received her guests upon a rug set with jewels to match.

All together, Montague judged this the "fastest" set he had yet encountered; they ate more and drank more and intrigued more openly. He had been slowly acquiring the special lingo of Society, but these people had so much more slang that he felt all lost again. A young lady who was gossiping to him about those present remarked that a certain youth was a "spasm"; and then, seeing the look of perplexity upon his face, she laughed, "I don't believe you know what I mean!" Montague replied that he had ventured to infer that she did not like him.

And then there was Mrs. Harper, who came from Chicago by way of London. Ten years ago Mrs. Harper had overwhelmed New York with the millions brought from her great department-store; and had then moved on, sighing for new worlds to conquer. When she had left Chicago, her grammar had been unexceptionable; but since she had been in England, she said "you ain't" and dropped all her g's; and when Montague brought down a bird at long range, she exclaimed, condescendingly, "Why, you're quite a dab at it!" He sat in the front seat of an automobile, and heard the great lady behind him referring to the sturdy Jersey farmers, whose ancestors had fought the British and Hessians all over the state, as "your peasantry."

It was an extraordinary privilege to have Mrs. Harper for a guest; "at home" she moved about in state recalling that of Queen Victoria, with flags and bunting on the way, and crowds of school children cheering. She kept up half a dozen establishments, and had a hundred thousand acres of game preserves in Scotland. She made a speciality of collecting jewels which had belonged to the romantic and picturesque queens of history. She appeared at the dance in a breastplate of diamonds covering the entire front of her bodice, so that she was literally clothed in light; and with her was her English friend, Mrs. Percy, who had accompanied her in her triumph through the courts and camps of Europe, and displayed a famous lorgnette-chain, containing one specimen of every rare and beautiful jewel known. Mrs. Percy wore a gown of cloth of gold tissue, covered with a fortune in Venetian lace, and made a tremendous sensation—until the rumour spread that it was a rehash of the costume which Mrs. Harper had worn at the Duchess of London's ball. The Chicago lady herself never by any chance appeared in the same costume twice.

Alice had a grand time at the Todds'; all the men fell in love with her—one in particular, a young chap named Fayette, quite threw himself at her feet. He was wealthy, but unfortunately he had made his money by eloping with a rich girl (who was one of the present party), and so, from a practical point of view, his attentions were not desirable for Alice.

Montague was left with the task of finding these things out for himself, for his brother devoted himself exclusively to Betty Wyman. The way these two disappeared between meals was a jest of the whole company; so that when they were on their way home, Montague felt called upon to make paternal inquiries.

"We're as much engaged as we dare to be," Oliver answered him.

"And when do you expect to marry her?"

"God knows," said he, "I don't. The old man wouldn't give her a cent."

"And you couldn't support her?"

"I? Good heavens, Allan—do you suppose Betty would consent to be poor?"

"Have you asked her?" inquired Montague.

"I don't want to ask her, thank you! I've not the least desire to live in a hovel with a girl who's been brought up in a palace."

"Then what do you expect to do?"

"Well, Betty has a rich aunt in a lunatic asylum. And then I'm making money, you know—and the old boy will have to relent in the end. And we're having a very good time in the meanwhile, you know."

"You can't be very much in love," said Montague—to which his brother replied cheerfully that they were as much in love as they felt like being.

This was on the train Monday morning. Oliver observed that his brother relapsed into a brown study, and remarked, "I suppose you're going back now to bury yourself in your books. You've got to give me one evening this week for a dinner that's important."

"Where's that?" asked the other.

"Oh, it's a long story," said Oliver. "I'll explain it to you some time. But first we must have an understanding about next week, also—I suppose you've not overlooked the fact that it's Christmas week. And you won't be permitted to do any work then."

"But that's impossible!" exclaimed the other.

"Nothing else is possible," said Oliver, firmly. "I've made an engagement for you with the Eldridge Devons up the Hudson—"

"For the whole week?"

"The whole week. And it'll be the most important thing you've done. Mrs. Winnie's going to take us all in her car, and you will make no end of indispensable acquaintances."

"Oliver, I don't see how in the world I can do it!" the other protested in dismay, and went on for several minutes arguing and explaining what he had to do. But Oliver contented himself with the assurance that where there's a will, there's a way. One could not refuse an invitation to spend Christmas with the Eldridge Devons!

And sure enough, there was a way. Mr. Hasbrook had mentioned to him that he had had considerable work done upon the case, and would have the papers sent round. And when Montague reached his office that morning, he found them there. There was a package of several thousand pages; and upon examining them, he found to his utter consternation that they contained a complete bill of complaint, with all the necessary references and citations, and a preliminary draught of a brief—in short, a complete and thoroughgoing preparation of his case. There could not have been less than ten or fifteen thousand dollars' worth of work in the papers; and Montague sat quite aghast, turning over the neatly typewritten sheets. He could indeed afford to attend Christmas house parties, if all his clients were to treat him like this!

He felt a little piqued about it—for he had noted some of these points for himself, and felt a little proud about them. Apparently he was to be nothing but a figure-head in the case! And he turned to the phone and called up Mr. Hasbrook, and asked him what he expected him to do with these papers. There was the whole case here; and was he simply to take them as they stood?

No one could have replied more considerately than did Mr. Hasbrook. The papers were for Montague's benefit—he would do exactly as he pleased with them. He might use them as they stood, or reject them altogether, or make them the basis for his own work—anything that appealed to his judgment would be satisfactory. And so Montague turned about and wrote an acceptance to the formal invitation which had come from the Eldridge Devons.

Later on in the day Oliver called up, and said that he was to go out to dinner the following evening, and that he would call for him at eight. "It's with the Jack Evanses," Oliver added. "Do you know them?"

Montague had heard the name, as that of the president of a chain of Western railroads. "Do you mean him?" he asked.

"Yes," said the other. "They're a rum crowd, but there's money in it. I'll call early and explain it to you."

But it was explained sooner than that. During the next afternoon Montague had a caller—none other than Mrs. Winnie Duval. Some one had left Mrs. Winnie some more money, it appeared; and there was a lot of red tape attached to it, which she wanted the new lawyer to attend to. Also, she said, she hoped that he would charge her a lot of money by way of encouraging himself. It was a mere bagatelle of a hundred thousand or so, from some forgotten aunt in the West.

The business was soon disposed of, and then Mrs. Winnie asked Montague if he had any place to go to for dinner that evening: which was the occasion of his mentioning the Jack Evanses. "O dear me!" said Mrs. Winnie, with a laugh. "Is Ollie going to take you there? What a funny time you'll have!"

"Do you know them?" asked the other.

"Heavens, no!" was the answer. "Nobody knows them; but everybody knows about them. My husband meets old Evans in business, of course, and thinks he's a good sort. But the family—dear me!"

"How much of it is there?"

"Why, there's the old lady, and two grown daughters and a son. The son's a fine chap, they say—the old man took him in hand and put him at work in the shops. But I suppose he thought that daughters were too much of a proposition for him, and so he sent them to a fancy school—and, I tell you, they're the most highly polished human specimens that ever you encountered!"

It sounded entertaining. "But what does Oliver want with them?" asked Montague, wonderingly.

"It isn't that he wants them—they want him. They're cumbers, you know—perfectly frantic. They've come to town to get into Society."

"Then you mean that they pay Oliver?" asked Montague.

"I don't know that," said the other, with a laugh. "You'll have to ask Ollie. They've a number of the little brothers of the rich hanging round them, picking up whatever plunder's in sight."

A look of pain crossed Montague's face; and she saw it, and put out her hand with a sudden gesture. "Oh!" she exclaimed, "I've offended you!"

"No," said he, "it's not that exactly—I wouldn't be offended. But I'm worried about my brother."

"How do you mean?"

"He gets a lot of money somehow, and I don't know what it means."

The woman sat for a few moments in silence, watching him. "Didn't he have any when he came here?" she asked.

"Not very much," said he.

"Because," she went on, "if he didn't, he certainly managed it very cleverly—we all thought he had."

Again there was a pause; then suddenly Mrs. Winnie said: "Do you know, you feel differently about money from the way we do in New York. Do you realize it?"

"I'm not sure," said he. "How do you mean?"

"You look at it in an old-fashioned sort of way—a person has to earn it—it's a sign of something he's done. It came to me just now, all in a flash—we don't feel that way about money. We haven't any of us earned ours; we've just got it. And it never occurs to us to expect other people to earn it—all we want to know is if they have it."

Montague did not tell his companion how very profound a remark he considered that; he was afraid it would not be delicate to agree with her. He had heard a story of a negro occupant of the "mourners' bench," who was voluble in confession of his sins, but took exception to the fervour with which the congregation said "Amen!"

"The Evanses used to be a lot funnier than they are now," continued Mrs. Winnie, after a while. "When they came here last year, they were really frightful. They had an English chap for social secretary—a younger son of some broken-down old family. My brother knew a man who had been one of their intimates in the West, and he said it was perfectly excruciating—this fellow used to sit at the table and give orders to the whole crowd: 'Your ice-cream fork should be at your right hand, Miss Mary.—One never asks for more soup, Master Robert.—And Miss Anna, always move your soup-spoon from you—that's better!'"

"I fancy I shall feel sorry for them," said Montague.

"Oh, you needn't," said the other, promptly. "They'll get what they want."

"Do you think so?"

"Why, certainly they will. They've got the money; and they've been abroad—they're learning the game. And they'll keep at it until they succeed—what else is there for them to do? And then my husband says that old Evans is making himself a power here in the East; so that pretty soon they won't dare offend him."

"Does that count?" asked the man.

"Well, I guess it counts!" laughed Mrs. Winnie. "It has of late." And she went on to tell him of the Society leader who had dared to offend the daughters of a great magnate, and how the magnate had retaliated by turning the woman's husband out of his high office. That was often the way in the business world; the struggles were supposed to be affairs of men, but oftener than not the moving power was a woman's intrigue. You would see a great upheaval in Wall Street, and it would be two of the big men quarrelling over a mistress; you would see some man rush suddenly into a high office—and that would be because his wife had sold herself to advance him.

Mrs. Winnie took him up town in her auto, and he dressed for dinner; and then came Oliver, and his brother asked, "Are you trying to put the Evanses into Society?"

"Who's been telling you about them?" asked the other.

"Mrs. Winnie," said Montague.

"What did she tell you?"

Montague went over her recital, which his brother apparently found satisfactory. "It's not as serious as that," he said, answering the earlier question. "I help them a little now and then."

"What do you do?"

"Oh, advise them, mostly—tell them where to go and what to wear. When they first came to New York, they were dressed like paraquets, you know. And"—here Oliver broke into a laugh—"I refrain from making jokes about them. And when I hear other people abusing them, I point out that they are sure to land in the end, and will be dangerous enemies. I've got one or two wedges started for them."

"And do they pay you for doing it?"

"You'd call it paying me, I suppose," replied the other. "The old man carries a few shares of stock for me now and then."

"Carries a few shares?" echoed Montague, and Oliver explained the procedure. This was one of the customs which had grown up in a community where people did not have to earn their money. The recipient of the favour put up nothing and took no risks; but the other person was supposed to buy some stock for him, and then, when the stock went up, he would send a cheque for the "profits." Many a man who would have resented a direct offer of money, would assent pleasantly when a powerful friend offered to "carry a hundred shares for him." This was the way one offered a tip in the big world; it was useful in the case of newspaper men, whose good opinion of a stock was desired, or of politicians and legislators, whose votes might help its fortunes. When one expected to get into Society, one must be prepared to strew such tips about him.

"Of course," added Oliver, "what the family would really like me to do is to get the Robbie Wallings to take them up. I suppose I could get round half a million of them if I could manage that."

To all of which Montague replied, "I see."

A great light had dawned upon him. So that was the way it was managed! That was why one paid thirty thousand a year for one's apartments, and thirty thousand more for a girl's clothes! No wonder it was better to spend Christmas week at the Eldridge Devons than to labour at one's law books!

"One more question," Montague went on. "Why are you introducing me to them?"

"Well," his brother answered, "it won't hurt you; you'll find it amusing. You see, they'd heard I had a brother; and they asked me to bring you. I couldn't keep you hidden for ever, could I?"

All this was while they were driving up town. The Evanses' place was on Riverside Drive; and when Montague got out of the cab and saw it looming up in the semi-darkness, he emitted an exclamation of wonder. It was as big as a jail!

"Oh, yes, they've got room enough," said Oliver, with a laugh. "I put this deal through for them—it's the old Lamson palace, you know."

They had the room; and likewise they had all the trappings of snobbery—Montague took that fact in at a glance. There were knee-breeches and scarlet facings and gold braid—marble balconies and fireplaces and fountains—French masters and real Flemish tapestry. The staircase of their palace was a winding one, and there was a white velvet carpet which had been specially woven for it, and had to be changed frequently; at the top of it was a white cashmere rug which had a pedigree of six centuries—and so on.

And then came the family: this tall, raw-boned, gigantic man, with weather-tanned face and straggling grey moustache—this was Jack Evans; and Mrs. Evans, short and pudgy, but with a kindly face, and not too many diamonds; and the Misses Evans,—stately and slender and perfectly arrayed. "Why, they're all right!" was the thought that came to Montague.

They were all right until they opened their mouths. When they spoke, you discovered that Evans was a miner, and that his wife had been cook on a ranch; also that Anne and Mary had harsh voices, and that they never by any chance said or did anything natural.

They were escorted into the stately dining-room—Henri II., with a historic mantel taken from the palace of Fontainebleau, and four great allegorical paintings of Morning, Evening, Noon, and Midnight upon the walls. There were no other guests—the table, set for six, seemed like a toy in the vast apartment. And in a sudden flash—with a start of almost terror—Montague realized what it must mean not to be in Society. To have all this splendour, and nobody to share it! To have Henri II. dining-rooms and Louis XVI. parlours and Louis XIV. libraries—and see them all empty! To have no one to drive with or talk with, no one to visit or play cards with—to go to the theatre and the opera and have no one to speak to! Worse than that, to be stared at and smiled at! To live in this huge palace, and know that all the horde of servants, underneath their cringing deference, were sneering at you! To face that—to live in the presence of it day after day! And then, outside of your home, the ever widening circles of ridicule and contempt—Society, with all its hangers-on and parasites, its imitators and admirers!

And some one had defied all that—some one had taken up the sword and gone forth to beat down that opposition! Montague looked at this little family of four, and wondered which of them was the driving force in this most desperate emprise!

He arrived at it by a process of elimination. It could not be Evans himself. One saw that the old man was quite hopeless socially; nothing could change his big hairy hands or his lean scrawny neck, or his irresistible impulse to slide down in his chair and cross his long legs in front of him. The face and the talk of Jack Evans brought irresistibly to mind the mountain trail and the prospector's pack-mule, the smoke of camp-fires and the odour of bacon and beans. Seventeen long years the man had tramped in deserts and mountain wildernesses, and Nature had graven her impress deep into his body and soul.

He was very shy at this dinner; but Montague came to know him well in the course of time. And after he had come to realize that Montague was not one of the grafters, he opened up his heart. Evans had held on to his mine when he had found it, and he had downed the rivals who had tried to take it away from him, and he had bought the railroads who had tried to crush him—and now he had come to Wall Street to fight the men who had tried to ruin his railroads. But through it all, he had kept the heart of a woman, and the sight of real distress was unbearable to him. He was the sort of man to keep a roll of ten-thousand-dollar bills in his pistol pocket, and to give one away if he thought he could do it without offence. And, on the other hand, men told how once when he had seen a porter insult a woman passenger on his line, he jumped up and pulled the bell-cord, and had the man put out on the roadside at midnight, thirty miles from the nearest town!

No, it was the women folks, he said to Montague, with his grim laugh. It didn't trouble him at all to be called a "noovoo rich"; and when he felt like dancing a shakedown, he could take a run out to God's country. But the women folks had got the bee in their bonnet. The old man added sadly that one of the disadvantages of striking it rich was that it left the women folks with nothing to do.

Nor was it Mrs. Evans, either. "Sarey," as she was called by the head of the house, sat next to Montague at dinner; and he discovered that with the very least encouragement, the good lady was willing to become homelike and comfortable. Montague gave the occasion, because he was a stranger, and volunteered the opinion that New York was a shamelessly extravagant place, and hard to get along in; and Mrs. Evans took up the subject and revealed herself as a good-natured and kindly personage, who had wistful yearnings for mush and molasses, and flap-jacks, and bread fried in bacon-grease, and similar sensible things, while her chef was compelling her to eat *paté de foie gras* in aspic, and milk-fed guinea-chicks, and *biscuits glacées Tortoni*. Of course she did not say that at dinner,—she made a game effort to play her part,—with the result of at least one diverting experience for Montague.

Mrs. Evans was telling him what a dreadful place she considered the city for young men; and how she feared to bring her boy here. "The men here have no morals at all," said she, and added earnestly, "I've come to the conclusion that Eastern men are naturally amphibious!"

Then, as Montague knitted his brows and looked perplexed, she added, "Don't you think so?" And he replied, with as little delay as possible, that he had never really thought of it before.

It was not until a couple of hours later that the light dawned upon him, in the course of a conversation with Miss Anne. "We met Lady Stonebridge at luncheon to-day," said that young person. "Do you know her?"

"No," said Montague, who had never heard of her.

"I think those aristocratic English women use the most abominable slang," continued Anne. "Have you noticed it?"

"Yes, I have," he said.

"And so utterly cynical! Do you know, Lady Stonebridge quite shocked mother—she told her she didn't believe in marriage at all, and that she thought all men were naturally polygamous!"

Later on, Montague came to know "Mrs. Sarey"; and one afternoon, sitting in her Petit Trianon drawing-room, he asked her abruptly, "Why in the world do you want to get into Society?" And the poor lady caught her breath, and tried to be indignant; and then, seeing that he was in earnest, and that she was cornered, broke down and confessed. "It isn't me," she said, "it's the gals." (For along with the surrender went a reversion to natural speech.) "It's Mary, and more particularly Anne."

They talked it over confidentially—which was a great relief to Mrs. Sarey's soul, for she was cruelly lonely. So far as she was concerned, it was not because she wanted Society, but because Society didn't want her. She flashed up in sudden anger, and clenched her fists, declaring that Jack Evans was as good a man as walked the streets of New York—and they would acknowledge it before he got through with them, too! After that she intended to settle down at home and be comfortable, and mend her husband's socks.

She went on to tell him what a hard road was the path of glory. There were hundreds of people ready to know them—but oh, such a riffraff! They might fill up their home with the hangers-on and the yellow, but no, they could wait. They had learned a lot since they set out. One very aristocratic lady had invited them to dinner, and their hopes had been high—but alas, while they were sitting by the fireplace, some one admired a thirty-thousand-dollar emerald ring which Mrs. Evans had on her finger, and she had taken it off and passed it about among the company, and somewhere it had vanished completely! And another person had invited Mary to a bridge-party, and though she had played hardly at all, her hostess had quietly informed her that she had lost a thousand dollars. And the great Lady Stonebridge had actually sent for her and told her that she could introduce her in some of the very best circles, if only she was willing to lose always! Mrs. Evans had possessed a very homely Irish name before she was married; and Lady Stonebridge had got five thousand dollars from her to use some great influence she possessed in the Royal College of Heralds, and prove that she was descended directly from the noble old family of Magennis, who had been the lords of Iveagh, way back in the fourteenth century. And now Oliver had told them that this imposing charter would not help them in the least!

In the process of elimination, there were the Misses Evans left. Montague's friends made many jests when they heard that he had met them—asking him if he meant to settle down. Major Venable went so far as to assure him that there was not the least doubt that either of the girls would take him in a second. Montague laughed, and answered that Mary was not so bad—she had a sweet face and was good-natured; but also, she was two years younger than Anne; and he could not get over the thought that two more years might make another Anne of her.

For it was Anne who was the driving force of the family! Anne who had planned the great campaign, and selected the Lamson palace, and pried the family loose from the primeval rocks of Nevada! She was cold as an iceberg, tireless, pitiless to others as to herself; for seventeen years her father had wandered and dug among the mountains; and for seventeen years, if need be, she would dig beneath the walls of the fortress of Society!

After Montague had had his heart to heart talk with the mother, Miss Anne Evans became very haughty toward him; whereby he knew that the old lady had told about it, and that the daughter resented his presumption. But to Oliver she laid bare her soul, and Oliver would come and tell his brother about it: how she plotted and planned and studied, and brought new schemes to him every week. She had some of the real people bought over to secret sympathy with her; if there was some especial favour which she asked for, she would set to work with the good-natured old man, and the person would have some important money service done him. She had the people of Society all marked—she was learning all their weaknesses, and the underground passages of their lives, and working patiently to find the key to her problem—some one family which was socially impregnable, but whose finances were in such a shape that they would receive the proposition to take up the Evanses, and definitely put them in. Montague used to look back upon all this with wonder and amusement—from those days in the not far distant future, when the papers had cable descriptions of the gowns of the Duchess of Arden, nee Evans, who was the bright particular star of the London social season!

CHAPTER XIV

Montague had written a reluctant letter to Major Thorne, telling him that he had been unable to interest anyone in his proposition, and that he was not in position to undertake it himself. Then, according to his brother's injunction, he left his money in the bank, and waited. There would be "something doing" soon, said Oliver.

And as they drove home from the Evanses', Oliver served notice upon him that this event might be expected any day. He was very mysterious about it, and would answer none of his brother's questions—except to say that it had nothing to do with the people they had just visited.

"I suppose," Montague remarked, "you have not failed to realize that Evans might play you false."

And the other laughed, echoing the words, "Might do it!" Then he went on to tell the tale of the great railroad builder of the West, whose daughter had been married, with elaborate festivities; and some of the young men present, thinking to find him in a sentimental mood, had asked him for his views about the market. He advised them to buy the stock of his road; and they formed a pool and bought, and as fast as they bought, he sold—until the little venture cost the boys a total of seven million and a half!

"No, no," Oliver added. "I have never put up a dollar for anything of Evans's, and I never shall.—They are simply a side issue, anyway," he added carelessly.

A couple of mornings later, while Montague was at breakfast, his brother called him up and said that he was coming round, and would go down town with him. Montague knew at once that that meant something serious, for he had never before known his brother to be awake so early.

They took a cab; and then Oliver explained. The moment had arrived—the time to take the plunge, and come up with a fortune. He could not tell much about it, for it was a matter upon which he stood pledged to absolute secrecy. There were but four people in the country who knew about it. It was the chance of a lifetime—and in four or five hours it would be gone. Three times before it had come to Oliver, and each time he had multiplied his capital several times; that he had not made millions was simply because he did not have enough money. His brother must take his word for this and simply put himself into his hands.

"What is it you want me to do?" asked Montague, gravely.

"I want you to take every dollar you have, or that you can lay your hands on this morning, and turn it over to me to buy stocks with."

"To buy on margin, you mean?"

"Of course I mean that," said Oliver. Then, as he saw his brother frown, he added, "Understand me, I have absolutely certain information as to how a certain stock will behave to-day."

"The best judges of a stock often make mistakes in such matters," said Montague.

"It is not a question of any person's judgment," was the reply. "It is a question of knowledge. The stock is to be MADE to behave so."

"But how can you know that the person who intends to make it behave may not be lying to you?"

"My information does not come from that person, but from a person who has no such interest—who, on the contrary, is in on the deal with me, and gains only as I gain."

"Then, in other words," said Montague, "your information is stolen?"

"Everything in Wall Street is stolen," was Oliver's concise reply.

There was a long silence, while the cab rolled swiftly on its way. "Well?" Oliver asked at last.

"I can imagine," said Montague, "how a man might intend to move a certain stock, and think that he had the power, and yet find that he was mistaken. There are so many forces, so many chances to be considered—it seems to me you must be taking a risk."

Oliver laughed. "You talk like a child," was his reply. "Suppose that I were in absolute control of a corporation, and that I chose to run it for purposes of market manipulation, don't you think I might come pretty near knowing what its stock was going to do?"

"Yes," said Montague, slowly, "if such a thing as that were conceivable."

"If it were conceivable!" laughed his brother. "And now suppose that I had a confidential man—a secretary, we'll say—and I paid him twenty thousand a year, and he saw chances to make a hundred thousand in an hour—don't you think he might conceivably try it?"

"Yes," said Montague, "he might. But where do you come in?"

"Well, if the man were going to do anything worth while, he'd need capital, would he not? And he'd hardly dare to look for any money in the Street, where a thousand eyes would be watching him. What more natural than to look out for some person who is in Society and has the ear of private parties with plenty of cash?"

And Montague sat in deep thought. "I see," he said slowly; "I see!" Then, fixing his eyes upon Oliver, he exclaimed, earnestly, "One thing more!"

"Don't ask me any more," protested the other. "I told you I was pledged—"

"You must tell me this," said Montague. "Does Bobbie Walling know about it?"

"He does not," was the reply. But Montague had known his brother long and intimately, and he could read things in his eyes. He knew that that was a lie. He had solved the mystery at last!

Montague knew that he had come to a parting of the ways. He did not like this kind of thing—he had not come to New York to be a stock-gambler. But what a difficult thing it would be to say so; and how unfair it was to be confronted with such an issue, and compelled to decide in a few minutes in a cab!

He had put himself in his brother's hands, and now he was under obligations to him, which he could not pay off. Oliver had paid all his expenses; he was doing everything for him. He had made all his difficulties his own, and all in frankness and perfect trust—upon the assumption that his brother would play the game with him. And now, at the critical moment, he was to face about, and say; "I do not like the game. I do not approve of your life!" Such a painful thing it is to have a higher moral code than one's friends!

If he refused, he saw that he would have to face a complete break; he could not go on living in the world to which he had been introduced. Fifty thousand had seemed an enormous fee, yet even a week or two had sufficed for it to come to seem inadequate. He would have to have many such fees, if they were to go on living at their present rate; and if Alice were to have a social career, and entertain her friends. And to ask Alice to give up now, and retire, would be even harder than to face his brother here in the cab.

Then came the temptation. Life was a battle, and this was the way it was being fought. If he rejected the opportunity, others would seize it; in fact, by refusing, he would be handing it to them. This great man, whoever he might be, who was manipulating stocks for his own convenience—could anyone in his senses reject a chance to wrench from him some part of his spoils? Montague saw the impulse of refusal dying away within him.

"Well?" asked his brother, finally.

"Oliver," said the other, "don't you think that I ought to know more about it, so that I can judge?"

"You could not judge, even if I told you all," said Oliver. "It would take you a long time to become familiar with the circumstances, as I am. You must take my word; I know it is certain and safe."

Then suddenly he unbuttoned his coat, and took out some papers, and handed his brother a telegram. It was dated Chicago, and read, "Guest is expected immediately.—HENRY." "That means, 'Buy Transcontinental this morning,'" said Oliver.

"I see," said the other. "Then the man is in Chicago?"

"No," was the reply. "That is his wife. He wires to her."

"—How much money have you?" asked Oliver, after a pause.

"I've most of the fifty thousand," the other answered, "and about thirty thousand we brought with us."

"How much can you put your hands on?"

"Why, I could get all of it; but part of the money is mother's, and I would not touch that."

The younger man was about to remonstrate, but Montague stopped him, "I will put up the fifty thousand I have earned," he said. "I dare not risk any more."

Oliver shrugged his shoulders. "As you please," he said. "You may never have another such chance in your life."

He dropped the subject, or at least he probably tried to. Within a few minutes, however, he was back at it again, with the result that by the time they reached the banking-district, Montague had agreed to draw sixty thousand.

They stopped at his bank. "It isn't open yet,—" said Oliver, "but the paying teller will oblige you. Tell him you want it before the Exchange opens."

Montague went in and got his money, in six new, crisp, ten-thousand-dollar bills. He buttoned them up in his inmost pocket, wondering a little, incidentally, at the magnificence of the place, and at the swift routine manner in which the clerk took in and paid out such sums as this. Then they drove to Oliver's bank, and he drew a hundred and twenty thousand; and then he paid off the cab, and they strolled down Broadway into Wall Street. It lacked a quarter of an hour of the time of the opening of the Exchange; and a stream of prosperous-looking men were pouring in from all the cars and ferries to their offices.

"Where are your brokers?" Montague inquired.

"I don't have any brokers—at least not for a matter such as this," said Oliver. And he stopped in front of one of the big buildings. "In there," he said, "are the offices of Hammond and Streeter—second floor to your left. Go there and ask for a member of the firm, and introduce yourself under an assumed name—"

"What!" gasped Montague.

"Of course, man—you would not dream of giving your own name! What difference will that make?"

"I never thought of doing such a thing," said the other.

"Well, think of it now."

But Montague shook his head. "I would not do that," he said.

Oliver shrugged his shoulders. "All right," he said; "tell him you don't care to give your name. They're a little shady—they'll take your money."

"Suppose they won't?" asked the other.

"Then wait outside for me, and I'll take you somewhere else."

"What shall I buy?"

"Ten thousand shares of Transcontinental Common at the opening price; and tell them to buy on the scale up, and to raise the stop; also to take your orders to sell over the 'phone. Then wait there until I come for you."

Montague set his teeth together and obeyed orders. Inside the door marked Hammond and Streeter a pleasant-faced young man advanced to meet him, and led him to a grey-haired and affable gentleman, Mr. Streeter. And Montague introduced himself as a stranger in town, from the South, and wishing to buy some stock. Mr. Streeter led him into an inner office and seated himself at a desk and drew some papers in front of him. "Your name, please?" he asked.

"I don't care to give my name," replied the other. And Mr. Streeter put down his pen.

"Not give your name?" he said.

"No," said Montague quietly.

"Why?"—said Mr. Streeter—"I don't understand—"

"I am a stranger in town," said Montague, "and not accustomed to dealing in stocks. I should prefer to remain unknown."

The man eyed him sharply. "Where do you come from?" he asked.

"From Mississippi," was the reply.

"And have you a residence in New York?"

"At a hotel," said Montague.

"You have to give some name," said the other.

"Any will do," said Montague. "John Smith, if you like."

"We never do anything like this," said the broker.

"We require that our customers be introduced. There are rules of the Exchange—there are rules—"

"I am sorry," said Montague; "this would be a cash transaction."

"How many shares do you want to buy?"

"Ten thousand," was the reply.

Mr. Streeter became more serious. "That is a large order," he said.

Montague said nothing.

"What do you wish to buy?" was the next question.

"Transcontinental Common," he replied.

"Well," said the other, after another pause-,-"we will try to accommodate you. But you will have to consider it—er—"

"Strictly confidential," said Montague.

So Mr. Streeter made out the papers, and Montague, looking them over, discovered that they called for one hundred thousand dollars.

"That is a mistake," he said. "I have only sixty thousand."

"Oh," said the other, "we shall certainly have to charge you a ten per cent, margin."

Montague was not prepared for this contingency; but he did some mental arithmetic. "What is the present price of the stock?" he asked.

"Fifty-nine and five-eighths," was the reply.

"Then sixty thousand dollars is more than ten per cent, of the market price," said Montague.

"Yes," said Mr. Streeter. "But in dealing with a stranger we shall certainly have to put a 'stop loss' order at four points above, and that would leave you only two points of safety—surely not enough."

"I see," said Montague—and he had a sudden appalling realization of the wild game which his brother had planned for him.

"Whereas," Mr. Streeter continued, persuasively, "if you put up ten per cent., you will have six points."

"Very well," said the other promptly. "Then please buy me six thousand shares."

So they closed the deal, and the papers were signed, and Mr. Streeter took the six new, crisp ten-thousand-dollar bills.

Then he escorted him to the outer office, remarking pleasantly on the way, "I hope you're well advised. We're inclined to be bearish upon Transcontinental ourselves—the situation looks rather squally."

These words were not worth the breath it took to say them; but Montague was not aware of this, and felt a painful start within. But he answered, carelessly, that one must take his chance, and sat down in one of the customer's chairs. Hammond and Streeter's was like a little lecture-hall, with rows of seats and a big blackboard in front, with the initials of the most important stocks in columns, and yesterday's closing prices above, on little green cards. At one side was a ticker, with two attendants awaiting the opening click.

In the seats were twenty or thirty men, old and young; most of them regular habitues, victims of the fever of the Street. Montague watched them, catching snatches of their whispered conversation, with its intricate and disagreeable slang. He felt intensely humiliated and uncomfortable—for he had got the fever of the Street into his own veins, and he could not conquer it. There were nasty shivers running up and down his spine, and his hands were cold.

He stared at the little figures, fascinated; they stood for some vast and tremendous force outside, which could not be controlled or even comprehended,—some merciless, annihilating force, like the lightning or the tornado. And he had put himself at the mercy of it; it might do its will with him! "Tr. C. 59 5/8" read the little pasteboard; and he had only six points of safety. If at any time in the day that figure should be changed to read "53 5/8"—then every dollar of Montague's sixty thousand would be gone for ever! The great fee that he had worked so hard for and rejoiced so greatly over—that would be all gone, and a slice out of his inheritance besides!

A boy put into his hand a little four-page paper—one of the countless news-sheets which different houses and interests distributed free for advertising or other purposes; and a heading "Transcontinental" caught his eye, among the paragraphs in the Day's Events. He read: "The directors' meeting of the Transcontinental R.R. will be held at noon. It is confidently predicted that the quarterly dividend will be passed, as it has been for the last three quarters. There is great dissatisfaction among the stock-holders. The stock has been decidedly weak, with no apparent inside support; it fell off three points just before closing yesterday, upon the news of further proceedings by Western state officials, and widely credited rumours of dissensions among the directors, with renewed opposition to the control of the Hopkins interests."

Ten o'clock came and went, and the ticker began its long journey. There was intense activity in Transcontinental, many thousands of shares changing hands, and the price swaying back and forth. When Oliver came in, in half an hour, it stood at 59 3/8.

"That's all right," said he. "Our time will not come till afternoon."

"But suppose we are wiped out before afternoon?" said the other.

"That is impossible," answered Oliver. "There will be big buying all the morning."

They sat for a while, nervous and restless. Then, by way of breaking the monotony, Oliver suggested that his brother might like to see the "Street." They went around the corner to Broad Street. Here at the head stood the Sub-treasury building, with all the gold of the government inside, and a Gatling gun in the tower. The public did not know it was there, but the financial men knew it, and it seemed as if they had huddled all their offices and banks and safe-deposit vaults under its shelter. Here, far underground, were hidden the two hundred millions of securities of the Oil Trust—in a huge six-hundred-ton steel vault, with a door so delicately poised that a finger could swing it on its hinges. And opposite to this was the white Grecian building of the Stock Exchange. Down the street were throngs of men within a roped arena, pushing, shouting, jostling; this was "the curb," where one could buy or sell small blocks of stock, and all the wild-cat mining and oil stocks which were not listed by the Exchange. Rain or shine, these men were always here; and in the windows of the neighbouring buildings stood others shouting quotations to them through megaphones, or signalling in deaf and dumb language. Some of these brokers wore coloured hats, so that they could be distinguished; some had offices far off, where men sat all day with strong glasses trained upon them. Everywhere was the atmosphere of speculation—the restless, feverish eyes; the quick, nervous gestures; the haggard, care-worn faces. For in this game every man was pitted against every other man; and the dice were loaded so that nine out of every ten were doomed in advance to ruin and defeat. They procured passes to the visitors' gallery of the Exchange. From here one looked down into a room one or two hundred feet square, its floor covered with a snowstorm of torn pieces of paper, and its air a babel of shouts and cries. Here were gathered perhaps two thousand men and boys; some were lounging and talking, but most were crowded about the various trading-posts, pushing, climbing over each other, leaping up, waving their hands and calling aloud. A "seat" in this exchange was worth about ninety-five thousand dollars, and so no one of these men was poor; but yet they came, day after day, to play their parts in this sordid arena, "seeking in sorrow for each other's joy": inventing a thousand petty tricks to outwit and deceive each other; rejoicing in a thousand petty triumphs; and spending their lives, like the waves upon the shore, a very symbol of human futility. Now and then a sudden impulse would seize them, and they would become like howling demons, surging about one spot, shrieking, gasping, clawing each other's clothing to pieces; and the spectator shuddered, seeing them as the victims of some strange and dreadful enchantment, which bound them to struggle and torment each other until they were worn out and grey.

But one felt these things only dimly, when he had put all his fortune into Transcontinental Common. For then he had sold his own soul to the enchanter, and the spell was upon him, and he hoped and feared and agonized with the struggling throng. Montague had no need to ask which was his "post"; for a mob of a hundred men were packed about it, with little whirls and eddies here and there on the outside. "Something doing to-day all right," said a man in his ear.

It was interesting to watch; but there was one difficulty—there were no quotations provided for the spectators. So the sight of this activity merely set them on edge with anxiety—something must be happening to their stock! Even Oliver was visibly nervous—after all, in the surest cases, the game was a dangerous one; there might be a big failure, or an assassination, or an earthquake! They rushed out and made for the nearest broker's office, where a glance at the board showed them Transcontinental at 60. They drew a long breath, and sat down again to wait.

That was about half-past eleven. At a quarter to twelve the stock went up an eighth, and then a quarter, and then another eighth. The two gripped their hands in excitement. Had the time come?

Apparently it had. A minute later the stock leaped to 61, on large buying. Then it went three-eighths more. A buzz of excitement ran through the office, and the old-timers sat up in their seats. The stock went another quarter.

Montague heard a man behind him say to his neighbour, "What does it mean?"

"God knows," was the answer; but Oliver whispered in his brother's ear, "I know what it means. The insiders are buying."

Somebody was buying, and buying furiously. The ticker seemed to set all other business aside and give its attention to the trading in Transcontinental. It was like a base-ball game, when one side begins to pile up runs, and the man in the coacher's box chants exultantly, and the dullest spectator is stirred—since no man can be indifferent to success. And as the stock went higher and higher, a little wave of excitement mounted with it, a murmur running through the room, and a thrill passing from person to person. Some watched, wondering if it would last, and if they had not better take on a little; then another point would be scored, and they would wish they had done it, and hesitate whether to do it now. But to others, like the Montagues, who "had some," it was victory, glorious and thrilling; their pulses leaped faster with every new change of the figures; and between times they reckoned up their gains, and hung between hope and dread for the new gains which were on the way, but not yet in sight.

There was little lull, and the boys who tended the board had a chance to rest. The stock was above 66; at which price, owing to the device of "pyramiding." Montague was on "velvet," to use the picturesque phrase of the Street. His earnings amounted to sixty thousand dollars, and even if the stock were to fall and he were to be sold out, he would lose nothing.

He wished to sell and realize his profits; but his brother gripped him fast by the arm. "No! no!" he said. "It hasn't really come yet!"

Some went out to lunch—to a restaurant where they could have a telephone on their table, so as to keep in touch with events. But the Montagues had no care about eating; they sat picturing the directors in session, and speculating upon a score of various eventualities. Things might yet go wrong, and all their profits would vanish like early snow-flakes—and all their capital with them. Oliver shook like a leaf, but he would not stir. "Stay game!" he whispered.

He took out his watch, and glanced at it. It was after two o'clock. "It may go over till to-morrow!" he muttered.—But then suddenly came the storm.

The ticker recorded a rise in the price of Transcontinental of a point and a half, upon a purchase of five thousand shares; and then half a point for two thousand more. After that it never stopped. It went a point at a time; it went ten points in about fifteen minutes. And babel broke loose in the office, and in several thousand other offices in the street, and spread to others all over the world. Montague had got up, and was moving here and there, because the tension was unendurable; and at the door of an inner office he heard some one at the telephone exclaiming, "For the love of God, can't you find out what's the matter?"—A moment later a man rushed in, breathless and wild-eyed, and his voice rang through the office, "The directors have declared a quarterly dividend of three per cent, and an extra dividend of two!"

And Oliver caught his brother by the arm and started for the door with him. "Get to your broker's," he said. "And if the stock has stopped moving, sell; and sell in any case before the close." And then he dashed away to his own headquarters.

At about half after three o'clock, Oliver came into Hammond and Streeter's, breathless, and with his hair and clothing dishevelled. He was half beside himself with exultation; and Montague was scarcely less wrought up—in fact he felt quite limp after the strain he had been through.

"What price did you get?" his brother inquired; and he answered, "An average of 78 3/8." There had been another sharp rise at the end, and he had sold all his stock without checking the advance.

"I got five-eighths," said Oliver. "O ye gods!"

There were some unhappy "shorts" in the office; Mr. Streeter was one of them. It was bitterness and gall to them to see the radiant faces of the two lucky ones; but the two did not even see this. They went out, half dancing, and had a drink or two to steady their nerves.

They would not actually get their money until the morrow; but Montague figured a profit of a trifle under a quarter of a million for himself. Of this about twenty thousand would go to make up the share of his unknown informant; the balance he considered would be an ample reward for his six hours' work that day.

His brother had won more than twice as much. But as they drove up home, talking over it in awe-stricken whispers, and pledging themselves to absolute secrecy, Oliver suddenly clenched his fist and struck his knee.

"By God!" he exclaimed. "If I hadn't been a fool and tried to save an extra margin, I could have had a million!"

CHAPTER XV

After such a victory one felt in a mood for Christmas festivities,—for music and dancing and all beautiful and happy things.

Such a thing, for instance, as Mrs. Winnie, when she came to meet him; clad in her best automobile coat, a thing of purest snowy ermine, so truly gorgeous that wherever she went, people turned and stared and caught their breath. Mrs. Winnie was a picture of joyful health, with a glow in her rich complexion, and a sparkle in her black eyes.

She sat in her big touring-car—in which one could afford to wear ermine. It was a little private self-moving hotel; in the limousine were seats for six persons, with revolving easy chairs, and berths for sleeping, and a writing-desk and a wash-stand, and a beautiful electric chandelier to light it at night. Its trimmings were of South American mahogany, and its upholstering of Spanish and Morocco leathers; it had a telephone with which one spoke to the driver; an ice-box and a lunch hamper—in fact, one might have spent an hour discovering new gimcracks in this magic automobile. It had been made especially for Mrs. Winnie a couple of years ago, and the newspapers said it had cost thirty thousand dollars; it had then been quite a novelty, but now "everybody" was getting them. In this car one might sit at ease, and laugh and chat, and travel at the rate of an express train; and with never a jar or a quiver, nor the faintest sound of any sort.

The streets of the city sped by them as if by enchantment. They went through the park, and out Riverside Drive, and up the river-road which runs out of Broadway all the way to Albany. It was a macadamized avenue, lined with beautiful and stately homes. As one went farther yet, he came to the great country estates-a whole district of hundreds of square miles given up to them. There were forests and lakes and streams; there were gardens and greenhouses filled with rare plants and flowers, and parks with deer browsing, and peacocks and lyre-birds strutting about. The road wound in and out among hills, the surfaces of which would be one unbroken lawn; and upon the highest points stood palaces of every conceivable style and shape.

One might find these great domains anywhere around the city, at a distance of from thirty to sixty miles; there were two or three hundred of them, and incredible were the sums of money which had been spent upon their decoration. One saw an artificial lake of ten thousand acres, made upon land which had cost several hundred dollars an acre; one saw gardens with ten thousand rose-bushes, and a quarter of a million dollars' worth of lilies from Japan; there was one estate in which had been planted a million dollars' worth of rare trees, imported from all over the world. Some rich men, who had nothing else to amuse them, would make their estates over and over again, changing the view about their homes as one changes the scenery in a play. Over in New Jersey the Hegans were building a castle upon a mountain-top, and had built a special railroad simply to carry the materials. Here, also, was the estate of the tobacco king, upon which three million dollars had been spent before the plans of the mansion had even been drawn; there were artificial lakes and streams, and fantastic bridges and statuary, and scores of little model plantations and estates, according to the whim of the owner. And here in the Pocantico Hills was the estate of the oil king, about four square miles, with thirty miles of model driveways; many car-loads of rare plants had been imported for its gardens, and it took six hundred men to keep it in order. There was a golf course, a little miniature Alps, upon which the richest man in the world pursued his lost health, with armed guards and detectives patrolling the place all day, and a tower with a search-light, whereby at night he could flood the grounds with light by pressing a button.

In one of these places lived the heir of the great house of Devon. His cousin dwelt in Europe, saying that America was not a fit place for a gentleman to live in. Each of them owned a hundred million dollars' worth of New York real estate, and drew their tribute of rents from the toil of the swarming millions of the city. And always, according to the policy of the family, they bought new real estate. They were directors of the great railroads tributary to the city, and in touch with the political machines, and in every other way in position to know what was under way: if a new subway were built to set the swarming millions free, the millions would find the land all taken up, and apartment-houses newly built for them—and the Devons were the owners. They had a score of the city's greatest hotels—and also slum tenements, and brothels and dives in the Tenderloin. They did not even have to know what they owned; they did not have to know anything, or do anything—they lived in their palaces, at home or abroad, and in their offices in the city the great rent-gathering machine ground on.

Eldridge Devon's occupation was playing with his country-place and his automobiles. He had recently sold all his horses, and turned his stables into a garage equipped with a score or so of cars; he was always getting a new one, and discussing its merits. As to Hudson Cliff, the estate, he had conceived the brilliant idea of establishing a gentleman's country-place which should be self-supporting—that is to say, which should furnish the luxuries and necessities of its owner's table for no more than it would have cost to buy them. Considering the prices usually paid, this was no astonishing feat, but Devon took a child's delight in it; he showed Montague his greenhouses, filled with rare flowers and fruits, and his model dairy, with marble stables and nickel plumbing, and attendants in white uniforms and rubber gloves. He was a short and very stout gentleman with red cheeks, and his conversation was not brilliant.

To Hudson Cliff came many of Montague's earlier acquaintances, and others whom he had not met before. They amused themselves in all the ways with which-he had become familiar at house-parties; likewise on Christmas Eve there were festivities for the children, and on Christmas night a costume ball, very beautiful and stately. Many came from New York to attend this, and others from the neighbourhood; and in returning calls, Montague saw others of these hill-top mansions.

Also, and most important of all, they played bridge—as they had played at every function which he had attended so far. Here Mrs. Winnie, who had rather taken him up, and threatened to supplant Oliver as his social guide and chaperon, insisted that no more excuses would be accepted; and so for two mornings he sat with her in one of the sun-parlours, and diligently put his mind upon the game. As he proved an apt pupil, he was then advised that he might take a trial plunge.

And so Montague came into touch with a new social phenomenon; perhaps on the whole the most significant and soul-disturbing phenomenon which Society had exhibited to him. He had just had the experience of getting a great deal of money without earning it, and was fresh from the disagreeable memories of it— the trembling and suspense, the burning lustful greed, the terrible nerve-devouring excitement. He had hoped that he would not soon have to go through such an experience again-and here was the prospect of an endless dalliance with it!

For that was the meaning of bridge; it was a penalty which people were paying for getting their money without earning it. The disease got into their blood, and they could no longer live without the excitement of gain and the hope of gain. So after their labours were over, when they were supposed to be resting and enjoying themselves, they would get together and torment themselves with an imitation struggle, mimicking the grim and dreadful gamble of business. Down in the Street, Oliver had pointed out to his brother a celebrated "plunger," who had sometimes won six or eight millions in a single day; and that man would play at stocks all morning, and "play the ponies" in the afternoon, and then spend the evening in a millionaires' gambling-house. And so it was with the bridge fiends.

It was a social plague; it had run through all Society, high and low. It had destroyed conversation and all good-fellowship—it would end by destroying even common decency, and turning the best people into vulgar gamblers.—Thus spoke Mrs. Billy Alden, who was one of the guests; and Montague thought that Mrs. Billy ought to know, for she herself was playing all the time.

Mrs. Billy did not like Mrs. Winnie Duval; and the beginning of the conversation was her inquiry why he let that woman corrupt him. Then the good lady went on to tell him what bridge had come to be; how people played it on the trains all the way from New York to San Francisco; how they had tables in their autos, and played while they were touring over the world. "Once," said she, "I took a party to see the America's Cup races off Sandy Hook; and when we got back to the pier, some one called, 'Who won?' And the answer was, 'Mrs. Billy's ahead, but we're going on this evening.' I took a party of friends through the Mediterranean and up the Nile, and we passed Venice and Cairo and the Pyramids and the Suez Canal, and they never once looked up—they were playing bridge. And you think I'm joking, but I mean just literally what I say. I know a man who was travelling from New York to Philadelphia, and got into a game with some strangers, and rode all the way to Palm Beach to finish it!"

Montague heard later of a well-known Society leader who was totally incapacitated that winter, from too much bridge at Newport; and she was passing the winter at Hot Springs and Palm Beach—and playing bridge there. They played it even in sanitariums, to which they had been driven by nervous breakdown. It was an occupation so exhausting to the physique of women that physicians came to know the symptoms of it, and before they diagnosed a case, they would ask, "Do you play bridge?" It had destroyed the last remnants of the Sabbath—it was a universal custom to have card-parties on that day.

It was a very expensive game, as they played it in Society; one might easily win or lose several thousand dollars in an evening, and there were many who could not afford this. If one did not play, he would be dropped from the lists of those invited; and when one entered a game, etiquette required him to stay in until it was finished. So one heard of young girls who had pawned their family plate, or who had sold their honour, to pay their bills at the game; and all Society knew of one youth who had robbed his hostess of her jewels and pawned them, and then taken her the tickets—telling her that her guests had robbed him. There were women received in the best Society, who lived as adventuresses pure and simple, upon their skill at the game; hostesses would invite rich guests and fleece them. Montague never forgot the sense of amazement and dismay with which he listened while first Mrs. Winnie and then his brother warned him that he must avoid playing with a certain aristocratic dame whom he met in this most aristocratic household—because she was such a notorious cheater!

"My dear fellow," laughed his brother, when he protested, "we have a phrase 'to cheat at cards like a woman.'" And then Oliver went on to tell him of his own first experience at cards in Society, when he had played poker with several charming young débutantes; they would call their hands and take the money without showing their cards, and he had been too gallant to ask to see them. But later he learned that this was a regular practice, and so he never played poker with women. And Oliver pointed out one of these girls to his brother—sitting, as beautiful as a picture and as cold as marble, with a half-smoked cigarette on the edge of the table, and whisky and soda and glasses of cracked ice beside her. Later on, as he chanced to be reading a newspaper, his brother leaned over his shoulder and pointed out another of the symptoms of the craze—an advertisement headed, "Your luck will change." It gave notice that at Rosenstein's Parlours, just off Fifth Avenue, one might borrow money upon expensive gowns and furs!

All during the ten days of this house-party, Mrs. Winnie devoted herself to seeing that Montague had a good time; Mrs. Winnie sat beside him at table—he found that somehow a convention had been established which assigned him to Mrs. Winnie as a matter of course. Nobody said anything to him about it, but knowing how relentlessly the affairs of other people were probed and analyzed, he began to feel exceedingly uncomfortable.

There came a time when he felt quite smothered by Mrs. Winnie; and immediately after lunch one day he broke away and went for a long walk by himself. This was the occasion of his meeting with an adventure.

An inch or two of snow had fallen, and lay gleaming in the sunlight. The air was keen, and he drank deep draughts of it, and went striding away over the hills for an hour or so. There was a gale blowing, and as he came over the summits it would strike him, and he would see the river white with foam. And then down in the valleys again all would be still.

Here, in a thickly wooded place, Montague's attention was arrested suddenly by a peculiar sound, a heavy thud, which seemed to shake the earth. It suggested a distant explosion, and he stopped for a moment and then went on, gazing ahead. He passed a turn, and then he saw a great tree which had fallen directly across the road.

He went on, thinking that this was what he had heard. But as he came nearer, he saw his mistake. Beyond the tree lay something else, and he began to run toward it. It was two wheels of an automobile, sticking up into the air.

He sprang upon the tree-trunk, and in one glance he saw the whole story. A big touring-car had swept round the sharp turn, and swerved to avoid the unexpected obstruction, and so turned a somersault into the ditch.

Montague gave a thrill of horror, for there was the form of a man pinned beneath the body of the car. He sprang toward it, but a second glance made him stop—he saw that blood had gushed from the man's mouth and soaked the snow all about. His chest was visibly crushed flat, and his eyes were dreadful, half-started from their sockets.

For a moment Montague stood staring, as if turned to stone. Then from the other side of the car came a moan, and he ran toward the sound. A second man lay in the ditch, moving feebly. Montague sprang to help him.

The man wore a heavy bearskin coat. Montague lifted him, and saw that he was a very elderly person, with a cut across his forehead, and a face as white as chalk. The other helped him to a position with his back against the bank, and he opened his eyes and groaned.

Montague knelt beside him, watching his breathing. He had a sense of utter helplessness—there was nothing he could think of to do, save to unbutton the man's coat and keep wiping the blood from his face.

"Some whisky," the stranger moaned. Montague answered that he had none; but the other replied that there was some in the car.

The slope of the bank was such that Montague could crawl under, and find the compartment with the bottle in it. The old man drank some, and a little colour came back to his face. As the other watched him, it came to him that this face was familiar; but he could not place it.

"How many were there with you?" Montague asked; and the man answered, "Only one."

Montague went over and made certain that the other man—who was obviously the chauffeur—was dead. Then he hurried down the road, and dragged some brush out into the middle of it, where it could be seen from a distance by any other automobile that came along; after which he went back to the stranger, and bound his handkerchief about his forehead to stop the bleeding from the cut.

The old man's lips were tightly set, as if he were suffering great pain. "I'm done for!" he moaned, again and again.

"Where are you hurt?" Montague asked.

"I don't know," he gasped. "But it's finished me! I know it—it's the last straw."

Then he closed his eyes and lay back. "Can't you get a doctor?" he asked.

"There are no houses very near," said Montague. "But I can run—"

"No, no!" the other interrupted, anxiously. "Don't leave me! Some one will come.—Oh, that fool of a chauffeur—why couldn't he go slow when I told him? That's always the way with them—they're always trying to show off."

"The man is dead," said Montague, quietly.

The other started upon his elbow. "Dead!" he gasped.

"Yes," said Montague. "He's under the car."

The old man's eyes had started wild with fright; and he caught Montague by the arm. "Dead!" he said. "O my God—and it might have been me!"

There was a moment's pause. The stranger caught his breath, and whispered again: "I'm done for! I can't stand it! it's too much!"

Montague had noticed when he lifted the man that he was very frail and slight of build. Now he could feel that the hand that held his arm was trembling violently. It occurred to him that perhaps the man was not really hurt, but that his nerves had been upset by the shock.

And he felt certain of this a moment later, when the stranger suddenly leaned forward, clutching him with redoubled intensity, and staring at him with wide, horror-stricken eyes.

"Do you know what it means to be afraid of death?" he panted. "Do you know what it means to be afraid of death?"

Then, without waiting for a reply, he rushed on—"No, no! You can't! you can't! I don't believe any man knows it as I do! Think of it—for ten years I've never known a minute when I wasn't afraid of death! It follows me around—it won't let me be! It leaps out at me in places, like this! And when I escape it, I can hear it laughing at me—for it knows I can't get away!"

The old man caught his breath with a choking sob. He was clinging to Montague like a frightened child, and staring with a wild, hunted look upon his face. Montague sat transfixed.

"Yes," the other rushed on, "that's the truth, as God hears me! And it's the first time I've ever spoken it in my life! I have to hide it—because men would laugh at me—they pretend they're not afraid! But I lie awake all night, and it's like a fiend that sits by my bedside! I lie and listen to my own heart—I feel it beating, and I think how weak it is, and what thin walls it has, and what a wretched, helpless thing it is to have your life depend on that!—You don't know what that is, I suppose."

Montague shook his head.

"You're young, you see," said the other. "You have health—everybody has health, except me! And everybody hates me—I haven't got a friend in the world!"

Montague was quite taken aback by the suddenness of this outburst. He tried to stop it, for he felt almost indecent in listening—it was not fair to take a man off his guard like this. But the stranger could not be stopped—he was completely unstrung, and his voice grew louder and louder.

"It's every word of it true," he exclaimed wildly. "And I can't stand it any more. I can't stand anything any more. I was young and strong once—I could take care of myself; and I said: I'll make money, I'll be master of other men! But I was a fool—I forgot my health. And now all the money on earth can't do me any good! I'd give ten million dollars to-day for a body like any other man's—and this—this is what I have!"

He struck his hands against his bosom. "Look at it!" he cried, hysterically. "This is what I've got to live in! It won't digest any food, and I can't keep it warm—there's nothing right with it! How would you like to lie awake at night and say to yourself that your teeth were decaying and you couldn't help it—your hair was falling out, and nobody could stop it? You're old and worn out—falling to pieces; and everybody hates you—everybody's waiting for you to die, so that they can get you out of the way. The doctors come, and they're all humbugs! They shake their heads and use long words—they know they can't do you any good, but they want their big fees! And all they do is to frighten you worse, and make you sicker than ever!"

There was nothing that Montague could do save to sit and listen to this outburst of wretchedness. His attempts to soothe the old man only had the effect of exciting him more.

"Why does it all have to fall on me?" he moaned. "I want to be like other people—I want to live! And instead, I'm like a man with a pack of hungry wolves prowling round him—that's what it's like! It's like Nature—hungry and cruel and savage! You think you know what life is; it seems so beautiful and gentle and pleasant—that's when you're on top! But now I'm down, and I KNOW what it is—it's a thing like a nightmare, that reaches out for you to clutch you and crush you! And you can't get away from it—you're helpless as a rat in a corner—you're damned—you're damned!" The miserable man's voice broke in a cry of despair, and he sank down in a heap in front of Montague, shaking and sobbing. The other was trembling slightly, and stricken with awe.

There was a long silence, and then the stranger lifted his tear-stained face, and Montague helped to support him. "Have a little more of the whisky," said he.

"No," the other answered feebly, "I'd better not."

"—My doctors won't let me have whisky," he added, after a while. "That's my liver. I've so many don'ts, you know, that it takes a note-book to keep track of them. And all of them together do me no good! Think of it—I have to live on graham crackers and milk—actually, not a thing has passed my lips for two years but graham crackers and milk."

And then suddenly, with a start, it came to Montague where he had seen this wrinkled old face before. It was Laura Hegan's uncle, whom the Major had pointed out to him in the dining-room of the Millionaires' Club! Old Henry S. Grimes, who was really only sixty, but looked eighty; and who owned slum tenements, and evicted more people in a month than could be crowded into the club-house!

Montague gave no sign, but sat holding the man in his arms. A little trickle of blood came from under the handkerchief and ran down his cheek; Montague felt him tremble as he touched this with his ringer.

"Is it much of a cut?" he asked.

"Not much," said Montague; "two or three stitches, perhaps."

"Send for my family physician," the other added. "If I should faint, or anything, you'll find his name in my card-case. What's that?"

There was the sound of voices down the road. "Hello!'" Montague shouted; and a moment later two men in automobile costume came running toward him. They stopped, staring in dismay at the sight which confronted them.

At Montague's suggestion they made haste to find a log by means of which they lifted the auto sufficiently to drag out the body of the chauffeur. Montague saw that it was quite cold.

He went back to old Grimes. "Where do you wish to go?" he asked.

The other hesitated. "I was bound for the Harrisons'—" he said.

"The Leslie Harrisons?" asked Montague. (They were people he had met at the Devons'.)

The other noticed his look of recognition. "Do you know them?" he asked.

"I do," said Montague.

"It isn't far," said the old man. "Perhaps I had best go there."—And then he hesitated for a moment; and catching Montague by the arm, and pulling him toward him, whispered, "Tell me—you-you won't tell—"

Montague, comprehending what he meant, answered, "It will be between us." At the same time he felt a new thrill of revulsion for this most miserable old creature.

They lifted him into the car; and because they delayed long enough to lay a blanket over the body of the chauffeur, he asked peevishly why they did not start. During the ten or fifteen minutes' trip he sat clinging to Montague, shuddering with fright every time they rounded a turn in the road.

They reached the Harrisons' place; and the footman who opened the door was startled out of his studied impassivity by the sight of a big bundle of bearskin in Montague's arms. "Send for Mrs. Harrison," said Montague, and laid the bundle upon a divan in the hall. "Get a doctor as quickly as you can," he added to a second attendant.

Mrs. Harrison came. "It's Mr. Grimes," said Montague; and then he heard a frightened exclamation, and turned and saw Laura Hegan, in a walking costume, fresh from the cold outside.

"What is it?" she cried. And he told her, as quickly as he could, and she ran to help the old man. Montague stood by, and later carried him upstairs, and waited below until the doctor came.

It was only when he set out for home again that he found time to think about Laura Hegan, and how beautiful she had looked in her furs. He wondered if it would always be his fate to meet her under circumstances which left her no time to be aware of his own existence.

At home he told about his adventure, and found himself quite a hero for the rest of the day. He was obliged to give interviews to several newspaper reporters, and to refuse to let one of them take his picture. Every one at the Devons' seemed to know old Harry Grimes, and Montague thought to himself that if the comments of this particular group of people were a fair sample, the poor wretch was right in saying that he had not a friend in the world.

When he came downstairs the next morning, he found elaborate accounts of the accident in the papers, and learned that Grimes had nothing worse than a scalp wound and a severe shock. Even so, he felt it was incumbent upon him to pay a visit of inquiry, and rode over shortly before lunch.

Laura Hegan came down to see him, wearing a morning gown of white. She confirmed the good news of the papers, and said that her uncle was resting quietly. (She did not say that his physician had come post-haste, with two nurses, and taken up his residence in the house, and that the poor old millionaire was denied even his graham crackers and milk). Instead she said that he had mentioned Montague's kindness particularly, and asked her to thank him. Montague was cynical enough to doubt this.

It was the first time that he had ever had any occasion to talk with Miss Hegan. He noticed her gentle and caressing voice, with the least touch of the South in it; and he was glad to find that it was possible for her to talk without breaking the spell of her serene and noble beauty. Montague stayed as long as he had any right to stay.

And all the way as he rode home he was thinking about Laura Hegan. Here for the first time was a woman whom he felt he should like to know; a woman with reserve and dignity, and some ideas in her life. And it was impossible for him to know her—because she was rich!

There was no dodging this fact—Montague did not even try. He had met women with fortunes already, and he knew how they felt about themselves, and how the rest of the world felt about them. They might wish in their hearts to be something else besides the keepers of a treasure-chest, but their wishes were futile; the money went with them, and they had to defend it against all comers. Montague recalled one heiress after another—débutantes, some of them, exquisite and delicate as butterflies—but under the surface as hard as chain-armour. All their lives they had been trained to think of themselves as representing money, and of every one who came near them as adventurers seeking money. In every word they uttered, in every glance and motion, one might read this meaning. And then he thought of Laura Hegan, with the fortune she would inherit; and he pictured what her life must be—the toadies and parasites and flatterers who would lay siege to her—the scheming mammas and the affectionate sisters and cousins who would plot to gain her confidence! For a man who was poor, and who meant to keep his self-respect, was there any possible conclusion except that she was entirely unknowable to him?

CHAPTER XVI

Montague came back to the city, and dug into his books again; while Alice gave her spare hours to watching the progress of the new gown in which she was to uphold the honour of the family at Mrs. Devon's opening ball. The great event was due in the next week and Society was as much excited about it as a family of children before Christmas. All whom Montague met were invited and all were going unless they happened to be in mourning. Their gossip was all of the disappointed ones, and their bitterness and heartburning.

Mrs. Devon's mansion was thrown open early on the eventful evening, but few would come until midnight. It was the fashion to attend the Opera first, and previous to that half a dozen people would give big dinners. He was a fortunate person who did not hear from his liver after this occasion; for at one o'clock came Mrs. Devon's massive supper, and then again at four o'clock another supper. To prepare these repasts a dozen extra chefs had been imported into the Devon establishment for a week—for it was part of the great lady's pride to permit no outside caterer to prepare anything for her guests.

Montague had never been able to get over his wonder at the social phenomenon known as Mrs. Devon. He came and took his chances in the jostling throngs; and except that he got into casual conversation with one of the numerous detectives whom he took for a guest he came off fairly well. But all the time that he was being passed about and introduced and danced with, he was looking about him and wondering. The grand staircase and the hall and parlours had been turned into tropical gardens, with palms and trailing vines, and azaleas and roses, and great vases of scarlet poinsettia, with hundreds of lights glowing through them. (It was said that this ball had exhausted the flower supply of the country as far south as Atlanta.) And then in the reception room one came upon the little old lady, standing' beneath a bower of orchids. She was clad in a robe of royal purple trimmed with silver, and girdled about with an armour-plate of gems. If one might credit the papers, the diamonds that were worn at one of these balls were valued at twenty million dollars.

The stranger was quite overwhelmed by all the splendour. There was a cotillion danced by two hundred gorgeously clad women and their partners—a scene so gay that one could only think of it as happening in a fairy legend, or some old romance of knighthood. Four sets of favours were given during this function, and jewels and objects of art were showered forth as if from a magician's wand. Mrs. Devon herself soon disappeared, but the riot of music and merry-making went on until near morning, and during all this time the halls and rooms of the great mansion were so crowded that one could scarcely move about.

Then one went home, and realized that all this splendour, and the human effort which it represented, had been for nothing but a memory! Nor would he get the full meaning of it if he failed to realize that it was simply one of thousands—a pattern which every one there would strive to follow in some function of his own. It was a signal bell, which told the world that the "season" was open. It loosed the floodgates of extravagance, and the torrent of dissipation poured forth. From then on there would be a continuous round of gaieties; one might have three banquets every single night—for a dinner and two suppers was now the custom, at entertainments! And filling the rest of one's day were receptions and teas and musicales—a person might take his choice among a score of opportunities, and never leave the circle he met at Mrs. Devon's. Nor was this counting the tens of thousands of aspirants and imitators all over the city; nor in a host of other cities, each with thousands of women who had nothing to do save to ape the ways of the Metropolis. The mind could not realize the volume of this deluge of destruction—it was a thing which stunned the senses, and thundered in one's ears like Niagara.

The meaning of it all did not stop with the people who poured it forth; its effects were to be traced through the whole country. There were hordes of tradesmen and manufacturers who supplied what Society bought, and whose study it was to induce people to buy as much as possible. And so they devised what were called "fashions"—little eccentricities of cut and material, which made everything go out of date quickly. There had once been two seasons, but now there were four; and through window displays and millions of advertisements the public was lured into the trap. The "yellow" journals would give whole pages to describing "What the 400 are wearing"; there were magazines with many millions of readers, which existed for nothing save to propagate these ideas. And everywhere, in all classes of Society, men and women were starving their minds and hearts, and straining their energies to follow this phantom of fashion; the masses were kept poor because of it, and the youth and hope of the world was betrayed by it. In country villages poor farmers' wives were trimming their bonnets over to be "stylish"; and servant-girls in the cities were wearing imitation sealskins, and shop-clerks and sempstresses selling themselves into brothels for the sake of ribbons and gilt jewellery.

It was the instinct of decoration, perverted by the money-lust. In the Metropolis the sole test of excellence was money, and the possession of money was the proof of power; and every natural desire of men and women had been tainted by this influence. The love of beauty, the impulse to hospitality, the joys of music and dancing and love—all these things had become simply means to the demonstration of money-power! The men were busy making more money—but their idle women had nothing in life save this mad race in display. So it had come about that the woman who could consume wealth most conspicuously—who was the most effective instrument for the destroying of the labour and the lives of other people—this was the woman who was most applauded and most noticed.

The most appalling fact about Society was this utter blind materialism. Such expectations as Montague had brought with him had been derived from the literature of Europe; in a grand monde such as this, he expected to meet diplomats and statesmen, scientists and explorers, philosophers and poets and painters. But one never heard anything about such people in Society. It was a mark of eccentricity to be interested in intellectual affairs, and one might go about for weeks and not meet a person with an idea. When these people read, it was a sugar-candy novel, and when they went to the play, it was a musical comedy. The one single intellectual product which it could point to as its own, was a rancid scandal-sheet, used mainly as a means of blackmail. Now and then some aspiring young matron of the "elite" would try to set up a salon after the fashion of the continent, and would gather a few feeble wits about her for a time. But for the most part the intellectual workers of the city held themselves severely aloof; and Society was left a little clique of people whose fortunes had become historic in a decade or two, and who got together in each other's palaces and gorged themselves, and gambled and gossiped about each other, and wove about their personalities a veil of awful and exclusive majesty.

Montague found himself thinking that perhaps it was not they who were to blame. It was not they who had set up wealth as the end and goal of things—it was the whole community, of which they were a part. It was not their fault that they had been left with power and nothing to use it for; it was not their fault that their sons and daughters found themselves stranded in the world, deprived of all necessity, and of the possibility of doing anything useful.

The most pitiful aspect of the whole thing to Montague was this "second generation" who were coming upon the scene, with their lives all poisoned in advance. No wrong which they could do to the world would ever equal the wrong which the world had done them, in permitting them to have money which they had not earned. They were cut off for ever from reality, and from the possibility of understanding life; they had big, healthy bodies, and they craved experience— and they had absolutely nothing to do. That was the real meaning of all this orgy of dissipation—this "social whirl" as it was called; it was the frantic chase of some new thrill, some excitement that would stir the senses of people who had nothing in the world to interest them. That was why they were building palaces, and flinging largesses of banquets and balls, and tearing about the country in automobiles, and travelling over the earth in steam yachts and private trains.

And first and last, the lesson of their efforts was, that the chase was futile; the jaded nerves would not thrill. The most conspicuous fact about Society was its unutterable and agonizing boredom; of its great solemn functions the shop-girl would read with greedy envy, but the women who attended them would be half asleep behind their jewelled fans. It was typified to Montague by Mrs. Billy Alden's yachting party on the Nile; yawning in the face of the Sphinx, and playing bridge beneath the shadow of the pyramids—and counting the crocodiles and proposing to jump in by way of "changing the pain"!

People attended these ceaseless rounds of entertainments, simply because they dreaded to be left alone. They wandered from place to place, following like a herd of sheep whatever leader would inaugurate a new diversion. One could have filled a volume with the list of their "fads." There were new ones every week—if Society did not invent them, the yellow journals invented them. There was a woman who had her teeth filled with diamonds; and another who was driving a pair of zebras. One heard of monkey dinners and pyjama dinners at Newport, of horse-back dinners and vegetable dances in New York. One heard of fashion-albums and autograph-fans and talking crows and rare orchids and reindeer meat; of bracelets for men and ankle rings for women; of "vanity-boxes" at ten and twenty thousand dollars each; of weird and repulsive pets, chameleons and lizards and king-snakes—there was one young woman who wore a cat-snake as a necklace. One would take to slumming and another to sniffing brandy through the nose; one had a table-cover made of woven roses, and another was wearing perfumed flannel at sixteen dollars a yard; one had inaugurated ice-skating in August, and another had started a class for the study of Plato. Some were giving tennis tournaments in bathing-suits, and playing leap-frog after dinner; others had got dispensations from the Pope, so that they might have private chapels and confessors; and yet others were giving "progressive dinners," moving from one restaurant to another—a cocktail and blue-points at Sherry's, a soup and Madeira at Delmonico's, some terrapin with amontillado at the Waldorf—and so on.

One of the consequences of the furious pace was that people's health broke down very quickly; and there were all sorts of bizarre ways of restoring it. One person would be eating nothing but spinach, and another would be living on grass. One would chew a mouthful of soup thirty-two times; another would eat every two hours, and another only once a week. Some went out in the early morning and walked bare-footed in the grass, and others went hopping about the floor on their hands and knees to take off fat. There were "rest cures" and "water cures," "new thought" and "metaphysical healing" and "Christian Science"; there was an automatic horse, which one might ride indoors, with a register showing the distance travelled. Montague met one man who had an electric machine, which cost thirty thousand dollars, and which took hold of his arms and feet and exercised him while he waited. He met a woman who told him she was riding an electric camel!

Everywhere one went there were new people, spending their money in new and incredible ways. Here was a man who had bought a chapel and turned it into a theatre, and hired professional actors, and persuaded his friends to come and see him act Shakespeare. Here was a woman who costumed herself after figures in famous paintings, with arrangements of roses and cherry leaves, and wreaths of ivy and laurel—and with costumes for her pet dogs to match! Here was a man who paid six dollars a day for a carnation four inches across; and a girl who wore a hat trimmed with fresh morning-glories, and a ball costume with swarms of real butterflies tied with silk threads; and another with a hat made of woven silver, with ostrich plumes forty inches long made entirely of silver films. Here was a man who hired a military company to drill all day long to prepare a floor for dancing; and another who put up a building at a cost of thirty thousand dollars to give a débutante dance for his daughter, and then had it torn down the day after. Here was a man who bred rattlesnakes and turned them loose by thousands, and had driven everybody away from the North Carolina estate of one of the Wallings. Here was a man who was building himself a yacht with a model dairy and bakery on board, and a French laundry and a brass band. Here was a million-dollar racing-yacht with auto-boats on it and a platoon of marksmen, and some Chinese laundrymen, and two physicians for its half-insane occupant. Here was a man who had bought a Rhine castle for three-quarters of a million, and spent as much in restoring it, and filled it with servants dressed in fourteenth-century costumes. Here was a five-million-dollar art collection hidden away where nobody ever saw it!

One saw the meaning of this madness most clearly in the young men of Society. Some were killing themselves and other people in automobile races at a hundred and twenty miles an hour. Some went in for auto-boats, mere shells of things, shaped like a knife-blade, that tore through the water at forty miles an hour. Some would hire professional pugilists to knock them out; others would get up dog-fights and bear-fights, and boxing matches with kangaroos. Montague was taken to the home of one young man who had given his life to hunting wild game in every corner of the globe, and would travel round the world for a new species to add to his museum of trophies. He had heard that Baron Rothschild had offered a thousand pounds for a "bongo," a huge grass-eating animal, which no white man had ever seen; and he had taken a year's trip into the interior, with a train of a hundred and thirty natives, and had brought out the heads of forty different species, including a bongo—which the Baron did not get! He met another who had helped to organize a balloon club, and two twenty-four-hour trips in the clouds. (This, by the way, was the latest sport—at Tuxedo they had races between balloons and automobiles; and Montague met one young lady who boasted that she had been up five times.) There was another young millionaire who sat and patiently taught Sunday School, in the presence of a host of reporters; there was another who set up a chain of newspapers all over the country and made war upon his class. There were others who went in for settlement work and Russian revolutionists—there were even some who called themselves Socialists! Montague thought that this was the strangest fad of all; and when he met one of these young men at an afternoon tea, he gazed at him with wonder and perplexity—thinking of the man he had heard ranting on the street-corner.

This was the "second generation." Appalling as it was to think of, there was a third growing up, and getting ready to take the stage. And with wealth accumulating faster than ever, who could guess what they might do? There were still in Society a few men and women who had earned their money, and had some idea of the toil and suffering that it stood for; but when the third generation had taken possession, these would all be dead or forgotten, and there would no longer be any link to connect them with reality!

In the light of this thought one was moved to watch the children of the rich. Some of these had inherited scores of millions of dollars while they were still in the cradle; now and then one of them would be presented with a million-dollar house for a birthday gift. When such a baby was born, the newspapers would give pages to describing its layette, with baby dresses at a hundred dollars each, and lace handkerchiefs at five dollars, and dressing-sets with tiny gold brushes and powder-boxes; one might see a picture of the precious object in a "Moses basket," covered with rare and wonderful Valenciennes lace.

This child would grow up in an atmosphere of luxury and self-indulgence; it would be bullying the servants at the age of six, and talking scandal and smoking cigarettes at twelve. It would be petted and admired and stared at, and paraded about in state, dressed up like a French doll; it would drink in snobbery and hate-fulness with the very air it breathed. One might meet in these great houses little tots not yet in their teens whose talk was all of the cost of things, and of the infe-riority of their neighbours. There was nothing in the world too good for them.— They had little miniature automobiles to ride about the country in, and blooded Arabian ponies, and doll-houses in real Louis Seize, with jewelled rugs and min-iature electric lights. At Mrs. Caroline Smythe's, Montague was introduced to a pale and anaemic-looking youth of thirteen, who dined in solemn state alone when the rest of the family was away, and insisted upon having all the footmen in attendance; and his unfortunate aunt brought a storm about her ears by forbidding the butler to take champagne upstairs into the nursery before lunch.

A little remark stayed in Montague's mind as expressing the attitude of Society toward such matters. Major Venable had chanced to remark jestingly that children were coming to understand so much nowadays that it was necessary for the ladies to be careful. To which Mrs. Vivie Patton answered, with a sudden access of seri-ousness: "I don't know—do you find that children have any morals? Mine haven't."

And then the fascinating Mrs. Vivie went on to tell the truth about her own children. They were natural-born savages, and that was all there was to it. They did as they pleased, and no one could stop them. The Major replied that nowadays all the world was doing as it pleased, and no one seemed to be able to stop it; and with that jest the conversation was turned to other matters. But Montague sat in silence, thinking about it—wondering what would happen to the world when it had fallen under the sway of this generation of spoiled children, and had adopted altogether the religion of doing as one pleased.

In the beginning people had simply done as they pleased spontaneously, and without thinking about it; but now, Montague discovered, the custom had spread to such an extent that it was developing a philosophy. There was springing up a new cult, whose devotees were planning to make over the world upon the plan of doing as one pleased. Because its members were wealthy, and able to command the talent of the world, the cult was developing an art, with a highly perfected technique, and a literature which was subtle and exquisite and alluring. Europe had had such a literature for a century, and England for a generation or two. And now America was having it, too!

Montague had an amusing insight into this one day, when Mrs. Vivie invited him to one of her "artistic evenings." Mrs. Vivie was in touch with a special set which went in for intellectual things, and included some amateur Bohemians and men of "genius." "Don't you come if you'll be shocked," she had said to him— "for Strathcona will be there."

Montague deemed himself able to stand a good deal by this time. He went, and found Mrs. Vivie and her Count (Mr. Vivie had apparently not been invited) and also the young poet of Diabolism, whose work was just then the talk of the town. He was a tall, slender youth with a white face and melancholy black eyes, and black locks falling in cascades about his ears; he sat in an Oriental corner, with a manuscript copied in tiny handwriting upon delicately scented "art paper," and tied with passionate purple ribbons. A young girl clad in white sat by his side and held a candle, while he read from this manuscript his unprinted (because unprintable) verses.

And between the readings the young poet talked. He talked about himself and his work—apparently that was what he had come to talk about. His words flowed like a swift stream, limpid, sparkling, incessant; leaping from place to place— here, there, quick as the play of light upon the water. Montague laboured to follow the speaker's ideas, until he found his mind in a whirl and gave it up. Afterward, when he thought it over, he laughed at himself; for Strathcona's ideas were not serious things, having relationship to truth—they were epigrams put together to dazzle the hearer, studies in paradox, with as much relation to life as fireworks. He took the sum-total of the moral experience of the human race, and turned it upside down and jumbled it about, and used it as bits of glass in a kaleidoscope. And the hearers would gasp, and whisper, "Diabolical!"

The motto of this "school" of poets was that there was neither good nor evil, but that all things were "interesting." After listening to Strathcona for half an hour, one felt like hiding his head, and denying that he had ever thought of having any virtue; in a world where all things were uncertain, it was presumptuous even to pretend to know what virtue was. One could only be what one was; and did not that mean that one must do as one pleased?

You could feel a shudder run through the company at his audacity. And the worst of it was that you could not dismiss it with a laugh; for the boy was really a poet—he had fire and passion, the gift of melodious ecstacy. He was only twenty, and in his brief meteor flight he had run the gamut of all experience; he had familiarized himself with all human achievement—past, present, and future. There was nothing any one could mention that he did not perfectly comprehend: the raptures of the saints, the consecration of the martyrs—yes, he had known them; likewise he had touched the depths of depravity, he had been lost in the innermost passages of the caverns of hell. And all this had been interesting—in its time; now he was sighing for new worlds of experience—say for unrequited love, which should drive him to madness.

It was at this point that Montague dropped out of the race, and took to studying from the outside the mechanism of this young poet's conversation. Strathcona flouted the idea of a moral sense; but in reality he was quite dependent upon it—his recipe for making epigrams was to take what other people's moral sense made them respect, and identify it with something which their moral sense made them abhor. Thus, for instance, the tale which he told about one of the members of his set, who was a relative of a bishop. The great man had occasion to rebuke him for his profligate ways, declaring in the course of his lecture that he was living off the reputation of his father; to which the boy made the crushing rejoinder: "It may be bad to live off the reputation of one's father, but it's better than living off the repu-tation of God."—This was very subtle and it was necessary to ponder it. God was dead; and the worthy bishop did not know it! But let him take a new God, who had no reputation, and go out into the world and make a living out of him!

Then Strathcona discussed literature. He paid his tribute to the "Fleurs de Mal" and the "Songs before Sunrise"; but most, he said, he owed to "the divine Oscar." This English poet of many poses and some vices the law had seized and flung into jail; and since the law is a thing so brutal and wicked that whoever is touched by it is made thereby a martyr and a hero, there had grown up quite a cult about the memory of "Oscar." All up-to-date poets imitated his style and his attitude to life; and so the most revolting of vices had the cloak of romance flung about them— were given long Greek and Latin names, and discussed with parade of learning as revivals of Hellenic ideals. The young men in Strathcona's set referred to each other as their "lovers"; and if one showed any perplexity over this, he was regard-ed, not with contempt—for it was not aesthetic to feel contempt—but with a slight lifting of the eyebrows, intended to annihilate.

One must not forget, of course, that these young people were poets, and to that extent were protected from their own doctrines. They were interested, not in life, but in making pretty verses about life; there were some among them who lived as cheerful ascetics in garret rooms, and gave melodious expression to devilish emo-tions. But, on the other hand, for every poet, there were thousands who were not poets, but people to whom life was real. And these lived out the creed, and wrecked their lives; and with the aid of the poet's magic, the glamour of melody and the fire divine, they wrecked the lives with which they came into contact. The new generation of boys and girls were deriving their spiritual sustenance from the poetry of Baudelaire and Wilde; and rushing with the hot impulsiveness of youth into the dreadful traps which the traders in vice prepared for them. One's heart bled to see them, pink-cheeked and bright-eyed, pursuing the hem of the Muse's robe in brothels and dens of infamy!

CHAPTER XVII

The social mill ground on for another month. Montague withdrew himself as much as his brother would let him; but Alice, was on the go all night and half the day. Oliver had sold his racing automobile to a friend—he was a man of family now, he said, and his wild days were over. He had got, instead, a limousine car for Alice; though she declared she had no need of it—if ever she was going to any place, Charlie Carter always begged her to use his. Charlie's siege was as persistent as ever, as Montague noticed with annoyance.

The great law case was going forward. After weeks of study and investigation, Montague felt that he had the matter well in hand; and he had taken Mr. Hasbrook's memoranda as a basis for a new work of his own, much more substantial. Bit by bit; as he dug into the subject, he had discovered a state of affairs in the Fidelity Company, and, indeed, in the whole insurance business and its allied realms of banking and finance, which shocked him profoundly. It was impossible for him to imagine how such conditions could exist and remain unknown to the public—more especially as every one in Wall Street with whom he talked seemed to know about them and to take them for granted.

His client's papers had provided him with references to the books; Montague had taken this dry material and made of it a protest which had the breath of life in it. It was a thing at which he toiled with deadly earnestness; it was not merely a struggle of one man to get a few thousand dollars, it was an appeal in behalf of millions of helpless people whose trust had been betrayed. It was the first step in a long campaign, which the young lawyer meant should force a great evil into the light of day.

He went over his bill of complaint with Mr. Hasbrook, and he was glad to see that the work he had done made its impression upon him. In fact, his client was a little afraid that some of his arguments might be too radical in tone—from the strictly legal point of view, he made haste to explain. But Montague reassured him upon this point.

And then came the day when the great ship was ready for launching. The news must have spread quickly, for a few hours after the papers in the suit had been filed, Montague received a call from a newspaper reporter, who told him of the excitement in financial circles, where the thing had fallen like a bomb. Montague explained the purpose of the suit, and gave the reporter a number of facts which he felt certain would attract attention to the matter. When he picked up the paper the next morning, however, he was surprised to find that only a few lines had been given to the case, and that his interview had been replaced by one with an unnamed official of the Fidelity, to the effect that the attack upon the company was obviously for black-mailing purposes.

That was the only ripple which Montague's work produced upon the surface of the pool; but there was a great commotion among the fish at the bottom, about which he was soon to learn.

That evening, while he was hard at work in his study, he received a telephone call from his brother. "I'm coming round to see you," said Oliver. "Wait for me."

"All right," said the other, and added, "I thought you were dining at the Wallings'."

"I'm there now," was the answer. "I'm leaving."

"What is the matter?" Montague asked.

"There's hell to pay," was the reply—and then silence.

When Oliver appeared, a few minutes later, he did not even stop to set down his hat, but exclaimed, "Allan, what in heaven's name have you been doing?"

"What do you mean?" asked the other.

"Why, that suit!"

"What about it?"

"Good God, man!" cried Oliver. "Do you mean that you really don't know what you've done?"

Montague was staring at him. "I'm afraid I don't," said he.

"Why, you're turning the world upside down!" exclaimed the other. "Everybody you know is crazy about it."

"Everybody I know!" echoed Montague. "What have they to do with it?"

"Why, you've stabbed them in the back!" half shouted Oliver. "I could hardly believe my ears when they told me. Robbie Walling is simply wild—I never had such a time in my life."

"I don't understand yet," said Montague, more and more amazed. "What has he to do with it?"

"Why, man," cried Oliver, "his brother's a director in the Fidelity! And his own interests—and all the other companies! You've struck at the whole insurance business!"

Montague caught his breath. "Oh, I see!" he said.

"How could you think of such a thing?" cried the other, wildly. "You promised to consult me about things—"

"I told you when I took this case," put in Montague, quickly.

"I know," said his brother. "But you didn't explain—and what did I know about it? I thought I could leave it to your common sense not to mix up in a thing like this."

"I'm very sorry," said Montague, gravely. "I had no idea of any such result."

"That's what I told Robbie," said Oliver. "Good God, what a time I had!"

He took his hat and coat and laid them on the bed, and sat down and began to tell about it. "I made him realize the disadvantage you were under," he said, "being a stranger and not knowing the ground. I believe he had an idea that you tried to get his confidence on purpose to attack him. It was Mrs. Robbie, I guess—you know her fortune is all in that quarter."

Oliver wiped the perspiration from his forehead. "My!" he said.—"And fancy what old Wyman must be saying about this! And what a time poor Betty must be having! And then Freddie Vandam—the air will be blue for half a mile round his place! I must send him a wire and explain that it was a mistake, and that we're getting out of it."

And he got up, to suit the action to the word. But half-way to the desk he heard his brother say, "Wait."

He turned, and saw Montague, quite pale. "I suppose by 'getting out of it,'" said the latter, "you mean dropping the case."

"Of course," was the answer.

"Well, then," he continued, very gravely,—"I can see that it's going to be hard, and I'm sorry. But you might as well understand me at the very beginning—I will never drop this case."

Oliver's jaw fell limp. "Allan!" he gasped.

There was a silence; and then the storm broke. Oliver knew his brother well enough to realize just how thoroughly he meant what he said; and so he got the full force of the shock all at once. He raved and swore and wrung his hands, and declaimed at his brother, saying that he had betrayed him, that he was ruining him—dumping himself and the whole family into the ditch. They would be jeered at and insulted—they would be blacklisted and thrown out of Society. Alice's career would be cut short—every door would be closed to her. His own career would die before it was born; he would never get into the clubs—he would be a pariah—he would be bankrupted and penniless. Again and again Oliver went over the situation, naming person after person who would be outraged, and describing what that person would do; there were the Wallings and the Venables and the Havens, the Vandams and the Todds and the Wymans—they were all one regiment, and Montague had flung a bomb into the centre of them!

It was very terrible to him to see his brother's rage and despair; but he had seen his way clear through this matter, and he knew that there was no turning back for him. "It is painful to learn that all one's acquaintances are thieves," he said. "But that does not change my opinion of stealing."

"But my God!" cried Oliver; "did you come to New York to preach sermons?"

To which the other answered, "I came to practise law. And the lawyer who will not fight injustice is a traitor to his profession."

Oliver threw up his hands in despair. What could one say to a sentiment such as that?

—But then again he came to the charge, pointing out to his brother the position in which he had placed himself with the Wallings. He had accepted their hospitality; they had taken him and Alice in, and done everything in the world for them—things for which no money could ever repay them. And now he had struck them!

But the only effect of that was to make Montague regret that he had ever had anything to do with the Wallings. If they expected to use their friendship to tie his hands in such a matter, they were people he would have left alone.

"But do you realize that it's not merely yourself you're ruining?" cried Oliver. "Do you know what you're doing to Alice?"

"That is harder yet for me," the other replied. "But I am sure that Alice would not ask me to stop."

Montague was firmly set in his own mind; but it seemed to be quite impossible for his brother to realize that this was the case. He would give up; but then, going back into his own mind, and facing the thought of this person and that, and the impossibility of the situation which would arise, he would return to the attack with new anguish in his voice. He implored and scolded, and even wept; and then he would get himself together again, and come and sit in front of his brother and try to reason with him.

And so it was that in the small hours of the morning, Montague, pale and nervous, but quite unshaken, was sitting and listening while his brother unfolded before him a picture of the Metropolis as he had come to see it. It was a city ruled by mighty forces—money-forces; great families and fortunes, which had held their sway for generations, and regarded the place, with all its swarming millions, as their birthright. They possessed it utterly—they held it in the hollow of their hands. Railroads and telegraphs and telephones—banks and insurance and trust companies—all these they owned; and the political machines and the legislatures, the courts and the newspapers, the churches and the colleges. And their rule was for plunder; all the streams of profit ran into their coffers. The stranger who came to their city succeeded as he helped them in their purposes, and failed if they could not use him. A great editor or bishop was a man who taught their doctrines; a great statesman was a man who made the laws for them; a great lawyer was one who helped them to outwit the public. Any man who dared to oppose them, they would cast out and trample on, they would slander and ridicule and ruin.

And Oliver came down to particulars—he named these powerful men, one after one, and showed what they could do. If his brother would only be a man of the world, and see the thing! Look at all the successful lawyers! Oliver named them, one after one—shrewd devisers of corporation trickery, with incomes of hundreds of thousands a year. He could not name the men who had refused to play the game—for no one had ever heard of them. But it was so evident what would happen in this case! His friends would cast him off; his own client would get his price—whatever it was—and then leave him in the lurch, and laugh at him! "If you can't make up your mind to play the game," cried Oliver, frantically, "at least you can give it up! There are plenty of other ways of getting a living—if you'll let me, I'll take care of you myself, rather than have you disgrace me. Tell me—will you do that? Will you quit altogether?"

And Montague suddenly leaped to his feet, and brought his fist down upon the desk with a bang. "No!" he cried; "by God, no!"

"Let me make you understand me once for all," he rushed on. "You've shown me New York as you see it. I don't believe it's the truth—I don't believe it for one single moment! But let me tell you this, I shall stay here and find out—and if it is true, it won't stop me! I shall stay here and defy those people! I shall stay and fight them till the day I die! They may ruin me,—I'll go and live in a garret if I have to,—but as sure as there's a God that made me, I'll never stop till I've opened the eyes of the people to what they're doing!"

Montague towered over his brother, white-hot and terrible. Oliver shrank from him—he never had seen such a burst of wrath from him before. "Do you understand me now?" Montague cried; and he answered, in a despairing voice, "Yes, yes."

"I see it's all up," he added weakly. "You and I can't pull together."

"No," exclaimed the other, passionately, "we can't. And we might as well give up trying. You have chosen to be a time-server and a lick-spittle, and I don't choose it! Do you think I've learned nothing in the time I've been here? Why, man, you used to be daring and clever—and now you never draw a breath without wondering if these rich snobs will like the way you do it! And you want Alice to sell herself to them—you want me to sell my career to them!"

There was a long pause. Oliver had turned very pale. And then suddenly his brother caught himself together, and said: "I'm sorry. I didn't mean to quarrel, but you've goaded me too much. I'm grateful for what you have tried to do for me, and I'll pay you back as soon as I can. But I can't go on with this game. I'll quit, and you can disown me to your friends—tell them that I've run amuck, and to forget they ever knew me. They'll hardly blame you for it—they know you too well for that. And as for Alice, I'll talk it out with her to-morrow, and let her decide for herself—if she wants to be a Society queen, she can put herself in your hands, and I'll get out of her way. On the other hand, if she approves of what I'm doing, why we'll both quit, and you won't have to bother with either of us."

That was the basis upon which they parted for the night; but like most resolutions taken at white heat, it was not followed literally. It was very hard for Montague to have to confront Alice with such a choice; and as for Oliver, when he went home and thought it over, he began to discover gleams of hope. He might make it clear to every one that he was not responsible for his brother's business vagaries, and take his chances upon that basis. After all, there were wheels within wheels in Society; and if the Robbie Wallings chose to break with him—why, they had plenty of enemies. There might even be interests which would be benefited by Allan's course, and would take him up.

Montague had resolved to write and break every engagement which he had made, and to sever his connection with Society at one stroke. But the next day his brother came again, with compromises and new protestations. There was no use going to the other extreme: he, Oliver, would have it out with the Wallings, and they might all go on their way as if nothing had happened.

So Montague made his début in the rôle of knight-errant. He went with many qualms and misgivings, uncertain how each new person would take it. The next evening he was promised for a theatre-party with Siegfried Harvey; and they had supper in a private room at Delmonico's, and there came Mrs. Winnie, resplendent as an apple tree in early April—and murmuring with bated breath, "Oh, you dreadful man, what have you been doing?"

"Have I been poaching on YOUR preserves?" he asked promptly.

"No, not mine," she said, "but—" and then she hesitated.

"On Mr. Duval's?" he asked.

"No," she said, "not his—but everybody else's! He was telling me about it to-day—there's a most dreadful uproar. He wanted me to try to find out what you were up to, and who was behind it."

Montague listened, wonderingly. Did Mrs. Winnie mean to imply that her husband had asked her to try to worm his business secrets out of him? That was what she seemed to imply. "I told him I never talked business with my friends," she said. "He can ask you himself, if he chooses. But what DOES it all mean, anyhow?"

Montague smiled at the naive inconsistency.

"It means nothing," said he, "except that I am trying to get justice for a client."

"But can you afford to make so many powerful enemies?" she asked.

"I've taken my chances on that," he replied.

Mrs. Winnie answered nothing, but looked at him with wondering admiration in her eyes. "You arc different from the men about you," she remarked, after a while-and her tone gave Montague to understand that there was one person who meant to stand by him.

But Mrs. Winnie Duval was not all Society. Montague was amused to notice with what suddenness the stream of invitations slacked up; it was necessary for Alice to give her calling list many revisions. Freddie Vandam had promised to invite them to his place on Long Island, and of course that invitation would never come; likewise they would never again see the palace of the Lester Todds, upon the Jersey mountain-top.

Oliver put in the next few days in calling upon people to explain his embarrassing situation. He washed his hands of his brother's affairs, he said; and his friends might do the same, if they saw fit. With the Robbie Wallings he had a stormy half hour, about which he thought it best to say little to the rest of the family. Robbie did not break with him utterly, because of their Wall Street Alliance; but Mrs. Robbie's feeling was so bitter, he said, that it would be best if Alice saw nothing of her for a while. He had a long talk with Alice, and explained the situation. The girl was utterly dumbfounded, for she was deeply grateful to Mrs. Robbie, and fond of her as well; and she could not believe that a friend could be so cruelly unjust to her.

The upshot of the whole situation was a very painful episode. A few days later Alice met Mrs. Robbie at a reception; and she took the lady aside, and tried to tell her how distressed and helpless she was. And the result was that Mrs. Robbie flew into a passion and railed at her, declaring in the presence of several people that she had sponged upon her and abused her hospitality! And so poor Alice came home, weeping and half hysterical.

All of which, of course, was like oil upon a fire; the heavens were lighted up with the conflagration. The next development was a paragraph in Society's scandal-sheet—telling with infinite gusto how a certain ultra-fashionable matron had taken up a family of stranded waifs from a far State, and introduced them into the best circles, and even gone so far as to give a magnificent dance in their honour; and how the discovery had been made that the head of the family had been secretly preparing an attack upon their business interests; and of the tearing of hair and gnashing of teeth which had followed—and the violent quarrel in a public place. The paragraph concluded with the prediction that the strangers would find themselves the centre of a merry social war.

Oliver was the first to show them this paper. But lest by any chance they should miss it, half a dozen unknown friends were good enough to mail them copies, carefully marked.—And then came Reggie Mann, who as free-lance and gossip-gatherer sat on the fence and watched the fun; Reggie wore a thin veil of sympathy over his naked glee, and brought them the latest reports from all portions of the battle-ground. Thus they were able to know exactly what everybody was saying about them—who was amused and who was outraged, and who proposed to drop them and who to take them up.

Montague listened for a while, but then he got tired of it, and went for a walk to escape it—but only to run into another trap. It was dark, and he was strolling down the Avenue, when out of a brilliantly lighted jewellery shop came Mrs. Billy Alden to her carriage. And she hailed him with an exclamation.

"You man," she cried, "what have you been doing?"

He tried to laugh it off and escape, but she took him by the arm, commanding, "Get in here and tell me about it."

So he found himself moving with the slow stream of vehicles on the Avenue, and with Mrs. Billy gazing at him quizzically and asking him if he did not feel like a hippopotamus in a frog-pond.

He replied to her raillery by asking her under which flag she stood. But there was little need to ask that, for anyone who was fighting a Walling became ipso facto a friend of Mrs. Billy's. She told Montague that if he felt his social position was imperilled, all he had to do was to come to her. She would gird on her armour and take the field.

"But tell me how you came to do it," she said.

He answered that there was very little to tell. He had taken up a case which was obviously just, but having no idea what a storm it would raise.

Then he noticed that his companion was looking at him sharply. "Do you really mean that's all there is to it?" she asked.

"Of course I do," said he, perplexed.

"Do you know," was her unexpected response, "I hardly know what to make of you. I'm afraid to trust you, on account of your brother."

Montague was embarrassed. "I don't know what you mean," he said.

"Everybody thinks there's some trickery in that suit," she answered.

"Oh," said Montague, "I see. Well, they will find out. If it will help you any to know it, I've been having no end of scenes with my brother."

"I'll believe you," said Mrs. Billy, genially. "But it seems strange that a man could have been so blind to a situation! I feel quite ashamed because I didn't help you myself!"

The carriage had stopped at Mrs. Billy's home, and she asked him to dinner. "There'll be nobody but my brother," she said,—"we're resting this evening. And I can make up to you for my negligence!"

Montague had no engagement, and so he went in, and saw Mrs. Billy's mansion, which was decorated in imitation of a Doge's palace, and met Mr. "Davy" Alden, a mild-mannered little gentleman who obeyed orders promptly. They had a comfortable dinner of half-a-dozen courses, and then retired to the drawing-room, where Mrs. Billy sank into a huge easy chair, with a decanter of whisky and some cracked ice in readiness beside it. Then from a tray she selected a thick black cigar, and placidly bit off the end and lighted it, and then settled back at her ease, and proceeded to tell Montague about New York, and about the great families who ruled it, and where and how they had got their money, and who were their allies and who their enemies, and what particular skeletons were hidden in each of their closets.

It was worth coming a long way to listen to Mrs. Billy tete-a-tete; her thoughts were vigorous, and her imagery was picturesque. She spoke of old Dan Waterman, and described him as a wild boar rooting chestnuts. He was all right, she said, if you didn't come under his tree. And Montague asked, "Which is his tree?" and she answered, "Any one he happens to be under at the time."

And then she came to the Wallings. Mrs. Billy had been in on the inside of that family, and there was nothing she didn't know about it; and she brought the members up, one by one, and dissected them, and exhibited them for Montague's benefit. They were typical bourgeois people, she said. They were burghers. They had never shown the least capacity for refinement—they ate and drank, and jostled other people out of the way. The old ones had been boors, and the new ones were cads.

And Mrs. Billy sat and puffed at her cigar. "Do you know the history of the family?" she asked. "The founder was a rough old ferryman. He fought his rivals so well that in the end he owned all the boats; and then some one discovered the idea of buying legislatures and building railroads, and he went into that. It was a time when they simply grabbed things—if you ever look into it, you'll find they're making fortunes to-day out of privileges that the old man simply sat down on and held. There's a bridge at Albany, for instance, to which they haven't the slightest right; my brother knows about it—they've given themselves a contract with their railroad by which they're paid for every passenger, and their profit every year is greater than the cost of the bridge. The son was the head of the family when I came in; and I found that he had it all arranged to leave thirty million dollars to one of his sons, and only ten million to my husband. I set to work to change that, I can tell you. I used to go around to see him, and scratch his back and tickle him and make him feel good. Of course the family went wild—my, how they hated me! They set old Ellis to work to keep me off—have you met Judge Ellis?"

"I have," said Montague.

"Well, there's a pussy-footed old hypocrite for you," said Mrs. Billy. "In those days he was Walling's business lackey—used to pass the money to the legislators and keep the wheels of the machine greased. One of the first things I said to the old man was that I didn't ask him to entertain my butler, and he mustn't ask me to entertain his valet—and so I forbid Ellis to enter my house. And when I found that he was trying to get between the old man and me, I flew into a rage and boxed his ears and chased him out of the room!"

Mrs. Billy paused, and laughed heartily over the recollection. "Of course that tickled the old man to death," she continued. "The Wallings never could make out how I managed to get round him as I did; but it was simply because I was honest with him. They'd come snivelling round, pretending they were anxious about his health; while I wanted his money, and I told him so."

The valiant lady turned to the decanter. "Have some Scotch?" she asked, and poured some for herself, and then went on with her story. "When I first came to New York," she said, "the rich people's houses were all alike—all dreary brown-stone fronts, sandwiched in on one or two city lots. I vowed that I would have a house with some room all around it—and that was the beginning of those palaces that all New York walks by and stares at. You can hardly believe it now—those houses were a scandal! But the sensation tickled the old man. I remember one day we walked up the Avenue to see how they were coming on; and he pointed with his big stick to the second floor, and asked, 'What's that?' I answered, 'It's a safe I'm building into the house.' (That was a new thing, too, in those days.)—'I'm going to keep my money in that,' I said. 'Bah!' he growled, 'when you're done with this house, you won't have any money left.'—'I'm planning to make you fill it for me,' I answered; and do you know, he chuckled all the way home over it!"

Mrs. Billy sat laughing softly to herself. "We had great old battles in those days," she said. "Among other things, I had to put the Wallings into Society. They were sneaking round on the outside when I came—licking people's boots and expecting to be kicked. I said to myself, I'll put an end to that—we'll have a show-down! So I gave a ball that made the whole country sit up and gasp—it wouldn't be noticed particularly nowadays, but then people had never dreamed of anything so gorgeous. And I made out a list of all the people I wanted to know in New York, and I said to myself: 'If you come, you're a friend, and if you don't come, you're an enemy.' And they all came, let me tell you! And there was never any question about the Wallings being in Society after that."

Mrs. Billy halted; and Montague remarked, with a smile, that doubtless she was sorry now that she had done it.

"Oh, no," she answered, with a shrug of her shoulders. "I find that all I have to do is to be patient—I hate people, and think I'd like to poison them, but if I only wait long enough, something happens to them much worse than I ever dreamed of. You'll be revenged on the Robbies some day."

"I don't want any revenge," Montague answered. "I've no quarrel with them—I simply wish I hadn't accepted their hospitality. I didn't know they were such little people. It seems hard to believe it."

Mrs. Billy laughed cynically. "What could you expect?" she said. "They know there's nothing to them but their money. When that's gone, they're gone—they could never make any more."

The lady gave a chuckle, and added: "Those words make me think of Davy's experience when he wanted to go to Congress! Tell him about it, Davy."

But Mr. Alden did not warm to the subject; he left the tale to his sister.

"He was a Democrat, you know," said she, "and he went to the boss and told him he'd like to go to Congress. The answer was that it would cost him forty thousand dollars, and he kicked at the price. Others didn't have to put up such sums, he said—why should he? And the old man growled at him, 'The rest have other things to give. One can deliver the letter-carriers, another is paid for by a corporation. But what can you do? What is there to you but your money?'—So Davy paid the money—didn't you, Davy?" And Davy grinned sheepishly.

"Even so," she went on, "he came off better than poor Devon. They got fifty thousand out of him, and sold him out, and he never got to Congress after all! That was just before he concluded that America wasn't a fit place for a gentleman to live in."

And so Mrs. Billy got started on the Devons! And after that came the Havens and the Wymans and the Todds—it was midnight before she got through with them all.

CHAPTER XVIII

The newspapers said nothing more about the Hasbrook suit; but in financial circles Montague had attained considerable notoriety because of it. And this was the means of bringing him a number of new cases.

But alas, there were no more fifty-thousand-dollar clients! The first caller was a destitute widow with a deed which would have entitled her to the greater part of a large city in Pennsylvania—only unfortunately the deed was about eighty years old. And then there was a poor old man who had been hurt in a street-car accident and had been tricked into signing away his rights; and an indignant citizen who proposed to bring a hundred suits against the traction trust for transfers refused. All were contingency cases, with the chances of success exceedingly remote. And Montague noticed that the people had come to him as a last resort, having apparently heard of him as a man of altruistic temper.

There was one case which interested him particularly, because it seemed to fit in so ominously with the grim prognosis of his brother. He received a call from an elderly gentleman, of very evident refinement and dignity of manner, who proceeded to unfold to him a most amazing story. Five or six years ago he had invented a storage-battery, which was the most efficient known. He had organised a company with three million dollars' capital to manufacture it, himself taking a third interest for his patents, and becoming president of the company. Not long afterward had come a proposal from a group of men who wished to organize a company to manufacture automobiles; they proposed to form an alliance which would give them the exclusive use of the battery. But these men were not people with whom the inventor cared to deal—they were traction and gas magnates widely known for their unscrupulous methods. And so he had declined their offer, and set to work instead to organize an automobile company himself. He had just got under way when he discovered that his rivals had set to work to take his invention away from him. A friend who owned another third share in his company had hypothecated his stock to help form the new company; and now came a call from the bank for more collateral, and he was obliged to sell out. And at the next stockholders' meeting it developed that their rivals had bought it, and likewise more stock in the open market; and they proceeded to take possession of the company, ousting the former president—and then making a contract with their automobile company to furnish the storage-battery at a price which left no profit for the manufacturers! And so for two years the inventor had not received a dollar of dividends upon his million dollars' worth of paper; and to cap the climax, the company had refused to sell the battery to his automobile company, and so that had gone into bankruptcy, and his friend was ruined also!

Montague went into the case very carefully, and found that the story was true. What interested him particularly in it was the fact that he had met a couple of these financial highwaymen in social life; he had come to know the son and heir of one of them quite well, at Siegfried Harvey's. This gilded youth was engaged to be married in a very few days, and the papers had it that the father-in-law had presented the bride with a cheque for a million dollars. Montague could not but wonder if it was the million that had been taken from his client!

There was to be a "bachelor dinner" at the Millionaires' on the night before the wedding, to which he and Oliver had been invited. As he was thinking of taking up his case, he went to his brother, saying that he wished to decline; but Oliver had been getting back his courage day by day, and declared that it was more important than ever now that he should hold his ground, and face his enemies—for Alice's sake, if not for his own. And so Montague went to the dinner, and saw deeper yet into the history of the stolen millions.

It was a very beautiful affair, in the beginning. There was a large private dining-room, elaborately decorated, with a string orchestra concealed in a bower of plants. But there were cocktails even on the side-board at the doorway; and by the time the guests had got to the coffee, every one was hilariously drunk. After each toast they would hurl their glasses over their shoulders. The purpose of a "bachelor dinner," it appeared, was a farewell to the old days and the boon companions; so there were sentimental and comic songs which had been composed for the occasion, and were received with whirlwinds of laughter.

By listening closely and reading between the lines, one might get quite a history of the young host's adventurous career. There was a house up on the West Side; and there was a yacht, with, orgies in every part of the world. There was the summer night in Newport harbour, when some one had hit upon the dazzling scheme of freezing twenty-dollar gold pieces in tiny blocks of ice, to be dropped down the girls' backs! And there was a banquet in a studio in New York, when a huge pie had been brought on, from which a half-nude girl had emerged, with a flock of canary birds about her! Then there was a damsel who had been wont to dance upon the tops of supper tables, clad in diaphanous costume; and who had got drunk after a theatre-party, and set out to smash up a Broadway restaurant. There was a cousin from Chicago, a wild lad, who made a speciality of this diversion, and whose mistresses were bathed in champagne.—Apparently there were numberless places in the city where such orgies were carried on continually; there were private clubs, and artists' "studios"—there were several allusions to a high tower, which Montague did not comprehend. Many such matters, however, were explained to him by an elderly gentleman who sat on his right, and who seemed to stay sober, no matter how much he drank. Incidentally he gravely advised Montague to meet one of the young host's mistresses, who was a "stunning" girl, and was in the market.

Toward morning the festivities changed to a series of wrestling-bouts; the young men stripped off their clothing and tore the table to pieces, and piled it out of the way in a corner, smashing most of the crockery in the process. Between the matches, champagne would be opened by knocking off the heads of the bottles; and this went on until four o'clock in the morning, when many of the guests were lying in heaps upon the floor.

Montague rode home in a cab with the elderly gentleman who had sat next to him; and on the way he asked if such affairs as this were common. And his companion, who was a "steel man" from the West, replied by telling him of some which he had witnessed at home. At Siegfried Harvey's theatre-party Montague had seen a popular actress in a musical comedy, which was then the most successful play running in New York. The house was sold out weeks ahead, and after the matinee you might observe the street in front of the stage-entrance blocked by people waiting to see the woman come out. She was lithe and supple, like a panther, and wore close-fitting gowns to reveal her form. It seemed that her play must have been built with one purpose in mind, to see how much lewdness could be put upon a stage without interference by the police.—And now his companion told him how this woman had been invited to sing at a banquet given by the magnates of a mighty Trust, and had gone after midnight to the most exclusive club in the town, and sung her popular ditty, "Won't you come and play with me?" The merry magnates had taken the invitation literally—with the result that the actress had escaped from the room with half her clothing torn off her. And a little while later an official of this trust had wished to get rid of his wife and marry a chorus-girl; and when public clamour had forced the directors to ask him to resign, he had replied by threatening to tell about this banquet!

The next day—or rather, to be precise, that same morning—Montague and Alice attended the gorgeous wedding. It was declared by the newspapers to be the most "important" social event of the week; and it took half a dozen policemen to hold back the crowds which filled the street. The ceremony took place at St. Cecilia's, with the stately bishop officiating, in his purple and scarlet robes. Inside the doors were all the elect, exquisitely groomed and gowned, and such a medley of delicious perfumes as not all the vales in Arcady could equal. The groom had been polished and scrubbed, and looked very handsome, though somewhat pale; and Montague could not but smile as he observed the best man, looking so very solemn, and recollected the drunken wrestler of a few hours before, staggering about in a pale blue undershirt ripped up the back.

The Montagues knew by this time whom they were to avoid. They were graciously taken under the wing of Mrs. Eldridge Devon—whose real estate was not affected by insurance suits; and the next morning they had the satisfaction of seeing their names in the list of those present—and even a couple of lines about Alice's costume. (Alice was always referred to as "Miss Montague"; it was very pleasant to be the "Miss Montague," and to think of all the other would-be Miss

Montagues in the city, who were thereby haughtily rebuked!) In the "yellow" papers there were also accounts of the trousseau of the bride, and of the wonderful gifts which she had received, and of the long honeymoon which she was to spend in the Mediterranean upon her husband's yacht. Montague found himself wondering if the ghosts of its former occupants would not haunt her, and whether she would have been as happy, had she known as much as he knew.

He found food for a good deal of thought in the memory of this banquet. Among the things which he had gathered from the songs was a hint that Oliver, also, had some secrets, which he had not seen fit to tell his brother. The keeping of young girls was apparently one of the established customs of the "little brothers of the rich"—and, for that matter, of many of the big brothers, also. A little later Montague had a curious glimpse into the life of this "half-world." He had occasion one evening to call up a certain financier whom he had come to know quite well-a man of family and a member of the church. There were some important papers to be signed and sent off by a steamer; and the great man's secretary said that he would try to find him. A minute or two later he called up Montague and asked him if he would be good enough to go to an address uptown. It was a house not far from Riverside Drive; and Montague went there and found his acquaintance, with several other prominent men of affairs whom he knew, conversing in a drawing-room with one of the most charming ladies he had ever met. She was exquisite to look at, and one of the few people in New York whom he had found worth listening to. He spent such an enjoyable evening, that when he was leaving, he remarked to the lady that he would like his cousin Alice to meet her; and then he noticed that she flushed slightly, and was embarrassed. Later on he learned to his dismay that the charming and beautiful lady did not go into Society.

Nor was this at all rare; on the contrary, if one took the trouble to make inquiries, he would find that such establishments were everywhere taken for granted. Montague talked about it with Major Venable; and out of his gossip storehouse the old gentleman drew forth a string of anecdotes that made one's hair stand on end. There was one all-powerful magnate, who had a passion for the wife of a great physician; and he had given a million dollars or so to build a hospital, and had provided that it should be the finest in the world, and that this physician should go abroad for three years to study the institutions of Europe! No conventions counted with this old man—if he saw a woman whom he wanted, he would ask for her; and women in Society felt that it was an honour to be his mistress. Not long after this a man who voiced the anguish of a mighty nation was turned out of several hotels in New York because he was not married according to the laws of South Dakota; but this other man would take a woman to any hotel in the city, and no one would dare oppose him!

And there was another, a great traction king, who kept mistresses in Chicago and Paris and London, as well as in New York; he had one just around the corner from his palatial home, and had an underground passage leading to it. And the Major told with glee how he had shown this to a friend, and the latter had remarked, "I'm too stout to get through there."—"I know it," replied the other, "else I shouldn't have told you!"

And so it went. One of the richest men in New York was a sexual degenerate, with half a dozen women on his hands all the time; he would send them cheques, and they would use these to blackmail him. This man's young wife had been shut up in a closet for twenty-four hours by her mother to compel her to marry him.— And then there was the charming tale of how he had gone away upon a mission of state, and had written long messages full of tender protestations, and given them to a newspaper correspondent to cable home "to his wife." The correspondent had thought it such a touching example of conjugal devotion that he told about it at a dinner-party when he came back; and he was struck by the sudden silence that fell. "The messages had been sent to a code address!" chuckled the Major. "And every one at the table knew who had got them!"

A few days after this, Montague received a telephone message from Siegfried Harvey, who said that he wanted to see him about a matter of business. He asked him to lunch at the Noonday Club; and Montague went—though not without a qualm. For it was in the Fidelity Building, the enemy's bailiwick: a magnificent structure with halls of white marble, and a lavish display of bronze. It occurred to Montague that somewhere in this structure people were at work preparing an answer to his charges; he wondered what they were saying.

The two had lunch, talking meanwhile about the coming events in Society, and about politics and wars; and when the coffee was served and they were alone in the room, Harvey settled his big frame back in his chair, and began:—

"In the first place," he said, "I must explain that I've something to say that is devilish hard to get into. I'm so much afraid of your jumping to a wrong conclusion in the middle of it—I'd like you to agree to listen for a minute or two before you think at all."

"All right," said Montague, with a smile. "Fire away."

And at once the other became grave. "You've taken a case against this company," he said. "And Ollie has talked enough to me to make me understand that you've done a plucky thing, and that you must be everlastingly sick of hearing from cowardly people who want you to drop it. I'd be very sorry to be classed with them, for even a moment; and you must understand at the outset that I haven't a particle of interest in the company, and that it wouldn't matter to me if I had. I don't try to use my friends in business, and I don't let money count with me in my social life. I made up my mind to take the risk of speaking to you about this case, simply because I happen to know one or two things about it that I thought you didn't know. And if that's so, you are at a great disadvantage; but in any case, please understand that I have no motive but friendship, and so if I am butting in, excuse me."

When Siegfried Harvey talked, he looked straight at one with his clear blue eyes, and there was no doubting his honesty. "I am very much obliged to you," said Montague. "Pray tell me what you have to say."

"All right," said the other. "It can be done very quickly. You have taken a case which involves a great many sacrifices upon your part. And I wondered if it had ever occurred to you to ask whether you might not be taken advantage of?"

"How do you mean?" asked Montague.

"Do you know the people who are behind you?" inquired the other. "Do you know them well enough to be sure what are their motives in the case?"

Montague hesitated, and thought. "No," he said, "I couldn't say that I do."

"Then it's just as I thought," replied Harvey. "I've been watching you—you are an honest man, and you're putting yourself to no end of trouble from the best of motives. And unless I'm mistaken, you're being used by men who are not honest, and whom you wouldn't work with if you knew their purposes."

"What purposes could they have?"

"There are several possibilities. In the first place, it might be a 'strike' suit—somebody who is hoping to be bought off for a big price. That is what nearly every one thinks is the case. But I don't; I think it's more likely some one within the company who is trying to put the administration in a hole."

"Who could that be?" exclaimed Montague, amazed.

"I don't know that. I'm not familiar enough with the situation in the Fidelity—it's changing all the time. I simply know that there are factions struggling for the control of it, and hating each other furiously, and ready to do anything in the world to cripple each other. You know that their forty millions of surplus gives an enormous power; I'd rather be able to swing forty millions in the Street than to have ten millions in my own right. And so the giants are fighting for the control of those companies; and you can't tell who's in and who's out—you can never know the real meaning of anything that happens in the struggle. All that you can be sure of is that the game is crooked from end to end, and that nothing that happens in it is what it pretends to be."

Montague listened, half dazed, and feeling as if the ground he stood on were caving beneath his feet.

"What do you know about those who brought you this case?" asked his companion, suddenly.

"Not much," he said weakly.

Harvey hesitated a moment. "Understand me, please," he said. "I've no wish to pry into your affairs, and if you don't care to say any more, I'll understand it perfectly. But I've heard it said that the man who started the thing was Ellis."

Montague, in his turn, hesitated; then he said, "That is correct—between you and me."

"Very good," said Harvey, "and that is what made me suspicious. Do you know anything about Ellis?"

"I didn't," said the other. "I've heard a little since."

"I can fancy so," said Harvey. "And I can tell you that Ellis is mixed up in life-insurance matters in all sorts of dubious ways. It seems to me that you have reason to be most careful where you follow him."

Montague sat with his hands clenched and his brows knitted. His friend's talk had been like a flash of lightning; it revealed huge menacing forms in the darkness about him. All the structure of his hopes seemed to be tottering; his case, that he had worked so hard over—his fifty thousand dollars that he had been so proud of! Could it be that he had been tricked, and had made a fool of himself?

"How in the world am I to know?" he cried.

"That is more than I can tell," said his friend. "And for that matter, I'm not sure that you could do anything now. All that I could do was to warn you what sort of ground you were treading on, so that you could watch out for yourself in future."

Montague thanked him heartily for that service; and then he went back to his office, and spent the rest of the day pondering the matter.

What he had heard had made a vast change in things. Before it everything had seemed simple; and now nothing was clear. He was overwhelmed with a sense of the utter futility of his efforts; he was trying to build a house upon quicksands. There was nowhere a solid spot upon which he could set his foot. There was nowhere any truth—there were only contending powers who used the phrases of truth for their own purposes! And now he saw himself as the world saw him,—a party to a piece of trickery,—a knave like all the rest. He felt that he had been tripped up at the first step in his career.

The conclusion of the whole matter was that he took an afternoon train for Albany; and the next morning he talked the matter out with the Judge. Montague had realized the need of going slowly, for, after all, he had no definite ground for suspicion; and so, very tactfully and cautiously he explained, that it had come to his ears that many people believed there were interested parties behind the suit of Mr. Hasbrook; and that this had made him uncomfortable, as he knew nothing whatever about his client. He had come to ask the Judge's advice in the matter.

No one could have taken the thing more graciously than did the great man; he was all kindness and tact. In the first place, he said, he had warned him in advance that enemies would attack him and slander him, and that all kinds of subtle means would be used to influence him. And he must understand that these rumours were part of such a campaign; it made no difference how good a friend had brought them to him—how could he know who had brought them to that friend?

The Judge ventured to hope that nothing that anyone might say could influence him to believe that he, the Judge, would have advised him to do anything improper.

"No," said Montague, "but can you assure me that there are no interested parties behind Mr. Hasbrook?"

"Interested parties?" asked the other.

"I mean people connected with the Fidelity or other insurance companies."

"Why, no," said the Judge; "I certainly couldn't assure you of that."

Montague looked surprised. "You mean you don't know?"

"I mean," was the answer, "that I wouldn't feel at liberty to tell, even if I did know."

And Montague stared at him; he had not been prepared for this frankness.

"It never occurred to me," the other continued, "that that was a matter which could make any difference to you."

"Why—" began Montague.

"Pray understand me, Mr. Montague," said the Judge. "It seemed to me that this was obviously a just case, and it seemed so to you. And the only other matter that I thought you had a right to be assured of was that it was seriously meant. Of that I felt assured. It did not seem to me of any importance that there might be interested individuals behind Mr. Hasbrook. Let us suppose, for instance, that there were some parties who had been offended by the administration of the Fidelity, and were anxious to punish it. Could a lawyer be justified in refusing to take a just case, simply because he knew of such private motives? Or, let us assume an extreme case—a factional fight within the company, as you say has been suggested to you. Well, that would be a case of thieves falling out; and is there any reason why the public should not reap the advantage of such a situation? The men inside the company are the ones who would know first what is going on; and if you saw a chance to use such an advantage in a just fight—would you not do it?"

So the Judge went on, gracious and plausible—and so subtly and exquisitely corrupting! Underneath his smoothly flowing sentences Montague could feel the presence of one fundamental thought; it was unuttered and even unhinted, but it pervaded the Judge's discourse as a mood pervades a melody. The young lawyer had got a big fee, and he had a nice easy case; and as a man of the world, he could not really wish to pry into it too closely. He had heard gossip, and felt that his reputation required him to be disturbed; but he had come, simply to be smoothed down the back and made at ease, and enabled to keep his fee without losing his good opinion of himself.

Montague quit, because he concluded that it was not worth while to try to make himself understood. After all, he was in the case now, and there was nothing to be gained by a breach. Two things he felt that he had made certain by the interview—first, that his client was a "dummy," and that it was really a case of thieves falling out; and second, that he had no guarantee that he might not be left in the lurch at any moment—except the touching confidence of the Judge in some parties unknown.

CHAPTER XIX

Montague came home with his mind made up that there was nothing he could do except to be more careful next time. For this mistake he would have to pay the price.

He had still to learn what the full price was. The day after his return there came a caller—Mr. John C. Burton, read his card. He proved to be a canvassing agent for the company which published the scandal-sheet of Society. They were preparing a de luxe account of the prominent families of New York; a very sumptuous affair, with a highly exclusive set of subscribers, at the rate of fifteen hundred dollars per set. Would Mr. Montague by any chance care to have his family included?

And Mr. Montague explained politely that he was a comparative stranger in New York, and would not belong properly in such a volume. But the agent was not satisfied with this. There might be reasons for his subscribing, even so; there might be special cases; Mr. Montague, as a stranger, might not realize the important nature of the offer; after he had consulted his friends, he might change his mind—and so on. As Montague listened to this series of broad hints, and took in the meaning of them, the colour mounted, to his cheeks—until at last he rose abruptly and bid the man good afternoon.

But then as he sat alone, his anger died away, and there was left only discomfort and uneasiness. And three or four days later he bought another issue of the paper, and sure enough, there was a new paragraph!

He stood on the street-corner reading it. The social war was raging hotly, it said; and added that Mrs. de Graffenried was threatening to take up the cause of the strangers. Then it went on to picture a certain exquisite young man of fashion who was rushing about among his friends to apologize for his brother's indiscretions. Also, it said, there was a brilliant social queen, wife of a great banker, who had taken up the cudgels.—And then came three sentences more, which made the blood leap like flame into Montague's cheeks:

"There have not been lacking comments upon her suspicious ardour. It has been noticed that since the advent of the romantic-looking Southerner, this restless lady's interest in the Babists and the trance mediums has waned; and now Society is watching for the denouement of a most interesting situation."

To Montague these words came like a blow in the face. He went on down the street, half dazed. It seemed to him the blackest shame that New York had yet shown him. He clenched his fists as he walked, whispering to himself, "The scoundrels!"

He realized instantly that he was helpless. Down home one would have thrashed the editor of such a paper; but here he was in the wolves' own country, and he could do nothing. He went back to his office, and sat down at the desk.

"My dear Mrs. Winnie," he wrote. "I have just read the enclosed paragraph, and I cannot tell you how profoundly pained I am that your kindness to us should have made you the victim of such an outrage. I am quite helpless in the matter, except to enable you to avoid any further annoyance. Please believe me when I say that we shall all of us understand perfectly if you think that we had best not meet again at present; and that this will make no difference whatever in our feelings."

This letter Montague sent by a messenger; and then he went home. Perhaps ten minutes after he arrived, the telephone bell rang—and there was Mrs. Winnie.

"Your note has come," she said. "Have you an engagement this evening?"

"No," he answered.

"Well," she said, "will you come to dinner?"

"Mrs. Winnie—" he protested.

"Please come," she said. "Please!"

"I hate to have you—" he began.

"I wish you to come!" she said, a third time.

So he answered, "Very well."

He went; and when he entered the house, the butler led him to the elevator, saying, "Mrs. Duval says will you please come upstairs, sir." And there Mrs. Winnie met him, with flushed cheeks and eager countenance.

She was even lovelier than usual, in a soft cream-coloured gown, and a crimson rose in her bosom. "I'm all alone to-night," she said, "so we'll dine in my apartments. We'd be lost in that big room downstairs."

She led him into her drawing-room, where great armfuls of new roses scattered their perfume. There was a table set for two, and two big chairs before the fire which blazed in the hearth. Montague noticed that her hand trembled a little, as she motioned him to one of them; he could read her excitement in her whole aspect. She was flinging down the gauntlet to her enemies!

"Let us eat first and talk afterward," she said, hurriedly. "We'll be happy for a while, anyway."

And she went on to be happy, in her nervous and eager way. She talked about the new opera which was to be given, and about Mrs. de Graffenried's new entertainment, and about Mrs. Ridgley-Clieveden's ball; also about the hospital for crippled children which she wanted to build, and about Mrs. Vivie Patton's rumoured divorce. And, meantime, the sphinx-like attendants moved here and there, and the dinner came and went. They took their coffee in the big chairs by the fire;

and the table was swept clear, and the servants vanished, closing the doors behind them.

Then Montague set his cup aside, and sat gazing sombrely into the fire. And Mrs. Winnie watched him. There was a long silence.

Suddenly he heard her voice. "Do you find it so easy to give up our friendship?" she asked.

"I didn't think about it's being easy or hard," he answered. "I simply thought of protecting you."

"And do you think that my friends are nothing to me?" she demanded. "Have I so very many as that?" And she clenched her hands with a sudden passionate gesture. "Do you think that I will let those wretches frighten me into doing what they want? I'll not give in to them—not for anything that Lelia can do!"

A look of perplexity crossed Montague's face. "Lelia?" he asked.

"Mrs. Robbie Walling!" she cried. "Don't you suppose that she is responsible for that paragraph?"

Montague started.

"That's the way they fight their battles!" cried Mrs. Winnie. "They pay money to those scoundrels to be protected. And then they send nasty gossip about people they wish to injure."

"You don't mean that!" exclaimed the man.

"Of course I do," cried she. "I know that it's true! I know that Robbie Walling paid fifteen thousand dollars for some trumpery volumes that they got out! And how do you suppose the paper gets its gossip?"

"I didn't know," said Montague. "But I never dreamed—"

"Why," exclaimed Mrs. Winnie, "their mail is full of blue and gold monogram stationery! I've known guests to sit down and write gossip about their hostesses in their own homes. Oh, you've no idea of people's vileness!"

"I had some idea," said Montague, after a pause.—"That was why I wished to protect you."

"I don't wish to be protected!" she cried, vehemently. "I'll not give them the satisfaction. They wish to make me give you up, and I'll not do it, for anything they can say!"

Montague sat with knitted brows, gazing into the fire. "When I read that paragraph," he said slowly. "I could not bear to think of the unhappiness it might cause you. I thought of how much it might disturb your husband—"

"My husband!" echoed Mrs. Winnie.

There was a hard tone in her voice, as she went on. "He will fix it up with them," she said,—"that's his way. There will be nothing more published, you can feel sure of that."

Montague sat in silence. That was not the reply he had expected, and it rather disconcerted him.

"If that were all—" he said, with hesitation. "But I could not know. I thought that the paragraph might disturb him for another reason—that it might be a cause of unhappiness between you and him—"

There was a pause. "You don't understand," said Mrs. Winnie, at last.

Without turning his head he could see her hands, as they lay upon her knees. She was moving them nervously. "You don't understand," she repeated.

When she began to' speak again, it was in a low, trembling voice. "I must tell you," she said; "I have felt sure that you did not know."

There was another pause. She hesitated, and her hands trembled; then suddenly she hurried on.—"I wanted you to know. I do not love my husband. I am not bound to him. He has nothing to say in my affairs."

Montague sat rigid, turned to stone. He was half dazed by the words. He could feel Mrs. Winnie's gaze fixed upon him; and he could feel the hot flush that spread over her throat and cheeks.

"It—it was not fair for you not to know," she whispered. And her voice died away, and there was again a silence. Montague was dumb.

"Why don't you say something?" she panted, at last; and he caught the note of anguish in her voice. Then he turned and stared at her, and saw her tightly clenched hands, and the quivering of her lips.

He was shocked quite beyond speech. And he saw her bosom heaving quickly, and saw the tears start into her eyes. Suddenly she sank down, and covered her face with her hands and broke into frantic sobbing.

"Mrs. Winnie!" he cried; and started to his feet.

Her outburst continued. He saw that she was shuddering violently. "Then you don't love me!" she wailed.

He stood trembling and utterly bewildered. "I'm so sorry!" he whispered. "Oh, Mrs. Winnie—I had no idea—"

"I know it! I know it!" she cried. "It's my fault! I was a fool! I knew it all the time. But I hoped—I thought you might, if you knew—"

And then again her tears choked her; she was convulsed with pain and grief.

Montague stood watching her, helpless with distress. She caught hold of the arm of the chair, convulsively, and he put his hand upon hers.

"Mrs. Winnie—" he began.

But she jerked her hand away and hid it. "No, no!" she cried, in terror. "Don't touch me!"

And suddenly she looked up at him, stretching out her arms. "Don't you understand that I love you?" she exclaimed. "You despise me for it, I know—but I can't help it. I will tell you, even so! It's the only satisfaction I can have. I have always loved you! And I thought—I thought it was only that you didn't understand. I was ready to brave all the world—I didn't care who knew it, or what anybody said. I thought we could be happy—I thought I could be free at last. Oh, you've no idea how unhappy I am—and how lonely—and how I longed to escape! And I believed that you—that you might—"

And then the tears gushed into Mrs. Winnie's eyes again, and her voice became the voice of a little child.

"Don't you think that you might come to love me?" she wailed.

Her voice shook Montague, so that he trembled to the depths of him. But his face only became the more grave.

"You despise me because I told you!" she exclaimed.

"No, no, Mrs. Winnie," he said. "I could not possibly do that—"

"Then—then why—" she whispered.—"Would it be so hard to love me?"

"It would be very easy," he said, "but I dare not let myself."

She looked at him piteously. "You are so cold—so merciless!" she cried.

He answered nothing, and she sat trembling. "Have you ever loved a woman?" she asked.

There was a long pause. He sat in the chair again. "Listen, Mrs. Winnie"—he began at last.

"Don't call me that!" she exclaimed. "Call me Evelyn—please."

"Very well," he said—"Evelyn. I did not intend to make you unhappy—if I had had any idea, I should never have seen you again. I will tell you—what I have never told anybody before. Then you will understand."

He sat for a few moments, in a sombre reverie.

"Once," he said, "when I was young, I loved a woman—a quadroon girl. That was in New Orleans; it is a custom we have there. They have a world of their own, and we take care of them, and of the children; and every one knows about it. I was very young, only about eighteen; and she was even younger. But I found out then what women are, and what love means to them. I saw how they could suffer. And then she died in childbirth—the child died, too."

Montague's voice was very low; and Mrs. Winnie sat with her hands clasped, and her eyes riveted upon his face. "I saw her die," he said. "And that was all. I have never forgotten it. I made up my mind then that I had done wrong; and that never again while I lived would I offer my love to a woman, unless I could devote all my life to her. So you see, I am afraid of love. I do not wish to suffer so much, or to make others suffer. And when anyone speaks to me as you did, it brings it all back to me—it makes me shrink up and wither."

He paused, and the other caught her breath.

"Understand me," she said, her voice trembling. "I would not ask any pledges of you. I would pay whatever price there was to pay—I am not afraid to suffer."

"I do not wish you to suffer," he said. "I do not wish to take advantage of any woman."

"But I have nothing in the world that I value!" she cried. "I would go away—I would give up everything, to be with a man like you. I have no ties—no duties—"

He interrupted her. "You have your husband—" he said.

And she cried out in sudden fury—"My husband!"

"Has no one ever told you about my husband?" she asked, after a pause.

"No one," he said.

"Well, ask them!" she exclaimed. "Meantime, take my word for it—I owe nothing to my husband."

Montague sat staring into the fire. "But consider my own case," he said. "*I* have duties—my mother and my cousin—"

"Oh, don't say any more!" cried the woman, with a break in her voice. "Say that you don't love me—that is all there is to say! And you will never respect me again! I have been a fool—I have ruined everything! I have flung away your friendship, that I might have kept!"

"No," he said.

But she rushed on, vehemently—"At least, I have been honest—give me credit for that! That is how all my troubles come—I say what is in my mind, and I pay the price for my blunders. It is not as if I were cold and calculating—so don't despise me altogether."

"I couldn't despise you," said Montague. "I am simply pained, because I have made you unhappy. And I did not mean to."

Mrs. Winnie sat staring ahead of her in a sombre reverie. "Don't think any more about it," she said, bitterly. "I will get over it. I am not worth troubling about. Don't you suppose I know how you feel about this world that I live in? And I'm part of it—I beat my wings, and try to get out, but I can't. I'm in it, and I'll stay in till I die; I might as well give up. I thought that I could steal a little joy—you have no idea how hungry I am for a little joy! You have no idea how lonely I am! And how empty my life is! You talk about your fear of making me unhappy; it's a grim jest—but I'll give you permission, if you can! I'll ask nothing—no promises, no sacrifices! I'll take all the risks, and pay all the penalties!"

She smiled through her tears, a sardonic smile. He was watching her, and she turned again, and their eyes met; again he saw the blood mount from her throat to her cheeks. At the same time came the old stirring of the wild beasts within him. He knew that the less time he spent in sympathizing with Mrs. Winnie, the better for both of them.

He had started to rise, and words of farewell were on his lips; when suddenly there came a knock upon the door.

Mrs. Winnie sprang to her feet. "Who is that?" she cried.

And the door opened, and Mr. Duval entered.

"Good evening," he said pleasantly, and came toward her.

Mrs. Winnie flushed angrily, and stared at him. "Why do you come here unannounced?" she cried.

"I apologize," he said—"but I found this in my mail—"

And Montague, in the act of rising to greet him, saw that he had the offensive clipping in his hand. Then he saw Duval give a start, and realized that the man had not been aware of his presence in the room.

Duval gazed from Montague to his wife, and noticed for the first time her tears, and her agitation. "I beg pardon," he said. "I am evidently trespassing."

"You most certainly are," responded Mrs. Winnie.

He made a move to withdraw; but before he could take a step, she had brushed past him and left the room, slamming the door behind her.

And Duval stared after her, and then he stared at Montague, and laughed. "Well! well! well!" he said.

Then, checking his amusement, he added, "Good evening, sir."

"Good evening," said Montague.

He was trembling slightly, and Duval noticed it; he smiled genially. "This is the sort of material out of which scenes are made," said he. "But I beg you not to be embarrassed—we won't have any scenes."

Montague could think of nothing to say to that.

"I owe Evelyn an apology," the other continued. "It was entirely an accident—this clipping, you see. I do not intrude, as a rule. You may make yourself at home in future."

Montague flushed scarlet at the words.

"Mr. Duval," he said, "I have to assure you that you are mistaken—"

The other stared at him. "Oh, come, come!" he said, laughing. "Let us talk as men of the world."

"I say that you are mistaken," said Montague again.

The other shrugged his shoulders. "Very well," he said genially. "As you please. I simply wish to make matters clear to you, that's all. I wish you joy with Evelyn. I say nothing about her—you love her. Suffice it that I've had her, and I'm tired of her; the field is yours. But keep her out of mischief, and don't let her make a fool of herself in public, if you can help it. And don't let her spend too much money—she costs me a million a year already.—Good evening, Mr. Montague."

And he went out. Montague, who stood like a statue, could hear him chuckling all the way down the hall.

At last Montague himself started to leave. But he heard Mrs. Winnie coming back, and he waited for her. She came in and shut the door, and turned toward him.

"What did he say?" she asked.

"He—was very pleasant," said Montague.

And she smiled grimly. "I went out on purpose," she said. "I wanted you to see him—to see what sort of a man he is, and how much 'duty' I owe him! You saw, I guess."

"Yes, I saw," said he.

Then again he started to go. But she took him by the arm. "Come and talk to me," she said. "Please!"

And she led him back to the fire. "Listen," she said. "He will not come here again. He is going away to-night—I thought he had gone already. And he does not return for a month or two. There will be no one to disturb us again."

She came close to him and gazed up into his face. She had wiped her tears away, and her happy look had come back to her; she was lovelier than ever.

"I took you by surprise," she said, smiling. "You didn't know what to make of it. And I was ashamed—I thought you would hate me. But I'm not going to be unhappy any more—I don't care at all. I'm glad that I spoke!"

And Mrs. Winnie put up her hands and took him by the lapels of his coat. "I know that you love me," she said; "I saw it in your eyes just now, before he came in: It is simply that you won't let yourself go. You have so many doubts and so many fears. But you will see that I am right; you will learn to love me. You won't be able to help it—I shall be so kind and good! Only don't go away—"

Mrs. Winnie was so close to him that her breath touched his cheek. "Promise me, dear," she whispered—"promise me that you won't stop seeing me—that you will learn to love me. I can't do without you!"

Montague was trembling in every nerve; he felt like a man caught in a net. Mrs. Winnie had had everything she ever wanted in her life; and now she wanted him! It was impossible for her to face any other thought.

"Listen," he began gently.

But she saw the look of resistance in his eyes, and she cried "No no—don't! I cannot do without you! Think! I love you! What more can I say to you? I cannot believe that you don't care for me—you HAVE been fond of me—I have seen it in your face. Yet you're afraid of me—why? Look at me—am I not beautiful to look at! And is a woman's love such a little thing—can you fling it away and trample upon it so easily? Why do you wish to go? Don't you understand—no one knows we are here—no one cares! You can come here whenever you wish—this is my place—mine! And no one will think anything about it. They all do it. There is nothing to be afraid of!"

She put her arms about him, and clung to him so that he could feel the beating of her heart upon his bosom. "Oh, don't leave me here alone to-night!" she cried.

To Montague it was like the ringing of an alarm-bell deep within his soul. "I must go," he said.

She flung back her head and stared at him, and he saw the terror and anguish in her eyes. "No, no!" she cried, "don't say that to me! I can't bear it—oh, see what I have done! Look at me! Have mercy on me!"

"Mrs. Winnie," he said, "you must have mercy on ME!"

But he only felt her clasp him more tightly. He took her by the wrists, and with quiet force he broke her hold upon him; her hands fell to her sides, and she stared at him, aghast.

"I must go," he said, again.

And he started toward the door. She followed him dumbly with her eyes.

"Good-bye," he said. He knew that there was no use of any more words; his sympathy had been like oil upon flames. He saw her move, and as he opened the door, she flung herself down in a chair and burst into frantic weeping. He shut the door softly and went away.

He found his way down the stairs, and got his hat and coat, and went out, unseen by anyone. He walked down the Avenue-and there suddenly was the giant bulk of St. Cecilia's lifting itself into the sky. He stopped and looked at it—it seemed a great tumultuous surge of emotion. And for the first time in his life it seemed to him that he understood why men had put together that towering heap of stone!

Then he went on home.

He found Alice dressing for a ball, and Oliver waiting for her. He went to his room, and took off his coat; and Oliver came up to him, and with a sudden gesture reached over to his shoulder, and held up a trophy.

He drew it out carefully, and measured the length of it, smiling mischievously in the meanwhile. Then he held it up to the light, to see the colour of it.

"A black one!" he cried. "Coal black!" And he looked at his brother, with a merry twinkle in his eyes. "Oh, Allan!" he chuckled.

Montague said nothing.

CHAPTER XX

It was about a week from the beginning of Lent, when there would be a lull in the city's gaieties, and Society would shift the scene of its activities to the country clubs, and to California and Hot Springs and Palm Beach. Mrs. Caroline Smythe invited Alice to join her in an expedition to the last-named place; but Montague interposed, because he saw that Alice had been made pale and nervous by three months of night-and-day festivities. Also, a trip to Florida would necessitate ten or fifteen thousand dollars' worth of new clothes; and these would not do for the summer, it appeared—they would be faded and passe by that time.

So Alice settled back to rest; but she was too popular to be let alone—a few days later came another invitation, this time from General Prentice and his family. They were planning a railroad trip—to be gone for a month; they would have a private train, and twenty five people in the party, and would take in California and Mexico—"swinging round the circle," as it was called. Alice was wild to go, and Montague gave his consent. Afterward he learned to his dismay that Charlie Carter was one of those invited, and he would have liked to have Alice withdraw; but she did not wish to, and he could not make up his mind to insist.

These train trips were the very latest diversion of the well-to-do; a year ago no one had heard of them, and now fifty parties were leaving New York every month. You might see a dozen of such hotel-trains at once at Palm Beach; there were some people who lived on board all the time, having special tracks built for them in pleasant locations wherever they stopped. One man had built a huge automobile railroad car, shaped like a ram, and having accommodation for sixty people. The Prentice train had four cars, one of them a "library car," finished in St. Iago mahogany, and provided with a pipe-organ. Also there were bath-rooms and a barber-shop, and a baggage car with two autos on board for exploring purposes.

Since the episode of Mrs. Winnie, Oliver had apparently concluded that his brother was one of the initiated. Not long afterward he permitted him to a glimpse into that side of his life which had been hinted at in the songs at the bachelors' dinner.

Oliver had planned to take Betty Wyman to the theatre; but Betty's grandfather had come home from the West unexpectedly, and so Oliver came round and took his brother instead.

"I was going to play a joke on her," he said. "We'll go to see one of my old flames."

It was a translation of a French farce, in which the marital infidelities of two young couples were the occasion of many mishaps. One of the characters was a waiting-maid, who was in love with a handsome young soldier, and was pursued by the husband of one of the couples. It was a minor part, but the young Jewish girl who played it had so many pretty graces and such a merry laugh that she made it quite conspicuous. When the act was over, Oliver asked him whose acting he liked best, and he named her.

"Come and be introduced to her," Oliver said.

He opened a door near their box. "How do you do, Mr. Wilson," he said, nodding to a man in evening dress, who stood near by. Then he turned toward the dressing-rooms, and went down a corridor, and knocked upon one of the doors. A voice called, "Come in," and he opened the door; and there was a tiny room, with odds and ends of clothing scattered about, and the girl, clad in corsets and under-skirt, sitting before a mirror. "Hello, Rosalie," said he.

And she dropped her powder-puff, and sprang up with a cry—"Ollie!" 'In a moment more she had her arms about his neck.

"Oh, you wretched man," she cried. "Why don't you come to see me any more? Didn't you get my letters?"

"I got some," said he. "But I've been busy. This is my brother, Mr. Allan Montague."

The other nodded to Montague, and said, "How do you do?"—but without letting go of Oliver. "Why don't you come to see me?" she exclaimed.

"There, there, now!" said Oliver, laughing good-naturedly. "I brought my brother along so that you'd have to behave yourself."

"I don't care about your brother!" exclaimed the girl, without even giving him another glance. Then she held Oliver at arm's length, and gazed into his face. "How can you be so cruel to me?" she asked.

"I told you I was busy," said he, cheerfully. "And I gave you fair warning, didn't I? How's Toodles?"

"Oh, Toodles is in raptures," said Rosalie. "She's got a new fellow." And then, her manner changing to one of merriment, she added: "Oh, Ollie! He gave her a diamond brooch! And she looks like a countess—she's hoping for a chance to wear it in a part!"

"You've seen Toodles," said Oliver, to his brother "She's in 'The Kaliph of Kamskatka.'".

"They're going on the road next week," said Rosalie. "And then I'll be all alone." She added, in a pleading voice: "Do, Ollie, be a good boy and take us out to-night. Think how long it's been since I've seen you! Why, I've been so good I don't know myself in the looking-glass. Please, Ollie!"

"All right," said he, "maybe I will."

"I'm not going to let you get away from me," she cried. "I'll come right over the footlights after you!"

"You'd better get dressed," said Oliver. "You'll be late."

He pushed aside a tray with some glasses on it, and seated himself upon a trunk; and Montague stood in a corner and watched Rosalie, while she powdered and painted herself, and put on an airy summer dress, and poured out a flood of gossip about "Toodles" and "Flossie" and "Grace" and some others. A few minutes later came a stentorian voice in the hallway: "Second act!" There were more embraces, and then Ollie brushed the powder from his coat, and went away laughing.

Montague stood for a few moments in the wings, watching the scene-shifters putting the final touches to the new set, and the various characters taking their positions. Then they went out to their seats. "Isn't she a jewel?" asked Oliver.

"She's very pretty," the other admitted.

"She came right out of the slums," said Oliver—"over on Rivington Street. That don't happen very often."

"How did you come to know her?" asked his brother.

"Oh, I picked her out. She was in a chorus, then. I got her first speaking part."

"Did you?" said the other, in surprise. "How did you do that?"

"Oh, a little money," was the reply. "Money will do most anything. And I was in love with her—that's how I got her."

Montague said nothing, but sat in thought.

"We'll take her out to supper and make her happy," added Oliver, as the curtain started up. "She's lonesome, I guess. You see, I promised Betty I'd reform."

All through that scene and the next one Rosalie acted for them; she was so full of verve and merriment that there was quite a stir in the audience, and she got several rounds of applause. Then, when the play was over, she extricated herself from the arms of the handsome young soldier, and fled to her dressing-room, and when Oliver and Montague arrived, she was half ready for the street.

They went up Broadway, and from a group of people coming out of another stage-entrance a young girl came to join them—an airy little creature with the face of a doll-baby, and a big hat with a purple feather on top. This was "Toodles"—otherwise known as Helen Gwynne; and she took Montague's arm, and they fell in behind Oliver and his companion.

Montague wondered what one said to a chorus-girl on the way to supper. Afterward his brother told him that Toodles had been the wife of a real-estate agent in a little town in Oklahoma, and had run away from respectability and boredom with a travelling theatrical company. Now she was tripping her part in the musical comedy which Montague had seen at Mrs. Lane's; and incidentally swearing devotion to a handsome young "wine-agent." She confided to Montague that she hoped the latter might see her that evening—he needed to be made jealous.

"The Great White Way" was the name which people had given to this part of Broadway; and at the head of it stood a huge hotel with flaming lights, and gorgeous marble and bronze, and famous paintings upon the walls and ceilings inside. At this hour every one of its many dining-rooms was thronged with supper-parties, and the place rang with laughter and the rattle of dishes, and the strains of several orchestras which toiled heroically in the midst of the uproar. Here they found a table, and while Oliver was ordering frozen poached eggs and quails in aspic, Montague sat and gazed about him at the revelry, and listened to the prattle of the little ex-sempstress from Rivington Street.

His brother had "got her," he said, by buying a speaking part in a play for her; and Montague recalled the orgies of which he had heard at the bachelors' dinner, and divined that here he was at the source of the stream from which they were fed. At the table next to them was a young Hebrew, whom Toodles pointed out as the son and heir of a great clothing manufacturer. He was "keeping" several girls, said she; and the queenly creature who was his vis-a-vis was one of the chorus in "The Maids of Mandalay." And a little way farther down the room was a boy with the face of an angel and the air of a prince of the blood—he had inherited a million and run away from school, and was making a name for himself in the Tenderloin. The pretty little girl all in green who was with him was Violet Pane, who was the artist's model in a new play that had made a hit. She had had a full-page picture of herself in the Sunday supplement of the "sporting paper" which was read here—so Rosalie remarked.

"Why don't you ever do that for me?" she added, to Oliver.

"Perhaps I will," said he, with a laugh. "What does it cost?"

And when he learned that the honour could be purchased for only fifteen hundred dollars, he said, "I'll do it, if you'll be good." And from that time on the last trace of worriment vanished from the face and the conversation of Rosalie.

As the champagne cocktails disappeared, she and Oliver became confidential. Then Montague turned to Toodles, to learn more about how the "second generation" was preying upon the women of the stage.

"A chorus-girl got from ten to twenty dollars a week," said Toodles; and that was hardly enough to pay for her clothes. Her work was very uncertain—she would spend weeks at rehearsal, and then if the play failed, she would get nothing. It was a dog's life; and the keys of freedom and opportunity were in the keeping of rich men, who haunted the theatres and laid siege to the girls. They would send in notes to them, or fling bouquets to them, with cards, or perhaps money, hidden in them. There were millionaire artists and bohemians who kept a standing order for seats in the front rows at opening performances; they had accounts with florists and liverymen and confectioners, and gave carte blanche to scores of girls who lent themselves to their purposes. Sometimes they were in league with the managers, and a girl who held back would find her chances imperilled; sometimes these men would even finance shows to give a chance to some favourite.

Afterward Toodles turned to listen to Oliver and his companion; and Montague sat back and gazed about the room. Next to him was a long table with a dozen, people at it; and he watched the buckets of champagne and the endless succession of fantastic-looking dishes of food, and the revellers, with their flushed faces and feverish eyes and loud laughter. Above all the tumult was the voice of the orchestra, calling, calling, like the storm wind upon the mountains; the music was wild and chaotic, and produced an indescribable sense of pain and confusion. When one realized that this same thing was going on in thousands of places in this district it seemed that here was a flood of dissipation that out-rivalled even that of Society.

It was said that the hotels of New York, placed end to end, would reach all the way to London; and they took care of a couple of hundred thousand people a day—a horde which had come from all over the world in search of pleasure and excitement. There were sight-seers and "country customers" from forty-five states; ranchers from Texas, and lumber kings from Maine, and mining men from Nevada. At home they had reputations, and perhaps families to consider; but once plunged into the whirlpool of the Tenderloin, they were hidden from all the world. They came with their pockets full of money; and hotels and restaurants, gambling-places and pool-rooms and brothels—all were lying in wait for them! So eager had the competition become that there was a tailoring establishment and a bank that were never closed the year round, except on Sunday.

Everywhere about one's feet the nets of vice were spread. The head waiter in one's hotel was a "steerer" for a "dive," and the house detective was "touting" for a gambling-place. The handsome woman who smiled at one in "Peacock Alley" was a "madame"; the pleasant-faced young man who spoke to one at the bar was on the look-out for customers for a brokerage-house next door. Three times in a single day in another of these great caravanserais Montague was offered "short change"; and so his eyes were opened to a new kind of plundering. He was struck by the number of attendants in livery who swarmed about him, and to whom he gave tips for their services. He did not notice that the boys in the wash-rooms and coat-rooms could not speak a word of English; he could not know that they were searched every night, and had everything taken from them, and that the Greek who hired them had paid fifteen thousand dollars a year to the hotel for the privilege.

So far had the specialization in evil proceeded that there were places of prostitution which did a telephone-business exclusively, and would send a woman in a cab to any address; and there were high-class assignation-houses, which furnished exquisite apartments and the services of maids and valets. And in this world of vice the modern doctrine of the equality of the sexes was fully recognized; there were gambling-houses and pool-rooms and opium-joints for women, and drinking-places which catered especially for them. In the "orange room" of one of the big hotels, you might see rich women of every rank and type, fingering the dainty leather-bound and gold-embossed wine cards. In this room alone were sold over ten thousand drinks every day; and the hotel paid a rental of a million a year to the Devon estate. Not far away the Devons also owned negro-dives, where, in the early hours of the morning, you might see richly-gowned white women drinking.

In this seething caldron of graft there were many strange ways of making money, and many strange and incredible types of human beings to be met. Once, in "Society," Montague had pointed out to him a woman who had been a "tattooed lady" in a circus; there was another who had been a confederate of gamblers upon the ocean steamships, and another who had washed dishes in a mining-camp. There was one of these great hotels whose proprietor had been a successful burglar; and a department-store whose owner had begun life as a "fence." In any crowd of these revellers you might have such strange creatures pointed out to you; a multimillionaire who sold rotten jam to the people; another who had invented opium soothing-syrup for babies; a convivial old gentleman who disbursed the "yellow dog fund" of several railroads; a handsome chauffeur who had run away with an heiress. 'Once a great scientist had invented a new kind of underwear, and had endeavoured to make it a gift to humanity; and here was a man who had seized upon it and made millions out of it! Here was a "trance medium," who had got a fortune out of an imbecile old manufacturer; here was a great newspaper proprietor, who published advertisements of assignations at a dollar a line; here was a cigar manufacturer, whose smug face was upon every billboard—he had begun as a tin manufacturer, and to avoid the duty, he had had his raw material cast in the form of statues, and brought them in as works of art!

And terrible and vile as were the sources from which the fortunes had been derived, they were no viler nor more terrible than the purposes for which they had been spent. Mrs. Vivie Patton had hinted to Montague of a "Decameron Club," whose members gathered in each others' homes and vied in the telling of obscene stories; Strathcona had told him about another set of exquisite ladies and gentlemen who gave elaborate entertainments, in which they dressed in the costumes of bygone periods, and imitated famous characters in history, and the vices and orgies of courts and camps. One heard of "Cleopatra nights" on board of yachts at Newport. There was a certain Wall Street "plunger," who had begun life as a mining man in the West; and when his customers came in town, he would hire a trolley-car, and take a load of champagne and half a dozen prostitutes, and spend the night careering about the country. This man was now quartered in one of the great hotels in New York; and in his apartments he would have prize fights and chicken fights; and bloodthirsty exhibitions called "purring matches," in which men tried to bark each other's shins; or perhaps a "battle royal," with a diamond scarf-pin dangling from the ceiling, and half a dozen negroes in a free-for-all fight for the prize.

No picture of the ways of the Metropolis would be complete which did not force upon the reluctant reader some realization of the extent to which new and hideous incitements to vice were spreading. To say that among the leisured classes such practices were raging like a pestilence would be no exaggeration. Ten years ago they were regarded with aversion by even the professionally vicious; but now the commonest prostitute accepted them as part of her fate. And there was no height to which they had not reached—ministers of state were enslaved by them; great fortunes and public events were controlled by them. In Washington there had been an ambassador whose natural daughter taught them in the houses of the great, until the scandal forced the minister's recall. Some of these practices were terrible in their effects, completely wrecking the victim in a short time; and physicians who studied their symptoms would be horrified to see them appearing in the homes of their friends.

And from New York, the centre of the wealth and culture of the country, these vices spread to every corner of it. Theatrical companies and travelling salesmen carried them; visiting merchants and sightseers acquired them. Pack-pedlers sold vile pictures and books—the manufacturing or importing of which was now quite an industry; one might read catalogues printed abroad in English, the contents of which would make one's flesh creep. There were cheap weeklies, costing ten cents a year, which were thrust into area-windows for servant-girls; there were yellow-covered French novels of unbelievable depravity for the mistress of the house. It was a curious commentary upon the morals of Society that upon the trains running to a certain suburban community frequented by the ultra-fashionable, the newsboys did a thriving business in such literature; and when the pastor of the fashionable church eloped with a Society girl, the bishop publicly laid the blame to the morals of his parishioners!

The theory was that there were two worlds, and that they were kept rigidly separate. There were two sets of women; one to be toyed with and flung aside, and the other to be protected and esteemed. Such things as prostitutes and kept women might exist, but people of refinement did not talk about them, and were not concerned with them. But Montague was familiar with the saying, that if you follow the chain of the slave, you will find the other end about the wrist of the master; and he discovered that the Tenderloin was wreaking its vengeance upon Fifth Avenue. It was not merely that the men of wealth were carrying to their wives and children the diseases of vice; they were carrying also the manners and the ideals.

Montague had been amazed by the things he had found in New York Society; the smoking and drinking and gambling of women, their hard and cynical views of life, their continual telling of coarse stories. And here, in this under-world, he had come upon the fountain head of the corruption. It was something which came to him in a sudden flash of intuition;—the barriers between the two worlds were breaking down!

He could picture the process in a hundred different forms. There was Betty Wyman. His brother had meant to take her to the theatre, to let her see Rosalie, by way of a joke! So, of course, Betty knew of his escapades, and of those of his set; she and her girl friends were whispering and jesting about them. Here sat Oliver, smiling and cynical, toying with Rosalie as a cat might toy with a mouse; and to-morrow he would be with Betty—and could anyone doubt any longer whence Betty had derived her attitude towards life? And the habits of mind that Oliver had taught her as a girl she would not forget as a wife; he might be anxious to keep her to himself, but there would be others whose interest was different.

And Montague recalled other things that he had seen or heard in Society, that he could put his finger upon, as having come out of this under-world. The more he thought of the explanation, the more it seemed to explain. This "Society," which had perplexed him—now he could describe it: its manners and ideals of life were those which he would have expected to find in the "fast" side of stage life.

It was, of course, the women who made Society, and gave it its tone; and the women of Society were actresses. They were actresses in their love of notoriety and display; in their taste in clothes and jewels, their fondness for cigarettes and champagne. They made up like actresses; they talked and thought like actresses. The only obvious difference was that the women of the stage were carefully selected—were at least up to a certain standard of physical excellence; whereas the women of Society were not selected at all, and some were lean, and some were stout, and some were painfully homely.

Montague recalled cases where the two sets had met as at some of the private entertainments. It was getting to be the fashion to hobnob with the stage people on such occasions; and he recalled how naturally the younger people took to this. Only the older women held aloof; looking down upon the women of the stage from an ineffable height, as belonging to a lower caste—because they were obliged to work for their livings. But it seemed to Montague, as he sat and talked with this poor chorus-girl, who had sold herself for a little pleasure, that it was easier to pardon her than the woman who had been born to luxury, and scorned those who produced her wealth.

But most of all, one's sympathies went out to a person who was not to be met in either of these sets; to the girl who had not sold herself, but was struggling for a living in the midst of this ravening corruption. There were thousands of self-respecting women, even on the stage; Toodles herself had been among them, she told Montague. "I kept straight for a long time," she said, laughing cheerfully—"and on ten dollars a week! I used to go out on the road, and then they paid me sixteen; and think of trying to live on one-night stands—to board yourself and stop at hotels and dress for the theatre—on sixteen a week, and no job half the year! And all that time—do you know Cyril Chambers, the famous church painter?"

"I've heard of him," said Montague.

"Well, I was with a show here on Broadway the next winter; and every night for six months he sent me a bunch of orchids that couldn't have cost less than seventy-five dollars! And he told me he'd open accounts for me in all the stores I chose, if I'd spend the next summer in Europe with him. He said I could take my mother or my sister with me—and I was so green in those days, I thought that must mean he didn't intend anything wrong!"

Toodles smiled at the memory. "Did you go?" asked the man.

"No," she answered. "I stayed here with a roof-garden show that failed. And I went to my old manager for a job, and he said to me, 'I can only pay you ten a week. But why are you so foolish?' 'How do you mean?' I asked; and he answered, 'Why don't you get a rich sweetheart? Then I could pay you sixty.' That's what a girl hears on the stage!"

"I don't understand," said Montague, perplexed. "Did he mean he could get money out of the man?"

"Not directly," said Toodles; "but tickets—and advertising. Why, men will hire front-row seats for a whole season, if they're interested in a girl in the show. And they'll take all their friends to see her, and she'll be talked about—she'll be somebody, instead of just nobody, as I was."

"Then it actually helps her on the stage!" said Montague.

"Helps her!" exclaimed Toodles. "My God! I've known a girl who'd been abroad with a tip-top swell—and had the gowns and the jewels to prove it—to come home and get into the front row of a chorus at a hundred dollars a week."

Toodles was cheerful and all unaware; and that only made the tragedy of it all one shade more black to Montague. He sat lost in sombre reverie, forgetting his companions, and the blare and glare of the place.

In the centre of this dining-room was a great cone-shaped stand, containing a display of food; and as they strolled out, Montague stopped to look at it. There were platters garnished with flowers and herbs, and containing roast turkeys and baked hams, jellied meats and game in aspic, puddings and tarts and frosted cakes—every kind of food-fantasticality imaginable. One might have spent an hour in studying it, and from top to bottom he would have found nothing simple, nothing natural. The turkeys had paper curls and rosettes stuck over them; the hams were covered with a white gelatine, the devilled crabs with a yellow mayonnaise-and all painted over in pink and green and black with landscapes and marine views—with "ships and shoes and sealing-wax and cabbages and kings." The jellied meats and the puddings were in the shape of fruits and flowers; and there were elaborate works of art in pink and white confectionery—a barn-yard, for instance, with horses and cows, and a pump, and a dairymaid—and one or two alligators.

And all this was changed every day! Each morning you might see a procession of a score of waiters bearing aloft a new supply. Montague remembered Betty Wyman's remark at their first interview, apropos of the whipped cream made into little curleques; how his brother had said, "If Allan were here, he'd be thinking about the man who fixed that cream, and how long it took him, and how he might have been reading 'The Simple Life'!"

He thought of that now; he stood here and gazed, and wondered about all the slaves of the lamp who served in this huge temple of luxury. He looked at the waiters—pale, hollow-chested, harried-looking men: he imagined the hordes of servants of yet lower kinds, who never emerged into the light of day; the men who washed the dishes, the men who carried the garbage, the men who shovelled the coal into the furnaces, and made the heat and light and power. Pent up in dim cellars, many stories under ground, and bound for ever to the service of sensuality—how terrible must be their fate, how unimaginable their corruption! And they were foreigners; they had come here seeking liberty. And the masters of the new country had seized them and pent them here!

From this as a starting-point his thought went on, to the hordes of toilers in every part of the world, whose fate it was to create the things which these blind revellers destroyed; the women and children in countless mills and sweatshops, who spun the cloth, and cut and sewed it; the girls who made the artificial flowers, who rolled the cigarettes, who gathered the grapes from the vines; the miners who dug the coal and the precious metals out of the earth; the men who watched in ten thousand signal-towers and engines, who fought the elements from the decks of ten thousand ships—to bring all these things here to be destroyed. Step by step, as the flood of extravagance rose, and the energies of the men were turned to the creation of futility and corruption—so, step by step, increased the misery and degradation of all these slaves of Mammon. And who could imagine what they would think about it—if ever they came to think?

And then, in a sudden flash, there came back to Montague that speech he had heard upon the street-corner, the first evening he had been in New York! He could hear again the pounding of the elevated trains, and the shrill voice of the orator; he could see his haggard and hungry face, and the dense crowd gazing up at him. And there came to him the words of Major Thorne:

"It means another civil war!"

CHAPTER XXI

Alice had been gone for a couple of weeks, and the day was drawing near when the Hasbrook case came up for trial. The Saturday before that being the date of the Mi-carême dance of the Long Island Hunt Club, Siegfried Harvey was to have a house-party for the week-end, and Montague accepted his invitation. He had been working hard, putting the finishing touches to his brief, and he thought that a rest would be good for him.

He and his brother went down upon Friday afternoon, and the first person he met was Betty Wyman, whom he had not seen for quite a while. Betty had much to say, and said it. As Montague had not been seen with Mrs. Winnie since the episode in her house, people had begun to notice the break, and there was no end of gossip; and Mistress Betty wanted to know all about it, and how things stood between them.

But he would not tell her, and so she saucily refused to tell him what she had heard. All the while they talked she was eyeing him quizzically, and it was evident that she took the worst for granted; also that he had become a much more interesting person to her because of it. Montague had the strangest sensations when he was talking with Betty Wyman; she was delicious and appealing, almost irresistible; and yet her views of life were so old! "I told you you wouldn't do for a tame cat!" she said to him.

Then she went on to talk to him about his case, and to tease him about the disturbance he had made.

"You know," she said, "Ollie and I were in terror—we thought that grandfather would be furious, and that we'd be ruined. But somehow, it didn't work out that way. Don't you say anything about it, but I've had a sort of a fancy that he must be on your side of the fence."

"I'd be glad to know it," said Montague, with a laugh—"I've been trying for a long time to find out who is on my side of the fence."

"He was talking about it the other day," said Betty, "and I heard him tell a man that he'd read your argument, and thought it was good."

"I'm glad to hear that," said Montague.

"So was I," replied she. "And I said to him afterward, 'I suppose you don't know that Allan Montague is my Ollie's brother.' And he did you the honour to say that he hadn't supposed any member of Ollie's family could have as much sense!"

Betty was staying with an aunt near by, and she went back before dinner. In the automobile which came for her was old Wyman himself, on his way home from the city; and as a snowstorm had begun, he came in and stood by the fire while his car was exchanged for a closed one from Harvey's stables. Montague did not meet him, but stood and watched him from the shadows-a mite of a man, with a keen and eager face, full of wrinkles. It was hard to realize that this little body held one of the great driving minds of the country. He was an intensely nervous and irritable man, bitter and implacable—by all odds the most hated and feared man in Wall Street. He was swift, imperious, savage as a hornet. "Directors at meetings that I attend vote first and discuss afterward," was one of his sayings that Montague had heard quoted. Watching him here by the fireside, rubbing his hands and chatting pleasantly, Montague had a sudden sense of being behind the scenes, of being admitted to a privilege denied to ordinary mortals—the beholding of royalty in everyday attire!

After dinner that evening Montague had a chat in the smoking-room with his host; and he brought up the subject of the Hasbrook case, and told about his trip to Washington, and his interview with Judge Ellis.

Harvey also had something to communicate. "I had a talk with Freddie Vandam about it," said he.

"What did he say?" asked Montague.

"Well," replied the other, with a laugh, "he's indignant, needless to say. You know, Freddie was brought up by his father to regard the Fidelity as his property, in a way. He always refers to it as 'my company.' And he's very high and mighty about it—it's a personal affront if anyone attacks it. But it was evident to me that he doesn't know who's behind this case."

"Did he know about Ellis?" asked Montague.

"Yes," said the other, "he had found out that much. It was he who told me that originally. He says that Ellis has been sponging off the company for years—he has a big salary that he never earns, and has borrowed something like a quarter of a million dollars on worthless securities."

Montague gave a gasp.

"Yes," laughed Harvey. "But after all, that's a little matter. The trouble with Freddie Vandam is that that sort of thing is all he sees; and so he'll never be able to make out the mystery. He knows that this clique or that in the company is plotting to get some advantage, or to use him for their purposes—but he never realizes how the big men are pulling the wires behind the scenes. Some day they'll throw him overboard altogether, and then he'll realize how they've played with him. That's what this Hasbrook case means, you know—they simply want to frighten him with a threat of getting the company's affairs into the courts and the newspapers."

Montague sat for a while in deep thought.

"What would you think would be Wyman's relation to the matter?" he asked, at last.

"I wouldn't know," said Harvey. "He's supposed to be Freddie's backer—but what can you tell in such a tangle?"

"It is certainly a mess," said Montague.

"There's no bottom to it," said the other. "Absolutely—it would take your breath away! Just listen to what Vandam told me to-day!"

And then Harvey named one of the directors of the Fidelity who was well known as a philanthropist. Having heard that the wife of one of his junior partners had met with an accident in childbirth, and that the doctor had told her husband that if she ever had another child, she would die, this man had asked, "Why don't you have her life insured?" The other replied that he had tried, and the companies had refused her. "I'll fix it for you," said he; and so they put in another application, and the director came to Freddie Vandam and had the policy put through "by executive order." Seven months later the woman died, and the Fidelity had paid her husband in full—a hundred thousand or two!

"That's what's going on in the insurance world!" said Siegfried Harvey.

And that was the story which Montague took with him to add to his enjoyment of the festivities at the country club. It was a very gorgeous affair; but perhaps the sombreness of his thoughts was to blame; the flowers and music and beautiful gowns failed entirely in their appeal, and he saw only the gluttony and drunkenness—more of it than ever before, it seemed to him.

Then, too, he had an unpleasant experience. He met Laura Hegan; and presuming upon her cordial reception of his visit, he went up and spoke to her pleasantly. And she greeted him with frigid politeness; she was so brief in her remarks and turned away so abruptly as almost to snub him. He went away quite bewildered. But later on he recalled the gossip about himself and Mrs. Winnie, and he guessed that that was the explanation of Miss Hegar's action.

The episode threw a shadow over his whole visit. On Sunday he went out into the country and tramped through a snowstorm by himself, filled with a sense of disgust for all the past, and of foreboding for the future. He hated this money-world, in which all that was worst in human beings was brought to the surface; he hated it, and wished that he had never set foot within its bounds. It was only by tramping until he was too tired to feel anything that he was able to master himself.

And then, toward dark, he came back, and found a telegram which had been forwarded from New York.

"Meet me at the Penna depot, Jersey City, at nine to-night. Alice."

This message, of course, drove all other thoughts from his mind. He had no time even to tell Oliver about it—he had to jump into an automobile and rush to catch the next train for the city. And all through the long, cold ride in ferry-boats and cabs he pondered this mystery. Alice's party had not been expected for two weeks yet; and only two days before there had come a letter from Los Angeles, saying that they would probably be a week over time. And here she was home again!

He found there was an express from the West due at the hour named; apparently, therefore, Alice had not come in the Prentice's train at all. The express was half an hour late, and so he paced up and down the platform, controlling his impatience as best he could. And finally the long train pulled in, and he saw Alice coming down the platform. She was alone!

"What does it mean?" were the first words he said to her.

"It's a long story," she answered. "I wanted to come home.";

"You mean you've come all the way from the coast by yourself!" he gasped.

"Yes," she said, "all the way."

"What in the world—" he began.

"I can't tell you here, Allan," she said. "Wait till we get to some quiet place."

"But," he persisted. "The Prentice? They let you come home alone?"

"They didn't know it," she said. "I ran away."

He was more bewildered than ever. But as he started to ask more questions, she laid a hand upon his arm. "Please wait, Allan," she said. "It upsets me to talk about it. It was Charlie Carter."

And so the light broke. He caught his breath and gasped, "Oh!"

He said not another word until they had crossed the ferry and settled themselves in a cab, and started. "Now," he said, "tell me."

Alice began. "I was very much upset," she said. "But you must understand, Allan, that I've had nearly a week to think it over, and I don't mind it now. So I want you please not to get excited about it; it wasn't poor Charlie's fault—he can't help himself. It was my mistake. I ought to have taken your advice and had nothing to do with him."

"Go on," said he; and Alice told her story.

The party had gone sight-seeing, and she had had a headache and had stayed in the car. And Charlie Carter had come and begun making love to her. "He had asked me to marry him already—that was at the beginning of the trip," she said. "And I told him no. After that he would never let me alone. And this time he went on in a terrible way—he flung himself down on his knees, and wept, and said he couldn't live without me. And nothing I could say did any good. At last he—he caught hold of me—and he wouldn't let me go. I was furious with him, and frightened. I had to threaten to call for help before he would stop. And so—you see how it was."

"I see," said Montague, gravely. "Go on."

"Well, after that I made up my mind that I couldn't stay anywhere where I had to see him. And I knew he would never go away without a scene. If I had asked Mrs. Prentice to send him away, there would have been a scandal, and it would have spoiled everybody's trip. So I went out, and found there was a train for the East in a little while, and I packed up my things, and left a note for Mrs. Prentice. I told her a story—I said I'd had a telegram that your mother was ill, and that I didn't want to spoil their good time, and had gone by myself. That was the best thing I could think of. I wasn't afraid to travel, so long as I was sure that Charlie couldn't catch up with me."

Montague said nothing; he sat with his hands gripped tightly.

"It seemed like a desperate thing to do," said Alice, nervously. "But you see, I was upset and unhappy. I didn't seem to like the party any more—I wanted to be home. Do you understand?"

"Yes," said Montague, "I understand. And I'm glad you are here."

They reached home, and Montague called up Harvey's and told his brother what had happened. He could hear Oliver gasp with astonishment. "That's a pretty how-do-you-do!" he said, when he had got his breath back; and then he added, with a laugh, "I suppose that settles poor Charlie's chances."

"I'm glad you've come to that conclusion," said the other, as he hung up the receiver.

This episode gave Montague quite a shock. But he had little time to think about it—the next morning at eleven o'clock his case was to come up for trial, and so all his thoughts were called away. This case had been the one real interest of his life for the last three months; it was his purpose, the thing for the sake of which he endured everything else that repelled him. And he had trained himself as an athlete for a great race; he was in form, and ready for the effort of his life. He went down town that morning with every fibre of him, body and mind, alert and eager; and he went into his office, and in his mail was a letter from Mr. Hasbrook. He opened it hastily and read a message, brief and direct and decisive as a sword-thrust:

"I beg to inform you that I have received a satisfactory proposition from the Fidelity Company. I have settled with them, and wish to withdraw the suit. Thanking you for your services, I remain, sincerely."

To Montague the thing came like a thunderbolt. He sat utterly dumbfounded—his hands went limp, and the letter fell upon the desk in front of him.

And at last, when he did move, he picked up the telephone, and told his secretary to call up Mr. Hasbrook. Then he sat waiting; and when the bell rang, picked up the receiver, expecting to hear Mr. Hasbrook's voice, and to demand an explanation. But he heard, instead, the voice of his own secretary: "Central says the number's been discontinued, sir."

And he hung up the receiver, and sat motionless again. The dummy had disappeared!

To Montague this incident meant a change in the prospect of his whole life. It was the collapse of all his hopes. He had nothing more to work for, nothing more to think about; the bottom had fallen out of his career!

He was burning with a sense of outrage. He had been tricked and made a fool of; he had been used and flung aside. And now there was nothing he could do—he was utterly helpless. What affected him most was his sense of the overwhelming magnitude of the powers which had made him their puppet; of the utter futility of the efforts that he or any other man could make against them. They were like elemental, cosmic forces; they held all the world in their grip, and a common man was as much at their mercy as a bit of chaff in a tempest.

All day long he sat in his office, brooding and nursing his wrath. He had moods when he wished to drop everything, to shake the dust of the city from his feet, and go back home and recollect what it was to be a gentleman. And then again he had fighting moods, when he wished to devote all his life to punishing the men who had made use of him. He would get hold of some other policy-holder in the Fidelity, one whom he could trust; he would take the case without pay, and carry it through to the end! He would force the newspapers to talk about it—he would force the people to heed what he said!

And then, toward evening, he went home, bitter and sore. And there was his brother sitting in his study, waiting for him.

"Hello," he said, and took off his coat, preparing his mind for one more ignominy—the telling of his misfortune to Oliver, and listening to his inevitable, "I told you so."

But Oliver himself had something to communicate something that would not bear keeping. He broke out at once—"Tell me, Allan! What in the world has happened between you and Mrs. Winnie?"

"What do you mean?" asked Montague, sharply.

"Why," said Oliver, "everybody is talking about some kind of a quarrel."

"There has been no quarrel," said Montague.

"Well, what is it, then?"

"It's nothing."

"It must be something!" exclaimed Oliver. "What do all the stories mean?"

"What stories?"

"About you two. I met Mrs. Vivie Patton just now, and she swore me to secrecy, and told me that Mrs. Winnie had told some one that you had made love to her so outrageously that she had to ask you to leave the house."

Montague shrunk as from a blow. "Oh!" he gasped.

"That's what she said," said he.

"It's a lie!" he cried.

"That's what I told Mrs. Vivie," said the other; "it doesn't sound like you—"

Montague had flushed scarlet. "I don't mean that!" he cried. "I mean that Mrs. Winnie never said any such thing."

"Oh," said Oliver, and he shrugged his shoulders. "Maybe not," he added. "But I know she's furious with you about something—everybody's talking about it. She tells people that she'll never speak to you again. And what I want to know is, why is it that you have to do things to make enemies of everybody you know?"

Montague said nothing; he was trembling with anger.

"What in the world did you do to her?" began the other. "Can't you trust me—-"

And suddenly Montague sprang to his feet. "Oh, Oliver," he exclaimed, "let me alone! Go away!"

And he went into the next room and slammed the door, and began pacing back and forth like a caged animal.

It was a lie! It was a lie! Mrs. Winnie had never said such a thing! He would never believe it—it was a nasty piece of backstairs gossip!

But then a new burst of rage swept over him What did it matter Whether it was true or not—whether anything was true or not? What did it matter if anybody had done all the hideous and loathsome things that everybody else said they had done? It was what everybody was saying! It was what everybody believed—what everybody was interested in! It was the measure of a whole society—their ideals and their standards! It was the way they spent their time, repeating nasty scandals about each other; living in an atmosphere of suspicion and cynicism, with endless whispering and leering, and gossip of lew intrigue.

A flood of rage surged up within him, and swept him, away—rage against the world into which he had come, and against himself for the part he had played in it. Everything seemed to have come to a head at once; and he hated everything— hated the people he had met, and the things they did, and the things they had tempted him to do. He hated the way he had got his money, and the way he had spent it. He hated the idleness and wastefulness, the drunkenness and debauchery, the meanness and the snobbishness.

And suddenly he turned and flung open the door of the room where Oliver still sat. And he stood in the doorway, exclaiming, "Oliver, I'm done with it!"

Oliver stared at him. "What do you mean?" he asked.

"I mean," cried his brother, "that I've had all I can stand of 'Society!' And I'm going to quit. You can go on—but I don't intend to take another step with you! I've had enough—and I think Alice has had enough, also. We'll take ourselves off your hands—we'll get out!"

"What are you going to do?" gasped Oliver.

"I'm going to give up these expensive apartments—give them up to-morrow, when our week is up. And I'm going to stop squandering money for things I don't want. I'm going to stop accepting invitations, and meeting people I don't like and don't want to know. I've tried your game—I've tried it hard, and I don't like it; and I'm going to get out before it's too late. I'm going to find some decent and simple place to live in; and I'm going down town to find out if there isn't some way in New York for a man to earn an honest living!"

THE MONEYCHANGERS

To Jack London

CHAPTER I

"I am," said Reggie Mann, "quite beside myself to meet this Lucy Dupree."

"Who told you about her?" asked Allan Montague.

"Ollie's been telling everybody about her," said Reggie. "It sounds really wonderful. But I fear he must have exaggerated."

"People seem to develop a tendency to exaggeration," said Montague, "when they talk about Lucy."

"I am in quite a state about her," said Reggie.

Allan Montague looked at him and smiled. There were no visible signs of agitation about Reggie. He had come to take Alice to church, and he was exquisitely groomed and perfumed, and wore a wonderful scarlet orchid in his buttonhole. Montague, lounging back in a big leather chair and watching him, smiled to himself at the thought that Reggie regarded Lucy as a new kind of flower, with which he might parade down the Avenue and attract attention.

"Is she large or small?" asked Reggie.

"She is about your size," said Montague,—which was very small indeed.

Alice entered at this moment in a new spring costume. Reggie sprang to his feet, and greeted her with his inevitable effusiveness.

When he asked, "Do you know her, too?"

"Who? Lucy?" asked Alice. "I went to school with her."

"Judge Dupree's plantation was next to ours," said Montague. "We all grew up together."

"There was hardly a day that I did not see her until she was married," said Alice. "She was married at seventeen, you know—to a man much older than herself."

"We have never seen her since that," added the other. "She has lived in New Orleans."

"And only twenty-two now," exclaimed Reggie. "All the wisdom of a widow and the graces of an ingénue!" And he raised his hands with a gesture of admiration.

"Has she got money?" he asked.

"She had enough for New Orleans," was the reply. "I don't know about New York."

"Ah well," he said meditatively, "there's plenty of money lying about."

He took Alice away to her devotions, leaving Montague to the memories which the mention of Lucy Dupree awakened.

Allan Montague had been in love with Lucy a half a dozen times in his life; it had begun when she was a babe in arms, and continued intermittently until her marriage. Lucy was a beauty of the creole type, with raven-black hair and gorgeous colouring; and Allan carried with him everywhere the face of joy, with the quick, mobile features across which tears and laughter chased like April showers across the sky.

Lucy was a tiny creature, as he had said, but she was a well-spring of abounding energy. She had been the life of a lonely household from the first hour, and all who came near her yielded to her spell. Allan remembered one occasion when he had entered the house and seen the grave and venerable chief justice of the State down upon his hands and knees, with Lucy on his back.

She was a born actress, everybody said. When she was no more than four, she would lie in bed when she should have been asleep, and tell herself tragic stories to make her weep. Before long she had discovered several chests full of the clothes which her mother had worn in the days when she was a belle of the old plantation society; and then Lucy would have tableaus and theatricals, and would astonish all beholders in the role of an Oriental princess or a Queen of the Night.

Her mother had died when she was very young, and she had grown up with only her father for a companion. Judge Dupree was one of the rich men of the neighbourhood, and he lavished everything upon his daughter; but people had said that Lucy would suffer for the lack of a woman's care, and the prophecy had been tragically fulfilled. There had come a man, much older than herself, but with a glamour of romance about him; and the wonder of love had suddenly revealed itself to Lucy, and swept her away as no emotion had ever done before.

One day she disappeared, and Montague had never seen her again. He knew that she had gone to New Orleans to live, and he heard rumours that she was very unhappy, that her husband was a spendthrift and a rake. Scarcely a year after her marriage Montague heard the story of his death by an accident while driving.

He had heard no more until a short time after his coming to New York, when the home papers had reported the death of Judge Dupree. And then a week or so ago had come a letter from Lucy, to his brother, Oliver Montague, saying that she was coming to New York, perhaps to live permanently, and asking him to meet her and to engage accommodations for her in some hotel.

Montague wondered what she would be like when he saw her again. He wondered what five years of suffering and experience would have done for her; whether it would have weakened her enthusiasm and dried up her springs of joy. Lucy grown serious was something that was difficult for him to imagine.

And then again would come a mood of doubt, when he distrusted the thrill which the memory of her brought. Would she be able to maintain her spell in competition with what life had brought him since?

His revery was broken by Oliver, who came in to ask him if he wished to go to meet her. "Those Southern trains are always several hours late," he said. "I told my man to go over and 'phone me."

"You are to have her in charge," said Montague; "you had better see her first. Tell her I will come in the evening." And so he went to the great apartment hotel—the same to which Oliver had originally introduced him. And there was Lucy.

She was just the same. He could see it in an instant; there was the same joyfulness, the same eagerness; there was the same beauty, which had made men's hearts leap up. There was not a line of care upon her features—she was like a perfect flower come to its fulness.

She came to him with both her hands outstretched. "Allan!" she cried, "Allan! I am so glad to see you!" And she caught his hands in hers and stood and gazed at him. "My, how big you have grown, and how serious! Isn't he splendid, Ollie?"

Oliver stood by, watching. He smiled drily. "He is a trifle too epic for me," he said.

"Oh, my, how wonderful it seems to see you!" she exclaimed. "It makes me think of fifty things at once. We must sit down and have a long talk. It will take me all night to ask you all the questions I have to."

Lucy was in mourning for her father, but she had contrived to make her costume serve as a frame for her beauty. She seemed like a flaming ruby against a background of black velvet. "Tell me how you have been," she rushed on. "And what has happened to you up here? How is your mother?"

"Just the same," said Montague; "she wants you to come around to-morrow morning."

"I will," said Lucy,—"the first thing, before I go anywhere. And Mammy Lucy! How is Mammy Lucy?"

"She is well," he replied. "She's beside herself to see you."

"Tell her I am coming!" said she. "I would rather see Mammy Lucy than the Brooklyn Bridge!"

She led him to a seat, placed herself opposite him, devouring him with her eyes. "It makes me seem like a girl again to see you," she said.

"Do you count yourself aged?" asked Montague, laughing.

"Oh, I feel old," said Lucy, with a sudden look of fear,—"you have no idea, Allan. But I don't want anybody to know about it!" And then she cried, eagerly, "Do you remember the swing in the orchard? And do you remember the pool where the big alligator lived? And the persimmons? And Old Joe?"

Allan Montague remembered all these things; in the course of the half hour that followed he remembered pretty nearly all the exciting adventures which he and Oliver and Lucy had had since Lucy was old enough to walk. And he told her the latest news about all their neighbours, and about all the servants whom she remembered. He told her also about his father's death, and how the house had been burned, and how they had sold the plantation and come North.

"And how are you doing, Allan?" she asked.

"I am practising law," he said. "I'm not making a fortune, but I'm managing to pay my bills. That is more than some other people do in this city."

"I should imagine it," said Lucy. "With all that row of shops on Fifth Avenue! Oh, I know I shall spend all that I own in the first week. And this hotel—why, it's perfectly frightful."

"Oliver has told you the prices, has he?" said Montague, with a laugh.

"He has taken my breath away," said Lucy. "How am I ever to manage such things?"

"You will have to settle that with him," said Montague. "He has taken charge, and he doesn't want me to interfere."

"But I want your advice," said Lucy. "You are a business man, and Ollie never was anything but a boy."

"Ollie has learned a good deal since he has been in New York," the other responded.

"I can tell you my side of the case very quickly," he went on after a moment's pause. "He brought me here, and persuaded me that this was how I ought to live if I wanted to get into Society. I tried it for a while, but I found that I did not like the things I had to do, and so I quit. You will find us in an apartment a couple of blocks farther from Fifth Avenue, and we only pay about one-tenth as much for it. And now, whether you follow me or Ollie depends upon whether you want to get into Society."

Lucy wrinkled her brows in thought. "I didn't come to New York to bury myself in a boarding-house," she said. "I do want to meet people."

"Well," said Montague, "Oliver knows a lot of them, and he will introduce you. Perhaps you will like them—I don't know. I am sure you won't have any difficulty in making them like you."

"Thank you, sir," said Lucy. "You are as ingenuous as ever!"

"I don't want to say anything to spoil your pleasure," said the other. "You will find out about matters for yourself. But I feel like telling you this—don't you be too ingenuous. You can't trust people quite so freely here as you did at home."

"Thank you," said Lucy. "Ollie has already been lecturing me. I had no idea it was such a serious matter to come to New York. I told him that widows were commonly supposed to know how to take care of themselves."

"I had a rather bad time of it myself, getting adjusted to things," said Montague, smiling. "So you must make allowances for my forebodings."

"I've told Lucy a little about it," put in Oliver, drily.

"He told me a most fascinating love story!" said Lucy, gazing at him with a mischievous twinkle in her eyes. "I shall certainly look out for the dazzling Mrs. Winnie."

"You may meet her to-morrow night," put in Oliver. "You are invited to dinner at Mrs. Billy Alden's."

"I have read about Mrs. Billy in the newspapers," said Lucy. "But I never expected to meet her. How in the world has Oliver managed to jump so into the midst of things?"

Oliver undertook to explain; and Montague sat by, smiling to himself over his brother's carefully expurgated account of his own social career. Oliver had evidently laid his plans to take charge of Lucy, and to escort her to a high seat upon the platform of Society.

"But tell me, all this will cost so much money!" Lucy protested. "And I don't want to have to marry one of these terrible millionaires."

She turned to Montague abruptly. "Have you got an office somewhere down town?" she asked. "And may I come to-morrow, and see you, and get you to be my business adviser? Old Mr. Holmes is dead, you know. He used to be father's lawyer, and he knew all about my affairs. He never thought it worth while to explain anything to me, so now I don't know very well what I have or what I can do."

"I will do all I can to help you," Montague answered.

"And you must be very severe with me," Lucy continued, "and not let me spend too much money, or make any blunders. That was the way Mr. Holmes used to do, and since he is dead, I have positively been afraid to trust myself about."

"If I am to play that part for you," said Montague, laughing, "I am afraid we'll very soon clash with my brother."

Montague had very little confidence in his ability to fill the part. As he watched Lucy, he had a sense of tragedy impending. He knew enough to feel sure that Lucy was not rich, according to New York standards of wealth; and he felt that the lure of the city was already upon her. She was dazzled by the vision of automobiles and shops and hotels and theatres, and all the wonders which these held out to her. She had come with all her generous enthusiasms; and she was hungry with a terrible hunger for life.

Montague had been through the mill, and he saw ahead so clearly that it was impossible for him not to try to guide her, and to save her from the worst of her mistakes. Hence arose a strange relationship between them; from the beginning Lucy made him her confidant, and told him all her troubles. To be sure, she never took his advice; she would say, with her pretty laugh, that she did not want him to keep her out of trouble, but only to sympathise with her afterwards. And Montague followed her; he told himself again and again that there was no excuse for Lucy; but all the while he was making excuses.

She went over the next morning to see Oliver's mother, and Mammy Lucy, who had been named after her grandmother. Then in the afternoon she went shopping with Alice—declaring that it was impossible for her to appear anywhere in New York until she had made herself "respectable." And then in the evening Montague called for her, and took her to Mrs. Billy Alden's Fifth Avenue palace.

On the way he beguiled the time by telling her about the terrible Mrs. Billy and her terrible tongue; and about the war between the great lady and her relatives, the Wallings. "You must not be surprised," he said, "if she pins you in a corner and asks all about you. Mrs. Billy is a privileged character, and the conventions do not apply to her."

Montague had come to take the Alden magnificence as a matter of course by this time, but he felt Lucy thrill with excitement at the vision of the Doge's palace, with its black marble carvings and its lackeys in scarlet and gold. Then came Mrs. Billy herself, resplendent in dark purple brocade, with a few ropes of pearls flung about her neck. She was almost tall enough to look over the top of Lucy's head, and she stood away a little so as to look at her comfortably.

"I tried to have Mrs. Winnie here for you," she said to Montague, as she placed him at her right hand. "But she was not able to come, so you will have to make out with me."

"Have you many more beauties like that down in Mississippi?" she asked, when they were seated. "If so, I don't see why you came up here."

"You like her, do you?" he asked.

"I like her looks," said Mrs. Billy. "Has she got any sense? It is quite impossible to believe that she's a widow. She needs someone to take care of her just the same."

"I will recommend her to your favour," said Montague. "I have been telling her about you."

"What have you told her?" asked Mrs. Billy, serenely,—"that I win too much money at bridge, and drink Scotch at dinner?" Then, seeing Montague blush furiously, she laughed. "I know it is true. I have caught you thinking it half a dozen times."

And she reached out for the decanter which the butler had just placed in front of her, and proceeded to help herself to her opening glass.

Montague told her all about Lucy; and, in the meantime, he watched the latter, who sat near the centre of the table, talking with Stanley Ryder. Montague had played bridge with this man once or twice at Mrs. Winnie's, and he thought to himself that Lucy could hardly have met a man who would embody in himself more of the fascinations of the Metropolis. Ryder was president of the Gotham Trust Company, an institution whose magnificent marble front was one of the sights of Fifth Avenue. He was a man a trifle under fifty, tall and distinguished-looking, with an iron-grey mustache, and the manners of a diplomat. He was not only a banker, he was also a man of culture; he had run away to sea in his youth, and he had travelled in every country of the world. He was also a bit of an author, in an amateur way, and if there was any book which he had not dipped into, it was not a book of which one would be apt to hear in Society. He could talk upon any subject, and a hostess who could secure Stanley Ryder for one of her dinner-parties generally counted upon a success. "He doesn't go out much, these busy days," said Mrs. Billy. "But I told him about your friend."

Now and then the conversation at the table would become general, and Montague noticed that it was always Ryder who led. His flashes of wit shot back and forth across the table; and those who matched themselves against him seldom failed to come off the worse. It was an unscrupulous kind of wit, dazzling and dangerous. Ryder was the type of man one met now and then in Society, who had adopted radical ideas for the sake of being distinguished. It was a fine thing for a man who had made a brilliant success in a certain social environment to shatter in his conversation all the ideals and conventions of that environment, and thus to reveal how little he really cared for the success which he had won.

It was very entertaining at a dinner-party; but Montague thought to himself with a smile how far was Stanley Ryder from the type of person one imagined as the head of an enormous and flourishing bank. When they had adjourned to the drawing-room, he capped the climax of the incongruity by going to the piano and playing a movement from some terrible Russian suite.

Afterwards Montague saw him stroll off to the conservatory with Lucy Dupree. There were two people too many for bridge, and that was a good excuse; but none the less Montague felt restless during the hours that he sat at table and let Mrs. Billy win his money.

After the ordeal was over and the party had broken up, he found his friend sitting by the side of the fountain in Mrs. Billy's conservatory, gazing fixedly in front of her, while Ryder at her side was talking.

"You met an interesting man," he said, when they had got settled in the carriage.

"One of the most extraordinary men I ever met," said Lucy, quickly. "I wish that you would tell me about him. Do you know him well?"

"I have heard him talk some, and I know him in a business way."

"Is he so very rich?" she asked.

"He has a few millions," said he. "And I suppose he is turning them over very rapidly. People say that he is a daring speculator."

"A speculator!" exclaimed Lucy. "Why, I thought that he was the president of a bank!"

"When you have been in New York awhile," said Montague, with a smile, "you will realise that there is nothing incompatible in the two."

Lucy was silent, a little staggered at the remark. "I am told," Montague added, with a smile, "that even Ryder's wife won't keep her money in the Gotham Trust."

Montague had not anticipated the effect of this remark. Lucy gave a sudden start. "His wife!" she exclaimed.

"Why, yes," said Montague. "Didn't you know that he was married?"

"No," said Lucy, in a low voice. "I did not."

There was a long silence. Finally she asked, "Why was not his wife invited to the dinner?"

"They seldom go out together," said Montague.

"Have they separated?" she asked.

"There is a new and fashionable kind of separation," was the answer. "They live in opposite sides of a large mansion, and meet on formal occasions."

"What sort of a woman is she?" asked Lucy,

"I don't know anything about her," he replied.

There was a silence again. Finally Montague said, "There is no cause to be sorry for him, you understand."

And Lucy touched his hand lightly with hers.

"That's all right, Allan," she said. "Don't worry. I am not apt to make the same mistake twice."

It seemed to Montague that there was nothing to be said after that.

CHAPTER II

Lucy wanted to come down to Montague's office to talk business with him; but he would not put her to that trouble, and called the next morning at her apartment before he went down town. She showed him all her papers; her father's will, with a list of his property, and also the accounts of Mr. Holmes, and the rent-roll of her properties in New Orleans. As Montague had anticipated, Lucy's affairs had not been well managed, and he had many matters to look into and many questions to ask. There were a number of mortgages on real estate and buildings, and, on the other hand, some of Lucy's own properties were mortgaged, a state of affairs which she was not able to explain. There were stocks in several industrial companies, of which Montague knew but little. Last and most important of all, there was a block of five thousand shares in the Northern Mississippi Railroad.

"You know all about that, at any rate," said Lucy. "Have you sold your own holdings yet?"

"No," said Montague. "Father wished me to keep the agreement as long as the others did."

"I am free to sell mine, am I not?" asked Lucy.

"I should certainly advise you to sell it," said Montague. "But I am afraid it will not be easy to find a purchaser."

The Northern Mississippi was a railroad with which Montague had grown up, so to speak; there was never a time in his recollection when the two families had not talked about it. It ran from Atkin to Opala, a distance of about fifty miles, connecting at the latter point with one of the main lines of the State. It was an enterprise which Judge Dupree had planned, as a means of opening up a section of country in the future of which he had faith.

It had been undertaken at a time when distrust of Wall Street was very keen in that neighbourhood; and Judge Dupree had raised a couple of million dollars among his own friends and neighbours, adding another half-million of his own, with a gentlemen's agreement among all of them that the road would not ask favours of Northern capitalists, and that its stock should never be listed on the Exchanges. The first president had been an uncle of Lucy's, and the present holder of the office was an old friend of the family's.

But the sectional pride which had raised the capital could not furnish the traffic. The towns which Judge Dupree had imagined did not materialise, and the little railroad did not keep pace with the progress of the time. For the last decade or so its properties had been depreciating and its earnings falling off, and it had been several years since Montague had drawn any dividends upon the fifty thousand dollars' worth of stock for which his father had paid par value.

He was reminded, as he talked about all this with Lucy, of a project which had been mooted some ten or twelve years ago, to extend the line from Atkin so as to connect with the plant of the Mississippi Steel Company, and give that concern a direct outlet toward the west. The Mississippi Steel Company had one of the half dozen largest plate and rail mills in the country, and the idea of directing even a small portion of its enormous freight was one which had incessantly tantalised the minds of the directors of the Northern Mississippi.

They had gone so far as to conduct a survey, and to make a careful estimate of the cost of the proposed extension. Montague knew about this, because it had chanced that he, together with Lucy's brother, who was now in California, had spent part of his vacation on a hunting trip, during which they had camped near the surveying party. The proposed line had to find its way through the Talula swamps, and here was where the uncertainty of the project came in. There were a dozen routes proposed, and Montague remembered how he had sat by the camp-fire one evening, and got into conversation with one of the younger men of the party, and listened to his grumbling about the blundering of the survey. It was his opinion that the head-surveyor was incompetent, that he was obstinately rejecting the best routes in favour of others which were almost impossible.

Montague had taken this gossip to his father, but he did not know whether his father had ever looked into the matter. He only knew that when the project for the proposed extension had been brought up at a stockholders' meeting, the cost of the work was found so great that it was impossible to raise the money. A proposal to go to the Mississippi Steel Company was voted down, because Mississippi Steel was in the hands of Wall Street men; and neither Judge Dupree nor General Montague had realised at that time the hopelessness of the plight of the little railroad.

All these matters were brought up in the conversation between Lucy and Montague. There was no reason, he assured her, why they should still hold on to their stock; if, by the proposed extension, or by any other plan, new capitalists could make a success of the company, it would be well to make some combination with them, or, better yet, to sell out entirely. Montague promised that he would take the matter in hand and see what he could do.

His first thought, as he went down town, was of Jim Hegan. "Come and see me sometime," Hegan had said, and Montague had never accepted the invitation. The Northern Mississippi would, of course, be a mere bagatelle to a man like Hegan, but who could tell what new plans he might be able to fit it into? Montague knew by the rumours in the street that the great financier had sold out all his holdings in two or three of his most important ventures.

He went at once to Hegan's office, in the building of one of the great insurance companies downtown. He made his way through corridors of marble to a gate of massively ornamented bronze, behind which stood a huge guardian in uniform, also massively ornamented. Montague generally passed for a big man, but this personage made him feel like an office-boy.

"Is Mr. Hegan in?" he asked.

"Do you call by appointment?" was the response.

"Not precisely," said Montague, producing a card. "Will you kindly send this to Mr. Hegan?"

"Do you know Mr. Hegan personally?" the man demanded.

"I do," Montague answered.

The other had made no sign, as far as Montague could make out, but at this moment a dapper young secretary made his appearance from the doors behind the gate. "Would you kindly state the business upon which you wish to see Mr. Hegan?" he said.

"I wish to see Mr. Hegan personally," Montague answered, with just a trifle of asperity, "If you will kindly take in this card, it will be sufficient."

He submitted with what grace he could to a swift inspection at the secretary's hands, wondering, in the meantime, if his new spring overcoat was sufficiently up-to-date to entitle him, in the secretary's judgment, to be a friend of the great man within. Finally the man disappeared with the card, and half a minute later came back, smiling effusively. He ushered Montague into a huge office with leather-cushioned chairs large enough to hold several people each, and too large for any one person to be comfortable in. There was a map of the continent upon the wall, across which Jim Hegan's railroads stretched like scarlet ribbons. There were also heads of bison and reindeer, which Hegan had shot himself.

Montague had to wait only a minute or two, and then he was escorted through a chain of rooms, and came at last to the magnate's inner sanctum. This was plain, with an elaborate and studied plainness, and Jim Hegan sat in front of a flat mahogany desk which had not a scrap of paper anywhere upon it.

He rose as the other came in, stretching out his huge form. "How do you do, Mr. Montague?" he said, and shook hands. Then he sat down in his chair, and settled back until his head rested on the back, and bent his great beetling brows, and gazed at his visitor.

The last time that Montague had met Hegan they had talked about horses, and about old days in Texas; but Montague was wise enough to realise that this had been in the evening. "I have come on a matter of business, Mr. Hegan," he said. "So I will be as brief as possible."

"A course of action which I do my best to pardon," was the smiling reply.

"I want to propose to you to interest yourself in the affairs of the Northern Mississippi Railroad," said the other.

"The Northern Mississippi?" said Hegan, knitting his brows. "I have never heard of it."

"I don't imagine that many people have," the other answered, and went on to tell the story of the line.

"I have five hundred shares of the stock myself," he said, "but it has been in my family for a long time, and I am perfectly satisfied to let it stay there. I am not making this proposition on my own account, but for a client who has a block of five thousand shares. I have here the annual reports of the road for several years, and some other information about its condition. My idea was that you might care to take the road, and make the proposed extension to the works of the Mississippi Steel Company."

"Mississippi Steel!" exclaimed Hegan. He had evidently heard of that.

"How long ago did you say it was that this plan was looked into?" he asked. And Montague told him the story of the survey, and what he himself had heard about it.

"That sounds curious," said Hegan, and bent his brows, evidently in deep thought. "I will look into the matter," he said, finally. "I have no plans of my own that would take me into that neighbourhood, but it may be possible that I can think of someone who would be interested. Have you any idea what your client wants for the thousand shares?"

"My client has put the matter into my hands," he answered. "The matter was only broached to me this morning, and I shall have to look further into the condition of the road. I should advise her to accept a fair offer—say seventy-five per cent of the par value of the stock."

"We can talk about that later," said Hegan, "if I can find the man for you." And Montague shook hands with him and left.

He stopped in on his way home in the evening to tell Lucy about the result of his interview. "We shall hear from him soon," he said. "I don't imagine that Hegan is a man who takes long to make up his mind."

"My prayers will be with him," said Lucy, with a laugh. Then she added, "I suppose I shall see you Friday night at Mr. Harvey's."

"I shan't come out until Saturday afternoon," said he. "I am very busy these days, working on a case. But I try to find time to get down to Siegfried Harvey's; I seem to get along with him."

"They tell me he goes in for horses," said Lucy.

"He has a splendid stable," he answered.

"It was good of Ollie to bring him round," said she. "I have certainly jumped into the midst of things. What do you think I'm going to do to-morrow?"

"I have no idea," he said.

"I have been invited to see Mr. Waterman's art gallery."

"Dan Waterman's!" he exclaimed. "How did that happen?"

"Mrs. Alden's brother asked me. He knows him, and got me the invitation. Wouldn't you like to go?"

"I shall be busy in court all day to-morrow," said Montague. "But I'd like to see the collection. I understand it's a wonderful affair,—the old man has spent all his spare time at it. You hear fabulous estimates of what it's cost him—four or five millions at the least."

"But why in the world does he hide it in a studio way up the Hudson?" cried Lucy.

The other shrugged his shoulders. "Just a whim," he said. "He didn't collect it for other people's pleasure."

"Well, so long as he lets me see it, I can't complain," said Lucy. "There are so many things to see in this city, I am sure I shall be busy for a year."

"You will get tired before you have seen half of them," he answered. "Everybody does."

"Do you know Mr. Waterman?" she asked.

"I have never met him," he said. "I have seen him a couple of times." And Montague went on to tell her of the occasion in the Millionaires' Club, when he had seen the Croesus of Wall Street surrounded by an attending throng of "little millionaires."

"I hope I shan't meet him," said Lucy. "I know I should be frightened to death."

"They say he can be charming when he wants to," replied Montague. "The ladies are fond of him."

On Saturday afternoon, when Montague went down to Harvey's Long Island home, his brother met him at the ferry.

"Allan," he began, immediately, "did you know that Lucy had come down here with Stanley Ryder?"

"Heavens, no!" exclaimed Montague. "Is Ryder down here?"

"He got Harvey to invite him," Oliver replied. "And I know it was for no reason in the world but to be with Lucy. He took her out in his automobile."

Montague was dumfounded.

"She never hinted it to me," he said.

"By God!" exclaimed Oliver, "I wonder if that fellow is going after Lucy!"

Montague stood for some time, lost in sombre thought. "I don't think it will do him much good," he said. "Lucy knows too much."

"Lucy has never met a man like Stanley Ryder!" declared the other. "He has spent all his life hunting women, and she is no match for him at all."

"What do you know about him?" asked Montague.

"What don't I know about him!" exclaimed the other. "He was in love with Betty Wyman once."

"Oh, my Lord!" exclaimed Montague.

"Yes," said Oliver, "and she told me all about it. He has as many tricks as a conjurer. He has read a lot of New Thought stuff, and he talks about his yearning soul, and every woman he meets is his affinity. And then again, he is a free thinker, and he discourses about liberty and the rights of women. He takes all the moralities and shuffles them up, until you'd think the noblest role a woman could play is that of a married man's mistress."

Montague could not forbear to smile. "I have known you to shuffle the moralities now and then yourself, Ollie," he said.

"Yes, that's all right," replied the other. "But this is Lucy. And somebody's got to talk to her about Stanley Ryder."

"I will do it," Montague answered.

He found Lucy in a cosy corner of the library when he came down to dinner. She was full of all the wonderful things that she had seen in Dan Waterman's art gallery. "And Allan," she exclaimed, "what do you think, I met him!"

"You don't mean it!" said he.

"He was there the whole afternoon!" declared Lucy. "And he never did a thing but be nice to me!"

"Then you didn't find him so terrible as you expected," said Montague.

"He was perfectly charming," said Lucy. "He showed me his whole collection and told me the history of the different paintings, and stories about how he got them. I never had such an experience in my life."

"He can be an interesting man when he chooses," Montague responded.

"He is marvellous!" said she. "You look at that lean figure, and the wizened-up old hawk's face, with the white hair all round it, and you'd think that he was in his dotage. But when he talks—I don't wonder men obey him!"

"They obey him!" said Montague. "No mistake about that! There is not a man in Wall Street who could live for twenty-four hours if old Dan Waterman went after him in earnest."

"How in the world does he do it?" asked Lucy. "Is he so enormously rich?"

"It is not the money he owns," said Montague; "it's what he controls. He is master of the banks; and no man can take a step in Wall Street without his knowing it if he wants to. And he can break a man's credit; he can have all his loans called. He can swing the market so as to break a man. And then, think of his power in Washington! He uses the Treasury as if it were one of his branch offices."

"It seems frightful," said Lucy. "And that old man—over eighty! I'm glad that I met him, at any rate."

She paused, seeing Stanley Ryder in the doorway. He was evidently looking for her. He took her in to dinner; and every now and then, when Montague stole a glance at her, he saw that Ryder was monopolising her attention.

After dinner they adjourned to the music-room, and Ryder played a couple of Chopin's Nocturnes. He never took his eyes from Lucy's face while he was playing. "I declare," remarked Betty Wyman in Montague's hearing, "the way Stanley Ryder makes love at the piano is positively indecent."

Montague dodged several invitations to play cards, and deliberately placed himself at Lucy's side for the evening. And when at last Stanley Ryder had gone away in disgust to the smoking-room, he turned to her and said, "Lucy, you must let me speak to you about this."

"I don't mind your speaking to me, Allan," she said; with a feeble attempt at a smile.

"But you must pay attention to me," he protested. "You really don't know the sort of man you are dealing with, or what people think about him."

She sat in silence, biting her lip nervously, while Montague told her, as plainly as he could, what Ryder's reputation was. All that she could answer was, "He is such an interesting man!"

"There are many interesting men," said he, "but you will never meet them if you get people talking about you like this."

Lucy clasped her hands together.

"Allan," she exclaimed, "I did my best to persuade him not to come out here. And you are right. I will do what you say—I will have nothing to do with him, honestly. You shall see! It's his own fault that he came, and he can find somebody else to entertain him while he's here."

"I wish that you would tell him plainly, Lucy," said Montague. "Never mind if he gets angry. Make him understand you—once for all."

"I will—I will!" she declared.

And Montague judged that she carried out her promise quickly, for the rest of the evening Ryder gave to entertaining the company. About midnight Montague chanced to look into the library, and he saw the president of the Gotham Trust in the midst of a group which was excitedly discussing divorce. "Marriage is a sin for which the church refuses absolution!" he heard Stanley Ryder exclaiming.

CHAPTER III

A few days after these incidents, Montague was waiting for a friend who was to come to dinner at his hotel. He was sitting in the lobby reading a paper, and he noticed an elderly gentleman with a grey goatee and rather florid complexion who passed down the corridor before him. A minute or two later he happened to glance up, and he caught this gentleman's eye.

The latter started, and a look of amazement came over his face. He came forward, saying, "I beg pardon, but is not this Allan Montague?"

"It is," said Montague, looking at him in perplexity.

"You don't remember me, do you?" said the other.

"I must confess that I do not," was the answer.

"I am Colonel Cole."

But Montague only knitted his brows in greater perplexity. "Colonel Cole?" he repeated.

"You were too young to remember me," the other said. "I have been at your house a dozen times. I was in your father's brigade."

"Indeed!" exclaimed Montague. "I beg your pardon."

"Don't mention it, don't mention it," said the other, taking a seat beside him. "It was really extraordinary that I should recall you. And how is your brother? Is he in New York?"

"He is," said Montague.

"And your mother? She is still living, I trust?"

"Oh, yes," said he. "She is in this hotel."

"It is really an extraordinary pleasure!" exclaimed the other. "I did not think I knew a soul in New York."

"You are visiting here?" asked Montague.

"From the West," said the Colonel.

"It is curious how things follow out," he continued, after a pause. "I was thinking about your father only this very day. I had a proposal from someone who wanted to buy some stock that I have—in the Northern Mississippi Railroad."

Montague gave a start. "You don't mean it!" he said.

"Yes," said the other. "Your father persuaded me to take some of the stock, away back in the old days. And I have had it ever since. I had forgotten all about it."

Montague smiled. "When you have disposed of yours," he said, "you might refer your party to me. I know of some more that is for sale."

"I have no doubt," said the Colonel. "But I fancy it won't fetch much now. I don't remember receiving any dividends."

There was a pause. "It is a curious coincidence," said the other. "I, too, have been thinking about the railroad. My friend, Mrs. Taylor, has just come up from New Orleans. She used to be Lucy Dupree."

The Colonel strove to recall. "Dupree?" he said.

"Judge Dupree's daughter," said Montague. "His brother, John Dupree, was the first president of the road."

"Oh, yes," said the Colonel. "Of course, of course! I remember the Judge now. Your father told me he had taken quite a lot of the stock."

"Yes, he was the prime mover in the enterprise."

"And who was that other gentleman?" said the Colonel, racking his brains. "The one who used to be so much in his house, and was so much interested in him—"

"You mean Mr. Lee Gordon?" said Montague.

"Yes, I think that was the name," the other replied.

"He was my father's cousin," said Montague. "He put so much money into the road that the family has been poor ever since."

"It was an unfortunate venture," said the Colonel. "It is too bad some of our big capitalists don't take it up and do something with it."

"That was my idea," said Montague. "I have broached it to one."

"Indeed?" said the Colonel. "Possibly that is where my offer came from. Who was it?"

"It was Jim Hegan," said Montague.

"Oh!" said the Colonel. "But of course," he added, "Hegan would do his negotiating through an agent."

"Let me give you my card," said the Colonel, after a pause. "It is possible that I may be able to interest someone in the matter myself. I have friends who believe in the future of the South. How many shares do you suppose you could get me, and what do you suppose they would cost?"

Montague got out a pencil and paper, and proceeded to recall as well as he could the location of the various holdings of Northern Mississippi. He and his new acquaintance became quite engrossed in the subject, and they talked it out from many points of view. By the time that Montague's friend arrived, the Colonel was in possession of all the facts, and he promised that he would write in a very few days.

And then, after dinner, Montague went upstairs and joined his mother. "I met an old friend of father's this evening," he said.

"Who was it?" she asked.

"Colonel Cole," he said, and Mrs. Montague looked blank.

"Colonel Cole?" she repeated.

"Yes, that was the name," said Montague. "Here is his card," and he took it out. "Henry W. Cole, Seattle, Washington," it read.

"But I never heard of him," said Mrs. Montague.

"Never heard of him!" exclaimed Montague. "Why, he has been at the house a dozen times, and he knew father and Cousin Lee and Judge Dupree and everyone."

But Mrs. Montague only shook her head. "He may have been at the house," she said, "but I am sure that I was never introduced to him."

Montague thought that it was strange, but he would never have given further thought to the matter, had it not been for something which occurred the next morning. He went to the office rather early, on account of important work which he had to get ready. He was the first to arrive, and he found the scrub-woman who cleaned the office just taking her departure.

It had never occurred to Montague before that such a person existed; and he turned in some surprise when she spoke to him.

"I beg pardon, sir," she said. "But there is something I have to tell you."

"What is it?" said he.

"There is someone trying to find out about you," said the woman.

"What do you mean?" he asked, in perplexity.

"Begging your pardon, sir," said the woman, "but there was a man came here this morning, very early, and he offered me money, sir, and he wanted me to save him all the papers that I took out of your scrap basket, sir."

Montague caught his breath. "Papers out of my scrap basket!" he gasped.

"Yes, sir," said the woman. "It is done now and then, sir,—we learn of such things, you know. And we are poor women,—they don't pay us very well. But you are a gentleman, sir, and I told him I would have nothing to do with it."

"What sort of a looking man was he?" Montague demanded.

"He was a dark chap, sir," said the other, "a sort of Jew like. He will maybe come back again."

Montague took out his purse and gave the woman a bill; and she stammered her thanks and went off with her pail and broom.

He shut the door and went and sat down at his desk, and stared in front of him, gasping, "My God!"

Then suddenly he struck his knee with an exclamation of rage. "I told him everything that I knew! Everything! He hardly had to ask me a question!"

But then again, wonder drowned every other emotion in him. "What in the world can he have wanted to know? And who sent him? What can it mean?"

He went back over his talk with the old gentleman from Seattle, trying to recall exactly what he had told, and what use the other could have made of the information. But he could not think very steadily, for his mind kept jumping back to the thought of Jim Hegan.

There could be but one explanation of all this. Jim Hegan had set detectives upon him! Nobody else knew anything about the Northern Mississippi Railroad, or wanted to know about it.

CHAPTER III

Jim Hegan! And Montague had met him socially at an entertainment—at Mrs. de Graffenried's! He had met him as one gentleman meets another, had shaken hands with him, had gone and talked with him freely and frankly! And then Hegan had sent a detective to worm his secrets from him, and had even tried to get at the contents of his trash basket!

There was only one resort that Montague could think of, in a case so perplexing. He sat down and wrote a note to his friend Major Venable, at the Millionaires' Club, saying that he was coming there to dinner, and would like to have the Major's company. And two or three hours later, when sufficient time had elapsed for the Major to have had his shave and his coffee and his morning newspaper, he rang for a messenger and sent the note.

The Major's reply was prompt. He had no engagement, and his stores of information and advice were at Montague's service. But his gout was bad, and his temper atrocious, and Montague must be warned in advance that his doctors permitted him neither mushrooms nor meat.

It always seemed to Montague that it could not be possible for a human face to wear a brighter shade of purple than the Major's; yet every time he met him, it seemed to him that the purple was a shade brighter. And it spread farther with every step the Major took. He growled and grumbled, and swore tremendous oaths under his breath, and the way the headwaiter and all his assistants scurried about the dining-room of the Club was a joy to the beholder.

Montague waited until the old gentleman had obtained his usual dry Martini, and until he had solved the problem of satisfying his appetite and his doctor. And then he told of his extraordinary experience.

"I felt sure that you could explain it, if anybody could," said he.

"But what is there to explain?" asked the other. "It simply means that Jim Hegan is interested in your railroad. What more could you want?"

"But he sent a detective after me!" gasped Montague.

"But that's all right," said the Major. "It is done every day. There are a half dozen big agencies that do nothing else. You are lucky if he hasn't had your telephone tapped, and read your telegrams and mail before you saw them."

Montague stared at him aghast. "A man like Jim Hegan!" he exclaimed. "And to a friend."

"A friend?" said the Major. "Pshaw! A man doesn't do business with friends. And, besides, Jim Hegan probably never knew anything about it. He turned the whole matter over to some subordinate, and told him to look it up, and he'll never give another thought to it until the facts are laid upon his desk. Some one of his men set to work, and he was a little clumsy about it—that's all."

"But why did he want to know about all my family affairs?"

"Why, he wanted to know how you were situated," said the other—"how badly you wanted to sell the stock. So when he came to do business with you, he'd have you where he wanted you, and he'd probably get fifty per cent off the price because of it. You'll be lucky if he doesn't have a few loans called on you at your bank."

The Major sat watching Montague, smiling at his naivete. "Where did you say this road was?" he asked. "In Mississippi?"

"Yes," said Montague.

"I was wondering about it," said the other. "It is not likely that it's Jim Hegan at all. I don't believe anybody could get him to take an interest in Southern railroads. He has probably mentioned it to someone else. What's your road good for, anyway?"

"We had a plan to extend it," said Montague.

"It would take but one or two millions to carry it to the main works of the Mississippi Steel Company."

The Major gave a start. "The Mississippi Steel Company!" he exclaimed.

"Yes," said Montague.

"Oh, my God!" cried the other.

"What is the matter?"

"Why in the world did you take a matter like that to Jim Hegan?" demanded Major Venable.

"I took it to him because I knew him," said Montague.

"But one doesn't take things to people because one knows them," said the Major. "One takes them to the right people. If Jim Hegan could have his way, he would wipe the Mississippi Steel Company off the map of the United States."

"What do you mean?"

"Don't you know," said the Major, "that Mississippi Steel is the chief competitor of the Trust? And old Dan Waterman organised the Steel Trust, and watches it all the time."

"But what's that got to do with Hegan?"

"Simply that Jim Hegan works with Waterman in everything."

Montague stared in dismay. "I see," he said.

"Of course!" said the Major. "My dear fellow, why don't you come to me before you do things like that? You should have gone to the Mississippi Steel people; and you should have gone quietly, and to the men at the top. For all you can tell, you may have a really big proposition that's been overlooked in the shuffle. What was that you said about the survey?"

And Montague told in detail the story of the aborted plan for an extension, and of his hunting trip, and what he had learned on it.

"Of course," said the Major, "you are in the heart of the thing right now. The Steel people balked your plan."

"How do you mean?" asked the other.

"They bought up the survey. And they've probably controlled your railroad ever since, and kept it down."

"But that's impossible! They've had nothing to do with it."

"Bah!" said the Major. "How could you know?"

"I know the president," said Montague. "He's an old friend of the family's."

"Yes," was the reply. "But suppose they have a mortgage on his business?"

CHAPTER III

"But why not buy the road and be done with it?" added Montague, in perplexity.

The other laughed. "I am reminded of a famous saying of Wyman's,—'Why should I buy stock when I can buy directors?'"

"It's those same people who are watching you now," he continued, after a pause. "Probably they think it is some move of the other side, and they are trying to run the thing down."

"Who owns the Mississippi Steel Company?" asked Montague.

"I don't know," said the Major. "I fancy that Wyman must have come into it somehow. Didn't you notice in the papers the other day that the contracts for furnishing rails for all his three transcontinental railroads had gone to the Mississippi Steel Company?"

"Sure enough!" exclaimed Montague.

"You see!" said the Major, with a chuckle. "You have jumped right into the middle of the frog pond, and the Lord only knows what a ruction you have stirred up! Just think of the situation for a moment. The Steel Trust is over-capitalised two hundred per cent. Because of the tariff it is able to sell its product at home for fifty per cent more than it charges abroad; and even so, it has to keep cutting its dividends! Its common stock is down to ten. It is cutting expenses on every hand, and of course it's turning out a rotten product. And now along comes Wyman, the one man in Wall Street who dares to shake his fist at old Dan Waterman; and he gives the newspapers all the facts about the bad steel rails that are causing smashups on his roads; and he turns all his contracts over to the Mississippi Steel Company, which is under-selling the Trust. The company is swamped with orders, and its plants are running day and night. And then along comes a guileless young fool with a little dinky railroad which he wants to run into the Company's back door-yard; and he takes the proposition to Jim Hegan!"

The Major arrived at his climax in a state of suppressed emotion, which culminated in a chuckle, which shook his rubicund visage and brought a series of twitches to his aching toe. As for Montague, he was duly humbled.

"What would you do now?" he asked, after a pause.

"I don't see that there's anything to do," said the Major, "except to hold on tight to your stock. Perhaps if you go on talking out loud about your extension, some of the Steel people will buy you out at your own price."

"I gave them a scare, anyhow," said Montague, laughing.

"I can wager one thing," said the other. "There has been a fine shaking up in somebody's office down town! There's a man who comes here every night, who's probably heard of it. That's Will Roberts."

And the Major looked about the dining-room. "Here he comes now," he said.

At the farther end of the room there had entered a tall, dark-haired man, with a keen expression and a brisk step. "Roberts the Silent," said the Major. "Let's have a try at him." And as the man passed near, he hailed him. "Hello! Roberts, where are you going? Let me introduce my friend, Mr. Allan Montague."

The man looked at Montague. "Good evening, sir," he said. "How are you, Venable?"

"Couldn't be worse, thank you," said the Major. "How are things with you on the Street?"

"Dull, very dull," said Roberts, as he passed on. "Matters look bad, I'm afraid. Too many people making money rapidly."

The Major chuckled. "A fine sentiment," he said, when Roberts had passed out of hearing—"from a man who has made sixty millions in the last ten years!"

"It did not appear that he had ever heard of me," said Montague.

"Oh, trust him for that!" said the Major. "He might have been planning to have your throat cut to-night, but you wouldn't have seen him turn an eyelid. He is that sort; he's made of steel himself, I believe."

He paused, and then went on, in a reminiscent mood, "You've read of the great strike, I suppose? It was Roberts put that job through. He made himself the worst-hated man in the country—Gad! how the newspapers and the politicians used to rage at him! But he stood his ground—he would win that strike or die in the attempt. And he very nearly did both, you know. An Anarchist came to his office and shot him twice; but he got the fellow down and nearly choked the life out of him, and he ran the strike on his sick-bed, and two weeks later he was back in his office again."

And now the Major's store-rooms of gossip were unlocked. He told Montague about the kings of Steel, and about the men they had hated and the women they had loved, and about the inmost affairs and secrets of their lives. William H. Roberts had begun his career in the service of the great iron-master, whose deadly rival he had afterwards become; and now he lived but to dispute that rival's claims to glory. Let the rival build a library, Roberts would build two. Let the rival put up a great office building, Roberts would buy all the land about it, and put up half a dozen, and completely shut out its light. And day and night "Roberts the Silent" was plotting and planning, and some day he would be the master of the Steel Trust, and his rival would be nowhere.

"They are lively chaps, the Steel crowd," said the Major, chuckling. "You will have to keep your eyes open when you do business with them."

"What would you advise me to do?" asked the other, smiling. "Set detectives after them?"

"Why not?" asked the Major, seriously. "Why not find out who sent that Colonel Cole to see you? And find out how badly he needs your little railroad, and make him pay for it accordingly."

"That is not QUITE in my line," said Montague.

"It's time you were learning," said the Major. "I can start you. I know a detective whom you can trust.—At any rate," he added cautiously, "I don't know that he's ever played me false."

Montague sat for a while in thought. "You said something about their getting after one's telephone," he observed. "Did you really mean that?"

"Of course," said the other.

"Do you mean to tell me that they could find out what goes over my 'phone?"

"I mean to tell you," was the reply, "that for two hundred and fifty dollars, I can get you a stenographic report of every word that you say over your 'phone for twenty-four hours, and of every word that anybody says to you."

"That sounds incredible!" said Montague. "Who does it?"

"Wire tappers. It's dangerous work, but the pay is big. I have a friend who once upon a time was putting through a deal in which the telephone company was interested, and they transferred his wire to another branch, and he finished up his business before the other side got on to the trick. To this day you'll notice that his telephone is 'Spring,' though every other 'phone in the neighbourhood is 'John.'"

"And mail, too?" asked Montague.

"Mail!" echoed the Major. "What's easier than that? You can hold up a man's mail for twenty-four hours and take a photograph of every letter. You can do the same with every letter that he mails, unless he is very careful. He can be followed, you understand, and every time he drops a letter, a blue or yellow envelope is dropped on top—for a signal to the post-office people."

"But then, so many persons would have to know about that!"

"Nothing of the kind. That's a regular branch of the post-office work. There are Secret Service men who are watching criminals that way all the time. And what could be easier than to pay one of them, and to have your enemy listed with the suspects?"

The Major smiled in amusement. It always gave him delight to witness Montague's consternation over his pictures of the city's corruption.

"There are things even stranger than that," he said. "I can introduce you to a man who's in this room now, who was fighting the Ship-building swindle, and he got hold of a lot of important papers, and he took them to his office, and sat by while his clerks made thirty-two copies of them. And he put the originals and thirty-one of the copies in thirty-two different safe-deposit vaults in the city, and took the other copy to his home in a valise. And that night burglars broke in, and the valise was missing. The next day he wrote to the people he was fighting, 'I was going to send you a copy of the papers which have come into my possession, but as you already have a copy, I will simply proceed to outline my proposition.' And that was all. They settled for a million or two."

The Major paused a moment and looked across the dining-room. "There goes Dick Sanderson," he said, pointing to a dapper young man with a handsome, smooth-shaven face. "He represents the New Jersey Southern Railroad. And one day another lawyer who met him at dinner remarked, 'I am going to bring a stockholders' suit against your road to-morrow.' He went on to outline the case, which was a big one. Sanderson said nothing, but he went out and telephoned to their agent in Trenton, and the next morning a bill went through both houses of the Legislature providing a statute of limitations that outlawed the case. The man who was the victim of that trick is now the Governor of New York State, and if you ever meet him, you can ask him about it."

There was a pause for a while; then suddenly the Major remarked, "Oh, by the way, this beautiful widow you have brought up from Mississippi—Mrs. Taylor—is that the name?"

"That's it," said Montague.

"I hear that Stanley Ryder has taken quite a fancy to her," said the other.

A grave look came upon Montague's face. "I am sorry, indeed, that you have heard it," he said.

"Why," said the other, "that's all right. He will give her a good time."

"Lucy is new to New York," said Montague. "I don't think she quite realises the sort of man that Ryder is."

The Major thought for a moment, then suddenly began to laugh. "It might be just as well for her to be careful," he said. "I happened to think of it—they say that Mrs. Stanley is getting ready to free herself from the matrimonial bond; and if your fascinating widow doesn't want to get into the newspapers, she had better be a little careful with her favours."

CHAPTER IV

Two or three days after this Montague met Jim Hegan at a directors' meeting. He watched him closely, but Hegan gave no sign of constraint. He was courteous and serene as ever. "By the way, Mr. Montague," he said, "I mentioned that railroad matter to a friend who is interested. You may hear from him in a few days."

"I am obliged to you," said the other, and that was all.

The next day was Sunday, and Montague came to take Lucy to church, and told her of this remark. He did not tell her about the episode with Colonel Cole, for he thought there was no use disturbing her.

She, for her part, had other matters to talk about. "By the way, Allan," she said, "I presume you know that the coaching parade is to-morrow."

"Yes," said he.

"Mr. Ryder has offered me a seat on his coach," said Lucy.—"I suppose you are going to be angry with me," she added quickly, seeing his frown.

"You said you would go?" he asked.

"Yes," said Lucy. "I did not think it would be any harm. It is such a public matter—"

"A public matter!" exclaimed Montague. "I should think so! To sit up on top of a coach for the crowds to stare at, and for thirty or forty newspaper reporters to take snap-shots of! And to have yourself blazoned as the fascinating young widow from Mississippi who was one of Stanley Ryder's party, and then to have all Society looking at the picture and winking and making remarks about it!"

"You take such a cynical view of everything," protested Lucy. "How can people help it if the crowds will stare, and if the newspapers will take pictures? Surely one cannot give up the pleasure of going for a drive—"

"Oh, pshaw, Lucy!" said Montague. "You have too much sense to talk like that. If you want to drive, go ahead and drive. But when a lot of people get together and pay ten or twenty thousand dollars apiece for fancy coaches and horses, and then appoint a day and send out notice to the whole city, and dress themselves up in fancy costumes and go out and make a public parade of themselves, they have no right to talk about driving for pleasure."

"Well," said she, dubiously, "it's nice to be noticed."

"It is for those who like it," said he; "and if a woman chooses to set out on a publicity campaign, and run a press bureau, and make herself a public character, why, that's her privilege. But for heaven's sake let her drop the sickly pretence that she is only driving beautiful horses, or listening to music, or entertaining her friends. I suppose a Society woman has as much right to advertise her personality as a politician or a manufacturer of pills; all I object to is the sham of it, the everlasting twaddle about her love of privacy. Take Mrs. Winnie Duval, for instance. You would think to hear her that her one ideal in life was to be a simple shepherdess and to raise flowers; but, as a matter of fact, she keeps a scrap-album, and if a week passes that the newspapers do not have some paragraphs about her doings, she begins to get restless."

Lucy broke into a laugh. "I was at Mrs. Robbie Walling's last night," she said. "She was talking about the crowds at the opera, and she said she was going to withdraw to some place where she wouldn't have to see such mobs of ugly people."

"Yes," said he. "But you can't tell me anything about Mrs. Robbie Walling. I have been there. There's nothing that lady does from the time she opens her eyes in the morning until the time she goes to bed the next morning that she would ever care to do if it were not for the mobs of ugly people looking on."

—"You seem to be going everywhere," said Montague, after a pause.

"Oh, I guess I'm a success," said Lucy. "I am certainly having a gorgeous time. I never saw so many beautiful houses or such dazzling costumes in my life."

"It's very fine," said Montague. "But take it slowly and make it last. When one has got used to it, the life seems rather dull and grey."

"I am invited to the Wymans' to-night," said Lucy,—"to play bridge. Fancy giving a bridge party on Sunday night!"

Montague shrugged his shoulders. "*Così fan tutti*," he said.

"What do you make of Betty Wyman?" asked the other.

"She is having a good time," said he. "I don't think she has much conscience about it."

"Is she very much in love with Ollie?" she asked.

"I don't know," he said. "I can't make them out. It doesn't seem to trouble them very much."

This was after church while they were strolling down the Avenue, gazing at the procession of new spring costumes.—"Who is that stately creature you just bowed to?" inquired Lucy.

"That?" said Montague. "That is Miss Hegan—Jim Hegan's daughter."

"Oh!" said Lucy. "I remember—Betty Wyman told me about her."

"Nothing very good, I imagine," said Montague, with a smile.

"It was interesting," said Lucy. "Fancy having a father with a hundred millions, and talking about going in for settlement work!"

"Well," he answered, "I told you one could get tired of the splurge."

Lucy looked at him quizzically. "I should think that kind of a girl would rather appeal to you," she said.

"I would like to know her very much," said he, "but she didn't seem to like me."

"Not like you!" cried the other. "Why, how perfectly outrageous!"

"It was not her fault," said Montague, smiling; "I am afraid I got myself a bad reputation."

"Oh, you mean about Mrs. Winnie!" exclaimed Lucy.

"Yes," said he, "that's it."

"I wish you would tell me about it," said she.

"There is nothing much to tell. Mrs. Winnie proceeded to take me up and make a social success of me, and I was fool enough to come when she invited me. Then the first thing I knew, all the gossips were wagging their tongues."

"That didn't do you any harm, did it?" asked Lucy.

"Not particularly," said he, shrugging his shoulders. "Only here is a woman whom I would have liked to know, and I don't know her. That's all."

Lucy gave him a sly glance. "You need a sister," she said, smiling. "Somebody to fight for you!"

* * *

According to Jim Hegan's prediction, it was not long before Montague received an offer. It came from a firm of lawyers of whom he had never heard. "We understand," ran the letter, "that you have a block of five thousand shares of the stock of the Northern Mississippi Railroad. We have a client on whose behalf we are authorised to offer you fifty thousand dollars cash for these shares. Will you kindly consult with your client, and advise us at your earliest convenience?"

He called up Lucy on the 'phone and told her that the offer had come.

"How much?" she asked eagerly.

"It is not satisfactory," he said. "But I would rather not discuss the matter over the 'phone. How can I arrange to see you?"

"Can't you send me up the letter by a messenger?" she asked.

"I could," said Montague, "but I would like to talk with you about it; and also I have that mortgage, and the other papers for you to sign. There are some things to be explained about these, also. Couldn't you come to my office this morning?"

"I would, Allan," she said, "but I have just made a most important engagement, and I don't know what to do about it."

"Couldn't it be postponed?" he asked.

"No," she said. "It's an invitation to join a party on Mr. Waterman's new yacht."

"The *Brünnhilde*!" exclaimed Montague. "You don't say so!"

"Yes, and I hate to miss it," said she.

"How long shall you be gone?" he asked.

"I shall be back sometime this evening," she answered. "We are going up the Sound. The yacht has just been put into commission, you know."

"Where is she lying?"

"Off the Battery. I am to be on board in an hour, and I was just about to start. Couldn't you possibly meet me there?"

"Yes," said Montague. "I will come over. I suppose they will wait a few minutes."

"I am half dying to know about the offer," said Lucy.

Montague had a couple of callers, which delayed him somewhat; finally he jumped into a cab and drove to the Battery.

Here, in the neighbourhood of Castle Garden, was a sheltered place popularly known as the "Millionaires' Basin," being the favourite anchorage of the private yachts of the "Wall Street flotilla." At this time of the year most of the great men had already moved out to their country places, and those of them who lived on the Hudson or up the Sound would come to their offices in vessels of every size, from racing motor-boats to huge private steamships. They would have their breakfasts served on board, and would have their secretaries and their mail.

Many of these yachts were floating palaces of incredible magnificence; one, upon which Montague had been a guest, had a glass-domed library extending entirely around its upper deck. This one was the property of the Lester Todds, and the main purpose it served was to carry them upon their various hunting trips; its equipment included such luxuries as a French laundry, a model dairy and poultry-yard, an ice-machine and a shooting-gallery.

And here lay the *Brünnhilde*, the wonderful new toy of old Waterman. Montague knew all about her, for she had just been completed that spring, and not a newspaper in the Metropolis but had had her picture, and full particulars about her cost. Waterman had purchased her from the King of Belgium, who had thought she was everything the soul of a monarch could desire. Great had been his consternation when he learned that the new owner had given orders to strip her down to the bare steel hull and refit and refurnish her. The saloon was now done with Louis Quinze decorations, said the newspapers. Its walls were panelled in satin-wood and inlaid walnut, and under foot were velvet carpets twelve feet wide and woven without seam. Its closets were automatically lighted, and opened at the touch of a button; even the drawers of its bureaus were upon ball-bearings. The owner's private bedroom measured the entire width of the vessel, twenty-eight feet, and opened upon a Roman bath of white marble.

Such was the *Brünnhilde*, Montague looked about him for one of the yacht's launches, but he could not find any, so he hailed a boatman and had himself rowed out. A man in uniform met him at the steps. "Is Mrs. Taylor on board?" he asked.

"She is," the other answered. "Is this Mr. Montague? She left word for you."

Montague had begun to ascend; but a half a second later he stopped short in consternation.

Through one of the portholes of the vessel he heard distinctly a muffled cry,— "Help! help!"

And he recognised the voice. It was Lucy's!

CHAPTER V

Montague hesitated only an instant. He sprang up to the deck. "Where is Mrs. Taylor?" he cried.

"She went below, sir," said the man, hesitating; but Montague sprang past him and down the companionway.

At the foot of the stairs he found himself in a broad entrance-hall, lighted by a glass dome above. He sprang toward a door which opened in the direction of the cry he had heard, and shouted aloud, "Lucy! Lucy!" He heard her answer beyond the doorway, and he seized the knob and tried it. The door was locked.

"Open the door!" he shouted.

There was no sound. "Open the door!" he called again, "or I'll break it down."

Suiting his action to the word, he flung his weight upon it. The barrier cracked; and then suddenly he heard a man's voice. "All right. Wait."

Someone fumbled at the knob; and Montague stood crouching and watching breathlessly, prepared for anything. The door opened, and he found himself confronted by Dan Waterman.

Montague recoiled a step in consternation; and the other strode out, and without a word went past him down the hall. There was just time enough for Montague to receive one look—of the most furious rage that he had ever seen upon a human face.

He rushed into the room. Lucy was standing at the farther end, leaning upon a table to support herself. Her clothing was in disarray, and her hair was falling about her ears; her face was flushed, and she was panting in great agitation.

"Lucy!" he gasped, running to her. She caught at his arm to steady herself.

"What is the matter?" he cried. She turned her face away, making not a sound.

For a minute or so he stood staring at her. Then she whispered, "Quick! let us go from here!"

And with a sudden movement of her hands, she swept her hair back from her forehead, and straightened her clothing, and started to the door, leaning upon her friend.

They went up to the deck, where the officer was still standing in perplexity.

"Mrs. Taylor wishes to go ashore," said Montague. "Will you get us a boat?"

"The launch will be back in a few minutes, sir—" the man began.

"We wish to go at once," said Montague. "Will you let us have one of those rowboats? Otherwise I shall hail that tug."

The man hesitated but a moment. Montague's voice was determined, and so he turned and gave orders to lower a small boat.

In the meantime, Lucy stood, breathing heavily, and gazing about her nervously. When at last they had left the yacht, he heard her sigh with relief.

They sat in silence until she had stepped upon the landing. Then she said, "Get me a cab, Allan."

He led her to the street and hailed a vehicle. When they were seated, Lucy sank back with a gasp. "Please don't ask me to talk, Allan," she said. And she made not another sound during the long drive to the hotel.

* * *

"Is there anything I can do for you?" he said, after he had seen her safely to her apartment.

"No," she answered. "I am all right. Wait for me."

She retired to her dressing-room, and when she came back, all traces of her excitement had been removed. Then she seated herself in a chair opposite Montague and gazed at him.

"Allan," she began, "I have been trying to think. What can I do to that man?"

"I am sure I don't know," he answered.

"Why, I can hardly believe that this is New York," she gasped. "I feel as though I had got back into the Middle Ages!"

"You forget, Lucy," he replied, "that I don't know what happened."

Again she fell silent. They sat staring at each other, and then suddenly she leaned back in her chair and began to laugh. Once she had started, burst after burst of merriment swept over her. "I try to stay angry, Allan!" she gasped. "It seems as if I ought to. But, honestly, it was perfectly absurd!"

"I am sure you'd much better laugh than cry," said he.

"I will tell you about it, Allan," the girl went on. "I know I shall have to tell somebody, or I shall simply explode. You will have to advise me about it, for I was never more bewildered in my life."

"Go ahead," said he. "Begin at the beginning."

"I told you how I met Waterman at his art gallery," said Lucy. "Mr. David Alden took me, and the old man was so polite, and so dignified—why, I never had the slightest idea! And then he wrote me a little note—in his own hand, mind you—inviting me to be one of a party for the first trip of the *Brünnhilde*. Of course, I thought it was all right. I told you I was going, you know, and you didn't have any objections either.

"I went down there, and the launch met me and took me on board, and a steward took me down into that room and left me, and a second later the old man himself came in. And he shut the door behind him and locked it!

"How do you do, Mrs. Taylor?' he said, and before I had a chance even to open my mouth and reply, he came to me and calmly put his arms around me.

"You can fancy my feelings. I was simply paralysed!

"Mr. Waterman?' I gasped.

"I didn't hear what he said; I was almost dazed with anger and fright. I remember I cried several times, 'Let me go!' but he paid not the slightest attention to me. He just held me tight in his arms.

"Finally I got myself together, a little. I didn't want to bite and scratch like a kitchen-wench. I tried to speak calmly.

"'Mr. Waterman,' I said, 'I want you to release me.'

"'I love you,' he said.

"'But I don't love you,' I protested. I remember thinking even then how absurd it sounded. I can't think of anything that wouldn't have sounded absurd in such a situation.

"'You will learn to love me,' he said. 'Many women have.'

"'I am not that sort of a woman,' I said. 'I tell you, you have made a mistake. Let me go.'

"'I want you,' he said. 'And when I want a thing, I get it. I never take any refusal—understand that. You don't realise the situation. It will be no disgrace to you. Women think it an honour to have me love them. Think what I can do for you. You can have anything you want. You can go anywhere you wish. I will never stint you.'

"I remember his going on like that for some time. And fancy, there I was! I might as well have been in the grip of a bear. You would not think it, you know, but he is terribly strong. I could not move. I could hardly think. I was suffocated, and all the time I could feel his breath on my face, and he was glaring into my eyes like some terrible wild beast.

"'Mr. Waterman,' I protested, 'I am not used to being treated in this way.'

"'I know, I know,' he said. 'If you were, I should not want you. But I am different from other men. Think of it—think of all that I have on my hands. I have no time to make love to women. But I love you. I loved you the minute I saw you. Is not that enough? What more can you ask?'

"'You have brought me here under false pretences,' I cried. 'You have taken cowardly advantage of me. If you have a spark of decency in you, you should be ashamed of yourself.'

"'Tut, tut,' he said, 'don't talk that kind of nonsense. You know the world. You are no spring chicken.'—Yes, he did, Allan—I remember that very phrase. And it made me so furious—you can't imagine! I tried to get away again, but the more I struggled, the more it seemed to enrage him. I was positively terrified. You know, I don't believe there was another person on board that yacht except his servants.

"'Mr. Waterman,' I cried, 'I tell you to take your hands off me. If you don't, I will make a disturbance. I will scream.'

"'It won't do you any good,' he said savagely.

"'But what do you want me to do?" I protested.

"'I want you to love me,' he said.

"And then I began to struggle again. I shouted once or twice,—I am not sure,—and then he clapped his hand over my mouth. Then I began to fight for my life. I really believe I would have scratched the old creature's eyes out if he had not heard you out in the hall. When you called my name, he dropped me and sprang back. I never saw such furious hatred on a man's countenance in my life.

"When I answered you, I tried to run to the door, but he stood in my way.

"'I will follow you!' he whispered. 'Do you understand me? I will never give you up!'

"And then you flung yourself against the door, and he turned and opened it and went out."

* * *

Lucy had turned scarlet over the recalling of the scene, and she was breathing quickly in her agitation. Montague sat staring in front of him, without a sound.

"Did you ever hear of anything like that in your life before?" she asked.

"Yes," said he, gravely, "I am sorry to say that I have heard of it several times. I have heard of things even worse."

"But what am I to do?" she cried. "Surely a man can't behave like that with impunity."

Montague said nothing.

"He is a monster!" cried Lucy. "I ought to have him put in jail."

Montague shook his head. "You couldn't do that," he said.

"I couldn't!" exclaimed the other. "Why not?"

"You couldn't prove it," said Montague.

"It would be your word against his, and they would take his every time. You can't go and have Dan Waterman arrested as you could any ordinary man. And think of the notoriety it would mean!"

"I would like to expose him," protested Lucy. "It would serve him right!"

"It would not do him the least harm in the world," said Montague. "I can speak quite positively there, for I have seen it tried. You couldn't get a newspaper in New York to publish that story. All that you could do would be to have yourself blazoned as an adventuress."

Lucy was staring, with clenched hands. "Why, I might as well be living in Turkey," she cried.

"Very nearly," said he. "There's an old man in this town who has spent his lifetime lending money and hoarding it; he has something like eighty or a hundred millions now, I believe, and once every six months or so you will read in the newspapers that some woman has made an attempt to blackmail him. That is because he does to every pretty girl who comes into his office just exactly what old Waterman did to you; and those who are arrested for blackmail are simply the ones who are so unwise as to make a disturbance."

"You see, Lucy," continued Montague, after a pause, "you must realise the situation. This man is a god in New York. He controls all the avenues of wealth; he can make or break any person he chooses. It is really the truth—I believe he could ruin any man in the city whom he chose to set out after. He can have anything that he wants done, so far as the police are concerned. It is simply a matter of paying them. And he is accustomed to rule in everything; his lightest whim is law. If he wants a thing, he buys it, and that is his attitude toward women. He is used to being treated as a master; women seek him, and vie for his favour. If you had been able to hold it, you might have had a million-dollar palace on Riverside Drive, or a cottage with a million-dollar pier at Newport. You might have had carte blanche at all the shops, and all the yachting trips and private trains that you wanted. That is all that other women want, and he could not understand what more you could want." Montague paused.

"Is that the way he spends his money?" Lucy asked.

"He buys everything he takes a fancy to," said Montague. "They say he spends five thousand dollars a day. One of the stories they tell in the clubs is that he loved the wife of a physician, and he gave a million dollars to found a hospital, and one of the conditions of the endowment was that this physician should go abroad for three years and study all the hospitals of Europe."

Lucy sat buried in thought. "Allan," she asked suddenly, "what do you suppose he meant by saying he would follow me? What could he do?"

"I don't know," said Allan, "it is something which we shall have to think over very carefully."

"He made a remark to me that I thought was very strange," she said. "I just happened to recall it. He said, 'You have no money. You cannot keep up the pace in New York. What you own is worth nothing.' Do you suppose, Allan, that he can know anything about my affairs?"

Montague was staring at her in consternation. "Lucy!" he exclaimed.

"What is it?" she cried.

"Nothing," he said; and he added to himself, "No, it is absurd. It could not be." The idea that it could have been Dan Waterman who had set the detectives to follow him seemed too grotesque for consideration. "It was nothing but a chance shot," he said to Lucy, "but you must be careful. He is a dangerous man."

"And I am powerless to punish him!" whispered Lucy, after a pause.

"It seems to me," said Montague, "that you are very well out of it. You will know better next time; and as for punishing him, I fancy that Nature will attend to that. He is getting old, you know; and they say he is morose and wretched."

"But, Allan!" protested Lucy. "I can't help thinking what would have happened to me if you had not come on board! I can't help thinking about other women who must have been caught in such a trap. Why, Allan, I would have been equally helpless—no matter what he had done!"

"I am afraid so," said he, gravely. "Many a woman has discovered it, I imagine. I understand how you feel, but what can you do about it? You can't punish men like Waterman. You can't punish them for anything they do, whether it is monopolising a necessity of life and starving thousands of people to death, or whether it is an attack upon a defenceless woman. There are rich men in this city who make it their diversion to answer advertisements and decoy young girls. A stenographer in my office told me that she had had over twenty positions in one year, and that she had left every one because some man in the office had approached her."

He paused for a moment. "You see," he added, "I have been finding out these things. You thought I was unreasonable, but I know what your dangers are. You are a stranger here; you have no friends and no influence, and so you will always be the one to suffer. I don't mean merely in a case like this, where it comes to the police and the newspapers; I mean in social matters—where it is a question of your reputation, of the interpretation which people will place upon your actions. They have their wealth and their prestige and their privileges, and they stand at bay. They are perfectly willing to give a stranger a good time, if the stranger has a pretty face and a lively wit to entertain them; but when you come to trespass, or to threaten their power, then you find out how they can hate you, and how mercilessly they will slander and ruin you!"

CHAPTER VI

Lucy's adventure had so taken up the attention of them both that they had forgotten all about the matter of the stock. Afterwards, however, Montague mentioned it, and Lucy exclaimed indignantly at the smallness of the offer.

"That is only ten cents on the dollar!" she cried. "You surely would not advise me to sell for that!"

"No, I should not," he answered. "I should reject the offer. It might be well, however, to set a price for them to consider."

They had talked this matter over before, and had agreed upon a hundred and eighty thousand dollars. "I think it will be best to state that figure," he said, "and give them to understand that it is final. I imagine they would expect to bargain, but I am not much of a hand at that, and would prefer to say what I mean and stick by it."

"Very well!" said Lucy, "you use your own judgment."

There was a pause; then Montague, seeing the look on Lucy's face, started to his feet. "It won't do you any good to think about to-day's mishap," he said. "Let's start over again, and not make any more mistakes. Come with me this evening. I have some friends who have been begging me to bring you around ever since you came."

"Who are they?" asked Lucy.

"General Prentice and his wife. Do you know of them?"

"I have heard Mr. Ryder speak of Prentice the banker. Is that the one you mean?"

"Yes," said Montague,—"the president of the Trust Company of the Republic. He was an old comrade of my father's, and they were the first people I met here in New York. I have got to know them very well since. I told them I would bring you up to dinner sometime, and I will telephone them, if you say so. I don't think it's a good idea for you to sit here by yourself and think about Dan Waterman."

"Oh, I don't mind it now," said Lucy. "But I will go with you, if you like."

* * *

They went to the Prentices'. There were the General himself, and Mrs. Prentice, and their two daughters, one of whom was a student in college, and the other a violinist of considerable talent. General Prentice was now over seventy, and his beard was snow-white, but he still had the erect carriage and the commanding presence of a soldier. Mrs. Prentice Montague had first met one evening when he had been their guest at the opera, and she had impressed him as a lady with a great many diamonds, who talked to him about other people while he was trying to listen to the music. But she was, as Lucy phrased it afterwards, "a motherly soul, when one got underneath her war-paint." She was always inviting Montague to her home and introducing him to people whom she thought would be of assistance to him.

Also there came that evening young Harry Curtiss, the General's nephew. Montague had never met him before, but he knew him as a junior partner in the firm of William E. Davenant, the famous corporation lawyer—the man whom Montague had found opposed to him in his suit against the Fidelity Insurance Company. Harry Curtiss, whom Montague was to know quite well before long, was a handsome fellow, with frank and winning manners. He had met Alice Montague at an affair a week or so ago, and he sent word that he was coming to see her.

After dinner they sat and smoked, and talked about the condition of the market. It was a time of great agitation in Wall Street. There had been a violent slump in stocks, and matters seemed to be going from bad to worse.

"They say that Wyman has got caught," said Curtiss, repeating one of the wild tales of the "Street." "I was talking with one of his brokers yesterday."

"Wyman is not an easy man to catch," said the General. "His own brokers are often the last men to know his real situation. There is good reason to believe that some of the big insiders are loaded up, for the public is very uneasy, as you know; but with the situation as it is just now in Wall Street, you can't tell anything. The men who are really on the inside have matters so completely in their own hands that they are practically omnipotent."

"You mean that you think this slump may be the result of manipulation?" asked Montague, wonderingly.

"Why not?" asked the General.

"It seems to be such a widespread movement," said Montague. "It seems incredible that any one man could cause such an upset."

"It is not one man," said the General, "it is a group of men. I don't say that it's true, mind you. I wouldn't be at liberty to say it even if I knew it; but there are certain things that I have seen, and I have my suspicions of others. And you must realise that a half-dozen men now control about ninety per cent of the banks of this city."

"Things will get worse before they get any better, I believe," said Curtiss, after a pause.

"Something has got to be done," replied the General. "The banking situation in this country at the present moment is simply unendurable; the legitimate banker is practically driven from the field by the speculator. A man finds himself in the position where he has either to submit to the dictation of such men, or else permit himself to be supplanted. It is a new element that has forced itself in. Apparently all a man needs in order to start a bank is credit enough to put up a building with marble columns and bronze gates. I could name you a man who at this moment owns eight banks, and when he started in, three years ago, I don't believe he owned a million dollars."

"But how in the world could he manage it?" gasped Montague.

"Just as I stated," said the General. "You buy a piece of land, with as big a mortgage as you can get, and you put up a million-dollar building and mortgage that. You start a trust company, and you get out imposing advertisements, and promise high rates of interest, and the public comes in. Then you hypothecate your stock in company number one, and you have your dummy directors lend you more money, and you buy another trust company. They call that pyramiding— you have heard the term, no doubt, with regard to stocks; it is a fascinating game to play with banks, because the more of them you get, the more prominent you become in the newspapers, and the more the public trusts you."

And the General went on to tell of some of the cases of which he knew. There was Stewart, the young Lochinvar out of the West. He had tried to buy the Trust Company of the Republic long ago, and so the General knew him and his methods. He had fought the Copper Trust to a standstill in Montana; the Trust had bought up the Legislature and both political machines, but Cummings had appealed to the public in a series of sensational campaigns, and had got his judges into office, and in the end the Trust had been forced to buy him out. And now he had come to New York to play this new game of bank-gambling, which paid even quicker profits than buying courts.—And then there was Holt, a sporting character, a vulgar man-about-town, who was identified with everything that was low and vile in the city; he, too, had turned his millions into banks.—And there was Cummings, the Ice King, who for years had financed the political machine in the city, and, by securing a monopoly of the docking-privileges, had forced all his rivals to the wall. He had set out to monopolise the coastwise steamship trade of the country, and had bought line after line of vessels by this same device of "pyramiding"; and now, finding that he needed still more money to buy out his rivals, he had purchased or started a dozen or so of trust companies and banks.

"Anyone ought to realise that such things cannot go on indefinitely," said the General. "I know that the big men realise it. I was at a directors' meeting the other day, and I heard Waterman remark that it would have to be ended very soon. Anyone who knows Waterman would not expect to get a second hint."

"What could he do?" asked Montague.

"Waterman!" exclaimed young Curtiss.

"He would find a way," said the General, simply. "That is the one hope that I see in the situation—the power of a conservative man like him."

"You trust him, then?" asked Montague.

"Yes," said the General, "I trust him.—One has to trust somebody."

"I heard a curious story," put in Harry Curtiss. "My uncle had dinner at the old man's house the other night, and asked him what he thought of the market. 'I can tell you in a sentence,' was the answer. 'For the first time in my life I don't own a security.'"

The General gave an exclamation of surprise. "Did he really say that?" he asked. "Then one can imagine that things will happen before long!"

"And one can imagine why the stock market is weak!" added the other, laughing.

At that moment the door of the dining-room was opened, and Mrs. Prentice appeared. "Are you men going to talk business all evening?" she asked. "If so, come into the drawing-room, and talk it to us."

They arose and followed her, and Montague seated himself upon a sofa with Mrs. Prentice and the younger man.

"What were you saying of Dan Waterman?" she asked of the latter.

"Oh, it's a long story," said Curtiss. "You ladies don't care anything about Waterman."

Montague had been watching Lucy out of the corner of his eye, and he could not forbear a slight smile.

"What a wonderful man he is!" said Mrs. Prentice. "I admire him more than any man I know of in Wall Street." Then she turned to Montague. "Have you met him?"

"Yes," said he; and added with a mischievous smile, "I saw him to-day."

"I saw him last Sunday night," said Mrs. Prentice, guilelessly. "It was at the Church of the Holy Virgin, where he passes the collection-plate. Isn't it admirable that a man who has as much on his mind as Mr. Waterman has, should still save time for the affairs of his church?"

And Montague looked again at Lucy, and saw that she was biting her lip.

CHAPTER VII

It was a week before Montague saw Lucy again. She came in to lunch with Alice one day, when he happened to be home early.

"I went to dinner at Mrs. Frank Landis's last night," she said. "And who do you think was there—your friend, Mrs. Winnie Duval."

"Indeed," said Montague.

"I had quite a long talk with her," said she. "I liked her very much."

"She is easy to like," he replied. "What did you talk about?"

"Oh, everything in the world but one thing," said Lucy, mischievously.

"What do you mean?" asked Montague.

"You, you goose," she answered. "Mrs. Winnie knew that I was your friend, and I had a feeling that every word she was saying was a message to you."

"Well, and what did she have to say to me?" he asked, smiling.

"She wants you to understand that she is cheerful, and not pining away because of you," was the answer. "She told me about all the things that she was interested in."

"Did she tell you about the Babubanana?"

"The what?" exclaimed Lucy.

"Why, when I saw her last," said Montague, "she was turning into a Hindoo, and her talk was all about Swamis, and Gnanis, and so on."

"No, she didn't mention them," said Lucy.

"Well, probably she has given it up, then," said he. "What is it now?"

"She has gone in for anti-vivisection."

"Anti-vivisection!"

"Yes," said the other; "didn't you see in the papers that she had been elected an honorary vice-president of some society or other, and had contributed several thousand dollars?"

"One cannot keep track of Mrs. Winnie in the newspapers," said Montague.

"Well," she continued, "she has heard some dreadful stories about how surgeons maltreat poor cats and dogs, and she would insist on telling me all about it. It was the most shocking dinner-table conversation imaginable."

"She certainly is a magnificent-looking creature," said Lucy, after a pause. "I don't wonder the men fall in love with her. She had her hair done up with some kind of a band across the front, and I declare she might have been an Egyptian princess."

"She has many roles," said Montague.

"Is it really true," asked the other, "that she paid fifty thousand dollars for a bath-tub?"

"She says she did," he answered. "The newspapers say it, too, so I suppose it is true. I know Duval told me with his own lips that she cost him a million dollars a year; but then that may have been because he was angry."

"Is he so rich as all that?" asked Lucy.

"I don't know how rich he is personally," said Montague. "I know he is one of the most powerful men in New York. They call him the 'System's' banker."

"I have heard Mr. Ryder speak of him," said she.

"Not very favourably, I imagine," said he, with a smile.

"No," said she, "they had some kind of a quarrel. What was the matter?"

"I don't know anything about it," was the answer. "But Ryder is a free lance, and a new man, and Duval works with the big men who don't like to have trespassers about."

Lucy was silent for a minute; her brows were knit in thought. "Is it really true that Mr. Ryder's position is so unstable? I thought the Gotham Trust Company was one of the largest institutions in the country. What are those huge figures that you see in their advertisements,—seventy millions—eighty millions—what is it?"

"Something like that," said Montague.

"And is not that true?" she asked.

"Yes, I guess that's true," he said. "I don't know anything about Ryder's affairs, you know—I simply hear the gossip. Everyone says he is playing a bold game. You take my advice, and keep your money somewhere else. You have to be doubly careful because you have enemies."

"Enemies?" asked Lucy, in perplexity.

"Have you forgotten what Waterman said to you?" Montague asked.

"You don't mean to tell me," cried she, "that you think that Waterman would interfere with Mr. Ryder on my account."

"It sounds incredible, I know," said Montague, "but such things have happened before this. If anyone knew the inside stories of the battles that have shaken Wall Street, he would find that many of them had some such beginning."

Montague said this casually, and with nothing in particular in mind. He was not watching his friend closely, and he did not see the effect which his words had produced upon her. He led the conversation into other channels; and he had entirely forgotten the matter the next day, when he received a telephone call from Lucy.

It had been a week since he had written to Smith and Hanson, the lawyers, in regard to the sale of her stock. "Allan," she asked, "no letter from those people yet?"

"Nothing at all," he answered.

"I was talking about it with a friend this morning, and he made a suggestion that I thought was important. Don't you think it might be well to find out whom they are representing?"

"What good would that do?" asked Montague.

"It might help us to get an idea of the prospects," said she. "I fancy they know who wants to sell the stock, and we ought to know who is thinking of buying it. Suppose you write them that you don't care to negotiate with agents."

"But I am in no position to do that," said Montague. "I have already set the people a figure, and they have not replied. We should only weaken our position by writing again. It would be much better to try to interest someone else."

"But I would like to know very much who made that offer," Lucy insisted. "I have heard rumours about the stock, and I really would like to know."

She reiterated this statement several times, and seemed to be very keen about it; Montague wondered a little who had been talking to her, and what she had heard. But warned by what the Major had told him, he did not ask these questions over the 'phone. He answered, finally, "I think you are making a mistake, but I will do what you wish."

So he sat down and wrote a note to Messrs. Smith and Hanson, and said that he would like to have a consultation with a member of their firm. He sent this note by messenger, and an hour or so later a wiry little person, with a much-wrinkled face and a shrewd look in his eyes, came into his office and introduced himself as Mr. Hanson.

"I have been talking with my client about the matter of the Northern Mississippi stock," said Montague. "You know, perhaps, that this road was organised under somewhat unusual circumstances; most of the stockholders were personal friends of our family. For this reason my client would prefer not to deal with an agent, if it can possibly be arranged. I wish to find out whether your client would consent to deal directly with the owner of the stock."

Montague finished what he had to say, although while he was speaking he noticed that Mr. Hanson was staring at him with very evident astonishment. Before he finished, this had changed to a slight sneer.

"What kind of a trick is this you are trying to play on me?" the man demanded.

Montague was too much taken aback to be angry. He simply stared. "I don't understand you," he said.

"You don't, eh?" said the other, laughing in his face. "Well, it seems I know more than you think I do."

"What do you mean?" asked Montague.

"Your client no longer has the stock that you are talking about," said the other.

Montague caught his breath. "No longer has the stock!" he gasped.

"Of course not," said Hanson. "She sold it three days ago." Then, unable to deny himself the satisfaction, he added, "She sold it to Stanley Ryder. And if you want to know any more about it, she sold it for a hundred and sixty thousand dollars, and he gave her a six months' note for a hundred and forty thousand."

Montague was utterly dumfounded. He could do nothing but stare.

It was evident to the other man that his emotion was genuine, and he smiled sarcastically. "Evidently, Mr. Montague," he said, "you have been permitting your client to take advantage of you."

Montague caught himself together, and bowed politely. "I owe you an apology, Mr. Hanson," he said, in a low voice. "I can only assure you that I was entirely helpless in the matter."

Then he rose and bade the man good morning.

When the door of his office was closed, he caught at the chair by his desk to steady himself, and stood staring in front of him. "To Stanley Ryder!" he gasped.

He turned to the 'phone, and called up his friend.

"Lucy," he said, "is it true that you have sold that stock?"

He heard her give a gasp. "Answer me!" he cried.

"Allan," she began, "you are going to be angry with me—"

"Please answer me!" he cried again. "Have you sold that stock?"

"Yes, Allan," she said, "I didn't mean—"

"I don't care to discuss the matter on the telephone," he said. "I will stop in to see you this afternoon on my way home. Please be in, because it is important." And then he hung up the receiver.

He called at the time he had set, and Lucy was waiting for him. She looked pale, and very much distressed. She sat in a chair, and neither arose to greet him nor spoke to him, but simply gazed into his face.

It was a very sombre face. "This thing has given me a great deal of pain," said Montague; "and I don't want to prolong it any more than necessary. I have thought the matter over, and my mind is made up, so there need be no discussion. It will not be possible for me to have anything further to do with your affairs."

Lucy gave a gasp: "Oh, Allan!"

He had a valise containing all her papers. "I have brought everything up to date," he said. "There are all the accounts, and the correspondence. Anyone will be able to find exactly how things stand."

"Allan," she said, "this is really cruel."

"I am very sorry," he answered, "but there is nothing else that I can do."

"But did I not have a right to sell that stock to Stanley Ryder?" she cried.

"You had a perfect right to sell it to anyone you pleased," he said. "But you had no right to ask me to take charge of your affairs, and then to keep me in the dark about what you had done."

"But, Allan," she protested, "I only sold it three days ago."

"I know that perfectly well," he said; "but the moment you made up your mind to sell it, it was your business to tell me. That, however, is not the point. You tried to use me as a cat's-paw to pull chestnuts out of the fire for Stanley Ryder."

He saw her wince under the words. "Is it not true?" he demanded. "Was it not he who told you to have me try to get that information?"

"Yes, Allan, of course it was he," said Lucy. "But don't you see my plight? I am not a business woman, and I did not realise—"

"You realised that you were not dealing frankly with me," he said. "That is all that I care about, and that is why I am not willing to continue to represent you. Stanley Ryder has bought your stock, and Stanley Ryder will have to be your adviser in the future."

He had not meant to discuss the matter with her any further, but he saw how profoundly he had hurt her, and the old bond between them held him still.

"Can't you understand what you did to me, Lucy?" he exclaimed. "Imagine my position, talking to Mr. Hanson, I knowing nothing and he knowing everything. He knew what you had been paid, and he even knew that you had taken a note."

Lucy stared at Montague with wide-open eyes. "Allan!" she gasped.

"You see what it means," he said. "I told you that you could not keep your doings secret. Now it will only be a matter of a few days before everybody who knows will be whispering that you have permitted Stanley Ryder to do this for you."

There was a long silence. Lucy sat staring before her. Then suddenly she faced Montague.

"Allan!" she cried. "Surely—you understand!"

She burst out violently, "I had a right to sell that stock! Ryder needed it. He is going to organise a syndicate, and develop the property. It was a simple matter of business."

"I have no doubt of it, Lucy," said Montague, in a low voice, "but how will you persuade the world of that? I told you what would happen if you permitted yourself to be intimate with a man like Stanley Ryder. You will find out too late what it means. Certainly that incident with Waterman ought to have opened your eyes to what people are saying."

Lucy gave a start, and gazed at him with horror in her eyes. "Allan!" she panted.

"What is it?" he asked.

"Do you mean to tell me that happened to me because Stanley Ryder is my friend?"

"Of course I do," said he. "Waterman had heard the gossip, and he thought that if Ryder was a rich man, he was a ten-times-richer man."

Montague could see the colour mount swiftly over Lucy's throat and face. She stood twisting her hands together nervously. "Oh, Allan!" she said. "That is monstrous!"

"It is not of my making. It is the way the world is. I found it out myself, and I tried to point it out to you."

"But it is horrible!" she cried. "I will not believe it. I will not yield to such things. I will not be coward enough to give up a friend for such a motive!"

"I know the feeling," said Montague. "I'd stand by you, if it were another man than Stanley Ryder. But I know him better than you, I believe."

"You don't, Allan, you can't!" she protested. "I tell you he is a good man! He is a man nobody understands—"

Montague shrugged his shoulders. "It is possible," he said. "I have heard that before. Many men are better than the things they do in this world; at any rate, they like to persuade themselves that they are. But you have no right to wreck your life out of pity for Ryder. He has made his own reputation, and if he had any real care for you, he would not ask you to sacrifice yourself to it."

"He did not ask me to," said Lucy. "What I have done, I have done of my own free will. I believe in him, and I will not believe the horrible things that you tell me."

"Very well," said Montague, "then you will have to go your own way."

He spoke calmly, though really his heart was wrung with grief. He knew exactly the sort of conversation by which Stanley Ryder had brought Lucy to this state of mind. He could have shattered the beautiful image of himself which Ryder had conjured up; but he could not bear to do it. Perhaps it was an instinct which guided him—he knew that Lucy was in love with the man, and that no facts that anyone could bring would make any difference to her. All he could say was, "You will have to find out for yourself."

And then, with one more look at her pitiful face of misery, he turned and went away, without even touching her hand.

CHAPTER VIII

It was now well on in May, and most of the people of Montague's acquaintance had moved out to their country places; and those who were chained to their desks had yachts or automobiles or private cars, and made the trip into the country every afternoon. Montague was invited to spend another week at Eldridge Devon's, where Alice had been for a week; but he could not spare the time until Saturday afternoon, when he made the trip up the Hudson in Devon's new three-hundred-foot steam-yacht, the Triton. Some unkind person had described Devon to Montague as "a human yawn"; but he appeared to have a very keen interest in life that Saturday afternoon. He had been seized by a sudden conviction that a new and but little advertised automobile had proven its superiority to any of the seventeen cars which he at present maintained in his establishment. He had got three of these new cars, and while Montague sat upon the quarter-deck of the Triton and gazed at the magnificent scenery of the river, he had in his ear the monotonous hum of Devon's voice, discussing annular ball-bearings and water-jacketed cylinders.

One of the new cars met them at Devon's private pier, and swept them over the hill to the mansion. The Devon place had never looked more wonderful to Montague than it did just then, with fruit trees in full blossom, and the wonder of springtime upon everything. For miles about one might see hillsides that were one unbroken stretch of luscious green lawn. But alas, Eldridge Devon had no interest in these hills, except to pursue a golf-ball over them. Montague never felt more keenly the pitiful quality of the people among whom he found himself than when he stood upon the portico of this house—a portico huge enough to belong to some fairy palace in a dream—and gazed at the sweeping vista of the Hudson over the heads of Mrs. Billy Alden and several of her cronies, playing bridge.

* * *

After luncheon, he went for a stroll with Alice, and she told him how she had been passing the time. "Young Curtiss was here for a couple of days," she said.

"General Prentice's nephew?" he asked.

"Yes. He told me he had met you," said she. "What do you think of him?"

"He struck me as a sensible chap," said Montague.

"I like him very much," said Alice. "I think we shall be friends. He is interesting to talk to; you know he was in a militia regiment that went to Cuba, and also he's been a cowboy, and all sorts of exciting things. We took a walk the other morning, and he told me some of his adventures. They say he's quite a successful lawyer."

"He is in a very successful firm," said Montague. "And he'd hardly have got there unless he had ability."

"He's a great friend of Laura Hegan's," said Alice. "She was over here to spend the day. She doesn't approve of many people, so that is a compliment."

Montague spoke of a visit which he had paid to Laura Hegan, at one of the neighbouring estates.

"I had quite a talk with her," said Alice. "And she invited me to luncheon, and took me driving. I like her better than I thought I would. Don't you like her, Allan?"

"I couldn't say that I really know her," said Montague. "I thought I might like her, but she did not happen to like me."

"But how could that be?" asked the girl.

Montague smiled. "Tastes are different," he said.

"But there must be some reason," protested Alice. "For she looks at many things in the same way that you do. I told her I thought she would be interested to talk to you."

"What did she say?" asked the other.

"She didn't say anything," answered Alice; and then suddenly she turned to him. "I am sure you must know some reason. I wish you would tell me."

"I don't know anything definite," Montague answered. "I have always imagined it had to do with Mrs. Winnie."

"With Mrs. Winnie!" exclaimed Alice, in perplexing wonder.

"I suppose she heard gossip and believed it," he added.

"But that is a shame!" exclaimed the girl. "Why don't you tell her the truth?"

"*I* tell her?" laughed Montague. "I have no reason for telling her. She doesn't care anything in particular about me."

He was silent for a moment or two. "I thought of it once or twice," he said. "For it made me rather angry at first. I saw myself going up to her, and startling her with the statement, 'What you believe about me is not true!' Then again, I thought I might write her a letter and tell her. But of course it would be absurd; she would never acknowledge that she had believed anything, and she would think I was impertinent."

"I don't believe she would do anything of the sort," Alice answered. "At least, not if she meant what she said to me. She was talking about people one met in Society, and how tiresome and conventional it all was. 'No one ever speaks the truth or deals frankly with you,' she said. 'All the men spend their time in paying you compliments about your looks. They think that is all a woman cares about. The more I come to know them, the less I think of them.'"

"That's just it," said Montague. "One cannot feel comfortable knowing a girl in her position. Her father is powerful, and some day she will be enormously rich herself; and the people who gather about her are seeking to make use of her. I was interested in her when I first met her. But when I learned more about the world in which she lives, I shrank from even talking to her."

"But that is rather unfair to her," said Alice. "Suppose all decent people felt that way. And she is really quite easy to know. She told me about some charities she is interested in. She goes down into the slums, on the East Side, and teaches poor children. It seemed to me a wonderfully daring sort of thing, but she laughed when I said so. She says those people are just the same as other people, when you come to know them; you get used to their ways, and then it does not seem so terrible and far off."

"I imagine it would be so," said Montague, with a smile.

"Her father came over to meet her," Alice added. "She said that was the first time he had been out of the city in six months. Just fancy working so hard, and with all the money he has! What in the world do you suppose he wants more for?"

"I don't suppose it is the money," said he. "It's the power. And when you have so much money, you have to work hard to keep other people from taking it away from you."

"He certainly looks as if he ought to be able to protect himself," said the girl. "His face is so grim and forbidding. You would hardly think he could smile, to look at him."

"He is very pleasant, when you know him," said Montague.

"He remembered you, and asked about you," said she. "Wasn't it he who was going to buy Lucy Dupree's stock?"

"I spoke to him about it," he answered, "but nothing came of it."

There was a moment's pause. "Allan," said Alice, suddenly, "what is this I hear about Lucy?"

"What do you mean?" he asked.

"People are talking about her and Mr. Ryder. I overheard Mrs. Landis yesterday. It's outrageous!"

Montague did not know what to say. "What can I do?" he asked.

"I don't know," said Alice, "but I think that Victoria Landis is a horrible woman. I know she herself does exactly as she pleases. And she tells such shocking stories—"

Montague said nothing.

"Tell me," asked the other, after a pause, "because you've given up Lucy's business affairs, are we to have nothing to do with her at all?"

"I don't know," he answered. "I don't imagine she will care to see me. I have told her about the mistake she's making, and she chooses to go her own way. So what more can I do?"

* * *

That evening Montague found himself settled on a sofa next to Mrs. Billy Alden. "What's this I hear about your friend, Mrs. Taylor?" she asked.

"I don't know," said he, abruptly.

"The fascinating widow seems to be throwing herself away," continued the other.

"What makes you say that?" he asked.

"Vivie Patton told me," said she. "She's an old flame of Stanley Ryder's, you know; and so I imagine it came directly from him."

Montague was dumb; he could think of nothing to say.

"It's too bad," said Mrs. Billy. "She is really a charming creature. And it will hurt her, you know—she is a stranger, and it's a trifle too sudden. Is that the Mississippi way?"

Montague forced himself to say, "Lucy is her own mistress." But his feeble impulse toward conversation was checked by Mrs. Billy's prompt response, "Vivie said she was Stanley Ryder's."

"I understand how you feel," continued the great lady, after a pause. "Everybody will be talking about it.—Your friend Reggie Mann heard what Vivie said, and he will see to that."

"Reggie Mann is no friend of mine," said Montague, abruptly.

There was a pause. "How in the world do you stand that man?" he asked, by way of changing the conversation.

"Oh, Reggie fills his place," was the reply. And Mrs. Billy gazed about the room. "You see all these women?" she said. "Take them in the morning and put half a dozen of them together in one room; they all hate each other like poison, and there are no men around, and there is nothing to do; and how are you to keep them from quarrelling?"

"Is that Reggie's role?" asked the other.

"Precisely. He sees a spark fly, and he jumps up and cracks a joke. It doesn't make any difference what he does—I've known him to crow like a rooster, or stumble over his own feet—anything to raise a laugh."

"Aren't you afraid these epigrams may reach your victim?" asked Montague, with a smile.

"That is what they are intended to do," was the reply.

"I judge you have not many enemies," added Mrs. Billy, after a pause.

"No especial ones," said he.

"Well," said she, "you should cultivate some. Enemies are the spice of life. I mean it, really," she declared, as she saw him smile.

"I had never thought of it," said he.

"Have you never known what it is to get into a really good fight? You see, you are conventional, and you don't like to acknowledge it. But what is there that wakes one up more than a good, vigorous hatred? Some day you will realise it— the chief zest in life is to go after somebody who hates you, and to get him down and see him squirm."

"But suppose he gets you down?" interposed Montague.

"Ah!" said she, "you mustn't let him! That is what you go into the fight for. Get after him, and do him first."

"It sounds rather barbarous," said he.

"On the contrary," was the answer, "it's the highest reach of civilisation. That is what Society is for—the cultivation of the art of hatred. It is the survival of the fittest in a new realm. You study your victim, you find out his weaknesses and his foibles, and you know just where to plant your sting. You learn what he wants, and you take it away from him. You choose your allies carefully, and you surround him and overwhelm him; then when you get through with him, you go after another."

And Mrs. Billy glanced about her at the exquisite assemblage in Mrs. Devon's Louis Seize drawing-room. "What do you suppose these people are here for to-night?" she asked.

CHAPTER IX

A week or two had passed, when one day Oliver called his brother on the 'phone. "Have you or Alice any engagement this evening?" he asked. "I want to bring a friend around to dinner."

"Who is it?" inquired Montague.

"Nobody you have heard of," said Oliver. "But I want you to meet him. You will think he's rather queer, but I will explain to you afterwards. Tell Alice to take my word for him."

Montague delivered the message, and at seven o'clock they went downstairs. In the reception room they met Oliver and his friend, and it was all that Montague could do to repress a look of consternation.

The name of the personage was Mr. Gamble. He was a little man, a trifle over five feet high, and so fat that one wondered how he could get about alone; his chin and neck were a series of rolls of fat. His face was round like a full moon, and out of it looked two little eyes like those of a pig. It was only after studying them for a while that one discovered that they twinkled shrewdly.

Mr. Gamble was altogether the vulgarest-looking personage that Alice Montague had ever met. He put out a fat little hand to her, and she touched it gingerly, and then gazed at Oliver and his brother in helpless dismay.

"Good evening. Good evening," he began volubly. "I am charmed to meet you. Mr. Montague, I have heard so much about you from your brother that I feel as if we were old friends."

There was a moment's pause. "Shall we go into the dining-room?" asked Montague.

He did not much relish the stares which would follow them, but he could see no way out of the difficulty. They went into the room and seated themselves, Montague wondering in a flash whether Mr. Gamble's arms would be long enough to reach to the table in front of him.

"A warm evening," he said, puffing slightly. "I have been on the train all day."

"Mr. Gamble comes from Pittsburg," interposed Oliver.

"Indeed?" said Montague, striving to make conversation. "Are you in business there?"

"No, I am out of business," said Mr. Gamble, with a smile. "Made my pile, so to speak, and got out. I want to see the world a bit before I get too old."

CHAPTER IX

The waiter came to take their orders; in the meantime Montague darted an indignant glance at his brother, who sat and smiled serenely. Then Montague caught Alice's eye, and he could almost hear her saying to him, "What in the world am I going to talk about?"

But it proved not very difficult to talk with the gentleman from Pittsburg. He appeared to know all the gossip of the Metropolis, and he cheerfully supplied the topics of conversation. He had been to Palm Beach and Hot Springs during the winter, and told about what he had seen there; he was going to Newport in the summer, and he talked about the prospects there. If he had the slightest suspicion of the fact that all his conversation was not supremely interesting to Montague and his cousin, he gave no hint of it.

After he had disposed of the elaborate dinner which Oliver ordered, Mr. Gamble proposed that they visit one of the theatres. He had a box all ready, it seemed, and Oliver accepted for Alice before Montague could say a word for her. He spoke for himself, however,—he had important work to do, and must be excused.

He went upstairs and shook off his annoyance and plunged into his work. Sometime after midnight, when he had finished, he went out for a breath of fresh air, and as he returned he found Oliver and his friend standing in the lobby of the hotel.

"How do you do, Mr. Montague?" said Gamble. "Glad to see you again."

"Alice has just gone upstairs," said Oliver. "We were going to sit in the cafe awhile. Will you join us?"

"Yes, do," said Mr. Gamble, cordially.

Montague went because he wanted to have a talk with Oliver before he went to bed that night.

"Do you know Dick Ingham?" asked Mr. Gamble, as they seated themselves at a table.

"The Steel man, you mean?" asked Montague. "No, I never met him."

"We were talking about him," said the other. "Poor chap—it really was hard luck, you know. It wasn't his fault. Did you ever hear the true story?"

"No," said Montague, but he knew to what the other referred. Ingham was one of the "Steel crowd," as they were called, and he had been president of the Trust until a scandal had forced his resignation.

"He is an old friend of mine," said Gamble; "he told me all about it. It began in Paris—some newspaper woman tried to blackmail him, and he had her put in jail for three months. And when she got out again, then the papers at home began to get stories about poor Ingham's cutting up. And the public went wild, and they made him resign—just imagine it!"

Gamble chuckled so violently that he was seized by a coughing spell, and had to signal for a glass of water.

"They've got a new scandal on their hands now," said Oliver.

"They're a lively crowd, the Steel fellows," laughed the other. "They want to make Davidson resign, too, but he'll fight them. He knows too much! You should hear his story!"

515

"I imagine it's not a very savoury one," said Montague, for lack of something to say.

"It's too bad," said the other, earnestly. "I have talked to them sometimes, but it don't do any good. I remember Davidson one night: 'Jim,' says he, 'a fellow gets a whole lot of money, and he buys him everything he wants, until at last he buys a woman, and then his trouble begins. If you're buying pictures, there's an end to it—you get your walls covered sooner or later. But you never can satisfy a woman.'" And Mr. Gamble shook his head. "Too bad, too bad," he repeated.

"Were you in the steel business yourself?" asked Montague, politely.

"No, no, oil was my line. I've been fighting the Trust, and last year they bought me out, and now I'm seeing the world."

Mr. Gamble relapsed into thought again. "I never went in for that sort of thing myself," he said meditatively; "I am a married man, I am, and one woman is enough for me."

"Is your family in New York?" asked Montague, in an effort to change the subject.

"No, no, they live in Pittsburg," was the answer. "I've got four daughters—all in college. They're stunning girls, I tell you—I'd like you to meet them, Mr. Montague."

"I should be pleased," said Montague, writhing inwardly. But a few minutes later, to his immense relief, Mr. Gamble arose, and bade him good night.

Montague saw him clamber laboriously into his automobile, and then he turned to his brother.

"Oliver," he asked, "what in the devil does this mean?"

"What mean?" asked Oliver, innocently.

"That man," exclaimed the other.

"Why, I thought you would like to meet him," said Oliver; "he is an interesting chap."

"I am in no mood for fooling," said his brother, angrily. "Why in the world should you insult Alice by introducing such a man to her?"

"Why, you are talking nonsense!" exclaimed Oliver; "he knows the best people—"

"Where did you meet him?" asked Montague.

"Mrs. Landis introduced him to me first. She met him through a cousin of hers, a naval officer. He has been living in Brooklyn this winter. He knows all the navy people."

"What is it, anyway?" demanded Montague, impatiently. "Is it some business affair that you are interested in?"

"No, no," said Oliver, smiling cheerfully—"purely social. He wants to be introduced about, you know."

"Are you going to put him into Society, by any chance?" asked the other, sarcastically.

"You are warm, as the children say," laughed his brother.

Montague stared at him. "Oliver, you don't mean it," he said. "That fellow in Society!"

"Sure," said Oliver, "if he wants to. Why not?"

"But his wife and his daughters!" exclaimed the other.

"Oh, that's not it—the family stays in Pittsburg. It's only himself this time. All the same," Oliver added, after a pause, "I'd like to wager you that if you were to meet Jim Gamble's four prize daughters, you'd find it hard to tell them from the real thing. They've been to a swell boarding-school, and they've had everything that money can buy them. My God, but I'm tired of hearing about their accomplishments!"

"But do you mean to tell me," the other protested, "that your friends will stand for a man like that?"

"Some of them will. He's got barrels of money, you know. And he understands the situation perfectly—he won't make many mistakes."

"But what in the world does he want?"

"Leave that to him."

"And you," demanded Montague; "you are getting money for this?"

Oliver smiled a long and inscrutable smile. "You don't imagine that I'm in love with him, I trust. I thought you'd be interested to see the game, that's why I introduced him."

"That's all very well," said the other. "But you have no right to inflict such a man upon Alice."

"Oh, stuff!" said Oliver. "She'll meet him at Newport this summer, anyway. How could I introduce him anywhere else, if I wasn't willing to introduce him here? He won't hurt Alice. He gave her a good time this evening, and I wager she'll like him before he gets through. He's really a good-natured chap; the chief trouble with him is that he gets confidential."

Montague relapsed into silence, and Oliver changed the subject. "It seems too bad about Lucy," he said. "Is there nothing we can do about it?"

"Nothing," said the other.

"She is simply ruining herself," said Oliver. "I've been trying to get Reggie Mann to have her introduced to Mrs. Devon, but he says he wouldn't dare to take the risk."

"No, I presume not," said Montague.

"It's a shame," said Oliver. "I thought Mrs. Billy Alden would ask her to Newport this summer, but now I don't believe she'll have a thing to do with her. Lucy will find she knows nobody except Stanley Ryder and his crowd. She has simply thrown herself away."

Montague shrugged his shoulders. "That's Lucy's way," he said.

"I suppose she'll have a good time," added the other. "Ryder is generous, at any rate."

"I hope so," said Montague.

"They say he's making barrels of money," said Oliver; then he added, longingly, "My God, I wish I had a trust company to play with!"

"Why a trust company particularly?" asked the other.

"It's the easiest graft that's going," said Oliver. "It's some dodge or other by which they evade the banking laws, and the money comes rolling in in floods. You've noticed their advertisements, I suppose?"

"I have noticed them," said Montague.

"He is adding something over a million a month, I hear."

"It sounds very attractive," said the other; and added, drily, "I suppose Ryder feels as if he owned it all."

"He might just as well own it," was the reply. "If I were going into Wall Street to make money, I'd rather have the control of fifty millions than the absolute ownership of ten."

"By the way," Oliver remarked after a moment, "the Prentices have asked Alice up to Newport. Alice seems to be quite taken with that young chap, Curtiss."

"He comes around a good deal," said Montague. "He seems a very decent fellow."

"No doubt," said the other. "But he hasn't enough money to take care of a girl like Alice."

"Well," he replied, "that's a question for Alice to consider."

CHAPTER X

ONE day, a month or so later, Montague, to his great surprise, received a letter from Stanley Ryder.

"Could you make it convenient to call at my office sometime this afternoon?" it read. "I wish to talk over with you a business proposition which I believe you will find of great advantage to yourself."

"I suppose he wants to buy my Northern Mississippi stock," he said to himself, as he called up Ryder on the 'phone, and made an appointment.

It was the first time that he had ever been inside the building of the Gotham Trust Company, and he gazed about him at the overwhelming magnificence—huge gates of bronze and walls of exquisite marble. Ryder's own office was elaborate and splendid, and he himself a picture of aristocratic elegance.

He greeted Montague cordially, and talked for a few minutes about the state of the market, and the business situation, in the meantime twirling a pencil in his hand and watching his visitor narrowly. At last he began, "Mr. Montague, I have for some time been working over a plan which I think will interest you."

"I shall be very pleased to hear of it," said Montague.

"Of course, you know," said Ryder, "that I bought from Mrs. Taylor her holdings in the Northern Mississippi Railroad. I bought them because I was of the opinion that the road ought to be developed, and I believed that I could induce someone to take the matter up. I have found the right parties, I think, and the plans are now being worked out."

"Indeed," said the other, with interest.

"The idea, Mr. Montague, is to extend the railroad according to the old plan, with which you are familiar. Before we took the matter up, we approached the holders of the remainder of the stock, most of whom, I suppose, are known to you. We made them, through our agents, a proposition to buy their stock at what we considered a fair price; and we have purchased about five thousand shares additional. The prices quoted on the balance were more than we cared to pay, in consideration of the very great cost of the improvements we proposed to undertake. Our idea is now to make a new proposition to these other shareholders. The annual stockholders' meeting takes place next month. At this meeting will be brought up the project for the issue of twenty thousand additional shares, with the understanding that as much of this new stock as is not taken by the present shareholders is to go to us. As I assume that few of them will take their allotments, that will give us control of the road; you can understand, of course, that our syndicate would not undertake the venture unless it could obtain control."

Montague nodded his assent to this.

"At this meeting," said Ryder, "we shall propose a ticket of our own for the new board of directors. We are in hopes that as our proposition will be in the interest of every stockholder, this ticket will be elected. We believe that the road needs a new policy, and a new management entirely; if a majority of the stockholders can be brought to our point of view, we shall take control, and put in a new president."

Ryder paused for a moment, to let this information sink into his auditor's mind; then, fixing his gaze upon him narrowly, he continued: "What I wished to see you about, Mr. Montague, was to make you a proposal to assist us in putting through this project. We should like you, in the first place, to act as our representative, in consultation with our regular attorneys. We should like you to interview privately the stockholders of the road, and explain to them our projects, and vouch for our good intentions. If you can see your way to undertake this work for us, we should be glad to place you upon the proposed board of directors; and as soon as we have matters in our hands, we should ask you to become president of the road."

Montague gave an inward start; but practice had taught him to keep from letting his surprise manifest itself very much. He sat for a minute in thought.

"Mr. Ryder," he said, "I am a little surprised at such a proposition from you, seeing that you know so little about me—"

"I know more than you suppose, Mr. Montague," said the other, with a smile. "You may rest assured that I have not broached such a matter to you without making inquiries, and satisfying myself that you were the proper person."

"It is very pleasant to be told that," said Montague. "But I must remind you, also, that I am not a railroad man, and have had no experience whatever in such matters—"

"It is not necessary that you should be a railroad man," was the answer. "One can hire talent of that kind at market prices. What we wish is a man of careful and conservative temper, and, above all, a man of thorough-going honesty; someone who will be capable of winning the confidence of the stockholders, and of keeping it. It seemed to us that you possessed these qualifications. Also, of course, you have the advantage of being familiar with the neighbourhood, and of knowing thoroughly the local conditions."

Montague thought for a while longer. "The offer is a very flattering one," he said, "and I need hardly tell you that it interests me. But before I could properly consider the matter, there is one thing I should have to know—that is, who are the members of this syndicate."

"Why would it be necessary to know that?" asked the other.

"Because I am to lend my reputation to their project, and I should have to know the character of the men that I was dealing with." Montague was gazing straight into the other's eyes.

"You will understand, of course," replied Ryder, "that in a matter of this sort it is necessary to proceed with caution. We cannot afford to talk about what we are going to do. We have enemies who will do what they can to check us at every step."

"Whatever you tell me will, of course, be confidential," said Montague.

"I understand that perfectly well," was the reply. "But I wished first to get some idea of your attitude toward the project—whether or not you would be at liberty to take up this work and to devote yourself to it."

"I can see no reason why I should not," Montague answered.

"It seems to me," said Ryder, "that the proposition can be judged largely upon its own merits. It is a proposition to put through an important public improvement; a road which is in a broken-down and practically bankrupt condition is to be taken up, and thoroughly reorganised, and put upon its feet. It is to have a vigorous and honest administration, a new and adequate equipment, and a new source of traffic. The business of the Mississippi Steel Company, as you doubtless know, is growing with extraordinary rapidity. All this, it seems to me, is a work about the advisability of which there can be no question."

"That is very true," said Montague, "and I will meet the persons who are interested and talk out matters with them; and if their plans are such as I can approve, I should be very glad to join with them, and to do everything in my power to make a success of the enterprise. As you doubtless know, I have five hundred shares of the stock myself, and I should be glad to become a member of the syndicate."

"That is what I had in mind to propose to you," said the other. "I anticipate no difficulty in satisfying you—the project is largely of my own originating, and my own reputation will be behind it. The Gotham Trust Company will lend its credit to the enterprise so far as possible."

Ryder said this with just a trifle of hauteur, and Montague felt that perhaps he had spoken too strenuously. No one could sit in Ryder's office and not be impressed by its atmosphere of magnificence; after all, it was here, and its seventy or eighty million dollars of deposits were real, and this serene and aristocratic gentleman was the master of them. And what reason had Montague for his hesitation, except the gossip of idle and cynical Society people?

Whatever doubts he himself might have, he needed to reflect but a moment to realise that his friends in Mississippi would not share them. If he went back home with the name of Stanley Ryder and the Gotham Trust Company to back him, he would come as a conqueror with tidings of triumph, and all the old friends of the family would rush to follow his suggestions.

Ryder waited awhile, perhaps to let these reflections sink in. Finally he continued: "I presume, Mr. Montague, that you know something about the Mississippi Steel Company. The steel situation is a peculiar one. Prices are kept at an altogether artificial level, and there is room for large profits to competitors of the Trust. But those who go into the business commonly find themselves unexpectedly handicapped. They cannot get the credit they want; orders overwhelm them in floods, but Wall Street will not put up money to help them. They find all kinds of powerful interests arrayed against them; there are raids upon their securities in the market, and mysterious rumours begin to circulate. They find suits brought against them which tend to injure their credit. And sometimes they will find important papers missing, important witnesses sailing for Europe, and so on. Then their most efficient employees will be bought up; their very bookkeepers and office-boys will be bribed, and all the secrets of their business passed on to their enemies. They will find that the railroads do not treat them squarely; cars will be slow in coming, and all kinds of petty annoyances will be practised. You know what the rebate is, and you can imagine the part which that plays. In these and a hundred other ways, the path of the independent steel manufacturer is made difficult. And now, Mr. Montague, this is a project to extend a railroad which will be of vast service to the chief competitor of the Steel Trust. I believe that you are man of the world enough to realise that this improvement would have been made long ago, if the Steel Trust had not been able to prevent it. And now, the time has come when that project is to be put through in spite of every opposition that the Trust can bring; and I have come to you because I believe that you are a man to be counted on in such a fight."

"I understand you," said Montague, quietly; "and you are right in your supposition."

"Very well," said Ryder. "Then I will tell you that the syndicate of which I speak is composed of myself and John S. Price, who has recently acquired control of the Mississippi Steel Company. You will find out without difficulty what Price's reputation is; he is the one man in the country who has made any real headway against the Trust. The business of the Mississippi Company has almost doubled in the past year, and there is no limit to what it can do, except the size of the plant and the ability of the railroads to handle its product. This new plan would have been taken up through the Company, but for the fact that the Company's capital and credit is involved in elaborate extensions. Price has furnished some of the capital personally, and I have raised the balance; and what we want now is an honest man to whom we can entrust this most important project, a man who will take the road in hand and put it on its feet, and make it of some service in the community. You are the man we have selected, and if the proposition appeals to you, why, we are ready to do business with you without delay."

For a minute or two Montague was silent; then he said: "I appreciate your confidence, Mr. Ryder, and what you say appeals to me. But the matter is a very important one to me, as you can readily understand, and so I will ask you to give me until to-morrow to make up my mind."

"Very well," said Ryder.

Montague's first thought was of General Prentice. "Come to me any time you need advice," the General had said; so Montague went down to his office. "Do you know anything about John S. Price?" he asked.

"I don't know him very well personally," was the reply. "I know him by reputation. He is a daring Wall Street operator, and he's been very successful, I am told."

"Price began life as a cowboy, I understand," continued the General, after a pause. "Then he went in for mines. Ten or fifteen years ago we used to know him as a silver man. Several years ago there was a report that he had been raiding Mississippi Steel, and had got control. That was rather startling news, for everybody knew that the Trust was after it. He seems to have fought them to a standstill."

"That sounds interesting," said Montague.

"Price was brought up in a rough school," said the General, with a smile. "He has a tongue like a whip-lash. I remember once I attended a creditors' meeting of the American Stove Company, which had got into trouble, and Price started off from the word go. 'Mr. Chairman,' he said, 'when I come into the office of an industrial corporation, and see a stock ticker behind the president's chair with the carpet worn threadbare in front of it, I know what's the matter with that corporation without asking another word.'"

"What do you want to know about him for?" asked the General, after he had got through laughing over this recollection.

"It's a case I'm concerned in," the other answered.

"I tell you who knows about him," said the General. "Harry Curtiss. William E. Davenant has done law business for Price."

"Is that so?" said Montague. "Then probably I shall meet Harry."

"I can tell you a better person yet," said the other, after a moment's thought. "Ask your friend Mrs. Alden; she knows Price intimately, I believe."

So Montague sent up a note to Mrs. Billy, and the reply came, "Come up to dinner. I am not going out." And so, late in the afternoon, he was ensconced in a big leather armchair in Mrs. Billy's private drawing-room, and listening to an account of the owner of the Mississippi Steel Company.

"Johnny Price?" said the great lady. "Yes, I know him. It all depends whether you are going to have him for a friend or an enemy. His mother was Irish, and he is built after her. If he happens to take a fancy to you, he'll die for you; and if you make him hate you, you will hear a greater variety of epithets than you ever supposed the language contained.—I first met him in Washington," Mrs. Billy went on, reminiscently; "that was fifteen years ago, when my brother was in Congress. I think I told you once how Davy paid forty thousand dollars for the nomination, and went to Congress. It was the year of a Democratic landslide, and they could have elected Reggie Mann if they had felt like it. I went to Washington to live the next winter, and Price was there with a whole army of lobbyists, fighting for free silver. That was before the craze, you know, when silver was respectable; and Price was the Silver King. I saw the inside of American government that winter, I can assure you."

"Tell me about it," said Montague.

"The Democratic party had been elected on a low tariff platform," said Mrs. Billy; "and it sold out bag and baggage to the corporations. Money was as free as water—my brother could have got his forty thousand back three times over. It was the Steel crowd that bossed the job, you know—William Roberts used to come down from Pittsburg every two or three days, and he had a private telephone wire the rest of the time. I have always said it was the Steel Trust that clamped the tariff swindle on the American people, and that's held it there ever since."

"What did Price do with his silver mines?" asked Montague.

"He sold them," said she, "and just in the nick of time. He was on the inside in the campaign of '96, and I remember one night he came to dinner at our house and told us that the Republican party had raised ten or fifteen million dollars to buy the election. 'That's the end of silver,' he said, and he sold out that very month, and he's been freelancing it in Wall Street ever since."

"Have you met him yet?" asked Mrs. Billy, after a pause.

"Not yet," he answered.

"He's a character," said she. "I've heard Davy tell about the first time he struck New York—as a miner, with huge wads of greenbacks in his pockets. He spent his money like a 'coal-oil Johnny,' as the phrase is—a hundred-dollar bill for a shine, and that sort of thing. And he'd go on the wildest debauches; you can have no idea of it."

"Is he that kind of a man?" said Montague.

"He used to be," said the other. "But one day he had something the matter with him, and he went to a doctor, and the doctor told him something, I don't know what, and he shut down like a steel trap. Now he never drinks a drop, and he lives on one meal a day and a cup of coffee. But he still goes with the old crowd—I don't believe there is a politician or a sporting-man in town that Johnny Price does not know. He sits in their haunts and talks with them until all sorts of hours in the morning, but I can never get him to come to my dinner-parties. 'My people are human,' he will say; 'yours are sawdust.' Sometime, if you want to see New York, just get Johnny Price to take you about and introduce you to his bookmakers and burglars!"

Montague meditated for a while over his friend's picture. "Somehow or other," he said, "it doesn't sound much like the president of a hundred-million-dollar corporation."

"That's all right," said Mrs. Billy, "but Price will be at his desk bright and early the next morning, and every man in the office will be there, too. And if you think he won't have his wits about him, just you try to fool him on some deal, and see. Let me tell you a little that I know about the fight he has made with the Mississippi Steel Company." And she went on to tell. The upshot of her telling was that Montague borrowed the use of her desk and wrote a note to Stanley Ryder. "From my inquiries about John S. Price, I gather that he makes steel. With the understanding that I am to make a railroad and carry his steel, I have concluded to accept your proposition, subject, of course, to a satisfactory arrangement as to terms."

CHAPTER XI

THE next morning Montague had an interview with John S. Price in his Wall Street office, and was retained as counsel in connection with the new reorganisation. He accepted the offer, and in the afternoon he called by appointment at the law-offices of William E. Davenant.

The first person Montague met there was Harry Curtiss, who greeted him with eagerness. "I was pleased to death when I heard that you were in on this deal," said he; "we shall have some work to do together."

About the table in the consultation room of Davenant's offices were seated Ryder and Price, and Montague and Curtiss, and, finally, William E. Davenant. Davenant was one of the half-dozen highest-paid corporation lawyers in the Metropolis. He was a tall, lean man, whose clothing hung upon him like rags upon a scare-crow. One of his shoulders was a trifle higher than the other, and his long neck invariably hung forward, so that his thin, nervous face seemed always to be peering about. One had a sense of a pair of keen eyes, behind which a restless brain was constantly plotting. Some people rated Davenant as earning a quarter of a million a year, and it was his boast that no one who made money according to plans which he approved had ever been made to give any of it up.

In curious contrast was the figure of Price, who looked like a well-dressed pugilist. He was verging on stoutness, and his face was round, but underneath the superfluous flesh one could see the jaw of a man of iron will. It was easy to believe that Price had fought his way through life. He spoke sharply and to the point, and he laid bare the subject with a few quick strokes, as of a surgeon's knife.

The first question was as to Montague's errand in the South. There was no need of buying more stock of the road, for if they got the new stock they would have control, and that was all they needed. Montague was to see those holders of the stock whom he knew personally, and to represent to them that he had succeeded in interesting some Northern capitalists in the road, and that they would undertake the improvements on condition that their board of directors should be elected. Price produced a list of the new directors. They consisted of Montague and Curtiss and Ryder and himself; a cousin of the latter's, and two other men, who, as he phrased it, were "accustomed to help me in that way." That left two places to be filled by Montague from among the influential holders of the stock.

"That always pleases," said Price, succinctly, "and at the same time we shall have an absolute majority."

There was to be voted an issue of a million dollars' worth of bonds, which the Gotham Trust Company would take; also a new issue of twenty thousand shares of stock, which was to be offered pro rata to the present stock-holders at fifty cents on the dollar. Montague was to state that his clients would take any which these stockholders did not want. He was to use every effort to keep the plan secret, and would make no attempt to obtain the stock-holders' list of the road. The reason for this came out a little later, when the subject of the old-time survey was broached.

"I must take steps to get hold of those plans," said Price. "In this, as well as everything else, we proceed upon the assumption that the present administration of the road is crooked."

The next matter to be considered was the charter. "When I get a charter for a railroad," said Price, "I get one that lets me do anything from building a toothpick factory to running flying-machines. But the fools who drew the charter of the Northern Mississippi got permission to build a railroad from Atkin to Opala. So we have to proceed to get an extension. While you are down there, Mr. Montague, you will see the job through with the Legislature."

Montague thought for a moment. "I don't believe that I have much influence with the Legislature," he began.

"That's all right," said Price, grimly. "We'll furnish the influence."

Here spoke Davenant. "It seems to me," he said, "that we can just as well arrange this matter without mentioning the Northern Mississippi Railroad at all. If the Steel people get wind of this, we are liable to have all sorts of trouble; the Governor is their man, as you know. The thing to do is to pass a blanket bill, providing that any public-service corporation whose charter antedates a certain period may extend its line within certain limits and under certain conditions, and so on. I think that I can draw a bill that will go through before anybody has an idea what it's about."

"Very good," said Price. "Do it that way."

And so they went, from point to point. Price laid down Montague's own course of procedure in a few brief sentences. They had just two weeks before the stock-holders' meeting, and it was arranged that he should start for Mississippi upon the following day.

When the conference was over, Montague rode up town with Harry Curtiss.

"What was that Davenant said about the Governor?" he asked, when they were seated in the train.

"Governor Hannis, you mean?" said the other. "I don't know so very much about it, but there's been some agitation down there against the railroads, and Waterman and the Steel crowd put in Governor Hannis to do nothing."

"It was rather staggering to me," said Montague, after a little thought. "I didn't say anything about it, but you know Governor Hannis is an old friend of my father's, and one of the finest men I ever knew."

"Oh, yes, I don't doubt that," said Curtiss, easily. "They put up these fine, respectable old gentlemen. Of course, he's simply a figure-head—he probably has no idea of what he's really doing. You understand, of course, that Senator Harmon is the real boss of your State."

"I have heard it said," said Montague. "But I never took much stock in such statements—"

"Humph!" said Curtiss. "You'd take it if you'd been in my boots. I used to do business for old Waterman's Southern railroads, and I've had occasion to take messages to Harmon once or twice. New York is the place where you find out about this game!"

"It's not a very pleasant game," said Montague, soberly.

"I didn't make the rules," said Curtiss. "You find you either have to play that way or else get out altogether."

The younger man relapsed into silence for a moment, then laughed to himself. "I know how you feel," he said. "I remember when I first came out of college, the twinges I used to have. I had my head full of all the beautiful maxims of the old Professor of Ethics. And they took me on in the legal department of the New York and Hudson Railroad, and we had a case—-some kind of a damage suit; and old Henry Corbin—their chief counsel, you know—gave me the papers, and then took out of his desk a typewritten list of the judges of the Supreme Court of the State. 'Some of them are marked with red,' he said; 'you can bring the case before any of them. They are our judges.' Just fancy, you know! And I as innocent as a spring chicken!"

"I should think things like that would get out in the end," said Montague.

Curtiss shrugged his shoulders. "How could you prove it?" he asked.

"But if a certain judge always decided in favour of the railroad—" began Montague.

"Oh, pshaw!" said Curtiss. "Leave that to the judge! Sometimes he'll decide against the railroad, but he'll make some ruling that the higher courts will be sure to upset, and by that time the other fellow will be tired out, and ready to quit. Or else—here's another way. I remember one case that I had that old Corbin told me I'd be sure to win, and I took eleven different exceptions, and the judge decided against me on every single one. I thought I was gone sure—but, by thunder, he instructed the jury in my favour! It took me a long time to see the shrewdness of that; you see, it goes to the higher courts, and they see that the judge has given the losing side every advantage, and has decided purely on the evidence. And of course they haven't the witnesses before them, and don't feel half so well able to judge of the evidence, and so they let the decision stand. There are more ways than one to skin a cat, you see!"

"It doesn't seem to leave much room for justice," said Montague.

To which the other responded, "Oh, hell! If you'd been in this business as long as I have, and seen all the different kinds of shysters that are trying to plunder the railroads, you'd not fret about justice. The way the public has got itself worked up just at present, you can win almost any case you can get before a jury, and there are men who spend all their time hunting up cases and manufacturing evidence."

Montague sat for a while in thought. He muttered, half to himself, "Governor Hannis! It takes my breath away!"

"Get Davenant to tell you about it," said Curtiss, with a laugh. "Maybe it's not so bad as I imagine. Davenant is cynical on the subject of governors, you know. He had an experience a few years ago, when he went up to Albany to try to get the Governor to sign a certain bill. The Governor went out of his office and left him, and Davenant noticed that a drawer of his desk was open, and he looked in, and there was an envelope with fifty brand-new one-thousand-dollar bills in it! He didn't know what they were there for, but this was a mighty important bill, and he concluded he'd take a chance. He put the envelope in his pocket; and then the Governor came back, and after some talk about the interests of the public, he told him he'd concluded to veto that bill. 'Very well,' Mr. Governor,' said the old man, 'I have only this to say,' and he took out the envelope. 'I have here fifty new one-thousand-dollar bills, which are yours if you sign that measure. On the other hand, if you refuse to sign it, I will take the bills to the newspaper men, and tell them what I know about how you got them.' And the Governor turned as white as a sheet, and, by God, he signed the bill and sent it off to the Legislature while Davenant waited! So you can see why he is sceptical about governors."

"I suppose," said Montague, "that was what Price meant when he said he'd furnish the influence."

"That was what he meant," said the other, promptly.

"I don't like the prospect," Montague responded.

The younger man shrugged his shoulders. "What are you going to do about it?" he asked. "Your political machines and your offices are in the hands of pea-nut-politicians and grafters who are looking for what's coming to them. If you want anything, you have to pay them for it, just the same as in any other business. You face the same situation every hour—'Pay or quit.'"

"Look," Curtiss went on, after a pause, "take our own case. Here we are, and we want to build a little railroad. It's an important work; it's got to be done. But we might haunt the lobbies of your State legislature for fifty years, and if we did-n't put up, we wouldn't get the charter. And, in the meantime, what do you suppose the Steel Trust would be doing?"

"Have you ever thought what such things will lead to?" asked Montague.

"I don't know," said Curtiss. "I've had a fancy that some day the business men of the country will have to go into politics and run it on business lines."

The other pondered the reply. "That sounds simple," he said. "But doesn't it mean the overthrow of Republican institutions?"

"I am afraid it would," said Curtiss. "But what's to be done?"

There was no answer.

"Do you know any remedy?" he persisted.

"No, I don't know any remedy," said Montague, "but I am looking for one. And I can tell you of this, for a start; I value this Republic more than I do any business I ever got into yet; and if I come to that dilemma, it will be the business that will give way."

Curtiss was watching him narrowly. He put his hand on his shoulder. "That's all right, old man," he said. "But take my advice, and don't let Davenant hear you say that."

"Why not?" asked the other.

The younger man rose from his seat. "Here's my station," he said. "The reason is—it might unsettle his ideas. He's a conservative Democrat, you know, and he likes to make speeches at banquets!"

CHAPTER XII

IN spite of his doubts, Montague returned to his old home, and put through the programme as agreed. Just as he had anticipated, he found that he was received as a conquering hero by the holders of the Northern Mississippi stock. He talked with old Mr. Lee, his cousin, and two or three others of his old friends, and he had no difficulty in obtaining their pledges for the new ticket. They were all interested, and eager about the future of the road.

He did not have to concern himself with the new charter. Davenant drew up the bill, and he wrote that a nephew of Senator Harmon's would be able to put it through without attracting any attention. All that Montague knew was that the bill passed, and was signed by the Governor.

And then came the day of the stockholders' meeting. He attended it, presenting proxies for the stock of Ryder and Price, and nominated his ticket, greatly to the consternation of Mr. Carter, the president of the road, who had been a lifelong friend of his family's. The new board of directors was elected by the votes of nearly three-fourths of the stock, and the new stock issue was voted by the same majority. As none of the former stockholders cared to take the new stock, Montague subscribed for the whole issue in the name of Ryder and Price, and presented a certified check for the necessary deposit.

The news of these events, of course, created great excitement in the neighbourhood; also it did not pass unobserved in New York. Northern Mississippi was quoted for the first time on the "curb," and there was quite a little trading; the stock went up nearly ten points in one day.

Montague received this information in a letter from Harry Curtiss. "You must be prepared to withstand the flatteries of the Steel crowd," he wrote. "They will be after you before long."

Montague judged that he would not mind facing the "Steel crowd"; but he was much troubled by an interview which he had to go through with on the day after the meeting. Old Mr. Carter came to see him, and gave him a feeble hand to shake, and sat and gazed at him with a pitiful look of unhappiness.

"Allan," he said, "I have been president of the Northern Mississippi for fifteen years, and I have served the road faithfully and devotedly. And now—I want you to tell me—what does this mean? Am I—"

Montague could not remember a time when Mr. Carter had not been a visitor at his father's home, and it was painful to see him in his helplessness. But there was nothing that could be done about it; he set his lips together.

"I am very sorry, Mr. Garter," he said; "but I am not at liberty to say a word to you about the plans of my clients."

"Am I to understand, then, that I am to be turned out of my position? I am to have no consideration for all that I have done? Surely—"

"I am very sorry," Montague said again, firmly,—"but the circumstances at the present time are such that I must ask you to excuse me from discussing the matter in any way."

A day or two later Montague received a telegram from Price, instructing him to go to Riverton, where the works of the Mississippi Steel Company were located, and to meet Mr. Andrews, the president of the Company. Montague had been to Riverton several times in his youth, and he remembered the huge mills, which were one of the sights of the State. But he was not prepared for the enormous development which had since taken place. The Mississippi Steel Company had now two huge Bessemer converters, in which a volcano of molten flame roared all day and night. It had bought up the whole western side of the town, and cleared away half a hundred ramshackle dwellings; and here were long rows of coke-ovens, and two huge rail-mills, and a plate-mill from which arose sounds like the crashing of the day of doom. Everywhere loomed rows of towering chimneys, and pillars of rolling black smoke. Little miniature railroad tracks ran crisscross about the yards, and engines came puffing and clanking, carrying blazing white ingots which the eye could not bear to face.

Opposite to the entrance of the stockaded yards, the Company had put up a new office building, and upon the top floor of this were the president's rooms.

"Mr. Andrews will be in on the two o'clock train," said his secretary, who was evidently expecting the visitor. "Will you wait in his office?"

"I think I should like to see the works, if you can arrange it for me," said Montague. And so he was provided with a pass and an attendant, and made a tour of the yards.

It was interesting to Montague to see the actual property of the Mississippi Steel Company. Sitting in comfortable offices in Wall Street and exchanging pieces of paper, one had a tendency to lose sight of the fact that he was dealing in material things and disposing of the destinies of living people. But Montague was now to build and operate a railroad—to purchase real cars and handle real iron and steel; and the thought was in his mind that at every step of what he did he wished to keep this reality in mind.

It was a July day, with not a cloud in the sky, and an almost tropical sun blazed down upon the works. The sheds and railroad tracks shimmered in the heat, and it seemed as if the cinders upon which one trod had been newly poured from a fire. In the rooms where the furnaces blazed, Montague could not penetrate at all; he could only stand in the doorway, shading his eyes from the glare. In each of these infernos toiled hundreds of grimy, smoke-stained men, stripped to the waist and streaming with perspiration.

He gazed down the long rows of the blast furnaces, great caverns through the cracks of which the molten steel shone like lightning. Here the men who worked had to have buckets of water poured over them continually, and they drank several gallons of beer each day. He went through the rail-mills, where the flaming white ingots were caught by huge rollers, and tossed about like pancakes, and flattened and squeezed, emerging at the other end in the shape of tortured red snakes of amazing length. At the far end of the mill one could see them laid out in long rows to cool; and as Montague stood and watched them, the thought came to him that these were some of the rails which Wyman had ordered, and which had been the cause of such dismay in the camp of the Steel Trust!

Then he went on to the plate-mill, where giant hammers resounded, and steel plates of several inches' thickness were chopped and sliced like pieces of cheese. Here the spectator stared about him in bewilderment and clung to his guide for safety; huge travelling cranes groaned overhead, and infernal engines made deafening clatter upon every side. It was a source of never ending wonder that men should be able to work in such confusion, with no sense of danger and no consciousness of all the uproar.

Montague's eye roamed from place to place; then suddenly it was arrested by a sight even unusually startling. Across on the other side of the mill was a steel shaft, which turned one of the largest of the rollers. It was high up in the air, and revolving with unimaginable speed, and Montague saw a man with an oil-can in his hand rest the top of a ladder upon this shaft, and proceed to climb up.

He touched his guide upon the arm and pointed. "Isn't that dangerous?" he shouted.

"It's against orders," said the man. "But they will do it."

And even while the words of a reply were upon his lips, something happened which turned the sound into a scream of horror. Montague stood with his hand still pointing, his whole body turned to stone. Instantaneously, as if by the act of a magician, the man upon the ladder had disappeared; and instead there was a hazy mist about the shaft, and the ladder tumbling to the ground.

No one else in the mill appeared to have noticed it. Montague's guide leaped forward, dodging a white-hot plate upon its journey to the roller, and rushed down the room to where the engineer was standing by his machinery. For a period which could not have been less than a minute, Montague stood staring at the horrible sight; and then slowly he saw what had been a mist beginning to define itself as the body of a man whirling about the shaft.

Then, as the machinery moved more slowly yet, and the din in the mill subsided, he saw several men raise the ladder again to the shaft and climb up. When the revolving had stopped entirely, they proceeded to cut the body loose; but Montague did not wait to see that. He was white and sick, and he turned and went outside.

He went away to another part of the yards and sat down in the shade of one of the buildings, and told himself that that was the way of life. All the while the din of the mills continued without interruption. A while later he saw four men go past, carrying a stretcher covered with a sheet. It dropped blood at every step, but Montague noticed that the men who passed it gave it no more than a casual glance. When he passed the plate-mill again, he saw that it was busy as ever; and when he went out at the front gate, he saw a man who had been pointed out to him as the foreman of the mill, engaged in picking another labourer from the group which was standing about.

He returned to the president's office, and found that Mr. Andrews had just arrived. A breeze was blowing through the office, but Andrews, who was stout, was sitting in his chair with his coat and vest off, vigorously wielding a palmleaf fan.

"How do you do, Mr. Montague?" he said. "Did you ever know such heat? Sit down—you look done up."

"I have just seen an accident in the mills," said Montague.

"Oh!" said the other. "Too bad. But one finds that steel can't be made without accidents. We had a blast-furnace explosion the other day, and killed eight. They are mostly foreigners, though—'hunkies,' they call them."

Then Andrews pressed a button, summoning his secretary.

"Will you please bring those plans?" he said; and to Montague's surprise he proceeded to spread before him a complete copy of the old reports of the Northern Mississippi survey, together with the surveyor's original drawings.

"Did Mr. Carter let you have them?" Montague asked; and the other smiled a dry smile.

"We have them," he said. "And now the thing for you to do is to have your own surveyors go over the ground. I imagine that when you get their reports, the proposition will look very different."

These were the instructions which came in a letter from Price the next day; and with the help of Andrews Montague made the necessary arrangements, and the next night he left for New York.

He arrived upon a Friday afternoon. He found that Alice had departed for her visit to the Prentices', and that Oliver was in Newport, also. There was an invitation from Mrs. Prentice to him to join them; as Price was away, he concluded that he would treat himself to a rest, and accordingly took an early train on Saturday morning.

Montague's initiation into Society had taken place in the winter-time, and he had yet to witness its vacation activities. When Society's belles and dames had completed a season's round of dinner-parties and dances, they were more or less near to nervous prostration, and Newport was the place which they had selected to retire to and recuperate. It was an old-fashioned New England town, not far from the entrance to Long Island Sound, and from a village with several grocery shops and a tavern, it had been converted by a magic touch of Society into the most famous and expensive resort in the world. Estates had been sold there for as much as a dollar a square foot, and it was nothing uncommon to pay ten thousand a month for a "cottage."

The tradition of vacation and of the country was preserved in such terms as "cottage." You would be invited to a "lawn-party," and you would find a blaze of illumination, and potted plants enough to fill a score of green-houses, and costumes and jewelled splendour suggesting the Field of the Cloth of Gold. You would be invited to a "picnic" at Gooseberry Point, and when you went there, you would find gorgeous canopies spread overhead, and velvet carpets under foot, and scores of liveried lackeys in attendance, and every luxury one would have expected in a Fifth Avenue mansion. You would take a cab to drive to this "picnic," and it would cost you five dollars; yet you must on no account go without a cab. Even if the destination was just around the corner, a stranger would commit a breach of the proprieties if he were to approach the house on foot.

Coming to Newport as Montague did, directly from the Mississippi Steel Mills, produced the strangest possible effect upon him. He had seen the social splurge in the Metropolis, and had heard the fabulous prices that people had paid for things. But these thousands and millions had seemed mere abstractions. Now suddenly they had become personified—he had seen where they came from, where all the luxury and splendour were produced! And with every glance that he cast at the magnificence about him, he thought of the men who were toiling in the blinding heat of the blast-furnaces.

Here was the palace of the Wymans, upon the laying out of the grounds of which a half million dollars had been spent; the stone wall which surrounded it was famous upon two continents, because it had cost a hundred thousand dollars. And it was to make steel rails for the Wymans that the slaves of the mills were toiling!

Here was the palace of the Eldridge Devons, with a greenhouse which had cost one hundred and fifty thousand dollars, and which merely supplied the daily needs of its owners. Here was the famous tulip tree, which had been dug up and brought a distance of fifty miles, at a cost of a thousand dollars. And Montague had seen in the making the steel for one of the great hotels of the Eldridge Devons!

And here was the Walling establishment, the "three-million-dollar palace on a desert," as Mrs. Billy Alden had described it. Montague had read of the famous mantel in its entrance hall, made from Pompeiian marble, and costing seventy-five thousand dollars. And the Wallings were the railroad kings who transported Mississippi Steel!

And from that his thoughts roamed on to the slaves of other mills, to the men and women and little children shut up to toil in shops and factories and mines for these people who flaunted their luxury about him. They had come here from every part of the country, with their millions drawn from every kind of labour. Here was the great white marble palace of the Johnsons—the ceilings, floors, and walls of its state apartments had all been made in France; its fences and gates, even its locks and hinges, had been made from special designs by famous artists. The

Johnsons were lords of railroads and coal, and ruled the state of West Virginia with a terrible hand. The courts and the legislature were but branches of old Johnson's office, and Montague knew of mining villages which were owned outright by the Company, and were like stockaded forts; the wretched toilers could not buy so much as a pint of milk outside of the Company store, and even the country doctor could not enter the gates without a pass.

And beyond that was the home of the Warfields, whose fortune came from great department stores, in which young girls worked for two dollars and a half a week, and eked out their existence by prostitution. And this was the summer that Warfield's youngest daughter was launched, and for her debutante dance they built a ballroom which cost thirty thousand dollars—and was torn down the day afterwards!

And beyond this, upon the cliffs, was the castle of the Mayers, whose fortunes came from coal.—Montague thought of the young man who had invented the device for the automatic weighing of coal as it was loaded upon steam-ships. Major Venable had hinted to him that the reason the Coal Trust would not consider it, was because they were selling short weight; and since then he had investigated the story, and learned that this was true, and that it was old Mayer himself who had devised the system. And here was his palace, and here were his sons and daughters—among the most haughty and exclusive of Society's entertainers!

So you might drive down the streets and point out the mansions and call the roll of the owners—kings of oil and steel and railroads and mines! Here everything was beauty and splendour. Here were velvet lawns and gardens of rare flowers, and dancing and feasting and merriment. It seemed very far from the sordid strife of commerce, from poverty and toil and death. But Montague carried with him the sight that he had seen in the plate-mill, the misty blur about the whirling shaft, and the shrouded form upon the stretcher, dripping blood.

* * *

He was so fortunate as to meet Alice and her friends upon the street, and he drove with them to the bathing beach which Society had purchased and maintained for its own exclusive use. The first person he saw here was Reggie Mann, who came and took possession of Alice. Reggie would not swim himself, because he did not care to exhibit his spindle legs; he was watching with disapproving eye the antics of Harry Percy, his dearest rival. Percy was a man about forty years of age, a cotillion-leader by profession; and he caused keen delight to the spectators upon the beach by wearing a monocle in the water.

They had lunch at the Casino, and then went for a sail in the Prentices' new racing yacht. It was estimated just at this time that there was thirty millions' worth of steam and sailing pleasure-craft in Newport harbour, and the bay was a wonderful sight that afternoon.

They came back rather early, however, as Alice had an engagement for a drive at six o'clock, and it was necessary for her to change her costume before she went. It was necessary to change it again before dinner, which was at eight o'clock; and Montague learned upon inquiry that it was customary to make five or six such changes during the day. The great ladies of Society were adepts in this art, and prided themselves upon the perfect system which enabled them to accomplish it.

All of Montague's New York acquaintances were here in their splendour: Miss Yvette Simpkins, with her forty trunks of new Paris costumes; Mrs. Billy Alden, who had just launched an aristocratic and exclusive bridge-club for ladies; Mrs. Winnie Duval, who had created a sensation by the rumour of her intention to introduce the simple life at Newport; and Mrs. Vivie Patton, whose husband had committed suicide as the only means of separating her from her Count.

It chanced to be the evening of Mrs. Landis's long-expected dinner-dance. When you went to the Landis mansion, you drove directly into the building, which had a court so large that a coach and four could drive around it. The entire ground floor was occupied by what were said to be the most elaborately equipped stables in the world. Your horses vanished magically through sliding doors at one side, and your carriage at the other side, and in front of you was the entrance to the private apartments, with liveried flunkies standing in state.

There were five tables at this dinner, each seating ten persons. There was a huge floral umbrella for the centrepiece, and an elaborate colour effect in flowers. During the dance, screens were put up concealing this end of the ballroom, and when they were removed sometime after midnight, the tables were found set for the supper, with an entirely new scenic effect.

They danced until broad daylight; Montague was told of parties at which the guests had adjourned in the morning to play tennis. All these people would be up by nine or ten o'clock the next day, and he would see them in the shops and at the bathing beach before noon. And this was Society's idea of "resting" from the labours of the winter season!

After the supper Montague was taken in charge by Mrs. Caroline Smythe, the lady who had once introduced him to her cats and dogs. Mrs. Smythe had become greatly interested in Mrs. Winnie's anti-vivisection crusade, and told him all about it while they strolled out upon the loggia of the Landis palace, and stood and watched the sunrise over the bay.

"Do you see that road back of us?" said Mrs. Smythe. "That is the one the Landises have just succeeded in closing. I suppose you've heard the story."

"No," said Montague, "I haven't heard it."

"It's the joke of Newport," said the lady. "They had to buy up the town council to do it. There was a sight-seers' bus that used to drive up that road every day, and the driver would rein up his horses and stand up and point with his whip.

"'This, ladies and gentlemen,' he'd say, 'is the home of the Landises, and just beyond there is the home of the Joneses. Once upon a time Mr. Smith had a wife and got tired of her, and Mr. Jones had a wife and got tired of her; so they both got divorces and exchanged, and now Mrs. Smith is living in Mr. Jones's house, and Mrs. Jones is living in Mr. Smith's. Giddap!'"

CHAPTER XIII

Alice was up early the next morning to go to church with Harry Curtiss, but Montague, who had really come to rest, was later in arising. Afterwards he took a stroll through the streets, watching the people. He was met by Mrs. De Graffenried, who, after her usual fashion, invited him to come round to lunch. He went, and met about forty other persons who had been invited in the same casual way, including his brother Ollie—and to his great consternation, Ollie's friend, Mr. Gamble!

Gamble was clad in a spotless yachting costume, which produced a most comical effect upon his expansive person. He greeted Montague with his usual effusiveness. "How do you do, Mr. Montague—how do you do?" he said. "I've been hearing about you since I met you last."

"In what way?" asked Montague.

"I understand that you have gone with the Mississippi Steel Company," said Gamble.

"After a fashion," the other assented.

"You want to be careful—you are dealing with a smooth crowd! Smoother even than the men in the Trust, I fancy." And the little man added, with a twinkle in his eye: "I'm accustomed to say there are two kinds of rascals in the oil business; there are the rascals who found they could rely upon each other, and they are in the Trust; and there are the rascals the devil himself couldn't rely upon, and they're the independents. I ought to know what I'm talking about, because I was an independent myself."

Mr. Gamble chuckled gleefully over this witticism, which was evidently one which he relied upon for the making of conversation. "How do you do, Captain?" he said, to a man who was passing. "Mr. Montague, let me introduce my friend Captain Gill."

Montague turned and faced a tall and dignified-looking naval officer. "Captain Henry Gill, of the Allegheny."

"How do you, Mr. Montague?" said the Captain.

"Oliver Montague's brother," added Gamble, by way of further introduction. And then, espying someone else coming whom he knew, he waddled off down the room, leaving Montague in conversation with the officer.

Captain Gill was in command of one of the half-dozen vessels which the government obligingly sent to assist in maintaining the gaieties of the Newport season. He was an excellent dancer, and a favourite with the ladies, and an old crony of Mrs. De Graffenried's. "Have you known Mr. Gamble long?" he asked, by way of making conversation.

"I met him once before," said Montague. "My brother knows him."

"Ollie seems to be a great favourite of his," said the Captain. "Queer chap."

Montague assented readily.

"I met him in Brooklyn," continued the other, seeming to feel that acquaintance with Gamble called for explanation. "He was quite chummy with the officers at the Navy Yard. Retired millionaires don't often fall in their way."

"I should imagine not," said Montague, smiling. "But I was surprised to meet him here."

"You'd meet him in heaven," said the other, with a laugh, "if he made up his mind that he wanted to go there. He is a good-natured personage; but I can tell you that anyone who thinks that Gamble doesn't know what he's about will make a sad mistake."

Montague thought of this remark at lunch, where he sat at table on the opposite side to Gamble. Next to him sat Vivie Fatten, who made the little man the victim of her raillery. It was not particularly delicate wit, but Gamble was tough, and took it all with a cheerful grin.

He was a mystery which Montague could not solve. To be sure he was rich, and spent his money like water; but then there was no scarcity of money in this crowd. Montague found himself wondering whether he was there because Mrs. De Graffenried and her friends liked to have somebody they could snub and wipe their feet upon. His eye ran down the row of people sitting at the table, and the contrast between them and Gamble was an amusing one. Mrs. De Graffenried was fond of the society of young people, and most of her guests were of the second or even the third generation. The man from Pittsburg seemed to be the only one there who had made his own money, and who bore the impress of the money struggle upon him. Montague smiled at the thought. He seemed the very incarnation of the spirit of oil; he was gross and unpleasant, while in the others the oil had been refined to a delicate perfume. Yet somehow he seemed the most human person there. No doubt he was crudely egotistical; and yet, if he was interested in himself, he was also interested in other people, while among Mrs. De Graffenried's intimates it was a sign of vulgarity to be interested in anything.

He seemed to have taken quite a fancy to Montague, for reasons best known to himself. He came up to him again, after the luncheon. "This is the first time you've been here, Oliver tells me," said he.

Montague assented, and the other added: "You'd better come and let me show you the town. I have my car here."

Montague had no engagement, and no excuse handy. "It's very good of you—" he began.

"All right," said Gamble. "Come on."

And he took him out and seated him in his huge red touring-car, which had a seat expressly built for its owner, not too deep, and very low, so that his fat little legs would reach the floor.

Gamble settled back in the cushions with a sigh. "Rum sort of a place this, ain't it?" said he.

"It's interesting for a short visit," said Montague.

"You can count me out of it," said the other. "I like to spend my summers in a place where I can take my coat off. And I prefer beer to champagne in hot weather, anyhow."

Montague did not reply.

"Such an ungodly lot of snobs a fellow does meet!" remarked his host, cheerily. "They have a fine time making fun of me—it amuses them, and I don't mind. Sometimes it does make you mad, though; you feel you'd like to make them swallow you, anyway. But then you think, What's the use of going after something you don't want, just because other people say you can't have it?"

It was on Montague's lips to ask, "Then why do you come here?" But he forbore.

The car sped on down the stately driveway, and his companion proceeded to point out the mansions and the people, and to discuss them in his own peculiar style.

"See that yellow brick house in there," said he. "That belongs to Allis, the railroad man. He used to live in Pittsburg, and I remember him thirty years ago, when he had one carriage for his three babies, and pushed them himself, by thunder. He was glad to borrow money from me then, but now he looks the other way when I go by.

"Allis used to be in the steel business six or eight years ago," Gamble continued, reminiscently. "Then he sold out—it was the real beginning of the forming of the Steel Trust. Did you ever hear that story?"

"Not that I know of," said Montague.

"Well," said the other, "if you are going to match yourself against the Steel crowd, it's a good idea to know about them. Did you ever meet Jim Stagg?"

"The Wall Street plunger?" asked Montague. "He's a mere name to me."

"His last exploit was to pull off a prize fight in one of the swell hotels in New York, and one nigger punched the other through a plate-glass mirror. Stagg comes from the wild West, you know, and he's wild as they make 'em—my God, I could tell you some stories about him that'd make your hair stand up! Perhaps you remember some time ago he raided Tennessee Southern in the market and captured it; and old Waterman testified that he took it away from him because he didn't consider he was a fit man to own it. As a matter of fact, that was just pure bluff, for Waterman uses him in little jobs like that all the time.—Well, six or eight years ago, Stagg owned a big steel plant out West; and there was a mill in Indiana, belonging to Allis, that interfered with their business. One time Stagg and some of his crowd had been on a spree for several days, and late one night they got to talking about Allis. 'Let's buy the——out,' said Stagg, so they ordered a special and a load of champagne, and away they went to the city in Indiana. They got to Allis's house about four o'clock in the morning, and they rang the bell and banged on the door, and after a while the butler came, half awake.

"'Is Allis in?' asked Stagg, and before the fellow could answer, the whole crowd pushed into the hall, and Stagg stood at the foot of the stairs and roared—he's got a voice like a bull, you know—'Allis, Allis, come down here!'

"Allis came to the head of the stairs in his nightshirt, half frightened to death.

"'Allis, we want to buy your steel plant,' said Stagg.

"'Buy my steel plant!' gasped Allis.

"'Sure, buy it outright! Spot cash! We'll pay you five hundred thousand for it.'

"'But it cost me over twelve hundred thousand,' said Allis.

"'Well, then, we'll pay you twelve hundred thousand,' said Stagg—'God damn you, we'll pay you fifteen hundred thousand!'

"'My plant isn't for sale,' said Allis.

"'We'll pay you two million!' shouted Stagg.

"'It isn't for sale, I tell you.'

"'We'll pay you two million and a half! Come on down here!'

"'Do you mean that?' gasped Allis. He could hardly credit his ears.

"'Come downstairs and I'll write you a check!' said Stagg. And so they hauled him down, and they bought his mill. Then they opened some more champagne, and Allis began to get good-natured, too.

"'There's only one thing the matter with my mill,' said he, 'and that's Jones's mill over in Harristown. The railroads give him rebates, and he undersells me.'

"'Well, damn his soul,' said Stagg, 'we'll have his mill, too.'

"And so they bundled into their special again, and about six o'clock in the morning they got to Harristown, and they bought another mill. And that started them, you know. They'd never had such fun in their lives before. It seems that Stagg had just cleaned up ten or twelve millions on a big Wall Street plunge, and they blew in every dollar, buying steel mills—and paying two or three prices for every one, of course."

Gamble paused and chuckled to himself. "What I'm telling you is the story that Stagg told me," said he. "And of course you've got to make allowances. He said he had no idea of what Dan Waterman had been planning, but I fancy that was a lie. Harrison of Pittsburg had been threatening to build a railroad of his own, and take away his business from Waterman's roads, and so there was nothing for Waterman to do but buy him out at three times what his mills were worth. He took the mills that Stagg had bought at the same time. Stagg had paid two or three prices, and Waterman paid him a couple of prices more, and then he passed them on to the American people for a couple of prices more than that."

Gamble paused. "That's where they get these fortunes," he added, waving his fat little hand. "Sometimes it makes a fellow laugh to think of it. Every concern they bought was overcapitalised to begin with; I doubt if two hundred million dollars' worth of honest dollars was ever put into the Steel Trust properties, and they capitalised it at a billion, and now they've raised it to a billion and a half! The men who pulled it off made hundreds of millions, and the poor public that bought the common stock saw it go down to six! They gave old Harrison a four-hundred-million-dollar mortgage on the property, and he sits back and grins, and wonders why a man can't die poor!"

Gamble's car was opposite one of the clubs. Suddenly he signalled his chauffeur to stop.

"Hello, Billy!" he called; and a young naval officer who was walking down the steps turned and came toward him.

"What have you been doing with yourself?" said Gamble. "Mr. Montague, my friend Lieutenant Long, of the Engineers. Where are you going, Billy?"

"Nowhere in particular," said the officer.

"Get in," said Gamble, pointing to the vacant seat between them. "I am showing Mr. Montague the town."

The other climbed in, and they went on. "The Lieutenant has just come up from Brooklyn," he continued. "Lively times we had in Brooklyn, didn't we, Billy? Tell me what you have been doing lately."

"I'm working hard," said the Lieutenant—"studying."

"Studying here in Newport?" laughed Gamble.

"That's easy enough when you belong to the Engineers," said the other. "We are working-men, and they don't want us at their balls."

"By the way, Gamble," he added, after a moment, "I was looking for you. I want you to help me."

"Me?" said Gamble.

"Yes," said the other. "I have just had notice from the Department that I am one of a board of five that has been appointed to draw up specifications for machine oil for the Navy."

"What can I do about it?" asked Gamble.

"I want you to help me draw them up."

"But I don't know anything about machine oil."

"You cannot possibly know less than I do," said the Lieutenant. "Surely, if you have been in the oil business, you can give me some sort of an idea about machine oil."

Gamble thought for a minute. "I might try," he said. "But would it be the proper thing for me to do? Of course, I'm out of the business myself; but I have friends who might bid for the contract."

"Well, your friends can take their chances with the rest," said the Lieutenant. "I am a friend, too, hang it. And how in the world am I to find out anything about oil?"

Gamble was silent again. "Well, I'll do what I can for you," he said, finally. "I'll write out what I know about the qualities of good oil, and you can use it as you think best."

"All right," said the Lieutenant, with relief.

"But you'll have to agree to say nothing about it," said Gamble. "It's a delicate matter, you understand."

"You may trust me for that," said the other, laughing. So the subject was dropped, and they went on with their ride.

Half an hour later Gamble set Montague down, at General Prentice's door, and he bade them farewell and went in.

The General was coming down the stairs. "Hello, Allan," he said. "Where have you been?"

"Seeing the place a little," said Montague.

"Come into the drawing-room," said the General. "There's a man in there you ought to know.

"One of the brainiest newspaper men in Wall Street," he added, as he went across the hall,—"the financial man of the Express."

Montague entered the room and was introduced to a powerfully built and rather handsome young fellow, who had not so long ago been centre-rush upon a famous football team. "Well, Bates," said the General, "what are you after now?"

"I'm trying to get the inside story of the failure of Grant and Ward," said Bates. "I supposed you'd know about it, if anyone did."

"I know about it," said the General, "but the circumstances are such that I'm not free to tell—at least, not for publication. I'll tell you privately, if you want to know."

"No," said Bates, "I'd rather you didn't do that; I can find it out somehow."

"Did you come all the way to Newport to see me?" asked the General.

"Oh, no, not entirely," said Bates. "I'm to get an interview with Wyman about the new bond issue of his road. What do you think of the market, General?"

"Things look bad to me," said Prentice. "It's a good time to reef sail."

Then Bates turned to Montague. "I think I passed you a while ago in the street," he said pleasantly. "You were with James Gamble, weren't you?"

"Yes," said Montague. "Do you know him?"

"Bates knows everybody," put in the General; "that's his specialty."

"I happen to know Gamble particularly well," said Bates. "I have a brother in his office in Pittsburg. What in the world do you suppose he is doing in Newport?"

"Just seeing the world, so he told me," said Montague. "He has nothing to do since his company sold out."

"Sold out!" echoed Bates. "What do you mean?"

"Why, the Trust has bought him out," said Montague.

The other stared at him. "What makes you think that?" he asked.

"He told me so himself," was the answer.

"Oh!" laughed the other. "Then it's just some dodge that he's up to!"

"You think he hasn't sold?"

"I don't think it, I know it," said Bates. "At any rate, he hadn't sold three days ago. I had a letter from my brother saying that they were expecting to land a big oil contract with the government that would put them on Easy Street for the next five years!"

Montague said no more. But he did some thinking. Experience had sharpened his wits, and by this time he knew a clew when he met it. A while later, when Bates had gone and his brother had come in with Alice, he got Oliver off in a corner and demanded, "How much are you to get out of that oil contract?"

The other stared at him in consternation. "Good heavens!" he exclaimed. "Did he tell you about it?"

"He told me some things," said Montague, "and I guessed the rest."

Oliver was watching him anxiously. "See here, Allan," he said, "you'll keep quiet about it!"

"I imagine I will," said the other. "It's none of my business, that I can see."

Then suddenly Oliver broke into a smile of amusement. "Say, Allan!" he exclaimed. "He's a clever dog, isn't he!"

"Very clever," admitted the other.

"He's been after that thing for six months, you know—and just as smooth and quiet! It's about the slickest game I ever heard of!"

"But how could he know what officers were to make out those specifications?"

"Oh, that's easy," said the other. "That was the beginning of the whole thing. They got a tip that the contract was to be let, and they had no trouble in finding out the names of the officers. That kind of thing is common, you know; the bureaus in Washington are rotten."

"I see," said Montague.

"Gamble's company is in a bad way," Oliver continued. "The Trust just about had it in a corner. But Gamble saw this chance, and he staked everything on it."

"But what's his idea?" asked the other. "What good will it do him to write the specifications?"

"There are five officers," said Oliver, "and he's been laying siege to every one of them. So now they are all his intimate friends, and every one of them has come to him for help! So there will go into Washington five sets of specifications, all different, but each containing one essential point. You see, Gamble's company has a peculiar kind of oil; it contains some ingredient or other—he told me the name, but I don't remember it now. It doesn't make it any better oil, and it doesn't make it any worse; but it's different from any other oil in the world. And now, don't you see—whatever other requirements are specified, this one quality will surely appear; and there will be only one company in the world that can bid. Of course they will name their own figure, and get a five-year contract."

"I see," said Montague, drily. "It's a beautiful scheme. And how much do you get out of it?"

"He paid me ten thousand at the start," said Oliver; "and I am to get five per cent of the first year's contract, whatever that may be. Gamble says his bid won't be less than half a million, so you see it was worth while!"

And Oliver chuckled to himself. "He's going home to-morrow," he added. "So my job is done. I'll probably never see him again—until his four prize daughters get ready for the market!"

CHAPTER XIV

Montague returned to New York and plunged into his work. The election at which he was scheduled to become president of the Northern Mississippi was not to come off for a month. Meantime there was no lack of work for him to do. It would, of course, be necessary for him to return to Mississippi to live, and he had to close up his affairs in New York. Also he wished to fit himself for the work of superintending a railroad. Through the courtesy of General Prentice, he was introduced to the president of one of the great transcontinental lines, and made a study of that official's office system. He went South again to inspect the work of the surveyors, and to consult with the engineers who had been selected for the work.

Price went ahead with his arrangements to take over the control of the road, without paying any attention to the old management. He sent for Montague one day, and introduced him to a Mr. Haskins, who was to be elected vice-president of the road. Haskins, he said, had formerly been general manager of the Tennessee Southern, and was a practical railroad man. Montague was to rely upon him for all the details of his work.

Haskins was a wiry, nervous little man, with a bad temper and a sarcastic tongue; he worshipped the gospel of efficiency, and in the consultations with him Montague got many curious lights upon the management of railroads. He learned, for instance, that a conspicuous item in the construction account was the money to be used in paying local government boards for right of way through towns and villages. Apparently no one even considered the possibility of securing the privilege by any other methods. Montague did not like the prospect, but he said nothing. Then again, the road was to purchase its rails and other necessaries from the Mississippi Steel Company, and apparently it was expected to pay a fancy price for these; it was not to ask for any of the discounts which were customary. Also Montague was troubled to learn that the secretary and treasurer of the road were to receive liberal salaries, and that no questions were to be asked, because they were relatives of Price.

All that he put up with; but matters came to a head about ten days before the election, when one day Haskins came to his office with the engineers' estimates, and with his own figures of the probable cost of the extension. Most of the figures were much higher than those which Montague had worked out for himself.

"We ought to do better on those contracts," he said, pointing to some of the items.

"I dare say we might," said Haskins; "but those contracts are to go to the Hill Manufacturing Company."

"I don't understand you," said Montague; "I thought that we were to advertise for bids."

"Yes," replied Haskins, "but that company is to get the contracts, all the same."

"You mean," asked Montague, "that we are not to give them to the lowest bidder?"

"I'm afraid not," said the other.

"Has Price said anything to you to that effect?"

"He has."

"But I don't understand," said Montague; "what is this Hill Manufacturing Company?"

And Haskins smiled. "It's a concern that Price has organised himself," he said.

Montague stared in amazement. "Price himself!" he gasped.

"His nephew is president of the company," added the other.

"Is it a new company?" Montague asked.

"Organised especially for the purpose," smiled the other.

"And what does it manufacture?"

"It doesn't manufacture anything; it simply sells."

"In other words," said Montague, "it's a device whereby Mr. Price proposes to rob the stockholders of the Northern Mississippi Railroad?"

"You can phrase it that way if you choose," said Haskins, quietly; "but I wouldn't advise you to let Price hear you."

"I thank you," responded Montague, and brought the interview to an end.

He took a day to think the matter over. It was not his habit to act upon impulse. He saw that the time had come for him to speak, but he wished to be sure of his course of action before he began. He had dinner at the Club that evening, and, seeing his friend Major Venable ensconced in a big leather chair in the reading-room, he went and sat down beside him.

"How do you do, Major?" he said. "I've got another case that I want to ask you some questions about."

"Always at your service," said the Major.

"It has to do with a railroad," said Montague. "Did you ever hear of such a thing as a railroad president organising a company to sell supplies to his own road?"

The Major smiled grimly. "Yes, I have heard of it," he said.

"Is it common?" asked Montague.

"Not so common as you might suppose," answered the other. "A railroad president is commonly not an important enough man to be permitted to do it. If it happens to be a big road, and the president is a power in it, why, then he may do it."

"I see," said Montague.

"That was Higgins's trick," said the Major. "Higgins used to go around making speeches to Sunday schools; he was the kind of man that the newspapers like to refer to as a model citizen and a leader of enterprise. His brothers, and his brothers-in-law, and his cousins, and all his family went into business in order to sell things to his railroads. I heard of one story—it has never come out, but it's very amusing. Every year the road would advertise its contract for stationery. It used about a million dollars' worth, and there'd be long and most elaborate specifications published—columns and columns. But sandwiched away somewhere in the middle of a paragraph was the provision that the paper must all bear a certain watermark; and that watermark was patented by one of Higgins's companies! It didn't even own so much as a mill—it sublet all the contracts. When Higgins died, he left eighty million dollars; but they juggled the records, and you read in all the newspapers that he left 'a few millions.' That was in Philadelphia, where you can do such things."

Montague sat thinking for a few moments. "But I can't see why they should do it in this case," he said. "The men who are doing it own nearly all of the stock of the road."

"What difference does that make?" asked the Major.

"Why, they are simply plundering their own property," said Montague.

"Tut!" was the reply. "What do they care about the value of the property? They'll unload it before the public finds out; and in the meantime they are probably manipulating the stock. That's the scheme they're working with the street railroads over in Brooklyn, for instance; the more irregular the dividends are, the more violently the stock fluctuates, and the better they like it."

"But this is the case of a railroad that is being built," said Montague; "and they are putting up the money to build it."

"Yes," said the Major, "of course; and then they are paying it back to themselves by this dodge; and they'll still have the stock, and whatever they can get for it will be profit. And if the State Legislature comes along and asks any impertinent questions, they can open their books and say: 'See, we have spent this much for improvements. This is the cost of the road; and if you reduce our freight-rates, you will cut off our dividends and confiscate our property.'"

And the Major gazed at Montague with a mischievous twinkle in his eye. "Besides," he said, "another thing. You say they are putting up the money. Are you sure it's their own money? Commonly the greater part of the cost of railroad building is paid by bonds, and they work those bonds off on banks and insurance companies and trust companies. Have you thought of that?"

"No, I hadn't," said Montague.

"I know very few men in Wall Street who use their own money," the Major added. "Take the case of Wyman, for instance. Wyman's railroad keeps a cash surplus of twenty or thirty millions, and Wyman uses that in Wall Street. And when he has made his profit, he takes it and salts it away in village improvement bonds all over the country. Do you see?"

"I see," said Montague. "It's a bad game for the small stockholder."

"It's a bad game for the small man of any sort," said the Major. "When I was young, I can remember, a man would save a little money and put it into an enterprise of some sort, and whatever the profits were, he would get his share of them. But now, you see, the big men have got control, and they are greedier than they used to be. There is nothing hurts them so much as to see the little fellow get any share of the profits, and they've all sorts of schemes for doing him out of it. I could take a week off and tell you about them. You are manufacturing soap, we will say. You find there are too many soap manufacturers and too much soap, and so you propose to combine, and put your rivals out of business, and monopolise the soap market. Your properties are already capitalised at twice what they cost you, because you are naturally hopeful, and that is what you expected they would earn; but now for this new combination you issue stock to the amount of three times this imagined value. Then you fill the street with rumours of the wonders of your soap combination, and all the privileges and monopolies that you've got, and you unload your stock on the public, we'll say at eighty. You may have sold all your stock, but you've still got control of the corporation. The public is helpless and unorganised, and your men are in. Then the Street begins to hear disturbing rumours about the soap trust, and your board of directors meet and declare that it is impossible to pay any dividends. There is great indignation among the stockholders, and an opposition is organised, but you set the clock an hour ahead, and elect your ticket before the other fellow comes around. Or perhaps the troubles have already knocked the stock down sufficiently low to satisfy you, and you buy a majority of it back. Then the public hears that a new interest has purchased the soap trust, and that a new and honest administration is to be elected; and once more there is hope for soap. You buy a few more plants, and issue more stocks and bonds, and soap begins to boom, and you sell once more. You can work that regularly every two or three years, for there is always a new crop of investors, and nobody but a few people in Wall Street can possibly keep track of what you are doing."

The Major paused for a while, and sat with a happy smile on his countenance. "You see," he said, "there are floods and floods of wealth, pouring into Wall Street from all over the country. It comes to me like a vision. The crops are growing, the mines and the mills and the factories are working, and here is all the money. People don't like to take it and hide it up their chimneys—few people have chimneys nowadays. They want to invest it; and so you prepare investments for them. Take the street railroads here in New York, for instance. What could be a safer investment than the street railroads of the Metropolis? An absolute monopoly, and traffic growing so fast that construction can't keep up with it. Profits are sure. So people buy street railway stocks and bonds. In this case it's the politicians who organise the construction companies; that's their share, in return for the franchises. The insiders have a new scheme—the best yet; it's like a Gatling gun against bows and arrows. They organise a syndicate, and get the franchises for nothing, and then sell them to the company for millions. They've even sold franchises they didn't own, and railroad lines that hadn't been built. You'll find some improvements charged for four or five times over, and the improvements haven't yet been made. First and last they have paid themselves about thirty million dollars. And, in the meantime, the poor stockholder wonders why he doesn't get his dividends!"

"That's the investment market," the Major continued after a pause; "but of course the biggest reservoirs of wealth are the insurance companies and the banks. It's there the real fortunes are made; you'll find you lose the greater part of your profits, unless you've got your own banks to take your bonds. I heard an amusing story the other day of a man who was manufacturing electrical supplies. He prides himself on being an honest business man, and having nothing to do with Wall Street. His company wanted to extend its business, and it issued a couple of hundred thousand dollars' worth of bonds, and went to the Fidelity Insurance Company and offered them at ninety. 'We aren't buying any bonds just at present,' said they, 'but suppose you try the National Trust Company.' So the man went there, and they offered him eighty for the bonds. That was the best he could do, and in the end he had to take it. And then the trust company turns the bonds over to the insurance company at par. I could name you half a dozen trust companies in New York that are simply syndicates of insurance people for the working of that little game."

The Major paused. "You see it?" he asked.

"Yes, I see," Montague replied.

"Is there a trust company by any chance back of this railroad you are talking of?"

"There is," said Montague; and the Major shrugged his shoulders.

"There you have it," he said. "By and by they will find their first bond issue inadequate to meet the cost of the proposed improvements. The estimates of the engineers will be found too low, and there will be another issue of bonds, and your president's company will get another contract. And then the first thing you know, your president will organise a manufacturing enterprise along the line of his road, and the road will give him secret rebates, and practically carry his goods free; or else he'll organise a private-car line, and make the road pay for the privilege of hauling his cars. Or perhaps he's already got some industrial concern, and is simply building the road as a side issue."

The Major stopped. He saw that Montague was staring at him with an expression of perplexity.

"What's the matter?" he asked.

"Good heavens, Major!" exclaimed the other. "Do you know what road I've been talking about?"

And the Major sank back in his chair and went into a fit of laughter. He laughed until he was purple in the face, and he could hardly find breath to speak.

"I really thought you did!" Montague protested. "It's exactly the situation."

"Oh, dear me!" said the Major, fishing for his pocket handkerchief to wipe the tears from his eyes. "Dear me! It makes me think of our district attorney's lemon story. Did you ever hear it?"

"No," said Montague, "I never did."

"It was one of the bright spots in a dreary reform campaign that we had a few years ago. It seems that our young crusader was giving his audience a few illustrations of how dishonest officials could make money in this city.

"'Let us imagine a case,' he said. 'You are an inspector of fruit, and there is a scarcity of lemons in New York. There are two ships full of lemons on the way, and one ship gets in twenty-four hours ahead. Now the law requires that the fruit be carefully inspected. If you are too careful about it, it will take more than twenty-four hours, and the owner of the cargo will lose a small fortune. So he comes to you and offers you a thousand or two, and you don't stop to open every crate of his lemons.'

"The district attorney told that story at a meeting, and the next morning the newspapers published it. That afternoon he happened to meet a fruit inspector, who was an old friend of his. 'Say, old man,' said the inspector, 'who the devil told you about those lemons?'"

The next morning Montague called at Price's office.

"Mr. Price," he said, "a matter has come up in my discussions with Mr. Haskins about which I thought it necessary to consult you immediately."

"What is it?" asked Price.

"Mr. Haskins informs me that it is understood that the Hill Manufacturing Company is to be favoured in the matter of contracts."

Montague was watching Price narrowly, and he saw his jaw set grimly, and a hostile look come upon his features. Price had been lounging back in his chair; now, slowly, he straightened himself up, as if to receive an attack.

"Well?" he asked.

"Is Mr. Haskins correct?" asked the other.

"He is correct."

"He also stated that you are interested in the company. Is that true?"

"That is true."

"He also stated that the company did not manufacture, but simply sold. Is that true?"

"Yes, that is true."

"Very well, Mr. Price," said Montague. "This is a matter about which we must have an understanding without delay. In my preliminary talks with you I was informed that it was your wish to find a man who should run the road honestly. The situation which you have just outlined to me does not seem to me consistent with that programme."

Montague was prepared for an angry response, but he saw the other make an effort and control himself.

"You must realise, Mr. Montague," he said, "that you are not very familiar with methods in the railroad world. This company of which you speak possesses advantages; it can secure better terms—" Price stopped.

"You mean that it can purchase goods more cheaply than the railroad itself can?" demanded Montague.

"In some cases," began the other.

"Very well, then," he answered. "In any case where it can obtain better terms, there can be no objection to its receiving the contract. But that does not agree with what Mr. Haskins told me; he gave me to understand that we were to prepare to pay a much higher price because it would be necessary to give the contracts to the Hill Manufacturing Company; and that was my reason for coming to see you. I wish to have a distinct understanding with you upon this point. While I am president of the Northern Mississippi Railroad, everything that is purchased by the road will be purchased in fair competition, and the concern which will give us the lowest price for the quality of goods we need will receive our order. That is a matter about which there must be left no possible room for misunderstanding. I trust I have made myself clear?"

"You have made yourself clear," said Price; and so the interview terminated.

CHAPTER XV

Montague went back to his work, but with a heart full of misgivings. He would have liked to persuade himself that that was the end of the episode, but he could not do it. He foresaw that his job as president of a railroad would not be a sinecure.

With all his forebodings, however, he was unprepared for the development which came the next day. Young Curtiss called him up, early in the morning, and asked him to wait at his office. A few minutes later he came in, with evident agitation upon his countenance.

"Montague," he said, "I have something important to tell you. I cannot leave you in ignorance about it. But before I begin, you must understand one thing—that I am taking my future in my hands by telling you. And you must promise me that you will never give the slightest hint that I have spoken to you."

"I will promise," said Montague. "What is it?"

"You must not even let on that you know," added the other. "Price would know that I told you."

"Oh, it's Price!" said Montague. "I'll promise to protect you. What is it?"

"He called up Davenant yesterday afternoon, and told him that you were not to be elected president of the road."

Montague gazed at him in dismay.

"He says you are to be dropped entirely," said the other. "Haskins is to be president. Davenant had to tell me, because I am one of the directors."

"So that's it," Montague whispered to himself.

"Do you know what's the matter?" asked Curtiss.

"Yes, I do," said Montague.

"What is it?"

"It's a long story—just some graft that I wouldn't stand for."

"Oh!" cried Curtiss, with sudden light. "Is it the Hill Manufacturing Company?"

"It is," said Montague.

It was Curtiss's turn to stare in amazement. "My God!" he gasped. "Do you mean that you have thrown up the sponge for that?"

"I haven't thrown up the sponge, by any means," was the answer. "But that's why Price wants to get rid of me."

"But, man!" cried the other. "How perfectly absurd!"

Montague fixed his glance upon him.

"Would you advise me to stand for it?" he asked.

"But, my dear fellow!" said Curtiss. "I've got some stock in that company my-self."

Montague sat in silence—he could think of nothing to say after that.

"What in the world do you suppose you have gone into?" protested the other. "A charity enterprise?" Then he stopped, seeing the look of pain upon his friend's face.

He put a hand upon his arm. "See here, old, man," he said, "this is too bad, honestly. I understand how you feel, and it's a great credit to you; but you are liv-ing in the world, and you have got to be practical. You can't expect to take a railroad and run it as if it were an orphan asylum. You can't expect to do business, if you're going to have notions like that. It's really a shame, to give up a work like this for such a reason."

Montague stiffened. "I assure you I haven't given up yet," he replied grimly.

"But what are you going to do?" protested the other.

"I am going to fight," said he.

"Fight?" echoed Curtiss. "But, man, you are perfectly helpless! Price and Ry-der own the road, and they will do as they please with it."

"You are one of the directors of the road," said Montague. "And you know the situation. You know the pledges upon which the election of the new board was secured. Will you vote for Haskins as president?"

"My God, Montague!" protested the other. "What a thing to ask of me! You know perfectly well that I have no power in the road. All the stock I own, Price gave me, and what can I do? Why, my whole career would be ruined if I were to oppose him."

"In other words," said Montague, "you are a dummy. You are willing to sell your name and your character for a block of stock. You take a position of trust, and you betray it."

The other's face hardened. "Oh, well," he said, "if that's the way you put it—"

"That's not the way I put it!" said Montague. "That is simply the fact."

"But," cried the other, "don't you realise that they have a majority, even with-out me?"

"Perhaps they have," said Montague; "but that is no reason why you should not do what is right."

Curtiss arose. "There is nothing more to be said," he remarked. "I am sorry you take it that way. I tried to do you a service."

"I appreciate that," said Montague, promptly. "For that I shall always be obliged to you."

"In this fight that you propose to make," said the other, "you must not forget that it is I who have brought you this information—"

"Do not trouble about that," said Montague; "I will protect you. No one shall ever know that I had the information."

Montague spent a half an hour pacing up and down his office in thought. Then he called his stenographer, and dictated a letter to his cousin, Mr. Lee, and to each of the three other persons whom he had approached in relation to their votes at the stockholders' meeting. "Certain matters have developed," he wrote, "in connection with the affairs of the Northern Mississippi Railroad, which make me unwilling to accept the position of president. It is also my intention to resign from the board of directors of the road, in which I find myself powerless to prevent the things of which I disapprove."

And then he went on to outline the plan which he intended to carry out, explaining that he offered to those whom he had been the means of influencing, the opportunity to go in with him upon equal terms. He requested them to communicate their decisions by telegraph; and two days later he had heard from them all, and was ready for business.

He called up Stanley Ryder, and made an appointment for an interview.

"Mr. Ryder," he said, "a few weeks ago you talked with me in this office, and asked me to assist you in electing your ticket for the Northern Mississippi Railroad. You said that you wished me to become president of the road, and that the reason for the request was that you wanted a man whom you could depend upon for efficient and honest management. I accepted your offer in good faith; and I have made all arrangements, and put in a great deal of hard work at the task of fitting myself for the position. Now I have learned from Mr. Price's own lips that he has organised a company for the purpose of exploiting the road for his own private benefit. I told him that I was unwilling to stand for anything of the sort. Since then I have been thinking the matter over, and I have concluded that this situation will make it impossible for me to cooperate with Mr. Price. I have concluded, therefore, that it would be best for me to resign my position as a member of the board of directors, and also to withdraw my candidacy as president."

Ryder had avoided Montague's gaze; he sat staring in front of him, and tapping nervously with a pencil upon his desk. It was some time before he answered.

"Mr. Montague," he said, finally, "I am very sorry indeed to hear your decision. But taking all the circumstances into consideration, it seems to me that perhaps it is a wise one."

Again there was a pause.

"You must permit me to thank you for what you have done," Ryder added. "And I trust that this unfortunate episode will not alter our personal relationship."

"Thank you," said Montague, coldly.

He had waited to see what Ryder would say. He waited again, having no mind to help him in his embarrassment.

"As I say," Ryder repeated, "I am very much obliged to you."

"I have no doubt of it," said Montague. "But I trust that you do not expect to end our relationship in any such simple way as that."

He saw Ryder's expression change. "What do you mean?" he asked.

"There is a matter of grave importance which has to be settled before we can part. As you know, I am personally the holder of five hundred shares of Northern Mississippi stock; and to that extent I am interested in the affairs of the road."

"Most certainly," said Ryder, quietly, "but I have nothing to do with that. As a stockholder of the road, you look to the board of directors."

"Besides being a stockholder myself," continued Montague, without heeding this remark, "I have also to consider the interests of the three persons whom I interviewed in your behalf. I was the means of inducing these people to vote for the board which you named. I was the means of inducing them to place themselves in the power of Mr. Price and yourself. This being the case, I consider that my honour is involved, and that I am responsible to them."

"What do you expect to do?" asked Ryder.

"I have written to them, informing them of my intention to withdraw. I have not told them the circumstances, but have simply indicated that I find myself powerless to prevent certain things to which I object. I have told them the course I intend to take, and offered them the opportunity to get out upon the same terms as myself. They have accepted the offer, and to-morrow I should receive their stock certificates, and their authorisation to dispose of them. I have my own certificates here; and I have to say that I consider you are under obligation to purchase this stock at the same price which you paid for the new stock; namely, fifty dollars a share."

Ryder stared at him. "Mr. Montague, you amaze me!" he said.

"I am sorry for that," said Montague. His voice was hard, and there was a grim look upon his face. He fixed his eyes upon Ryder. "Nevertheless," he said, "it will be necessary for you to take the stock."

"I am sorry to have to say it," said Ryder, "but this seems to me impertinent."

"The total number of shares," said Montague, "is thirty-five hundred, and the price of them is one hundred and seventy-five thousand dollars."

The two gazed at each other. Ryder saw the look in Montague's eyes, and he did not repeat his sneer.

"May I ask," he inquired, in a low voice, "what reason you have to believe that I will comply with this extraordinary request?"

"I have a very good reason, as I believe you will perceive," said Montague. "You and Mr. Price have purchased this railroad, and you wish to plunder it. That is your privilege—apparently it is the custom here in Wall Street to play tricks upon the investing public. But you cannot play them upon me, because I know too much."

"May I know what you propose to do?" asked Ryder.

"You certainly may," said the other. "I propose to fight. Until you have purchased my stock and the stock of my friends, I shall remain a director in the railroad, and also a candidate for the position of president. I shall make a contest at the next directors' meeting, and if I fail in my purpose there, I shall carry the fight before the public. I flatter myself that my reputation will count for something in my old home; you will not be able to carry matters with quite the same high hand in Mississippi as you are accustomed to in New York. Also, I shall fight you in the courts. I don't happen to know just what is the law in regard to the plundering of a public-service corporation by its own directors, but I shall be very much surprised if I cannot find some ground upon which to put a stop to it. Also, as you know, I am in possession of facts regarding the means whereby you got your new privileges from the State Legislature—"

Ryder was glaring at him in rage. "Mr. Montague," he cried, "this is black-mail!"

"You may call it that if you please," said the other. "I shall not be afraid to face the charge, if you should see fit to bring it in the courts."

Ryder started to reply, then caught his breath and gasped. When he spoke again, he had mastered himself. "It seems to me a most extraordinary thing," he said. "Surely, Mr. Montague, you cannot feel at liberty to make public what you learned from Mr. Price and myself while you were acting as our confidential adviser! Surely you cannot have forgotten the pledge of secrecy which you gave me here in this office!"

"I have not forgotten it," answered Montague. "And I have considered the matter with the greatest care. I consider that it is you who have violated a pledge. I believe that your violation was a deliberate one—that you had intended it from the very beginning. You assured me that you wished an honest administration of the road. I don't believe that you ever did wish it; I believe that you had no thought whatever except to use me as your tool to secure the control of the railroad, without buying out the remaining stockholders. Having accomplished that purpose, you are perfectly willing to have me retire. In fact, I have made up my mind that you never intended that I should be president—I have all along been suspicious about it. But I can assure you that you have struck the wrong man; you cannot play with me in any such manner. I have no idea whatever of retiring from the railroad and permitting you and Mr. Price to exploit it, and to deprive me of the value of my holdings—"

Montague was going on, but the other interrupted him quickly. "I recognise the justice of what you say there, Mr. Montague," said he. "So far as your own shares are concerned, you are entitled to be bought out. I am sure that that is a fair basis—"

"On the contrary," said Montague, "it's a basis the suggestion of which I take as an insult. I have been the means of placing other people at your mercy. My reputation and my promises were used for that purpose, and to whatever I am entitled, they are entitled equally. There can be no possible settlement except the one which I have offered you."

Ryder could think of nothing more to say. He sat staring at the other. And Montague, who had no desire to prolong the interview, arose abruptly.

"I do not expect you to decide this matter immediately," he said. "I presume that you will wish to consult with Mr. Price. I have made known my terms to you, and I have nothing more to say. Either you will accept the terms, or I shall drop everything else, and prepare to fight you at every step. I expect to receive the stock by this evening's mail, and I am obliged to ask you to favour me with a decision by to-morrow noon, so that we can close the matter up without delay."

And with that he bowed formally and took his departure.

The next morning's mail brought him a letter from William E. Davenant. "My dear Mr. Montague," it read. "It is reported to me that you have thirty-five hundred shares of the stock of the Northern Mississippi Railroad which you desire to sell at fifty dollars a share. If you will bring the stock to my office to-day, I shall be glad to purchase it."

Having received the letters from the South, Montague went immediately. Davenant was formal; but Montague could catch a humorous twinkle in his eye, which seemed to say, quite confidentially, that he appreciated the joke.

"That ends the matter," he said, as he blotted the last of Montague's signatures. "And I trust you will permit me to say, Mr. Montague, that I consider you an exceedingly capable business man."

"I appreciate the compliment," replied Montague, drily.

CHAPTER XVI

Montague was now a gentleman of leisure, comparatively speaking. He had two cases on his hands, but they did not occupy his time as had the prospect of running a railroad. They were contingency cases, and as they were against large corporations, Montague saw a lean year ahead of him. He smiled bitterly to himself as he realised that the only thing which had given him the courage to break with Price and Ryder had been the money which he and his brother Oliver had won by means of a Wall Street "tip."

He received a letter from Alice. "I am going to remain a couple of weeks longer in Newport," she wrote. "Who do you think has invited me—Laura Hegan. She has been perfectly lovely to me, and I go to her place next week. You will be interested to know that I had a long talk with her about you; I took occasion to tell her a few things that she ought to know. She was very nice about it. I am hoping that you will come up for another week end before I leave here. Harry Curtiss is going to spend his vacation here; you might come with him."

Montague smiled to himself as he read this letter. He did not go with Curtiss. But the heat of the city was stifling, and the thought of the surf and the country was alluring, and he went up by way of the Sound one Friday night.

He was invited to dinner at the Hegans'. Jim Hegan was there himself—for the first occasion in three years. Mrs. Hegan declared that it was only because she had gone down to New York and fetched him.

It was the first time that Montague had ever been with Hegan for any length of time. He watched him with interest, for the man was a fascinating problem to him. He was so calm and serene—always courteous and friendly. But what was there behind the mask, Montague wondered. For forty years this man had toiled and fought in the arena of Wall Street, and with only one purpose and one thought in life, so far as Montague knew—the piling up of money. Jim Hegan indulged himself in none of the pleasures of rich men. He had no hobbies, and he seldom went into company. In his busy times it was said that he would use a dozen secretaries, and wear them all out. He was a gigantic engine which drove all day and all night—a machine for the making of money.

Montague did not care much for money himself, and he wondered about it. What did the man want it for? What did he expect to accomplish by it? What was the moral code, the outlook upon life, of a man who gave all his time to heaping up money? What reason did he give to himself for his own career? Some reason he must have, or he could not be so calm and cheerful. Or could it be that he had no thoughts about it at all? Was it simply a blind instinct with him? Was he an animal whose nature it was to make money, and who was untroubled by any scruples? This last idea seemed rather uncanny to Montague; he found himself watching Jim Hegan with a kind of awe; thinking of him as some terrible elemental force, blind and unconscious, like the lightning or the tornado.

For Jim Hegan was one of the wreckers. His fortune had been made by the methods which Major Venable had outlined, by buying aldermen and legislatures and governors; by getting franchises for nothing and selling them for millions; by organising huge swindles and unloading them upon the public. And here he sat upon the veranda of his home, in the twilight of an August evening, smoking a cigar and telling about an orphan asylum he had founded!

He was cheerful and kindly; he was even benevolent. And could it be that he had no idea of the trail of ruin and distress which he had left behind him? Montague found himself possessed by a sudden desire to penetrate beneath that reserve; to spring at the man and surprise him with some sudden question; to get at the reality of him, to know him as he was. This air of power and masterfulness, surely that must be the mask that he wore. And how was he to himself? When he was alone with his own conscience? Surely there must come doubt and wonder, unhappiness and loneliness! Surely, then, the lives that he had wrecked must come back to plague him! Surely the memories of treachery and cruelty must make him wince!

And from Hegan, Montague's thoughts went to his daughter. She, too, was serene and stately; Montague wondered what was in her mind. How much did she know about her father's career? Surely she could not have persuaded herself that all that she had heard was calumny. There might be question about this offence or that, but of the great broad facts there could be no question. And did she justify it and excuse it; or was she, too, secretly unhappy? And was this the reason for her pride, and for her bitter speeches? It was a continual topic of chatter in Society, how Laura Hegan had withdrawn herself from all of her mother's affairs, and was interesting herself in work in the slums. Could it be that Nemesis had overtaken Jim Hegan in the form of his daughter? That she was the conscience by which he was to be tormented?

Jim Hegan never talked about his affairs. In all the time that Montague spent with him during his two days at Newport, he gave just one hint for the other to go upon. "Money?" he remarked, that evening. "I don't care about money. Money is just chips to me."

Life was a game, and the chips were dollars! What he had played for was power! And suddenly Montague seemed to see the career of this man, unrolled before him like a panorama. He had begun life as an office-boy; and above him were all the heights of business and finance; and the ladder by which to scale them was money. There were rivals with whom he fought; and the overcoming of these rivals had occupied all his time and his thought. If he had bought legislatures, it was because his rivals were trying to buy them. And perhaps then he did not even know that he was a wrecker; perhaps he would not have believed it if anyone had told him! He had travelled all the long journey of his life, trampling out opposition and crushing everything before him, nourishing in his heart the hope that some day, when he had attained to mastery, when there were no more rivals to oppose and thwart him—then he would be free to do good. Then he would no longer have to be a wrecker!

And perhaps that was the meaning of his pitiful little effort—an orphan asylum! It seemed to Montague that the gods must shake with Olympian laughter when they contemplated the spectacle of Jim Hegan and his orphan asylum: Jim Hegan, who could have filled a score of orphan asylums with the children of the men whom he had driven to ruin and suicide!

These thoughts were seething in Montague's mind, and they would not let him rest. Perhaps it was just as well that he did not stay too long that evening. After all, what was the use? Jim Hegan was what circumstances had made him. Vain was the dream of peace and well doing—there was always another rival! There was a new battle on just at present, if one might believe the gossip of the Street; Hegan and Wyman were at each other's throats. They would fight out their quarrel, and there was no way to prevent them—even though they pulled down the pillars of the nation about each other's heads.

As to just what these men were doing in their struggles, Montague got new information every day. The next morning, while he was sitting on the piazza of one of the hotels watching the people, he recognised a familiar face, and greeted the young engineer, Lieutenant Long, who came and sat down beside him.

"Well," said Montague, "have you heard anything from our friend Gamble?"

"He's back in the bosom of his family again," said the young officer. "He got tired of the splurge."

"Great fellow, Gamble," said Montague.

"I liked him very much," said the Lieutenant. "He's not beautiful to look at, but his heart's in the right place."

Montague thought for a moment, then asked, "Did he ever send you your oil specifications?"

"You bet he did!" said the other. "And say, they were great! The Department will think I'm an expert."

"Indeed," said Montague.

"It was a precious lucky thing for me," said the officer. "I'd have been in quite a predicament, you know."

He paused for a moment. "You cannot imagine," he said, "the position that we naval officers are in. Do you know, I think some word must have got out about that contract."

"You don't say so," said Montague, with interest.

"I do. By gad, I thought of writing to headquarters about it. I was approached no less than three times!"

"Indeed!"

"Fancy," said the officer. "A young chap got himself introduced to me by one of my friends here. He stuck by me the whole evening, and afterwards, as we were strolling home, he opened up on me in this fashion. He'd heard from a friend in Washington that I was one of those who had been asked to write specifications for the oil contracts of the Navy; and he had some friends who were interested in oil, and who might be able to advise me. He hinted that it might be a good thing for me. Just think of it!"

"I can imagine it was unpleasant."

"I tell you, it sets a man to thinking," said the Lieutenant. "You know the men in our service are exposed to that sort of thing all the time, and some of them are trying to live a good deal higher than their incomes warrant. It's a thing that we've all got to look out for; I can stand graft in politics and in business, but when it comes to the Army and Navy—I tell you, that's where I'm ready to fight."

Montague said nothing. He could think of nothing to say.

"Gamble said something about your being interested in a fight against the Steel Trust," said the other. "Is that so?"

"It was so," replied Montague. "I'm out of it now."

"What we were saying made me think of the Steel Trust," said the Lieutenant. "We get some glimpses of that concern in the Navy, you know."

"I hadn't thought of that," said Montague.

"Ask any man in the service about it," said the Lieutenant. "It's an old scar that we carry around in our souls—it won't heal. I mean the armour-plate frauds."

"Sure enough!" said Montague. He carried a long list of indictments against the steel kings in his mind; but he had forgotten this one.

"I know about it particularly," the other continued, "because my father was on the board of investigation fifteen years ago. I am disposed to be a little keen on the subject, because what he found out at that time practically caused his death."

Montague darted a keen glance at the young officer, who sat gazing ahead in sombre thought. "Fancy how a naval man feels," he said. "We are told that our ships are going to the Pacific, and any hour the safety of the nation may depend upon them! And they are covered with rotten armour plate that was made by old Harrison, and sold to the Government for four or five times what it cost. Take one case that I know about—the Oregon. I've got a brother on board her to-day. During the Spanish War the whole country was watching her and praying for her. And I could go on board that battleship and put my finger on the spot in her conning-tower that has a series of blow-holes straight through the middle of it—holes that old Harrison had drilled through and plugged up with an iron bar. If ever that plate was struck by a shell, it would splinter like so much glass."

Montague listened, half dazed. "Can one see that?" he cried.

"See it? No!" said the officer. "It's all on the inside of the plate, of course. When they got through with their dirty work, they would treat the surface, and who would ever know the difference?"

"But then, how can YOU know it?" asked Montague.

"I?" said the other. "Because my father had laid before him the history of that plate from the hour it was made until it was put in: the original copies of the doctored shop records, and the affidavits of the man who did the work. He had the same thing in a hundred other cases. I know the man who has the papers at this day."

"You see," continued the Lieutenant, after a pause, "the Government's specifications required that each plate should undergo an elaborate set of treatments; and the shop records of each plate were kept. But, of course, it cost enormous sums to get these treatments right, and even then hundreds of the plates would be bad. So when the shop records came up to the office, young Ingham and Davidson would go over them and edit them and bring them up to standard—that's the way those brilliant young fellows made all the money that they are spending on chorus girls and actresses to-day. They would have these shop records recopied, but they did not always tear up the old ones, and somebody in the office hid them, and that was how the Government got hold of the story."

"It sounds almost incredible!" exclaimed Montague.

"Take the story of plate H619, of the Oregon," said the Lieutenant. "That was one of a whole group of plates, which was selected for the ballistic tests at Indian Head. After it had been selected, it was taken back into the company's shops at night, and secretly retreated three times. And then of course it passed the tests, and the whole group was passed with it!"

"What was done about it?" Montague asked.

"Nothing much was ever done about it," said the other. "The Government could not afford to let the real facts get out. But, of course, the insiders in the Navy knew it, and the memory will last as long as the ships last. As I say, it killed my father."

"But weren't the men punished at all?"

"There was a Board appointed to try the case, and they awarded the Government about six hundred thousand dollars' damages. There's a man here in this hotel now who could tell you that story straight from the inside." And the Lieutenant paused and looked about him. Suddenly he stood up, and went to the railing and called to a man who was passing on the other side of the street.

"Hello, Bates," he said, "come here."

"Oh! Bates of the Express!" said Montague.

"You know him, do you?" asked the Lieutenant. "Hello, Bates! Have they put you on the Society notes?"

"I'm hunting interviews," replied the other. "How do you do, Mr. Montague? Glad to see you again."

"Come up," said the Lieutenant, "and have a seat."

"I was talking to Mr. Montague about the armour-plate frauds," he added, when the other had drawn up a chair. "I told him you knew the story of the Government's investigation. Bates comes from Pittsburg, you know."

"Yes, I know it," Montague replied.

"That was the first newspaper story I ever worked on," said Bates. "Of course, the Pittsburg papers didn't print the facts, but I got them all the same. And afterwards I came to know intimately a lawyer in Pittsburg who had charge of a secret investigation; and every time I read in the newspapers that old Harrison has given a new library, it sets my blood to boiling all over again."

"I sometimes think," put in the other, "that if somebody could be found to tell that story to the American people, they would rise up and drive the old scoundrel out of the country."

"You could never bring it home to him," said Bates; "he's too cunning for that. He has always turned his dirty work over to other people. You remember during the big strike how he ran away and left the job to William Roberts; and after it was all over, he came back smiling."

"And then buying out the Government to keep himself from being punished!" said the Lieutenant, savagely.

Montague turned and looked at him. "What is that?"

"That is the story that Bates's lawyer friend can tell," was the reply. "The board of officers awarded six hundred thousand dollars' damages to the Government; and the case was appealed to the President of the United States, and he sold out the Navy!"

"Sold it out!" gasped Montague.

The officer shrugged his shoulders. "That's what I call it," he said. "One day old Harrison startled the country by making a speech in support of the President's policy of tariff reform; and the next day the lawyer got word that the award was to be scaled down about seventy-five per cent!"

"And then," added Bates, "William Roberts came down from Pittsburg, and bought up the Democratic party in Congress; and so the country got neither the damages nor the tariff reform. And then a few years later old Harrison sold out to the Steel Trust, and got off with a four-hundred-million-dollar mortgage on the American people!"

Bates sank back in his chair. "It's not a very pleasant topic for a holiday afternoon," he said. "But I can't forget about it. It's this kind of thing that does it, you know—this." And he waved his hand about at the gay assemblage. "The women spending their money on dresses and diamonds, and the men tearing the country to pieces to get it. You'll hear people talk about it—they say these idle rich harm nobody but themselves; but I tell you they spread a trail of corruption wherever they go. Don't you believe that, Mr. Montague?"

"I believe it," said he.

"Take these New England towns," said Bates; "and look at the people in them. The ones who had any energy got up and went West years ago; and those who are left haven't any jaw-bones. Did you ever notice it? And it's just the same, wherever this pleasure crowd comes; it turns the men into boarding-house keepers and lackeys, and the girls into waitresses and prostitutes."

"They learn to take tips!" put in the Lieutenant.

"Everything they've got is for sale to city people," said Bates. "Politically, there isn't a rottener little corner in the whole United States of America than this same Rhode Island—and how much that's saying, you can imagine. You can buy votes on election day as you'd buy herrings, and there's not the remotest effort at reform, nor any hope of it."

"You speak bitterly," said Montague.

"I am bitter," said Bates. "But it doesn't often break out. I hold my tongue, and stew in my own juice. We newspaper men see the game, you know. We are behind the scenes, and we see the sawdust put into the dolls. We have to work in this rottenness all the time, and some of us don't like it, I can tell you. But what can we do?"

He shrugged his shoulders. "I spend my time getting facts together, and nine times out of ten my newspaper won't print them."

"I should think you'd quit," said the other, in a low voice.

"What better can I do?" asked the reporter. "I have the facts; and once in a while there comes an explosion, and I get my chance. So I stick at the job. I can't but believe that if you keep putting these things before the people, sometime, sooner or later, they will do something. Sometime there will come a man who has a conscience and a voice, and who won't sell out. Don't you think so, Mr. Montague?"

"Yes," said Montague, "I think so."

CHAPTER XVII

The summer wore on. At the end of August Alice returned from Newport for a couple of days, having some shopping to do before she joined the Prentices at their camp in the Adirondacks.

Society had here a new way of enjoying itself. People built themselves elaborate palaces in the wilderness, and lived in a fantastic kind of rusticity, with every luxury of civilisation included. For this life one needed an entirely separate wardrobe, with doeskin hunting-boots and mountain-climbing skirts—all very picturesque and expensive. It reminded Montague of a jest that he had heard about Mrs. Vivie Patton, whose husband had complained of the expensiveness of her costumes, and requested her to wear simpler dresses. "Very well," she said, "I will get a lot of simple dresses immediately."

Alice spent one evening at home, and she took her cousin into her confidence. "I've an idea, Allan, that Harry Curtiss is going to ask me to marry him. I thought it was right to tell you about it."

"I've had a suspicion of it," said Montague, smiling.

"Harry has a feeling you don't like him," said the girl. "Is that true?"

"No," replied Montague, "not precisely that." He hesitated.

"I don't understand about it," she continued. "Do you think I ought not to marry him?"

Montague studied her face. "Tell me," he said, "have you made up your mind to marry him?"

"No," she answered, "I cannot say that I have."

"If you have," he added, "of course there is no use in my talking about it."

"I wish you would tell me just what happened between you and him," exclaimed the girl.

"It was simply," said Montague, "that I found that Curtiss was doing, in a business way, something which I considered improper. Other people are doing it, of course—he has that excuse."

"Well, he has to earn a living," said Alice.

"I know," said the other; "and if he marries, he will have to earn still more of a living. He will only place himself still tighter in the grip of these forces of corruption."

"But what did he do?" asked Alice, anxiously. Montague told her the story.

"But, Allan," she said, "I don't see what there is so very bad about that. Don't Ryder and Price own the railroad?"

"They own some of it," said Montague. "Other people own some."

"But the other people have to take their chances," protested the girl; "if they choose to have anything to do with men like that."

"You are not familiar with business," said the other, "and you don't appreciate the situation. Curtiss was elected a director—he accepted a position of trust."

"He simply did it as a favour to Price," said she. "If he hadn't done it, Price would only have got somebody else. As you say, Allan, I don't understand much about it, but it seems to me it isn't fair to blame a young man who has to make his way in the world, and who simply does what he finds everybody else doing. Of course, you know best about your own affairs; but it always did seem to me that you go out of your way to look for scruples."

Montague smiled sadly. "That sounds very much like what he said, Alice. I guess you have made up your mind to marry him, after all."

Alice set out, accompanied by Oliver, who was bound for Bertie Stuyvesant's imitation baronial castle, in another part of the mountains. Betty Wyman was also to be there, and Oliver was to spend a full month. But three days later Montague received a telegram, saying that his brother would arrive in New York shortly after eight that morning, and to wait at his home for him. Montague suspected what this meant; and he had time enough to think it over and make up his mind. "Well?" he said, when Oliver came in. "It's come again, has it?"

"Yes," said Oliver, "it has."

"Another 'sure thing'?"

"Dead sure. Are you coming in?" Oliver asked, after a moment.

Montague shook his head. "No," he said. "I think once was enough for me."

"You don't mean that, Allan!" protested the other.

"I mean it," was the reply.

"But, my dear fellow, that is perfectly insane! I have information straight from the inside—it's as certain as the sunrise!"

"I have no doubt of that," responded Montague. "But I am through with gambling in Wall Street. I've seen enough of it, Oliver, and I'm sick of it. I don't like the emotions it causes in me—I don't like the things it makes me do."

"You found the money came in useful, didn't you?" said Oliver, sarcastically.

"Yes, I can use what I've got."

"And when that's gone?"

"I don't know about that yet. But I'll find some way that I like better."

"All right," said Oliver; "it's your own lookout. I will make my own little pile."

They rode down town in a cab together. "Where does your information come from this time?" asked Montague.

"The same source," was the reply.

"And is it Transcontinental again?"

"No," said Oliver; "it's another stock."

"What is it?"

"It's Mississippi Steel," was the answer.

Montague turned and stared at him. "Mississippi Steel!" he gasped.

"Why, yes," said Oliver. "What's that to you?" he added, in perplexity.

"Mississippi Steel!" Montague ejaculated again. "Why, didn't you know about my relations with the Northern Mississippi Railroad?"

"Of course," said Oliver; "but what's that got to do with Mississippi Steel?"

"But it's Price who is managing the deal—the man who owns the Mississippi Steel Company!"

"Oh," said the other, "I had forgotten that." Oliver's duties in Society did not give him much time to ask about his brother's affairs.

"Allan," he added quickly, "you won't say anything about it!"

"It's none of my business now," answered the other. "I'm out of it. But naturally I am interested to know. What is it—a raid on the stock?"

"It's going down," said Oliver.

Montague sat staring ahead of him. "It must be the Steel Trust," he whispered, half to himself.

"Nothing more likely," was the reply. "My tip comes from that direction."

"Do you suppose they are going to try to break Price?"

"I don't know; I guess they could do it if they made up their mind to."

"But he owns a majority of the stock!" said Montague. "They can't take it away from him outright."

"Not if he's got it locked up in his safe," was the reply; "and if he's got no debts or obligations. But suppose he's overextended; and suppose some bank has loaned him money on the stock—what then?"

Montague was now keenly interested. He went with his brother while the latter drew his money from the bank, and called at his brokers and ordered them to sell Mississippi Steel. The other was called away then by an engagement in court, which occupied him for several hours; when he came out, he made for the nearest ticker, and the first figures he saw were Mississippi Steel—quoted at nearly twenty points below the price of the morning!

The bare figures were eloquent to him of many tragedies; they brought before him half a dozen different personalities, with their triumphs and despairs. He could read in them the story of a Titan struggle. Oliver had made his killing; but what of Price and Ryder? Montague knew that most of Price's stock was hypothecated at the Gotham Trust. And now what would become of it? And what would become of the Northern Mississippi?

He bought the afternoon papers. Their columns were full of the sensational events of the day. The bottom had dropped out of Mississippi Steel, as they phrased it. The wildest rumours were afloat. The Company was known to be making enormous extensions, and it was said to have overreached itself; there were whispers that its officers had been speculating, that the Company would be unable to meet the next quarterly payment upon its bonds, that a receivership would be necessary. There were hints that the concern was to be taken over by the Trust, but this was vigorously denied by officers of the latter.

All of which had come like a bolt out of the blue. To Montague it was an amazing and terrible thing. It counted little to him that he was out of the struggle himself; that he no longer had anything to lose personally. He was like a man who had been through an earthquake, and who stood and stared at a gaping crack in the ground. Even though he was safe at the moment, he could not forget that this was the earth upon which he had to spend the rest of his life, and that the next crack might open where he stood.

Montague could not see that there was the least chance for Price and Ryder; he pictured them bowled clean out, and he would not have been surprised to read that they were ruined. But apparently they weathered the storm. The episode passed with no more than a crop of rumours. Mississippi Steel did not go back, however; and he noticed that Northern Mississippi stock had also "gone off" eight or ten points on the curb.

It was a period of great anxiety in the financial world. Men felt the unrest, even though they could not give definite reasons. There had been several panics in the stock market throughout the summer; and leading financiers and railroad presidents seemed to have got the habit of prognosticating the ruin of the country every time they made a speech at a banquet.

But apparently men could not agree about the causes of the trouble. Some insisted that it was owing to the speeches of the President, to his attacks upon the great business interests of the country. Others maintained that the world's supply of capital was inadequate, and pointed out the destruction of great wars and earthquakes and fires. Others argued that there was not enough currency to do the country's business. Now and again there rose above the din the shrill voice of some radical who declared that the stock collapses had been brought about deliberately; but such statements seemed so preposterous that they were received with ridicule whenever they were heeded at all. To Montague the idea that there were men in the country sufficiently powerful to wreck its business, and sufficiently unscrupulous to use their power—the idea seemed to him sensational and absurd.

But he had a talk about it one evening with Major Venable, who laughed at him. The Major named half a dozen men—Waterman and Duval and Wyman among them—who controlled ninety per cent of the banks in the Metropolis. They controlled all three of the big insurance companies, with their resources of four or five hundred million dollars; one of them controlled a great transcontinental railroad system, which alone kept a twenty-or thirty-million dollar "surplus" for stock-gambling purposes.

"If any two or three of those men were to make up their minds," declared the Major, "they could wreck the business of this country in a day. If there were stocks they wanted to pick up, they could knock them to any price they chose."

"How would they do it?" asked the other.

"There are many ways. You noticed that the last big slump began with the worst scarcity of money the Street has known for years. Now suppose those men should gradually accumulate a lot of cash in the banks, and make an agreement to withdraw it at a certain hour. Suppose that the banks that they own, and the banks where they own directors, and the insurance companies which they control—suppose they all did the same! Can't you imagine the scurrying around for money, the calling in of loans, the rush to realise on holdings? And when you have a public as nervous as ours is, when you have credit stretched to the breaking-point, and everybody involved—don't you see the possibilities?"

"It seems like playing with dynamite," said Montague.

"It's not as bad as it might be," was the answer. "We are saved by the fact that these big men don't get together. There are too many jealousies and quarrels. Waterman wants easy money, and gets the Treasury Department to lend ten millions; Wyman, on the other hand, wants high prices, and he goes into the Street and borrows fifteen millions; and so it goes. There are a half dozen big banking groups in the city—"

"They are still competing, then?" asked Montague.

"Oh, yes," said the Major. "For instance, they fight for the patronage of the out-of-town banks. The banks all over the country send their reserves to New York; it's a matter of four or five hundred million dollars, and that's an enormous power. Some of the big banks are agents for one or two thousand institutions, and there's the keenest kind of struggle going on. It's not an easy thing to follow, of course; but they offer all kinds of secret advantages—there's more graft in it than you'd find in Russia."

"I see," said Montague.

"There's only one thing about which the banks are agreed," continued the other. "That is their hatred of the independent trust companies. You see, the national banks have to keep twenty-five per cent reserve, while the trust companies only keep five per cent. Consequently they do a faster business, and they offer four per cent, and advertise widely, and they are simply driving the banks to the wall. There are over fifty of them in this city alone, and they've got over a billion of the people's money. And, mark my word, that is where you'll see blood spilled before long."

And Montague was destined to remember the prophecy.

A couple of days later occurred an incident which gave him a new light upon the situation. His brother came around one afternoon, with a letter in his hand. "Allan," he said, "what do you make of this?"

Montague glanced at it, and saw that it was from Lucy Dupree.

"My dear Ollie," it read. "I find myself in an embarrassing position, owing to the fact that some business arrangements upon which I had counted have fallen through. The money which I brought with me to New York is nearly all gone, and, as you can understand, my position as a stranger is a difficult one. I have a note which Stanley Ryder gave me for my stock. It is for a hundred and forty thousand dollars, and is due in three months. It occurred to me that you might know someone who has some ready cash, and who would like to purchase the note. I should be very glad to sell it for a hundred and thirty thousand. Please do not mention it except in confidence."

"Now, what in the world do you suppose that means?" said Oliver.

The other stared at him. "I am sure I can't imagine," he replied.

"How much money did Lucy have when she came here?"

"She had three or four thousand dollars. But then, she got ten thousand from Stanley Ryder when he bought that stock."

"She can't have spent any such sum of money!" exclaimed Oliver.

"She may have invested it," said the other, thoughtfully.

"Invested nothing!" exclaimed Oliver.

"But that's not what puzzles me," said Montague. "Why doesn't Ryder discount the note himself?"

"That's just it! What business has he letting Lucy hawk his notes about the town?"

"Maybe he doesn't know it. Maybe she's trying to keep her affairs from him."

"Nonsense!" Oliver replied. "I don't believe anything of the sort. What I think is that Stanley Ryder is doing it himself."

"How do you mean?" asked Montague, in perplexity.

"I believe that he is trying to get his own note discounted. I don't believe that Lucy would ever come to us of herself. She'd starve first. She's too proud."

"But Stanley Ryder!" protested Montague. "The president of the Gotham Trust Company!"

"That's all right," said Oliver. "It's his own note, and not the Trust Company's; and I'll wager you he's hard up for cash. There was a big realty company that failed the other day, and I saw that Ryder was one of the stockholders. And he's been hit by that Mississippi Steel slump, and I'll wager you he's scurrying around to raise money. It's just like Lucy, too. Before he gets through, he'll take every dollar she owns."

Montague said nothing for a minute or two. Suddenly he clenched his hands. "I must go up and see her," he said.

Lucy had moved from the expensive hotel to which Oliver had taken her, and rented an apartment on Riverside Drive. Montague went up early the next morning.

She came and stood in the doorway of the drawing-room and looked at him. He saw that she was paler than she had been, and with lines of pain upon her face.

"Allan!" she said. "I thought you would come some day. How could you stay away so long?"

"I didn't think you would care to see me," he said.

She did not answer. She came and sat down, continuing to gaze at him, with a kind of fear in her eyes.

Suddenly he stretched out his hands to her. "Lucy!" he exclaimed. "Won't you come away from here? Won't you come, before it is too late?"

"Where can I go?" she asked.

"Anywhere!" he said. "Go back home."

"I have no home," she answered.

"Go away from Stanley Ryder," said Montague. "He has no right to let you throw yourself away."

"He has not let me, Allan," said Lucy. "You must not blame him—I cannot bear it." She stopped.

"Lucy," he said, after a pause, "I saw that letter you wrote to Oliver."

"I thought so," said she. "I asked him not to. It wasn't fair—"

"Listen," he said. "Will you tell me what that means? Will you tell me honestly?"

"Yes, I will tell you," she said, in a low voice.

"I will help you if you are in trouble," he continued; "but I will not help Stanley Ryder. If you are permitting him to use you—"

"Allan!" she gasped, in sudden excitement. "You don't think that he knew I wrote?"

"Yes, I thought it," said he.

"Oh, how could you!" she cried.

"I knew that he was in trouble."

"Yes, he is in trouble, and I wanted to help him, if I could. It was a crazy idea, I know; but it was all I could think of."

"Oh, I understand," said Montague.

"And don't you see that I cannot leave him?" exclaimed Lucy. "Now of all times—when he needs help—when his enemies have surrounded him? I'm the only person in the world who cares anything about him—who really understands him—"

Montague could think of nothing to say.

"I know how it hurts you," said Lucy, "and don't think that I have not cared. It is a thought that never leaves me! But some day I know that you will understand; and the rest of the world—I don't care what the world says."

"All right, Lucy," he answered, sadly. "I see that I can't be of any help to you. I won't trouble you any more."

CHAPTER XVIII

Another month passed by. Montague was buried in his work, and he caught but faint echoes of the storm that rumbled in the financial world. It was a thing which he thought of with wonder in future times—that he should have had so little idea of what was coming. He seemed to himself like some peasant who digs with bent head in a field, while armies are marshalling for battle all around him; and who is startled suddenly by the crash of conflict, and the bursting of shells about his head.

There came another great convulsion of the stock market. Stewart, the young Lochinvar out of the West, made an attempt to corner copper. One heard wild rumours in relation to the crash which followed. Some said that a traitor had sold out the pool; others, that there had been a quarrel among the conspirators. However that might be, copper broke, and once more there were howling mobs on the curb, and a shudder throughout the financial district. Then suddenly, like a thunderbolt, came tidings that a conference of the big bankers had decreed that the young Lochinvar should be forced out of his New York banks. There were rumours that other banks were involved, and that there were to be more conferences. Then a couple of days later came the news that all the banks of Cummings the Ice King were in trouble, and that he too had been forced from the field.

Montague had never seen anything like the excitement in Wall Street. Everyone he met had a new set of rumours, wilder than the last. It was as if a great rift in the earth had suddenly opened before the eyes of the banking community. But Montague was at an important crisis in a suit which he had taken up against the Tobacco Trust; and he had no idea that he was in any way concerned in what was taking place. The newspapers were all making desperate efforts to allay the anxiety—they said that all the trouble was over, that Dan Waterman had come to the rescue of the imperilled institutions. And Montague believed what he read, and went his way.

Three or four days after the crisis had developed, he had an engagement to dine with his friend Harvey. Montague was tired after a long day in court, and as no one else was coming, and he did not intend to dress, he walked up town from his office to Harvey's hotel, a place of entertainment much frequented by Society people. Harvey rented an entire floor, and had had it redecorated especially to suit his taste.

"How do you do, Mr. Montague?" said the clerk, when he went to the desk. "Mr. Harvey left a note for you."

Montague opened the envelope, and read a hurried scrawl to the effect that Harvey had just got word that a bank of which he was a director was in trouble, and that he would have to attend a meeting that evening. He had telephoned both to Montague's office and to his hotel, without being able to find him.

Montague turned away. He had no place to go, for his own family was out of town; consequently he strolled into the dining-room and ate by himself. Afterwards he came out into the lobby, and bought several evening papers, and stood glancing over the head-lines.

Suddenly a man strode in at the door, and he looked up. It was Winton Duval, the banker; Montague had never seen him since the time when they had parted in Mrs. Winnie's drawing-room. He did not see Montague, but strode past, his brows knit in thought, and entered one of the elevators.

A moment later Montague heard a voice at his side. "How do you do, Mr. Montague?"

He turned. It was Mr. Lyon, the manager of the hotel, whom Siegfried Harvey had once introduced to him. "Have you come to attend the conference?" said he.

"Conference?" said Montague. "No."

"There's a big meeting of the bankers here to-night," remarked the other. "It's not supposed to be known, so don't mention it.—How do you do, Mr. Ward?" he added, to a man who went past. "That's David Ward."

"Ah," said Montague. Ward was known in the Street by the nickname of Waterman's "office-boy." He was a high-salaried office-boy—Waterman paid him a hundred thousand a year to manage one of the big insurance companies for him.

"So he's here, is he?" said Montague.

"Waterman is here himself," said Lyon. "He came in by the side entrance. It's something especially secret, I gather—they've rented eight rooms upstairs, all connecting. Waterman will go in at one end, and Duval at the other, and so the reporters won't know they're together!"

"So that's the way they work it!" said Montague, with a smile.

"I've been looking for some of the newspaper men," Lyon added. "But they don't seem to have caught on."

He strolled away, and Montague stood watching the people in the lobby. He saw Jim Hegan come and enter the elevator, in company with an elderly man whom he recognised as Bascom, the president of the Empire Bank, Waterman's own institution. He saw two other men whom he knew as leading bankers of the System; and then, as he glanced toward the desk, he saw a tall, broad-shouldered man, who had been talking to the clerk, turn around, and reveal himself as his friend Bates, of the Express.

"Humph!" thought Montague. "The newspaper men are 'on,' after all."

He saw Bates's glance sweep the lobby and rest upon him. Montague made a movement of greeting with his hand, but Bates did not reply. Instead, he strolled toward him, went by without looking at him, and, as he passed, whispered in a low, quick voice, "Please come into the writing-room!"

Montague stood for a moment, wondering; then he followed. Bates went to a corner of the room and seated himself. Montague joined him.

The reporter darted a quick glance about, then began hastily: "Excuse me, Mr. Montague, I didn't want anyone to see us talking. I want to ask you to do me a favour."

"What is it?"

"I'm running down a story. It is something very important. I can't explain it to you now, but I want to get a certain room in this hotel. You have an opportunity to do me the service of a lifetime. I'll explain it to you as soon as we are alone."

"What do you want me to do?" asked Montague.

"I want to rent room four hundred and seven," said Bates. "If I can't get four hundred and seven, I want five hundred and seven, or six hundred and seven. I daren't ask for it myself, because the clerk knows me. But he'll let you have it."

"But how shall I ask for it?" said Montague.

"Just ask," said Bates; "it will be all right."

Montague looked at him. He could see that his friend was labouring under great excitement.

"Please! please!" he whispered, putting his hand on Montague's arm. And Montague said, "All right."

He got up and strolled into the lobby again, and went to the desk.

"Good evening, Mr. Montague," said the clerk. "Mr. Harvey hasn't returned."

"I know it," said Montague. "I would like to get a room for the evening. I would like to be near a friend. Could I get a room on the fourth floor?"

"Fourth?" said the clerk, and turned to look at his schedule on the wall. "Whereabouts—front or back?"

"Have you four hundred and five?" asked Montague.

"Four hundred and five? No, that's rented. We have four hundred and one— four hundred and six, on the other side of the hall—four hundred and seven—"

"I'll take four hundred and seven," said Montague.

"Four dollars a day," said the clerk, as he took down the key.

Not having any baggage, Montague paid in advance, and followed the boy to the elevator. Bates followed him, and another man, a little wiry chap, carrying a dress-suit case, also entered with them, and got out at the fourth floor.

The boy opened the door, and the three men entered the room. The boy turned on the light, and proceeded to lower the shades and the windows, and to do enough fixing to earn his tip. Then he went out, closing the door behind him; and Bates sank upon the bed and put his hands to his forehead and gasped, "Oh, my God."

The young man who accompanied him had set down his suit-case, and he now sat down on one of the chairs, and proceeded to lean back and laugh hilariously.

Montague stood staring from one to the other.

"My God, my God!" said Bates, again. "I hope I may never go through with a job like this—-I believe my hair will be grey before morning!"

"You forget that you haven't told me yet what's the matter," said Montague.

"Sure enough," said Bates.

And suddenly he sat up and stared at him.

"Mr. Montague," he exclaimed, "don't go back on us! You've no idea how I've been working—and it will be the biggest scoop of a lifetime. Promise me that you won't give us away!"

"I cannot promise you," said Montague, laughing in spite of himself, "until you tell me what it is."

"I'm afraid you are not going to like it," said Bates. "It was a mean trick to play on you, but I was desperate. I didn't dare take the risk myself, and Rodney wasn't dressed for the occasion."

"You haven't introduced your friend," said Montague.

"Oh, excuse me," said Bates. "Mr. Rodney, one of our office-men."

"And now tell me about it," said Montague, taking a seat.

"It's the conference," said Bates. "We got a tip about it an hour or so ago. They meet in the room underneath us."

"What of it?" asked Montague.

"We want to find out what's going on," said Bates.

"But how?"

"Through the window. We've got a rope here." And Bates pointed toward the suitcase.

Montague stared at him, dumfounded. "A rope!" he gasped. "You are going to let him down from the window?"

"Sure thing," said Bates; "it's a rear window, and quite safe."

"But for Heaven's sake, man!" gasped the other, "suppose the rope breaks?"

"Oh, it won't break," was the reply; "we've got the right sort of rope."

"But how will you ever get him up again?" Montague exclaimed.

"That's all right," said Bates; "he can climb up, or else we can let him down to the ground. We've got rope enough."

"But suppose he loses his grip! Suppose—"

"That's all right," said Bates, easily. "You leave that to Rodney. He's nimble— he began life as a steeple-jack. That's why I picked him."

Rodney grinned. "I'll take my chances," he said.

Montague gazed from one to the other, unable to think of another word to say.

"Tell me, Mr. Bates," he asked finally, "do you often do this in your profession?"

"I've done it once before," was the reply. "I wanted some photographs in a murder case. I've often tried back windows, and fire-escapes, and such things. I used to be a police reporter, you know, and I learned bad habits."

"But," said Montague, "suppose you were caught?"

"Oh, pshaw!" said he. "The office would soon fix that up. The police never bother a newspaper man."

There was a pause. "Mr. Montague," said Bates, earnestly, "I know this is a tough proposition—but think what it means. We get word about this conference. Waterman is here—and Duval—think of that! Dan Waterman and the Oil Trust getting together! The managing editor sent for me himself, and he said, 'Bates, get that story.' And what am I to do? There's about as much chance of my finding out what goes on in that conference—"

He stopped. "Think of what it may mean, Mr. Montague," he cried. "They will decide on to-morrow's moves! It may turn the stock market upside down. Think of what you could do with the information!"

"No," said Montague, shaking his head; "don't go at me that way."

Bates was gazing at him. "I beg your pardon," he said; "but then maybe you have interests of your own; or your friends—surely this situation—"

"No, not that either," said Montague, smiling; and Bates broke into a laugh.

"Well, then," he said, "just for the sport of it! Just to fool them!"

"That's more like it," said Montague.

"Of course, it's your room," said Bates. "You can stop us, if you insist. But you needn't stay if you don't want to. We'll take all the risk; and you may be sure that if we were caught, the hotel would suppress it. You can trust me to clear your name—"

"I'll stay," said Montague. "I'll see it through."

Bates jumped up and stretched out his hand. "Good!" he cried. "Put it there!"

In the meantime, Rodney pounced upon the dress-suit case, and opened it, taking out a coil of wire rope, very light and flexible, and a short piece of board. He proceeded to make a loop with the rope, and in this he fixed the board for a seat. He then took the blankets from the bed and folded them. He took out a pair of heavy calfskin gloves, which he tossed to Bates, and a ball of twine, one end of which he tied about his wrist. He tossed the ball on the floor, and then turned out the lights in the room, raised the shade of the window, and placed the bundle of blankets upon the sill.

"All ready," he said.

Bates put on the gloves and seized the rope, and Rodney adjusted the seat under his thighs. "You hold the blankets, if you will be so good, Mr. Montague, and keep them in place, if you can."

And Bates uncoiled some of the rope, and passed it over the top of the large bureau which stood beside the window. He brought the rope down to the middle of the body of the bureau, so that by this means he could diminish the pull of Rodney's weight.

"Steady now," said the latter; and he climbed over the sill, and, holding on with his hands, gradually put his weight against the rope.

"Now! All ready," he whispered.

Bates grasped the line, and, bracing his knees against the bureau, paid the rope out inch by inch. Montague held the blankets in place in the corner, and Rodney's shoulders and head gradually disappeared below the sill. He was still holding on with his hands, however.

"All right," he whispered, and let go, and slowly the rope slid past.

Montague's heart was beating fast with excitement, but Bates was calm and businesslike. After he had let out several turns of the rope, he stopped and whispered, "Look out now."

Montague leaned over the sill. He could see a stream of light from the window below him. Rodney was standing upon the cornice at the top of the window.

"Lower," said Montague, as he drew in his head, and once more Bates paid out.

"Now," he whispered, and Montague looked again. Rodney had cleverly pushed himself by the corner of the cornice, and kept himself at one side of the window, so that he would not be visible from the inside of the room. He made a frantic signal with his hand, and Montague drew back and whispered, "Lower!"

The next time he looked out, Rodney was standing upon the sill of the window, leaning to one side.

"Now, make fast," muttered Bates. And while he held the rope, Montague took it and wound it again around the bureau, and then carried it over and made it fast to the leg of the bath-tub.

"I guess that will hold all right," said Bates; and he went to the window and picked up the ball of cord, the other end of which was tied around Rodney's wrist.

"This is for signals," he said. "Morse telegraph."

"Good heavens!" gasped Montague. "You didn't leave much to chance."

"Couldn't afford to," said Bates. "Keep still!"

Montague saw that the hand which held the cord was being jerked.

"W-i-n-d-o-w o-p-e-n," said Bates; and added, "By the Lord! we've got them!"

CHAPTER XIX

Montague brought a couple of chairs, and the two seated themselves at the window for a long wait.

"How did you learn about this conference?" asked Montague.

"Be careful," whispered the other in his ear. "We mustn't make a noise, because Rodney will need quiet to hear them."

Montague saw that the cord was jerking again. Bates spelled out the letters one by one.

"W-a-t-e-r-m-a-n. D-u-v-a-l. He's telling us who's there. David Ward. Hegan. Prentice."

"Prentice!" whispered Montague. "Why, he's up in the Adirondacks!"

"He came down on a special train to-day," whispered the other. "Ward telegraphed him—I think that's where we got our tip. Henry Patterson. He's the real head of the Oil Trust now. Bascom of the Empire Bank. He's Waterman's man."

"You can imagine from that list that there's something big going on," Bates muttered; and he spelled the names of several other bankers, heads of the most important institutions in Wall Street.

"Talking about Stewart," spelled out Rodney.

"That's ancient history," muttered Bates. "He's a dead one."

"P-r-i-c-e," spelled Rodney.

"Price!" exclaimed Montague.

"Yes," said the other. "I saw him down in the lobby. I rather thought he'd come."

"But to a conference with Waterman!" exclaimed Montague.

"That's all right," said Bates. "Why not?"

"But they are deadly enemies!"

"Oh," said the other, "you don't want to let yourself believe things like that."

"What do you mean?" protested Montague. "Do you suppose they're not enemies?"

"I certainly do suppose it," said Bates.

"But, man! I can give you positive facts that prove they are."

"For every fact that you bring," laughed the other, "I can bring half a dozen to show you they are not."

"But that is perfectly absurd!" began Montague.

"Hush," said Bates, and he waited while the string jerked.

"I-c-e," spelled Rodney.

"That's Cummings—another dead one," said Bates. "My Lord, but they did him up brown!"

"Who did it?" asked Montague.

"Waterman," answered the other. "The Steamship Trust was competing with his New England railroads, and now it's in the hands of a receiver. Before long you'll hear that he's gathered it in."

"Then you think this last smash-up was planned?" said he.

"Planned! My Heavens, man, it was the greatest gobbling up of the little fish that I have ever known since I've been in Wall Street!"

"And it was Waterman?"

"With the Oil Trust. They were after young Stewart. You see, he beat them out in Montana, and they had to buy him off for ten million dollars. But he was fool enough to come to New York and go in for banking; and now they've got his banks, and a good part of his ten millions as well!"

"It takes a man's breath away," said Montague.

"Just save your breath-you'll need it to-night," said Bates, drily.

The other sat in thought for a moment. "We were talking about Price," he whispered. "Do you mean John S. Price?"

"There is only one Price that I know of," was the reply.

"And you don't believe that he and Waterman are enemies?"

"I mean that Price is simply one of Waterman's agents in every big thing he does."

"But, man! Doesn't he own the Mississippi Steel Company?"

"He owns it for Waterman," said Bates.

"But that is impossible," cried Montague. "Isn't Waterman interested in the Steel Trust? And isn't Mississippi Steel its chief competitor?"

"It is supposed to be," said the other. "But that is simply a bluff to fool the public. There has been no real competition between them ever since four years ago, when Price raided the stock and captured it for Waterman."

Montague was staring at his friend, almost speechless with amazement.

"Mr. Bates," he said, "it happens that I was very recently connected with Price and the Mississippi Steel Company in a very intimate way; and I know most positively that what you say is not true."

"It's very hard to answer a statement like that," Bates responded. "I'd have to know just what your facts are. But they'd have to be very convincing indeed to make an impression upon me, for I ran that story down pretty thoroughly. I got it straight from the inside, and I got all the details of it. I nailed Price down, right in his own office. The only trouble was that my people wouldn't print the facts."

It was some time before Montague spoke again. He was groping around in his own mind, trying to grasp the significance of what Bates had said.

"But Price was fighting Waterman!" he whispered. "The whole crowd were fighting him! That was the whole purpose of what they were doing. It had no sense otherwise."

"But are you sure?" asked the other. "Think it over. Suppose they were only pretending to fight."

There was a silence again.

"Mind you," Bates added, "I am only speaking about Price himself. I don't know about any people he may have been with. He may have been deceiving them—he may have been leading them into a trap—"

And suddenly Montague clutched the arms of his chair. He sat staring ahead of him, struck dumb by the thought which the other's words had brought to him. "My God," he gasped; and again, and yet again, "My God!"

It seemed to unroll before him, in vista after vista. Price deceiving Ryder! leading him into that Northern Mississippi deal; getting him to lend money upon the stock of the Mississippi Steel Company; promising, perhaps, to support the stock in the market, and helping to smash it instead! Twisting Ryder around his finger, crushing him—and why? And why?

Montague's thoughts stopped still. It was as if he had found himself suddenly confronted by a bottomless abyss. He shrank back from it. He could not face the thought in his own mind. Waterman! It was Dan Waterman! It was something which he had planned! It was the vengeance that he had threatened! He had been all this time plotting it, setting his nets about Ryder's feet!

It was an idea so wild and so horrible that Montague fought it off. He pushed it away from him, again and again. No, no, it could not be!

And yet, why not? He had always felt certain in his own mind that that detective had come from Waterman. The old man had set to work to find out about Lucy and her affairs, the first time that he had ever laid eyes on her. And then suddenly Montague saw the face of volcanic fury that had flashed past him on board the *Brünnhilde*. "You will hear from me again," the old man had said; and now, all these months of silence—and at last he heard!

Why not? Why not? Montague kept asking himself. After all, what did he know about the Mississippi Steel Company? What had he ever seen to prove that it was actually competing with the Trust? What had he even heard, except what Stanley Ryder had told him; and what more likely than that Ryder was simply repeating what Price had said?

Montague had forgotten all about his present situation in the rush of thoughts which had come to him. The cord had been jerking again, and had spelled out the names of several more of the masters of the city who had arrived; but he had not heard their names. "What object would there be," he asked, "in keeping the fact a secret—I mean that Price was Waterman's agent?"

"Object!" exclaimed Bates. "Good Heavens, and with the public half crazy about monopolies, and the President making such a fight! If it were known that the Steel Trust had gathered in its last big competitor, you can't tell what the Government might do!"

"I see," said Montague. "And how long has this been?"

"Four years," was the reply; "all they're waiting for is some occasion like this, when they can put the Company in a hole, and pose as benefactors in taking it over."

"I see," said Montague, again.

"Listen," said Bates, and leaned out of the window. He could catch faintly the sounds of a deep voice in the consultation room.

"W-a-t-e-r-m-a-n," spelled Rodney.

"I guess business has begun," whispered Bates.

"Situation intolerable," spelled Rodney. "End wildcat banking."

"That means end of opposition to me," was the other's comment.

"Duval assents," continued Rodney.

The two in the window were on edge by this time. It was tantalising to have to wait several minutes, and then get only such snatches.

"But they'll get past the speech-making pretty soon," whispered Bates; and indeed they did.

The next two words which the cord spelled out made Montague sit up and clutch the arms of his chair again.

"Gotham Trust!"

"Ah!" whispered Bates. Montague made not a sound.

"Ryder misusing," spelled the cord.

Bates seized his companion by the arm, and leaned close to him. "By the Lord!" he whispered breathlessly, "I wonder if they're going to smash the Gotham Trust!"

"Refuse clearing," spelled Rodney; and Montague felt Bates's hand trembling. "They refuse to clear for Ryder!" he panted.

Montague was beyond all speech; he sat as if turned to stone.

"To-morrow morning," spelled the cord.

Bates could hardly keep still for his excitement.

"Do you catch what that means?" he whispered. "The Clearing-house is to throw out the Gotham Trust!"

"Why, they'll wreck it!" panted the other.

"My God, my God, they're mad!" cried Bates. "Don't they realise what they'll do? There'll be a panic such as New York has never seen before! It will bring down every bank in the city! The Gotham Trust! Think of it!—the Gotham Trust!"

"Prentice objects," came Rodney's next message.

"Objects!" exclaimed Bates, striking his knee in repressed excitement. "I should think he might object. If the Gotham Trust goes down, the Trust Company of the Republic won't live for twenty-four hours."

"Afraid," spelled the cord. "Patterson angry."

"Much he has to lose," muttered Bates.

Montague started up and began to pace the room. "Oh, this is horrible, horrible!" he exclaimed.

Through all the images of the destruction and suffering which Bates's words brought up before him, his thoughts flew back to a pale and sad-faced little woman, sitting alone in an apartment up on the Riverside. It was to her that it all came back; it was for her that this terrible drama was being enacted. Montague could picture the grim, hawk-faced old man, sitting at the head of the council board, and laying down the law to the masters of the Metropolis. And this man's thoughts, too, went back to Lucy—his and Montague's alone, of all those who took part in the struggle!

"Waterman protect Prentice," spelled Rodney. "Insist turn out Ryder. Withdraw funds."

"There's no doubt of it," whispered Bates; "they can finish him if they choose. But oh, my Lord, what will happen in New York to-morrow!'

"Ward protect legitimate banks," was the next message.

"The little whelp!" sneered Bates. "By legitimate banks he means those that back his syndicates. A lot of protecting he will do!"

But then the newspaper man in Bates rose to the surface. "Oh, what a story," he whispered, clenching his hands, and pounding his knees. "Oh, what a story!"

Montague carried away but a faint recollection of the rest of Rodney's communications; he was too much overwhelmed by his own thoughts. Bates, however, continued to spell out the words; and he caught the statement that General Prentice, who was a director in the Gotham Trust, was to vote against any plan to close the doors of that institution. While they were after it, they were going to finish it.

Also he caught the sentence, "Panic useful, curb President!" And he heard Bates's excited exclamations over that. "Did you catch that?" he cried. "That's Waterman! Oh, the nerve of it! We are in at the making of history to-night, Mr. Montague."

Perhaps half an hour later, Montague, standing beside Bates, saw his hand jerked violently several times.

"That means pull up!" cried he. "Quick!"

And he seized the rope. "Put your weight on it," he whispered. "It will hold."

They proceeded to haul. Rodney helped them by catching hold of the cornice of the window and lifting himself. Then there was a moment of great straining, during which Montague held his breath; after which the weight grew lighter again. Rodney had got his knees upon the cornice.

A few moments later his fingers appeared, clutching the edge of the sill. He swung himself up, and Montague and Bates grasped him under the arms, and fairly jerked him into the room.

He staggered to his feet; and there was a moment's pause, while all three caught their breath. Then Rodney leaped at Bates, and grasped him by the shoulders. "Old man!" he cried. "We landed them! We landed them!"

"We landed them!" laughed the other in exultation.

"Oh, what a scoop!" shouted Rodney. "There was never one like it."

The two were like schoolboys in their glee. They hugged each other, and laughed and danced about. But it was not long before they became serious again. Montague turned on the lights, and pulled down the window; and Rodney stood there, with his clothing dishevelled and his face ablaze with excitement, and talked to them.

"Oh, you can't imagine that scene!" he said. "It makes my hair stand on end to think of it. Just fancy—I was not more than twenty feet from Dan Waterman, and most of the time he seemed to be glaring right at me. I hardly dared wink, for fear he'd notice; and I thought every instant he would jump up and run to the window. But there he sat, and pounded on the table, and glared about at those fellows, and laid down the law to them."

"I've heard him talk," said Bates. "I know how it is."

"Why, he fairly knocked them over!" said the other. "You could have heard a pin drop when he got through. Oh, it was a mad thing to see!"

"I've hardly been able to get my breath," said Bates. "I can't believe it."

"They have no idea what it will mean," said Montague.

"They know," said Rodney; "but they don't care. They've smelt blood. That's about the size of it—they were like a lot of hounds on the trail. You should have seen Waterman, with that lean, hungry face of his. 'The time has come,' said he. 'There's no one here but has known that sooner or later this work had to be done. We must crush them, once and for all time!' And you should have seen him turn on Prentice, when he ventured a word."

"Prentice doesn't like it, then?" asked Montague.

"I should think he wouldn't!" put in Bates.

"Waterman said he'd protect him," said Rodney. "But he must place himself absolutely in their hands. It seems that the Trust Company of the Republic has a million dollars with the Gotham Trust, and that's to be withdrawn."

"Imagine it!" gasped Bates.

"And wait!" exclaimed the other; "then they got on to politics. I would have given one arm if I could have got a photograph of Dan Waterman at that moment—just to spread it before the American people and ask them what they thought of it! David Ward had made the remark that 'A little trouble mightn't have a bad effect just now.' And Waterman brought down his fist on the table. 'This country needs a lesson,' he cried. 'There's been too much abuse of responsible men, and there's been too much wild talk in high places. If the people get a little taste of hard times, they'll have something else to think about besides abusing those who have made the prosperity of the country; and it seems to me, gentlemen, that we have it in our power to put an end to this campaign of radicalism.'"

"Think of it, think of it!" gasped Bates. "The old devil!"

"And then Duval chimed in, with a laugh, 'To put it in a nutshell, gentlemen, we are going to smash Ryder and scare the President!'"

"Was the conference over?" asked Bates, after a moment's pause.

"All but the hand-shakes," said the other. "I didn't dare to stay while they were moving about."

And Bates started suddenly to his feet. "Come!" he said. "We haven't any time to waste. Our work isn't done yet, by a long sight."

He proceeded to untie the rope and coil it up. Rodney took the blanket and put it on the bed, covering it with the spread, so as to conceal the holes which had been worn by the rope. He wound up the ball of cord, and dropped it into the bag with the rest of the stuff. Bates took his hat and coat and started for the door.

"You will excuse us, Mr. Montague," he said. "You can understand that this story will need a lot of work."

"I understand," said Montague.

"We'll try to thank you by and by," added the other. "Come around after the paper goes to press, and we'll have a celebration."

CHAPTER XX

They went out; and Montague waited a minute or two, to give them a chance to get out of the way, and then he rang the elevator bell and entered the car.

It stopped again at the next floor, and he gave a start of excitement. As the door opened, he saw a group of men, with Duval, Ward, and General Prentice among them. He moved behind the elevator man, so that none of them should notice him.

Montague had caught one glimpse of the face of General Prentice. It was deathly pale. The General said not a word to anyone, but went out into the corridor. The other hesitated for a moment, then, with a sudden resolution, he turned and followed. As his friend passed out of the door, he stepped up beside him.

"Good evening, General," he said. The General turned and stared at him, half in a daze.

"Oh, Montague!" he said. "How are you?"

"Very well," said Montague.

In the street outside, among a group of half a dozen automobiles, he recognised the General's limousine car.

"Where are you going?" he asked.

"Home," was the reply.

"I'll ride with you, if you like," said Montague. "I've something to say to you."

"All right," said the General. He could not very well have refused, for Montague had taken him by the arm and started toward the car; he did not intend to be put off.

He helped the General in, got in himself, and shut to the door behind him. Prentice sat staring in front of him, still half in a daze.

Montague watched him for a minute or so. Then suddenly he leaned toward him, and said, "General, why do you let them persuade you to do it?"

"Hey?" said the other.

"I say," repeated Montague, "why do you let them persuade you?"

The other turned and stared at him, with a startled look in his eyes.

"I know all about what has happened," said Montague. "I know what went on at that conference."

"What do you mean?" gasped the General.

"I know what they made you promise to do. They are going to wreck the Gotham Trust Company."

The General was dumfounded. "Why!" he gasped. "How? Who told you? How could you—"

Montague had to wait a minute or two until his friend had got over his dismay.

"I cannot help it," he burst out, finally. "What can I do?"

"You can refuse to play their game!" exclaimed Montague.

"But don't you suppose that they would do it just the same? And how long do you suppose that I would last, if I refused them?"

"But think of what it means!" cried Montague. "Think of the ruin! You will bring everything about your head."

"I know, I know!" cried the General, in a voice of anguish. "Don't think that I haven't realised it—don't think that I haven't fought against it! But I am helpless, utterly helpless."

He turned upon Montague, and caught his sleeve with a trembling hand. "I never thought that I would live to face such an hour," he exclaimed. "To despise myself—to be despised by all the world! To be browbeaten, and insulted, and dragged about—"

The old man paused, choking with excess of emotion. "Look at me!" he cried, with sudden vehemence. "Look at me! You think that I am a man, a person of influence in the community, the head of a great institution in which thousands of people have faith. But I am nothing of the kind. I am a puppet—I am a sham—I am a disgrace to myself and to the name I bear!"

And suddenly he clasped his hands over his face, and bowed his head, so that Montague should not see his grief.

There was a long silence. Montague was dumb with horror. He felt that his mere presence was an outrage.

Finally the General looked up again. He clenched his hand, and mastered himself.

"I have chosen my part," he said. "I must play it through. What I feel about it makes no difference."

Montague again said nothing.

"I have no right to inflict my grief upon you," the General continued. "I have no right to try to excuse myself. There is no turning back now. I am Dan Waterman's man, and I do his bidding."

"But how can you have got into such a position?" asked Montague.

"A friend of mine organised the Trust Company of the Republic. He asked me to become president, because I had a name that would be useful to him. I accepted—he was a man I knew I could trust. I managed the business properly, and it prospered; and then, three years ago, the control was bought by other men. That was when the crisis came. I should have resigned. But I had my family to think of; I had friends who were involved; I had interests that I could not leave. And I stayed—and that is all. I found that I had stayed to be a puppet, a figurehead. And now it is too late."

"But can't you withdraw now?" asked Montague.

"Now?" echoed the General. "Now, in the most critical moment, when all my friends are hanging upon me? There is nothing that my enemies would like better, for they could lay all their sins at my door. They would class me with Stewart and Ryder."

"I see," said Montague, in a low voice.

"And now the crisis comes, and I find out who my real master is. I am told to do this, and do that, and I do it. There are no threats; I understand without any. Oh, my God, Mr. Montague, if I should tell you of some of the things that I have seen in this city—of the indignities that I have seen heaped upon men, of the deeds to which I have seen them driven. Men whom you think of as the most honourable in the community—men who have grown grey in the service of the public! It is too brutal, too horrible for words!"

There was a long silence.

"And there is nothing you can do?" asked Montague.

"Nothing," he answered.

"Tell me, General, is your institution sound?"

"Perfectly sound."

"And you have done nothing improper?"

"Nothing."

"Then why should you fear Waterman?"

"Why?" exclaimed the General. "Because I am liable for eighty per cent of my deposits, and I have only five per cent of reserves."

"I see!" said Montague.

"It is a choice between Stanley Ryder and myself," added the other. "And Stanley Ryder will have to fight his own battle."

There was nothing more said. Each of the men sat buried in his own thoughts, and the only sound was the hum of the automobile as it sped up Broadway.

Montague was working out another course of action. He moved to another seat in the car where he could see the numbers upon the street lamps as they flashed by; and at last he touched the General upon the knee. "I will leave you at the next corner," he said.

The General pressed the button which signalled his chauffeur, and the car drew up at the curb. Montague descended.

"Good night, General," he said.

"Good night," said the other, in a faint voice. He did not offer to take Montague's hand. The latter closed the door of the car, and it sped away up the street.

Then he crossed over and went down to the River drive, and entered Lucy's apartment house.

"Is Mrs. Taylor in?" he asked of the clerk.

"I'll see," said the man. Montague gave his name and added, "Tell her it is very important."

Lucy came to the door herself, clad in an evening gown.

One glance at his haggard face was enough to tell her that something was wrong. "What is it, Allan?" she cried.

He hung up his hat and coat, and went into the drawing-room.

"What is it, Allan?" she cried again.

"Lucy, do you know where Stanley Ryder is?" he asked.

"Yes," she answered, and added quickly, "Oh! it's some bad news!"

"It is," said he. "He must be found at once."

She stared at him for a moment, hesitating; then, her anxiety overcoming every other emotion, she said, "He is in the next room."

"Call him," said Montague.

Lucy ran to the door. "Come in. Quickly!" she called, and Ryder appeared.

Montague saw that he was very pale; and there was nothing left of his air of aristocratic serenity.

"Mr. Ryder," he began, "I have just come into possession of some news which concerns you very closely. I felt that you ought to know. There is to be a directors' meeting to-morrow morning, at which it is to be decided that the bank which clears for the Gotham Trust Company will discontinue to do it."

Ryder started as if he had been shot; his face turned grey. There was no sound except a faint cry of fright from Lucy.

"My information is quite positive," continued Montague. "It has been determined to wreck your institution!"

Ryder caught at a chair to support himself. "Who? Who?" he stammered.

"It is Duval and Waterman," said Montague.

"Dan Waterman!" It was Lucy who spoke.

Montague turned to look at her, and saw her eyes, wide open with terror.

"Yes, Lucy," he said.

"Oh, oh!" she gasped, choking; then suddenly she cried wildly, "Tell me! I don't understand—what does it mean?"

"It means that I am ruined," exclaimed Ryder.

"Ruined?" she echoed.

"Absolutely!" he said. "They've got me! I knew they were after me, but I didn't think they'd dare!"

He ended with a furious imprecation; but Montague had kept his eyes fixed upon Lucy. It was her suffering that he cared about.

He heard her whisper, under her breath, "It's for me!" And then again, "It's for me!"

"Lucy," he began; but suddenly she put up her hand, and rushed toward him.

"Hush! he doesn't know!" she panted breathlessly. "I haven't told him."

And then she turned toward Ryder again. "Oh, surely there must be some way," she cried, wildly. "Surely—"

Ryder had sunk down in a chair and buried his face in his hands. "Ruined!" he exclaimed. "Utterly ruined! I won't have a dollar left in the world."

"No, no," cried Lucy, "it cannot be!" And she put her hands to her forehead, striving to think. "It must be stopped. I'll go and see him. I'll plead with him."

"You must not, Lucy!" cried Montague, starting toward her.

But again she whirled upon him. "Not a word!" she whispered, with fierce intensity. "Not a word!"

And she rushed into the next room, and half a minute later came back with her hat and wrap.

"Allan," she said, "tell them to call me a cab!"

He tried to protest again; but she would not hear him. "You can ride with me," she said. "You can talk then. Call me a cab! Please—save me that trouble."

He gave the message: and Lucy, meanwhile, stood in the middle of the room, twisting her hands together nervously.

"Now, Allan, go downstairs," she said; "wait for me there." And after another glance at the broken figure of Ryder, he took his hat and coat and obeyed.

Montague spent his time pacing back and forth in the entrance-hall. The cab arrived, and a minute later Lucy appeared, wearing a heavy veil. She went straight to the vehicle, and sprang in, and Montague followed. She gave the driver the address of Waterman's great marble palace over by the park; and the cab started.

Then suddenly she turned upon Montague, speaking swiftly and intensely.

"I know what you are going to say," she cried. "But you must spare me—and you must spare yourself. I am sorry that you should have to know this—God knows that I could not help it! But it cannot be undone. And there is no other way out of it. I must go to him, and try to save Ryder!"

"Lucy," he began, "listen to me—"

"I don't want to listen to you," she cried wildly—almost hysterically. "I cannot bear to be argued with. It is too hard for me as it is!"

"But think of the practical side of it!" he cried. "Do you imagine that you can stop this huge machine that Waterman has set in motion?"

"I don't know, I don't know!" she exclaimed, choking back a sob. "I can only do what I can. If he has any spark of feeling in him—I'll get down on my knees to him, I will beg him—"

"But, Lucy! think of what you are doing. You go there to his house at night! You put yourself into his power!"

"I don't care, Allan—I am not afraid of him. I have thought about myself too long. Now I must think about the man I love."

Montague did not answer, for a moment. "Lucy," he said at last, "will you tell me how you have thought of yourself in one single thing?"

"Yes, yes—I will!" she cried, vehemently. "I have known all along that Waterman was following me. I have been haunted by the thought of him—I have felt his power in everything that has befallen us. And I have never once told Ryder of his peril!"

"That was more a kindness to him—" began the other.

"No, no!" panted Lucy; and she caught his coat sleeve in her trembling hands. "You see, you see—you cannot even imagine it of me! I kept it a secret—because I was afraid!"

"Afraid?" he echoed.

"I was afraid that Ryder would leave me! I was afraid that he would give me up! And I loved him too much!—Now," she rushed on—"you see what kind of a person I have been! And I can sit here, and tell you that! Is there anything that can make me ashamed after that? Is there anything that can degrade me after that? And what is there left for me to do but go to Waterman and try to undo what I have done?"

Montague was speechless, before the agony of her humiliation.

"You see!" she whispered.

"Lucy," he began, protesting.

But suddenly she caught him by the arm. "Allan," she whispered, "I know that you have to try to stop me. But it is no use, and I must do it! And I cannot bear to hear you—it makes it too hard for me. My course is chosen, and nothing in the world can turn me; and I want you to go away and leave me. I want you to go— right now! I am not afraid of Waterman; I am not afraid of anything that he can do. I am only afraid of you, and your unhappiness. I want you to leave me to my fate! I want you to stop thinking about me!"

"I cannot do it, Lucy," he said.

She reached up and pulled the signal cord; and the cab came to a halt.

"I want you to get out, Allan!" she cried wildly. "Please get out, and go away."

He started to protest again; but she pushed him away in frenzy. "Go, go!" she cried; and half dazed, and scarcely realising what he did, he gave way to her and stepped out into the street.

"Drive!" she called to the man, and shut the door; and Montague found himself standing on a driveway in the park, with the lights of the cab disappearing around a turn.

CHAPTER XXI

Montague started to walk. He had no idea where he went; his mind was in a whirl, and he was lost to everything about him. He must have spent a couple of hours wandering about the park and the streets of the city; when at last he stopped and looked about him, he was on a lighted thoroughfare, and a big clock in front of a jewellery store was pointing to the hour of two.

He looked around. Immediately across the street was a building which he recognised as the office of the Express; and in a flash he thought of Bates. "Come in after the paper has gone to press," the latter had said.

He went in and entered the elevator.

"I want to see Mr. Bates, a reporter," he said.

"City-room," said the elevator man; "eleventh floor."

Montague confronted a very cross and sleepy-looking office-boy. "Is Mr. Bates in?" he asked.

"I dunno," said the boy, and slowly let himself down from the table upon which he had been sitting. Montague produced a card, and the boy disappeared. "This way," he said, when he returned; and Montague found himself in a huge room, crowded with desks and chairs. Everything was in confusion; the floor was literally buried out of sight in paper.

Montague observed that there were only about a dozen men in the room; and several of these were putting on their coats. "There he is, over there," said the office-boy.

He looked and saw Bates sitting at a desk, with his head buried in his arms. "Tired," he thought to himself.

"Hello, Bates," he said; then, as the other looked up, he gave a start of dismay.

"What's the matter?" he cried.

It was half a minute before Bates replied. His voice was husky. "They sold me out," he whispered.

"What!" gasped the other.

"They sold me out!" repeated Bates, and struck the table in front of him. "Cut out the story, by God! Did me out of my scoop!

"Look at that, sir," he added, and shoved toward Montague a double column of newspaper proofs, with a huge head-line, "Gotham Trust Company to be

Wrecked," and the words scrawled across in blue pencil, "Killed by orders from the office."

Montague could scarcely find words to reply. He drew up a chair and sat down. "Tell me about it," he said.

"There's nothing much to tell," said Bates. "They sold me out. They wouldn't print it."

"But why didn't you take it elsewhere?" asked the other.

"Too late," said Bates; "the scoundrels—they never even let me know!" He poured out his rage in a string of curses.

Then he told Montague the story.

"I was in here at half-past ten," he said, "and I reported to the managing editor. He was crazy with delight, and told me to go ahead—front page, double column, and all the rest. So Rodney and I set to work. He did the interview, and I did all the embroidery—oh, my God, but it was a story! And it was read, and went through; and then an hour or two ago, just when the forms were ready, in comes old Hodges—he's one of the owners, you know—and begins nosing round. 'What's this?' he cries, and reads the story; and then he goes to the managing editor. They almost had a fight over it. 'No paper that I am interested in shall ever print a story like that!' says Hodges; and the managing editor threatens to resign, but he can't budge him. The first thing I knew of it was when I got this copy; and the paper had already gone to press."

"What do you suppose was the reason for it?" asked Montague, in wonder.

"Reason?" echoed Bates. "The reason is Hodges; he's a crook. 'If we publish that story,' he said, 'the directors of the bank will never meet, and we'll bear the onus of having wrecked the Gotham Trust Company.' But that's all a bluff, and he knew it; we could prove that that conference took place, if it ever came to a fight."

"You were quite safe, it seems to me," said Montague.

"Safe?" echoed Bates. "We had the greatest scoop that a newspaper ever had in this country—if only the Express were a newspaper. But Hodges isn't publishing the news, you see; he's serving his masters, whoever they are. I knew that it meant trouble when he bought into the Express. He used to be managing editor of the Gazette, you know; and he made his fortune selling the policy of that paper—its financial news is edited to this very hour in the offices of Wyman's bankers, and I can prove it to anybody who wants me to. That's the sort of proposition a man's up against; and what's the use of gathering the news?"

And Bates rose up with an oath, kicking away the chair behind him. "Come on," he said; "let's get out of here. I don't know that I'll ever come back."

Montague spent another hour wandering about with Bates, listening to his opinion of the newspapers of the Metropolis. Then, utterly exhausted, he went home; but not to sleep. He sat in a chair for an hour or two, his mind besieged by images of ruin and destruction. At last he lay down, but he had not closed his eyes when daylight began to stream into the room.

At eight o'clock he was up again and at the telephone. He called up Lucy's apartment house.

"I want to speak to Mrs. Taylor," he said.

"She is not in," was the reply.

"Will you ring up the apartment?" asked Montague. "I will speak to the maid."

"This is Mr. Montague," he said, when he heard the woman's voice. "Where is Mrs. Taylor?"

"She has not come back, sir," was the reply.

Montague had some work before him that day which could not be put off. Accordingly he bathed and shaved, and had some coffee in his room, and then set out for his office. Even at that early hour there were crowds in the financial district, and another day's crop of rumours had begun to spring. He heard nothing about the Gotham Trust Company; but when he left court at lunch time, the newsboys on the street were shouting the announcement of the action of the bank directors. Lucy had failed in her errand, then; the blow had fallen!

There was almost a panic on the Exchange that day, and the terror and anxiety upon the faces of the people who thronged the financial district were painful to see. But the courts did not suspend, even on account of the Gotham Trust; and Montague had an important case to argue. He came out on the street late in the afternoon, and though it was after banking hours, he saw crowds in front of a couple of the big trust companies, and he read in the papers that a run upon the Gotham Trust had begun.

At his office he found a telegram from his brother Oliver, who was still in the Adirondacks: "Money in Trust Company of the Republic. Notify me of the slightest sign of trouble."

He replied that there was none; and, as he rode up in the subway, he thought the problem over, and made up his own mind. He had a trifle over sixty thousand dollars in Prentice's institution—more than half of all he owned. He had Prentice's word for it that the Company was in a sound condition, and he believed it. He made up his mind that he would not be one of those to be stampeded, whatever might happen.

He dined quietly at home with his mother; then he took his way up town again to Lucy's apartment; for he was haunted by the thought of her, and could not rest. He had read in the late evening papers that Stanley Ryder had resigned from the Gotham Trust Company.

"Is Mrs. Taylor in?" he asked, and gave his name.

"Mrs. Taylor says will you please to wait, sir," was the reply. And Montague sat down in the reception-room. A couple of minutes later, the hall-boy brought him a note.

He opened it and read these words, in a trembling hand:—

"Dear Allan: It is good of you to try to help me, but I cannot bear it. Please go away. I do not want you to think about me. Lucy."

Montague could read the agony between those lines; but there was nothing he could do about it. He went over to Broadway, and started to walk down town.

He felt that he must have someone to talk to, to take his mind off these things. He thought of the Major, and went over to the club, but the storm had routed out even the Major, it appeared. He was just off to attend some conference, and had only time to shake hands with Montague, and tell him to "trim sail."

Then he thought of Bates, and went down to the office of the Express. He found Bates hard at work, seated at a table in his shirt-sleeves, and with stacks of papers around him.

"I can always spare time for a chat," he said, as Montague offered to go.

"I see you came back," observed the other.

"I'm like an old horse in a tread mill," answered Bates. "What else is there for me to do?"

He leaned back in his chair, and put his thumbs in his armholes. "Well," he remarked, "they made their killing."

"They did, indeed," said Montague.

"And they're not satisfied yet," exclaimed the other. "They're on another trail!"

"What!" cried Montague.

"Listen," said Bates. "I went in to see David Ward about the action of the Clearinghouse Committee; Gary—he's the Despatch man—was with me. Ward talked for half an hour, as he always does; he told us all about the gallant efforts which the bankers were making to stem the tide, and he told us that the Trust Company of the Republic was in danger and that an agreement had been made to try to save it. Mind you, there's not been the least sign of trouble for the company.' 'Shall we print that?' asked Gary. 'Surely,' said Ward. 'But it will make trouble,' said Gary. 'That's all right,' said Ward. 'It's a fact. So print it.' Now what do you think of that?"

Montague sat rigid. "But I thought they had promised to protect Prentice!" he exclaimed.

"Yes," said Bates, grimly; "and now they throw him down."

"Do you suppose Waterman knew that?"

"Why, of course; Ward is no more than one of his clerks."

"And will the Despatch print it, do you suppose?"

"I don't know why not," said the other. "I asked Gary if he was going to put it in, and he said 'Yes.' 'It will make another panic,' I said, and he answered, 'Panics are news.'"

Montague said nothing for a minute or two. Finally he remarked, "I have good reason to believe that the Trust Company of the Republic is perfectly sound."

"I have no doubt of it," was the reply.

"Then why—" He stopped.

Bates shrugged his shoulders. "Ask Waterman," he said. "It's some quarrel or other; he wants to put the screws on somebody. Perhaps it's simply that two trust companies will scare the President more than one; or perhaps it's some stock he wants to break. I've heard it said that he has seventy-five millions laid by to pick up bargains with; and I shouldn't wonder if it was true."

There was a moment's pause. "And by the way," Bates added, "the Oil Trust has made another haul! The Electric Manufacturing Company is in trouble—that's a rival of one of their enterprises! Doesn't it all fit together beautifully?"

Montague thought for a moment or two. "This is rather important news to me," he said; "I've got money in the Trust Company of the Republic. Do you suppose they are going to let it go down?"

"I talked it over with Rodney," the other replied. "He says Waterman was quite explicit in his promises to see Prentice through. And there's one thing you can say about old Dan—for all his villainies, he never breaks his word. So I imagine he'll save it."

"But then, why give out this report?" exclaimed the lawyer.

"Don't you see?" said Bates. "He wants a chance to save it."

Montague's jaw fell. "Oh!" he said.

"It's as plain as the nose on your face," said Bates. "That story will come out to-morrow morning, and everybody will say it was the blunder of a newspaper reporter; and then Waterman will come forward and do the rescue act. It'll be just like a play."

"It's taking a long chance," said Montague, and added, "I had thought of telling Prentice, who's an intimate friend of mine; but I don't suppose it will do him any good."

"Poor old Prentice can't help himself," was the reply. "All you can do is to make him lose a night's sleep."

Montague went out, with a new set of problems to ponder. As he went home, he passed the magnificent building of the Gotham Trust Company, where there stood a long line of people who had prepared to spend the night. All the afternoon a frantic mob had besieged the doors, and millions of dollars had been withdrawn in a few hours. Montague knew that by the time he got down town the next morning there would be another such mob in front of the Trust Company of the Republic; but he was determined to stand by his own resolve. However, he had sent a telegram to Oliver, warning him to return at once.

He went home and found there another letter from Lucy Dupree.

"Dear Allan," she wrote. "No doubt you have heard the news that Ryder has been forced out of the Gotham Trust. But I have accomplished part of my purpose—Waterman has promised that he will put him on his feet again after this trouble is over. In the meantime, I am told to go away. This is for the best; you will remember that you yourself urged me to go. Ryder cannot see me, because the newspaper reporters are following him so closely.

"I beg of you not to try to find me. I am hateful in my own sight, and you will never see me again. There is one last thing that you can do for me. Go to Stanley Ryder and offer him your help—I mean your advice in straightening out his affairs. He has no friends now, and he is in a desperate plight. Do this for me. Lucy."

CHAPTER XXII

At eight the next morning the train from the Adirondacks arrived, and Montague was awakened by his brother at the telephone. "Have you seen this morning's Despatch?" was Oliver's first word.

"I haven't seen it," said Montague; "but I know what's in it."

"About the Trust Company of the Republic?" asked Oliver.

"Yes," said the other. "I was told the story before I telegraphed you."

"But my God, man," cried Oliver—"then why aren't you down town?"

"I'm going to let my money stay."

"What?"

"I believe that the institution is sound; and I am not going to leave Prentice in the lurch. I telegraphed you, so that you could do as you chose."

It was a moment or two before Oliver could find words to reply.

"Thanks!" he said. "You might have done a little more—sent somebody down to keep a place in line for me. You're out of your mind, but there's no time to talk about it now. Good-by." And so he rang off.

Montague dressed and had his breakfast; in the meantime he glanced over a copy of the Despatch, where, in the account of the day's events, he found the fatal statements about the Trust Company of the Republic. It was very interesting to Montague to read these newspapers and see the picture of events which they presented to the public. They all told what they could not avoid telling—that is, the events which were public matters; but they never by any chance gave a hint of the reasons for the happenings—you would have supposed that all these upheavals in the banking world were so many thunderbolts which had fallen from the heavens above. And each day they gave more of their space to insisting that the previous day's misfortunes were the last—that by no chance could there be any more thunderbolts to fall.

When he went down town, he rode one station farther than usual in order to pass the Trust Company of the Republic. He found a line of people extending halfway round the block, and in the minute that he stood watching there were a score or more added to it. Police were patrolling up and down—it was not many hours later that they were compelled to adopt the expedient of issuing numbered tickets to those who waited in the line.

Montague walked on toward the front, looking for his brother. But he had not gone very far before he gave an exclamation of amazement. He saw a short, stout, grey-haired figure, which he recognised, even by its back. "Major Venable!" he gasped.

The Major whirled about. "Montague!" he exclaimed. "My God, you are just in time to save my life!"

"What do you want?" asked the other.

"I want a chair!" gasped the Major, whose purple features seemed about to burst with his unwonted exertions. "I've been standing here for two hours. In another minute more I should have sat down on the sidewalk."

"Where can I get a chair?" asked Montague, biting his tongue in order to repress his amusement.

"Over on Broadway," said the Major. "Go into one of the stores, and make somebody sell you one. Pay anything—I don't care."

So Montague went back, and entered a leather-goods store, where he saw several cane-seated chairs. He was free to laugh then all he pleased; and he explained the situation to one of the clerks, who demurred at five dollars, but finally consented for ten dollars to take the risk of displeasing his employer. For fifty cents more Montague found a boy to carry it, and he returned in triumph to his venerable friend.

"I never expected to see you in a position like this," he remarked. "I thought you always knew things in advance."

"By the Lord, Montague!" muttered the other, "I've got a quarter of a million in this place."

"I've got about one-fourth as much myself," said Montague.

"What!" cried the Major. "Then what are you doing?"

"I'm going to leave it in," said Montague. "I have reason to know that that report in the Despatch is simply a blunder, and that the institution is sound."

"But, man, there'll be a run on it!" sputtered the old gentleman.

"There will, if everybody behaves like you. You don't need your quarter of a million to pay for your lunch, do you?"

The Major was too much amazed to find a reply.

"You put your money in a trust company," the other continued, "and you know that it only keeps five per cent reserve, and is liable to pay a hundred per cent of its deposits. How can you expect it to do that?"

"I don't expect it," said the Major, grimly; "I expect to be among the five per cent." And he cast his eye up the line, and added, "I rather think I am."

Montague went on ahead, and found his brother, with only about a score of people ahead of him. Apparently not many of the depositors of the Trust Company read their newspapers before eight o'clock in the morning.

"Do you want a chair, too?" asked Montague. "I just got one for the Major."

"Is he here, too?" exclaimed Oliver. "Good Heavens! No, I don't want a chair," he added, "I'll get through early. But, Allan, tell me—what in the world is the matter? Do you really mean that your money is still in here?"

"It's here," the other answered. "There's no use arguing about it—come over to the office when you get your money."

"I got the train just by half a minute," said Oliver. "Poor Bertie Stuyvesant didn't get up in time, and he's coming on a special—he's got about three hundred thousand in here. It was to pay for his new yacht."

"I guess some of the yacht-makers won't be quite so busy from now on," remarked the other, as he moved away.

That afternoon he heard the story of how General Prentice, as a director of the Gotham Trust, had voted that the institution should not close its doors, and then, as president of the Trust Company of the Republic, had sent over and cashed a check for a million dollars. None of the newspapers printed that story, but it ran from mouth to mouth, and was soon the jest of the whole city. Men said that it was this act of treachery which had taken the heart out of the Gotham Trust Company directors, and led to the closing of its doors.

Such was the beginning of the panic as Montague saw it. It had all worked out beautifully, according to the schedule. The stock market was falling to pieces—some of the leading stocks were falling several points between transactions, and Wyman and Hegan and the Oil and Steel people were hammering the market and getting ready for the killing. And at the same time, representatives of Waterman in Washington were interviewing the President, and setting before him the desperate plight of the Mississippi Steel Company. Already the structure of the country's finances was tottering; and here was one more big failure threatening. Realising the desperate situation, the Steel Trust was willing to do its part to save the country—it would take over the Mississippi Steel Company, provided only that the Government would not interfere. The desired promise was given; and so that last of Waterman's purposes was accomplished.

But there was one factor in the problem upon which few had reckoned, and that was the vast public which furnished all the money for the game—the people to whom dollars were not simply gamblers' chips, but to whom they stood for the necessities of life; business men who must have them to pay their clerks on Saturday afternoon; working-men who needed them for rent and food; helpless widows and orphans to whom they meant safety from starvation. These unhappy people had no means of knowing that financial institutions, which were perfectly sound and able to pay their depositors, might be wrecked deliberately in a gamblers' game. When they heard that banks were tottering, and were being besieged for money, they concluded that there must be real danger—that the long-predicted crash must be at hand. They descended upon Wall Street in hordes—the whole financial district was packed with terrified crowds, and squads of policemen rode through upon horseback in order to keep open the streets.

"Somebody asked for a dollar," was the way one banker phrased it. Wall Street had been doing business with pieces of paper; and now someone asked for a dollar, and it was discovered that the dollar had been mislaid.

It was an experience for which the captains of finance were not entirely prepared; they had forgotten the public. It was like some great convulsion of nature, which made mockery of all the powers of men, and left the beholder dazed and terrified. In Wall Street men stood as if in a valley, and saw far up above them the starting of an avalanche; they stood fascinated with horror, and watched it gathering headway; saw the clouds of dust rising up, and heard the roar of it swelling, and realised that it was a matter of only a second or two before it would be upon them and sweep them to destruction.

The lines of people before the Gotham Trust and the Trust Company of the Republic were now blocks in length; and every hour one heard of runs upon new institutions. There were women wringing their hands and crying in nervous excitement; there were old people, scarcely able to totter; there were people who had risen from sick-beds, and who stood all through the day and night, shivering in the keen October winds.

Runs had begun on the savings banks also; over on the East Side the alarm had reached the ignorant foreign population. It had spread with the speed of lightning all over the country; already there were reports of runs in other cities, and from thousands and tens of thousands of banks in East and South and West came demands upon the Metropolis for money. And there was no money anywhere.

And so the masters of the Banking Trust realised to their annoyance that the monster which they had turned loose might get beyond their control. Runs were beginning upon institutions in which they themselves were concerned. In the face of madness such as this, even the twenty-five per cent reserves of the national banks would not be sufficient. The moving of the cotton and grain crops had taken hundreds of millions from New York; and there was no money to be got by any chance from abroad. Everywhere they turned, they faced this appalling scarcity of money; nothing could be sold, no money could be borrowed. The few who had succeeded in getting their cash were renting safe-deposit boxes and hiding the actual coin.

And so, all their purposes having been accomplished, the bankers set to work to stem the tide. Frantic telegrams were sent to Washington, and the Secretary of the Treasury deposited six million dollars in the national banks of the Metropolis, and then came on himself to consult.

Men turned to Dan Waterman, who was everywhere recognised as the master of the banking world. The rivalry of the different factions ceased in the presence of this peril; and Waterman became suddenly a king, with practically absolute control of the resources of every bank in the city. Even the Government placed itself in his hands; the Secretary of the Treasury became one of his clerks, and bank presidents and financiers came crowding into his office like panic-stricken children. Even the proudest and most defiant men, like Wyman and Hegan, took his orders and listened humbly to his tirades.

All these events were public history, and one might follow them day by day in the newspapers. Waterman's earlier acts had been planned and carried out in darkness. No one knew, no one had the faintest suspicion. But now newspaper reporters attended the conferences and trailed Waterman about wherever he went, and the public was invited to the wonderful spectacle of this battle-worn veteran, rousing himself for one last desperate campaign and saving the honour and credit of the country.

The public hung upon his lightest word, praying for his success. The Secretary of the Treasury sat in the Sub-Treasury building near his office, and poured out the funds of the Government under his direction. Thirty-two million dollars in all were thus placed with the national banks; and from all these institutions Waterman drew the funds which he poured into the vaults of the imperilled banks and trust companies. It was a time when one man's peril was every man's, and none might stand alone. And Waterman was a despot, imperious and terrible. "I have taken care of my bank," said one president; "and I intend to shut myself up in it and wait until the storm is over." "If you do," Waterman retorted, "I will build a wall around you, and you will never get out of it again!" And so the banker contributed the necessary number of millions.

The fight centred around the imperilled Trust Company of the Republic. It was recognised by everyone that if Prentice's institution went down, it would mean defeat. Longer and longer grew the line of waiting depositors; the vaults were nearly empty. The cashiers adopted the expedient of paying very slowly—they would take half an hour or more to investigate a single check; and thus they kept going until more money arrived. The savings banks of the city agreed unanimously to close their doors, availing themselves of their legal right to demand sixty days before paying. The national banks resorted to the expedient of paying with clearing-house certificates. The newspapers preached confidence and cheered the public—even the newsboys were silenced, so that their shrill cries might no longer increase the public excitement. Groups of mounted policemen swept up and down the streets, keeping the crowds upon the move.

And so at last came the fateful Thursday, the climax of the panic. A pall seemed to have fallen upon Wall Street. Men ran here and there, bareheaded and pale with fright. Upon the floor of the Stock Exchange men held their breath. The market was falling to pieces. All sales had stopped; one might quote any price one chose, for it was impossible to borrow a dollar. Interest rates had gone to one hundred and fifty per cent to two hundred per cent; a man might have offered a thousand per cent for a large sum and not obtained it. The brokers stood about, gazing at each other in utter despair. Such an hour had never before been known.

All this time the funds of the Government had been withheld from the Exchange. The Government must not help the gamblers, everyone insisted. But now had come the moment when it seemed that the Exchange must be closed. Thousands of firms would be ruined, the business of the country would be paralysed. There came word that the Pittsburg Exchange had closed. So once more the terrified magnates crowded into Waterman's office. Once more the funds of the Government were poured into the banks; and from the banks they came to Waterman; and within a few minutes after the crisis had developed, the announcement was made that Dan Waterman would lend twenty-five million dollars at ten per cent.

So the peril was averted. Brokers upon the floor wept for joy, and cheers rang through all the Street. A mob of men gathered in front of Waterman's office, singing a chorus of adulation.

All these events Montague followed day by day. He was passing through Wall Street that Thursday afternoon, and he heard the crowds singing. He turned away, bitter and sick at heart. Could a more tragic piece of irony have been imagined than this—that the man, who of all men had been responsible for this terrible calamity, should be heralded before the whole country as the one who averted it! Could there have been a more appalling illustration of the way in which the masters of the Metropolis were wont to hoodwink its blind and helpless population?

There was only one man to whom Montague could vent his feelings; only one man besides himself who knew the real truth. Montague got the habit, when he left his work, of stopping at the Express building, and listening for a few minutes to the grumbling of Bates.

Bates would have each day's news fresh from the inside; not only the things which would be printed on the morrow, but the things which would never be printed anywhere. And he and Montague would feed the fires of each other's rage. One day it would be one of the Express's own editorials, in which it was pointed out that the intemperate speeches and reckless policies of the President were now bearing their natural fruit; another day it would be a letter from a prominent clergyman, naming Waterman as the President's successor.

Men were beside themselves with wonder at the generosity of Waterman in lending twenty-five millions at ten per cent. But it was not his own money—it was the money of the national banks which he was lending; and this was money which the national banks had got from the Government, and for which they paid the Government no interest at all. There was never any graft in the world so easy as the national bank graft, declared Bates. These smooth gentlemen got the people's money to build their institutions. They got the Government to deposit money with them, and they paid the Government nothing, and charged the people interest for it. They had the privilege of issuing a few hundred millions of bank-notes, and they charged interest for these and paid the Government nothing. And then, to cap the climax, they used their profits to buy up the Government! They filled the Treasury Department with their people, and when they got into trouble, the Sub-Treasury was emptied into their vaults. And in the face of all this, the people agitated for postal savings banks, and couldn't get them. In other countries the people had banks where they could put their money with absolute certainty; for no one had ever known such a thing as a run upon a postal bank.

"Sometimes," said Bates, "it seems almost as if our people were hypnotised. You saw all this life insurance scandal, Mr. Montague; and there's one simple and obvious remedy for all the evils—if we had Government life insurance, it could never fail, and there'd be no surplus for Wall Street gamblers. It sounds almost incredible—but do you know, I followed that agitation as I don't believe any other man in this country followed it—and from first to last I don't believe that one single suggestion of that remedy was ever made in print!"

A startled look had come upon Montague's face as he listened. "I don't believe I ever thought of it myself!" he exclaimed.

And Bates shrugged his shoulders. "You see!" he said. "So it goes."

CHAPTER XXIII

Montague had taken a couple of days to think over Lucy's last request. It was a difficult commission; but he made up his mind at last that he would make the attempt. He went up to Ryder's home and presented his card.

"Mr. Ryder is very much occupied, sir—" began the butler, apologetically.

"This is important," said Montague. "Take him the card, please." He waited in the palatial entrance-hall, decorated with ceilings which had been imported intact from old Italian palaces.

At last the butler returned. "Mr. Ryder says will you please see him upstairs, sir?"

Montague entered the elevator, and was taken to Ryder's private apartments. In the midst of the drawing-room was a great library table, covered with a mass of papers; and in a chair in front of it sat Ryder.

Montague had never seen such dreadful suffering upon a human countenance. The exquisite man of fashion had grown old in a week.

"Mr. Ryder," he began, when they were alone, "I received a letter from Mrs. Taylor, asking me to come to see you."

"I know," said Ryder. "It was like her; and it is very good of you."

"If there is any way that I can be of assistance," the other began.

But Ryder shook his head. "No," he said; "there is nothing."

"If I could give you my help in straightening out your own affairs—"

"They are beyond all help," said Ryder. "I have nothing to begin on—I have not a dollar in the world."

"That is hardly possible," objected Montague.

"It is literally true!" he exclaimed. "I have tried every plan—I have been over the thing and over it, until I am almost out of my mind." And he glanced about him at the confusion of papers, and leaned his forehead in his hands in despair.

"Perhaps if a fresh mind were to take it up," suggested Montague. "It is difficult to see how a man of your resources could be left without anything—"

"Everything I have is mortgaged," said the other. "I have been borrowing money right and left. I was counting on profits—I was counting on increases in value. And now see—everything is wiped out! There is not value enough left in anything to cover the loans."

"But surely, Mr. Ryder, this slump is merely temporary. Values must be restored—"

"It will be years, it will be years! And in the meantime I shall be forced to sell. They have wiped me out—they have destroyed me! I have not even money to live on."

Montague sat for a few moments in thought. "Mrs. Taylor wrote me that Waterman—" he began.

"I know, I know!" cried the other. "He had to tell her something, to get what he wanted."

Montague said nothing.

"And suppose he does what he promised?" continued the other. "He has done it before—but am I to be one of Dan Waterman's lackeys?"

There was a silence. "Like John Lawrence," continued Ryder, in a low voice. "Have you heard of Lawrence? He was a banker—one of the oldest in the city. And Waterman gave him an order, and he defied him. Then he broke him; took away every dollar he owned. And the man came to him on his knees. 'I've taught you who is your master,' said Waterman. 'Now here's your money.' And now Lawrence fawns on him, and he's got rich and fat. But all his bank exists for is to lend money when Waterman is floating a merger, and call it in when he is buying."

Montague could think of nothing to reply to that.

"Mr. Ryder," he began at last, "I cannot be of much use to you now, because I haven't the facts. All I can tell you is that I am at your disposal. I will give you my best efforts, if you will let me. That is all I can say."

And Ryder looked up, the light shining on his white, wan face. "Thank you, Mr. Montague," he said. "It is very good of you. It is a help, at least, to hear a word of sympathy. I—I will let you know—"

"All right," said Montague, rising. He put out his hand, and Ryder took it tremblingly. "Thank you," he said again.

And the other turned and went out. He went down the great staircase by himself. At the foot he passed the butler, carrying a tray with some coffee.

He stopped the man. "Mr. Ryder ought not to be left alone," he said. "He should have his physician."

"Yes, sir," began the other, and then stopped short. From the floor above a pistol shot rang out and echoed through the house.

"Oh, my God!" gasped the butler, staggering backward.

He half dropped and half set the tray upon a chair, and ran wildly up the steps. Montague stood for a moment or two as if turned to stone. He saw another servant run out of the dining-room and up the stairs. Then, with a sudden impulse, he turned and went to the door.

"I can be of no use," he thought to himself; "I should only drag Lucy's name into it." And he opened the door, and went quietly down the steps.

In the newspapers the next morning he read that Stanley Ryder had shot himself in the body, and was dying.

And that same morning the newspapers in Denver, Colorado, told of the suicide of a mysterious woman, a stranger, who had gone to a room in one of the hotels and taken poison. She was very beautiful; it was surmised that she must be an actress. But she had left not a scrap of paper or a clew of any sort by which she could be identified. The newspapers printed her photograph; but Montague did not see the Denver newspapers, and so to the day of his death he never knew what had been the fate of Lucy Dupree.

The panic was stopped, but the business of the country lay in ruins. For a week its financial heart had ceased to beat, and through all the arteries of commerce, and every smallest capillary, there was stagnation. Hundreds of firms had failed, and the mills and factories by the thousands were closing down. There were millions of men out of work. Throughout the summer the railroads had been congested with traffic, and now there were a quarter of a million freight cars laid by. Everywhere were poverty and suffering; it was as if a gigantic tidal wave of distress had started from the Metropolis and rolled over the continent. Even the oceans had not stopped it; it had gone on to England and Germany—it had been felt even in South America and Japan.

One day, while Montague was still trembling with the pain of his experience, he was walking up the Avenue, and he met Laura Hegan coming from a shop to her carriage.

"Mr. Montague," she exclaimed, and stopped with a frank smile of greeting. "How are you?"

"I am well," he answered.

"I suppose," she added, "you have been very busy these terrible days."

"I have been more busy observing than doing," he replied.

"And how is Alice?"

"She is well. I suppose you have heard that she is engaged."

"Yes," said Miss Hegan. "Harry told me the first thing. I was perfectly delighted."

"Are you going up town?" she added. "Get in and drive with me."

He entered the carriage, and they joined the procession up the Avenue. They talked for a few minutes, then suddenly Miss Hegan said, "Won't you and Alice come to dinner with us some evening this week?"

Montague did not answer for a moment.

"Father is home now," Miss Hegan continued. "We should like so much to have you."

He sat staring in front of him. "No," he said at last, in a low voice. "I would rather not come."

His manner, even more than his words, struck his companion. She glanced at him in surprise.

"Why?" she began, and stopped. There was a silence.

"Miss Hegan," he said at last, "I might make conventional excuses. I might say that I have engagements; that I am very busy. Ordinarily one does not find it worth while to tell the truth in this social world of ours. But somehow I feel impelled to deal frankly with you."

He did not look at her. Her eyes were fixed upon him in wonder. "What is it?" she asked.

And he replied, "I would rather not meet your father again."

"Why! Has anything happened between you and father?" she exclaimed in dismay.

"No," he answered; "I have not seen your father since I had lunch with you in Newport."

"Then what is it?"

He paused a moment. "Miss Hegan," he began, "I have had a painful experience in this panic. I have lived through it in a very dreadful way. I cannot get over it—I cannot get the images of suffering out of my mind. It is a very real and a very awful thing to me—this wrecking of the lives of tens of thousands of people. And so I am hardly fitted for the amenities of social life just at present."

"But my father!" gasped she. "What has he to do with it?"

"Your father," he answered, "is one of the men who were responsible for that panic. He helped to make it; and he profited by it."

She started forward, clenching her hands and staring at him wildly. "Mr. Montague!" she exclaimed.

He did not reply.

There was a long pause. He could hear her breath coming quickly.

"Are you sure?" she whispered.

"Quite sure," said he.

Again there was silence.

"I do not know very much about my father's affairs," she began, at last. "I cannot reply to what you say. It is very dreadful."

"Please understand me, Miss Hegan," said he. "I have no right to force such thoughts upon you; and perhaps I have made a mistake—"

"I should have preferred that you should tell me the truth," she said quickly.

"I believed that you would," he answered. "That was why I spoke."

"Was what he did so very dreadful?" asked the girl, in a low voice.

"I would prefer not to answer," said he. "I cannot judge your father. I am simply trying to protect myself. I'm afraid of the grip of this world upon me. I have followed the careers of so many men, one after another. They come into it, and it lays hold of them, and before they know it, they become corrupt. What I have seen here in the Metropolis has filled me with dismay, almost with terror. Every fibre of me cries out against it; and I mean to fight it—to fight it all my life. And so I do not care to make terms with it socially. When I have seen a man doing what I believe to be a dreadful wrong, I cannot go to his home, and shake his hand, and smile, and exchange the commonplaces of life with him."

It was a long time before Miss Hegan replied. Her voice was trembling.

"Mr. Montague," she said, "you must not think that I have not been troubled by these things. But what can one do? What is the remedy?"

"I do not know," he answered. "I wish that I did know. I can only tell you this, that I do not intend to rest until I have found out."

"What are you going to do?" she asked.

He replied: "I am going into politics. I am going to try to teach the people."

KING COAL

TO
MARY CRAIG KIMBROUGH

To whose persistence in the perilous task of tearing her husband's manuscript to pieces, the reader is indebted for the absence of most of the faults from this book.

INTRODUCTION

Upton Sinclair is one of the not too many writers who have consecrated their lives to the agitation for social justice, and who have also enrolled their art in the service of a set purpose. A great and non-temporizing enthusiast, he never flinched from making sacrifices. Now and then he attained great material successes as a writer, but invariably he invested and lost his earnings in enterprises by which he had hoped to ward off injustice and to further human happiness. Though disappointed time after time, he never lost faith nor courage to start again.

As a convinced socialist and eager advocate of unpopular doctrines, as an exposer of social conditions that would otherwise be screened away from the public eye, the most influential journals of his country were as a rule arraigned against him. Though always a poor man, though never willing to grant to publishers the concessions essential for many editions and general popularity, he was maliciously represented to be a carpet knight of radicalism and a socialist millionaire. He has several times been obliged to change his publisher, which goes to prove that he is no seeker of material gain.

Upton Sinclair is one of the writers of the present time most deserving of a sympathetic interest. He shows his patriotism as an American, not by joining in hymns to the very conditional kind of liberty peculiar to the United States, but by agitating for infusing it with the elixir of real liberty, the liberty of humanity. He does not limit himself to a dispassionate and entertaining description of things as they are. But in his appeals to the honour and good-fellowship of his compatriots, he opens their eyes to the appalling conditions under which wage-earning slaves are living by the hundreds of thousands. His object is to better these unnatural conditions, to obtain for the very poorest a glimpse of light and happiness, to make even them realise the sensation of cosy well-being and the comfort of knowing that justice is to be found also for them.

This time Upton Sinclair has absorbed himself in the study of the miner's life in the lonesome pits of the Rocky Mountains, and his sensitive and enthusiastic mind has brought to the world an American parallel to GERMINAL, Emile Zola's technical masterpiece.

The conditions described in the two books are, however, essentially different. While Zola's working-men are all natives of France, one meets in Sinclair's book a motley variety of European emigrants, speaking a Babel of languages and therefore debarred from forming some sort of association to protect themselves against being exploited by the anonymous limited Company. Notwithstanding this natural bar against united action on the part of the wage-earning slaves, the Company feels far from at ease and jealously guards its interests against any attempt of organising the men.

A young American of the upper class, with great sympathy for the downtrodden and an honest desire to get a first-hand knowledge of their conditions in order to help them, decides to take employment in a mine under a fictitious name and dressed like a working-man. His unusual way of trying to obtain work arouses suspicion. He is believed to be a professional strike-leader sent out to organise the miners against their exploiters, and he is not only refused work, but thrashed mercilessly. When finally he succeeds in getting inside, he discovers with growing indignation the shameless and inhuman way in which those who unearth the black coal are being exploited.

These are the fundamental ideas of the book, but they give but a faint notion of the author's poetic attitude. Most beautifully is this shown in Hal's relation to a young Irish girl, Red Mary. She is poor, and her daily life harsh and joyless, but nevertheless her wonderful grace is one of the outstanding features of the book. The first impression of Mary is that of a Celtic Madonna with a tender heart for little children. She develops into a Valküre of the working-class, always ready to fight for the worker's right.

The last chapters of the book give a description of the miners' revolt against the Company. They insist upon their right to choose a deputy to control the weighing-in of the coal, and upon having the mines sprinkled regularly to prevent explosion. They will also be free to buy their food and utensils wherever they like, even in shops not belonging to the Company.

In a postscript Sinclair explains the fundamental facts on which his work of art has been built up. Even without the postscript one could not help feeling convinced that the social conditions he describes are true to life. The main point is that Sinclair has not allowed himself to become inspired by hackneyed phrases that bondage and injustice and the other evils and crimes of Kingdoms have been banished from Republics, but that he is earnestly pointing to the honeycombed ground on which the greatest modern money-power has been built. The fundament of this power is not granite, but mines. It lives and breathes in the light, because it has thousands of unfortunates toiling in the darkness. It lives and has its being in proud liberty because thousands are slaving for it, whose thraldom is the price of this liberty.

This is the impression given to the reader of this exciting novel.
GEORG BRANDES.

BOOK ONE — THE DOMAIN OF KING COAL

SECTION 1.

The town of Pedro stood on the edge of the mountain country; a straggling assemblage of stores and saloons from which a number of branch railroads ran up into the canyons, feeding the coal-camps. Through the week it slept peacefully; but on Saturday nights, when the miners came trooping down, and the ranchmen came in on horseback and in automobiles, it wakened to a seething life.

At the railroad station, one day late in June, a young man alighted from a train. He was about twenty-one years of age, with sensitive features, and brown hair having a tendency to waviness. He wore a frayed and faded suit of clothes, purchased in a quarter of his home city where the Hebrew merchants stand on the sidewalks to offer their wares; also a soiled blue shirt without a tie, and a pair of heavy boots which had seen much service. Strapped on his back was a change of clothing and a blanket, and in his pockets a comb, a toothbrush, and a small pocket mirror.

Sitting in the smoking-car of the train, the young man had listened to the talk of the coal-camps, seeking to correct his accent. When he got off the train he proceeded down the track and washed his hands with cinders, and lightly powdered some over his face. After studying the effect of this in his mirror, he strolled down the main street of Pedro, and, selecting a little tobacco-shop, went in. In as surly a voice as he could muster, he inquired of the proprietress, "Can you tell me how to get to the Pine Creek mine?"

The woman looked at him with no suspicion in her glance. She gave the desired information, and he took a trolley and got off at the foot of the Pine Creek canyon, up which he had a thirteen-mile trudge. It was a sunshiny day, with the sky crystal clear, and the mountain air invigourating. The young man seemed to be happy, and as he strode on his way, he sang a song with many verses:

> "Old King Coal was a merry old soul,
>   And a merry old soul was he;
> He made him a college all full of knowledge—
>   Hurrah for you and me!
>
> "Oh, Liza-Ann, come out with me,
>   The moon is a-shinin' in the monkey-puzzle tree;

Oh, Liza-Ann, I have began
  To sing you the song of Harrigan!

"He keeps them a-roll, this merry old soul—
  The wheels of industree;
A-roll and a-roll, for his pipe and his bowl
  And his college facultee!

"Oh, Mary-Jane, come out in the lane,
  The moon is a-shinin' in the old pecan;
Oh, Mary-Jane, don't you hear me a-sayin'
  I'll sing you the song of Harrigan!

"So hurrah for King Coal, and his fat pay-roll,
  And his wheels of industree!
Hurrah for his pipe, and hurrah for his bowl—
  And hurrah for you and me!

"Oh, Liza-Ann, come out with me,
  The moon is a-shinin'—"

And so on and on—as long as the moon was a-shinin' on a college campus. It was a mixture of happy nonsense and that questioning with which modern youth has begun to trouble its elders. As a marching tune, the song was a trifle swift for the grades of a mountain canyon; Warner could stop and shout to the canyon-walls, and listen to their answer, and then march on again. He had youth in his heart, and love and curiosity; also he had some change in his trousers' pocket, and a ten dollar bill, for extreme emergencies, sewed up in his belt. If a photographer for Peter Harrigan's General Fuel Company could have got a snap-shot of him that morning, it might have served as a "portrait of a coal-miner" in any "prosperity" publication.

But the climb was a stiff one, and before the end the traveller became aware of the weight of his boots, and sang no more. Just as the sun was sinking up the canyon, he came upon his destination—a gate across the road, with a sign upon it:

PINE CREEK COAL CO.
PRIVATE PROPERTY
TRESPASSING FORBIDDEN

Hal approached the gate, which was of iron bars, and padlocked. After standing for a moment to get ready his surly voice, he kicked upon the gate and a man came out of a shack inside.

"What do you want?" said he.

"I want to get in. I'm looking for a job."

"Where do you come from?"

"From Pedro."

"Where you been working?"

"I never worked in a mine before."

"Where did you work?"

"In a grocery-store."

"What grocery-store?"

"Peterson & Co., in Western City."

The guard came closer to the gate and studied him through the bars.

"Hey, Bill!" he called, and another man came out from the cabin. "Here's a guy says he worked in a grocery, and he's lookin' for a job."

"Where's your papers?" demanded Bill.

Every one had told Hal that labour was scarce in the mines, and that the companies were ravenous for men; he had supposed that a workingman would only have to knock, and it would be opened unto him. "They didn't give me no papers," he said, and added, hastily, "I got drunk and they fired me." He felt quite sure that getting drunk would not bar one from a coal camp.

But the two made no move to open the gate. The second man studied him deliberately from top to toe, and Hal was uneasily aware of possible sources of suspicion. "I'm all right," he declared. "Let me in, and I'll show you."

Still the two made no move. They looked at each other, and then Bill answered, "We don't need no hands."

"But," exclaimed Hal, "I saw a sign down the canyon—"

"That's an old sign," said Bill.

"But I walked all the way up here!"

"You'll find it easier walkin' back."

"But—it's night!"

"Scared of the dark, kid?" inquired Bill, facetiously.

"Oh, say!" replied Hal. "Give a fellow a chance! Ain't there some way I can pay for my keep—or at least for a bunk to-night?"

"There's nothin' for you," said Bill, and turned and went into the cabin.

The other man waited and watched, with a decidedly hostile look. Hal strove to plead with him, but thrice he repeated, "Down the canyon with you." So at last Hal gave up, and moved down the road a piece and sat down to reflect.

It really seemed an absurdly illogical proceeding, to post a notice, "Hands Wanted," in conspicuous places on the roadside, causing a man to climb thirteen miles up a mountain canyon, only to be turned off without explanation. Hal was convinced that there must be jobs inside the stockade, and that if only he could get at the bosses he could persuade them. He got up and walked down the road a quarter of a mile, to where the railroad-track crossed it, winding up the canyon. A train of "empties" was passing, bound into the camp, the cars rattling and bumping as the engine toiled up the grade. This suggested a solution of the difficulty.

It was already growing dark. Crouching slightly, Hal approached the cars, and when he was in the shadows, made a leap and swung onto one of them. It took but a second to clamber in, and he lay flat and waited, his heart thumping.

Before a minute had passed he heard a shout, and looking over, he saw the Cerberus of the gate running down a path to the track, his companion, Bill, just behind him. "Hey! come out of there!" they yelled; and Bill leaped, and caught the car in which Hal was riding.

The latter saw that the game was up, and sprang to the ground on the other side of the track and started out of the camp. Bill followed him, and as the train passed, the other man ran down the track to join him. Hal was walking rapidly, without a word; but the Cerberus of the gate had many words, most of them unprintable, and he seized Hal by the collar, and shoving him violently, planted a kick upon that portion of his anatomy which nature has constructed for the reception of kicks. Hal recovered his balance, and, as the man was still pursuing him, he turned and aimed a blow, striking him on the chest and making him reel.

Hal's big brother had seen to it that he knew how to use his fists; he now squared off, prepared to receive the second of his assailants. But in coal-camps matters are not settled in that primitive way, it appeared. The man halted, and the muzzle of a revolver came suddenly under Hal's nose. "Stick 'em up!" said the man.

This was a slang which Hal had never heard, but the meaning was inescapable; he "stuck 'em up." At the same moment his first assailant rushed at him, and dealt him a blow over the eye which sent him sprawling backward upon the stones.

<h1 style="text-align:center">SECTION 2.</h1>

When Hal came to himself again he was in darkness, and was conscious of agony from head to toe. He was lying on a stone floor, and he rolled over, but soon rolled back again, because there was no part of his back which was not sore. Later on, when he was able to study himself, he counted over a score of marks of the heavy boots of his assailants.

He lay for an hour or two, making up his mind that he was in a lock-up, because he could see the starlight through iron bars. He could hear somebody snoring, and he called half a dozen times, in a louder and louder voice, until at last, hearing a growl, he inquired, "Can you give me a drink of water?"

"I'll give you hell if you wake me up again," said the voice; after which Hal lay in silence until morning.

A couple of hours after daylight, a man entered his cell. "Get up," said he, and added a prod with his foot. Hal had thought he could not do it, but he got up.

"No funny business now," said his jailer, and grasping him by the sleeve of his coat, marched him out of the cell and down a little corridor into a sort of office, where sat a red-faced personage with a silver shield upon the lapel of his coat. Hal's two assailants of the night before stood nearby.

"Well, kid?" said the personage in the chair. "Had a little time to think it over?"

"Yes," said Hal, briefly.

"What's the charge?" inquired the personage, of the two watchmen.

"Trespassing and resisting arrest."

"How much money you got, young fellow?" was, the next question.

Hal hesitated.

"Speak up there!" said the man.

"Two dollars and sixty-seven cents," said Hal—"as well as I can remember."

"Go on!" said the other. "What you givin' us?" And then, to the two watchmen, "Search him."

"Take off your coat and pants," said Bill, promptly, "and your boots."

"Oh, I say!" protested Hal.

"Take 'em off!" said the man, and clenched his fists. Hal took 'em off, and they proceeded to go through the pockets, producing a purse with the amount stated, also a cheap watch, a strong pocket knife, the tooth-brush, comb and mirror, and two white handkerchiefs, which they looked at contemptuously and tossed to the spittle-drenched floor.

They unrolled the pack, and threw the clean clothing about. Then, opening the pocket-knife, they proceeded to pry about the soles and heels of the boots, and to cut open the lining of the clothing. So they found the ten dollars in the belt, which they tossed onto the table with the other belongings. Then the personage with the shield announced, "I fine you twelve dollars and sixty-seven cents, and your watch and knife." He added, with a grin, "You can keep your snot-rags."

"Now see here!" said Hal, angrily. "This is pretty raw!"

"You get your duds on, young fellow, and get out of here as quick as you can, or you'll go in your shirt-tail."

But Hal was angry enough to have been willing to go in his skin. "You tell me who you are, and your authority for this procedure?"

"I'm marshal of the camp," said the man.

"You mean you're an employé of the General Fuel Company? And you propose to rob me—"

"Put him out, Bill," said the marshal. And Hal saw Bill's fists clench.

"All right," he said, swallowing his indignation. "Wait till I get my clothes on." And he proceeded to dress as quickly as possible; he rolled up his blanket and spare clothing, and started for the door.

"Remember," said the marshal, "straight down the canyon with you, and if you show your face round here again, you'll get a bullet through you."

So Hal went out into the sunshine, with a guard on each side of him as an escort. He was on the same mountain road, but in the midst of the company-village. In the distance he saw the great building of the breaker, and heard the incessant roar of machinery and falling coal. He marched past a double lane of company houses and shanties, where slattern women in doorways and dirty children digging in the dust of the roadside paused and grinned at him—for he limped as he walked, and it was evident enough what had happened to him.

Hal had come with love and curiosity. The love was greatly diminished—evidently this was not the force which kept the wheels of industry a-roll. But the curiosity was greater than ever. What was there so carefully hidden inside this coal-camp stockade?

Hal turned and looked at Bill, who had showed signs of humour the day before. "See here," said he, "you fellows have got my money, and you've blacked my eye and kicked me blue, so you ought to be satisfied. Before I go, tell me about it, won't you?"

"Tell you what?" growled Bill.

"Why did I get this?"

"Because you're too gay, kid. Didn't you know you had no business trying to sneak in here?"

"Yes," said Hal; "but that's not what I mean. Why didn't you let me in at first?"

"If you wanted a job in a mine," demanded the man, "why didn't you go at it in the regular way?"

"I didn't know the regular way."

"That's just it. And we wasn't takin' chances with you. You didn't look straight."

"But what did you think I was? What are you afraid of?"

"Go on!" said the man. "You can't work me!"

Hal walked a few steps in silence, pondering how to break through. "I see you're suspicious of me," he said. "I'll tell you the truth, if you'll let me." Then, as the other did not forbid him, "I'm a college boy, and I wanted to see life and shift for myself a while. I thought it would be a lark to come here."

"Well," said Bill, "this ain't no foot-ball field. It's a coal-mine."

Hal saw that his story had been accepted. "Tell me straight," he said, "what did you think I was?"

"Well, I don't mind telling," growled Bill. "There's union agitators trying to organise these here camps, and we ain't taking no chances with 'em. This company gets its men through agencies, and if you'd went and satisfied them, you'd 'a been passed in the regular way. Or if you'd went to the office down in Pedro and got a pass, you'd 'a been all right. But when a guy turns up at the gate, and looks like a dude and talks like a college perfessor, he don't get by, see?"

"I see," said Hal. And then, "If you'll give me the price of a breakfast out of my money, I'll be obliged."

"Breakfast is over," said Bill. "You sit round till the pinyons gets ripe." He laughed; but then, mellowed by his own joke, he took a quarter from his pocket and passed it to Hal. He opened the padlock on the gate and saw him out with a grin; and so ended Hal's first turn on the wheels of industry.

SECTION 3.

Hal Warner started to drag himself down the road, but was unable to make it. He got as far as a brooklet that came down the mountain-side, from which he might drink without fear of typhoid; there he lay the whole day, fasting. Towards evening a thunder-storm came up, and he crawled under the shelter of a rock, which was no shelter at all. His single blanket was soon soaked through, and he passed a night almost as miserable as the previous one. He could not sleep, but he could think, and he thought about what had happened to him. "Bill" had said that a coal mine was not a foot-ball field, but it seemed to Hal that the net impress of the two was very much the same. He congratulated himself that his profession was not that of a union organiser.

At dawn he dragged himself up, and continued his journey, weak from cold and unaccustomed lack of food. In the course of the day he reached a power-station near the foot of the canyon. He did not have the price of a meal, and was afraid to beg; but in one of the group of buildings by the roadside was a store, and he entered and inquired concerning prunes, which were twenty-five cents a pound. The price was high, but so was the altitude, and as Hal found in the course of time, they explained the one by the other—not explaining, however, why the altitude of the price was always greater than the altitude of the store. Over the counter he saw a sign: "We buy scrip at ten per cent discount." He had heard rumours of a state law forbidding payment of wages in "scrip"; but he asked no questions, and carried off his very light pound of prunes, and sat down by the roadside and munched them.

Just beyond the power-house, down on the railroad track, stood a little cabin with a garden behind it. He made his way there, and found a one-legged old watchman. He asked permission to spend the night on the floor of the cabin; and seeing the old fellow look at his black eye, he explained, "I tried to get a job at the mine, and they thought I was a union organiser."

"Well," said the man, "I don't want no union organisers round here."

"But I'm not one," pleaded Hal.

"How do I know what you are? Maybe you're a company spy."

"All I want is a dry place to sleep," said Hal. "Surely it won't be any harm for you to give me that."

"I'm not so sure," the other answered. "However, you can spread your blanket in the corner. But don't you talk no union business to me."

Hal had no desire to talk. He rolled himself in his blanket and slept like a man untroubled by either love or curiosity. In the morning the old fellow gave him a slice of corn bread and some young onions out of his garden, which had a more delicious taste than any breakfast that had ever been served him. When Hal thanked his host in parting, the latter remarked: "All right, young fellow, there's one thing you can do to pay me, and that is, say nothing about it. When a man has grey hair on his head and only one leg, he might as well be drowned in the creek as lose his job."

Hal promised, and went his way. His bruises pained him less, and he was able to walk. There were ranch-houses in sight—it was like coming back suddenly to America!

SECTION 4.

Hal had now before him a week's adventures as a hobo: a genuine hobo, with no ten dollar bill inside his belt to take the reality out of his experiences. He took stock of his worldly goods and wondered if he still looked like a dude. He recalled that he had a smile which had fascinated the ladies; would it work in combination with a black eye? Having no other means of support, he tried it on susceptible looking housewives, and found it so successful that he was tempted to doubt the wisdom of honest labour. He sang the Harrigan song no more, but instead the words of a hobo-song he had once heard:

"Oh, what's the use of workin' when there's women in the land?"

The second day he made the acquaintance of two other gentlemen of the road, who sat by the railroad-track toasting some bacon over a fire. They welcomed him, and after they had heard his story, adopted him into the fraternity and instructed him in its ways of life. Pretty soon he made the acquaintance of one who had been a miner, and was able to give him the information he needed before climbing another canyon.

"Dutch Mike" was the name this person bore, for reasons he did not explain. He was a black-eyed and dangerous-looking rascal, and when the subject of mines and mining was broached, he opened up the flood-gates of an amazing reservoir of profanity. He was through with that game—Hal or any other God-damned fool might have his job for the asking. It was only because there were so many natural-born God-damned fools in the world that the game could be kept going. "Dutch Mike" went on to relate dreadful tales of mine-life, and to summon before him the ghosts of one pit-boss after another, consigning them to the fires of eternal perdition.

"I wanted to work while I was young," said he, "but now I'm cured, an' fer good." The world had come to seem to him a place especially constructed for the purpose of making him work, and every faculty he possessed was devoted to foiling this plot. Sitting by a camp-fire near the stream which ran down the valley, Hal had a merry time pointing out to "Dutch Mike" how he worked harder at dodging work than other men worked at working. The hobo did not seem to mind that, however—it was a matter of principle with him, and he was willing to make sacrifices for his convictions. Even when they had sent him to the work-house, he had refused to work; he had been shut in a dungeon, and had nearly died on a diet of bread and water, rather than work. If everybody would do the same, he said, they would soon "bust things."

Hal took a fancy to this spontaneous revolutionist, and travelled with him for a couple of days, in the course of which he pumped him as to details of the life of a miner. Most of the companies used regular employment agencies, as the guard had mentioned; but the trouble was, these agencies got something from your pay for a long time—the bosses were "in cahoots" with them. When Hal wondered if this were not against the law, "Cut it out, Bo!" said his companion. "When you've had a job for a while, you'll know that the law in a coal-camp is what your boss tells you." The hobo went on to register his conviction that when one man has the giving of jobs, and other men have to scramble for them, the law would never have much to say in the deal. Hal judged this a profound observation, and wished that it might be communicated to the professor of political economy at Harrigan.

On the second night of his acquaintance with "Dutch Mike," their "jungle" was raided by a constable with half a dozen deputies; for a determined effort was being made just then to drive vagrants from the neighbourhood—or to get them to work in the mines. Hal's friend, who slept with one eye open, made a break in the darkness, and Hal followed him, getting under the guard of the raiders by a foot-ball trick. They left their food and blankets behind them, but "Dutch Mike" made light of this, and lifted a chicken from a roost to keep them cheerful through the night hours, and stole a change of underclothing off a clothes-line the next day. Hal ate the chicken, and wore the underclothing, thus beginning his career in crime.

Parting from "Dutch Mike," he went back to Pedro. The hobo had told him that saloon-keepers nearly always had friends in the coal-camps, and could help a fellow to a job. So Hal began enquiring, and the second one replied, Yes, he would give him a letter to a man at North Valley, and if he got the job, the friend would deduct a dollar a month from his pay. Hal agreed, and set out upon another tramp up another canyon, upon the strength of a sandwich "bummed" from a ranch-house at the entrance to the valley. At another stockaded gate of the General Fuel Company he presented his letter, addressed to a person named O'Callahan, who turned out also to be a saloon-keeper.

The guard did not even open the letter, but passed Hal in at sight of it, and he sought out his man and applied for work. The man said he would help him, but would have to deduct a dollar a month for himself, as well as a dollar for his friend in Pedro. Hal kicked at this, and they bartered back and forth; finally, when Hal turned away and threatened to appeal directly to the "super," the saloon-keeper compromised on a dollar and a half.

"You know mine-work?" he asked.

"Brought up at it," said Hal, made wise, now, in the ways of the world.

"Where did you work?"

Hal named several mines, concerning which he had learned something from the hoboes. He was going by the name of "Joe Smith," which he judged likely to be found on the payroll of any mine. He had more than a week's growth of beard to disguise him, and had picked up some profanity as well.

The saloon-keeper took him to interview Mr. Alec Stone, pit-boss in Number Two mine, who inquired promptly: "You know anything about mules?"

"I worked in a stable," said Hal, "I know about horses."

"Well, mules is different," said the man. "One of my stable-men got the colic the other day, and I don't know if he'll ever be any good again."

"Give me a chance," said Hal. "I'll manage them."

The boss looked him over. "You look like a bright chap," said he. "I'll pay you forty-five a month, and if you make good I'll make it fifty."

"All right, sir. When do I start in?"

"You can't start too quick to suit me. Where's your duds?"

"This is all I've got," said Hal, pointing to the bundle of stolen underwear in his hand.

"Well, chuck it there in the corner," said the man; then suddenly he stopped, and looked at Hal, frowning. "You belong to any union?"

"Lord, no!"

"Did you *ever* belong to any union?"

"No, sir. Never."

The man's gaze seemed to imply that Hal was lying, and that his secret soul was about to be read. "You have to swear to that, you know, before you can work here."

"All right," said Hal, "I'm willing."

"I'll see you about it to-morrow," said the other. "I ain't got the paper with me. By the way, what's your religion?"

"Seventh Day Adventist."

"Holy Christ! What's that?"

"It don't hurt," said Hal. "I ain't supposed to work on Saturdays, but I do."

"Well, don't you go preachin' it round here. We got our own preacher—you chip in fifty cents a month for him out of your wages. Come ahead now, and I'll take you down." And so it was that Hal got his start in life.

SECTION 5.

The mule is notoriously a profane and godless creature; a blind alley of Nature, so to speak, a mistake of which she is ashamed, and which she does not permit to reproduce itself. The thirty mules under Hal's charge had been brought up in an environment calculated to foster the worst tendencies of their natures. He soon made the discovery that the "colic" of his predecessor had been caused by a mule's hind foot in the stomach; and he realised that he must not let his mind wander for an instant, if he were to avoid this dangerous disease.

These mules lived their lives in the darkness of the earth's interior; only when they fell sick were they taken up to see the sunlight and to roll about in green pastures. There was one of them called "Dago Charlie," who had learned to chew tobacco, and to rummage in the pockets of the miners and their "buddies." Not knowing how to spit out the juice, he would make himself ill, and then he would swear off from indulgence. But the drivers and the pit-boys knew his failing, and would tempt "Dago Charlie" until he fell from grace. Hal soon discovered this moral tragedy, and carried the pain of it in his soul as he went about his all-day drudgery.

He went down the shaft with the first cage, which was very early in the morning. He fed and watered his charges, and helped to harness them. Then, when the last four hoofs had clattered away, he cleaned out the stalls, and mended harness, and obeyed the orders of any person older than himself who happened to be about.

Next to the mules, his torment was the "trapper-boys," and other youngsters with whom he came into contact. He was a newcomer, and so they hazed him; moreover, he had an inferior job—there seemed to their minds to be something humiliating and comic about the task of tending mules. These urchins came from a score of nations of Southern Europe and Asia; there were flat-faced Tartars and swarthy Greeks and shrewd-eyed little Japanese. They spoke a compromise language, consisting mainly of English curse words and obscenities; the filthiness which their minds had spawned was incredible to one born and raised in the sunlight. They alleged obscenities of their mothers and their grandmothers; also of the Virgin Mary, the one mythological character they had heard of. Poor little creatures of the dark, their souls grimed and smutted even more quickly and irrevocably than their faces!

Hal had been advised by his boss to inquire for board at "Reminitsky's." He came up in the last car, at twilight, and was directed to a dimly lighted building of corrugated iron, where upon inquiry he was met by a stout Russian, who told him he could be taken care of for twenty-seven dollars a month, this including a cot in a room with eight other single men. After deducting a dollar and a half a month for his saloon-keepers, fifty cents for the company clergyman and a dollar for the company doctor, fifty cents a month for wash-house privileges and fifty cents for a sick and accident benefit fund, he had fourteen dollars a month with which to clothe himself, to found a family, to provide himself with beer and tobacco, and to patronise the libraries and colleges endowed by the philanthropic owners of coal mines.

Supper was nearly over at Reminitsky's when he arrived; the floor looked like the scene of a cannibal picnic, and what food was left was cold. It was always to be this way with him, he found, and he had to make the best of it. The dining-room of this boarding-house, owned and managed by the G. F. C., brought to his mind the state prison, which he had once visited—with its rows of men sitting in silence, eating starch and grease out of tin-plates. The plates here were of crockery half an inch thick, but the starch and grease never failed; the formula of Reminitsky's cook seemed to be, When in doubt add grease, and boil it in. Even ravenous as Hal was after his long tramp and his labour below ground, he could hardly swallow this food. On Sundays, the only time he ate by daylight, the flies swarmed over everything, and he remembered having heard a physician say that an enlightened man should be more afraid of a fly than of a Bengal tiger. The boarding-house provided him with a cot and a supply of vermin, but with no blanket, which was a necessity in the mountain regions. So after supper he had to seek out his boss, and arrange to get credit at the company-store. They were willing to give a certain amount of credit, he found, as this would enable the camp-marshal to keep him from straying. There was no law to hold a man for debt—but Hal knew by this time how much a camp-marshal cared for law.

SECTION 6.

For three days Hal toiled in the bowels of the mine, and ate and pursued vermin at Reminitsky's. Then came a blessed Sunday, and he had a couple of free hours to see the sunlight and to get a look at the North Valley camp. It was a village straggling along more than a mile of the mountain canyon. In the centre were the great breaker-buildings, the shaft-house, and the power-house with its tall chimneys; nearby were the company-store and a couple of saloons. There were several boarding-houses like Reminitsky's, and long rows of board cabins containing from two to four rooms each, some of them occupied by several families. A little way up a slope stood a school-house, and another small one-room building which served as a church; the clergyman belonging to the General Fuel Company denomination. He was given the use of the building, by way of start over the saloons, which had to pay a heavy rental to the company; it seemed a proof of the innate perversity of human nature that even in spite of this advantage, heaven was losing out in the struggle against hell in the coal-camp.

As one walked through this village, the first impression was of desolation. The mountains towered, barren and lonely, scarred with the wounds of geologic ages. In these canyons the sun set early in the afternoon, the snow came early in the fall; everywhere Nature's hand seemed against man, and man had succumbed to her power. Inside the camps one felt a still more cruel desolation—that of sordidness and animalism. There were a few pitiful attempts at vegetable-gardens, but the cinders and smoke killed everything, and the prevailing colour was of grime. The landscape was strewn with ash-heaps, old wire and tomato-cans, and smudged and smutty children playing.

There was a part of the camp called "shanty-town," where, amid miniature mountains of slag, some of the lowest of the newly-arrived foreigners had been permitted to build themselves shacks out of old boards, tin, and sheets of tar-paper. These homes were beneath the dignity of chicken-houses, yet in some of them a dozen people were crowded, men and women sleeping on old rags and blankets on a cinder floor. Here the babies swarmed like maggots. They wore for the most part a single ragged smock, and their bare buttocks were shamelessly upturned to the heavens. It was so the children of the cave-men must have played, thought Hal; and waves of repulsion swept over him. He had come with love and curiosity, but both motives failed here. How could a man of sensitive nerves, aware of the refinements and graces of life, learn to love these people, who were an affront to his every sense—a stench to his nostrils, a jabbering to his ear, a procession of deformities to his eye? What had civilisation done for them? What could it do? After all, what were they fit for, but the dirty work they were penned up to do? So spoke the haughty race-consciousness of the Anglo-Saxon, contemplating these Mediterranean hordes, the very shape of whose heads was objectionable.

But Hal stuck it out; and little by little new vision came to him. First of all, it was the fascination of the mines. They were old mines—veritable cities tunnelled out beneath the mountains, the main passages running for miles. One day Hal stole off from his job, and took a trip with a "rope-rider," and got through his physical senses a realisation of the vastness and strangeness and loneliness of this labyrinth of night. In Number Two mine the vein ran up at a slope of perhaps five degrees; in part of it the empty cars were hauled in long trains by an endless rope, but coming back loaded, they came of their own gravity. This involved much work for the "spraggers," or boys who did the braking; it sometimes meant runaway cars, and fresh perils added to the everyday perils of coal-mining.

The vein varied from four to five feet in thickness; a cruelty of nature which made it necessary that the men at the "working face"—the place where new coal was being cut—should learn to shorten their stature. After Hal had squatted for a while and watched them at their tasks, he understood why they walked with head and shoulders bent over and arms hanging down, so that, seeing them coming out of the shaft in the gloaming, one thought of a file of baboons. The method of getting out the coal was to "undercut" it with a pick, and then blow it loose with a charge of powder. This meant that the miner had to lie on his side while working, and accounted for other physical peculiarities.

Thus, as always, when one understood the lives of men, one came to pity instead of despising. Here was a separate race of creatures, subterranean, gnomes, pent up by society for purposes of its own. Outside in the sunshine-flooded canyon, long lines of cars rolled down with their freight of soft-coal; coal which would go to the ends of the earth, to places the miner never heard of, turning the wheels of industry whose products the miner would never see. It would make precious silks for fine ladies, it would cut precious jewels for their adornment; it would carry long trains of softly upholstered cars across deserts and over mountains; it would drive palatial steamships out of wintry tempests into gleaming tropic seas. And the fine ladies in their precious silks and jewels would eat and sleep and laugh and lie at ease—and would know no more of the stunted creatures of the dark than the stunted creatures knew of them. Hal reflected upon this, and subdued his Anglo-Saxon pride, finding forgiveness for what was repulsive in these people—their barbarous, jabbering speech, their vermin-ridden homes, their bare-bottomed babies.

SECTION 7.

It chanced before many days that Hal got a holiday, relieving the monotony of his labours as stableman: an accidental holiday, not provided for in his bargain with the pit-boss. Something went wrong with the ventilating-course in Number Two, and he began to notice a headache, and heard the men grumbling that their lamps were burning low. Then, as matters began to get serious, orders came to get the mules to the surface.

Which meant an amusing adventure. The delight of Hal's pets at seeing the sunlight was irresistibly comic. They could not be kept from lying down and rolling on their backs in the cinder-strewn street; and when they were corralled in a distant part of the camp where actual grass grew, they abandoned themselves to rapture like a horde of school children at a picnic.

So Hal had a few free hours; and being still young and not cured of idle curiosities, he climbed the canyon wall to see the mountains. As he was sliding down again, toward evening, a vivid spot of colour was painted into his picture of mine-life; he found himself in somebody's back yard, and being observed by somebody's daughter, who was taking in the family wash. It was a splendid figure of a lass, tall and vigorous, with the sort of hair that in polite circles is called auburn, and that flaming colour in the cheeks which is Nature's recompense to people who live where it rains all the time. She was the first beautiful sight Hal had seen since he had come up the canyon, and it was only natural that he should be interested. It seemed to him that, so long as the girl stared, he had a right to stare back. It did not occur to him that he too was a pleasing sight—that the mountain air had given colour to his cheeks and a shine to his gay brown eyes, while the mountain winds had blown his wavy brown hair.

"Hello," said she, at last, in a warm voice, unmistakably Irish.

"Hello yourself," said Hal, in the accepted dialect; then he added, with more elegance, "Pardon me for trespassing on your wash."

Her grey eyes opened wider. "Go on!" she said.

"I'd rather stay," said Hal. "It's a beautiful sunset."

"I'll move, so ye can see it better." She carried her armful of clothes over and dropped them into the basket.

"No," said Hal, "it's not so fine now. The colours have faded."

She turned and gazed at him again. "Go on wid ye! I been teased about my hair since before I could talk."

"'Tis envy," said Hal, dropping into her way of speech; and he came a few steps nearer, so that he could inspect the hair more closely. It lay above her brow in undulations which were agreeable to the decorative instinct, and a tight heavy braid of it fell over her shoulders and swung to her waist-line. He observed the shoulders, which were sturdy, obviously accustomed to hard labour; not conforming to accepted romantic standards of femininity, yet having an athletic grace of their own. They were covered with a faded blue calico dress, unfortunately not entirely clean; also, the young man noticed, there was a rent in one shoulder through which a patch of skin was visible. The girl's eyes, which had been following his, became defiant; she tossed a piece of her washing over the shoulder, where it stayed through the balance of the interview.

"Who are ye?" she demanded, suddenly.

"My name's Joe Smith. I'm a stableman in Number Two."

"And what were ye doin' up there, if a body might ask?" She lifted her grey eyes to the bare mountainside, down which he had come sliding in a shower of loose stones and dirt.

"I've been surveying my empire," said he.

"Your what?"

"My empire. The land belongs to the company, but the landscape belongs to him who cares for it."

She tossed her head a little. "Where did ye learn to talk like ye do?"

"In another life," said he—"before I became a stableman. Not in entire forgetfulness, but trailing clouds of glory did I come."

For a moment she wrestled with this. Then a smile broke upon her face. "Sure, 'tis like a poetry-book! Say some more!"

"*O, singe fort, so suess und fein*!" quoted Hal—and saw her look puzzled.

"Aren't you American?" she inquired; and he laughed. To speak a foreign language in North Valley was not a mark of culture!

"I've been listening to the crowd at Reminitsky's," he said, apologetically.

"Oh! You eat there?"

"I go there three times a day. I can't say I eat very much. Could you live on greasy beans?"

"Sure," laughed the girl, "the good old pertaties is good enough for me."

"I should have said you lived on rose leaves!" he observed.

"Go on wid ye! 'Tis the blarney-stone ye been kissin'!"

"'Tis no stone I'd be wastin' my kisses on."

"Ye're gettin' bold, Mister Smith. I'll not listen to ye." And she turned away, and began industriously taking her clothes from the line. But Hal did not want to be dismissed. He came a step closer.

"Coming down the mountain-side," he said, "I found something wonderful. It's bare and grim up there, but I came on a sheltered corner where the sun shone, and there was a wild rose. Only one! I thought to myself, 'So roses grow, even in the loneliest parts of the world!'"

"Sure, 'tis a poetry-book again!" she cried. "Why didn't ye bring the rose?"

"There is a poetry-book that tells us to 'leave the wild-rose on its stalk.' It will go on blooming there; but if one were to pluck it, it would wither in a few hours."

He had meant nothing more by this than to keep the conversation going. But her answer turned the tide of their acquaintance.

"Ye can never be sure, lad. Perhaps to-night a storm may come and blow it to pieces. Perhaps if ye'd pulled it and been happy, 'twould 'a been what the rose was for."

Whatever of unconscious patronage there had been in the poet's attitude was lost now in the eternal mystery. Whether the girl knew it—or cared—she had won the woman's first victory. She had caught the man's mind and pinned it with curiosity. What did this wild rose of the mining camps mean?

The wild rose, apparently unconscious that she had said anything epoch-making, was busy with the wash; and meantime Hal Warner studied her features and pondered her words. From a lady of sophistication they would have meant only one thing, an invitation; but in this girl's clear grey eyes was nothing of wantonness, only pain. But what was this pain in the face and words of one so young, so eager and alive? Was it the melancholy of her race, the thing one got in old folk-songs? Or was it a new and special kind of melancholy, engendered in mining-camps in the far West of America?

The girl's countenance was as intriguing as her words. Her grey eyes were set under sharply defined dark brows, which did not match her hair. Her lips also were sharply defined, and straight, almost without curves, so that it seemed as if her mouth had been painted in carmine upon her face. These features gave her, when she stared at you, an aspect vivid and startling, bold, with a touch of defiance. But when she smiled, the red lips would curve into gentler lines, and the grey eyes would become wistful, and seemingly darker in colour. Winsome indeed, but not simple, was this Irish lass!

SECTION 8.

Hal asked the name of his new acquaintance, and she told him it was Mary Burke. "Ye've not been here long, I take it," she said, "or ye'd have heard of 'Red Mary.' 'Tis along of this hair."

"I've not been here long," he answered, "but I shall hope to stay now—along of this hair! May I come to see you some time, Miss Burke?"

She did not reply, but glanced at the house where she lived. It was an unpainted, three room cabin, more dilapidated than the average, with bare dirt and cinders about it, and what had once been a picket-fence, now falling apart and being used for stove-wood. The windows were cracked and broken, and upon the roof were signs of leaks that had been crudely patched.

"May I come?" he made haste to ask again—so that he would not seem to look too critically at her home.

"Perhaps ye may," said the girl, as she picked up the clothes basket. He stepped forward, offering to carry it, but she did not give it up. Holding it tight, and looking him defiantly in the face, she said, "Ye may come, but ye'll not find it a happy place to visit, Mr. Smith. Ye'll hear soon enough from the neighbours."

"I don't think I know any of your neighbours," said he.

There was sympathy in his voice; but her look was no less defiant. "Ye'll hear about it, Mr. Smith; but ye'll hear also that I hold me head up. And 'tis not so easy to do that in North Valley."

"You don't like the place?" he asked; and he was amazed by the effect of this question, which was merely polite. It was as if a storm cloud had swept over the girl's face. "I hate it! 'Tis a place of fear and devils!"

He hesitated a moment; then, "Will you tell me what you mean by that when I come?"

But "Red Mary" was winsome again. "When ye come, Mr. Smith, I'll not be entertaining ye with troubles. I'll put on me company manner, and we'll go out for a nice walk, if ye please."

All the way as he walked back to Reminitsky's to supper, Hal thought about this girl; not merely her pleasantness to the eye, so unexpected in this place of desolation, but her personality, which baffled him—the pain that seemed always just beneath the surface of her thoughts, the fierce pride which flashed out at the slightest suggestion of sympathy, the way she had of brightening when he spoke the language of metaphor, however trite. How had she come to know about poetry-books? He wanted to know more about this miracle of Nature—this wild rose blooming on a bare mountain-side!

SECTION 9.

There was one of Mary Burke's remarks upon which Hal soon got light—her statement that North Valley was a place of fear. He listened to the tales of these underworld men, until it came so that he shuddered with dread each time that he went down in the cage.

There was a wire-haired and almond eyed Korean, named Cho, a "rope-rider" in Hal's part of the mine. He was one of those who had charge of the long trains of cars, called "trips," which were hauled through the main passage-ways; the name "rope-rider" came from the fact that he sat on the heavy iron ring to which the rope was attached. He invited Hal to a seat with him, and Hal accepted, at peril of his job as well as of his limbs. Cho had picked up what he fondly thought was English, and now and then one could understand a word. He pointed upon the ground, and shouted above the rattle of the cars: "Big dust!" Hal saw that the ground was covered with six inches of coal-dust, while on the old disused walls one could write his name in it. "Much blow-up!" said the rope-rider; and when the last empty cars had been shunted off into the working-rooms, and he was waiting to make up a return "trip," he laboured with gestures to explain what he meant. "Load cars. Bang! Bust like hell!"

Hal knew that the mountain air in this region was famous for its dryness; he learned now that the quality which meant life to invalids from every part of the world meant death to those who toiled to keep the invalids warm. Driven through the mines by great fans, this air took out every particle of moisture, and left coal dust so thick and dry that there were fatal explosions from the mere friction of loading-shovels. So it happened that these mines were killing several times as many men as other mines throughout the country.

Was there no remedy for this, Hal asked, talking with one of his mule-drivers, Tim Rafferty, the evening after his ride with Cho. There was a remedy, said Tim—the law required sprinkling the mines with "adobe-dust"; and once in Tim's life, he remembered this law's being obeyed. There had come some "big fellows" inspecting things, and previous to their visit there had been an elaborate campaign of sprinkling. But that had been several years ago, and now the apparatus was stored away, nobody knew where, and one heard nothing about sprinkling.

It was the same with precautions against gas. The North Valley mines were especially "gassy," it appeared. In these old rambling passages one smelt a stink as of all the rotten eggs in all the barn-yards of the world; and this sulphuretted hydrogen was the least dangerous of the gases against which a miner had to contend. There was the dreaded "choke-damp," which was odourless, and heavier than air. Striking into soft, greasy coal, one would open a pocket of this gas, a deposit laid up for countless ages, awaiting its predestined victim. A man might sink to sleep as he lay at work, and if his "buddy," or helper, happened to be out of sight, and to delay a minute too long, it would be all over with the man. And there was the still more dreaded "fire-damp," which might wreck a whole mine, and kill scores and even hundreds of men.

Against these dangers there was a "fire-boss," whose duty was to go through the mine, testing for gas, and making sure that the ventilating-course was in order, and the fans working properly. The "fire-boss" was supposed to make his rounds in the early morning, and the law specified that no one should go to work till he had certified that all was safe. But what if the "fire-boss" overslept himself, or happened to be drunk? It was too much to expect thousands of dollars to be lost for such a reason. So sometimes one saw men ordered to their work, and sent down grumbling and cursing. Before many hours some of them would be prostrated with headache, and begging to be taken out; and perhaps the superintendent would not let them out, because if a few came, the rest would get scared and want to come also.

Once, only last year, there had been an accident of that sort. A young mule-driver, a Croatian, told Hal about it while they sat munching the contents of their dinner-pails. The first cage-load of men had gone down into the mine, sullenly protesting; and soon afterwards some one had taken down a naked light, and there had been an explosion which had sounded like the blowing up of the inside of the world. Eight men had been killed, the force of the explosion being so great that some of the bodies had been wedged between the shaft wall and the cage, and it had been necessary to cut them to pieces to get them out. It was them Japs that were to blame, vowed Hal's informant. They hadn't ought to turn them loose in coal mines, for the devil himself couldn't keep a Jap from sneaking off to get a smoke.

So Hal understood how North Valley was a place of fear. What tales the old chambers of these mines could have told, if they had had voices! Hal watched the throngs pouring in to their labours, and reflected that according to the statisticians of the government eight or nine of every thousand of them were destined to die violent deaths before a year was out, and some thirty more would be badly injured. And they knew this, they knew it better than all the statisticians of the government; yet they went to their tasks! Reflecting upon this, Hal was full of wonder. What was the force that kept men at such a task? Was it a sense of duty? Did they understand that society had to have coal and that some one had to do the "dirty work" of providing it? Did they have a vision of a future, great and wonderful, which was to grow out of their ill-requited toil? Or were they simply fools or cowards, submitting blindly, because they had not the wit nor the will to do otherwise? Curiosity held him, he wanted to understand the inner souls of these silent and patient armies which through the ages have surrendered their lives to other men's control.

637

SECTION 10.

Hal was coming to know these people; to see them no longer as a mass, to be despised or pitied in bulk, but as individuals, with individual temperaments and problems, exactly like people in the world of the sunlight. Mary Burke and Tim Rafferty, Cho the Korean and Madvik the Croatian—one by one these individualities etched themselves into the foreground of Hal's picture, making it a thing of life, moving him to sympathy and fellowship. Some of these people, to be sure, were stunted and dulled to a sordid ugliness of soul and body—but on the other hand, some of them were young, and had the light of hope in their hearts, and the spark of rebellion.

There was "Andy," a boy of Greek parentage; Androkulos was his right name—but it was too much to expect any one to get that straight in a coal-camp. Hal noticed him at the store, and was struck by his beautiful features, and the mournful look in his big black eyes. They got to talking, and Andy made the discovery that Hal had not spent all his time in coal-camps, but had seen the great world. It was pitiful, the excitement that came into his voice; he was yearning for life, with its joys and adventures—and it was his destiny to sit ten hours a day by the side of a chute, with the rattle of coal in his ears and the dust of coal in his nostrils, picking out slate with his fingers. He was one of many scores of "breaker-boys."

"Why don't you go away?" asked Hal.

"Christ! How I get away? Got mother, two sisters."

"And your father?" So Hal made the discovery that Andy's father had been one of those men whose bodies had had to be cut to pieces to get them out of the shaft. Now the son was chained to the father's place, until his time too should come!

"Don't want to be miner!" cried the boy. "Don't want to get *kil-lid*!"

He began to ask, timidly, what Hal thought he could do if he were to run away from his family and try his luck in the world outside. Hal, striving to remember where he had seen olive-skinned Greeks with big black eyes in this beautiful land of the free, could hold out no better prospect than a shoe-shining parlour, or the wiping out of wash-bowls in a hotel-lavatory, handing over the tips to a fat padrone.

Andy had been to school, and had learned to read English, and the teacher had loaned him books and magazines with wonderful pictures in them; now he wanted more than pictures, he wanted the things which they portrayed. So Hal came face to face with one of the difficulties of mine-operators. They gathered a population of humble serfs, selected from twenty or thirty races of hereditary bondsmen; but owing to the absurd American custom of having public-schools, the children of this population learned to speak English, and even to read it. So they became too good for their lot in life; and then a wandering agitator would get in, and all of a sudden there would be hell. Therefore in every coal-camp had to be another kind of "fire-boss," whose duty it was to guard against another kind of explosions—not of carbon monoxide, but of the human soul.

The immediate duties of this office in North Valley devolved upon Jeff Cotton, the camp-marshal. He was not at all what one would have expected from a person of his trade—lean and rather distinguished-looking, a man who in evening clothes might have passed for a diplomat. But his mouth would become ugly when he was displeased, and he carried a gun with six notches upon it; also he wore a deputy-sheriff's badge, to give him immunity for other notches he might wish to add. When Jeff Cotton came near, any man who was explosive went off to be explosive by himself. So there was "order" in North Valley, and it was only on Saturday and Sunday nights, when the drunks had to be suppressed, or on Monday mornings when they had to be haled forth and kicked to their work, that one realised upon what basis this "order" rested.

Besides Jeff Cotton, and his assistant, "Bud" Adams, who wore badges, and were known, there were other assistants who wore no badges, and were not supposed to be known. Coming up in the cage one evening, Hal made some remark to the Croatian mule-driver, Madvik, about the high price of company-store merchandise, and was surprised to get a sharp kick on the ankle. Afterwards, as they were on their way to supper, Madvik gave him the reason. "Red-faced feller, Gus. Look out for him—company spotter."

"Is that so?" said Hal, with interest. "How do you know?"

"I know. Everybody know."

"He don't look like he had much sense," said Hal—who had got his idea of detectives from Sherlock Holmes.

"No take much sense. Go pit-boss, say, 'Joe feller talk too much. Say store rob him.' Any damn fool do that. Hey?"

"To be sure," admitted Hal. "And the company pays him for it?"

"Pit-boss pay him. Maybe give him drink, maybe two bits. Then pit-boss come to you: 'You shoot your mouth off too much, feller. Git the hell out of here!' See?"

Hal saw.

"So you go down canyon. Then maybe you go 'nother mine. Boss say, 'Where you work?' You say 'North Valley.' He say, 'What your name?' You say, 'Joe Smith.' He say, 'Wait.' He go in, look at paper; he come out, say, 'No job!' You say, 'Why not?' He say, 'Shoot off your mouth too much, feller. Git the hell out of here!' See?"

"You mean a black-list," said Hal.

"Sure, black-list. Maybe telephone, find out all about you. You do anything bad, like talk union"—Madvik had dropped his voice and whispered the word "union"—"they send your picture—don't get job nowhere in state. How you like that?"

SECTION 11.

Before long Hal had a chance to see this system of espionage at work, and he began to understand something of the force which kept these silent and patient armies at their tasks. On a Sunday morning he was strolling with his mule-driver friend Tim Rafferty, a kindly lad with a pair of dreamy blue eyes in his coal-smutted face. They came to Tim's home, and he invited Hal to come in and meet his family. The father was a bowed and toil-worn man, but with tremendous strength in his solid frame, the product of many generations of labour in coal-mines. He was known as "Old Rafferty," despite the fact that he was well under fifty. He had been a pit-boy at the age of nine, and he showed Hal a faded leather album with pictures of his ancestors in the "oul' country"—men with sad, deeply lined faces, sitting very stiff and solemn to have their presentments made permanent for posterity.

The mother of the family was a gaunt, grey-haired woman, with no teeth, but with a warm heart. Hal took to her, because her home was clean; he sat on the family door-step, amid a crowd of little Rafferties with newly-washed Sunday faces, and fascinated them with tales of adventures cribbed from Clark Russell and Captain Mayne Reid. As a reward he was invited to stay for dinner, and had a clean knife and fork, and a clean plate of steaming hot potatoes, with two slices of salt pork on the side. It was so wonderful that he forthwith inquired if he might forsake his company boarding-house and come and board with them.

Mrs. Rafferty opened wide her eyes. "Sure," exclaimed she, "do you think you'd be let?"

"Why not?" asked Hal.

"Sure, 't would be a bad example for the others."

"Do you mean I *have* to board at Reminitsky's?"

"There be six company boardin'-houses," said the woman.

"And what would they do if I came to you?"

"First you'd get a hint, and then you'd go down the canyon, and maybe us after ye."

"But there's lots of people have boarders in shanty-town," objected Hal.

"Oh! Them wops! Nobody counts them—they live any way they happen to fall. But you started at Reminitsky's, and 't would not be healthy for them that took ye away."

"I see," laughed Hal. "There seem to be a lot of unhealthy things hereabouts."

"Sure there be! They sent down Nick Ammons because his wife bought milk down the canyon. They had a sick baby, and it's not much you get in this thin stuff at the store. They put chalk in it, I think; any way, you can see somethin' white in the bottom."

"So you have to trade at the store, too!"

"I thought ye said ye'd worked in coal-mines," put in Old Rafferty, who had been a silent listener.

"So I have," said Hal. "But it wasn't quite that bad."

"Sure," said Mrs. Rafferty, "I'd like to know where 'twas then—in this country. Me and me old man spent weary years a-huntin'."

Thus far the conversation had proceeded naturally; but suddenly it was as if a shadow passed over it—a shadow of fear. Hal saw Old Rafferty look at his wife, and frown and make signs to her. After all, what did they know about this handsome young stranger, who talked so glibly, and had been in so many parts of the world?

"'Tis not complainin' we'd be," said the old man.

And his wife made haste to add, "If they let peddlers and the like of them come in, 'twould be no end to it, I suppose. We find they treat us here as well as anywhere."

"'Tis no joke, the life of workin' men, wherever ye try it," added the other; and when young Tim started to express an opinion, they shut him up with such evident anxiety that Hal's heart ached for them, and he made haste to change the subject.

SECTION 12.

On the evening of the same Sunday Hal went to pay his promised call upon Mary Burke. She opened the front door of the cabin to let him in, and even by the dim rays of the little kerosene lamp, there came to him an impression of cheerfulness. "Hello," she said—just as she had said it when he had slid down the mountain into the family wash. He followed her into the room, and saw that the impression he had got of cheerfulness came from Mary herself. How bright and fresh she looked! The old blue calico, which had not been entirely clean, was newly laundered now, and on the shoulder where the rent had been was a neat patch of unfaded blue.

There being only three rooms in Mary's home, two of these necessarily bedrooms, she entertained her company in the kitchen. The room was bare, Hal saw—there was not even so much as a clock by way of ornament. The only charm the girl had been able to give to it, in preparation for company, was that of cleanness. The board floor had been newly sanded and scrubbed; the kitchen table also had been scrubbed, and the kettle on the stove, and the cracked tea-pot and bowls on the shelf. Mary's little brother and sister were in the room: Jennie, a dark-eyed, dark-haired little girl, frail, with a sad, rather frightened face; and Tommie, a round headed youngster, like a thousand other round headed and freckle-faced boys. Both of them were now sitting very straight in their chairs, staring at the visitor with a certain resentment, he thought. He suspected that they had been included in the general scrubbing. Inasmuch as it had been uncertain just when the visitor would come, they must have been required to do this every night, and he could imagine family disturbances, with arguments possibly not altogether complimentary to Mary's new "feller."

There seemed to be a certain uneasiness in the place.

Mary did not invite her company to a seat, but stood irresolute; and after Hal had ventured a couple of friendly remarks to the children, she said, abruptly, "Shall we be takin' that walk that we spoke of, Mr. Smith?"

"Delighted!" said Hal; and while she pinned on her hat before the broken mirror on the shelf, he smiled at the children and quoted two lines from his Harrigan song—

"Oh, Mary-Jane, come out in the lane,

The moon is a-shinin' in the old pecan!"

Tommie and Jennie were too shy to answer, but Mary exclaimed, "'Tis in a tin-can ye see it shinin' here!"

They went out. In the soft summer night it was pleasant to stroll under the moon—especially when they had come to the remoter parts of the village, where there were not so many weary people on door-steps and children playing noisily. There were other young couples walking here, under the same moon; the hardest day's toil could not so sap their energies that they did not feel the spell of this soft summer night.

Hal, being tired, was content to stroll and enjoy the stillness; but Mary Burke sought information about the mysterious young man she was with. "Ye've not worked long in coal-mines, Mr. Smith?" she remarked.

Hal was a trifle disconcerted. "How did you find that out?"

"Ye don't look it—ye don't talk it. Ye're not like anybody or anything around here. I don't know how to say it, but ye make me think more of the poetry-books."

Flattered as Hal was by this naïve confession, he did not want to talk of the mystery of himself. He took refuge in a question about the "poetry-books." "I've read some," said the girl; "more than ye'd have thought, perhaps." This with a flash of her defiance.

He asked more questions, and learned that she, like the Greek boy, "Andy," had come under the influence of that disturbing American institution, the public-school; she had learned to read, and the pretty young teacher had helped her, lend-ing her books and magazines. Thus she had been given a key to a treasure-house, a magic carpet on which to travel over the world. These similes Mary herself used—for the Arabian Nights had been one of the books that were loaned to her. On rainy days she would hide behind the sofa, reading at a spot where the light crept in—so that she might be safe from small brothers and sisters!

Joe Smith had read these same books, it appeared; and this seemed remarkable to Mary, for books cost money and were hard to get. She explained how she had searched the camp for new magic carpets, finding a "poetry-book" by Longfellow, and a book of American history, and a story called "David Copperfield," and last and strangest of all, another story called "Pride and Prejudice." A curious freak of fortune—the prim and sentimentally quivering Jane Austen in a coal-camp in a far Western wilderness! An adventure for Jane, as well as for Mary!

What had Mary made of it, Hal wondered. Had she revelled, shop-girl fashion, in scenes of pallid ease? He learned that what she had made of it was despair. This world outside, with its freedom and cleanness, its people living gracious and worth-while lives, was not for her; she was chained to a scrub-pail in a coal-camp. Things had got so much worse since the death of her mother, she said. Her voice had become dull and hard—Hal thought that he had never heard a young voice express such hopelessness.

"You've never been anywhere but here?" he asked.

"I been in two other camps," she said—"first the Gordon, and then East Run. But they're all alike."

"But you've been down to the towns?"

"Only for a day, once or twice a year. Once I was in Sheridan, and in a church I heard a lady sing."

She stopped for a moment, lost in this memory. Then suddenly her voice changed—and he could imagine in the darkness that she had tossed her head defiantly. "I'll not be entertainin' company with my troubles! Ye know how tiresome that is when ye hear it from somebody else—like my next-door neighbour, Mrs. Zamboni. D' ye know her?"

"No," said Hal.

"The poor old lady has troubles enough, God knows. Her man's not much good—he's troubled with the drink; and she's got eleven childer, and that's too many for one woman. Don't ye think so?"

She asked this with a naïveté which made Hal laugh. "Yes," he said, "I do."

"Well, I think people'd help her more if she'd not complain so! And half of it in the Slavish language, that a body can't understand!" So Mary began to tell funny things about Mrs. Zamboni and her other polyglot neighbours, imitating their murdering of the Irish dialect. Hal thought her humour was naïve and delightful, and he led her on to more cheerful gossip during the remainder of their walk.

SECTION 13.

But then, as they were on their way home, tragedy fell upon them. Hearing a step behind them, Mary turned and looked; then catching Hal by the arm, she drew him into the shadows at the side, whispering to him to be silent. The bent figure of a man went past them, lurching from side to side.

When he had turned and gone into the house, Mary said, "It's my father. He's ugly when he's like that." And Hal could hear her quick breathing in the darkness.

So that was Mary's trouble—the difficulty in her home life to which she had referred at their first meeting! Hal understood many things in a flash—why her home was bare of ornament, and why she did not invite her company to sit down. He stood silent, not knowing what to say. Before he could find the word, Mary burst out, "Oh, how I hate O'Callahan, that sells the stuff to my father! His home with plenty to eat in it, and his wife dressin' in silk and goin' down to mass every Sunday, and thinkin' herself too good for a common miner's daughter! Sometimes I think I'd like to kill them both."

"That wouldn't help much," Hal ventured.

"No, I know—there'd only be some other one in his place. Ye got to do more than that, to change things here. Ye got to get after them that make money out of O'Callahan."

So Mary's mind was groping for causes! Hal had thought her excitement was due to humiliation, or to fear of a scene of violence when she reached home; but she was thinking of the deeper aspects of this terrible drink problem. There was still enough unconscious snobbery in Hal Warner for him to be surprised at this phenomenon in a common miner's daughter; and so, as at their first meeting, his pity was turned to intellectual interest.

"They'll stop the drink business altogether some day," he said. He had not known that he was a Prohibitionist; he had become one suddenly!

"Well," she answered, "they'd best stop it soon, if they don't want to be too late. 'Tis a sight to make your heart sick to see the young lads comin' home staggerin', too drunk even to fight."

Hal had not had time to see much of this aspect of North Valley. "They sell to boys?" he asked.

"Sure, who's to care? A boy's money's as good as a man's."

"But I should think the company—"

"The company lets the saloon-buildin'—that's all the company cares."

"But they must care something about the efficiency of their hands!"

"Sure, there's plenty more where they come from. When ye can't work, they fire ye, and that's all there is to it."

"And is it so easy to get skilled men?"

"It don't take much skill to get out coal. The skill is in keepin' your bones whole—and if you can stand breakin' 'em, the company can stand it."

They had come to the little cabin. Mary stood for a moment in silence. "I'm talkin' bitter again!" she exclaimed suddenly. "And I promised ye me company manner! But things keep happening to set me off." And she turned abruptly and ran into the house. Hal stood for a moment wondering if she would return; then, deciding that she had meant that as good night, he went slowly up the street.

He fought against a mood of real depression, the first he had known since his coming to North Valley. He had managed so far to keep a certain degree of aloofness, that he might see this industrial world without prejudice. But to-night his pity for Mary had involved him more deeply. To be sure, he might be able to help her, to find her work in some less crushing environment; but his mind went on to the question—how many girls might there be in mining-camps, young and eager, hungering for life, but crushed by poverty, and by the burden of the drink problem?

A man walked past Hal, greeting him in the semi-darkness with a nod and a motion of the hand. It was the Reverend Spragg, the gentleman who was officially commissioned to combat the demon rum in North Valley.

Hal had been to the little white church the Sunday before, and heard the Reverend Spragg preach a doctrinal sermon, in which the blood of the lamb was liberally sprinkled, and the congregation heard where and how they were to receive compensation for the distresses they endured in this vale of tears.

What a mockery it seemed! Once, indubitably, people had believed such doctrines; they had been willing to go to the stake for them. But now nobody went to the stake for them—on the contrary, the company compelled every worker to contribute out of his scanty earnings towards the preaching of them. How could the most ignorant of zealots confront such an arrangement without suspicion of his own piety? Somewhere at the head of the great dividend-paying machine that was called the General Fuel Company must be some devilish intelligence that had worked it all out, that had given the orders to its ecclesiastical staff: "We want the present—we leave you the future! We want the bodies—we leave you the souls! Teach them what you will about heaven—so long as you let us plunder them on earth!"

In accordance with this devil's program, the Reverend Spragg might denounce the demon rum, but he said nothing about dividends based on the renting of rum-shops, nor about local politicians maintained by company contributions, plus the profits of wholesale liquor. He said nothing about the conclusions of modern hygiene, concerning over-work as a cause of the craving for alcohol; the phrase "industrial drinking," it seemed, was not known in General Fuel Company theology! In fact, when you listened to such a sermon, you would never have guessed that the hearers of it had physical bodies at all; certainly you would never have guessed that the preacher had a body, which was nourished by food produced by the overworked and under-nourished wage-slaves whom he taught!

SECTION 14.

For the most part the victims of this system were cowed and spoke of their wrongs only in whispers; but there was one place in the camp, Hal found, where they could not keep silence, where their sense of outrage battled with their fear. This place was the solar plexus of the mine-organism, the centre of its nervous energies; to change the simile, it was the judgment-seat, where the miner had sentence passed upon him—sentence either to plenty, or to starvation and despair.

This place was the "tipple," where the coal that came out of the mine was weighed and recorded. Every digger, as he came from the cage, made for this spot. There was a bulletin-board, and on it his number, and the record of the weights of the cars he had sent out that day. And every man, no matter how ignorant, had learned enough English to read those figures.

Hal had gradually come to realise that here was the place of drama. Most of the men would look, and then, without a sound or glance about, would slouch off with drooping shoulders. Others would mumble to themselves—or, what amounted to the same thing, would mumble to one another in barbarous dialects. But about one in five could speak English; and scarcely an evening passed that some man did not break loose, shaking his fist at the sky, or at the weigh-boss—behind the latter's back. He might gather a knot of fellow-grumblers about him; it was to be noted that the camp-marshal had the habit of being on hand at this hour.

It was on one of these occasions that Hal first noticed Mike Sikoria, a grizzle-haired old Slovak, who had spent twenty years in the mines of these regions. All the bitterness of all the wrongs of all these years welled up in Old Mike, as he shouted his score aloud: "Nineteen, twenty-two, twenty-four, twenty! Is that my weight, Mister? You want me to believe that's my weight?"

"That's your weight," said the weigh-boss, coldly.

"Well, by Judas, your scale is off, Mister! Look at them cars—them cars is big! You measure them cars, Mister—seven feet long, three and a half feet high, four feet wide. And you tell me them don't go but twenty?"

"You don't load them right," said the boss.

"Don't load them right?" echoed the old miner; he became suddenly plaintive, as if more hurt than angered by such an insinuation. "You know all the years I work, and you tell me I don't know a load? When I load a car, I load him like a miner, I don't load him like a Jap, that don't know about a mine! I put it up—I chunk it up like a stack of hay. I load him square—like that." With gestures the old fellow was illustrating what he meant. "See there! There's a ton on the top, and a ton and a half on the bottom—and you tell me I get only nineteen, twenty!"

"That's your weight," said the boss, implacably.

"But, Mister, your scale is wrong! I tell you I used to get my weight. I used to get forty-five, forty-six on them cars. Here's my buddy—ask him if it ain't so. What is it, Bo?"

"Um m m-mum," said Bo, who was a negro—though one could hardly be sure of this for the coal-dust on him.

"I can't make a living no more!" exclaimed the old Slovak, his voice trembling and his wizened dark eyes full of pleading. "What you think I make? For fifteen days, fifty cents! I pay board, and so help me God, Mister—and I stand right here—I swear for God I make fifty cents. I dig the coal and I ain't got no weight, I ain't got nothing! Your scale is wrong!"

"Get out!" said the weigh-boss, turning away.

"But, Mister!" cried Old Mike, following behind him, and pouring his whole soul into his words. "What is this life, Mister? You work like a burro, and you don't get nothing for it! You burn your own powder—half a dollar a day powder—what you think of that? Crosscut—and you get nothing! Take the skip and a pillar, and you get nothing! Brush—and you get nothing! Here, by Judas, a poor man, going and working his body to the last point, and blood is run out! You starve me to death, I say! I have got to have something to eat, haven't I?"

And suddenly the boss whirled upon him. "Get the hell out of here!" he shouted. "If you don't like it, get your time and quit. Shut your face, or I'll shut it for you."

The old man quailed and fell silent. He stood for a moment more, biting his whiskered lips nervously; then his shoulders sank together, and he turned and slunk off, followed by his negro helper.

SECTION 15.

Old Mike boarded at Reminitsky's, and after supper was over, Hal sought him out. He was easy to know, and proved an interesting acquaintance. With the help of his eloquence Hal wandered through a score of camps in the district. The old fellow had a temper that he could not manage, and so he was always on the move; but all places were alike, he said—there was always some trick by which a miner was cheated of his earnings. A miner was a little business man, a contractor who took a certain job, with its expenses and its chance of profit or loss. A "place" was assigned to him by the boss—and he undertook to get out the coal from it, being paid at the rate of fifty-five cents a ton for each ton of clean coal. In some "plac-es" a man could earn good money, and in others he would work for weeks, and not be able to keep up with his store-account.

It all depended upon the amount of rock and slate that was found with the coal. If the vein was low, the man had one or two feet of rock to take off the ceiling, and this had to be loaded on separate cars and taken away. This work was called "brushing," and for it the miner received no pay. Or perhaps it was necessary to cut through a new passage, and clean out the rock; or perhaps to "grade the bot-tom," and lay the ties and rails over which the cars were brought in to be loaded; or perhaps the vein ran into a "fault," a broken place where there was rock instead of coal—and this rock must be hewed away before the miner could get at the coal. All such work was called "dead-work," and it was the cause of unceasing war. In the old days the company had paid extra for it; now, since they had got the upper hand of the men, they were refusing to pay. And so it was important to the miner to have a "place" assigned him where there was not so much of this dead work. And the "place" a man got depended upon the boss; so here, at the very outset, was endless opportunity for favouritism and graft, for quarrelling, or "keeping in" with the boss. What chance did a man stand who was poor and old and ugly, and could not speak English good? inquired old Mike, with bitterness. The boss stole his cars and gave them to other people; he took the weight off the cars, and gave them to fellows who boarded with him, or treated him to drinks, or otherwise cur-ried favour with him.

"I work five days in the Southeastern," said Mike, "and when I work them five days, so help me God, brother, if I don't get up out of this chair, fifteen cents I was still in the hole yet. Fourteen inches of rock! And the Mr. Bishop—that is the superintendent—I says, 'Do you pay something for that rock?' 'Huh?' says he. 'Well,' I says, 'if you don't pay nothing for the rock, I don't go ahead with it. I ain't got no place to put that rock.' 'Get the hell out of here,' says he, and when I started to fight he pull gun on me. And then I go to Cedar Mountain, and the super give me work there, and he says, 'You go Number Four,' and he says, 'Rail is in Number Three, and the ties.' And he says, 'I pay you for it when you put it in.' So I take it away and I put it in, and I work till twelve o'clock. Carried the three pair of rails and the ties, and I pulled all the spikes—"

"Pulled the spikes?" asked Hal.

"Got no good spikes. Got to use old spikes, what you pull out of them old ties. So then I says, 'What is my half day, what you promise me?' Says he, 'You ain't dug no coal yet!' 'But, mister,' says I, 'you promise me pay to pull them spikes and put in them ties!' Says he, 'Company pay nothin' for dead work—you know that,' says he, and that is all the satisfaction I get."

"And you didn't get your half day's pay?"

"Sure I get nothin'. Boss do just as he please in coal mine."

SECTION 16.

There was another way, Old Mike explained, in which the miner was at the mercy of others; this was the matter of stealing cars. Each miner had brass checks with his number on them, and when he sent up a loaded car, he hung one of these checks on a hook inside. In the course of the long journey to the tipple, some one would change the check, and the car was gone. In some mines, the number was put on the car with chalk; and how easy it was for some one to rub it out and change it! It appeared to Hal that it would have been a simple matter to put a number padlock on the car, instead of a check; but such an equipment would have cost the company one or two hundred dollars, he was told, and so the stealing went on year after year.

"You think it's the bosses steal these cars?" asked Hal.

"Sometimes bosses, sometimes bosses' friend—sometimes company himself steal them from miners." In North Valley it was the company, the old Slovak insisted. It was no use sending up more than six cars in one day, he declared; you could never get credit for more than six. Nor was it worth while loading more than a ton on a car; they did not really weigh the cars, the boss just ran them quickly over the scales, and had orders not to go above a certain average. Mike told of an Italian who had loaded a car for a test, so high that he could barely pass it under the roof of the entry, and went up on the tipple and saw it weighed himself, and it was sixty-five hundred pounds. They gave him thirty-five hundred, and when he started to fight, they arrested him. Mike had not seen him arrested, but when he had come out of the mine, the man was gone, and nobody ever saw him again. After that they put a door onto the weigh-room, so that no one could see the scales.

The more Hal listened to the men and reflected upon these things, the more he came to see that the miner was a contractor who had no opportunity to determine the size of the contract before he took it on, nor afterwards to determine how much work he had done. More than that, he was obliged to use supplies, over the price and measurements of which he had no control. He used powder, and would find himself docked at the end of the month for a certain quantity, and if the quantity was wrong, he would have no redress. He was charged a certain sum for "black-smithing"—the keeping of his tools in order; and he would find a dollar or two deducted from his account each month, even though he had not been near the blacksmith shop.

Let any business-man in the world consider the proposition, thought Hal, and say if he would take a contract upon such terms! Would a man undertake to build a dam, for example, with no chance to measure the ground in advance, nor any way of determining how many cubic yards of concrete he had to put in? Would a grocer sell to a customer who proposed to come into the store and do his own weighing—and meantime locking the grocer outside? Merely to put such questions was to show the preposterousness of the thing; yet in this district were fifteen thousand men working on precisely such terms.

Under the state law, the miner had a right to demand a check-weighman to protect his interest at the scales, paying this check-weighman's wages out of his own earnings. Whenever there was any public criticism about conditions in the coal-mines, this law would be triumphantly cited by the operators; and one had to have actual experience in order to realise what a bitter mockery this was to the miner.

In the dining-room Hal sat next to a fair-haired Swedish giant named Johannson, who loaded timbers ten hours a day. This fellow was one who indulged in the luxury of speaking his mind, because he had youth and huge muscles, and no family to tie him down. He was what is called a "blanket-stiff," wandering from mine to harvest-field and from harvest-field to lumber-camp. Some one broached the subject of check-weighmen to him, and the whole table heard his scornful laugh. Let any man ask for a check-weighman!

"You mean they would fire him?" asked Hal.

"Maybe!" was the answer. "Maybe they make him fire himself."

"How do you mean?"

"They make his life one damn misery till he go."

So it was with check-weighman—as with scrip, and with company stores, and with all the provisions of the law to protect the miner against accidents. You might demand your legal rights, but if you did, it was a matter of the boss's temper. He might make your life one damn misery till you went of your own accord. Or you might get a string of curses and an order, "Down the canyon!"—and likely as not the toe of a boot in your trouser-seat, or the muzzle of a revolver under your nose.

SECTION 17.

Such conditions made the coal-district a place of despair. Yet there were men who managed to get along somehow, and to raise families and keep decent homes. If one had the luck to escape accident, if he did not marry too young, or did not have too many children; if he could manage to escape the temptations of liquor, to which overwork and monotony drove so many; if, above all, he could keep on the right side of his boss—why then he might have a home, and even a little money on deposit with the company.

Such a one was Jerry Minetti, who became one of Hal's best friends. He was a Milanese, and his name was Gerolamo, which had become Jerry in the "melting-pot." He was about twenty-five years of age, and what is unusual with the Italians, was of good stature. Their meeting took place—as did most of Hal's social experiences—on a Sunday. Jerry had just had a sleep and a wash, and had put on a pair of new blue overalls, so that he presented a cheering aspect in the sunlight. He walked with his head up and his shoulders square, and one could see that he had few cares in the world.

But what caught Hal's attention was not so much Jerry as what followed at Jerry's heels; a perfect reproduction of him, quarter-size, also with a newly-washed face and a pair of new blue overalls. He too had his head up, and his shoulders square, and he was an irresistible object, throwing out his heels and trying his best to keep step. Since the longest strides he could take left him behind, he would break into a run, and getting close under his father's heels, would begin keeping step once more.

Hal was going in the same direction, and it affected him like the music of a military band; he too wanted to throw his head up and square his shoulders and keep step. And then other people, seeing the grin on his face, would turn and watch, and grin also. But Jerry walked on gravely, unaware of this circus in the rear.

They went into a house; and Hal, having nothing to do but enjoy life, stood waiting for them to come out. They returned in the same procession, only now the man had a sack of something on his shoulder, while the little chap had a smaller load poised in imitation. So Hal grinned again, and when they were opposite him, he said, "Hello."

"Hello," said Jerry, and stopped. Then, seeing Hal's grin, he grinned back; and Hal looked at the little chap and grinned, and the little chap grinned back. Jerry, seeing what Hal was grinning at, grinned more than ever; so there stood all three in the middle of the road, grinning at one another for no apparent reason.

"Gee, but that's a great kid!" said Hal.

"Gee, you bet!" said Jerry; and he set down his sack. If some one desired to admire the kid, he was willing to stop any length of time.

"Yours?" asked Hal.

"You bet!" said Jerry, again.

"Hello, Buster!" said Hal.

"Hello yourself!" said the kid. One could see in a moment that he had been in the "melting-pot."

"What's your name?" asked Hal.

"Jerry," was the reply.

"And what's his name?" Hal nodded towards the man—

"Big Jerry."

"Got any more like you at home?"

"One more," said Big Jerry. "Baby."

"He ain't like me," said Little Jerry. "He's little."

"And you're big?" said Hal.

"He can't walk!"

"Neither can you walk!" laughed Hal, and caught him up and slung him onto his shoulder. "Come on, we'll ride!"

So Big Jerry took up his sack again, and they started off; only this time it was Hal who fell behind and kept step, squaring his shoulders and flinging out his heels. Little Jerry caught onto the joke, and giggled and kicked his sturdy legs with delight. Big Jerry would look round, not knowing what the joke was, but enjoying it just the same.

They came to the three-room cabin which was Both Jerrys' home; and Mrs. Jerry came to the door, a black-eyed Sicilian girl, who did not look old enough to have even one baby. They had another bout of grinning, at the end of which Big Jerry said, "You come in?"

"Sure," said Hal.

"You stay supper," added the other. "Got spaghetti."

"Gee!" said Hal. "All right, let me stay, and pay for it."

"Hell, no!" said Jerry. "You no pay!"

"No! No pay!" cried Mrs. Jerry, shaking her pretty head energetically.

"All right," said Hal, quickly, seeing that he might hurt their feelings. "I'll stay if you're sure you have enough."

"Sure, plenty!" said Jerry. "Hey, Rosa?"

"Sure, plenty!" said Mrs. Jerry.

"Then I'll stay," said Hal. "You like spaghetti, Kid?"

"Jesus!" cried Little Jerry.

Hal looked about him at this Dago home. It was a tome in keeping with its pretty occupant. There were lace curtains in the windows, even shinier and whiter than at the Rafferties; there was an incredibly bright-coloured rug on the floor, and bright coloured pictures of Mount Vesuvius and of Garibaldi on the walls. Also there was a cabinet with many interesting treasures to look at—a bit of coral and a conch-shell, a shark's tooth and an Indian arrow-head, and a stuffed linnet with a glass cover over him. A while back Hal would not have thought of such things as especially stimulating to the imagination; but that was before he had begun to spend five-sixths of his waking hours in the bowels of the earth.

He ate supper, a real Dago supper; the spaghetti proved to be real Dago spaghetti, smoking hot, with tomato sauce and a rich flavour of meat-juice. And all through the meal Hal smacked his lips and grinned at Little Jerry, who smacked his lips and grinned back. It was all so different from feeding at Reminitsky's pig-trough, that Hal thought he had never had such a good supper in his life before. As for Mr. and Mrs. Jerry, they were so proud of their wonderful kid, who could swear in English as good as a real American, that they were in the seventh heaven.

When the meal was over, Hal leaned back and exclaimed, just as he had at the Rafferties', "Lord, how I wish I could board here!"

He saw his host look at his wife. "All right," said he. "You come here. I board you. Hey, Rosa?"

"Sure," said Rosa.

Hal looked at them, astonished. "You're sure they'll let you?" he asked.

"Let me? Who stop me?"

"I don't know. Maybe Reminitsky. You might get into trouble."

Jerry grinned. "I no fraid," said he. "Got friends here. Carmino my cousin. You know Carmino?"

"No," said Hal.

"Pit-boss in Number One. He stand by me. Old Reminitsky go hang! You come here, I give you bunk in that room, give you good grub. What you pay Reminitsky?"

"Twenty-seven a month."

"All right, you pay me twenty-seven, you get everything good. Can't get much stuff here, but Rosa good cook, she fix it."

Hal's new friend—besides being a favourite of the boss—was a "shot-firer"; it was his duty to go about the mine at night, setting off the charges of powder which the miners had got ready by day. This was dangerous work, calling for a skilled man, and it paid pretty well; so Jerry got on in the world and was not afraid to speak his mind, within certain limits. He ignored the possibility that Hal might be a company spy, and astonished him by rebellious talk of the different kinds of graft in North Valley, and at other places he had worked since coming to America as a boy. Minetti was a Socialist, Hal learned; he took an Italian Socialist paper, and the clerk at the post-office knew what sort of paper it was, and would "josh" him about it. What was more remarkable, Mrs. Minetti was a Socialist also;

that meant a great deal to a man, as Jerry explained, because she was not under the domination of a priest.

658

SECTION 18.

Hal made the move at once, sacrificing part of a month's board, which Reminitsky would charge against his account with the company. But he was willing to pay for the privilege of a clean home and clean food. To his amusement he found that in the eyes of his Irish friends he was losing caste by going to live with the Minettis. There were most rigid social lines in North Valley, it appeared. The Americans and English and Scotch looked down upon the Welsh and Irish; the Welsh and Irish looked down upon the Dagoes and Frenchies; the Dagoes and Frenchies looked down upon Polacks and Hunkies, these in turn upon Greeks, Bulgarians and "Montynegroes," and so on through a score of races of Eastern Europe, Lithuanians, Slovaks, and Croatians, Armenians, Roumanians, Rumelians, Ruthenians—ending up with Greasers, niggers, and last and lowest, Japs.

It was when Hal went to pay another call upon the Rafferties that he made this discovery. Mary Burke happened to be there, and when she caught sight of him, her grey eyes beamed with mischief. "How do ye do, Mr. Minetti?" she cried.

"How do ye do, Miss Rosetti?" he countered.

"You lika da spagett?"

"You no lika da spagett?"

"I told ye once," laughed the girl—"the good old pertaties is good enough for me!"

"And you remember," said he, "what I answered?"

Yes, she remembered! Her cheeks took on the colour of the rose-leaves he had specified as her probable diet.

And then the Rafferty children, who had got to know Hal well, joined in the teasing. "Mister Minetti! Lika da spagetti!" Hal, when he had grasped the situation, was tempted to retaliate by reminding them that he had offered to board with the Irish, and been turned down; but he feared that the elder Rafferty might not appreciate this joke, so instead he pretended to have supposed all along that the Rafferties were Italians. He addressed the elder Rafferty gravely, pronouncing the name with the accent on the second syllable—"Signer Rafferti"; and this so amused the old man that he chuckled over it at intervals for an hour. His heart warmed to this lively young fellow; he forgot some of his suspicions, and after the youngsters had been sent away to bed, he talked more or less frankly about his life as a coal-miner.

"Old Rafferty" had once been on the way to high station. He had been made tipple-boss at the San José mine, but had given up his job because he had thought that his religion did not permit him to do what he was ordered to do. It had been a crude proposition of keeping the men's score at a certain level, no matter how much coal they might send up; and when Rafferty had quit rather than obey such orders, he had had to leave the mine altogether; for of course everybody knew why he had quit, and his mere presence had the effect of keeping discontent alive.

"You think there are no honest companies at all?" Hal asked.

The old man answered, "There be some, but 'tis not so easy as ye might think to be honest. They have to meet each other's prices, and when one short-weights, the others have to. 'Tis a way of cuttin' wages without the men findin' it out; and there be people that do not like to fall behind with their profits." Hal found himself thinking of old Peter Harrigan, who controlled the General Fuel Company, and had made the remark: "I am a great clamourer for dividends!"

"The trouble with the miner," continued Old Rafferty, "is that he has no one to speak for him. He stands alone—"

During this discourse, Hal had glanced at "Red Mary," and noticed that she sat with her arms on the table, her sturdy shoulders bowed in a fashion which told of a hard day's toil. But here she broke into the conversation; her voice came suddenly, alive with scorn: "The trouble with the miner is that he's a *slave!*"

"Ah, now—" put in the old man, protestingly.

"He has the whole world against him, and he hasn't got the sense to get together—to form a union, and stand by it!"

There fell a sudden silence in the Rafferty home. Even Hal was startled—for this was the first time during his stay in the camp that he had heard the dread word "union" spoken above a whisper.

"I know!" said Mary, her grey eyes full of defiance. "Ye'll not have the word spoken! But some will speak it in spite of ye!"

"'Tis all very well," said the old man. "When ye're young, and a woman too—"

"A woman! Is it only the women that can have courage?"

"Sure," said he, with a wry smile, "'tis the women that have the tongues, and that can't be stopped from usin' them. Even the boss must know that."

"Maybe so," replied Mary. "And maybe 'tis the women have the most to suffer in a coal-camp; and maybe the boss knows that." The girl's cheeks were red.

"Mebbe so," said Rafferty; and after that there was silence, while he sat puffing his pipe. It was evident that he did not care to go on, that he did not want union speeches made in his home. After a while Mrs. Rafferty made a timid effort to change the course of the talk, by asking after Mary's sister, who had not been well; and after they had discussed remedies for the ailments of children, Mary rose, saying, "I'll be goin' along."

Hal rose also. "I'll walk with you, if I may," he said.

"Sure," said she; and it seemed that the cheerfulness of the Rafferty family was restored by the sight of a bit of gallantry.

SECTION 19.

They strolled down the street, and Hal remarked, "That's the first word I've heard here about a union."

Mary looked about her nervously. "Hush!" she whispered.

"But I thought you said you were talking about it!"

She answered, "'Tis one thing, talkin' in a friend's house, and another outside. What's the good of throwin' away your job?"

He lowered his voice. "Would you seriously like to have a union here?"

"Seriously?" said she. "Didn't ye see Mr. Rafferty—what a coward he is? That's the way they are! No, 'twas just a burst of my temper. I'm a bit crazy to-night—something happened to set me off."

He thought she was going on, but apparently she changed her mind. Finally he asked, "What happened?"

"Oh, 'twould do no good to talk," she answered; and they walked a bit farther in silence.

"Tell me about it, won't you?" he said; and the kindness in his tone made its impression.

"'Tis not much ye know of a coal-camp, Joe Smith," she said. "Can't ye imagine what it's like—bein' a woman in a place like this? And a woman they think good-lookin'!"

"Oh, so it's that!" said he, and was silent again. "Some one's been troubling you?" he ventured after a while.

"Sure! Some one's always troublin' us women! Always! Never a day but we hear it. Winks and nudges—everywhere ye turn."

"Who is it?"

"The bosses, the clerks—anybody that has a chance to wear a stiff collar, and thinks he can offer money to a girl. It begins before she's out of short skirts, and there's never any peace afterwards."

"And you can't make them understand?"

"I've made them understand me a bit; now they go after my old man."

"What?"

"Sure! D'ye suppose they'd not try that? Him that's so crazy for liquor, and can never get enough of it!"

"And your father?—" But Hal stopped. She would not want that question asked!

She had seen his hesitation, however. "He was a decent man once," she declared. "'Tis the life here, that turns a man into a coward. 'Tis everything ye need, everywhere ye turn—ye have to ask favours from some boss. The room ye work in, the dead work they pile on ye; or maybe 'tis more credit ye need at the store, or maybe the doctor to come when ye're sick. Just now 'tis our roof that leaks—so bad we can't find a dry place to sleep when it rains."

"I see," said Hal. "Who owns the house?"

"Sure, there's none but company houses here."

"Who's supposed to fix it?"

"Mr. Kosegi, the house-agent. But we gave him up long ago—if he does anything, he raises the rent. Today my father went to Mr. Cotton. He's supposed to look out for the health of the place, and it seems hardly healthy to keep people wet in their beds."

"And what did Cotton say?" asked Hal, when she stopped again.

"Well, don't ye know Jeff Cotton—can't ye guess what he'd say? 'That's a fine girl ye got, Burke! Why don't ye make her listen to reason?' And then he laughed, and told me old father he'd better learn to take a hint. 'Twas bad for an old man to sleep in the rain—he might get carried off by pneumonia."

Hal could no longer keep back the question, "What did your father do?"

"I'd not have ye think hard of my old father," she said, quickly. "He used to be a fightin' man, in the days before O'Callahan had his way with him. But now he knows what a camp-marshal can do to a miner!"

SECTION 20.

Mary Burke had said that the company could stand breaking the bones of its men; and not long after Number Two started up again, Hal had a chance to note the truth of this assertion.

A miner's life depended upon the proper timbering of the room where he worked. The company undertook to furnish the timbers, but when the miner needed them, he would find none at hand, and would have to make the mile-long trip to the surface. He would select timbers of the proper length, and would mark them—the understanding being that they were to be delivered to his room by some of the labourers. But then some one else would carry them off—here was more graft and favouritism, and the miner might lose a day or two of work, while meantime his account was piling up at the store, and his children might have no shoes to go to school. Sometimes he would give up waiting for timbers, and go on taking out coal; so there would be a fall of rock—and the coroner's jury would bring in a verdict of "negligence," and the coal-operators would talk solemnly about the impossibility of teaching caution to miners. Not so very long ago Hal had read an interview which the president of the General Fuel Company had given to a newspaper, in which he set forth the idea that the more experience a miner had the more dangerous it was to employ him, because he thought he knew it all, and would not heed the wise regulations which the company laid down for his safety!

In Number Two mine there were some places being operated by the "room and pillar" method; the coal being taken out as from a series of rooms, the portion corresponding to the walls of the rooms being left to uphold the roof. These walls are the "pillars"; and when the end of the vein is reached, the miner begins to work backwards, "pulling the pillars," and letting the roof collapse behind him. This is a dangerous task; as he works, the man has to listen to the drumming sounds of the rock above his head, and has to judge just when to make his escape. Sometimes he is too anxious to save a tool; or sometimes the collapse comes without warning. In that case the victim is seldom dug out; for it must be admitted that a man buried under a mountain is as well buried as a company could be expected to arrange it.

In Number Two mine a man was caught in this way. He stumbled as he ran, and the lower half of his body was pinned fast; the doctor had to come and pump opiates into him, while the rescue crew was digging him loose. The first Hal knew of the accident was when he saw the body stretched out on a plank, with a couple of old sacks to cover it. He noticed that nobody stopped for a second glance. Going up from work, he asked his friend Madvik, the mule driver, who answered, "Lit'uanian feller—got mash." And that was all. Nobody knew him, and nobody cared about him.

It happened that Mike Sikoria had been working nearby, and was one of those who helped to get the victim out. Mike's negro "buddy" had been in too great haste to get some of the rock out of the way, and had got his hand crushed, and would not be able to work for a month or so. Mike told Hal about it, in his broken English. It was a terrible thing to see a man trapped like that, gasping, his eyes almost popping out of his head. Fortunately he was a young fellow, and had no family.

Hal asked what they would do with the body; the answer was they would bury him in the morning. The company had a piece of ground up the canyon.

"But won't they have an inquest?" he inquired.

"Inques'?" repeated the other. "What's he?"

"Doesn't the coroner see the body?"

The old Slovak shrugged his bowed shoulders; if there was a coroner in this part of the world, he had never heard of it; and he had worked in a good many mines, and seen a good many men put under the ground. "Put him in a box and dig a hole," was the way he described the procedure.

"And doesn't the priest come?"

"Priest too far away."

Afterwards Hal made inquiry among the English-speaking men, and learned that the coroner did sometimes come to the camp. He would empanel a jury consisting of Jeff Cotton, the marshal, and Predovich, the Galician Jew who worked in the company store, and a clerk or two from the company's office, and a couple of Mexican labourers who had no idea what it was all about. This jury would view the corpse, and ask a couple of men what had happened, and then bring in a verdict: "We find that the deceased met his death from a fall of rock caused by his own fault." (In one case they had added the picturesque detail: "No relatives, and damned few friends!")

For this service the coroner got a fee, and the company got an official verdict, which would be final in case some foreign consul should threaten a damage suit. So well did they have matters in hand that nobody in North Valley had ever got anything for death or injury; in fact, as Hal found later, there had not been a damage suit filed against any coal-operator in that county for twenty-three years!

This particular, accident was of consequence to Hal, because it got him a chance to see the real work of mining. Old Mike was without a helper, and made the proposition that Hal should take the job. It was better than a stableman's, for it paid two dollars a day.

"But will the boss let me change?" asked Hal.

"You give him ten dollar, he change you," said Mike.

"Sorry," said Hal, "I haven't got ten dollars."

"You give him ten dollar credit," said the other.

And Hal laughed. "They take scrip for graft, do they?"

"Sure they take him," said Mike.

"Suppose I treat my mules bad?" continued the other. "So I can make him change me for nothing!"

"He change you to hell!" replied Mike. "You get him cross, he put us in bad room, cost us ten dollar a week. No, sir—you give him drink, say fine feller, make him feel good. You talk American—give him jolly!"

SECTION 21.

Hal was glad of this opportunity to get better acquainted with his pit-boss. Alec Stone was six feet high, and built in proportion, with arms like hams—soft with fat, yet possessed of enormous strength. He had learned his manner of handling men on a sugar-plantation in Louisiana—a fact which, when Hal heard it, explained much. Like a stage-manager who does not heed the real names of his actors, but calls them by their character-names, Stone had the habit of addressing his men by their nationalities: "You, Polack, get that rock into the car! Hey, Jap, bring them tools over here! Shut your mouth, now, Dago, and get to work, or I'll kick the breeches off you, sure as you're alive!"

Hal had witnessed one occasion when there was a dispute as to whose duty it was to move timbers. There was a great two-handled cross-cut saw lying on the ground, and Stone seized it and began to wave it, like a mighty broadsword, in the face of a little Bohemian miner. "Load them timbers, Hunkie, or I'll carve you into bits!" And as the terrified man shrunk back, he followed, until his victim was flat against a wall, the weapon swinging to and fro under his nose after the fashion of "The Pit and the Pendulum." "Carve you into pieces, Hunkie! Carve you into stew-meat!" When at last the boss stepped back, the little Bohemian leaped to load the timbers.

The curious part about it to Hal was that Stone seemed to be reasonably good-natured about such proceedings. Hardly one time in a thousand did he carry out his bloodthirsty threats, and like as not he would laugh when he had finished his tirade, and the object of it would grin in turn—but without slackening his frightened efforts. After the broad-sword waving episode, seeing that Hal had been watching, the boss remarked, "That's the way you have to manage them wops." Hal took this remark as a tribute to his American blood, and was duly flattered.

He sought out the boss that evening, and found him with his feet upon the railing of his home. "Mr. Stone," said he, "I've something I'd like to ask you."

"Fire away, kid," said the other.

"Won't you come up to the saloon and have a drink?"

"Want to get something out of me, hey? You can't work me, kid!" But nevertheless he slung down his feet from the railing, and knocked the ashes out of his pipe and strolled up the street with Hal.

"Mr. Stone," said Hal, "I want to make a change."

"What's that? Got a grouch on them mules?"

"No, sir, but I got a better job in sight. Mike Sikoria's buddy is laid up, and I'd like to take his place, if you're willing."

"Why, that's a nigger's place, kid. Ain't you scared to take a nigger's place?"

"Why, sir?"

"Don't you know about hoodoos?"

"What I want," said Hal, "is the nigger's pay."

"No," said the boss, abruptly, "you stick by them mules. I got a good stable-man, and I don't want to spoil him. You stick, and by and by I'll give you a raise. You go into them pits, the first thing you know you'll get a fall of rock on your head, and the nigger's pay won't be no good to you."

They came to the saloon and entered. Hal noted that a silence fell within, and every one nodded and watched. It was pleasant to be seen going out with one's boss.

O'Callahan, the proprietor, came forward with his best society smile and joined them, and at Hal's invitation they ordered whiskies. "No, you stick to your job," continued the pit-boss. "You stay by it, and when you've learned to manage mules, I'll make a boss out of you, and let you manage men."

Some of the bystanders tittered. The pit-boss poured down his whiskey, and set the glass on the bar. "That's no joke," said he, in a tone that every one could hear. "I learned that long ago about niggers. They'd say to me, 'For God's sake, don't talk to our niggers like that. Some night you'll have your house set afire.' But I said, 'Pet a nigger, and you've got a spoiled nigger.' I'd say, 'Nigger, don't you give me any of your imp, or I'll kick the breeches off you.' And they knew I was a gentleman, and they stepped lively."

"Have another drink," said Hal.

The pit-boss drank, and becoming more sociable, told nigger stories. On the sugar-plantations there was a rush season, when the rule was twenty hours' work a day; when some of the niggers tried to shirk it, they would arrest them for swearing or crap-shooting, and work them as convicts, without pay. The pit-boss told how one "buck" had been brought before the justice of the peace, and the charge read, "being cross-eyed"; for which offence he had been sentenced to sixty days' hard labour. This anecdote was enjoyed by the men in the saloon—whose race-feelings seemed to be stronger than their class-feelings.

When the pair went out again, it was late, and the boss was cordial. "Mr. Stone," began Hal, "I don't want to bother you, but I'd like first rate to get more pay. If you could see your way to let me have that buddy's job, I'd be more than glad to divide with you."

"Divide with me?" said Stone. "How d'ye mean?" Hal waited with some apprehension—for if Mike had not assured him so positively, he would have expected a swing from the pit-boss's mighty arm.

"It's worth about fifteen a month more to me. I haven't any cash, but if you'd be willing to charge off ten dollars from my store-account, it would be well worth my while."

They walked for a short way in silence. "Well, I'll tell you," said the boss, at last; "that old Slovak is a kicker—one of these fellows that thinks he could run the mine if he had a chance. And if you get to listenin' to him, and think you can come to me and grumble, by God—"

"That's all right, sir," put in Hal, quickly. "I'll manage that for you—I'll shut him up. If you'd like me to, I'll see what fellows he talks with, and if any of them are trying to make trouble, I'll tip you off."

"Now that's the talk," said the boss, promptly. "You do that, and I'll keep my eye on you and give you a chance. Not that I'm afraid of the old fellow—I told him last time that if I heard from him again, I'd kick the breeches off him. But when you got half a thousand of this foreign scum, some of them Anarchists, and some of them Bulgars and Montynegroes that's been fightin' each other at home—"

"I understand," said Hal. "You have to watch 'em."

"That's it," said the pit-boss. "And by the way, when you tell the store-clerk about that fifteen dollars, just say you lost it at poker."

"I said ten dollars," put in Hal, quickly.

"Yes, I know," responded the other. "But *I* said fifteen!"

SECTION 22.

Hal told himself with satisfaction that he was now to do the real work of coal-mining. His imagination had been occupied with it for a long time; but as so often happens in the life of man, the first contact with reality killed the results of many years' imagining. It killed all imagining, in fact; Hal found that his entire stock of energy, both mental and physical, was consumed in enduring torment. If any one had told him the horror of attempting to work in a room five feet high, he would not have believed it. It was like some of the dreadful devices of torture which one saw in European castles, the "iron maiden" and the "spiked collar." Hal's back burned as if hot irons were being run up and down it; every separate joint and muscle cried aloud. It seemed as if he could never learn the lesson of the jagged ceiling above his head—he bumped it and continued to bump it, until his scalp was a mass of cuts and bruises, and his head ached till he was nearly blind, and he would have to throw himself flat on the ground.

Then old Mike Sikoria would grin. "I know. Like green mule! Some day get tough!"

Hal recalled the great thick callouses on the flanks of his former charges, where the harness rubbed against them. "Yes, I'm a 'green mule,' all right!"

It was amazing how many ways there were to bruise and tear one's fingers, loading lumps of coal into a car. He put on a pair of gloves, but these wore through in a day. And then the gas, and the smoke of powder, stifling one; and the terrible burning of the eyes, from the dust and the feeble light. There was no way to rub these burning eyes, because everything about one was equally dusty. Could anybody have imagined the torment of that—any of those ladies who rode in soft-ly upholstered parlour-cars, or reclined upon the decks of steam-ships in gleaming tropic seas?

Old Mike was good to his new "buddy." Mike's spine was bent and his hands were hardened by forty years of this sort of toil, so he could do the work of two men, and entertain his friend with comments into the bargain. The old fellow had the habit of talking all the time, like a child; he would talk to his helper, to him-self, to his tools. He would call these tools by obscene and terrifying names—but with entire friendliness and good humour. "Get in there, you son-of-a-gun!" he would say to his pick. "Come along here, you wop!" he would say to his car. "In with you, now, you old buster!" he would say to a lump of coal. And he would lecture Hal on the details of mining. He would tell stories of successful days, or of terrible mishaps. Above all he would tell about rascality—cursing the "G. F. C.," its foremen and superintendents, its officials, directors and stock-holders, and the world which permitted such a criminal institution to exist.

Noon-time would come, and Hal would lie upon his back, too worn to eat. Old Mike would sit munching; his abundant whiskers came to a point on his chin, and as his jaws moved, he looked for all the world like an aged billy-goat. He was a kind-hearted and anxious old billy-goat, and sought to tempt his buddy with a bit of cheese or a swig of cold coffee. He believed in eating—no man could keep up steam if he did not stoke the furnace. Failing in this, he would try to divert Hal's mind, telling stories of mining-life in America and Russia. He was most proud to have an "American feller" for a buddy, and tried to make the work as easy as possible, for fear lest Hal might quit.

Hal did not quit; but he would drag himself out towards night, so exhausted that he would fall asleep in the cage. He would fall asleep at supper, and go in and sink down on his cot and sleep like a log. And oh, the torture of being routed out before daybreak! Having to shake the sleep out of his head, and move his creaking joints, and become aware of the burning in his eyes, and the blisters and sores on his hands!

It was a week before he had a moment that was not pain; and he never got fully used to the labour. It was impossible for any one to work so hard and keep his mental alertness, his eagerness and sensitiveness; it was impossible to work so hard and be an adventurer—to be anything, in fact, but a machine. Hal had heard that phrase of contempt, "the inertia of the masses," and had wondered about it. He no longer wondered, he knew. Could a man be brave enough to protest to a pit-boss when his body was numb with weariness? Could he think out a definite conclusion as to his rights and wrongs, and back his conclusion with effective action, when his mental faculties were paralysed by such weariness of body?

Hal had come here, as one goes upon the deck of a ship in mid-ocean, to see the storm. In this ocean of social misery, of ignorance and despair, one saw up-turned, tortured faces, writhing limbs and clutching hands; in one's ears was a storm of lamentation, upon one's cheek a spray of blood and tears. Hal found himself so deep in this ocean that he could no longer find consolation in the thought that he could escape whenever he wanted to: that he could say to himself, It is sad, it is terrible—but thank God, I can get out of it when I choose! I can go back into the warm and well-lighted saloon and tell the other passengers how picturesque it is, what an interesting experience they are missing!

SECTION 23.

During these days of torment, Hal did not go to see "Red Mary"; but then, one evening, the Minettis' baby having been sick, she came in to ask about it, bringing what she called "a bit of a custard" in a bowl. Hal was suspicious enough of the ways of men, especially of business-men; but when it came to women he was without insight—it did not occur to him as singular that an Irish girl with many troubles at home should come out to nurse a Dago woman's baby. He did not reflect that there were plenty of sick Irish babies in the camp, to whom Mary might have taken her "bit of a custard." And when he saw the surprise of Rosa, who had never met Mary before, he took it to be the touching gratitude of the poor!

There are, in truth, many kinds of women, with many arts, and no man has time to learn them all. Hal had observed the shop-girl type, who dress themselves with many frills, and cast side-long glances, and indulge in fits of giggles to attract the attention of the male; he was familiar with the society-girl type, who achieve the same end with more subtle and alluring means. But could there be a type who hold little Dago babies in their laps, and call them pretty Irish names, and feed them custard out of a spoon? Hal had never heard of that kind, and he thought that "Red Mary" made a charming picture—a Celtic madonna with a Sicilian infant in her arms.

He noticed that she was wearing the same faded blue calico-dress with a patch on the shoulder. Man though he was, he realised that dress is an important consideration in the lives of women. He was tempted to suspect that this blue calico might be the only dress that Mary owned; but seeing it newly laundered every time, he concluded that she must have at least one other. At any rate, here she was, crisp and fresh-looking; and with the new shining costume, she had put on the long promised "company manner": high spirits and badinage, precisely like any belle of the world of luxury, who powders and bedecks herself for a ball. She had been grim and complaining in former meetings with this interesting young man; she had frightened him away, apparently; perhaps she could win him back by womanliness and good humour.

She rallied him upon his battered scalp and his creaking back, telling him he looked ten years older—which he was fully prepared to believe. Also she had fun with him for working under a Slovak—another loss of caste, it appeared! This was a joke the Minettis could share in—especially Little Jerry, who liked jokes.

He told Mary how Joe Smith had had to pay fifteen dollars for his new job, besides several drinks at O'Callahan's. Also he told how Mike Sikoria had called Joe his "green mule." Little Jerry complained about the turn of events, for in the old days Joe had taught him a lot of fine new games—and now he was sore, and would not play them. Also, in the old days he had sung a lot of jolly songs, full of the most fascinating rhymes. There was a song about a "monkey puzzle tree"! Had Mary ever seen that kind of tree? Little Jerry never got tired of trying to imagine what it might look like.

The Dago urchin stood and watched gravely while Mary fed the custard to the baby; and when two or three spoonfuls were held out to him, he opened his mouth wide, and afterwards licked his lips. Gee, that was good stuff!

When the last taste was gone, he stood gazing at Mary's shining coronet. "Say," said he, "was your hair always like that?"

Hal and Mary burst into laughter, while Rosa cried "Hush!" She was never sure what this youngster would say next.

"Sure, did ye think I painted it?" asked Mary.

"I didn't know," said Little Jerry. "It looks so nice and new." And he turned to Hal. "Ain't it?"

"You bet," said Hal, and added, "Go on and tell her about it. Girls like compliments."

"Compliments?" echoed Little Jerry. "What's that?"

"Why," said Hal, "that's when you say that her hair is like the sunrise, and her eyes are like twilight, or that she's a wild rose on a mountain-side."

"Oh," said the Dago urchin, somewhat doubtfully. "Anyhow," he added, "she make nice custard!"

SECTION 24.

The time came for Mary to take her departure, and Hal got up, wincing with pain, to escort her home. She regarded him gravely, having not realised before how seriously he was suffering. As they walked along she asked, "Why do ye do such work, when ye don't have to?"

"But I *do* have to! I have to earn a living!"

"Ye don't have to earn it that way! A bright young fellow like you—an American!"

"Well," said Hal, "I thought it would be interesting to see coal mining."

"Now ye've seen it," said the girl—"now quit!"

"But it won't do me any harm to go on for a while!"

"Won't it? How can ye know? When any day they may carry you out on a plank!"

Her "company manner" was gone; her voice was full of bitterness, as it always was when she spoke of North Valley. "I know what I'm tellin' ye, Joe Smith. Didn't I lose two brothers in it—as fine lads as ye'd find anywhere in the world! And many another lad I've seen go in laughin', and come out a corpse—or what is worse, for workin' people, a cripple. Sometimes I'd like to go and stand at the pit-mouth in the mornin' and cry to them, 'Go back, go back! Go down the canyon this day! Starve, if ye have to, beg if ye have to, only find some other work but coal-minin'!'"

Her voice had risen to a passion of protest; when she went on a new note came into it—a note of personal terror. "It's worse now—since you came, Joe! To see ye settin' out on the life of a miner—you, that are young and strong and different. Oh, go away, Joe, go away while ye can!"

He was astonished at her intensity. "Don't worry about me, Mary," he said. "Nothing will happen to me. I'll go away after a while."

The path was irregular, and he had been holding her arm as they walked. He felt her trembling, and went on again, quickly, "It's not I that should go away, Mary. It's yourself. You hate the place—it's terrible for you to have to live here. Have you never thought of going away?"

She did not answer at once, and when she did the excitement was gone from her voice; it was flat and dull with despair. "'Tis no use to think of me. There's nothin' I can do—there's nothin' any girl can do when she's poor. I've tried—but 'tis like bein' up against a stone wall. I can't even save the money to get on a train with! I've tried it—I been savin' for two years—and how much d'ye think I got, Joe? Seven dollars! Seven dollars in two years! No—ye can't save money in a place where there's so many things that wring the heart. Ye may hate them for being cowards—but ye must help when ye see a man killed, and his family turned out without a roof to cover them in the winter-time!"

"You're too tender-hearted, Mary."

"No, 'tis not that! Should I go off and leave me own brother and sister, that need me?"

"But you could earn money and send it to them."

"I earn a little here—I do cleanin' and nursin' for some that need me."

"But outside—couldn't you earn more?"

"I could get a job in a restaurant for seven or eight a week, but I'd have to spend more, and what I sent home would not go so far, with me away. Or I could get a job in some other woman's home, and work fourteen hours a day for it. But, Joe, 'tis not more drudgery I want, 'tis somethin' fair to look upon—somethin' of my own!" She flung out her arms suddenly like one being stifled. "Oh, I want somethin' that's fair and clean!"

Again he felt her trembling. Again the path was rough, and having an impulse of sympathy, he put his arm about her. In the world of leisure, one might indulge in such considerateness, and he assumed it would not be different with a miner's daughter. But then, when she was close to him, he felt, rather than heard, a sob.

"Mary!" he whispered; and they stopped. Almost without realising it, he put his other arm about her, and in a moment more he felt her warm breath on his cheek, and she was trembling and shaking in his embrace. "Joe! Joe!" she whispered. "*You* take me away!"

She was a rose in a mining-camp, and Hal was deeply moved. The primrose path of dalliance stretched fair before him, here in the soft summer night, with a moon overhead which bore the same message as it bore in the Italian gardens of the leisure-class. But not many minutes passed before a cold fear began to steal over Hal. There was a girl at home, waiting for him; and also there was the resolve which had been growing in him since his coming to this place—a resolve to find some way of compensation to the poor, to repay them for the freedom and culture he had taken; not to prey upon them, upon any individual among them. There were the Jeff Cottons for that!

"Mary," he pleaded, "we mustn't do this."

"Why not?"

"Because—I'm not free. There is some one else."

He felt her start, but she did not draw away.

"Where?" she asked, in a low voice.

"At home, waiting for me."

"And why didn't ye tell me?"

"I don't know."

Hal realised in a moment that the girl had ground of complaint against him. According to the simple code of her world, he had gone some distance with her; he had been seen to walk out with her, he had been accounted her "fellow." He had led her to talk to him of herself—he had insisted upon having her confidences. And these people who were poor did not have subtleties, there was no room in their lives for intellectual curiosities, for Platonic friendships or philanderings. "Forgive me, Mary!" he said.

She made no answer; but a sob escaped her, and she drew back from his arms—slowly. He struggled with an impulse to clasp her again. She was beautiful, warm with life—and so much in need of happiness!

But he held himself in check, and for a minute or two they stood apart. Then he asked, humbly, "We can still be friends, Mary, can't we? You must know—I'm so *sorry*!"

But she could not endure being pitied. "'Tis nothin'," she said. "Only I thought I was going to get away! That's what ye mean to me."

<h1 align="center">SECTION 25.</h1>

Hal had promised Alec Stone to keep a look-out for trouble-makers; and one evening the boss stopped him on the street, and asked him if he had anything to report. Hal took the occasion to indulge his sense of humour.

"There's no harm in Mike Sikoria," said he. "He likes to shoot off his head, but if he's got somebody to listen, that's all he wants. He's just old and grouchy. But there's another fellow that I think would bear watching."

"Who's that?" asked the boss.

"I don't know his last name. They call him Gus and he's a 'cager.' Fellow with a red face."

"I know," said Stone—"Gus Durking."

"Well, he tried his best to get me to talk about unions. He keeps bringing it up, and I think he's some kind of trouble-maker."

"I see," said the boss. "I'll get after him."

"You won't say I told you," said Hal, anxiously.

"Oh, no—sure not." And Hal caught the trace of a smile on the pit-boss's face.

He went away, smiling in his turn. The "red-faced feller. Gus," was the person Madvik had named as being a "spotter" for the company!

There were ins and outs to this matter of "spotting," and sometimes it was not easy to know what to think. One Sunday morning Hal went for a walk up the canyon, and on the way he met a young chap who got to talking with him, and after a while brought up the question of working-conditions in North Valley. He had only been there a week, he said, but everybody he had met seemed to be grumbling about short weight. He himself had a job as an "outside man," so it made no difference to him, but he was interested, and wondered what Hal had found.

Straightway came the question, was this really a workingman, or had Alec Stone set some one to spying upon his spy. This was an intelligent fellow, an American—which in itself was suspicious, for most of the new men the company got in were from "somewhere East of Suez."

Hal decided to spar for a while. He did not know, he said, that conditions were any worse here than elsewhere. You heard complaints, no matter what sort of job you took.

Yes, said the stranger, but matters seemed to be especially bad in the coal-camps. Probably it was because they were so remote, and the companies owned everything in sight.

"Where have you been?" asked Hal, thinking that this might trap him.

But the other answered straight; he had evidently worked in half a dozen of the camps. In Mateo he had paid a dollar a month for wash-house privileges, and there had never been any water after the first three men had washed. There had been a common wash-tub for all the men, an unthinkably filthy arrangement. At Pine Creek—Hal found the very naming of the place made his heart stand still—at Pine Creek he had boarded with his boss, but the roof of the building leaked, and everything he owned was ruined; the boss would do nothing—yet when the boarder moved, he lost his job. At East Ridge, this man and a couple of other fellows had rented a two room cabin and started to board themselves, in spite of the fact that they had to pay a dollar-fifty a sack for potatoes and eleven cents a pound for sugar at the company store. They had continued until they made the discovery that the water supply had run short, and that the water for which they were paying the company a dollar a month was being pumped from the bottom of the mine, where the filth of mules and men was plentiful!

Hal forced himself to remain non-committal; he shook his head and said it was too bad, but the workers always got it in the neck, and he didn't see what they could do about it. So they strolled back to the camp, the stranger evidently baffled, and Hal, for his part, feeling like the reader of a detective story at the end of the first chapter. Was this young man the murderer, or was he the hero? One would have to read on in the book to find out!

SECTION 26.

Hal kept his eye upon his new acquaintance, and perceived that he was talking with others. Before long the man tackled Old Mike; and Mike of course could not refuse an invitation to grumble, though it came from the devil himself. Hal decided that something must be done about it.

He consulted his friend Jerry, who, being a radical, might have some touchstone by which to test the stranger. Jerry sought him out at noon-time, and came back and reported that he was as much in the dark as Hal. Either the man was an agitator, seeking to "start something," or else he was a detective sent in by the company. There was only one way to find out—which was for some one to talk freely with him, and see what happened to that person!

After some hesitation, Hal decided that he would be the victim. It rewakened his love of adventure, which digging in a coal-mine had subdued in him. The mysterious stranger was a new sort of miner, digging into the souls of men; Hal would countermine him, and perhaps blow him up. He could afford the experiment better than some others—better, for example, than little Mrs. David, who had already taken the stranger into her home, and revealed to him the fact that her husband had been a member of the most revolutionary of all miners' organisations, the South Wales Federation.

So next Sunday Hal invited the stranger for another walk. The man showed reluctance—until Hal said that he wanted to talk to him. As they walked up the canyon, Hal began, "I've been thinking about what you said of conditions in these camps, and I've concluded it would be a good thing if we had a little shaking up here in North Valley."

"Is that so?" said the other.

"When I first came here, I used to think the men were grouchy. But now I've had a chance to see for myself, and I don't believe anybody gets a square deal. For one thing, nobody gets full weight in these mines—at least not unless he's some favourite of the boss. I'm sure of it, for I've tried all sorts of experiments with my partner. We've loaded a car extra light, and got eighteen hundredweight, and then we've loaded one high and solid, so that we'd know it had twice as much in it— but all we ever got was twenty-two and twenty-three. There's just no way you can get over that—though everybody knows those big cars can be made to hold two or three tons."

"Yes, I suppose they might," said the other.

"And if you get the smallest piece of rock in, you get a 'double-O,' sure as fate; and sometimes they say you got rock in when you didn't. There's no law to make them prove it."

"No, I suppose not."

"What it comes to is simply this—they make you think they are paying fifty-five a ton, but they've secretly cut you down to thirty-five. And yesterday at the company-store I paid a dollar and a half for a pair of blue overalls that I'd priced in Pedro for sixty cents."

"Well," said the other, "the company has to haul them up here, you know!"

So, gradually, Hal made the discovery that the tables were turned—the mysterious personage was now occupied in holding *him* at arm's length! For some reason, Hal's sudden interest in industrial justice had failed to make an impression.

So his career as a detective came to an inglorious end. "Say, man!" he exclaimed "What's your game, anyhow?"

"Game?" said the other, quietly. "How do you mean?"

"I mean, what are you here for?"

"I'm here for two dollars a day—the same as you, I guess."

Hal began to laugh. "You and I are like a couple of submarines, trying to find each other under water. I think we'd better come to the surface to do our fighting."

The other considered the simile, and seemed to like it. "You come first," said he. But he did not smile. His quiet blue eyes were fixed on Hal with deadly seriousness.

"All right," said Hal; "my story isn't very thrilling. I'm not an escaped convict, I'm not a company spy, as you may be thinking. Nor am I a 'natural born' coal-miner. I happen to have a brother and some friends at home who think they know about the coal-industry, and it got on my nerves, and I came to see for myself. That's all, except that I've found things interesting, and want to stay on a while, so I hope you aren't a 'dick'!"

The other walked in silence, weighing Hal's words. "That's not exactly what you'd call a usual story," he remarked, at last.

"I know," replied Hal. "The best I can say for it is that it's true."

"Well," said the stranger, "I'll take a chance on it. I have to trust somebody, if I'm ever to get anywhere. I picked you out because I liked your face." He gave Hal another searching look as he walked. "Your smile isn't that of a cheat. But you're young—so let me remind you of the importance of secrecy in this place."

"I'll keep mum," said Hal; and the stranger opened a flap inside his shirt, and drew out a letter which certified him to be Thomas Olson, an organiser for the United Mine-Workers, the great national union of the coal-miners!

SECTION 27.

Hal was so startled by this discovery that he stopped in his tracks and gazed at the man. He had heard a lot about "trouble-makers" in the camps, but so far the only kind he had seen were those hired by the company to make trouble for the men. But now, here was a union organiser! Jerry had suggested the possibility, but Hal had not thought of it seriously; an organiser was a mythological creature, whispered about by the miners, cursed by the company and its servants, and by Hal's friends at home. An incendiary, a fire-brand, a loudmouthed, irresponsible person, stirring up blind and dangerous passions! Having heard such things all his life, Hal's first impulse was of distrust. He felt like the one-legged old switchman who had given him a place to sleep, after his beating at Pine Creek, and who had said, "Don't you talk no union business to me!"

Seeing Hal's emotion, the organiser gave an uneasy laugh. "While you're hoping I'm not a 'dick,' I trust you understand I'm hoping *you're* not one."

Hal's answer was to the point. "I was taken for an organiser once," he said, and his hands sought the seat of his ancient bruises.

The other laughed. "You got off with a beating? You were lucky. Down in Alabama, not so long ago, they tarred and feathered one of us."

Dismay came upon Hal's face; but after a moment he too began to laugh. "I was just thinking about my brother and his friends—what they'd have said if I'd come home from Pine Creek in a coat of tar and feathers!"

"Possibly," ventured the other, "they'd have said you got what you deserved."

"Yes, that seems to be their attitude. That's the rule they apply to all the world—if anything goes wrong with you, it must be your own fault. It's a land of equal opportunity."

"And you'll notice," said the organiser, "that the more privileges people have had, the more boldly they talk that way."

Hal began to feel a sense of comradeship with this stranger, who was able to understand one's family troubles! It had been a long time since Hal had talked with any one from the outside world, and he found it a relief to his mind. He remembered how, after he had got his beating, he had lain out in the rain and congratulated himself that he was not what the guards had taken him for. Now he was curious about the psychology of an organiser. A man must have strong convictions to follow that occupation!

He made the remark, and the other answered, "You can have my pay any time you'll do my work. But let me tell you, too, it isn't being beaten and kicked out of camp that bothers one most; it isn't the camp-marshal and the spy and the black-list. Your worst troubles are inside the heads of the fellows you're trying to help! Have you ever thought what it would mean to try to explain things to men who speak twenty different languages?"

"Yes, of course," said Hal. "I wonder how you ever get a start."

"Well, you look for an interpreter—and maybe he's a company spy. Or maybe the first man you try to convert reports you to the boss. For, of course, some of the men are cowards, and some of them are crooks; they'll sell out the next fellow for a better 'place'—maybe for a glass of beer."

"That must have a tendency to weaken your convictions," said Hal.

"No," said the other, in a matter of fact tone. "It's hard, but one can't blame the poor devils. They're ignorant—kept so deliberately. The bosses bring them here, and have a regular system to keep them from getting together. And of course these European peoples have their old prejudices—national prejudices, religious prejudices, that keep them apart. You see two fellows, one you think is exactly as miserable as the other—but you find him despising the other, because back home he was the other's superior. So they play into the bosses' hands."

SECTION 28.

They had come to a remote place in the canyon, and found themselves seats on a flat rock, where they could talk in comfort.

"Put yourself in their place," said the organiser. "They're in a strange country, and one person tells them one thing, and another tells them something else. The masters and their agents say: 'Don't trust the union agitators. They're a lot of grafters, they live easy and don't have to work. They take your money and call you out on strike, and you lose your jobs and your home; they sell you out, maybe, and go on to some other place to repeat the same trick.' And the workers think maybe that's true; they haven't the wit to see that if the union leaders are corrupt, it must be because the bosses are buying them. So you see, they're completely bedevilled; they don't know which way to turn."

The man was speaking quietly, but there was a little glow of excitement in his face. "The company is forever repeating that these people are satisfied—that it's we who are stirring them up. But are they satisfied? You've been here long enough to know!"

"There's no need to discuss that," Hal answered. "Of course they're not satisfied! They've seemed to me like a lot of children crying in the dark—not knowing what's the matter with them, or who's to blame, or where to turn for help."

Hal found himself losing his distrust of this man. He did not correspond in any way to Hal's imaginary picture of a union organiser; he was a blue-eyed, clean-looking young American, and instead of being wild and loud-mouthed, he seemed rather wistful. He had indignation, of course, but it did not take the form of ranting or florid eloquence; and this repression was making its appeal to Hal, who, in spite of his democratic impulses, had the habits of thought of a class which shrinks from noisiness and over-emphasis.

Also Hal was interested in his attitude towards the weaknesses of working-people. The "inertia" of the poor, which caused so many people to despair for them—their cowardice and instability—these were things about which Hal had heard all his life. "You can't help them," people would say. "They're dirty and lazy, they drink and shirk, they betray each other. They've always been like that." The idea would be summed up in a formula: "You can't change human nature!" Even Mary Burke, herself one of the working-class, spoke of the workers in this angry and scornful way. But Olson had faith in their manhood, and went ahead to awaken and teach them.

To his mind the path was clear and straight. "They must be taught the lesson of solidarity. As individuals, they're helpless in the power of the great corporations; but if they stand together, if they sell their labour as a unit—then they really count for something." He paused, and looked at the other inquiringly. "How do you feel about unions?"

Hal answered, "They're one of the things I want to find out about. You hear this and that—there's so much prejudice on each side. I want to help the under dog, but I want to be sure of the right way."

"What other way is there?" And Olson paused. "To appeal to the tender hearts of the owners?"

"Not exactly; but mightn't one appeal to the world in general—to public opinion? I was brought up an American, and learned to believe in my country. I can't think but there's some way to get justice. Maybe if the men were to go into politics—"

"Politics?" cried Olson. "My God! How long have you been in this place?"

"Only a couple of months."

"Well, stay till November, and see what they do with the ballot-boxes in these camps!"

"I can imagine, of course—"

"No, you can't. Any more than you could imagine the graft and the misery!"

"But if the men should take to voting together—"

"How *can* they take to voting together—when any one who mentions the idea goes down the canyon? Why, you can't even get naturalisation papers, unless you're a company man; they won't register you, unless the boss gives you an O. K. How are you going to make a start, unless you have a union?"

It sounded reasonable, Hal had to admit; but he thought of the stories he had heard about "walking delegates," all the dreadful consequences of "union domination." He had not meant to go in for unionism!

Olson was continuing. "We've had laws passed, a whole raft of laws about coal-mining—the eight-hour law, the anti-scrip law, the company-store law, the mine-sprinkling law, the check-weighman law. What difference has it made in North Valley that there are such laws on the statute-books? Would you ever even know about them?"

"Ah, now!" said Hal. "If you put it that way—if your movement is to have the law enforced—I'm with you!"

"But how will you get the law enforced, except by a union? No individual man can do it—it's 'down the canyon' with him if he mentions the law. In Western City our union people go to the state officials, but they never do anything—and why? They know we haven't got the men behind us! It's the same with the politicians as it is with the bosses—the union is the thing that counts!"

Hal found this an entirely new argument. "People don't realise that idea—that men have to be organised to get their *legal* rights."

And the other threw up his hands with a comical gesture. "My God! If you want to make a list of the things that people don't realise about us miners!"

SECTION 29.

Olson was eager to win Hal, and went on to tell all the secrets of his work. He sought men who believed in unions, and were willing to take the risk of trying to convert others. In each place he visited he would get a group together, and would arrange some way to communicate with them after he left, smuggling in propaganda literature for distribution. So there would be the nucleus of an organisation. In a year or two they would have such a nucleus in every camp, and then they would be ready to come into the open, calling meetings in the towns, and in places in the canyons to which the miners would flock. So the flame of revolt would leap up; men would join the movement faster than the companies could get rid of them, and they would make a demand for their rights, backed with the threat of a strike throughout the entire district.

"You understand," added Olson, "we have a legal right to organise—even though the bosses disapprove. You need not stand back on that score."

"Yes," said Hal; "but it occurs to me that as a matter of tactics, it would be better here in North Valley if you chose some issue there's less controversy about; if, for instance, you'd concentrate on getting a check-weighman."

The other smiled. "We'd have to have a union to back the demand; so what's the difference?"

"Well," argued Hal, "there are prejudices to be reckoned with. Some people don't like the idea of a union—they think it means tyranny and violence—"

The organiser laughed. "You aren't convinced but that it does yourself, are you! Well, all I can tell you is, if you want to tackle the job of getting a check-weighman in North Valley, I'll not stand in your way!"

Here was an idea—a real idea! Life had grown dull for Hal since he had become a buddy, working in a place five feet high. This would promise livelier times!

But was it a thing he wanted to do? So far he had been an observer of conditions in this coal-camp. He had convinced himself that conditions were cruel, and he had pretty well convinced himself that the cruelty was needless and deliberate. But when it came to a question of an action to be taken—then he hesitated, and old prejudices and fears made themselves heard. He had been told that labour was "turbulent" and "lazy," that it had to be "ruled with a strong hand"; now, was he willing to weaken the strong hand, to ally himself with those who "fomented labour troubles"?

But this would not be the same thing, he told himself. This suggestion of Olson's was different from trade unionism, which might be a demoralising force, leading the workers from one demand to another, until they were seeking to "dominate industry." This would be merely an appeal to the law, a test of that honesty and fair dealing to which the company everywhere laid claim. If, as the bosses proclaimed, the workers were fully protected by the check-weighman law; if, as all the world was made to believe, the reason there was no check-weighman was simply because the men did not ask for one—why, then there would be no harm done. If on the other hand a demand for a right that was not merely a legal right, but a moral right as well—if that were taken by the bosses as an act of rebellion against the company—well, Hal would understand a little more about the "turbulence" of labour! If, as Old Mike and Johannson and the rest maintained, the bosses would "make your life one damn misery" till you left—then he would be ready to make a few damn miseries for the bosses in return!

"It would be an adventure," said Hal, suddenly.

And the other laughed. "It would that!"

"You're thinking I'll have another Pine Creek experience," Hal added. "Well, maybe so—but I have to try things out for myself. You see, I've got a brother at home, and when I think about going in for revolution, I have imaginary arguments with him. I want to be able to say 'I didn't swallow anybody's theories; I tried it for myself, and this is what happened.'"

"Well," replied the organiser, "that's all right. But while you're seeking education for yourself and your brother, don't forget that I've already got my education. I *know* what happens to men who ask for a check-weighman, and I can't afford to sacrifice myself proving it again."

"I never asked you to," laughed Hal. "If I won't join your movement, I can't expect you to join mine! But if I can find a few men who are willing to take the risk of making a demand for a check-weighman—that won't hurt your work, will it?"

"Sure not!" said the other. "Just the opposite—it'll give me an object lesson to point to. There are men here who don't even know they've a legal right to a check-weighman. There are others who know they don't get their weights, but aren't sure its the company that's cheating them. If the bosses should refuse to let any one inspect the weights, if they should go further and fire the men who ask it—well, there'll be plenty of recruits for my union local!"

"All right," said Hal. "I'm not setting out to recruit your union local, but if the company wants to recruit it, that's the company's affair!" And on this bargain the two shook hands.

BOOK TWO — THE SERFS OF KING COAL

SECTION 1.

Hal was now started upon a new career, more full of excitements than that of stableman or buddy, with perils greater than those of falling rock or the hind feet of mules in the stomach. The inertia which overwork produces had not had time to become a disease with him; youth was on his side, with its zest for more and yet more experience. He found it thrilling to be a conspirator, to carry about with him secrets as dark and mysterious as the passages of the mine in which he worked.

But Jerry Minetti, the first person he told of Tom Olson's purpose in North Valley, was older in such thrills. The care-free look which Jerry was accustomed to wear vanished abruptly, and fear came into his eyes. "I know it come some day," he exclaimed—"trouble for me and Rosa!"

"How do you mean?"

"We get into it—get in sure. I say Rosa, 'Call yourself Socialist—what good that do? No help any. No use to vote here—they don't count no Socialist vote, only for joke!' I say, 'Got to have union. Got to strike!' But Rosa say, 'Wait little bit. Save little bit money, let children grow up. Then we help, no care if we no got any home.'"

"But we're not going to start a union now!" objected Hal. "I have another plan for the present."

Jerry, however, was not to be put at ease. "No can wait!" he declared. "Men no stand it! I say, 'It come some day quick—like blow-up in mine! Somebody start fight, everybody fight.'" And Jerry looked at Rosa, who sat with her black eyes fixed anxiously upon her husband. "We get into it," he said; and Hal saw their eyes turn to the room where Little Jerry and the baby were sleeping.

Hal said nothing—he was beginning to understand the meaning of rebellion to such people. He watched with curiosity and pity the struggle that went on; a struggle as old as the soul of man—between the voice of self-interest, of comfort and prudence, and the call of duty, of the ideal. No trumpet sounded for this conflict, only the still small voice within.

After a while Jerry asked what it was Hal and Olson had planned; and Hal explained that he wanted to make a test of the company's attitude toward the check-weighman law. Hal thought it a fine scheme; what did Jerry think?

Jerry smiled sadly. "Yes, fine scheme for young feller—no got family!"

"That's all right," said Hal, "I'll take the job—I'll be the check-weighman."

"Got to have committee," said Jerry—"committee go see boss."

"All right, but we'll get young fellows for that too—men who have no families. Some of the fellows who live in the chicken-coops in shanty-town. They won't care what happens to them."

But Jerry would not share Hal's smile. "No got sense 'nough, them fellers. Take sense to stick together." He explained that they would need a group of men to stand back of the committee; such a group would have to be organised, to hold meetings in secret—it would be practically the same thing as a union, would be so regarded by the bosses and their spotters. And no organisation of any sort was permitted in the camps. There had been some Serbians who had wanted to belong to a fraternal order back in their home country, but even that had been forbidden. If you wanted to insure your life or your health, the company would attend to it— and get the profit from it. For that matter, you could not even buy a post-office money-order, to send funds back to the old country; the post-office clerk, who was at the same time a clerk in the company-store, would sell you some sort of a store-draft.

So Hal was facing the very difficulties about which Olson had warned him. The first of them was Jerry's fear. Yet Hal knew that Jerry was no "coward"; if any man had a contempt for Jerry's attitude, it was because he had never been in Jerry's place!

"All I'll ask of you now is advice," said Hal. "Give me the names of some young fellows who are trustworthy, and I'll get their help without anybody sus- pecting you."

"You my boarder!" was Jerry's reply to this.

So again Hal was "up against it." "You mean that would get you into trouble?"

"Sure! They know we talk. They know I talk Socialism, anyhow. They fire me sure!"

"But how about your cousin, the pit-boss in Number One?"

"He no help. May be get fired himself. Say damn fool—board check- weighman!"

"All right," said Hal. "Then I'll move away now, before it's too late. You can say I was a trouble-maker, and you turned me off."

The Minettis sat gazing at each other—a mournful pair. They hated to lose their boarder, who was such good company, and paid them such good money. As for Hal, he felt nearly as bad, for he liked Jerry and his girl-wife, and Little Jer- ry—even the black-eyed baby, who made so much noise and interrupted conversation!

"No!" said Jerry. "I no run, away! I do my share!"

"That's all right," replied Hal. "You do your share—but not just yet. You stay on in the camp and help Olson after I'm fired. We don't want the best men put out at once."

So, after further argument, it was decided, and Hal saw little Rosa sink back in her chair and draw a deep breath of relief. The time for martyrdom was put off;

her little three-roomed cabin, her furniture and her shining pans and her pretty white lace curtains, might be hers for a few weeks longer!

SECTION 2.

Hal went back to Reminitsky's boarding-house; a heavy sacrifice, but not without its compensations, because it gave him more chance to talk with the men.

He and Jerry made up a list of those who could be trusted with the secret: the list beginning with the name of Mike Sikoria. To be put on a committee, and sent to interview a boss, would appeal to Old Mike as the purpose for which he had been put upon earth! But they would not tell him about it until the last minute, for fear lest in his excitement he might shout out the announcement the next time he lost one of his cars.

There was a young Bulgarian miner named Wresmak who worked near Hal. The road into this man's room ran up an incline, and he had hardly been able to push his "empties" up the grade. While he was sweating and straining at the task, Alec Stone had come along, and having a giant's contempt for physical weakness, began to cuff him. The man raised his arm—whether in offence or to ward off the blow, no one could be sure; but Stone fell upon him and kicked him all the way down the passage, pouring out upon him furious curses. Now the man was in another room, where he had taken out over forty car-loads of rock, and been allowed only three dollars for it. No one who watched his face when the pit-boss passed would doubt that this man would be ready to take his chances in a movement of protest.

Then there was a man whom Jerry knew, who had just come out of the hospital, after contact with the butt-end of the camp-marshal's revolver. This was a Pole, who unfortunately did not know a word of English; but Olson, the organiser, had got into touch with another Pole, who spoke a little English, and would pass the word on to his fellow-countryman. Also there was a young Italian, Rovetta, whom Jerry knew and whose loyalty he could vouch for.

There was another person Hal thought of—Mary Burke. He had been deliberately avoiding her of late; it seemed the one safe thing to do—although it seemed also a cruel thing, and left his mind ill at ease. He went over and over what had happened. How had the trouble got started? It is a man's duty in such cases to take the blame upon himself; but a man does not like to take blame upon himself, and he tries to make it as light as possible. Should Hal say that it was because he had been too officious that night in helping Mary where the path was rough? She had not actually needed such help, she was quite as capable on her feet as he! But he had really gone farther than that—he had had a definite sentimental impulse; and he had been a cad—he should have known all along that all this girl's discontent, all the longing of her starved soul, would become centred upon him, who was so "different," who had had opportunity, who made her think of the "poetry-books"!

But here suddenly seemed a solution of the difficulty; here was a new interest for Mary, a safe channel in which her emotions could run. A woman could not serve on a miners' committee, but she would be a good adviser, and her sharp tongue would be a weapon to drive others into line. Being aflame with this enterprise, Hal became impersonal, man-fashion—and so fell into another sentimental trap! He did not stop to think that Mary's interest in the check-weighman movement might be conditioned in part by a desire to see more of him; still less did it occur to him that he might be glad for a pretext to see Mary.

No, he was picturing her in a new role, an activity more inspiriting than cooking and nursing. His "poetry-book" imagination took fire; he gave her a hope and a purpose, a pathway with a goal at the end. Had there not been women leaders in every great proletarian movement?

He went to call on her, and met her at the door of her cabin. "'Tis a cheerin' sight to see ye, Joe Smith!" she said. And she looked him in the eye and smiled.

"The same to you, Mary Burke!" he answered.

She was game, he saw; she was going to be a "good sport." But he noticed that she was paler than when he had seen her last. Could it be that these gorgeous Irish complexions ever faded? He thought that she was thinner too; the old blue calico seemed less tight upon her.

Hal plunged into his theme. "Mary, I had a vision of you to-day!"

"Of me, lad? What's that?"

He laughed. "I saw you with a glory in your face, and your hair shining like a crown of gold. You were mounted on a snow-white horse, and wore a robe of white, soft and lustrous—like Joan of Arc, or a leader in a suffrage parade. You were riding at the head of a host—I've still got the music in my ears, Mary!"

"Go on with ye, lad—what's all this about?"

"Come in and I'll tell you," he said.

So they went into the bare kitchen, and sat in bare wooden chairs—Mary folding her hands in her lap like a child who has been promised a fairy-story. "Now hurry," said she. "I want to know about this new dress ye're givin' me. Are ye tired of me old calico?"

He joined in her smile. "This is a dress you will weave for yourself, Mary, out of the finest threads of your own nature—out of courage and devotion and self-sacrifice."

"Sure, 'tis the poetry-book again! But what is it ye're really meanin'?"

He looked about him. "Is anybody here?"

"Nobody."

But instinctively he lowered his voice as he told his story. There was an organiser of the "big union" in the camp, and he was going to rouse the slaves to protest.

The laughter went out of Mary's face. "Oh! It's that!" she said, in a flat tone. The vision of the snow-white horse and the soft and lustrous robe was gone. "Ye can never do anything of that sort here!"

"Why not?"

"'Tis the men in this place. Don't ye remember what I told ye at Mr. Rafferty's? They're cowards!"

"Ah, Mary, it's easy to say that. But it's not so pleasant being turned out of your home—"

"Do ye have to tell me that?" she cried, with sudden passion. "Haven't I seen that?"

"Yes, Mary; but I want to *do* something—"

"Yes, and haven't I wanted to do something? Sure, I've wanted to bite off the noses of the bosses!"

"Well," he laughed, "we'll make that a part of our programme." But Mary was not to be lured into cheerfulness; her mood was so full of pain and bewilderment that he had an impulse to reach out and take her hand again. But he checked that; he had come to divert her energies into a safe channel!

"We must waken these men to resistance, Mary!"

"Ye can't do it, Joe—not the English-speakin' men. The Greeks and the Bulgars, maybe—they're fightin' at home, and they might fight here. But the Irish never—never! Them that had any backbone went out long ago. Them that stayed has been made into boot-licks. I know them, every man of them. They grumble, and curse the boss, but then they think of the blacklist, and they go back and cringe at his feet."

"What such men want—"

"'Tis booze they want, and carousin' with the rotten women in the coal-towns, and sittin' up all night winnin' each other's money with a greasy pack of cards! They take their pleasure where they find it, and 'tis nothin' better they want."

"Then, Mary, if that's so, don't you see it's all the more reason for trying to teach them? If not for their own sakes, for the sake of their children! The children, mustn't grow up like that! They are learning English, at least—"

Mary gave a scornful laugh. "Have ye been up to that school?"

He answered no; and she told him there were a hundred and twenty children packed in one room, three in a seat, and solid all round the wall. She went on, with swift anger—the school was supposed to be paid for out of taxes, but as nobody owned any property but the company, it was all in the company's hands. The school-board consisted of Mr. Cartwright, the mine-superintendent, and Jake Predovich, a clerk in the store, and the preacher, the Reverend Spraggs. Old Spraggs would bump his nose on the floor if the "super" told him to.

"Now, now!" said Hal, laughing. "You're down on him because his grandfather was an Orangeman!"

SECTION 3.

Mary Burke had been suckled upon despair, and the poison of it was deep in her blood. Hal began to realise that it would be as hard to give her a hope as to rouse the workers whom she despised. She was brave enough, no doubt, but how could he persuade her to be brave for men who had no courage for themselves?

"Mary," he said, "in your heart you don't really hate these people. You know how they suffer, you pity them for it. You give their children your last cent when they need it—"

"Ah, lad!" she cried, and he saw tears suddenly spring into her eyes. "'Tis because I love them so that I hate them! Sometimes 'tis the bosses I would murder, sometimes 'tis the men. What is it ye're wantin' me to do?"

And then, even before he could answer, she began to run over the list of her acquaintances in the camp. Yes, there was one man Hal ought to talk to; he would be too old to join them, but his advice would be invaluable, and they could be sure he would never betray them. That was old John Edstrom, a Swede from Minnesota, who had worked in this district from the time the mines had first started up. He had been active in the great strike eight years ago, and had been black-listed, his four sons with him. The sons were scattered now to the four parts of the world, but the father had stayed nearby, working as a ranch-hand and railroad la-bourer, until a couple of years ago, during a rush season, he had got a chance to come back into the mines.

He was old, old, declared Mary—must be sixty. And when Hal remarked that that did not sound so frightfully aged, she answered that one seldom heard of a man being able to work in a coal-mine at that age; in fact, there were not many who managed to live to that age. Edstrom's wife was dying now, and he was hav-ing a hard time.

"'Twould not be fair to let such an old gentleman lose his job," said Mary. "But at least he could give ye good advice."

So that evening the two of them went to call on John Edstrom, in a tiny un-painted cabin in "shanty-town," with a bare earth floor, and a half partition of rough boards to hide his dying wife from his callers. The woman's trouble was cancer, and this made calling a trying matter, for there was a fearful odour in the place. For some time it was impossible for Hal to force himself to think about an-ything else; but finally he overcame this weakness, telling himself that this was a war, and that a man must be ready for the hospital as well as for the parade-ground.

He looked about, and saw that the cracks of Edstrom's cabin were stopped with rags, and the broken windowpanes mended with brown paper. The old man had evidently made an effort to keep the place neat, and Hal noticed a row of books on a shelf. Because it was cold in these mountain regions at night, even in September, the old man had a fire in the little cast-iron stove, and sat huddled by it. There were only a few hairs left on his head, and his scrubby beard was as white as anything could be in a coal-camp. The first impression of his face was of its pallor, and then of the benevolence in the faded dark eyes; also his voice was gentle, like a caress. He rose to greet his visitors, and put out to Hal a trembling hand, which resembled the paw of some animal, horny and misshapen. He made a move to draw up a bench, and apologised for his unskillful house-keeping. It occurred to Hal that a man might be able to work in a coal-mine at sixty, and not be able to work in it at sixty-one.

Hal had requested Mary to say nothing about his purpose, until after he had a chance to judge for himself. So now the girl inquired about Mrs. Edstrom. There was no news, the man answered; she was lying in a stupor, as usual. Dr. Barrett had come again, but all he could do was to give her morphine. No one could do any more, the doctor declared.

"Sure, he'd not know it if they could!" sniffed Mary.

"He's not such a bad one, when he's sober," said Edstrom, patiently.

"And how often is that?" sniffed Mary again. She added, by way of explanation to Hal, "He's a cousin of the super."

Things were better here than in some places, said Edstrom. At Harvey's Run, where he had worked, a man had got his eye hurt, and had lost it through the doctor's instrument slipping; broken arms and legs had been set wrong, and either the men had to go through life as cripples, or go elsewhere and have the bones re-broken and reset, It was like everything else—the doctor was a part of the company machine, and if you had too much to say about him, it was down the canyon with you. You not only had a dollar a month taken out of your pay, but if you were injured, and he came to attend you, he would charge whatever extra he pleased.

"And you have to pay?" asked Hal.

"They take it off your account," said the old man.

"Sometimes they take it when he's done nothin' at all," added Mary. "They charged Mrs. Zamboni twenty-five dollars for her last baby—and Dr. Barrett never set foot across her door till three hours after the baby was in my arms!"

SECTION 4.

The talk went on. Wishing to draw the old man out, Hal spoke of various troubles of the miners, and at last he suggested that the remedy might be found in a union. Edstrom's dark eyes studied him, and then turned to Mary. "Joe's all right," said the girl, quickly. "You can trust him."

Edstrom made no direct answer to this, but remarked that he had once been in a strike. He was a marked man, now, and could only stay in the camp so long as he attended strictly to his own affairs. The part he had played in the big strike had never been forgotten; the bosses had let him work again, partly because they had needed him at a rush time, and partly because the pit-boss happened to be a personal friend.

"Tell him about the big strike," said Mary. "He's new in this district."

The old man had apparently accepted Mary's word for Hal's good faith, for he began to narrate those terrible events which were a whispered tradition of the camps. There had been a mighty effort of ten thousand slaves for freedom; and it had been crushed with utter ruthlessness. Ever since these mines had been started, the operators had controlled the local powers of government, and now, in the emergency, they had brought in the state militia as well, and used it frankly to drive the strikers back to work. They had seized the leaders and active men, and thrown them into jail without trial or charges; when the jails would hold no more, they kept some two hundred in an open stockade, called a "bull-pen," and finally they loaded them into freight-cars, took them at night out of the state, and dumped them off in the midst of the desert without food or water.

John Edstrom had been one of these men. He told how one of his sons had been beaten and severely injured in jail, and how another had been kept for weeks in a damp cellar, so that he had come out crippled with rheumatism for life. The officers of the state militia had done these things; and when some of the local authorities were moved to protest, the militia had arrested them—even the judges of the civil courts had been forbidden to sit, under threat of imprisonment. "To hell with the constitution!" had been the word of the general in command; his subordinate had made famous the saying, "No habeas corpus; we'll give them post-mortems!"

Tom Olson had impressed Hal with his self-control, but this old man made an even deeper impression upon him. As he listened, he became humble, touched with awe. Incredible as it might seem, when John Edstrom talked about his cruel experiences, it was without bitterness in his voice, and apparently without any in his heart. Here, in the midst of want and desolation, with his family broken and scattered, and the wolf of starvation at his door, he could look back upon the past without hatred of those who had ruined him. Nor was this because he was old and feeble, and had lost the spirit of revolt; it was because he had studied economics, and convinced himself that it was an evil system which blinded men's eyes and poisoned their souls. A better day was coming, he said, when this evil system would be changed, and it would be possible for men to be merciful to one another.

At this point in the conversation, Mary Burke gave voice once more to her corroding despair. How could things ever be changed? The bosses were mean-hearted, and the men were cowards and traitors. That left nobody but God to do the changing—and God had left things as they were for such a long time!

Hal was interested to hear how Edstrom dealt with this attitude. "Mary," he said, "did you ever read about ants in Africa?"

"No," said she.

"They travel in long columns, millions and millions of them. And when they come to a ditch, the front ones fall in, and more and more of them on top, till they fill up the ditch, and the rest cross over. We are ants, Mary."

"No matter how many go in," cried the girl, "none will ever get across. There's no bottom to the ditch!"

He answered: "That's more than any ant can know. Mary. All they know is to go in. They cling to each other's bodies, even in death; they make a bridge, and the rest go over."

"I'll step one side!" she declared, fiercely. "I'll not throw meself away."

"You may step one side," answered the other—"but you'll step back into line again. I know you better than you know yourself, Mary."

There was silence in the little cabin. The winds of an early fall shrilled outside, and life suddenly seemed to Hal a stern and merciless thing. He had thought in his youthful fervour it would be thrilling to be a revolutionist; but to be an ant, one of millions and millions, to perish in a bottomless ditch—that was something a man could hardly bring himself to face! He looked at the bowed figure of this white haired toiler, vague in the feeble lamplight, and found himself thinking of Rembrandt's painting, the Visit of Emmaus: the ill-lighted room in the dirty tavern, and the two ragged men, struck dumb by the glow of light about the forehead of their table-companion. It was not fantastic to imagine a glow of light about the forehead of this soft-voiced old man!

"I never had any hope it would come in my time," the old man was saying gently. "I did use to hope my boys might see it—but now I'm not sure even of that. But in all my life I never doubted that some day the working-people will cross over to the promised land. They'll no longer be slaves, and what they make won't be wasted by idlers. And take it from one who knows, Mary—for a workingman or woman not to have that faith, is to have lost the reason for living."

Hal decided that it would be safe to trust this man, and told him of his check-weighman plan. "We only want your advice," he explained, remembering Mary's warning. "Your sick wife—"

But the old man answered, sadly, "She's almost gone, and I'll soon be following. What little strength I have left might as well be used for the cause."

<h1 style="text-align:center">SECTION 5.</h1>

This business of conspiracy was grimly real to men whose living came out of coal; but Hal, even at the most serious moments, continued to find in it the thrill of romance. He had read stories of revolutionists, and of the police who hunted them. That such excitements were to be had in Russia, he knew; but if any one had told him they could be had in his own free America, within a few hours' journey of his home city and his college-town, he could not have credited the statement.

The evening after his visit to Edstrom, Hal was stopped on the street by his boss. Encountering him suddenly, Hal started, like a pick-pocket who runs into a policeman.

"Hello, kid," said the pit-boss.

"Hello, Mr. Stone," was the reply.

"I want to talk to you," said the boss.

"All right, sir." And then, under his breath, "He's got me!"

"Come up to my house," said Stone; and Hal followed, feeling as if hand-cuffs were already on his wrists.

"Say," said the man, as they walked, "I thought you were going to tell me if you'd heard any talk."

"I haven't heard any, sir."

"Well," continued Stone, "you want to get busy; there's sure to be kickers in every coal-camp." And deep within, Hal drew a sigh of relief. It was a false alarm!

They came to the boss's house, and he took a chair on the piazza and motioned Hal to take another. They sat in semi-darkness, and Stone dropped his voice as he began. "What I want to talk to you about now is something else—this election."

"Election, sir?"

"Didn't you know there was one? The Congressman in this district died, and there's a special election three weeks from next Tuesday."

"I see, sir." And Hal chuckled inwardly. He would get the information which Tom Olson had recommended to him!

"You ain't heard any talk about it?" inquired the pit-boss.

"Nothing at all, sir. I never pay much attention to politics—it ain't in my line."

"Well, that's the way I like to hear a miner talk!" said the pit-boss, with heartiness. "If they all had sense enough to leave politics to the politicians, they'd be a sight better off. What they need is to tend to their own jobs."

"Yes, sir," agreed Hal, meekly—"like I had to tend to them mules, if I didn't want to get the colic."

The boss smiled appreciatively. "You've got more sense than most of 'em. If you'll stand by me, there'll be a chance for you to move up in the world."

"Thank you, Mr. Stone," said Hal. "Give me a chance."

"Well now, here's this election. Every year they send us a bunch of campaign money to handle. A bit of it might come your way."

"I could use it, I reckon," said Hal, brightening visibly. "What is it you want?"

There was a pause, while Stone puffed on his pipe. He went on, in a businesslike manner. "What I want is somebody to feel things out a bit, and let me know the situation. I thought it better not to use the men that generally work for me, but somebody that wouldn't be suspected. Down in Sheridan and Pedro they say the Democrats are making a big stir, and the company's worried. I suppose you know the 'G. F. C.' is Republican."

"I've heard so."

"You might think a congressman don't have much to do with us, way off in Washington; but it has a bad effect to have him campaigning, telling the men the company's abusing them. So I'd like you just to kind o' circulate a bit, and start the men on politics, and see if any of them have been listening to this MacDougall talk. (MacDougall's this here Democrat, you know.) And I want to find out whether they've been sending in literature to this camp, or have any agents here. You see, they claim the right to come in and make speeches, and all that sort of thing. North Valley's an incorporated town, so they've got the law on their side, in a way, and if we shut 'em out, they make a howl in the papers, and it looks bad. So we have to get ahead of them in quiet ways. Fortunately there ain't any hall in the camp for them to meet in, and we've made a local ordinance against meetings on the street. If they try to bring in circulars, something has to happen to them before they get distributed. See?"

"I see," said Hal; he thought of Tom Olson's propaganda literature!

"We'll pass the word out,—it's the Republican the company wants elected; and you be on the lookout and see how they take it in the camp."

"That sounds easy enough," said Hal. "But tell me, Mr. Stone, why do you bother? Do so many of these wops have votes?"

"It ain't the wops so much. We get them naturalised on purpose—they vote our way for a glass of beer. But the English-speaking men, or the foreigners that's been here too long, and got too big for their breeches—they're the ones we got to watch. If they get to talking politics, they don't stop there; the first thing you know, they're listening to union agitators, and wanting to run the camp."

"Oh yes, I see!" said Hal, and wondered if his voice sounded right.

But the pit-boss was concerned with his own troubles. "As I told Si Adams the other day, what I'm looking for is fellows that talk some new lingo—one that nobody will ever understand! But I suppose that would be too easy. There's no way to keep them from learning some English!"

Hal decided to make use of this opportunity to perfect his education. "Surely, Mr. Stone," he remarked, "you don't have to count any votes if you don't want to!"

"Well, I'll tell you," replied Stone; "it's a question of the easiest way to manage things. When I was superintendent over to Happy Gulch, we didn't waste no time on politics. The company was Democratic at that time, and when election night come, we wrote down four hundred votes for the Democratic candidates. But the first thing we knew, a bunch of fellers was taken into town and got to swear they'd voted the Republican ticket in our camp. The Republican papers were full of it, and some fool judge ordered a recount, and we had to get busy over night and mark up a new lot of ballots. It gave us a lot of bother!"

The pit-boss laughed, and Hal joined him discreetly.

"So you see, you have to learn to manage. If there's votes for the wrong candidate in your camp, the fact gets out, and if the returns is too one-sided, there's a lot of grumbling. There's plenty of bosses that don't care, but I learned my lesson that time, and I got my own method—that is not to let any opposition start. See?"

"Yes, I see."

"Maybe a mine-boss has got no right to meddle in politics—but there's one thing he's got the say about, and that is who works in his mine. It's the easiest thing to weed out—weed out—" Hal never forgot the motion of beefy hands with which Alec Stone illustrated these words. As he went on, the tones of his voice did not seem so good-natured as usual. "The fellows that don't want to vote my way can go somewhere else to do their voting. That's all I got to say on politics!"

There was a brief pause, while Stone puffed on his pipe. Then it may have occurred to him that it was not necessary to go into so much detail in breaking in a political recruit. When he resumed, it was in a good-natured tone of dismissal. "That's what you do, kid. To-morrow you get a sprained wrist, so you can't work for a few days, and that'll give you a chance to bum round and hear what the men are saying. Meantime, I'll see you get your wages."

"That sounds all right," said Hal; but showing only a small part of his satisfaction!

The pit-boss rose from his chair and knocked the ashes from his pipe. "Mind you—I want the goods. I've got other fellows working, and I'm comparing 'em. For all you know, I may have somebody watching you."

"Yes," said Hal, and grinned cheerfully. "I'll not fail to bear that in mind."

SECTION 6.

The first thing Hal did was to seek out Tom Olson and narrate this experience. The two of them had a merry time over it. "I'm the favourite of a boss now!" laughed Hal.

But the organiser became suddenly serious. "Be careful what you do for that fellow."

"Why?"

"He might use it on you later on. One of the things they try to do if you make any trouble for them, is to prove that you took money from them, or tried to."

"But he won't have any proofs."

"That's my point—don't give him any. If Stone says you've been playing the political game for him, then some fellow might remember that you did ask him about politics. So don't have any marked money on you."

Hal laughed. "Money doesn't stay on me very long these days. But what shall I say if he asks me for a report?"

"You'd better put your job right through, Joe—so that he won't have time to ask for any report."

"All right," was the reply. "But just the same, I'm going to get all the fun there is, being the favourite of a boss!"

And so, early the next morning when Hal went to his work he proceeded to "sprain his wrist." He walked about in pain, to the great concern of Old Mike; and when finally he decided that he would have to lay off, Mike followed him half way to the shaft, giving him advice about hot and cold cloths. Leaving the old Slovak to struggle along as best he could alone, Hal went out to bask in the wonderful sunshine of the upper world, and the still more wonderful sunshine of a boss's favour.

First he went to his room at Reminitsky's, and tied a strip of old shirt about his wrist, and a clean handkerchief on top of that; by this symbol he was entitled to the freedom of the camp and the sympathy of all men, and so he sallied forth.

Strolling towards the tipple of Number One, he encountered a wiry, quick-moving little man, with restless black eyes and a lean, intelligent face. He wore a pair of common miner's "jumpers," but even so, he was not to be taken for a workingman. Everything about him spoke of authority.

"Morning, Mr. Cartwright," said Hal.

"Good morning," replied the superintendent; then, with a glance at Hal's bandage, "You hurt?"

"Yes, sir. Just a bit of sprain, but I thought I'd better lay off."

"Been to the doctor?"

"No, sir. I don't think it's that bad."

"You'd better go. You never know how bad a sprain is."

"Right, sir," said Hal. Then, as the superintendent was passing, "Do you think, Mr. Cartwright, that MacDougall stands any chance of being elected?"

"I don't know," replied the other, surprised. "I hope not. You aren't going to vote for him, are you?"

"Oh, no. I'm a Republican—born that way. But I wondered if you'd heard any MacDougall talk."

"Well, I'm hardly the one that would hear it. You take an interest in politics?"

"Yes, sir—in a way. In fact, that's how I came to get this wrist."

"How's that? In a fight?"

"No, sir; but you see, Mr. Stone wanted me to feel out sentiment in the camp, and he told me I'd better sprain my wrist and lay off."

The "super," after staring at Hal, could not keep from laughing. Then he looked about him. "You want to be careful, talking about such things."

"I thought I could surely trust the superintendent," said Hal, drily.

The other measured him with his keen eyes; and Hal, who was getting the spirit of political democracy, took the liberty of returning the gaze. "You're a wide-awake young fellow," said Cartwright, at last. "Learn the ropes here, and make yourself useful, and I'll see you're not passed over."

"All right, sir—thank you."

"Maybe you'll be made an election-clerk this time. That's worth three dollars a day, you know."

"Very good, sir." And Hal put on his smile again. "They tell me you're the mayor of North Valley."

"I am."

"And the justice of the peace is a clerk in your store. Well, Mr. Cartwright, if you need a president of the board of health or a dog catcher, I'm your man—as soon, that is, as my wrist gets well."

And so Hal went on his way. Such "joshing" on the part of a "buddy" was of course absurdly presumptuous; the superintendent stood looking after him with a puzzled frown upon his face.

SECTION 7.

Hal did not look back, but turned into the company-store. "North Valley Trading Company" read the sign over the door; within was a Serbian woman pointing out what she wanted to buy, and two little Lithuanian girls watching the weighing of a pound of sugar. Hal strolled up to the person who was doing the weighing, a middle-aged man with a yellow moustache stained with tobacco-juice. "Morning, Judge."

"Huh!" was the reply from Silas Adams, justice of the peace in the town of North Valley.

"Judge," said Hal, "what do you think about the election?"

"I don't think about it," said the other. "Busy weighin' sugar."

"Anybody round here going to vote for MacDougall?"

"They better not tell me if they are!"

"What?" smiled Hal. "In this free American republic?"

"In this part of the free American republic a man is free to dig coal, but not to vote for a skunk like MacDougall." Then, having tied up the sugar, the "J. P." whittled off a fresh chew from his plug, and turned to Hal. "What'll you have?"

Hal purchased half a pound of dried peaches, so that he might have an excuse to loiter, and be able to keep time with the jaws of the Judge. While the order was being filled, he seated himself upon the counter. "You know," said he, "I used to work in a grocery."

"That so? Where at?"

"Peterson & Co., in American City." Hal had told this so often that he had begun to believe it.

"Pay pretty good up there?"

"Yes, pretty fair." Then, realising that he had no idea what would constitute good pay in a grocery, Hal added, quickly, "Got a bad wrist here!"

"That so?" said the other.

He did not show much sociability; but Hal persisted, refusing to believe that any one in a country store would miss an opening to discuss politics, even with a miner's helper. "Tell me," said he, "just what is the matter with MacDougall?"

"The matter with him," said the Judge, "is that the company's against him." He looked hard at the young miner. "You meddlin' in politics?" he growled. But the young miner's gay brown eyes showed only appreciation of the earlier response;

so the "J. P." was tempted into specifying the would-be congressman's vices. Thus conversation started; and pretty soon the others in the store joined in—"Bob" Johnson, bookkeeper and post-master, and "Jake" Predovich, the Galician Jew who was a member of the local school-board, and knew the words for staple groceries in fifteen languages.

Hal listened to an exposition of the crimes of the political opposition in Pedro County. Their candidate, MacDougall, had come to the state as a "tin-horn gambler," yet now he was going around making speeches in churches, and talking about the moral sentiment of the community. "And him with a district chairman keeping three families in Pedro!" declared Si Adams.

"Well," ventured Hal, "if what I hear is true, the Republican chairman isn't a plaster saint. They say he was drunk at the convention—"

"Maybe so," said the "J. P." "But we ain't playin' for the prohibition vote; and we ain't playin' for the labour vote—tryin' to stir up the riff-raff in these coal-camps, promisin' 'em high wages an' short hours. Don't he know he can't get it for 'em? But he figgers he'll go off to Washington and leave us here to deal with the mess he's stirred up!"

"Don't you fret," put in Bob Johnson—"he ain't goin' to no Washin'ton."

The other two agreed, and Hal ventured again, "He says you stuff the ballot-boxes."

"What do you suppose his crowd is doin' in the cities? We got to meet 'em some way, ain't we?"

"Oh, I see," said Hal, naïvely. "You stuff them worse!"

"Sometimes we stuff the boxes, and sometimes we stuff the voters." There was an appreciative titter from the others, and the "J. P." was moved to reminiscence. "Two years ago I was election clerk, over to Sheridan, and we found we'd let 'em get ahead of us—they had carried the whole state. 'By God,' said Alf. Raymond, 'we'll show 'em a trick from the coal-counties! And there won't be no recount business either!' So we held back our returns till the rest had come in, and when we seen how many votes we needed, we wrote 'em down. And that settled it."

"That seems a simple method," remarked Hal. "They'll have to get up early to beat Alf."

"You bet you!" said Si, with the complacency of one of the gang. "They call this county the 'Empire of Raymond.'"

"It must be a cinch," said Hal—"being the sheriff, and having the naming of so many deputies as they need in these coal-camps!"

"Yes," agreed the other. "And there's his wholesale liquor business, too. If you want a license in Pedro county, you not only vote for Alf, but you pay your bills on time!"

"Must be a fortune in that!" remarked Hal; and the Judge, the Post-master and the School-commissioner appeared like children listening to a story of a feast. "You bet you!"

"I suppose it takes money to run politics in this county," Hal added.

"Well, Alf don't put none of it up, you can bet! That's the company's job."

This from the Judge; and the School-commissioner added, "De coin in dese camps is beer."

"Oh, I see!" laughed Hal. "The companies buy Alf's beer, and use it to get him votes!"

"Sure thing!" said the Post-master.

At this moment he happened to reach into his pocket for a cigar, and Hal observed a silver shield on the breast of his waistcoat. "That a deputy's badge?" he inquired, and then turned to examine the School-commissioner's costume. "Where's yours?"

"I git mine ven election comes," said Jake, with a grin.

"And yours, Judge?"

"I'm a justice of the peace, young feller," said Silas, with dignity.

Leaning round, and observing a bulge on the right hip of the School-commissioner, Hal put out his hand towards it. Instinctively the other moved his hand to the spot.

Hal turned to the Post-master. "Yours?" he asked.

"Mine's under the counter," grinned Bob.

"And yours, Judge?"

"Mine's in the desk," said the Judge.

Hal drew a breath. "Gee!" said he. "It's like a steel trap!" He managed to keep the laugh on his face, but within he was conscious of other feelings than those of amusement. He was losing that "first fine careless rapture" with which he had set out to run with the hare and the hounds in North Valley!

<h1 style="text-align:center">SECTION 8.</h1>

Two days after this beginning of Hal's political career, it was arranged that the workers who were to make a demand for a check-weighman should meet in the home of Mrs. David. When Mike Sikoria came up from the pit that day, Hal took him aside and told him of the gathering. A look of delight came upon the old Slovak's face as he listened; he grabbed his buddy by the shoulders, crying, "You mean it?"

"Sure meant it," said Hal. "You want to be on the committee to go and see the boss?"

"*Pluha biedna*!" cried Mike—which is something dreadful in his own language. "By Judas, I pack up my old box again!"

Hal felt a guilty pang. Should he let this old man into the thing? "You think you'll have to move out of camp?" he asked.

"Move out of state this time! Move back to old country, maybe!" And Hal realised that he could not stop him now, even if he wanted to. The old fellow was so much excited that he hardly ate any supper, and his buddy was afraid to leave him alone, for fear he might blurt out the news.

It had been agreed that those who attended the meeting should come one by one, and by different routes. Hal was one of the first to arrive, and he saw that the shades of the house had been drawn, and the lamps turned low. He entered by the back door, where "Big Jack" David stood on guard. "Big Jack," who had been a member of the South Wales Federation at home, made sure of Hal's identity, and then passed him in without a word.

Inside was Mike—the first on hand. Mrs. David, a little black-eyed woman with a never-ceasing tongue, was bustling about, putting things in order; she was so nervous that she could not sit still. This couple had come from their birth-place only a year or so ago, and had brought all their wedding presents to their new home—pictures and bric-a-brac and linen. It was the prettiest home Hal had so far been in, and Mrs. David was risking it deliberately, because of her indignation that her husband had had to foreswear his union in order to get work in America.

The young Italian, Rovetta, came, then old John Edstrom. There being not chairs enough in the house, Mrs. David had set some boxes against the wall, covering them with cloth; and Hal noticed that each person took one of these boxes, leaving the chairs for the later comers. Each one as he came in would nod to the others, and then silence would fall again.

When Mary Burke entered, Hal divined from her aspect and manner that she had sunk back into her old mood of pessimism. He felt a momentary resentment. He was so thrilled with this adventure; he wanted everybody else to be thrilled—especially Mary! Like every one who has not suffered much, he was repelled by a condition of perpetual suffering in another. Of course Mary had good reasons for her black moods—but she herself considered it necessary to apologise for what she called her "complainin'"! She knew that he wanted her to help encourage the others; but here she was, putting herself in a corner and watching this wonderful proceeding, as if she had said: "I'm an ant, and I stay in line—but I'll not pretend I have any hope in it!"

Rosa and Jerry had insisted on coming, in spite of Hal's offer to spare them. After them came the Bulgarian, Wresmak; then the Polacks, Klowoski and Zamierowski. Hal found these difficult names to remember, but the Polacks were not at all sensitive about this; they would grin good-naturedly while he practised, nor would they mind if he gave it up and called them Tony and Pete. They were humble men, accustomed all their lives to being driven about. Hal looked from one to another of their bowed forms and toil-worn faces, appearing more than ever sombre and mournful in the dim light; he wondered if the cruel persecution which had driven them to protest would suffice to hold them in line.

Once a newcomer, having misunderstood the orders, came to the front door and knocked; and Hal noted that every one started, and some rose to their feet in alarm. Again he recognised the atmosphere of novels of Russian revolutionary life. He had to remind himself that these men and women, gathered here like criminals, were merely planning to ask for a right guaranteed them by the law!

The last to come was an Austrian miner named Huszar, with whom Olson had got into touch. Then, it being time to begin, everybody looked uneasily at everybody else. Few of them had conspired before, and they did not know quite how to set about it. Olson, the one who would naturally have been their leader, had deliberately stayed away. They must run this check-weighman affair for themselves!

"Somebody talk," said Mrs. David at last; and then, as the silence continued, she turned to Hal. "You're going to be the check-weighman. You talk."

"I'm the youngest man here," said Hal, with a smile. "Some older fellow talk."

But nobody else smiled. "Go on!" exclaimed old Mike; and so at last Hal stood up. It was something he was to experience many times in the future; because he was an American, and educated, he was forced into a position of leadership.

"As I understand it, you people want a check-weighman. Now, they tell me the pay for a check-weighman should be three dollars a day, but we've got only seven miners among us, and that's not enough. I will offer to take the job for twenty-five cents a day from each man, which will make a dollar-seventy-five, less than what I'm getting now as a buddy. If we get thirty men to come in, then I'll take ten cents a day from each, and make the full three dollars. Does that seem fair?"

"Sure!" said Mike; and the others added their assent by word or nod.

"All right. Now, there's nobody that works in this mine but knows the men don't get their weight. It would cost the company several hundred dollars a day to give us our weight, and nobody should be so foolish as to imagine they'll do it without a struggle. We've got to make up our minds to stand together."

"Sure, stand together!" cried Mike.

"No get check-weighman!" exclaimed Jerry, pessimistically.

"Not unless we try, Jerry," said Hal.

And Mike thumped his knee. "Sure try! And get him too!"

"Right!" cried "Big Jack." But his little wife was not satisfied with the response of the others. She gave Hal his first lesson in the drilling of these polyglot masses.

"Talk to them. Make them understand you!" And she pointed them out one by one with her finger: "You! You! Wresmak, here, and you, Klowoski, and you, Zam—you other Polish fellow. Want check-weighman. Want to get all weight. Get all our money. Understand?"

"Yes, yes!"

"Get committee, go see super! Want check-weighman. Understand? Got to have check-weighman! No back down, no scare."

"No—no scare!" Klowoski, who understood some English, explained rapidly to Zamierowski; and Zamierowski, whose head was still plastered where Jeff Cotton's revolver had hit it, nodded eagerly in assent. In spite of his bruises, he would stand by the others, and face the boss.

This suggested another question. "Who's going to do the talking to the boss?"

"You do that," said Mrs. David, to Hal.

"But I'm the one that's to be paid. It's not for me to talk."

"No one else can do it right," declared the woman.

"Sure—got to be American feller!" said Mike.

But Hal insisted. If he did the talking, it would look as if the check-weighman had been the source of the movement, and was engaged in making a good paying job for himself.

There was discussion back and forth, until finally John Edstrom spoke up. "Put me on the committee."

"You?" said Hal. "But you'll be thrown out! And what will your wife do?"

"I think my wife is going to die to-night," said Edstrom, simply.

He sat with his lips set tightly, looking straight before him. After a pause he went on: "If it isn't to-night, it will be to-morrow, the doctor says; and after that, nothing will matter. I shall have to go down to Pedro to bury her, and if I have to stay, it will make little difference to me, so I might as well do what I can for the rest of you. I've been a miner all my life, and Mr. Cartwright knows it; that might have some weight with him. Let Joe Smith and Sikoria and myself be the ones to go and see him, and the rest of you wait, and don't give up your jobs unless you have to."

<h1 style="text-align:center">SECTION 9.</h1>

Having settled the matter of the committee, Hal told the assembly how Alec Stone had asked him to spy upon the men. He thought they should know about it; the bosses might try to use it against him, as Olson had warned. "They may tell you I'm a traitor," he said. "You must trust me."

"We trust you!" exclaimed Mike, with fervour; and the others nodded their agreement.

"All right," Hal answered. "You can rest sure of this one thing—if I get onto that tipple, you're going to get your weights!"

"Hear, hear!" cried "Big Jack," in English fashion. And a murmur ran about the room. They did not dare make much noise, but they made clear that that was what they wanted.

Hal sat down, and began to unroll the bandage from his wrist. "I guess I'm through with this," he said, and explained how he had come to wear it.

"What?" cried Old Mike. "You fool me like that?" And he caught the wrist, and when he had made sure there was no sign of swelling upon it, he shook it so that he almost sprained it really, laughing until the tears ran down his cheeks. "You old son-of-a-gun!" he exclaimed. Meantime Klowoski was telling the story to Zamierowski, and Jerry Minetti was explaining it to Wresmak, in the sort of pidgin-English which does duty in the camps. Hal had never seen such real laughter since coming to North Valley.

But conspirators cannot lend themselves long to merriment. They came back to business again. It was agreed that the hour for the committee's visit to the superintendent should be quitting-time on the morrow. And then John Edstrom spoke, suggesting that they should agree upon their course of action in case they were offered violence.

"You think there's much chance of that?" said some one.

"Sure there be!" cried Mike Sikoria. "One time in Cedar Mountain we go see boss, say air-course blocked. What you think he do them fellers? He hit them one lick in nose, he kick them three times in behind, he run them out!"

"Well," said Hal, "if there's going to be anything like that, we must be ready."

"What you do?" demanded Jerry.

It was time for Hal's leadership. "If he hits me one lick in the nose," he declared, "I'll hit him one lick in the nose, that's all."

There was a bit of applause at this. That was the way to talk! Hal tasted the joys of his leadership. But then his fine self-confidence met with a sudden check—a "lick in the nose" of his pride, so to speak. There came a woman's voice from the corner, low and grim: "Yes! And get ye'self killed for all your trouble!"

He looked towards Mary Burke, and saw her vivid face, flushed and frowning. "What do you mean?" he asked. "Would you have us turn and run away?"

"I would that!" said she. "Rather than have ye killed, I would! What'll ye do if he pulls his gun on ye?"

"Would he pull his gun on a committee?"

Old Mike broke in again. "One time in Barela—ain't I told you how I lose my cars? I tell weigh-boss somebody steal my cars, and he pull gun on me, and he say, 'Get the hell off that tipple, you old billy-goat, I shoot you full of holes!'"

Among his class-mates at college, Hal had been wont to argue that the proper way to handle a burglar was to call out to him, saying, "Go ahead, old chap, and help yourself; there's nothing here I'm willing to get shot for." What was the value of anything a burglar could steal, in comparison with a man's own life? And surely, one would have thought, this was a good time to apply the plausible theory. But for some reason Hal failed even to remember it. He was going ahead, precisely as if a ton of coal per day was the one thing of consequence in life!

"What shall we do?" he asked. "We don't want to back out."

But even while he asked the question, Hal was realising that Mary was right. His was the attitude of the leisure-class person, used to having his own way; but Mary, though she had a temper too, was pointing the lesson of self-control. It was the second time to-night that she had injured his pride. But now he forgave her in his admiration; he had always known that Mary had a mind and could help him! His admiration was increased by what John Edstrom was saying—they must do nothing that would injure the cause of the "big union," and so they must resolve to offer no physical resistance, no matter what might be done to them.

There was vehement argument on the other side. "We fight! We fight!" declared Old Mike, and cried out suddenly, as if in anticipation of the pain in his injured nose. "You say me stand that?"

"If you fight back," said Edstrom, "we'll all get the worst of it. The company will say we started the trouble, and put us in the wrong. We've got to make up our mind to rely on moral force."

So, after more discussion, it was agreed; every man would keep his temper— that is, if he could! So they shook hands all round, pledging themselves to stand firm. But, when the meeting was declared adjourned, and they stole out one by one into the night, they were a very sober and anxious lot of conspirators.

SECTION 10.

Hal slept but little that night. Amid the sounds of the snoring of eight of Reminitsky's other boarders, he lay going over in his mind various things which might happen on the morrow. Some of them were far from pleasant things; he tried to picture himself with a broken nose, or with tar and feathers on him. He recalled his theory as to the handling of burglars. The "G. F. C." was a burglar of gigantic and terrible proportions; surely this was a time to call out, "Help yourself!" But instead of doing it, Hal thought about Edstrom's ants, and wondered at the power which made them stay in line.

When morning came, he went up into the mountains, where a man may wander and renew his moral force. When the sun had descended behind the mountain-tops, he descended also, and met Edstrom and Sikoria in front of the company office.

They nodded a greeting, and Edstrom told Hal that his wife had died during the day. There being no undertaker in North Valley, he had arranged for a woman friend to take the body down to Pedro, so that he might be free for the interview with Cartwright. Hal put his hand on the old man's shoulder, but attempted no word of condolence; he saw that Edstrom had faced the trouble and was ready for duty.

"Come ahead," said the old man, and the three went into the office. While a clerk took their message to the inner office, they stood for a couple of minutes, shifting uneasily from one foot to the other, and turning their caps in their hands in the familiar manner of the lowly.

At last Mr. Cartwright appeared in the doorway, his small sparely-built figure eloquent of sharp authority. "Well, what's this?" he inquired.

"If you please," said Edstrom, "we'd like to speak to you. We've decided, sir, that we want to have a check-weighman."

"*What?*" The word came like the snap of a whip.

"We'd like to have a check-weighman, sir."

There was a moment's silence. "Come in here." They filed into the inner office, and he shut the door.

"Now. What's this?"

Edstrom repeated his words again.

"What put that notion into your heads?"

"Nothing, sir; only we thought we'd be better satisfied."

"You think you're not getting your weight?"

"Well, sir, you see—some of the men—we think it would be better if we had the check-weighman. We're willing to pay for him."

"Who's this check-weighman to be?"

"Joe Smith, here."

Hal braced himself to meet the other's stare. "Oh! So it's you!" Then, after a moment, "So that's why you were feeling so gay!"

Hal was not feeling in the least gay at the moment; but he forebore to say so. There was a silence.

"Now, why do you fellows want to throw away your money?" The superintendent started to argue with them, showing the absurdity of the notion that they could gain anything by such a course. The mine had been running for years on its present system, and there had never been any complaint. The idea that a company as big and as responsible as the "G. F. C." would stoop to cheat its workers out of a few tons of coal! And so on, for several minutes.

"Mr. Cartwright," said Edstrom, when the other had finished, "you know I've worked all my life in mines, and most of it in this district. I am telling you something I know when I say there is general dissatisfaction throughout these camps because the men feel they are not getting their weight. You say there has been no public complaint; you understand the reason for this—"

"What is the reason?"

"Well," said Edstrom, gently, "maybe you don't know the reason—but anyway we've decided that we want a check-weighman."

It was evident that the superintendent had been taken by surprise, and was uncertain how to meet the issue. "You can imagine," he said, at last, "the company doesn't relish hearing that its men believe it's cheating them—"

"We don't say the company knows anything about it, Mr. Cartwright. It's possible that some people may be taking advantage of us, without either the company or yourself having anything to do with it. It's for your protection as well as ours that a check-weighman is needed."

"Thank you," said the other, drily. His tone revealed that he was holding himself in by an effort. "Very well," he added, at last. "That's enough about the matter, if your minds are made up. I'll give you my decision later."

This was a dismissal, and Mike Sikoria turned humbly, and started to the door. But Edstrom was one of the ants that did not readily "step one side"; and Mike took a glance at him, and then stepped back into line in a hurry, as if hoping his delinquency had not been noted.

"If you please, Mr. Cartwright," said Edstrom, "we'd like your decision, so as to have the check-weighman start in the morning."

"What? You're in such a hurry?"

"There's no reason for delay, sir. We've selected our man, and we're ready to pay him."

"Who are the men who are ready to pay him? Just you two"

"I am not at liberty to name the other men, sir."

"Oh! So it's a secret movement!"

"In a way—yes, sir."

"Indeed!" said the superintendent, ominously. "And you don't care what the company thinks about it!"

"It's not that, Mr. Cartwright, but we don't see anything for the company to object to. It's a simple business arrangement—"

"Well, if it seems simple to you, it doesn't to me," snapped the other. And then, getting himself in hand, "Understand me, the company would not have the least objection to the men making sure of their weights, if they really think it's necessary. The company has always been willing to do the right thing. But it's not a matter that can be settled off hand. I will let you know later."

Again they were dismissed, and again Old Mike turned, and Edstrom also. But now another ant sprang into the ditch. "Just when will you be prepared to let the check-weighman begin work, Mr. Cartwright?" asked Hal.

The superintendent gave him a sharp look, and again it could be seen that he made a strong effort to keep his temper. "I'm not prepared to say," he replied. "I will let you know, as soon as convenient to me. That's all now." And as he spoke he opened the door, putting something into the action that was a command.

"Mr. Cartwright," said Hal, "there's no law against our having a check-weighman, is there?"

The look which these words drew from the superintendent showed that he knew full well what the law was. Hal accepted this look as an answer, and continued, "I have been selected by a committee of the men to act as their check-weighman, and this committee has duly notified the company. That makes me a check-weighman, I believe, Mr. Cartwright, and so all I have to do is to assume my duties." Without waiting for the superintendent's answer, he walked to the door, followed by his somewhat shocked companions.

SECTION 11.

At the meeting on the night before it had been agreed to spread the news of the check-weighman movement, for the sake of its propaganda value. So now when the three men came out from the office, there was a crowd waiting to know what had happened; men clamoured questions, and each one who got the story would be surrounded by others eager to hear. Hal made his way to the boarding-house, and when he had finished his supper, he set out from place to place in the camp, telling the men about the check-weighman plan and explaining that it was a legal right they were demanding. All this while Old Mike stayed on one side of him, and Edstrom on the other; for Tom Olson had insisted strenuously that Hal should not be left alone for a moment. Evidently the bosses had given the same order; for when Hal came out from Reminitsky's, there was "Jake" Predovich, the store-clerk, on the fringe of the crowd, and he followed wherever Hal went, doubtless making note of every one he spoke to.

They consulted as to where they were to spend the night. Old Mike was nervous, taking the activities of the spy to mean that they were to be thugged in the darkness. He told horrible stories of that sort of thing. What could be an easier way for the company to settle the matter? They would fix up some story; the world outside would believe they had been killed in a drunken row, perhaps over some woman. This last suggestion especially troubled Hal; he thought of the people at home. No, he must not sleep in the village! And on the other hand he could not go down the canyon, for if he once passed the gate, he might not be allowed to repass it.

An idea occurred to him. Why not go *up* the canyon? There was no stockade at the upper end of the village—nothing but wilderness and rocks, without even a road.

"But where we sleep?" demanded Old Mike, aghast.

"Outdoors," said Hal.

"*Pluha biedna*! And get the night air into my bones?"

"You think you keep the day air in your bones when you sleep inside?" laughed Hal.

"Why don't I, when I shut them windows tight, and cover up my bones?"

"Well, risk the night air once," said Hal. "It's better than having somebody let it into you with a knife."

"But that fellow Predovich—he follow us up canyon too!"

"Yes, but he's only one man, and we don't have to fear him. If he went back for others, he'd never be able to find us in the darkness."

Edstrom, whose notions of anatomy were not so crude as Mike's, gave his support to this suggestion; so they got their blankets and stumbled up the canyon in the still, star-lit night. For a while they heard the spy behind them, but finally his footsteps died away, and after they had moved on for some distance, they believed they were safe till daylight. Hal had slept out many a night as a hunter, but it was a new adventure to sleep out as the game!

At dawn they rose, and shook the dew from their blankets, and wiped it from their eyes. Hal was young, and saw the glory of the morning, while poor Mike Sikoria groaned and grumbled over his stiff and aged joints. He thought he had ruined himself forever, but he took courage at Edstrom's mention of coffee, and they hurried down to breakfast at their boarding-house.

Now came a critical time, when Hal had to be left by himself. Edstrom was obliged to go down to see to his wife's funeral; and it was obvious that if Mike Sikoria were to lay off work, he would be providing the boss with an excuse for firing him. The law which provided for a check-weighman had failed to provide for a check-weighman's body-guard!

Hal had announced his programme in that flash of defiance in Cartwright's office. As soon as work started up, he went to the tipple. "Mr. Peters," he said, to the tipple-boss, "I've come to act as check-weighman."

The tipple-boss was a man with a big black moustache, which made him look like the pictures of Nietzsche. He stared at Hal, frankly dumbfounded. "What the devil?" said he.

"Some of the men have chosen me check-weighman," explained Hal, in a business-like manner. "When their cars come up, I'll see to their weights."

"You keep off this tipple, young fellow!" said Peters. His manner was equally business-like.

So the would-be check-weighman came out and sat on the steps to wait. The tipple was a fairly public place, and he judged he was as safe there as anywhere. Some of the men grinned and winked at him as they went about their work; several found a chance to whisper words of encouragement. And all morning he sat, like a protestant at the palace-gates of a mandarin in China, It was tedious work, but he believed that he would be able to stand it longer than the company.

SECTION 12.

In the middle of the morning a man came up to him—"Bud" Adams, a younger brother of the "J. P.," and Jeff Cotton's assistant. Bud was stocky, red-faced, and reputed to be handy with his fists. So Hal rose up warily when he saw him.

"Hey, you," said Bud. "There's a telegram at the office for you."

"For me?"

"Your name's Joe Smith, ain't it?"

"Yes."

"Well, that's what it says."

Hal considered for a moment. There was no one to be telegraphing Joe Smith. It was only a ruse to get him away.

"What's in the telegram?" he asked.

"How do I know?" said Bud.

"Where is it from?"

"I dunno that."

"Well," said Hal, "you might bring it to me here."

The other's eyes flew open. This was not a revolt, it was a revolution! "Who the hell's messenger boy do you think I am?" he demanded.

"Don't the company deliver telegrams?" countered Hal, politely. And Bud stood struggling with his human impulses, while Hal watched him cautiously. But apparently those who had sent the messenger had given him precise instructions; for he controlled his wrath, and turned and strode away.

Hal continued his vigil. He had his lunch with him; and was prepared to eat alone—understanding the risk that a man would be running who showed sympathy with him. He was surprised, therefore, when Johannson, the giant Swede, came and sat down by his side. There also came a young Mexican labourer, and a Greek miner. The revolution was spreading!

Hal felt sure the company would not let this go on. And sure enough, towards the middle of the afternoon, the tipple-boss came out and beckoned to him. "Come here, you!" And Hal went in.

The "weigh-room" was a fairly open place; but at one side was a door into an office. "This way," said the man.

But Hal stopped where he was.

"This is where the check-weighman belongs, Mr. Peters."

"But I want to talk to you."

"I can hear you, sir." Hal was in sight of the men, and he knew that was his only protection.

The tipple-boss went back into the office; and a minute later Hal saw what had been intended. The door opened and Alec Stone came out.

He stood for a moment looking at his political henchman. Then he came up. "Kid," he said, in a low voice, "you're overdoing this. I didn't intend you to go so far."

"This is not what you intended, Mr. Stone," answered Hal.

The pit-boss came closer yet. "What you looking for, kid? What you expect to get out of this?"

Hal's gaze was unwavering. "Experience," he replied.

"You're feeling smart, sonny. But you'd better stop and realise what you're up against. You ain't going to get away with it, you know; get that through your head—you ain't going to get away with it. You'd better come in and have a talk with me."

There was a silence.

"Don't you know how it'll be, Smith? These little fires start up—but we put 'em out. We know how to do it, we've got the machinery. It'll all be forgotten in a week or two, and then where'll you be at? Can't you see?"

As Hal still made no reply, the other's voice dropped lower. "I understand your position. Just give me a nod, and it'll be all right. You tell the men that you've watched the weights, and that they're all right. They'll be satisfied, and you and me can fix it up later."

"Mr. Stone," said Hal, with intense gravity, "am I correct in the impression that you are offering me a bribe?"

In a flash, the man's self-control vanished. He thrust his huge fist within an inch of Hal's nose, and uttered a foul oath. But Hal did not remove his nose from the danger-zone, and over the fist a pair of angry brown eyes gazed at the pit-boss. "Mr. Stone, you had better realise this situation. I am in dead earnest about this matter, and I don't think it will be safe for you to offer me violence."

For a moment or two the man continued to glare at Hal; but it appeared that he, like Bud Adams, had been given instructions. He turned abruptly and strode back into the office.

Hal stood for a bit, until he had made sure of his composure. After which he strolled over towards the scales. A difficulty had occurred to him for the first time—that he did not know anything about the working of coal-scales.

But he was given no time to learn. The tipple-boss reappeared. "Get out of here, fellow!" said he.

"But you invited me in," remarked Hal, mildly.

"Well, now I invite you out again."

And so the protestant resumed his vigil at the mandarin's palace-gates.

<h1 style="text-align:center">SECTION 13.</h1>

When the quitting-whistle blew, Mike Sikoria came quickly to join Hal and hear what had happened. Mike was exultant, for several new men had come up to him and offered to join the check-weighman movement. The old fellow was not sure whether this was owing to his own eloquence as a propagandist, or to the fine young American buddy he had; but in either case he was equally proud. He gave Hal a note which had been slipped into his hand, and which Hal recognised as coming from Tom Olson. The organiser reported that every one in the camp was talking check-weighman, and so from a propaganda standpoint they could count their move a success, no matter what the bosses might do. He added that Hal should have a number of men stay with him that night, so as to have witnesses if the company tried to "pull off anything." "And be careful of the new men," he added; "one or two of them are sure to be spies."

Hal and Mike discussed their programme for the second night. Neither of them were keen for sleeping out again—the old Slovak because of his bones, and Hal because he saw there were now several spies following them about. At Reminitsky's, he spoke to some of those who had offered their support, and asked them if they would be willing to spend the night with him in Edstrom's cabin. Not one shrank from this test of sincerity; they all got their blankets, and repaired to the place, where Hal lighted the lamp and held an impromptu check-weighman meeting—and incidentally entertained himself with a spy-hunt!

One of the new-comers was a Pole named Wojecicowski; this, on top of Zamierowski, caused Hal to give up all effort to call the Poles by their names. "Woji" was an earnest little man, with a pathetic, tired face. He explained his presence by the statement that he was sick of being robbed; he would pay his share for a check-weighman, and if they fired him, all right, he would move on, and to hell with them. After which declaration he rolled up in a blanket and went to snoring on the floor of the cabin. That did not seem to be exactly the conduct of a spy.

Another was an Italian, named Farenzena; a dark-browed and sinister-looking fellow, who might have served as a villain in any melodrama. He sat against the wall and talked in guttural tones, and Hal regarded him with deep suspicion. It was not easy to understand his English, but finally Hal managed to make out the story he was telling—that he was in love with a "fanciulla," and that the "fanciulla" was playing with him. He had about made up his mind that she was a co-quette, and not worth bothering with, so he did not care any curses if they sent him down the canyon. "Don't fight for fanciulla, fight for check-weighman!" he concluded, with a growl.

Another volunteer was a Greek labourer, a talkative young chap who had sat with Hal at lunch-time, and had given his name as Apostolikas. He entered into fluent conversation with Hal, explaining how much interested he was in the check-weighman plan; he wanted to know just what they were going to do, what chance of success they thought they had, who had started the movement and who was in it. Hal's replies took the form of little sermons on working-class solidarity. Each time the man would start to "pump" him, Hal would explain the importance of the present issue to the miners, how they must stand by one another and make sacrifices for the good of all. After he had talked abstract theories for half an hour, Apostolikas gave up and moved on to Mike Sikoria, who, having been given a wink by Hal, talked about "scabs," and the dreadful things that honest working-men would do to them. When finally the Greek grew tired again, and lay down on the floor, Hal moved over to Old Mike and whispered that the first name of Apostolikas must be Judas!

<h1 style="text-align:center">SECTION 14.</h1>

Old Mike went to sleep quickly; but Hal had not worked for several days, and had exciting thoughts to keep him awake. He had been lying quiet for a couple of hours, when he became aware that some one was moving in the room. There was a lamp burning dimly, and through half-closed eyes he made out one of the men lifting himself to a sitting position. At first he could not be sure which one it was, but finally he recognised the Greek.

Hal lay motionless, and after a minute or so he stole another look and saw the man crouching and listening, his hands still on the floor. Through half opened eye-lids Hal continued to steal glimpses, while the other rose and tip-toed towards him, stepping carefully over the sleeping forms.

Hal did his best to simulate the breathing of sleep: no easy matter, with the man stooping over him, and a knife-thrust as one of the possibilities of the situation. He took the chance, however; and after what seemed an age, he felt the man's fingers lightly touch his side. They moved down to his coat-pocket.

"Going to search me!" thought Hal; and waited, expecting the hand to travel to other pockets. But after what seemed an interminable period, he realised that Apostolikas had risen again, and was stepping back to his place. In a minute more he had lain down, and all was still in the cabin.

Hal's hand moved to the pocket, and his fingers slid inside. They touched something, which he recognised instantly as a roll of bills.

"I see!" thought he. "A frame-up!" And he laughed to himself, his mind going back to early boyhood—to a dilapidated trunk in the attic of his home, containing story-books that his father had owned. He could see them now, with their worn brown covers and crude pictures: "The Luck and Pluck Series," by Horatio Alger; "Live or Die," "Rough and Ready," etc. How he had thrilled over the story of the country-boy who comes to the city, and meets the villain who robs his employer's cash-drawer and drops the key of it into the hero's pocket! Evidently some one connected with the General Fuel Company had read Horatio Alger!

Hal realised that he could not be too quick about getting those bills out of his pocket. He thought of returning them to "Judas," but decided that he would save them for Edstrom, who was likely to need money before long. He gave the Greek half an hour to go to sleep, then with his pocket-knife he gently picked out a hole in the cinders of the floor and buried the money as best he could. After which he wormed his way to another place, and lay thinking.

SECTION 15.

Would they wait until morning, or would they come soon? He was inclined to the latter guess, so he was only slightly startled when, an hour or two later, he heard the knob of the cabin-door turned. A moment later came a crash and the door was burst open, with the shoulder of a heavy man behind it.

The room was in confusion in a second. Men sprang to their feet, crying out; others sat up bewildered, still half asleep. The room was bright from an electric torch in the hands of one of the invaders. "There's the fellow!" cried a voice, which Hal instantly recognised as belonging to Jeff Cotton, the camp-marshal. "Stick 'em up, there! You, Joe Smith!" Hal did not wait to see the glint of the marshal's revolver.

There followed a silence. As this drama was being staged for the benefit of the other men, it was necessary to give them time to get thoroughly awake, and to get their eyes used to the light. Meantime Hal stood, his hands in the air. Behind the torch he could make out the faces of the marshal, Bud Adams, Alec Stone, Jake Predovich, and two or three others.

"Now, men," said Cotton, at last, "you are some of the fellows that want a check-weighman. And this is the man you chose. Is that right?"

There was no answer.

"I'm going to show you the kind of fellow he is. He came to Mr. Stone here and offered to sell you out."

"It's a lie, men," said Hal, quietly.

"He took some money from Mr. Stone to sell you out!" insisted the marshal.

"It's a lie," said Hal, again.

"He's got that money now!" cried the other.

And Hal cried, in turn, "They are trying to frame something on me, boys! Don't let them fool you!"

"Shut up," commanded the marshal; then, to the men, "I'll show you. I think he's got that money on him now. Jake, search him."

The store-clerk advanced.

"Watch out, boys!" exclaimed Hal. "They will put something in my pockets." And then to Old Mike, who had started angrily forward, "It's all right, Mike! Let them alone!"

"Jake, take off your coat," ordered Cotton. "Roll up your sleeves. Show your hands."

It was for all the world like the performance of a prestidigitator. The little Jew took off his coat and rolled up his sleeves above his elbows. He exhibited his hands to the audience, turning them this way and that; then, keeping them out in front of him, he came slowly towards Hal, like a hypnotist about to put him to sleep.

"Watch him!" said Cotton. "He's got that money on him, I know."

"Look sharp!" cried Hal. "If it isn't there, they'll put it there."

"Keep your hands up, young fellow," commanded the marshal. "Keep back from him there!" This last to Mike Sikoria and the other spectators, who were pressing nearer, peering over one another's shoulders.

It was all very serious at the time, but afterwards, when Hal recalled the scene, he laughed over the grotesque figure of Predovich searching his pockets while keeping as far away from him as possible, so that every one might know that the money had actually come out of Hal's pocket. The searcher put his hands first in the inside pockets, then in the pockets of Hal's shirt. Time was needed to build up this climax!

"Turn around," commanded Cotton; and Hal turned, and the Jew went through his trouser-pockets. He took out in turn Hal's watch, his comb and mirror, his handkerchief; after examining them and holding them up, he dropped them onto the floor. There was a breathless hush when he came to Hal's purse, and proceeded to open it. Thanks to the greed of the company, there was nothing in the purse but some small change. Predovich closed it and dropped it to the floor.

"Wait now! He's not through!" cried the master of ceremonies. "He's got that money somewhere, boys! Did you look in his side-pockets, Jake?"

"Not yet," said Jake.

"Look sharp!" cried the marshal; and every one craned forward eagerly, while Predovich stooped down on one knee, and put his hand into one coat pocket and then into the other.

He took his hand out again, and the look of dismay upon his face was so obvious that Hal could hardly keep from laughing. "It ain't dere!" he declared.

"What?" cried Cotton, and they stared at each other. "By God, he's got rid of it!"

"There's no money on me, boys!" proclaimed Hal. "It's a job they are trying to put over on us."

"He's hid it!" shouted the marshal. "Find it, Jake!"

Then Predovich began to search again, swiftly, and with less circumstance. He was not thinking so much about the spectators now, as about all that good money gone for nothing! He made Hal take off his coat, and ripped open the lining; he unbuttoned the trousers and felt inside; he thrust his fingers down inside Hal's shoes.

But there was no money, and the searchers were at a standstill. "He took twenty-five dollars from Mr. Stone to sell you out!" declared the marshal. "He's managed to get rid of it somehow."

"Boys," cried Hal, "they sent a spy in here, and told him to put money on me." He was looking at Apostolikas as he spoke; he saw the man start and shrink back.

"That's him! He's a scab!" cried Old Mike. "He's got the money on him, I bet!" And he made a move towards the Greek.

So the camp-marshal realised suddenly that it was time to ring down the curtain on this drama. "That's enough of this foolishness," he declared. "Bring that fellow along here!" And in a flash a couple of the party had seized Hal's wrists, and a third had grabbed him by the collar of his shirt. Before the miners had time to realise what was happening, they had rushed their prisoner out of the cabin.

The quarter of an hour which followed was an uncomfortable one for the would-be check-weighman. Outside, in the darkness, the camp-marshal was free to give vent to his rage, and so was Alec Stone. They poured out curses upon him, and kicked him and cuffed him as they went along. One of the men who held his wrists twisted his arm, until he cried out with pain; then they cursed him harder, and bade him hold his mouth. Down the dark and silent street they went swiftly, and into the camp-marshal's office, and upstairs to the room which served as the North Valley jail. Hal was glad enough when they left him here, slamming the iron door behind them.

SECTION 16.

It had been a crude and stupid plot, yet Hal realised that it was adapted to the intelligence of the men for whom it was intended. But for the accident that he had stayed awake, they would have found the money on him, and next morning the whole camp would have heard that he had sold out. Of course his immediate friends, the members of the committee, would not have believed it; but the mass of the workers would have believed it, and so the purpose of Tom Olson's visit to North Valley would have been balked. Throughout the experiences which were to come to him, Hal retained his vivid impression of that adventure; it served to him as a symbol of many things. Just as the bosses had tried to bedevil him, to destroy his influence with his followers, so later on he saw them trying to bedevil the labour-movement, to confuse the intelligence of the whole country.

Now Hal was in jail. He went to the window and tried the bars—but found that they had been made for such trials. Then he groped his way about in the darkness, examining his prison, which proved to be a steel cage built inside the walls of an ordinary room. In one corner was a bench, and in another corner another bench, somewhat broader, with a mattress upon it. Hal had read a little about jails—enough to cause him to avoid this mattress. He sat upon the bare bench, and began to think.

It is a fact that there is a peculiar psychology incidental to being in jail; just as there is a peculiar psychology incidental to straining your back and breaking your hands loading coal-cars in a five foot vein; and another, and quite different psychology, produced by living at ease off the labours of coal-miners. In a jail, you have first of all the sense of being an animal; the animal side of your being is emphasised, the animal passions of hatred and fear are called into prominence, and if you are to escape being dominated by them, it can only be by intense and concentrated effort of the mind. So, if you are a thinking man, you do a great deal of thinking in a jail; the days are long, and the nights still longer—you have time for all the thoughts you can have.

The bench was hard, and seemed to grow harder. There was no position in which it could be made to grow soft. Hal got up and paced about, then he lay down for a while, then got up and walked again; and all the while he thought, and all the while the jail-psychology was being impressed upon his mind.

First, he thought about his immediate problem. What were they going to do to him? The obvious thing would be to put him out of camp, and so be done with him; but would they rest content with that, in their irritation at the trick he had played? Hal had heard vaguely of that native American institution, the "third degree," but had never had occasion to think of it as a possibility in his own life. What a difference it made, to think of it in that way!

Hal had told Tom Olson that he would not pledge himself to organise a union, but that he would pledge himself to get a check-weighman; and Olson had laughed, and seemed quite content—apparently assuming that it would come to the same thing. And now, it rather seemed that Olson had known what he was talking about. For Hal found his thoughts no longer troubled with fears of labour union domination and walking delegate tyranny; on the contrary, he became suddenly willing for the people of North Valley to have a union, and to be as tyrannical as they knew how! And in this change, though Hal had no idea of it, he was repeating an experience common among reformers; many of whom begin as mild and benevolent advocates of some obvious bit of justice, and under the operation of the jail-psychology are made into blazing and determined revolutionists. "Eternal spirit of the chainless mind," says Byron. "Greatest in dungeons Liberty thou art!"

The poet goes on to add that "When thy sons to fetters are confined—" then "Freedom's fame finds wings on every wind." And just as it was in Chillon, so it seemed to be in North Valley. Dawn came, and Hal stood at the window of his cell, and heard the whistle blow and saw the workers going to their tasks, the toil-bent, pallid faced creatures of the underworld, like a file of baboons in the half-light. He waved his hand to them, and they stopped and stared, and then waved back; he realised that every one of those men must be thinking about his imprisonment, and the reason for it—and so the jail-psychology was being communicated to them. If any of them cherished distrust of unions, or doubt of the need of organisation in North Valley—that distrust and that doubt were being dissipated!

—There was only one thing discouraging about the matter, as Hal thought it over. Why should the bosses have left him here in plain sight, when they might so easily have put him into an automobile, and whisked him down to Pedro before daylight? Was it a sign of the contempt they felt for their slaves? Did they count upon the sight of the prisoner in the window to produce fear instead of resentment? And might it not be that they understood their workers better than the would-be check-weighman? He recalled Mary Burke's pessimism about them, and anxiety gnawed at his soul; and—such is the operation of the jail-psychology—he fought against this anxiety. He hated the company for its cynicism, he clenched his hands and set his teeth, desiring to teach the bosses a lesson, to prove to them that their workers were not slaves, but men!

SECTION 17.

Toward the middle of the morning, Hal heard footsteps in the corridor outside, and a man whom he did not know opened the barred door and set down a pitcher of water and a tin plate with a hunk of bread on it. When he started to leave, Hal spoke: "Just a minute, please."

The other frowned at him.

"Can you give me any idea how long I am to stay in here?"

"I cannot," said the man.

"If I'm to be locked up," said Hal, "I've certainly a right to know what is the charge against me."

"Go to blazes!" said the other, and slammed the door and went down the corridor.

Hal went to the window again, and passed the time watching the people who went by. Groups of ragged children gathered, looking up at him, grinning and making signs—until some one appeared below and ordered them away.

As time passed, Hal became hungry. The taste of bread, eaten alone, becomes speedily monotonous, and the taste of water does not relieve it; nevertheless, Hal munched the bread, and drank the water, and wished for more.

The day dragged by; and late in the afternoon the keeper came again, with another hunk of bread and another pitcher of water. "Listen a moment," said Hal, as the man was turning away.

"I got nothin' to say to you," said the other.

"I have something to say to you," pleaded Hal. "I have read in a book—I forget where, but it was written by some doctor—that white bread does not contain the elements necessary to the sustaining of the human body."

"Go on!" growled the jailer. "What yer givin' us?"

"I mean," explained Hal, "a diet of bread and water is not what I'd choose to live on."

"What would yer choose?"

The tone suggested that the question was a rhetorical one; but Hal took it in good faith. "If I could have some beefsteak and mashed potatoes—"

The door of the cell closed with a slam whose echoes drowned out the rest of that imaginary menu. And so once more Hal sat on the hard bench, and munched his hunk of bread, and thought jail-thoughts.

When the quitting-whistle blew, he stood at the window, and saw the groups of his friends once again, and got their covert signals of encouragement. Then darkness fell, and another long vigil began.

It was late; Hal had no means of telling how late, save that all the lights in the camps were out. He made up his mind that he was in for the night, and had settled himself on the floor with his arm for a pillow, and had dozed off to sleep, when suddenly there came a scraping sound against the bars of his window. He sat up with a start, and heard another sound, unmistakably the rustling of paper. He sprang to the window, where by the faint light of the stars he could make out something dangling. He caught at it; it seemed to be an ordinary note-book, such as stenographers use, tied on the end of a pole.

Hal looked out, but could see no one. He caught hold of the pole and jerked it, as a signal; and then he heard a whisper which he recognised instantly as Rovetta's. "Hello! Listen. Write your name hundred times in book. I come back. Understand?"

The command was a sufficiently puzzling one, but Hal realised that this was no time for explanations. He answered, "Yes," and broke the string and took the notebook. There was a pencil attached, with a piece of cloth wrapped round the point to protect it.

The pole was withdrawn, and Hal sat on the bench, and began to write, three or four times on a page, "Joe Smith—Joe Smith—Joe Smith." It is not hard to write "Joe Smith," even in darkness, and so, while his hand moved, Hal's mind was busy with this mystery. It was fairly to be assumed that his committee did not want his autograph to distribute for a souvenir; they must want it for some vital purpose, to meet some new move of the bosses. The answer to this riddle was not slow in coming: having failed in their effort to find money on him, the bosses had framed up a letter, which they were exhibiting as having been written by the would-be check-weigh-man. His friends wanted his signature to disprove the authenticity of the letter.

Hal wrote a free and rapid hand, with a generous flourish; he felt sure it would be different from Alec Stone's idea of a working-boy's scrawl. His pencil flew on and on—"Joe Smith—Joe Smith—" page after page, until he was sure that he had written a signature for every miner in the camp, and was beginning on the buddies. Then, hearing a whistle outside, he stopped and sprang to the window.

"Throw it!" whispered a voice; and Hal threw it. He saw a form vanish up the street, after which all was quiet again. He listened for a while, to see if he had roused his jailer; then he lay down on the bench—and thought more jail-thoughts!

SECTION 18.

Morning came, and the mine-whistle blew, and Hal stood at the window again. This time he noticed that some of the miners on their way to work had little strips of paper in their hands, which strips they waved conspicuously for him to see. Old Mike Sikoria came along, having a whole bunch of strips in his hands, which he was distributing to all who would take them. Doubtless he had been warned to proceed secretly, but the excitement of the occasion had been too much for him; he capered about like a young spring lamb, and waved the strips at Hal in plain sight of all the world.

Such indiscreet behaviour met the return it invited. As Hal watched, he saw a stocky figure come striding round the corner, confronting the startled old Slovak. It was Bud Adams, the mine-guard, and his hard fists were clenched, and his whole body gathered for a blow. Mike saw him, and was as if suddenly struck with paralysis; his toil-bent shoulders sunk together, and his hands fell to his sides—his fingers opening, and his precious strips of paper fluttering to the ground. Mike stared at Bud like a fascinated rabbit, making no move to protect himself.

Hal clutched the bars, with an impulse to leap to his friend's defence. But the expected blow did not fall; the mine-guard contented himself with glaring ferociously, and giving an order to the old man. Mike stooped and picked up the papers—the process taking him some time, as he was unable or unwilling to take his eyes off the mine-guard's. When he got them all in his hands, there came another order, and he gave them up to Bud. After which he fell back a step, and the other followed, his fists still clenched, and a blow seeming about to leap from him every moment. Mike receded another step, and then another—so the two of them backed out of sight around the corner. Men who had been witnesses of this little drama turned and slunk off, and Hal was given no clue as to its outcome.

A couple of hours afterwards, Hal's jailer came up, this time without any bread and water. He opened the door and commanded the prisoner to "come along." Hal went downstairs, and entered Jeff Cotton's office.

The camp-marshal sat at his desk with a cigar between his teeth. He was writing, and he went on writing until the jailer had gone out and closed the door. Then he turned his revolving chair and crossed his legs, leaning back and looking at the young miner in his dirty blue overalls, his hair tousled and his face pale from his period of confinement. The camp-marshal's aristocratic face wore a smile. "Well, young fellow," said he, "you've been having a lot of fun in this camp."

"Pretty fair, thank you," answered Hal.

"Beat us out all along the line, hey?" Then, after a pause, "Now, tell me, what do you think you're going to get out of it?"

"That's what Alec Stone asked me," replied Hal. "I don't think it would do much good to explain. I doubt if you believe in altruism any more than Stone does."

The camp-marshal took his cigar from his mouth, and flicked off the ashes. His face became serious, and there was a silence, while he studied Hal. "You a union organiser?" he asked, at last.

"No," said Hal.

"You're an educated man; you're no labourer, that I know. Who's paying you?"

"There you are! You don't believe in altruism."

The other blew a ring of smoke across the room. "Just want to put the company in the hole, hey? Some kind of agitator?"

"I am a miner who wants to be a check-weighman."

"Socialist?"

"That depends upon developments here."

"Well," said the marshal, "you're an intelligent chap, that I can see. So I'll lay my hand on the table and you can study it. You're not going to serve as check-weighman in North Valley, nor any other place that the 'G. F. C.' has anything to do with. Nor are you going to have the satisfaction of putting the company in a hole. We're not even going to beat you up and make a martyr of you. I was tempted to do that the other night, but I changed my mind."

"You might change the bruises on my arm," suggested Hal, in a pleasant voice.

"We're going to offer you the choice of two things," continued the marshal, without heeding this mild sarcasm. "Either you will sign a paper admitting that you took the twenty-five dollars from Alec Stone, in which case we will fire you and call it square; or else we will prove that you took it, in which case we will send you to the pen for five or ten years. Do you get that?"

Now when Hal had applied for the job of check-weighman, he had been expecting to be thrown out of the camp, and had intended to go, counting his education complete. But here, as he sat and gazed into the marshal's menacing eyes, he decided suddenly that he did not want to leave North Valley. He wanted to stay and take the measure of this gigantic "burglar," the General Fuel Company.

"That's a serious threat, Mr. Cotton," he remarked. "Do you often do things like that?"

"We do them when we have to," was the reply.

"Well, it's a novel proposition. Tell me more about it. What will the charge be?"

"I'm not sure about that—we'll put it up to our lawyers. Maybe they'll call it conspiracy, maybe blackmail. They'll make it whatever carries a long enough sentence."

"And before I enter my plea, would you mind letting me see the letter I'm supposed to have written."

"Oh, you've heard about the letter, have you?" said the camp-marshal, lifting his eyebrows in mild surprise. He took from his desk a sheet of paper and handed it to Hal, who read:

"Dere mister Stone, You don't need worry about the check-wayman. Pay me twenty five dollars, and I will fix it right. Yours try, Joe Smith."

Having taken in the words of the letter, Hal examined the paper, and perceived that his enemies had taken the trouble, not merely to forge a letter in his name, but to have it photographed, to have a cut made of the photograph, and to have it printed. Beyond doubt they had distributed it broadcast in the camp. And all this in a few hours! It was as Olson had said—a regular system to keep the men bedevilled.

SECTION 19.

Hal took a minute or so to ponder the situation. "Mr. Cotton," he said, at last. "I know how to spell better than that. Also my handwriting is a bit more fluent."

There was a trace of a smile about the marshal's cruel lips. "I know," he replied. "I've not failed to compare them."

"You have a good secret-service department!" said Hal.

"Before you get through, young fellow, you'll discover that our legal department is equally efficient."

"Well," said Hal, "they'll need to be; for I don't see how you can get round the fact that I'm a check-weighman, chosen according to the law, and with a group of the men behind me."

"If that's what you're counting on," retorted Cotton, "you may as well forget it. You've got no group any more."

"Oh! You've got rid of them?"

"We've got rid of the ring-leaders."

"Of whom?"

"That old billy-goat, Sikoria, for one."

"You've shipped him?"

"We have."

"I saw the beginning of that. Where have you sent him?"

"That," smiled the marshal, "is a job for *your* secret-service department!"

"And who else?"

"John Edstrom has gone down to bury his wife. It's not the first time that dough-faced old preacher has made trouble for us, but it'll be the last. You'll find him in Pedro—probably in the poor-house."

"No," responded Hal, quickly—and there came just a touch of elation in his voice—"he won't have to go to the poor-house at once. You see, I've just sent twenty-five dollars to him."

The camp-marshal frowned. "Really!" Then, after a pause, "You *did* have that money on you! I thought that lousy Greek had got away with it!"

"No. Your knave was honest. But so was I. I knew Edstrom had been getting short weight for years, so he was the one person with any right to the money."

This story was untrue, of course; the money was still buried in Edstrom's cabin. But Hal meant for the old miner to have it in the end, and meantime he wanted to throw Cotton off the track.

"A clever trick, young man!" said the marshal. "But you'll repent it before you're through. It only makes me more determined to put you where you can't do us any harm."

"You mean in the pen? You understand, of course, it will mean a jury trial. You can get a jury to do what you want?"

"They tell me you've been taking an interest in politics in Pedro County. Haven't you looked into our jury-system?"

"No, I haven't got that far."

The marshal began blowing rings of smoke again.

"Well, there are some three hundred men on our jury-list, and we know them all. You'll find yourself facing a box with Jake Predovich as foreman, three company-clerks, two of Alf Raymond's saloon-keepers, a ranchman with a mortgage held by the company-bank, and five Mexicans who have no idea what it's all about, but would stick a knife into your back for a drink of whiskey. The District Attorney is a politician who favours the miners in his speeches, and favours us in his acts; while Judge Denton, of the district court, is the law partner of Vagleman, our chief-counsel. Do you get all that?"

"Yes," said Hal. "I've heard of the 'Empire of Raymond'; I'm interested to see the machinery. You're quite open about it!"

"Well," replied the marshal, "I want you to know what you're up against. We didn't start this fight, and we're perfectly willing to end it without trouble. All we ask is that you make amends for the mischief you've done us."

"By 'making amends,' you mean I'm to disgrace myself—to tell the men I'm a traitor?"

"Precisely," said the marshal.

"I think I'll have a seat while I consider the matter," said Hal; and he took a chair, and stretched out his legs, and made himself elaborately comfortable. "That bench upstairs is frightfully hard," said he, and smiled mockingly upon the camp-marshal.

SECTION 20.

When this conversation was continued, it was upon a new and unexpected line. "Cotton," remarked the prisoner, "I perceive that you are a man of education. It occurs to me that once upon a time you must have been what the world calls a gentleman."

The blood started into the camp-marshal's face. "You go to hell!" said he.

"I did not intend to ask questions," continued Hal. "I can well understand that you mightn't care to answer them. My point is that, being an ex-gentleman, you may appreciate certain aspects of this case which would be beyond the understanding of a nigger-driver like Stone, or an efficiency expert like Cartwright. One gentleman can recognise another, even in a miner's costume. Isn't that so?"

Hal paused for an answer, and the marshal gave him a wary look. "I suppose so," he said.

"Well, to begin with, one gentleman does not smoke without inviting another to join him."

The man gave another look. Hal thought he was going to consign him to hades once more; but instead he took a cigar from his vest-pocket and held it out.

"No, thank you," said Hal, quietly. "I do not smoke. But I like to be invited."

There was a pause, while the two men measured each other.

"Now, Cotton," began the prisoner, "you pictured the scene at my trial. Let me carry on the story for you. You have your case all framed up, your hand-picked jury in the box, and your hand-picked judge on the bench, your hand-picked prosecuting-attorney putting through the job; you are ready to send your victim to prison, for an example to the rest of your employés. But suppose that, at the climax of the proceedings, you should make the discovery that your victim is a person who cannot be sent to prison?"

"Cannot be sent to prison?" repeated the other. His tone was thoughtful. "You'll have to explain."

"Surely not to a man of your intelligence! Don't you know, Cotton, there are people who cannot be sent to prison?"

The camp-marshal smoked his cigar for a bit. "There are some in this county," said he. "But I thought I knew them all."

"Well," said Hal, "has it never occurred to you that there might be some in this *state*?"

There followed a long silence. The two men were gazing into each other's eyes; and the more they gazed, the more plainly Hal read uncertainty in the face of the marshal.

"Think how embarrassing it would be!" he continued. "You have your drama all staged—as you did the night before last—only on a larger stage, before a more important audience; and at the *dénouement* you find that, instead of vindicating yourself before the workers in North Valley, you have convicted yourself before the public of the state. You have shown the whole community that you are law-breakers; worse than that—you have shown that you are jack-asses!"

This time the camp-marshal gazed so long that his cigar went out. And meantime Hal was lounging in his chair, smiling at him strangely. It was as if a transformation was taking place before the marshal's eyes; the miner's "jumpers" fell away from Hal's figure, and there was a suit of evening-clothes in their place!

"Who the devil are you?" cried the man.

"Well now!" laughed Hal. "You boast of the efficiency of your secret service department! Put them at work upon this problem. A young man, age twenty-one, height five feet ten inches, weight one hundred and fifty-two pounds, eyes brown, hair chestnut and rather wavy, manner genial, a favourite with the ladies—at least that's what the society notes say—missing since early in June, supposed to be hunting mountain-goats in Mexico. As you know, Cotton, there's only one city in the state that has any 'society,' and in that city there are only twenty-five or thirty families that count. For a secret service department like that of the 'G. F. C.', that is really too easy."

Again there was a silence, until Hal broke it. "Your distress is a tribute to your insight. The company is lucky in the fact that one of its camp-marshals happens to be an ex-gentleman."

Again the other flushed. "Well, by God!" he said, half to himself; and then, making a last effort to hold his bluff—"You're kidding me!"

"'Kidding,' as you call it, is one of the favourite occupations of society, Cotton. A good part of our intercourse consists of it—at least among the younger set."

Suddenly the marshal rose. "Say," he demanded, "would you mind going back upstairs for a few minutes?"

Hal could not restrain his laughter at this. "I should mind it very much," he said. "I have been on a bread and water diet for thirty-six hours, and I should like very much to get out and have a breath of fresh air."

"But," said the other, lamely, "I've got to send you up there."

"That's another matter," replied Hal. "If you send me, I'll go, but it's your look-out. You've kept me here without legal authority, with no charge against me, and without giving me an opportunity to see counsel. Unless I'm very much mistaken, you are liable criminally for that, and the company is liable civilly. That is your own affair, of course. I only want to make clear my position—when you ask me would I *mind* stepping upstairs, I, answer that I would mind very much indeed."

The camp-marshal stood for a bit, chewing nervously on his extinct cigar. Then he went to the door. "Hey, Gus!" he called. Hal's jailer appeared, and Cotton whispered to him, and he went away again. "I'm telling him to get you some food, and you can sit and eat it here. Will that suit you better?"

"It depends," said Hal, making the most of the situation. "Are you inviting me as your prisoner, or as your guest?"

"Oh, come off!" said the other.

"But I have to know my legal status. It will be of importance to my lawyers."

"Be my guest," said the camp-marshal.

"But when a guest has eaten, he is free to go out, if he wishes to!"

"I will let you know about that before you get through."

"Well, be quick. I'm a rapid eater."

"You'll promise you won't go away before that?"

"If I do," was Hal's laughing reply, "it will be only to my place of business. You can look for me at the tipple, Cotton!"

SECTION 21.

The marshal went out, and a few moments later the jailer came back, with a meal which presented a surprising contrast to the ones he had previously served. There was a tray containing cold ham, a couple of soft boiled eggs, some potato salad, and a cup of coffee with rolls and butter.

"Well, well!" said Hal, condescendingly. "That's even nicer than beefsteak and mashed potatoes!" He sat and watched, not offering to help, while the other made room for the tray on the table in front of him. Then the man stalked out, and Hal began to eat.

Before he had finished, the camp-marshal returned. He seated himself in his revolving chair, and appeared to be meditative. Between bites, Hal would look up and smile at him.

"Cotton," said he, "you know there is no more certain test of breeding than table-manners. You will observe that I have not tucked my napkin in my neck, as Alec Stone would have done."

"I'm getting you," replied the marshal.

Hal set his knife and fork side by side on his plate. "Your man has overlooked the finger-bowl," he remarked. "However, don't bother. You might ring for him now, and let him take the tray."

The camp-marshal used his voice for a bell, and the jailer came. "Unfortunately," said Hal, "when your people were searching me, night before last, they dropped my purse, so I have no tip for the waiter."

The "waiter" glared at Hal as if he would like to bite him; but the camp-marshal grinned. "Clear out, Gus, and shut the door," said he.

Then Hal stretched his legs and made himself comfortable again. "I must say I like being your guest better than being your prisoner!"

There was a pause.

"I've been talking it over with Mr. Cartwright," began the marshal. "I've got no way of telling how much of this is bluff that you've been giving me, but it's evident enough that you're no miner. You may be some newfangled kind of agitator, but I'm damned if I ever saw an agitator that had tea-party manners. I suppose you've been brought up to money; but if that's so, why you want to do this kind of thing is more than I can imagine."

"Tell me, Cotton," said Hal, "did you never hear of *ennui*?"

"Yes," replied the other, "but aren't you rather young to be troubled with that complaint?"

"Suppose I've seen others suffering from it, and wanted to try a different way of living from theirs?"

"If you're what you say, you ought to be still in college."

"I go back for my senior year this fall."

"What college?"

"You doubt me still, I see!" said Hal, and smiled. Then, unexpectedly, with a spirit which only moonlit campuses and privilege could beget, he chanted:

> "Old King Coal was a merry old soul,
>   And a merry old soul was he;
> He made him a college, all full of knowledge—
>   Hurrah for you and me!"

"What college is that?" asked the marshal. And Hal sang again:

> "Oh, Liza-Ann, come out with me,
> The moon is a-shinin' in the monkey-puzzle tree!
> Oh, Liza-Ann, I have began
> To sing you the song of Harrigan!"

"Well, well!" commented the marshal, when the concert was over. "Are there many more like you at Harrigan?"

"A little group—enough to leaven the lump."

"And this is your idea of a vacation?"

"No, it isn't a vacation; it's a summer-course in practical sociology."

"Oh, I see!" said the marshal; and he smiled in spite of himself.

"All last year we let the professors of political economy hand out their theories to us. But somehow the theories didn't seem to correspond with the facts. I said to myself, 'I've got to check them up.' You know the phrases, perhaps—individualism, *laissez faire*, freedom of contract, the right of every man to work for whom he pleases. And here you see how the theories work out—a camp-marshal with a cruel smile on his face and a gun on his hip, breaking the laws faster than a governor can sign them."

The camp-marshal decided suddenly that he had had enough of this "tea-party." He rose to his feet to cut matters short. "If you don't mind, young man," said he, "we'll get down to business!"

SECTION 22.

He took a turn about the room, then he came and stopped in front of Hal. He stood with his hands thrust into his pockets, with a certain jaunty grace that was out of keeping with his occupation. He was a handsome devil, Hal thought—in spite of his dangerous mouth, and the marks of dissipation on him.

"Young man," he began, with another effort at geniality. "I don't know who you are, but you're wide awake; you've got your nerve with you, and I admire you. So I'm willing to call the thing off, and let you go back and finish that course at college."

Hal had been studying the other's careful smile. "Cotton," he said, at last, "let me get the proposition clear. I don't have to say I took that money?"

"No, we'll let you off from that."

"And you won't send me to the pen?"

"No. I never meant to do that, of course. I was only trying to bluff you. All I ask is that you clear out, and give our people a chance to forget."

"But what's there in that for me, Cotton? If I had wanted to run away, I could have done it any time during the last eight or ten weeks."

"Yes, of course, but now it's different. Now it's a matter of my consideration."

"Cut out the consideration!" exclaimed Hal. "You want to get rid of me, and you'd like to do it without trouble. But you can't—so forget it."

The other was staring, puzzled. "You mean you expect to stay here?"

"I mean just that."

"Young man, I've had enough of this! I've got no more time to play. I don't care who you are, I don't care about your threats. I'm the marshal of this camp, and I have the job of keeping order in it. I say you're going to get out!"

"But, Cotton," said Hal, "this is an incorporated town! I have a right to walk on the streets—exactly as much right as you."

"I'm not going to waste time arguing. I'm going to put you into an automobile and take you down to Pedro!"

"And suppose I go to the District Attorney and demand that he prosecute you?"

"He'll laugh at you."

"And suppose I go to the Governor of the state?"

"He'll laugh still louder."

"All right, Cotton; maybe you know what you're doing; but I wonder—I wonder just how sure you feel. Has it never occurred to you that your superiors might not care to have you take these high-handed steps?"

"My superiors? Who do you mean?"

"There's one man in the state you must respect—even though you despise the District Attorney and the Governor. That is Peter Harrigan."

"Peter Harrigan?" echoed the other; and then he burst into a laugh. "Well, you *are* a merry lad!"

Hal continued to study him, unmoved. "I wonder if you're sure! He'll stand for everything you've done."

"He will!" said the other.

"For the way you treat the workers? He knows you are giving short weights."

"Oh hell!" said the other. "Where do you suppose he got the money for your college?"

There was a pause; at last the marshal asked, defiantly, "Have you got what you want?"

"Yes," replied Hal. "Of course, I thought it all along, but it's hard to convince other people. Old Peter's not like most of these Western wolves, you know; he's a pious high-church man."

The marshal smiled grimly. "So long as there are sheep," said he, "there'll be wolves in sheep's clothing."

"I see," said Hal. "And you leave them to feed on the lambs!"

"If any lamb is silly enough to be fooled by that old worn-out skin," remarked the marshal, "it deserves to be eaten."

Hal was studying the cynical face in front of him. "Cotton," he said, "the shepherds are asleep; but the watch-dogs are barking. Haven't you heard them?"

"I hadn't noticed."

"They are barking, barking! They are going to wake the shepherds! They are going to save the sheep!"

"Religion don't interest me," said the other, looking bored; "your kind any more than Old Peter's."

And suddenly Hal rose to his feet. "Cotton," said he, "my place is with the flock! I'm going back to my job at the tipple!" And he started towards the door.

SECTION 23.

Jeff Cotton sprang forward. "Stop!" he cried.

But Hal did not stop.

"See here, young man!" cried the marshal. "Don't carry this joke too far!" And he sprang to the door, just ahead of his prisoner. His hand moved toward his hip.

"Draw your gun, Cotton," said Hal; and, as the marshal obeyed, "Now I will stop. If I obey you in future, it will be at the point of your revolver."

The marshal's mouth was dangerous-looking. "You may find that in this country there's not so much between the drawing of a gun and the firing of it!"

"I've explained my attitude," replied Hal. "What are your orders?"

"Come back and sit in this chair."

So Hal sat, and the marshal went to his desk, and took up the telephone. "Number seven," he said, and waited a moment. "That you, Tom? Bring the car right away."

He hung up the receiver, and there followed a silence; finally Hal inquired, "I'm going to Pedro?"

There was no reply.

"I see I've got on your nerves," said Hal. "But I don't suppose it's occurred to you that you deprived me of my money last night. Also, I've an account with the company, some money coming to me for my work? What about that?"

The marshal took up the receiver and gave another number. "Hello, Simpson. This is Cotton. Will you figure out the time of Joe Smith, buddy in Number Two, and send over the cash. Get his account at the store; and be quick, we're waiting for it. He's going out in a hurry." Again he hung up the receiver.

"Tell me," said Hal, "did you take that trouble for Mike Sikoria?"

There was silence.

"Let me suggest that when you get my time, you give me part of it in scrip. I want it for a souvenir."

Still there was silence.

"You know," persisted the prisoner, tormentingly, "there's a law against paying wages in scrip."

The marshal was goaded to speech. "We don't pay in scrip."

"But you do, man! You know you do!"

"We give it when they ask their money ahead."

"The law requires you to pay them twice a month, and you don't do it. You pay them once a month, and meantime, if they need money, you give them this imitation money!"

"Well, if it satisfies them, where's your kick?"

"If it doesn't satisfy them, you put them on the train and ship them out?"

The marshal sat in silence, tapping impatiently with his fingers on the desk.

"Cotton," Hal began, again, "I'm out for education, and there's something I'd like you to explain to me—a problem in human psychology. When a man puts through a deal like this, what does he tell himself about it?"

"Young man," said the marshal, "if you'll pardon me, you are getting to be a bore."

"Oh, but we've got an automobile ride before us! Surely we can't sit in silence all the way!" After a moment he added, in a coaxing tone, "I really want to learn, you know. You might be able to win me over."

"No!" said Cotton, promptly. "I'll not go in for anything like that!"

"But why not?"

"Because, I'm no match for you in long-windedness. I've heard you agitators before, you're all alike: you think the world is run by talk—but it isn't."

Hal had come to realise that he was not getting anywhere in his duel with the camp-marshal. He had made every effort to get somewhere; he had argued, threatened, bluffed, he had even sung songs for the marshal! But the marshal was going to ship him out, that was all there was to it.

Hal had gone on with the quarrel, simply because he had to wait for the automobile, and because he had endured indignities and had to vent his anger and disappointment. But now he stopped quarrelling suddenly. His attention was caught by the marshal's words, "You think the world is run by talk!" Those were the words Hal's brother always used! And also, the marshal had said, "You agitators!" For years it had been one of the taunts Hal had heard from his brother, "You will turn into one of these agitators!" Hal had answered, with boyish obstinacy, "I don't care if I do!" And now, here the marshal was calling him an agitator, seriously, without an apology, without the license of blood relationship. He repeated the words, "That's what gets me about you agitators—you come in here trying to stir these people up—"

So that was the way Hal seemed to the "G. F. C."! He had come here intending to be a spectator, to stand on the deck of the steamer and look down into the ocean of social misery. He had considered every step so carefully before he took it! He had merely tried to be a check-weighman, nothing more! He had told Tom Olson he would not go in for unionism; he had had a distrust of union organisers, of agitators of all sorts—blind, irresponsible persons who went about stirring up dangerous passions. He had come to admire Tom Olson—but that had only partly removed his prejudices; Olson was only one agitator, not the whole lot of them!

But all his consideration for the company had counted for nothing; likewise all his efforts to convince the marshal that he was a leisure-class person. In spite of all Hal's "tea-party manners," the marshal had said, "You agitators!" What was he judging by, Hal wondered. Had he, Hal Warner, come to look like one of these blind, irresponsible persons? It was time that he took stock of himself!

Had two months of "dirty work" in the bowels of the earth changed him so? The idea was bound to be disconcerting to one who had been a favourite of the ladies! Did he talk like it?—he who had been "kissing the Blarney-stone!" The marshal had said he was "long-winded!" Well, to be sure, he had talked a lot; but what could the man expect—having shut him up in jail for two nights and a day, with only his grievances to brood over! Was that the way real agitators were made—being shut up with grievances to brood over?

Hal recalled his broodings in the jail. He had been embittered; he had not cared whether North Valley was dominated by labour unions. But that had all been a mood, the same as his answer to his brother; that was jail psychology, a part of his summer course in practical sociology. He had put it aside; but apparently it had made a deeper impression upon him than he had realised. It had changed his physical aspect! It had made him look and talk like an agitator! It had made him "irresponsible," "blind!"

Yes, that was it! All this dirt, ignorance, disease, this knavery and oppression, this maiming of men in body and soul in the coal-camps of America—all this did not exist—it was the hallucination of an "irresponsible" brain! There was the evidence of Hal's brother and the camp-marshal to prove it; there was the evidence of the whole world to prove it! The camp-marshal and his brother and the whole world could not be "blind!" And if you talked to them about these conditions, they shrugged their shoulders, they called you a "dreamer," a "crank," they said you were "off your trolley"; or else they became angry and bitter, they called you names; they said, "You agitators!"

SECTION 24.

The camp-marshal of North Valley had been "agitated" to such an extent that he could not stay in his chair. All the harassments of his troubled career had come pouring into his mind. He had begun pacing the floor, and was talking away, regardless of whether Hal listened or not.

"A campful of lousy wops! They can't understand any civilised language, they've only one idea in the world—to shirk every lick of work they can, to fill up their cars with slate and rock and blame it on some other fellow, and go off to fill themselves with booze. They won't work fair, they won't fight fair—they fight with a knife in the back! And you agitators with your sympathy for them—why the hell do they come to this country, unless they like it better than their own?"

Hal had heard this question before; but they had to wait for the automobile—and being sure that he was an agitator now, he would make all the trouble he could! "The reason is obvious enough," he said. "Isn't it true that the 'G. F. C.' employs agents abroad to tell them of the wonderful pay they get in America?"

"Well, they get it, don't they? Three times what they ever got at home!"

"Yes, but it doesn't do them any good. There's another fact which the 'G. F. C.' doesn't mention—that the cost of living is even higher than the wages. Then, too, they're led to think of America as a land of liberty; they come, hoping for a better chance for themselves and their children; but they find a camp-marshal who's off in his geography—who thinks the Rocky Mountains are somewhere in Russia!"

"I know that line of talk!" exclaimed the other. "I learned to wave the starry flag when I was a kid. But I tell you, you've got to get coal mined, and it isn't the same thing as running a Fourth of July celebration. Some church people make a law they shan't work on Sunday—and what comes of that? They have thirty-six hours to get soused in, and so they can't work on Monday!"

"Surely there's a remedy, Cotton! Suppose the company refused to rent buildings to saloon-keepers?"

"Good God! You think we haven't tried it? They go down to Pedro for the stuff, and bring back all they can carry—inside them and out. And if we stop that—then our hands move to some other camps, where they can spend their money as they please. No, young man, when you have such cattle, you have to drive them! And it takes a strong hand to do it—a man like Peter Harrigan. If there's to be any coal, if industry's to go on, if there's to be any progress—"

"We have that in our song!" laughed Hal, breaking into the camp-marshal's discourse—

> "He keeps them a-roll, that merry old soul—
>   The wheels of industree;
> A-roll and a-roll, for his pipe and his bowl
>   And his college facultee!"

"Yes," growled the marshal. "It's easy enough for you smart young chaps to make verses, while you're living at ease on the old man's bounty. But that don't answer any argument. Are you college boys ready to take over his job? Or these Democrat politicians that come in here, talking fool-talk about liberty, making labour laws for these wops—"

"I begin to understand," said Hal. "You object to the politicians who pass the laws, you doubt their motives—and so you refuse to obey. But why didn't you tell me sooner you were an anarchist?"

"Anarchist?" cried the marshal. "*Me* an anarchist?"

"That's what an anarchist is, isn't it?"

"Good God! If that isn't the limit! You come here, stirring up the men—a union agitator, or whatever you are—and you know that the first idea of these people, when they do break loose, is to put dynamite in the shafts and set fire to the buildings!"

"Do they do that?" There was surprise in Hal's tone.

"Haven't you read what they did in the last big strike? That dough-faced old preacher, John Edstrom, could tell you. He was one of the bunch."

"No," said Hal, "you're mistaken. Edstrom has a different philosophy. But others did, I've no doubt. And since I've been here, I can understand their point of view entirely. When they set fire to the buildings, it was because they thought you and Alec Stone might be inside."

The marshal did not smile.

"They want to destroy the properties," continued Hal, "because that's the only way they can think of to punish the tyranny and greed of the owners. But, Cotton, suppose some one were to put a new idea into their heads; suppose some one were to say to them, 'Don't destroy the properties—*take them!*'"

The other stared. "Take them! So that's your idea of morality!"

"It would be more moral than the method by which Peter got them in the beginning."

"What method is that?" demanded the marshal, with some appearance of indignation. "He paid the market-price for them, didn't he?"

"He paid the market-price for politicians. Up in Western City I happen to know a lady who was a school-commissioner when he was buying school-lands from the state—lands that were known to contain coal. He was paying three dollars an acre, and everybody knew they were worth three thousand."

"Well," said Cotton, "if you don't buy the politicians, you wake up some fine morning and find that somebody else has bought them. If you have property, you have to protect it."

"Cotton," said Hal, "you sell Old Peter your time—but surely you might keep part of your brains! Enough to look at your monthly pay-check and realise that you too are a wage-slave, not much better than the miners you despise."

The other smiled. "My check might be bigger, I admit; but I've figured over it, and I think I have an easier time than you agitators. I'm top-dog, and I expect to stay on top."

"Well, Cotton, on that view of life, I don't wonder you get drunk now and then. A dog-fight, with no faith or humanity anywhere! Don't think I'm sneering at you—I'm talking out of my heart to you. I'm not so young, nor such a fool, that I haven't had the dog-fight aspect of things brought to my attention. But there's something in a fellow that insists he isn't all dog; he has at least a possibility of something better. Take these poor under-dogs sweating inside the mountain, risking their lives every hour of the day and night to provide you and me with coal to keep us warm—to 'keep the wheels of industry a-roll'—"

SECTION 25.

These were the last words Hal spoke. They were obvious enough words, yet when he looked back upon the coincidence, it seemed to him a singular one. For while he was sitting there chatting, it happened that the poor under-dogs inside the mountain were in the midst of one of those experiences which make the romance and terror of coal-mining. One of the boys who were employed underground, in violation of the child labour law, was in the act of bungling his task. He was a "spragger," whose duty it was to thrust a stick into the wheel of a loaded car to hold it; and he was a little chap, and the car was in motion when he made the attempt. It knocked him against the wall—and so there was a load of coal rolling down grade, pursued too late by half a dozen men. Gathering momentum, it whirled round a curve and flew from the track, crashing into timbers and knocking them loose. With the timbers came a shower of coal-dust, accumulated for decades in these old workings; and at the same time came an electric light wire, which, as it touched the car, produced a spark.

And so it was that Hal, chatting with the marshal, suddenly felt, rather than heard, a deafening roar; he felt the air about him turn into a living thing which struck him a mighty blow, hurling him flat upon the floor. The windows of the room crashed inward upon him in a shower of glass, and the plaster of the ceiling came down on his head in another shower.

When he raised himself, half stunned, he saw the marshal, also on the floor; these two conversationalists stared at each other with horrified eyes. Even as they crouched, there came a crash above their heads, and half the ceiling of the room came toward them, with a great piece of timber sticking through. All about them were other crashes, as if the end of the world had come.

They struggled to their feet, and rushing to the door, flung it open, just as a jagged piece of timber shattered the side-walk in front of them. They sprang back again, "Into the cellar!" cried the marshal, leading the way to the back-stairs.

But before they had started down these stairs, they realised that the crashing had ceased. "What is it?" gasped Hal, as they stood.

"Mine-explosion," said the other; and after a few seconds they ran to the door again.

The first thing they saw was a vast pillar of dust and smoke, rising into the sky above them. It spread before their dazed eyes, until it made night of everything about them. There was still a rain of lighter debris pattering down over the village; as they stared, and got their wits about them, remembering how things had looked before this, they realised that the shaft-house of Number One had disappeared.

"Blown up, by God!" cried the marshal; and the two ran out into the street, and looking up, saw that a portion of the wrecked building had fallen through the roof of the jail above their heads.

The rain of debris had now ceased, but there were clouds of dust which covered the two men black; the clouds grew worse, until they could hardly see their way at all. And with the darkness there fell silence, which, after the sound of the explosion and the crashing of debris, seemed the silence of death.

For a few moments Hal stood dazed. He saw a stream of men and boys pouring from the breaker; while from every street there appeared a stream of women; women old, women young—leaving their cooking on the stove, their babies in the crib, with their older children screaming at their skirts, they gathered in swarms about the pit-mouth, which was like the steaming crater of a volcano.

Cartwright, the superintendent, appeared, running toward the fan-house. Cotton joined him, and Hal followed. The fan-house was a wreck, the giant fan lying on the ground a hundred feet away, its blades smashed. Hal was too inexperienced in mine-matters to get the full significance of this; but he saw the marshal and the superintendent stare blankly at each other, and heard the former's exclamation, "That does for us!" Cartwright said not a word; but his thin lips were pressed together, and there was fear in his eyes.

Back to the smoking pit-mouth the two men hurried, with Hal following. Here were a hundred, two hundred women crowded, clamouring questions all at once. They swarmed about the marshal, the superintendent, the other bosses—even about Hal, crying hysterically in Polish and Bohemian and Greek. When Hal shook his head, indicating that he did not understand them, they moaned in anguish, or shrieked aloud. Some continued to stare into the smoking pit-mouth; others covered the sight from their eyes, or sank down upon their knees, sobbing, praying with uplifted hands.

Little by little Hal began to realise the full horror of a mine-disaster. It was not noise and smoke and darkness, nor frantic, wailing women; it was not anything above ground, but what was below in the smoking black pit! It was men! Men whom Hal knew, whom he had worked with and joked with, whose smiles he had shared; whose daily life he had come to know! Scores, possibly hundreds of them, they were down here under his feet—some dead, others injured, maimed. What would they do? What would those on the surface do for them? Hal tried to get to Cotton, to ask him questions; but the camp-marshal was surrounded, besieged. He was pushing the women back, exclaiming, "Go away! Go home!"

What? Go home? they cried. When their men were in the mine? They crowded about him closer, imploring, shrieking.

"Get out!" he kept exclaiming. "There's nothing you can do! There's nothing anybody can do yet! Go home! Go home!" He had to beat them back by force, to keep them from pushing one another into the pit-mouth.

Everywhere Hal looked were women in attitudes of grief: standing rigid, staring ahead of them as if in a trance; sitting down, rocking to and fro; on their knees with faces uplifted in prayer; clutching their terrified children about their skirts. He saw an Austrian woman, a pitiful, pale young thing with a ragged grey shawl about her head, stretching out her hands and crying: "Mein Mann! Mein Mann!" Presently she covered her face, and her voice died into a wail of despair: "O, mein Mann! O, mein Mann!" She turned away, staggering about like some creature that has received a death wound. Hal's eyes followed her; her cry, repeated over and over incessantly, became the leit-motif of this symphony of horror.

He had read about mine-disasters in his morning newspaper; but here a mine-disaster became a thing of human flesh and blood. The unendurable part of it was the utter impotence of himself and of all the world. This impotence became clearer to him each moment—from the exclamations of Cotton and of the men he questioned. It was monstrous, incredible—but it was so! They must send for a new fan, they must wait for it to be brought in, they must set it up and get it into operation; they must wait for hours after that while smoke and gas were cleared out of the main passages of the mine; and until this had been done, there was nothing they could do—absolutely nothing! The men inside the mine would stay. Those who had not been killed outright would make their way into the remoter chambers, and barricade themselves against the deadly "after damp." They would wait, without food or water, with air of doubtful quality—they would wait and wait, until the rescue-crew could get to them!

SECTION 26.

At moments in the midst of this confusion, Hal found himself trying to recall who had worked in Number One, among the people he knew. He himself had been employed in Number Two, so he had naturally come to know more men in that mine. But he had known some from the other mine—Old Rafferty for one, and Mary Burke's father for another, and at least one of the members of his check-weighman group—Zamierowski. Hal saw in a sudden vision the face of this patient little man, who smiled so good-naturedly while Americans were trying to say his name. And Old Rafferty, with all his little Rafferties, and his piteous efforts to keep the favour of his employers! And poor Patrick Burke, whom Hal had never seen sober; doubtless he was sober now, if he was still alive!

Then in the crowd Hal encountered Jerry Minetti, and learned that another man who had been down was Farenzena, the Italian whose "fanciulla" had played with him; and yet another was Judas Apostolikas—having taken his thirty pieces of silver with him into the deathtrap!

People were making up lists, just as Hal was doing, by asking questions of others. These lists were subject to revision—sometimes under dramatic circumstances. You saw a woman weeping, with her apron to her eyes; suddenly she would look up, give a piercing cry, and fling her arms about the neck of some man. As for Hal, he felt as if he were encountering a ghost when suddenly he recognised Patrick Burke, standing in the midst of a group of people. He went over and heard the old man's story—how there was a Dago fellow who had stolen his timbers, and he had come up to the surface for more; so his life had been saved, while the timber-thief was down there still—a judgment of Providence upon mine-miscreants!

Presently Hal asked if Burke had been to tell his family. He had run home, he said, but there was nobody there. So Hal began pushing his way through the throngs, looking for Mary, or her sister Jennie, or her brother Tommie. He persisted in this search, although it occurred to him to wonder whether the family of a hopeless drunkard would appreciate the interposition of Providence in his behalf.

He encountered Olson, who had had a narrow escape, being employed as a surface-man near the hoist. All this was an old story to the organiser, who had worked in mines since he was eight years old, and had seen many kinds of disaster. He began to explain things to Hal, in a matter of fact way. The law required a certain number of openings to every mine, also an escape-way with ladders by which men could come out; but it cost good money to dig holes in the ground.

At this time the immediate cause of the explosion was unknown, but they could tell it was a "dust explosion" by the clouds of coke-dust, and no one who had been into the mine and seen its dry condition would doubt what they would find when they went down and traced out the "force" and its effects. They were supposed to do regular sprinkling, but in such matters the bosses used their own judgment.

Hal was only half listening to these explanations. The thing was too raw and too horrible to him. What difference did it make whose fault it was? The accident had happened, and the question was now how to meet the emergency! Underneath Olson's sentences he heard the cry of men and boys being asphyxiated in dark dungeons—he heard the wailing of women, like a surf beating on a distant shore, or the faint, persistent accompaniment of muted strings: "O, mein Mann! O, mein Mann!"

They came upon Jeff Cotton again. With half a dozen men to help him, he was pushing back the crowd from the pit-mouth, and stretching barbed wired to hold them back. He was none too gentle about it, Hal thought; but doubtless women are provoking when they are hysterical. He was answering their frenzied questions, "Yes, yes! We're getting a new fan. We're doing everything we can, I tell you. We'll get them out. Go home and wait."

But of course no one would go home. How could a woman sit in her house, or go about her ordinary tasks of cooking or washing, while her man might be suffering asphyxiation under the ground? The least she could do was to stand at the pit-mouth—as near to him as she could get! Some of them stood motionless, hour after hour, while others wandered through the village streets, asking the same people, over and over again, if they had seen their loved ones. Several had turned up, like Patrick Burke; there seemed always a chance for one more.

SECTION 27.

In the course of the afternoon Hal came upon Mary Burke on the street. She had long ago found her father, and seen him off to O'Callahan's to celebrate the favours of Providence. Now Mary was concerned with a graver matter. Number Two Mine was in danger! The explosion in Number One had been so violent that the gearing of the fan of the other mine, nearly a mile up the canyon, had been thrown out of order. So the fan had stopped; and when some one had gone to Alec Stone, asking that he bring out the men, Stone had refused. "What do ye think he said?" cried Mary. "What do ye think? 'Damn the men! Save the mules!'"

Hal had all but lost sight of the fact that there was a second mine in the village, in which hundreds of men and boys were still at work. "Wouldn't they know about the explosion?" he asked.

"They might have heard the noise," said Mary. "But they'd not know what it was; and the bosses won't tell them till they've got out the mules."

For all that he had seen in North Valley, Hal could hardly credit that story. "How do you know it, Mary?"

"Young Rovetta just told me. He was there, and heard it with his own ears."

He was staring at her. "Let's go and make sure," he said, and they started up the main street of the village. On the way they were joined by others—for already the news of this fresh trouble had begun to spread. Jeff Cotton went past them in an automobile, and Mary exclaimed, "I told ye so! When ye see him goin', ye know there's dirty work to be done!"

They came to the shaft-house of Number Two, and found a swarm of people, almost a riot. Women and children were shrieking and gesticulating, threatening to break into the office and use the mine-telephone to warn the men themselves. And here was the camp-marshal driving them back. Hal and Mary arrived in time to see Mrs. David, whose husband was at work in Number Two, shaking her fist in the marshal's face and screaming at him like a wild-cat. He drew his revolver upon her; and at this Hal started forward. A blind fury seized him—he would have thrown himself upon the marshal.

But Mary Burke stopped him, flinging her arms about him, and pinning him by main force. "No, no!" she cried. "Stay back, man! D'ye want to get killed?"

He was amazed at her strength. He was amazed also at the vehemence of her emotion. She was calling him a crazy fool, and names even more harsh. "Have ye no more sense than a woman? Running into the mouth of a revolver like that!"

The crisis passed in a moment, for Mrs. David fell back, and then the marshal put up his weapon. But Mary continued scolding Hal, trying to drag him away. "Come on now! Come out of here!"

"But, Mary! We must do something!"

"Ye can do nothin', I tell ye! Ye'd ought to have sense enough to know it. I'll not let ye get yeself murdered! Come away now!" And half by force and half by cajoling, she got him farther down the street.

He was trying to think out the situation. Were the men in Number Two really in danger? Could it be possible that the bosses would take such a chance in cold blood? And right at this moment, with the disaster in the other mine before their eyes! He could not believe it; and meantime Mary, at his side, was declaring that the men were in no real danger—it was only Alec Stone's brutal words that had set her crazy.

"Don't ye remember the time when the air-course was blocked before, and ye helped to get up the mules yeself? Ye thought nothin' of it then, and 'tis the same now. They'll get everybody out in time!"

She was concealing her real feelings in order to keep him safe; he let her lead him on, while he tried to think of something else to do. He would think of the men in Number Two; they were his best friends, Jack David, Tim Rafferty, Wresmak, Androkulos, Klowoski. He would think of them, in their remote dungeons—breathing bad air, becoming sick and faint—in order that mules might be saved! He would stop in his tracks, and Mary would drag him on, repeating over and over, "Ye can do nothin'! Nothin'!" And then he would think, What could he do? He had put up his best bluff to Jeff Cotton a few hours earlier, and the answer had been the muzzle of the marshal's revolver in his face. All he could accomplish now would be to bring himself to Cotton's attention, and be thrust out of camp forthwith.

SECTION 28.

They came to Mary's home; and next door was the home of the Slav woman, Mrs. Zamboni, about whom in the past she had told him so many funny stories. Mrs. Zamboni had had a new baby every year for sixteen years, and eleven of these babies were still alive. Now her husband was trapped in Number One, and she was distracted, wandering about the streets with the greater part of her brood at her heels. At intervals she would emit a howl like a tortured animal, and her brood would take it up in various timbres. Hal stopped to listen to the sounds, but Mary put her fingers into her ears and fled into the house. Hal followed her, and saw her fling herself into a chair and burst into hysterical weeping. And suddenly Hal realised what a strain this terrible affair had been upon Mary. It had been bad enough to him—but he was a man, and more able to contemplate sights of horror. Men went to their deaths in industry and war, and other men saw them go and inured themselves to the spectacle. But women were the mothers of these men; it was women who bore them in pain, nursed them and reared them with endless patience—women could never become inured to the spectacle! Then too, the women's fate was worse. If the men were dead, that was the end of them; but the women must face the future, with its bitter memories, its lonely and desolate struggle for existence. The women must see the children suffering, dying by slow stages of deprivation.

Hal's pity for all suffering women became concentrated upon the girl beside him. He knew how tenderhearted she was. She had no man in the mine, but some day she would have, and she was suffering the pangs of that inexorable future. He looked at her, huddled in her chair, wiping away her tears with the hem of her old blue calico. She seemed unspeakably pathetic—like a child that has been hurt. She was sobbing out sentences now and then, as if to herself: "Oh, the poor women, the poor women! Did ye see the face of Mrs. Jonotch? She'd jumped into the smoking pit-mouth if they'd let her!"

"Don't suffer so, Mary!" pleaded Hal—as if he thought she could stop.

"Let me alone!" she cried. "Let me have it out!" And Hal, who had had no experience with hysteria, stood helplessly by.

"There's more misery than I ever knew there was!" she went on. "'Tis everywhere ye turn, a woman with her eyes burnin' with suffering wondering if she'll ever see her man again! Or some mother whose lad may be dying and she can do nothin' for him!"

"And neither can you do anything, Mary," Hal pleaded again. "You're only sorrowing yourself to death."

"Ye say that to me?" she cried. "And when ye were ready to let Jeff Cotton shoot ye, because you were so sorry for Mrs. David! No, the sights here nobody can stand."

He could think of nothing to answer. He drew up a chair and sat by her in silence, and after a while she began to grow calmer, and wiped away her tears, and sat gazing dully through the doorway into the dirty little street.

Hal's eyes followed hers. There were the ash-heaps and tomato-cans, there were two of Mrs. Zamboni's bedraggled brood, poking with sticks into a dump-heap—looking for something to eat, perhaps, or for something to play with. There was the dry, waste grass of the road-side, grimy with coal-dust, as was everything else in the village. What a scene!—And this girl's eyes had never a sight of anything more inspiring than this. Day in and day out, all her life long, she looked at this scene! Had he ever for a moment reproached her for her "black moods"? With such an environment could men or women be cheerful—could they dream of beauty, aspire to heights of nobility and courage, to happy service of their fellows? There was a miasma of despair over this place; it was not a real place—it was a dream-place—a horrible, distorted nightmare! It was like the black hole in the ground which haunted Hal's imagination, with men and boys at the bottom of it, dying of asphyxiation!

Suddenly it came to Hal—he wanted to get away from North Valley! To get away at all costs! The place had worn down his courage; slowly, day after day, the sight of misery and want, of dirt and disease, of hunger, oppression, despair, had eaten the soul out of him, had undermined his fine structure of altruistic theories. Yes, he wanted to escape—to a place where the sun shone, where the grass grew green, where human beings stood erect and laughed and were free. He wanted to shut from his eyes the dust and smoke of this nasty little village; to stop his ears to that tormenting sound of women wailing: "O, mein Mann! O, mein Mann!"

He looked at the girl, who sat staring before her, bent forward, her arms hanging limply over her knees.

"Mary," he said, "you must go away from here! It's no place for a tenderhearted girl to be. It's no place for any one!"

She gazed at him dully for a moment. "It was me that was tellin' *you* to go away," she said, at last. "Ever since ye came here I been sayin' it! Now I guess ye know what I mean."

"Yes," he said, "I do, and I want to go. But I want you to go too."

"D'ye think 'twould do me any good, Joe?" she asked. "D'ye think 'twould do me any good to get away? Could I ever forget the sights I've seen this day? Could I ever have any real, honest happiness anywhere after this?"

He tried to reassure her, but he was far from reassured himself. How would it be with him? Would he ever feel that he had a right to happiness after this? Could he take any satisfaction in a pleasant and comfortable world, knowing that it was based upon such hideous misery? His thoughts went to that world, where careless, pleasure-loving people sought gratification of their desires. It came to him suddenly that what he wanted more than to get away was to bring those people here, if only for a day, for an hour, that they might hear this chorus of wailing women!

SECTION 29.

Mary made Hal swear that he would not get into a fight with Cotton; then they went to Number Two. They found the mules coming up, and the bosses promising that in a short while the men would be coming. Everything was all right—there was not a bit of danger! But Mary was afraid to trust Hal, in spite of his promise, so she lured him back to Number One.

They found that a rescue-car had just arrived from Pedro, bringing doctors and nurses, also several "helmets." These "helmets" were strange looking contrivances, fastened over the head and shoulders, air-tight, and provided with oxygen sufficient to last for an hour or more. The men who wore them sat in a big bucket which was let down the shaft with a windlass, and every now and then they pulled on a signal-cord to let those on the surface know they were alive. When the first of them came back, he reported that there were bodies near the foot of the shaft, but apparently all dead. There was heavy black smoke, indicating a fire somewhere in the mine; so nothing more could be done until the fan had been set up. By reversing the fan, they could draw out the smoke and gases and clear the shaft.

The state mine-inspector had been notified, but was ill at home, and was sending one of his deputies. Under the law this official would have charge of all the rescue work, but Hal found that the miners took no interest in his presence. It had been his duty to prevent the accident, and he had not done so. When he came, he would do what the company wanted.

Some time after dark the workers began to come out of Number Two, and their women, waiting at the pit-mouth, fell upon their necks with cries of thankfulness. Hal observed other women, whose men were in Number One, and would perhaps never come out again, standing and watching these greetings with wistful, tear-filled eyes. Among those who came out was Jack David, and Hal walked home with him and his wife, listening to the latter abuse Jeff Cotton and Alec Stone, which was an education in the vocabulary of class-consciousness. The little Welsh woman repeated the pit-boss's saying, "Damn the men, save the mules!" She said it again and again—it seemed to delight her like a work of art, it summed up so perfectly the attitude of the bosses to their men! There were many other people repeating that saying, Hal found; it went all over the village, in a few days it went all over the district. It summed up what the district believed to be the attitude of the coal-operators to the workers!

Having got over the first shock of the disaster, Hal wanted information, and he questioned Big Jack, a solid and well-read man who had given thought to every aspect of the industry. In his quiet, slow way, he explained to Hal that the frequency of accidents in this district was not due to any special difficulty in operating these mines, the explosiveness of the gases or the dryness of the atmosphere. It was merely the carelessness of those in charge, their disregard of the laws for the protection of the men. There ought to be a law with "teeth" in it—for example, one providing that for every man killed in a coal-mine his heirs should receive a thousand dollars, regardless of who had been to blame for the accident. Then you would see how quickly the operators would get busy and find remedies for the "unusual" dangers!

As it was, they knew that no matter how great their culpability, they could get off with slight loss. Already, no doubt, their lawyers were on the spot, and by the time the first bodies were brought out, they would be fixing things up with the families. They would offer a widow a ticket back to the old country; they would offer a whole family of orphaned children, maybe fifty dollars, maybe a hundred dollars—and it would be a case of take it or leave it. You could get nothing from the courts; the case was so hopeless that you could not even find a lawyer to make the attempt. That was one reform in which the companies believed, said "Big Jack," with sarcasm; they had put the "shyster lawyer" out of business!

SECTION 30.

There followed a night and then another day of torturing suspense. The fan came, but it had to be set up before anything could be done. As volumes of black smoke continued to pour from the shaft, the opening was made tight with a board and canvas cover; it was necessary, the bosses said, but to Hal it seemed the climax of horror. To seal up men and boys in a place of deadly gases!

There was something peculiarly torturing in the idea of men caught in a mine; they were directly under one's feet, yet it was impossible to get to them, to communicate with them in any way! The people on top yearned to them, and they, down below, yearned back. It was impossible to forget them for even a few minutes. People would become abstracted while they talked, and would stand staring into space; suddenly, in the midst of a crowd, a woman would bury her face in her hands and burst into tears, and then all the others would follow suit.

Few people slept in North Valley during those two nights. They held mourning parties in their homes or on the streets. Some house-work had to be done, of course, but no one did anything that could be left undone. The children would not play; they stood about, silent, pale, like wizened-up grown people, over-mature in knowledge of trouble. The nerves of every one were on edge, the self-control of every one balanced upon a fine point.

It was a situation bound to be fruitful in imaginings and rumours, stimulated to those inclined to signs and omens—the seers of ghosts, or those who went into trances, or possessed second sight or other mysterious gifts. There were some living in a remote part of the village who declared they had heard explosions under the ground, several blasts in quick succession. The men underground were setting off dynamite by way of signalling!

In the course of the second day Hal sat with Mary Burke upon the steps of her home. Old Patrick lay within, having found the secret of oblivion at O'Callahan's. Now and then came the moaning of Mrs. Zamboni, who was in her cabin with her brood of children. Mary had been in to feed them, because the distracted mother let them starve and cry. Mary was worn out, herself; the wonderful Irish complexion had faded, and there were no curves to the vivid lips. They had been sitting in silence, for there was nothing to talk of but the disaster—and they had said all there was to say about that. But Hal had been thinking while he watched Mary.

"Listen, Mary," he said, at last; "when this thing is over, you must really come away from here. I've thought it all out—I have friends in Western City who will give you work, so you can take care of yourself, and of your brother and sister too. Will you go?"

But she did not answer. She continued to gaze indifferently into the dirty little street.

"Truly, Mary," he went on. "Life isn't so terrible everywhere as it is here. Come away! Hard as it is to believe, you'll forget all this. People suffer, but then they stop suffering; it's nature's way—to make them forget."

"Nature's way has been to beat me dead," said she.

"Yes, Mary. Despair can become a disease, but it hasn't with you. You're just tired out. If you'll try to rouse yourself—" And he reached over and caught her hand with an attempt at playfulness. "Cheer up, Mary! You're coming away from North Valley."

She turned and looked at him. "Am I?" she asked, impassively; and she went on studying his face. "Who are ye, Joe Smith? What are ye doin' here?"

"Working in a coal-mine," he laughed, still trying to divert her.

But she went on, as gravely as before. "Ye're no working man, that I know. And ye're always offering me help! Ye're always sayin' what ye can do for me!" She paused and there came some of the old defiance into her face. "Joe, ye can have no idea of the feelin's that have got hold of me just now. I'm ready to do something desperate; ye'd best be leavin' me alone, Joe!"

"I think I understand, Mary. I would hardly blame you for anything you did."

She took up his words eagerly. "Wouldn't ye, Joe? Ye're sure? Then what I want is to get the truth from ye. I want ye to talk it out fair!"

"All right, Mary. What is it?"

But her defiance had vanished suddenly. Her eyes dropped, and he saw her fingers picking nervously at a fold of her dress. "About us, Joe," she said. "I've thought sometimes ye cared for me. I've thought ye liked to be with me—not just because ye were sorry for me, but because of *me*. I've not been sure, but I can't help thinkin' it's so. Is it?"

"Yes, it is," he said, a little uncertainly. "I *do* care for you."

"Then is it that ye don't care for that other girl all the time?"

"No," he said, "it's not that."

"Ye can care for two girls at the same time?"

He did not know what to say. "It would seem that I can, Mary."

She raised her eyes again and studied his face. "Ye told me about that other girl, and I been wonderin', was it only to put me off? Maybe it's me own fault, but I can't make meself believe in that other girl, Joe!"

"You're mistaken, Mary," he answered, quickly. "What I told you was true."

"Well, maybe so," she said, but there was no conviction in her tone. "Ye come away from her, and ye never go where she is or see her—it's hard to believe ye'd do that way if ye were very close to her. I just don't think ye love her as much as

ye might. And ye say you do care some for me. So I've thought—I've wondered—
"

She stopped, forcing herself to meet his gaze: "I been tryin' to work it out! I know ye're too good a man for me, Joe. Ye come from a better place in life, ye've a right to expect more in a woman—"

"It's not that, Mary!"

But she cut him short. "I know that's true! Ye're only tryin' to save my feelin's. I know ye're better than me! I've tried hard to hold me head up, I've tried a long time not to let meself go to pieces. I've even tried to keep cheerful, telling meself I'd not want to be like Mrs. Zamboni, forever complainin'. But 'tis no use tellin' yourself lies! I been up to the church, and heard the Reverend Spragg tell the people that the rich and poor are the same in the sight of the Lord. And maybe 'tis so, but I'm not the Lord, and I'll never pretend I'm not ashamed to be livin' in a place like this."

"I'm sure the Lord has no interest in keeping you here—" he began.

But she broke in, "What makes it so hard to bear is knowin' there's so many wonderful things in the world, and ye can never have them! 'Tis as if ye had to see them through a pane of glass, like in the window of a store. Just think, Joe Smith—once, in a church in Sheridan, I heard a lady sing beautiful music; once in my whole lifetime! Can ye guess what it meant to me?"

"Yes, Mary, I can."

"But I had that all out with meself—years ago. I knew the price a workin' girl has to pay for such things, and I said, I'll not let meself think about them. I've hated this place, I've wanted to get away—but there's only one way to go, to let some man take ye! So I've stayed; I've kept straight, Joe. I want ye to believe that."

"Of course, Mary!"

"No! It's not been 'of course'! It means ye have to fight with temptations. It's many a time I've looked at Jeff Cotton, and thought about the things I need! And I've done without! But now comes the thing a woman wants more than all the other things in the world!"

She paused, but only for a moment. "They tell ye to love a man of your own class. Me old mother said that to me, before she died. But suppose ye didn't happen to? Suppose ye'd stopped and thought what it meant, havin' one baby after another, till ye're worn out and drop—like me old mother did? Suppose ye knew good manners when ye see them—ye knew interestin' talk when ye heard it!" She clasped her hands suddenly before her, exclaiming, "Ah, 'tis something different ye are, Joe—so different from anything around here! The way ye talk, the way ye move, the gay look in your eyes! No miner ever had that happy look, Joe; me heart stops beatin' almost when ye look at me!" She stopped with a sharp catching of her breath, and he saw that she was struggling for self-control. After a moment she exclaimed, defiantly: "But they'd tell ye, be careful, ye daren't love that kind of man; ye'd only have your heart broken!"

There was silence. For this problem the amateur sociologist had no solution at hand—whether for the abstract question, or for its concrete application!

SECTION 31.

Mary forced herself to go on. "This is how I've worked it out, Joe! I said to meself, 'Ye love this man; and it's his *love* ye want—nothin' else! If he's got a place in the world, ye'd only hold him back—and ye'd not want to do that. Ye don't want his name, or his friends, or any of those things—ye want *him*!' Have ye ever heard of such a thing as that?"

Her cheeks were flaming, but she continued to meet his gaze. "Yes, I've heard of it," he answered, in a low voice.

"What would ye say to it? Is it honest? The Reverend Spragg would say 'twas the devil, no doubt; Father O'Gorman, down in Pedro, would call it mortal sin; and maybe they know—but I don't! I only know I can't stand it any more!"

Tears sprang to her eyes, and she cried out suddenly, "Oh, take me away from here! Take me away and give me a chance, Joe! I'll ask nothing, I'll never stand in your way; I'll work for ye, I'll cook and wash and do everything for ye, I'll wear my fingers to the bone! Or I'll go out and work at some job, and earn my share. And I'll make ye this promise—if ever ye get tired and want to leave me, ye'll not hear a word of complaint!"

She made no conscious appeal to his senses; she sat gazing at him honestly through her tears, and that made it all the harder to answer her.

What could he say? He felt the old dangerous impulse—to take the girl in his arms and comfort her. When finally he spoke it was with an effort to keep his voice calm. "I'd say yes, Mary, if I thought it would work."

"It *would* work! It would, Joe! Ye can quit when ye want to. I mean it!"

"There's no woman lives who can be happy on such terms, Mary. She wants her man, and she wants him to herself, and she wants him always; she's only deluding herself if she believes anything else. You're over-wrought now, what you've seen in the last few days has made you wild—"

"No!" she exclaimed. "'Tis not only that! I been thinkin' about it for weeks."

"I know. You've been thinking, but you wouldn't have spoken if it hadn't been for this horror." He paused for a moment, to renew his own self-possession. "It won't do, Mary," he declared. "I've seen it tried more than once, and I'm not so old either. My own brother tried it once, and ruined himself."

"Ah, ye're afraid to trust me, Joe!"

"No, it's not that; what I mean is—he ruined his own heart, he made himself selfish. He took everything, and gave nothing. He's much older than I, so I've had a chance to see its effect on him. He's cold, he has no faith, even in his own nature; when you talk to him about making the world better he tells you you're a fool."

"It's another way of bein' afraid of me," she insisted. "Afraid you'd ought to marry me!"

"But, Mary—there's the other girl. I really love her, and I'm promised to her. What can I do?"

"'Tis that I've never believed you loved her," she said, in a whisper. Her eyes fell and she began picking nervously again at the faded blue dress, which was smutted and grease-stained, perhaps from her recent effort with Mrs. Zamboni's brood. Several times Hal thought she was going to speak, but she shut her lips tightly again; he watched her, his heart aching.

When finally she spoke, it was still in a whisper, and there was a note of humility he had never heard from her before. "Ye'll not be wantin' to speak to me, Joe, after what I've said."

"Oh, Mary!" he exclaimed, and caught her hand, "don't say I've made you more unhappy! I want to help you! Won't you let me be your friend—your real, true friend? Let me help you to get out of this trap; you'll have a chance to look about, you'll find a way to be happy—the whole world will seem different to you then, and you'll laugh at the idea that you ever wanted me!"

SECTION 32.

The two of them went back to the pit-mouth. It had been two days since the disaster, and still the fan had not been started, and there was no sign of its being started. The hysteria of the women was growing, and there was a tension in the crowds. Jeff Cotton had brought in a force of men to assist him in keeping order. They had built a fence of barbed wire about the pit-mouth and its approaches, and behind this wire they walked—hard-looking citizens with policemen's "billies," and the bulge of revolvers plainly visible on their hips.

During this long period of waiting, Hal had talks with members of his check-weighman group. They told what had happened while he was in jail, and this reminded him of something which had been driven from his mind by the explosion. Poor old John Edstrom was down in Pedro, perhaps in dire need. Hal went to the old Swede's cabin that night, climbed through a window, and dug up the buried money. There were five five-dollar bills, and he put them in an envelope, addressed them in care of General Delivery, Pedro, and had Mary Burke take them to the post office and register them.

The hours dragged on, and still there was no sign of the pit-mouth being opened. There began to be secret gatherings of the miners and their wives to complain at the conduct of the company; and it was natural that Hal's friends who had started the check-weighman movement, should take the lead in these. They were among the most intelligent of the workers, and saw farther into the meaning of events. They thought, not merely of the men who were trapped under ground at this moment, but of thousands of others who would be trapped through years to come. Hal, especially, was pondering how he could accomplish something definite before he left the camp; for of course he would have to leave soon—Jeff Cotton would remember him, and carry out his threat to get rid of him.

Newspapers had come in, with accounts of the disaster, and Hal and his friends read these. It was evident that the company had been at pains to have the accounts written from its own point of view. There existed some public sensitiveness on the subject of mine-disasters in this state. The death-rate from accidents was seen to be mounting steadily; the reports of the state mine inspector showed six per thousand in one year, eight and a half in the next, and twenty-one and a half in the next. When fifty or a hundred men were killed in a single accident, and when such accidents kept happening, one on the heels of another, even the most callous public could not help asking questions. So in this case the "G. F. C." had been careful to minimise the loss of life, and to make excuses. The accident had been owing to no fault of the company's; the mine had been regularly sprinkled, both with water and adobe dust, and so the cause of the explosion must have been the carelessness of the men in handling powder.

In Jack David's cabin one night there arose a discussion as to the number of men entombed in the mine. The company's estimate of the number was forty, but Minetti and Olson and David agreed that this was absurd. Any man who went about in the crowds could satisfy himself that there were two or three times as many unaccounted for. And this falsification was deliberate, for the company had a checking system, whereby it knew the name of every man in the mine. But most of these names were unpronounceable Slavish, and the owners of the names had no friends to mention them—at least not in any language understood by American newspaper editors.

It was all a part of the system, declared Jack David: its purpose and effect being to enable the company to go on killing men without paying for them, either in money or in prestige. It occurred to Hal that it might be worth while to contradict these false statements—almost as worth while as to save the men who were at this moment entombed. Any one who came forward to make such a contradiction would of course be giving himself up to the black-list; but then, Hal regarded himself as a man already condemned to that penalty.

Tom Olson spoke up. "What would you do with your contradiction?"

"Give it to the papers," Hal answered.

"But what papers would print it?"

"There are two rival papers in Pedro, aren't there?"

"One owned by Alf Raymond, the sheriff-emperor, and the other by Vagleman, counsel for the 'G. F. C.' Which one would you try?"

"Well then, the outside papers—those in Western City. There are reporters here now, and some one of them would surely take it."

Olson answered, declaring that they would not get any but labour and Socialist papers to print such news. But even that was well worth doing. And Jack David, who was strong for unions and all their activities, put in, "The thing to do is to take a regular census, so as to know exactly how many are in the mine."

The suggestion struck fire, and they agreed to set to work that same evening. It would be a relief to do something, to have something in their minds but despair. They passed the word to Mary Burke, to Rovetta, Klowoski, and others; and at eleven o'clock the next morning they met again, and the lists were put together, and it was found that no less than a hundred and seven men and boys were positively known to be inside Number One.

SECTION 33.

As it happened, however, discussion of this list and the method of giving it to the world was cut short by a more urgent matter. Jack David came in with news of fresh trouble at the pit-mouth. The new fan was being put in place; but they were slow about it, so slow that some people had become convinced that they did not mean to start the fan at all, but were keeping the mine sealed to prevent the fire from spreading. A group of such malcontents had presumed to go to Mr. Carmichael, the deputy state mine-inspector, to urge him to take some action; and the leader of these protestants, Huszar, the Austrian, who had been one of Hal's check-weighman group, had been taken into custody and marched at double-quick to the gate of the stockade!

Jack David declared furthermore that he knew a carpenter who was working in the fan-house, and who said that no haste whatever was being made. All the men at the fan-house shared that opinion; the mine was sealed, and would stay sealed until the company was sure the fire was out.

"But," argued Hal, "if they were to open it, the fire would spread; and wouldn't that prevent rescue work?"

"Not at all," declared "Big Jack." He explained that by reversing the fan they could draw the smoke up through the air-course, which would clear the main passages for a time. "But, you see, some coal might catch fire, and some timbers; there might be falls of rock so they couldn't work some of the rooms again."

"How long will they keep the mine sealed?" cried Hal, in consternation.

"Nobody can say. In a big mine like that, a fire might smoulder for a week."

"Everybody be dead!" cried Rosa Minetti, wringing her hands in a sudden access of grief.

Hal turned to Olson. "Would they possibly do such a thing?"

"It's been done—more than once," was the organiser's reply.

"Did you never hear about Cherry, Illinois?" asked David. "They did it there, and more than three hundred people lost their lives." He went on to tell that dreadful story, known to every coal-miner. They had sealed the mine, while women fainted and men tore their clothes in frenzy—some going insane. They had kept it sealed for two weeks, and when they opened it, there were twenty-one men still alive!

"They did the same thing in Diamondville, Wyoming," added Olson. "They built up a barrier, and when they took it away they found a heap of dead men, who had crawled to it and torn their fingers to the bone trying to break through."

"My God!" cried Hal, springing to his feet. "And this man Carmichael—would he stand for that?"

"He'd tell you they were doing their best," said "Big Jack." "And maybe he thinks they are. But you'll see—something'll keep happening; they'll drag on from day to day, and they'll not start the fan till they're ready."

"Why, it's murder!" cried Hal.

"It's business," said Tom Olson, quietly.

Hal looked from one to another of the faces of these working people. Not one but had friends in that trap; not one but might be in the same trap to-morrow!

"You have to stand it!" he exclaimed, half to himself.

"Don't you see the guards at the pit-mouth?" answered David. "Don't you see the guns sticking out of their pockets?"

"They bring in more guards this morning," put in Jerry Minetti. "Rosa, she see them get off."

"They know what they doin'!" said Rosa. "They only fraid we find it out! They told Mrs. Zamboni she keep away or they send her out of camp. And old Mrs. Jonotch—her husband and three sons inside!"

"They're getting rougher and rougher," declared Mrs. David. "That big fellow they call Pete, that came up from Pedro—the way he's handling the women is a shame!"

"I know him," put in Olson; "Pete Hanun. They had him in Sheridan when the union first opened headquarters. He smashed one of our organisers in the mouth and broke four of his teeth. They say he has a jail-record."

All through the previous year at college Hal had listened to lectures upon political economy, filled with the praises of a thing called "Private Ownership." This Private Ownership developed initiative and economy; it kept the wheels of industry a-roll, it kept fat the pay-rolls of college faculties; it accorded itself with the sacred laws of supply and demand, it was the basis of the progress and prosperity wherewith America had been blessed. And here suddenly Hal found himself face to face with the reality of it; he saw its wolfish eyes glaring into his own, he felt its smoking hot breath in his face, he saw its gleaming fangs and claw-like fingers, dripping with the blood of men and women and children. Private Ownership of coal-mines! Private Ownership of sealed-up entrances and non-existent escape-ways! Private Ownership of fans which did not start, of sprinklers which did not sprinkle. Private Ownership of clubs and revolvers, and of thugs and ex-convicts to use them, driving away rescuers and shutting up agonised widows and orphans in their homes! Oh, the serene and well-fed priests of Private Ownership, chanting in academic halls the praises of the bloody Demon!

Suddenly Hal stopped still. Something had risen in him, the existence of which he had never suspected. There was a new look upon his face, his voice was deep as a strong man's when he spoke: "I am going to make them open that mine!"

They looked at him. They were all of them close to the border of hysteria, but they caught the strange note in his utterance. "I am going to make them open that mine!"

"How?" asked Olson.

"The public doesn't know about this thing. If the story got out, there'd be such a clamour, it couldn't go on!"

"But how will you get it out?"

"I'll give it to the newspapers! They can't suppress such a thing—I don't care how prejudiced they are!"

"But do you think they'd believe what a miner's buddy tells them?" asked Mrs. David.

"I'll find a way to make them believe me," said Hal. "I'm going to make them open that mine!"

SECTION 34.

In the course of his wanderings about the camp, Hal had observed several wide-awake looking young men with notebooks in their hands. He could see that these young men were being made guests of the company, chatting with the bosses upon friendly terms; nevertheless, he believed that among them he might find one who had a conscience—or at any rate who would yield to the temptation of a "scoop." So, leaving the gathering at Mrs. David's, Hal went to the pit-mouth, watching out for one of these reporters; when he found him, he followed him for a while, desiring to get him where no company "spotter" might interfere. At the first chance, he stepped up, and politely asked the reporter to come into a side street, where they might converse undisturbed.

The reporter obeyed the request; and Hal, concealing the intensity of his feelings, so as not to repel the other, let it be known that he had worked in North Valley for some months, and could tell much about conditions in the camp. There was the matter of adobe-dust, for example. Explosions in dry mines could be prevented by spraying the walls with this material. Did the reporter happen to know that the company's claim to have used it was entirely false?

No, the reporter answered, he did not know this. He seemed interested, and asked Hal's name and occupation. Hal told him "Joe Smith," a "buddy," who had recently been chosen as check-weighman. The reporter, a lean and keen-faced young man, asked many questions—intelligent questions; incidentally he mentioned that he was the local correspondent of the great press association whose stories of the disaster were sent to every corner of the country. This seemed to Hal an extraordinary piece of good fortune, and he proceeded to tell this Mr. Graham about the census which some of the workers had taken; they were able to give the names of a hundred and seven men and boys who were inside the mine. The list was at Mr. Graham's disposal if he cared to see it. Mr. Graham seemed more interested than ever, and made notes in his book.

Another thing, more important yet, Hal continued; the matter of the delay in getting the fan started. It had been three days since the explosion, but there had been no attempt at entering the mine. Had Mr. Graham seen the disturbance at the pit-mouth that morning? Did he realise that a man had been thrown out of camp merely because he had appealed to the deputy state mine-inspector? Hal told what so many had come to believe—that the company was saving property at the expense of life. He went on to point out the human meaning of this—he told about old Mrs. Rafferty, with her failing health and her eight children; about Mrs. Zamboni, with eleven children; about Mrs. Jonotch, with a husband and three sons in the mine. Led on by the reporter's interest, Hal began to show some of his feeling. These were human beings, not animals; they loved and suffered, even though they were poor and humble!

"Most certainly!" said Mr. Graham. "You're right, and you may rest assured I'll look into this."

"There's one thing more," said Hal. "If my name is mentioned, I'll be fired, you know."

"I won't mention it," said the other.

"Of course, if you can't publish the story without giving its source—"

"I'm the source," said the reporter, with a smile. "Your name would not add anything."

He spoke with quiet assurance; he seemed to know so completely both the situation and his own duty in regard to it, that Hal felt a thrill of triumph. It was as if a strong wind had come blowing from the outside world, dispelling the miasma which hung over this coal-camp. Yes, this reporter *was* the outside world! He was the power of public opinion, making itself felt in this place of knavery and fear! He was the voice of truth, the courage and rectitude of a great organisation of publicity, independent of secret influences, lifted above corruption!

"I'm indebted to you," said Mr. Graham, at the end, and Hal's sense of victory was complete. What an extraordinary chance—that he should have run into the agent of the great press association! The story would go out to the great world of industry, which depended upon coal as its life-blood. The men in the factories, the wheels of which were turned by coal—the travellers on trains which were moved by coal—they would hear at last of the sufferings of those who toiled in the bowels of the earth for them! Even the ladies, reclining upon the decks of palatial steamships in gleaming tropic seas—so marvellous was the power of modern news-spreading agencies, that these ladies too might hear the cry for help of these toilers, and of their wives and little ones! And from this great world would come an answer, a universal shout of horror, of execration, that would force even old Peter Harrigan to give way! So Hal mused—for he was young, and this was his first crusade.

He was so happy that he was able to think of himself again, and to realise that he had not eaten that day. It was noon-time, and he went into Reminitsky's, and was about half through with the first course of Reminitsky's two-course banquet, when his cruel disillusioning fell upon him!

He looked up and saw Jeff Cotton striding into the dining-room, making straight for him. There was blood in the marshal's eye, and Hal saw it, and rose, instinctively.

"Come!" said Cotton, and took him by the coat-sleeve and marched him out, almost before the rest of the diners had time to catch their breath.

Hal had no opportunity now to display his "tea-party manners" to the camp-marshal. As they walked, Cotton expressed his opinion of him, that he was a skunk, a puppy, a person of undesirable ancestry; and when Hal endeavoured to ask a question—which he did quite genuinely, not grasping at once the meaning of what was happening—the marshal bade him "shut his face," and emphasised the command by a twist at his coat-collar. At the same time two of the huskiest mine-guards, who had been waiting at the dining-room door, took him, one by each arm, and assisted his progress.

They went down the street and past Jeff Cotton's office, not stopping this time. Their destination was the railroad-station, and when Hal got there, he saw a train standing. The three men marched him to it, not releasing him till they had jammed him down into a seat.

"Now, young fellow," said Cotton, "we'll see who's running this camp!"

By this time Hal had regained a part of his self-possession. "Do I need a ticket?" he asked.

"I'll see to that," said the marshal.

"And do I get my things?"

"You save some questions for your college professors," snapped the marshal.

So Hal waited; and a minute or two later a man arrived on the run with his scanty belongings, rolled into a bundle and tied with a piece of twine. Hal noted that this man was big and ugly, and was addressed by the camp-marshal as "Pete."

The conductor shouted, "All aboard!" And at the same time Jeff Cotton leaned over towards Hal and spoke in a menacing whisper: "Take this from me, young fellow; don't stop in Pedro, move on in a hurry, or something will happen to you on a dark night."

After which he strode down the aisle, and jumped off the moving train. But Hal noticed that Pete Hanun, the breaker of teeth, stayed on the car a few seats behind him.

BOOK THREE — THE HENCHMEN OF KING COAL

SECTION 1.

It was Hal's intention to get to Western City as quickly as possible to call upon the newspaper editors. But first he must have money to travel, and the best way he could think of to get it was to find John Edstrom. He left the train, followed by Pete Hanun; after some inquiry, he came upon the undertaker who had buried Edstrom's wife, and who told him where the old Swede was staying, in the home of a labouring-man nearby.

Edstrom greeted him with eager questions: Who had been killed? What was the situation? Hal told in brief sentences what had happened. When he mentioned his need of money, Edstrom answered that he had a little, and would lend it, but it was not enough for a ticket to Western City. Hal asked about the twenty-five dollars which Mary Burke had sent by registered mail; the old man had heard nothing about it, he had not been to the post-office. "Let's go now!" said Hal, at once; but as they were starting downstairs, a fresh difficulty occurred to him. Pete Hanun was on the street outside, and it was likely that he had heard about this money from Jeff Cotton; he might hold Edstrom up and take it away.

"Let me suggest something," put in the old man. "Come and see my friend Ed MacKellar. He may be able to give us some advice—even to think of some way to get the mine open." Edstrom explained that MacKellar, an old Scotchman, had been a miner, but was now crippled, and held some petty office in Pedro. He was a persistent opponent of "Alf" Raymond's machine, and they had almost killed him on one occasion. His home was not far away, and it would take little time to consult him.

"All right," said Hal, and they set out at once. Pete Hanun followed them, not more than a dozen yards behind, but did not interfere, and they turned in at the gate of a little cottage. A woman opened the door for them, and asked them into the dining-room where MacKellar was sitting—a grey-haired old man, twisted up with rheumatism and obliged to go about on crutches.

Hal told his story. As the Scotchman had been brought up in the mines, it was not necessary to go into details about the situation. When Hal told his idea of appealing to the newspapers, the other responded at once, "You won't have to go to Western City. There's a man right here who'll do the business for you; Keating, of the *Gazette*."

"The Western City *Gazette?*" exclaimed Hal. He knew this paper; an evening journal selling for a cent, and read by working-men. Persons of culture who referred to it disposed of it with the adjective "yellow."

"I know," said MacKellar, noting Hal's tone. "But it's the only paper that will publish your story anyway."

"Where is this Keating?"

"He's been up at the mine. It's too bad you didn't meet him."

"Can we get hold of him now?"

"He might be in Pedro. Try the American Hotel."

Hal went to the telephone, and in a minute was hearing for the first time the cheery voice of his friend and lieutenant-to-be, "Billy" Keating. In a couple of minutes more the owner of the voice was at MacKellar's door, wiping the perspiration from his half-bald forehead. He was round-faced, like a full moon, and as jolly as Falstaff; when you got to know him better, you discovered that he was loyal as a Newfoundland dog. For all his bulk, Keating was a newspaper man, every inch of him "on the job."

He started to question the young miner as soon as he was introduced, and it quickly became clear to Hal that here was the man he was looking for. Keating knew exactly what questions to ask, and had the whole story in a few minutes. "By thunder!" he cried. "My last edition!" And he pulled out his watch, and sprang to the telephone. "Long distance," he called; then, "I want the city editor of the Western City *Gazette*. And, operator, please see if you can't rush it through. It's very urgent, and last time I had to wait nearly half an hour."

He turned back to Hal, and proceeded to ask more questions, at the same time pulling a bunch of copy-paper from his pocket and making notes. He got all Hal's statements about the lack of sprinkling, the absence of escape-ways, the delay in starting the fan, the concealing of the number of men in the mine. "I knew things were crooked up there!" he exclaimed. "But I couldn't get a lead! They kept a man with me every minute of the time. You know a fellow named Predovich?"

"I do," said Hal. "The company store-clerk; he once went through my pockets."

Keating made a face of disgust. "Well, he was my chaperon. Imagine trying to get the miners to talk to you with that sneak at your heels! I said to the superintendent, 'I don't need anybody to escort me around your place.' And he looked at me with a nasty little smile. 'We wouldn't want anything to happen to you while you're in this camp, Mr. Keating.' 'You don't consider it necessary to protect the lives of the other reporters,' I said. 'No,' said he; 'but the *Gazette* has made a great many enemies, you know.' 'Drop your fooling, Mr. Cartwright,' I said. 'You propose to have me shadowed while I'm working on this assignment?' 'You can put it that way,' he answered, 'if you think it'll please the readers of the *Gazette*.'"

"Too bad we didn't meet!" said Hal. "Or if you'd run into any of our check-weighman crowd!"

"Oh! You know about that check-weighman business!" exclaimed the reporter. "I got a hint of it—that's how I happened to be down here to-day. I heard there was a man named Edstrom, who'd been shut out for making trouble; and I thought if I could find him, I might get a lead."

Hal and MacKellar looked at the old Swede, and the three of them began to laugh. "Here's your man!" said MacKellar.

"And here's your check-weighman!" added Edstrom, pointing to Hal.

Instantly the reporter was on his job again; he began to fire another series of questions. He would use that check-weighman story as a "follow-up" for the next day, to keep the subject of North Valley alive. The story had a direct bearing on the disaster, because it showed what the North Valley bosses were doing when they should have been looking after the safety of their mine. "I'll write it out this afternoon and send it by mail," said Keating; he added, with a smile, "That's one advantage of handling news the other papers won't touch—you don't have to worry about losing your 'scoops'!"

<h1 style="text-align:center">SECTION 2.</h1>

Keating went to the telephone again, to worry "long distance"; then, grumbling about his last edition, he came back to ask more questions about Hal's experiences. Before long he drew out the story of the young man's first effort in the publicity game; at which he sank back in his chair, and laughed until he shook, as the nursery-rhyme describes it, "like a bowlful of jelly."

"Graham!" he exclaimed. "Fancy, MacKellar, he took that story to Graham!"

The Scotchman seemed to find it equally funny; together they explained that Graham was the political reporter of the *Eagle*, the paper in Pedro which was owned by the Sheriff-emperor. One might call him Alf Raymond's journalistic jackal; there was no job too dirty for him.

"But," cried Hal, "he told me he was correspondent for the Western press association!"

"He's that, too," replied Billy.

"But does the press association employ spies for the 'G. F. C.'?"

The reporter answered, drily, "When you understand the news game better, you'll realise that the one thing the press association cares about in a correspondent is that he should have respect for property. If respect for property is the backbone of his being, he can learn what news is, and the right way to handle it."

Keating turned to the Scotchman. "Do you happen to have a typewriter in the house, Mr. MacKellar?"

"An old one," said the other—"lame, like myself."

"I'll make out with it. I'd ask this young man over to my hotel, but I think he'd better keep off the streets as much as possible."

"You're right. If you take my advice, you'll take the typewriter upstairs, where there's no chance of a shot through the window."

"Great heavens!" exclaimed Hal. "Is this America, or mediaeval Italy?"

"It's the Empire of Raymond," replied MacKellar. "They shot my friend Tom Burton dead while he stood on the steps of his home. He was opposing the machine, and had evidence about ballot-frauds he was going to put before the Grand Jury."

While Keating continued to fret with "long distance," the old Scotchman went on trying to impress upon Hal the danger of his position. Quite recently an organiser of the miners' union had been beaten up in broad day-light and left insensible on the sidewalk; MacKellar had watched the trial and acquittal of the two thugs who had committed this crime—the foreman of the jury being a saloon-keeper one of Raymond's heelers, and the other jurymen being Mexicans, unable to comprehend a word of the court proceedings.

"Exactly such a jury as Jeff Cotton promised me!" remarked Hal, with a feeble attempt at a smile.

"Yes," answered the other; "and don't make any mistake about it, if they want to put you away, they can do it. They run the whole machine here. I know how it is, for I had a political job myself, until they found they couldn't use me."

The old Scotchman went on to explain that he had been elected justice of peace, and had tried to break up the business of policemen taking money from the women of the town; he had been forced to resign, and his enemies had made his life a torment. Recently he had been candidate for district judge on the Progressive ticket, and told of his efforts to carry on a campaign in the coal-camps—how his circulars had been confiscated, his posters torn down, his supporters "kangarooed." It was exactly as Alec Stone, the pit-boss, had explained to Hal. In some of the camps the meeting-halls belonged to the company; in others they belonged to saloon-keepers whose credit depended upon Alf Raymond. In the few places where there were halls that could be hired, the machine had gone to the extreme of sending in rival entertainments, furnishing free music and free beer in order to keep the crowds away from MacKellar.

All this time Billy Keating had been chafing and scolding at "long distance." Now at last he managed to get his call, and silence fell in the room. "Hello, Pringle, that you? This is Keating. Got a big story on the North Valley disaster. Last edition put to bed yet? Put Jim on the wire. Hello, Jim! Got your book?" And then Billy, evidently talking to a stenographer, began to tell the story he had got from Hal. Now and then he would stop to repeat or spell a word; once or twice Hal corrected him on details. So, in about a quarter of an hour, they put the job through; and Keating turned to Hal.

"There you are, son," said he. "Your story'll be on the street in Western City in a little over an hour; it'll be down here as soon thereafter as they can get telephone connections. And take my advice, if you want to keep a whole skin, you'll be out of Pedro when that happens!"

<h1>SECTION 3.</h1>

When Hal spoke, he did not answer Billy Keating's last remark. He had been listening to a retelling of the North Valley disaster over the telephone; so he was not thinking about his skin, but about a hundred and seven men and boys buried inside a mine.

"Mr. Keating," said he, "are you sure the *Gazette* will print that story?"

"Good Lord!" exclaimed the other. "What am I here for?"

"Well, I've been disappointed once, you know."

"Yes, but you got into the wrong camp. We're a poor man's paper, and this is what we live on."

"There's no chance of its being 'toned down'?"

"Not the slightest, I assure you."

"There's no chance of Peter Harrigan's suppressing it?"

"Peter Harrigan made his attempts on the *Gazette* long ago, my boy."

"Well," said Hal, "and now tell me this—will it do the work?"

"In what way?"

"I mean—in making them open the mine."

Keating considered for a moment. "I'm afraid it won't do much."

Hal looked at him blankly. He had taken it for granted the publication of the facts would force the company to move. But Keating explained that the *Gazette* read mainly by working-people, and so had comparatively little influence. "We're an afternoon paper," he said; "and when people have been reading lies all morning, it's not easy to make them believe the truth in the afternoon."

"But won't the story go to other papers—over the country, I mean?"

"Yes, we have a press service; but the papers are all like the *Gazette*—poor man's papers. If there's something very raw, and we keep pounding away for a long time, we can make an impression; at least we limit the amount of news the Western press association can suppress. But when it comes to a small matter like sealing up workingmen in a mine, all we can do is to worry the 'G. F. C.' a little."

So Hal was just where he had begun! "I must find some other plan," he exclaimed.

"I don't see what you can do," replied the other.

There was a pause, while the young miner pondered. "I had thought of going up to Western City and appealing to the editors," he said, a little uncertainly.

"Well, I can tell you about that—you might as well save your car-fare. They wouldn't touch your story."

"And if I appealed to the Governor?"

"In the first place, he probably wouldn't see you. And if he did, he wouldn't do anything. He's not really the Governor, you know; he's a puppet put up there to fool you. He only moves when Harrigan pulls a string."

"Of course I knew he was Old Peter's man," said Hal. "But then"—and he concluded, somewhat lamely, "What *can* I do?"

A smile of pity came upon the reporter's face. "I can see this is the first time you've been up against 'big business.'" And then he added, "You're young! When you've had more experience, you'll leave these problems to older heads!" But Hal failed to get the reporter's sarcasm. He had heard these exact words in such deadly seriousness from his brother! Besides, he had just come from scenes of horror.

"But don't you see, Mr. Keating?" he exclaimed. "It's impossible for me to sit still while those men die?"

"I don't know about your sitting still," said the other. "All I know is that all your moving about isn't going to do them any good."

Hal turned to Edstrom and MacKellar. "Gentlemen," he said, "listen to me for a minute." And there was a note of pleading in his voice—as if he thought they were deliberately refusing to help him! "We've got to do something about this. We've *got* to do something! I'm new at the game, as Mr. Keating says; but you aren't. Put your minds on it, gentlemen, and help me work out a plan!"

There was a long silence. "God knows," said Edstrom, at last. "I'd suggest something if I could."

"And I, too," said MacKellar. "You're up against a stone-wall, my boy. The government here is simply a department of the 'G. F. C.' The officials are crooks—company servants, all of them."

"Just a moment now," said Hal. "Let's consider. Suppose we had a real government—what steps would we take? We'd carry such a case to the District Attorney, wouldn't we?"

"Yes, no doubt of it," said MacKellar.

"You mentioned him before," said Hal. "He threatened to prosecute some mine-superintendents for ballot-frauds, you said."

"That was while he was running for election," said MacKellar.

"Oh! I remember what Jeff Cotton said—that he was friendly to the miners in his speeches, and to the companies in his acts."

"That's the man," said the other, drily.

"Well," argued Hal, "oughtn't I go to him, to give him a chance, at least? You can't tell, he might have a heart inside him."

"It isn't a heart he needs," replied MacKellar; "it's a back-bone."

"But surely I ought to put it up to him! If he won't do anything, at least I'll put him on record, and it'll make another story for you, won't it, Mr. Keating?"

"Yes, that's true," admitted the reporter. "What would you ask him to do?"

"Why, to lay the matter before the Grand Jury; to bring indictments against the North Valley bosses."

"But that would take a long time; it wouldn't save the men in the mine."

"What might save them would be the threat of it." MacKellar put in. "I don't think any threat of Dick Barker's would count for that much. The bosses know they could stop him."

"Well, isn't there somebody else? Shouldn't I try the courts?"

"What courts?"

"I don't know. You tell me."

"Well," said the Scotchman, "to begin at the bottom, there's a justice of the peace."

"Who's he?"

"Jim Anderson, a horse-doctor. He's like any other J.P. you ever knew—he lives on petty graft."

"Is there a higher court?"

"Yes, the district court; Judge Denton. He's the law-partner of Vagleman, counsel for the 'G. F. C.' How far would you expect to get with him?"

"I suppose I'm clutching at straws," said Hal. "But they say that's what a drowning man does. Anyway, I'm going to see these people, and maybe out of the lot of them I can find one who'll act. It can't do any harm!"

The three men thought of some harm it might do; they tried to make Hal consider the danger of being slugged Or shot. "They'll do it!" exclaimed MacKellar. "And no trouble for them—they'll prove you were stabbed by a drunken Dago, quarrelling over some woman."

But Hal had got his head set; he believed he could put this job through before his enemies had time to lay any plans. Nor would he let any of his friends accompany him; he had something more important for both Edstrom and Keating to do—and as for MacKellar, he could not get about rapidly enough. Hal bade Edstrom go to the post-office and get the registered letter, and proceed at once to change the bills. It was his plan to make out affidavits, and if the officials here would not act, to take the affidavits to the Governor. And for this he would need money. Meantime, he said, let Billy Keating write out the check-weighman story, and in a couple of hours meet him at the American Hotel, to get copies of the affidavits for the *Gazette*.

Hal was still wearing the miner's clothes he had worn on the night of his arrest in Edstrom's cabin. But he declined MacKellar's offer to lend him a business-suit; the old Scotchman's clothes would not fit him, he knew, and it would be better to make his appeal as a real miner than as a misfit gentleman.

These matters being settled, Hal went out upon the street, where Pete Hanun, the breaker of teeth, fell in behind him. The young miner at once broke into a run, and the other followed suit, and so the two of them sped down the street, to the wonder of people on the way. As Hal had had practice as a sprinter, no doubt Pete was glad that the District Attorney's office was not far away!

<h1 style="text-align:center">SECTION 4.</h1>

Mr. Richard Parker was busy, said the clerk in toe outer office; for which Hal was not sorry, as it gave him a chance to get his breath. Seeing a young man flushed and panting, the clerk stared with curiosity; but Hal offered no explanation, and the breaker of teeth waited on the street outside.

Mr. Parker received his caller in a couple of minutes. He was a well-fed gentleman with generous neck and chin, freshly shaved and rubbed with talcum powder. His clothing was handsome, his linen immaculate; one got the impression of a person who "did himself well." There were papers on his desk, and he looked preoccupied.

"Well?" said he, with a swift glance at the young miner.

"I understand that I am speaking to the District Attorney of Pedro County?"

"That's right."

"Mr. Parker, have you given any attention to the circumstances of the North Valley disaster?"

"No," said Mr. Parker. "Why?"

"I have just come from North Valley, and I can give you information which may be of interest to you. There are a hundred and seven people entombed in the mine, and the company officials have sealed it, and are sacrificing those lives."

The other put down the correspondence, and made an examination of his caller from under his heavy eyelids. "How do you know this?"

"I left there only a few hours ago. The facts are known to all the workers in the camp."

"You are speaking from what you heard?"

"I am speaking from what I know at first hand. I saw the disaster, I saw the pit-mouth boarded over and covered with canvas. I know a man who was driven out of camp this morning for complaining about the delay in starting the fan. It has been over three days since the explosion, and still nothing has been done."

Mr. Parker proceeded to fire a series of questions, in the sharp, suspicious manner customary to prosecuting officials. But Hal did not mind that; it was the man's business to make sure.

Presently he demanded to know how he could get corroboration of Hal's statements.

"You'll have to go up there," was the reply.

"You say the facts are known to the men. Give me the names of some of them."

"I have no authority to give their names, Mr. Parker."

"What authority do you need? They will tell me, won't they?"

"They may, and they may not. One man has already lost his job; not every man cares to lose his job."

"You expect me to go up there on your bare say-so?"

"I offer you more than my say-so. I offer an affidavit."

"But what do I know about you?"

"You know that I worked in North Valley—or you can verify the fact by using the telephone. My name is Joe Smith, and I was a miner's helper in Number Two."

But that was not sufficient, said Mr. Parker; his time was valuable, and before he took a trip to North Valley he must have the names of witnesses who would corroborate these statements.

"I offer you an affidavit!" exclaimed Hal. "I say that I have knowledge that a crime is being committed—that a hundred and seven human lives are being sacrificed. You don't consider that a sufficient reason for even making inquiry?"

The District Attorney answered again that he desired to do his duty, he desired to protect the workers in their rights; but he could not afford to go off on a "wild goose chase," he must have the names of witnesses. And Hal found himself wondering. Was the man merely taking the first pretext for doing nothing? Or could it be that an official of the state would go as far as to help the company by listing the names of "trouble-makers"?

In spite of his distrust, Hal was resolved to give the man every chance he could. He went over the whole story of the disaster. He took Mr. Parker up to the camp, showed him the agonised women and terrified children crowding about the pit-mouth, driven back with clubs and revolvers. He named family after family, widows and mothers and orphans. He told of the miners clamouring for a chance to risk their lives to save their fellows. He let his own feelings sweep him along; he pleaded with fervour for his suffering friends.

"Young man," said the other, breaking in upon his eloquence, "how long have you been working in North Valley?"

"About ten weeks."

"How long have you been working in coal-mines?"

"That was my first experience."

"And you think that in ten weeks you have learned enough to entitle you to bring a charge of 'murder' against men who have spent their lives in learning the business of mining?"

"As I have told you," exclaimed Hal, "it's not merely my opinion; it's the opinion of the oldest and most experienced of the miners. I tell you no effort whatever is being made to save those men! The bosses care nothing about their men! One of them, Alec Stone, was heard by a crowd of people to say, 'Damn the men! Save the mules!'"

"Everybody up there is excited," declared the other. "Nobody can think straight at present—you can't think straight yourself. If the mine's on fire, and if the fire is spreading to such an extent that it can't be put out—"

"But, Mr. Parker, how can you say that it's spreading to such an extent?"

"Well, how can you say that it isn't?"

There was a pause. "I understand there's a deputy mine-inspector up there," said the District Attorney, suddenly. "What's his name?"

"Carmichael," said Hal.

"Well, and what does *he* say about it?"

"It was for appealing to him that the miner, Huszar, was turned out of camp."

"Well," said Mr. Parker—and there came a note into his voice by which Hal knew that he had found the excuse he sought—"Well, it's Carmichael's business, and I have no right to butt in on it. If he comes to me and asks for indictments, I'll act—but not otherwise. That's all I have to say about it."

And Hal rose. "Very well, Mr. Parker," said he. "I have put the facts before you. I was told you wouldn't do anything, but I wanted to give you a chance. Now I'm going to ask the Governor for your removal!" And with these words the young miner strode out of the office.

SECTION 5.

Hal went down the street to the American Hotel, where there was a public stenographer. When this young woman discovered the nature of the material he proposed to dictate, her fingers trembled visibly; but she did not refuse the task, and Hal proceeded to set forth the circumstances of the sealing of the pit-mouth of Number One Mine at North Valley, and to pray for warrants for the arrest of Enos Cartwright and Alec Stone. Then he gave an account of how he had been selected as check-weighman and been refused access to the scales; and with all the legal phraseology he could rake up, he prayed for the arrest of Enos Cartwright and James Peters, superintendent and tipple-boss at North Valley, for these offences. In another affidavit he narrated how Jeff Cotton, camp-marshal, had seized him at night, mistreated him, and shut him in prison for thirty-six hours without warrant or charge; also how Cotton, Pete Hanun, and two other parties by name unknown, had illegally driven him from the town of North Valley, threatening him with violence; for which he prayed the arrest of Jeff Cotton, Pete Hanun, and the two parties unknown.

Before this task was finished, Billy Keating came in, bringing the twenty-five dollars which Edstrom had got from the post-office. They found a notary public, before whom Hal made oath to each document; and when these had been duly inscribed and stamped with the seal of the state, he gave carbon copies to Keating, who hurried off to catch a mail-train which was just due. Billy would not trust such things to the local post-office; for Pedro was the hell of a town, he declared. As they went out on the street again they noticed that their body-guard had been increased by another husky-looking personage, who made no attempt to conceal what he was doing.

Hal went around the corner to an office bearing the legend, "J.W. Anderson, Justice of the Peace."

Jim Anderson, the horse-doctor, sat at his desk within. He had evidently chewed tobacco before he assumed the ermine, and his reddish-coloured moustache still showed the stains. Hal observed such details, trying to weigh his chances of success. He presented the affidavit describing his treatment in North Valley, and sat waiting while His Honour read it through with painful slowness.

"Well," said the man, at last, "what do you want?"

"I want a warrant for Jeff Cotton's arrest."

The other studied him for a minute. "No, young fellow," said he. "You can't get no such warrant here."

"Why not?"

"Because Cotton's a deputy-sheriff; he had a right to arrest you."

"To arrest me without a warrant?"

"How do you know he didn't have a warrant?"

"He admitted to me that he didn't."

"Well, whether he had a warrant or not, it was his business to keep order in the camp."

"You mean he can do anything he pleases in the camp?"

"What I mean is, it ain't my business to interfere. Why didn't you see Si Adams, up to the camp?"

"They didn't give me any chance to see him."

"Well," replied the other, "there's nothing I can do for you. You can see that for yourself. What kind of discipline could they keep in them camps if any fellow that had a kick could come down here and have the marshal arrested?"

"Then a camp-marshal can act without regard to the law?"

"I didn't say that."

"Suppose he had committed murder—would you give a warrant for that?"

"Yes, of course, if it was murder."

"And if you knew that he was in the act of committing murder in a coal-camp—would you try to stop him?"

"Yes, of course."

"Then here's another affidavit," said Hal; and he produced the one about the sealing of the mine. There was silence while Justice Anderson read it through.

But again he shook his head. "No, you can't get no such warrants here."

"Why not?"

"Because it ain't my business to run a coal-mine. I don't understand it, and I'd make a fool of myself if I tried to tell them people how to run their business."

Hal argued with him. Could company officials in charge of a coal-mine commit any sort of outrage upon their employés, and call it running their business? Their control of the mine in such an emergency as this meant the power of life and death over a hundred and seven men and boys; could it be that the law had nothing to say in such a situation? But Mr. Anderson only shook his head; it was not his business to interfere. Hal might go up to the court-house and see Judge Denton about it. So Hal gathered up his affidavits and went out to the street again—where there were now three husky-looking personages waiting to escort him.

SECTION 6.

The district court was in session and Hal sat for a while in the court-room, watching Judge Denton. Here was another prosperous and well-fed appearing gentleman, with a rubicund visage shining over the top of his black silk robe. The young miner found himself regarding both the robe and the visage with suspicion. Could it be that Hal was becoming cynical, and losing his faith in his fellow man? What he thought of, in connection with the Judge's appearance, was that there was a living to be made sitting on the bench, while one's partner appeared before the bench as coal-company counsel!

In an interval of the proceedings, Hal spoke to the clerk, and was told that he might see the judge at four-thirty; but a few minutes later Pete Hanun came in and whispered to this clerk. The clerk looked at Hal, then he went up and whispered to the Judge. At four-thirty, when the court was declared adjourned, the Judge rose and disappeared into his private office; and when Hal applied to the clerk, the latter brought out the message that Judge Denton was too busy to see him.

But Hal was not to be disposed of in that easy fashion. There was a side door to the court-room, with a corridor beyond it, and while he stood arguing with the clerk he saw the rubicund visage of the Judge flit past.

He darted in pursuit. He did not shout or make a disturbance; but when he was close behind his victim, he said, quietly, "Judge Denton, I appeal to you for justice!"

The Judge turned and looked at him, his countenance showing annoyance. "What do you want?"

It was a ticklish moment, for Pete Hanun was at Hal's heels, and it would have needed no more than a nod from the Judge to cause him to collar Hal. But the Judge, taken by surprise, permitted himself to parley with the young miner; and the detective hesitated, and finally fell back a step or two.

Hal repeated his appeal. "Your Honour, there are a hundred and seven men and boys now dying up at the North Valley mine. They are being murdered, and I am trying to save their lives!"

"Young man," said the Judge, "I have an urgent engagement down the street."

"Very well," replied Hal, "I will walk with you and tell you as you go." Nor did he give "His Honour" a chance to say whether this arrangement was pleasing to him; he set out by his side, with Pete Hanun and the other two men some ten yards in the rear.

Hal told the story as he had told it to Mr. Richard Parker; and he received the same response. Such matters were not easy to decide about; they were hardly a Judge's business. There was a state official on the ground, and it was for him to decide if there was violation of law.

Hal repeated his statement that a man who made a complaint to this official had been thrown out of camp. "And I was thrown out also, your Honour."

"What for?"

"Nobody told me what for."

"Tut, tut, young man! They don't throw men out without telling them the reason!"

"But they *do*, your Honour! Shortly before that they locked me up in jail, and held me for thirty-six hours without the slightest show of authority."

"You must have been doing something!"

"What I had done was to be chosen by a committee of miners to act as their check-weighman."

"Their check-weighman?"

"Yes, your Honour. I am informed there's a law providing that when the men demand a check-weighman, and offer to pay for him, the company must permit him to inspect the weights. Is that correct?"

"It is, I believe."

"And there's a penalty for refusing?"

"The law always carries a penalty, young man."

"They tell me that law has been on the statute-books for fifteen or sixteen years, and that the penalty is from twenty-five to five hundred dollars fine. It's a case about which there can be no dispute, your Honour—the miners notified the superintendent that they desired my services, and when I presented myself at the tipple, I was refused access to the scales; then I was seized and shut up in jail, and finally turned out of the camp. I have made affidavit to these facts, and I think I have the right to ask for warrants for the guilty men."

"Can you produce witnesses to your statements?"

"I can, your Honour. One of the committee of miners, John Edstrom, is now in Pedro, having been kept out of his home, which he had rented and paid for. The other, Mike Sikoria, was also thrown out of camp. There are many others at North Valley who know all about it."

There was a pause. Judge Denton for the first time took a good look at the young miner at his side; and then he drew his brows together in solemn thought, and his voice became deep and impressive. "I shall take this matter under advisement. What is your name, and where do you live?"

"Joe Smith, your Honour. I'm staying at Edward MacKellar's, but I don't know how long I'll be able to stay there. There are company thugs watching the place all the time."

"That's wild talk!" said the Judge, impatiently.

"As it happens," said Hal, "we are being followed by three of them at this moment—one of them the same Pete Hanun who helped to drive me out of North Valley. If you will turn your head you will see them behind us."

But the portly Judge did not turn his head.

"I have been informed," Hal continued, "that I am taking my life in my hands by my present course of action. I believe I'm entitled to ask for protection."

"What do you want me to do?"

"To begin with, I'd like you to cause the arrest of the men who are shadowing me."

"It's not my business to cause such arrests. You should apply to a policeman."

"I don't see any policeman. Will you tell me where to find one?"

His Honour was growing weary of such persistence. "Young man, what's the matter with you is that you've been reading dime novels, and they've got on your nerves!"

"But the men are right behind me, your Honour! Look at them!"

"I've told you it's not my business, young man!"

"But, your Honour, before I can find a policeman I may be dead!"

The other appeared to be untroubled by this possibility.

"And, your Honour, while you are taking these matters under advisement, the men in the mine will be dead!"

Again there was no reply.

"I have some affidavits here," said Hal. "Do you wish them?"

"You can give them to me if you want to," said the other.

"You don't ask me for them?"

"I haven't yet."

"Then just one more question—if you will pardon me, your Honour. Can you tell me where I can find an honest lawyer in this town—a man who might be willing to take a case against the interests of the General Fuel Company?"

There was a silence—a long, long silence. Judge Denton, of the firm of Denton and Vagleman, stared straight in front of him as he walked. Whatever complicated processes might have been going on inside his mind, his judicial features did not reveal them. "No, young man," he said at last, "it's not my business to give you information about lawyers." And with that the judge turned on his heel and went into the Elks' Club.

SECTION 7.

Hal stood and watched the portly figure until it disappeared; then he turned back and passed the three detectives, who stopped. He stared at them, but made no sign, nor did they. Some twenty feet behind him, they fell in and followed as before.

Judge Denton had suggested consulting a policeman; and suddenly Hal noticed that he was passing the City Hall, and it occurred to him that this matter of his being shadowed might properly be brought to the attention of the mayor of Pedro. He wondered what the chief magistrate of such a "hell of a town" might be like; after due inquiry, he found himself in the office of Mr. Ezra Perkins, a mild-mannered little gentleman who had been in the undertaking-business, before he became a figure-head for the so-called "Democratic" machine.

He sat pulling nervously at a neatly trimmed brown beard, trying to wriggle out of the dilemma into which Hal put him. Yes, it might possibly be that a young miner was being followed on the streets of the town; but whether or not this was against the law depended on the circumstances. If he had made a disturbance in North Valley, and there was reason to believe that he might be intending trouble, doubtless the company was keeping track of him. But Pedro was a law-abiding place, and he would be protected in his rights so long as he behaved himself.

Hal replied by citing what MacKellar had told him about men being slugged on the streets in broad day-light. To this Mr. Perkins answered that there was uncertainty about the circumstances of these cases; anyhow, they had happened before he became mayor. His was a reform administration, and he had given strict orders to the Chief of Police that there were to be no more incidents of the sort.

"Will you go with me to the Chief of Police and give him orders now?" demanded Hal.

"I do not consider it necessary," said Mr. Perkins.

He was about to go home, it seemed. He was a pitiful little rodent, and it was a shame to torment him; but Hal stuck to him for ten or twenty minutes longer, arguing and insisting—until finally the little rodent bolted for the door, and made his escape in an automobile. "You can go to the Chief of Police yourself," were his last words, as he started the machine; and Hal decided to follow the suggestion. He had no hope left, but he was possessed by a kind of dogged rage. He *would* not let go!

Upon inquiry of a passer-by, he learned that police headquarters was in this same building, the entrance being just round the corner. He went in, and found a man in uniform writing at a desk, who stated that the Chief had "stepped down the street." Hal sat down to wait, by a window through which he could look out upon the three gunmen loitering across the way.

The man at the desk wrote on, but now and then he eyed the young miner with that hostility which American policemen cultivate toward the lower classes. To Hal this was a new phenomenon, and he found himself suddenly wishing that he had put on MacKellar's clothes. Perhaps a policeman would not have noticed the misfit!

The Chief came in. His blue uniform concealed a burly figure, and his moustache revealed the fact that his errand down the street had had to do with beer. "Well, young fellow?" said he, fixing his gaze upon Hal.

Hal explained his errand.

"What do you want me to do?" asked the Chief, in a decidedly hostile voice.

"I want you to make those men stop following me."

"How can I make them stop?"

"You can lock them up, if necessary. I can point them out to you, if you'll step to the window."

But the other made no move. "I reckon if they're follerin' you, they've got some reason for it. Have you been makin' trouble in the camps?" He asked this question with sudden force, as if it had occurred to him that it might be his duty to lock up Hal.

"No," said Hal, speaking as bravely as he could—"no indeed, I haven't been making trouble. I've only been demanding my rights."

"How do I know what you been doin'?"

The young miner was willing to explain, but the other cut him short. "You behave yourself while you're in this town, young feller, d'you see? If you do, nobody'll bother you."

"But," said Hal, "they've already threatened to bother me."

"What did they say?"

"They said something might happen to me on a dark night."

"Well, so it might—you might fall down and hit your nose."

The Chief was pleased with this wit, but only for a moment. "Understand, young feller, we'll give you your rights in this town, but we got no love for agitators, and we don't pretend to have. See?"

"You call a man an agitator when he demands his legal rights?"

"I ain't got time to argue with you, young feller. It's no easy matter keepin' order in coal-camps, and I ain't going to meddle in the business. I reckon the company detectives has got as good a right in this town as you."

There was a pause. Hal saw that there was nothing to be gained by further discussion with the Chief. It was his first glimpse of the American policeman as he appears to the labouring man in revolt, and he found it an illuminating experience. There was dynamite in his heart as he turned and went out to the street; nor was the amount of the explosive diminished by the mocking grins which he noted upon the faces of Pete Hanun and the other two husky-looking personages.

SECTION 8.

Hal judged that he had now exhausted his legal resources in Pedro; the Chief of Police had not suggested any one else he might call upon, so there seemed nothing he could do but go back to MacKellar's and await the hour of the night train to Western City. He started to give his guardians another run, by way of working off at least a part of his own temper; but he found that they had anticipated this difficulty. An automobile came up and the three of them stepped in. Not to be outdone, Hal engaged a hack, and so the expedition returned in pomp to MacKellar's.

Hal found the old cripple in a state of perturbation. All that afternoon his telephone had been ringing; one person after another had warned him—some pleading with him, some abusing him. It was evident that among them were people who had a hold on the old man; but he was undaunted, and would not hear of Hal's going to stay at the hotel until train-time.

Then Keating returned, with an exciting tale to tell. Schulman, general manager of the "G. F. C.," had been sending out messengers to hunt for him, and finally had got him in his office, arguing and pleading, cajoling and denouncing him by turns. He had got Cartwright on the telephone, and the North Valley superintendent had laboured to convince Keating that he had done the company a wrong. Cartwright had told a story about Hal's efforts to hold up the company for money. "Incidentally," said Keating, "he added the charge that you had seduced a girl in his camp."

Hal stared at his friend. "Seduced a girl!" he exclaimed.

"That's what he said; a red-headed Irish girl."

"Well, damn his soul!"

There followed a silence, broken by a laugh from Billy. "Don't glare at me like that. *I* didn't say it!"

But Hal continued to glare, nevertheless. "The dirty little skunk!"

"Take it easy, sonny," said the fat man, soothingly. "It's quite the usual thing, to drag in a woman. It's so easy—for of course there always *is* a woman. There's one in this case, I suppose?"

"There's a perfectly decent girl."

"But you've been friendly with her? You've been walking around where people can see you?"

"Yes."

"So you see, they've got you. There's nothing you can do about a thing of that sort."

"You wait and see!" Hal burst out.

The other gazed curiously at the angry young miner. "What'll you do? Beat him up some night?"

But the young miner did not answer. "You say he described the girl?"

"He was kind enough to say she was a red-headed beauty, and with no one to protect her but a drunken father. I could understand that must have made it pretty hard for her, in one of these coal-camps." There was a pause. "But see here," said the reporter, "you'll only do the girl harm by making a row. Nobody believes that women in coal-camps have any virtue. God knows, I don't see how they do have, considering the sort of men who run the camps, and the power they have."

"Mr. Keating," said Hal, "did *you* believe what Cartwright told you?"

Keating had started to light a cigar. He stopped in the middle, and his eyes met Hal's. "My dear boy," said he, "I didn't consider it my business to have an opinion."

"But what did you say to Cartwright?"

"Ah! That's another matter. I said that I'd been a newspaper man for a good many years, and I knew his game."

"Thank you for that," said Hal. "You may be interested to know there isn't any truth in the story."

"Glad to hear it," said the other. "I believe you."

"Also you may be interested to know that I shan't drop the matter until I've made Cartwright take it back."

"Well, you're an enterprising cuss!" laughed the reporter. "Haven't you got enough on your hands, with all the men you're going to get out of the mine?"

SECTION 9.

Billy Keating went out again, saying that he knew a man who might be willing to talk to him on the quiet, and give him some idea what was going to happen to Hal. Meantime Hal and Edstrom sat down to dinner with MacKellar. The family were afraid to use the dining-room of their home, but spread a little table in the upstairs hall. The distress of mind of MacKellar's wife and daughter was apparent, and this brought home to Hal the terror of life in this coal-country. Here were American women, in an American home, a home with evidences of refinement and culture; yet they felt and acted as if they were Russian conspirators, in terror of Siberia and the knout!

The reporter was gone a couple of hours; when he came back, he brought news. "You can prepare for trouble, young fellow."

"Why so?"

"Jeff Cotton's in town."

"How do you know?"

"I saw him in an automobile. If he left North Valley at this time, it was for something serious, you may be sure."

"What does he mean to do?"

"There's no telling. He may have you slugged; he may have you run out of town and dumped out in the desert; he may just have you arrested."

Hal considered for a moment. "For slander?"

"Or for vagrancy; or on suspicion of having robbed a bank in Texas, or murdered your great-grandmother in Tasmania. The point is, he'll keep you locked up till this trouble has blown over."

"Well," said Hal, "I don't want to be locked up. I want to go up to Western City. I'm waiting for the train."

"You may have to wait till morning," replied Keating. "There's been trouble on the railroad—a freight-car broke down and ripped up the track; it'll be some time before it's clear."

They discussed this new problem back and forth. MacKellar wanted to get in half a dozen friends and keep guard over Hal during the night; and Hal had about agreed to this idea, when the discussion was given a new turn by a chance remark of Keating's. "Somebody else is tied up by the railroad accident. The Coal King's son!"

"The Coal King's son?" echoed Hal.

"Young Percy Harrigan. He's got a private car here—or rather a whole train. Think of it—dining-car, drawing-room car, two whole cars with sleeping apartments! Wouldn't you like to be a son of the Coal King?"

"Has he come on account of the mine-disaster?"

"Mine-disaster?" echoed Keating. "I doubt if he's heard of it. They've been on a trip to the Grand Canyon, I was told; there's a baggage-car with four automobiles."

"Is Old Peter with them?"

"No, he's in New York. Percy's the host. He's got one of his automobiles out, and was up in town—two other fellows and some girls."

"Who's in his party?"

"I couldn't find out. You can see, it might be a story for the *Gazette*—the Coal King's son, coming by chance at the moment when a hundred and seven of his serfs are perishing in the mine! If I could only have got him to say a word about the disaster! If I could even have got him to say he didn't know about it!"

"Did you try?"

"What am I a reporter for?"

"What happened?"

"Nothing happened; except that he froze me stiff."

"Where was this?"

"On the street. They stopped at a drug-store, and I stepped up. 'Is this Mr. Percy Harrigan?' He was looking into the store, over my head. 'I'm a reporter,' I said, 'and I'd like to ask you about the accident up at North Valley.' 'Excuse me,' he said, in a tone—gee, it makes your blood cold to think of it! 'Just a word,' I pleaded. 'I don't give interviews,' he answered; and that was all—he continued looking over my head, and everybody else staring in front of them. They had turned to ice at my first word. If ever I felt like a frozen worm!"

There was a pause.

"Ain't it wonderful," reflected Billy, "how quick you can build up an aristocracy! When you looked at that car, the crowd in it and the airs they wore, you'd think they'd been running the world since the time of William the Conqueror. And Old Peter came into this country with a pedlar's pack on his shoulders!"

"We're hustlers here," put in MacKellar.

"We'll hustle all the way to hell in a generation more," said the reporter. Then, after a minute, "Say, but there's one girl in that bunch that was the real thing! She sure did get me! You know all those fluffy things they do themselves up in—soft and fuzzy, makes you think of spring-time orchards. This one was exactly the colour of apple-blossoms."

"You're susceptible to the charms of the ladies?" inquired Hal, mildly.

"I am," said the other. "I know it's all fake, but just the same, it makes my little heart go pit-a-pat. I always want to think they're as lovely as they look."

Hal's smile became reminiscent, and he quoted:

> "Oh Liza-Ann, come out with me,

The moon is a-shinin' in the monkey-puzzle tree!"

Then he stopped, with a laugh. "Don't wear your heart on your sleeve, Mr. Keating. She wouldn't be above taking a peck at it as she passed."

"At me? A worm of a newspaper reporter?"

"At you, a man!" laughed Hal. "I wouldn't want to accuse the lady of posing; but a lady has her role in life, and has to keep her hand in."

There was a pause. The reporter was looking at the young miner with sudden curiosity. "See here," he remarked, "I've been wondering about you. How do you come to know so much about the psychology of the leisure class?"

"I used to have money once," said Hal. "My family's gone down as quickly as the Harrigans have come up."

SECTION 10.

Hal went on to question Keating about the apple-blossom girl. "Maybe I could guess who she is. What colour was her hair?"

"The colour of molasses taffy when you've pulled it," said Billy; "but all fluffy and wonderful, with star-dust in it. Her eyes were brown, and her cheeks pink and cream."

"She had two rows of pearly white teeth, that flashed at you when she smiled?"

"She didn't smile, unfortunately."

"Then her brown eyes gazed at you, wide open, full of wonder?"

"Yes, they did—only it was into the drug-store window."

"Did she wear a white hat of soft straw, with a green and white flower garden on it, and an olive green veil, and maybe cream white ribbons?"

"By George, I believe you've seen her!" exclaimed the reporter.

"Maybe," said Hal. "Or maybe I'm describing the girl on the cover of one of the current magazines!" He smiled; but then, seeing the other's curiosity, "Seriously, I think I do know your young lady. If you announce that Miss Jessie Arthur is a member of the Harrigan party, you won't be taking a long chance."

"I can't afford to take any chance at all," said the reporter. "You mean Robert Arthur's daughter?"

"Heiress-apparent of the banking business of Arthur and Sons," said Hal. "It happens I know her by sight."

"How's that?"

"I worked in a grocery-store where she used to come."

"Whereabouts?"

"Peterson and Company, in Western City."

"Oho! And you used to sell her candy."

"Stuffed dates."

"And your little heart used to go pit-a-pat, so that you could hardly count the change?"

"Gave her too much, several times!"

"And you wondered if she was as good as she was beautiful! One day you were thrilled with hope, the next you were cynical and bitter—till at last you gave up in despair, and ran away to work in a coal-mine!"

They laughed, and MacKellar and Edstrom joined in. But suddenly Keating became serious again. "I ought to be away on that story!" he exclaimed. "I've got to get something out of that crowd about the disaster. Think what copy it would make!"

"But how can you do it?"

"I don't know; I only know I ought to be trying. I'll hang round the train, and maybe I can get one of the porters to talk."

"Interview with the Coal King's porter!" chuckled Hal. "How it feels to make up a multi-millionaire's bed!"

"How it feels to sell stuffed dates to a banker's daughter!" countered the other.

But suddenly it was Hal's turn to become serious. "Listen, Mr. Keating," said he, "why not let *me* interview young Harrigan?"

"*You?*"

"Yes! I'm the proper person—one of his miners! I help to make his money for him, don't I? I'm the one to tell him about North Valley."

Hal saw the reporter staring at him in sudden excitement; he continued: "I've been to the District Attorney, the Justice of the Peace, the District Judge, the Mayor and the Chief of Police. Now, why shouldn't I go to the Owner?"

"By thunder!" cried Billy. "I believe you'd have the nerve!"

"I believe I would," replied Hal, quietly.

The other scrambled out of his chair, wild with delight. "I dare you!" he exclaimed.

"I'm ready," said Hal.

"You mean it?"

"Of course I mean it."

"In that costume?"

"Certainly. I'm one of his miners."

"But it won't go," cried the reporter. "You'll stand no chance to get near him unless you're well dressed."

"Are you sure of that? What I've got on might be the garb of a railroad-hand. Suppose there was something out of order in one of the cars—the plumbing, for example?"

"But you couldn't fool the conductor or the porter."

"I might be able to. Let's try it."

There was a pause, while Keating thought. "The truth is," he said, "it doesn't matter whether you succeed or not—it's a story if you even make the attempt. The Coal King's son appealed to by one of his serfs! The hard heart of Plutocracy rejects the cry of Labour!"

"Yes," said Hal, "but I really mean to get to him. Do you suppose he's got back to the train yet?"

"They were starting to it when I left."

"And where *is* the train?"

"Two or three hundred yards east of the station, I was told."

MacKellar and Edstrom had been listening enthralled to this exciting conversation. "That ought to be just back of my house," said the former.

"It's a short train—four parlour-cars and a baggage-car," added Keating. "It ought to be easy to recognise."

The old Scotchman put in an objection. "The difficulty may be to get out of this house. I don't believe they mean to let you get away to-night."

"By Jove, that's so!" exclaimed Keating. "We're talking too much—let's get busy. Are they watching the back door, do you suppose?"

"They've been watching it all day," said MacKellar.

"Listen," broke in Hal—"I've an idea. They haven't tried to interfere with your going out, have they, Mr. Keating?"

"No, not yet."

"Nor with you, Mr. MacKellar?"

"No, not yet," said the Scotchman.

"Well," Hal suggested, "suppose you lend me your crutches?"

Whereat Keating gave an exclamation of delight. "The very thing!"

"I'll take your over-coat and hat," Hal added. "I've watched you get about, and I think I can give an imitation. As for Mr. Keating, he's not easy to mistake."

"Billy, the fat boy!" laughed the other. "Come, let's get on the job!"

"I'll go out by the front door at the same time," put in Edstrom, his old voice trembling with excitement. "Maybe that'll help to throw them off the track."

SECTION 11.

They had been sitting upstairs in MacKellar's room. Now they rose, and were starting for the stairs, when suddenly there came a ring at the front door bell. They stopped and stared at one another. "There they are!" whispered Keating.

And MacKellar sat down suddenly, and held out his crutches to Hal. "The hat and coat are in the front hall," he exclaimed. "Make a try for it!" His words were full of vigour, but like Edstrom, his voice was trembling. He was no longer young, and could not take adventure gaily.

Hal and Keating ran downstairs, followed by Edstrom. Hal put on the coat and hat, and they went to the back door, while at the same time Edstrom answered the bell in front.

The back door opened into a yard, and this gave, through a side gate, into an alley. Hal's heart was pounding furiously as he began to hobble along with the crutches. He had to go at MacKellar's slow pace—while Keating, at his side, started talking. He informed "Mr. MacKellar," in a casual voice, that the *Gazette* was a newspaper which believed in the people's cause, and was pledged to publish the people's side of all public questions. Discoursing thus, they went out of the gate and into the alley.

A man emerged from the shadows and walked by them. He passed within three feet of Hal, and peered at him, narrowly. Fortunately there was no moon; Hal could not see the man's face, and hoped the man could not see his.

Meantime Keating was proceeding with his discourse. "You understand, Mr. MacKellar," he was saying, "sometimes it's difficult to find out the truth in a situation like this. When the interests are filling their newspapers with falsehoods and exaggerations, it's a temptation for us to publish falsehoods and exaggerations on the other side. But we find in the long run that it pays best to publish the truth, Mr. MacKellar—we can stand by it, and there's no come-back."

Hal, it must be admitted, was not paying much attention to this edifying sermon. He was looking ahead, to where the alley debouched onto the street. It was the street behind MacKellar's house, and only a block from the railroad-track.

He dared not look behind, but he was straining his ears. Suddenly he heard a shout, in John Edstrom's voice. "Run! Run!"

In a flash, Hal dropped the two crutches, and started down the alley, Keating at his heels. They heard cries behind them, and a voice, sounding quite near, commanded, "Halt!" They had reached the end of the alley, and were in the act of swerving, when a shot rang out and there was a crash of glass in a house beyond them on the far side of the street.

Farther on was a vacant lot with a path running across it. Following this, they dodged behind some shanties, and came to another street—and so to the railroad tracks. There was a long line of freight-cars before them, and they ran between two of these, and climbing over the couplings, saw a great engine standing, its headlight gleaming full in their eyes. They sprang in front of it, and alongside the train, passing a tender, then a baggage-car, then a parlour-car.

"Here we are!" exclaimed Keating, who was puffing like a bellows.

Hal saw that there were only three more cars to the train; also, he saw a man in a blue uniform standing at the steps. He dashed towards him. "Your car's on fire!" he cried.

"What?" exclaimed the man. "Where?"

"Here!" cried Hal; and in a flash he had sprung past the other, up the steps and into the car.

There was a long, narrow corridor, to be recognised as the kitchen portion of a dining-car; at the other end of this corridor was a swinging door, and to this Hal leaped. He heard the conductor shouting to him to stop, but he paid no heed. He slipped off his over-coat and hat; and then, pushing open the door, he entered a brightly lighted apartment—and the presence of the Coal King's son.

SECTION 12.

White linen and cut glass of the dining-saloon shone brilliantly under electric lights, softened to the eye by pink shades. Seated at the tables were half a dozen young men and as many young ladies, all in evening costume; also two or three older ladies. They had begun the first course of their meal, and were laughing and chatting, when suddenly came this unexpected visitor, clad in coal-stained miner's jumpers. He was not disturbing in the manner of his entry; but immediately behind him came a fat man, perspiring, wild of aspect, and wheezing like an old fashioned steam-engine; behind him came the conductor of the train, in a no less evident state of agitation. So, of course, conversation ceased. The young ladies turned in their chairs, while several of the young men sprang to their feet.

There followed a silence: until finally one of the young men took a step forward. "What's this?" he demanded, as one who had a right to demand.

Hal advanced towards the speaker, a slender youth, correct in appearance, but not distinguished looking. "Hello, Percy!" said Hal.

A look of amazement came upon the other's face. He stared, but seemed unable to believe what he saw. And then suddenly came a cry from one of the young ladies; the one having hair the colour of molasses taffy when you've pulled it—but all fluffy and wonderful, with stardust in it. Her cheeks were pink and cream, and her brown eyes gazed, wide open, full of wonder. She wore a dinner gown of soft olive green, with a cream white scarf of some filmy material thrown about her bare shoulders.

She had started to her feet. "It's Hal!" she cried.

"Hal Warner!" echoed young Harrigan. "Why, what in the world—?"

He was interrupted by a clamour outside. "Wait a moment," said Hal, quietly. "I think some one else is coming in."

The door was pushed violently open. It was pushed so violently that Billy Keating and the conductor were thrust to one side; and Jeff Cotton appeared in the entrance.

The camp-marshal was breathless, his face full of the passion of the hunt. In his right hand he carried a revolver. He glared about him, and saw the two men he was chasing; also he saw the Coal King's son, and the rest of the astonished company. He stood, stricken dumb.

The door was pushed again, forcing him aside, and two more men crowded in, both of them carrying revolvers in their hands. The foremost was Pete Hanun, and he also stood staring. The "breaker of teeth" had two teeth of his own missing, and when his prize-fighter's jaw dropped down, the deficiency became conspicuous. It was probably his first entrance into society, and he was like an overgrown boy caught in the jam-closet.

Percy Harrigan's manner became distinctly imperious. "What does this mean?" he demanded.

It was Hal who answered. "I am seeking a criminal, Percy."

"What?" There were little cries of alarm from the women.

"Yes, a criminal; the man who sealed up the mine."

"Sealed up the mine?" echoed the other. "What do you mean?"

"Let me explain. First, I will introduce my friends. Harrigan, this is my friend Keating."

Billy suddenly realised that he had a hat on his head. He jerked it off; but for the rest, his social instincts failed him. He could only stare. He had not yet got all his breath.

"Billy's a reporter," said Hal. "But you needn't worry—he's a gentleman, and won't betray a confidence. You understand, Billy."

"Y—yes," said Billy, faintly.

"And this," said Hal, "is Jeff Cotton, camp-marshal at North Valley. I suppose you know, Percy, that the North Valley mines belong to the 'G. F. C.' Cotton, this is Mr. Harrigan."

Then Cotton remembered his hat; also his revolver, which he tried to get out of sight behind his back.

"And this," continued Hal, "is Mr. Pete Hanun, by profession a breaker of teeth. This other gentleman, whose name I don't know, is presumably an assistant-breaker." So Hal went on, observing the forms of social intercourse, his purpose being to give his mind a chance to work. So much depended upon the tactics he chose in this emergency! Should he take Percy to one side and tell him the story quietly, leaving it to his sense of justice and humanity? No, that was not the way one dealt with the Harrigans! They had bullied their way to the front; if anything were done with them, it would be by force! If anything were done with Percy, it would be by laying hold of him before these guests, exposing the situation, and using their feelings to coerce him!

The Coal King's son was asking questions again. What was all this about? So Hal began to describe the condition of the men inside the mine. "They have no food or water, except what they had in their dinner-pails; and it's been three days and a half since the explosion! They are breathing bad air; their heads are aching, the veins swelling in their foreheads; their tongues are cracking, they are lying on the ground, gasping. But they are waiting—kept alive by the faith they have in their friends on the surface, who will try to get to them. They dare not take down the barriers, because the gases would kill them at once. But they know the rescuers will come, so they listen for the sounds of axes and picks. That is the situation."

Hal stopped and waited for some sign of concern from young Harrigan. But no such sign was given. Hal went on:

"Think of it, Percy! There is one old man in that mine, an Irishman who has a wife and eight children waiting to learn about his fate. I know one woman who has a husband and three sons in the mine. For three days and a half the women and children have been standing at the pit-mouth; I have seen them sitting with their heads sunk upon their knees, or shaking their fists, screaming curses at the criminal who is to blame."

There was a pause. "The criminal?" inquired young Harrigan. "I don't understand!"

"You'll hardly be able to believe it; but nothing has been done to rescue these men. The criminal has nailed a cover of boards over the pit-mouth, and put tarpaulin over it—sealing up men and boys to die!"

There was a murmur of horror from the diners.

"I know, you can't conceive such a thing. The reason is, there's a fire in the mine; if the fan is set to working, the coal will burn. But at the same time, some of the passages could be got clear of smoke, and some of the men could be rescued. So it's a question of property against lives; and the criminal has decided for the property. He proposes to wait a week, two weeks, until the fire has been smothered; *then* of course the men and boys will be dead."

There was a silence. It was broken by young Harrigan. "Who has done this?"

"His name is Enos Cartwright."

"But who *is* he?"

"Just now when I said that I was seeking the criminal, I misled you a little, Percy. I did it because I wanted to collect my thoughts." Hal paused: when he continued, his voice was sharper, his sentences falling like blows. "The criminal I've been telling you about is the superintendent of the mine—a man employed and put in authority by the General Fuel Company. The one who is being chased is not the one who sealed up the mine, but the one who proposed to have it opened. He is being treated as a malefactor, because the laws of the state, as well as the laws of humanity, have been suppressed by the General Fuel Company; he was forced to seek refuge in your car, in order to save his life from thugs and gunmen in the company's employ!"

SECTION 13.

Knowing these people well, Hal could measure the effect of the thunderbolt he had hurled among them. They were people to whom good taste was the first of all the virtues; he knew how he was offending them. If he was to win them to the least extent, he must explain his presence here—a trespasser upon the property of the Harrigans.

"Percy," he continued, "you remember how you used to jump on me last year at college, because I listened to 'muck-rakers.' You saw fit to take personal offence at it. You knew that their tales couldn't be true. But I wanted to see for myself, so I went to work in a coal-mine. I saw the explosion; I saw this man, Jeff Cotton, driving women and children away from the pit-mouth with blows and curses. I set out to help the men in the mine, and the marshal rushed me out of camp. He told me that if I didn't go about my business, something would happen to me on a dark night. And you see—this is a dark night!"

Hal waited, to give young Harrigan a chance to grasp this situation and to take command. But apparently young Harrigan was not aware of the presence of the camp-marshal and his revolver. Hal tried again:

"Evidently these men wouldn't have minded killing me; they fired at me just now. The marshal still has the revolver and you can smell the powder-smoke. So I took the liberty of entering your car, Percy. It was to save my life, and you'll have to excuse me."

The Coal King's son had here a sudden opportunity to be magnanimous. He made haste to avail himself of it. "Of course, Hal," he said. "It was quite all right to come here. If our employés were behaving in such fashion, it was without authority, and they will surely pay for it." He spoke with quiet certainty; it was the Harrigan manner, and before it Jeff Cotton and the two mine-guards seemed to wither and shrink.

"Thank you, Percy," said Hal. "It's what I knew you'd say. I'm sorry to have disturbed your dinner-party—"

"Not at all, Hal; it was nothing of a party."

"You see, Percy, it was not only to save myself, but the people in the mine! They are dying, and every moment is precious. It will take a day at least to get to them, so they'll be at their last gasp. Whatever's to be done must be done at once."

Again Hal waited—until the pause became awkward. The diners had so far been looking at him; but now they were looking at young Harrigan, and young Harrigan felt the change.

"I don't know just what you expect of me, Hal. My father employs competent men to manage his business, and I certainly don't feel that I know enough to give them any suggestions." This again in the Harrigan manner; but it weakened before Hal's firm gaze. "What can I do?"

"You can give the order to open the mine, to reverse the fan and start it. That will draw out the smoke and gases, and the rescuers can go down."

"But Hal, I assure you I have no authority to give such an order."

"You must *take* the authority. Your father's in the East, the officers of the company are in their beds at home; you are here!"

"But I don't understand such things, Hal! I don't know anything of the situation—except what you tell me. And while I don't doubt your word, any man may make a mistake in such a situation."

"Come and see for yourself, Percy! That's all I ask, and it's easy enough. Here is your train, your engine with steam up; have us switched onto the North Valley branch, and we can be at the mine in half an hour. Then—let me take you to the men who know! Men who've been working all their lives in mines, who've seen accidents like this many times, and who will tell you the truth—that there's a chance of saving many lives, and that the chance is being thrown away to save some thousands of dollars' worth of coal and timbers and track."

"But even if that's true, Hal, I have no *power*!"

"If you come there, you can cut the red-tape in one minute. What those bosses are doing is a thing that can only be done in darkness!"

Under the pressure of Hal's vehemence, the Harrigan manner was failing; the Coal King's son was becoming a bewildered and quite ordinary youth. But there was a power greater than Hal behind him. He shook his head. "It's the old man's business, Hal. I've no right to butt in!"

The other, in his desperate need, turned to the rest of the party. His gaze, moving from one face to another, rested upon the magazine-cover countenance, with the brown eyes wide open, full of wonder.

"Jessie! What do you think about it?"

The girl started, and distress leaped into her face. "How do you mean, Hal?"

"Tell him he ought to save those lives!"

The moments seemed ages as Hal waited. It was a test, he realised. The brown eyes dropped. "I don't understand such things, Hal!"

"But, Jessie, I am explaining them! Here are men and boys being suffocated to death, in order to save a little money. Isn't that plain?"

"But how can I *know*, Hal?"

"I'm giving you my word, Jessie. Surely I wouldn't appeal to you unless I knew."

Still she hesitated. And there came a swift note of feeling into his voice: "Jessie, dear!"

As if under a spell, the girl's eyes were raised to his; he saw a scarlet flame of embarrassment spreading over her throat and cheeks. "Jessie, I know—it seems an intolerable thing to ask! You've never been rude to a friend. But I remember once you forgot your good manners, when you saw a rough fellow on the street beating an old drudge-horse. Don't you remember how you rushed at him—like a wild thing! And now—think of it, dear, here are old drudge-creatures being tortured to death; but not horses—working-men!"

Still the girl gazed at him. He could read grief, dismay in her eyes; he saw tears steal from them, and stream down her cheeks. "Oh, I don't know, I don't *know!*" she cried; and hid her face in her hands, and began to sob aloud.

SECTION 14.

There was a painful pause. Hal's gaze travelled on, and came to a grey-haired lady in a black dinner-gown, with a rope of pearls about her neck. "Mrs. Curtis! Surely *you* will advise him!"

The grey-haired lady started—was there no limit to his impudence? She had witnessed the torturing of Jessie. But Jessie was his fiancée; he had no such claim upon Mrs. Curtis. She answered, with iciness in her tone: "I could not undertake to dictate to my host in such a matter."

"Mrs. Curtis! You have founded a charity for the helping of stray cats and dogs!" These words rose to Hal's lips; but he did not say them. His eyes moved on. Who else might help to bully a Harrigan?

Next to Mrs. Curtis sat Reggie Porter, with a rose in the button-hole of his dinner-jacket. Hal knew the rôle in which Reggie was there—a kind of male chaperon, an assistant host, an admirer to the wealthy, a solace to the bored. Poor Reggie lived other people's lives, his soul perpetually a-quiver with other people's excitements, with gossip, preparations for tea-parties, praise of tea-parties past. And always the soul was pushing; calculating, measuring opportunities, making up in tact and elegance for distressing lack of money. Hal got one swift glimpse of the face; the sharp little black moustaches seemed standing up with excitement, and in a flash of horrible intuition Hal read the situation—Reggie was expecting to be questioned, and had got ready an answer that would increase his social capital in the Harrigan family bank!

Across the aisle sat Genevieve Halsey: tall, erect, built on the scale of a statue. You thought of the ox-eyed Juno, and imagined stately emotions; but when you came to know Genevieve, you discovered that her mind was slow, and entirely occupied with herself. Next to her was Bob Creston, smooth-shaven, rosy-cheeked, exuding well-being—what is called a "good fellow," with a wholesome ambition to win cups for his athletic club, and to keep up the score of his rifle-team of the state militia. Jolly Bob might have spoken, out of his good heart; but he was in love with a cousin of Percy's, Betty Gunnison, who sat across the table from him—and Hal saw her black eyes shining, her little fists clenched tightly, her lips pressed white. Hal understood Betty—she was one of the Harrigans, working at the Harrigan family task of making the children of a pack-pedlar into leaders in the "younger set!"

Next sat "Vivie" Cass, whose talk was of horses and dogs and such ungirlish matters; Hal had discussed social questions in her presence, and heard her view expressed in one flashing sentence—"If a man eats with his knife, I consider him my personal enemy!" Over her shoulder peered the face of a man with pale eyes and yellow moustaches—Bert Atkins, cynical and world-weary, whom the papers referred to as a "club-man," and whom Hal's brother had called a "tame cat." There was "Dicky" Everson, like Hal, a favourite of the ladies, but nothing more; "Billy" Harris, son of another "coal man"; Daisy, his sister; and Blanche Vagleman, whose father was Old Peter's head lawyer, whose brother was the local counsel, and publisher of the Pedro *Star*.

So Hal's eyes moved from face to face, and his mind from personality to personality. It was like the unrolling of a scroll; a panorama of a world he had half forgotten. He had no time for reflection, but one impression came to him, swift and overwhelming. Once he had lived in this world and taken it as a matter of course. He had known these people, gone about with them; they had seemed friendly, obliging, a good sort of people on the whole. And now, what a change! They seemed no longer friendly! Was the change in them? Or was it Hal who had become cynical—so that he saw them in this terrifying new light, cold, and unconcerned as the stars about men who were dying a few miles away!

Hal's eyes came back to the Coal King's son, and he discovered that Percy was white with anger. "I assure you, Hal, there's no use going on with this. I have no intention of letting myself be bulldozed."

Percy's gaze shifted with sudden purpose to the camp-marshal. "Cotton, what do you say about this? Is Mr. Warner correct in his idea of the situation?"

"You know what such a man would say, Percy!" broke in Hal.

"I don't," was the reply. "I wish to know. What is it, Cotton?"

"He's mistaken, Mr. Harrigan." The marshal's voice was sharp and defiant.

"In what way?"

"The company's doing everything to get the mine open, and has been from the beginning."

"Oh!" And there was triumph in Percy's voice. "What is the cause of the delay?"

"The fan was broken, and we had to send for a new one. It's a job to set it up—such things can't be done in an hour."

Percy turned to Hal. "You see! There are two opinions, at least!"

"Of course!" cried Betty Gunnison, her black eyes snapping at Hal. She would have said more, but Hal interrupted, stepping closer to his host. "Percy," he said, in a low voice, "come back here, please. I have a word to say to you alone."

There was just a hint of menace in Hal's voice; his gaze went to the far end of the car, a space occupied only by two negro waiters. These retired in haste as the young men moved towards them; and so, having the Coal King's son to himself, Hal went in to finish this fight.

<h1 style="text-align:center">SECTION 15.</h1>

Percy Harrigan was known to Hal, as a college-boy is known to his class-mates. He was not brutal, like his grim old father; he was merely self-indulgent, as one who had always had everything; he was weak, as one who had never had to take a bold resolve. He had been brought up by the women of the family, to be a part of what they called "society"; in which process he had been given high notions of his own importance. The life of the Harrigans was dominated by one painful memory—that of a pedlar's pack; and Hal knew that Percy's most urgent purpose was to be regarded as a real and true and freehanded aristocrat. It was this knowledge Hal was using in his attack.

He began with apologies, attempting to soothe the other's anger. He had not meant to make a scene like this; it was the gunmen who had forced it, putting his life in danger. It was the very devil, being chased about at night and shot at! He had lost his nerve, really; he had forgot what little manners he had been able to keep as a miner's buddy. He had made a spectacle of himself; good Lord yes, he realised how he must seem!

—And Hal looked at his dirty miner's jumpers, and then at Percy. He could see that Percy was in hearty agreement thus far—he had indeed made a spectacle of himself, and of Percy too! Hal was sorry about this latter, but here they were, in a pickle, and it was certainly too late now. This story was out—there could be no suppressing it! Hal might sit down on his reporter-friend, Percy might sit down on the waiters and the conductor and the camp-marshal and the gunmen—but he could not possibly sit down on all his friends! They would talk about nothing else for weeks! The story would be all over Western City in a day—this amazing, melodramatic, ten-twenty-thirty story of a miner's buddy in the private car of the Coal King's son!

"And you must see, Percy," Hal went on, "it's the sort of thing that sticks to a man. It's the thing by which everybody will form their idea of you as long as you live!"

"I'll take my chances with my friends' criticism," said the other, with some attempt at the Harrigan manner.

"You can make it whichever kind of story you choose," continued Hal, implacably. "The world will say, He decided for the dollars; or it will say, He decided for the lives. Surely, Percy, your family doesn't need those particular dollars so badly! Why, you've spent more on this one train-trip!"

And Hal waited, to give his victim time to calculate.

The result of the thinking was a question worthy of Old Peter. "What are *you* getting out of this?"

"Percy," said Hal, "you must *know* I'm getting nothing! If you can't understand it otherwise, say to yourself that you are dealing with a man who's irresponsible. I've seen so many terrible things—I've been chased around so much by camp-marshals—why, Percy, that man Cotton has six notches on his gun! I'm simply crazy!" And into the brown eyes of this miner's buddy came a look wild enough to convince a stronger man than Percy Harrigan. "I've got just one idea left in the world, Percy—to save those miners! You make a mistake unless you realise how desperate I am. So far I've done this thing incog! I've been Joe Smith, a miner's buddy. If I'd come out and told my real name—well, maybe I wouldn't have made them open the mine, but at least I'd have made a lot of trouble for the G. F. C.! But I didn't do it; I knew what a scandal it would make, and there was something I owed my father. But if I see there's no other way, if it's a question of letting those people perish, I'll throw everything else to the winds. Tell your father that; tell him I threatened to turn this man Keating loose and blow the thing wide open— denounce the company, appeal to the Governor, raise a disturbance and get arrested on the street, if necessary, in order to force the facts before the public. You see, I've got the facts, Percy! I've been there and seen with my own eyes. Can't you realise that?"

The other did not answer, but it was evident that he realised.

"On the other hand, see how you can fix it, if you choose. You were on a pleasure trip when you heard of this disaster; you rushed up and took command, you opened the mine, you saved the lives of your employés. That is the way the papers will handle it."

Hal, watching his victim intently, and groping for the path to his mind, perceived that he had gone wrong. Crude as the Harrigans were, they had learned that it is not aristocratic to be picturesque.

"All right then!" said Hal, quickly. "If you prefer, you needn't be mentioned. The bosses up at the camp have the reporters under their thumbs, they'll handle the story any way you want it. The one thing I care about is that you run your car up and see the mine opened. Won't you do it, Percy?"

Hal was gazing into the other's eyes, knowing that life and death for the miners hung upon his nod. "Well? What is the answer?"

"Hal," exclaimed Percy, "my old man will give me hell!"

"All right; but on the other hand, *I'll* give you hell; and which will be worse?"

Again there was a silence. "Come along, Percy! For God's sake!" And Hal's tone was desperate, alarming.

And suddenly the other gave way. "All right!"

Hal drew a breath. "But mind you!" he added. "You're not going up there to let them fool you! They'll try to bluff you out—they may go as far as to refuse to obey you. But you must stand by your guns—for, you see, I'm going along, I'm going to see that mine open. I'll never quit till the rescuers have gone down!"

"Will they go, Hal?"

"Will they go? Good God, man, they're clamouring for the chance to go! They've almost been rioting for it. I'll go with them—and you, too, Percy—the whole crowd of us idlers will go! When we come out, we'll know something about the business of coal-mining!"

"All right, I'm with you," said the Coal King's son.

SECTION 16.

Hal never knew what Percy said to Cartwright that night; he only knew that when they arrived at the mine the superintendent was summoned to a consultation, and half an hour later Percy emerged smiling, with the announcement that Hal Warner had been mistaken all along; the mine authorities had been making all possible haste to get the fan ready, with the intention of opening the mine at the earliest moment. The work was now completed, and in an hour or two the fan was to be started, and by morning there would be a chance of rescuers getting in. Percy said this so innocently that for a moment Hal wondered if Percy himself might not believe it. Hal's position as guest of course required that he should graciously pretend to believe it, consenting to appear as a fool before the rest of the company.

Percy invited Hal and Billy Keating to spend the night in the train; but this Hal declined. He was too dirty, he said; besides, he wanted to be up at daylight, to be one of the first to go down the shaft. Percy answered that the superintendent had vetoed this proposition—he did not want any one to go down but experienced men, who could take care of themselves. When there were so many on hand ready and eager to go, there was no need to imperil the lives of amateurs.

At the risk of seeming ungracious, Hal declared that he would "hang around" and see them take the cover off the pit-mouth. There were mourning parties in some of the cabins, where women were gathered together who could not sleep, and it would be an act of charity to take them the good news.

Hal and Keating set out; they went first to the Rafferties', and saw Mrs. Rafferty spring up and stare at them, and then scream aloud to the Holy Virgin, waking all the little Rafferties to frightened clamour. When the woman had made sure that they really knew what they were talking about, she rushed out to spread the news, and so pretty soon the streets were alive with hurrying figures, and a crowd gathered once more at the pit-mouth.

Hal and Keating went on to Jerry Minetti's. Out of a sense of loyalty to Percy, Hal did no more than repeat Percy's own announcement, that it had been Cartwright's intention all along to have the mine opened. It was funny to see the effect of this statement—the face with which Jerry looked at Hal! But they wasted no time in discussion; Jerry slipped into his clothes and hurried with them to the pit-mouth.

Sure enough, a gang was already tearing off the boards and canvas. Never since Hal had been in North Valley had he seen men working with such a will! Soon the great fan began to stir, and then to roar, and then to sing; and there was a crowd of a hundred people, roaring and singing also.

It would be some hours before anything more could be done; and suddenly Hal realised that he was exhausted. He and Billy Keating went back to the Minetti cabin, and spreading themselves a blanket on the floor, lay down with sighs of relief. As for Billy, he was soon snoring; but to Hal there came sudden reaction from all the excitement, and sleep was far from him.

An ocean of thoughts came flooding into his mind: the world outside, *his* world, which he had banished deliberately for several months, and which he had so suddenly been compelled to remember! It had seemed so simple, what he had set out to do that summer: to take another name, to become a member of another class, to live its life and think its thoughts, and then come back to his own world with a new and fascinating adventure to tell about! The possibility that his own world, the world of Hal Warner, might find him out as Joe Smith, the miner's buddy—that was a possibility which had never come to his mind. He was like a burglar, working away at a job in darkness, and suddenly finding the room flooded with light.

He had gone into the adventure, prepared to find things that would shock him; he had known that somehow, somewhere, he would have to fight the "system." But he had never expected to find himself in the thick of the class-war, leading a charge upon the trenches of his own associates. Nor was this the end, he knew; this war would not be settled by the winning of a trench! Lying here in the darkness and silence, Hal was realising what he had got himself in for. To employ another simile, he was a man who begins a flirtation on the street, and wakes up next morning to find himself married.

It was not that he had regrets for the course he had taken with Percy. No other course had been thinkable. But while Hal had known these North Valley people for ten weeks, he had known the occupants of Percy's car for as many years. So these latter personalities loomed large in his consciousness, and here in the darkness their thoughts about him, whether actively hostile or passively astonished, laid siege to the defences of his mind.

Particularly he found himself wrestling with Jessie Arthur. Her face rose up before him, appealing, yearning. She had one of those perfect faces, which irresistibly compel the soul of a man. Her brown eyes, soft and shining, full of tenderness; her lips, quick to tremble with emotion; her skin like apple-blossoms, her hair with star-dust in it! Hal was cynical enough about coal-operators and mine-guards, but it never occurred to him that Jessie's soul might be anything but what these bodily charms implied. He was in love with her; and he was too young, too inexperienced in love to realise that underneath the sweetness of girlhood, so genuine and so lovable, might lie deep, unconscious cruelty, inherited and instinctive—the cruelty of caste, the hardness of worldly prejudice. A man has to come to middle age, and to suffer much, before he understands that the charms of women, those rare and magical perfections of eyes and teeth and hair, that softness of skin and delicacy of feature, have cost labour and care of many generations, and imply inevitably that life has been feral, that customs and conventions have been murderous and inhuman.

Jessie had failed Hal in his desperate emergency. But now he went over the scene, and told himself that the test had been an unfair one. He had known her since childhood, and loved her, and never before had he seen an act or heard a word that was not gracious and kind. But—so he told himself—she gave her sympathy to those she knew; and what chance had she ever had to know working-people? He must give her the chance; he must compel her, even against her will, to broaden her understanding of life! The process might hurt her, it might mar the unlined softness of her face, but nevertheless, it would be good for her—it would be a "growing pain"!

So, lying there in the darkness and silence, Hal found himself absorbed in long conversation with his sweetheart. He escorted her about the camp, explaining things to her, introducing her to this one and that. He took others of his private-car friends and introduced them to his North Valley friends. There were individuals who had qualities in common, and would surely hit it off! Bob Creston, for example, who was good at a "song and dance"—he would surely be interested in "Blinky," the vaudeville specialist of the camp! Mrs. Curtis, who liked cats, would find a bond of sisterhood with old Mrs. Nagle, who lived next door to the Minettis, and kept five! And even Vivie Cass, who hated men who ate with their knives—she would be driven to murder by the table-manners of Reminitsky's boarders, but she would take delight in "Dago Charlie," the tobacco-chewing mule which had once been Hal's pet! Hal could hardly wait for daylight to come, so that he might begin these efforts at social amalgamation!

SECTION 17.

Towards dawn Hal fell asleep; he was awakened by Billy Keating, who sat up yawning, at the same time grumbling and bewailing. Hal realised that Billy also had discovered troubles during the night. Never in all his career as a journalist had he had such a story; never had any man had such a story—and it must be killed!

Cartwright had got the reporters together late the night before and told them the news—that the company had at last succeeded in getting the mine ready to be opened; also that young Mr. Harrigan was there in his private train, prompted by his concern for the entombed miners. The reporters would mention his coming, of course, but were requested not to "play it up," nor to mention the names of Mr. Harrigan's guests. Needless to say they were not told that the "buddy" who had been thrown out of camp for insubordination had turned out to be the son of Edward S. Warner, the "coal magnate."

A fine, cold rain was falling, and Hal borrowed an old coat of Jerry's and slipped it on. Little Jerry clamoured to go with him, and after some controversy Hal wrapped him in a shawl and slung him onto his shoulder. It was barely daylight, but already the whole population of the village was on hand at the pit-mouth. The helmet-men had gone down to make tests, so the hour of final revelation was at hand. Women stood with wet shawls about their hunched shoulders, their faces white and strained, their suspense too great for any sort of utterance. A ghastly thought it was, that while they were shuddering in the wet, their men below might be expiring for lack of a few drops of water!

The helmet-men, coming up, reported that lights would burn at the bottom of the shaft; so it was safe for men to go down without helmets, and the volunteers of the first rescue party made ready. All night there had been a clattering of hammers, where the carpenters were working on a new cage. Now it was swung from the hoist, and the men took their places in it. When at last the hoist began to move, and the group disappeared below the surface of the ground, you could hear a sigh from a thousand throats, like the moaning of wind in a pine-tree. They were leaving women and children above, yet not one of these women would have asked them to stay—such was the deep unconscious bond of solidarity which made these toilers of twenty nations one!

It was a slow process, letting down the cage; on account of the danger of gas, and the newness of the cage, it was necessary to proceed a few feet at a time, waiting for a pull upon the signal-cord to tell that the men were all right. After they had reached the bottom, there would be more time, no one could say how long, before they came upon survivors with signs of life in them. There were bodies near the foot of the shaft, according to the reports of the helmet-men, but there was no use delaying to bring these up, for they must have been dead for days. Hal saw a crowd of women clamouring about the helmet-men, trying to find out if these bodies had been recognised. Also he saw Jeff Cotton and Bud Adams at their old duty of driving the women back.

The cage returned for a second load of men. There was less need of caution now; the hoist worked quickly, and group after group of men with silent, set faces, and pickaxes and crow-bars and shovels in their hands, went down into the pit of terror. They would scatter through the workings, testing everywhere ahead of them with safety-lamps, and looking for barriers erected by the imprisoned men for defence against the gases. As they hammered on these barriers, perhaps they would hear the signals of living men on the other side; or they would break through in silence, and find men too far gone to make a sound, yet possibly with the spark of life still in them.

One by one, Hal's friends went down—"Big Jack" David, and Wresmak, the Bohemian, Klowoski, the Pole, and finally Jerry Minetti. Little Jerry waved his hand from his perch on Hal's shoulder; while Rosa, who had come out and joined them, was clinging to Hal's arm, silent, as if her soul were going down in the cage. There went blue-eyed Tim Rafferty to look for his father, and black-eyed "Andy," the Greek boy, whose father had perished in a similar disaster years ago; there went Rovetta, and Carmino, the pit-boss, Jerry's cousin. One by one their names ran through the crowd, as of heroes marching out to battle.

SECTION 18.

Looking about, Hal saw some of the guests of the Harrigan party. There was Vivie Cass, standing under an umbrella with Bert Atkins; and there was Bob Creston with Dicky Everson. These two had on mackintoshes and water-proof hats, and were talking to Cartwright; tall, immaculate men, who seemed like creatures of another world beside the stunted and coal-smutted miners.

Seeing Hal, they moved over to him. "Where did you get the kid?" inquired Bob, his rosy, smooth-shaven face breaking into a smile.

"I picked him up," said Hal, giving Little Jerry a toss and sliding him off his shoulder.

"Hello, kid!" said Bob.

And the answer came promptly, "Hello, yourself!" Little Jerry knew how to talk American; he was a match for any society man! "My father's went down in that cage," said he, looking up at the tall stranger, his bright black eyes sparkling.

"Is that so!" replied the other. "Why don't you go?"

"My father'll get 'em out. He ain't afraid o' nothin', my father!"

"What's your father's name?"

"Big Jerry."

"Oho! And what'll you be when you grow up?"

"I'm goin' to be a shot-firer."

"In this mine?"

"You bet not!"

"Why not?"

Little Jerry looked mysterious. "I ain't tellin' all I know," said he.

The two young fellows laughed. Here was education for them! "Maybe you'll go back to the old country?" put in Dicky Everson.

"No, sir-ee!" said Little Jerry. "I'm American."

"Maybe you'll be president some day."

"That's what my father says," replied the little chap—"president of a miners' union."

Again they laughed; but Rosa gave a nervous whisper and caught at the child's sleeve. That was not the sort of thing to say to mysterious and rich-looking strangers! "This is Little Jerry's mother, Mrs. Minetti," put in Hal, by way of reassuring her.

"Glad to meet you, Mrs. Minetti," said the two young men, taking off their hats with elaborate bows; they stared, for Rosa was a pretty object as she blushed and made her shy response. She was much embarrassed, having never before in her life been bowed to by men like these.

And here they were greeting Joe Smith as an old friend, and calling him by a strange name! She turned her black Italian eyes upon Hal in inquiry, and he felt a flush creeping over him. It was almost as uncomfortable to be found out by North Valley as to be found out by Western City!

The men talked about the rescue-work, and what Cartwright had been telling of its progress. The fire was in one of the main passages, and was burning out the timbering, spreading rapidly under the draft from the reversed fan. There could be little hope of rescue in this part of the mine, but the helmet-men would defy the heat and smoke in the burned out passages. They knew how likely was the collapse of such portions of the mine; but also they knew that men had been working here before the explosion. "I must say they're a game lot!" remarked Dicky.

A group of women and children were gathered about to listen, their shyness overcome by their torturing anxiety for news. They made one think of women in war-time, listening to the roar of distant guns and waiting for the bringing in of the wounded. Hal saw Bob and Dicky glance now and then at the ring of faces about them; they were getting something of this mood, and that was a part of what he had desired for them.

"Are the others coming out?" he asked.

"I don't know," said Bob. "I suppose they're having breakfast. It's time we went in."

"Won't you come with us?" added Dicky.

"No, thanks," replied Hal, "I've an engagement with the kid here." And he gave Little Jerry's hand a squeeze. "But tell some of the other fellows to come. They'll be interested in these things."

"All right," said the two, as they moved away.

SECTION 19.

After allowing a sufficient time for the party in the dining-car to finish breakfast, Hal went down to the tracks, and induced the porter to take in his name to Percy Harrigan. He was hoping to persuade Percy to see the village under other than company chaperonage; he heard with dismay the announcement that the party had arranged to depart in the course of a couple of hours.

"But you haven't seen anything at all!" Hal protested.

"They won't let us into the mine," replied the other. "What else is there we can do?"

"I wanted you to talk to the people and learn something about conditions here. You ought not to lose this chance, Percy!"

"That's all right, Hal, but you might understand this isn't a convenient time. I've got a lot of people with me, and I've no right to ask them to wait."

"But can't they learn something also, Percy?"

"It's raining," was the reply; "and ladies would hardly care to stand round in a crowd and see dead bodies brought out of a mine."

Hal got the rebuke. Yes, he had grown callous since coming to North Valley; he had lost that delicacy of feeling, that intuitive understanding of the sentiments of ladies, which he would surely have exhibited a short time earlier in his life. He was excited about this disaster; it was a personal thing to him, and he lost sight of the fact that to the ladies of the Harrigan party it was, in its details, merely sordid and repelling. If they went out in the mud and rain of a mining-village and stood about staring, they would feel that they were exhibiting, not human compassion, but idle curiosity. The sights they would see would harrow them to no purpose; and incidentally they would be exposing themselves to distressing publicity. As for offering sympathy to widows and orphans—well, these were foreigners mostly, who could not understand what was said to them, and who might be more embarrassed than helped by the intrusion into their grief of persons from an alien world.

The business of offering sympathy had been reduced to a system by the civilisation which these ladies helped to maintain; and, as it happened, there was one present who was familiar with this system. Mrs. Curtis had already acted, so Percy informed Hal; she had passed about a subscription-paper, and in a couple of minutes over a thousand dollars had been pledged. This would be paid by check to the "Red Cross," whose agents would understand how to distribute relief among such sufferers. So the members of Percy's party felt that they had done the proper and delicate thing, and might go their ways with a quiet conscience.

"The world can't stop moving just because there's been a mine-disaster," said the Coal King's son. "People have engagements they must keep."

And he went on to explain what these engagements were. He himself had to go to a dinner that evening, and would barely be able to make it. Bert Atkins was to play a challenge match at billiards, and Mrs. Curtis was to attend a committee meeting of a woman's club. Also it was the last Friday of the month; had Hal forgotten what that meant?

After a moment Hal remembered—the "Young People's Night" at the country club! He had a sudden vision of the white colonial mansion on the mountain-side, with its doors and windows thrown wide, and the strains of an orchestra floating out. In the ball-room the young ladies of Percy's party would appear—Jessie, his sweetheart, among them—gowned in filmy chiffons and laces, floating in a mist of perfume and colour and music. They would laugh and chatter, they would flirt and scheme against one another for the sovereignty of the ball-room—while here in North Valley the sobbing widows would be clutching their mangled dead in their arms! How strange, how ghastly it seemed! How like the scenes one read of on the eve of the French Revolution!

SECTION 20.

Percy wanted Hal to come away with the party. He suggested this tactfully at first, and then, as Hal did not take the hint, he began to press the matter, showing signs of irritation. The mine was open now—what more did Hal want? When Hal suggested that Cartwright might order it closed again, Percy revealed the fact that the matter was in his father's hands. The superintendent had sent a long telegram the night before, and an answer was due at any moment. Whatever the answer ordered would have to be done.

There was a grim look upon Hal's face, but he forced himself to speak politely. "If your father orders anything that interferes with the rescuing of the men—don't you see, Percy, that I have to fight him?"

"But how *can* you fight him?"

"With the one weapon I have—publicity."

"You mean—" Percy stopped, and stared.

"I mean what I said before—I'd turn Billy Keating loose and blow this whole story wide open."

"Well, by God!" cried young Harrigan. "I must say I'd call it damned dirty of you! You said you'd not do it, if I'd come here and open the mine!"

"But what good does it do to open it, if you close it again before the men are out?" Hal paused, and when he went on it was in a sincere attempt at apology. "Percy, don't imagine I fail to appreciate the embarrassments of this situation. I know I must seem a cad to you—more than you've cared to tell me. I called you my friend in spite of all our quarrels. All I can do is to assure you that I never intended to get into such a position as this."

"Well, what the hell did you want to come here for? You knew it was the property of a friend—"

"That's the question at issue between us, Percy. Have you forgotten our arguments? I tried to convince you what it meant that you and I should own the things by which other people have to live. I said we were ignorant of the conditions under which our properties were worked, we were a bunch of parasites and idlers. But you laughed at me, called me a crank, an anarchist, said I swallowed what any muck-raker fed me. So I said: 'I'll go to one of Percy's mines! Then, when he tries to argue with me, I'll have him!' That was the way the thing started—as a joke. But then I got drawn into things. I don't want to be nasty, but no man with a drop of red blood in his veins could stay in this place a week without wanting to fight! That's why I want you to stay—you ought to stay, to meet some of the people and see for yourself."

"Well, I can't stay," said the other, coldly. "And all I can tell you is that I wish you'd go somewhere else to do your sociology."

"But where could I go, Percy? Somebody owns everything. If it's a big thing, it's almost certain to be somebody we know."

Said Percy, "If I might make a suggestion, you could have begun with the coal-mines of the Warner Company."

Hal laughed. "You may be sure I thought of that, Percy. But see the situation! If I was to accomplish my purpose, it was essential that I shouldn't be known. And I had met some of my father's superintendents in his office, and I knew they'd recognise me. So I *had* to go to some other mines."

"Most fortunate for the Warner Company," replied Percy, in an ugly tone.

Hal answered, gravely, "Let me tell you, I don't intend to leave the Warner Company permanently out of my sociology."

"Well," replied the other, "all I can say is that we pass one of their properties on our way back, and nothing would please me better than to stop the train and let you off!"

SECTION 21.

Hal went into the drawing-room car. There were Mrs. Curtis and Reggie Porter, playing bridge with Genevieve Halsey and young Everson. Bob Creston was chatting with Betty Gunnison, telling her what he had seen outside, no doubt. Bert Atkins was looking over the morning paper, yawning. Hal went on, seeking Jessie Arthur, and found her in one of the compartments of the car, looking out of the rain-drenched window—learning about a mining-camp in the manner permitted to young ladies of her class.

He expected to find her in a disturbed state of mind, and was prepared to apologise. But when he met the look of distress she turned upon him, he did not know just where to begin. He tried to speak casually—he had heard she was going away. But she caught him by the hand, exclaiming: "Hal, you are coming with us!"

He did not answer for a moment, but sat down by her. "Have I made you suffer so much, Jessie?"

He saw tears start into her eyes. "Haven't you *known* you were making me suffer? Here I was as Percy's guest; and to have you put such questions to me! What could I say? What do I know about the way Mr. Harrigan should run his business?"

"Yes, dear," he said, humbly. "Perhaps I shouldn't have drawn you into it. But the matter was so complicated and so sudden. Can't you understand that, and forgive me? Everything has turned out so well!"

But she did not think that everything had turned out well. "In the first place, for you to be here, in such a plight! And when I thought you were hunting mountain-goats in Mexico!"

He could not help laughing; but Jessie had not even a smile. "And then—to have you drag our love into the thing, there before every one!"

"Was that really so terrible, Jessie?"

She looked at him with amazement. That he, Hal Warner, could have done such a thing, and not realise how terrible it was! To put her in a position where she had to break either the laws of love or the laws of good-breeding! Why, it had amounted to a public quarrel. It would be the talk of the town—there was no end to the embarrassment of it!

"But, sweetheart!" argued Hal. "Try to see the reality of this thing—think about those people in the mine. You really *must* do that!"

She looked at him, and noticed the new, grim lines that had come upon his youthful face. Also, she caught the note of suppressed passion in his voice. He was pale and weary looking, in dirty clothes, his hair unkempt and his face only half washed. It was terrifying—as if he had gone to war.

"Listen to me, Jessie," he insisted. "I want you to know about these things. If you and I are ever to make each other happy, you must try to grow up with me. That was why I was glad to have you here—you would have a chance to see for yourself. Now I ask you not to go without seeing."

"But I have to go, Hal. I can't ask Percy Harrigan to stay and inconvenience everybody!"

"You can stay without him. You can ask one of the ladies to chaperon you."

She gazed at him in dismay. "Why, Hal! What a thing to suggest!"

"Why so?"

"Think how it would look!"

"I can't think so much about looks, dear—"

She broke in: "Think what Mamma would say!"

"She wouldn't like it, I know—"

"She would be wild! She would never forgive either of us. She would never forgive any one who stayed with me. And what would Percy say, if I came here as his guest, and stayed to spy on him and his father? Don't you see how preposterous it would be?"

Yes, he saw. He was defying all the conventions of her world, and it seemed to her a course of madness. She clutched his hands in hers, and the tears ran down her cheeks.

"Hal," she cried, "I can't leave you in this dreadful place! You look like a ghost, and a scarecrow, too! I want you to go and get some decent clothes and come home on this train."

But he shook his head. "It's not possible, Jessie."

"Why not?"

"Because I have a duty to do here. Can't you understand, dear? All my life, I've been living on the labour of coal-miners, and I've never taken the trouble to go near them, to see how my money was got!"

"But, Hal! These aren't your people! They are Mr. Harrigan's people!"

"Yes," he said, "but it's all the same. They toil, and we live on their toil, and take it as a matter of course."

"But what can one *do* about it, Hal?"

"One can understand it, if nothing else. And you see what I was able to do in this case—to get the mine open."

"Hal," she exclaimed, "I can't understand you! You've become so cynical, you don't believe in any one! You're quite convinced that these officials meant to murder their working people! As if Mr. Harrigan would let his mines be run that way!"

"Mr. Harrigan, Jessie? He passes the collection plate at St. George's! That's the only place you've ever seen him, and that's all you know about him."

"I know what everybody says, Hal! Papa knows him, and my brothers—yes, your own brother, too! Isn't it true that Edward would disapprove what you're doing?"

"Yes, dear, I fear so."

"And you set yourself up against them—against everybody you know! Is it reasonable to think the older people are all wrong, and only you are right? Isn't it at least possible you're making a mistake? Think about it—honestly, Hal, for my sake!"

She was looking at him pleadingly; and he leaned forward and took her hand. "Jessie," he said, his voice trembling, "I *know* that these working people are oppressed; I know it, because I have been one of them! And I know that such men as Peter Harrigan, and even my own brother, are to blame! And they've got to be faced by some one—they've got to be made to see! I've come to see it clearly this summer—that's the job I have to do!"

She was gazing at him with her wide-open, beautiful eyes; underneath her protests and her terror, she was thrilling with awe at this amazing madman she loved. "They will *kill* you!" she cried.

"No, dearest—you don't need to worry about that—I don't think they'll kill me."

"But they shot at you!"

"No, they shot at Joe Smith, a miner's buddy. They won't shoot at the son of a millionaire—not in America, Jessie."

"But some dark night—"

"Set your mind at rest," he said, "I've got Percy tied up in this, and everybody knows it. There's no way they could kill me without the whole story's coming out—and so I'm as safe as I would be in my bed at home!"

SECTION 22.

Hal was still possessed by his idea that Jessie must be taught—she must have knowledge forced upon her, whether she would or no. The train would not start for a couple of hours, and he tried to think of some use he could make of that precious interval. He recalled that Rosa Minetti had returned to her cabin to attend to her baby. A sudden vision came to him of Jessie in that little home. Rosa was sweet and good, and assuredly Little Jerry was a "winner."

"Sweetheart," he said, "I wish you'd come for a walk with me."

"But it's raining, Hal!"

"It won't hurt you to spoil one dress; you have plenty."

"I'm not thinking of that—"

"I *wish* you'd come."

"I don't feel comfortable about it, Hal. I'm here as Percy's guest, and he mightn't like—"

"I'll ask him if he objects to your taking a stroll," he suggested, with pretended gravity.

"No, no! That would make it worse!" Jessie had no humour whatever about these matters.

"Well, Vivie Cass was out, and some of the others are going. He hasn't objected to that."

"I know, Hal. But he knows they're all right."

Hal laughed. "Come on, Jessie. Percy won't hold you for my sins! You have a long train journey before you, and some fresh air will be good for you."

She saw that she must make some concession to him, if she was to keep any of her influence over him.

"All right," she said, with resignation, and disappeared and returned with a heavy veil over her face, to conceal her from prying reportorial eyes; also an equipment of mackintosh, umbrella and overshoes, against the rain. The two stole out of the car, feeling like a couple of criminals.

Skirting the edge of the throng about the pit-mouth, they came to the muddy, unpaved quarter in which the Italians had their homes; he held her arm, steering her through the miniature sloughs and creeks. It was thrilling to him to have her with him thus, to see her sweet face and hear her voice full of love. Many a time he had thought of her here, and told her in his imagination of his experiences!

He told her now—about the Minetti family, and how he had met Big and Little Jerry on the street, and how they had taken him in, and then been driven by fear to let him go again. He told his check-weighman story, and was telling how Jeff Cotton had arrested him; but they came to the Minetti cabin, and the terrifying narrative was cut short.

It was Little Jerry who came to the door, with the remains of breakfast distributed upon his cheeks; he stared in wonder at the mysteriously veiled figure. Entering, they saw Rosa sitting in a chair nursing her baby. She rose in confusion; but she did not quite like to turn her back upon her guests, so she stood trying to hide her breast as best she could, blushing and looking very girlish and pretty.

Hal introduced Jessie, as an old friend who was interested to meet his new friends, and Jessie threw back her veil and sat down. Little Jerry wiped off his face at his mother's command, and then came where he could stare at this incredibly lovely vision.

"I've been telling Miss Arthur what good care you took of me," said Hal to Rosa. "She wanted to come and thank you for it."

"Yes," added Jessie, graciously. "Anybody who is good to Hal earns my gratitude."

Rosa started to murmur something; but Little Jerry broke in, with his cheerful voice, "Why you call him Hal? His name's Joe!"

"Ssh!" cried Rosa. But Hal and Jessie laughed—and so the process of Americanising Little Jerry was continued.

"I've got lots of names," said Hal. "They called me Hal when I was a kid like you."

"Did *she* know you then?" inquired Little Jerry.

"Yes, indeed."

"Is she your girl?"

Rosa laughed shyly, and Jessie blushed, and looked charming. She realised vaguely a difference in manners. These people accepted the existence of "girls," not concealing their interest in the phenomenon.

"It's a secret," warned Hal. "Don't you tell on us!"

"I can keep a secret," said Little Jerry. After a moment's pause he added, dropping his voice, "You gotta keep secrets if you work in North Valley."

"You bet your life," said Hal.

"My father's a Socialist," continued the other, addressing Jessie; then, since one thing leads on to another, "My father's a shot-firer."

"What's a shot-firer?" asked Jessie, by way of being sociable.

"Jesus!" exclaimed Little Jerry. "Don't you know nothin' about minin'?"

"No," said Jessie. "You tell me."

"You couldn't get no coal without a shot-firer," declared Little Jerry. "You gotta get a good one, too, or maybe you bust up the mine. My father's the best they got."

"What does he do?"

"Well, they got a drill—long, long, like this, all the way across the room; and they turn it and bore holes in the coal. Sometimes they got machines to drill, only we don't like them machines, 'cause it takes the men's jobs. When they got the holes, then the shot-firer comes and sets off the powder. You gotta have—" and here Little Jerry slowed up, pronouncing each syllable very carefully—"per-miss-i-ble powder—what don't make no flame. And you gotta know just how much to put in. If you put in too much, you smash the coal, and the miner raises hell; if you don't put in enough, you make too much work for him, an' he raises hell again. So you gotta get a good shot-firer."

Jessie looked at Hal, and he saw that her dismay was mingled with genuine amusement. He judged this a good way for her to get her education, so he proceeded to draw out Little Jerry on other aspects of coal-mining: on short weights and long hours, grafting bosses and camp-marshals, company-stores and boarding-houses, Socialist agitators and union organisers. Little Jerry talked freely of the secrets of the camp. "It's all right for you to know," he remarked gravely. "You're Joe's girl!"

"You little cherub!" exclaimed Jessie.

"What's a cherub?" was Little Jerry's reply.

SECTION 23.

So the time passed in a way that was pleasant. Jessie was completely won by this little Dago mine-urchin, in spite of all his frightful curse-words; and Hal saw that she was won, and was delighted by the success of this experiment in social amalgamation. He could not read Jessie's mind, and realise that underneath her genuine delight were reservations born of her prejudices, the instinctive cruelty of caste. Yes, this little mine chap was a cherub, now; but how about when he grew big? He would grow ugly and coarse-looking, in ten years one would not know him from any other of the rough and dirty men of the village. Jessie took the fact that common people grow ugly as they mature as a proof that they are, in some deep and permanent way, the inferiors of those above them. Hal was throwing away his time and strength, trying to make them into something which Nature had obviously not intended them to be! She decided to make that point to Hal on their way back to the train. She realised that he had brought her here to educate her; like all the rest of the world, she resented forcible education, and she was not without hope that she might turn the tables and educate Hal.

Pretty soon Rosa finished nursing the baby, and Jessie remarked the little one's black eyes. This topic broke down the mother's shyness, and they were chatting pleasantly, when suddenly they heard sounds outside which caused them to start up. It was a clamour of women's voices; and Hal and Rosa sprang to the door. Just now was a critical time, when every one was on edge for news.

Hal threw open the door and called to those outside "What is it?" There came a response, in a woman's voice, "They've found Rafferty!"

"Alive?"

"Nobody knows yet."

"Where?"

"In Room Seventeen. Eleven of them—Rafferty, and young Flanagan, and Johannson, the Swede. They're near dead—can't speak, they say. They won't let anybody near them."

Other voices broke in; but the one which answered Hal had a different quality; it was a warm, rich voice, unmistakably Irish, and it held Jessie's attention. "They've got them in the tipple-room, and the women want to know about their men, and they won't tell them. They're beatin' them back like dogs!"

There was a tumult of weeping, and Hal stepped out of the cabin, and in a minute or so he entered again, supporting on his arm a girl, clad in a faded blue calico dress, and having a head of very conspicuous red hair. She seemed half fainting, and kept moaning that it was horrible, horrible. Hal led her to a chair, and she sank into it and hid her face in her hands, sobbing, talking incoherently between her sobs.

Jessie stood looking at this girl. She felt the intensity of her excitement, and shared it; yet at the same time there was something in Jessie that resented it. She did not wish to be upset about things like this, which she could not help. Of course these unfortunate people were suffering; but—what a shocking lot of noise the poor thing was making! A part of the poor thing's excitement was rage, and Jessie realised that, and resented it still more. It was as if it were a personal challenge to her; the same as Hal's fierce social passions, which so bewildered and shocked her.

"They're beatin' the women back like dogs!" the girl repeated.

"Mary," said Hal, trying to soothe her, "the doctors will be doing their best. The women couldn't expect to crowd about them!"

"Maybe they couldn't; but that's not it, Joe, and ye know it! They been bringin' up dead bodies, some they found where the explosion was—blown all to pieces. And they won't let anybody see them. Is that because of the doctors? No, it ain't! It's because they want to tell lies about the number killed! They want to count four or five legs to a man! And that's what's drivin' the women crazy! I saw Mrs. Zamboni, tryin' to get into the shed, and Pete Hanun caught her by the breasts and shoved her back. 'I want my man!' she screamed. 'Well, what do you want him for? He's all in pieces!' 'I want the pieces!' 'What good'll they do you? Are you goin' to eat him?'"

There were cries of horror now, even from Jessie; and the strange girl hid her face in her hands and began to sob again. Hal put his hand gently on her arm.

"Mary," he pleaded, "it's not so bad—at least they're getting the people out."

"How do ye know what they're doin'? They might be sealin' up parts of the mine down below! That's what makes it so horrible—nobody knows what's happenin'! Ye should have heard poor Mrs. Rafferty screamin'. Joe, it went through me like a knife. Just think, it's been half an hour since they brought him up, and the poor lady can't be told if her man is alive."

SECTION 24.

Hal stood for a few moments in thought. He was surprised that such things should be happening while Percy Harrigan's train was in the village. He was considering whether he should go to Percy, or whether a hint to Cotton or Cartwright would not be sufficient.

"Mary," he said, in a quiet voice, "you needn't distress yourself so. We can get better treatment for the women, I'm sure."

But her sobbing went on. "What can ye do? They're bound to have their way!"

"No," said Hal. "There's a difference now. Believe me—something can be done. I'll step over and have a word with Jeff Cotton."

He started towards the door; but there came a cry: "Hal!" It was Jessie, whom he had almost forgotten in his sudden anger at the bosses.

At her protest he turned and looked at her; then he looked at Mary. He saw the latter's hands fall from her tear-stained face, and her expression of grief give way to one of wonder. "Hal!"

"Excuse me," he said, quickly. "Miss Burke, this is my friend, Miss Arthur." Then, not quite sure if this was a satisfactory introduction, he added, "Jessie, this is my friend, Mary."

Jessie's training could not fail in any emergency. "Miss Burke," she said, and smiled with perfect politeness. But Mary said nothing, and the strained look did not leave her face.

In the first excitement she had almost failed to notice this stranger; but now she stared, and realisation grew upon her. Here was a girl, beautiful with a kind of beauty hardly to be conceived of in a mining-camp; reserved, yet obviously expensive—even in a mackintosh and rubber-shoes. Mary was used to the expensiveness of Mrs. O'Callahan, but here was a new kind of expensiveness, subtle and compelling, strangely unconscious. And she laid claim to Joe Smith, the miner's buddy! She called him by a name hitherto unknown to his North Valley associates! It needed no word from Little Jerry to guide Mary's instinct; she knew in a flash that here was the "other girl."

Mary was seized with sudden acute consciousness of the blue calico dress, patched at the shoulder and stained with grease-spots; of her hands, big and rough with hard labour; of her feet, clad in shoes worn sideways at the heel, and threatening to break out at the toes. And as for Jessie, she too had the woman's instinct;

she too saw a girl who was beautiful, with a kind of beauty of which she did not approve, but which she could not deny—the beauty of robust health, of abounding animal energy. Jessie was not unaware of the nature of her own charms, having been carefully educated to conserve them; nor did she fail to make note of the other girl's handicaps—the patched and greasy dress, the big rough hands, the shoes worn sideways. But even so, she realised that "Red Mary" had a quality which she lacked—that beside this wild rose of a mining-camp, she, Jessie Arthur, might possibly seem a garden flower, fragile and insipid.

She had seen Hal lay his hand upon Mary's arm, and heard her speak to him. She called him Joe! And a sudden fear had leaped into Jessie's heart.

Like many girls who have been delicately reared, Jessie Arthur knew more than she admitted, even to herself. She knew enough to realise that young men with ample means and leisure are not always saints and ascetics. Also, she had heard the remark many times made that these women of the lower orders had "no morals." Just what did such a remark mean? What would be the attitude of such a girl as Mary Burke—full-blooded and intense, dissatisfied with her lot in life—to a man of culture and charm like Hal? She would covet him, of course; no woman who knew him could fail to covet him. And she would try to steal him away from his friends, from the world to which he belonged, the future of happiness and ease to which he was entitled. She would have powers—dark and terrible powers, all the more appalling to Jessie because they were mysterious. Might they possibly be able to overcome even the handicap of a dirty calico dress, of big rough hands and shoes worn sideways?

These reflections, which have taken many words to explain, came to Jessie in one flash of intuition. She understood now, all at once, the incomprehensible phenomenon—that Hal should leave friends and home and career, to come and live amid this squalor and suffering! She saw the old drama of the soul of man, heaven and hell contending for mastery of it; and she knew that she was heaven, and that this "Red Mary" was hell.

She looked at Hal. He seemed to her so fine and true; his face was frank, he was the soul of honourableness. No, it was impossible to believe that he had yielded to such a lure! If that had been the case, he would never have brought her to this cabin, he would never have taken a chance of her meeting the girl. No; but he might be struggling against temptation, he might be in the toils of it, and only half aware of it. He was a man, and therefore blind; he was a dreamer, and it would be like him to idealise this girl, calling her naïve and primitive, thinking that she had no wiles! Jessie had come just in time to save him! And she would fight to save him—using wiles more subtle than those at the command of any mining-camp hussy!

SECTION 25.

It was the surging up in Jessie Arthur of that instinctive self, the creature of hereditary cruelty, of the existence of which Hal had no idea. She drew back, and there was a quiet *hauteur* in her tone as she spoke. "Hal, come here, please."

He came; and she waited until he was close enough for intimacy, and then said, "Have you forgotten you have to take me back to the train?"

"Can't you come with me for a few minutes?" he pleaded. "It would have such a good effect if you did."

"I can't go into that crowd," she answered; and suddenly her voice trembled, and the tears came into her sweet brown eyes. "Don't you know, Hal, that I couldn't stand such terrible sights? This poor girl—she is used to them—she is hardened! But I—I—oh, take me away, take me away, dear Hal!" This cry of a woman for protection came with a familiar echo to Hal's mind. He did not stop to think—he was moved by it instinctively. Yes, he had exposed the girl he loved to suffering! He had meant it for her own good, but even so, it was cruel!

He stood close to her, and saw the love-light in her eyes; he saw the tears, the trembling of her sensitive chin. She swayed to him, and he caught her in his arms—and there, before these witnesses, she let him press her to him, while she sobbed and whispered her distress. She had been shy of caresses hitherto, watched and admonished by an experienced mother; certainly she had never before made what could by the remotest stretch of the imagination be considered an advance towards him. But now she made it, and there was a cry of triumph in her soul as she saw that he responded to it. He was still hers—and these low people should know it, this "other girl" should know it!

Yet, in the midst of this very exultation, Jessie Arthur really felt the grief she expressed for the women of North Valley; she really felt horror at the story of Mrs. Zamboni's "man": so intricate is the soul of woman, so puzzling that faculty, older than the ages, which enables her to be hysterical, and at the same time to be guided in the use of that hysteria by deep and infallible calculation.

But she made Hal realise that it was necessary for him to take her away. He turned to Mary Burke and said, "Miss Arthur's train is leaving in a short time. I'll have to take her hack, and then I'll go to the pit-mouth with you and see what I can do."

"Very well," Mary answered; and her voice was hard and cold. But Hal did not notice this. He was a man, and not able to keep up with the emotions of one woman—to say nothing of two women at the same time.

He took Jessie out, and all the way hack to the train she fought a desperate fight to get him away from here. She no longer even suggested that he get decent clothing; she was willing for him to come as he was, in his coal-stained mining-jumpers, in the private train of the Coal King's son. She besought him in the name of their affection. She threatened him that if he did not come, this might be the last time they would meet. She even broke down in the middle of the street, and let him stand there in plain sight of miners' wives and children, and of possible newspaper reporters, holding her in his arms and comforting her.

Hal was much puzzled; but he would not give way. The idea of going off in Percy Harrigan's train had come to seem morally repulsive to him; he hated Percy Harrigan's train, and Percy Harrigan also, he declared. And Jessie saw that she was only making him unreasonable—that before long he might be hating her. With her instinctive *savoir faire*, she brought up his suggestion that she might find some one to chaperon her, and stay with him at North Valley until he was ready to come away.

Hal's heart leaped at that; he had no idea what was in her mind—the certainty that no one of the ladies of the Harrigan party would run the risk of offending her host by staying under such circumstances.

"You mean it, sweetheart?" he cried, happily.

She answered, "I mean that I love you, Hal."

"All right, dear!" he said. "We'll see if we can arrange it."

But as they walked on, she managed, without his realising it, to cause him to reflect upon the effect of her staying. She was willing to do it, if it was what he wanted; but it would injure, perhaps irrevocably, his standing with her parents. They would telegraph her to come at once; and if she did not obey, they would come by the next train. So on, until at last Hal was moved to withdraw his own suggestion. After all, what was the use of her staying, if her mind was on the people at home, if she would simply keep him in hot water? Before the conversation was over Hal had become clear in his mind that North Valley was no place for Jessie Arthur, and that he had been a fool to think he could bring the two together.

She tried to get him to promise to leave as soon as the last man had been brought out of the mine. He answered that he intended to leave then, unless some new emergency should arise. She tried to get an unqualified promise; and failing in that, when they had nearly got to the train she suddenly made a complete surrender. Let him do what he pleased—but let him remember that she loved him, that she needed him, that she could not do without him. No matter what he might do, no matter what people might say about him, she believed in him, she would stand by him. Hal was deeply touched, and took her in his arms again and kissed her tenderly under the umbrella, in the presence of the wondering stares of several urchins with coal-smutted faces. He pledged anew his love for her, assuring her that no amount of interest in mining-camps should ever steal him from her.

Then he put her on the train, and shook hands with the departing guests. He was so very sombre and harassed-looking that the young men forbore to "kid" him as they would otherwise have done. He stood on the station-platform and saw the train roll away—and felt, to his own desperate bewilderment, that he hated these friends of his boyhood and youth. His reason protested against it; he told himself there was nothing they could do, no reason on earth for them to stay—and yet he hated them. They were hurrying off to dance and flirt at the country club— while he was going back to the pit-mouth, to try to get Mrs. Zamboni the right to inspect the pieces of her "man"!

BOOK FOUR — THE WILL OF KING COAL

SECTION 1.

The pit of death was giving up its secrets. The hoist was busy, and cage-load after cage-load came up, with bodies dead and bodies living and bodies only to be classified after machines had pumped air into them for a while. Hal stood in the rain and watched the crowd and thought that he had never witnessed a scene so compelling to pity and terror. The silence that would fall when any one appeared who might have news to tell! The sudden shriek of anguish from some woman whose hopes were struck dead! The moans of sympathy that ran through the crowd, alternating with cheers at some good tidings, shaking the souls of the multitude as a storm of wind shakes a reed-field!

And the stories that ran through the camp—brought up from the underground world—stories of incredible sufferings, and of still more incredible heroisms! Men who had been four days without food or water, yet had resisted being carried out of the mine, proposing to stay and help rescue others! Men who had lain together in the darkness and silence, keeping themselves alive by the water which seeped from the rocks overhead, taking turns lying face upwards where the drops fell, or wetting pieces of their clothing and sucking out the moisture! Members of the rescue parties would tell how they knocked upon the barriers, and heard the faint answering signals of the imprisoned men; how madly they toiled to cut through, and how, when at last a little hole appeared, they heard the cries of joy, and saw the eyes of men shining from the darkness, while they waited, gasping, for the hole to grow bigger, so that water and food might be passed in!

In some places they were fighting the fire. Long lines of hose had been sent down, and men were moving forward foot by foot, as the smoke and steam were sucked out ahead of them by the fan. Those who did this work were taking their lives in their hands, yet they went without hesitation. There was always hope of finding men in barricaded rooms beyond.

Hal sought out Jeff Cotton at the entrance to the tipple-room, which had been turned into a temporary hospital. It was the first time the two had met since the revelation in Percy's car, and the camp-marshal's face took on a rather sheepish grin. "Well, Mr. Warner, you win," he remarked; and after a little arguing he agreed to permit a couple of women to go into the tipple-room and make a list of the injured, and go out and give the news to the crowd. Hal went to the Minettis to ask Mary Burke to attend to this; but Rosa said that Mary had gone out after he and Miss Arthur had left, and no one knew where she was. So Hal went to Mrs. David, who consented to get a couple of friends, and do the work without being called a "committee." "I won't have any damned committees!" the camp-marshal had declared.

So the night passed, and part of another day. A clerk from the office came to Hal with a sealed envelope, containing a telegram, addressed in care of Cartwright. "I most urgently beg of you to come home at once. It will be distressing to Dad if he hears what has happened, and it will not be possible to keep the matter from him for long."

As Hal read, he frowned; evidently the Harrigans had got busy without delay! He went to the office and telephoned his answer. "Am planning to leave in a day or two. Trust you will make an effort to spare Dad until you have heard my story."

This message troubled Hal. It started in his mind long arguments with his brother, and explanations and apologies to his father. He loved the old man tenderly. What a shame if some emissary of the Harrigans were to get to him to upset him with misrepresentations!

Also these ideas had a tendency to make Hal homesick; they brought more vividly to his thoughts the outside world, with its physical allurements—there being a limit to the amount of unwholesome meals and dirty beds and repulsive sights a man of refinement can force himself to endure. Hal found himself obsessed by a vision of a club dining-room, with odours of grilled steaks and hot rolls, and the colours of salads and fresh fruits and cream. The conviction grew suddenly strong in him that his work in North Valley was nearly done!

Another night passed, and another day. The last of the bodies had been brought out, and the corpses shipped down to Pedro for one of those big wholesale funerals which are a feature of mine-life. The fire was out, and the rescue-crews had given place to a swarm of carpenters and timbermen, repairing the damage and making the mine safe. The reporters had gone; Billy Keating having clasped Hal's hand, and promised to meet him for luncheon at the club. An agent of the "Red Cross" was on hand, and was feeding the hungry out of Mrs. Curtis's subscription-list. What more was there for Hal to do—except to bid good-bye to his friends, and assure them of his help in the future?

First among these friends was Mary Burke, whom he had had no chance to talk to since the meeting with Jessie. He realised that Mary had been deliberately avoiding him. She was not in her home, and he went to inquire at the Rafferties', and stopped for a good-bye chat with the old woman whose husband he had saved.

Rafferty was going to pull through. His wife had been allowed in to see him, and tears rolled down her shrunken cheeks as she told about it. He had been four days and nights blocked up in a little tunnel, with no food or water, save for a few drops of coffee which he had shared with other men. He could still not speak, he could hardly move a hand; but there was life in his eyes, and his look had been a greeting from the soul she had loved and served these thirty years and more. Mrs.

Rafferty sang praises to the Rafferty God, who had brought him safely through these perils; it seemed obvious that He must be more efficient than the Protestant God of Johannson, the giant Swede, who had lain by Rafferty's side and given up the ghost.

But the doctor had stated that the old Irishman would never be good to work again; and Hal saw a shadow of terror cross the sunshine of Mrs. Rafferty's rejoicing. How could a doctor say a thing like that? Rafferty was old, to be sure; but he was tough—and could any doctor imagine how hard a man would try who had a family looking to him? Sure, he was not the one to give up for a bit of pain now and then! Besides him, there was only Tim who was earning; and though Tim was a good lad, and worked steady, any doctor ought to know that a big family could not be kept going on the wages of one eighteen-year-old pit-boy. As for the other lads, there was a law that said they were too young to work. Mrs. Rafferty thought there should be some one to put a little sense into the heads of them that made the laws—for if they wanted to forbid children to work in coal-mines, they should surely provide some other way to feed the children.

Hal listened, agreeing sympathetically, and meantime watching her, and learning more from her actions than from her words. She had been obedient to the teachings of her religion, to be fruitful and multiply; she had fed three grown sons into the maw of industry, and had still eight children and a man to care for. Hal wondered if she had ever rested a single minute of daylight in all her fifty-four years. Certainly not while he had been in her house! Even now, while praising the Rafferty God and blaming the capitalist law-makers, she was getting a supper, moving swiftly, silently, like a machine. She was lean as an old horse that has toiled across a desert; the skin over her cheek-bones was tight as stretched rubber, and cords stood out in her wrists like piano-wires.

And now she was cringing before the spectre of destitution. He asked what she would do about it, and saw the shadow of terror cross her face again. There was one recourse from starvation, it seemed—to have her children taken from her, and put in some institution! At the mention of this, one of the special nightmares of the poor, the old woman began to sob and cry again that the doctor was wrong; he would see, and Hal would see—Old Rafferty would be back at his job in a week or two!

SECTION 2.

Hal went out on the street again. It was the hour which would have been sunset in a level region; the tops of the mountains were touched with a purple light, and the air was fresh and chill with early fall. Down the darkening streets he saw a gathering of men; there was shouting, and people running towards the place, so he hurried up, with the thought in his mind, "What's the matter now?" There were perhaps a hundred men crying out, their voices mingling like the sound of waves on the sea. He could make out words: "Go on! Go on! We've had enough of it! Hurrah!"

"What's happened?" he asked, of some one on the outskirts; and the man, recognising him, raised a cry which ran through the throng: "Joe Smith! He's the boy for us! Come in here, Joe! Give us a speech!"

But even while Hal was asking questions, trying to get the situation clear, other shouts had drowned out his name. "We've had enough of them walking over us!" And somebody cried, more loudly, "Tell us about it! Tell it again! Go on!"

A man was standing upon the steps of a building at one side. Hal stared in amazement; it was Tim Rafferty. Of all people in the world—Tim, the light-hearted and simple, Tim of the laughing face and the merry Irish blue eyes! Now his sandy hair was tousled and his features distorted with rage. "Him near dead!" he yelled. "Him with his voice gone, and couldn't move his hand! Eleven years he's slaved for them, and near killed in an accident that's their own fault—every man in this crowd knows it's their own fault, by God!"

"Sure thing! You're right!" cried a chorus of voices "Tell it all!"

"They give him twenty-five dollars and his hospital expenses—and what'll his hospital expenses be? They'll have him out on the street again before he's able to stand. You know that—they done it to Pete Cullen!"

"You bet they did!"

"Them damned lawyers in there—gettin' 'em to sign papers when they don't know what they're doin'. An' me that might help him can't get near! By Christ, I say it's too much! Are we slaves, or are we dogs, that we have to stand such things?"

"We'll stand no more of it!" shouted one. "We'll go in there and see to it ourselves!"

"Come on!" shouted another. "To hell with their gunmen!"

Hal pushed his way into the crowd. "Tim!" he cried. "How do you know this?"

"There's a fellow in there seen it."

"Who?"

"I can't tell you—they'd fire him; but it's somebody you know as well as me. He come and told me. They're beatin' me old father out of damages!"

"They do it all the time!" shouted Wauchope, an English miner at Hal's side. "That's why they won't let us in there."

"They done the same thing to my father!" put in another voice. Hal recognised Andy, the Greek boy.

"And they want to start Number Two in the mornin'!" yelled Tim. "Who'll go down there again? And with Alec Stone, him that damns the men and saves the mules!"

"We'll not go back in them mines till they're safe!" shouted Wauchope. "Let them sprinkle them—or I'm done with the whole business."

"And let 'em give us our weights!" cried another. "We'll have a check-weighman, and we'll get what we earn!"

So again came the cry, "Joe Smith! Give us a speech, Joe! Soak it to 'em! You're the boy!"

Hal stood helpless, dismayed. He had counted his fight won—and here was another beginning! The men were looking to him, calling upon him as the boldest of the rebels. Only a few of them knew about the sudden change in his fortunes.

Even while he hesitated, the line of battle had swept past him; the Englishman, Wauchope, sprang upon the steps and began to address the throng. He was one of the bowed and stunted men, but in this emergency he developed sudden lung-power. Hal listened in astonishment; this silent and dull-looking fellow was the last he would have picked for a fighter. Tom Olson had sounded him out, and reported that he would hear nothing, so they had dismissed him from mind. And here he was, shouting terrible defiance!

"They're a set of robbers and murderers! They rob us everywhere we turn! For my part, I've had enough of it! Have you?"

There was a roar from every one within reach of his voice. They had all had enough.

"All right, then—we'll fight them!"

"Hurrah! Hurrah! We'll have our rights!"

Jeff Cotton came up on the run, with "Bud" Adams and two or three of the gunmen at his heels. The crowd turned upon them, the men on the outskirts clenching their fists, showing their teeth like angry dogs. Cotton's face was red with rage, but he saw that he had a serious matter in hand; he turned and went for more help—and the mob roared with delight. Already they had begun their fight! Already they had won their first victory!

SECTION 3.

The crowd moved down the street, shouting and cursing as it went. Some one started to sing the Marseillaise, and others took it up, and the words mounted to a frenzy:

> "To arms! To arms, ye brave!
> March on, march on, all hearts resolved
> On victory or death!"

There were the oppressed of many nations in this crowd; they sang in a score of languages, but it was the same song. They would sing a few bars, and the yells of others would drown them out. "March on! March on! All hearts resolved!" Some rushed away in different directions to spread the news, and very soon the whole population of the village was on the spot; the men waving their caps, the women lifting up their hands and shrieking—or standing terrified, realising that babies could not be fed upon revolutionary singing.

Tim Rafferty was raised up on the shoulders of the crowd and made to tell his story once more. While he was telling it, his old mother came running, and her shrieks rang above the clamour: "Tim! Tim! Come down from there! What's the matter wid ye?" She was twisting her hands together in an agony of fright; seeing Hal, she rushed up to him. "Get him out of there, Joe! Sure, the lad's gone crazy! They'll turn us out of the camp, they'll give us nothin' at all—and what'll become of us? Mother of God, what's the matter with the b'y?" She called to Tim again; but Tim paid no attention, if he heard her. Tim was on the march to Versailles!

Some one shouted that they would go to the hospital to protect the injured men from the "damned lawyers." Here was something definite, and the crowd moved in that direction, Hal following with the stragglers, the women and children, and the less bold among the men. He noticed some of the clerks and salaried employés of the company; presently he saw Jeff Cotton again, and heard him ordering these men to the office to get revolvers.

"Big Jack" David came along with Jerry Minetti, and Hal drew back to consult with them. Jerry was on fire. It had come—the revolt he had been looking for-ward to for years! Why were they not making speeches, getting control of the men and organising them?

Jack David voiced uncertainty. They had to consider if this outburst could mean anything permanent.

Jerry answered that it would mean what they chose to make it mean. If they took charge, they could guide the men and hold them together. Wasn't that what Tom Olson had wanted?

No, said the big Welshman, Olson had been trying to organise the men secretly, as preliminary to a revolt in all the camps. That was quite another thing from an open movement, limited to one camp. Was there any hope of success for such a movement? If not, they would be foolish to start, they would only be making sure of their own expulsion.

Jerry turned to Hal. What did he think?

And so at last Hal had to speak. It was hard for him to judge, he said. He knew so little about labour matters. It was to learn about them that he had come to North Valley. It was a hard thing to advise men to submit to such treatment as they had been getting; but on the other hand, any one could see that a futile outbreak would discourage everybody, and make it harder than ever to organise them.

So much Hal spoke; but there was more in his mind, which he could not speak. He could not say to these men, "I am a friend of yours, but I am also a friend of your enemy, and in this crisis I cannot make up my mind to which side I owe allegiance. I'm bound by a duty of politeness to the masters of your lives; also, I'm anxious not to distress the girl I am to marry!" No, he could not say such things. He felt himself a traitor for having them in his mind, and he could hardly bring himself to look these men in the eye. Jerry knew that he was in some way connected with the Harrigans; probably he had told the rest of Hal's friends, and they had been discussing it and speculating about the meaning of it. Suppose they should think he was a spy?

So Hal was relieved when Jack David spoke firmly. They would only be playing the game of the enemy if they let themselves be drawn in prematurely. They ought to have the advice of Tom Olson.

Where was Olson? Hal asked; and David explained that on the day when Hal had been thrown out of camp, Olson had got his "time" and set out for Sheridan, the local headquarters of the union, to report the situation. He would probably not come back; he had got his little group together, he had planted the seed of revolt in North Valley.

They discussed back and forth the problem of getting advice. It was impossible to telephone from North Valley without everything they said being listened to; but the evening train for Pedro left in a few minutes, and "Big Jack" declared that some one ought to take it. The town of Sheridan was only fifteen or twenty miles from Pedro, and there would be a union official there to advise them; or they might use the long distance telephone, and persuade one of the union leaders in Western City to take the midnight train, and be in Pedro next morning.

Hal, still hoping to withdraw himself, put this task off on Jack David. They emptied out the contents of their pockets, so that he might have funds enough, and the big Welshman darted off to catch the train. In the meantime Jerry and Hal agreed to keep in the background, and to seek out the other members of their group and warn them to do the same.

SECTION 4.

This programme was a convenient one for Hal; but as he was to find almost at once, it had been adopted too late. He and Jerry started after the crowd, which had stopped in front of one of the company buildings; and as they came nearer they heard some one making a speech. It was the voice of a woman, the tones rising clear and compelling. They could not see the speaker, because of the throng, but Hal recognised her voice, and caught his companion by the arm. "It's Mary Burke!"

Mary Burke it was, for a fact; and she seemed to have the crowd in a kind of frenzy. She would speak one sentence, and there would come a roar from the throng; she would speak another sentence, and there would come another roar. Hal and Jerry pushed their way in, to where they could make out the words of this litany of rage.

"Would they go down into the pit themselves, do ye think?"

"They would not!"

"Would they be dressed in silks and laces, do ye think?"

"They would not!"

"Would they have such fine soft hands, do ye think?"

"They would not!"

"Would they hold themselves too good to look at ye?"

"They would not! They would not!"

And Mary swept on: "If only ye'd stand together, they'd come to ye on their knees to ask for terms! But ye're cowards, and they play on your fears! Ye're traitors, and they buy ye out! They break ye into pieces, they do what they please with ye—and then ride off in their private cars, and leave gunmen to beat ye down and trample on your faces! How long will ye stand it? How long?"

The roar of the mob rolled down the street and back again. "We'll not stand it! We'll not stand it!" Men shook their clenched fists, women shrieked, even children shouted curses. "We'll fight them! We'll slave no more for them!"

And Mary found a magic word. "We'll have a union!" she shouted. "We'll get together and stay together! If they refuse us our rights, we'll know what to answer—we'll have a *strike!*"

There was a roar like the crashing of thunder in the mountains. Yes, Mary had found the word! For many years it had not been spoken aloud in North Valley, but now it ran like a flash of gunpowder through the throng. "Strike! Strike! Strike! Strike!" It seemed as if they would never have enough of it. Not all of them had understood Mary's speech, but they knew this word, "Strike!" They translated and proclaimed it in Polish and Bohemian and Italian and Greek. Men waved their caps, women waved their aprons—in the semi-darkness it was like some strange kind of vegetation tossed by a storm. Men clasped one another's hands, the more demonstrative of the foreigners fell upon one another's necks. "Strike! Strike! Strike!"

"We're no longer slaves!" cried the speaker. "We're men—and we'll live as men! We'll work as men—or we'll not work at all! We'll no longer be a herd of cattle, that they can drive about as they please! We'll organise, we'll stand together—shoulder to shoulder! Either we'll win together, or we'll starve and die together! And not a man of us will yield, not a man of us will turn traitor! Is there anybody here who'll scab on his fellows?"

There was a howl, which might have come from a pack of wolves. Let the man who would scab on his fellows show his dirty face in that crowd!

"Ye'll stand by the union?"

"We'll stand by it!"

"Ye'll swear?"

"We'll swear!"

She flung her arms to heaven with a gesture of passionate adjuration. "Swear it on your lives! To stick to the rest of us, and never a man of ye give way till ye've won! Swear! *Swear!*"

Men stood, imitating her gesture, their hands stretched up to the sky. "We swear! We swear!"

"Ye'll not let them break ye! Ye'll not let them frighten ye!"

"No! No!"

"Stand by your word, men! Stand by it! 'Tis the one chance for your wives and childer!" The girl rushed on—exhorting with leaping words and passionate out-flung arms—a tall, swaying figure of furious rebellion. Hal listened to the speech and watched the speaker, marvelling. Here was a miracle of the human soul, here was hope born of despair! And the crowd around her—they were sharing the wonderful rebirth; their waving arms, their swaying forms responded to Mary as an orchestra to the baton of a leader.

A thrill shook Hal—a thrill of triumph! He had been beaten down himself, he had wanted to run from this place of torment; but now there was hope in North Valley—now there would be victory, freedom!

Ever since he had come to the coal-country, the knowledge had been growing in Hal that the real tragedy of these people's lives was not their physical suffering, but their mental depression—the dull, hopeless misery in their minds. This had been driven into his consciousness day by day, both by what he saw and by what others told him. Tom Olson had first put it into words: "Your worst troubles are inside the heads of the fellows you're trying to help!" How could hope be given to men in this environment of terrorism? Even Hal himself, young and free as he was, had been brought to despair. He came from a class which is accustomed to say, "Do this," or "Do that," and it will be done. But these mine-slaves had never known that sense of power, of certainty; on the contrary, they were accustomed to having their efforts balked at every turn, their every impulse to happiness or achievement crushed by another's will.

But here was this miracle of the human soul! Here was hope in North Valley! Here were the people rising—and Mary Burke at their head! It was his vision come true—Mary Burke with a glory in her face, and her hair shining like a crown of gold! Mary Burke mounted upon a snow-white horse, wearing a robe of white, soft and lustrous—like Joan of Arc, or a leader in a suffrage parade! Yes, and she was at the head of a host, he had the music of its marching in his ears!

Underneath Hal's jesting words had been a real vision, a real faith in this girl. Since that day when he had first discovered her, a wild rose of the mining-camp taking in the family wash, he had realised that she was no pretty young working-girl, but a woman with a mind and a personality. She saw farther, she felt more deeply than the average of these wage-slaves. Her problem was the same as theirs, yet more complex. When he had wanted to help her and had offered to get her a job, she had made clear that what she craved was not merely relief from drudgery, but a life with intellectual interest. So then the idea had come to him that Mary should become a teacher, a leader of her people. She loved them, she suffered for them and with them, and at the same time she had a mind that was capable of seeking out the causes of their misery. But when he had gone to her with plans of leadership, he had been met by her corroding despair; her pessimism had seemed to mock his dreams, her contempt for these mine-slaves had belittled his efforts in their behalf and in hers.

And now, here she was taking up the role he had planned for her! Her very soul was in this shouting throng, he thought. She had lived the lives of these people, shared their every wrong, been driven to rebellion with them. Being a mere man, Hal missed one important point about this startling development; he did not realise that Mary's eloquence was addressed, not merely to the Rafferties and the Wauchopes, and the rest of the North Valley mine-slaves, but to a certain magazine-cover girl, clad in a mackintosh and a pale green hat and a soft and filmy and horribly expensive motoring veil!

<h1 style="text-align:center">SECTION 5.</h1>

Mary's speech was brought to a sudden end. A group of the men had moved down the street, and there arose a disturbance there. The noise of it swelled louder, and more people began to move in that direction. Mary turned to look, and all at once the whole throng surged down the street.

The trouble was at the hospital. In front of this building was a porch, and on it Cartwright and Alec Stone were standing, with a group of the clerks and office-employés, among whom Hal saw Predovich, Johnson, the postmaster, and Si Adams. At the foot of the steps stood Tim Rafferty, with a swarm of determined men at his back. He was shouting, "We want them lawyers out of there!"

The superintendent himself had undertaken to parley with him. "There are no lawyers in here, Rafferty."

"We don't trust you!" And the crowd took up the cry: "We'll see for ourselves!"

"You can't go into this building," declared Cartwright.

"I'm goin' to see my father!" shouted Tim. "I've got a right to see my father, ain't I?"

"You can see him in the morning. You can take him away, if you want to. We've no desire to keep him. But he's asleep now, and you can't disturb the others."

"You weren't afraid to disturb them with your damned lawyers!" And there was a roar of approval—so loud that Cartwright's denial could hardly be heard.

"There have been no lawyers near him, I tell you."

"It's a lie!" shouted Wauchope. "They been in there all day, and you know it. We mean to have them out."

"Go on, Tim!" cried Andy, the Greek boy, pushing his way to the front. "Go on!" cried the others; and thus encouraged, Rafferty started up the steps.

"I mean to see my father!" As Cartwright caught him by the shoulder, he yelled, "Let me go, I say!"

It was evident that the superintendent was trying his best not to use violence; he was ordering his own followers back at the same time that he was holding the boy. But Tim's blood was up; he shoved forward, and the superintendent, either striking him or trying to ward off a blow, threw him backwards down the steps.

There was an uproar of rage from the throng; they surged forward, and at the same time some of the men on the porch drew revolvers.

The meaning of that situation was plain enough. In a moment more the mob would be up the steps, and there would be shooting. And if once that happened, who could guess the end? Wrought up as the crowd was, it might not stop till it had fired every company building, perhaps not until it had murdered every company representative.

Hal had resolved to keep in the back-ground, but he saw that to keep in the back-ground at that moment would be an act of cowardice, almost a crime. He sprang forward, his cry rising above the clamour. "Stop, men! Stop!"

There was probably no other man in North Valley who could have got himself heeded at that moment. But Hal had their confidence, he had earned the right to be heard. Had he not been to prison for them, had they not seen him behind the bars? "Joe Smith!" The cry ran from one end of the excited throng to the other.

Hal was fighting his way forward, shoving men to one side, imploring, commanding silence. "Tim Rafferty! Wait!" And Tim, recognising the voice, obeyed.

Once clear of the press, Hal sprang upon the porch, where Cartwright did not attempt to interfere with him.

"Men!" he cried. "Hold on a moment! This isn't what you want! You don't want a fight!" He paused for an instant; but he knew that no mere negative would hold them at that moment. They must be told what they did want. Just now he had learned the particular words that would carry, and he proclaimed them at the top of his voice: "What you want is a union! A *strike!*"

He was answered by a roar from the crowd, the loudest yet. Yes, that was what they wanted! A strike! And they wanted Joe Smith to organise it, to lead it. He had been their leader once, he had been thrown out of camp for it. How he had got back they were not quite clear—but here he was, and he was their darling. Hurrah for him! They would follow him to hell and back!

And wasn't he the boy with the nerve! Standing there on the porch of the hospital, right under the very noses of the bosses, making a union speech to them, and the bosses never daring to touch him! The crowd, realising this situation, went wild with delight. The English-speaking men shouted assent to his words; and those who could not understand, shouted because the others did.

They did not want fighting—of course not! Fighting would not help them! What would help them was to get together, and stand a solid body of free men. There would be a union committee, able to speak for all of them, to say that no man would go to work any more until justice was secured! They would have an end to the business of discharging men because they asked for their rights, of blacklisting men and driving them out of the district because they presumed to want what the laws of the state awarded them!

SECTION 6.

How long could a man expect to stand on the steps of a company building, with a super and a pit-boss at his back, and organise a union of mine-workers? Hal realised that he must move the crowd from that perilous place.

"You'll do what I say, now?" he demanded; and when they agreed in chorus, he added the warning: "There'll be no fighting! And no drinking! If you see any man drunk to-night, sit on him and hold him down!"

They laughed and cheered. Yes, they would keep straight. Here was a job for sober men, you bet!

"And now," Hal continued, "the people in the hospital. We'll have a committee go in and see about them. No noise—we don't want to disturb the sick men. We only want to make sure nobody else is disturbing them. Some one will go in and stay with them. Does that suit you?"

Yes, that suited them.

"All right," said Hal. "Keep quiet for a moment."

And he turned to the superintendent. "Cartwright," said he, "we want a committee to go in and stay with our people." Then, as the superintendent started to expostulate, he added, in a low voice, "Don't be a fool, man! Don't you see I'm trying to save your life?"

The superintendent knew how bad it would be for discipline to let Hal carry his point with the crowd; but also he saw the immediate danger—and he was not sure of the courage and shooting ability of book-keepers and stenographers.

"Be quick, man!" exclaimed Hal. "I can't hold these people long. If you don't want hell breaking loose, come to your senses."

"All right," said Cartwright, swallowing his dignity.

And Hal turned to the men and announced the concession. There was a shout of triumph.

"Now, who's to go?" said Hal, when he could be heard again; and he looked about at the upturned faces. There Were Tim and Wauchope, the most obvious ones; but Hal decided to keep them under his eye. He thought of Jerry Minetti and of Mrs. David—but remembered his agreement with "Big Jack," to keep their own little group in the back-ground. Then he thought of Mary Burke; she had already done herself all the harm she could do, and she was a person the crowd would trust. He called her, and called Mrs. Ferris, an American woman in the crowd. The two came up the steps, and Hal turned to Cartwright.

"Now, let's have an understanding," he said. "These people are going in to stay with the sick men, and to talk to them if they want to, and nobody's going to give them any orders but the doctors and nurses. Is that right?"

"All right," said the superintendent, sullenly.

"Good!" said Hal. "And for God's sake have a little sense and stand by your word; this crowd has had all it can endure, and if you do any more to provoke it, the consequences will be on you. And while you're about it, see that the saloons are closed and kept closed until this trouble is settled. And keep your people out of the way—don't let them go about showing their guns and making faces."

Without waiting to hear the superintendent's reply, Hal turned to the throng, and held up his hand for silence. "Men," he said, "we have a big job to do—we're going to organise a union. And we can't do it here in front of the hospital. We've made too much noise already. Let's go off quietly, and have our meeting on the dump in back of the power-house. Does that suit you?"

They answered that it suited them; and Hal, having seen the two women passed safely into the hospital, sprang down from the porch to lead the way. Jerry Minetti came to his side, trembling with delight; and Hal clutched him by the arm and whispered, excitedly, "Sing, Jerry! Sing them some Dago song!"

SECTION 7.

They got to the place appointed without any fighting. And meantime Hal had worked out in his mind a plan for communicating with this polyglot horde. He knew that half the men could not understand a word of English, and that half the remainder understood very little. Obviously, if he was to make matters clear to them, they must be sorted out according to nationality, and a reliable interpreter found for each group.

The process of sorting proved a slow one, involving no end of shouting and good-natured jostling—Polish here, Bohemian here, Greek here, Italian here! When this job had been done, and a man found from each nationality who understood enough English to translate to his fellows, Hal started in to make a speech. But before he had spoken many sentences, pandemonium broke loose. All the interpreters started interpreting at the same time—and at the top of their lungs; it was like a parade with the bands close together! Hal was struck dumb; then he began to laugh, and the various audiences began to laugh; the orators stopped, perplexed—then they too began to laugh. So wave after wave of merriment rolled over the throng; the mood of the assembly was changed all at once, from rage and determination to the wildest hilarity. Hal learned his first lesson in the handling of these hordes of child-like people, whose moods were quick, whose tempers were balanced upon a fine point.

It was necessary for him to make his speech through to the end, and then move the various audiences apart, to be addressed by the various interpreters. But then arose a new difficulty. How could any one control these floods of eloquence? How be sure that the message was not being distorted? Hal had been warned by Olson of company detectives who posed as workers, gaining the confidence of men in order to incite them to violence. And certainly some of these interpreters were violent-looking, and one's remarks sounded strange in their translations!

There was the Greek orator, for example; a wild man, with wild hair and eyes, who tore all his passions to tatters. He stood upon a barrel-head, with the light of two pit-lamps upon him, and some two score of his compatriots at his feet; he waved his arms, he shook his fists, he shrieked, he bellowed. But when Hal, becoming uneasy, went over and asked another English-speaking Greek what the orator was saying, the answer was that he was promising that the law should be enforced in North Valley!

Hal stood watching this perfervid little man, a study in the possibilities of gesture. He drew back his shoulders and puffed out his chest, almost throwing himself backwards off the barrel-head; he was saying that the miners would be able to live like men. He crouched down and bowed his head, moaning; he was telling them what would happen if they gave up. He fastened his fingers in his long black hair and began tugging desperately; he pulled, and then stretched out his empty hands; he pulled again, so hard that it almost made one cry out with pain to watch him. Hal asked what that was for; and the answer was, "He say, 'Stand by union! Pull one hair, he come out; pull all hairs, no come out'!" It carried one back to the days of Aesop and his fables!

Tom Olson had told Hal something about the technique of an organiser, who wished to drill these ignorant hordes. He had to repeat and repeat, until the dullest in his audience had grasped his meaning, had got into his head the all-saving idea of solidarity. When the various orators had talked themselves out, and the audiences had come back to the cinder-heap, Hal made his speech all over again, in words of one syllable, in the kind of pidgin-English which does duty in the camps. Sometimes he would stop to reinforce it with Greek or Italian or Slavish words he had picked up. Or perhaps his eloquence would inflame some one of the interpreters afresh, and he would wait while the man shouted a few sentences to his compatriots. It was not necessary to consider the possibility of boring any one, for these were patient and long-suffering men, and now desperately in earnest.

They were going to have a union; they were going to do the thing in regular form, with membership cards and officials chosen by ballot. So Hal explained to them, step by step. There was no use organising unless they meant to stay organised. They would choose leaders, one from each of the principal language groups; and these leaders would meet and draw up a set of demands, which would be submitted in mass-meeting, and ratified, and then presented to the bosses with the announcement that until these terms were granted, not a single North Valley worker would go back into the pits.

Jerry Minetti, who knew all about unions, advised Hal to enroll the men at once; he counted on the psychological effect of having each man come forward and give in his name. But here at once they met a difficulty encountered by all would-be organisers—lack of funds. There must be pencils and paper for the enrollment; and Hal had emptied his pockets for Jack David! He was forced to borrow a quarter, and send a messenger off to the store. It was voted by the delegates that each member as he joined the union should be assessed a dime. There would have to be some telegraphing and telephoning if they were going to get help from the outside world.

A temporary committee was named, consisting of Tim Rafferty, Wauchope and Hal, to keep the lists and the funds, and to run things until another meeting could be held on the morrow; also a body-guard of a dozen of the sturdiest and most reliable men were named to stay by the committee. The messenger came back with pads and pencils, and sitting on the ground by the light of pit-lamps, the interpreters wrote down the names of the men who wished to join the union, each man in turn pledging his word for solidarity and discipline. Then the meeting was declared adjourned till daylight of the morrow, and the workers scattered to their homes to sleep, with a joy and sense of power such as few of them had ever known in their lives before.

SECTION 8.

The committee and its body-guard repaired to the dining-room of Reminit-sky's, where they stretched themselves out on the floor; no one attempted to interfere with them, and while the majority snored peacefully, Hal and a small group sat writing out the list of demands which were to be submitted to the bosses in the morning. It was arranged that Jerry should go down to Pedro by the early morning train, to get into touch with Jack David and the union officials, and report to them the latest developments. Because the officials were sure to have detectives following them, Hal warned Jerry to go to MacKellar's house, and have MacKellar bring "Big Jack" to meet him there. Also Jerry must have MacKellar get the *Gazette* on the long distance phone, and tell Billy Keating about the strike.

A hundred things like this Hal had to think of; his head was a-buzz with them, so that when he lay down to sleep he could not. He thought about the bosses, and what they might be doing. The bosses would not be sleeping, he felt sure!

And then came thoughts about his private-car friends; about the strangeness of this plight into which he had got himself! He laughed aloud in a kind of desperation as he recalled Percy's efforts to get him away from here. And poor Jessie! What could he say to her now?

The bosses made no move that night; and when morning came, the strikers hurried to the meeting-place, some of them without even stopping for breakfast. They came tousled and unkempt, looking anxiously at their fellows, as if unable to credit the memory of the bold thing they had done on the night before. But finding the committee and its body-guard on hand and ready for business, their courage revived, they felt again the wonderful sentiment of solidarity which had made men of them. Pretty soon speech-making began, and cheering and singing, which brought out the laggards and the cowards. So in a short while the move-ment was in full swing, with practically every man, woman and child among the workers present.

Mary Burke came from the hospital, where she had spent the night. She looked weary and bedraggled, but her spirit of battle had not slumped. She reported that she had talked with some of the injured men, and that many of them had signed "releases," whereby the company protected itself against even the threat of a law-suit. Others had refused to sign, and Mary had been vehement in warning them to stand out. Two other women volunteered to go to the hospital, in order that she might have a chance to rest; but Mary did not wish to rest, she did not feel as if she could ever rest again.

The members of the newly-organised union proceeded to elect officers. They sought to make Hal president, but he was shy of binding himself in that irrevocable way, and succeeded in putting the honour off on Wauchope. Tim Rafferty was made treasurer and secretary. Then a committee was chosen to go to Cartwright with the demands of the men. It included Hal, Wauchope, and Tim; an Italian named Marcelli, whom Jerry had vouched for; a representative of the Slavs and one of the Greeks—Rusick and Zammakis, both of them solid and faithful men. Finally, with a good deal of laughter and cheering, the meeting voted to add Mary Burke to this committee. It was a new thing to have a woman in such a role, but Mary was the daughter of a miner and the sister of a breaker-boy, and had as good a right to speak as any one in North Valley.

SECTION 9.

Hal read the document which had been prepared the night before. They demanded the right to have a union without being discharged for it. They demanded a check-weighman, to be elected by the men themselves. They demanded that the mines should be sprinkled to prevent explosions, and properly timbered to prevent falls. They demanded the right to trade at any store they pleased. Hal called attention to the fact that every one of these demands was for a right guaranteed by the laws of the state; this was a significant fact, and he urged the men not to include other demands. After some argument they voted down the proposition of the radicals, who wanted a ten per cent. increase in wages. Also they voted down the proposition of a syndicalist-anarchist, who explained to them in a jumble of English and Italian that the mines belonged to them, and that they should refuse all compromise and turn the bosses out forthwith.

While this speech was being delivered, young Rovetta pushed his way through the crowd and drew Hal to one side. He had been down by the railroad-station and seen the morning train come in. From it had descended a crowd of thirty or forty men, of that "hard citizen" type which every miner in the district could recognise at the first glance. Evidently the company officials had been keeping the telephone-wires busy that night; they were bringing in, not merely this train-load of guards, but automobile loads from other camps—from the Northeastern down the canyon, and from Barela, in a side canyon over the mountain.

Hal told this news to the meeting, which received it with howls of rage. So that was the bosses' plan! Hot-heads sprang upon the cinder-heap, half a dozen of them trying to make speeches at once. The leaders had to suppress these too impetuous ones by main force; once more Hal gave the warning of "No fighting!" They were going to have faith in their union; they were going to present a solid front to the company, and the company would learn the lesson that intimidation would not win a strike.

So it was agreed, and the committee set out for the company's office, Wauchope carrying in his hand the written demands of the meeting. Behind the committee marched the crowd in a solid mass; they packed the street in front of the office, while the heroic seven went up the steps and passed into the building. Wauchope made inquiry for Mr. Cartwright, and a clerk took in the message.

They stood waiting; and meanwhile, one of the office-people, coming in from the street, beckoned to Hal. He had an envelope in his hand, and gave it over without a word. It was addressed, "Joe Smith," and Hal opened it, and found within a small visiting card, at which he stared. "Edward S. Warner, Jr."!

For a moment Hal could hardly believe the evidence of his eyesight. Edward in North Valley! Then, turning the card over, he read, in his brother's familiar handwriting, "I am at Cartwright's house. I must see you. The matter concerns Dad. Come instantly."

Fear leaped into Hal's heart. What could such a message mean?

He turned quickly to the committee and explained. "My father's an old man, and had a stroke of apoplexy three years ago. I'm afraid he may be dead, or very ill. I must go."

"It's a trick!" cried Wauchope excitedly.

"No, not possibly," answered Hal. "I know my brother's handwriting. I must see him."

"Well," declared the other, "we'll wait. We'll not see Cartwright until you get back."

Hal considered this. "I don't think that's wise," he said. "You can do what you have to do just as well without me."

"But I wanted you to do the talking!"

"No," replied Hal, "that's your business, Wauchope. You are the president of the union. You know what the men want, as well as I do; you know what they complain of. And besides, there's not going to be any need of talking with Cartwright. Either he's going to grant our demands or he isn't."

They discussed the matter back and forth. Mary Burke insisted that they were pulling Hal away just at the critical moment! He laughed as he answered. She was as good as any man when it came to an argument. If Wauchope showed signs of weakening, let her speak up!

SECTION 10.

So Hal hurried off, and climbed the street which led to the superintendent's house, a concrete bungalow set upon a little elevation overlooking the camp. He rang the bell, and the door opened, and in the entrance stood his brother.

Edward Warner was eight years older than Hal; the perfect type of the young American business man. His figure was erect and athletic, his features were regular and strong, his voice, his manner, everything about him spoke of quiet decision, of energy precisely directed. As a rule, he was a model of what the tailor's art could do, but just now there was something abnormal about his attire as well as his manner.

Hal's anxiety had been increasing all the way up the street. "What's the matter with Dad?" he cried.

"Dad's all right," was the answer—"that is, for the moment."

"Then what—?"

"Peter Harrigan's on his way back from the East. He's due in Western City to-morrow. You can see that something will be the matter with Dad unless you quit this business at once."

Hal had a sudden reaction from his fear. "So that's all!" he exclaimed.

His brother was gazing at the young miner, dressed in sooty blue overalls, his face streaked with black, his wavy hair all mussed. "You wired me you were going to leave here, Hal!"

"So I was; but things happened that I couldn't foresee. There's a strike."

"Yes; but what's that got to do with it?" Then, with exasperation in his voice, "For God's sake, Hal, how much farther do you expect to go?"

Hal stood for a few moments, looking at his brother. Even in a tension as he was, he could not help laughing. "I know how all this must seem to you, Edward. It's a long story; I hardly know how to begin."

"No, I suppose not," said Edward, drily.

And Hal laughed again. "Well, we agree that far, at any rate. What I was hoping was that we could talk it all over quietly, after the excitement was past. When I explain to you about conditions in this place—"

But Edward interrupted. "Really, Hal, there's no use of such an argument. I have nothing to do with conditions in Peter Harrigan's camps."

The smile left Hal's face. "Would you have preferred to have me investigate conditions in the Warner camps?" Hal had tried to suppress his irritation, but there was simply no way these two could get along. "We've had our arguments about these things, Edward, and you've always had the best of me—you could tell me I was a child, it was presumptuous of me to dispute your assertions. But now—well, I'm a child no longer, and we'll have to meet on a new basis."

Hal's tone, more than his words, made an impression. Edward thought before he spoke. "Well, what's your new basis?"

"Just now I'm in the midst of a strike, and I can hardly stop to explain."

"You don't think of Dad in all this madness?"

"I think of Dad, and of you too, Edward; but this is hardly the time—"

"If ever in the world there was a time, this is it!"

Hal groaned inwardly. "All right," he said, "sit down. I'll try to give you some idea how I got swept into this."

He began to tell about the conditions he had found in this stronghold of the "G. F. C." As usual, when he talked about it, he became absorbed in its human aspects; a fervour came into his tone, he was carried on, as he had been when he tried to argue with the officials in Pedro. But his eloquence was interrupted, even as it had been then; he discovered that his brother was in such a state of exasperation that he could not listen to a consecutive argument.

It was the old, old story; it had been thus as far back as Hal could remember. It seemed one of the mysteries of nature, how she could have brought two such different temperaments out of the same parentage. Edward was practical and positive; he knew what he wanted in the world, and he knew how to get it; he was never troubled with doubts, nor with self-questioning, nor with any other superfluous emotions; he could not understand people who allowed that sort of waste in their mental processes. He could not understand people who got "swept into things."

In the beginning, he had had with Hal the prestige of the elder brother. He was handsome as a young Greek god, he was strong and masterful; whether he was flying over the ice with sure, strong strokes, or cutting the water with his glistening shoulders, or bringing down a partridge with the certainty and swiftness of a lightning stroke, Edward was the incarnation of Success. When he said that one's ideas were "rot," when he spoke with contempt of "mollycoddles"—then indeed one suffered in soul, and had to go back to Shelley and Ruskin to renew one's courage.

The questioning of life had begun very early with Hal; there seemed to be something in his nature which forced him to go to the roots of things; and much as he looked up to his wonderful brother, he had been made to realise that there were sides of life to which this brother was blind. To begin with, there were religious doubts; the distresses of mind which plague a young man when first it dawns upon him that the faith he has been brought up in is a higher kind of fairytale. Edward had never asked such questions, apparently. He went to church, because it was the thing to do; more especially because it was pleasing to the young lady he wished to marry to have him put on stately clothes, and escort her to a beautiful place of music and flowers and perfumes, where she would meet her friends, also in stately clothes. How abnormal it seemed to Edward that a young man should give up this pleasant custom, merely because he could not be sure that Jonah had swallowed a whale!

But it was when Hal's doubts attacked his brother's week-day religion—the religion of the profit-system—that the controversy between them had become deadly. At first Hal had known nothing about practical affairs, and it had been Edward's duty to answer his questions. The prosperity of the country had been built up by strong men; and these men had enemies—evil-minded persons, animated by jealousy and other base passions, seeking to tear down the mighty structure. At first this devil-theory had satisfied the boy; but later on, as he had come to read and observe, he had been plagued by doubts. In the end, listening to his brother's conversation, and reading the writings of so-called "muck-rakers," the realisation was forced upon him that there were two types of mind in the controversy—those who thought of profits, and those who thought of human beings.

Edward was alarmed at the books Hal was reading; he was still more alarmed when he saw the ideas Hal was bringing home from college. There must have been some strange change in Harrigan in a few years; no one had dreamed of such ideas when Edward was there! No one had written satiric songs about the faculty, or the endowments of eminent philanthropists!

In the meantime Edward Warner Senior had had a paralytic stroke, and Edward Junior had taken charge of the company. Three years of this had given him the point of view of a coal-operator, hard and set for a life-time. The business of a coal-operator was to buy his labour cheap, to turn out the maximum product in the shortest time, and to sell the product at the market price to parties whose credit was satisfactory. If a concern was doing that, it was a successful concern; for any one to mention that it was making wrecks of the people who dug the coal, was to be guilty of sentimentality and impertinence.

Edward had heard with dismay his brother's announcement that he meant to study industry by spending his vacation as a common labourer. However, when he considered it, he was inclined to think that the idea might not be such a bad one. Perhaps Hal would not find what he was looking for; perhaps, working with his hands, he might get some of the nonsense knocked out of his head!

But now the experiment had been made, and the revelation had burst upon Edward that it had been a ghastly failure. Hal had not come to realise that labour was turbulent and lazy and incompetent, needing a strong hand to rule it; on the contrary, he had become one of these turbulent ones himself! A champion of the lazy and incompetent, an agitator, a fomenter of class-prejudice, an enemy of his own friends, and of his brother's business associates!

Never had Hal seen Edward in such a state of excitement. There was something really abnormal about him, Hal realised; it puzzled him vaguely while he talked, but he did not understand it until his brother told how he had come to be here. He had been attending a dinner-dance at the home of a friend, and Percy

Harrigan had got him on the telephone at half past eleven o'clock at night. Percy had had a message from Cartwright, to the effect that Hal was leading a riot in North Valley; Percy had painted the situation in such lurid colours that Edward had made a dash and caught the midnight train, wearing his evening clothes, and without so much as a tooth-brush with him!

Hal could hardly keep from bursting out laughing. His brother, his punctilious and dignified brother, alighting from a sleeping-car at seven o'clock in the morning, wearing a dress suit and a silk hat! And here he was, Edward Warner Junior, the fastidious, who never paid less than a hundred and fifty dollars for a suit of clothes, clad in a "hand-me-down" for which he had expended twelve dollars and forty-eight cents in a "Jew-store" in a coal-town!

SECTION 11.

But Edward would not stop for a single smile; his every faculty was absorbed in the task he had before him, to get his brother out of this predicament, so dangerous and so humiliating. Hal had come to a town owned by Edward's business friends, and had proceeded to meddle in their affairs, to stir up their labouring people and imperil their property. That North Valley was the property of the General Fuel Company—not merely the mines and the houses, but likewise the people who lived in them—Edward seemed to have no doubt whatever; Hal got only exclamations of annoyance when he suggested any other point of view. Would there have been any town of North Valley, if it had not been for the capital and energy of the General Fuel Company? If the people of North Valley did not like the conditions which the General Fuel Company offered them, they had one simple and obvious remedy—to go somewhere else to work. But they stayed; they got out the General Fuel Company's coal, they took the General Fuel Company's wages—

"Well, they've stopped taking them now," put in Hal.

All right, that was their affair, replied Edward. But let them stop because they wanted to—not because outside agitators put them up to it. At any rate, let the agitators not include a member of the Warner family!

The elder brother pictured old Peter Harrigan on his way back from the East; the state of unutterable fury in which he would arrive, the storm he would raise in the business world of Western City. Why, it was unimaginable, such a thing had never been heard of! "And right when we're opening up a new mine—when we need every dollar of credit we can get!"

"Aren't we big enough to stand off Peter Harrigan?" inquired Hal.

"We have plenty of other people to stand off," was the answer. "We don't have to go out of our way to make enemies."

Edward spoke, not merely as the elder brother, but also as the money-man of the family. When the father had broken down from over-work, and had been changed in one terrible hour from a driving man of affairs into a childish and pathetic invalid, Hal had been glad enough that there was one member of the family who was practical; he had been perfectly willing to see his brother shoulder these burdens, while he went off to college, to amuse himself with satiric songs. Hal had no responsibilities, no one asked anything of him—except that he would not throw sticks into the wheels of the machine his brother was running. "You are living by the coal industry! Every dollar you spend comes from it—"

"I know it! I know it!" cried Hal. "That's the thing that torments me! The fact that I'm living upon the bounty of such wage-slaves—"

"Oh, cut it out!" cried Edward. "That's not what I mean!"

"I know—but it's what *I* mean! From now on I mean to know about the people who work for me, and what sort of treatment they get. I'm no longer your kid-brother, to be put off with platitudes."

"You know ours are union mines, Hal—"

"Yes, but what does that mean? How do we work it? Do we give the men their weights?"

"Of course! They have their check-weighmen."

"But then, how do we compete with the operators in this district, who pay for a ton of three thousand pounds?"

"We manage it—by economy."

"Economy? I don't see Peter Harrigan wasting anything here!" Hal paused for an answer, but none came. "Do we buy the check-weighmen? Do we bribe the labour leaders?"

Edward coloured slightly. "What's the use of being nasty, Hal? You know I don't do dirty work."

"I don't mean to be nasty, Edward; but you must know that many a business-man can say he doesn't do dirty work, because he has others do it for him. What about politics, for instance? Do we run a machine, and put our clerks and bosses into the local offices?"

Edward did not answer, and Hal persisted, "I mean to know these things! I'm not going to be blind any more!"

"All right, Hal—you can know anything you want; but for God's sake, not now! If you want to be taken for a man, show a man's common sense! Here's Old Peter getting back to Western City to-morrow night! Don't you know that he'll be after me, raging like a mad bull? Don't you know that if I tell him I can do nothing—that I've been down here and tried to pull you away—don't you know he'll go after Dad?"

Edward had tried all the arguments, and this was the only one that counted. "You must keep him away from Dad!" exclaimed Hal.

"You tell me that!" retorted the other. "And when you know Old Peter! Don't you know he'll get at him, if he has to break down the door of the house? He'll throw the burden of his rage on that poor old man! You've been warned about it clearly; you know it may be a matter of life and death to keep Dad from getting excited. I don't know what he'd do; maybe he'd fly into a rage with you, maybe he'd defend you. He's old and weak, he's lost his grip on things. Anyhow, he'd not let Peter abuse you—and like as not he'd drop dead in the midst of the dispute! Do you want to have that on your conscience, along with the troubles of your work-ingmen friends?"

SECTION 12.

Hal sat staring in front of him, silent. Was it a fact that every man had something in his life which palsied his arm, and struck him helpless in the battle for social justice?

When he spoke again, it was in a low voice. "Edward, I'm thinking about a young Irish boy who works in these mines. He, too, has a father; and this father was caught in the explosion. He's an old man, with a wife and seven other children. He's a good man, the boy's a good boy. Let me tell you what Peter Harrigan has done to them!"

"Well," said Edward, "whatever it is, it's all right, you can help them. They won't need to starve."

"I know," said Hal, "but there are so many others; I can't help them all. And besides, can't you see, Edward—what I'm thinking about is not charity, but *justice*. I'm sure this boy, Tim Rafferty, loves his father just exactly as much as I love my father; and there are other old men here, with sons who love them—"

"Oh, Hal, for Christ's sake!" exclaimed Edward, in a sort of explosion. He had no other words to express his impatience. "Do you expect to take all the troubles in the world on your shoulders?" And he sprang up and caught the other by the arm. "Boy, you've got to come away from here!"

Hal got up, without answering. He seemed irresolute, and his brother started to draw him towards the door. "I've got a car here. We can get a train in an hour—"

Hal saw that he had to speak firmly. "No, Edward," he said. "I can't come just yet."

"I tell you you *must* come!"

"I can't. I made these men a promise!"

"In God's name—what are these men to you? Compared with your own father!"

"I can't explain it, Edward. I've talked for half an hour, and I don't think you've even heard me. Suffice it to say that I see these people caught in a trap—and one that my whole life has helped to make. I can't leave them in it. What's more, I don't believe Dad would want me to do it, if he understood."

The other made a last effort at self-control. "I'm not going to call you a sentimental fool. Only, let me ask you one plain question. What do you think you can *do* for these people?"

"I think I can help to win decent conditions for them."

"Good God!" cried Edward; he sighed, in his agony of exasperation. "In Peter Harrigan's mines! Don't you realise that he'll pick them up and throw them out of here, neck and crop—the whole crew, every man in the town, if necessary?"

"Perhaps," answered Hal; "but if the men in the other mines should join them—if the big union outside should stand by them—"

"You're dreaming, Hal! You're talking like a child! I talked to the superintendent here; he had telegraphed the situation to Old Peter, and had just got an answer. Already he's acted, no doubt."

"Acted?" echoed Hal. "How do you mean?" He was staring at his brother in sudden anxiety.

"They were going to turn the agitators out, of course."

"*What?* And while I'm here talking!"

Hal turned toward the door. "You knew it all the time!" he exclaimed. "You kept me here deliberately!"

He was starting away, but Edward sprang and caught him. "What could you have done?"

"Turn me loose!" cried Hal, angrily.

"Don't be a fool, Hal! I've been trying to keep you out of the trouble. There may be fighting."

Edward threw himself between Hal and the door, and there was a sharp struggle. But the elder man was no longer the athlete, the young bronzed god; he had been sitting at a desk in an office, while Hal had been doing hard labour. Hal threw him to one side, and in a moment more had sprung out of the door, and was running down the slope.

<h1 style="text-align:center">SECTION 13.</h1>

Coming to the main street of the village, Hal saw the crowd in front of the office. One glance told him that something had happened. Men were running this way and that, gesticulating, shouting. Some were coming in his direction, and when they saw him they began to yell to him. The first to reach him was Klowoski, the little Pole, breathless; gasping with excitement. "They fire our committee!"

"Fire them?"

"Fire 'em out! Down canyon!" The little man was waving his arms in wild gestures; his eyes seemed about to start out of his head. "Take 'em off! Whole bunch fellers—gunmen! People see them—come out back door. Got ever'body's arm tied. Gunmen fellers hold 'em, don't let 'em holler, can't do nothin'! Got them cars waitin'—what you call?—"

"Automobiles?"

"Sure, got three! Put ever'body in, quick like that—they go down road like wind! Go down canyon, all gone! They bust our strike!" And the little Pole's voice ended in a howl of despair.

"No, they won't bust our strike!" exclaimed Hal. "Not yet!"

Suddenly he was reminded of the fact that his brother had followed him—puffing hard, for the run had been strenuous. He caught Hal by the arm, exclaiming, "Keep out of this, I tell you!"

Thus while Hal was questioning Klowoski, he was struggling half-unconsciously, to free himself from his brother's grasp. Suddenly the matter was forced to an issue, for the little Polack emitted a cry like an angry cat, and went at Edward with fingers outstretched like claws. Hal's dignified brother would have had to part with his dignity, if Hal had not caught Klowoski's onrush with his other arm. "Let him alone!" he said. "It's my brother!" Whereupon the little man fell back and stood watching in bewilderment.

Hal saw Androkulos running to him. The Greek boy had been in the street back of the office, and had seen the committee carried off; nine people had been taken—Wauchope, Tim Rafferty, and Mary Burke, Marcelli, Zammakis and Rusick, and three others who had served as interpreters on the night before. It had all been done so quickly that the crowd had scarcely realised what was happening.

Now, having grasped the meaning of it, the men were beside themselves with rage. They shook their fists, shouting defiance to a group of officials and guards who were visible upon the porch of the office-building. There was a clamour of shouts for revenge.

Hal could see instantly the dangers of the situation; he was like a man watching the burning fuse of a bomb. Now, if ever, this polyglot horde must have leadership—wise and cool and resourceful leadership.

The crowd, discovering his presence, surged down upon him like a wave. They gathered round him, howling. They had lost the rest of their committee, but they still had Joe Smith. Joe Smith! Hurrah for Joe! Let the gunmen take him, if they could! They waved their caps, they tried to lift him upon their shoulders, so that all could see him.

There was clamour for a speech, and Hal started to make his way to the steps of the nearest building, with Edward holding on to his coat. Edward was jostled; he had to part with his dignity—but he did not part with his brother. And when Hal was about to mount the steps, Edward made a last desperate effort, shouting into his ear, "Wait a minute! Wait! Are you going to try to talk to this mob?"

"Of course. Don't you see there'll be trouble if I don't?"

"You'll get yourself killed! You'll start a fight, and get a lot of these poor devils shot! Use your common sense, Hal; the company has brought in guards, and they are armed, and your people aren't."

"That's exactly why I have to speak!"

The discussion was carried on under difficulties, the elder brother clinging to the younger's arm, while the younger sought to pull free, and the mob shouted with a single voice, "Speech! Speech!" There were some near by who, like Klowoski, did not relish having this stranger interfering with their champion, and showed signs of a disposition to "mix in"; so at last Edward gave up the struggle, and the orator mounted the steps and faced the throng.

SECTION 14.

Hal raised his arms as a signal for silence.

"Boys," he cried, "they've kidnapped our committee. They think they'll break our strike that way—but they'll find they've made a mistake!"

"They will! Right you are!" roared a score of voices.

"They forget that we've got a union. Hurrah for our North Valley union!"

"Hurrah! Hurrah!" The cry echoed to the canyon-walls.

"And hurrah for the big union that will back us—the United Mine-Workers of America!"

Again the yell rang out; again and again. "Hurrah for the union! Hurrah for the United Mine-Workers!" A big American miner, Ferris, was in the front of the throng, and his voice beat in Hal's ears like a steam-siren.

"Boys," Hal resumed, when at last he could be heard, "use your brains a moment. I warned you they would try to provoke you! They would like nothing better than to start a scrap here, and get a chance to smash our union! Don't forget that, boys, if they can make you fight, they'll smash the union, and the union is our only hope!"

Again came the cry: "Hurrah for the union!" Hal let them shout it in twenty languages, until they were satisfied.

"Now, boys," he went on, at last, "they've shipped out our committee. They may ship me out in the same way—"

"No, they won't!" shouted voices in the crowd. And there was a bellow of rage from Ferris. "Let them try it! We'll burn them in their beds!"

"But they *can* ship me out!" argued Hal. "You *know* they can beat us at that game! They can call on the sheriff, they can get the soldiers, if necessary! We can't oppose them by force—they can turn out every man, woman and child in the village, if they choose. What we have to get clear is that even that won't crush our union! Nor the big union outside, that will be backing us! We can hold out, and make them take us back in the end!"

Some of Hal's friends, seeing what he was trying to do, came to his support. "No fighting! No violence! Stand by the union!" And he went on to drive the lesson home; even though the company might evict them, the big union of the four hundred and fifty thousand mine-workers of the country would feed them, it would call out the rest of the workers in the district in sympathy. So the bosses, who thought to starve and cow them into submission, would find their mines lying permanently idle. They would be forced to give way, and the tactics of solidarity would triumph.

So Hal went on, recalling the things Olson had told him, and putting them into practice. He saw hope in their faces again, dispelling the mood of resentment and rage.

"Now, boys," said he, "I'm going in to see the superintendent for you. I'll be your committee, since they've shipped out the rest."

The steam-siren of Ferris bellowed again: "You're the boy! Joe Smith!"

"All right, men—now mind what I say! I'll see the super, and then I'll go down to Pedro, where there'll be some officers of the United Mine-workers this morning. I'll tell them the situation, and ask them to back you. That's what you want, is it?"

That was what they wanted. "Big union!"

"All right. I'll do the best I can for you, and I'll find some way to get word to you. And meantime you stand firm. The bosses will tell you lies, they'll try to deceive you, they'll send spies and trouble-makers among you—but you hold fast, and wait for the big union."

Hal stood looking at the cheering crowd. He had time to note some of the faces upturned to him. Pitiful, toil-worn faces they were, each making its separate appeal, telling its individual story of deprivation and defeat. Once more they were transfigured, shining with that wonderful new light which he had seen for the first time the previous evening. It had been crushed for a moment, but it flamed up again; it would never die in the hearts of men—once they had learned the power it gave. Nothing Hal had yet seen moved him so much as this new birth of enthusiasm. A beautiful, a terrible thing it was!

Hal looked at his brother, to see how he had been moved. What he saw on his brother's face was satisfaction, boundless relief. The matter had turned out all right! Hal was coming away!

Hal turned again to the men; somehow, after his glance at Edward, they seemed more pitiful than ever. For Edward typified the power they were facing—the unseeing, uncomprehending power that meant to crush them. The possibility of failure was revealed to Hal in a flash of emotion, overwhelming him. He saw them as they would be, when no leader was at hand to make speeches to them. He saw them waiting, their life-long habit of obedience striving to reassert itself; a thousand fears besetting them, a thousand rumours preying upon them—wild beasts set on them by their cunning enemies. They would suffer, not merely for themselves, but for their wives and children—the very same pangs of dread that Hal suffered when he thought of one old man up in Western City, whose doctors had warned him to avoid excitement.

If they stood firm, if they kept their bargain with their leader, they would be evicted from their homes, they would face the cold of the coming winter, they would face hunger and the black-list. And he, meantime—what would he be doing? What was his part of the bargain? He would interview the superintendent for them, he would turn them over to the "big union"—and then he would go off to his own life of ease and pleasure. To eat grilled steaks and hot rolls in a perfectly appointed club, with suave and softly-moving servitors at his beck! To dance at the country club with exquisite creatures of chiffon and satin, of perfume and sweet smiles and careless, happy charms! No, it was too easy! He might call that his duty to his father and brother, but he would know in his heart that it was treason to life; it was the devil, taking him onto a high mountain and showing him all the kingdoms of the earth!

Moved by a sudden impulse, Hal raised his hands once more. "Boys," he said, "we understand each other now. You'll not go back to work till the big union tells you. And I, for my part, will stand by you. Your cause is my cause, I'll go on fighting for you till you have your rights, till you can live and work as men! Is that right?"

"That's right! That's right!"

"Very good, then—we'll swear to it!" And Hal raised his hands, and the men raised theirs, and amid a storm of shouts, and a frantic waving of caps, he made them the pledge which he knew would bind his own conscience. He made it deliberately, there in his brother's presence. This was no mere charge on a trench, it was enlisting for a war! But even in that moment of fervour, Hal would have been frightened had he realised the period of that enlistment, the years of weary and desperate conflict to which he was pledging his life.

SECTION 15.

Hal descended from his rostrum, and the crowds made way for him, and with his brother at his side he went down the street to the office building, upon the porch of which the guards were standing. His progress was a triumphal one; rough voices shouted words of encouragement in his ears, men jostled and fought to shake his hand or to pat him on the back; they even patted Edward and tried to shake his hand, because he was with Hal, and seemed to have his confidence. Afterwards Hal thought it over and was merry. Such an adventure for Edward!

The younger man went up the steps of the building and spoke to the guards. "I want to see Mr. Cartwright."

"He's inside," answered one, not cordially. With Edward following, Hal entered, and was ushered into the private office of the superintendent.

Having been a working-man, and class-conscious, Hal was observant of the manners of mine-superintendents; he noted that Cartwright bowed politely to Edward, but did not include Edward's brother. "Mr. Cartwright," he said, "I have come to you as a deputation from the workers of this camp."

The superintendent did not appear impressed by the announcement.

"I am instructed to say that the men demand the redress of four grievances before they return to work. First—"

Here Cartwright spoke, in his quick, sharp way. "There's no use going on, sir. This company will deal only with its men as individuals. It will recognise no deputations."

Hal's answer was equally quick. "Very well, Mr. Cartwright. In that case, I come to you as an individual."

For a moment the superintendent seemed nonplussed.

"I wish to ask four rights which are granted to me by the laws of this state. First, the right to belong to a union, without being discharged for it."

The other had recovered his manner of quiet mastery. "You have that right, sir; you have always had it. You know perfectly well that the company has never discharged any one for belonging to a union."

The man was looking at Hal, and there was a duel of the eyes between them. A cold anger moved Hal. His ability to endure this sort of thing was at an end. "Mr. Cartwright," he said, "you are the servant of one of the world's greatest actors; and you support him ably."

The other flushed and drew back; Edward put in quickly: "Hal, there's nothing to be gained by such talk!"

"He has all the world for an audience," persisted Hal. "He plays the most stupendous farce—and he and all his actors wearing such solemn faces!"

"Mr. Cartwright," said Edward, with dignity, "I trust you understand that I have done everything I can to restrain my brother."

"Of course, Mr. Warner," replied the superintendent. "And you must know that I, for my part, have done everything to show your brother consideration."

"Again!" exclaimed Hal. "This actor is a genius!"

"Hal, if you have business with Mr. Cartwright—"

"He showed me consideration by sending his gunmen to seize me at night, drag me out of a cabin, and nearly twist the arm off me! Such humour never was!"

Cartwright attempted to speak—but looking at Edward, not at Hal. "At that time—"

"He showed me consideration by having me locked up in jail and fed on bread and water for two nights and a day! Can you beat that humour?"

"At that time I did not know—"

"By forging my name to a letter and having it circulated in the camp! Finally—most considerate of all—by telling a newspaper man that I had seduced a girl here!"

The superintendent flushed still redder. "*No!*" he declared.

"*What?*" cried Hal. "You didn't tell Billy Keating of the *Gazette* that I had seduced a girl in North Valley? You didn't describe the girl to him—a red-haired Irish girl?"

"I merely said, Mr. Warner, that I had heard certain rumours—"

"*Certain* rumours, Mr. Cartwright? The certainty was all of your making! You made a definite and explicit statement to Mr. Keating—"

"I did not!" declared the other.

"I'll soon prove it!" And Hal started towards the telephone on Cartwright's desk.

"What are you going to do, Hal?"

"I am going to get Billy Keating on the wire, and let you hear his statement."

"Oh, rot, Hal!" cried Edward. "I don't care anything about Keating's statement. You know that at that time Mr. Cartwright had no means of knowing who you were."

Cartwright was quick to grasp this support. "Of course not, Mr. Warner! Your brother came here, pretending to be a working boy—"

"Oh!" cried Hal. "So that's it! You think it proper to circulate slanders about working boys in your camp?"

"You have been here long enough to know what the morals of such boys are."

"I have been here long enough, Mr. Cartwright, to know that if you want to go into the question of morals in North Valley, the place for you to begin is with the bosses and guards you put in authority, and allow to prey upon women."

Edward broke in: "Hal, there's nothing to be gained by pursuing this conversation. If you have any business here, get it over with, for God's sake!"

Hal made an effort to recover his self-possession. He came back to the demands of the strike—but only to find that he had used up the superintendent's self-possession. "I have given you my answer," declared Cartwright, "I absolutely decline any further discussion."

"Well," said Hal, "since you decline to permit a deputation of your men to deal with you in plain, business-like fashion, I have to inform you as an individual that every other individual in your camp refuses to work for you."

The superintendent did not let himself be impressed by this elaborate sarcasm. "All I have to tell you, sir, is that Number Two mine will resume work in the morning, and that any one who refuses to work will be sent down the canyon before night."

"So quickly, Mr. Cartwright? They have rented their homes from the company, and you know that according to the company's own lease they are entitled to three days' notice before being evicted!"

Cartwright was so unwise as to argue. He knew that Edward was hearing, and he wished to clear himself. "They will not be evicted by the company. They will be dealt with by the town authorities."

"Of which you yourself are the head?"

"I happen to have been elected mayor of North Valley."

"As mayor of North Valley, you gave my brother to understand that you would put me out, did you not?"

"I asked your brother to persuade you to leave."

"But you made clear that if he could not do this, you would put me out?"

"Yes, that is true."

"And the reason you gave was that you had had instructions by telegraph from Mr. Peter Harrigan. May I ask to what office Mr. Harrigan has been elected in your town?"

Cartwright saw his difficulty. "Your brother misunderstood me," he said, crossly.

"Did you misunderstand him, Edward?"

Edward had walked to the window in disgust; he was looking at tomato-cans and cinder-heaps, and did not see fit to turn around. But the superintendent knew that he was hearing, and considered it necessary to cover the flaw in his argument. "Young man," said he, "you have violated several of the ordinances of this town."

"Is there an ordinance against organising a union of the miners?"

"No; but there is one against speaking on the streets."

"Who passed that ordinance, if I may ask?"

"The town council."

"Consisting of Johnson, postmaster and company-store clerk; Ellison, company book-keeper; Strauss, company pit-boss; O'Callahan, company saloon-keeper. Have I the list correct?"

Cartwright did not answer.

"And the fifth member of the town council is yourself, ex-officio—Mr. Enos Cartwright, mayor and company-superintendent."

Again there was no answer.

"You have an ordinance against street-speaking; and at the same time your company owns the saloon-buildings, the boarding-houses, the church and the school. Where do you expect the citizens to do their speaking?"

"You would make a good lawyer, young man. But we who have charge here know perfectly well what you mean by 'speaking'!"

"You don't approve, then, of the citizens holding meetings?"

"I mean that we don't consider it necessary to provide agitators with opportunity to incite our employés."

"May I ask, Mr. Cartwright, are you speaking as mayor of an American community, or as superintendent of a coal-mine?"

Cartwright's face had been growing continually redder. Addressing Edward's back, he said, "I don't see any reason why this should continue."

And Edward was of the same opinion. He turned. "Really, Hal—"

"But, Edward! A man accuses your brother of being a law-breaker! Have you hitherto known of any criminal tendencies in our family?"

Edward turned to the window again and resumed his study of the cinder-heaps and tomato-cans. It was a vulgar and stupid quarrel, but he had seen enough of Hal's mood to realise that he would go on and on, so long as any one was indiscreet enough to answer him.

"You say, Mr. Cartwright, that I have violated the ordinance against speaking on the street. May I ask what penalty this ordinance carries?"

"You will find out when the penalty is exacted of you."

Hal laughed. "From what you said just now, I gather that the penalty is expulsion from the town! If I understand legal procedure, I should have been brought before the justice of the peace—who happens to be another company store-clerk. Instead of that, I am sentenced by the mayor—or is it the company superintendent? May I ask how that comes to be?"

"It is because of my consideration—"

"When did I ask consideration?"

"Consideration for your brother, I mean."

"Oh! Then your ordinance provides that the mayor—or is it the superintendent?—may show consideration for the brother of a law-breaker, by changing his penalty to expulsion from the town. Was it consideration for Tommie Burke that caused you to have his sister sent down the canyon?"

Cartwright clenched his hands. "I've had all I'll stand of this!"

He was again addressing Edward's back; and Edward turned and answered, "I don't blame you, sir." Then to Hal, "I really think you've said enough!"

"I hope I've said enough," replied Hal—"to convince you that the pretence of American law in this coal-camp is a silly farce, an insult and a humiliation to any man who respects the institutions of his country."

"You, Mr. Warner," said the superintendent, to Edward, "have had experience in managing coal-mines. You know what it means to deal with ignorant foreigners, who have no understanding of American law—"

Hal burst out laughing. "So you're teaching them American law! You're teaching them by setting at naught every law of your town and state, every constitutional guarantee—and substituting the instructions you get by telegraph from Peter Harrigan!"

Cartwright turned and walked to the door. "Young man," said he, over his shoulder, "it will be necessary for you to leave North Valley this morning. I only hope your brother will be able to persuade you to leave without trouble." And the bang of the door behind him was the superintendent's only farewell.

SECTION 17.

Edward turned upon his brother. "Now what the devil did you want to put me through a scene like that for? So undignified! So utterly uncalled for! A quarrel with a man so far beneath you!"

Hal stood where the superintendent had left him. He was looking at his brother's angry face. "Was that all you got out of it, Edward?"

"All that stuff about your private character! What do you care what a fellow like Cartwright thinks about you?"

"I care nothing at all what he thinks, but I care about having him use such a slander. That's one of their regular procedures, so Billy Keating says."

Edward answered, coldly, "Take my advice, and realise that when you deny a scandal, you only give it circulation."

"Of course," answered Hal. "That's what makes me so angry. Think of the girl, the harm done to her!"

"It's not up to you to worry about the girl."

"Suppose that Cartwright had slandered some woman friend of yours. Would you have felt the same indifference?"

"He'd not have slandered any friend of mine; I choose my friends more carefully."

"Yes, of course. What that means is that you choose them among the rich. But I happen to be more democratic in my tastes—"

"Oh, for heaven's sake!" cried Edward. "You reformers are all alike—you talk and talk and talk!"

"I can tell you the reason for that, Edward—a man like you can shut his eyes, but he can't shut his ears!"

"Well, can't you let up on me for awhile—long enough to get out of this place? I feel as if I were sitting on the top of a volcano, and I've no idea when it may break out again."

Hal began to laugh. "All right," he said; "I guess I haven't shown much appreciation of your visit. I'll be more sociable now. My next business is in Pedro, so I'll go that far with you. There's one thing more—"

"What is it?"

"The company owes me money—"

"What money?"

"Some I've earned."

It was Edward's turn to laugh. "Enough to buy you a shave and a bath?"

He took out his wallet, and pulled off several bills; and Hal, watching him, realised suddenly a change which had taken place in his own psychology. Not merely had he acquired the class-consciousness of the working-man, he had acquired the money-consciousness as well. He was actually concerned about the dollars the company owed him! He had earned those dollars by back- and heart-breaking toil, lifting lumps of coal into cars; the sum was enough to keep the whole Rafferty family alive for a week or two. And here was Edward, with a smooth brown leather wallet full of ten- and twenty-dollar bills, which he peeled off without counting, exactly as if money grew on trees, or as if coal came out of the earth and walked into furnaces to the sound of a fiddle and a flute!

Edward had of course no idea of these abnormal processes going on in his brother's mind. He was holding out the bills. "Get yourself some decent things," he said. "I hope you don't have to stay dirty in order to feel democratic?"

"No," answered Hal; and then, "How are we going?"

"I've a car waiting, back of the office."

"So you had everything ready!" But Edward made no answer; afraid of setting off the volcano again.

SECTION 18.

They went out by the rear door of the office, entered the car, and sped out of the village, unseen by the crowd. And all the way down the canyon Edward pleaded with Hal to drop the controversy and come home at once. He brought up the tragic question of Dad again; when that did not avail, he began to threaten. Suppose Hal's money-resources were to be cut off, suppose he were to find himself left out of his father's will—what would he do then? Hal answered, without a smile, "I can always get a job as organiser for the United Mine-Workers."

So Edward gave up that line of attack. "If you won't come," he declared, "I'm going to stay by you till you do!"

"All right," said Hal. He could not help smiling at this dire threat. "But if I take you about and introduce you to my friends, you must agree that what you hear shall be confidential."

The other made a face of disgust. "What the devil would I want to talk about your friends for?"

"I don't know what might happen," said Hal. "You're going to meet Peter Harrigan and take his side, and I can't tell what you might conceive it your duty to do."

The other exclaimed, with sudden passion, "I'll tell you right now! If you try to go back to that coal-camp, I swear to God I'll apply to the courts and have you shut up in a sanitarium. I don't think I'd have much trouble in persuading a judge that you're insane."

"No," said Hal, with a laugh—"not a judge in this part of the world!"

Then, after studying his brother's face for a moment, it occurred to him that it might be well not to let such an idea rest unimpeached in Edward's mind. "Wait," said he, "till you meet my friend Billy Keating, of the *Gazette*, and hear what he would do with such a story! Billy is crazy to have me turn him loose to 'play up' my fight with Old Peter!" The conversation went no farther—but Hal was sure that Edward would "put that in his pipe and smoke it."

They came to the MacKellar home in Pedro, and Edward waited in the automobile while Hal went inside. The old Scotchman welcomed him warmly, and told him what news he had. Jerry Minetti had been there that morning, and MacKellar at his request had telephoned to the office of the union in Sheridan, and ascertained that Jack David had brought word about the strike on the previous evening. All parties had been careful not to mention names, for "leaks" in the telephone were notorious, but it was clear who the messenger had been. As a result of the message, Johann Hartman, president of the local union of the miners, was now at the American Hotel in Pedro, together with James Moylan, secretary of the district organisation—the latter having come down from Western City on the same train as Edward.

This was all satisfactory; but MacKellar added a bit of information of desperate import—the officers of the union declared that they could not support a strike at the present time! It was premature, it could lead to nothing but failure and discouragement to the larger movement they were planning.

Such a possibility Hal had himself realised at the outset. But he had witnessed the new birth of freedom at North Valley, he had seen the hungry, toil-worn faces of men looking up to him for support; he had been moved by it, and had come to feel that the union officials must be moved in the same way. "They've simply got to back it!" he exclaimed. "Those men must not be disappointed! They'll lose all hope, they'll sink into utter despair! The labour men must realise that—I must make them!"

The old Scotchman answered that Minetti had felt the same way. He had flung caution to the winds, and rushed over to the hotel to see Hartman and Moylan. Hal decided to follow, and went out to the automobile.

He explained matters to his brother, whose comment was, Of course! It was what he had foretold. The poor, mis-guided miners would go back to their work, and their would-be leader would have to admit the folly of his course. There was a train for Western City in a couple of hours; it would be a great favour if Hal would arrange to take it.

Hal answered shortly that he was going to the American Hotel. His brother might take him there, if he chose. So Edward gave the order to the driver of the car. Incidentally, Edward began asking about clothing-stores in Pedro. While Hal was in the hotel, pleading for the life of his newly-born labour union, Edward would seek a costume in which he could "feel like a human being."

SECTION 19.

Hal found Jerry Minetti with the two officials in their hotel-room: Jim Moylan, district secretary, a long, towering Irish boy, black-eyed and black-haired, quick and sensitive, the sort of person one trusted and liked at the first moment; and Johann Hartman, local president, a grey-haired miner of German birth, reserved and slow-spoken, evidently a man of much strength, both physical and moral. He had need of it, any one could realise, having charge of a union headquarters in the heart of this "Empire of Raymond"!

Hal first told of the kidnapping of the committee. This did not surprise the officials, he found; it was the thing the companies regularly did when there was threat of rebellion in the camps. That was why efforts to organise openly were so utterly hopeless. There was no chance for anything but a secret propaganda, maintained until every camp had the nucleus of an organisation.

"So you can't back this strike!" exclaimed Hal.

Not possibly, was Moylan's reply. It would be lost as soon as it was begun. There was no slightest hope of success until a lot of organisation work had been done.

"But meantime," argued Hal, "the union at North Valley will go to pieces!"

"Perhaps," was the reply. "We'll only have to start another. That's what the labour movement is like."

Jim Moylan was young, and saw Hal's mood. "Don't misunderstand us!" he cried. "It's heartbreaking—but it's not in our power to help. We are charged with building up the union, and we know that if we supported everything that looked like a strike, we'd be bankrupt the first year. You can't imagine how often this same thing happens—hardly a month we're not called on to handle such a situation."

"I can see what you mean," said Hal. "But I thought that in this case, right after the disaster, with the men so stirred—"

The young Irishman smiled, rather sadly. "You're new at this game," he said. "If a mine-disaster was enough to win a strike, God knows our job would be easy. In Barela, just down the canyon from you, they've had three big explosions—they've killed over five hundred men in the past year!"

Hal began to see how, in his inexperience, he had lost his sense of proportion.

He looked at the two labour leaders, and recalled the picture of such a person which he had brought with him to North Valley—a hot headed and fiery agitator, luring honest workingmen from their jobs. But here was the situation exactly reversed! Here was he in a blaze of excitement—and two labour leaders turning the fire-hose on him! They sat quiet and business-like, pronouncing a doom upon the slaves of North Valley. Back to their black dungeons with them!

"What can we tell the men?" he asked, making an effort to repress his chagrin.

"We can only tell them what I'm telling you—that we're helpless, till we've got the whole district organised. Meantime, they have to stand the gaff; they must do what they can to keep an organisation."

"But all the active men will be fired!"

"No, not quite all—they seldom get them all."

Here the stolid old German put in. In the last year the company had turned out more than six thousand men because of union activity or suspicion of it.

"*Six thousand!*" echoed Hal. "You mean from this one district?"

"That's what I mean."

"But there aren't more than twelve or fifteen thousand men in the district!"

"I know that."

"Then how can you ever keep an organisation?"

The other answered, quietly, "They treat the new men the same as they treated the old."

Hal thought suddenly of John Edstrom's ants! Here they were—building their bridge, building it again and again, as often as floods might destroy it! They had not the swift impatience of a youth of the leisure-class, accustomed to having his own way, accustomed to thinking of freedom and decency and justice as necessities of life. Much as Hal learned from the conversation of these men, he learned more from their silences—the quiet, matter-of-fact way they took things which had driven him beside himself with indignation. He began to realise what it would mean to stand by his pledge to those poor devils in North Valley. He would need more than one blaze of excitement; he would need brains and patience and discipline, he would need years of study and hard work!

SECTION 20.

Hal found himself forced to accept the decision of the labour-leaders. They had had experience, they could judge the situation. The miners would have to go back to work, and Cartwright and Alec Stone and Jeff Cotton would drive them as before! All that the rebels could do was to try to keep a secret organisation in the camp.

Jerry Minetti mentioned Jack David. He had gone back this morning, without having seen the labour-leaders. So he might escape suspicion, and keep his job, and help the union work.

"How about you?" asked Hal. "I suppose you've cooked your goose."

Jerry had never heard this phrase, but he got its meaning. "Sure thing!" said he. "Cooked him plenty!"

"Didn't you see the 'dicks' down stairs in the lobby?" inquired Hartman.

"I haven't learned to recognise them yet."

"Well, you will, if you stay at this business. There hasn't been a minute since our office was opened that we haven't had half a dozen on the other side of the street. Every man that comes to see us is followed back to his camp and fired that same day. They've broken into my desk at night and stolen my letters and papers; they've threatened us with death a hundred times."

"I don't see how you make any headway at all!"

"They can never stop us. They thought when they broke into my desk, they'd get a list of our organisers. But you see, I carry the lists in my head!"

"No small task, either," put in Moylan. "Would you like to know how many organisers we have at work? Ninety-seven. And they haven't caught a single one of them!"

Hal heard him, amazed. Here was a new aspect of the labour movement! This quiet, resolute old "Dutchy," whom you might have taken for a delicatessen-proprietor; this merry-eyed Irish boy, whom you would have expected to be escorting a lady to a firemen's ball——they were captains of an army of sappers who were undermining the towers of Peter Harrigan's fortress of greed!

Hartman suggested that Jerry might take a chance at this sort of work. He would surely be fired from North Valley, so he might as well send word to his family to come to Pedro. In this way he might save himself to work as an organiser; because it was the custom of these company "spotters" to follow a man back to his camp and there identify him. If Jerry took a train for Western City, they would be thrown off the track, and he might get into some new camp and do organising among the Italians. Jerry accepted this proposition with alacrity; it would put off the evil day when Rosa and her little ones would be left to the mercy of chance.

They were still talking when the telephone rang. It was Hartman's secretary in Sheridan, reporting that he had just heard from the kidnapped committee. The entire party, eight men and Mary Burke, had been taken to Horton, a station not far up the line, and put on the train with many dire threats. But they had left the train at the next stop, and declared their intention of coming to Pedro. They were due at the hotel very soon.

Hal desired to be present at this meeting, and went downstairs to tell his brother. There was another dispute, of course. Edward reminded Hal that the scenery of Pedro had a tendency to monotony; to which Hal could only answer by offering to introduce his brother to his friends. They were men who could teach Edward much, if he would consent to learn. He might attend the session with the committee—eight men and a woman who had ventured an act of heroism and been made the victims of a crime. Nor were they bores, as Edward might be thinking! There was blue-eyed Tim Rafferty, for example, a silent, smutty-faced gnome who had broken out of his black cavern and spread unexpected golden wings of oratory; and Mary Burke, of whom Edward might read in that afternoon's edition of the Western City *Gazette*—a "Joan of Arc of the coal-camps," or something equally picturesque. But Edward's mood was not to be enlivened. He had a vision of his brother's appearance in the paper as the companion of this Hibernian Joan!

Hal went off with Jerry Minetti to what his brother described as a "hash-house," while Edward proceeded in solitary state to the dining-room of the American Hotel. But he was not left in solitary state; pretty soon a sharp-faced young man was ushered to a seat beside him, and started up a conversation. He was a "drummer," he said; his "line" was hardware, what was Edward's? Edward answered coldly that he had no "line," but the young man was not rebuffed— apparently his "line" had hardened his sensibilities. Perhaps Edward was interested in coal-mines? Had he been visiting the camps? He questioned so persistently, and came back so often to the subject, that at last it dawned over Edward what this meant—he was receiving the attention of a "spotter!" Strange to say, the circumstance caused Edward more irritation against Peter Harrigan's regime than all his brother's eloquence about oppression at North Valley.

SECTION 21.

Soon after dinner the kidnapped committee arrived, bedraggled in body and weary in soul. They inquired for Johann Hartman, and were sent up to the room, where there followed a painful scene. Eight men and a woman who had ventured an act of heroism and been made the victims of a crime could not easily be persuaded to see their efforts and sacrifices thrown on the dump-heap, nor were they timid in expressing their opinions of those who were betraying them.

"You been tryin' to get us out!" cried Tim Rafferty. "Ever since I can remember you been at my old man to help you—an' here, when we do what you ask, you throw us down!"

"We never asked you to go on strike," said Moylan.

"No, that's true. You only asked us to pay dues, so you fellows could have fat salaries."

"Our salaries aren't very fat," replied the young leader, patiently. "You'd find that out if you investigated."

"Well, whatever they are, they go on, while ours stop. We're on the streets, we're done for. Look at us—and most of us has got families, too! I got an old mother an' a lot of brothers and sisters, an' my old man done up an' can't work. What do you think's to become of us?"

"We'll help you out a little, Rafferty—"

"To hell with you!" cried Tim. "I don't want your help! When I need charity, I'll go to the county. They're another bunch of grafters, but they don't pretend to be friends to the workin' man."

Here was the thing Tom Olson had told Hal at the outset—the workingmen bedevilled, not knowing whom to trust, suspecting the very people who most desired to help them. "Tim," he put in, "there's no use talking like that. We have to learn patience—"

And the boy turned upon Hal. "What do you know about it? It's all a joke to you. You can go off and forget it when you get ready. You've got money, they tell me!"

Hal felt no resentment at this; it was what he heard from his own conscience. "It isn't so easy for me as you think, Tim. There are other ways of suffering besides not having money—"

"Much sufferin' you'll do—with your rich folks!" sneered Tim.

There was a murmur of protest from others of the committee.

"Good God, Rafferty!" broke in Moylan. "We can't help it, man—we're just as helpless as you!"

"You say you're helpless—but you don't even try!"

"*Try?* Do you want us to back a strike that we know hasn't a chance? You might as well ask us to lie down and let a load of coal run over us. We can't win, man! I tell you we can't *win*! We'd only be throwing away our organisation!"

Moylan became suddenly impassioned. He had seen a dozen sporadic strikes in this district, and many a dozen young strikers, homeless, desolate, embittered, turning their disappointment on him. "We might support you with our funds, you say—we might go on doing it, even while the company ran the mine with scabs. But where would that land us, Rafferty? I seen many a union on the rocks—and I ain't so old either! If we had a bank, we'd support all the miners of the country, they'd never need to work again till they got their rights. But this money we spend is the money that other miners are earnin'—right now, down in the pits, Rafferty, the same as you and your old man. They give us this money, and they say, 'Use it to build up the union. Use it to help the men that aren't organised—take them in, so they won't beat down our wages and scab on us. But don't waste it, for God's sake; we have to work hard to make it, and if we don't see results, you'll get no more out of us.' Don't you see how that is, man? And how it weighs on us, worse even then the fear that maybe we'll lose our poor salaries—though you might refuse to believe anything so good of us? You don't need to talk to me like I was Peter Harrigan's son. I was a spragger when I was ten years old, and I ain't been out of the pits so long that I've forgot the feeling. I assure you, the thing that keeps me awake at night ain't the fear of not gettin' a living, for I give myself a bit of education, working nights, and I know I could always turn out and earn what I need; but it's wondering whether I'm spending the miners' money the best way, whether maybe I mightn't save them a little misery if I hadn't 'a' done this or had 'a' done that. When I come down on that sleeper last night, here's what I was thinking, Tim Rafferty—all the time I listened to the train bumping—'Now I got to see some more of the suffering, I got to let some good men turn against us, because they can't see why we should get salaries while they get the sack. How am I going to show them that I'm working for them—working as hard as I know how—and that I'm not to blame for their trouble?'"

Here Wauchope broke in. "There's no use talking any more. I see we're up against it. We'll not trouble you, Moylan."

"You trouble me," cried Moylan, "unless you stand by the movement!"

The other laughed bitterly. "You'll never know what I do. It's the road for me—and you know it!"

"Well, wherever you go, it'll be the same; either you'll be fighting for the union, or you'll be a weight that we have to carry."

The young leader turned from one to another of the committee, pleading with them not to be embittered by this failure, but to turn it to their profit, going on with the work of building up the solidarity of the miners. Every man had to make his sacrifices, to pay his part of the price. The thing of importance was that every man who was discharged should be a spark of unionism, carrying the flame of revolt to a new part of the country. Let each one do his part, and there would soon be no place to which the masters could send for "scabs."

SECTION 22.

There was one member of this committee whom Hal watched with especial anxiety——Mary Burke. She had not yet said a word; while the others argued and protested, she sat with her lips set and her hands clenched. Hal knew what rage this failure must bring to her. She had risen and struggled and hoped, and the result was what she had always said it would be—nothing! Now he saw her, with eyes large and dark with fatigue, fixed on this fiery young labour-leader. He knew that a war must be going on within her. Would she drop out entirely now? It was the test of her character—as it was the test of the characters of all of them.

"If only we're strong enough and brave enough," Jim Moylan was saying, "we can use our defeats to educate our people and bring them together. Right now, if we can make the men at North Valley see what we're doing, they won't go back beaten, they won't be bitter against the union, they'll only go back to wait. And ain't that a way to beat the bosses—to hold our jobs, and keep the union alive, till we've got into all the camps, and can strike and win?"

There was a pause; then Mary spoke. "How're you meanin' to tell the men?" Her voice was without emotion, but nevertheless, Hal's heart leaped. Whether Mary had any hope or not, she was going to stay in line with the rest of the ants!

Johann Hartman explained his idea. He would have circulars printed in several languages and distributed secretly in the camp, ordering the men back to work. But Jerry met this suggestion with a prompt no. The people would not believe the circulars, they would suspect the bosses of having them printed. Hadn't the bosses done worse than that, "framing up" a letter from Joe Smith to balk the check-weighman movement? The only thing that would help would be for some of the committee to get into the camp and see the men face to face.

"And it got to be quick!" Jerry insisted. "They get notice to work in morning, and them that don't be fired. They be the best men, too—men we want to save."

Other members of the committee spoke up, agreeing with this. Said Rusick, the Slav, slow-witted and slow-spoken, "Them fellers get mighty damn sore if they lose their job and don't got no strike." And Zammakis, the Greek, quick and nervous, "We say strike; we got to say no strike."

What could they do? There was, in the first place, the difficulty of getting away from the hotel, which was being watched by the "spotters." Hartman suggested that if they went out all together and scattered, the detectives could not follow all of them. Those who escaped might get into North Valley by hiding in the "empties" which went up to the mine.

But Moylan pointed out that the company would be anticipating this; and Rusick, who had once been a hobo, put in: "They sure search them cars. They give us plenty hell, too, when they catch us."

Yes, it would be a dangerous mission. Mary spoke again. "Maybe a lady could do it better."

"They'd beat a lady," said Minetti.

"I know, but maybe a lady might fool them. There's some widows that came to Pedro for the funerals, and they're wearin' veils that hide their faces. I might pretend to be one of them and get into the camp."

The men looked at one another. There was an idea! The scowl which had stayed upon the face of Tim Rafferty ever since his quarrel with Moylan, gave place suddenly to a broad grin.

"I seen Mrs. Zamboni on the street," said he. "She had on black veils enough to hide the lot of us."

And here Hal spoke, for the first time since Tim Rafferty had silenced him. "Does anybody know where to find Mrs. Zamboni?"

"She stay with my friend, Mrs. Swajka," said Rusick.

"Well," said Hal, "there's something you people don't know about this situation. After they had fired you, I made another speech to the men, and made them swear they'd stay on strike. So now I've got to go back and eat my words. If we're relying on veils and things, a man can be fixed up as well as a woman."

They were staring at him. "They'll beat you to death if they catch you!" said Wauchope.

"No," said Hal, "I don't think so. Anyhow, it's up to me"—he glanced at Tim Rafferty—"because I'm the only one who doesn't have to suffer for the failure of our strike."

There was a pause.

"I'm sorry I said that!" cried Tim, impulsively.

"That's all right, old man," replied Hal. "What you said is true, and I'd like to do something to ease my conscience." He rose to his feet, laughing. "I'll make a peach of a widow!" he said. "I'm going up and have a tea-party with my friend Jeff Cotton!"

SECTION 23.

Hal proposed going to find Mrs. Zamboni at the place where she was staying; but Moylan interposed, objecting that the detectives would surely follow him. Even though they should all go out of the hotel at once, the one person the detective would surely stick to was the arch-rebel and trouble-maker, Joe Smith. Finally they decided to bring Mrs. Zamboni to the room. Let her come with Mrs. Swajka or some other woman who spoke English, and go to the desk and ask for Mary Burke, explaining that Mary had borrowed money from her, and that she had to have it to pay the undertaker for the burial of her man. The hotel-clerk might not know who Mary Burke was; but the watchful "spotters" would gather about and listen, and if it was mentioned that Mary was from North Valley, some one would connect her with the kidnapped committee.

This was made clear to Rusick, who hurried off, and in the course of half an hour returned with the announcement that the women were on the way. A few minutes later came a tap on the door, and there stood the black-garbed old widow with her friend. She came in; and then came looks of dismay and horrified exclamations. Rusick was requesting her to give up her weeds to Joe Smith!

"She say she don't got nothing else," explained the Slav.

"Tell her I give her plenty money buy more," said Hal.

"Ai! Jesu!" cried Mrs. Zamboni, pouring out a sputtering torrent.

"She say she don't got nothing to put on. She say it ain't good to go no clothes!"

"Hasn't she got on a petticoat?"

"She say petticoat got holes!"

There was a burst of laughter from the company, and the old woman turned scarlet from her forehead to her ample throat. "Tell her she wrap up in blankets," said Hal. "Mary Burke buy her new things."

It proved surprisingly difficult to separate Mrs. Zamboni from her widow's weeds, which she had purchased with so great an expenditure of time and tears. Never had a respectable lady who had borne sixteen children received such a proposition; to sell the insignia of her grief—and here in a hotel room, crowded with a dozen men! Nor was the task made easier by the unseemly merriment of the men. "Ai! Jesu!" cried Mrs. Zamboni again.

"Tell her it's very, very important," said Hal. "Tell her I must have them." And then, seeing that Rusick was making poor headway, he joined in, in the compromise-English one learns in the camps. "Got to have! Sure thing! Got to hide! Quick! Get away from boss! See? Get killed if no go!"

So at last the frightened old woman gave way. "She say all turn backs," said Rusick. And everybody turned, laughing in hilarious whispers, while, with Mary Burke and Mrs. Swajka for a shield, Mrs. Zamboni got out of her waist and skirt, putting a blanket round her red shoulders for modesty's sake. When Hal put the garments on, there was a foot to spare all round; but after they had stuffed two bed pillows down in the front of him, and drawn them tight at the waist-line, the disguise was judged more satisfactory. He put on the old lady's ample if ragged shoes, and Mary Burke set the widow's bonnet on his head and adjusted the many veils; after that Mrs. Zamboni's own brood of children would not have suspected the disguise.

It was a merry party for a few minutes; worn and hopeless as Mary had seemed, she was possessed now by the spirit of fun. But then quickly the laughter died. The time for action had come. Mary Burke said that she would stay with what was left of Mrs. Zamboni, to answer the door in case any of the hotel people or the detectives should come. Hal asked Jim Moylan to see Edward, and say that Hal was writing a manifesto to the North Valley workers, and would not be ready to leave until the midnight train.

These things agreed upon, Hal shook hands all round, and the eleven men left the room at once, going down stairs and through the lobby, scattering in every direction on the streets. Mrs. Swajka and the pseudo-Mrs. Zamboni followed a minute later—and, as they anticipated, found the lobby swept clear of detectives.

<h1 style="text-align:center">SECTION 24.</h1>

Bidding Mrs. Swajka farewell, Hal set out for the railroad station. But before he had gone a block from the hotel, he ran into his brother, coming straight towards him.

Edward's face wore a bored look; his very manner of carrying the magazine under his arm said that he had selected it in a last hopeless effort against the monotony of Pedro. Such a trick of fate, to take a man of important affairs, and immure him at the mercy of a maniac in a God-forsaken coal-town! What did people do in such a hole? Pay a nickel to look at moving pictures of cow-boys and counterfeiters?

Edward's aspect was too much for Hal's sense of humour. Besides, he had a good excuse; was it not proper to make a test of his disguise, before facing the real danger in North Valley?

He placed himself in the path of his brother's progress, and in Mrs. Zamboni's high, complaining tones, began, "Mister!"

Edward stared at the interrupting black figure. "Mister, you Joe Smith's brother, hey?"

The question had to be repeated before Edward gave his grudging answer. He was not proud of the relationship.

"Mister," continued the whining voice, "my old man got blow up in mine. I get five pieces from my man what I got to bury yesterday in grave-yard. I got to pay thirty dollar for bury them pieces and I don't got no more money left. I don't got no money from them company fellers. They come lawyer feller and he say maybe I get money for bury my man, if I don't jay too much. But, Mister, I got eleven children I got to feed, and I don't got no more man, and I don't find no new man for old woman like me. When I go home I hear them children crying and I don't got no food, and them company-stores don't give me no food. I think maybe you Joe Smith's brother you good man, maybe you sorry for poor widow-woman, you maybe give me some money, Mister, so I buy some food for them children."

"All right," said Edward. He pulled out his wallet and extracted a bill, which happened to be for ten dollars. His manner seemed to say, "For heaven's sake, here!"

Mrs. Zamboni clutched the bill with greedy fingers, but was not appeased. "You got plenty money, Mister! You rich man, hey! You maybe give me all them moneys, so I got plenty feed them children? You don't know them company-stores, Mister, them prices is way up high like mountains; them children is hungry, they cry all day and night, and one piece money don't last so long. You give me some more piece moneys, Mister——hey?"

"I'll give you one more," said Edward. "I need some for myself." He pulled off another bill.

"What you need so much, Mister? You don't got so many children, hey? And you got plenty more money home, maybe!"

"That's all I can give you," said the man. He took a step to one side, to get round the obstruction in his path.

But the obstruction took a step also—and with surprising agility. "Mister, I thank you for them moneys. I tell them children I get moneys from good man. I like you, Mister Smith, you give money for poor widow-woman—you nice man."

And the dreadful creature actually stuck out one of her paws, as if expecting to pat Edward on the cheek, or to chuck him under the chin. He recoiled, as from a contagion; but she followed him, determined to do something to him, he could not be sure what. He had heard that these foreigners had strange customs!

"It's all right! It's nothing!" he insisted, and fell back—at the same time glancing nervously about, to see if there were spectators of this scene.

"Nice man, Mister! Nice man!" cried the old woman, with increasing cordiality. "Maybe some day I find man like you, Mr. Edward Smith—so I don't stay widow-woman no more. You think maybe you like to marry nice Slavish woman, got plenty nice children?"

Edward, perceiving that the matter was getting desperate, sprang to one side. It was a spring which should have carried him to safety; but to his dismay the Slavish widow sprang also—her claws caught him under the arm-pit, and fastening in his ribs, gave him a ferocious pinch. After which the owner of the claws went down the street, not looking back, but making strange gobbling noises, which might have been the weeping of a bereaved widow in Slavish, or might have been almost anything else.

SECTION 25.

The train up to North Valley left very soon, and Hal figured that there would be just time to accomplish his errand and catch the last train back. He took his seat in the car without attracting attention, and sat in his place until they were approaching their destination, the last stop up the canyon. There were several of the miners' women in the car, and Hal picked out one who belonged to Mrs. Zamboni's nationality, and moved over beside her. She made place, with some remark; but Hal merely sobbed softly, and the woman felt for his hand to comfort him. As his hands were clasped together under the veils, she patted him reassuringly on the knee.

At the boundary of the stockaded village the train stopped, and Bud Adams came through the car, scrutinising every passenger. Seeing this, Hal began to sob again, and murmured something indistinct to his companion—which caused her to lean towards him, speaking volubly in her native language. "Bud" passed by.

When Hal came to leave the train, he took his companion's arm; he sobbed some more, and she talked some more, and so they went down the platform, under the very eyes of Pete Hanun, the "breaker of teeth." Another woman joined them, and they walked down the street, the women conversing in Slavish, apparently without a suspicion of Hal.

He had worked out his plan of action. He would not try to talk with the men secretly—it would take too long, and he might be betrayed before he had talked with a sufficient number. One bold stroke was the thing. In half an hour it would be supper-time, and the feeders would gather in Reminitsky's dining-room. He would give his message there!

Hal's two companions were puzzled that he passed the Zamboni cabin, where presumably the Zamboni brood were being cared for by neighbours. But he let them make what they could of this, and went on to the Minetti home. To the astonished Rosa he revealed himself, and gave her husband's message—that she should take herself and the children down to Pedro, and wait quietly until she heard from him. She hurried out and brought in Jack David, to whom Hal explained matters. "Big Jack's" part in the recent disturbance had apparently not been suspected; he and his wife, with Rovetta, Wresmak, and Klowoski, would remain as a nucleus through which the union could work upon the men.

The supper-hour was at hand, and the pseudo-Mrs. Zamboni emerged and toddled down the street. As she passed into the dining-room of the boarding-house, men looked at her, but no one spoke. It was the stage of the meal where everybody was grabbing and devouring, in the effort to get the best of his grabbing and devouring neighbours. The black-clad figure went to the far end of the room; there was a vacant chair, and the figure pulled it back from the table and climbed upon it. Then a shout rang through the room: "Boys! Boys!"

The feeders looked up, and saw the widow's weeds thrown back, and their leader, Joe Smith, gazing out at them. "Boys! I've come with a message from the union!"

There was a yell; men leaped to their feet, chairs were flung back, falling with a crash to the floor. Then, almost instantly, came silence; you could have heard the movement of any man's jaws, had any man continued to move them.

"Boys! I've been down to Pedro and seen the union people. I knew the bosses wouldn't let me come back, so I dressed up, and here I am!"

It dawned upon them, the meaning of this fantastic costume; there were cheers, laughter, yells of delight.

But Hal stretched out his hands, and silence fell again. "Listen to me! The bosses won't let me talk long, and I've something important to say. The union leaders say we can't win a strike now."

Consternation came into the faces before him. There were cries of dismay. He went on:

"We are only one camp, and the bosses would turn us out, they'd get in scabs and run the mines without us. What we must have is a strike of all the camps at once. One big union and one big strike! If we walked out now, it would please the bosses; but we'll fool them—we'll keep our jobs, and keep our union too! You are members of the union, you'll go on working for the union! Hooray for the North Valley union!"

For a moment there was no response. It was hard for men to cheer over such a prospect! Hal saw that he must touch a different chord.

"We mustn't be cowards, boys! We've got to keep our nerve! I'm doing my part—it took nerve to get in here! In Mrs. Zamboni's clothes, and with two pillows stuffed in front of me!"

He thumped the pillows, and there was a burst of laughter. Many in the crowd knew Mrs. Zamboni—it was what comedians call a "local gag." The laughter spread, and became a gale of merriment. Men began to cheer: "Hurrah for Joe! You're the girl! Will you marry me, Joe?" And so, of course, it was easy for Hal to get a response when he shouted, "Hurrah for the North Valley union!"

Again he raised his hands for silence, and went on again. "Listen, men. They'll turn me out, and you're not going to resist them. You're going to work and keep your jobs, and get ready for the big strike. And you'll tell the other men what I say. I can't talk to them all, but you tell them about the union. Remember, there are people outside planning and fighting for you. We're going to stand by the union, all of us, till we've brought these coal-camps back into America!" There was a cheer that shook the walls of the room. Yes, that was what they wanted—to live in America!

A crowd of men had gathered in the doorway, attracted by the uproar; Hal noticed confusion and pushing, and saw the head and burly shoulders of his enemy, Pete Hanun, come into sight.

"Here come the gunmen, boys!" he cried; and there was a roar of anger from the crowd. Men turned, clenching their fists, glaring at the guard. But Hal rushed on, quickly:

"Boys, hear what I say! Keep your heads! I can't stay in North Valley, and you know it! But I've done the thing I came to do, I've brought you the message from the union. And you'll tell the other men—tell them to stand by the union!"

Hal went on, repeating his message over and over. Looking from one to another of these toil-worn faces, he remembered the pledge he had made them, and he made it anew: "I'm going to stand by you! I'm going on with the fight, boys!"

There came more disturbance at the door, and suddenly Jeff Cotton appeared, with a couple of additional guards, shoving their way into the room, breathless and red in the face from running.

"Ah, there's the marshal!" cried Hal. "You needn't push, Cotton, there's not going to be any trouble. We are union men here, we know how to control ourselves. Now, boys, we're not giving up, we're not beaten, we're only waiting for the men in the other camps! We have a union, and we mean to keep it! Three cheers for the union!"

The cheers rang out with a will: cheers for the union, cheers for Joe Smith, cheers for the widow and her weeds!

"You belong to the union! You stand by it, no matter what happens! If they fire you, you take it on to the next place! You teach it to the new men, you never let it die in your hearts! In union there is strength, in union there is hope! Never forget it, men—*Union*!"

The voice of the camp-marshal rang out. "If you're coming, young woman, come now!"

Hal dropped a shy curtsey. "Oh, Mr. Cotton! This is so sudden!" The crowd howled; and Hal descended from his platform. With coquettish gesturing he replaced the widow's veils about his face, and tripped mincingly across the dining-room. When he reached the camp-marshal, he daintily took that worthy's arm, and with the "breaker of teeth" on the other side, and Bud Adams bringing up the rear, he toddled out of the dining-room and down the street.

Hungry men gave up their suppers to behold that sight. They poured out of the building, they followed, laughing, shouting, jeering. Others came from every direction—by the time the party had reached the depot, a good part of the population of the village was on hand; and everywhere went the word, "It's Joe Smith! Come back with a message from the union!" Big, coal-grimed miners laughed till the tears made streaks on their faces; they fell on one another's necks for delight at this trick which had been played upon their oppressors.

Even Jeff Cotton could not withhold his tribute. "By God, you're the limit!" he muttered. He accepted the "tea-party" aspect of the affair, as the easiest way to get rid of his recurrent guest, and avert the possibilities of danger. He escorted the widow to the train and helped her up the steps, posting escorts at the doors of her car; nor did the attentions of these gallants cease until the train had moved down the canyon and passed the limits of the North Valley stockade!

SECTION 26.

Hal took off his widow's weeds; and with them he shed the merriment he had worn for the benefit of the men. There came a sudden reaction; he realised that he was tired.

For ten days he had lived in a whirl of excitement, scarcely stopping to sleep. Now he lay back in the car-seat, pale, exhausted; his head ached, and he realised that the sum-total of his North Valley experience was failure. There was left in him no trace of that spirit of adventure with which he had set out upon his "summer course in practical sociology." He had studied his lessons, tried to recite them, and been "flunked." He smiled a bitter smile, recollecting the careless jesting that had been on his lips as he came up that same canyon:

> "He keeps them a-roll, that merry old soul—
> The wheels of industree;
> A-roll and a-roll, for his pipe and his bowl
> And his college facultee!"

The train arrived in Pedro, and Hal took a hack at the station and drove to the hotel. He still carried the widow's weeds rolled into a bundle. He might have left them in the train, but the impulse to economy which he had acquired during the last ten weeks had become a habit. He would return them to Mrs. Zamboni. The money he had promised her might better be used to feed her young ones. The two pillows he would leave in the car; the hotel might endure the loss!

Entering the lobby, the first person Hal saw was his brother, and the sight of that patrician face made human by disgust relieved Hal's headache in part. Life was harsh, life was cruel; but here was weary, waiting Edward, that boon of comic relief!

Edward demanded to know where the devil he had been; and Hal answered, "I've been visiting the widows and orphans."

"Oh!" said Edward. "And while I sit in this hole and stew! What's that you've got under your arm?"

Hal looked at the bundle. "It's a souvenir of one of the widows," he said, and unrolled the garments and spread them out before his brother's puzzled eyes. "A lady named Mrs. Swajka gave them to me. They belonged to another lady, Mrs. Zamboni, but she doesn't need them any more."

"What have *you* got to do with them?"

"It seems that Mrs. Zamboni is going to get married again." Hal lowered his voice, confidentially. "It's a romance, Edward—it may interest you as an illustration of the manners of these foreign races. She met a man on the street, a fine, fine man, she says—and he gave her a lot of money. So she went and bought herself some new clothes, and she wants to give these widow's weeds to the new man. That's the custom in her country, it seems—her sign that she accepts him as a suitor."

Seeing the look of wonderment growing on his brother's face, Hal had to stop for a moment to keep his own face straight. "If that man wasn't serious in his intention, Edward, he'll have trouble, for I know Mrs. Zamboni's emotional nature. She'll follow him about everywhere—"

"Hal, that creature is insane!" And Edward looked about him nervously, as if he thought the Slavish widow might appear suddenly in the hotel lobby to demonstrate her emotional nature.

"No," replied Hal, "it's just one of those differences in national customs." And suddenly Hal's face gave way. He began to laugh; he laughed, perhaps more loudly than good form permitted.

Edward was much annoyed. There were people in the lobby, and they were staring at him. "Cut it out, Hal!" he exclaimed. "Your fool jokes bore me!" But nevertheless, Hal could see uncertainty in his brother's face. Edward recognised those widow's weeds. And how could he be sure about the "national customs" of that grotesque creature who had pinched him in the ribs on the street?

"Cut it out!" he cried again.

Hal, changing his voice suddenly to the Zamboni key, exclaimed: "Mister, I got eight children I got to feed, and I don't got no more man, and I don't find no new man for old woman like me!"

So at last the truth in its full enormity began to dawn upon Edward. His consternation and disgust poured themselves out; and Hal listened, his laughter dying. "Edward," he said, "you don't take me seriously even yet!"

"Good God!" cried the other. "I believe you're really insane!"

"You were up there, Edward! You heard what I said to those poor devils! And you actually thought I'd go off with you and forget about them!"

Edward ignored this. "You're really insane!" he repeated. "You'll get yourself killed, in spite of all I can do!"

But Hal only laughed. "Not a chance of it! You should have seen the tea-party manners of the camp-marshal!"

SECTION 27.

Edward would have endeavoured to carry his brother away forthwith, but there was no train until late at night; so Hal went upstairs, where he found Moylan and Hartman with Mary Burke and Mrs. Zamboni, all eager to hear his story. As the members of the committee, who had been out to supper, came straggling in, the story was told again, and yet again. They were almost as much delighted as the men in Reminitsky's. If only all strikes that had to be called off could be called off as neatly as that!

Between these outbursts of satisfaction, they discussed their future. Moylan was going back to Western City, Hartman to his office in Sheridan, from which he would arrange to send new organisers into North Valley. No doubt Cartwright would turn off many men—those who had made themselves conspicuous during the strike, those who continued to talk union out loud. But such men would have to be replaced, and the union knew through what agencies the company got its hands. The North Valley miners would find themselves mysteriously provided with union literature in their various languages; it would be slipped under their pillows, or into their dinner-pails, or the pockets of their coats while they were at work.

Also there was propaganda to be carried on among those who were turned away; so that, wherever they went, they would take the message of unionism. There had been a sympathetic outburst in Barela, Hal learned—starting quite spontaneously that morning, when the men heard what had happened at North Valley. A score of workers had been fired, and more would probably follow in the morning. Here was a job for the members of the kidnapped committee; Tim Rafferty, for example—would he care to stay in Pedro for a week or two, to meet such men, and give them literature and arguments?

This offer was welcome; for life looked desolate to the Irish boy at this moment. He was out of a job, his father was a wreck, his family destitute and helpless. They would have to leave their home, of course; there would be no place for any Rafferty in North Valley. Where they would go, God only knew; Tim would become a wanderer, living away from his people, starving himself and sending home his pitiful savings.

Hal was watching the boy, and reading these thoughts. He, Hal Warner, would play the god out of a machine in this case, and in several others equally pitiful. He had the right to sign his father's name to checks, a privilege which he believed he could retain, even while undertaking the role of Haroun al Raschid in a mine-disaster. But what about the mine-disasters and abortive strikes where there did not happen to be any Haroun al Raschid at hand? What about those people, right in North Valley, who did not happen to have told Hal of their affairs? He perceived that it was only by turning his back and running that he would escape from his adventure with any portion of his self-possession. Truly, this fair-seeming and wonderful civilisation was like the floor of a charnel-house or a field of battle; anywhere one drove a spade beneath its surface, he uncovered horrors, sights for the eyes and stenches for the nostrils that caused him to turn sick!

There was Rusick, for example; he had a wife and two children, and not a dollar in the world. In the year and more that he had worked, faithfully and persistently, to get out coal for Peter Harrigan, he had never once been able to get ahead of his bill for the necessities of life at Old Peter's store. All his belongings in the world could be carried in a bundle on his back, and whether he ever saw these again would depend upon the whim of old Peter's camp-marshal and guards. Rusick would take to the road, with a ticket purchased by the union. Perhaps he would find a job and perhaps not; in any case, the best he could hope for in life was to work for some other Harrigan, and run into debt at some other company-store.

There was Hobianish, a Serbian, and Hernandez, a Mexican, of whom the same things were true, except that one had four children and the other six. Bill Wauchope had only a wife—their babies had died, thank heaven, he said. He did not seem to have been much moved by Jim Moylan's pleadings; he was down and out; he would take to the road, and beat his way to the East and back to England. They called this a free country! By God, if he were to tell what had happened to him, he could not get an English miner to believe it!

Hal gave these men his real name and address, and made them promise to let him know how they got along. He would help a little, he said; in his mind he was figuring how much he ought to do. How far shall a man go in relieving the starvation about him, before he can enjoy his meals in a well-appointed club? What casuist will work out this problem—telling him the percentage he shall relieve of the starvation he happens personally to know about, the percentage of that which he sees on the streets, the percentage of that about which he reads in government reports on the rise in the cost of living. To what extent is he permitted to close his eyes, as he walks along the streets on his way to the club? To what extent is he permitted to avoid reading government reports before going out to dinner-dances with his fiancée? Problems such as these the masters of the higher mathematics have neglected to solve; the wise men of the academies and the holy men of the churches have likewise failed to work out the formulas; and Hal, trying to obtain them by his crude mental arithmetic, found no satisfaction in the results.

SECTION 28.

Hal wanted a chance to talk to Mary Burke; they had had no intimate talk since the meeting with Jessie Arthur, and now he was going away, for a long time. He wanted to find out what plans Mary had for the future, and—more important yet—what was her state of mind. If he had been able to lift this girl from despair, his summer course in practical sociology had not been all a failure!

He asked her to go with him to say good-bye to John Edstrom, whom he had not seen since their unceremonious parting at MacKellar's, when Hal had fled to Percy Harrigan's train. Downstairs in the lobby Hal explained his errand to his waiting brother, who made no comment, but merely remarked that he would follow, if Hal had no objection. He did not care to make the acquaintance of the Hibernian Joan of Arc, and would not come close enough to interfere with Hal's conversation with the lady; but he wished to do what he could for his brother's protection. So there set out a moon-light procession—first Hal and Mary, then Edward, and then Edward's dinner-table companion, the "hardware-drummer!"

Hal was embarrassed in beginning his farewell talk with Mary. He had no idea how she felt towards him, and he admitted with a guilty pang that he was a little afraid to find out! He thought it best to be cheerful, so he started to tell her how fine he thought her conduct during the strike. But she did not respond to his remarks, and at last he realised that she was labouring with some thoughts of her own.

"There's somethin' I got to say to ye!" she began, suddenly. "A couple of days ago I knew how I meant to say it, but now I don't."

"Well," he laughed, "say it as you meant to."

"No; 'twas bitter—and now I'm on my knees before ye."

"Not that I want you to be bitter," said Hal, still laughing, "but it's I that ought to be on my knees before you. I didn't accomplish anything, you know."

"Ye did all ye could—and more than the rest of us. I want ye to know I'll never forget it. But I want ye to hear the other thing, too!"

She walked on, staring before her, doubling up her hands in agitation. "Well?" said he, still trying to keep a cheerful tone.

"Ye remember that day just after the explosion? Ye remember what I said about—about goin' away with ye? I take it back."

"Oh, of course!" said he, quickly. "You were distracted, Mary—you didn't know what you were saying."

"No, no! That's not it! But I've changed my mind; I don't mean to throw meself away."

"I told you you'd see it that way," he said. "No man is worth it."

"Ah, lad!" said she. "'Tis the fine soothin' tongue ye have—but I'd rather ye knew the truth. 'Tis that I've seen the other girl; and I hate her!"

They walked for a bit in silence. Hal had sense enough to realise that here was a difficult subject. "I don't want to be a prig, Mary," he said gently; "but you'll change your mind about that, too. You'll not hate her; you'll be sorry for her."

She laughed—a raw, harsh laugh. "What kind of a joke is that?"

"I know—it may seem like one. But it'll come to you some day. You have a wonderful thing to live and fight for; while she"—he hesitated a moment, for he was not sure of his own ideas on this subject—"she has so many things to learn; and she may never learn them. She'll miss some fine things."

"I know one of the fine things she does not mean to miss," said Mary, grimly; "that's Mr. Hal Warner." Then, after they had walked again in silence: "I want ye to understand me, Mr. Warner—"

"Ah, Mary!" he pleaded. "Don't treat me that way! I'm Joe."

"All right," she said, "Joe ye shall be. 'Twill remind ye of a pretty adventure— bein' a workin' man for a few weeks. Well, that's a part of what I have to tell ye. I've got my pride, even if I'm only a poor miner's daughter; and the other day I found out me place."

"How do you mean?" he asked.

"Ye don't understand? Honest?"

"No, honest," he said.

"Ye're stupid with women, Joe. Ye didn't see what the girl did to me! 'Twas some kind of a bug I was to her. She was not sure if I was the kind that bites, but she took no chances—she threw me off, like that." And Mary snapped her hand, as one does when troubled with a bug.

"Ah, now!" pleaded Hal. "You're not being fair!"

"I'm bein' just as fair as I've got it in me to be, Joe. I been off and had it all out. I can see this much—'tis not her fault, maybe—'tis her class; 'tis all of ye—the very best of ye, even yeself, Joe Smith!"

"Yea," he replied, "Tim Rafferty said that."

"Tim said too much—but a part of it was true. Ye think ye've come here and been one of us workin' people. But don't your own sense tell you the difference, as if it was a canyon a million miles across—between a poor ignorant creature in a minin' camp, and a rich man's daughter, a lady? Ye'd tell me not to be ashamed of poverty; but would ye ever put me by the side of her—for all your fine feelin's of friendship for them that's beneath ye? Didn't ye show that at the Minettis'?"

"But don't you see, Mary—" He made an effort to laugh. "I got used to obeying Jessie! I knew her a long time before I knew you."

"Ah, Joe! Ye've a kind heart, and a pleasant way of speakin'. But wouldn't it interest ye to know the real truth? Ye said ye'd come out here to learn the truth!"

And Hal answered, in a low voice, "Yes," and did not interrupt again.

<h1 style="text-align:center">SECTION 29.</h1>

Mary's voice had dropped low, and Hal thought how rich and warm it was when she was deeply moved. She went on:

"I lived all me life in minin' camps, Joe Smith, and I seen men robbed and beaten, and women cryin' and childer hungry. I seen the company, like some great wicked beast that eat them up. But I never knew why, or what it meant—till that day, there at the Minettis'. I'd read about fine ladies in books, ye see; but I'd never been spoke to by one, I'd never had to swallow one, as ye might say. But there I did—and all at once I seemed to know where the money goes that's wrung out of the miners. I saw why people were robbin' us, grindin' the life out of us—for fine ladies like that, to keep them so shinin' and soft! 'Twould not have been so bad, if she'd not come just then, with all the men and boys dyin' down in the pits—dyin' for that soft, white skin, and those soft, white hands, and all those silky things she swished round in. My God, Joe—d'ye know what she seemed to me like? Like a smooth, sleek cat that has just eat up a whole nest full of baby mice, and has the blood of them all over her cheeks!"

Mary paused, breathing hard. Hal kept silence, and she went on again: "I had it out with meself, Joe! I don't want ye to think I'm any better than I am, and I asked meself this question—Is it for the men in the pits that ye hate her with such black murder? Or is it for the one man ye want, and that she's got? And I knew the answer to that! But then I asked meself another question, too—Would ye be like her if ye could? Would ye do what she's doin' right now—would ye have it on your soul? And as God hears me, Joe, 'tis the truth I speak—I'd not do it! No, not for the love of any man that ever walked on this earth!"

She had lifted her clenched fist as she spoke. She let it fall again, and strode on, not even glancing at him. "Ye might try a thousand years, Joe, and ye'd not realise the feelin's that come to me there at the Minettis'. The shame of it—not what she done to me, but what she made me in me own eyes! Me, the daughter of a drunken old miner, and her—I don't know what her father is, but she's some sort of princess, and she knows it. And that's the thing that counts, Joe! 'Tis not that she has so much money, and so many fine things; that she knows how to talk, and I don't, and that her voice is sweet, and mine is ugly, when I'm ragin' as I am now. No—'tis that she's so *sure!* That's the word I found to say it; she's sure—sure—*sure!* She has the fine things, she's always had them, she has a right to have them!

And I have a right to nothin' but trouble, I'm hunted all day by misery and fear, I've lost even the roof over me head! Joe, ye know I've got some temper—I'm not easy to beat down; but when I'd got through bein' taught me place, I went off and hid meself, I ground me face in the dirt, for the black rage of it! I said to meself, 'Tis true! There's somethin' in her better than me! She's some kind of finer creature.—Look at these hands!" She held them out in the moonlight, with a swift, passionate gesture. "So she's a right to her man, and I'm a fool to have ever raised me eyes to him! I have to see him go away, and crawl back into me leaky old shack! Yes, that's the truth! And when I point it out to the man, what d'ye think he says? Why, he tells me gently and kindly that I ought to be sorry for her! Christ! did ye ever hear the like of that?"

There was a long silence. Hal could not have said anything now, if he had wished to. He knew that this was what he had come to seek! This was the naked soul of the class-war!

"Now," concluded Mary, with clenched hands, and a voice that corresponded, "now, I've had it out. I'm no slave; I've just as good a right to life as any lady. I know I'll never have it, of course; I'll never wear good clothes, nor live in a decent home, nor have the man I want; but I'll know that I've done somethin' to help free the workin' people from the shame that's put on them. That's what the strike done for me, Joe! The strike showed me the way. We're beat this time, but somehow it hasn't made the difference ye might think. I'm goin' to make more strikes before I quit, and they won't all of them be beat!"

She stopped speaking; and Hal walked beside her, stirred by a conflict of emotions. His vision of her was indeed true; she would make more strikes! He was glad and proud of that; but then came the thought that while she, a girl, was going on with the bitter war, he, a man, would be eating grilled beefsteaks at the club!

"Mary," he said, "I'm ashamed of myself—"

"That's not it, Joe! Ye've no call to be ashamed. Ye can't help it where ye were born—"

"Perhaps not, Mary. But when a man knows he's never paid for any of the things he's enjoyed all his life, surely the least he can do is to be ashamed. I hope you'll try not to hate me as you do the others."

"I never hated ye, Joe! Not for one moment! I tell ye fair and true, I love ye as much as ever. I can say it, because I'd not have ye now; I've seen the other girl, and I know ye'd never be satisfied with me. I don't know if I ought to say it, but I'm thinkin' ye'll not be altogether satisfied with her, either. Ye'll be unhappy either way—God help ye!"

The girl had read deeply into his soul in this last speech; so deeply that Hal could not trust himself to answer. They were passing a street-lamp, and she looked at him, for the first time since they had started on their walk, and saw harassment in his face. A sudden tenderness came into her voice. "Joe," she said; "ye're lookin' bad. 'Tis good ye're goin' away from this place!"

He tried to smile, but the effort was feeble.

"Joe," she went on, "ye asked me to be your friend. Well, I'll be that!" And she held out the big, rough hand.

He took it. "We'll not forget each other, Mary," he said. There was a catch in his voice.

"Sure, lad!" she exclaimed. "We'll make another strike some day, just like we did at North Valley!"

Hal pressed the big hand; but then suddenly, remembering his brother stalking solemnly in the rear, he relinquished the clasp, and failed to say all the fine things he had in his mind. He called himself a rebel, but not enough to be sentimental before Edward!

<h1 style="text-align:center">SECTION 30.</h1>

They came to the house where John Edstrom was staying. The labouring man's wife opened the door. In answer to Hal's question, she said, "The old gentleman's pretty bad."

"What's the matter with him?"

"Didn't you know he was hurt?"

"No. How?"

"They beat him up, sir. Broke his arm, and nearly broke his head."

Hal and Mary exclaimed in chorus, "Who did it? When?"

"We don't know who did it. It was four nights ago."

Hal realised it must have happened while he was escaping from MacKellar's. "Have you had a doctor for him?"

"Yes, sir; but we can't do much, because my man is out of work, and I have the children and the boarders to look after."

Hal and Mary ran upstairs. Their old friend lay in darkness, but he recognised their voices and greeted them with a feeble cry. The woman brought a lamp, and they saw him lying on his back, his head done up in bandages, and one arm bound in splints. He looked really desperately bad, his kindly old eyes deep-sunken and haggard, and his face—Hal remembered what Jeff Cotton had called him, "that dough-faced old preacher!"

They got the story of what had happened at the time of Hal's flight to Percy's train. Edstrom had shouted a warning to the fugitives, and set out to run after them; when one of the mine-guards, running past him, had fetched him a blow over the eye, knocking him down. He had struck his head upon the pavement, and lain there unconscious for many hours. When finally some one had come upon him, and summoned a policeman, they had gone through his pockets, and found the address of this place where he was staying written on a scrap of paper. That was all there was to the story—except that Edstrom had refrained from sending to MacKellar for help, because he had felt sure they were all working to get the mine open, and he did not feel he had the right to put his troubles upon them.

Hal listened to the old man's feeble statements, and there came back to him a surge of that fury which his North Valley experience had generated in him. It was foolish, perhaps; for to knock down an old man who had been making trouble was a comparatively slight exercise of the functions of a mine-guard. But to Hal it seemed the most characteristic of all the outrages he had seen; it was an expression of the company's utter blindness to all that was best in life. This old man, who was so gentle, so patient, who had suffered so much, and not learned to hate, who had kept his faith so true! What did his faith mean to the thugs of the General Fuel Company? What had his philosophy availed him, his saintliness, his hopes for mankind? They had fetched him one swipe as they passed him, and left him lying—alive or dead, it was all the same.

Hal had got some satisfaction out of his little adventure in widowhood, and some out of Mary's self-victory; but there, listening to the old man's whispered story, his satisfaction died. He realised again the grim truth about his summer's experience—that the issue of it had been defeat. Utter, unqualified defeat! He had caused the bosses a momentary chagrin; but it would not take them many hours to realise that he had really done them a service in calling off the strike for them. They would start the wheels of industry again, and the workers would be just where they had been before Joe Smith came to be stableman and buddy among them. What was all the talk about solidarity, about hope for the future; what would it amount to in the long run, the daily rolling of the wheels of industry? The workers of North Valley would have exactly the right they had always had— the right to be slaves, and if they did not care for that, the right to be martyrs!

Mary sat holding the old man's hand and whispering words of passionate sympathy, while Hal got up and paced the tiny attic, all ablaze with anger. He resolved suddenly that he would not go back to Western City; he would stay here, and get an honest lawyer to come, and set out to punish the men who were guilty of this outrage. He would test out the law to the limit; if necessary, he would begin a political fight, to put an end to coal-company rule in this community. He would find some one to write up these conditions, he would raise the money and publish a paper to make them known! Before his surging wrath had spent itself, Hal Warner had actually come out as a candidate for governor, and was overturning the Republican machine—all because an unidentified coal-company detective had knocked a dough-faced old miner into the gutter and broken his arm!

SECTION 31.

In the end, of course, Hal had to come down to practical matters. He sat by the bed and told the old man tactfully that his brother had come to see him and had given him some money. This brother had plenty of money, so Edstrom could be taken to the hospital; or, if he preferred, Mary could stay near here and take care of him. They turned to the landlady, who had been standing in the doorway; she had three boarders in her little home, it seemed, but if Mary could share a bed with the landlady's two children, they might make out. In spite of Hal's protest, Mary accepted this offer; he saw what was in her mind—she would take some of his money, because of old Edstrom's need, but she would take just as little as she possibly could.

John Edstrom of course knew nothing of events since his injury, so Hal told him the story briefly—though without mentioning the transformation which had taken place in the miner's buddy. He told about the part Mary had played in the strike; trying to entertain the poor old man, he told how he had seen her mounted upon a snow-white horse, and wearing a robe of white, soft and lustrous, like Joan of Arc, or the leader of a suffrage parade.

"Sure," said Mary, "he's forever callin' attention to this old dress!"

Hal looked; she was wearing the same blue calico. "There's something mysterious about that dress," said he. "It's one of those that you read about in fairy-stories, that forever patch themselves, and keep themselves new and starchy. A body only needs one dress like that!"

"Sure, lad," she answered. "There's no fairies in coal-camps—unless 'tis meself, that washes it at night, and dries it over the stove, and irons it next mornin'."

She said this with unwavering cheerfulness; but even the old miner lying in pain on the cot could realise the tragedy of a young girl's having only one old dress in her love-hunting season. He looked at the young couple, and saw their evident interest in each other; after the fashion of the old, he was disposed to help along the romance. "She may need some orange blossoms," he ventured, feebly.

"Go along with ye!" laughed Mary, still unwavering.

"Sure," put in Hal, with hasty gallantry, "'tis a blossom she is herself! A rose in a mining-camp—and there's a dispute about her in the poetry-books. One tells you to leave her on her stalk, and another says to gather ye rosebuds while ye may, old time is still a-flying!"

"Ye're mixin' me up," said Mary. "A while back I was ridin' on a white horse."

"I remember," said Old Edstrom, "not so far back, you were an ant, Mary."

Her face became grave. To jest about her personal tragedy was one thing, to jest about the strike was another. "Yes, I remember. Ye said I'd stay in the line! Ye were wiser than me, Mr. Edstrom."

"That's one of the things that come with being old, Mary." He moved his gnarled old hand toward hers. "You're going on, now?" he asked. "You're a unionist now, Mary?"

"I am that!" she answered, promptly, her grey eyes shining.

"There's a saying," said he—"once a striker, always a striker. Find a way to get some education for yourself, Mary, and when the big strike comes you'll be one of those the miners look to. I'll not be here, I know—the young people must take my place."

"I'll do my part," she answered. Her voice was low; it was a kind of benediction the old man was giving her.

The woman had gone downstairs to attend to her children; she came back now to say that there was a gentleman at the door, who wanted to know when his brother was coming. Hal remembered suddenly—Edward had been pacing up and down all this while, with no company but a "hardware drummer!" The younger brother's resolve to stay in Pedro had already begun to weaken somewhat, and now it weakened still further; he realised that life is complex, that duties conflict! He assured the old miner again of his ability to see that he did not suffer from want, and then he bade him farewell for a while.

He started out, and Mary went as far as the head of the stairway with him. He took the girl's big, rough hand in his—this time with no one to see. "Mary," he said, "I want you to know that nothing will make me forget you; and nothing will make me forget the miners."

"Ah, Joe!" she cried. "Don't let them win ye away from us! We need ye so bad!"

"I'm going back home for a while," he answered, "but you can be sure that no matter what happens in my life, I'm going to fight for the working people. When the big strike comes, as we know it's coming in this coal-country, I'll be here to do my share."

"Sure lad," she said, looking him bravely in the eye, "and good-bye to ye, Joe Smith." Her eyes did not waver; but Hal noted a catch in her voice, and he found himself with an impulse to take her in his arms. It was very puzzling. He knew he loved Jessie Arthur; he remembered the question Mary had once asked him— could he be in love with two girls at the same time? It was not in accord with any moral code that had been impressed upon him, but apparently he could!

SECTION 32.

He went out to the street, where his brother was pacing up and down in a ferment. The "hardware drummer" had made another effort to start a conversation, and had been told to go to hell—no less!

"Well, are you through now?" Edward demanded, taking out his irritation on Hal.

"Yes," replied the other. "I suppose so." He realised that Edward would not be concerned about Edstrom's broken arm.

"Then, for God's sake, get some clothes on and let's have some food."

"All right," said Hal. But his answer was listless, and the other looked at him sharply. Even by the moonlight Edward could see the lines in the face of his younger brother, and the hollows around his eyes. For the first time he realised how deeply these experiences were cutting into the boy's soul. "You poor kid!" he exclaimed, with sudden feeling. But Hal did not answer; he did not want sympathy, he did not want anything!

Edward made a gesture of despair. "God knows, I don't know what to do for you!"

They started back to the hotel, and on the way Edward cast about in his mind for a harmless subject of conversation. He mentioned that he had foreseen the shutting up of the stores, and had purchased an outfit for his brother. There was no need to thank him, he added grimly; he had no intention of travelling to Western City in company with a hobo.

So the young miner had a bath, the first real one in a long time. (Never again would it be possible for ladies to say in Hal Warner's presence that the poor might at least keep clean!) He had a shave; he trimmed his finger-nails, and brushed his hair, and dressed himself as a gentleman. In spite of himself he found his cheerfulness partly restored. A strange and wonderful sensation—to be dressed once more as a gentleman. He thought of the saying of the old negro, who liked to stub his toe, because it felt so good when it stopped hurting!

They went out to find a restaurant, and on the way one last misadventure befell Edward. Hal saw an old miner walking past, and stopped with a cry: "Mike!" He forgot all at once that he was a gentleman; the old miner forgot it also. He stared for one bewildered moment, then he rushed at Hal and seized him in the hug of a mountain grizzly.

"My buddy! My buddy!" he cried, and gave Hal a prodigious thump on the back. "By Judas!" And he gave him a thump with the other hand. "Hey! you old son-of-a-gun!" And he gave him a hairy kiss!

But in the very midst of these raptures it dawned over him that there was something wrong about his buddy. He drew back, staring. "You got good clothes! You got rich, hey?"

Evidently the old fellow had heard no rumour concerning Hal's secret. "I've been doing pretty well," Hal said.

"What you work at, hey?"

"I been working at a strike in North Valley."

"What's that? You make money working at strike?"

Hal laughed, but did not explain. "What you working at?"

"I work at strike too—all alone strike."

"No job?"

"I work two days on railroad. Got busted track up there. Pay me two-twenty-five a day. Then no more job."

"Have you tried the mines?"

"What? Me? They got me all right! I go up to San José. Pit-boss say, 'Get the hell out of here, you old groucher! You don't get no more jobs in this district!'"

Hal looked Mike over, and saw that his dirty old face was drawn and white, belying the feeble cheerfulness of his words. "We're going to have something to eat," he said. "Won't you come with us?"

"Sure thing!" said Mike, with alacrity. "I go easy on grub now."

Hal introduced "Mr. Edward Warner," who said "How do you do?" He accepted gingerly the calloused paw which the old Slovak held out to him, but he could not keep the look of irritation from his face. His patience was utterly exhausted. He had hoped to find a decent restaurant and have some real food; but now, of course, he could not enjoy anything, with this old gobbler in front of him.

They entered an all-night lunch-room, where Hal and Mike ordered cheese-sandwiches and milk, and Edward sat and wondered at his brother's ability to eat such food. Meantime the two cronies told each other their stories, and Old Mike slapped his knee and cried out with delight over Hal's exploits. "Oh, you buddy!" he exclaimed; then, to Edward, "Ain't he a daisy, hey?" And he gave Edward a thump on the shoulder. "By Judas, they don't beat my buddy!"

Mike Sikoria had last been seen by Hal from the window of the North Valley jail, when he had been distributing the copies of Hal's signature, and Bud Adams had taken him in charge. The mine-guard had marched him into a shed in back of the power-house, where he had found Kauser and Kalovac, two other fellows who had been arrested while helping in the distribution.

Mike detailed the experience with his usual animation. "'Hey, Mister Bud,' I say, 'if you going to send me down canyon, I want to get my things.' 'You go to hell for your things,' says he. And then I say, 'Mister Bud, I want to get my time.' And he says, 'I give you plenty time right here!' And he punch me and throw me over. Then he grab me up' again and pull me outside, and I see big automobile waiting, and I say, 'Holy Judas! I get ride in automobile! Here I am, old fellow fifty-seven years old, never been in automobile ride all my days. I think always I die and never get in automobile ride!' We go down canyon, and I look round and see them mountains, and feel nice cool wind in my face, and I say, 'Bully for you, Mister Bud, I don't never forget this automobile. I don't have such good time any day all my life.' And he say, 'Shut your face, you old wop!' Then we come out on prairie, we go up in Black Hills, and they stop, and say, 'Get out here, you sons o' guns.' And they leave us there all alone. They say, 'You come back again, we catch you and we rip the guts out of you!' They go away fast, and we got to walk seven hours, us fellers, before we come to a house! But I don't mind that, I begged some grub, and then I got job mending track; only I don't find out if you get out of jail, and I think maybe I lose my buddy and never see him no more."

Here the old man stopped, gazing affectionately at Hal. "I write you letter to North Valley, but I don't hear nothing, and I got to walk all the way on railroad track to look for you."

How was it? Hal wondered. He had encountered naked horror in this coal-country—yet here he was, not entirely glad at the thought of leaving it! He would miss Old Mike Sikoria, his hairy kiss and his grizzly-bear hug!

He struck the old man dumb by pressing a twenty-dollar bill into his hand. Also he gave him the address of Edstrom and Mary, and a note to Johann Hartman, who might use him to work among the Slovaks who came down into the town. Hal explained that he had to go back to Western City that night, but that he would never forget his old friend, and would see that he had a good job. He was trying to figure out some occupation for the old man on his father's country-place. A pet grizzly!

Train-time came, and the long line of dark sleepers rolled in by the depot-platform. It was late—after midnight; but, nevertheless, there was Old Mike. He was in awe of Hal now, with his fine clothes and his twenty-dollar bills; but, nevertheless, under stress of his emotion, he gave him one more hug, and one more hairy kiss. "Good-bye, my buddy!" he cried. "You come back, my buddy! I don't forget my buddy!" And when the train began to move, he waved his ragged cap, and ran along the platform to get a last glimpse, to call a last farewell. When Hal turned into the car, it was with more than a trace of moisture in his eyes.

POSTSCRIPT

From previous experiences the writer has learned that many people, reading a novel such as "King Coal," desire to be informed as to whether it is true to fact. They write to ask if the book is meant to be so taken; they ask for evidence to convince themselves and others. Having answered thousands of such letters in the course of his life, it seems to the author the part of common-sense to answer some of them in advance.

"King Coal" is a picture of the life of the workers in unorganised labour-camps in many parts of America, The writer has avoided naming a definite place, for the reason that such conditions are to be found as far apart as West Virginia, Alabama, Michigan, Minnesota, and Colorado. Most of the details of his picture were gathered in the last-named state, which the writer visited on three occasions during and just after the great coal-strike of 1913-14. The book gives a true picture of conditions and events observed by him at this time. Practically all the characters are real persons, and every incident which has social significance is not merely a true incident, but a typical one. The life portrayed in "King Coal" is the life that is lived to-day by hundreds of thousands of men, women and children in this "land of the free."

The reader who wishes evidence may be accommodated. There was never a strike more investigated than the Colorado coal-strike. The material about it in the writer's possession cannot be less than eight million words, the greater part of it sworn testimony taken under government supervision. There is, first, the report of the Congressional Committee, a government document of three thousand closely printed pages, about two million words; an equal amount of testimony given before the U. S. Commission on Industrial Relations, also a government document; a special report on the Colorado strike, prepared for the same commission, a book of 189 pages, supporting every contention of this story; about four hundred thousand words of testimony given before a committee appointed at the suggestion of the Governor of Colorado; a report made by the Rev. Henry A. Atkinson, who investigated the strike as representative of the Federal Council of the Churches of Christ in America, and of the Social Service Commission of the Congregational Churches; the report of an elaborate investigation by the Colorado state militia; the bulletins issued by both sides during the controversy; the testimony given at various coroners' inquests; and, finally, articles by different writers to be found in the files of *Everybody's Magazine*, the *Metropolitan Magazine*, the *Survey*, *Harper's Weekly*, and *Collier's Weekly*, all during the year 1914.

The writer prepared a collection of extracts from these various sources, meaning to publish them in this place; but while the manuscript was in the hands of the publishers, there appeared one document, which, in the weight of its authority, seemed to discount all others. A decision was rendered by the Supreme Court of the State of Colorado, in a case which included the most fundamental of the many issues raised in "King Coal." It is not often that the writer of a novel of contemporary life is so fortunate as to have the truth of his work passed upon and estab-established by the highest judicial tribunal of the community!

In the elections of November, 1914, in Huerfano County, Colorado, J. B. Farr, Republican candidate for re-election as sheriff, a person known throughout the coal-country as "the King of Huerfano County," was returned as elected by a majority of 329 votes. His rival, the Democratic candidate, contested the election, alleging "malconduct, fraud and corruption." The district court found in Farr's favour, and the case was appealed on error to the Supreme Court of the State. On June 21st, 1916, after Farr had served nearly the whole of his term of office, the Supreme Court handed down a decision which unseated him and the entire ticket elected with him, finding in favour of the opposition ticket in all cases and upon all grounds charged.

The decision is long—about ten thousand words, and its legal technicalities would not interest the reader. It will suffice to reprint the essential paragraphs. The reader is asked to give these paragraphs careful study, considering, not merely the specific offence denounced by the court, but its wider implications. The offence was one so unprecedented that the justices of the court, men chosen for their learning in the history of offences, were moved to say: "We find no such example of fraud within the books, and must seek the letter and spirit of the law in a free government, as a scale in which to weigh such conduct." And let it be noted, this "crime without a name" was not a crime of passion, but of policy; it was a crime deliberately planned and carried out by profit-seeking corporations of enormous power. Let the reader imagine the psychology of the men of great wealth who ordered this crime, as a means of keeping and increasing their wealth; let him realise what must be the attitude of such men to their helpless workers; and then let him ask himself whether there is any act portrayed in "King Coal" which men of such character would shrink from ordering.

The Court decision first gives an outline of the case, using for the most part the statements of the counsel for the defendant, Farr; so that for practical purposes the following may be taken as the coal companies' own account of their domain: "Round the shaft of each mine are clustered the tipple, the mine office, the shops, sheds and outbuildings; and huddled close by, within a stone's throw, cottages of the miners built on the land of, and owned by, the mining company. All the dwellers in the camp are employés of the mine. There is no other industry. This is 'the camp.' Of the eight 'closed camps' it appears that practically the same conditions existed in all of them, and those conditions were in general that members of the United Mine Workers of America, their organisers or agitators, were prevented from coming into the camps, so far as it was possible to keep them out, and to this end guards were stationed about them. Of the eight 'closed camps' one of them, 'Walsen,' was, and at the time of the trial still was, enclosed by a fence erected at the beginning of the strike in October, 1913: Rouse and Cameron were partly, but never entirely, enclosed by fences. It is admitted that all persons entering these camps and precincts were required by the companies to have passes, and it is contended that this was an 'industrial necessity.'"

The Court then goes on as follows:

"The Federal troops entered the district in May of 1914, and the testimony is in agreement that no serious acts of violence occurred thereafter, and that order was preserved up to and subsequent to the election, and to the time of this trial.

"It was under this condition that in July, 1914, the Board of County Commissioners changed certain of the election precincts so as to constitute each of such camps an election precinct, and with but one exception where a few ranches were included, these precincts were made to conform to the fences and lines around each camp, protected by fences in some instances and with armed guards in all cases. Thus each election precinct by this unparalleled act of the commissioners was placed exclusively within and upon the private grounds and under the private control of a coal corporation, which autocratically declared who should and who should not enter upon the territory of this political entity of the state, so purposely bounded by the county commissioners.

"With but one exception all the lands and buildings within each of these election precincts as so created, were owned or controlled by the coal corporations; every person resident within such precincts was an employé of these private corporations or their allied companies, with the single exception: every judge, clerk or officer of election with the exception of a saloon keeper, and partner of Farr, was an employé of the coal-companies.

"The polling places were upon the grounds, and in the buildings of these companies; the registration lists were kept within the private offices or buildings of such companies, and used and treated as their private property.

"Thus were the public election districts and the public election machinery turned over to the absolute domination and imperial control of private coal corporations, and used by them as absolutely and privately as were their mines, to and for their own private purposes, and upon which public territory no man might enter for either public or private purpose, save and except by the express permission of these private corporations.

"This right to determine who should enter such so called election precincts, appears from the record to have been exercised as against all classes; merchants, tradesmen or what not, and whether the business of such person was public or private. Indeed, it appears that in one instance the governor and adjutant general of the state while on official business, were denied admission to one of these closed camps. And that on the day of election, the Democratic watchers and challengers for Walsen Mine precinct, one of which was Neelley, the Democratic candidate for sheriff, were forced to seek and secure a detail of Federal soldiers to escort them into the precinct and to the polls, and that such soldiers remained as such guard during the day and a part of the night....

"But if there was any doubt concerning the condition of the closed camps and precincts, and the exclusion of representatives of the Democratic party from discussing the issues of the campaign within the precincts comprising the closed camps, it is entirely removed by the testimony of the witness Weitzel, for contestee (Farr). He testified that he was a resident of Pueblo, and was manager of the Colorado Fuel and Iron Company; that Rouse, Lester, Ideal, Cameron, Walsen, Pictou and McNally are camps under his jurisdiction. That he had general charge of the camps and that there was no company official in Colorado superior to him in this respect except the president; that the superintendent and other employés are under his supervision; that the Federal troops came about the 1st of May, 1914, and continued until January, 1915. That in all those camps he tried to keep out the people who were antagonistic to the company's interests; that it was private property and so treated by his company; that through him the company and its officials assumed to exercise authority as to who might or who might not enter; that if persons could assure or satisfy the man at the gate, or the superintendent that they were not connected with the United Mine Workers, or in their employ as agitators, they were let into the camp. That 'no one we were fighting against got in for social intercourse or any other'; that he and officials under him assumed to pass upon the question of whether or not any person coming there came for the purpose of agitation. That Mr. Mitchell, the chairman of the Democratic committee, as he recalled it, was identified with the agitators, ran a newspaper and was connected either directly or indirectly with the United Mine Workers; that Mr. Neelley, Democratic candidate for sheriff, was identified with the strikers, and that he would be considered as an objectionable character. That when the Federal troops came, they restored peace and normal conditions; there was no rioting after that, there was no fear on the part of the company when the Federal soldiers were here, except fear of agitation. Asked if he guarded the camp against discussion, against the espousal of the cause of the company, he replied, 'We didn't encourage it.' The company would not encourage organisers to come into the camp, no matter how peacefully they conducted themselves; that the company did not permit men to come into the camp to discuss with the employés certain principles, or to carry on arguments with them or to appeal to their reason, or to discuss with them things along reasonable lines, because it was known from experience that if they were allowed to come in they would resort to threats of violence. They might not resort to any violence at the time, but it might result in the people becoming frightened and leaving, and they were anxious to hold their employés. He was asked whether or not one had business there depended upon the decision of the official in charge; he replied that the superintendent probably would inquire of him what his business was. That any one that Farr asked for a permit to enter the camp would likely get it....

"There was but one attempt to hold a political meeting in the closed precincts. Joseph Patterson, who attempted to hold this meeting, testifies concerning it as follows:

"Was at a political meeting at Oakview. Had been a warm, personal friend of Mr. Jones, the assistant superintendent of the Oakview mine, and had written him a letter asking the courtesy of holding a political meeting. On Saturday evening received a letter that he could hold such meeting. On the day previous to the meeting witness received a 'phone message from the assistant superintendent, in which the latter inquired whether witness was coming up there to cause any trouble, and witness replied, certainly not, and if the superintendent felt that way they would not come. Had advised the superintendent that he and others were going to hold a political meeting for the Democratic party. Jones, the superintendent, stated that witness should come to the office that night before he went to the school house for the purpose of the meeting; when witness arrived at the meeting there were about six or eight English speaking people and a dozen to fourteen Mexicans. The superintendent, Mr. Morgan, and Mr. Price, were outside of the door most of the time. Witness noticed that the first few fellows that came toward the school house, the superintendent stopped and talked with them and they turned back to the camp. This happened several times: as soon as they talked with Morgan they turned back. After he saw that, witness went into the school house and said that it was no use to hold any meeting; that it seemed that nobody was allowed to come. This meeting was supposed to be in a public school house on the company property. Had to get permission from the superintendent of the Oakview mining Company to hold said political meeting."....

"It appears that the number of registered voters in the closed precincts was very largely in excess of the number of votes cast, and this of itself was sufficient to demand an open and fair investigation as to the qualifications of the alleged voters.

"It appears from the testimony that in these closed precincts many of those who voted were unable to speak or read the English language, and that in numerous instances, the election judges assisted such, by marking the ballots for them in violation of the law. Again, it appears that the ballots were printed so that.... (The decision here goes on to explain in detail a device whereby the ballot was so printed that voting could be controlled with the help of a card device.) Thus such voters were not choosing candidates, but, under the direction of the companies, were simply placing the cross where they found the particular letter R on the ballot, so that the ballot was not an expression of opinion or judgment, not an intelligent exercise of suffrage, but plainly a dictated coal company vote, as much so as if the agents of these companies had marked the ballots without the intervention of the voter. No more fraudulent and infamous prostitution of the ballot is conceivable....

"Counsel contend that the closed precincts were an 'industrial necessity,' and for such reason the conduct of the coal companies during the campaign was justified. However such conduct may be viewed when confined to the private property of such corporations in their private operation, the fact remains that there is no justification when they were dealing with such territory after it had been dedicated to a public use, and particularly involving the right of the people to exercise their duties and powers as electors in a popular government.

"The fact appears that the members of the board of county commissioners and all other county officers were Republicans, and as stated by counsel for the contestees, the success of the Republican candidates was considered by the coal companies, vital to their interests. The close relationship of the coal companies and the Republican officials and candidates appears to have been so marked both before and during the campaign, as to justify the conclusion that such officers regarded their duty to the coal companies as paramount to their duty to the public service. To say that the closed precincts were not so created to suit the convenience and interests of these corporations, or that they were not so formed with the advice and consent of these corporations, is to discredit human intelligence, and to deny human experience. The plain purpose of the formation of the new precincts was that the coal companies might have opportunity to conduct and control the elections therein, just as such elections were conducted. The irresistible conclusion is that these close precincts were so formed by the county commissioners with the connivance of the representatives of the coal companies, if not by their express command.

"There can be no free, open and fair election as contemplated by the constitution, where private industrial corporations so throttle public opinion, deny the free exercise of choice by sovereign electors, dictate and control all election officers, prohibit public discussion of public questions, and imperially command what citizens may and what citizens may not, peacefully and for lawful purposes, enter upon election or public territory....

"We find no such example of fraud within the books, and must seek the letter and spirit of the law in a free government, as a scale in which to weigh such conduct....

"The denial of the right of peaceful assemblage, can have been for no other purpose than to influence the election. There was no disturbance in any of these precincts after they were created, up to the time of the election, and up to the time of this trial. The Federal troops were present at all times to preserve the peace and to protect life and property. There was no reason to anticipate any disturbance. Therefore this bold denial was an inexcusable and corrupt violation of the natural and inalienable rights of the citizens.

"The defence relies not upon conflicting evidence, but upon the contention that the conduct of the election was justified as an 'industrial necessity.'

"We have heard much in this state in recent years as to the denial of inherent and constitutional rights of citizens being justified by 'military necessity,' but this we believe is the first time in our experience when the violation of the fundamental rights of freemen has been attempted to be justified by the plea of 'industrial necessity.'

"Even if we were to concede that there may be some palliation in the plea of military necessity on the theory that such acts purport to be acts of the government itself, through its military arm and with the purpose of preserving the public peace and safety: yet that a private corporation, with its privately armed forces, may violate the most sacred right of the citizenship of the state and find lawful excuse in the plea of private 'industrial necessity' savours too much of anarchy to find approval by courts of justice.

"This case clearly comes within another exception to the rule, in that it is plain that the findings were influenced by the bias and prejudice of the trial judge.

"A careful reading of the record discloses the rejection by the court of so much palpably pertinent and competent testimony offered by the contestors, as to force the conclusion that the trial judge was influenced by bias and prejudice, to the extent at least, charged in the application for a change of venue, and sufficient in itself to justify a reversal of judgment....

"For the foregoing reasons the judgment of the court in each case before us, is reversed, and the entire poll in the said precincts of Niggerhead, Ravenwood, Walsen Mine, Oakview, Pryor, Rouse and Cameron is annulled, and held for naught, and the election in each of said precincts is hereby set aside. This leaves a substantial and unquestioned majority for each of the contestors in the county, and which entitles each contestor to be declared elected to the office for which he was a candidate.

"We find further, that J. B. Farr, the defendant in error, was not and is not the duly elected sheriff of Huerfano county, and that E. L. Neelley, the plaintiff in error, was and is the duly elected sheriff of said county. It is therefore ordered that the said county, and that the said E. L. Neelley, immediately and upon qualification as required by law, enter and discharge the duties of the said office of sheriff of Huerfano county...."

So much for the court opinion upon coal-camp politics. In relation thereto, the writer has only one comment to offer. Let the reader not drop the matter with the idea that because one set of corrupt officials have been turned out of office in one American county, therefore justice has been vindicated, and there is no longer need to be concerned about the conditions portrayed in "King Coal." The defeat of the "King of Huerfano County" is but one step in a long road which the miners of Colorado have to travel if ever they are to be free men. The industrial power of the great corporations remains untouched by this decision; and this power is greater than any political power ever wielded by the government of Huerfano County, or even of the state of Colorado. This industrial power is a deep, far-spreading root; and so long as it is allowed to thrive, it will send up again and again the poisonous plant of political "malconduct, fraud and corruption." The citizens and workers of such industrial communities, whether in Colorado, in West Virginia, Alabama, Michigan or Minnesota, in the Chicago stock-yards, the steel-mills of Pittsburg, the woollen-mills of Lawrence or the silk-mills of Paterson, will find that they have neither peace nor freedom, until they have abolished the system of production for profit, and established in the field of industry what they are supposed to have already in the field of politics—a government of the people, by the people, for the people.

NOTE: On the day that the author finished the reading of the proofs of "King Coal," the following item appeared in his daily newspaper:

COLORADO MINE WORKERS ASK LEAVE TO STRIKE
[BY A. P. NIGHT WIRE]

DENVER (Colo.), June 14.—Officers of the United Mine Workers representing members of that organisation employed by the Colorado Fuel and Iron Company, have telegraphed their national officers asking permission to strike.

At the morning session a resolution was adopted expressing disapprobation of the action of J. F. Welborn, president of the fuel company, for failure to attend the meeting, which was a part of the "peace programme" to prevent industrial differences in the State during the war.

The grievances of the men, according to John McLennan, spokesman for them, centre about the operation of the so-called "Rockefeller plan" at the mines. McLennan said the failure of Mr. Welborn to attend the meeting and discuss these grievances with the men precipitated the strike agitation.

THEY CALL ME CARPENTER

A Tale of the Second Coming

To
Charles F. Nevens
True and devoted friend

I

The beginning of this strange adventure was my going to see a motion picture which had been made in Germany. It was three years after the end of the war, and you'd have thought that the people of Western City would have got over their war-phobias. But apparently they hadn't; anyway, there was a mob to keep anyone from getting into the theatre, and all the other mobs started from that. Before I tell about it, I must introduce Dr. Karl Henner, the well-known literary critic from Berlin, who was travelling in this country, and stopped off in Western City at that time. Dr. Henner was the cause of my going to see the picture, and if you will have a moment's patience, you will see how the ideas which he put into my head served to start me on my extraordinary adventure.

You may not know much about these cultured foreigners. Their manners are like softest velvet, so that when you talk to them, you feel as a Persian cat must feel while being stroked. They have read everything in the world; they speak with quiet certainty; and they are so old—old with memories of racial griefs stored up in their souls. I, who know myself for a member of the best clubs in Western City, and of the best college fraternity in the country—I found myself suddenly indisposed to mention that I had helped to win the battle of the Argonne. This foreign visitor asked me how I felt about the war, and I told him that it was over, and I bore no hard feelings, but of course I was glad that Prussian militarism was finished. He answered: "A painful operation, and we all hope that the patient may survive it; also we hope that the surgeon has not contracted the disease." Just as quietly as that.

Of course I asked Dr. Henner what he thought about America. His answer was that we had succeeded in producing the material means of civilization by the ton, where other nations had produced them by the pound. "We intellectuals in Europe have always been poor, by your standards over here. We have to make a very little food support a great many ideas. But you have unlimited quantities of food, and—well, we seek for the ideas, and we judge by analogy they must exist—"

"But you don't find them?" I laughed.

"Well," said he, "I have come to seek them."

This talk occurred while we were strolling down our Broadway, in Western City, one bright afternoon in the late fall of 1921. We talked about the picture which Dr. Henner had recommended to me, and which we were now going to see.

It was called "The Cabinet of Dr. Caligari," and was a "futurist" production, a strange, weird freak of the cinema art, supposed to be the nightmare of a madman. "Being an American," said Dr. Henner, "you will find yourself asking, 'What good does such a picture do?' You will have the idea that every work of art must serve some moral purpose." After a pause, he added: "This picture could not possibly have been produced in America. For one thing, nearly all the characters are thin." He said it with the flicker of a smile—"One does not find American screen actors in that condition. Do your people care enough about the life of art to take a risk of starving for it?"

Now, as a matter of fact, we had at that time several millions of people out of work in America, and many of them starving. There must be some intellectuals among them, I suggested; and the critic replied: "They must have starved for so long that they have got used to it, and can enjoy it—or at any rate can enjoy turning it into art. Is not that the final test of great art, that it has been smelted in the fires of suffering? All the great spiritual movements of humanity began in that way; take primitive Christianity, for example. But you Americans have taken Christ, the carpenter—"

I laughed. It happened that at this moment we were passing St. Bartholomew's Church, a great brown-stone structure standing at the corner of the park. I waved my hand towards it. "In there," I said, "over the altar, you may see Christ, the carpenter, dressed up in exquisite robes of white and amethyst, set up as a stained glass window ornament. But if you'll stop and think, you'll realize it wasn't we Americans who began that!"

"No," said the other, returning my laugh, "but I think it was you who finished him up as a symbol of elegance, a divinity of the respectable inane."

Thus chatting, we turned the corner, and came in sight of our goal, the Excelsior Theatre. And there was the mob!

II

At first, when I saw the mass of people, I thought it was the usual picture crowd. I said, with a smile, "Can it be that the American people are not so dead to art after all?" But then I observed that the crowd seemed to be swaying this way and that; also there seemed to be a great many men in army uniforms. "Hello!" I exclaimed. "A row?"

There was a clamor of shouting; the army men seemed to be pulling and pushing the civilians. When we got nearer, I asked of a bystander, "What's up?" The answer was: "They don't want 'em to go in to see the picture."

"Why not?"

"It's German. Hun propaganda!"

Now you must understand, I had helped to win a war, and no man gets over such an experience at once. I had a flash of suspicion, and glanced at my companion, the cultured literary critic from Berlin. Could it possibly be that this smooth-spoken gentleman was playing a trick upon me—trying, possibly, to get something into my crude American mind without my realizing what was happening? But I remembered his detailed account of the production, the very essence of "art for art's sake." I decided that the war was three years over, and I was competent to do my own thinking.

Dr. Henner spoke first. "I think," he said, "it might be wiser if I did not try to go in there."

"Absurd!" I cried. "I'm not going to be dictated to by a bunch of imbeciles!"

"No," said the other, "you are an American, and don't have to be. But I am a German, and I must learn."

I noted the flash of bitterness, but did not resent it. "That's all nonsense, Dr. Henner!" I argued. "You are my guest, and I won't—"

"Listen, my friend," said the other. "You can doubtless get by without trouble; but I would surely rouse their anger, and I have no mind to be beaten for nothing. I have seen the picture several times, and can talk about it with you just as well."

"You make me ashamed of myself," I cried—"and of my country!"

"No, no! It is what you should expect. It is what I had in mind when I spoke of the surgeon contracting the disease. We German intellectuals know what war means; we are used to things like this." Suddenly he put out his hand. "Good-bye."

"I will go with you!" I exclaimed. But he protested—that would embarrass him greatly. I would please to stay, and see the picture; he would be interested later on to hear my opinion of it. And abruptly he turned, and walked off, leaving me hesitating and angry.

At last I started towards the entrance of the theatre. One of the men in uniform barred my way. "No admittance here!"

"But why not?"

"It's a German show, and we aint a-goin' to allow it."

"Now see here, buddy," I countered, none too good-naturedly, "I haven't got my uniform on, but I've as good a right to it as you; I was all through the Argonne."

"Well, what do you want to see Hun propaganda for?"

"Maybe I want to see what it's like."

"Well, you can't go in; we're here to shut up this show!"

I had stepped to one side as I spoke, and he caught me by the arm. I thought there had been talk enough, and gave a sudden lurch, and tore my arm free. "Hold on here!" he shouted, and tried to stop me again; but I sprang through the crowd towards the box-office. There were more than a hundred civilians in or about the lobby, and not more than twenty or thirty ex-service men maintaining the blockade; so a few got by, and I was one of the lucky ones. I bought my ticket, and entered the theatre. To the man at the door I said: "Who started this?"

"I don't know, sir. It's just landed on us, and we haven't had time to find out."

"Is the picture German propaganda?"

"Nothing like that at all, sir. They say they won't let us show German pictures, because they're so much cheaper; they'll put American-made pictures out of business, and it's unfair competition."

"Oh!" I exclaimed, and light began to dawn. I recalled Dr. Henner's remark about producing a great many ideas out of a very little food; assuredly, the American picture industry had cause to fear competition of that sort! I thought of old "T-S," as the screen people call him for short—the king of the movie world, with his roll of fat hanging over his collar, and his two or three extra chins! I thought of Mary Magna, million dollar queen of the pictures, contriving diets and exercises for herself, and weighing with fear and trembling every day!

III

It was time for the picture to begin, so I smoothed my coat, and went to a seat, and was one of perhaps two dozen spectators before whom "The Cabinet of Dr. Caligari" received its first public showing in Western City. The story had to do with a series of murders; we saw them traced by a young man, and fastened bit by bit upon an old magician and doctor. As the drama neared its climax, we discovered this doctor to be the head of an asylum for the insane, and the young man to be one of the inmates; so in the end the series of adventures was revealed to us as the imaginings of a madman about his physician and keepers. The settings and scenery were in the style of "futurist" art—weird and highly effective. I saw it all in the light of Dr. Henner's interpretation, the product of an old, perhaps an over-ripe culture. Certainly no such picture could have been produced in America! If I had to choose between this and the luxurious sex-stuff of Mary Magna—well, I wondered. At least, I had been interested in every moment of "Dr. Caligari," and I was only interested in Mary off the screen. Several times every year I had to choose between mortally hurting her feelings, and watching her elaborate "vamping" through eight or ten costly reels.

I had read many stories and seen a great many plays, in which the hero wakes up in the end, and we realize that we have been watching a dream. I remembered "Midsummer Night's Dream," and also "Looking Backward." An old, old device of art; and yet always effective, one of the most effective! But this was the first time I had ever been taken into the dreams of a lunatic. Yes, it was interesting, there was no denying it; grisly stuff, but alive, and marvelously well acted. How Edgar Allen Poe would have revelled in it! So thinking, I walked towards the exit of the theatre, and a swinging door gave way—and upon my ear broke a clamor that might have come direct from the inside of Dr. Caligari's asylum. "Ya, ya. Boo, boo! German propaganda! Pay your money to the Huns! For shame on you! Leave your own people to starve, and send your cash to the enemy."

I stopped still, and whispered to myself, "My God!" During all the time—an hour or more—that I had been away on the wings of imagination, these poor boobs had been howling and whooping outside the theatre, keeping the crowds away, and incidentally working themselves into a fury! For a moment I thought I would go out and reason with them; they were mistaken in the idea that there was anything about the war, anything against America in the picture. But I realized that they were beyond reason. There was nothing to do but go my way and let them rave.

But quickly I saw that this was not going to be so easy as I had fancied. Right in front of the entrance stood the big fellow who had caught my arm; and as I came toward him I saw that he had me marked. He pointed a finger into my face, shouting in a fog-horn voice: "There's a traitor! Says he was in the service, and now he's backing the Huns!"

I tried to have nothing to do with him, but he got me by the arm, and others were around me. "Yein, yein, yein!" they shouted into my ear; and as I tried to make my way through, they began to hustle me. "I'll shove your face in, you damned Hun!"—a continual string of such abuse; and I had been in the service, and seen fighting!

I never tried harder to avoid trouble; I wanted to get away, but that big fellow stuck his feet between mine and tripped me, he lunged and shoved me into the gutter, and so, of course, I made to hit him. But they had me helpless; I had no more than clenched my fist and drawn back my arm, when I received a violent blow on the side of my jaw. I never knew what hit me, a fist or a weapon. I only felt the crash, and a sensation of reeling, and a series of blows and kicks like a storm about me.

I ask you to believe that I did not run away in the Argonne. I did my job, and got my wound, and my honorable record. But there I had a fighting chance, and here I had none; and maybe I was dazed, and it was the instinctive reaction of my tormented body—anyhow, I ran. I staggered along, with the blows and kicks to keep me moving. And then I saw half a dozen broad steps, and a big open doorway; I fled that way, and found myself in a dark, cool place, reeling like a drunken man, but no longer beaten, and apparently no longer pursued. I was falling, and there was something nearby, and I caught at it, and sank down upon a sort of wooden bench.

IV

I had run into St. Bartholomew's Church; and when I came to—I fear I cut a pitiful figure, but I have to tell the truth—I was crying. I don't think the pain of my head and face had anything to do with it, I think it was rage and humiliation; my sense of outrage, that I, who had helped to win a war, should have been made to run from a gang of cowardly rowdies. Anyhow, here I was, sunk down in a pew of the church, sobbing as if my heart was broken.

At last I raised my head, and holding on to the pew in front, looked about me. The church was apparently deserted. There were dark vistas; and directly in front of me a gleaming altar, and high over it a stained glass window, with the afternoon sun shining through. You know, of course, the sort of figures they have in those windows; a man in long robes, white, with purple and gold; with a brown beard, and a gentle, sad face, and a halo of light about the head. I was staring at the figure, and at the same time choking with rage and pain, but clenching my hands, and making up my mind to go out and follow those brutes, and get that big one alone and pound his face to a jelly. And here begins the strange part of my adventure; suddenly that shining figure stretched out its two arms to me, as if imploring me not to think those vengeful thoughts!

I knew, of course, what it meant; I had just seen a play about delirium, and had got a whack on the head, and now I was delirious myself. I thought I must be badly hurt; I bowed my reeling head in my arms, and began to sob like a kid, out loud, and without shame. But somehow I forgot about the big brute, and his face that I wanted to pound; instead, I was ashamed and bewildered, a queer hysterical state with a half dozen emotions mixed up. The Caligari story was in it, and the lunatic asylum; I've got a cracked skull, I thought, and my mind will never get right again! I sat, huddled and shuddering; until suddenly I felt a quiet hand on my shoulder, and heard a gentle voice saying: "Don't be afraid. It is I."

Now, I shall waste no time telling you how amazed I was. It was a long time before I could believe what was happening to me; I thought I was clean off my head. I lifted my eyes, and there, in the aisle of the most decorous church of St. Bartholomew, standing with his hand on my head, was the figure out of the stained glass window! I looked at him twice, and then I looked at the window. Where the figure had been was a great big hole with the sun shining through!

We know the power of suggestion, and especially when one taps the deeps of the unconscious, where our childhood memories are buried. I had been brought up in a religious family, and so it seemed quite natural to me that while that hand lay on my head, the throbbing and whirling should cease, and likewise the fear. I became perfectly quiet, and content to sit under the friendly spell. "Why were you crying?" asked the voice, at last.

I answered, hesitatingly, "I think it was humiliation."

"Is it something you have done?"

"No. Something that was done to me."

"But how can a man be humiliated by the act of another?"

I saw what he meant; and I was not humiliated any more.

The stranger spoke again. "A mob," he said, "is a blind thing, worse than madness. It is the beast in man running away with his master."

I thought to myself: how can he know what has happened to me? But then I reflected, perhaps he saw them drive me into the church! I found myself with a sudden, queer impulse to apologize for those soldier boys. "We had some terrible fighting," I cried. "And you know what wars do—to the minds of the people, I mean."

"Yes," said the stranger, "I know, only too well."

I had meant to explain this mob; but somehow, I decided that I could not. How could I make him understand moving picture shows, and German competition, and ex-service men out of jobs? There was a pause, and he asked, "Can you stand up?"

I tried and found that I could. I felt the side of my jaw, and it hurt, but somehow the pain seemed apart from myself. I could see clearly and steadily; there were only two things wrong that I could find—first, this stranger standing by my side, and second, that hole in the window, where I had seen him standing so many Sunday mornings!

"Are you going out now?" he asked. As I hesitated, he added, tactfully, "Perhaps you would let me go with you?"

Here was indeed a startling proposition! His costume, his long hair—there were many things about him not adapted to Broadway at five o'clock in the afternoon! But what could I say? It would be rude to call attention to his peculiarities. All I could manage was to stammer: "I thought you belonged in the church."

"Do I?" he replied, with a puzzled look. "I'm not sure. I have been wondering—am I really needed here? And am I not more needed in the world?"

"Well," said I, "there's one thing certain." I pointed up to the window. "That hole is conspicuous."

"Yes, that is true."

"And if it should rain, the altar would be ruined. The Reverend Dr. Lettuce-Spray would be dreadfully distressed. That altar cloth was left to the church in the will of Mrs. Elvina de Wiggs, and God knows how many thousands of dollars it cost."

"I suppose that wouldn't do," said the stranger. "Let us see if we can't find something to put there."

He started up the aisle, and through the chancel. I followed, and we came into the vestry-room, and there on the wall I noticed a full length, life-sized portrait of old Algernon de Wiggs, president of the Empire National Bank, and of the Western City Chamber of Commerce. "Let us see if he would fill the place," said the stranger; and to my amazement he drew up a chair, and took down the huge picture, and carried it, seemingly without effort, into the church.

He stepped upon the altar, and lifted the portrait in front of the window. How he got it to stay there I am not sure—I was too much taken aback by the procedure to notice such details. There the picture was; it seemed to fit the window exactly, and the effect was simply colossal. You'd have to know old de Wiggs to appreciate it—those round, puffy cheeks, with the afternoon sun behind them, making them shine like two enormous Jonathan apples! Our leading banker was clad in decorous black, as always on Sunday mornings, but in one place the sun penetrated his form—at one side of his chest. My curiosity got the better of me; I could not restrain the question, "What is that golden light?"

Said the stranger: "I think that is his heart."

"But that can't be!" I argued. "The light is on his right side; and it seems to have an oblong shape—exactly as if it were his wallet."

Said the other: "Where the treasure is, there will the heart be also."

VI

We passed out through the arched doorway, and Broadway was before us. I had another thrill of distress—a vision of myself walking down this crowded street with this extraordinary looking personage. The crowds would stare at us, the street urchins would swarm about us, until we blocked the traffic and the police ran us in! So I thought, as we descended the steps and started; but my fear passed, for we walked and no one followed us—hardly did anyone even turn his eyes after us.

I realized in a little while how this could be. The pleasant climate of Western City brings strange visitors to dwell here; we have Hindoo swamis in yellow silk, and a Theosophist college on a hill-top, and people who take up with "nature," and go about with sandals and bare legs, and a mane of hair over their shoulders. I pass them on the street now and then—one of them carries a shepherd's crook! I remember how, a few years ago, my Aunt Caroline, rambling around looking for something to satisfy her emotions, took up with these queer ideas, and there came to her front door, to the infinite bewilderment of the butler, a mild-eyed prophet in pastoral robes, and with a little newspaper bundle in his hand. This, spread out before my aunt, proved to contain three carrots and two onions, carefully washed, and shining; they were the kindly fruits of the earth, and of the prophet's own labor, and my old auntie was deeply touched, because it appeared that this visitor was a seer, the sole composer of a mighty tome which is to be found in the public library, and is known as the "Eternal Bible."

So here I was, strolling along quite as a matter of course with my strange acquaintance. I saw that he was looking about, and I prepared for questions, and wondered what they would be. I thought that he must naturally be struck by such wonders as automobiles and crowded street-cars. I failed to realize that he would be thinking about the souls of the people.

Said he, at last: "This is a large city?"

"About half a million."

"And what quarter are we in?"

"The shopping district."

"Is it a segregated district?"

"Segregated? In what way?"

"Apparently there are only courtesans."

I could not help laughing. "You are misled by the peculiarities of our feminine fashions—details with which you are naturally not familiar—"

"Oh, quite the contrary," said he, "I am only too familiar with them. In childhood I learned the words of the prophet: 'Because the daughters of Zion are haughty, and walk with stretched forth necks and wanton eyes, walking and mincing as they go, and making a tinkling with their feet; therefore the Lord will smite with a scab the crown of the head of the daughters of Zion, and the Lord will discover their secret parts. In that day the Lord will take away the bravery of their tinkling ornaments about their feet, and their cauls, and their round tires like the moon, the chains, and the bracelets, and the mufflers, the bonnets, and the ornaments of the legs, and the headbands, and the tablets, and the earrings, and nose jewels, the changeable suits of apparel, and the mantles, and the wimples, and the crisping pins, the glasses, and the fine linen, and the hoods, and the veils. And it shall come to pass that instead of sweet smell there shall be stink; and instead of a girdle a rent; and instead of well set hair, baldness; and instead of a stomacher a girding of sackcloth; and burning instead of beauty.'"

From the point of view of literature this might be great stuff; but on the corner of Broadway and Fifth Street at the crowded hours it was unusual, to say the least. My companion was entering into the spirit of it in a most alarming way; he was half chanting, his voice rising, his face lighting up. "'Thy men shall fall by the sword, and thy mighty in the war. And her gates shall lament and mourn; and she being desolate shall sit upon the ground.'"

"Be careful!" I whispered. "People will hear you!"

"But why should they not?" He turned on me a look of surprise. "The people hear me gladly." And he added: "The common people."

Here was an aspect of my adventure which had not occurred to me before. "My God!" I thought. "If he takes to preaching on street corners!" I realized in a flash—it was exactly what he would be up to! A panic seized me; I couldn't stand that; I'd have to cut and run!

I began to speak quickly. "We must get across this street while we have time; the traffic officer has turned the right way now." And I began explaining our remarkable system of traffic handling.

But he stopped me in the middle. "Why do we wish to cross the street, when we have no place to go?"

"I have a place I wish to take you to," I said; "a friend I want you to meet. Let us cross." And while I was guiding him between the automobiles, I was desperately trying to think how to back up my lie. Who was there that would receive this incredible stranger, and put him up for the night, and get him into proper clothes, and keep him off the soap-box?

Truly, I was in an extraordinary position! What had I done to get this stranger wished onto me? And how long was he going to stay with me? I found myself recalling the plight of Mary who had a little lamb!

Fate had me in its hands, and did not mean to consult me. We had gone less than a block further when I heard a voice, "Hello! Billy!" I turned. Oh, Lord! Oh,

Lord! Of all the thankless encounters—Edgerton Rosythe, moving picture critic of the Western City "Times." Precisely the most cynical, the most profane, the most boisterous person in a cynical and profane and boisterous business! And he had me here, in full daylight, with a figure just out of a stained glass window in St. Bartholomew's Church!

VII

"Hello, Billy! Who's your good-looking friend?" Rosythe was in full sail before a breeze of his own making.

How could I answer. "Why—er—"

The stranger spoke. "They call me Carpenter."

"Ah!" said the critic. "Mr. Carpenter, delighted to meet you." He gave the stranger a hearty grip of the hand. "Are you on location?"

"Location?" said the other; and Rosythe shot an arrow of laughter towards me. Perhaps he knew about the vagaries of my Aunt Caroline; anyhow, he would have a fantastic tale to tell about me, and was going to exploit it to the limit!

I made a pitiful attempt to protect my dignity. "Mr. Carpenter has just arrived," I began&&

"Just arrived, hey?" said the critic. "Oviparous, viviparous, or oviviparous?" He raised his hand; actually, in the glory of his wit, he was going to clap the stranger on the shoulder!

But his hand stayed in the air. Such a look as came on Carpenter's face! "Hush!" he commanded. "Be silent!" And then: "Any man will join in laughter; but who will join in disease?"

"Hey?" said Rosythe; and it was my turn to grin.

"Mr. Carpenter has just done me a great service," I explained. "I got badly mauled in the mob—"

"Oh!" cried the other. "At the Excelsior Theatre!" Here was something to talk about, to cover his bewilderment. "So you were in it! I was watching them just now."

"Are they still at it?"

"Sure thing!"

"A fine set of boobs," I began—

"Boobs, nothing!" broke in the other. "What do you suppose they're doing?"

"Saving us from Hun propaganda, so they told me."

"The hell of a lot they care about Hun propaganda! They are earning five dollars a head."

"What?"

"Sure as you're born!"

"You really know that?"

"Know it? Pete Dailey was at a meeting of the Motion Picture Directors' Association last night, and it was arranged to put up the money and hire them. They're a lot of studio bums, doing a real mob scene on a real location!"

"Well, I'll be damned!" I said. "And what about the police?"

"Police?" laughed the critic. "Would you expect the police to work free when the soldiers are paid? Why, Jesus Christ——"

"I beg pardon?" said Carpenter.

"Why—er—" said Rosythe; and stopped, completely bluffed.

"You ought not swear," I remarked, gravely; and then, "I must explain. I got pounded by that mob; I was knocked quite silly, and this gentleman found me, and healed me in a wonderful way."

"Oh!" said the critic, with genuine interest. "Mind cure, hey? What line?"

I was about to reply, but Carpenter, it appeared, was able to take care of himself. "The line of love," he answered, gently.

"See here, Rosythe," I broke in, "I can't stand on the street. I'm beginning to feel seedy again. I think I'll have a taxi."

"No," said the critic. "Come with me. I'm on the way to pick up the missus. Right around the corner—a fine place to rest." And without further ado he took me by the arm and led me along. He was a good-hearted chap inside; his rowdyisms were just the weapons of his profession. We went into an office building, and entered an elevator. I did not know the building, or the offices we came to. Rosythe pushed open a door, and I saw before me a spacious parlor, with birds of paradise of the female sex lounging in upholstered chairs. I was led to a vast plush sofa, and sank into it with a sigh of relief.

The stranger stood beside me, and put his hand on my head once more. It was truly a miracle, how the whirling and roaring ceased, and peace came back to me; it must have shown in my face, for the moving picture critic of the Western City "Times" stood watching me with a quizzical smile playing over his face. I could read his thoughts, as well as if he had uttered them: "Regular Svengali stuff, by God!"

VIII

I was so comfortable there, I did not care what happened. I closed my eyes for a while; then I opened them and gazed lazily about the place. I noted that all the birds of paradise were watching Carpenter. With one accord their heads had turned, and their eyes were riveted upon him. I found myself thinking. "This man will make a hit with the ladies!" Like the swamis, with their soft brown skins, and their large, dark, cow-like eyes!

There had been silence in the place. But suddenly we all heard a moan; I felt Carpenter start, and his hand left my head. A dozen doors gave into this big parlor—all of them closed. We perceived that the sound came through the door nearest to us. "What is it?" I asked, of Rosythe.

"God knows," said he; "you never can tell, in this place of torment."

I was about to ask, "What sort of place is it?" But the moan came again, louder, more long drawn out: "O-o-o-o-o-o-o-o-oh!" It ended in a sort of explosion, as if the maker of it had burst.

Carpenter turned, and took two steps towards the door; then he stopped, hesitating. My eyes followed him, and then turned to the critic, who was watching Carpenter, with a broad grin on his face. Evidently Rosythe was going to have some fun, and get his revenge!

The sound came again—louder, more harrowing. It came at regular intervals, and each time with the explosion at the end. I watched Carpenter, and he was like a high-spirited horse that hears the cracking of a whip over his head. The creature becomes more restless, he starts more quickly and jumps farther at each sound. But he is puzzled; he does not know what these lashes mean, or which way he ought to run.

Carpenter looked from one to another of us, searching our faces. He looked at the birds of paradise in the lounging chairs. Not one of them moved a muscle—save only those muscles which caused their eyes to follow him. It was no concern of theirs, this agony, whatever it was. Yet, plainly, it was the sound of a woman in torment: "O-o-o-o-o-o-o-o-oh!"

Carpenter wanted to open that door. His hand would start towards it; then he would turn away. Between the two impulses he was presently pacing the room; and since there was no one who appeared to have any interest in what he might say, he began muttering to himself. I would catch a phrase: "The fate of woman!" And again: "The price of life!" I would hear the terrible, explosive wail:

"O-o-o-o-o-o-o-o-oh!" And it would wring a cry out of the depths of Carpenter's soul: "Oh, have mercy!"

In the beginning, the moving picture critic of the Western City "Times" had made some effort to restrain his amusement. But as this performance went on, his face became one enormous, wide-spreading grin; and you can understand, that made him seem quite devilish. I saw that Carpenter was more and more goaded by it. He would look at Rosythe, and then he would turn away in aversion. But at last he made an effort to conquer his feelings, and went up to the critic, and said, gently: "My friend: for every man who lives on earth, some woman has paid the price of life."

"The price of life?" repeated the critic, puzzled.

Carpenter waved his hand towards the door. "We confront this everlasting mystery, this everlasting terror; and it is not becoming that you should mock."

The grin faded from the other's face. His brows wrinkled, and he said: "I don't get you, friend. What can a man do?"

"At least he can bow his heart; he can pay his tribute to womanhood."

"You're too much for me," responded Rosythe. "The imbeciles choose to go through with it; it's their own choice."

Said Carpenter: "You have never thought of it as the choice of God?"

"Holy smoke!" exclaimed the critic. "I sure never did!"

At that moment one of the doors was opened. Rosythe turned his eyes. "Ah, Madame Planchet!" he cried. "Come tell us about it!"

IX

A stoutish woman out of a Paris fashion-plate came trotting across the room, smiling in welcome: "Meester Rosythe!" She had black earrings flapping from each ear, and her face was white, with a streak of scarlet for lips. She took the critic by his two hands, and the critic, laughing, said: "Respondez, Madame! Does God bring the ladies to this place?"

"Ah, surely, Meester Rosythe! The god of beautee, he breengs them to us! And the leetle god with the golden arrow, the rosy cheeks and the leetle dimple—the dimple that we make heem for two hundred dollars a piece—eh, Meester Rosythe? He breengs the ladies to us!"

The critic turned. "Madame Planchet, permit me to introduce Mr. Carpenter. He is a man of wonder, he heals pain, and does it by means of love."

"Oh, how eenteresting! But what eef love heemself ees pain—who shall heal that, eh, Meester Carpentair?"

"O-o-o-o-o-o-o-o-h!" came the moan.

Said Rosythe: "Mr. Carpenter thinks you make the ladies suffer too much. It worries him."

"Ah, but the ladies do not mind! Pain? What ees eet? The lady who makes the groans, she cannot move, and so she ees unhappy. Also, she likes to have her own way, she ees a leetle—what you say?—spoilt. But her troubles weel pass; she weel be beautiful, and her husband weel love her more, and she weel be happy."

"O-o-o-o-o-o-o-o-oh!" from the other room; and Madame Planchet prattled away: "I say to them, Make plenty of noises! Eet helps! No one weel be afraid, for all here are worshippers of the god of beautee—all weel bear the pains that he requires. Eh, Meester Carpentair?"

Carpenter was staring at her. I had not before seen such intensity of concentration on his face. He was trying to understand this situation, so beyond all believing.

"I weel tell you something," said Madame Planchet, lowering her voice confidentially. "The lady what you hear—that ees Meeses T-S. You know Meester T-S, the magnate of the peectures?"

Carpenter did not say whether he knew or not.

"They come to me always, the peecture people; to me. The magician, the deputee of the god of beautee. Polly Pretty, she comes, and Dolly Dimple, she comes, and Lucy Love, she comes, and Betty Belle Bird. They come to me for the hair, and for the eyes, and for the complexion. You are a workair of miracles yourself—but can you do what I do? Can you make the skeen all new? Can you make the old young?"

"O-o-o-o-o-o-o-o-oh!"

"Mary Magna, she comes to me, and she breengs me her old grandmother, and she says, 'Madame,' she says, 'make her new from the waist up, for you can nevair tell how the fashions weel change, and what she weel need to show.' Ha, ha, ha, she ees wittee, ees the lovely Mary! And I take the old lady, and her wrinkles weel be gone, and her skeen weel be soft like a leetle baby's, and in her cheeks weel be two lovely dimples, and she weel dance with the young boys, and they weel not know her from her grandchild—ha, ha, ha!—ees eet not the wondair?"

I knew by now where I was. I had heard many times of Madame Planchet's beauty-parlors. I sat, wondering; should I take Carpenter by the arm, and lead him gently out? Or should I leave him to fight his own fight with modern civilization?

"O-o-o-o-o-o-o-o-oh!"

Madame turned suddenly upon me. "I know you, Meester Billee," she said. "I have seen you with Mees Magna! Ah, naughtee boy! You have the soft, fine hair—you should let it grow—eight inches we have to have, and then you can come to me for the permanent wave. So many young men come to me for the permanent wave! You know eet? Meester Carpentair, you see, he has let hees hair grow, and he has the permanent wave—eet could not be bettair eef I had done eet myself. I say always, 'My work ees bettair than nature, I tell nature by the eemper-fections.' Eh, voila?"

I am not sure whether it was for the benefit of me or of Carpenter. The deputee of the god of beautee was moved to volunteer a great revelation. "Would you like to see how we make eet—the permanent wave? I weel show you Messes T-S. But you must not speak—she would not like eet if I showed her to gentlemen. But her back ees turned and she cannot move. We do not let them see the apparatus, be-cause eet ees rather frightful, eet would make them seek. You will be very steel, eh?"

"Mum's the word, Madame," said Rosythe, speaking for the three of us.

"O-o-o-o-o-o-o-o-oh!" moaned the voice.

"First, I weel tell you," said Madame. "For the complete wave we wind the hair in tight leetle coils on many rods. Eet ees very delicate operations—every hair must be just so, not one crooked, not one must we skeep. Eet takes a long time—two hours for the long hair; and eet hurts, because we must pull eet so tight. We wrap each coil een damp cloths, and we put them een the contacts, and we turn on the eelectreeceetee—and then eet ees many hours that the hair ees baked, ees cooked een the proper curves, eh? Now, very steel, eef you please!"

And softly she opened the door.

X

Before us loomed what I can only describe as a mountain of red female flesh. This flesh-mountain had once apparently been slightly covered by embroidered silk lingerie, but this was now soaked in moisture and reduced to the texture of wet tissue paper. The top of the flesh-mountain ended in an amazing spectacle. It appeared as if the head had no hair whatever; but starting from the bare scalp was an extraordinary number of thin rods, six inches or so in length. These rods stood out in every direction, and being of gleaming metal, they gave to the head the aspect of some bright Phoebus Apollo, known as the "far-darter;" or shall I say some fierce Maenad with electric snakes having nickel-plated skins; or shall I say some terrific modern war-god, pouring poison gases from a forest of chemical tubes? Over the top of the flesh-mountain was a big metal object, a shining concave dome with which all the tubes connected; so that a stranger to the procedure could not have felt sure whether the mountain was holding up the dome, or was dangling from it. A piece of symbolism done by a maniac artist, whose meaning no one could fathom!

From the dome there was given heat; so from the pores of the flesh-mountain came perspiration. I could not say that I actually saw perspiration flowing from any particular pore; it is my understanding that pores are small, and do not squirt visible jets. What I could say is that I saw little trickles uniting to form brooks, and brooks to form rivers, which ran down the sides of the flesh-mountain, and mingled in an ocean on the floor.

Also I observed that flesh-mountains when exposed to heat do not stand up of their own consistency, but have a tendency to melt and flatten; it was necessary that this bulk should be supported, so there were three attendants, one securely braced under each armpit, and the third with a more precarious grip under the mountain's chin. Every thirty seconds or so the heaving, sliding mass would emit one of those explosive groans: "O-o-o-o-o-oh!" Then it would collapse, an avalanche would threaten to slide, and the living caryatids would shove and struggle.

Said Madame Planchet, in her stage-whisper: "The serveece of the young god of beautee!" And my fancy took flight. I saw proud vestals tending sacred flames on temple-clad islands in blue Grecian seas; I saw acolytes waving censers, and grave, bearded priests walking in processions crowned with myrtle-wreaths. I wondered if ever since the world began, the young god of beautee looking down from his crystal throne had beheld a stranger ritual of adoration!

Silently we drew back from the door-way, and Madame closed the door, reducing the promethean groans and the strong ammoniacal odors. I did not see the face of Carpenter, because he had turned it from us. Rosythe favored me with a smile, and whispered, "Your friend doesn't care for beautee!" Then he added, "What do you suppose he meant by that stuff about 'the price of life' and 'the choice of God?'"

"Didn't you really get it?" I asked.

"I'm damned if I did."

"My dear fellow," I said, "you didn't tell us what sort of place this was; and Carpenter thought it must be a maternity-ward."

The moving picture critic of the Western City "Times" gave me one wild look; then from his throat there came a sound like the sudden bleat of a young sheep in pain. It caused Carpenter to start, and Madame Planchet to start, and for the first time since we entered the place, the birds of paradise gave signs of life elsewhere than in the eye-muscles. The sheep gave a second bleat, and then a third, and Rosythe, red in the face and apparently choking, turned and fled to the corridor.

Madame Planchet drew me apart and said: "Meester Billee, tell me something. Ees eet true that thees gentleman ees a healer? He takes away the pains?"

"He did it for me," I answered.

"He ees vairy handsome, eh, Meester Billee?"

"Yes, that is true."

"I have an idea; eet ees a wondair." She turned to my friend. "Meester Carpentair, they tell me that you heal the pains. I think eet would be a vairy fine thing eef you would come to my parlor and attend the ladies while I give them the permanent wave, and while I skeen them, and make them the dimples and the sweet smiles. They suffer so, the poor dears, and eef you would seet and hold their hands, they would love eet, they would come every day for eet, and you would be famous, and you would be reech. You would meet—oh, such lovely ladies! The best people in the ceety come to my beauty parlors, and they would adore you, Meester Carpentair—what do you say to eet?"

It struck me as curious, as I looked back upon it; Madame Planchet so far had not heard the sound of Carpenter's voice. Now she forced him to speak, but she did not force him to look at her. His gaze went over her head, as if he were seeing a vision; he recited:

"Because the daughters of Zion are haughty, and walk with stretched forth necks and wanton eyes, walking and mincing as they go, and making a tinkling with their feet; therefore the Lord will smite with a scab the crown of the head of the daughters of Zion, and the Lord will discover their secret parts."

"Oh, mon Dieu!" cried Madame Planchet.

"In that day the Lord will take away the bravery of their twinkling ornaments about their feet, and their cauls, and their round tires like the moon, the chains, and the bracelets, and the mufflers, the bonnets, and the ornaments of the legs, and the headbands, and the tablets, and the earrings, the rings and nose jewels, the changeable suits of apparel, and the mantles, and the wimples, and the crisping pins, the glasses, and the fine linen, and the hoods, and the veils. And it shall come to pass that instead of sweet smell there shall be stink; and instead of a girdle a rent; and instead of well set hair, baldness; and instead of a stomacher a girding of sackcloth: and burning instead of beauty."

And at that moment the door from the corridor was flung open, and Mary Magna came in.

XI

"My God, will you look who's here! Billy, wretched creature, I haven't laid eyes on you for two months! Do you have to desert me entirely, just because you've fallen in love with a society girl with the face of a Japanese doll-baby? What's the matter with me, that I lose my lovers faster than I get them? Edgerton Rosythe, come in here—you've got a good excuse, I admit—I'm almost as much scared of your wife as you are yourself. But still, I'd like a chance to get tired of some man first. Hello, Planchet, how's my old grannie making out in your scalping-shop? Say, would you think it would take three days labor for half a dozen Sioux squaws to pull the skin off one old lady's back? And a week to tie up the corners of her mouth and give her a permanent smile! 'Why, grannie,' I said, 'good God, it would be cheaper to hire Charlie Chaplin to walk round in front of you all the rest of your life!' And—why, what's this? For the love of Peter, somebody introduce me to this gentleman. Is he a friend of yours, Billy? Carpenter? Excuse me, Mr. Carpenter, but we picture people learn to talk about our faces and our styles, and it isn't every day I come on a million dollars walking round on two legs. Who does the gentleman work for?"

The storm of Mary Magna stopped long enough for her to stare from one to another of us. "What? You mean nobody's got him? And you all standing round here, not signing any contracts? You, Edgerton—you haven't run to the telephone to call up Eternal City? Well, as it happens, T-S is going to be here in five minutes—his wife is being made beautiful once again somewhere in this scalping-shop. Take my advice, Mr. Carpenter, and don't sign today—the price will go up several hundred per week as long as you hold off."

Mary stopped again; and this was most unusual, for as a general rule she never stopped until somebody or something stopped her. But she was fascinated by the spectacle of Carpenter. "My good God! Where did he come from? Why, it seems like—I'm trying to think—yes, it's the very man! Listen, Billy; you may not believe it, but I was in a church a couple of weeks ago. I went to see Roxanna Riddle marry that grand duke fellow. It was in a big church over by the park—St. Bartholomew's, they call it. I sat looking at a stained glass window over the altar, and Billy, I swear I believe this Mr. Carpenter came down from that window!"

"Maybe he did, Mary," I put in.

"But I'm not joking! I tell you he's the living, speaking image of that figure. Come to think of it, he isn't speaking, he hasn't said a word! Tell me, Mr. Carpenter, have you got a voice, or are you only a close up from 'The Servant in the House' or 'Ben Hur'? Say something, so I can get a line on you!"

Again I stood wondering; how would Carpenter take this? Would he bow his head and run before a hail-storm of feminine impertinence? Would she "vamp" him, as she did every man who came near her? Or would this man do what no man alive had yet been able to do—reduce her to silence?

He smiled gently; and I saw that she had vamped him this much, at least—he was going to be polite! "Mary," he said, "I think you are carrying everything but the nose jewels."

"Nose jewels? What a horrid idea! Where did you get that?"

"When you came in, I was quoting the prophet Isaiah. Some eighty generations of ladies have lived on earth since his day, Mary; they have won the ballot, but apparently they haven't discovered anything new in the way of ornaments. Some of the prophet's words may be strange to you, but if you study them you will see that you've got everything he lists: 'their tinkling ornaments about their feet, and their cauls, and their round tires like the moon, the chains, and the bracelets, and the mufflers, the bonnets, and the ornaments of the legs, and the headbands, and the tablets, and the earrings, the rings, and nose jewels, the changeable suits of apparel, and the mantles, and the wimples, and the crisping pins, the glasses, and the fine linen, and the hoods, and the veils.'"

As Carpenter recited this list, his eyes roamed from one part to another of the wondrous "get up" of Mary Magna. You can imagine her facing him—that bold and vivid figure which you have seen as "Cleopatra" and "Salome," as "Dubarry" and "Anne Boleyn," and I know not how many other of the famous courtesans and queens of history. In daily life her style and manner is every bit as staggering; she is a gorgeous brunette, and wears all the colors there are—when she goes down the street it is like a whole procession with flags. I'll wager that, apart from her jewels, which may or may not have been real, she was carrying not less than five thousand dollars worth of stuff that fall afternoon. A big black picture hat, with a flower garden and parts of an aviary on top—but what's the use of going over Isaiah's list?

"Everything but the nose jewels," said Carpenter, "and they may be in fashion next week."

"How about the glasses?" put in Rosythe, entering into the fun.

"Oh, shucks!" said I, protecting my friend. "Turn out the contents of your vanity-bag, Mary."

"And the crisping-pins?" laughed the critic.

"Hasn't Madame Planchet just shown us those?"

All this while Mary had not taken her eyes off Carpenter. "So you are really one of those religious fellows!" she exclaimed. "You'll know exactly what to do without any directing! How perfectly incredible!" And at that appropriate moment T-S pushed open the door and waddled in!

<h1 style="text-align:center">XII</h1>

You know the screen stars, of course; but maybe you do not know those larger celestial bodies, the dark and silent and invisible stars from which the shining ones derive their energies. So, permit me to introduce you to T-S, the trade abbreviation for a name which nobody can remember, which even his secretaries have to keep typed on a slip of paper just above their machine—Tszchniczklefritszch. He came a few years ago from Ruthenia, or Rumelia, or Roumania—one of those countries where the consonants are so greatly in excess of the vowels. If you are as rich as he, you call him Abey, which is easy; otherwise, you call him Mr. T-S, which he accepts as a part of his Americanization.

He is shorter than you or I, and has found that he can't grow upward, but can grow without limit in all lateral directions. There is always a little more of him than his clothing can hold, and it spreads out in rolls about his collar. He has a yellowish face, which turns red easily. He has small, shiny eyes, he speaks atrocious English, he is as devoid of culture as a hairy Ainu, and he smells money and goes after it like a hog into a swill-trough.

"Hello, everybody! Madame, vere's de old voman?

"She ees being dressed—"

"Vell, speed her up! I got no time. I got—Jesus Christ!"

"Yes, exactly," said Mary Magna.

The great man of the pictures stood rooted to the spot. "Vot's dis? Some joke you people playin' on me?" He shot a suspicious glance from one to another of us.

"No," said Mary, "he's real. Honest to God!"

"Oh! You bring him for an engagement. Vell, I don't do no business outside my office. Send him to see Lipsky in de mornin'."

"He hasn't asked for an engagement," said Mary.

"Oh, he ain't. Vell, vot's he hangin' about for? Been gittin' a permanent vave? Ha, ha, ha!"

"Cut it out, Abey," said Mary Magna. "This is a gentleman, and you must be decent. Mr. Carpenter, meet Mr. T-S."

"Carpenter, eh? Vell, Mr. Carpenter, if I vas to make a picture vit you I gotta spend a million dollars on it—you know you can't make no cheap skate picture fer a ting like dat, if you do you got a piece o' cheese. It'd gotta be a costume picture, and you got shoost as much show to market vun o' dem today as you got vit a pauper's funeral. I spend all dat money, and no show to git it back, and den you actors tink I'm makin' ten million a veek off you—"

"Cut it out, Abey!" broke in Mary. "Mr. Carpenter hasn't asked anything of you."

"Oh, he ain't, hey? So dat's his game. Vell, he'll find maybe I can vait as long as de next feller. Ven he gits ready to talk business, he knows vere Eternal City is, I guess. Vot's de matter, Madame, you got dat old voman o' mine melted to de chair?"

"I'll see, I'll see, Meester T-S," said Madame, hustling out of the room.

Mary came up to the great man. "See here, Abey," she said, in a low voice, "you're making the worst mistake of your life. Apparently this man hasn't been discovered. When he is, you know what'll happen."

"Vere doss he come from?"

"I don't know. Billy here brought him. I said he must have come out of a stained glass window in St. Bartholomew's Church."

"Oho, ho!" said T-S.

"Anyhow, he's new, and he's too good to keep. The paper's 'll get hold of him sure. Just look at him!"

"But, Mary, can he act?"

"Act? My God, he don't have to act! He only has to look at you, and you want to fall at his feet. Go be decent to him, and find out what he wants."

The great man surveyed the figure of the stranger appraisingly. Then he went up to him. "See here, Mr. Carpenter, maybe I could make you famous. Vould you like dat?"

"I have never thought of being famous," was the reply.

"Vell, you tink of it now. If I hire you, I make you de greatest actor in de vorld. I make it a propaganda picture fer de churches, dey vould show it to de headens in China and in Zululand. I make you a contract fer ten years, and I pay you five hunded dollars a veek, vedder you vork or not, and you vouldn't have to vork so much, because I don't catch myself makin' a million dollar feature picture vit gawd amighty and de angels in it for no regular veekly releases. Maybe you find some cheap skate feller vit some vild cat company vot promise you more; but he sells de picture and makes over de money to his vife's brudders, and den he goes bust, and vere you at den, hey? Mary Magna, here, she tell you, if you git a contract vit old Abey, it's shoost like you got libbidy bonds. I make dat lovely lady a check every veek fer tirty-five hunded dollars, an' I gotta sign it vit my own hand, and I tell you it gives me de cramps to sign so much money all de time, but I do it, and you see all dem rings and ribbons and veils and tings vot she buys vit de money, she looks like a jeweler's shop and a toy-store all rolled into vun goin' valkin' down de street."

"Mr. Carpenter was just scolding me for that," said Mary. "I've an idea if you pay him a salary, he'll feed it to the poor."

"If I pay it," said T-S, "it's his, and he can feed it to de dicky-birds if he vants to. Vot you say, Mr. Carpenter?"

I was waiting with curiosity to hear what he would say; but at that moment the door from the "maternity-room" was opened, and the voice of Madame Planchet broke in: "Here she ees!" And the flesh-mountain appeared, with the two caryatids supporting her.

XIII

"My Gawd!" gasped Mrs. T-S. "I'm dyin'!"

Her husband responded, beaming, "So you gone and done it again!"

Said Mrs. T-S: "I'll never do it no more!"

Said the husband: "Y'allus say dat. Fergit it, Maw, you're all right now, you don't have to have your hair frizzed fer six mont's!"

Said Mrs. T-S: "I gotta lie down. I'm dyin', Abey, I tell you. Lemme git on de sofa."

Said the husband: "Now, Maw, we gotta git to dinner—"

"I can't eat no dinner."

"Vot?" There was genuine alarm in the husband's voice. "You can't eat no dinner? Sure you gotta eat your dinner. You can't live if you don't eat. Come along now, Maw."

"O-o-o-o-o-o-o-o-oh!"

T-S went and stood before her, and a grin came over his face. "Sure, now, ain't it fine? Say, Mary, look at dem lovely curves. Billy, shoost look here! Vy, she looks like a kid again, don't she! Madame, you're a daisy—you sure deliver de goods."

Madame Planchet beamed, and the flesh-mountain was feebly cheered. "You like it, Abey?"

"Sure, I like it! Maw, it's grand! It's like I got a new girl! Come on now, git up, we go git our dinner, and den we gotta see dem night scenes took. Don't forgit, we're payin' two tousand men five dollars apiece tonight, and we gotta git our money out of 'em." Then, taking for granted that this settled it, he turned to the rest. "You come vit us, Mary?"

"I must wait for my grannie."

"Sure, you leave your car fer grannie, and you come vit us, and we git some dinner, and den we see dem mob scenes took. You come along, Mr. Carpenter, I gotta have some talk vit you. And you, Billy? And Rosythe—come, pile in."

"I have to wait for the missus," said the critic. "We have a date."

"Vell," said T-S, and he went up close. "You do me a favor, Rosythe; don't say nuttin' about dis fellow Carpenter tonight. I feed him and git him feelin' good, and den I make a contract vit him, and I give you a front page telegraph story, see?"

"All right," said the critic.

"Mum's de vord now," said the magnate; and he waddled out, and the two car-yatids lifted the flesh-mountain, and half carried it to the elevator, and Mary walked with Carpenter, and I brought up the rear.

The car of T-S was waiting at the door, and this car is something special. It is long, like a freight-car, made all of shining gun-metal, or some such material; the huge wheels are of solid metal, and the fenders are so big and solid, it looks like an armored military car. There is an extra wheel on each side, and two more locked on to the rear. There is a chauffeur in uniform, and a footman in uniform, just to open the doors and close them and salute you as you enter. Inside, it is all like the sofas in Madame's scalping shop; you fall into them, and soft furs enfold you, and you give a sigh of Contentment, "O-o-o-o-o-o-oh!"

"Prince's," said T-S to the chauffeur, and the palace on wheels began to glide along. It occurred to me to wonder that T-S was not embarrassed to take Carpenter to a fashionable eating-place. But I could read his thoughts; everybody would assume that he had been "on location" with one of his stars; and anyhow, what the hell? Wasn't he Abey Tszchniczklefritszch?

"Wor-r-r-r! Wor-r-r-r-r!" snarled the horn of the car; and I could understand the meaning of this also. It said: "I am the car of Abey Tszchniczklefritszch, king of the movies, future king of the world. Get the hell out o' my way!" So we sped through the crowded streets, and pedestrians scattered like autumn leaves before a storm. "My Gawd, but I'm hungry!" said T-S. "I ain't had nuttin' to eat since lunch-time. How goes it, Maw? Feelin' better? Vell, you be all right ven you git your grub."

So we came to Prince's, and drew up before the porte-cochere, and found our-selves confronting an adventure. There was a crowd before the place, a surging throng half-way down the block, with a whole line of policemen to hold them back. Over the heads of the crowd were transparencies, frame boxes with canvas on, and lights inside, and words painted on them. "Hello!" cried T-S. "Vot's dis?"

Suddenly I recalled what I had read in the morning's paper. The workers of the famous lobster palace had gone on strike, and trouble was feared. I told T-S, and he exclaimed: "Oh, hell! Ain't we got troubles enough vit strikers in de studios, vitout dey come spoilin' our dinner?"

The footman had jumped from his seat, and had the door open, and the great man began to alight. At that moment the mob set up a howl. "For shame! For shame! Unfair! Don't go in there! They starve their workers! They're taking the bread out of our mouths! Scabs! Scabs!"

I got out second, and saw a spectacle of haggard faces, shouting menaces and pleadings; I saw hands waved wildly, one or two fists clenched; I saw the police, shoving against the mass, poking with their sticks, none too gently. A poor devil in a waiter's costume stretched out his arms to me, yelling in a foreign dialect: "You take de food from my babies!" The next moment the club of a policeman came down on his head, crack. I heard Mary scream behind me, and I turned, just in the nick of time. Carpenter was leaping toward the policeman, crying, "Stop!"

XIII

There was no chance to parley in this emergency. I grabbed Carpenter in a foot-ball tackle. I got one arm pinned to his side, and Mary, good old scout, got the other as quickly. She is a bit of an athlete—has to keep in training for those hoochie-coochies and things she does, when she wins the love of emperors and sultans and such-like world-conquerors. Also, when we got hold of Carpenter, we discovered that he wasn't much but skin and bones anyhow. We fairly lifted him up and rushed him into the restaurant; and after the first moment he stopped resisting, and let us lead him between the aisles of diners, on the heels of the toddling T-S. There was a table reserved, in an alcove, and we brought him to it, and then waited to see what we had done.

XIV

Carpenter turned to me-and those sad but everchanging eyes were flashing. "You have taken a great liberty!"

"There wasn't any time to argue," I said. "If you knew what I know about the police of Western City and their manners, you wouldn't want to monkey with them."

Mary backed me up earnestly. "They'd have mashed your face, Mr. Carpenter."

"My face?" he repeated. "Is not a man more than his face?"

You should have heard the shout of T-S! "Vot? Ain't I shoost offered you five hunded dollars a veek fer dat face, and you vant to go git it smashed? And fer a lot o' lousy bums dat vont vork for honest vages, and vont let nobody else vork! Honest to Gawd, Mr. Carpenter, I tell you some stories about strikes vot we had on our own lot—you vouldn't spoil your face for such lousy sons-o'-guns—"

"Ssh, Abey, don't use such langwich, you should to be shamed of yourself!" It was Maw, guardian of the proprieties, who had been extracted from the car by the footman, and helped to the table.

"Vell, Mr. Carpenter, he dunno vot dem fellers is like—"

"Sit down, Abey!" commanded the old lady. "Ve ain't ordered no stump speeches fer our dinner."

We seated ourselves. And Carpenter turned his dark eyes on me. "I observe that you have many kinds of mobs in your city," he remarked. "And the police do interfere with some of them."

"My Gawd!" cried T-S. "You gonna have a lot o' bums jumpin' on people ven dey try to git to dinner?"

Said Carpenter: "Mr. Rosythe said that the police would not work unless they were paid. May I ask, who pays them to work here? Is it the proprietor of the restaurant?"

"Vell," cried T-S, "ain't he gotta take care of his place?"

"As a matter of fact," said I, laughing, "from what I read in the 'Times' this morning, I gather that an old friend of Mr. Carpenter's has been paying in this case."

Carpenter looked at me inquiringly.

"Mr. Algernon de Wiggs, president of the Chamber of Commerce, issued a statement denouncing the way the police were letting mobs of strikers interfere with business, and proposing that the Chamber take steps to stop it. You remember de Wiggs, and how we left him?"

"Yes, I remember," said Carpenter; and we exchanged a smile over that trick we had played.

I could see T-S prick forward his ears. "Vot? You know de Viggs?"

"Mr. Carpenter possesses an acquaintance with our best society which will astonish you when you realize it."

"Vy didn't you tell me dat?" demanded the other; and I could complete the sentence for him: "Somebody has offered him more money!"

Here the voice of Maw was heard: "Ain't we gonna git nuttin' to eat?"

So for a time the problem of capital and labor was put to one side. There were two waiters standing by, very nervous, because of the strike. T-S grabbed the card from one, and read off a list of food, which the waiter wrote down. Maw, who was learning the rudiments of etiquette, handed her card to Mary, who gave her order, and then Maw gave hers, and I gave mine, and there was only Carpenter left.

He was sitting, his dark eyes roaming here and there about the dining-room. Prince's, as you may know, is a gorgeous establishment: too much so for my taste—it has almost as much gilded moulding as if T-S had designed it for a picture palace. In front of Carpenter's eyes sat a dame with a bare white back, and a rope of big pearls about it, and a tiara of diamonds on top; and beyond her were more dames, and yet more, and men in dinner-coats, putting food into red faces. You and I get used to such things, but I could understand that to a stranger it must be shocking to see so many people feeding so expensively.

"Vot you vant to order, Mr. Carpenter?" demanded T-S; and I waited, full of curiosity. What would this man choose to eat in a "lobster palace"?

Carpenter took the card from his host and studied it. Apparently he had no difficulty in finding the most substantial part of the menu. "I'll have prime ribs of beef," said he; "and boiled mutton with caper sauce; and young spring turkey; and squab en casserole; and milk fed guinea fowl—" The waiter, of course, was obediently writing down each item. "And planked steak with mushrooms; and braised spare ribs—"

"My Gawd!" broke in the host.

"And roast teal duck; and lamb kidneys—"

"Fer the love o' Mike, Mr. Carpenter, you gonna eat all dat?"

"No; of course not."

"Den vot you gonna do vit it?"

"I'm going to take it to the hungry men outside."

Well, sir, you'd have thought the world had stopped turning round, so still it was. The two waiters nearly dropped their order-pads and their napkins; they did drop their jaws, and Mrs. T-S's permanent wave seemed about to go flat.

"Oh, hell!" cried T-S at last. "You can't do it!"

"I can't?"

"You can't order only vot you gonna eat."

"But then, I don't want anything. I'm not hungry."

"But you can't sit here like a dummy, man!" He turned to the waiter. "You bring him de same vot you bring me. Unnerstand? And git a move on, cause I'm starvin'. Fade out now!" And the waiter turned and fled.

XV

The proprietor of Eternal City wiped his perspiring forehead with his napkin, and started rather hurriedly to make conversation. I understood that he wanted to enjoy his dinner, and proposed to talk about something pleasant in the meantime. "I vonna tell you about dis picture ve're goin' to see took, Mr. Carpenter. I vant you should see de scale we do tings on, ven we got a big subjic. Y'unnerstand, dis is a feature picture ve're makin' now; a night picture, a big mob scene.".

"Mob scene?" said Carpenter. "You have so many mobs in this world of yours!"

"Vell, sure," said T-S. "You gotta take dis vorld de vay you find it. Y'can't change human nature, y'know. But dis vot you're gonna see tonight is only a play mob, y'unnerstand."

"That is what seems strangest of all to me," said the other, thoughtfully. "You like mobs so well that you make imitation ones!"

"Vell, de people, dey like to see crowds in a picture, and dey like to see action. If you gonna have a big picture, you gotta spend de money."

"Why not take this real mob that is outside the door?"

"Ha, ha, ha! Ve couldn't verk dat very good, Mr. Carpenter. Ve gotta have it in de right set; and ven you git a real mob, it don't alvays do vot you vant exactly! Besides, you can't take night pictures unless you got your lights and everyting. No, ve gotta make our mobs to order; we got two tousand fellers hired—"

"What Mr. Rosythe called 'studio bums'? You have that many?"

"Sure, we could git ten tousand if de set vould hold 'em. Dis picture is called 'De Tale o' Two Cities,' and it's de French revolution. It's about a feller vot takes anodder feller's place and gits his head cut off; and say, dere's a sob story in it vot's a vunder. Ven dey brought me de scenario, I says, 'Who's de author?' Dey says, 'It's a guy named Charles Dickens.' 'Dickens?' says I. 'Vell, I like his verk. Vot's his address?' And Lipsky, he says, says he, 'Dey tell me he stays in a place called Vestminster Abbey, in England.' 'Vell,' says I, 'send him a cablegram and find out vot he'll take fer an exclusive contract.' So we sent a cablegram to Charles Dickens, Vestminster Abbey, England, and we didn't git no answer, and come to find out, de boys in de studios vas havin' a laugh on old Abey, because dis guy Dickens is some old time feller, and de Abbey is vere dey got his bones. Vell, dey can have deir fun—how de hell's a feller like me gonna git time to know about writers? Vy, only twelve years ago, Maw here and me vas carryin' pants in a push-cart fer a livin', and we didn't know if a book vas top-side up or bottom—ain't it, Maw?"

Maw certified that it was—though I thought not quite so eagerly as her husband. There were five little T-S's growing up, and bringing pressure to let the dead past stay buried, in Vestminster Abbey or wherever it might be.

The waiter brought the dinner, and spread it before us. And T-S tucked his napkin under both ears, and grabbed his knife in one hand and his fork in the other, and took a long breath, and said: "Good-bye, folks. See you later!" And he went to work.

<h1 style="text-align:center">XVI</h1>

For five minutes or so there was no sound but that of one man's food going in and going down. Then suddenly the man stopped, with his knife and fork upright on the table in each hand, and cried: "Mr. Carpenter, you ain't eatin' nuttin'!"

The stranger, who had apparently been in a daydream, came suddenly back to Prince's. He looked at the quantities of food spread about him. "If you'd only let me take a little to those men outside!" He said it pleadingly.

But T-S tapped imperiously on the table, with both his knife and fork together. "Mr. Carpenter, eat your dinner! Eat it, now, I say!" It was as if he were dealing with one of the five little T-S's. And Carpenter, strange as it may seem, obeyed. He picked up a bit of bread, and began to nibble it, and T-S went to work again.

There was another five minutes of silence; and then the picture magnate stopped, with a look of horror on his face. "My Gawd! He's cryin'!" Sure enough, there were two large tears trickling, one down each cheek of the stranger, and dropping on the bread he was putting into his mouth!

"Look here, Mr. Carpenter," protested T-S. "Is it dem strikers?"

"I'm sorry; you see—"

"Now, honest, man, vy should you spoil your dinner fer a bunch o' damn lousy loafers—"

"Abey, vot a vay to talk at a dinner-party!" broke in Maw.

And then suddenly Mary Magna spoke. It was a strange thing, though I did not realize it until afterwards. Mary, the irrepressible, had hardly said one word since we left the beauty parlors! Mary, always the life of dinner parties, was sitting like a woman who had seen the ghost of a dead child; her eyes following Carpenter's, her mind evidently absorbed in probing his thoughts.

"Abey!" said she, with sudden passion, of a sort I'd never seen her display before. "Forget your grub for a moment, I have something to say. Here's a man with a heart full of love for other people—while you and I are just trying to see what we can get out of them! A man who really has a religion—and you're trying to turn him into a movie doll! Try to get it through your skull, Abey!"

The great man's eyes were wide open. "Holy smoke, Mary! Vot's got into you?" And suddenly he almost shrieked. "Lord! She's cryin' too!"

"No, I'm not," declared Mary, vialiantly. But there were two drops on her cheeks, so big that she was forced to wipe them away. "It's just a little shame, that's all. Here we sit, with three times as much food before us as we can eat; and all over this city are poor devils with nothing to eat, and no homes to go to—don't you know that's true, Abey? Don't you know it, Maw?"

"Looka here, kid," said the magnate; "you know vot'll happen to you if you git to broodin' over tings? You git your face full o' wrinkles—you already gone and spoilt your make-up."

"Shucks, Abey," broke in Maw, "vot you gotta do vit dat? Vy don't you mind your own business?"

"Mind my own business? My own business, you say? Vell, I like to know vot you call my business! Ven I got a contract to pay a girl tirty-five hunded dollars a veek fer her face, and she goes and gits it all wrinkles, I ask any jury, is it my business or ain't it? And if a feller vants to pull de tremulo stop fer a lot o' hoboes and Bullsheviki, and goes and spills his tears into his soup—"

It sounded fierce; but Mary apparently knew her Abey; also, she saw that Maw was starting to cry. "There's no use trying to bluff me, Abey. You know as well as I do there are hungry people in this city, and no fault of theirs. You know, too, you eat twice what you ought to, because I've heard the doctor tell you. I'm not blaming you a bit more than I do myself—me, with two automobiles, and a whole show-window on my back." And suddenly she turned to Carpenter. "What can we do?"

He answered: "Here, men gorge themselves; in Russia they are eating their dead."

T-S dropped his knife and fork, and Maw gave a gulp. "Oh, my Gawd!"

"There are ten million people doomed to starve. Their children eat grass, and their bellies swell up and their legs dwindle to broom-sticks; they stagger and fall into the ditches, and other children tear their flesh and devour it."

"O-o-o-o-o-o-o-oh!" wailed Maw; and the diners at Prince's began to stare.

"Now looka here!" cried T-S, wildly. "I say dis ain't no decent way to behave at a party. I say it ain't on de level to be a feller's guest, and den jump on him and spoil his dinner. See here, Mr. Carpenter, I tell you vot I do. You be good and eat your grub, so it don't git vasted, and I promise you, tomorrow I go and hunt up strike headquarters, and give dem a check fer a tousand dollars, and if de damn graftin' leaders don't hog it, dey all git someting to eat. And vot's more, I send a check fer five tousand to de Russian relief. Now ain't dat square? Vot you say?"

"What I say is, Mr. T-S, I cannot be the keeper of another man's conscience. But I'll try to eat, so as not to be rude."

And T-S grunted, and went back to his feeding; and the stranger made a pretense of eating, and we did the same.

XVII

It happens that I was brought up in a highly conscientious family. To my dear mother, and to her worthy sisters, there is nothing in the world more painful than what they call a "scene"—unless possibly it is what they call a "situation." And here we had certainly had a "scene," and still had a "situation." So I sat, racking my brains to think of something safe to talk about. I recalled that T-S had had pretty good success with his "Tale of Two Cities" as a topic of conversation, so I began:

"Mr. Carpenter, the spectacle you are going to see this evening is rather re-markable from the artistic point of view. One of the greatest scenic artists of Paris has designed the set, and the best judges consider it a real achievement, a land-mark in moving picture work."

"Tell me about it," said Carpenter; and I was grateful for his tone of interest.

"Well, I don't know how much you know about picture making—"

"You had better explain everything."

"Well, Mr. T-S has built a large set, representing a street scene in Paris over a century ago. He has hired a thousand men—"

"Two tousand!" broke in T-S.

"In the advertisements?" I suggested, with a smile.

"No, no," insisted the other. "Two tousand, really. In de advertisements, five tousand."

"Well," said I, "these men wear costumes which T-S has had made for them, and they pretend to be a mob. They have been practicing all day, and by now they know what to do. There is a man with a megaphone, shouting orders to them, and enormous lights playing upon them, so that men with cameras can take pictures of the scene. It is very vivid, and as a portrayal of history, is truly educational."

"And when it is done—what becomes of the men?"

Utterly hopeless, you see! We were right back on the forbidden ground! "How do you mean?" I evaded.

"I mean, how do they live?"

"Dey got deir five dollars, ain't dey?" It was T-S, of course.

"Yes, but that won' last very long, will it? What is the cost of this dinner we are eating?"

The magnate of the movies looked to the speaker, and then burst into a laugh. "Ho, ho, ho! Dat's a good vun!"

Said I, hastily: "Mr. T-S means that there are cheaper eating places to be found."

"Well," said Carpenter, "why don't we find one?"

"It's no use, Billy. He thinks it's up to me to feed all de bums on de lot. Is dat it, Mr. Carpenter?"

"I can't say, Mr. T-S; I don't know how many there are, and I don't know how rich you are."

"Vell, dey got five million out o' verks in this country now, and if I vanted to bust myself, I could feed 'em vun day, maybe two. But ven I got done, dey vouldn't be nobody to make pictures, and somebody vould have to feed old Abey—or maybe me and Maw could go back to carryin' pants in a push cart! If you tink I vouldn't like to see all de hungry fed, you got me wrong, Mr. Carpenter; but vot I learned is dis—if you stop fer all de misery you see in de vorld about you, you vouldn't git novhere."

"Well," said Carpenter, "what difference would that make?"

The proprietor of Eternal City really wanted to make out the processes of this abnormal mind. He wrinkled his brows, and thought very hard over it.

"See here, Mr. Carpenter," he began at last, "I tink you got hold o' de wrong feller. I'm a verkin' man, de same as any mechanic on my lot. I verked ever since I vas a liddle boy, and if I eat too much now, maybe it's because I didn't get enough ven I vas liddle. And maybe I got more money dan vot I got a right to, but I know dis—I ain't never had enough to do half vot I vant to! But dere's plenty fellers got ten times vot I got, and never done a stroke o' vork fer it. Dey're de vuns y'oughter git after!"

Said Carpenter: "I would, if I knew how."

"Dey's plenty of 'em right in dis room, I bet." And Mary added: "Ask Billy; he knows them all!"

"You flatter me, Mary," I laughed.

"Ain't dey some of 'em here?" demanded T-S.

"Yes, that's true. There are some not far away, who are developing a desire to meet Mr. Carpenter, unless I miss the signs."

"Vere are dey at?" demanded T-S.

"I won't tell you that," I laughed, "because you'd turn and stare into their faces."

"So he vould!" broke in Maw. "How often I gotta tell you, Abey? You got no more manners dan if you vas a jimpanzy."

"All right," said the magnate, grinning good naturedly. "I'll keep a-eatin' my dinner. Who is it?"

"It's Mrs. Parmelee Stebbins," said I. "She boasts a salon, and has to have what are called lions, and she's been watching Mr. Carpenter out of the corner of her eye ever since he came into the room—trying to figure out whether he's a lion, or only an actor. If his skin were a bit dark, she would be sure he was an Eastern potentate; as it, she's afraid he's of domestic origin, in which case he's vulgar. The company he keeps is against him; but still—Mrs. Stebbins has had my eye three times, hoping I would give her a signal, I haven't given it, so she's about to leave."

"Vell, she can go to hell!" said T-S, keeping his promise to devote himself to his dinner. "I offered Parmelee Stebbins a tird share in 'De Pride o' Passion' fer a hunded tousand dollars, and de damn fool turned me down, and de picture has made a million and a quarter a'ready."

"Well," said I, "he's probably paying for it by sitting up late to buy the city council on this new franchise grab of his; and so he hasn't kept his date to dine with his expensive family at Prince's. Here is Miss Lucinda Stebbins; she's engaged to Babcock, millionaire sport and man about town, but he's taking part in a flying race over the Rocky Mountains tonight, and so Lucinda feels bored, and she knows the vaudeville show is going to be tiresome, but still she doesn't want to meet any freaks. She has just said to her mother that she can't see why a person in her mother's position can't be content to meet proper people, but always has to be getting herself into the newspapers with some new sort of nut."

"My Gawd, Billy!" cried Maw. "You got a dictaphone on dem people?"

"No, but I know the type so well, I can tell by their looks. Lucinda is thinking about their big new palace on Grand Avenue, and she regards everyone outside her set as a burglar trying to break in. And then there's Bertie Stebbins, who's thinking about a new style of collar he saw advertised to-day, and how it would look on him, and what impression it would make on his newest girl."

It was Mary who spoke now: "I know that little toad. I've seen him dancing at the Palace with Dorothy Doodles, or whatever her name is."

"Well," said I, "Mrs. Stebbins runs the newer set—those who hunt sensations, and make a splurge in the papers. It costs like smoke, of course—" And suddenly I stopped. "Look out!" I whispered. "Here she comes!"

XVIII

I heard Maw catch her breath, and I heard Maw's husband give a grunt. Then I rose. "How are you, Billy?" gurgled a voice—one of those voices made especially for social occasions. "Wretched boy, why do you never come to see us?"

"I was coming to-morrow," I said—for who could prove otherwise? "Mrs. Stebbins, permit me to introduce Mrs. Tszchniczklefritszch."

"Charmed to meet you, I'm sure," said Mrs. Stebbins. "I've heard my husband speak of your husband so often. How well you are looking, Mrs.—"

She stopped; and Maw, knowing the terrors of her name, made haste to say something agreeable. "Yes, ma'am; dis country agrees vit me fine. Since I come here, I've rode and et, shoost rode and et."

"And Mr. T-S," said I.

"Howdydo, Mr. T-S?"

"Pretty good, ma'am," said T-S. He had been caught with his mouth full, and was making desperate efforts to swallow.

A singular thing is the power of class prestige! Here was Maw, a good woman, according to her lights, who had worked hard all her life, and had achieved a colossal and astounding success. She had everything in the world that money could buy; her hair was done by the best hair-dresser, her gown had been designed by the best costumer, her rings and bracelets selected by the best jeweller; and yet nothing was right, no power on earth could make it right, and Maw knew it, and writhed the consciousness of it. And here was Mrs. Parmelee Stebbins, who had never done a useful thing in all her days—except you count the picking out of a rich husband; yet Mrs. Stebbins was "right," and Maw knew it, and in the presence of the other woman she was in an utter panic, literally quivering in every nerve. And here was old T-S, who, left to himself, might have really meant what he said, that Mrs. Stebbins could go to hell; but because he was married, and loved his wife, he too trembled, and gulped down his food!

Mrs. Stebbins is one of those American matrons who do not allow marriage and motherhood to make vulgar physical impressions upon them. Her pale blue gown might have been worn by her daughter; her cool grey eyes looked out through a face without a wrinkle from a soul without a care. She was a patroness of art and intellect; but never did she forget her fundamental duty, the enhancing of the prestige of a family name. When she was introduced to a screen-actress, she was gracious, but did not forget the difference between an actress and a lady. When she was introduced to a strange man who did not wear trousers, she took it quite as an everyday matter, revealing no trace of vulgar human curiosity.

There came Bertie, full grown, but not yet out of the pimply stage, and still conscious of the clothes which he had taken such pains to get right. Bertie's sister remained in her seat, refusing naughtily to be compromised by her mother's vagaries; but Bertie had a purpose, and after I had introduced him round, I saw what he wanted—Mary Magna! Bertie had a vision of himself as a sort of sporting prince in this movie world. His social position would make conquests easy; it was a sort of Christmas-tree, all a-glitter with prizes.

I was standing near, and heard the beginning of their conversation. "Oh, Miss Magna, I'm so pleased to meet you. I've heard so much about you from Miss Dulles."

"Miss Dulles?"

"Yes; Dorothy Dulles."

"I'm sorry. I don't think I ever heard of her."

"What? Dorothy Dulles, the screen actress?"

"No, I can't place her."

"But—but she's a star!"

"Well, but you know, Mr. Stebbins—there are so many stars in the heavens, and not all of them visible to the eye."

I turned to Bertie's mamma. She had discovered that Carpenter looked even more thrilling on a close view; he was not a stage figure, but a really grave and impressive personality, exactly the thing to thrill the ladies of the Higher Arts Club at their monthly luncheon, and to reflect prestige upon his discoverer. So here she was, inviting the party to share her box at the theatre; and here was T-S explaining that it couldn't be done, he had got to see his French revolution pictures took, dey had five tousand men hired to make a mob. I noted that Mrs. Stebbins received the "advertising" figures on the production!

The upshot of it was that the great lady consented to forget her box at the theatre, and run out to the studios to see the mob scenes for the "The Tale of Two Cities." T-S hadn't quite finished his dinner, but he waved his hand and said it was nuttin', he vouldn't keep Mrs. Stebbins vaitin'. He beckoned the waiter, and signed his magic name on the check, with a five-dollar bill on top for a tip. Mrs. Stebbins collected her family and floated to the door, and our party followed.

I expected another scene with the mob; but I found that the street had been swept clear of everything but policemen and chauffeurs. I knew that this must have meant rough work on the part of the authorities, but I said nothing, and hoped that Carpenter would not think of it. The Stebbins car drew up by the porte-cochere; and suddenly I discovered why the wife of the street-car magnate was known as a "social leader." "Billy," she said, "you come in our car, and bring Mr. Carpenter; I have something to talk to you about." Just that easily, you see! She wanted something, so she asked for it!

I took Carpenter by the arm and put him in. Bertie drove, the chauffeur sitting in the seat beside him. "Beat you to it!" called Bertie, with his invincible arrogance, and waved his hand to the picture magnate as we rolled away.

974

XIX

As it happened, we made a poor start. Turning the corner into Broadway, we found ourselves caught in the jam of the theatre traffic, and our car was brought to a halt in front of the "Empire Varieties." If you have been on any Broadway between the Atlantic and Pacific oceans, you can imagine the sight; the flaring electric signs, the pictures of the head line artists, the people waiting to buy tickets, and the crowds on the sidewalk pushing past. There was one additional feature, a crowd of "rah-rah boys," with yellow and purple flags in their hands, and the glory of battle in their eyes. As our car halted, the cheer-leader gave a signal, and a hundred throats let out in unison:

> "Rickety zim, rickety zam,
> Brickety, stickety, slickety slam!
> Wallybaloo! Billybazoo!
> We are the boys for a hullabaloo—Western City!"

It sounded all the more deafening, because Bertie, in the front seat, had joined in.

"Hello!" said I. "We must have won the ball-game!"

"You *bet* we did!" said Bertie, in his voice of bursting self-importance.

"Ball-game?" asked Carpenter.

"Foot-ball," said I. "Western City played Union Tech today. Wonder what the score was."

The cheer leader seemed to take the words out of my mouth. Again the hundred voices roared:

> "What was the score?
> Seventeen to four!
> Who got it in the neck?
> Union Tech!
> Who took the kitty?
> Western City!"

Then more waving of flags, and yells for our prize captain and our agile quarter-back: "Rah, rah, rah, Jerry Wilson! Rah, rah, rah, Harriman! Western City, Western City, Western City! W-E-S-T-E-R-N-C-I-T-Y! Western City!"

You have heard college yells, no doubt, and can imagine the tempo of these cries, the cumulative rush of the spelled out letters, the booming roar at the end. The voice of Bertie beat back from the wind-shield with devastating effect upon our ears; and then our car rolled on, and the clamor died away, and I answered the questions of Carpenter. "They are college boys. They have won a game with another college, and are celebrating the victory."

"But," said the other, "how do they manage to shout all together that way?"

"Oh, they've practiced that, of course."

"You mean—they gather and practice making those noises?"

"Surely."

"They make them in cold blood?"

I laughed. "Well, the blood of youth is seldom entirely cold. They imagine the victory while they rehearse, no doubt."

When Carpenter spoke again, it was half to himself. "You make your children into mobs! You train them for it!"

"It really isn't that bad," I replied. "It's all in good temper—it's their play."

"Yes, yes! But what is play but practice for reality? And how shall love be learned in savage war-dances?"

They tell us that we have a new generation of young people since the war; a generation which thinks for itself, and has its own way. I was an advocate of this idea in the abstract, but I must admit that I was startled by the concrete case which I now encountered. Bertie suddenly looked round from his place in the driver's seat. "Say," he demanded, in a grating voice, "where was that guy raised?"

"Bertie *dear*!" cried his mother. "Don't be rude!"

"I'm not being rude," replied the other. "I just want to know where he got his nut ideas."

"Bertie *dear*!" cried the mother, again; and you knew that for eighteen or nineteen years she had been crying "Bertie *dear*!"—in a tone in which rebuke was tempered by fatuous maternal admiration. And all the time, Bertie had gone on doing what he pleased, knowing that in her secret heart his mother was smiling with admiration of his masterfulness, taking it as one more symptom of the greatness of the Stebbins line. I could see him in early childhood, stamping on the floor and commanding his governess to bring him a handkerchief—and throwing his shoe at her when she delayed!

Presently it was Lucinda's turn. Lucinda, you understand, was in revolt against the social indignity which her mother had inflicted upon her. When Carpenter had entered the car, she had looked at him once, with a deliberate stare, then lifted her chin, ignoring my effort to introduce him to her. Since then she had sat silent, cold, and proud. But now she spoke. "Mother, tell me, do we have to meet those horrid fat old Jews again?"

Mrs. Stebbins wisely decided that this was not a good time to explore the soul of a possible Eastern potentate. Instead, she elected to talk for a minute or two about a lawn fete she was planning to give next week for the benefit of the Polish relief. "Poland is the World's Bulwark against Bolshevism," she explained; and then added: "Bertie *dear*, aren't you driving recklessly?"

Bertie turned his head. "Didn't you hear me tell that old sheeny I was going to beat him to it?"

"But, Bertie *dear*, this street is crowded!"

"Well, let them look out for themselves!"

But a few seconds later it appeared as if the son and heir of the Stebbins family had decided to take his mother's advice. The car suddenly slowed up—so suddenly as to slide us out of our seats. There was a grinding of brakes, and a bump of something under the wheels; then a wild stream from the sidewalk, and a half-stifled cry from the chauffeur. Mrs. Stebbins gasped, "Oh, my God!" and put her hands over her face; and Lucinda exclaimed, in outraged irritation, "Mamma!" Carpenter looked at me, puzzled, and asked, "What is the matter?"

XX

The accident had happened in an ill-chosen neighborhood: one of those crowded slum quarters, swarming with Mexicans and Italians and other foreigners. Of course, that was the only neighborhood in which it could have happened, because it is only there that children run wild in the streets at night. There was one child under the front wheels, crushed almost in half, so that you could not bear to look at it, to say nothing of touching it; and there was another, struck by the fender and knocked into the gutter. There was an old hag of a woman standing by, with her hands lifted into the air, shrieking in such a voice of mingled terror and fury as I had never heard in my life before. It roused the whole quarter; there were people running out of twenty houses, I think, before one of us could get out of the car.

The first person out was Carpenter. He took one glance at the form under the car, and saw there was no hope there; then he ran to the child in the gutter and caught it into his arms. The poor people who rushed to the scene found him sitting on the curb, gazing into the pitiful, quivering little face, and whispering grief-stricken words. There was a street-lamp near, so he could see the face of the child, and the crowd could see him.

There came a woman, apparently the mother of the dead child. She saw the form under the car, and gave a horrified scream, and fell into a faint. There came a man, the father, no doubt, and other relatives; there was a clamoring, frantic throng, swarming about the car and about the victims. I went to Carpenter, and asked, "Is it dead?" He answered, "It will live, I think." Then, seeing that the crowd was likely to stifle the little one, he rose. "Where does this child live?" he asked, and some one pointed out the house, and he carried his burden into it. I followed him, and it was fortunate that I did so, because of the part I was able to play.

I saw him lay the child upon a couch, and put his hands upon its forehead, and close his eyes, apparently in prayer. Then, noting the clamor outside growing louder, I went to the door and looked out, and found the Stebbins family in a frightful predicament. The mob had dragged Bertie and the chauffeur outside the car, and were yelling menaces and imprecations into their faces; poor Bertie was shouting back, that it wasn't his fault, how could *he* help it? But they thought he might have helped coming into their quarter with his big rich car; why couldn't he stay in his own part of the city, and kill the children of the rich? A man hit him a blow in the face and knocked him over; his mother shrieked, and leaped out to help him, and half a dozen women flung themselves at her, and as many men at the chauffeur. There was a pile of bricks lying handy, and no doubt also knives in the pockets of these foreign men; I believe the little party would have been torn to pieces, had it not occurred to me to run into the house and summon Carpenter.

Why did I do it? I think because I had seen how the crowd gave way before him with the child in his arms. Anyhow, I knew that I could do nothing alone, and before I could find a policeman it might be many times too late. I told Carpenter what was happening, and he rose, and ran out to the street.

It was like magic, of course. To these poor foreigners, Catholics most of them, he did not suggest a moving picture actor on location; he suggested something serious and miraculous. He called to the crowd, stretching out his arms, and they gave way before him, and he walked into them, and when he got to the struggling group he held his arms over them, and that was all there was to it.

Except, of course, that he made them a speech. Seeing that he was saving Bertie Stebbins' life, it was no more than fair that he should have his own way, and that a member of the younger generation should listen in unprotesting silence to a discourse, the political and sociological implications of which must have been very offensive to him. And Bertie listened; I think he would not have made a sound, even if he could have, after the crack in the face he had got.

"My people," said Carpenter, "what good would it do you to kill these wretches? The blood-suckers who drain the life of the poor are not to be killed by blows. There are too many of them, and more of them grow in place of those who die. And what is worse, if you kill them, you destroy in yourselves that which makes you better than they, which gives you the right to life. You destroy those virtues of patience and charity, which are the jewels of the poor, and make them princes in the kingdom of love. Let us guard our crown of pity, and not acquire the vices of our oppressors. Let us grow in wisdom, and find ways to put an end to the world's enslavement, without the degradation of our own hearts. For so many ages we have been patient, let us wait but a little longer, and find the true way! Oh, my people, my beloved poor, not in violence, but in solidarity, in brotherhood, lies the way! Let us bid the rich go on, to the sure damnation which awaits them. Let us not soil our hands with their blood!"

He spread out his arms again, majestically. "Stand back! Make way for them!"

Not all the crowd understood the words, but enough of them did, and set the example. In dead silence they withdrew from the sides and front of the car. The body of the dead child had been dragged out of the way and laid on the sidewalk, covered by a coat; and so Carpenter said to the Stebbins family: "The road is clear before you. Step in." Half dazed, the four people obeyed, and again Carpenter raised his voice. "Drinkers of human blood, devourers of human bodies, go your way! Go forward to that doom which history prepares for parasites!"

The engine began to purr, and the car began to move. There was a low mutter from the crowd, a moan of fury and baffled desire; but not a hand was lifted, and the car shot away, and disappeared down the street, leaving Carpenter standing on the curb, making a Socialist speech to a mob of greasers and dagoes.

XXI

When he stopped speaking, it was because a woman pressed her way through the crowd, and caught one of his hands. "Master, my baby!" she sobbed. "The little one that was hurt!" So Carpenter said to the crowd, "The sick child needs me. I must go in." They started to press after him, and he added, "You must not come into the room. The child will need air." He went inside, and knelt once more by the couch, and put his hand on the little one's forehead. The mother, a frail, dark Mexican woman, crouched at the foot, not daring to touch either the man or the child, but staring from one to the other, pressing her hands together in an agony of dread.

The little one opened his eyes, and gazed up. Evidently he liked what he saw, for he kept on gazing, and a smile spread over his features, a wistful and tender and infinitely sad little smile, of a child who perhaps never had a good meal in his lifetime. "Nice man!" he whispered; and the woman, hearing his voice again, began sobbing wildly, and caught Carpenter's free hand and covered it with her tears. "It is all right," said he; "all right, all right! He will get well—do not be afraid." He smiled back at the child, saying: "It is better now; you will not have so much pain." To me he remarked, "What is there so lovely as a child?"

The people thronging the doorway spread word what was going on, and there were shouts of excitement, and presently the voice of a woman, clamoring for admission. The throng made way, and she brought a bundle in her arms, which being unfolded proved to contain a sick baby. I never knew what was the matter with it; I don't suppose the mother knew, nor did Carpenter seem to care. The woman knelt at his feet, praying to him; but he bade her stand up, and took the child from her, and looked into its face, and then closed his eyes in prayer. When he handed back the burden, a few minutes later, she gazed at it. Something had happened, or at least she thought it had happened, for she gave a cry of joy, and fell at Carpenter's feet again, and caught the hem of his garment with one hand and began to kiss it. The rumor spread outside, and there were more people clamoring. Before long, filtering into the room, came the lame, and the halt, and the blind.

I had been reading not long ago of the miracles of Lourdes, so I knew in a general way what to expect. I know that modern science vindicates these things, demonstrating that any powerful stimulus given to the unconscious can awaken new vital impulses, and heal not merely the hysterical and neurotic, but sometimes actual physical ailments. Of course, to these ignorant Mexicans and Italians, there was no possible excitement so great as that caused by Carpenter's appearance and behavior. I understood the thing clearly; and yet, somehow, I could not watch it without being startled—thrilled in a strange, uncomfortable way.

And later on I had company in these unaccustomed emotions; the crowd gave way, and who should come into the room but Mary Magna! She did not speak to either of us, but slipped to one side and stood in silence—while the crowd watched her furtively out of the corner of its eyes, thinking her some foreign princess, with her bold, dark beauty and her costly attire. I went over to her, whispering, "How did you get here?" She explained that, when we did not arrive at the studios, she had called up the Stebbins home and learned about the accident. "They warned me not to come here, because this man was a terrible Bolshevik; he made a blood-thirsty speech to the mob. What did he say?"

I started to tell; but I was interrupted by a piercing shriek. A sick and emaciated young girl with paralyzed limbs had been carried into the room. They had laid her on the couch, from which the child had been taken away, and Carpenter had put his hands upon her. At once the girl had risen up—and here she stood, her hands flung into the air, literally screaming her triumphant joy. Of course the crowd took it up—these primitive people are always glad of a chance to make a big noise, so the whole room was in a clamor, and Carpenter had hard work to extract himself from the throng which wished to touch his hands and his clothing, and to worship him on their knees.

He came over to us, and smiled. "Is not this better than acting, Mary?

"Yes, surely—if one can do it."

Said he: "Everyone could do it, if they knew."

"Is that really true?" she asked, with passionate earnestness.

"There is a god in every man, and in every woman."

"Why don't they know it, then?"

"There is a god, and also a beast. The beast is old, and familiar, and powerful; the god is new, and strange, and afraid. Because of his fear, the beast kills him."

"What is the beast?"

"His name is self; and he has many forms. In men he is greed; in women he is vanity, and goes attired in much raiment—the chains, and the bracelets, and the mufflers—"

"Oh, don't!" cried Mary, wildly.

"Very well, Mary; I won't." And he didn't. But, looking at Mary, it seemed that she was just as unhappy as if he had.

He turned to an old man who had hobbled into the room on crutches. "Poor old comrade! Poor old friend!" His voice seemed to break with pity. "They have worked you like an old mule, until your skin is cracked and your joints grown hard; but they have not been so kind to you as to an old mule—they have left you to suffer!"

To a pale young woman who staggered towards him, coughing, he cried: "What can I do for you? They are starving you to death! You need food—and I have no food to give!" He raised his arms, in sudden wrath. "Bring forth the masters of this city, who starve the poor, while they themselves riot in wantonness!"

But the members of the Chamber of Commerce and of the Bankers' Association of Western City were not within hearing, nor are their numbers as a rule to be found in the telephone book. Carpenter looked about the place, now lined pretty well with cripples and invalids. Only a couple of hours of spreading rumor had been needed to bring them forth, unholy and dreadful secrets, dragged from the dark corners and back alley-ways of these tenements. He gazed from one crooked and distorted face to another, and put his hand to his forehead with a gesture of despair. "No, no!" he said. "It is of no use!" He lifted his voice, calling once more to the masters of the city. "You make them faster than I can heal them! You make them by machinery—and he who would help them must break the machine!"

He turned to me; and I was startled, for it was as if he had been inside my mind. "I know, it will not be easy! But remember, I broke the empire of Rome!"

That was his last flare. "I can do no more," he whispered. "My power is gone from me; I must rest." And his voice gave way. "I beg you to go, unhappy poor of the world! I have done all that I can do for you tonight."

And silently, patiently, as creatures accustomed to the voice of doom, the sick and the crippled began to hobble and crawl from the room.

<h1 style="text-align:center">XXII</h1>

He sat on the edge of the couch, gazing into space, lost in tragic thought; and Mary and I sat watching him, not quite certain whether we ought to withdraw with the rest. But he did not seem aware of our presence, so we stayed.

In our world it is not considered permissible for people to remain in company without talking. If the talk lags, we have to cast hurriedly about in our minds for something to say—it is called "making conversation." But Carpenter evidently did not know about this custom, and neither of us instructed him. Once or twice I stole a glance at Mary, marvelling at her. All her life she had been a conversational volcano, in a state of perpetual eruption; but now, apparently she passed judgment on her own remarks, and found them not worth making.

In the doorway of the room appeared the little boy who had been knocked down by the car. He looked at Carpenter, and then came towards him. When Carpenter saw him, a smile of welcome came upon his face; he stretched out an arm, and the little fellow nestled in it. Other children appeared in the doorway, and soon he had a group about him, sitting on his knees and on the couch. They were little gutter-urchins, but he, seemingly, was interested in knowing their names and their relationships, what they learned in school, and what games they played. I think he had Bertie's foot-ball crowd in mind, for he said: "Some day they will teach you games of love and friendship, instead of rivalry and strife."

Presently the mother of the household appeared. She was distressed, because it did not seem possible that a great man should be interested in the prattle of children, when he had people like us, evidently rich people, to talk to. "You will bother the master," she said, in Spanish. He seemed to understand, and answered, "Let the children stay with me. They teach me that the world might be happy."

So the prattle went on, and the woman stood in the doorway, with other women behind her, all beaming with delight. They had known all their lives there was something especially remarkable about these children; and here was their pride confirmed! When the little ones laughed, and the stranger laughed with them, you should have seen the pleasure shining from a doorway full of dusky Mexican faces!

But after a while one of the children began to rub his eyes, and the mother exclaimed—it was so late! The children had stayed awake because of the excitement, but now they must go to bed. She bundled them out of the room, and presently came back, bearing a glass of milk and a plate with bread and an orange on it. The master might be hungry, she said, with a humble little bow. In her halting English she offered to bring something to us, but she did not suppose we would care for poor people's food. She took it for granted that "poor people's food" was what Carpenter would want; and apparently she was right, for he ate it with relish. Meantime he tried to get the woman to sit on the couch beside him; but she would not sit in his presence—or was it in the presence of Mary and me? I had a feeling, as she withdrew, that she might have been glad to chat with him, if a million-dollar movie queen and a spoiled young club man had not been there to claim prior rights.

XXIII

So presently we three were alone once more; and Mary, gazing intently with those big dark eyes that the public knows so well, opened up: "Tell me, Mr. Carpenter! Have you ever been in love?"

I was startled, but if Carpenter was, he gave no sign. "Mary," he said, "I have been in grief." Then thinking, perhaps, that he had been abrupt, he added: "You, Mary—you have been in love?"

She answered: "No." I'm not sure if I said anything out loud, but my thought was easy to read, and she turned upon me. "You don't know what love is. But a woman knows, even though she doesn't act it."

"Well, of course," I replied; "if you want to go into metaphysics—"

"Metaphysics be damned!" said Mary, and turned again to Carpenter.

Said he: "A good woman like you—"

"*Me*?" cried Mary. And she laughed, a wild laugh. "Don't hit me when you've got me down! I've sold myself for every job I ever got; I sold myself for every jewel you saw on me this afternoon. You notice I've got them off now!"

"I don't understand, Mary," he said, gently. "Why does a woman like you sell herself?"

"What else has she got? I was a rat in a tenement. I could have been a drudge, but I wasn't made for that. I sold myself for a job in a store, and then for ribbons to be pretty, and then for a place in the chorus, and then for a speaking part—so on all the way. Now I portray other women selling themselves. They get fancy prices, and so do I, and that makes me a 'star.' I hope you'll never see my pictures."

I sat watching this scene, marvelling more than ever. That tone in Mary Magna's voice was a new one to me; perhaps she had not used it since she played her last "speaking part!" I thought to myself, there was a crisis impending in the screen industry.

Said Carpenter: "What are you going to do about it, Mary?"

"What can I do? My contract has seven years to run."

"Couldn't you do something honest? I mean, couldn't you tell an honest story in your pictures?"

"Me? My God! Tell that to T-S, and watch his face! Why, they hunt all the world over for some new kind of clothes for me to take off; they search all history for some war I can cause, some empire I can wreck. Me play an honest woman? The public would call it a joke, and the screen people would call it indecent."

Carpenter got up, and began to pace the room. "Mary," said he, "I once lived under the Roman empire—"

"Yes, I know. I was Cleopatra, and again I was Nero's mistress while he watched the city burning."

"Rome was rough, and crude, and poor, Mary. Rome was nothing to this. This is Satan on my Father's throne, making new worlds for himself." He paced the room again, then turned and said: "I don't understand this world. I must know more about it, if I am to save it!" There was such grief, such selfless pity in his voice as he repeated this: "I must know more!"

"You know everything!" exclaimed Mary, suddenly. "You are all wisdom!"

But he went on, speaking as if to himself, pondering his problem: "To serve others, yet not to indulge them; for the cause of their enslavment is that they have accepted service without return. And how shall one preach patience to the poor, when the masters make such preaching a new means of enslavement?" He looked at me, as if he thought that I could answer his question. Then with sudden energy he exclaimed: "I must meet those who are in rebellion against enslavement! Tomorrow I want to meet the strikers—all the strikers in your city."

"You'll have your hands full," I said—for I was a coward, and wanted to keep him out of it.

"How shall I find them?" he persisted.

"I don't know; I suppose their headquarters are at the Labor Temple."

"I will go there. Meantime, I fear I shall have to be alone. I need to think about the things I have learned."

"Where are you going to stay?"

"I don't know."

Said Mary, hesitatingly: "My car is outside—"

He answered: "In ancient days I saw the young patricians drive through the streets in their chariots; no, I shall not ride with them again."

Said I: "I have an apartment at the club, with plenty of room—"

"No, no, friend. I have seen enough of the masters of this city. From now on, if you want to see me, you will find me among the poor."

"If I may meet you in the morning," I said—"to show you to the Labor Temple—" Yes, I would see him through!

"By all means," said he. "But you must come early, for I cannot delay."

"Where shall I come?"

"Come here. I am sure these people will give me shelter." He looked about him. "I suspect that some of them sleep in this room; but they have a little porch outside, and if they will let me stay there I shall be alone, which is what I want now." After a moment, he added, "What I wish to do is to pray. Have you ever tried prayer, Mary?"

She answered, simply, "I wouldn't know how."

"Come to me, and I will teach you," he said.

XXIV

I went early next morning, but not early enough. The Mexican woman told me that "the master" had waited, and finally had gone. He had asked the way to the Labor Temple, and left word that I would find him there. So I stepped back into my taxi, and told the driver to take the most direct route.

Meantime I kept watch for my friend, and I did not have to watch very long. There was a crowd ahead, the street was blocked, and a premonition came to me: "Good Lord, I'm too late—he's got into some new mess!" I leaned out of the window, and sure enough, there he was standing on the tail-end of a truck, haranguing a crowd which packed the street from one line of houses to the other. "And before he got half way to the Labor Temple!" I thought to myself.

I got out, and paid the driver of the taxi, and pushed into the crowd. Now and then I caught a few words of what Carpenter was telling them, and it seemed quite harmless—that they were all brothers, that they should love one another, and not do one another injustice. What could there have been that made him think it necessary to deliver this message before breakfast? I looked about, noting that it was the Hebrew quarter of the city, plastered with signs with queer, spattered-up letters. I thought: "Holy smoke! Is he going to convert the Jews?"

I pushed my way farther into the crowd, and saw a policeman, and went up to him. "Officer, what's this all about?" I spoke as one wearing the latest cut of clothes, and he answered accordingly. "Search me! They brought us out on a riot call, but when we got here, it seems to have turned into a revival meeting."

I got part of the story from this policeman, and part from a couple of bystanders. It appeared that some Jewish lady, getting her shopping done early, had complained of getting short weight, and the butcher had ordered her out of his shop, and she had stopped to express her opinion of profiteers, and he had thrown her out, and she had stood on the sidewalk and shrieked until all the ladies in this crowded quarter had joined her. Their fury against soaring prices and wages that never kept up with them, had burst all bounds, and they had set out to clean up the butcher-shop with the butcher. So there was Carpenter, on his way to the Labor Temple, with another mob to quell!

"You know how it is," said the policeman. "It really does cost these poor devils a lot to live, and they say prices are going down, but I can't see it anywhere but in the papers."

"Well," said I, "I guess you were glad enough to have somebody do this job."

He grinned. "You bet! I've tackled crowds of women before this, and you don't like to hit them, but they claw into your face if you don't. I guess the captain will let this bird spout for a bit, even if he does block the traffic."

We listened for a minute. "Bear in mind, my friends, I am come among you; and I shall not desert you. I give you my justice, I give you my freedom. Your cause is my cause, world without end. Amen."

"Now wouldn't that jar you?" remarked the "copper." "Holy Christ, if you'd hear some of the nuts we have to listen to on street-corners! What do you suppose that guy thinks he can do, dressed up in Abraham's nightshirt?"

Said Carpenter: "The days of the exploiter are numbered. The thrones of the mighty are tottering, and the earth shall belong to them that labor. He that toils not, neither shall he eat, and they that grow fat upon the blood of the people— they shall grow lean again."

"Now what do you think o' that?" demanded the guardian of authority. "If that ain't regular Bolsheviki talk, then I'm dopy. I'll bet the captain don't stand much more of that."

Fortunately the captain's endurance was not put to the test. The orator had reached the climax of his eloquence. "The kingdom of righteousness is at hand. The word will be spoken, the way will be made clear. Meantime, my people, I bid you go your way in peace. Let there be no more disturbance, to bring upon you the contempt of those who do not understand your troubles, nor share the heart-break of the poor. My people, take my peace with you!" He stretched out his arms in invocation, and there was a murmur of applause, and the crowd began slowly to disperse.

Which seemed to remind my friend the policeman that he had authority to ex-ercise. He began to poke his stick into the humped backs of poor Jewish tailors, and into the ample stomachs of fat Jewish housewives. "Come on now, get along with you, and let somebody else have a bit o' the street." I pushed my way for-ward, by virtue of my good clothes, and got through the press about Carpenter, and took him by the arm, saying, "Come on now, let's see if we can't get to the Labor Temple."

XXV

There was a crowd following us, of course; and I sought to keep Carpenter busy in conversation, to indicate that the crowd was not wanted. But before we had gone half a block I felt some one touch me on the arm, and heard a voice, saying, "I beg pardon, I'm a reporter for the 'Evening Blare'."

Now, of course, I had known this must come; I had realized that I would be getting myself in for it, if I went to join Carpenter that morning. I had planned to warn him, to explain to him what our newspapers are; but how could I have foreseen that he was going to get into a riot before breakfast, and bring out the police reserves and the police reporters?

"Excuse us," I said, coldly. "We have something urgent—"

"I just want to get something of this gentleman's speech—"

"We are on our way to the Labor Temple. If you will come there in a couple of hours, we will give you an interview."

"But I must have a story for our first edition, that goes to press before that."

I had Carpenter by the arm, and kept him firmly walking. I could not get rid of the reporter, but I was resolved to get my warning spoken, regardless of anything. Said I: "This is a matter extremely urgent for you to understand, Mr. Carpenter. This young man represents a newspaper, and anything you say to him will be read in the course of a few hours by perhaps a hundred thousand people. If it is found especially senational, the Continental Press may put it on its wires, and it will go to several hundred papers all over the country—"

"Twelve hundred and thirty-seven papers," corrected the young man.

"So you see, it is necessary that you should be careful what you say—far more so than if you were speaking to a handful of Mexican laborers or Jewish house-wives."

Said Carpenter: "I don't understand what you mean. When I speak, I speak the truth."

"Yes, of course," I replied—and meantime I was racking my poor wits figuring out how to present this strange acquaintance of mine most tactfully to the world. I knew the reporter would not tarry long; he would grab a few sentences, and rush away to telephone them in.

"I'll tell you what I'm free to tell," I began. "This gentleman is a healer, a man of very remarkable gifts. Mental healing, you understand."

"I get you," said the reporter. "Some religion?"

"Mr. Carpenter teaches a new religion."

"I see. A sort of prophet! And where does he come from?"

I tried to evade. "He has just arrived—"

But the blood-hound of the press was not going to be evaded. "Where do you come from, sir?" he demanded, of Carpenter.

To which Carpenter answered, promptly: "From God."

"From God? Er—oh, I see. From God! Most interesting! How long ago, may I ask?"

"Yesterday."

"Oh! That is indeed extraordinary! And this mob that you've just been addressing—did you use some kind of mind cure on them?"

I could see the story taking shape; the headlines flamed before my mind's eye—streamer heads, all the way across the sheet, after the fashion of our evening papers:

PROPHET FRESH FROM GOD QUELLS MOB

XXVI

I came to a sudden decision in this crisis. The sensible thing to do was to meet the issue boldly, and take the job of launching Carpenter under proper auspices. He really was a wonderful man, and deserved to be treated decently.

I addressed the reporter again. "Listen. This gentleman is a man of remarkable gifts, and does not take money for them; so, if you are going to tell about him at all, do it in a dignified way."

"Of course! I had no other idea—"

"Your city editor might have another idea," I remarked, drily. "Permit me to introduce myself." I gave him my name, and saw him start.

"You mean *the* Mr.—" Then, giving me a swift glance, he decided it was not necessary to complete the question.

Said I: "Here is my card," and handed it to him.

He glanced at it, and said, "I'll be very glad to explain matters to the desk, and see that the story is handled exactly as you wish."

"Thank you," I replied. "Now, yesterday I was caught in that mob at the picture theatre, and knocked nearly insensible. This gentleman found me, and healed me almost instantly. Naturally, I am grateful, and as I find that he is a teacher, who aids the poor, and will not take money from anyone, I want to thank him publicly, and help to make him known."

"Of course, of course!" said the reporter; and before my mind's eye flashed a new set of headlines:

WEALTHY CLUBMAN MIRACULOUSLY HEALED

Or perhaps it would be a double head:

CLUBMAN, SLUGGED BY MOB, HEALED BY PROPHET
WEALTHY SCION, VICTIM OF PICTURE RIOT, RESTORED BY MAN
FRESH FROM GOD

I thought that was sensation enough, and that the interview would end; but alas for my hopes! Said that blood-hound of the press: "Will you give public healings to the people, Mr. Carpenter?"

To which Carpenter answered: "I am not interested in giving healings."

"What? Why not?"

"Worldly and corrupt people ask me to do miracles, to prove my power to them. But the proof I bring to the world is a new vision and a new hope."

"Oh, I see! Your religion! May I ask about it?"

"You are the first; the world will follow you. Say to the people that I have come to understand the nature and causes of their mobs."

"Mobs?" said the puzzled young blood-hound.

"I wish to understand a land which is governed by mobs; I wish to know, who lives upon the madness of others."

"You have been studying a mob this morning?" inquired the reporter.

"I ask, why do the police of Mobland put down the mobs of the poor, and not the mobs of the rich? I ask, who pays the police, and who pays the mobs."

"I see! You are some kind of radical!" And with sickness of soul I saw another headline before my mind's eye:

WEALTHY CLUBMAN AIDS BOLSHEVIK PROPHET

I hastened to break in: "Mr. Carpenter is not a radical; he is a lover of man." But then I realized, that did not sound just right. How the devil was I to describe this man? How came it that all the phrases of brotherhood and love had come to be tainted with "radicalism"? I tried again: "He is a friend of peace."

"Oh, really!" observed the reporter. "A pacifist, hey?" And I thought: "Damn the hound!" I knew, of course, that he had the rest of the formula in his head: "Pro-German!" Out loud I said: "He teaches brotherhood."

But the hound was not interested in my generalities and evasions. "Where have you seen mobs of the rich, Mr. Carpenter?"

"I have seen them whirling through the streets in automobiles, killing the children of the poor."

"You have seen that?"

"I saw it last night."

Now, I had inspected our "Times" and our "Examiner" that morning, and noted that both, in their accounts of the accident, had given only the name of the chauffeur, and suppressed that of the owner. I understood what an amount of social and financial pressure that feat had taken; and here was Carpenter about to spoil it! I laid my hand on his arm, saying: "My friend, you were a guest in that car. You are not at liberty to talk about it."

I expected to be argued with; but Carpenter apparently conceded my point, for he fell silent. It was the young reporter who spoke. "You were in an auto accident, I judge? We had only one report of a death, and that was caused by Mrs. Stebbins' car. Were you in that?" Then, as neither Carpenter nor I replied, he laughed. "It doesn't matter, because I couldn't use the story. Mr. Stebbins is one of our 'sacred cows.' Good-day, and thank you."

He started away; and suddenly all my terror of newspaper publicity overwhelmed me. I simply could not face the public as guardian of a Bolshevik! I shouted: "Young man!" And the reporter turned, respectfully, to listen. "I tell you, Mr. Carpenter is *not* a radical! Get that clear!" And to the young man's skeptical half-smile I exclaimed: "He's a Christian!" At which the reporter laughed out loud.

XXVII

We got to the Labor Temple, and found the place in a buzz of excitement, over what had occurred in front of Prince's last night. I had suspected rough work on the part of the police, and here was the living evidence—men with bandages over cracked heads, men pulling open their shirts or pulling up their sleeves to show black and blue bruises. In the headquarters of the Restaurant Workers we found a crowd, jabbering in a dozen languages about their troubles; we learned that there were eight in jail, and several in the hospital, one not expected to live. All that had been going on, while we sat at table gluttonizing—and while tears were running down Carpenter's cheeks!

It seemed to me that every third man in the crowd had one of the morning's newspapers in his hand—the newspapers which told how a furious mob of armed ruffians had sought to break its way into Prince's, and had with difficulty been driven off by the gallant protectors of the law. A man would read some passage which struck him as especially false; he would tell what he had seen or done, and he would crumple the paper in his hand and cry. "The liars! The dirty liars!"—adding adjectives not suitable for print.

I realized more than ever that I had made a mistake in letting Carpenter get into this place. It was no resort for anybody who wanted to be patriotic, or happy about the world. All sorts of wonderful promises had been made to labor, to persuade it to win the war; and now labor came with the blank check, duly filled out according to its fancy—and was in process of being kicked downstairs. Wages were being "liquidated," as the phrase had it; and there was an endless succession of futile strikes, all pitiful failures. You must understand that Western City is the home of the "open shop;" the poor devils who went on strike were locked out of the factories, and slugged off the streets; their organizations were betrayed by spies, and their policies dedeviled by provocateurs. And all the mass of misery resulting seemed to have crowded into one building this bright November morning; pitiful figures, men and women and even a few children—for some had been turned out of their homes, and had no place to go; ragged, haggard, and underfed; weeping, some of them, with pain, or lifting their clenched hands in a passion of impotent fury. My friend T-S, the king of the movies, with all his resources, could not have made a more complete picture of human misery—nor one more fitted to work on the sensitive soul of a prophet, and persuade him that capitalist America was worse than imperial Rome.

The arrival of Carpenter attracted no particular attention. The troubles of these people were too recent for them to be aware of anything else. All they wanted was some one to tell their troubles to, and they quickly found that this stranger was available for the purpose. He asked many questions, and before long had a crowd about him—as if he were some sort of government commissioner, conducting an investigation. It was an all day job, apparently; I hung round, trying to keep myself inconspicuous.

Towards noon came a boy with newspapers, and I bought the early edition of the "Evening Blare." Yes, there it was—all the way across the front page; not even a big fire at the harbor and an earthquake in Japan had been able to displace it. As I had foreseen, the reporter had played up the most sensational aspects of the matter: Carpenter announced himself as a prophet only twenty-four hours out of God's presence, and proved it by healing the lame and the halt and the blind— and also by hypnotising everyone he spoke to, from a wealthy young clubman to a mob of Jewish housewives. Incidentally he denounced America as "Mobland," and called it a country governed by madmen.

I took the paper to him, thinking to teach him a little worldly prudence. Said I: "You remember, I tried to keep out that stuff about mobs—"

He took the sheet from my hands and looked at the headlines. I saw his nostrils dilate, and his eyes flash. "Mobs? This paper is a mob! It is the worst of your mobs!" And it fell to the floor, and he put his foot on the flaring print.

Said he: "You talk about mobs—listen to this." Then, to one of the group about him: "Tell how they mobbed you!" The man thus addressed, a little Russian tailor named Korwsky, narrated in his halting English that he was the secretary of the tailors' union, and they had a strike, and a few days ago their offices had been raided at night, the door "jimmed" open and the desk rifled of all the papers and records. Evidently it had been done by the bosses or their agents, for nothing had been taken but papers which would be of use against the strike. "Dey got our members' list," said Korwsky. "Dey send people to frighten 'em back to verk! Dey call loans, dey git girls fired from stores if dey got jobs—dey hound 'em every way!"

The speaker went on to declare that no such job could have been pulled off without the police knowing; yet they made no move to arrest the criminals. His voice trembled with indignation; and Carpenter turned to me.

"You have mobs that come at night, with dark lanterns and burglars' tools!"

I had noticed among the men talking to Carpenter one who bore a striking resemblance to him. He was tall and not too well nourished; but instead of the prophet's robes of white and amethyst, he wore the clothes of a working-man, a little too short in the sleeves; and where Carpenter had a soft and silky brown beard, this man had a skinny Adam's apple that worked up and down. He was something of an agitator, I judged, and he appeared to have a religious streak. "I am a Christian," I heard him say; "but one of the kind that speak out against injustice. And I can show you Bible texts for it," he insisted. "I can prove it by the word of God."

This man's name was James, and I learned that he was one of the striking carpenters. The prophet turned to him, and said: "Tell him your story." So the other took from his pocket a greasy note-book, and produced a newspaper clipping, quoting an injunction which Judge Wollcott had issued against his union. "Read that," said he; but I answered that I knew about it. I remember hearing my uncle laughing over the matter at the dinner-table, saying that "Bobbie" Wollcott had forbidden the strikers to do everything but sit on air and walk on water. And now I got another view of "Bobbie," this time from a prophet fresh from God. Said the prophet: "Your judges are mobs!"

XXVIII

Soon after the noon-hour, there pushed his way into the crowd a young man, whom I recognized as one of the secretaries of T-S. He was looking for me, and told me in a whisper that his employer was downstairs in his car, and wanted to see Mr. Carpenter and myself about something important. He did not want to come up, because it was too conspicuous. Would we come down and take a little drive? I answered that I should be willing, but I knew Carpenter would not—he had been in an automobile accident the night before, and had refused to ride again.

Then, said the secretary, was there some room where we could meet? I went to one of the officials, and asked for a vacant room where I could talk about a private matter with a friend. I managed to separate Carpenter from his crowd and took him to the room, and presently Everett, the secretary, came with T-S.

The great man shook hands cordially with both of us; then, looking round to make sure that no one heard us, he began: "Mr. Carpenter, I told you I vould give a tousand dollars to dese strikers."

The other's face, which had looked so grey and haggard, was suddenly illumined as if by his magical halo. "I had forgotten it! There are so many hungry in there; I have been watching them, wondering when they would be fed."

"All right," said T-S. "Here you are." And reaching into his pocket, he produced a wad of new shiny hundred dollar notes, folded together. "Count 'em."

Carpenter took the money in his hand. "So this is it!" he said. He looked at it, as if he were inspecting some strange creature from the wilds of Patagonia.

"It's de real stuff," said T-S, with a grin.

"The stuff for which men sell their souls, and women their virtue! For which you starve and beat and torture one another—"

"Ain't it pretty?" said the magnate, not a bit embarrassed.

The other began reading the writing on the notes—as you may remember having done in some far-off time of childhood. "Whose picture is this?" he asked.

"I dunno," said the magnate. "De Secretary of de Treasury, I reckon."

"But," said the other, "why not your picture, Mr. T-S?"

"Mine?"

"Of course."

"My picture on de money?"

"Why not? You are the one who makes it, and enables everyone else to make it."

It was one of those brand new ideas that come only to geniuses and children. I could see that T-S had never thought of it before; also, that he found it interesting to think of. Carpenter went on: "If your picture was on it, then every one would know what it meant. People would say: 'Render unto T-S the things that are T-S's.' When you were paying off your mobs, you would pay them with your own money, and whenever they spent it, the people would bow to Caesar—I mean to T-S."

He said it without the trace of a smile; and T-S had no idea there was a smile anywhere in the neighborhood. In a business-like tone he said: "I'll tink about it." Then he went on: "You give it to de strikers—"

But Carpenter interrupted: "It was you who were going to give it. I cannot give nor take money."

"You mean you von't take it to dem?"

"I couldn't possibly do it, Mr. T-S."

"But, man—"

"Your promise was that *you* would come and give it. Now do so."

"But, Mr. Carpenter, if I vas to do such a ting, it vould cost me a million dollars. I vould git into a row vit de Merchants' and Manufacturers' Association, dey vould boycott my business, dey vould give me a black eye all over de country. You dunno vot you're askin', Mr. Carpenter."

"I understand then—you are in business alliance with men who are starving these people into submission, and you are afraid to help them? Afraid to feed the poor!" The far-off, wondering look came again to his face. "The world is organized!" he said, to himself. "There is a mob of masters! What can I do to save the people?"

T-S was unchanged in his cheerful good-nature. "You give dem a tousand dollars and you help a lot. Nobody can do it all."

But Carpenter was not satisfied; he shook his head, sadly. "Please take this," he said, and pressed the roll of bills back into the hands of the astounded magnate!

XXIX

However, T-S had come there to get something that day, and I thought I knew what it was. He swallowed his consternation, and all the rest of his emotions. "Now, now, Mr. Carpenter! Ve ain't a-goin' to quarrel about a ting like dat. Dem fellers is hungry, and de money vill give dem vun good feed. Ve git somebody to bring it to dem, and we be friends shoost de same. Billy, maybe you could give it, hey?"

I drew back with a laugh. "You don't get me into your quarrels!"

"Vell," said T-S—and suddenly he had an inspiration. "I know. I git Mary Magna to give it! She's a voman!"

Carpenter turned with sudden wonder. "Then women are permitted to have hearts?"

"Shoost so, Mr. Carpenter! Ha, ha, ha! Ve business fellers—my Gawd, if you knew vot business is, you'd vunder we got hearts enough to keep our blood movin'."

"Business," said Carpenter, still pondering. "Then it's business—"

"Yes, business—" put in T-S. "Dat's it!" And he lowered his voice, and looked round once more. "It's time we vas talkin' business now! Mr. Carpenter, I be frank vit you, I put all my cards on de table. I seen de papers shoost now, vot vunderful tings you do—healin' de sick and quellin' de mobs and all dat—and I tink I gotta raise my offer, Mr. Carpenter. If you sign a contract I got here in my pocket, I pay you a tousand dollars a veek. Vot you say, my friend?"

Carpenter did not say anything, and so the magnate began to expatiate upon the artistic triumphs he would achieve. "I make such a picture fer you as de vorld never seen before. You can do shoost vot you vant in dat story—all de tings you like to do, and nuttin' you didn't like. I never said dat to no man before, but I know you now, Mr. Carpenter, and all I ask you is to heal de sick and quell de mobs, shoost like today. I pledge you my vord—I put it in de contract if you say so—I make nuttin' but Bible pictures."

"That is very kind of you, Mr. T-S, and I thank you for the compliment; but I fear you will have to get some one else to play my part."

Said T-S: "I vant you to tink, Mr. Carpenter, vot it vould mean if you had a tousand dollars every week. You could feed all de babies of de strikers. I vouldn't care vot you did—you could feed my own strikers, ven I git some at Eternal City. A tousand dollars a veek is an awful pile o' money to have!"

"I know that, my friend."

"And vot's more, I pay you five tousand cash on de signin' of de contract. You can go right in now vit dese strikers—maybe you could beat Prince's vit all dat money!" Then, as Carpenter still shook his head: "I give you vun more raise, my friend—but dat's de last, you gotta believe me. I pay you fifteen hunded a veek. I aint ever paid so much money to a green actor in my life before, and I don't tink anybody else in de business ever did."

But still Carpenter shook his head!

"Vould you mind tellin' me vy, Mr. Carpenter?"

"Not at all. You tell me that I may quell mobs for you. But there are mobs in your business that I could not quell."

"Vot mobs?"

"Among others, yourself."

"Me?"

"Yes—you are a mob; a mob of money! You storm the souls of men, and of women too. It will take a stronger force than I to quell you."

"I don't git you," said T-S, helplessly; but then, thinking it over a bit, he went on: "I guess I'm a vulgar feller, Mr. Carpenter, and maybe all my pictures ain't vot you call high-brow. But if I had a man like you to vork vit, I could make vot you call real educational pictures. You're vot dey call a prophet, you got a message fer de vorld; vell, vy don't you let me spread it fer you? If you use my machinery, you can talk to a billion people. Dat's no joke—if dey is dat many alive, I bring 'em to you; I bring de Japs and de Chinks and de niggers—de vooly-headed savages vot vould eat your missionaries if you sent 'em. I offer you de whole vorld, Mr. Carpenter; and you vould be de boss!"

Carpenter became suddenly grave. "My friend," said he, "a long time ago there was a prophet, and he was offered the world. The story is told us—'Again, the devil taketh him up into an exceeding high mountain, and sheweth him all the kingdoms of the world, and the glory of them; and saith unto him, All these things will I give thee, if thou wilt fall down and worship me.' You recall that story, Mr. T-S?"

"No," said T-S, "I ain't vun o' dese litry fellers." But he realized that the story was not complimentary to him, and he showed his chagrin. "I tell you vun ting, Mr. Carpenter, if you vas to know me better, you vouldn't call me a devil."

And suddenly the other put his hand on the great man's shoulder. "I believe that, my friend; I hate the sin but love the sinner—And so, suppose you come to lunch with me?"

"Lunch?" said T-S, taken aback.

"I went to dinner with you last night. Now you come to lunch with me."

"Vere at, Mr. Carpenter?"

Said Carpenter: "When I went with you, I did not ask where."

Carpenter signed to me and to Everett, the secretary, and the four of us went out of the room. I was as much mystified as the picture magnate, but I held my peace, and Carpenter led us to the elevator, and down to the street. "No," said he, to T-S, "there is no need to get into your car. The place is just around the corner." And he put his arm in that of the magnate, and led him down the street— somewhat to the embarrassment of his victim, for there was a crowd following us. People had read the afternoon papers by now, and it was no longer possible to walk along unheeded, with a prophet only twenty-four hours from God, who healed the sick and quelled mobs before breakfast. But T-S set his teeth and bore it—hoping this might be the way to land his contract.

XXX

We turned the corner, and soon I saw what was before us, and almost cried out with glee. It was really too good to be true! Carpenter, in the course of his talks with strikers, had learned where their soup-kitchen was located, the relief-headquarters where their families were being fed; and he now had the sublime audacity to take the picture magnate to lunch among them!

The place was an empty warehouse, fitted with long tables, and benches made of planks that were old and full of splinters. Here in rows of twenty or thirty were seated men and women and children, mixed together; before each one a bowl of not very thick soup, and a hunk of bread, and a tin cup full of hot brown liquid, politely taken for coffee. It was a meal which would have been spurned by any of the "studio bums" of T-S's mob-scenes; but now T-S was going to be a good sport, and sit on a splintery plank and eat it!

Nor was that all. As we pushed our way into the place, Carpenter turned to the magnate, and without a trace of embarrassment, said: "You understand, Mr. T-S, I have no money. But we must pay—"

"Oh, sure!" said T-S, quickly. "I'll pay!"

"Thank you," said the other; and he turned to an official of the union with whom he had got acquainted in the course of the morning. He introduced us all, not forgetting the secretary, and then said: "Mr. T-S is the moving picture producer, and wants to have lunch with you, if you will consent."

"Oh, sure!" said the official, cordially.

"He will pay for it," added Carpenter. "He has brought along a thousand dollars for that purpose."

T-S started as if some one had struck him; and the official started too. "WHAT?"

"He will pay a thousand dollars," declared Carpenter. "It is a fact, and you may tell the people, if you wish."

"My Gawd, no!" cried T-S wildly.

But the official did not heed him. He faced the crowd and stretched out his arms. "Boys! Boys! This is Mr. T-S, the picture producer, and he's come to lunch with us, and he's going to pay a thousand dollars for it!"

There was a moment of amazed silence, then a roar from the company. Men leaped to their feet and yelled. And there stood poor T-S-not enjoying the ovation!

"Give it to them," whispered Carpenter; and the magnate, thus held up, took out the roll of bills, and turned it over to the trembling official, who leaped onto a chair and waved the miracle before the crowd. "A thousand dollars! A thousand dollars!" He counted it over before their eyes and called, louder than ever, "A thousand dollars!"

Carpenter, followed by T-S and the secretary and myself, went down the line of tables, shaking hands with many on the way, and being patted on the back by others. Also T-S shook hands, and was patted. Seats were found for us, and food was brought—double portions of it, as if to make the plight of the poor magnate even more absurd! I watched him out of the corner of my eye; he enjoyed that costly meal just about as much as Carpenter had enjoyed the one at Prince's last night!

However, he was game, and spilled no tears into his soup; and Carpenter ate with honest appetite, having had no breakfast. The strikers about us ate as if they had missed both breakfast and supper; they laughed and chatted and made jokes with us—you would have thought they were celebrating the winning of the strike and the end of all their troubles. In the midst of the meal I noted two well-dressed young men by the door, asking questions; I chuckled to myself, seeing more head-lines—double ones, and extra size:

PROPHET OF GOD VAMPS MOVIE KING MAGNATE OF SCREEN PAYS THOUSAND FOR LUNCH

But I knew that T-S had never yet paid a thousand dollars without getting something for it, and I was not surprised when, after he had gulped down his meal, he turned to his host and, disregarding the company and the excitement, demanded, "Now, Mr. Carpenter, tell me, do I git de contract?"

Carpenter had had his jest, and was through with it. He answered, gravely: "You must understand me, Mr. T-S. You don't want a contract with me."

"I don't?"

"If I were to sign it, it would not be a week before you would be sorry, and would be asking me to release you."

"Vy is dat, Mr. Carpenter?"

"Because I am going to do things which will make me quite useless to you in a business way."

"Dat can't be true, Mr. Carpenter!"

"It is true, and you will realize it soon. I assure you, it won't be a day before you will be ashamed of having known me."

T-S was gazing at the speaker, not certain whether this was something very terrible, or only a polite evasion. "Mr. Carpenter," he answered, "if all de vorld vas to give you up, I vouldn't!"

Said Carpenter: "I tell you, before the cock crows again, you will deny three times that you know me." And then, without awaiting response from the amazed T-S, he turned to speak to the man on the other side of him.

The magnate of the pictures sat silent, evidently frightened. At last he turned to me and asked, "Vot you tink he meant by dat, Billy?"

I answered: "I think he meant that you are to play the part of Peter."

"Peter? Peter Pan?"

"No; St. Peter, who denied his master."

"Vell," said T-S, patiently, "you know, I ain't vun o' dese litry fellers."

"I'll tell it to you some time," I continued. "It's kind of funny. If he's right, you are going to be the first pope, and sit at the golden gate, holding the keys of heaven."

"My Gawd!" said T-S.

"And you've made a record in the movies." I added. "You've played Satan and St. Peter, both on the same day! That is 'doubling' with a vengeance!"

XXXI

When I got back to the Labor Temple, I learned that there was to be a mass-meeting of the strikers this Saturday evening. It had been planned some days ago, and now was to be turned into a protest against police violence and "government by injunction." There was a cheap afternoon paper which professed sympathy with the workers, and this published a manifesto, signed by a number of labor leaders, summoning their followers to make clear that they would no longer submit to "Cossack rule."

It appeared now that these leaders were considering inviting Carpenter to become one of the speakers at their meeting. Two of them came up to me. I had heard this stranger speak, and did I think he could hold an audience? I gave assurance; he was a man of dignity, and would do them credit. They were afraid the newspapers would represent him as a freak, but of course their meeting would hardly fare very well in the papers anyhow. One of them asked, cautiously, how much of an extremist was he? Labor leaders were having a hard time these days to hold down the "reds," and the employers were not giving them any help. Did I think Carpenter would support the "reds"? I answered that I didn't know the labor movement well enough to judge, but one thing they could be sure of, he was a man of peace, and would not preach any sort of violence.

The matter was settled a little later, when Mary Magna drove up to the Labor Temple in her big limousine. Mary, for the first time in the memory of anyone who knew her, was without her war-paint; dressed like a Quakeress—a most uncanny phenomenon! She had not a single jewel on; and before long I learned why—she had taken all she owned to a jeweler that morning, and sold them for something over six thousand dollars. She brought the money to the fund for the babies of the strikers; nor did she ask anyone else to hand it in for her. It was Mary's fashion to look the world in the eye and say what she was doing.

T-S was still hanging about, and at first he tried to check this insane extravagance, but then he thought it over and grinned, saying, "I git my tousand dollars back in advertising!" When I pointed out to him what would be the interpretation placed by newspaper gossip on Mary's intervention in the affairs of Carpenter, he grinned still more widely. "Ain't he got a right to be in love vit Mary? All de vorld's in love vit Mary!" And of course, there was a newspaper reporter standing by his side, so that this remark went out to the world as semi-official comment!

You understand that by this time the second edition of the papers was on the streets, and it was known that the new prophet was at the Labor Temple. Curiosity seekers came filtering in, among them half a dozen more reporters, and as many camera men. After that, poor Carpenter could get no peace at all. Would he please say if he was going to do any more healing? Would he turn a little more to the light—just one second, thank you. Would he mind making a group with Miss Magna and Mr. T-S and the "wealthy young scion"? Would he consent to step outside for some moving pictures, before the light got too dim? It was a new kind of mob—a ravening one, making all dignity and thought impossible. In the end I had to mount guard and fight the publicity-hounds away. Was it likely this man would go out and pose for cameras, when he had just refused fifteen hundred dollars a week from Mr. T-S to do that very thing? And then more excitement! Had he really refused such an offer? The king of the movies admitted that he had!

We live in an age of communication; we can send a bit of news half way round the world in a few seconds, we can make it known to a whole city in a few hours. And so it was with this "prophet fresh from God"; in spite of himself, he was seized by the scruff of the neck and flung up to the pinnacle of fame! He had all the marvels of a lifetime crowded into one day—enough to fill a whole newspaper with headlines!

And the end was not yet. Suddenly there was a commotion in the crowd, and a man pushed his way through—Korwsky, the secretary of the tailor's union, who, learning of Carpenter's miracles, had rushed all the way home, and got a friend with a delivery wagon, and brought his half-grown son post-haste. He bore him now in his arms, and poured out to Carpenter the pitiful tale of his paralyzed limbs. Such a gentle, good child he was; no one ever heard a complaint; but he had not been able to stand up for five years.

So, of course, Carpenter put his hands upon the child, and closed his eyes in prayer; and suddenly he put him down to the ground and cried: "Walk!" The lad stared at him, for one wild moment, while people caught their breath; then, with a little choking cry, he took a step. There came a shout from the spectators, and then—Bang!—a puff as if a gun had gone off, and a flash of light, and clouds of white smoke rolling to the ceiling.

Women screamed, and one or two threatened to faint; but it was nothing more dangerous than the cameraman of the Independent Press Service, who had hired a step-ladder, and got it set up in a corner of the room, ready for any climax! A fine piece of stage management, said his jealous rivals; others in the crowd were sure it was a put up job between Carpenter and Korwsky. But the labor leaders knew the little tailor, and they believed. After that there was no doubt about Carpenter's being a speaker at the mass-meeting!

XXXII

It came time when the rest of us were ready for dinner, but Carpenter said that he wanted to pray. Apparently, whenever he was tired, and had work to do he prayed. He told me that he would find his own way to Grant Hall, the place of the mass-meeting; but somehow, I didn't like the idea of his walking through the streets alone. I said I would call for him at seven-thirty and made him promise not to leave the Labor Temple until that hour.

I cast about in my mind for a body-guard, and bethought me of old Joe. His name is Joseph Camper, and he played centre-rush with my elder brother in the days before they opened up the game, and when beef was what counted. Old Joe has shoulders like the biggest hams in a butcher shop, and you can trust him like a Newfoundland dog. I knew that if I asked him not to let anybody hurt my friend, he wouldn't—and this regardless of the circumstance of my friend's not wearing pants. Old Joe knows nothing about religion or sociology—only wrestling and motor-cars, and the price of wholesale stationery.

So I phoned him to meet me, and we had dinner, and at seven-thirty sharp our taxi crew drew up at the Labor Temple. Half a minute later, who should come walking down the street but Everett, T-S's secretary! "I thought I'd take the liberty," he said, apologetically. "I thought Mr. Carpenter might say something worth while, and you'd be glad to have a transcript of his speech."

"Why, that's very kind of you," I answered, "I didn't know you were interested in him."

"Well, I didn't know it myself, but I seem to be; and besides, he told me to follow him."

I went upstairs, and found the stranger waiting in the room where I had left him. I put myself on one side of him, and the ex-centre-rush on the other, with Everett respectfully bringing up the rear, and so we walked to Grant Hall. Many people stared at us, and a few followed, but no one said anything—and thank God, there was nothing resembling a mob! I took my prophet to the stage entrance of the hall, and got him into the wings; and there was a pathetically earnest lady waiting to give him a tract on the horrors of vivisection, and an old gentleman with a white beard and palsied hands, inviting him to a spiritualistic seance. Funniest of all, there was Aunt Caroline's prophet, the author of the "Eternal Bible," with his white robes and his permanent wave, and his little tribute of carrots and onions wrapped in a newspaper. I decided that these were Carpenter's own kind of troubles, and I left him to attend to them, and strolled out to have a look at the audience.

The hall was packed, both the floor and the galleries; there must have been three thousand people. I noted a big squad of police, and wondered what was coming; for in these days you can never tell whether any public meeting is to be allowed to start, and still less if it is to be allowed to finish. However, the crowd was orderly, the only disturber being some kind of a Socialist trying to sell literature.

I saw Mary Magna come in, with Laura Lee, another picture actress, and Mrs. T-S. They found seats; and I looked for the magnate, and saw him talking to some one near the door. I strolled back to speak to him, and recognized the other man as Westerly, secretary of the Merchants' and Manufacturers' Association. I knew what he was there for—to size up this new disturber Of the city's peace, and perhaps to give the police their orders.

It was not my wish to overhear the conversation, but it worked out that way, partly because it is hard not to overhear T-S, and partly because I stopped in surprise at the first words: "Good Gawd, Mr. Vesterly, vy should I vant to give money to strikers? Dat's nuttin' but fool newspaper talk. I vent to see de man, because Mary Magna told me he vas a vunderful type, and I said I'd pay him a tousand dollars on de contract. You know vot de newspapers do vit such tings!"

"Then the man isn't a friend of yours?" said the other.

"My Gawd, do I make friends vit every feller vot I hire because he looks like a character part?"

At this point there came up Rankin, one of T-S's directors. "Hello!" said he. "I thought I'd come to hear your friend the prophet."

"Friend?" said T-S. "Who told you he's a friend o' mine?"

"Why, the papers said—"

"Vell, de papers 're nutty!"

And then came one of the strikers who had been in the soup-kitchen—a fresh young fellow, proud to know a great man. "How dy'do, Mr. T-S? I hear our friend, Mr. Carpenter, is going—"

"Cut out dis friend stuff!" cried T-S, irritably. "He may be yours—he ain't mine!"

I strolled up. "Hello, T-S!" I said.

"Oh, Billy! Hello!"

"So you've denied him three times!"

"Vot you mean?"

"Three times—and the cock hasn't crowed yet! That man's a prophet for sure, T-S!"

The magnate pretended not to understand, but the deep flush on his features gave him away.

"How dy'do, Mr. Westerly," I said. "What do you think of Mr. T-S in the role of the first pope?"

"You mean he's going to act?" inquired the other, puzzled.

"Come off!" exclaimed Rankin, who knew better, of course.

"He's going to be St. Peter," I insisted, "and hold the keys to the golden gate. He's planning a religious play, you know, for this fellow Carpenter. Maybe he might cast Mr. Westerly for a part—say Pontius Pilate."

"Ha, ha, ha!" said the secretary of our "M. and M." "Pretty good! Ha, ha, ha! Gimme a chance at these bunk-shooters—I'll shut 'em up, you bet!"

XXXIII

The chairman of the meeting was a man named Brown, the president of the city's labor council. He was certainly respectable enough, prosy and solemn. But he was deeply moved on this question of clubbing strikers' heads; and you could see that the crowd was only waiting for a chance to shout its indignation. The chairman introduced the president of the Restaurant Workers, a solid citizen whom you would have taken for a successful grocer. He told about what had happened last night at Prince's; and then he told about the causes of the strike, and the things that go on behind the scenes in big restaurants. I had been to Prince's many times in my life, but I had never been behind the scenes, nor had I ever before been to a labor-meeting. I must admit that I was startled. The things they put into the hashes! And the distressing habit of unorganized waiters, when robbed of their tips or otherwise ill-treated, to take it out by spitting into the soup!

A couple of other labor men spoke, and then came James, the carpenter with a religious streak. He had a harsh, rasping voice, and a way of poking a long bony finger at the people he was impressing. He was desperately in earnest, and it caused him to swallow a great deal, and each time his Adam's apple would jump up. "I'm going to read you a newspaper clipping," he began; and I thought it was Judge Wollcott's injunction again, but it was a story about one of our social leaders, Mrs. Alinson Pakenham, who has four famous Pekinese spaniels, worth six thousand dollars each, and weighing only eight ounces—or is it eighty ounces?— I'm not sure, for I never was trusted to lift one of the wretched little brutes. Anyhow, their names are Fe, Fi, Fo, and Fum, and they have each their own attendant, and the four have a private limousine in which to travel, and they dine off a service of gold plate. And here were hundreds of starving strikers, with their wives, also starving; and a couple of thousand other workers in factories and on ranches who were in process of having their wages "deflated." The orator quoted a speech of Algernon de Wiggs before the Chamber of Commerce, declaring that the restoration of prosperity, especially in agriculture, depended upon "deflation," and this alone; and suddenly James, the carpenter with a religious streak, launched forth:

"Go to now, you rich men, weep and howl for your miseries that are coming upon you! Your riches are corrupted, and your garments are moth-eaten! Your gold and silver is cankered; and the rust on it shall be a witness against you, and shall eat your flesh as if it were fire. You have heaped treasure together for the last days. Behold the hire of the laborers, who have reaped your fields; you have kept it back by fraud, and the cries of the reapers have entered into the ears of the Lord! You have lived in pleasure on the earth, and been wanton; you have nourished your hearts, as in a day of slaughter. You have condemned and killed the just—"

At this point in the tirade, my old friend the ex-centre-rush, who was standing in the wings with me, turned and whispered: "For God's sake, Billy, what kind of a Goddamn Bolshevik stunt is this, anyhow?"

I answered: "Hush, you dub! He's quoting from the Bible!"

XXXIV

President Brown of the Western City Labor Council arose to perform his next duty as chairman. Said he:

"The next speaker is a stranger to most of you, and he is also a stranger to me. I do not know what his doctrine is, and I assume no responsibility for it. But he is a man who has proven his friendship for labor, not by words, but by very unusual deeds. He is a man of remarkable personality, and we have asked him to make what suggestions he can as to our problems. I have pleasure in introducing Mr. Carpenter."

Whereupon the prophet fresh from God arose from his chair, and come slowly to the front of the platform. There was no applause, but a silence made part of curiosity and part of amazement. His figure, standing thus apart, was majestic; and I noted a curious thing—a shining as of light about his head. It was so clear and so beautiful that I whispered to Old Joe: "Do you see that halo?"

"Go on, Billy!" said the ex-centre-rush. "You're getting nutty!"

"But it's plain as day, man!"

I felt some one touch my arm, and saw the little lady of the anti-vivisection tracts peering past me. "Do you see his aura?" she whispered, excitedly.

"Is that what it is?"

"Yes. It's purple. That denotes spirituality."

I thought to myself, "Good Lord, am I getting to be that sort?"

Carpenter began to speak, quietly, in his grave, measured voice. "My brothers!" He waited for some time, as if that were enough; as if all the problems of life would be solved, if only men would understand those two words. "My brothers: I am, as your chairman says, a stranger to this world of yours. I do not understand your vast machines and your complex arts. But I know the souls of men and women; when I meet greed, and pride, and cruelty, the enslavements of the flesh, they cannot lie to me. And I have walked about the streets of your city, and I know myself in the presence of a people wandering in a wilderness. My children!—broken-hearted, desolate, and betrayed—poorest when you are rich, loneliest when you throng together, proudest when you are most ignorant—my people, I call you into the way of salvation!"

He stretched out his arms to them, and on his face and in his whole look was such anguish, that I think there was no man in that whole great throng so rooted in self-esteem that he was not shaken with sudden awe. The prophet raised his hands in invocation: "Let us pray!" He bowed his head, and many in the audience did the same. Others stared at him in bewilderment, having long ago forgotten how to pray. Here and there some one snickered.

"Oh, God, Our Father, we, Thy lost children, return to Thee, the Giver of Life. We bring our follies and our greeds, and cast them at Thy feet. We do not like the life we have lived. We wish to be those things which for long ages we have dreamed in vain. Wilt Thou show the way?"

His hands sank to his sides, and he raised his head. "Such is the prayer. What is the answer? It has been made known: Ask, and it shall be given you; seek, and ye shall find; knock, and it shall be opened unto you. For everyone that asketh receiveth; and he that seeketh findeth; and to him that knocketh it shall be opened.—These are ancient words, by many forgotten. What do they mean? They mean that we are children of our Father, and not slaves of earthly masters. Would a man make a slave of his own child? And shall man be more righteous than his Creator?

"My brothers: You are hungry, and in need, and your children cry for bread; do I bid you feed them upon words? Not so; but the life of men is made by the will of men, and that which exists in steel and stone existed first in thought. If your thought is mean and base, your world is a place of torment; if your thought is true and generous, your world is free.

"There was once a man who owned much land, and upon it he built great factories, and many thousand men toiled for him, and he grew fat upon the product of their labor, and his heart was high. And it came to pass that his workers rebelled; and he hired others, and they shot down the workers, so that the rest returned to their labor. And the master said: The world is mine, and none can oppose me. But one day there arose among the workers a man who laughed. And his laughter spread, until all the thousands were laughing; they said, We are laughing at the thought that we should work and you take the fruit of our labor. He ordered his troops to shoot them, but his troops were also laughing, and he could not withstand the laughter of so many men; he laughed also, and said, let us end this foolish thing.

"Is there a man among you who can say, I am worthy of freedom? That man shall save the world. And I say to you: Make ready your hearts for brotherhood; for the hour draws near, and it is a shameful thing when man is not worthy of his destiny. A man may serve with his body, and yet be free, but he that is a slave in his soul admires the symbols of mastery, and lusts after its fruits.

"What are the fruits of mastery? They are pride and pomp, they are luxury and wantoness and the shows of power. And who is there among you that can say to himself, these things have no roots in my heart? That man is great, and the deliverance of the world is the act of his will."

XXXV

The speaker paused, and turned; his gaze swept the platform, and those seated on it. Said he: "You are the representatives of organized labor. I do not know your organization, therefore I ask: For what are you united? Is it to follow in the footsteps of your masters, and bind others as they have bound you?"

He waited for an answer, and the chairman, upon whom his gaze was fixed, cried, "No!" Others also cried, "No!" and the audience took it up with fervor. Carpenter turned to them. "Then I say to you: Break down in your hearts and in the hearts of your fellows the worship of those base things which mastership has brought into the world. If a man pile up food while others starve, is not this evil? If a woman deck herself with clothing to her own discomfort, is not this folly? And if it be folly, how shall it be admired by you, to whom it brings starvation and despair?

"Before me sit young women of the working class. Say to yourselves: I tear from my fingers the jewels which are the blood and tears of my fellow-men; I wash the paint from my face, and from my head and my bosom I take the silly feathers and ribbons. I dare to be what I am. I dare to speak truth in a world of lies. I dare to deal honestly with men and women.

"Before me sit young men of the working-class. I say to you: Love honest women. Do not love harlots, nor imitations of harlots. Do not admire the idle women of the ruling class, nor those who ape them, and thereby glorify them. Do not admire languid limbs and pouting lips and the signs of haughtiness and vanity, your own enslavements.

"A tree is known by the fruit it gives; and the masters are known by the lives they give to their servants. They are known by misery and unemployment, by plague and famine, by wars, and the slaughter of the people. Let judgment be pronounced upon them!

"You have heard it said: Each for himself, and the devil take the hindmost. But I say to you: Each for all, and the hindmost is your charge. I say to you: If a man will not work, let him be the one that hungers; if he will not serve, let him be your criminal. For if one man be idle, another man has been robbed; and if any man make display of wealth, that man has the flesh of his brothers in his stomach. Verily, he that lives at ease while others starve has blood-guilt upon him; and he that despises his fellows has committed the sin for which there is no pardon. He that lives for his own glory is a wolf, and vengeance will hunt him down; but he that loves justice and mercy, and labors for these things, dwells in the bosom of my Father.

"Do not think that I am come to bring you ease and comfort; I am come to bring strife and discontent to this world. For the time of martyrdom draws near, and from your Father alone can you draw the strength to endure your trials. You are hungry, but you will be starved; you are prisoned in mills and mines, but you will be walled up in dungeons; you are beaten with whips, but you will be beaten with clubs, your flesh will be torn by bullets, your skin will be burned with fire and your lungs poisoned with deadly gases—such is the dominion of this world. But I say to you, resist in your hearts, and none can conquer you, for in the hearts of men lies the past and the future, and there is no power but love.

"You say: The world is evil, and men are base; why should I die for them? Oh, ye of little faith, how many have died for you, and would you cheat mankind? If there is to be goodness in the world, some one must begin; who will begin with me?

"My brothers: I am come to lead you into the way of justice. I bid you follow; not in passion and blind excitement, but as men firm in heart and bent upon service. For the way of self-love is easy, while the way of justice is hard. But some will follow, and their numbers will grow; for the lives of men have grown ill beyond enduring, and there must be a new birth of the spirit. Think upon my message; I shall speak to you again, and the compulsion of my law will rest upon you. The powers of this world come to an end, but the power of good will is everlasting, and the body can sooner escape from its own shadow than mankind can escape from brotherhood."

He ceased, and a strange thing happened. Half the crowd rose to its feet; and they cried, "Go, on!" Twice he tried to retire to his seat, but they cried, "Go on, go on!" Said he, "My brothers, this is not my meeting, there are other speakers—" But they cried, "We want to hear you!" He answered, "You have your policies to decide, and your leaders must have their say. But I will speak to you again to-morrow. I am told that your city permits street speaking on Western City Street on Sundays. In the morning I am going to church, to see how they worship my Father in this city of many mobs; but at noon I will hold a meeting on the corner of Fifth and Western City Streets, and if you wish, you may hear me. Now I ask you to excuse me, for I am weary." He stood for a moment, and I saw that, although he had never raised his voice nor made a violent gesture, his eyes were dark and hollow with fatigue, and drops of sweat stood upon his forehead.

He turned and left the platform, and Old Joe and I hurried around to join him. We found him with Korwsky the little Russian tailor whose son he had healed. Korwsky claimed him to spend the night at his home; the friend with the delivery wagon was on hand, and they were ready to start. I asked Carpenter to what church he was going in the morning, and he startled me by the reply, "St. Bartholomew's." I promised that I would surely be on hand, and then Old Joe and I set out to walk home.

XXXV

"Well?" said I. "What do you think of him?"

The ex-centre-rush walked for a bit before he answered. "You know, Billy boy," said he, "we do lead rotten useless lives."

"Good Lord!" I thought; it was the first sign of a soul I had ever noted in Old Joe! "Why," I argued, "you sell paper, and that's useful, isn't it?"

"I don't know whether it is or not. Look at what's printed on it—mostly advertisements and bunk." And again we walked for a bit. "By the way," said the ex-centre-rush, "before he got through, I saw that aura, or whatever you call it. I guess I'm getting nutty, too!"

XXXVI

The first thing I did on Sunday morning was to pick up the "Western City Times," to see what it had done to Carpenter. I found that he had achieved the front page, triple column, with streamer head all the way across the page:

PROPHET IN TOWN, HEALS SICK, RAVES AT RICH AMERICA IS MOBLAND, ALLEGED IN RED RIOT OF TALK

There followed a half page story about Carpenter's strenuous day in Western City, beginning with a "Bolshevik stump speech" to a mob of striking tailors. It appears that the prophet had gone to the Hebrew quarter of the city, and finding a woman railing at a butcher because of "alleged extortion," had begun a speech, inciting a mob, so that the police reserves had to be called out, and a riot was narrowly averted. From there the prophet had gone to the Labor Temple, announcing himself to the reporters as "fresh from God," with a message to "Mobland," his name for what he prophesied America would be under his rule. He had then healed a sick boy, the performance being carefully staged in front of moving picture cameras. The account of the "Times" did not directly charge that the performance was a "movie stunt," but it described it in a mocking way which made it obviously that. The paper mentioned T-S in such a way as to indicate him as the originator of the scheme, and it had fun with Mary Magna, pawning her paste jewels. It published the flash-light picture, and also a picture of Carpenter walking down the street, trailed by his mob.

In another column was the climax, the "red riot of talk" at Grant Hall. James, the striking carpenter, had indulged in virulent and semi-insane abuse of the rich; after which the new prophet had stirred the mob to worse frenzies. The "Times" quoted sample sentences, such as: "Do not think that I am come to bring you ease and comfort; I am come to bring strife and disorder to this world."

I turned to the editorial page, and there was a double-column leader, made extra impressive by leads. "AN INFAMOUS BLASPHEMY," was the heading. Perhaps you have a "Times" in your own city; if so, you will no doubt recognize the standard style:

"For many years this newspaper has been pointing out to the people of Western City the accumulating evidence that the men who manipulate the forces of organized labor are Anarchists at heart, plotting to let loose the torch of red revolution over this fair land. We have clearly showed their nefarious purpose to overthrow the Statue of Liberty and set up in its place the Dictatorship of the Walking Delegate. But, evil as we thought them, we were naive enough to give them credit for an elemental sense of decency. Even though they had no respect for the works of man, we thought at least they would spare the works of God, the most sacred symbols of divine revelation to suffering humanity. But yesterday there occurred in this city a performance which for shameless insolence and blasphemous perversion exceeds anything but the wildest flight of a devil's imagination, and reveals the bosses of the Labor Trust as wanton defilers of everything that decent people hold precious and holy.

"What was the spectacle? A moving picture producer, moved by blind, and we trust unthinking lust for gain, produces in our midst an alleged 'prophet,' dressed in a costume elaborately contrived to imitate and suggest a Sacred Presence which our respect for religion forbids us to name; he brings this vile, perverted creature forward, announcing himself to the newspapers as 'fresh from God,' and mouthing phrases of social greed and jealousy with which for the past few years the Hun-agents and Hun-lovers in our midst have made us only too sickenly familiar. This monstrous parody of divine compassion is escorted to that headquarters of Pro-Germanism and red revolution, the Labor Temple, and there performs, in the presence of moving picture cameras, a grotesque parody upon the laying on of hands and the healing of the sick. The 'Times' presents a photograph of this incredible infamy. We apologize to our readers for thus aiding the designs of cunning publicity-seekers, but there is no other way to make clear to the public the gross affront to decency which has been perpetrated, and the further affronts which are being planned. This appears to be a scheme for making a moving picture 'star'; this 'Carpenter'—note the silly pun—is to become the latest sensation in million dollar movie dolls, and the American public is to be invited to pay money to witness a story of sacred things played by a real 'prophet' and worker of 'miracles'!"

"But the worst has yet to be told. The masters of the Labor Trust, not to be outdone in bidding for unholy notoriety, had the insolence to invite this blasphemous charlatan to their riot of revolutionary ranting called a 'protest meeting.' He and other creatures of his ilk, summoning the forces which are organizing red ruin in our city, proceed to rave at the police and the courts for denying to mobs of strikers the right to throw brickbats at honest workers looking for jobs, and to hold the pistol of the boycott at the heads of employers who dare to stand for American liberty and democracy! We have heard much mouthing of class venom and hate in this community, but never have our ears been affronted by anything so unpardonable as this disguising of the doctrine of Lenin and Trotsky in the robes of Christian revelation. This 'prophet fresh from God,' as he styles himself, is a man of peace and brotherly love—oh, yes, of course! We know these wolves in sheeps' clothing, these pacifists and lovers of man with the gold of the Red International in their pockets, and slavering from their tongues the fine phrases of idealism which conveniently protect them from the strong hand of the law! We have seen their bloody work for four years in Russia, and we tell them that if they expect to prepare the confiscation of property and the nationalization of women in this country while disguising themselves in moving picture imitations of religion, they are grossly underestimating the intelligence of the red-blooded citizens of this great republic. We shall be much mistaken if the order-loving and patriotic people of our Christian community do not find a way to stamp their heel upon this vile viper before its venom shall have poisoned the air we breathe."

XXXVII

Then I picked up the "Examiner." Our "Examiner" does not go in so much for moral causes; it is more interested in getting circulation, for which it relies upon sensation, and especially what it calls "heart interest," meaning sex. It had found what it wanted in this story, as you may judge by the headlines:

MOVIE QUEEN PAWNS JEWELS FOR PROPHET OF GOD

Then followed a story of which Mary Magna was the centre, with T-S and myself for background. The reporter had hunted out the Mexican family with which Carpenter had spent the night, and he drew a touching picture of Carpenter praying over Mary in this humble home, and converting her to a better life. Would the "million dollar vamp," as the "Examiner" called her, now take to playing only religious parts? Mary was noncommittal on the point; and pending her decision, the "Examiner" published her portraits in half a dozen of her most luxurious roles—for example, as Salome after taking off the seventh veil. Side by side with Carpenter, that had a real "punch," you may believe!

The telephone rang, and there was the voice of T-S, fairly raving. He didn't mind the "Examiner" stuff; that was good business, but that in the "Times"—he was going to sue the "Times" for a million dollars, by God, and would I back him in his claim that he had not put Carpenter up to the healing business?

After a bit, the magnate began apologizing for his repudiation of the prophet. He was in a position, just now with these hard times, where the Wall Street crowd could ruin him if he got in bad with them. And then he told me a curious story. Last night, after the meeting, young Everett, his secretary, had come to him and asked if he could have a couple of months' leave of absence without pay. He was so much interested in Carpenter that he wanted to follow him and help him!

"Y' know, Billy," said the voice over the phone, "y' could a' knocked me over vit a fedder! Dat young feller, he vas alvays so quiet, and such a fine business feller, I put him in charge of all my collections. I said to him, 'Vot you gonna do?' And he said, 'I gonna learn from Mr. Carpenter.' Says I, 'Vot you gonna learn?' and he says, 'I gonna learn to be a better man.' Den he vaits a minute, and he says, 'Mr. T-S, he *told* me to foller him!' J' ever hear de like o' dat?"

"What did you say?"

"Vot could I say? I vanted to say, 'Who's givin' you de orders?' But I couldn't, somehow! I hadda tell him to go ahead, and come back before he forgot all my business."

I dressed, and had my breakfast, and drove to St. Bartholomew's. It was a November morning, bright and sunny, as warm as summer; and it is always such a pleasure to see that goodly company of ladies and gentlemen, so perfectly groomed, so perfectly mannered, breathing a sense of peace and well being. Ah, that wonderful sense of well being! "God's in His Heaven, all's right with the world!" And what a curious contrast with the Labor Temple! For a moment I doubted Carpenter; surely these ladies with their decorative bonnets, their sweet perfumes, their gowns of rose and lilac and other pastel shades—surely they were more important life-products than women in frowsy and dowdy imitation clothes! Surely it was better to be serene and clean and pleasant, than to be terrible and bewildered, sick and quarrelsome! I was seized by a frenzy, a sort of instinctive animal lust for this life of ease and prettiness. No matter if those dirty, raucous-voiced hordes of strikers, and others of their "ilk"—as the "Times" phrased it—did have to wash my clothes and scrub my floors, just so that *I* stayed clean and decent!

I bowed to a score or two of the elegant ladies, and to their escorts in shiny top hats and uncreased kid gloves, and went into the exquisite church with its glowing stained glass window, and looked up over the altar—and there stood Carpenter! I tell you, it gave me a queer shock. There he was, up in the window, exactly where he had always been; I thought I had suddenly wakened from a dream. There had been no "prophet fresh from God," no mass-meeting at Grant Hall, no editorial in the "Times"! But suddenly I heard a voice at my elbow: "Billy, what is this awful thing you've been doing?" It was my Aunt Caroline, and I asked what she meant, and she answered, "That terrible prophet creature, and getting your name into the papers!"

So I knew it was true, and I walked with my dear, sweet old auntie down the aisle, and there sat Aunt Jennie, with her two lanky girls who have grown inches every time I run into them; and also Uncle Timothy. Uncle Timothy was my guardian until I came of age, so I am a little in awe of him, and now I had to listen to his whispered reproaches—it being the first principle of our family never to "get into the papers." I told him that it wasn't my fault I had been knocked down by a mob, and surely I couldn't help it if this man Carpenter found me while I was unconscious, and made me well. Nor could I fail to be polite to my benefactor, and try to help him about. My Uncle Timothy was amazed, because he had accepted the "Times" story that it was all a "movie" hoax. Everybody will tell you in Western City that they "never believe a word they read in the 'Times'"; but of course they do—they have to believe something, and what else have they?

I was trying to think about that picture over the altar. Of course, they would naturally have replaced it! I wondered who had found old de Wiggs up there; I wondered if he knew about it, and if he had any idea who had played that prank. I looked to his pew; yes, there he sat, rosy and beaming, bland as ever! I looked for old Peter Dexter, president of the Dexter Trust Company—yes, he was in his pew, wizened and hunched up, prematurely bald. And Stuyvesant Gunning, of the Fidelity National—they were all here, the masters of the city's finance and the pil-pillars of "law and order." Some wag had remarked if you wanted to call directors' meeting after the service, you could settle all the business of Western City in St. Bartholomew's!

The organ pealed and the white-robed choir marched in, bearing the golden crosses, and followed by the Reverend Dr. Lettuce-Spray, smooth-shaven, plump and beautiful, his eyes bent reverently on the floor. They were singing with fervor that most orthodox of hymns:

The church's one foundation Is Jesus Christ, her Lord.

It is a beautiful old service, as you may know, and I had been taught to love it and thrill to it as a little child, and we never forget those things. Peace and propriety are its keynotes; order and dignity, combined with sensuous charm. Everyone knows his part, and it moves along like a beautiful machine. I knelt and prayed, and then sat and listened, and then stood and sang—over and over for perhaps three-quarters of an hour. We came to the hymn which precedes the sermon, and turning to the number, we obediently proclaimed:

The Son of God goes forth to war A kingly crown to gain: His blood-red banner streams afar: Who follows in His train?

During the singing of the last verse, the Reverend Lettuce-Spray had moved silently into the pulpit. After the choir had sung "Amen," he raised his hands in invocation—and at that awesome moment I saw Carpenter come striding up the aisle!

<h1 style="text-align:center">XXXVIII</h1>

He knew just where he was going, and walked so fast that before anyone had time to realize what was happening, he was on the altar steps, and facing the congregation. You could hear the gasp of amazement; he was so absolutely identical with the painted figure over his head, that if he had remained still, you could not have told which was painting and which was flesh and blood. The rector in the pulpit stood with his mouth open, staring as if seeing a ghost.

The prophet stretched out both his hands, and pointed two accusing fingers at the congregation. His voice rang out, stern and commanding: "Let this mockery cease!" Again he cried: "What do ye with my Name?" And pointing over his head: "Ye crucify me in stained glass!"

There came murmurs from the congregation, the first mutterings of a storm. "Oh! Outrageous! Blasphemy!"

"Blasphemy?" cried Carpenter. "Is it not written that God dwelleth not in temples made with hands? Ye have built a temple to Mammon, and defile the name of my Father therein!"

The storm grew louder. "This is preposterous!" exclaimed my uncle Timothy at my side. And the Reverend Lettuce-Spray managed to find his voice. "Sir, whoever you are, leave this church!"

Carpenter turned upon him. "You give orders to me—you who have brought back the moneychangers into my Father's temple?" And suddenly he faced the congregation, crying in a voice of wrath: "Algernon de Wiggs! Stand up!"

Strange as it may seem, the banker rose in his pew; whether under the spell of Carpenter's majestic presence, or preparing to rush at him and throw him out, I could not be sure. The great banker's face was vivid scarlet.

And Carpenter pointed to another part of the congregation. "Peter Dexter! Stand up!" The president of the Dexter Trust Company also arose, trembling as if with palsy, mumbling something, one could not tell whether protest or apology.

"Stuyvesant Gunning! Stand up!" And the president of the Fidelity National obeyed. Apparently Carpenter proposed to call the whole roll of financial directors; but the procedure was halted suddenly, as a tall, white-robed figure strode from its seat near the choir. Young Sidney Simpkinson, assistant to the rector, went up to Carpenter and took him by the arm.

"Leave this house of God," he commanded.

XXXVIII

The other faced him. "It is written, Thou shalt not take the name of the Lord thy God in vain, for the Lord will not hold him guiltless that taketh His name in vain."

Young Simpkinson wasted no further words in parley. He was an advocate of what is known as "muscular Christianity," and kept himself in trim playing on the parish basket-ball team. He flung his strong arms about Carpenter, and half carrying him, half walking him, took him down the steps and down the aisle. As he went, Carpenter was proclaiming: "It is written, My house shall be called a house of prayer; but ye have made it a den of thieves. He that steals little is called a pickpocket, but he that steals much is called a pillar of the church. Verily, he that deprives the laborer of the fruit of his toil is more dangerous than he that robs upon the highway; and he that steals the state and the powers of government is the father of all thieves."

By that time, the prophet had been hustled two-thirds down the aisle; and then came a new development. Unobserved by anyone, a number of Carpenter's followers had come with him into the church; and these, seeing the way he was being handled, set up a cry: "For shame! For shame!" I saw Everett, secretary to T-S, and Korwsky, secretary of the tailor's union; I saw some one leap at Everett and strike him a ferocious blow in the teeth, and two other men leap upon the little Russian and hurl him to the ground.

I started up, involuntarily. "Oh, shame! Shame!" I cried, and would have rushed out into the aisle. But I had to pass my uncle, and he had no intention of letting me make myself a spectacle. He threw his arms about me, and pinned me against the pew in front; and as he is one of the ten ranking golfers at the Western City Country Club, his embrace carried authority. I struggled, but there I stayed, shouting, "For shame! For shame!" and my uncle exclaiming, in a stern whisper, "Shut up! Sit down, you fool!" and my Aunt Caroline holding onto my coat-tails, crying, and my aunt Jennie threatening to faint.

The melee came quickly to an end, for the men of the congregation seized the half dozen disturbers and flung them outside, and mounted guard to make sure they did not return. I sank back into my seat, my worthy uncle holding my arm tightly with both hands, lest I should try to make my escape over the laps of Aunt Caroline and Aunt Jennie.

All this time the Reverend Lettuce-Spray had been standing in the pulpit, making no sound. Now, as the congregation settled back into order, he said, with the splendid, conscious self-possession of one who can remain "equal to the occasion": "We will resume the service." And he opened his portfolio, and spread out his manuscript before him, and announced:

"Our text for the morning is the fifth chapter of the gospel according to St. Matthew, the thirty-ninth and fortieth verses: 'But I say unto you, that ye resist not evil: but whosoever shall smite thee on thy right cheek, turn to him the other also. And if any man shall sue thee at law, and take away thy coat, let him have thy cloak also.'"

XXXIX

I sat through the sermon, and the offertory, and the recessional. After that my uncle tried to detain me, to warn and scold me; but he no longer used physical force, and nothing but that would have held me. At the door I asked one of the ushers what had become of the prophet, thinking he might be in jail. But the answer was that the gang had gone off, carrying their wounded; so I ran round the corner to where my car was parked, and within ten minutes I was on Western City Street, where Carpenter had announced that he would speak.

There had been nothing said about the proposed meeting in the papers, and no one knew about it save those who had been present at Grant Hall. But it looked as if they had told everyone they knew, and everyone they had told had come. The wide street was packed solid for a block, and in the midst of this throng stood Carpenter, upon a wagon, making a speech.

There was no chance to get near, so I bethought me of an alley which ran parallel to the street. There was an obscure hotel on the street, and I entered it through the rear entrance, and had no trouble in persuading the clerk to let me join some of the guests of the hotel who were watching the scene from the second story windows.

The first thing which caught my attention was the figure of Everett, seated on the floor of the wagon from which the speech was being made. I saw that his face was covered with blood; I learned later that he had three teeth knocked out, and his nose broken. Nevertheless, there he was with his stenographer's notebook, taking down the prophet's words. He told me afterwards that he had taken even what Carpenter said in the church. "I've an idea he won't last very long," was the way he put it; "and if they should get rid of him, every word he's said will be precious. Anyhow, I'm going to get what I can."

Also I saw Korwsky, lying on the floor of the wagon, evidently knocked out; and two other men whom I did not know, nursing battered and bloody faces. Having taken all that in at a glance, I gave my attention to what Carpenter was saying.

He was discussing churches and those who attend them. Later on, my attention was called to the curious fact that his discourse was merely a translation into modern American of portions of the twenty-third chapter of St. Matthew; a free adaptation of those ancient words to present day practices and conditions. But I had no idea of this while I listened; I was shocked by what seemed to me a furious tirade, and the guests of the hotel were even more shocked—I think they would have taken to throwing things out of the windows at the orator, had it not been for their fear of the crowd. Said Carpenter:

"The theologians and scholars and the pious laymen fill the leisure class churches, and it would be all right if you were to listen to what they preach, and do that; but don't follow their actions, for they never practice what they preach. They load the backs of the working-classes with crushing burdens, but they themselves never move a finger to carry a burden, and everything they do is for show. They wear frock-coats and silk hats on Sundays, and they sit at the speakers' tables at the banquets of the Civic Federation, and they occupy the best pews in the churches, and their doings are reported in all the papers; they are called leading citizens and pillars of the church. But don't you be called leading citizens, for the only useful man is the man who produces. (Applause.) And whoever exalts himself shall be abased, and whoever humbles himself shall be exalted.

"Woe unto you, doctors of divinity and Catholics, hypocrites! for you shut up the kingdom of heaven against men; you don't go in yourself and you don't let others go in. Woe unto you, doctors of divinity and Presbyterians, hypocrites! for you foreclose mortgages on widows' houses, and for a pretense you make long prayers. For this you will receive the greater damnation! Woe unto you, doctors of divinity and Methodists, hypocrites! for you send missionaries to Africa to make one convert, and when you have made him, is twice as much a child of hell as yourselves. (Applause.) Woe unto you, blind guides, with your subtleties of doctrine, your transubstantiation and consubstantiation and all the rest of it; you fools and blind! Woe unto you, doctors of divity and Episcopalians, hypocrites! for you drop your checks into the collection-plate and you pay no heed to the really important things in the Bible, which are justice and mercy and faith in goodness. You blind guides, who choke over a fly and swallow a flivver! (Laughter.) Woe unto you, doctors of divinity and Anglicans, hypocrites! for you dress in immaculate clothing kept clean by the toil of frail women, but within you are full of extortion and excess. You blind high churchmen, clean first your hearts, so that the clothes you wear may represent you. Woe unto you, doctors of divinity and Baptists, hypocrites! for you are like marble tombs which appear beautiful on the outside, but inside are full of dead men's bones and all uncleanness. Even so you appear righteous to men, but inside you are full of hypocrisy and iniquity. (Applause.) Woe unto you doctors of divinity and Unitarians, hypocrites! because you erect statues to dead reformers, and put wreaths upon the tombs of old-time martyrs. You say, if we had been alive in those days, we would not have helped to kill those good men. That ought to show you how to treat us at present. (Laughter.) But you are the children of those who killed the good men; so go ahead and kill us too! You serpents, you generation of vipers, how can you escape the damnation of hell?"

<h1 style="text-align:center">XL</h1>

When Carpenter stopped speaking, his face was dripping with sweat, and he was pale. But the eager crowd would not let him go. They began to ask him questions. There were some who wanted to know what he meant by saying that he came from God, and some who wanted to know whether he believed in the Christian religion. There were others who wanted to know what he thought about political action, and if he really believed that the capitalists would give up without using force. There was a man who had been at the relief kitchen, and noted that he ate soup with meat in it, and asked if this was not using force against one's fellow creatures. The old gentleman who represented spiritualism was on hand, asking if the dead are still alive, and if so, where are they?

Then, before the meeting was over, there came a sick man to be healed; and others, pushing their way through the crowd, clamoring about the wagon, seeking even to touch the hem of Carpenter's garments. After a couple of hours of this he announced that he was worn out. But it was a problem to get the wagon started; they could only move slowly, the driver calling to the people in front to make room. So they went down the street, and I got into my car and followed at a distance. I did not know where they were going, and there was nothing I could do but creep along—a poor little rich boy with a big automobile and nobody to ride in it, or to pay any attention to him.

The wagon drove to the city jail; which rather gave me a start, because I had been thinking that the party might be arrested at any minute, on complaint to the police from the church. But apparently this did not trouble Carpenter. He wished to visit the strikers who had been arrested in front of Prince's restaurant. He and several others stood before the heavy barred doors asking for admission, while a big crowd gathered and stared. I sat watching the scene, with phrases learned in earliest childhood floating through my mind: "I was sick, and ye visited me; I was in prison, and ye came unto me."

But it appeared that Sunday was not visitors' day at the jail, and the little company was turned away. As they climbed back into the wagon, I saw two husky fellows come from the jail, a type one learns to know as plain clothes men. "Why won't they let him in?" cried some one in the crowd; and one of the detectives looked over his shoulder, with a sneering laugh: "We'll let him in before long, don't you worry!"

XL

The wagon took up its slow march again. It was a one-horse express-cart, belonging, as I afterwards learned, to a compatriot of Korwsky the tailor. This man, Simon Karlin, earned a meager living for himself and his family by miscellaneous delivery in his neighborhood; but now he was so fascinated with Carpenter that he had dropped everything in order to carry the prophet about. I mention it, because next day in the newspapers there was much fun made of this imitation man of God riding about town in a half broken-down express-wagon, hauled by a rickety and spavined old nag.

The company drove to one of the poorer quarters of the city, and stopped before a workingman's cottage on a street whose name I had never heard before. I learned that it was the home of James, the striking carpenter, and on the steps were his wife and a brood of half a dozen children, and his old father and mother, and several other people unidentified. There were many who had walked all the way following the wagon, and others gathered quickly, and besought the prophet to speak to them, and to heal their sick. Apparently his whole life was to consist of that kind of thing, for he found it hard to refuse any request. But finally he told them he must be quiet, and went inside, and James mounted guard at the door, and I sat in my car and waited until the crowd had filtered away. There was no good reason why I should have been admitted, but James apparently was glad to see me, and let me join the little company that was gathered in his home.

There was Everett, who had now washed the blood off his face, but had not been able to put back his lost teeth, nor to heal the swollen mass that had once been his upper lip and nose. And there was Korwsky, who was now able to sit up and smile feebly, and two other men, whose names I did not learn, nursing battered faces. Carpenter prayed over them all, and they became more cheerful, and eager to talk about the adventure, each telling over what had happened to him. I noted that Everett, in spite of what must have been intense pain, was still faithfully taking down every word the prophet uttered.

It had been known that Carpenter was to honor this house with his presence, and the family were all dressed in their best, and had got together a supper, in spite of hard times and strikes. We had sandwiches and iced tea and a slice of pie for each of us, and I was interested to observe that the prophet, tired as he was, liked to laugh and chat over his food, exactly like any uninspired human being. He never failed to get the children around him and tell them stories, and hear their bright laughter.

XLI

But, of course, serious things kept intruding. Karlin the express driver, had a sick wife, and Carpenter heard about her and insisted upon going to see her. Apparently there was no end to this business of the poor being sick. It was a new thing to me—this world swarming with dirty and miserable and distracted people. Of course, I had known about "the poor," but always either in the abstract, or else as an individual, or a family, that one could help. But here was a new world, thickly peopled, swarming; that was the terrible part of it—the vastness of it, the thickness of the population in these regions of "the poor." It was like some sort of delirium; like being lost in a wilderness, of which the trees were miseries, and deformities, and pains! I could understand to the full Carpenter's feeling when he put his hands to his forehead, exclaiming: "There is so much to do and so few to do it! Pray to God, that he will send some to help us!"

When he returned from Simon Karlin's, he brought with him the latter's wife, whom he had healed of a fever; and here was another of the company whom he insisted upon helping—"Comrade" Abell, one of the men I had noticed at the meeting last night, and who appeared to be done up. This man, I learned, was secretary of the Socialist local of Western City. I had known there were Socialists in the city, just as I knew there were poor, but I had never seen one, and was curious about Abell. He was a lawyer; and that might suggest to you a certain type of person, brisk and well dressed—but apparently Socialist lawyers are not true to type. Comrade Abell was a shy, timid little man, with black hair straggling about his ears, and sometimes into his eyes. He had a gentle, pathetic face, and his voice was melancholy and caressing. He was clad in a frock coat of black broadcloth, which had once been appropriate for Sunday; but I should judge it had been worn for twenty years, for it was green about the collar and the cuffs and button-holes.

Comrade Abell's office and also his home were in a second story, over a grocery-store in this neighborhood, and here also was a little hall used as a meeting-place by the Socialists. Every Saturday night Abell and two or three of his friends conducted a soap-box meeting on Western City Street, and gave away propaganda leaflets and sold a few pamphlets and books. He had had quite a supply of literature of all kinds at his office, nearly two thousand dollars worth, he told Carpenter, but a few months previously the place had been mobbed. A band of ex-service men, accompanied by a few police and detectives, had raided it and terrified the wife and children by breaking down the doors and throwing the contents of desks and bureaus out on the floor. They had dumped the literature into a truck and carted it away, and after two or three weeks they had dumped it back again, having found nothing criminal in it. "But they ruined it so that it can't be sold!" broke in James, indignantly. "Most of it was bought on credit, and how can we pay for it."

James was also a Socialist, it appeared, while Korwsky and his friend Karlin advocated "industrial action," and these fell to arguing over "tactics," while Carpenter asked questions, so as to understand their different points of view. Presently Korwsky was called out of the room, and came back with an announcement which he evidently considered grave. John Colver was in the neighborhood, and wanted to know if Carpenter would meet him.

"Who is John Colver?" asked the prophet. And it was explained that this was a dangerous agitator, now under sentence of twenty years in jail, but out on bail pending the appeal of his case to the supreme court. Colver was a "wobbly," well known as one of their poets. Said Korwsky, "He tinks you vouldn't like to know him, because if de spies find it out, dey vould git after you."

"I will meet any man," said Carpenter. "My business is to meet men." And so in a few minutes the terrible John Colver was escorted into the room.

Now, every once in a while I had read in the "Times" how another bunch of these I.W.W's. were put on trial, and how they were insolent to the judge, and how it was proved they had committed many crimes, and how they were sentenced to fourteen years in State's prison under our criminal syndicalism act. Needless to say, I had never seen one of these desperate men; but I had a quite definite idea what they looked like—dark and sinister creatures, with twisted mouths and furtive eyes. I knew that, because I had seen a couple of moving picture shows in which they figured. But now for the first time I met one, and behold, he was an open-faced, laughing lad, with apple cheeks and two most beautiful rows of even white teeth that gleamed at you!

"Fellow-worker Carpenter!" he cried; and caught the prophet by his two hands. "You are an old friend of ours, though you may not know it! We drink a toast to you in our jungles."

"Is that so?" said Carpenter.

"I suppose I really have no right to see you," continued the other, "because I'm shadowed all the time, and you know my organization is outlawed."

"Why is it outlawed?"

"Well," said Colver, "they say we burn crops and barns, and drive copper-nails into fruit-trees, and spikes into sawmill lumber."

"And do you do that?"

Colver laughed his merry laugh. "We do it just as often as you act for the movies, Fellow-worker Carpenter!"

"I see," said Carpenter. "What do you really do?"

"What we really do is to organize the unskilled workers."

"For what do you organize them?"

"So that they will be able to run the industries when the system of greed breaks down of its own rottenness."

"I see," said the prophet, and he thought for a moment. "It is a slave revolt!"

"Exactly," said the other.

"I know what they do to slave revolts, my brother. You are fortunate if they only send you to prison."

"They do plenty more than that," said Colver. "I will give you our pamphlet, 'Drops of Blood,' and you may read about some of the lynching and tarring and feathering and shooting of Mobland." His eyes twinkled. "That's a dandy name you've hit on! I shall be surprised if it doesn't stick."

Carpenter went on questioning, bent upon knowing about this outlaw organization and its members. It was clear before long that he had taken a fancy to young John Colver. He made him sit beside him, and asked to hear some of his poetry, and when he found it really vivid and beautiful, he put his arm about the young poet's shoulders. Again I found memories of old childhood phrases stirring in my mind. Had there not once been a disciple named John, who was especially beloved?

XLII

Presently the young agitator began telling about an investigation he had been making in the lumber country of the Northwest. He was writing a pamphlet on the subject of a massacre which had occurred there. A mob of ex-soldiers had stormed the headquarters of the "wobblies," and the latter had defended themselves, and killed two or three of their assailants. A news agency had sent out over the country a story to the effect that the "wobblies" had made an unprovoked assault upon the ex-soldiers. "That's what the papers do to us!" said John Colver. "There have been scores of mobbings as a result, and just now it may be worth a man's life to be caught carrying a red card in any of these Western states."

So there was the subject of non-resistance, and I sat and listened with strangely mingled feelings of sympathy and repulsion, while this group of rebels of all shades and varieties argued whether it was really possible for the workers to get free without some kind of force. Carpenter, it appeared, was the only one in the company who believed it possible. The gentle Comrade Abell was obliged to admit that the Socialists, in using political action, were really resorting to force in a veiled form. They sought to take possession of the state by voting; but the state was an instrument of force, and would use force to carry out its will. "You are an anarchist!" said the Socialist lawyer, addressing Carpenter.

To my surprise Carpenter was not shocked by this.

"If I admit no power but love," said he, "how can I have anything to do with government?"

More visitors called, and were admitted, and presently the little room was packed with people, and a regular meeting was in progress. I heard more strange ideas than I had ever known existed in the world. I tried not to be offended; but I thought there ought to be at least a few words said for plain ordinary human beings who carry no labels, so I ventured now and then to put in a mild suggestion—for example, that there were quite a few people in the world who did not love all their neighbors, and could not be persuaded to love them all at once, and it might be necessary to put just a little restraint upon them for a time. Again I suggested, maybe the workers were not yet sufficiently educated to run the industries, they might need some help from the present masters. "Just a little more education," I ventured—

And John Colver laughed, the first ugly laugh I had heard from him. "Education by the masters? Education at the end of a club!"

"My boy," I argued, "I know there are plenty of employers who are rough, but there are others who are good men, who would like to change the system, would like to do something, if they knew what it was. But who will tell them what to do? Take me, for example. I have a great deal of wealth which I have not earned; but what can I do about it? What do you say, Mr. Carpenter?"

I turned to him, as the true authority; and the others also turned to him. He answered, without hesitation: "Sell everything that you have and give it to the unemployed."

"But," said I, "would that really solve the problem. They would spend it, and we should be right where we were before."

Said Carpenter: "They are unemployed because you have taken from them wealth which you have not earned. Give it back to them."

And then, seeing that I was not satisfied, he added: "How hard it is for a rich man to understand the meaning of social justice! Indeed, it would be easier for a strike leader to get the truth published in your 'Times', than for a rich man to understand what the word social justice means."

The company laughed, and I subsided, and let the wave of conversation roll by. It was only later that I realized the part I had just been playing. It had been easy for me to recognize T-S as St. Peter, but I had not known myself as that rich young man who had asked for advice, and then rejected it. "When he heard this, he was very sorrowful; for he was very rich." Yes, I had found my place in the story!

XLIII

You may believe that next morning my first thought was to get hold of the "Times" and see what they had done to my prophet. Sure enough, there he was on the front page, three columns wide, with the customary streamer head:

MOB OF ANARCHISTS RAID ST. BARTHOLMEW'S
PROPHET AND RAGGED HORDE BREAK UP CHURCH SERVICES

I skimmed over the story quickly; I noted that Carpenter was represented as having tried to knock down the Reverend Mr. Simpkinson, and that the prophet's followers had assaulted members of the congregation. I confess to some relief upon discovering that my own humble part in the adventure had not been mentioned. I suspected that my Uncle Timothy must have been busy at the telephone on Sunday evening! But then I turned to the "Examiner," and alas, there I was! "A certain rich young man," rising up to protect an incendiary prophet! I remembered that my Uncle Timothy had had a violent row with the publisher of the "Examiner" a year or two ago, over some political appointment!

The "Times" had another editorial, two columns, double leaded. Yesterday the paper had warned the public what to expect; today it saw the prophecies justified, and what it now wished to know was, had Western City a police department, or had it not? "How much longer do our authorities propose to give rein to this firebrand imposter? This prophet of God who rides about town in a broken-down express-wagon, and consorts with movie actresses and red agitators! Must the police wait until his seditious doctrines have fanned the flames of mob violence beyond control? Must they wait until he has gathered all the others of his ilk, the advocates of lunacy and assassination about him, and caused an insurrection of class envy and hate? We call upon the authorities of our city to act and act at once; to put this wretched mountebank behind bars where he belongs, and keep him there."

There was another aspect of this matter upon which the "Times" laid emphasis. After long efforts on the part of the Chamber of Commerce and other civic organizations, Western City had been selected as the place for the annual convention of the Mobland Brigade. In three days this convention would be called to order, and already the delegates were pouring in by every train. What impression would they get of law and order in this community? Was this the purpose for which they had shed their blood in a dreadful war—that their country might be affronted by the ravings of an impious charlatan? What had the gold-star mothers of Western City to say to this? What did the local post of the Mobland Brigade propose to do to save the fair name of their city? Said the "Times": "If our supine authorities refuse to meet this emergency, we believe there are enough 100% Americans still among us to protect the cause of public decency, and to assert the right of Christian people to worship their God without interference from the Dictatorship of the Lunatic Asylum."

Now, I had been so much interested in Carpenter and his adventures that I had pretty well overlooked this matter of the Mobland Brigade and its convention. I belong to the Brigade myself, and ought to have been serving on the committee of arrangements; instead of which, here I was chasing around trying to save a prophet, who, it appeared, really wanted to get into trouble! Yes, the Brigade was coming; and I could foresee what would happen when a bunch of these wild men encountered Carpenter's express wagon on the street!

XLIV

I swallowed a hasty cup of coffee, and drove in a taxi to the Labor Temple. Carpenter had said he would be there early in the morning, to help with the relief work again. I went to the rooms of the Restaurant Workers, and found that he had not yet arrived. I noticed a group of half a dozen men standing near the door, and there seemed something uncordial in the look they gave me. One of them came toward me, the same who had sought my advice about permitting Carpenter to speak at the mass meeting. "Good morning," he said; and then: "I thought you told me this fellow Carpenter was not a red?"

"Well," said I, taken by surprise, "is he?"

"God Almighty!" said the other. "What do you call this?" And he held up a copy of the "Times." "Going in and shouting in the middle of a church service, and trying to knock down a clergyman!"

I could not help laughing in the man's face. "So even you labor men believe what you read in the 'Times'! It happens I was present in the church myself, and I assure you that Carpenter offered no resistance, and neither did anyone else in his group. You remember, I told you he was a man of peace, and that was all I told you."

"Well," said the other, somewhat more mildly, "even so, we can't stand for this kind of thing. That's no way to accomplish anything. A whole lot of our members are Catholics, and what will they make of carryings-on like this? We're trying to persuade people that we're a law-abiding organization, and that our officials are men of sense."

"I see," said I. "And what do you mean to do about it?"

"We have called a meeting of our executive committee this morning, and are going to adopt a resolution, making clear to the public that we knew nothing about this church raid, and that we don't stand for such things. We would never have permitted this man Carpenter to speak on our platform, if we had known about his ideas."

I had nothing to say, and I said it. The other was watching me uneasily. "We hear the man proposes to come back to our relief kitchen. Is that so?"

"I believe he does; and I suppose you would rather he didn't. Is that it?" The other admitted that was it, and I laughed. "He has had his thousand dollars worth of hospitality, I suppose."

"Well, we don't want to hurt his feelings," said the other. "Of gourse our members are having a hard time, and we were glad to get the money, but it would be better if our central organization were to contribute the funds, rather than to have us pay such a price as this newspaper publicity."

"Then let your committee vote the money, and return it to Mr. T-S, and also to Mary Magna."

It took the man sometime to figure out a reply to this proposition. "We have no objection to Mr. T-S coming here," he said, "or Miss Magna either."

"That is," said I, "so long as they obey the law, and don't get in bad with the Western City 'Times'!" After a moment I added, "You may make your mind easy. I will go downstairs and wait for Mr. Carpenter, and tell him he is not wanted."

And so I left the Labor Temple and walked up and down on the sidewalk in front. It was really rather unreasonable of me to be annoyed with this labor man for having voiced the same point of view of "common sense" which I had been defending to Carpenter's group on the previous evening. Also, I was obliged to admit to myself that if I were a labor leader, trying to hold together a group of half-educated men in the face of public sentiment such as existed in this city, I might not have the same carefree, laughing attitude towards life as a certain rich young man whose pockets were stuffed with unearned increments.

To this mood of tolerance I had brought myself, when I saw a white robe come round the corner, arm in arm with a frock coat of black broadcloth. Also there came Everett, looking still more ghastly, his nose and lip having become purple, and in places green. Also there was Korwsky, and two other men; Moneta, a young Mexican cigarmaker out of work, and a man named Hamby, who had turned up on the previous evening, introducing himself as a pacifist who had been arrested and beaten up during the war. Somehow he did not conform to my idea of a pacifist, being a solid and rather stoutish fellow, with nothing of the idealist about him. But Carpenter took him, as he took everybody, without question or suspicion.

XLV

I joined the group, and made clear to them, as tactfully as I could, that they were not wanted inside. Comrade Abell threw up his hands. "Oh, those labor skates!" he cried. "Those miserable, cowardly, grafting politicians! Thinking about nothing but keeping themselves respectable, and holding on to their fat, comfortable salaries!"

"Vell, vat you expect?" cried Korwsky. "You git de verkin' men into politics, and den you blame dem fer bein' politicians!"

"Nothing was said about returning the money, I suppose?" remarked Everett, in a bitter tone.

"Something was said," I replied. "I said it. I don't think the money will be returned."

Then Carpenter spoke. "The money was given to feed the hungry," said he. "If it is used for that purpose, we can ask no more. And if men set out to preach a new doctrine, how can they expect to be welcomed at once? We have chosen to be outcasts, and must not complain. Let us go to the jail. Perhaps that is the place for us." So the little group set out in a new direction.

On the way we talked about the labor movement, and what was the matter with it. Comrade Abell said that Carpenter was right, the fundamental trouble was that the workers were imbued with the psychology of their masters. They would strike for this or that improvement in their condition, and then go to the polls and vote for the candidates of their masters. But Korwsky was more vehement; he was an industrial unionist, and thought the present craft unions worse than nothing.

Little groups of labor aristocrats, seking to benefit themselves at the expense of the masses, the unorganized, unskilled workers and the floating population of casual labor! That was why those "skates" at the Labor Temple has so little enthusiasm for Carpenter and his doctrine of brotherhood! In this country where every man was trying to climb up on the face of some other man!

Our little group had come out on Broadway. It attracted a good deal of attention, and a number of curiosity seekers were beginning to trail behind us. "We'll get a crowd again, and Carpenter 'll be making a speech," I thought; and as usual I faced a moral conflict. Should I stand by, or should I sneak away, and preserve the dignity of my family?

Suddenly came a sound of music, fifes and drums. It burst on our ears from round the corner, shrill and lively—"The Girl I Left Behind Me." Carpenter, who was directly in front of me, stopped short, and seemed to shrink away from what was coming, until his back was against the show-window of a department-store, and he could shrink no further.

It was a company of ex-service men in uniform; one or two hundred, carrying rifles with fixed bayonets which gleamed in the sunshine. There were two fifers and two drummers at their head, and also two flags, one the flag of the Brigade, and the other the flag of Mobland. I remembered having noted in the morning papers that the national commander of the brigade was to arrive in town this morning, and no doubt this was a delegation to do him honor.

The marchers swept down on us, and past us, and I watched the prophet. His eyes were wide, his whole face expressing anguish. "Oh God, my Father!" he whispered, and seemed to quiver with each thud of the tramping feet on the pavement. After the storm had passed, he stood motionless, the pain still in his face "It is Rome! It is Rome!" he murmured.

"No," said I, "it is Mobland."

He went on, as if he had not heard me. "Rome! Eternal Rome! Rome that never dies!" And he turned upon me his startled eyes. "Even the eagles!"

For a moment I was puzzled; but then I remembered the golden eagle with wings outspread, that perches on top of our national banner. "We only use one eagle," I said, somewhat feebly.

To which he answered, "The soul of one eagle is the same as the soul of two."

Now, I had felt quite certain that Carpenter would not get along very well with the Brigade, and I was more than ever decided that he must be got out of the way somehow or other. But meantime, the first task was to get him away from this crowd which was rapidly collecting. Already he was in the full tide of a speech. "Those sharp spears! Can you not see them thrust into the bowels of human beings? Can you not see them dripping with the blood of your brothers?"

I whispered to Everett, thinking him one among this company of enthusiasts who might have a little common sense left. "We had better get him away from here!" And Everett put his hand gently on the prophet's shoulder, and said, "The prisoners in the jail are hoping for us." I took him by the other arm, and we began to lead him down the street. When we had once got him going, we walked him faster and faster, until presently the crowd was trailing out into a string of idlers and curiosity seekers, as before.

XLVI

The party came to the city jail, and knocked for admission. But no doubt the authorities had taken consultation in the meantime, and there was no admission for prophets. The party stood on the steps, baffled and bewildered, a pitiful and pathetic little group.

For my part, I thought it just as well that Carpenter had not got inside, for I knew what he would find there. It happens that my Aunt Jennie belongs to a couple of women's clubs, and they have been making a fuss about our city jail; they have kept on making it for many years, but apparently without accomplishing anything. The place was built a generation ago, for a city of perhaps one-tenth our present size; it is old and musty, and the walls are so badly cracked that it has been condemned by the building department. It is so crowded that half a dozen men sometimes sleep on the floor of a single cell. They are devoured by vermin, and lie in semi-darkness, some of them shivering with cold and others half suffocated. They stay there, sometimes for many months unheeded, because the courts are crowded, and if Comrade Abell's word may be taken in the matter, every poor man is assumed to be guilty until he is proven innocent. I have heard Aunt Jennie arguing the matter with considerable energy. Our banks are housed in palaces, and our Chamber of Commerce and our Merchants and Manufacturers and our Real Estate Exchange and all the rest of our boosters have commodious and expensive quarters; but our prisoners lie in torment, and no one boosts for them.

Did Carpenter know these things? Had the strikers or his little company of agitators, told him about them? Suddenly he said, "Let us pray;" and there on the steps of the jail he raised his hands in invocation, and prayed for all prisoners and captives. And when he finished, Comrade Abell suddenly lifted his voice and began to sing. I would not have supposed that so big a voice could have come out of so frail a body; but I was reminded that Abell had been practicing on soap-boxes a good part of his life. He was one of these shouting evangelists—only his gospel was different. He sang:

> Arise, ye pris'ners of starvation!
> Arise, ye wretched of the earth!
> For justice thunders condemnation,
> A better world's in birth.

I think I would have shuddered, even more than I did, if I had known the name of this song; if I had realized that this group of fanatics were sounding the dread Internationale on the steps of our city jail! I suspect that what saved them was the fact that the guardians of the jail had no more idea what it was than I had!

The group had sung a couple of verses, when the iron-barred doors were opened, and a policeman stepped out. He addressed Carpenter, who was not singing. "Tell that bunch of nuts of yours to can the yowling."

To which Carpenter replied: "I tell you that if these men should hold their peace, the stones of your jail would immediately cry out!" And he turned, and looked up and down the streets of the city, and suddenly I saw that he was weeping. "Oh, Mobland, Mobland! If you had known even at this time the way of justice! But the way is hid from your eyes, and you will not see it, and now the hour is coming, the horrors of the class war are upon you, ruin and destruction are at hand! Your towers of pride shall fall, your own children shall destroy you; they shall not leave you one stone upon another, because you knew not the time for justice when it came."

The doors of the jail opened again, and three or four more policemen came out, with clubs in their hands. "Get along, now!" they said roughly, and began poking the prophet and his disciples in the back; they poked them down the stairs and along the street for a block or so—until they were sure the ears of the jail inmates would no longer be troubled by offensive sounds. But still they did not arrest them, and I marveled, wondering how long it could go on. I had an uneasy feeling that the longer the climax was postponed, the more severe it would be.

There was quite a crowd following us now, hoping that something sensational would happen. And presently a woman saw us, and rushed into the house, and came out leading a blind man, and appealing to Carpenter to restore his sight; and when he stopped to do this, there were a couple of newspaper men, and an operator with a camera, and more excitement and more crowds! So we started to walk again, and came to Main Street, which in our city is given up to ten cent picture-shows, and pawn-brokers, and old clothes shops, and eating-stands for working-men. A block or so distant we saw a mass of people, and something warned me— my heart sank into my boots. Another mob!

XLVII

There was shouting, and people running from every direction. The throng would surge back, and a few run from it. "What's the matter?" I cried to one of these, and the answer was, "They're cleaning out the reds!" Comrade Abell, who knew the neighborhood, exclaimed in dismay, "It's Erman's Book Store!"

"Who's doing this?" I asked of another bystander, and the answer was, "The Brigade! They're cleaning up the city before the convention!" And Comrade Abell clasped his hands to his forehead, and wailed in despair, "It's because they've been selling the 'Liberator'! Erman told me last week he'd been warned to stop selling it!"

Now, I don't know whether or not Carpenter had ever heard of this radical monthly. But he knew that here was a mob, and people in trouble, and he shook off the hands which sought to restrain him, and pushed his way into the throng, which gave way before him, either from respect or from curiosity. I learned later that some of the mob had dragged the bookseller and his two clerks out by the rear entrance, and were beating them pretty severely. But fortunately Carpenter did not see this. All he saw were a dozen or so ex-soldiers in uniform carrying armfuls of magazines and books out into a little square, which was made by the oblique intersection of two avenues. They were dumping the stuff into a pile, and a man with a five gallon can was engaged in pouring kerosene over it.

"My friend," said Carpenter, "what is this that you do?"

The other turned upon him and stared. "What the hell you got to do with it? Get out of the way there!" And to emphasize his words he slopped a jet of kerosene over the prophet's robes.

Said Carpenter: "Do you know what a book is? One of your poets has described it as the precious life-blood of a great spirit, embalmed and preserved to all posterity."

The other laughed scornfully. "Was he talkin' about Bolsheviki books, you reckon?"

Said Carpenter: "Are you one that should be set to judge books? Have you read these that you are about to destroy?" And as the other, paying no attention, knelt down to strike a match and light the pyre, he cried, in a louder voice: "Behold what a thing is war! You have been trained to kill your fellow men; the beast has been let loose in your heart, and he raves within!"

"One of these God-damn pacifists, eh?" cried the ex-soldier; and he dropped his matches and sprang up with fists clenched. Carpenter faced him without flinching; there was something so majestic about him, the man did not strike him, he merely put his spread hand against the prophet's chest and shoved him violently. "Get back out of the way!"

I well knew the risk I was taking, but I could not refrain. "Now, look here, buddy!" I began; and the soldier whirled upon me. "You one of these Huns, too?"

"I was all through the Argonne," I said quickly. "And I belong to the Brigade."

"Oh ho! Well, pitch in here, and help carry out this bloody Arnychist literature!"

I was about to answer, but Carpenter's voice rang out again. He had turned and stretched out his arms to the crowd, and we both stopped to listen to his words.

"Shall ye be wolves, or shall ye be men? That is the choice, and ye have chosen wolfhood. The blood of your brothers is upon your hands, and murder in your hearts. You have trained your young men to be killers of their brothers, and now they know only the law of madness."

There were a dozen ex-doughboys in sound of this discourse, and I judged they would not stand much of it. Suddenly one of them began to chant; and the rest took it up, half laughing, half shouting:

> Rough! Tough!
> We're the stuff!
> We want to fight and we can't get enough!

And after that:

> Hail! Hail! The gang's all here!
> We're going to get the Kaiser!

The crowd joined in, and the words of the prophet were completely drowned out. A moment later I heard a gruff voice behind me. "Make way here!" There came a policeman, shoving through. "What's all this about?"

The fellow with the kerosene can spoke up: "Here's this damn Arnychist prophet been incitin' the crowd and preachin' sedition! You better take him along, officer, and put him somewhere he'll be safe, because me and my buddies won't stand no more Bolsheviki rantin'."

It seemed ludicrous when I looked back upon it; though at the moment I did not appreciate the funny side. Here was a group of men engaged in raiding a book-store, beating up the proprietor and his clerks, and burning a thousand dollars worth of books and magazines on the public street; but the policeman did not see a bit of that, he had no idea that any such thing was happening! All he saw was a prophet, in a white nightgown dripping with kerosene, engaged in denouncing war! He took him firmly by the arm, saying, "Come along now! I guess we've heard enough o' this;" and he started to march Carpenter down the street.

"Take me too!" cried Moneta, the Mexican, beside himself with excitement; and the policeman grabbed him with the other hand, and the three set out to march.

XLVIII

I no longer had any impulse to interfere. In truth I was glad to see the policeman, considering that his worst might be better than the mob's best. About half
the crowd followed us, but the singing died away, and that gave Comrade Abell
his chance. He was walking directly behind the policeman, and suddenly he raised
his voice, and all the rest of the way to the station-house he provided marching
tunes: first the Internationale, and then the Reg Flag, and then the Marseillaise:

> Ye sons of toil, awake to glory!
> Hark, hark! What myriads bids you rise!
> Your children, wives, and grand sires hoary—
> Behold their tears and hear their cries!

When we came to the station house, the policeman gave Moneta a shove and
told him to get along; he had not done anything, and was denied the honor of being arrested. The officer pushed Carpenter through the door, and bade the rest of
us keep out.

Said Abell: "I am an attorney."

"The hell you are!" said the other. "I thought you were an opery singer."

"I'm a practicing attorney," said Abell, "and I represent the man you have arrested. I presume I have a right to enter."

"And I am a prospective bondsman," I stated, with sudden inspiration. "So let
me in also."

We entered, and the policeman led his prisoner to the sergeant at the desk. The
latter asked the charge, and was told, "Disturbing the peace and blocking traffic."

"Now, sergeant," said I, "this is preposterous. All this prisoner did was to try to
stop a mob from destroying property."

"You can tell all that to the magistrate in the morning," said the sergeant.

"What is the bail?" I demanded.

"You are prepared to put up bail?"

I answered that I was; and then for the first time Carpenter spoke. "You mean
you wish to pay money to secure my release? Let there be no money paid for me."

"Let me explain, Mr. Carpenter," I pleaded. "You will accomplish nothing by
spending the night in a police cell. You will have no opportunity to talk with the
prisoners. They will keep you by yourself."

He answered, "My Father will be with me." And gazing into the face of the sergeant, he demanded, "Do you think you can build a cell to which my Father cannot come?"

The officer was an old hand, with a fringe of grey hair around his bald head, and no doubt he had been asked many queer questions in his day. His response was to inquire the prisoner's name; and when the prisoner kept haughty silence, he wrote down "John Doe Carpenter," and proceeded: "Where do you live?"

Said Carpenter: "The foxes have holes, and the birds of the air have nests, but he that espouses the cause of justice has no home in a world of greed."

So the sergeant wrote: "No address," and nodded to a jailer, who took the prophet by the arm and led him away through a steel-barred door.

Abell and I went outside and joined the rest of the group. None of us knew just what to do—with the exception of Everett, who sat on the steps with his notebook, and made me repeat to him word for word what Carpenter had said!

XLIX

Comrade Abell told us where the police-court was located, and we agreed to be there at nine o'clock next morning. Then I parted from the rest, and walked until I met a taxi and drove to my rooms.

I felt desolate and forlorn. Nothing in my old life had any interest for me. This was the afternoon when I usually went to the Athletic Club to box; but now I found myself wondering, what would Carpenter say to such imitation fighting? I decided I would stay by myself for a while, and take a walk and think things over. I had been dissatisfied with my life for a long time; the glamor had begun to wear off the excitement of youth, and I had begun to suspect that my life was idle and vain. Now I knew that it was: and also I knew that the world was a place of torment and woe.

I returned late in the afternoon, and a few minutes afterwards my telephone rang, and I discovered that somebody else was dissatisfied with life.

"Hello, Billy," said the voice of T-S. "I see dat feller Carpenter is in jail. Vy don't you bail him out?"

"He won't let me," I said.

"Vell, maybe it might be a good ting to leave him in jail a veek, till dis Brigade convention gits over."

"Funny!" said I. "I had the same idea!"

"Listen," continued the other, "I been feelin' awful bad because I told dem fellers I didn't know him. D' you suppose he knows I said dat, Billy?"

"Well," said I, "he knew you were going to say it, so probably he knows you said it."

"Vell," said T-S, "maybe you laugh at me, but I been tinkin' I tell dem fellows to go to hell."

"What fellows?"

"De whole damn vorld! Billy, I like dat feller Carpenter! I never met a feller like him before. You tink he vould let me go to see him in de jail?"

"I'm sure he'd be glad to see you," I said; "if the jailers didn't object."

"Sure, I fix de jailers all right!"

"But T-S," I added, "I don't believe he'll sign any contract."

"Contract nuttin'," said T-S. "I shoost vant to see him, Billy. Is dere anyting I could do fer him?"

I thought for a moment; then I said: "You might do something for one of his friends, and that's young Everett. He got pretty badly hurt, and he's sticking at the job of taking down all Carpenter's speeches. He ought to have a surgeon, and also a first class stenographer to take turns with him. Have you got another man like him?"

"I dunno," said T-S. "You don't find a young feller like Matt Everett everyday."

I started. "What do you say is his name?"

"Matthew," said T-S. "Vy you ask?"

"Nothing," said I; "just a coincidence!"

Our conversation ended with the remark by T-S that he would call up the station-house and arrange to see Carpenter. Five minutes later the telephone rang again, and I heard the magnate's voice: "Billy, dey say he's been bailed out!"

"What?" I cried. "He declared he wouldn't have it done."

"Somebody done it vitout askin' him! De money vas paid, and dey turned him out!"

"Who did it?"

"Guess!"

"You mean it was you?"

"I vouldn't 'a dared. I only shoost found out about it. Mary Magna done it, and she's took him avay somevere."

"Good Lord!" I exclaimed; and before my mind's eye flashed another headline:

FAIR FILM STAR FREES LOVE-CULT PROPHET

I promised to try to find out about the prophet at once. "He won't get away," I said, "because he doesn't ride in automobiles, and he and Mary can't walk very far on the street without the newspapers finding them!"

I took my telephone-book, and looked up the name Abell. It is an unusual name, and there was only one attorney bearing it. (I was struck by the fact that the first name of this attorney was Mark.) I called him on the phone, and heard the familiar gentle voice. Yes, Comrade Carpenter had just arrived, and Miss Magna was with him. They were going to have a little party, and they would be glad to have me come. Yes, Mr. T-S would be welcome, of course. So then I called up the magnate of the pictures, and not without an inward smile, conferred on him the gracious permission to spend the evening at the headquarters of Local Western City of the Socialist Party!

L

When I got to the meeting-place I found that a feast had been spread. I don't know where the money came from; maybe it was Bolshevik gold, as the enemy charged, or maybe it was the ill-gotten gains of a "million dollar movie vamp." Anyhow, there was a table spread with a couple of cloths that were clean, if ragged, and on them flowers and fruit. Carpenter was seated at the head of the table, and I noted to my surprise that he had on a beautiful robe of snow-white linen, instead of the one he had formerly worn, which was not only stained with kerosene but filthy with the dust of the streets. I learned that Mrs. T-S had brought this festal garment—a simple matter for her, because in movie studios they have wardrobe rooms where they turn out any sort of costume imaginable.

This robe was so striking that it created a little controversy. James, the carpenter, who had an ascetic spirit, considered it necessary to speak plainly, and point out that Mrs. T-S would have done better to take the money and give it to the poor. But the prophet answered: "Let this woman alone. She has done a good thing. The poor you have always with you, but me you have only for a short time. This woman has helped to make our feast happy, and men will tell about it in future years."

But that did not satisfy the ascetic James, who retired to his corner grumbling. "I know, we're going to start a new church—the same old graft all over again! A man has no business to say a thing like that. The first thing you know, they'll be taking the widow's mite to buy silk and velvet dresses for him and golden goblets for him to drink from! And then, before you know it they'll be setting him up in stained glass windows, and priests'll be wearing jewelled robes, and saying it's all right, and quoting his words!" I perceived that it wasn't so easy for a prophet to manage a bunch of disciples in these modern days!

The controversy did not seem to trouble Mrs. T-S, who was waddling about, perfectly happy in the kitchen—doing the things she would have done all the time, if her husband's social position had not required her to keep a dozen servants. Also, I noted to my great astonishment that Mary Magna, instead of taking a place at the prophet's right hand, according to the prerogative of queens, had put on a plain apron and was helping "Maw" and Mrs. Abell. More surprising yet, T-S had seated himself inconspicuously at the foot of the table, while at the prophet's right hand there sat a convict with a twenty year jail sentence hanging over him—John Colver, the "wobbly" poet! Again an ancient phrase learned in childhood came floating through my mind: "He hath put down the mighty from their seats, and exalted them of low degree!"

Somehow word had been got to all the little group of agitators of various shades. There was Korwsky, the secretary of the tailors' union—whose first name I learned was Luka; also his fellow Russian, the express-driver,—Simon Karlin, and Tom Moneta, the young Mexican cigar-maker. There was Matthew Everett, free to be a guest on this occasion, because T-S had brought along another stenographer. There was Mark Abell, and another Socialist, a young Irishman named Andy Lynch, a veteran of the late war who had come home completely cured of militarism, and was now spending his time distributing Socialist leaflets, and preaching to the workers wherever he could get two or three to listen. Also there was Hamby, the pacifist whom I did not like, and a second I. W. W., brought by Colver—a lad named Philip, who had recently been indicted by the grand jury, and was at this moment a fugitive from justice with a price upon his head.

The door of the room was opened, and another man came in; a striking figure, tall and gaunt, with old and pitifully untidy clothing, and a half month's growth of beard upon his chin. He wore an old black hat, frayed at the edges; but under this hat was a face of such gentleness and sadness that it made you think of Carpenter's own. Withal, it was a Yankee face—of that lean, stringy kind that we know so well. The newcomer's eyes fell upon Carpenter, and his face lighted; he set down an old carpet-bag that he was carrying, and stretched out his two hands, and went to him. "Carpenter! I've been looking for you!"

And Carpenter answered, "My brother!" And the two clasped hands, and I thought to myself with astonishment, "How does Carpenter know this man?"

Presently I whispered to Abell, "Who is he?" I learned that he was one I had heard of in the papers—Bartholomew Howard, the "millionaire hobo;" he was grandson and heir of one of our great captains of industry, and had taken literally the advice of the prophet, to sell all that he had and give it to the unemployed. He traveled over the country, living among the hobos and organizing them into his Brotherhood. Now you would have thought that he and Carpenter had known each other all their lives; as I watched them, I found myself thinking: "Where are the clergy and the pillars of St. Bartholomew's Church?" There were none of them at this supper-party!

LI

T-S had stopped at a caterer's on his way to the gathering, and had done his humble best in the form of a strawberry short-cake almost half as large around as himself; also several bottles of purple color, with the label of grape juice. When the company gathered at the table and these bottles were opened, they made a suspicious noise, and so we all made jokes, as people have the habit of doing in these days of getting used to prohibition. I noticed that Carpenter laughed at the jokes, and seemed to enjoy the whole festivity.

It happened that fate had placed me next to James, so I listened to more asceticism. "He oughtn't to do things like this! People will say he likes to eat rich food and to drink. It's bad for the movement for such things to be said."

"Cheer up, my friend!" I laughed. "Even the Bolsheviks have a feast now and then, when they can get it."

"You'll see what the newspapers do with this tomorrow," growled the other; "then you won't think it so funny."

"Forget it!" I said. "There aren't any reporters here."

"No," said he, "but there are spies here, you may be sure. There are spies everywhere, nowadays. You'll see!"

Presently Carpenter called on some of the company for speeches. Would Bartholomew tell about the unemployed, what their organization was doing, and what were their plans? And after that he asked John Colver, who sat on his right hand, to recite some of his verses. John and his friend Philip, a blue eyed, freckle-faced lad who looked as if he might be in high school, told stories about the adventures of outlaw agitators. For several months these two had been traveling the country as "blanket stiffs," securing employment in lumber-camps and mines, gathering the workers secretly in the woods to listen to the new gospel of deliverance. The employers were organized on a nation-wide scale everywhere throughout the country, and the workers with their feeble craft unions were like men using bows and arrows against machine-guns. There must be One Big Union—that was the slogan, and if you preached it, you went every hour in peril of such a fate that you counted fourteen years in jail as comparatively a happy ending.

Said Carpenter: "It is not such a bad thing for a cause to have its preachers go to jail."

"Well," said the lad of the blue eyes and the freckled face, "we try to keep a few outside, to tell what the rest are in for!"

Later on, I remember, John Colver told a funny story about this pal of his. The story had to do with grape juice instead of with propaganda, but it appealed to me because it showed the gay spirit of these lads. The two of them had sought refuge from a storm in a barn, and there, lying buried in the hay with the rain pouring down on the roof, they had heard the farmer coming to milk his cows. The man had evidently just parted from his wife, and there had been a quarrel; but the farmer hadn't dared to say what he wanted to, so now he took it out on the cows! "Na! na! na!" he shouted, with furious vehemence. "That's it! Go on! Nag, nag, nag! Don't stop, or I might manage to get a word in! Yes, I'm late, of course I'm late! Do you expect me to drive by the clock? Maybe I did forget the sugar! Maybe I've got nothing on my mind but errands! Whiskey? Maybe it's whiskey, and maybe it's gin, and maybe it's grape-juice!" The farmer set down his milk-pail and his lantern, and shook his clenched fist at the patient cattle. "I'm a man, I am, and I'll have you understand I'm master in my own house! I'll drink if I feel like drinking, I'll stop and chat with my neighbors if I feel like stopping, I'll buy sugar if I remember to buy it, and if you don't like it, you can buy your own!" And so on— becoming more inspired with his own eloquence—or maybe with the whiskey, or the gin, or the grape-juice; until young Philip became so filled with the spirit of the combat that he popped up out of the hay and shouted, "Good for you, old man! Stand up for your rights! Don't let her down you! Hurrah for men!" And the astounded farmer stood staring with his mouth open, while the two "wobbles" leaped up and fled from the barn, so convulsed with laughter they hardly noticed the floods of rain pouring down upon them.

<h1 style="text-align:center">LII</h1>

But, of course, it wasn't long before this little company became serious again. Carpenter told Franklin that he ought not stay here; he, Carpenter, was too conspicuous a figure, the authorities were certain to be watching him. Korwsky backed him up. There were sure to be spies here! They would never leave such a man unwatched. They would set to work to get something on him, and if they couldn't get it they would make it. When Carpenter asked what he meant, he explained, "Dey'll plant dynamite in de place vere you are, or dey'll fake up some letters to show you been plannin' violence."

"And do people believe such things?" asked Carpenter.

"Believe dem?" cried Korwsky. "If dey see it in de papers, dey believe it—sure dey do!"

The prophet answered, "Let a man live so that the world will believe him and not his enemies." Then he added a startling remark. "There is one among us who will betray me."

Of course, they all looked at one another in consternation. They were deeply distressed, and each tried in turn—"Comrade," or "Brother," or "Fellow-worker," or whatever term they used—"is it I?" Presently the sturdy looking fellow named Hamby, who called himself a pacifist, asked, "Is it I?" And Carpenter answered, quietly, "You have said it."

Then, of course, some of the others started up; they wanted to throw him out, but Carpenter bade them sit down again, saying, "Let things take their course; for the powers of this world will perish more quickly if they are permitted to kill themselves."

Apparently he saw no reason why this episode should be permitted to interfere with the festivities. Mary Magna came in laughing, bearing the strawberry short-cake, and set it on the table and proceeded to portion it out. When it was served, Carpenter said, "I shall not be with you much longer, my friends; but you will remember me when you see this beautiful red fruit on top of a cake; and also you will think of me and my message when you taste rich purple grape-juice that has perhaps stayed a day or two too long in the bottle!"

Some of the company laughed, but others of them had tears in their eyes; and I noticed that in the midst of the merriment the fellow Hamby got up and slipped out of the room. Not long after that the company began to disperse for various reasons. Karlin explained that his old horse had been working all day, and had had no supper. Colver was uneasy, not for himself, but for his friend, and I saw him start every time the door was opened. Also, T-S was having some night-scenes taken, and he and Mary were to see the work. Finally Carpenter dismissed the company, with the statement that he wished to retire to Comrade Abell's private office to pray; and Abell and his friend Lynch and the young Mexican said they would watch and wait for him. The rest of us took our departure, not without misgivings and sorrow in our hearts.

LIII

Now, you may find it hard to believe a confession which I have put off making—the fact that at this time I was engaged to be married. There was a certain member of what is called the "younger set," whom I had given reason to expect that I would think about her at least once in a while. But here for precisely three days I had been chasing about at the skirts of a prophet fresh from God, getting my name into the newspapers in scandalous fashion, and not daring even to call the young lady on the telephone and make apologies. That evening there was a dinner-dance at her home, and I supposed I was supposed to be there; but no one had bothered to invite me, and as a matter of fact I would not have known of the affair if I had not seen the announcement in the papers. I was too late for the dinner, but I got myself a taxicab, and drove to my room and changed my clothes, and hurried in my own car to the dance.

You would not be interested in the fact that when I arrived I was treated as an unwelcome guest, and Miss Betty even went so far as to remind me that I had not been invited. But after I had pleaded, she consented to dance with me; and so for an hour or two I tried to forget there were any people in the world who had anything to do but be happy. Just as I was succeeding, the butler came, calling me to the telephone, and I answered, and who should it be but Old Joe!

My surprise became consternation at his first words: "Billy, your friend Carpenter is in peril!"

"What do you mean?"

"They are going to get him tonight."

"Good God! How do you know?"

"It's a long story, and no time to tell it. Somebody's tipped me off. Where can I meet you? Every minute is precious."

"Where are you?" I asked, and learned that he was at his home, not far away. I said I would come there, and I hurried to Betty and had another scene with her, and left her weeping, vowing that she would never see me again. I ran out and jumped into my car—and I would hate to tell what I did to the speed laws of Western City. Suffice it to say that a few minutes later I was in Old Joe's den, and he was telling me his story.

Part of it I got then, and part of it later, but I might as well tell it all at once and be done with it. It happened that at the restaurant where Old Joe and I had dined before we went to the mass-meeting, he had met a girl whom he knew too well, after the fashion of young men about town. In greeting her on the way out, he had told her he was going to hear the new prophet and had laughingly suggested that the meeting was free. The girl, out of idle curiosity, had come, and had been touched by Carpenter's physical, if not by his moral charms. It chanced that this girl was living with a man who stood high in the secret service department of "big business" in our city; so she had got the full story of what was being planned against Carpenter. That afternoon, it appeared, there had been a meeting between Algernon de Wiggs, president of our Chamber of Commerce, and Westerly, secretary of our "M. and M.," and Gerald Carson, organizer of our "Boosters' League." These three had put up six thousand dollars, and turned it over to their secret service agents, with instructions that Carpenter's agitations in Western City were to be ended inside of twenty-four hours.

A plan had been worked out, every detail of which had been phoned to Old Joe. A group of ex-service men, members of the Brigade, had been hired to seize the prophet and treat him to a tar and feathering. It had not taken much to move them to action, for the afternoon papers were full of accounts of Carpenter's speech on Main Street, his denunciation of war, and of soldiers as "murderers" and "wolves."

But that was not all, said Old Joe; and I saw that his hand was trembling as he spoke. It appeared that there was an "operative" named Hamby, who was one of Carpenter's followers.

"By God!" I burst out, in sudden fury. "I was sure that fellow was a crook!"

"Yes," said the other. "He's been telephoning in regular reports as to Carpenter's doings. And now it's been arranged that he is to put an infernal machine in the Socialist headquarters where Carpenter has been staying!"

I was almost speechless. "You mean—to blow them up?"

"No, to blow up their reputations. Hamby is to lure Carpenter out to the street, and when the gang grabs him, Hamby will fire a shot, and there will be three or four secret agents in the crowd, who will incite the others, and see to it that Carpenter is lynched instead of being tarred and feathered!"

LIV

So there was the layout; and now, what was to be done? The first thing was to call Abell on the phone, and see if anything had happened. I picked up the receiver; but alas, the report was, "No answer." I urged "central" to try several times, but all I could get was, "I am ringing them." Carpenter, no doubt, was praying. What were the others doing? I kept on trying, but finally gave up.

Could the mob have taken them away? But Old Joe answered, no, a definite hour had been set. The ex-service men were to gather on the stroke of midnight. We had nearly an hour yet.

My first thought was that we should hurry to the Socialist headquarters and get Carpenter out of the way. But my friend pointed out that the place was certain to be watched, and we might find ourselves held up by the armed detectives; they would hardly take a chance of letting their prey escape at this hour. Also, I realized there was no use figuring on any plan that involved spiriting Carpenter away quietly, by the roof, or a rear entrance, or anything of that sort. He would insist on staying and facing his enemies.

I put my wits to work. We needed a good-sized crowd; we needed, in fact, a mob of our own. And suddenly the word brought to me an inspiration; that mob which T-S had drilled at Eternal City! I recalled that a year or so ago I had been lured to sit through a very dull feature picture which the magnate had made, showing the salvation of our country by the Ku Klux Klan; and I knew enough about studio methods to be sure they had not thrown away the costumes, but would have them stored. Here was the way to save our prophet! Here was the way to get what one wanted in Mobland!

I picked up the receiver and called Eternal City. Yes, Mr. T-S was there, but he was "on the lot" and could not be disturbed. I gave my name, and stated that it was a matter of life and death; Mr. T-S must come to the phone instantly. A couple of minutes later I heard his voice, and told him the situation, and also my scheme. He must come himself, to make sure that his orders were obeyed; he must bring several bus-loads of men, clad in the full regalia of Mobland's great Secret Society; and they must arrive at Abell's place precisely on the stroke of midnight. The men must be paid five dollars apiece, and be told that if they succeeded in bringing away the prophet unharmed, they would each get ten dollars extra. "I will put up that money," I said to T-S; but to my surprise he cried: "You ain't gonna put up nuttin'! God damn dem fellers, I'll beat 'em if it costs me a million!" So I realized that the prophet had made one more convert!

"Have you got that bus with the siren?" I asked; and when he answered, yes, I said, "Let that be the signal. When we hear it, Joe and I will bring Carpenter down to the street, and if the Brigade is there, it's up to you to persuade them you're the bigger mob!"

Then Old Joe and I ran down to my car, and drove at full speed to the Socialist headquarters; and on the way we worked out our own plan of campaign. The real danger-point was Hamby, the secret agent, and we must manage to put him out of the way. Despite his pose of "pacifism," he was certain to be armed, said Old Joe; yet we must take a chance, and do the job unarmed. If we should get into a shooting-scrape, they would certainly put it onto us; and they would make it a hanging matter, too.

I named over the members of Carpenter's party who had stayed with him. Andy Lynch, the ex-soldier, was probably a useful man, and we would get his help. We would get rid of Hamby, and then we would wait for T-S and his siren. By the time these plans were thoroughly talked out, we had reached the building in which the headquarters were located. There were lights in the main room upstairs, and the door which led up to them was open. The street was apparently deserted, and we did not stop to look for any "operatives," but left our machine and stole quietly upstairs and into the room.

LV

Comrade Abell sat at the table, with his head bowed in his arms, sound asleep. Lynch, the ex-soldier, and Tom Moneta, the Mexican, were lying on the floor snoring. And on a chair near the doorway, watching the scene, sat Hamby, wide awake. We knew he was awake, because he leaped to his feet the instant we entered the door. "Oh, it's you!" he said, recognizing me; I noted the alarm in his voice.

I beckoned to him, softly. "Come here a moment;" and he came out into the ante-room. At the same time Old Joe stepped across the big room, and stooped down and waked up Lynch. We had agreed that Joe was to give Lynch a whispered explanation of the situation, while I kept Hamby busy.

"Where is Mr. Carpenter?" I asked.

"He's in the private office, praying."

"Well," said I, "there's a sick woman who needs help very badly. I wonder if we'd better disturb him."

"I don't know," said Hamby. "I've been here an hour, and haven't heard a sound. Maybe he's asleep."

I was uncertain what I should do, and I elaborately explained my uncertainty. Of course, praying was an important and useful occupation, and I knew that the prophet laid great stress upon it, and all of us who loved him so dearly must respect his wishes.

"Yes, of course," said Hamby.

Yet at the same time, I continued, this woman was very ill, a case of ptomaine poisoning—

"Do you think he can cure that?" asked Hamby guilelessly; and at that moment Old Joe and Lynch came from the big room. Hamby started to turn, but he was too late. Old Joe's arms went around him, and Hamby's two elbows were clamped to his sides, in a grip which more than one professional wrestler in our part of the world has found it impossible to break. At the same time I stooped on my knees and grasped the man's two wrists; because we were taking no chances of his gun. Lynch, the ex-soldier, had a cloth, taken from the big table, and he flung this over the head of the "pacifist" and stifled his cries.

I took a revolver from his hip-pocket, but Joe was not satisfied. "Search him carefully," said he, and so I discovered another weapon in a side-pocket. Then I made hasty search in a big closet of the room, and found a lot of bundles of books and magazines tied with stout cords. I took the cords, and we bound the "pacifist's" wrists and ankles, and put a gag in his mouth, and then we felt sure he was really a pacifist. We carried him to the closet and laid him on the floor, where a humorous idea came to us. These bundles of magazines and books were no doubt the ones which the mob had confiscated from Comrade Abell. Since they were no longer saleable, they might as well be put to some use, so I gathered armfuls of them and distributed them over the form of Hamby, until there was no longer a trace of him visible.

And while I was doing this, I noticed in one corner of the closet, under the bundles, a wooden box about a foot square. Upon trying to lift it, I discovered that it weighed several times as much as it should have weighed if it had contained printed matter. "Here's our infernal machine," I whispered, and I picked it up gingerly, and tiptoed out of the room, and back to the kitchen, and down a rear stairway of the building. I unlocked the door and opened it—and there, crouching in the shadows alongside the door, just as I expected, I saw a man.

"Hello!" I whispered.

"Hello!" said he, badly startled.

"Here's something belonging to Hamby. He wants me to give it to you. Be careful, it's heavy." I deposited the box in his hands, and shut the door, and turned the lock again, and groped my way upstairs, chuckling to myself as I imagined the man's plight. He would not know what to make of this incident, and I had an idea he would not be able to find out, because he could not leave his post. Nor would he have much time to figure over the matter; for when I got back to the light, I looked at my watch, and it lacked just three minutes to twelve.

I found that Lynch and Old Joe had shut the pacifist in the closet, and were in the ante-room waiting for me. I whispered that everything was all right. A moment later we heard a sound in the big room, and peered in, and saw a door at the far end open—and there was Carpenter, standing with his white robes gleaming in the light. After a moment I realized that they gleamed even more than was natural; I perceived once more that strange "aura" which had been noticed at the mass-meeting; and by means of it I noticed an even more startling thing. There were drops of sweat on Carpenter's forehead, as always when he had labored intensely in his soul. This time I saw that the drops were large, and they were drops of blood!

A trembling seized me. I was awe-stricken before this man—afraid to go on with what I was doing, and equally afraid to back out. I remained staring helplessly, and saw him approach the sleeping figures, and stand looking at them. "Could you not watch with me one hour?" he said, in his gentle, sad voice; and he put his hand on Comrade Abell's shoulder, with the words: "The time has come."

Abell started to his feet, and began to apologize. The other said nothing, but stooped and waked Moneta. And at that moment I heard the shrill blast of a whistle outside on the street! "There's the Brigade!" whispered Old Joe.

LVI

I ran down the stairs, and peered through the doorway, and sure enough, there were four or five automobiles stopped before the headquarters, having approached from opposite direction. I stood just long enough to see a crowd of men in khaki uniforms jumping out; then I ran back, and leaving Old Joe and Lynch to keep guard at the top of the stairs, I walked in and greeted Carpenter.

He expressed no surprise at seeing me. Evidently his thoughts were on other things. For my part, I was trembling with excitement, so that my knees would barely hold me. How long would it be before T-S and his crowd appeared? I could figure the time it should take them to drive from Eternal City; but suppose something held them up? How long would the ex-service men stay out on the street, waiting for Hamby to answer their signal? Surely not many minutes! They would storm the place, and hunt out their victim for themselves. And suppose they should carry him off before the others arrived?

I had Hamby's two revolvers in my pocket. Should we use them, or not? The thought hit me all of a sudden; and apparently it hit Old Joe at the same moment. "Give me those guns, Billy," he whispered, and I put them obediently into his hands, and he went quickly into the rear rooms. At the end of a minute, he returned, saying, "I unloaded them and threw them out of the back window." And even as he spoke, the silence of the night outside was shattered by the scream of that siren, which served to warn people out of the way when T-S was moving his companies about "on location."

I went up to Carpenter. I didn't enjoy telling him a lie; in fact, I had an idea that one couldn't lie to him successfully. But I tried it. "Mr. Carpenter, Hamby left a message; he had to go downstairs, and said he wanted to see you. Would you come down and meet him?"

"Ah, yes!" said Carpenter. And he walked to the door and down the stairs without another word. The rest of us followed him; Abell and Moneta first, they being innocent and unsuspicious; and then Lynch, and then Joe and I.

The prophet stepped out to the street, and was instantly surrounded by a group of a dozen ex-service men, two of whom grasped him by the arms. He did not lift a hand, nor even make a sound. Comrade Abell, of course, started to cry out in protest; Moneta, the Mexican, reverted to his ancestors. His hand flashed to an inside pocket, and a knife leaped out. A soldier had hold of him, and Moneta shouted, "Stand back, or I cut off your ears." At which Carpenter turned, and in a stern, commanding voice proclaimed: "Let no man use force in my behalf! They who use force shall perish by force." Moneta stood still; and of course Lynch and Old Joe and I stood still; and the dozen men about Carpenter started to lead him away to their automobiles.

But they did not get very far. Upon the silence of the street a voice rang out. Ordinarily, one would have known it was the voice of a woman; but in this place, under these exciting circumstances, it seemed the voice of a supernatural being. It almost sang the words; it was like a silver bugle calling across a battle-field— glorious, thrilling, hypnotic. "Make way-y-y-y for the Grand Imperial Kle-e-e-agle of the Ku-u Klux Klan!" Every one was startled; but I think I was startled more that the rest, for I knew the voice! Mary Magna had taken another speaking part!

I was on the steps of the building, so I could see over the heads of the crowd. There were four of the big busses from Eternal City, two having approached from each direction. Some fifty figures had descended from them, and others were still descending, each one clad in a voluminous white robe, with a white hood over the head, and two black holes for eyes, and another for the nose. These figures had spread out in a half moon, entirely surrounding the little mob of ex-service men, and penning them against the wall of the building. In the center of the half moon, standing a few feet in advance, was the figure of the "Grand Imperial Kleagle," with a red star upon the forehead of the white hood, and shrouded white arms stretched out, and in one hand a magic wand with a red light on the end. This wand was waving over the Brigade members, and had apparently its full supernatural effect, for one and all they stood rooted to the spot, staring with wide-open eyes.

LVII

The grand-opera voice raised again its silver chant: "Give way, all mobs! Yield! Retire! Abdicate!—Bow down-n-n-n-n! Make way for the Mob of Mobs, the irresistible, imperial, superior super-mob! Hearken to the Lord High Chief Commanding Dragon of the Esoteric Cohorts, the Exalted Immortal Grand Imperial Kleagle of the Ku Klux Klan!"

Then the Grand Imperial Kleagle turned and addressed the white-robed throng in a voice of sharp command: "Klansmen! Remember your oath! The hour of Judgment is here! The guilty wretch cowers! The grand insuperable sentence has been spoken! Coelum animum imperiabilis senescat! Similia similibus per quantum imperator. Inexorabilis ingenium parasimilibua esperantur! Saeva itnparatus ignotum indignatio! Salvo! Suppositio! Indurato! Klansmen, kneel!"

As one man, the host fell upon its knees.

"Klansmen, swear! Si fractus illibatur orbis, impavidum ferient ruinae! You have heard the sentence. What is the penalty? Is it death?"

And a voice in the crowd cried "Death!" And the others took it up; there was a roar: "Death! Death!"

Said the Grand Imperial Kleagle: "Arma virumque cano, tou poluphlesboiou thalasses!" Then, facing the staring ex-servicemen: "Tetlathi mater erne kai anaskeo ko-omeneper!"

Finally the Grand Imperial Kleagle pointed her shrouded white arm at Carpenter, who stood, as pale as death, but unflinchingly. "Death to all traitors!" she cried. "Death to all agitators! Death to all enemies of the Ku Klux Klan! Condemnatus! Incomparabilis! Ingenientis exequatur! Let the Loyal High Inexorable Guardians and the Grand Holy Seneschals of the Klan advance!"

Six shrouded figures stepped out from the crowd. Said the Grand Imperial Kleagle: "Possess yourselves of the body of this guilty wretch!" And to the ex-servicemen: "Yield up this varlet to the High Secret Court-martial of the Klan, which alone has power to punish such as he."

What the bewildered members of the Brigade made of all this hocus-pocus I had no idea. Afterwards, when the adventure was over, I asked Mary, "Where in the world did you get that stuff?" And she told me how she had once acted in a children's comedy, in which there was an old magician who spent his time putting spells on people. She had had to witness his incantations eight or ten times a week for nearly a year, so of course the phrases had got fixed in her memory, and they had served just as well to impress these grown-up children.

Or perhaps the ex-servicemen thought this might be a further plan of those who had employed them. Whatever they thought, it was obvious that they were hopelessly outnumbered. There could be nothing for a mob to do but yield to a Super-mob; and they yielded. Those who were in front of Carpenter stepped back, and the Loyal High Inexorable Guardians and the Grand Holy Seneschals took Carpenter by the arms and led him away. Apparently they were going to overlook the rest of us; but Old Joe and Lynch and myself took Abell and Moneta by the shoulders and shoved them along, past the ex-service men and into the midst of the "Klansmen."

There was no need to consider dignity after that. We hustled Carpenter to the nearest of the busses, and put him in; the Grand Imperial Kleagle followed, and the rest of us clambered in after her. Sitting up beside the driver, watching the scene, was T-S, beaming with delight; he got me by the hand and wrung it. I could not speak, my teeth were literally chattering with excitement. Carpenter, sitting in the seat behind us, must have realized by now the meaning of this scandalous adventure; but he said not a word, and the white-gowned Klansmen piled in behind him, and the siren shrieked out into the night, and the bus backed to the corner, and turned and sped off; and all the way to Eternal City, T-S and I and Old Joe slapped one another on the back and roared with laughter, and the rest of the Klansmen roared with laughter—all save the Grand Imperial Kleagle, who sat by Carpenter's side, and was discovered to be weeping.

LVIII

T-S and I had exchanged a few whispered words, and decided that we would take Carpenter to his place, which was a few miles in the country from Eternal City. He would be as safe there as anywhere I could think of. When we had got to the studios, we discharged our Klansmen, and arranged to send Old Joe to his home, and the three disciples to a hotel for the night; then I invited Carpenter to step into T-S's car. He had not spoken a word, and all he said now was, "I wish to be alone."

I answered: "I am taking you to a place where you may be alone as long as you choose." So he entered the car, and a few minutes later T-S and I were escorting him into the latter's showy mansion.

We were getting to be rather scared now, for Carpenter's silence was forbidding. But again he said: "I wish to be alone." We took him upstairs to a bed-room, and shut him in and left him—but taking the precaution to lock the door.

Downstairs, we stood and looked at each other, feeling like two school-boys who had been playing truant, and would soon have to face the teacher. "You stay here, Billy!" insisted the magnate. "You gotta see him in de mornin'! I von't!"

"I'll stay," I said, and looked at my watch. It was after one o'clock. "Give me an alarm-clock," I said, "because Carpenter wakes with the birds, and we don't want him escaping by the window."

So it came about that at daybreak I tapped on Carpenter's door, softly, so as not to waken him if he were asleep. But he answered, "Come in;" and I entered, and found him sitting by the window, watching the dawn.

I stood timidly in the middle of the room, and began: "I realize, of course, Mr. Carpenter, that I have taken a very great liberty with you—"

"You have said it," he replied; and his eyes were awful.

"But," I persisted, "if you knew what danger you were in—"

Said he: "Do you think that I came to Mobland to look for a comfortable life?"

"But," I pleaded, "if you only knew that particular gang! Do you realize that they had planted an infernal machine, a dynamite bomb, in that room? And all the world was to read in the newspapers this morning that you had been conspiring to blow up somebody!"

Said Carpenter: "Would it have been the first time that I have been lied about?"

"Of course," I argued, "I know what I have done—"

"You can have no idea what you have done. You are too ignorant."

I bowed my head, prepared to take my punishment. But at once Carpenter's voice softened. "You are a part of Mobland," he said; "you cannot help yourself. In Mobland it is not possible for even a martyrdom to proceed in an orderly way."

I gazed at him a moment, bewildered. "What's the good of a martyrdom?" I cried.

"The good is, that men can be moved in no other way; they are in that childish stage of being, where they require blood sacrifice."

"But what kind of martyrdom!" I argued. "So undignified and unimpressive! To have hot tar smeared over your body, and be hanged by the neck like a common criminal!"

I realized that this last phrase was unfortunate. Said Carpenter: "I am used to being treated as a common criminal."

"Well," said I, in a voice of despair, "of course, if you're absolutely bent on being hanged—if you can't think of anything you would prefer—"

I stopped, for I saw that he had covered his face with his hands. In the silence I heard him whisper: "I prayed last night that this cup might pass from me; and apparently my prayer has been answered."

"Well," I said, deciding to cheer up, "you see, I have only been playing the part of Providence. Let me play it just a few days longer, until this mob of crazy soldier-boys has got out of town again. I am truly ashamed for them, but I am one of them myself, so I understand them. They really fought and won a war, you see, and they are full of the madness of it, the blind, intense passions—"

Carpenter was on his feet. "I know!" he exclaimed. "I know! You need not tell me about that! I do not blame your soldier-boys. I blame the men who incite them—the old men, the soft-handed men, who sit back in office-chairs and plan madness for the world! What shall be the punishment of these men?"

"They're a hard crowd—" I admitted.

"I have seen them! They are stone-faced men! They are wolves with machinery! They are savages with polished fingernails! And they have made of the land a place of fools! They have made it Mobland!"

I did not try to answer him, but waited until the storm of his emotion passed. "You are right, Mr. Carpenter. But that is the fact about our world, and you cannot change it—"

Carpenter flung out his arm at me. "Let no man utter in my presence the supreme blasphemy against life!"

So, of course, I was silent; and Carpenter went and sat at the window again, and watched the dawn.

At last I ventured: "All that your friends ask, Mr. Carpenter, is that you will wait until this convention of the ex-soldiers has got out of town. After that, it may be possible to get people to listen to you. But while the Brigade is here, it is impossible. They are rough, and they are wild; they are taking possession of the city, and will do what they please. If they see you on the streets, they will inflict indignities upon you, they will mishandle you—"

Said Carpenter: "Do not fear those who kill the body, but fear those who kill the soul."

So again I fell silent; and presently he remarked: "My brother, I wish to be alone."

Said I: "Won't you please promise, Mr. Carpenter—"

He answered: "I make promises only to my Father. Let me be."

LIX

I went downstairs, and there was T-S, wandering around like a big fat monk in a purple dressing gown. And there was Maw, also—only her dressing gown was rose-pink, with white chrysanthemums on it. It took a lot to get those two awake at six o'clock in the morning, you may be sure; but there they were, very much worried. "Vot does he say?" cried the magnate.

"He won't say what he is going to do."

"He von't promise to stay?"

"He won't promise anything."

"Vell, did you lock de door?"

I answered that I had, and then Maw put in, in a hurry: "Billy, you gotta stay here and take care of him! If he vas to gome downstairs and tell me to do someting, I vould got to do it!"

I promised; and a little later they got ready a cup of coffee and a glass of milk and some rolls and butter and fruit, and I had the job of taking up the tray and setting it in the prophet's room. When I came in, I tried to say cheerfully, "Here's your breakfast," and not to show any trace of my uneasiness.

Carpenter looked at me, and said: "You had the door locked?"

I summoned my nerve, and answered, "Yes."

Said he: "What is the difference to me between being your prisoner and being the prisoner of your rulers?"

Said I: "Mr. Carpenter, the difference is that we don't intend to hang you."

"And how long do you propose to keep me here?"

"For about four days," I said; "until the convention disbands. If you will only give me your word to wait that time, you may have the freedom of this beautiful place, and when the period is over, I pledge you every help I can give to make known your message to the people."

I waited for an answer, but none came, so I set down the tray and went out, locking the door again. And downstairs was one of T-S's secretaries, with copies of the morning newspapers, and I picked up a "Times," and there was a headline, all the way across the page:

KU KLUX KLAN KIDNAPS KARPENTER RANTING RED PROPHET
DISAPPEARS IN TOOTING AUTOS

I understood, of course, that the secret agency which had engineered the mobbing of the prophet would have had their stories all ready for our morning newspapers—stories which played up to the full the finding of an infernal machine, and an unprovoked attack upon ex-service men by the armed followers of the "Red Prophet." But now all this was gone, and instead was a story glorifying the Klansmen as the saviors of the city's good name. It was evident that up to the hour of going to press, neither of the two newspapers had any idea but that the white robed figures were genuine followers of the "Grand Imperial Kleagle." The "Times" carried at the top of its editorial page a brief comment in large type, congratulating the people of Western City upon the promptness with which they had demonstrated their devotion to the cause of law and order.

But of course the truth about our made-to-order mob could not be kept very long. When you have hired a hundred moving-picture actors to share in the greatest mystery of the age, it will not be many hours before your secret has got to the newspaper offices. As a matter of fact, it wasn't two hours before the "Evening Blare" was calling the home of the movie magnate to inquire where he had taken the kidnapped prophet; there was no use trying to deny anything, said the editor, diplomatically, because too many people had seen the prophet transferred to Mr. T-S's automobile. Of course T-S's secretary, who answered the phone, lied valiantly; but here again, we knew the truth would leak. There were servants and chauffeurs and gardeners, and all of them knew that the white robed mystery was somewhere on the place. They would be offered endless bribes—and some of them would accept!

In the course of the next hour or two there were a dozen newspaper reporters besieging the mansion, and camera men taking pictures of it, and even spying with opera glasses from a distance. Before my mind's eye flashed new headlines:

MOVIE MAGNATE HIDES MOB PROPHET FROM LAW

This was an aspect of the matter which we had at first overlooked. Carpenter was due at Judge Ponty's police-court at nine o'clock that morning. Was he going? demanded the reporters, and if not, why not? Mary Magna no doubt would be willing to sacrifice the two hundred dollars bail that she had put up; but the judge had a right to issue a bench warrant and send a deputy for the prisoner. Would he do it?

Behind the scenes of Western City's government there began forthwith a tremendous diplomatic duel. Who it was that wanted Carpenter dragged out of his hiding-place, we could not be sure, but we knew who it was that wanted him to stay hidden! I called up my uncle Timothy, and explained the situation. It wasn't worth while for him to waste his breath scolding, I was going to stand by my prophet. If he wanted to put an end to the scandal, let him do what he could to see that the prophet was let alone.

"But, Billy, what can I do?" he cried. "It's a matter of the law."

I answered: "Fudge! You know perfectly well there's no magistrate or judge in this city that won't do what he's told, if the right people tell him. What I want you to do is to get busy with de Wiggs and Westerly and Carson, and the rest of the big gang, and persuade them that there's nothing to be gained by dragging Carpenter out of his hiding-place."

What did they want anyway? I argued. They wanted the agitation stopped. Well, we had stopped it, and without any bloodshed. If they dragged the prophet out from concealment, and into a police court, they would only have more excitement, more tumult, ending nobody could tell how.

I called up several other people who might have influence; and meanwhile T-S was over at his office in Eternal City, pleading over the telephone with the editors of afternoon papers. They had got the Red Prophet out of the way during the convention, and why couldn't they let well enough alone? Wasn't there news enough, with five or ten thousand war-heroes coming to town, without bothering about one poor religious freak?

When you shoot a load of shot at a duck, and the bird comes tumbling down, you do not bother to ask which particular shot it was that hit the target. And so it was with these frantic efforts of ours. One shot must have hit, for at eleven o'clock that morning, when the case of John Doe Carpenter versus the Commonwealth of Western City was reached in Judge Ponty's court, and the bailiff called the name of the defendant and there was no answer, the magistrate in a single sentence declared the bail forfeited, and passed on to the next case without a word. And all three of our afternoon newspapers reported this incident in an obscure corner on an inside page. The Red Prophet was dead and buried!

IX

I took up Carpenter's lunch at one o'clock, and discovered, to my dismay, that he had not tasted his breakfast. I ventured to speak to him; but he sat on a chair, gazing ahead of him and paying no attention to me, so I left him alone. At six o'clock in the evening I took up his dinner, and discovered that he had not touched either breakfast or lunch; but still he had nothing to say, so I took back the dinner, and went downstairs, and said to T-S: "We've got ourselves in for a hunger strike!"

Needless to say, under the circumstances we did not very heartily enjoy our own dinner. And T-S, neglecting his important business, stayed around; getting up out of one chair and walking nowhere, and then sitting down in another chair. I did the same, and after we had exchanged chairs a dozen times—it being then about eight o'clock in the evening—I said: "By the way, hadn't you better call up the morning papers and persuade them to be decent." So T-S seated himself at the telephone, and asked for the managing editor of the Western City "Times," and I sat and listened to the conversation.

It began with a reminder of the amount of advertising space which Eternal City consumed in the "Times" in the course of a year, and also the amount of its pay-roll in the community. It wasn't often that T-S asked favors, but he wanted to ask one now; he wanted the "Times" to let up on this prophet business, and especially about the prophet's connection with the moving picture industry. Everything was quiet now, the prophet wasn't bothering anybody—

Suddenly, at the height of his eloquence, T-S stopped; and it seemed to me as if he jumped a foot out of his chair. "VOT!" And then, "Vy man, you're crazy!" He turned upon me, his eyes wide with dismay. "Billy! Dey got a report—Carpenter is shoost now speakin' to a mob on de steps of de City Hall!"

The magnate did not wait to see me jump out of my chair or to hear my exclamations, but turned again to the telephone. "My Gawd, man! Vot do I know about it? De feller vas up in his room two hours ago ven we took him his dinner! He vouldn't eat it, he vouldn't speak—"

That was the last I heard, having bolted out of the room, and upstairs. I found Carpenter's door locked; I opened it, and rushed in. The place was empty! The bird had flown!

How had he got out? Had he climbed through the window and slid down a rain-spout in his prophetic robes? Had he won the heart of some servant? Had some newspaper reporter or agent of our enemies used bribery? I rushed downstairs, and got my car from the garage; and all the way to the city I spent my time in such futile speculations. How Carpenter, having escaped from the house, had managed to get into town so quickly—that was much easier to figure out; for our highways are full of motor traffic, and almost any driver will take in a stranger.

I came to the city. Even outside the crowded district, the traffic was held up for a minute or two at every corner; so I found time to look about, and to realize that the Brigade had got to town. All day special trains had been pouring into the city, literally dozens of them by every road; and now the streets were thronged with men in uniform, marching arm in arm, shouting, chanting war-cries, roaming in search of adventure. Tomorrow was the first day of the convention, the day of the big parade: tonight was a night of riot. Everything in town was free to ex-service men—and to all others who could borrow or buy a uniform. The spirit of the occasion was set forth in a notice published on the editorial page of the "Times":

"Hello, bo! Have a cigarette. Take another one. Take anything you see around the place.

"The town is yours. Take it into camp with you. Scruff it up to your heart's content. Order it about. Let it carry grub to you. Have it shine your shoes. Hand it your coat and tell it to hold it until the show is over.

"We are all waiting your orders. Shove us back if we crowd. Push us off the street. Give us your grip and tell us where to deliver it. Any errands? Call us. If you want to go anywhere, don't ask for directions. Just jump into the car and tell us where you're bound for.

"Let's have another one before we part. Put up your money; it's no good here. This one's on Western City."

I saw that it was not going to be possible to drive through the jam, so I put my car in a parking place, and set out for the City Hall on foot. On the way I observed that the invitation of the "Times" had been accepted; the Brigade had taken possession of the town. It was just about possible to walk on the down-town streets; there were solid masses of noisy, pushing people, every other man in uniform. Evidently there had been a tacit agreement to repeal the Eighteenth amendment to the Constitution for the next three days; bootleggers had drawn up their trucks and automobiles along the curbs, and corn-whiskey, otherwise known as "white lightnin'," was freely sold. You would meet a man with a bottle in his hand, and the effects of other bottles in his face, who would embrace you and offer you a drink; in the same block you would meet another man who would invite you to buy drinks for everybody in sight. The town had apparently agreed that no invitation should be declined. If the great Republic of Mobland had been unable to make for its returned war-heroes the new world which it had promised them—if it could not even give them back the jobs they had had before they left—surely the least it could do was to get them drunk!

And several times in each block you would have to get off the sidewalk for a group of ten or twenty flushed, dishevelled men, playing the great national game of craps. "Roll the bones!" they would shout, completely ignoring the throngs which surged about them. Each had his pile of bills and silver laid out on the pavement, and his bottle of "white lightnin';" now and then one would take a swig, and now and then one would start singing:

> All we do is sign the pay-roll—
> And we don't get a goddam cent.

You would go a little farther, and find a couple of automobiles trying to get past, and a merry crowd amusing itself throwing large waste cans in front of them. Some one would shout: "Who won the war?" And the answer would come booming: "The goddam slackers;" or maybe it would be, "The goddam officers." The crowd would move along, starting to chant the favorite refrain:

> You're in the army now,
> You're not behind the plow—;
> You son-of-a—,
> You'll never get rich—
> You're in the army now!

And from farther down the street would come a chorus from another crowd of marchers:

> I got a girl in Baltimore,
> The street-car runs right by her door.

Every now and then you would come on a fist-fight, or maybe a fight with bottles, and a crowd, laughing and whooping, engaged in pulling the warriors apart and sitting on them. Through a mile or two of this kind of thing I made my way, my heart sinking deeper with misgiving. I got within a couple of blocks of the City Hall, and then suddenly I came upon the thing I dreaded—my friend Carpenter in the hands of the mob!

LXI

They had got hold of a canvas-covered wagon, of the type of the old "prairie-schooner." You still find these camped by our roadsides now and then, with no-mad families in them; and evidently one of these families had been so ill advised as to come to town for the convention. The rioters had hoisted their victim on top of the wagon, having first dumped a gallon of red paint over his head, so that everyone might know him for the Red Prophet they had been reading about in the papers. They had tied a long rope to the shaft of the wagon, and one or two hundred men had hold of it, and were hauling it through the streets, dancing and singing, shouting murder-threats against the "reds." Some ran ahead, to clear the traffic; and then came the wagon, lumbering and rocking, so that the prophet was thrown from side to side. Fortunately there was a hole in the canvas, and he could hold to one of the wooden ribs.

The cortege came opposite to me. On each side was a guard of honor, a line of men walking in lock-step, each with his hands on the shoulders of the one in front; they had got up a sort of chant: "Hi! Hi! The Bolsheviki prophet! Hi! Hi! The Bolsheviki prophet!" And others would yell, "I won't work! I won't work!"—this being our Mobland nickname for the I.W.W. Some one had daubed the letters on the sides of the wagon, using the red paint; and a drunken fellow standing near me shook his clenched fist at the wretch on top and bellowed in a fog-horn voice: "Hey, there, you goddam Arnychist, if you're a prophet, come down from that there wagon and cure my venereal disease!" There was a roar of laughter from the throng, and the drunken fellow liked the sensation so well that he walked alongside, shouting his challenge again and again.

Then I heard a crash behind me, and a clatter of falling glass; I turned to see a soldier, inside the Royal Hotel, engaged in chopping out the plate-glass window of the lobby with a chair. There were twenty or thirty uniformed men behind him, who wanted to get out and see the fun; but the door of the hotel was blocked by the crowd, so they were seeking a direct route to the goal of their desires.

I knew, of course, there was nothing I could do; one might as well have tried to stop a hurricane by blowing one's breath. Carpenter had wanted martyrdom, and now he was going to get it—of the peculiar kind and in the peculiar fashion of our free and independent and happy-go-lucky land. We have had many agitators and disturbers of our self-satisfaction, and they have all "got theirs," in one form or another; but there had never been one who had done quite so much to make himself odious as this "Bolsheviki prophet," who was now "getting his." "Treat 'em rough!" runs the formula of the army; and I fell in step, watching, and thinking that later I might serve as one of the stretcher-bearers.

Half way down the block we came to the Palace Hotel, and uniformed men came pouring out of that. I heard the shrieks of a woman, and put my foot on the edge of a store-window, and raised myself up by an awning, to see over the heads of the crowd. Half a dozen rowdies had got hold of a girl; I don't know what she had done—maybe her skirts were too short, or maybe she had been saucy to one of the gang; anyhow, they were tearing her clothes to shreds, and having done this gaily, they took her on their shoulders, and ran her out to the wagon, and tossed her up beside the Red Prophet. "There's a girl for you!" they yelled; and the drunken fellow who wanted Carpenter to cure him, suddenly thought of a new witticism: "Hey, you goddam Bolsheviki, why don't you nationalize her?" Men laughed and whooped over that; some of them were so tickled that they danced about and waved their arms in the air. For, you see, they knew all the details concerning the "nationalization of women in Russia," and also they had read in the papers about Mary Magna, and Carpenter's fondness for picture-actresses and other gay ladies. He stretched out his hand to the girl, to save her from falling off; and at this there went up such a roar from the mob, that it made me think of wild beasts in the arena. So to my whirling brain came back the words that Carpenter had spoken: "It is Rome! It is Rome! Rome that never dies!"

The cortege came to the "Hippodrome," which is our biggest theatre, and which, like everything else, had declared open house for Brigade members during the convention. Some one in the crowd evidently knew the building, and guided the procession down a side street, to the stage-entrance. They have all kinds of shows in the "Hippodrome," and have a driveway by which they bring in automobiles, or war-chariots, or wild animals in cages, or whatever they will. Now the mob stormed the entrance, and brushed the door-keepers to one side, and unbolted and swung back the big gates, and a swarm of yelling maniacs rushed the lumbering prairie-schooner up the slope into the building.

The unlucky girl rolled off at this point, and somebody caught her, and mercifully carried her to one side. The wagon rolled on; the advance guard swept everything out of the way, scenery as well as stage-hands and actors, and to the vast astonishment of an audience of a couple of thousand people, the long string of rope-pullers marched across the stage, and after them came the canvas-covered vehicle with the red-painted letters, and the red-painted victim clinging to the top. The khaki-clad swarm gathered about him, raising their deafening chant: "Hi! Hi! The Bolsheviki prophet. Hi! Hi! The Bolsheviki prophet!"

I had got near enough so that I could see what happened. I don't know whether Carpenter fainted; anyhow, he slipped from his perch, and a score of upraised hands caught him. Some one tore down a hanging from the walls of the stage set, and twenty or thirty men formed a cirfcle about it, and put the prophet in the middle of it, and began to toss him ten feet up into the air and catch him and throw him again.

And that was all I could stand—I turned and went out by the rear entrance of the theatre. The street in back was deserted; I stood there, with my hands clasped to my head, sick with disgust; I found myself repeating out loud, over and over again, those words of Carpenter: "It is Rome! It is Rome! Rome that never dies!"

A moment later I heard a crash of glass up above me; I ducked, just in time to avoid a shower of it. Then I looked up, and to my consternation saw the red-painted head and the red and white shoulders of Carpenter suddenly emerging. The shoulders were quickly followed by the rest of him; but fortunately there was a narrow shed between him and the ground. He struck the shed, and rolled, and as he fell, I caught him, and let him down without harm.

LXII

I expected to find my prophet nearly dead; I made ready to get him onto my shoulders and find some place to hide him. But to my surprise he started to his feet. I could not see much of him, because of the streams of paint; but I could see enough to realize that his face was contorted with fury. I remembered that gentle, compassionate countenance; never had I dreamed to see it like this!

He raised his clenched hands. "I meant to die for this people! But now—let them die for themselves!" And suddenly he reached out to me in a gesture of frenzy. "Let me get away from them! Anywhere, anyway! Let me go back where I was—where I do not see, where I do not hear, where I do not think! Let me go back to the church!"

With these words he started to run down the street; hauling up his long robes—never would I have dreamed that a prophet's bare legs could flash so quickly, that he could cover the ground at such amazing speed! I set out after him; I had stuck to him thus far, and meant to be in at the finish, whatever it was. We came out on Broadway again, and there were more crowds of soldier boys; the prophet sped past them, like a dog with a tin-can tied to its tail. He came to a cross-street, and dodged the crowded traffic, and I also got through, knocking pedestrians this way and that. People shouted, automobiles tooted; the soldiers whooped on the trail. I began to get short of breath, a little dizzy; the buildings seemed to rock before me, there were mobs everywhere, and hands clutching at me, nearly upsetting me. But still I followed my prophet with the bare flying legs; we swept around another corner, and I saw the goal to which the tormented soul was racing—St. Bartholomew's!

He went up the steps three at a time, and I went up four at a time behind him. He flung open the door and vanished inside; when I got in, he was half way up the aisle. I saw people in the church start up with cries of amazement; some grabbed me, but I broke away—and saw my prophet give three tremendous leaps. The first took him up the altar-steps; the second took him onto the altar; the third took him up into the stained-glass window.

And there he turned and faced me. His paint-smeared robes fell down about his bare legs, his convulsed and angry face became as gentle and compassionate as the paint would permit. With a wave of his hand, he signalled me to stand back and let him alone. Then the hand sank to his side, and he stood motionless. Exhausted, dizzy, I fell against one of the pews, and then into a seat, and bowed my head in my arms.

LXIII

I don't know just how much time passed after that. I felt a hand on my shoulder, and realized that some one was shaking me. I had a horror of hands reaching out for me, so I tried to get away from this one; but it persisted, and there was a voice, saying, "You must get up, my friend. It's time we closed. Are you ill?"

I raised my head; and first I glanced at the figure above the altar. It was perfectly motionless; and—incredible as it may seem—there was no trace of red paint upon either the face or the robes! The figure was dignified and serene, with a halo of light about its head—in short, it was the regulation stained glass figure that I had gazed at through all my childhood.

"What is the matter?" asked the voice at my side; and I looked up, and discovered the Reverend Mr. Simpkinson. He recognized me, and cried: "Why, Billy! For heaven sake, what has happened?"

I was dazed, and put my hand to my jaw. I realized that my head was aching, and that the place I touched was sore. "I—I—-" I stammered. "Wait a minute." And then, "I think I was hurt." I tried to get my thoughts together. Had I been dreaming; and if so, how much was dream and how much was reality? "Tell me," I said, "is there a moving picture theatre near this church?"

"Why, yes," said he. "The Excelsior."

"And—was there some sort of riot?"

"Yes. Some ex-soldiers have been trying to keep people from going in there. They are still at it. You can hear them."

I listened. Yes, there was a murmur of voices outside. So I realized what had happened to me. I said: "I was in that mob, and I got beaten up. I was knocked pretty nearly silly, and fled in here."

"Dear me!" exclaimed the clergyman, his amiable face full of concern. He took me by my shoulders and helped me to my feet.

"I'm all right now," I said—"except that my jaw is swollen. Tell me, what time is it?"

"About six o'clock."

"For goodness sake!" I exclaimed. "I dreamed all that in an hour! I had the strangest dream—even now I can't make up my mind what was dream and what really happened." I thought for a moment. "Tell me, is there a convention of the Brigade—that is, I mean, of the American Legion in Western City now?"

"No," said the other; "at least, not that I've heard of. They've just held their big convention in Kansas City."

"Oh, I see! I remember—I read about it in the 'Nation.' They were pretty riotous—made a drunken orgy of it."

"Yes," said the clergyman. "I've heard that. It seems too bad."

"One thing more. Tell me, is there a picture of Mr. de Wiggs in the vestry-room?"

"Good gracious, no!" laughed the other. "Was that one of the things you dreamed? Maybe you're thinking of the portrait they are showing at the Academy."

"By George, that's it!" I said. "I patched the thing up out of all the people I know, and all the things I've read in the papers! I had been talking to a German critic, Dr. Henner—or wait a moment! Is he real? Yes, he came before I went to see the picture. He'll be entertained to hear about it. You see, the picture was supposed to be the delirium of a madman, and when I got this whack on the jaw, I set to work to have a delirium of my own, just as I had seen on the screen. It was the most amazing thing—so real, I mean. Every person I think of, I have to stop and make sure whether I really know them, or whether I dreamed them. Even you!"

"Was I in it?" laughed Mr. Simpkinson. "What did I do?"

But I decided I'd better not tell him. "It wasn't a polite dream," I said. "Let me see if I can walk now." I started down the aisle. "Yes, I'm all right."

"Do you suppose that crowd will bother you again? Perhaps I'd better go with you," said the apostle of muscular Christianity.

"No, no," I said. "They're not after me especially. I'll slip away in the other direction."

So I bade Mr. Simpkinson good-bye, and went out on the steps, and the fresh air felt good to me. I saw the crowd down the street; the ex-service men were still pushing and shouting, driving people away from the theatre. I stopped for one glance, then hurried away and turned the corner. As I was passing an office building, I saw a big limousine draw up. The door opened, and a woman stepped out: a bold, dark, vivid beauty, bedecked with jewels and gorgeous raiment of many sorts; a big black picture hat, with a flower garden and parts of an aviary on top—

Her glance lit on me. "My God! Will you look who's here!" She came to me with her two hands stretched out. "Billy, wretched creature, I haven't laid eyes on you for two months! Do you have to desert me entirely, just because you've fallen in love with a society girl with the face of a Japanese doll-baby? What's the matter with me, that I lose my lovers faster than I get them? I just met Edgerton Rosythe; he's got a good excuse, I admit—I'm almost as much scared of his wife as he is himself. But still, I'd like a chance to get tired of some man first! Want to come upstairs with me, and see what Planchet's doing to my old grannie in her scalping-shop? Say, would you think it would take three days' labor for half a dozen Sioux squaws to pull the skin off one old lady's back? And a week to tie up the corners of her mouth and give her a permanent smile! 'Why, grannie,' I said, 'good God, it would be cheaper to hire Charlie Chaplin to walk around in front of you all the rest of your life.' But the old girl was bound to be beautiful, so I said to Planchet, 'Make her new from the waist up, Madame, for you never can tell how the fashions'll change, and what she'll need to show.'"

And so I knew that I was back in the real world.

**The Palliser Novels, Volume One, Including: Can You For-
give Her? Phineas Finn and the Eustace Diamonds
Anthony Trollope**
Benediction Classics, 2013
1200 pages
ISBN: 978-1-78139-407-6

Available from www.amazon.com, www.amazon.co.uk

The Palliser Novels make up Trollope's second major series, which overlap with
the first major series - the Barsetshire novels. These stories are concerned with
politics, featuring the wealthy, industrious Plantagenet Palliser and his wonderfully impulsive and even richer wife Lady Glencora. These books bear all the
hallmarks of Trollope's later works, blending dark cynicism with wit and a sharp
awareness of human nature.

The complete Palliser novels include:

**The Palliser Novels, Volume Two, Including: Phineas Re-
dux, the Prime Minister and the Duke's Children
Anthony Trollope**
Benediction Classics, 2013
1134 pages
ISBN: 978-1-78139-408-3

Available from www.amazon.com, www.amazon.co.uk

The Palliser Novels make up Trollope's second major series, which overlap with
the first major series - the Barsetshire novels. These stories are concerned with
politics, featuring the wealthy, industrious Plantagenet Palliser and his wonderfully impulsive and even richer wife Lady Glencora. These books bear all the
hallmarks of Trollope's later works, blending dark cynicism with wit and a sharp
awareness of human nature.

The complete Palliser novels include:

Can You Forgive Her? (1865)
Phineas Finn (1869)
The Eustace Diamonds (1873)
Phineas Redux (1874)
The Prime Minister (1876)
The Duke's Children (1880)

Metamorphosis and The Trial
Franz Kafka
Benediction Classics, 2013
224 pages
ISBN: 978-1-78139-377-2

Available from www.amazon.com, www.amazon.co.uk

Franz Kafka (1883 - 1924) was born into a German
speaking Jewish family in Prague. He wrote in German and is regarded as one of
the most influential authors of the 20th century. His works examine the themes of
transformation, alienation, bullying and the characters are given insuperable
quests.

This book contains two of his most famous stories - "Metamorphosis" and "The
Trial".

Metamorphosis begins like this:
"One morning, when Gregor Samsa woke from troubled dreams, he found himself
transformed in his bed into a horrible vermin. He lay on his armour-like back, and
if he lifted his head a little he could see his brown belly, slightly domed and divided by arches into stiff sections. The bedding was hardly able to cover it and
seemed ready to slide off any moment. His many legs, pitifully thin compared
with the size of the rest of him, waved about helplessly as he looked."

The story is harrowing, but funny in a dark way, it explores the themes of alienation - the guilt, inadequacy and anguish of transformation. Samsa's predicament is
perhaps the predicament we all face at times, and especially if we suffer illness or
disability. This is one of the most influential books of all time.

The Trail also starts with a stark problem:
"Someone must have been telling lies about Josef K., he knew he had done nothing wrong but, one morning, he was arrested. Every day at eight in the morning
he was brought his breakfast by Mrs. Grubach's cook - Mrs. Grubach was his
landlady - but today she didn't come."

We never find out what Josef K was arrested for, he is a respected worker in a
bank and he has to defend himself against a charge about which he can get no information. This is a terrifying tale but again is comic at times. It explores the
nightmare of excessive bureaucracy, hold onto your hat because this book is a
psychological roller-coaster.

Also from Benediction Books …
Wandering Between Two Worlds: Essays on Faith and Art
Anita Mathias
Benediction Books, 2007
152 pages
ISBN: 0955373700

Available from www.amazon.com, www.amazon.co.uk

In these wide-ranging lyrical essays, Anita Mathias writes, in lush, lovely prose, of her naughty Catholic childhood in Jamshedpur, India; her large, eccentric family in Mangalore, a sea-coast town converted by the Portuguese in the sixteenth century; her rebellion and atheism as a teenager in her Himalayan boarding school, run by German missionary nuns, St. Mary's Convent, Nainital; and her abrupt religious conversion after which she entered Mother Teresa's convent in Calcutta as a novice. Later rich, elegant essays explore the dualities of her life as a writer, mother, and Christian in the United States-- Domesticity and Art, Writing and Prayer, and the experience of being "an alien and stranger" as an immigrant in America, sensing the need for roots.

About the Author

Anita Mathias is the author of *Wandering Between Two Worlds: Essays on Faith and Art*. She has a B.A. and M.A. in English from Somerville College, Oxford University, and an M.A. in Creative Writing from the Ohio State University, USA. Anita won a National Endowment of the Arts fellowship in Creative Non-fiction in 1997. She lives in Oxford, England with her husband, Roy, and her daughters, Zoe and Irene.

Anita's website:
    http://www.anitamathias.com, and
Anita's blog Dreaming Beneath the Spires:
    http://dreamingbeneaththespires.blogspot.com

The Church That Had Too Much
Anita Mathias
Benediction Books, 2010
52 pages
ISBN: 9781849026567

Available from www.amazon.com, www.amazon.co.uk

The Church That Had Too Much was very well-intentioned. She wanted to love God, she wanted to love people, but she was both hampered by her muchness and the abundance of her possessions, and beset by ambition, power struggles and snobbery. Read about the surprising way The Church That Had Too Much began to resolve her problems in this deceptively simple and enchanting fable.

About the Author

Anita Mathias is the author of *Wandering Between Two Worlds: Essays on Faith and Art*. She has a B.A. and M.A. in English from Somerville College, Oxford University, and an M.A. in Creative Writing from the Ohio State University, USA. Anita won a National Endowment of the Arts fellowship in Creative Non-fiction in 1997. She lives in Oxford, England with her husband, Roy, and her daughters, Zoe and Irene.

Anita's website:
    http://www.anitamathias.com, and
Anita's blog Dreaming Beneath the Spires:
    http://dreamingbeneaththespires.blogspot.com